BETH BOLDEN

Bite Me

BETH BOLDEN

Chapter One

The crash woke Miles up, the sharp metallic clang of stainless steel against the deeper, resonating thud of the wood floor.

Almost certain dents in his favorite copper pot—*check*.

Scratches in the hardwood floor their landlord would definitely freak about—*check*.

Bruises his roommates would inevitably punish him for? Still in question, though if Xander's exaggerated howl of pain was any indication, Miles Costa thought those were inevitable.

"Goddamn it, Miles," Xander exclaimed loudly, as Miles dragged his head up from where it had landed in a slump of exhaustion only a few hours before on his marble pastry slab. If he was a betting man, he'd definitely bet that the fine grain of the marble was imprinted on his cheek.

He probably shouldn't have fallen asleep in the kitchen after filming the video, and he definitely shouldn't have piled those pans in such a precarious pile to dry after washing them. Inspiration had struck midway through the dinner service last night, and he'd been in too much of a rush to work out the intricacies of the recipe in his head to care much about the consequences of yet another late-night/early-morning filming marathon.

"At least I washed the pans out?" Through his tired squint, Miles could just make out Xander's disgruntled expression. He was annoyed, not pissed off, which boded well for Miles. He was also pretty sure that Xander had a few crumbs clinging to his chin, which meant that he'd already sampled some of last night's experiments.

Having eaten one over the sink just past 4 a.m., Miles knew just how fantastic those tarts were. Xander's forgiveness was no longer an uncertainty, but an inevitability.

"Good, huh?" Miles asked with a grin. After culinary school, working in many good kitchens, before finally moving to the *great* kitchen at Terroir, and then ending up with three chefs as roommates, he knew all about the culinary ego. Sure, he had one, but constantly crowing about how talented he was got exhausting. He normally preferred the food to do the talking for him—but in this case, distracting Xander from the fact that he'd used the kitchen until 4 a.m. *again*, was way more important.

"You film these too?" Xander asked ruefully. He reached for another tart, not even trying to be subtle.

Miles remembered when they'd first met, and Xander, all that ego barely restrained, had looked down his nose at pastry. He'd claimed to not even like sweets, but now he was chowing down on Miles' tarts like there weren't about a hundred more packed away in neatly stacked Tupperware.

It was particularly sweet to convert someone who didn't appreciate his craft, just like he enjoyed bringing the skill of his craft to the masses. Even the masses who didn't necessarily appreciate it, but watched his videos anyway.

"Of course I did."

Xander might have been converted to liking Miles' tarts, but Miles knew he probably wasn't ever going to understand why he filmed himself making them, and posted them to social media. For Xander, it felt too much like a magician giving away his secrets for free.

Xander might want the cultured and erudite to enjoy his food, but he didn't want to teach them how to make it.

He shook his head. "You're wasting your time," he said.

Miles was tired. It couldn't be any later than 8 a.m.—because that was when Xander took his run every day—and that meant he'd gotten only a handful of hours of sleep on a marble slab that wasn't quite the same as his feather pillow. He had a fierce crick in his neck, and he had to be at work in two hours for prep.

Which was why he nicked the tart from Xander's fingers, and popped the remains in his own mouth. "But it's my time," Miles said, and made a shooing motion. "Now go jog like a good boy."

Xander made a face, shrugged, and then turned away, shutting the door behind him a little louder than normal. Miles might be worried things would be weird between them, but they worked fourteen-hour days at one of the most exacting restaurants in the world, and after going through Chef's bullshit each shift, nothing ever seemed weird for long.

Miles bent down and started gathering his pots. Yes, there was definitely a dent in his favorite copper sugar pan. Damnit. He'd just got the sink filled with soapy water so he could wash them again when his other roommate wandered in.

Wyatt was rubbing the sleep out of his eyes, but they lit up when they saw the Tupperware containers. "You filmed last night?" he asked, popping the lid off. "Oh, these are pretty. Raspberry and strawberry?"

Wyatt's nose was legendary. He could sometimes tell the separate ingredients in a dish just from the aroma, and always by taste. Sometimes Miles enjoyed trying to stump him, but today, he just nodded, then turned back to his sink full of pots.

"Delicious," Wyatt pronounced through a mouthful of pastry cream and flaky tart shell. "I never would have dreamt of doing just raspberry and straw-berry. Mixed berry is so middle-class housewife. But you elevated it."

Since he had his back to his roommate, Wyatt couldn't see Miles roll his eyes. Every chef he knew believed they were as high class as the restaurant they worked with. He would be the first to tell anybody that Terroir was special, because it was. Chef Bastian Aquino had built something one of a kind deep in the heart of the Napa Valley, and then maintained it—which, Miles knew, was most of the struggle. But most of the chefs he knew also came from decidedly low or middle-class origins. And they wanted to forget them as quickly as possible.

But Miles had lots of good memories of his childhood, and the dreaded "mixed berry" had shown up lots of times in bundt cakes and muffins and as far as he was concerned, it was a classic. He'd just used a little of the technique he'd spent so many years perfecting to make it even better.

"Wish we could get marionberries here," Miles said, because he wasn't going to tell Wyatt, who was one of his best friends, that he was full of shit. He'd already antagonized Xander this morning, and he tried to only piss off one of his roommates per day.

"Chef could," Wyatt said. Miles rolled his eyes again. Chef could get *any-thing*, because he was Bastian Aquino, and a god of American cuisine. Pans washed, he started drying them one at a time, because he wasn't letting them air dry in a precarious pile again. His precious copper sugar pot might not survive another tumble.

"At the farmer's market," Miles clarified, which Wyatt must have known he meant. Chef was only vaguely aware of Miles' "little internet experiment," as his boss had termed it, and as far as Miles was concerned, it was going to stay that way. He wasn't going to go around name-dropping Bastian Aquino to get some marionberries.

Wyatt might, but then Wyatt was a fucking idiot.

"They're good just as they are," Wyatt said complacently, which as far as Miles was concerned was Wyatt's biggest drawback as a chef. He rested on his laurels. He made the vision in his head, and if it matched, declared it done and perfect.

Miles knew his own personal drawback was that no recipe was ever truly done. The tarts *would* be better with a single marionberry resting on the glossy surface of the pink pastry cream. They'd not only look better, they'd taste better too.

Putting the last pan away, Miles turned back to Wyatt. "I'm going in at eleven. What about you?"

"Just got a text. Bunch of artichokes came in. Lots of prep today. So I'm going in early." Wyatt flashed him a carefree smile that belied the fact that he'd be spending approximately the next sixteen hours at the restaurant, deep in the bowels of the kitchen. "But your tarts were a great start. Breakfast of champions."

"You're welcome," Miles said, wiping his hands on a towel.

"Go get some sleep. You look like the walking dead. And not that hot one with the bow and arrows either."

Miles didn't look in the mirror when he walked back to his room, but he considered it for a brief moment. He probably did look like hell, nothing like that admittedly very hot man from *The Walking Dead*. He *should* go take another catnap, but he wanted to get the tart video posted before his shift started.

He spent the next two hours editing his footage, and without even watching it all the way through, posted it to his page, *Pastry by Miles*. He took a lightning-quick shower, jumped on his bike, and was walking through the back door to the kitchens at Terroir right on time for his prep shift to start.

Part of the beauty of posting a video before a shift began was that there was no time to check hits or views or comments or anything at all. He was deep in prep, waist-high in white chocolate lemon mousse pyramids when René, the head pastry chef, stopped in front of his station.

René was sort of a dick, but almost all the chefs that reached his level were, so Miles mostly didn't hold it against him.

"Did you put the rosemary in the cream while it steeped?" René asked, like Miles hadn't been making these all summer. Terroir was considered one of the best restaurants in the world, and René wasn't a terrible innovator—it wasn't like they were making hot fudge lava cake or anything—but sometimes his desserts were a little obvious. Miles had also discovered the hard way that René wasn't a huge fan of anyone having an idea other than him. If this wasn't Terroir and the best job anyone at his level could hope to have, Miles would have left long ago, but here he still was, fielding René's stupid questions and creating white chocolate lemon mousse pyramids.

And it should have been thyme, not rosemary, as far as he was concerned. But nobody had ever asked Miles and that wasn't about to change.

"Yes, Chef," Miles answered respectfully, but didn't glance up from his work.

"Good," René said, and then lingered in front of his station, which made Miles nervous. René lingering didn't usually mean good things; it usually meant a great deal of unexpected work, and Miles was already tired.

"Your new video," René said, and Miles couldn't help but tense. René knew about the videos but he'd never imagined René might watch one.

He'd had to tell René, and René's boss, Chef Aquino, what he was doing with *Pastry by Miles*, because he figured it was better to beg permission now than to be fired later. Chef Aquino hadn't cared, because it wasn't about him, and René had only insisted that the desserts he created be Miles' ideas and Miles' ideas alone.

That was perfectly fine by him, because the site had originally been created because he'd been creatively stymied at work, so he had zero intention of ever posting a white chocolate lemon mousse pyramid to *Pastry by Miles*.

"Yes, Chef?" Miles said, glancing up when René didn't spit it out right away. His dark beady eyes seemed to grow even beadier. Or maybe Miles had just been up three quarters of the night baking. It was hard to say exactly.

"It was good." René's voice was gruff, like he could barely bring himself to say anything positive. "An innovative concept."

So much of his job was biting his tongue, and Miles kept right on biting it. "Thank you."

"I might mention to Chef Aquino that we could use it as a special next weekend."

Miles had to tamp down his excitement so it wouldn't show. It wouldn't be a surprise to see Chef taking some poor *sous* apart for not cooking the scallops to perfection, but celebrating in the Terroir kitchen? Out of the question.

"That would be good," Miles said, and because he was too tired not to, took a risk. "I didn't even realize you watched the videos, sir."

René had turned to move on, but looked back at Miles' question. "I don't," he said. "Chef Aquino recommended I watch it. Apparently he really enjoyed it. He said he was seeing it all over his Twitter feed."

Miles couldn't hold back his smile at that. He might not enjoy the reign of Chef René but he very much respected Chef Aquino. And all over Chef's Twitter feed? He knew his videos were popular, but he'd never heard of them spreading that quickly before. He wished he could put his pastry bag down and look at his phone, but he still had a good hour left and these pyramids needed to chill before the dinner service started.

He'd check his phone on his break.

When he finally finished the white chocolate lemon mousse pyramids, and they were nestled in the blast chiller, the crick in his neck was much worse than it had been that morning. Trying to stretch it out, he detoured into the tiny locker room next to the dishwashers. Grabbing his phone out of his locker, he was floored by how many notifications he had—and he'd anticipated having a ton.

Chef Aquino hearing about his video and seeing it on his timeline had been a pretty good hint that his video had gone viral. The avalanche of notifications he was trying to sort through proved it.

After fifteen minutes, Miles felt overwhelmed and for the first time ever, he was relieved his break was over. It felt like he'd barely touched the growing mountain of comments and shares and likes.

He couldn't put his finger on why the sudden flash of white hot popularity bothered him, but as he was dusting the mousse pyramids with edible gold, it hit him.

Pastry by Miles had never been about becoming popular. It had been an expression of his creative side that had been stifled at Terroir—a necessary outlet that he paid attention to in fits and starts. He didn't post videos weekly, or even regularly, but he must have hit a nerve because each video he posted seemed to exponentially increase his social media reach.

It was, Miles decided, a serendipitous symptom of something he enjoyed doing. He'd still record the videos if nobody but his little sister watched them.

"Costa," a voice bellowed across the kitchen. Miles glanced up and tensed. It was Xander, his short brown hair covered by a bandana festooned with chili peppers, and he had his phone in his hand.

"What do you want?" he asked shortly, and far more quietly than Xander. It was just like Xander to believe that even in another chef's kitchen—even in *Chef Aquino's* kitchen—he could do whatever the fuck he wanted.

Sometimes Xander pushed his buttons, and all Miles wanted to do was push them back. But Miles always remembered he was a roommate and a friend, and even worse a co-worker, before he punched Xander in the face.

"You didn't tell me you were famous," he said, coming to stand over by the tray of pyramids. Miles set his brush on the lid of the gold dust with a steady hand.

"I'm not famous," Miles said, even though the notifications blowing up his phone might argue otherwise.

"I don't know," Xander said skeptically, "when my aunt in New Jersey texts me to say she thinks our kitchen is a pit, I sorta feel like you are."

Miles stared at his friend. "You don't have an aunt in New Jersey."

"But I *could*," Xander said blithely.

"You're an asshole," Miles said, scowling as he picked his brush back up. "Now go away, I have to finish these. Don't you have about a thousand artichokes to break down?"

"Roughly two thousand," Xander announced cheerfully.

Miles shook his head in disbelief. Not at the artichokes—that didn't surprise him at all because Chef Aquino was a famous perfectionist and a closet sadist—but at how happy Xander seemed to be about them.

"Did you have sex?" Miles demanded quietly. "Is that what this obnoxious cheerfulness is about?"

Xander just laughed. "You look tired. You should get some sleep, Costa." He sauntered away without ever answering Miles' question.

"You shouldn't let him get to you," Kian said. Kian was Miles' third roommate—Napa was insanely expensive and the only way Miles could afford a halfway decent kitchen with halfway decent light was to split the rent four ways.

"Easy for you to say," Miles retorted.

"I had a tart. Actually two," Kian confessed. "They were awesome."

Miles had a soft spot for Kian. He reminded him a lot of his little sister, Gina. Except that Kian was male and tough as nails because he was the bottom of the food chain in Terroir's kitchen. Miles had no idea how Kian even survived the diabolical tasks Chef Aquino put on his plate. Miles usually thought women were usually way tougher than men, but what Kian put up with put Gina to shame regularly. And Gina was a freshman in college.

"Thank you," Miles acknowledged. Kian was way more respectful than Xander, and had kept his distance so Miles could pick his brush up and get back to his careful, artful dusting of the pyramids. Chef René might not make crazily innovative desserts, but he was a stickler for presentation. Every single one of his desserts was a work of art.

"Xander's just jealous, you know. He has a secret, desperate yearning to be famous."

"It's not so secret," Miles said darkly. "In fact, it's hard to miss."

Kian burst out laughing. "True."

"You're too nice to him."

"I'm too nice to everyone," Kian said, which was also true. "I'll leave you alone to your geometric wonders."

When Miles finally finished the dinner service, he had gold dust under his fingernails and a shit ton of sleepy grit in his eyes. He tossed his bike into the back of Kian's little hatchback, and barely remembered his head hitting the pillow.

His phone blared shrilly, interrupting Miles' deep dreamless sleep.

His hand shot out of the covers and grabbed what he thought might be the shape of his phone. Not bothering to look at the screen, he blindly pressed the answer button.

"What," he barked. It better not be Xander, waking him up to go for a jog. Or Kian, trying to be cute and failing.

"You're famous!" his little sister Gina sang into the speaker, sounding even brighter than she normally did.

Miles groaned and fell back to his pillow. "What time is it?"

"I waited until nine, at least," Gina said. "I've got a class in five, I just wanted to tell you that you're famous, in case you missed it somehow."

"You'd be surprised," Miles told her wryly, because he'd pulled an extra-long shift and then fallen asleep. He hadn't exactly had time in the last twenty-four hours to wrap his head around his sudden, inexplicable fame.

"What class?" he asked before she could tell him the breadth of what he'd neglected by choosing sleep. He didn't get a lot of time to talk to Gina since she'd started at Cal in the fall, and he'd missed their chats.

"Philosophy 101," Gina said, and he could hear her eye roll.

"Not enjoying it?" he asked. He'd chosen to go to culinary school instead of college, and it had absolutely been the right choice for him, but he was thrilled at the brave step Gina was taking. She was one of his favorite people—smart and funny and bright as the sun—and she was the first of his family to go to college. He couldn't think of anyone better suited to fight for what she deserved.

"Oh, it's plenty dumb at points," Gina said. "Like whether we're actually not here, but figments of someone's imagination. Of *course* we're actually here. It's just . . ."

Miles heard her pause, and he was still wiping the sleepy cobwebs from his brain so it took him a long second to catch up to why she was hesitating. "What is it?" he finally asked. "What happened?" He was still, and would always be, a big brother.

"There's this guy," she said, frustration evident in her voice. "He argues with *everything* I say. I'm not sure he even agrees with what he's saying, but it doesn't seem to matter."

"He sounds like an ass." What he sounded like was a guy with a crush on Miles' baby sister, and no idea how to go about getting her attention like an adult. Miles wanted to punch him in the face.

"He definitely is," Gina said, and though she didn't say it, Miles could hear the hesitation in her tone. She didn't think he was an ass at all. And just like that, Miles realized that she probably wouldn't be his baby sister for much longer. At least not in her mind. She was eighteen and in college and discovering the world.

"I've got to go," Gina continued, "but don't think I didn't notice you changed the subject. We still need to talk about *you*, big bro."

"Someday," Miles said.

"Sooner rather than later," Gina insisted.

After she hung up, Miles hesitated before unlocking his phone again. Did he even want to look? When he finally did, he grimaced. If the avalanche of notifications yesterday had been daunting, the pile this morning was insurmountable.

He wasn't sure if it was a good or a bad thing that René had told him he wouldn't need to be in until four today.

He debated whether he wanted coffee or not—not a real debate, more like whether Miles wanted to pull on pants and stumble into the kitchen—and he'd just about made up his mind that coffee was required if he was going to slog through his phone when there was a knock on the door.

Miles pushed his hair back and grabbed a pair of loose sweats on the floor by the bed. Pulling them on, he opened the door to Kian's way too bright smile.

It was hard to scowl at all that cheerfulness, but Miles was a pro and managed it just fine.

"I brought you coffee," Kian said, extending a cup filled to the brim. "Two sugars, dark as sludge."

Miles eyed his roommate suspiciously. "Why are you being so nice to me?"

"I'm always nice." This was partly true. Kian was definitely the nicest of his roommates. Xander and Wyatt could be assholes on a good day. But Kian had a sort of apprehensive puppy dog thing going on this morning, and Miles was naturally suspicious, but he wasn't usually wrong.

"Have you looked at your phone?" Kian asked, sounding way too much like Gina for Miles' peace of mind. If Kian hadn't emphatically expressed his preference for the male sex, Miles might have thought about introducing them.

"Sort of."

Kian shot him a frank look. "Take a closer look," was all he said. "Last I saw, Martha Stewart retweeted it, and then Snoop Dogg picked it up too."

Miles' jaw dropped open. "Snoop Dogg retweeted my video?"

"I mean, have you even watched that cooking show he hosts with Martha?" Kian rambled, as Miles clumsily unlocked his phone after three tries and sat down on the bed, coffee abandoned to the bedside table as he scrolled through some of his notifications.

"I don't get it," Miles finally said, looking up and realizing that Kian was still expectantly standing in the doorway. "Most viral stuff has a good hook. This was a video of me . . . baking tarts."

"But you've never showed yourself as much as you did in this one," Kian pointed out. "And, honestly, you looked pretty cute and intense, hair falling in your face, and I think at one point you might've had some raspberry puree smeared across your cheek."

Miles stared at his friend.

"You did watch it before you posted it, didn't you?" Kian asked awkwardly. He was so young—okay, not that much younger than Miles, but in your twenties, sometimes three years felt like an eternity—and sort of naïve. Very naïve, depending on the moment.

"Technically yes." Miles thought back to the morning two days ago when he'd gotten approximately three hours of sleep on a marble slab and decided he might not have been entirely coherent enough to do the editing justice. "But I was a little tired at the time. I probably thought the raspberry puree gave me a sort of rakish charm."

"It totally did," Kian said, very loyally. Kian was much nicer than Xander. Since Xander had yet to give him shit over the puree that must mean he hadn't seen it yet. Miles hoped that state continued for a long time, though considering the way the video was spreading, he probably wouldn't get that lucky.

"So I looked . . . funny?" Miles asked, unable to keep the desperation out of his tone.

"No, no," Kian corrected quickly. "You just look really intense and cute and driven. It's a good video, and people like it for the right reasons, I promise. Plus, the tarts look delicious—and they tasted even better, by the way."

"Okay." Miles took a deep breath. "Is it totally weird if I didn't want this to happen?"

Kian's gaze grew sympathetic. "Uh, no. It's a lot of scrutiny. I'm not sure Chef Aquino will like it, if I'm being totally honest."

That was something Miles had not even considered. Chef Aquino was notoriously driven by his gigantic ego. Where Terroir was concerned, he didn't like anybody else stealing the spotlight. Especially a lowly pastry assistant.

"He seemed okay with it two days ago," Miles said.

"Miles," Kian said, "*Snoop Dogg* retweeted it. He's probably not okay with it now."

Miles had difficulty wrapping his head around Chef Aquino even knowing who Snoop Dogg was, never mind caring what he thought of the video, but Kian was almost always right when it came to Chef Aquino. Chef had hand-picked Kian from his culinary school's graduating class and had taken him on as a special assistant. From what Miles could figure out, that mostly meant that Kian got to bear the brunt of their overbearing boss. But no matter how many times Chef yelled at Kian, or generally embarrassed him in front of the rest of the staff, Kian still worshipped him.

Personally, Miles thought there might be a little more than hero worship going on there, but he wasn't going to open that bag of worms anytime soon. If Kian was smart, he'd get over it and move on. If Kian wasn't smart, he'd eventually get chewed up and spit out by their illustrious leader. Miles liked Kian a lot, and hoped the kid could keep his head on straight.

"Well, I'll find out tonight," Miles said. "I don't have to go in 'til four though." He already knew what he'd be doing the rest of the day, and even though he knew he should be celebrating his success, all he felt was a mild dread. He hadn't set out to become popular or famous, and he wasn't sure how this video would ultimately impact his fairly simple life. A life he liked *because* it was simple.

"Drink your coffee," Kian ordered. "I'll see you tonight."

Miles slunk into the staff entrance at Terroir at fifteen minutes to four. He'd drunk three cups of Kian's excellent coffee, almost fully cleared out his notifications, and had even had a little time to start wrapping his head around what had just happened to him.

With a decent night's sleep and some high-quality caffeine in him, Miles found he could actually enjoy the really positive comments to the video. Especially flattering, though bordering on creepy in some moments, were the many people who seemed to want to pick him up. Men and women both, and Miles realized that he'd never outright stated on his *Pastry by Miles* page that he was gay. Oh well, it wasn't like he was taking anybody up on any of the offers—even the ones that seemed particularly attractive. And there had been more than a few of those.

His only real concern remained Chef Aquino's developing reaction to the video's unexpected success. Kian hadn't texted him any red alerts during the afternoon, so Miles could only pray that Chef Aquino was still okay with it. He was even harboring a secret hope that the popularity of the video had only made Chef more determined to feature the tart as a special dessert.

"Costa," Chef René barked out as he caught sight of him slinking into the break room to put his bag in his locker.

"Yes, Chef?" Miles asked.

"There's someone to see you," he said.

"Chef Aquino?" Miles began to sweat a little under his whites.

Chef René shook his head. "No, someone else. They're on the terrace, waiting for you."

Miles definitely was sweating now. Was he going to be fired? He'd done good work here—nothing innovative, because Chef René wasn't that kind of chef—but he'd created solid and consistent product. He'd never even explicitly stated in his videos that he worked at Terroir, though a few commenters had voiced their suspicions that he did when he'd mentioned working at a famous restaurant. He'd never confirmed anything, but even though there were a lot of top-notch restaurants in Napa, there was only one with Michelin stars, and that was Terroir.

He walked through the empty restaurant, the tables already sparkling with glassware and silver, out the side door, and onto the terrace. Terroir overlooked some of the vineyards Napa was famous for, and the terrace was one of the most prized dining areas in California—probably in the whole United States. Trellised ivy and grapevines wound around the brick stonework of the building, and even though the terrace was technically outside, every inch was swept and pristine. Miles thought Chef Aquino probably even frightened the bugs away.

There was a man on the end of the terrace, sampling a cheese platter, with a glass of sparkling wine at his elbow. He had dark hair, shaved close, and a broad set of muscular shoulders that his white t-shirt only seemed to emphasize. He looked up with dark, intense eyes as Miles approached.

"You're Reed Ryan," Miles said, before the man could introduce himself. He couldn't believe he hadn't recognized him the second he'd spotted him. Xander worshipped the man something fierce, both for his incredible culinary expertise and also because he was seriously hot. Miles had teased Xander more times than he could count about hanging a poster of Reed Ryan above his bed, and now he was here, in the flesh.

Xander was going to eat his heart out when he discovered who'd come to see Miles. He'd never mock *Pastry by Miles* ever again, not if the site drew Reed Ryan up to Napa.

"And you're Miles." Reed stood and offered a firm handshake. "Sit down." He gestured to the glass. "Would you like some wine?"

Miles shook his head. "Sorry, but no, I'm on shift tonight."

"Right, of course," Reed said. "Well, I'm sure you're wondering why I asked to meet with you."

Miles was desperately curious. He knew Reed had closed his famous Chicago restaurant, Garnet, and had disappeared for a year or so, reappearing on the West Coast, but he couldn't remember what it was that Reed was doing now. Xander had certainly told him, probably more than once, but Miles blocked out most of the shit Xander said.

"I didn't realize you'd opened another restaurant," Miles said as Reed selected a chunk of brie and popped it in his mouth.

"I haven't," Reed said. "I'm the culinary producer at *Five Points*." *Five Points* was a pop culture and sports website that had been recently branching into short culinary video series.

Miles now remembered all those rants Xander had subjected him to about Reed Ryan wasting all his talent by selling out.

"I've been following *Pastry by Miles* for awhile," Reed continued, picking through the thinly sliced meats on the tray. "I had always planned to offer you a show on our site, but after the last forty-eight hours, I decided I'd better get up here and do it before someone else beat me to the punch."

"A show on *Five Points*?" Miles asked skeptically. "You teach people how to bake bread out of melted ice cream. How to make edible cookie dough out of garbanzo beans. *Pastry by Miles* is a serious pastry blog."

Reed shot Miles a very frank look. "I'm a serious chef, Mr. Costa. I want to make a serious pastry show. Believe it or not, I have higher ambitions than teaching the masses how to make a dessert with three ingredients or less. I want to teach them what good pastry is about. And I think you're exactly the person to do that."

Garnet had been legendary in the food scene. It was hard to picture a Reed Ryan who didn't take the culinary arts very seriously. But there was still a whisper in the back of his head that *he'd* be selling out if he quit to film a show for *Five Points*. He wouldn't be able to come back to Terroir. His job wouldn't be waiting for him. Chef Aquino might let him go, but he'd never forgive Miles for moving on, no matter how unfair that might be.

"How much input would I have into the show?" Miles asked, because that, more than anything else, felt very important. He wasn't going to dumb down his ideas for anybody. He wasn't going to be subject to someone else's vision, not if he was going to take the drastic step of walking away from employment at one of the very best restaurants in the world.

"There would be a producer. Me, maybe, or someone else. Maybe my assistant, Evan. I've been looking to promote him, and your show would be a great fit. But the process at *Five Points* is collaborative." He paused. "I said it before, but I'll say it again. I don't have any intention of dumbing down your skill. I want something accessible, but elevated. I want you to teach people about pastry."

When he'd begun *Pastry by Miles*, he'd wanted to share his creativity with people who weren't just his roommates or his family. He'd wanted a way to express his vision without being constantly shut down.

"How long do I have to think about it?" Miles asked.

"As long as you need," Reed said. "But I guarantee there will be others after me. That video was *very* good, Mr. Costa. I'll email you over a sample contract with compensation attached. But everything is negotiable."

"Thanks, I'll be in touch," Miles said, getting to his feet, his fingers already itching to check his email and see how much Reed was offering him to leave Terroir and everything familiar. "I've got to get back to my prep."

If he detoured through the locker room and grabbed his phone to check his email, who could blame him? He scrolled through Reed's email, and his jaw dropped open at the offering bid for fifteen episodes. That was two years of salary at Terroir, plus there were stipulations about housing and moving costs *and* additional bonuses if certain benchmarks were met.

Miles hadn't gotten into the culinary business to make money—most chefs weren't rich, or even close to rich, but he couldn't deny the money held an attractive appeal.

Later, as he was making yet another tray of white chocolate lemon mousse pyramids, sure he would be dreaming about gold dust, Miles thought that the money paled in comparison to the opportunity to do whatever he wanted, whenever he wanted. True creative vision. And extra bonus: no more white chocolate lemon mousse pyramids and no more gold dust.

Miles biked home because it was a gorgeous night—clear and with just the right amount of briskness in the air. He couldn't deny he was avoiding his friends because they'd try to talk him out of leaving. Especially Xander, because he was the most vocal of the three—though Miles knew he'd get arguments from all of them. They knew just how special finding a place at Terroir was, and then how much work and determination and thick skin went into staying there.

It wouldn't be something they'd want him to give up lightly, but Miles realized as he pulled into the drive that he'd been ready to move on for awhile now. Why else feel compelled to start *Pastry by Miles* at all? He shouldn't need to come home from a long, exhausting shift, and bake. As far as Miles was concerned, he should feel creatively fulfilled at the position he'd worked his ass off for.

And if that wasn't the case anymore, then he *should* move on. It was the right thing to do, Miles knew as he walked into the house, but it didn't make telling his friends any easier.

It was after midnight, and they'd all worked at least ten hours today, but when he walked into the living room, Xander and Wyatt were on the couch, and Kian was sprawled next to them on the floor. The TV was tuned to ESPN, which meant Wyatt had picked the channel, but when Miles walked in, he muted it.

Three sets of eyes swiveled his direction.

"So Reed Ryan came to see you today?" Xander's statement was phrased like a question, but it wasn't like Miles could deny it. He slumped into an old chair and let his bag fall to the floor.

"Yeah, he came to see me."

Xander scooted to the edge of the couch. "And you didn't come get me?"

"It wasn't that kind of visit." Miles hesitated and then continued before Xander could reload again. "Listen, I know you're all going to try to talk me out of it, and that's fine, but I've made up my mind. I'm giving my two weeks tomorrow."

Xander and Wyatt didn't look all that surprised, but Kian turned to him, accusation and dismay all over his delicate features. "You're really going to quit? I heard people talking, saying you might, and that's why Reed Ryan came by, but I didn't believe them. I couldn't believe them. Miles, you've more than earned your place at Terroir."

"I've earned it yeah, but that doesn't mean I enjoy it."

Sacrilege, to admit he didn't love every chef's dream job, but it felt so good to finally say it out loud.

"You really mean that," Wyatt said with disbelief. "It's not the money? I was sure Ryan threw a bunch of money at you."

He had, and maybe Miles should have used that reason, instead of the truth. But the more he thought about it, the more he realized how all of them had been restricted and restrained by Chef Aquino's iron-clad rule. Every single one of them had their own point of view as a chef, and none of them were expressing it.

And Miles couldn't help but think that was just sad.

"Someday, you're going to understand, I promise," he said.

Kian made a scoffing noise, and Wyatt rolled his eyes.

Xander didn't say a word. Miles supposed he should be relieved that Xander was so unusually quiet, but Xander was also one of his best friends. And for someone who loved to argue and express all his opinions, all the time, the silence was sort of galling. Like Xander had already given up on him.

"I'm sorry I'm going to leave you without a fourth roommate," Miles added, though he knew with the addition of Kian eight months ago, it wouldn't be as tough of a financial hardship.

"We'll manage," Wyatt said.

Xander scowled, and Miles just couldn't help himself. "Aren't you even going to attempt to change my mind?" he asked, but Xander just shrugged.

"You've already made up your mind. It would be a waste of breath."

Miles got to his feet. "I'll see you guys tomorrow, I'm wiped." And he realized as he headed towards his room, that he'd only have two more weeks of waking up and heading into the restaurant with his friends.

On the flip side, he only had two more weeks of Chef René's insultingly obvious questions and only two more weeks of white chocolate lemon mousse pyramids.

Chapter Two

Evan Patterson was used to people not understanding his choices.

When his boss had asked if he wanted to come with him to a world-famous restaurant, renowned throughout the globe for its food and its ambiance, to meet with the man whose show he would very likely be producing, it had been easy to turn Reed down.

It wasn't Evan's pitch that was going to win Miles Costa over to the idea of leaving Terroir and everything he knew behind; it was Reed Ryan, culinary star a little dented and tarnished but still present and still glowing.

"But you'll be working with him. Closely. Don't you want to meet him?" Reed had protested. A token protest. He was great in the kitchen, and also great at inspiring his underlings to follow in his culinary footsteps, but he was not good at business. Evan was and they both knew it, so it usually wasn't very tough to convince Reed that Evan was right.

"I've already met him," Evan had said, pointing to his laptop screen, where he'd been compiling a dossier on Miles Costa. A dossier he'd started long before the latest *Pastry by Miles'* video had gone viral.

So Reed had gone to Terroir alone, and come back to a signed contract, and an assistant who was now officially a producer.

Evan's decisions might be considered strange, but nobody could ever argue with the results.

Reed recognized this and also Evan's value, which was why Evan had already decided not to usurp his job eventually. Evan needed Reed to be the esteemed figurehead, and while everyone was oohing and aahing over Reed's big muscles and all his culinary credibility, Evan would be behind the scenes, getting shit done.

The promotion was nice though, and Evan had every intention of paying back his boss and mentor's faith in him in spades.

Evan straightened his shirt and glanced over at his boss, who was scribbling on a piece of paper as he leaned over the receptionist's desk. Either a new idea for *Dream Team*, the one show Reed still produced, or a new recipe he'd just thought of. Evan returned his attention to the elevator and its closed doors.

He'd planned very carefully for this day. Not just after he'd been hired for the *Five Points* internship. Not just after he'd gotten into college. Not just after he'd won valedictorian at high school graduation. He'd known much earlier than that, that one day he'd be someone people looked to, that people followed, at a place where he would be taken seriously.

All those other days had been stepping stones to *this* day.

The elevator doors dinged open, depositing Miles Costa on the carpet in front of him.

Evan had been studying Miles for months. He didn't vet dates with as much scrutiny as he had Miles Costa—which probably explained his extensive date-less drought—and he'd expected very little surprise facing him for the first time.

But Miles did surprise him. Shocked him, in fact. He walked up, his cloudy gray eyes lazy but direct, dark wavy hair a tousled mass on his head, and Evan felt a thrill in a place he'd never felt a thrill before.

He'd known Miles was handsome and very possibly charismatic. That was one of the reasons he'd been an easy selection as a candidate. He had a way of making you like him that was subtle and easy—you just slid right in.

Evan didn't just slide, he catapulted.

"Miles Costa," the man in front of him said, extending a hand. Evan was dimly aware of Reed straightening next to him, and shoving the paper in his pocket.

Evan reached out and shook Miles' hand, and even though his brain felt sluggish and distracted by the way Miles' lips tilted up in a half smirk, managed to introduce himself. "Evan Patterson."

Miles turned to Reed, and they shook hands "How badly did Aquino take it?" Reed asked. "I didn't hear from him so he must not have been too pissed off."

The gray eyes turned thoughtful, and Evan swore he saw a little worry there, but before he could look closer, it was gone. He told himself he was watching so carefully not because Miles was so carelessly handsome, but because he needed to figure out how Miles Costa ticked so he could control him.

"Actually," Miles said, "he wasn't all that pissed."

"Well, we're really happy you're at *Five Points*," Reed said warmly. He could be socially awkward; in fact, Evan was almost certain he had social anxiety, but he had gotten better at hiding it. Evan also recognized when Reed was passing the torch onto him, and he stepped in, smoothly, like they'd discussed it ahead of time even though they hadn't.

"I've been watching *Pastry by Miles* almost since the very beginning," Evan said. "What Reed told you is true. You've been on our radar for a long time."

"I'm honestly excited to be here. I'm looking forward to something different, if I'm being honest."

Reed chuckled. "Well, you and Evan will get along like a house on fire then. He's sort of unapologetically blunt."

It was true, but Reed didn't need to go around sharing all of Evan's secrets during the first five minutes. "Don't you have that meeting?" he asked his boss pointedly. He didn't have a meeting, but Evan knew how happy Reed would be to escape. This was the part of his job that he didn't love.

"Right, well, I just wanted to stop by and say welcome, and we're so happy you're here," Reed said. "Evan will take good care of you. He'll give you a tour and show you your office and the kitchen. And then you two can get started."

Evan was watching closely, or he might not have noticed Miles' eyes grow cloudier. "Thanks again," Miles said, voice normal. Except that Evan didn't think he'd imagined any of the undercurrents running through his new partner.

Miles might have a laid-back, casual attitude, but Evan had a feeling that there was a lot more to him than met the eye.

"Let's start with a tour," Evan said, trying to tone down his own tendency to take control over everything. "I'm sure you're dying to see the kitchen."

"Sounds good to me," Miles said casually.

They went on a quick tour of the office, with Evan pointing out the bathrooms, the conference rooms, Evan's cubicle, and Miles', which was right next door. Miles looked around the tiny box, setting his messenger bag on the small desk, and Evan wished he could read minds as his new partner took in his surroundings.

He was exceptionally difficult to read, and Evan didn't like that at all. He wanted to know where he stood. The unknown was a scary place, full of pitfalls and potential failure lingering at the end like a bad smell.

"We film at a local studio," Evan said as they entered the kitchens. "We don't have the room or the resources here, but eventually we're going to move to a bigger space and we'll build our own soundstage. So we do all our prep here, practicing and perfecting the rundown of the show, and then we film the final product at the other studio."

The other man glanced around the kitchen, his eyes not missing a thing, from the commercial appliances to the long stainless steel counters.

"I filmed with way less than this at my house," Miles pointed out. "Maybe we could figure out how to do small stuff here."

Evan didn't want to tell him that it had *looked* like Miles filmed in an unprofessional environment and that part of the bonus of signing with *Five Points* was his production value was going to undergo a significant upgrade.

"We'll see," was all Evan said. He wasn't willing to promise anything more. They had certain standards at *Five Points*, and Evan not only intended to honor them, but to exceed them. And there was no way they could do that with some sort of cobbled-together video they did in the test kitchens.

"Reed runs the kitchens, then?" Miles asked. Evan wasn't sure he liked the hopeful note in Miles' voice, because he needed Miles to like him—for purely professional reasons, of course. But even as he insisted on this to himself, Evan knew he was lying.

Evan could admit that complicated an already potentially complex business partnership, but Evan was also willing to be flexible if it meant great results. *Dream Team*, the first show *Five Points* had done, had paired together two people already in a relationship, and even though the culinary side was well-developed, the reason it had such a high viewership was how charming Landon Patton and Quentin Maxwell were together. *Dream Team* had changed Evan's perspective about what could and what could not work in a TV environment.

"Reed is the executive producer and the director of the test kitchens, yes," Evan said. "But the day-to-day manager of the kitchens is Lucy. If you need anything specific, you ask her."

Miles glanced over, and Evan's skin burned as his gaze skimmed over him. "And you?"

"Me?" Evan clarified, proud that his voice hadn't come out squeaking, like he'd regressed about a dozen years. He'd won his confidence with a shit ton of hard work, and he didn't like how this man dismantled it so easily. It was infuriating.

"Your position here," Miles clarified.

Evan was not thrilled. Reed was supposed to have covered all this stuff in the contract and Miles was already supposed to know they were going to be working together closely. Evan wasn't supposed to have to break it to him.

"I'm the producer of your show. We're going to be working together. A lot."

One discernible emotion out of the man in the last fifteen minutes, and it had to be dismay at being paired with Evan.

"Reed didn't tell me that you had any culinary experience. I assumed he'd be my producer, since he has the background," Miles said, and Evan realized that this was the laid-back Miles' way of issuing a protest at who he'd been stuck with.

Evan liked this even less. His ego was smarting more than he wanted to admit. He hadn't ever anticipated that *Miles Costa*, that super cute guy who he'd been admiring for months, would be such a jerk.

"I have a degree in business, with an emphasis on marketing," Evan said, trying to tamp down the testy edge to his voice. "I've also been Reed's assistant for almost two years. I know how to produce a successful program."

Miles shot him an almost pitying look. As if the degree Evan had worked his ass off for meant nothing. "But do you know anything about pastry?"

"You do," Evan said, and the confidence he felt was genuine. The way Miles had always been able to pare down difficult concepts and explain them was brilliant. He'd be great at showing a brand-new audience how to bake in a way they hadn't experienced before. And Evan's job was to provide that audience.

On paper, they were a great team, something that Reed had unhesitatingly stated more than once. But now that he and Miles were standing in front of each other, Evan wondered if he and Reed had made a miscalculation.

They hadn't taken into consideration that Miles Costa was quite possibly a culinary snob who didn't like to bother with anyone lacking his training.

"Right," Miles said, and he did not look convinced.

Evan decided this wasn't the right moment to argue the point and definitely not the right place—right in the middle of a kitchen that he'd never used, so he changed the subject. "Let's swing by IT and get your laptop."

Miles followed and didn't argue so Evan took that as a success, then dropped him at his cubicle, with a promise to get him for their first brainstorming session in a few hours. Reed had already promised to take Miles by the cafeteria for lunch. Maybe after spending time with a chef of Reed's culinary pedigree, and realizing how committed *Five Points* was to authenticity, Miles would soften his stance.

After a quick lunch at his desk, Evan went to the bathroom to wash his hands and to give himself a pep talk in the mirror.

Opportunities like this didn't come around very often and he wasn't going to blow the first big one he'd ever been handed. Once they started working on Miles' show, he would see that Evan was just as committed as he was to making it a success.

When he returned to his cubicle to grab his laptop and to fetch Miles next door, for a split second, Evan considered leaving behind all the prep work he'd been doing on his vision of *Pastry by Miles*.

But all of it was important market research and branding. Stuff that Miles needed, whether he admitted it or not. Stuff he needed to develop if he wanted to expand beyond retweets by Snoop Dogg.

It had been very clear to Evan from the beginning of *Pastry by Miles* that Miles had no real marketing plan, and that's all this was, Evan justified to himself. He took the folder and hated that Miles had made him question his motives.

"What did you think of the cafeteria?" Evan asked as they set up in one of the smaller meeting rooms.

Miles wrinkled his nose. "It was okay, I guess."

Reed had been appalled when he'd first started at *Five Points* at the quality of the building's cafeteria, and had worked hard to improve the quality of the food they served. They still didn't do everything well, but they'd made huge strides. It was definitely better than anything that Evan could cook himself. Which, he realized, was the root of Miles' problem.

It wasn't too hard to imagine him feeling regret at taking this step, but Evan still believed they could make this work. There was a reason they'd been spending months looking over the market and the talent available, and had ultimately decided on Miles.

"Maybe you can give Reed some suggestions on how to improve," Evan said. "He doesn't technically run the food service, but he has a lot of influence and works with them frequently."

"We already discussed it," Miles said, making it very clear that he was done discussing food-related topics with someone who apparently couldn't understand them. Which was going to make the next two hours rather difficult.

Evan decided there was no point in further procrastinating. "I thought it might be helpful to start with a rundown of the videos you've produced so far, and talk about where we might make improvements, and what facets we would want to keep for your show here."

But instead of just *agreeing*, Miles shoved his long, tapered fingers through dark curls and pinned Evan with an adversarial look that Evan knew he should have found entirely obnoxious, but instead of simply being annoying, it was intense and left Evan feeling unsettled. Exposed. Warmer than he liked.

"So you bring me in here," Miles said, "and claim you want me so badly to sign with you, so badly you send a famous chef to meet with me, then when I agree to film videos for you, you stick me with some marketing guru who doesn't know anything about pastry who wants to change everything." He leaned back and folded his arms. "Why?"

"I didn't send anyone," Evan argued. "Reed wanted to go, and he's the boss." Technically true, but also partly a lie.

"I think you'd understand, being some marketing expert, what false advertising is. You lured me here with Reed, because you knew I'd never agree to work with you."

"You're working with me because your show needs to improve its marketing angle and develop some polish," Evan said through gritted teeth. "And I bet you that's what Reed told you when you complained to him at lunch."

Miles gave a short bark of laughter. "Sort of, yeah." For the first time, Evan felt the spark of Miles' natural charm. He wanted to pettily reject it, but also bask in the novelty of experiencing it for the first time in person.

"You want things to be perfect, even if they're unstudied in their perfection," Evan said, pulling out every persuasive technique he'd learned in a lifetime of bad living situations. "I can help you with that."

Miles looked intrigued, but not completely convinced, but Evan decided that maybe it would be better to show, not tell. "For example," he said, pulling out his notes from the folder he'd brought in, "you experimented with a lot of different camera angles and placements while you were filming. Every episode is slightly different. I can help figure out the best one and then standardize it. Do you want to be featured on camera? Not on camera? Just a pair of hands?"

"Someone told me my last video was so successful because I was on it more," Miles said, but he sounded skeptical.

Evan did not want to say that *yes*, everyone ate up that footage because there was nothing hotter than a good-looking person absorbed in what they were creating. Even to the point of missing a smear of pink pastry cream across one chiseled cheekbone.

"There were definitely factors that helped that video spread virally," Evan said. "I can help you recreate them."

Miles nodded. It wasn't exactly enthusiastic, but it was something, and even Evan couldn't work with nothing.

"I didn't think I'd care if people watched my videos or not," Miles admitted, and Evan barely restrained from doing a little cheer at the man *finally* revealing something about what he was looking for from this partnership, "but I liked it. I started making them for me, and I never thought about my audience. But then a million people watched the last one, and that was pretty cool."

"Try five point six million," Evan said.

"Jesus, I had no idea it was that high."

Evan realized that Miles wasn't being humble; he really had no idea what his stats were like. And that did shed some light on how the man ticked. He lived for his work and his kitchen.

"So you didn't get into this for the fame, obviously," Evan said. "Why did you start?"

Evan couldn't believe it, but Miles flushed. It was almost very nearly a blush. Evan felt his own skin flame hotter in response. "I was bored at work, if you could believe it. And my sister missed seeing me bake. So I posted it for her, really." Miles went a tiny bit darker red and Evan had a sudden visceral image of their bare skin pressed together, damp and warm. "It sounds silly, doesn't it? I made the first video just for my sister, and five point six million people saw the last one."

"It's actually pretty incredible." Evan paused. "And it's just the beginning. The sky's the limit."

Miles leaned back in his chair, and actually laughed. "You really mean that."

Evan rolled his eyes. "Like Reed said, I'm annoyingly honest." What Evan didn't say was that he had believed in Miles almost as much as he'd always believed in himself. The belief was currently a little tarnished, but Evan knew it wouldn't take much encouragement from Miles to bring it—or his ill-advised crush—back to their former states.

Considering how far they'd gotten in the last five minutes by just *talking*, Evan decided they could do an analysis of the old videos later. He didn't want to do anything to remind Miles that he was the interloper trying to take over the show he'd started as a way of keeping in touch with his sister.

That was sort of cute, actually. It made Evan wish that he knew how to bake. Or that he'd had a sister.

Still, it was better to stick to non-confrontational topics. So Evan opened up his internet browser, and another food site that did videos. He turned the screen so Miles could see it. "I didn't know they let you watch those," Miles said wryly. "Aren't they the enemy?"

"It's research," Evan said. "We're going to go through these videos and you tell me everything you like and everything you don't."

Evan figured that criticizing other people would probably keep Miles from going rogue until Evan could figure out a new way to plan the next season of *Pastry by Miles*.

Evan came home to his apartment—and tried not to think of Miles doing the same, only a door away. The first thing he did was pour himself a very large glass of wine.

It was a Tuesday but he had fucking earned this wine. Miles had spent almost three hours complaining about everything in the other videos. He had lots to say, though most of his criticism was culinary-based. Even though the plan was to keep Miles focused on other people than Evan, every time Miles had pointed out something that was wrong, he'd pointedly glanced over at Evan. Basically, he was never going to let Evan forget that his degree was in business and not croissants.

Usually Evan did some form of work in the evenings, but tonight he didn't even want to open his laptop. Miles had managed to make Evan hate his job, albeit temporarily. He was a horrid pain in the ass, and Evan tried to dig up some motivation because he needed to find a way out of this situation. *Not out,* Evan corrected, *he wasn't going to give Miles what he wanted and quit.*

No, he needed to figure out a way to change up the dynamic. He needed something to put Miles at ease and stop feeling like he needed to fight Evan all the time. Goddamn it, he wanted Miles to like him. Even if it wasn't ever in *that* way.

Tomorrow had to be better than today was. If it was any worse, Evan was seriously considering smacking Miles for being an asshole. And that wouldn't make Miles like him any more than he already didn't.

Evan's stomach grumbled, and he opened his fridge with a glare and a wrench. Empty, of course. A half-empty bottle of orange juice and a sad glass jar of mustard adorned the shelves. He was going to need to order in, again. And then it hit him.

He needed to emphasize to Miles that they agreed food was at the center of his videos. What better way to convince him than to put him back in the kitchen?

Pizza first, Evan thought, *plan later.*

Miles poured himself a big glass of red wine and thought, *I fucking earned this.*

He'd known this transition would be hard. He'd spent his entire professional life in prestigious restaurant kitchens where marketing was something the PR reps dealt with so diners would pay hundreds of dollars to eat at the latest and greatest.

Miles had personally always thought of it as an inside joke, something completely made up. Not something real and concrete that people spent time and effort to research. He sort of figured that he'd design the show, film the episodes, and then the marketing guys would come in and figure out what sort of bullshit they needed to say about it so people would watch.

As it turned out, that was not how it worked at all. It turned out that Miles was going to be saddled with some marketing "expert" who would be criticizing and forcing him into changing everything along the way until the end result only vaguely resembled Miles' initial vision.

That Evan guy was determined, Miles thought as he opened his fridge and perused the contents. Cute, because Miles was human and he couldn't avoid thinking it more than once today, but annoyingly determined.

At lunch, Reed had said they'd had the fridge and pantry stocked for him. And it had definitely been done with a chef in mind, with a plethora of fresh ingredients. The apartment itself felt like an accidental luxury, all open rooms and this enormous kitchen with fantastic natural light.

Miles had planned on coming back to his apartment and getting so drunk that he wouldn't have to think about Evan's sour milk expression every time Miles opened his mouth—or his light-brown, crème brulee eyes that reminded Miles of one of his favorite desserts. But maybe there was something he could do to make tomorrow marginally better. Maybe there was a way he could win Evan over to his side. Maybe there was a way to control Evan other than disparaging him. It wouldn't be a hardship, Miles thought as he sipped the wine, he was good-looking, and Miles was attracted to him. Of course, Miles was attracted to most good-looking men, but with all the couples at *Five Points*, there wasn't a reason not to act on it. It wasn't against the rules. He could see Evan flustered and warm, bow tie dangling, sleeves rolled up, a slight dusting of flour on his cheek. Lips swollen pink from Miles' mouth.

It would be easy. Maybe too easy.

Miles turned back to the fridge. Maybe there was a way to kill two birds with one stone.

Chapter Three

"I've been looking for you." Miles looked up to see his brand-new partner standing in the doorway of his cubicle. He still wasn't sure how he felt about the cubicle thing, but he definitely knew how he felt about Evan. Miles gave himself a little mental pat on the back for the annoyed edge in Evan's voice, and then another that he was ignoring how incredible Evan's ass looked in those tight jeans.

Maybe it was petty or childish, but it felt so satisfying. Miles had spent time around lots of egotistical perfectionists over the years, but none of them had ever had a stick up their ass quite the same way Evan Patterson did.

"I've been sitting right here. For at least an hour." Miles leaned back, and enjoyed the way Evan's face struggled to find control. He also just plain enjoyed Evan's face, but those gorgeous brown eyes or his blond hair, and not even the slim, cute body he was showcasing in those skinny jeans could entice Miles to get in bed with someone so uptight.

Evan walked into the cubicle, and glanced down at Miles' laptop screen. He pointed to the left of the laptop, where a neon-green Post-it note read, "Join me in the kitchen when you get here," in what must be Evan's neat handwriting.

Miles thought Evan could have sold his handwriting to some font website, and hipsters would be falling all over themselves to buy it.

"Oh, I didn't see that." Miles didn't even attempt to sound convincing. Anyway, they both knew he was lying.

Evan crossed his arms and his eyes shot bullets. It made him look cuter—and also more terrifying, if you were into that sort of thing. Which Miles was not.

Definitely not. He'd told himself last night that he wasn't going to try to seduce Evan to control him. This morning, the prospect looked a lot more appealing.

Or maybe that was just Evan.

"What have you even been doing?" Evan asked.

This was the opening Miles had been dying for. "I'm so glad you asked. I decided to do a little show-and-tell experiment."

Evan didn't look convinced. Or amused. Which only amused Miles further. He wasn't usually such an asshole, but he wasn't going to share control of *Pastry by Miles* with anyone, especially a marketing "expert" like Evan. He'd only had to be in his new partner's presence for approximately ten point two seconds to realize that Evan was the kind that didn't give up easily. Thus, Miles' attitude shift to being as annoying as possible. Miles had a little sister; there was no way Evan could hold out against the pain and suffering Miles could bring him.

Miles clicked on the video he'd been working on. Evan watched it soundlessly and Miles watched Evan. Other than a very subtle eye twitch, Miles gave Evan a handful of points for reigning in his explosion of annoyance.

"You filmed an episode of your show in your apartment last night," Evan stated.

"I did," Miles said unrepentantly.

"You made a Twinkie."

"Actually," Miles drawled, "it's better known as a Ding Dong. And it's a *homemade* Ding Dong. I don't know if you've ever tried the store-bought version, but this one is infinitely better. Tastes a whole lot less like cardboard."

Evan's eye was twitching harder.

"A Ding Dong," he repeated in disbelief. "How did you even film this? With your phone?"

"Yep," Miles admitted happily. "Rigged it up on one of those fake house plants with some duct tape. Had to drop by Reed's office this morning and let him know how much I appreciated such a stocked apartment. And not just the fridge."

"That was me," Evan said. "I stocked your apartment." He was looking like he'd love to march right over and un-stock it. Miles was delighted. He'd anticipated how this might go, and it was going better than even his wildest expectations. He ignored the little voice that said just how much he'd enjoy it if Evan lost it and threw him down on the desk.

He also ignored what came next in that little fantasy.

Miles shot Evan his most charming smile, but the recipient did not look particularly charmed. "Oh, thank you. It all came in handy, as you can see."

"I can definitely see that." Evan leaned down, and Miles caught a whiff of his cologne. Something tart and lemony. It suited him. "Now you're going to come with me to the kitchen, and we're going to figure out how to work together. On a video of you doing something impressive that isn't a Ding Dong."

"You don't think that would be cute?" Miles asked, and thought maybe he'd taken it a step too far because the look on Evan's face was suddenly not playing around. Having worked in very tough kitchens and then Terroir, Miles was used to people wanting to kill him. He was not used to people who looked like they wanted to kill him slowly, and might enjoy it the whole time.

"Okay," Miles added. "I can do that." He was still chalking this up as a win because anything that put that look on a man's face was worth the effort it took to rig up a phone on a fake ficus tree.

"I know this isn't easy for either of us. But I do think we can make it work." Evan looked like he was repeating something out of a handbook for crisis management. The problem was that he also looked like he meant it. Miles tried to ignore the pulse of guilt at how he'd deliberately tried to rile him up, and mostly failed.

"If you say so," Miles said. He didn't see either of them relinquishing control to the other anytime soon, and he had a feeling that Evan liked compromise just as much as Miles did—basically, not at all.

"I do." Miles was pretty sure Evan was grinding his teeth together. Then he turned and stomped right out of the cubicle.

Miles was still seeing that look of Evan's—the one that promised a slow and painful death if he didn't follow—so he followed.

And if that also meant he got a nice back view of those skinny jeans, he wasn't exactly complaining.

They got to the kitchen, and Evan breezed right by the schedule board that he'd so helpfully and earnestly pointed out yesterday. Miles had just enough time to see that they definitely had not been scheduled for this morning.

Evan stopped by one of the long counters, and gave Miles a frank look that shouldn't have been hot, but apparently was. Miles didn't have a history of liking confrontational men, but either his tastes had changed, or he apparently found Evan a lot more attractive than he wanted to admit.

"Let's see what you can do," Evan said. He gestured around the kitchen. "This is your domain. Bake me something."

Miles ignored the jibe about what he could do. It wasn't worth his time to refute it, and they both knew it. Bastian Aquino wouldn't tolerate someone in his kitchen who didn't know what he was doing.

"What do you like?"

"Me?" Evan sounded disbelieving, like he couldn't imagine Miles wanting to personally bake him something. And honestly, Miles didn't want to, but he had a feeling there was only so much he could fight back against this arrangement without making Reed pissed at him. Reed, while admittedly giving up Garnet, was still *Reed Ryan*. The thought of pissing him off was not a pleasant one.

"You said, and I quote, 'bake me something.' Tell me what you like."

Evan waved a hand. "Oh, I don't really like sweets. So, anything, I guess. It doesn't matter."

There was roaring in his ears as Miles tried to process this statement. "You . . . don't . . . like . . . sweets."

"Are you deaf *and* intractable?" Evan asked archly.

"No, I'm just trying not to . . . cry or something," Miles muttered. "You realize what I create isn't exactly the same as a bag of M&M's or bag of Oreo cookies."

"Of course I do."

Miles tried to keep his temper leashed. It wasn't easy, probably because it felt like Evan was pushing all his buttons, even the ones he liked having pushed. "Tell me what you might like if you liked sweets."

"Apparently once when I was four I ate a whole bag of Reese's peanut butter cups. I vomited them all up afterwards, but I did eat them." Evan didn't even act like this was a horrifying memory.

"Perfect," Miles said, the finished product already emerging in his mind. His recipes usually started with the end product, and worked backward. Each step was a way to achieve what he'd already conceived in his head.

Right now, he was imagining a fluffy deeply peanut butter-y cookie, dotted with the sharp bitterness of dark chocolate chunks.

Evan whipped out a pad and started writing. "What are you doing?" Miles demanded.

"Taking notes," Evan claimed. "This whole experiment is to figure out how you work. I already know how I work. The end goal is to try to mesh something together of the two."

Miles raised a dubious eyebrow. "You really think we can compromise?"

"Not really," Evan admitted. "But I've never given up, ever. I'm not about to start." He hesitated. "What are you doing now?"

"Standing here?"

Evan made a grumpy sound that shouldn't have been as cute as it was. "In your head, silly. What are you *thinking*?"

Miles had never talked about his process before. Everyone had a slightly different one, and nobody usually cared about the intricacies, as long as the end result was good. "I usually construct an idea of what I'm baking in my head first. Then work backwards to figure out the exact recipe steps."

Scribbling away in his notebook, Evan nodded. "What's the idea you're creating today?"

"Peanut butter cookie with dark chocolate chunks," Miles said.

"Now that wasn't so hard," Evan shot back with a sly, challenging look that Miles told himself he hated. He never lied to himself, but he knew he was now.

"Supplies?" Miles asked, changing the subject. He didn't want to trade flirty quips; he wanted to prove to Evan that there was no way they could figure out how to work together.

"What, you haven't already familiarized yourself with the kitchen layout and pantry?" Evan snarked right back. He definitely sounded bitter over Miles filming his own video.

Okay, he probably deserved that. Though baking that Ding Dong had been pretty damn satisfying—almost as satisfying as Evan's reaction to it—it was still on the tip of his tongue to apologize. Only the thought of leaving Terroir, moving to LA, and somehow losing control of *Pastry by Miles* in the process, kept him silent. Ignoring why his base instinct was yelling at him to treat Evan nicer, he trailed after the other man, who pointed out the tucked-away pantry and the big commercial fridges against the far wall.

Evan returned to his pad, scribbling with his eyes down as Miles methodically went through and picked out his ingredients. Setting everything on the counter and beginning to sort through so he could get his *mise en place* set up, he glanced over at his partner.

He knew Evan wasn't going to tell him and so there was no point in asking, but Miles found he couldn't help the question. "What are you writing?"

Evan didn't even glance up. "Terrible, dreadful things."

Miles rolled his eyes.

"I thought you'd already deigned this experiment a failure before it even began," Evan continued. "So why do you even care?"

"Maybe I want to know all the terrible, dreadful things."

Evan looked up and even across the room, his dark eyes felt piercing, right through all the skin and muscle and into his chest.

"First off, you spent probably four hours making homemade Ding Dongs. I'm not sure you deserve to know."

"Six," Miles said, and it was technically true, but it also did what he'd intended, which was to get Evan's attention away from that stupid notebook again.

"What?" Evan demanded. "You spent *six* hours on those stupid Ding Dongs?" He sounded even more affronted than he had when he'd first found out about them.

Miles shrugged. "I'm a perfectionist. I have to make a recipe more than once to get it right."

"How many times usually?"

"Last night? Four. Today? We'll just have to see."

"Well, you have the kitchen for three more hours today," Evan said unrepentantly. "So it's however many batches of cookies you can bake in that time."

"Only three?" Miles knew he was pouting. He was also painfully aware that they had bridged a snarky, sharped-edged back-and-forth that vaguely resembled flirting.

"It would have been four if you didn't waste an hour this morning not coming to the kitchen when I told you to."

Miles returned his focus to the mixing bowl in front of him. If he only had three hours, he needed to focus, and stop bantering with Evan. If that was even what they were doing. Maybe it wasn't bantering if it was one-sided. And Miles was sure it was one-sided. Evan didn't look like anything ever distracted him from work.

Especially someone Evan intended to control. He talked big about compromise, but Miles had a feeling that Evan had zero experience compromising. Probably as far as Evan was concerned, all compromise meant was that you'd conceded.

Miles wasn't great at it either, but even if he had been, he couldn't do it here. Not with *Pastry by Miles*. Not when he was taking such a risk in leaving the restaurant industry. If he failed here, he might not be able to get another plum job like the one he'd had at Terroir. And Miles knew he'd never get his job at Terroir back.

He wasn't even sure he wanted it back, if it came to that, but the phantom sting of potential failure made him turn away from the temptation Evan presented, and back to his mixing bowl.

Evan was a distraction, and almost certainly the enemy. Even worse, Miles was beginning to realize he might like him more than he hated him.

Miles was fascinating to watch as he worked. Evan was trying to spend more of his time scribbling down notes and ideas versus staring at the other man like a creeper, but it was hard because he totally had a thing for competent people. Watching Miles was like competence porn; he was so instinctual and confident, it was very hard to look away once you'd started.

He'd been trying to keep his questions to a minimum in order to give genius a chance to work uninterrupted. Evan might have been worried about Miles unconsciously changing his process because he was being observed, but there was an innate certainty in every movement he made. Besides, Evan thought darkly, Miles had had zero compunction about demonstrating exactly what he thought of Evan's involvement in this project.

Rigging up a phone in a fake ficus. Evan didn't know what he could have said or done to make someone so desperate to prove themselves. What Miles didn't realize was that while Evan was committed to making a successful show that appealed to a wide range of audience members, he was also committed to producing a show that Miles could be proud of.

The problem, Evan thought, his eyes returning again to a pair of graceful hands as they cracked eggs, was they were both too determined to be in charge.

It was Evan's natural position, and while he wasn't sure it was Miles', Miles was clearly determined not to relinquish creative control.

Evan still believed they could find a compromise they could both be happy with; the problem lay with convincing Miles of that fact. And, considering what Miles had done when he thought he'd been backed into a corner, it was not going to be easy.

Evan didn't need easy—he'd been living the hard way for as long as he could remember—but easy still would have been nice. It also would have been nice if

Miles had returned even an iota of the interest that Evan was trying to forget he felt. But clearly, Evan was alone there.

He usually didn't let himself feel regret, but if he had, he might have wallowed in it a very tiny bit. He might have also wondered what could have been if they'd met in a bar, or a coffee shop or even on Grindr, and *Pastry by Miles* hadn't been this big, looming, impossible thing between them.

Evan looked down and realized he'd doodled a heart in the margin of his notebook. He scribbled it out with such hard pen strokes, the paper tore. When he looked up, Miles was watching him, amusement tilting up the corner of his lips.

"You writing more terrible, dreadful things?" Miles asked.

Ha. If he only knew just how terrible they were. Evan shook his head. "Just an idea that wouldn't work out."

"Those are usually the best sort of ideas," Miles observed.

This was definitely not Evan's experience. Of course, he'd made a habit of always doing the stuff that people said was impossible. Go to school while working three jobs? Transition his part-time internship at *Five Points* into a full-time, paid position? Take care of himself and others when most guys his age were barely able to handle the former?

Unlike the saying, yeah, he'd definitely broken a sweat, but he'd still done it. But those were all things that he didn't share about himself. Especially not at work. Miles would find out that he was a former intern sooner or later—hopefully later, if Evan got lucky—but the rest was going to stay firmly locked away.

"Trust me, this one isn't," Evan said. Because getting Miles to be able to stand him professionally seemed like a tall enough order; to convince him to like him personally wasn't even under consideration.

Miles seemed to digest this as he poured vanilla from a bottle into the mixer. He wasn't measuring, and Evan couldn't help it. "You're not measuring anything," he asked. "How do we replicate the recipe if we don't know the proportions?"

"This is just a test batch. I'll adjust from here," Miles said. "Besides, I might not be measuring everything out, but I know how much I'm adding."

Of course he did. Evan knew odd things turned him on, but finding it hot that Miles was a human measuring cup was weird, even for him.

"Force of habit," Miles added, with a bashful, lopsided smile that would have made Evan's insides clench if he'd let them.

"Must come in pretty handy," Evan said.

"Yeah, at home, for sure. But at the restaurant, we measured everything. Had to follow every recipe to the letter."

"You didn't like that?" Evan was surprised; Miles struck him as a chef who didn't do wild experimentation.

"I hated it," Miles admitted. "I get that diners look for consistency, especially at a restaurant like Terroir, but it got really old. Sometimes I felt like I couldn't take a step out of place without having a ton of bricks come down on me."

"That's why you took this job," Evan said, realizing very quickly what had driven Miles to accept their offer. "You were bored."

"No," Miles corrected. "I was bored so I started *Pastry by Miles*. I was insane, that's why I took this job."

Evan couldn't dignify that with a response, but when he glanced up, he saw that Miles was actually smiling still. "Seriously?" Evan demanded.

"I made you a video of me baking a Ding Dong," Miles said, "do you really think insanity scares me off?"

"Obviously not."

"It's just like I said. Sometimes, the worst ideas are the best ones." Miles folded in the dark chocolate chunks he'd just been chopping off the big block. "Dark chocolate, as dark as I'm using, is probably going to be complete shit in this recipe, but I'm trying it anyway."

Evan's jaw dropped a little. "You think those aren't going to be good? Then why are you making them?" It seemed like a total waste of time and resources to bake something Miles didn't think was going to be good. But he'd done it anyway.

Clearly, this was part of the reason why they hadn't gotten along right away. They both had very different ideas of how to go about a project.

"Because I thought they might actually be brilliant, and I had to know. I made those strawberry raspberry tarts that everyone loved so much eight times before I was happy with them." He gave a careless shrug.

Evan realized that Miles really did not care how long something took before he declared it finished. In a terrible premonition, he could see blown budgets, billowing grocery bills, and an intractable chef whose perfectionism somehow eclipsed Evan's own.

It was not a pretty picture of the future. Even if Evan had been inclined to let Miles take over and control *Pastry by Miles*, he couldn't let it happen because Miles wasn't just fooling around in his own kitchen. There was a lot more on the line now, including, Evan thought with a mental shudder, *his* job.

"How long are they going to bake for?" Evan asked, eyeing the filling cookie sheet with trepidation. If these weren't outstanding, they were going to have to go through this process as many times as Miles wanted until he was satisfied.

"Ten minutes, give or take," Miles said.

Evan scribbled that number down, next to the list of ingredients Miles had used. Miles might be lackadaisical about measurements, but the point of this show was to make what he did accessible to the regular viewer. That meant recipes—proven, tested, *reliable* recipes—that accompanied each video.

"Did you just write that down?"

Evan glanced up at Miles' incredulous voice. "Of course I wrote it down. You might not be measuring, but we need to provide a recipe for the cookies to everyone who watches the video."

Miles wiped his hands deliberately on the towel he'd draped across his shoulder. Evan, in a moment of unbelievably weak hormones, thought it made him look like a romantically temperamental chef. *Delete the romantic part of that*, Evan thought to himself morosely, and braced himself for another round of, "I'm a big fancy chef and I know better than you do because I took a class on how to chop an onion."

"I didn't realize we were doing that," Miles said.

Evan couldn't help but explode. "Of course we're doing that," Evan ground out. "How do you think this site makes the money to pay you? Hits. And you get hits by directing people to the recipe and the site, where we sell ads that pay for all of this."

Miles rolled his eyes. "I'm not an idiot."

The problem was Evan had a temper. A temper that he'd spend a lifetime hiding and controlling and stuffing back into its little box, but a temper nonetheless. And Miles was the most tempting target for it that Evan had run across in a long time.

"Then don't behave like one," he snapped, all too aware that Miles' laid-back, infuriating, patronizing personality was breaking him, a little bit at a time.

Evan did not like being broken. He'd learned to assert control over himself because he didn't always have control over his environment, and Miles, with his annoyingly good looks and bullshit attitude, was taking him right back to a time Evan never wanted to revisit.

Miles didn't say a word, merely turned back towards the counter and began piling dishes into the sink. Evan returned to his notebook and scribbled out the line he'd written about compromise. There was going to be no compromise.

He would prove to Miles, one day at a time, that he was the one who was in charge of this show, and it was Miles' job to develop the recipes in a reasonable timeframe, and then stand in front of the camera and charm the women of the world into attempting his recipes.

It would happen because Evan had never failed in his life and he wasn't about to start now. If that meant he had to become an asshole to meet Miles' asshole, and forever ditch the hope that something could have grown between them, so be it.

Miles ran some hot water over the dishes in the sink as the first batch of cookies baked, and then began to re-assemble the ingredients for a new batch. He hadn't tasted the first ones yet, because they weren't out of the oven, but he didn't need to. He'd never made a recipe that couldn't be further perfected.

And Evan could just pry his head out of that exasperatingly cute ass and get with the program.

Ever since marching the two of them into the kitchen, he'd been making noise about compromise, but Miles knew one thing for sure—Evan had never compromised in his life, and he wasn't about to start now. The sour-milk look on his face after Miles had confessed to redoing the strawberry raspberry tarts told him everything he needed to know. There was no way Evan was going to let him be true either to his vision or his training. And sharing recipes! Miles didn't feel comfortable with that at all. The point of *Pastry by Miles* had never been to make the food accessible to anyone. It had been to express his point of view.

Having to dumb down his processes so the common person could follow along was not something that Miles was interested in doing.

The alarm on the oven beeped, and Miles sauntered off to take a look. The cookies were baking nicely, looking fluffy and full in the middles, and just browning around the outside. He opened the door, pressed on one lightly, and decided it could use another minute. He wanted a firm, cake-y cookie on the inside, but with crisp outer edges.

Miles didn't have to look over his shoulder to know that Evan was writing this all down. He could hear his pen scratching across the pages as if he was doing it right next to his ear. He put in another thirty seconds, just to fuck with him.

He fully expected Evan to loudly and emphatically inquire what good thirty seconds of oven time would accomplish (almost nothing) but his section of the kitchen remained quiet. Miles knew it wouldn't last.

Pulling the cookies out of the oven, he slid them across the counter, and went to grab a spatula and a cooling rack in the equipment pantry. Returning, he saw Evan had moved closer, bending over the pan, finger outstretched, as if he was going to duplicate Miles' movement from earlier.

"Don't touch those," Miles growled. "They're not cool yet."

"You touched them," Evan said, straightening, and looking him right in the eye. Always challenging. Miles wondered if he was even capable of anything else. He had a sudden, blinding idea that sex with him would be fantastic. All that drive and passion and certainness focused on him.

"Yeah, but I knew what I was doing. You don't." Miles acted casual, like he wasn't reeling from the idea of sex and Evan. Frankly, he probably would have thought of it before now, if they hadn't fought from almost the first moment. Miles knew he was attracted to Evan; it had only been a matter of time before he considered it.

"You've made that abundantly clear," Evan sniffed.

"Then don't touch if you don't know," Miles said, trying to keep his temper and rapidly failing.

Evan threw his hands up. "They're just cookies," he said.

"Yeah, and you've made it pretty damn obvious that I have a limited number of attempts to get them right. So," he said, his voice growing hard around the edges, "don't touch."

"For the record," Evan said, returning to his pad and pen, "you're an ass."

Miles knew he really wasn't. Except maybe he was being one now, just a tiny bit. And only because if he didn't assert firm boundaries now, he was going to lose the thing that mattered most to a professional chef: his reputation.

He shoved the spatula under a cookie and transported it to the cooling rack. He repeated this with the rest of the cookies, and then went back to the mixer. "You're making a new batch before you even taste these?" Evan asked incredulously.

Miles refused to even look up from what he was doing. Evan was just trying to get under his skin—trying and unfortunately succeeding.

"Actually," Evan continued, and there was the clear munching sound of a cookie being eaten, "these are actually pretty good."

Miles turned around, to see Evan's mouth full of chewed cookie. "I told you not to touch."

"You did," Evan said. "I'm terrible at rules. Sorry." He didn't sound apologetic at all.

Miles reached over, and grabbed a cookie himself, taking an experimental bite.

"I thought you didn't like sweets," he said.

"I don't," Evan said. "These don't exactly make me change my mind, but they're not bad."

They were more than "not bad," in Miles' expert opinion. They had good crumb, good texture, a solid amount of peanut butter taste, and the dark chocolate was an interesting juxtaposition with the richness of the batter. He made a note to add more salt next time, and to change to semi-sweet chocolate. It had been a decent first try, but he could make better cookies than this.

Chapter Four

"How do you think it's going?" Reed asked, leaning back in his desk chair, looking relaxed because he had no idea how it was actually going.

Evan had a feeling that if he had an inkling, his question wouldn't have been nearly so casual.

"Uh, it's . . . well . . . it could be going better." Evan believed one hundred percent in being truthful and straightforward in business, but he genuinely liked Reed and wanted Reed to not only appreciate his professional skills but to like him too. And the truth about how Miles felt about him and his ideas didn't reflect well on Evan at all.

"What happened?" Reed still didn't look worried. Evan didn't want to tell him he should be, but he really *should* be.

"We're still trying to come to an agreement about the direction of the show," Evan said with diplomacy.

Reed finally frowned, and sat up straighter in his chair. "The direction? I thought we talked about this."

"*We* did." Evan paused. "Miles is very committed to having complete creative control over the content of the show."

"And he does, right?" Reed asked.

Evan nodded. "I keep telling him that there's a very happy middle ground between the production and marketing and the vision he has, but he's not really interested in compromise. Of any kind."

"Do you want me to talk to him?" Reed asked, sounding very much like he did not want to moderate the discussion.

That might be the right way to proceed, but Evan didn't want to fix his problems with Miles by just dragging him in front of their boss and pointing at the part in his contract that said he retained creative control, but had relinquished production control to a *Five Points* representative.

Because that wouldn't really solve anything, and if Evan knew anything about this business, it would only lead to terrible shows that nobody ever wanted to watch.

He didn't just want to successfully produce *Pastry by Miles*—he wanted it to be a fucking smash.

"No. I want to try to fix this without forcing you to intervene."

"Okay, how about this," Reed said, and Evan was reminded that not only did he manage sixteen employees and sub-contractors at *Five Points,* but that he'd very successfully run a high-end restaurant with a full staff in Chicago. "What is Miles' point of view?"

Evan slumped back in his chair. "I'm a super special pastry chef who makes rainbows and orgasms but I won't tell you how to make them. You need to bow down to my superior ability; I'm not going to actually teach you. You just watch my videos to bask in my cute hair and dimples and imagine you could make pastries like I do."

Evan ignored that this attitude of Miles' was what had attracted him in the first place. Or that he'd wanted to be the one Miles gave rainbows and orgasms to.

Reed chuckled. "I hate to tell you that nearly every chef is like that, to some extent."

"Oh, and I forgot," Evan added. "You must also let me follow my beautiful chef muse, even if that means baking fifteen batches of cookies. When the first batch was plenty fine."

"I thought I smelled cookies," Reed said, then sighed. "I warned you this is how chefs are."

"You did. But I've worked with them before—you, and Quentin and even others. And nobody has ever been this stubborn and difficult."

"You've never worked with me in a kitchen before," Reed corrected warmly. "Trust me when I say that I'm probably way more difficult than Miles."

Evan was plenty loyal to his boss, but he was also a realist. "How would I convince you to compromise?"

"Tell me your vision for *Pastry by Miles.*"

That was the easiest thing Reed had asked since he had sat down. Reed had seen him walking by the open door of his office and had waved him in to discuss the progress of their newest show. Evan had learned after working for Reed for over two years that he hated formal meetings and much preferred organic conversations.

Evan had been actively trying to avoid this organic conversation, but the only way to get to the break room was to walk by Reed's office.

"I want a great pastry chef who is willing and *wanting* to teach the housewives and teenagers and bored retirees how to bake with skill and conviction. I want clear, easy-to-follow recipes, paring down difficult concepts to easy steps. Miles should want to help people, not condescend to them."

Reed didn't say anything for a long moment. "Finding a compromise there is going to be tough, Evan."

Evan knew it. It was why he had spent the last two hours alternatively wanting to beat Miles' head and his own against a wall.

"But I think there's hope in even the most dire situation," Reed continued, which Evan thought was probably total bullshit. He was probably just hoping that they didn't kill each other in the next few months. Evan had read that leadership manual before. "But if you do need me to intervene, just say the word."

"I will," Evan said, getting up from his chair and feeling more frustrated than he had before sitting down. It was well and good to be able to accomplish the impossible on a regular basis because he put his head down and got shit done, but it would've been nice for Reed to acknowledge just how impossible of a task this was.

Unfortunately, the task began with convincing Miles to consider compromising his artistic vision. And Evan had no freaking idea how to do that.

Reed wished him luck again, and Evan stepped into the hallway and right into Mr. Artistic Vision himself, thunderclouds in his eyes.

"What the fuck do you think you were doing in there?" Miles demanded, in a hushed, angry whisper that was not nearly as effective as he probably thought it was. He sounded raw, almost betrayed. Which, as far as Evan was concerned, was a serious overreaction.

"None of your business," Evan said.

Miles gaped at him. "You really mean that, don't you? You really mean to make me some sort of pastry Julia Child Joan of Arc, don't you?"

Evan rolled his eyes. "The problem with eavesdropping is that you have no context for anything I said."

"Oh, no, I heard it all," Miles challenged. "I heard what you said about me. All about my insufferable ego. And then how you want to bring it down to earth. *Bury it.* That's never going to happen."

It had been a long day. Scratch that—it had been a long *two* days, and the blame for that could be laid directly at the feet of the man in front of him. Without Miles' ego, they could've already been working towards filming their first episode. Instead, Evan was trying to figure out a way to placate it all the damn time. All while not trying to fantasize about what he looked like bent over the kitchen counter.

"Listen," Evan said, grabbing Miles by the forearm and dragging him further down the hall towards the break room, which was certain to be empty at this hour in the early evening. When he reached the room, he dropped Miles' arm like it had stung him. Touching was bad. Touching would expose what he really wanted.

"Listen," he repeated. "I am sick of your bullshit. I'm trying to get something done here, and instead of you even trying to listen, you just keep pontificating about how fucking awesome you are. Get over your damn self."

"Me?" Miles retorted. He pushed a finger right against Evan's chest and pushed him back towards the soda machine. Caught off guard, Evan's back hit the machine and he couldn't escape before Miles crowded right in front of him.

This close, his eyes were definitely thunderclouds. It shouldn't have been sexy; it sort of was.

"Definitely you. You're ninety-nine point nine percent of the problem here," Evan argued.

"You walk around like the hottest thing in chinos, all spreadsheets and calculators and stupid bow ties," Miles muttered. "You don't know a *damn thing*. You don't even like dessert!"

"Not even yours," Evan retorted, which was only sort of true. He shouldn't, but he wanted to taste Miles' dessert more than ever.

Not just his desserts if he was being completely honest.

Miles' brows drew together like two dark slashes against his olive skin. "You're an asshole."

Evan found himself almost pinned and almost breathless. And only mostly because of the argument he was currently having. "It takes one to know one."

Evan could see that he was breathing hard, fists clenched together at his sides. Evan had never considered the possibility that Miles might punch him, because Miles worked in a kitchen, for god's sake, physical violence couldn't be up his alley, and yet, he seemed tempted to do it.

Evan got it. He'd been punched more than once growing up because he was an asshole. Or maybe because he was smarter than his parent of the week, or this month's brother.

"I'm not doing this with you," Miles finally spat out. "I'm not going to let you ruin me."

"Ditto," Evan said. And between the two of them, he was definitely convinced that he was the more determined of the two. After all, look at what he'd forcibly put behind him. Nobody was more motivated than he was to do this job and to do it to everyone's satisfaction.

He had already come to terms with the knowledge he'd never be able to satisfy Miles. There was no point crying over that spilt milk.

Miles had at least three inches on him, and he leaned in, expression both intense and inscrutable. "Are you even going to tell me what you were doing in Reed's office? I heard you complaining about me."

Complaining? Evan hadn't even gotten started complaining. "At Reed's request, I was giving him a fair assessment of our situation."

"I'm not an egotistical prick!" Miles said hotly. Evan knew just how hot it was, because he could practically feel Miles' very firm thigh pushing against his own. He didn't know how they'd suddenly gotten so close, but he wasn't sure he could complain about it.

Not for the first time, Evan was surprised that his own weakness for someone who did *not* deserve it kept cropping up. He should have been pissed as hell that Miles was attempting to use his height to try to intimidate him. The only problem was it was more of a turn-on than anything else.

Evan wasn't usually this conflicted, and he hated it.

"Then stop acting like it," Evan said. "You've been acting like hot shit ever since you arrived. I don't care if I never went to culinary school, I'm not a moron. I know it sounds crazy, but we might even learn to like working together."

Miles' breath stopped short. They were so close, Evan could hear it, and feel the lack of it against his cheek. There was an awful, horrific pause of total silence, like Miles was contemplating how completely insane it was for them to ever like working together.

Or maybe he was figuring out that Evan had just let one of his closely held secrets slip. He'd wanted so fucking badly for them to be friends. To like working together. To maybe, in some faraway fantasy vision, find something even deeper.

Now Miles probably knew, and Miles was probably disgusted.

Of course, he didn't look disgusted. He was staring at Evan, at his mouth actually, and there wasn't a hint of disgust to be seen.

Evan tensed as Miles' hands slammed on the wall behind him, bracketing his head. And before Evan could demand to be released, Miles' mouth was on his.

It was probably the angriest kiss Evan had ever had. It was raw and anguished and bizarre. Miles' lips crushed against his, moving hotly, desperately, like he had to convince himself or maybe even both of them, that there was no way in hell they could ever get along.

But we're kissing, Evan thought helplessly.

It was nothing like Evan had imagined it would happen. Part of him wanted to slap Miles for doing it now, when they wanted to kill each other. Part of him wanted to melt into Miles, and show him just how much he'd wanted him from the very first moment of *Pastry by Miles*.

It was a problem.

Abruptly, it ended. Really, before it could even begin—or at least before it could begin being anything other than angry and intense. Miles' breath was coming hard now, in fast, furious little pants. His eyes were slanted to the side, like he couldn't even bear looking at Evan. Like maybe he *was* disgusted.

That thought pushed Evan over the limit and he tumbled right off the cliff. He set the heel of his hand against Miles' chest and shoved him, hard, pushing him away. "Get your shit together and start acting like a professional," Evan said.

Miles shook his head, blank confusion still written all over his face. His stupid, cute face. He turned and walked away, leaving Evan shook up and pissed off, his blood hot with no convenient outlet.

That wasn't the worst of the offenses he could lay at Miles' feet, but it sure as hell felt like the worst right now.

The accusation and his lips burned all the way to Napa.

Miles had stormed right out of the *Five Points* offices, and had caught a ride right to the rental car office, where he used some of his signing bonus to rent a car.

He spent the next six hours contemplating every way that he could make Evan pay for his words and trying to forget how Evan's mouth had felt under his. He didn't know how the kiss had even happened, only that it had happened and that his world felt rocked by it.

He hit the town limits right around eleven, and headed straight to Terroir, where, as he'd expected, employees were beginning to drift out the back door.

Wyatt and Xander walked out first, unsurprisingly, because Bastian Aquino could never bear for Kian to be one of the first out of the door.

Miles rolled down the car window and whistled. Xander's head turned his direction, and his jaw dropped.

"What are you doing here?" Xander asked, jogging over to the car. "Aren't you supposed to be Julia Child-ing in LA?"

"That's not a verb," Wyatt said, joining them. "Julia Child is a person, not an action."

"If you're Miles, it is," Xander said, and it wasn't surprising to hear that rough edge of disapproval in his friend's voice, but it hurt anyway.

He'd given up the camaraderie and Terroir for what exactly? Some uptight prick who wanted to make everyone a world-class pastry chef? Miles didn't know what he'd been thinking. To be frank, Miles still didn't know what the fuck he was thinking.

"So why are you even here?" Wyatt asked.

Miles forced himself to shrug casually. "Let's go home, open some wine, and I'll tell you about it."

But as the others piled into Miles' compact rental, he didn't even know how to begin telling them about it. *I thought I'd go to LA and run the town the moment I showed up? I thought I'd get to call all the shots, and now that I can't, I'm freaking out and pulling the ego card? I'm going around kissing my producer when he tells me to get my ego in check?*

What stung the most about Evan's accusations was that they weren't so far from the truth; they hit right in the tender, honest parts of himself. He was being a bratty unprofessional. He was panicking, and that explained some of it, but he was way out of his element and he didn't trust Evan enough to let him guide them in the right direction.

How could you trust someone who made you kiss them even when you didn't like them?

And how could Miles possibly trust him when all Evan wanted to do was teach every man, woman, and child how to make world-class desserts, *and* he didn't even like them?

There was an exclusivity that surrounded chefs like Miles and Wyatt and Xander, and sometimes even Kian. It was a cult that was cultivated by chefs like Bastian Aquino. And what it proclaimed, loud and clear, was that not everybody could join. You had to pass the tests. You had to prove yourself. You couldn't just turn on YouTube and walk in. There was a blood, sweat, and tears barrier that had to be crossed first. It was what made Bastian able to charge hundreds of dollars for a single meal. If everyone could make it, then everyone might, and they would all be out of a job.

Miles hadn't made the rules, but he was expected to live by them. And some upstart guy with spreadsheets and a marketing degree and tight khakis that made Miles' dick ache wasn't going to make him break them.

He'd been gone from the house they'd all shared for less than a week, but already Miles felt nostalgic as they all collapsed on the various sitting surfaces in the living room. They all had their special spot, and Miles still got the particularly comfy corner of the couch.

"Don't worry," Xander said with a roll of his eyes. "I haven't appropriated it yet. I couldn't get comfy in it because the dents in it still match your skinny ass."

Miles never thought he'd miss Xander's snide little comments, but he'd take Xander's mostly open hostility over Evan's insidious back-stabbing manipulation. Even thinking of him now and the innocent openness of his expression right after Miles had caught him red-handed burned.

"I figure this is as good a time as any to open this," Wyatt said, walking into the living room holding a dusty bottle.

"Nate gave that to you, didn't he?" Kian asked, because he hadn't had *that* sort of boyfriend yet, and was still blissfully naïve. Miles and Xander were both too smart to bring up that Nate, Wyatt's asshole sommelier ex-boyfriend, had given him the bottle in his hands.

"Fuck that asshole, anyway," Xander said.

Wyatt's expression grew wistful. "I know you all hated him, but he wasn't so bad."

"Quick," Miles said, "let's drink the wine before Wyatt changes his mind and waxes nostalgic about his relationship with Nate."

"More like waxes nostalgic about what great wine Nate would always buy," Xander added.

Wyatt raised an eyebrow. "Do you want me to open this or not?"

"We've been staring at it for more than six months," Xander said. "And nine before that, when you were still together and you felt obligated to drink it with that dick. Open the fucking wine."

Wyatt made a face but started opening the wine anyway.

"Kian broke our fourth red wine glass," Xander explained when Wyatt brought out three wine glasses and a champagne flute.

"It wasn't my fault!" Kian exclaimed, though out of a kitchen, he was notoriously clumsy.

"And the sky isn't blue," Xander retorted.

Miles took the glass Wyatt handed him, and did a showy little swirl. He wasn't a sommelier like Nate, but he'd taken a few classes about wine, and he could tell from the bouquet that it was pretty good. Maybe not as good as Nate had sworn it was, he thought as he sipped, but pretty damn good.

The problem was that Nate had always oversold everything—and that included himself. It had been a very good day when Wyatt had finally shown him the door. And, *bonus*, he'd gotten to keep the birthday gift Nate had given him a few months before.

"Dish," Wyatt said, leaning forward, elbows on his knees, blue eyes bright in the dim room. "I wouldn't have opened this wine if I didn't think it would loosen your tongue."

Miles tipped his glass in a faux toast. "You're a real giver."

"Seriously," Xander complained. "What the fuck are you doing back here?"

Miles didn't even know where to begin. He didn't want to talk about Evan, but everything started with him. "You know how we all really liked Nate at first, and it took us a long time—some of us a *very* long time—to realize he was a tool?" A round of nods. They'd all been happy when Wyatt had started dating Nate. He was decent and had access to better wine than any of them could afford. Plus, nobody else had dated anyone seriously during the time they'd all lived together. Xander was too mean to date anyone, Miles liked to keep things more casual, and from the very beginning, Kian had this unfortunate crush on their boss he continually denied but was obvious from about a hundred miles away.

"Well," Miles continued, "that isn't what happened with my producer. I pretty much hated him right away." This hadn't really been true then, and it definitely wasn't true now. But it made for a simpler story. Definitely easier than explaining that his feelings were intense and confused. Too difficult to try to explore, even with his best friends.

Kian made an aborted shocked noise. Kian was also too young and too naïve to ever hate anyone at first sight.

"I don't buy it," Xander inserted cynically. "You don't hate anyone right away. That's me, not you."

This was unfortunately true. Miles' first impression of Evan hadn't been hatred; it had been vague interest at his cute ass and velvety brown eyes. And he'd seemed nice and eager to please. Even if nothing he said had particularly pleased Miles.

"You haven't met him," was all Miles said. They'd already had to discuss Nate tonight; they didn't need to rehash all of Miles' poor romantic judgement too—*and* they didn't even know the half of it.

"I can't believe you only lasted two days," Wyatt said with a shake of his head. It sounded like a Xander comment, and it stung.

"I'm not *back*," Miles retorted. But he knew how it looked. He knew how good it felt; how comfortable and routine to sit on this couch and drink a glass of wine and bullshit with his three friends.

Like he'd slid right back into the same life he'd already acknowledged he'd grown out of.

There was nothing to do but take a big gulp of wine, and appreciate the acidic burn.

"Does this mean you have to pay back the money?" Xander asked.

Miles knew he wasn't going to pay back a dime. He was tied up, metaphorically and legally. The rest of his glass of wine slid down his throat with none of the ceremony Wyatt's ex-boyfriend would have required.

He got up from the comfy corner of the couch; suddenly it didn't fit the same way it had. He walked in the kitchen, which looked a little barer without Miles' precious copper pots. The thought stung, and he turned away, towards the sad little cabinet that contained their meager liquor collection—most of which they'd kept to be used in Miles' desserts.

He grabbed the half-full bottle of knockoff Kahlua, and returned to the living room. This time, he didn't take the corner on the couch, but settled on the edge of the arm.

"What are you doing?" Kian asked. Only Kian wouldn't recognize a meltdown requiring alcohol, Miles thought bleakly.

"Getting drunk," Miles said, at the same time as Xander added, "Trying to forget he's already made his bed."

Miles glared over at Xander. It was a little rawer than usual, because he'd already taken two swigs of the terrible Kahlua knockoff and if he'd thought Nate's wine had burned going down, it had nothing on this shit.

"You can't come back," Xander said by way of explanation, and his casual shrug burned even more than the wine and the bad Kahlua combined.

Miles took another long drink, straight from the bottle. "Anyone joining me?"

Wyatt laughed. "We all have to work tomorrow. Unlike you, apparently."

Miles could only imagine Evan's affronted expression when he didn't turn up the next morning, and then the exaggerated annoyance when he used his key to check Miles' apartment and discovered he wasn't there.

He could also imagine the smug edge to his annoyance. How Evan would imagine that Miles had conceded victory.

Miles let more booze slide down his throat and snapped his fingers in Kian's direction. "Go get your laptop."

A wrinkle appeared between Kian's blond brows. "I really don't think you should be making a video now, Miles."

Miles frowned. "I'm not making a video, I'm writing a fucking email."

Xander looked concerned now. A sure sign that everyone was convinced Miles was melting down. Even Miles was convinced, but he didn't give a shit anymore.

He waved with the plastic bottle. He should've stopped at the store and bought some half-decent booze to lose it with. "I'm not going to actually send it," he claimed. "I just want to write it. That's why I'm using Kian's laptop. It never fucking stays connected to the Wi-Fi."

The glance Wyatt gave him was galling. "I don't think this is a good idea."

Miles finished the bottle with a gross belch that tasted of pretty good red wine and bad Kahlua and definite regrets. "It's the best fucking idea I've had in awhile."

Kian must have been at least partially convinced—or maybe he was trying to distract Miles from the liquor cabinet—because he went and got his laptop and reluctantly handed it over.

Miles traded the laptop for the empty Kahlua bottle, which Kian took with a dubious look and an even more dubious sniff.

"You're a snob," Miles told him with a shake of his head.

"I just don't get it," Kian said earnestly. "You're—okay, you *were*—a chef at one of the best restaurants in the world. How can you even stomach bad liquor like that?"

Miles was booting up the laptop and was so focused on the white-hot ball of rage lighting his way that he nearly missed Xander's answer.

"Kian," he said much more patiently than usual, "you wouldn't. But sometimes you want it to burn going down."

That was the goddamn truth.

Miles wanted to burn the whole world down, starting with his taste buds and his throat and his stomach. Next stop, Evan's infuriating ego.

Not once, not *once* in his whole fucking career, had anyone—either a superior or a head chef or co-worker—ever had reason to call him unprofessional.

Miles wanted to burn Evan down because he'd dared to say it out loud and mean it. Even worse, he was *right*.

He opened Kian's browser. The Wi-Fi was currently working, but it was only a matter of time before it went on the fritz. The most consistent thing in this entire house was the inconsistency of Kian's Wi-Fi. It was something Miles was counting on, because while he wanted to mentally deep fry Evan, he wasn't ready to deep fry his career.

Nobody, even Evan Patterson, was enough motivation for Miles to throw away everything he'd killed himself to achieve.

"Are you really sure about this?" Kian asked. He sounded worried. His voice echoed the look on Wyatt's face. Even Xander didn't look completely convinced. Probably because none of them had consumed half a bottle of faux Kahlua.

Knock-off Kahlua was apparently the key to saying *fuck it* to the world.

"Definitely," Miles said. The adrenaline from his fight hours ago with Evan was still coursing through him. It was a physical impossibility but something about Evan kept him alight. Miles didn't want to look too carefully at what that might be. He zoned right onto the outrage and bypassed the rest right by.

"Dear Evan," Miles said out loud as he typed. Badly, but he wasn't sending this, so it didn't matter. This letter was only for him, an attempt to exorcise all his rage. Tomorrow he'd go skulking back to LA, tail sort-of between his legs, maybe not ready to apologize but conceptually ready to compromise. He wasn't ready to face the kiss yet, but he was sure Evan would want to pretend like it hadn't happened.

But first . . . revenge.

Kian opened his mouth to try to say something else, but Miles talked right over him. "Dear Evan," he repeated, "I really hate your face. It's a big fat fucking lie. Earnest and trustworthy when you're really a big backstabber."

"Maybe you shouldn't repeat 'big' twice in one sentence," Xander inserted.

Miles shot him a hot glare. "This isn't a fucking essay, you idiot."

Xander just shrugged, and Miles felt the room begin to spin as he tried to focus on his face. But he dug down deep and returned to his email.

"How about horrible backstabber?" Wyatt suggested.

"Thanks, Mr. Thesaurus," Miles retorted. His fingers were flying over the keys, insulting everything from Evan's stupid bow ties to fake marketing genius to his cute ass—okay maybe that last one wasn't quite an insult. But Miles was trying. He didn't mention the kiss, but it was right there, hidden between the lines. The one thing he wasn't saying.

The problem was the more he wrote, the colder the fire grew, until it felt just about ready to smolder right out. This had been a fucking fantastic idea. He'd managed to exorcise the last of his anger, and he'd really be able to return and try to salvage this whole thing.

And then . . .

"Oh, shit," Miles said, dread spinning through him faster than quicksilver. Certainly faster than the rage had spread. And unlike the rage, it made him sick. Or maybe that was the Kahlua.

"What happened?" Kian asked, scrambling to get over to where Miles sat on the floor with the laptop. Something in Miles' voice must have told him something terrible had happened, because he could move quick when he wanted to, and he was moving fast now.

"I pressed enter," Miles said in a small voice.

"Oh shit," Kian said, which was unusual for him because like the Boy Scout he'd been, he almost never swore.

"What?" Xander was scrambling now, trying to join Miles and Kian as they stared unbelieving at the laptop screen.

"I think Miles sent the email," Kian said carefully.

"What?" Wyatt exclaimed. "How could that even happen?"

"I forgot to mention, I think I fixed the Wi-Fi," Kian said, and he sounded wretched. Not nearly as wretched as Miles felt, and in some other universe, it might have helped that Kian felt bad, but in this one, it didn't. It didn't at all.

His brain was one long fuzzy slow-rolling image of Evan, all peppy and morning-person, opening his email tomorrow and being confronted with one insult after another, most of which weren't even true. Miles didn't even want to think about the spelling and grammar errors. No doubt Evan would return it to him, marked up with a red pen. His eyes would be red too, because as frustrating as he was, he wasn't immune or cold.

He *cared*. He'd wanted a Joan of Arc Julia Child, and all he'd gotten was the asshole half of Gordon Ramsay.

It didn't feel fair at all, even if Miles didn't really like him. It really wasn't fair if Miles decided he *did* like him.

"Maybe we can take the email back," Kian suggested, trying for hope and landing somewhere north of despair.

"Take the email back?" Xander sneered. "It's a good thing you're not on a career path that requires any sort of technical skills. The email is gone."

"Gone," Miles repeated hopelessly.

Someone shoved a bottle in his hand. He took a swig. It was worse even than the fake Kahlua, some sort of sickly sweet orange liquor, but Miles didn't even care anymore. He wanted oblivion because maybe that would kill the shame.

Chapter Five

His mouth tasted like a Russian and a Spaniard had fought over a rotten orange and lost. As Miles gradually fell towards consciousness, he knew only one thing: he'd never be able to drink White Russians or Spanish Coffees ever again. For a split second, that was something to seriously mourn. And then it all came roaring back: the fight, the drive back to Napa, the wine and bitch session with his friends, and then the email from hell. Followed by the faux Kahlua and the fake orange liquor and what he was pretty sure was a drag of shame into the bathroom.

Yep, Miles realized, that was definitely the edge of the toilet his face was resting on. It was a good thing too, because as soon as he got ambitious enough to open one sleep-crusted eye, he got instantly, horrifically sick.

Miles wiped his mouth and settled back on the toilet seat, which thanks to Xander's OCD tendencies, was spotless. It was also a whole lot more comfortable than he'd imagined. And conveniently close to the toilet bowl, which might be making another rapid appearance in his life at any moment.

Why had he come here? He'd known his life here was done—even if the friendships weren't. Had he come so his best friends could plump his ego, even though they'd never done it before? Had he come here so they could clean his wounds? Salve his pride? He wasn't sure, though he knew the decision to get drunk and write the email had been the worst of the bunch.

Never mind that he'd never intended to send it. It was enough that he'd written it, spelling errors and odes to Evan's ass and all. And now Evan had most likely already seen it. The thought was enough to send him back to the toilet, retching helplessly because he'd already thrown most of his stomach up already.

He was fucked, and not even in the fun way.

A brisk knock sounded on the door. He ignored it. He wasn't in any mood for Xander's resigned "you've fucked up your life" bullshit.

"What?" Miles croaked when they didn't go away but instead knocked again, with way more determination. Definitely more determination than Miles felt. He was only determined not to die, and it was feeling pretty touch and go at the moment.

"Miles, are you okay?" It was Kian, and he sounded a hell of a lot more sympathetic than Miles deserved. As far as he was concerned, he wasn't worthy of any of it.

"No," he croaked. Might as well be honest.

"Open the door," Kian said.

"You open it," Miles retorted.

"You locked it, you idiot." That was Wyatt, who was even more protective over Kian than Miles was. "There's someone here to see you."

It was probably Reed, here to fire Miles and demand all his signing bonus back. Some of which he'd already spent on a stupid rental car to come up here and bitch at his friends about how hard he had it. Miles wanted to vomit again, but nothing came. Somehow that felt like the final indignity.

"He's wearing a bow tie, Miles."

Oh god. Even worse. Evan had come here in person. Probably after reading the email. He was definitely here to commit a murder on the parts of Miles that weren't already dead, and he wasn't sure his friends would be inclined to stop him.

Then Miles remembered the kiss, and wondered if he could stay in here forever. He didn't know if he could face Evan, considering what he'd done and then what he'd said.

But Miles knew he should drag himself off the floor and give Evan an opportunity for the murdering to begin.

It was a several-minutes-long process, gently and carefully unfolding his aching body from the position over the toilet, and then hefting himself up using the counter. He flipped on the light and only screamed a little bit, either at the brightness or the horrible image the mirror confronted him with.

He stole Xander's toothbrush and splashed some water on his face, and tried to fix his hair. It was a useless exercise, but Miles guessed it didn't really matter anyway. Nobody would care what his hair looked like when he was dead.

Unlocking the door, Miles braced himself, but it was only Kian standing outside, a worried crease between his brows. "What are you doing?" Kian hissed.

"I wish I knew," he admitted.

"Well, figure your shit out. Your partner you just insulted ten ways from Sunday is here."

"How did he even get here so fast?" Miles wondered, even though the thinking hurt his brain. It could only be mid-morning because Kian hadn't left for Terroir yet.

Kian just shrugged. "He's in the kitchen."

Miles gingerly felt his way to the kitchen, and when he arrived, was ironically confronted by a vision of what he'd just insulted—or praised. He wasn't sure. But there Evan was, back to him, in another pair of those tight khakis.

It wasn't fair. Nothing was fair.

"So this is where the magic all began," Evan said without turning. Miles didn't think he was a particularly heavy breather, but maybe Evan had sold his soul for magic powers so he could kill Miles and get away with it.

"I'm not sure it was very magical," Miles said, and all of a sudden he didn't know if they were talking about *Pastry by Miles* or their kiss. He took a breath and tried to steady himself. He wanted to cry and apologize and tell Evan just how sorry he was, but there was something deep inside holding it all back. Pride? Ego? Shame? "How did you even know I was here?"

"You used your corporate credit card, it wasn't very hard to track you," Evan said, and there was a hint of a sneer in his tone. Like Miles must be incredibly stupid to not be able to keep his credit cards straight—and Miles thought he was probably right. It *was* stupid and would have topped his most embarrassing list, if not for the email.

That was going to win for a very long time. Possibly forever.

Evan turned around. "God," he said, and there was definitely an audible sneer now, "you look even worse than you smell."

"Thanks," Miles said stiffly.

If he had any embarrassment left, he'd be cringing right now.

"I guess Reed sent you up to fire me," Miles said, uncomfortable with even vaguely referring to the email. He'd already been rightly accused of being unprofessional; he didn't even know what this behavior was. A complete aber-ration. A panic-induced, ego-driven freak-out. But no, that wasn't even right, because if his ego was where it was supposed to be, he would have spent this morning working to contradict Evan's words, not support them.

Evan ignored the reference. "I came here to get you, not to fire you," he said. "We have work to do, and you're not where you're supposed to be."

It was even tougher to face Evan, knowing he was right. Maybe not on every count, but on every count that mattered. Sure Evan shouldn't have gone blabbing to Reed, and maybe he should have shared his plans in a less autocratic way, but he'd at least been trying to work out some sort of compromise.

What had Miles been trying to do? Get drunk and write an ode to how much he hated Evan's face but loved his ass?

"Okay," Miles said.

Evan looked skeptical. "Just . . . okay? No arguments?"

"Some . . . discussion can be good for creativity. But you're right, I'm not where I'm supposed to be." Miles had definitely learned that during this little unplanned trip. He was done in Napa, at least for now. He still wasn't a hundred percent convinced he was supposed to be at *Five Points* either, but he'd given his word, and that had used to mean something to Miles.

So he'd go back and no matter how daunting it was for Miles to try to live up to Evan's Joan of Arc Julia Child label, he'd give it his best shot. Basic cooperation was the least he could do after how he'd just insulted Evan.

It turned out part of how Evan had gotten here so quickly was that he hadn't driven.

"What's this?" Miles asked, as the black Lincoln pulled into one of the side private airstrips by the Napa airport.

With a quick phone call, Evan had efficiently arranged for Miles' rental to be picked up and for their travel arrangements. Miles hadn't been listening because he'd still been trying not to vomit. He'd sort of assumed Evan had come up overnight using the car service so he could grab a few hours of sleep.

Apparently not. Miles knew that he had to stop assuming things when it came to Evan, because each wrong assumption was growing more embarrassing, and he didn't have any extra to spare.

"A favor," Evan said succinctly as the car stopped in front of a small white jet.

The driver grabbed their bags from the trunk and followed Evan and Miles to the small set of stairs leading to the aircraft.

"What, no check-in? No ticketing gate?" Miles knew he sounded stupid, but Evan's calm silence, which had lasted from their departure from the rental house to the present was nerve-wracking. He couldn't tell when Evan was going to finally explode and tell him off for the things he'd said.

Evan stayed quiet, and climbed the stairs. The captain was waiting for them at the top, dressed in a navy-blue uniform. It was only then that Miles glimpsed an insignia featuring a fish with particularly nasty teeth on his breast pocket. And he realized whose jet this must be.

Embarrassment felt like a mild word in comparison to what he felt now. He'd heard rumors that someone in the upper management of *Five Points* was married to Colin O'Connor, the famous Miami Piranhas quarterback, but since he didn't really follow sports, he'd assumed those were just rumors.

He'd been so wrong. He and Evan were currently ensconced in comfortable blue-and-white-striped seats with tiny light-blue piranhas woven right into the fabric.

"None of the above," Evan finally said with satisfaction as he took in Miles' stupefied expression. "First class all the way."

Even calling this first class was being modest, and even though they'd only met a few days before, Miles didn't think Evan tended towards humility.

He could only think that this was yet another way for Evan to put him, subtly or firmly, back in his place. A little flare of anger that he knew he had no right to feel burned through him.

He'd been puking less than an hour ago, and his mouth still vaguely tasted like rotten oranges. It was enough of a reminder to swallow back down the retort he'd just been about to dish back. Back at the rental house, he'd made himself a vow that he'd be professional, no matter what, even if Evan pushed his buttons.

How could Miles have forgotten how good Evan was at pushing them?

It didn't matter, he told himself resolutely, he was going to be a professional. After the email, he owed Evan at least that much.

"I guess I should be grateful you came to get me then," Miles said, leaning back into the soft leather captain's chair, trying to act like it was something he did every day.

Evan just rolled his eyes and got to his feet, walking over to a little cleverly disguised refrigerator under one of the gleaming wood accents. Clearly he'd been on this plane before, and that stung even more.

He turned back towards Miles and he had two bottles of water in his hands. He tossed one in Miles' direction. "Thought you might still be feeling it," Evan said. "We're about to take off soon. This might help."

His voice was blunt, but his message was at least semi-sympathetic. It confused Miles, whose head was still pounding. "I wouldn't expect you to care much," he said. He kept expecting Evan to mention the email. Or the kiss. Or both, together, as two actions that didn't make any sense put together.

"I don't," Evan said, with an even blunter delivery. "But Mr. Wheeler will skin me alive if you puke all over his plane."

Miles took a sip of water, grateful even though the anger he kept trying to tamp down kept cropping up. "Trust me, it's all gone. You can keep your skin intact." He ignored the voice inside his head that decided this was a great time to mention what gorgeous skin it was. And that it might be soft if Miles was ever allowed to touch it.

"What a relief," Evan retorted disdainfully.

The desire fizzled. Dealing with Evan was confusing and exhausting and he was already worn out.

He heard Evan rustling around and then the all too familiar staccato punch of fingertips on a keyboard. He was working again, even though they were on a private plane. Miles was grateful though, because that meant he might have more time to gather himself for the apology he still needed to make.

Too many damn things were floating in the air around them and until they addressed them, he didn't know how they would ever get anything done.

I really hate your face. It's a big fat fucking lie.

He'd just close his eyes for a minute, to collect himself, and then he'd figure out his apology. It wouldn't be as complicated as a *Napoleon* or his famous *Paris-Brest* even. Pastry was difficult, people were easy—usually, anyway.

"Rise and shine, sweetheart." The voice, edged with derision, could only belong to one person.

Miles' eyes snapped open and Evan's face swam into view.

I really hate your face.

What a joke his little drunken charade was turning out to be.

"Are we back?" Miles asked groggily as he pulled himself upright. The chairs were so cushy it felt like they were sinking their padded claws into you.

"We're back." Evan was already facing the door, bag in hand, looking so proper and together that Miles wanted to swear. No doubt his hair, already a wreck, was a rat's nest on his head, and he didn't want to think what his clothes smelled like.

"Great." Miles tried to sound enthused, but definitely didn't pull it off.

"Don't worry," Evan said, not even bothering to glance back, "we'll drop you off at your place first, so you can wash that horrific smell off. And then you'll be coming in. We have work to do."

"I would've come back today, I swear," Miles said, because the apology was still an unformed, cloudy mirage in his head and he couldn't seem to wring solid, concrete words from it.

"Of course you would have," Evan said in clipped tones.

Miles knew he was lying.

True to his word, Miles was dropped off at his apartment. He showered, letting the hot water beat him into defeat. As he got ready, his face frosted in the foggy mirror, he told himself that he could be a professional. He'd been a complete professional every single day of his career until he'd come to *Five Points*. Letting fear get the best of him was stupid.

By the time he'd walked to the office, his head was a little clearer and he'd discovered a deep-seated determination not to let Evan push any more of his buttons.

He'd just settled in with his laptop to check the email he'd missed when Evan popped his head around the corner of his cubicle.

"Marketing meeting in the conference room, you're already five minutes late," was all he said in clipped, straightforward tones.

Personally, Miles thought every meeting they'd had so far could be categorized as a "marketing meeting," but Evan just tilted his head, tempting Miles to challenge him. And Miles wasn't stupid. If Reed knew about the email, he'd already be fired.

Reed might preach more touchy-feely now, but he was still the same man who had run Garnet with a velvet-covered iron fist and the expectation that everyone brought their A game every single day. Which meant that Evan hadn't told him about the email.

Miles didn't like blackmail, whether it was inferred or directly stated, but he couldn't be pissed because he'd handed it to Evan on a silver platter.

"Fine," Miles ground out, and picked up his laptop to follow Evan.

When Evan opened the door to the conference room, he was a little shocked to find it was full. Lots of employees, including Reed, were sitting around the table. He and Evan were able to grab two of the last free seats right before it started.

What followed was the most interminably boring bunch of bullshit that Miles had ever sat through. There were multiple presenters, and everybody had slide decks with more charts and keywords and strategies than Miles had ever wanted to see.

His head was still pounding behind his eyes and he'd barely gotten any sleep, but every time he even briefly considered closing his eyes, he saw Reed sitting across the table, taking attentive notes and asking questions that seemed to be relevant.

Plus, there was Evan beside him, no doubt ready to pick up on any wavering from Miles.

It was like being bored to death.

When the torture was finally over, Reed stopped by and clapped Miles on the shoulder. "I couldn't believe it when Evan said you'd expressed interest in coming to one of these. I only come because I don't have a choice. But I guess you really meant it when you said you wanted to reach the people."

Miles could only nod mutely. Miserably. In acute pain and wishing he could inflict even a tiny bit of it on the man next to him.

He couldn't. Never mind his own vow to stay professional, he knew if he took even the tiniest step out of line, Evan would bat him right back with the email.

Grinding his teeth together, Miles forced himself to smile. "Working in the kitchens doesn't give me many opportunities to see stuff like this," he said, which was all true. And he'd been one hundred percent okay with that situation.

"I'm impressed," Reed said, and he sounded it too, which was even worse. Normally Miles craved approbation from his bosses, but not like this. Not for something he basically loathed.

Miles didn't have to look over at Evan to see the smug smile on his face as Reed departed.

"Lunch?" Miles asked, aware of how desperate he sounded. He didn't really care about food yet, but coffee was going to be a necessity.

"We have another meeting," Evan said.

"I didn't really have to come to this one," Miles said slowly as they walked towards one of the smaller meeting rooms. "Did I?"

Evan just shrugged. "I thought it would be educational."

"If you understand what they're saying, probably it would have been," Miles grumbled. It was clear that Evan wasn't going to trip up and admit that the meeting had been clear punishment for the email—or maybe for the kiss—or that he was essentially blackmailing Miles into compliance.

Evan was too smart for that, which Miles sort of admired and definitely hated.

"So, what's this meeting about?" Miles said, slumping into a chair.

"We only have a few short weeks to plan your first slate of episodes before we have to film," Evan said, and that hard, determined edge to his voice was back. "We need a plan of attack. *Now.*"

"Okay, tell me what you think Joan of Arc Julia Child would do," Miles said, because he might as well hear the worst of it, all completely spelled out.

Evan flipped open a folder. "I'm glad you finally asked." Even this statement was pointed at the end, like he was insinuating Miles should have asked that right away. And frankly, Miles probably should have. Except it wasn't entirely Miles' fault because he'd never really done this before. As his producer, wasn't it Evan's job to guide him?

Miles watched Evan as he gathered papers and tried to bury the seething resentment that somehow Evan had wanted him to fail. But that didn't make any sense either, because hadn't Evan picked him? Not Reed?

Miles didn't know what to think anymore. So he decided that if he'd asked the question, he might as well listen.

"Joan of Arc Julia Child, as you put it, is essentially a pastry course built into the first season. Each episode is a dessert that showcases a particular type of technique, and we work forward from there. The idea is to build on knowledge, but I'd like it to be accessible to anyone, at the same time."

Miles ran a hand through his hair. "That's what I've been trying to tell you, it *can't* be accessible to just anyone."

"Why not?" Evan retorted. "Anyone who can read can follow a recipe."

"It's not all about following a recipe," Miles countered. "Or else we'd just be publishing recipes online, and not filming videos. There's technique that you can't teach through words."

"Then *teach*," Evan challenged, dark eyes spiking with temper across the table. "Or . . . is that something you aren't capable of?"

"What I'm trying to fucking tell you is that I don't care about people learning how to bake," Miles said, all too aware that even though he was trying to listen, trying to understand, he was beginning to lose the control over his temper. It was funny, even Xander had never provoked it the way Evan did. Until this job, Miles would have insisted he didn't even have a real temper.

"Then what do you want to do?" Evan questioned, still even and calm.

"I want to bake what I want to bake," Miles said testily.

"Why can't we do both? It's not that great of a restriction, showcasing one technique each episode. And it's not like you didn't have restrictions at Terroir."

"Yeah, well there's a reason I'm not working there anymore," Miles mumbled.

"So, if I asked you what you wanted, you'd tell me you want to make videos that don't do anything except look pretty and impressive. Bolster your ego, so to speak."

Miles had never thought of it that way before, but put the way Evan did, he certainly sounded like a petty egomaniac. It wasn't an attractive look, and they both knew it.

They both knew Evan was going to win this round.

And really, Miles justified to himself, Evan was sort of right. There was a small restriction on each episode, but there wasn't any reason he couldn't go a little wild and crazy. And maybe the wilder and the crazier he went, he might pay back Evan for painting him into this corner.

"No," Miles said. "That's not really me." He could tell from Evan's face that he was definitely not convinced of that. "We'll try it your way."

It didn't sting as much he'd expected, saying those words, but Evan's smug face still needed something—a punch maybe? But that wasn't right either, Miles thought as Evan started taking notes. No, something else, something to surprise him.

It shouldn't have surprised him when the thought of kissing Evan popped into his head. Evan already had an ass he admired—which unfortunately they were both aware of now—but nothing would probably drive Mr. Bow Ties up the creek more than something messy and complicated, which was what all sexual relationships were, as far as Miles was concerned.

Definitely worth considering, Miles thought.

Miles landed on the couch with a heavy oof. It had been an extremely long day and he was exhausted but he still dragged out his phone from his back pocket. He felt a pulse of shame when he noticed that he hadn't texted Gina since telling her with many emojis and exclamations that he was moving to LA. Of course, she hadn't texted or called him either, but she was in college. He'd never been but he had a feeling you were so tired when you finally hit your bed, regular correspondence was basically impossible.

His fingers hesitated over the keys. Finally, he typed out a quick, **you free to talk?** and sent it.

He was so tired, it was a genuine worry that he might fall asleep before she replied, but instead, the phone rang almost immediately, jerking him awake.

"Big brother," Gina crowed on the other end of the phone. Miles switched it over to speaker and laid the phone on his chest. "Long time no talk."

"How is your philosophy class? Did it improve at all?"

She laughed, and he couldn't believe how much better he felt, just hearing her voice and her high-pitched giggle. Something tight in his chest loosened.

"No, not really." She paused. "What's up?"

Miles felt a little bad about not talking to her for three weeks and then dumping his horrible situation on her, asking for her advice, but he couldn't go to Xander or Wyatt. Kian would look at him uncomprehendingly. There was only one person he always felt he could go to, and she was listening right now.

"I think I fucked up, Gee."

"Do you think it was a mistake to move to LA?" she asked quietly.

"No. Yes. I don't know. That's not exactly it. LA was the right choice, I don't think I shouldn't have come. But everything after I showed up. That's the problem."

She sighed, sounding like she'd been around the block a hundred times and knew the score. "Who is he?"

"How do you know it's a he?" Miles squawked. "It could be the job. It could be my boss."

"No. Definitely not. Because *one*, you're ridiculously good at your job—crazy intimidating good, if I'm being honest—so there's no way it's the job. *Two*, you already told me your boss was Reed Ryan, and he didn't ever strike me as an asshole you couldn't get along with. I mean, you get along with *Xander*."

Miles regretted introducing his sister to Xander for so many reasons.

"Did Xander tell you about his crush on Reed? Is that how you know about him?"

Miles could feel her disapproval radiating through the phone line. Even her silences could say a hundred words. He'd always envied that about her. He knew he tended to be both too open and not open enough; charming but opaque.

"Don't you remember when he was on *Kitchen Wars*?" Gina asked, referring to a reality TV show that Miles vaguely remembered and definitely hadn't watched. The name probably only sounded familiar because Xander had likely DVRed it and then had refused to delete it. Especially if Reed had starred in it.

"No?"

"Right," Gina said with amusement, "I always forget that it's Xander who has a crush on Reed, not you."

"Thankfully not. Considering he's now my boss," Miles retorted. He really hoped he had distracted her from the topic at hand—the mysterious *he* she had already correctly identified—by the topic change. He'd initially wanted to ask her advice, but now that he was talking to her, he realized he didn't know what he would even ask her. Besides, talking to her had already made him feel better, like none of this was truly permanently fucked, and he could still salvage it.

He loved his little sister a whole damn lot.

"So, who is he?" she persisted, and Miles groaned out loud.

"You're not very good at subtle," Gina pointed out with a laugh. "I can always see you changing the subject from a mile away. So who is he?"

"He's my producer," Miles reluctantly admitted.

"And?"

"And I was stupid." Miles didn't really want to detail every way he'd messed up with Evan, but knowing Gina, she'd drag it out of him.

"Big bro," Gina said patiently, "you're stupid about a hundred times a day. Did you hit on him? You hit on him, didn't you. Like five seconds after meeting him."

He couldn't exactly blame Gina for coming to that conclusion, because if he hadn't been so on edge when arriving at *Five Points*, he probably would have taken one look at Evan and done exactly that. But he'd been scared and worried and apprehensive, and so afraid those would show, he'd done the exact opposite.

"Not exactly," Miles hedged. "I sort of insulted him. And then kept insulting him."

He could tell Gina was speechless because there was a long, loaded silence.

"Who are you and what have you done with my brother?" Gina finally asked.

"He was afraid he was out of his depth and acted like an idiot," Miles said.

"Then he should *apologize*," Gina reprimanded, sounding so much like their mom, Miles had to do a double take.

"Yeah, he didn't do that," Miles said.

"So, he should start there," Gina said. "And then he should definitely stop referring to himself in the third person, because that makes him sound even weirder than he already is."

"Noted," Miles said with a laugh. He definitely felt lighter. He wasn't sure how he could even begin to apologize to Evan for what he'd said, but he knew Gina's advice was sound. It was Gina. It couldn't be anything else.

"Good," Gina said.

"How is that guy in your philosophy class?" Miles asked.

Gina groaned. Miles couldn't help but think that the sound they had both made when confronted with their nemeses—Miles with Evan, and Gina with Philosophy Class Guy—were eerily similar.

That could be because they were related, or it could be for an entirely different reason.

"Believe me, I feel you," Miles said.

"How can you want to kiss someone and kill them all in the same breath?" Gina demanded to know.

"I really don't know. When I figure it out, I'll get back to you." He paused. "And no kissing! I like to think of you as one of those nuns in the *Sound of Music*."

He could hear the force of Gina's eye roll over the phone. "You're an idiot," she said. But there was so much love in her voice, he squeezed his eyes shut against the sudden wave of emotion.

"I miss you, Gee," he said. "We need to figure out a way to hang out. Soon."

"Soon," she promised. "But I've got a midterm to study for, so I'd better go."

"Good luck on your test," he said.

"Thank you." She hesitated. "And, Miles?"

"Yeah?"

"Just fucking apologize."

Miles knew it would be so much smarter to just listen to his sister, but he already knew he wouldn't. The only way he intended to apologize, after the way Evan had manipulated and blackmailed him today, would be if he could leverage it as a way to control the producer.

After all, he'd never admitted to being a smart man, only a driven, determined one.

Chapter Six

As far as Evan was concerned, Miles' agreement to do things his way was just a little too easy.

Sure, he'd strong-armed him, half-drunk and one hundred percent nasty-smelling, like an orchard gone bad, into Colin O'Connor's jet, then dragged him to the marketing meeting that Reed regularly said was the worst day of his week, all while walking a delicate line between outright and only inferred blackmail.

And sure, he'd had to wake up at six this morning after a mostly sleepless night, tossing and turning and agonizing over what Miles had meant by kissing him. And then he'd had to read the email Miles had clearly gotten wasted and then written, probably because he'd kissed him and didn't know what to do about it. But in between the not-very-imaginative and poorly written insults had been some insights into both Miles-the-Chef and Miles-the-Man.

After all, was something really insulting when it started with the playground taunt of "I really hate your face"?

Evan didn't really think so.

Even if Evan had actually been offended by the email, he still would have used the material the same way. The sick look on Miles' face this morning hadn't just been the bad liquor talking; he'd clearly been overwrought with guilt and confused as hell.

Guilt, Evan thought with satisfaction as he swept into the *Five Points* kitchens the next morning, was the best fucking motivator in the whole world. Better than love or revenge or whatever petty shit those comic book villains were always preaching about.

They could keep their world domination via childhood insecurity. Evan was going to take guilt and shame right to the bank.

Lucy, the kitchen manager, called out good morning from her spot on the other side of the gigantic space, where she was probably writing up next week's kitchen schedule. Even if she hadn't been, Evan still would have smiled big and waved. As it was, he smiled extra big because it was a fucking fantastic morning.

His espresso had been the perfect blend of hot milk and bitter, rich coffee and he'd slept like a baby the night before. But most importantly, he'd finally fixed his problem.

"Hey."

Evan looked up to see his fixed problem staring at him inscrutably.

"You look better," Evan said judiciously. Now that Miles was no longer a thorn in his side, Evan was fine with being civil. Besides, Miles could hardly look worse than he'd looked yesterday. So his statement also had the bonus ring of truth.

"Actual sleep and no booze works wonders," Miles pointed out.

There had been a tiny worried part of Evan that had been concerned that after a good night's sleep, Miles might recant his agreement of the day before. Or even worse, decide he wanted to talk about the two major events of the last forty-eight hours. But when Miles stayed silent, Evan forged on with his plan.

"I'm going to suggest," Evan said, "that we use the peanut butter dark chocolate cookie recipe as our first episode of the series. It's a strong introduction to your point of view as a chef—your sort of high-end, low-end combo that you used with the strawberry raspberry tarts that went viral—and it's a great introduction to basic concepts of baking, like creaming together butter and sugar and sifting dry ingredients."

Miles looked grudgingly impressed. "That's not a bad idea."

Evan couldn't quite help the chiding look he shot Miles' direction. He had a problem being a little smug after he knew he'd won, and this morning was no exception. "If you'd give me half a chance, you'd learn that I have more than a few of those."

"I told you yesterday I'd listen," Miles said, a grumpy expression crossing his face. But unlike the inscrutable, lofty frowns of earlier this week, this one was almost adorable. Like a pissed-off cat.

"We talked yesterday about you coming up with a list of higher concepts you thought would come across good on video."

Miles pulled a crumpled piece of paper out of his jeans and slid it across the counter. It was a sunny morning and the tall windows in the kitchen were all open, lightening his eyes and making them tougher for Evan to read. But if he had a guess, Miles looked the way Evan felt: smug.

Scanning the list, Evan had to admit that Miles had done a really good job. Which didn't surprise him all that much, because he'd personally selected Miles for a reason. They'd gotten off to a bit of a bumpy start, but there was no reason everything couldn't go smoothly from now on.

"This is good," Evan said.

"Don't sound so surprised."

Evan glanced up, surprised at the hard, defensive edge to Miles' voice.

"I know I haven't shown it here, but I'm a professional," Miles said and there it was again—the little thread of shame for the way he'd behaved earlier.

Evan couldn't have planned it better if he'd orchestrated the whole damn thing. He wanted to break into a song and dance of victory.

"Of course you are." Okay, if he sounded a little patronizing, then it was payback for, "I really hate your face."

"Which of these would be good for the next episode in the series?" Evan continued.

"They're actually in order—or the order I'd suggest they be in," Miles said, shoving his hands in his pockets.

"Thoughtful," Evan said approvingly. "Next up is chocolate croissants?"

Miles nodded. "And even better, last night I thought of an even better way we can learn to cooperate."

Later, Evan would come to think of this moment as the one where he stumbled and fell over his own ego.

"You're teaching me all about marketing," Miles said, oh-so-innocently—so innocently that Evan should have realized what was coming, but he was too busy celebrating such an easy win. He should have known that anything too easy to believe was just that—*too damn easy*. "And so I thought I could teach you how to bake. Starting with these recipes. You want me to teach an average person. I figure," Miles said, flashing another one of those charming smiles that made the housewives across America fall in love with him, "you're about as average as it gets."

Evan didn't know whether to be pissed off or very reluctantly admiring over the way he'd just been out-maneuvered. It was almost a masterstroke of genius, and from the lack of smugness emanating from Mr. Ego, it was hard to tell if he even realized he'd struck gold.

As far as Evan was concerned, that was the worst part of all. If you were going to meet Evan on a field of victory and snatch it out from under him, then you'd better be damn aware you'd done it.

"Average?" Evan asked, definitely conscious of how his voice crept up at the end of the word.

"If you want me to teach anyone, then I sure as hell better be able to teach *you*," Miles said. And suddenly, there was just a flash of the egotistical chef Evan had come to know.

Evan had never failed at anything in his life. He definitely wasn't about to start now.

"Sure," he said breezily. "I'm sure you can teach me."

Evan had fully expected another kitchen session observing Miles and taking notes. He hadn't anticipated touching anything—unless it riled Miles up again—and so he'd worn one of his favorite bow ties, a beautiful summer-blue plaid.

The last thing he expected was Miles to take a few steps closer, and reach up, resting one of those slim, capable hands on his shoulder, then edge towards his throat. Evan might have worried Miles was finally going to strangle him, except those fingers were hesitant but sure of their destination, which was his bow tie.

"This needs to go," Miles said, and Evan wasn't sure he imagined it, but his voice seemed lower, almost gravelly. Earthy. Evan might have imagined it was sexual, but he couldn't quite reconcile the Miles who wrote, "I really hate your face," and had kissed him like he was attacking him, to someone who might be sexually interested in him. It didn't compute.

And yet here Miles was, fingers capably and nimbly undoing his bow tie and gracefully tugging it out of his collar. He still couldn't seem to form words—maybe that was the sheer shock of Miles choosing to touch him, maybe it was that his actions fulfilled so much of what Evan had daydreamed about before they'd ever met—and he stood in silence as Miles thumbed open one collar button and the next, with efficient movements.

If Evan hadn't had sexual fantasies about Miles' hands before now, he definitely was going to now.

Miles Costa was undressing him.

It seemed too unreal to be actually happening, but Evan could feel the floor under his feet, and the brush of Miles' breath on the skin he'd exposed.

"There," Miles said softly, and Evan swore his voice wobbled for a second. "Much better."

"I thought it was the khakis you didn't like." Evan knew only the most shocking event would have forced him to refer to the email and the things Miles had said to him. He figured his slip was pretty justified, considering what had just happened.

"They're distracting," Miles said, but instead of continuing that line of thought, he turned away and headed towards the supply pantry, leaving Evan confused and sort of bereft. He wondered that if Miles kissed him again, if it would still be so angry.

He didn't think it would be.

When Miles returned, he was carrying an apron, which he handed to Evan. "You don't wear one of these," Evan said skeptically. It turned out he was far more interested in Miles undressing him than encouraging him to put more clothes on. And that was definitely a problem.

Miles gestured to his worn t-shirt and jeans. "Besides," he added, "I'm the professional, remember? I'm teaching you."

Evan shouldn't have found anything endearing about Miles bringing up one of their main conflicts, but there was a self-conscious, almost wry, edge to his voice that made it obvious how embarrassed he was about the whole thing.

And he *should* be embarrassed about that email, Evan thought as he plucked the apron from Miles' hand with barely another glance. "If it's a requirement, I'll be happy to wear it."

He only looked down after he'd tied it around his waist. "Wait," he stuttered, "this isn't . . . this didn't come from the kitchen."

"Kiss the Cook" was emblazoned across the front in bright red letters. Miles only grinned, the curve of his bottom lip all the evidence Evan needed that he was far too pleased with himself.

It occurred to Evan then that while Miles had come in today, prepared to deal and to compromise, he'd made some plans of his own. Teaching Evan to cook wasn't a spontaneous idea he'd just come up with. He'd planned for this to happen, even to the extent of buying and bringing this ugly apron in for Evan to wear.

"Looks good," was all Miles said before he turned away, but that was enough. Evan had already seen the amusement in his gray eyes, and he had to force down the answering blush.

"Thank you," Evan said stiffly.

He would've had to be dead not to be affected by some of the things Miles said and did. The reluctant attraction he felt had come through loud and strong, in between all the silly insults and the angry kiss. But Evan already knew it would be dangerous to let Miles kiss him again. Maybe too dangerous, especially not when Miles had just proved that he was perfectly capable of arranging his own manipulative plans. Evan would never know if anything that developed between them was real or if it was just Miles trying to gain the upper hand in their power struggle.

That was why it couldn't happen at all.

Evan picked up the paper Miles had scribbled the show ideas on and pointed at the first line. He needed to remind both of them that this was a professional—not personal—relationship. "This is what we're doing today?" He hesitated, already thinking of how he'd stumble over the French. "*Pain au chocolat?*"

"*Oui, pain au chocolat,*" Miles answered absently, absorbed as he arranged the ingredients he'd just fetched from the pantry on a rolling cart.

Unlike Evan, French rolled off Miles' tongue naturally. Evan was reminded that one of the bullet points on his resume was several years studying and working in Paris at one of the great *patisseries* there.

Evan had never been to Europe. His childhood had definitely never afforded him a chance to travel, and he'd spent his entire adult life clawing his way up by his fingernails. There had never been time or money to indulge any of his fantasies.

Hearing Miles speak such careless and perfect French was another reminder of how different they were, and how Miles could never find out just how different.

"Do you speak fluently?" Evan asked before he could swallow the question back. Like he needed any more vivid dreams of those long, pliant fingers running across his skin, hypnotic murmurs of French in his ear.

"Not as much as I should," Miles admitted. There was a hint of a smile on his lips, like he knew what Evan was thinking—and he couldn't, Evan knew that, but there was still a fearful thrill that he might still figure it out. "Everyone kept speaking English."

"Well that was a waste," Evan said.

"I'm assuming you don't," Miles said.

Obviously Evan didn't. The way he'd butchered the pronunciation of the recipe name would have given that away instantly. He spoke a little Spanish, because you'd have to be painfully isolated not to pick up some, and also because he'd taken the language courses required by his university.

"It's a goal of mine to learn another language," Evan said.

Miles rolled his eyes. "Of course it is."

Evan was instantly reminded of all those years of being made fun of because he'd had the nerve to excel in school, because he'd had the nerve to want *better* for himself. Why wasn't that cool? Why did Miles, who'd certainly done some excelling of his own, find that lame?

But Evan had long learned there was no point in asking those questions. He'd do whatever he believed he needed to do, damn everyone else. He pushed the hurt away because there was no point in wondering why Miles would judge him for it too.

"What are *pain au chocolat*?" he asked, carefully attempting to copy Miles' effortless accent.

"Chocolate croissants," Miles said. "And they're important because learning how to make pastry dough is vital to French baking. Also because they're delicious *and* impressive."

Evan was definitely impressed but he kept his lips pressed tightly together because he wasn't about to tell Miles that.

"We begin," Miles continued, "by putting the basic dough together." He gestured to a gigantic glass bowl that he'd placed on the counter.

Evan walked over to the bowl. He was only going to follow instructions and mix some stuff together in a bowl. How hard could this really be?

"I don't suppose you have this recipe written down yet," Evan said.

Miles smiled and leaned against the counter, a little closer than Evan felt comfortable with, his gray eyes the warmest they'd been since he'd arrived at *Five Points*. He was a long, lean temptation and Evan needed him a little further away. A little more unattainable.

"I'll walk you through it," Miles promised. "Flour first." He pointed to a big metal bin.

Evan tugged it over to the bowl and opened the latch. "How much?"

"Four cups." Miles pointed to a variety of measuring cups and spoons that he'd laid out at the workstation.

Picking up the cup measure, Evan tried not to be self-conscious as Miles watched him intently measure out four cups of the flour and dump it into the bowl.

"No," was all Miles said, picking up the bowl and dumping all the flour back in the container. "There's a way to measure flour correctly when baking." He leaned over and suddenly was right in Evan's personal bubble, forearm brushing against his chest and plucked the measuring cup from his hand. Despite fighting his attraction, Evan knew he was breathing heavier, while Miles, who was just as close, didn't seem to be affected at all. Evan didn't know whether to remind himself of what Miles had said in the email or to try to forget it completely and believe the charade Miles was playing at.

"We fluff up the flour first," Miles said, voice casual but precise as he took the metal cup in his hand and with a few flicks of his wrist, churned up the flour. "We want it light but uniform. Flour can clump together, making the measurement imprecise."

Then he handed the cup back to Evan. Flour sifted gently over his fingers as he dipped his hand into the container and tried to replicate Miles' movements. "Now," Miles said, snagging Evan's wrist, his fingers making a loose bracelet around it, "you dip the cup in and level it off with your other hand."

Flour was coating both their hands now, specks sifting down across the counter as Miles guided Evan's movements. Finally there were four new cups of flour in the bowl. The amount seemed very similar to Evan, but Miles was the expert, and if he said this was how flour should be measured, then he'd do it.

"Half cup of cold water," Miles said, releasing his wrist gently, more flour sifting to the counter, to the floor, even onto Miles' jeans. He seemed unconcerned. Evan hadn't thought he'd ever be grateful for the apron, but he sort of was.

Evan sorted through the selection of measuring cups, and he'd just found the right one when Miles' voice stopped him again. "Nope," he said. "Those are just for dry ingredients." He gestured to the nestled glass measuring cups on the side. "*These* are for wet ingredients, like water."

Not about to let Miles stop him again, Evan slowly measured water from the faucet into the cup, ducking down so his eyes could double-check the liquid had rested exactly at the little red line.

Miles gave an approving little nod as he poured the water into the flour. "Same amount of milk," he said, and Evan dutifully measured that too.

"Wait," he said, as he was pouring the milk in, "didn't you make all sorts of excuses when I asked you the other day about measuring? You didn't measure anything in those cookies."

"You've got to learn the rules to break them," Miles said a little smugly.

Evan was tempted to tell him he was an asshole, but that wasn't exactly in the spirit of cooperation and compromise they were working on right now. Plus, if he'd actually said it, it probably would have come out disgruntled but endeared, like he found Miles' insistence on teaching Evan how to measure kind of adorable.

And it wasn't. Not even a little bit. His heart just hadn't gotten the memo from his brain yet.

He dutifully measured out the sugar, and then the salt, per Miles' specific instructions, and then poured out the packet of yeast into the bowl.

"Last ingredient," Miles said, pushing over a small glass bowl filled with butter. "This is really important—more important than measuring things right. Some recipes call for room temperature butter. Others call for cold butter. You need to make sure you follow the instructions. That can make or break a recipe."

"Like I have a recipe I'm actually following," Evan grumbled.

Four days ago, Miles probably would have shot something grumpy and ill-tempered right back, but this time his smile was as soft as the butter. "You're following *my* recipe," he said, and his voice edged just enough on proprietary that despite all his good intentions, Evan went hot all over. It felt like he'd just been blasted by the heat from an open oven, but there wasn't one. Only Miles.

How had Evan ever thought he was cold and unfriendly? The man could melt chocolate at a hundred paces. Evan wanted to believe it had something to do with their unspoken attraction, but he knew better. It didn't have anything to do with him. Not really. It was all about who was going to be in control, and Miles just wanted it that bad.

Badly enough to bother charming Evan, when, if Miles had been paying attention at all, Evan had been charmed—despite his best intentions—from day one. From the first moment he'd watched a *Pastry by Miles* episode, if he was being painfully honest.

"Well, what does *your* recipe say?" It was stupid to flirt back, but Miles' charm made it too easy.

"Soft," Miles murmured, easing closer, and *god*, yes, that was his finger, brushing casually yet purposefully against Evan's arm. He was probably touching more flour than skin, but even that teasing touch was enough to shoot lightning up his nerves.

It nearly killed him, but Evan took a step away, disguising his need to put some breathing room in between him and the gorgeous man next to him by grabbing a thin flexible spatula from the pile of equipment Miles had set out earlier.

"Just plop it in?" Evan asked and even he was impressed by how cool he sounded when the reality was so much different.

Miles still smiled though, like he knew the truth, and Evan hiding it only added an extra edge of anticipation. "Yep, right in the bowl. And then we get to the fun part."

Evan was almost afraid to ask what the fun part was. But he did because he needed to have some kind of plan of how to resist Miles going forward. "What's that?"

"You mix it up." Miles eyed the spatula in Evan's hand. "And not with that."

"With my hands?" Evan squeaked. "Isn't that unsanitary?"

"Not if you wash them first," Miles said.

Evan did, spending a lot of time unnecessarily scrubbing, like a dose of water and soap could extinguish the fire that Miles kept trying to start.

"You're trying to clean them, not take the skin off," Miles pointed out, leaning over near the sink, eyes bright with amusement. Evan kept telling himself that Miles couldn't read his mind or understand why he was doing anything, but it was getting tougher to believe it.

"Just want to make sure they're clean of laptop cooties before I shove them in the bowl," Evan retorted, reaching for the paper towels next to the sink.

"But laptop cooties are my favorite," Miles said, his lips forming a crooked, lopsided smile and his eyes crinkling.

This was the most blatant lie Miles had told him yet, and it had the opposite effect than he'd probably anticipated. Instead of enchanted, Evan felt cold and clammy, like he'd just sobered up.

No matter how much he liked Miles—and desperately wanted Miles to like him back—the truth was Miles was only trying to charm him so he could have the upper hand. Miles thought the stuff Evan did with his laptop was pointless and a waste of time.

"How should I mix this?" This time it was easy for Evan to drag his attention back to the task. He should have been happier, but he wasn't.

Miles' expression was perplexed. "Mix . . . it?"

"Never mind," Evan huffed. "I'll figure it out." He stuck his hands in and started swirling the ingredients together. Way too quickly his fingers were caked with the sticky flour mixture.

"Wait," Miles said and Evan hesitated, still fingers-deep in the gluey mass. "I think . . . I think maybe we need to approach this differently."

Evan hoped the glare he shot the other man said pointedly that he had *tried* to ask ahead of time, and Miles hadn't understood.

"I know, I know," Miles murmured as he approached Evan, a little like he was trying to calm an upset dog, "it'll be fine. We'll figure it out."

"I don't think so," Evan retorted. "I think we're pretty fucked." His voice wobbled on the last word as Miles reached in and plucked out one of Evan's hands. Whenever Miles was in the kitchen, his own hands were always quick and efficient—certain. Now, he took his time, carefully and thoroughly cleaning off the caked-on mass of sticky flour off each finger.

It couldn't be impersonal, because there was so much touching—way too much touching for Evan's peace of mind—but it felt even more intimate with Miles bent over his fingers, so meticulously making sure every bit of the "dough" was off, his lashes dark against his cheeks as he concentrated on the task.

"I'm sure . . . I'm sure I could manage," Evan stuttered helplessly. He was caught. Literally. Metaphorically.

"Almost done," Miles said, his soft voice still roughly hypnotic, pinning Evan in place even further. He could have moved. He could have protested—he *should* have protested. But the truth was he didn't want to stop touching Miles, even if it didn't mean what he wanted it to.

"Why don't we start over?" Evan asked. "We've got lots of ingredients."

"Because I was slow and you were too fast? There's no reason to. We can salvage this." Miles glanced up, his gray eyes almost green in the light, and it was like he could see right through Evan and all his token protests. Like he meant something else by his words. Like maybe he was admitting he'd been too slow out of the gate and was just now catching up.

"There," he finally said, releasing the second hand. The sticky mass was mostly gone, but Evan knew he needed to wash them off still. And then they needed to do whatever Miles came up with to salvage the half-mixed ingredients.

But he didn't move, and neither did Miles, even though their hips had somehow aligned. If they took a step closer, more than just their fingers would touch. Evan had a sudden flash of memory: Miles crowding him close against the wall when they'd argued only a few days ago. Then, he'd been hot with anger and the indignity of having Miles push him around. Now, the anger had faded and all that remained was an indelible memory of Miles' body against his. And the memory was filled with a whole different kind of heat.

It was annoying that even when Miles was an ass, Evan somehow found him irresistible. Evan figured that must be a commentary on his poor taste in men. Nice men didn't register; it was only when someone went out of their way to be a dick that he paid attention.

"I didn't mean it," Miles murmured, and that was the worst of all, because that was his doughy fingers brushing his cheek, and if he leaned in another few inches, they might be kissing.

The very last thing on earth that Evan wanted to discuss was the email, and he definitely didn't want it to be used against him, especially not when it was only fair and equitable that Evan get to use it against Miles.

After all, it hadn't been Evan who'd up and run away and then gotten drunk and written a nearly incoherent email filled with vague insults and even vaguer compliments.

The good news was it was the push Evan needed to pull away and put some space between them. He turned towards the sink and told himself that he imagined Miles' disappointed face. "Tell me," Evan said briskly, scrubbing with more cold water, "how do we fix it?"

"I don't know, I'm trying," Miles said, and there was too much raw honesty in his voice.

Evan looked up and his own was sharp in response. "I meant the dough."

"Oh. The dough. Right."

Evan ignored how sulky Miles sounded. Was that all he thought he needed to do to fix things between them? Some charming lines and some vague flirting? And a few moments where he considered kissing Evan again?

Yeah, *no*.

Miles had made Evan's life hell since he'd showed up at *Five Points*, and then he'd gone out of his way to insult him.

Finishing up with his hands, Evan wet a paper towel and scrubbed at his face, sure that Miles' fingers had left some traces of flour even though they'd only brushed his skin for a split second. It had been long enough.

When Evan returned to the workspace, Miles was staring into the bowl like it held all the mysteries of the universe. "I think if we mix with a spatula to get the mixture into a rough dough then we can knead it by hand."

Evan picked up the spatula and gently, carefully mixed the dough until it came together into a ball. He wasn't taking any more chances for Miles to ingratiate himself. Mistakes were an opportunity for Miles, and Evan wasn't giving him any additional openings.

"That's good," Miles said. The murmured intimacy in his voice had lessened somewhat, and Evan *was* glad. It was exhausting to fight the attraction all the time. Sometimes he just wanted to get some stuff done without all the distraction.

Shoving his hands back into the dough, Evan copied Miles' demonstrated kneading techniques until Miles pronounced it ready, and got another bowl out, to set the dough into. It went into the freezer to chill.

"What now?" Evan asked.

"Have you ever eaten a croissant?" Miles asked.

"Of course I have." Evan tapped a foot impatiently. It felt like they'd wasted hours, even though it had only barely been one, if the clock on the far side of the kitchen wasn't lying to him.

"Then you know about the flaky layers it has. We need to create that, and to do that, we use a sheet of cold butter, folded in between layers of dough. When the croissants bake, the butter evaporates and creates pockets of air in the dough."

"Which makes it flaky." This baking thing, Evan thought, was a lot more complicated than he'd realized. He re-thought what Miles had said. "A *sheet* of butter?"

Miles shrugged at Evan's astonishment and pulled over a single sheet of waxed paper, on which was spread a thick even layer of butter. "I came in early and made this, and chilled it," he said. "It needs to be very cold, or else it'll all just melt into the dough. It's like pie dough."

When Evan continued to look at him blankly, Miles continued. "You know, like the pies you bake on Thanksgiving? You need cold fat mixed into the dough to prevent it from being tough."

Evan knew what Miles was getting at, and while he had no intention of sharing just how far his Thanksgivings had been from family pie-making, he couldn't exactly pretend like he knew what Miles was talking about.

"We always had store-bought," Evan said, which was only partially a lie. He remembered years when he'd been fortunate and lucky to get a piece of store-bought pie. Homemade pie was a figment of his imagination, a dream that he'd never gotten to share.

"It's the same concept," Miles said. "The water in the butter or the lard evaporates in the heat of the oven, leaving the dough pocketed and airy. Here," he handed a rolling pin to Evan, "let's roll out the butter a little while the dough finishes chilling."

Evan felt like he did a really good job getting the butter perfectly flat and even, as Miles grabbed the dough. Finally, his A-plus personality and perfectionist instincts were coming in handy in the kitchen.

The dough was far trickier to roll out. Miles kept tossing flour on the marble and insisting Evan flour his hands and the pin so many times that he was sure that flour had made it past the apron to his clothes beneath. Good thing he didn't have any other meetings scheduled for today.

When Miles felt like he had the dough flattened enough, they worked together to carefully transport the butter from the wax paper to the dough rectangle. This time, Miles didn't offer to lick the residual butter off his fingers, and Evan shouldn't have been disappointed, but he was a little.

He certainly thought about offering to return the favor as Miles lifted one of his hands to his mouth for a surreptitious lick. But that would be insane and Evan prided himself on his sanity.

"Now, fold the sides of the dough over the butter, like a Christmas present." Evan held his breath and waited for Miles to try the same thing he had with the Thanksgiving pies, but he didn't. Which meant nobody else in the office had blabbed and Miles didn't know yet. A small blessing.

"We're done?" Evan asked hopefully after the folding was complete.

Miles shot him an incredulous look. "Not even close. The dough needs to be re-chilled, and then we'll re-fold to make more layers. And then rinse and repeat."

Jaw dropping, Evan stared incredulously at the man next to him. "How many rinse and repeats?"

"Four? We'll see how it looks at four," Miles said, piling up bowls together and walking over to the sink. "Pastry isn't a race to see how fast you can get something on a plate."

"Or in my stomach," Evan grumbled. "Am I allowed to work at non-baking tasks in between layers?"

Miles waved a hand as he started running hot water in the dishes. "Whatever you want."

Checking email usually didn't fill Evan with quite so much excitement or anticipation, but he was so ready to get back to the familiar, he nearly forgot to take off his flour-dusted apron before venturing back to his cubicle to retrieve his laptop and his notes.

He could only imagine what the reactions would have been if he hadn't detoured to quickly shed the ugly apron and brush off his clothes. He left the bow tie lying on the counter next to his notepad, and considered it a worthy sacrifice for a little bit of Miles' trust.

The problem was that Miles wasn't just after trust. That much was becoming very obvious, and even though it was difficult to imagine a world in which Evan could resist him forever, he still had to make a decision about giving in.

What would it mean? What would it look like? How could he make sure he maintained the upper hand while giving in?

Since he'd turned eighteen, Evan had been professionally ambitious and personally careful. It was a combination that served him well until now, and he saw no reason to throw caution to the wind. If he was going to let Miles—and himself, if he was being very honest—have their way, he needed to at least do it on his own terms, in his own way.

Laptop in hand, Evan swung by the restroom and when he was washing up, gave his face only the most perfunctory look over. Even with the briefest glance, his flushed cheeks and bright eyes gave away the story.

Miles evoked all sorts of emotions in him—frustration and annoyance and impatience, but also something warmer and more indefinable. Something he'd always avoided because he wasn't sure he could control it, and until this moment, that had felt like the scariest risk he could have taken.

This time it felt scarier *not* to take it, like he didn't know what he was missing out on if he let it pass him by.

Chapter Seven

When Evan left the kitchen to grab his laptop, Miles did the dishes and stared at his reflection in the window in front of the sink.

There was no shame in needing to give yourself a pep talk every now and again, but Miles felt weird that he didn't need any sort of pep talk at all. Didn't people usually need to psych themselves up when required to cozy up to someone for mercenary reasons? James Bond never flinched, but James Bond was a manwhore with zero conscience.

Miles didn't like to think he was that sort of person, but when faced with the prospect of using Evan's attraction to give himself the upper hand all he felt was pure, unadulterated excitement. He knew his own feelings about Evan were conflicted, but maybe the lack of shame he was feeling meant he wasn't really conflicted at all.

He was pretty sure that meant his heart or his mind or maybe just his dick was engaged on some level. *And that made it better, didn't it?* his conscience insisted.

It wasn't going to be all for show, on some level it was real for Miles and that should have been all the green light he needed to close the deal. But instead of prodding him into action, the thought made him hold back when Evan returned to the kitchen with his laptop and that stupid folder bulging with notes, half of which seemed to be pages torn from the precious notebook that barely ever left his side.

It was the same sky blue as the bow tie he'd removed earlier, and they both sat, innocent but inherently dangerous, on the kitchen counter.

"Do you want to go over some of the stuff I have?" Evan asked, and unlike his normal, ball-busting certainty, he seemed hesitant. Like maybe he'd reconsidered just how good of an idea so much flirting was.

Miles' dick certainly thought the flirting had been fantastic, and nothing in the world had been hotter than uptight, always-confident Evan uncertainly digging his hands into a bowl of dough and looking to Miles for instructions on how to deal with it.

He hadn't realized that was going to be a turn-on, but Miles wasn't stupid. It added a flair of authenticity to the charm he was trying to pour on, so he used it.

The real question was if it only had the ring of truth or it *was* the truth. Miles had claimed, not even a week ago, that he could never be attracted to a man with such a stick up his ass. He was not happy to discover he might have been wrong.

The only explanation was that Evan, like any decent mold, grew on you after awhile.

"What do we need to go over?" Miles tried to play it casual, but he sounded equal parts apprehensive and excited.

"Oh, tons of stuff. A whole bunch of tiny details, all pointless by themselves, but it all needs to be decided."

"Like?"

Miles had spent most of his teenage and adult life playing it casual with guys he liked. He didn't do serious relationships, or usually relationships at all. He'd never felt the need because casual came naturally to him.

Casual was not coming easy to him now, as he sidled up to where Evan was perched on a stool, sorting through his folders. He leaned against the counter, and railed at himself for looking like some sort of practiced gigolo.

Maybe he *was* James Bond, he'd just never realized it.

Evan wrinkled his nose. "You don't have to be so tense. I'm not *telling* you the decisions, we're making them together."

"Right, yeah, of course."

Costa, he told himself firmly, *you sound like a fucking moron. You can barely string together a sentence. When did he get to you like this?*

Apparently between one breath and the next, in the time it had taken for Evan to stick his fingers in the dough and then throw Miles a single beseeching look.

Miles wasn't James Bond, he was a romance novel heroine straight out of the bodice-ripping 1980s.

"For example," Evan said, pulling out a single sheet with a bunch of scribbles, "how do you feel about the title?"

Evan had very straight posture, his spine stiff even when he was sitting on one of those uncomfortable stools. Miles had never really noticed before, or if he had, he'd marked it off as a character flaw, but now he couldn't stop noticing. And all that ramrod posture made him want to do was tear off Evan's shirt and see what his back looked like, pale and firm, as he bent over the kitchen counter.

Maybe it was Miles who was the bodice ripper.

"The title?" Miles was having difficulty giving coherent answers, and Evan was looking at him a little like he was crazy. More than usual, anyway.

"Of your show. *Pastry by Miles?*"

"I'm not changing the name."

"I know that," Evan coaxed, "but what about a subtitle for this first season?"

"What, like *Pastry by Miles: Joan of Arc Julia Child Teaches You How to Bake?*"

"Not exactly," Evan sniffed.

"Then what?"

"Like, *Pastry by Miles: Baking 101.*"

"I sort of like that," Miles admitted begrudgingly. There was a part of him that still recoiled in horror, of course. He wasn't Joan of Arc Julia Child; there was a part of him who was always going to be an inherently selfish slave to his own creativity. But the idea of helping others find their potential was growing on him. He'd drink another bottle of faux Kahlua if Evan found out, though.

"I thought you might." Miles told himself that Evan's smug tone of voice was not in any way attractive. He wasn't very convincing.

"What else?"

"Well, I took the liberty of having the graphics department make some mockups of the new title, just to see what you thought."

Evan pulled some other brightly colored pages out of his folder and slid them across the workspace.

Miles knew graphics were not his strong suit. The logo he'd pulled together last year for *Pastry by Miles* was barely acceptable. Which was why it was so easy to get excited about having a professional take a crack at it—or at least that was what he used to justify it to himself.

"These are great," he said, leaning over and carefully examining the options one at a time.

"We can change them, or mix them, or really, anything we can think of. If you don't like any of them, we can even start over," Evan rambled, and Miles looked up at him, and realized, like a light turning on in a pitch-black room, that he was nervous. Uncertain. Worried that Miles wouldn't be happy with his initiative.

That was to be expected, because Miles hadn't been happy with any of his initiatives until now. It was completely Miles' fault that Evan worried about his reaction—because, and this was a bitter pill to swallow—none of Miles' reactions had exactly been reassuring.

Obviously, Miles had seen Evan before, but at this moment, it was like he was seeing him for the very first time, separate from his own fear-tinted glasses. It felt like he'd just been dunked in very cold water.

"I think some of these could really work," Miles said.

Evan smiled, any momentary lapses in self-confidence gone. "Agreed. This one is my favorite," he said, pulling one particular graphic, the font curling around a series of rainbow-tinted circles that evoked the famous French *macarons*. A series of episodes that Miles had done on *macarons* inspired by famous adult beverages had been very popular; probably his most popular episodes before the strawberry raspberry tarts. He still got people messaging him that they'd never thought of making a strawberry margarita *macaron*, or one inspired by a White Russian, but that he'd changed the way they saw pastry.

Those comments had probably been part of the problem, Miles realized. Somehow he'd gotten insufferably smug. There was self-assurance and then there was conceited arrogance. Somehow he'd fallen on the wrong side of that line.

He wanted to apologize—to his credit, not for the first time this week—but that apology, like all his others, still stuck in his throat.

"Did you know that three quarters of *Five Points* clamored for Reed to make those *macarons*?" Evan asked, almost to himself, like of course Miles knew.

"Did he?" Miles asked.

The expression on Evan's face grew conspiratorial, and it shouldn't have been so cute, but it was, undeniably. He leaned closer, bending over the drawings between them. "Reed claimed he was too busy, but his boyfriend, Jordan, admitted to me that he spent three weeks trying to perfect them, and finally gave up."

Reed Ryan had attempted to duplicate his recipes and failed? Miles didn't know whether to be flattered or embarrassed. Suddenly it seemed very stupid to not provide people who wanted to duplicate his creations the recipe.

And sure, he'd worked at Terroir, but Miles had always prided himself as being laid-back and down-to-earth, at least as far as chefs went. He certainly had never been as bad as Bastian Aquino, whose ego he'd gotten to witness with a front row seat.

"*Macarons* are tricky," Miles said, which wasn't a lie. They were notoriously difficult to master, and even he sometimes baked batches that just didn't turn out for reasons he could never pinpoint. "I'll make some this weekend and bring them in." He hesitated, because even though Evan had claimed not to like sweets, maybe he could extend a peace offering in lieu of an actual apology. "Did you want to try a particular flavor?"

Evan shot him a triumphant look, like he'd just been waiting for Miles to ask. "The lemon drop. Of course."

It felt as easy as breathing to reach forward and trace the bright yellow circle on the logo. "One of my favorites."

Evan just sniffed. "Well, you have *some* taste, apparently."

"Does that mean I should pick that particular logo?" Miles challenged. But he couldn't help but miss that the sniping they were doing today was far more playful and anticipatory than the sniping of the last two weeks.

It left Miles breathless and fairly certain that he had almost nothing in common with James Bond after all.

"If you want to. It's ultimately your show. But," Evan said, with more than a little defiance in his own voice, "it's the best choice, by far."

"And probably the idea that you came up with," Miles finished smoothly.

Evan looked surprised and annoyed—definitely not as pleased as Miles had hoped when he'd thrown that line out. "So much shock I can do my job properly," he retorted.

"I figured they put the best with the best."

Evan just rolled his eyes. "And there's the Miles Costa I've grown to know."

"Be nice, or you won't get any *macarons*. Or any *pain au chocolat*."

This time Evan seemed to completely forget that he didn't like sweets, because he sighed with exasperation at Miles' threat. "What?" he asked defensively. "They're taking an eternity to make, surely I should get something out of all this time and effort."

The beeper on Miles' phone went off, pinging loudly. "And that's our cue for more time and effort. Time to re-fold the dough."

This time Evan didn't make a movement to go grab the dough from the blast chiller, but Miles let him go, as he scribbled more into his notebook, seemingly absorbed in making notes on the new logo.

It was an easy five minutes of work for Miles, who got twitchy if he couldn't get his hands into some sort of dough every day.

When he got back to where Evan was perched, he had opened his laptop and was typing furiously into an email window. Miles peered over his shoulder. "Anything good?" he asked.

"Sending some final notes to the graphic designer," Evan said. "I told her to bump the brightness of the colors up a bit, I want something bright and almost candy-colored. And to make the font a bit less fanciful. I feel like the rainbow *macarons* are enough on that front. She'll probably send a few options for us to look at."

Miles rubbed his neck and tried not to look sheepish. "I'm not very good at this part, I should probably default to your expertise."

It was worth admitting that he wasn't very good at something to see Evan's face light up. "Of course," he chirped happily. "If you're sure you trust me not to pick something hideous."

"You picked me, didn't you?"

Evan's smile evolved into a self-satisfied smirk. "That's right, I did. Besides, in case you were worried, I have fantastic taste."

"What else do you have for me?" Miles asked.

"Do you watch *Dream Team*?" Evan shot the question over as he typed furiously away at his laptop. Miles knew enough to see he wasn't working on another email. It was hard to bite back the sudden demand that Evan tell him what he was writing—it wasn't easy to trust Evan when he'd said all that to Reed—but Miles knew he needed to.

"*Dream Team*? The cooking show with that baker from LA and Landon Patton? The one where they spent three quarters of the time flirting and not actually cooking?"

"That's the one." Evan didn't look up. "They're gearing up for rehearsals in the next week, because the next season of their show starts filming."

"And?"

Evan looked up, and he didn't look thrilled. "And that means our kitchen time goes way down, because they're stars and we're the low men on the totem pole."

"What?" Miles demanded. How was he supposed to create recipes and test them and make sure he was able to actually teach people if he didn't have access to the kitchen?

"Believe me, I know. How are you supposed to create recipes if you can't get in the kitchen?"

Miles stared. "That was fucking eerie. How did you know I was thinking that?"

Evan shrugged. "You're predictable. Chef, kitchen time—more important than anything else. It's not hard to connect the dots."

"So what are we going to do about it?" Miles asked, trying to keep his voice level. Evan might be responsible for some things he didn't like, but he wasn't responsible for this. This was, apparently, out of his control. "I'm assuming, since you're you, you have some sort of plan to deal with this."

"Yes," Evan said. "Of course I do. Even though I just found out about this."

"Just now?"

Evan shot him a challenging look over his laptop screen. "Literally thirty seconds ago."

"Oh, so that *was* an email you were typing so angrily," Miles said.

"No. Well. Yes. Sort of. I was sending a message to Reed. Getting permission for us to work from home. Or rather, permission for us to work from *your* home. You've got a good kitchen. Not fantastic, but it should be good enough for our purposes." Evan skewered Miles with another incredibly direct look. "After all, you made that Twinkie at home, didn't you?"

"It was a Ding Dong," Miles corrected.

"Whatever." Evan threw up his hands in frustration. "This is my solution. I wish I had something else, but it's what we've got."

"Would begging help?" Miles asked. "I can be pretty persuasive."

Evan's incredulous glance didn't instantly puncture his ego. Nope. Not at all.

"Okay," he admitted, "*usually* I can be pretty persuasive. Better?"

Evan gave a sharp nod. He was still typing like each key he hit was a punch in the face of the people who had demoted their kitchen time to zip, nada, *nil*.

"No," Evan finally said, with a sigh, fingers finally drifting off the keyboard, "it wouldn't help. *Dream Team* trumps all."

It wasn't like he hadn't heard of *Dream Team*—Miles didn't live under a rock. But he hadn't really paid attention to how popular it was. Or cared, until he was suddenly faced with losing the kitchen time he needed.

"We can work around this, right?" Miles asked, and he didn't even try to hide the desperate edge to his voice. The part of him that was still terrified and needed any reassurance he could get. He'd never imagined asking for it from Evan, of all people, but maybe that had been his problem when they'd first met.

"Of course we can. Working from your place, and we'll still get some time in here but it'll be shorter and it'll be either early or late."

The one thing Miles felt confident about was that Evan was definitely as committed as he was to making this show a success. Of course how they got to that success was still up for debate, but he could never doubt Evan's commitment.

The timer on his phone dinged again, and Miles went to the fridge to pull out the dough. It felt right to be working on something right now, as they tried to muddle through this new hurdle. Whenever he'd struggled with anything cropping up in his life, he'd always gone to the kitchen.

In the kitchen, if you put flour with leavening, you got dough, and if you baked the dough, you got bread and pastries and rolls. There was a logically reassuring certainty about baking—like Miles was asserting control when he didn't have any.

"How many more rinse and repeats do we have left?" Evan asked, not even looking up from his laptop.

"One more, and then they bake," Miles said.

"I find it difficult to believe that anything is worth all this," he said primly.

"Wait and see," Miles insisted.

"You keep saying that." Evan rolled his eyes. Miles couldn't even see his whole face, but he'd begun to discover just what Evan's voice sounded like when his face did that cute little scrunchy thing that always accompanied an eye roll.

Miles shouldn't, but he couldn't help imagining feeding Evan little bites of hot, flaky, buttery pastry dotted with the rich, dark chocolate and him moaning with pleasure as the flavors hit his tongue. He couldn't help it because he was just a man and Evan was wearing him down with each cute scrunchy face and every snarky retort.

Miles was befuddled because those weren't supposed to be things that attracted him. They weren't supposed to be things that attracted anyone. But somehow those things—and a growing list of others—had caught him and now he wasn't just flirting because he was trying to out-James Bond James Bond. He was flirting because he couldn't do anything else.

And that was a problem, mostly because Miles had been incredibly dumb and had kissed him like he was trying to eat him alive and then had sent an email that would have turned off the most understanding and forgiving of people.

Evan was definitely not that understanding or forgiving.

"Miles, Miles, *Miles*." Evan's voice hit him suddenly and Miles realized that while he'd been daydreaming, trying to figure out how to get Evan to eat from his fingers and *like it* and also forget all about that very unforgettable email, he'd been trying to get his attention.

"Sorry," he said.

Evan threw his hands up in frustration. "Did you hear anything I just said?"

"No?" Miles put on his most charming sheepish expression and hoped that would melt the exasperation on Evan's face. It didn't. Not even a dent.

"I said, tomorrow we should get what you need at your apartment to make it baking-friendly."

"Right, yes, we can do that." Miles realized after he'd said it that *we* had to be a misnomer. Because Evan had no clue what he needed at his apartment to make it "baking-friendly," whatever that meant.

"You'll put the list together?"

Miles saw an opening and even though this attraction confused the hell out of him, it didn't confuse him enough to not take advantage of it. "You said, *we*," he said, with a faux leer that Xander had once said made him look like a creeper. But that was Xander, and Miles took everything he said with a massive grain of salt.

The look in Evan's eyes when he glanced up was dismissive. "Like I would know what you need to bake stuff," he said. "You make the list, and we'll go get the stuff tomorrow. You—list; me—corporate credit card."

"Let me guess, you're also in charge of the budget."

"Yes, and no. Reed just sent me a message and said we could work from your place, *and* he'd foot anything that didn't seem excessive." Evan looked rather self-satisfied at that, and Miles couldn't blame him. He also couldn't deny that even though a week ago, that smug look would have made him crazy, today, all it did was make him want to wipe it off. With his mouth.

It wasn't so much a problem as it was . . . complicated.

The timer on his phone went off again, and this time he dragged Evan off his barstool, ignoring the pulse of electricity under his skin when his fingers closed around Evan's forearm.

He was slender, but he had muscle tone under all that smooth skin, and that was an image that Miles didn't need to have when he was trying to explain to Evan how to roll out the dough for the final steps.

"A big rectangle, like this-ish," Miles said, gesturing with his hands. Evan just stood there, looking at him levelly, his arms crossed across his chest, which might be a way he stood all the time, but right now, only emphasized to Miles that he'd somehow missed that Evan was all lean muscle he desperately wanted to see.

He'd thought this was complicated, but the more he sunk into this new understanding of Evan, the more difficult Miles realized the situation really was. Because he wanted him, much more than he'd ever imagined.

"Maybe you should give me an actual dimension," Evan retorted frostily.

"We'll work on that," Miles coaxed. "It'll be great, just . . . more flour. Lots of flour. We don't want the dough to stick to the counter."

"Not after we've spent four hours in this torture chamber," Evan snarked.

Miles knew it had been frustrating at points, but he thought they'd had a pretty solid morning. He was a little offended that Evan had just referred to the kitchen as a torture chamber. Because that made Miles the head torturer. Yeah, complicated was probably an understatement.

"Just . . . flour the damn counter," Miles said.

Evan did as instructed, but only after tying the apron back on, which surprised Miles. That had been a silently acknowledged instrument of torture (apparently) and here Evan was, voluntarily putting it back on. Of course, he was probably more worried about the state of his clothes than the stupid apron.

The rolling went pretty well; Evan had good technique; he was slow and careful and even with the pressure. Miles stood a little ways behind him, and made all the right encouraging noises and tried not to check out his ass in those pants.

He remembered a point when he'd made fun of those khakis. Now he just wanted to worship them. Or at least what they contained.

"How's that?" Evan asked, standing back and eyeing the rectangle of dough critically. Like this was a life-and-death situation. And baking could be tricky, you often had to be extremely precise, but this was the easy part of the whole thing. It was tough to fuck this up, but Evan never let up on himself for a single second. He had the most A-plus personality that Miles had ever encountered.

"It's fine," Miles said, and pointed to the knife. "Now trim the edges, and cut into four equal strips."

Instead of grabbing the knife, Evan turned around and there was fire and brimstone flashing in his eyes. Miles stood there shocked, because even at the worst, even when they'd been trading insults in the break room and even after Miles had sent him the worst email in the history of emails, Evan hadn't looked at him like that.

"Do you mean to tell me," Evan said, voice low and frustrated, "that we're only getting *four* croissants out of this?"

Miles knew he should have doubled the recipe. But it had seemed easier at the beginning to keep things small and relatively simpler.

"Uh, yes?" He remembered after answering that Evan was easily within reach of both a knife and a rolling pin. Both of which he could use to extract his revenge on Miles.

"*Are you insane?*" Evan hissed. "*Four fucking hours on four croissants?*"

"I thought it was more about the experience and the journey. Besides, you said you don't even like sweets." Miles was torn between groveling and also throwing up an arm to protect against the inevitable attack with the rolling pin, which Evan was still gripping.

"I don't." Evan was still shooting fire from his eyes. It shouldn't have been sexy; it was. Miles couldn't explain that or anything else that had happened today, but logic was overrated. Maybe he should just go with it.

"Right, well, let's continue cutting the dough then. Four even strips." Miles wanted to power through this, and maybe then they could finally get them in the oven, and he could see his fantasy come to life. Evan, putting his food in his mouth.

"This is ridiculous," Evan ground out. But he still turned back to the work surface and began to cut the dough.

"Noted," Miles retorted. But he knew the difference was stark. This time, he sounded amused and not angry. Not like before. He wondered if Evan was paying close enough attention to care. Or if it even mattered.

Evan didn't say anything else, just absorbed the instructions on how to roll up the chocolate bar in the middle of each dough strip, and then brush with a beaten egg.

"And now, *finally*, the oven," Miles said.

"Why do people even do this?" Evan wondered, and Miles thought it was probably a rhetorical question, but he was going to answer it anyway. At least so Evan might absorb some of why baking was so vital to Miles.

"Because once you've tasted the real thing, not the chemical-flavored, soggy, sunken artificial croissant, you won't want anything else."

"I thought you were going to feed me some sort of bullshit about pride in your work."

"That was next." Miles smiled weakly.

"Right, how long in the oven?" Evan asked, picking up the tray and walking it over to the oven. Miles was only a little ashamed, but the sight of him holding a tray of baked goods was undeniably a turn-on.

"Fifteen minutes," Miles said.

Evan absorbed that, and then immediately ripped off the apron. "I'll be right back."

Thirteen minutes later—Miles totally didn't time Evan on his watch or anything, because that would be creepy—he returned, holding two cups of coffee. From the good coffee place that was a block further than the Starbucks in the first floor of the building.

"I figured if we were having first class *pain au chocolat*, we might as well indulge in better coffee." Evan handed Miles his cup with a shrug, like he was trying to downplay his gesture. Maybe he was just trying to downplay that it meant anything deeper.

But Miles already believed it went deeper.

"Thank you," he said, right as the timer went off.

The *pain au chocolat* came out of the oven a beautiful burnished golden brown, crisp edges, with the scent of butter and chocolate wafting through the air.

Evan stared at the tray and seemed to be fighting himself. "Don't you want to have one?" Miles asked innocently. He'd been sure Evan would be on the pan before they even cooled, desperate and eager to prove to Miles that he was wrong. That it wasn't worth the time and effort to bake a *pain au chocolat* from scratch.

"Maybe we should wait for them to cool a minute," Evan said.

"They're perfect just like this," Miles argued. Reached over and deposited one in Evan's palm.

"Hot," Evan complained, but he still lifted the pastry to his mouth and took a single bite. In Miles' fantasy he'd been feeding him in tantalizing little bites, waiting until Evan begged him for more. But this was good too.

Evan's eyes drifted over the first bite, and the expression on his face as he chewed and swallowed was *very* good. There was undeniable bliss, and Miles knew if he'd been able to hold it back, he would have. It made the success even sweeter.

"Good?" Miles asked innocently.

Setting the pastry on the counter with careful, deliberate movements, Evan turned towards Miles. There was something conflicted in his face, like he was doing all of this against his better judgement.

Miles understood that feeling far too well.

"How do you do that?" Evan asked plaintively.

"Do what?"

Evan threw his hands up. "Be so damn good at this. Win me over to your side when I know just how much I want you to be wrong and I know just how stubborn I am."

Miles took a step closer even though Evan's expression was telling him he'd better stay right where he was. "You wanted the best," he said, and his voice was shaky. "Why are you so disappointed you got it?"

"I'm not, I'm not," Evan tried to protest, but he'd already said enough and the green light was flashing in Miles' head. Evan might pretend to be aloof and uninterested, and might fight this every inch of the way, but he felt the exact same pull Miles did. And this time, Miles wasn't going to fuck it up by being angry.

It wasn't going to go away; in fact, it was only getting stronger. Miles usually acted on instinct, and he did now. There were only three steps between him and Evan, and he crossed them in a blink but he still hesitated when he'd reached his destination.

Evan's eyes were huge in his face, wide and shocked as Miles slid a hand around the back of his collar. But he didn't pull away and he didn't say no. Miles had been sure he'd need to argue his case harder, spend longer trying to erase the memory of their first kiss and then the email.

But instead Evan held his ground and held Miles' gaze and waited for him to close the distance between them.

Miles kissed him. It took an achingly long moment for Evan to respond, to reciprocate. A heart-stopping moment when Miles thought that maybe he'd judged everything wrong and that hadn't been the green light he'd secretly been dying for.

Then Evan's mouth moved against his, sluggish and hesitant at first, and then his tongue was slipping between his lips and he tasted just as he'd expected—like chocolate and coffee and butter—and like nothing he'd ever anticipated—sharp and charged, like the red wine that grew high up in the hills of Mount Veeder at the edge of the valley.

It was fierce and hot and the power of it blew out every fuse in his head, giving Miles no time to get his kissing shit together. His hands had just drifted up Evan's arms, and he was wondering if it was too soon to go for his cock, when Evan suddenly pulled away. His face was flushed, his eyes on the floor.

But he was breathing hard, the rhythm an echo of the ricochet of Miles' heartbeat.

The only thing Miles could think was that he needed another chance, another shot, because that couldn't be the last time it ever happened between them. A week ago he hadn't even liked this man, and now he couldn't get enough of him.

Had Evan changed or was it Miles who was irrevocably altered? He didn't know, and he wasn't sure it mattered.

"This isn't happening," Evan said resolutely before Miles could catch up and make sure that he knew everything he'd done was definitely okay. More than okay. Actually, perfectly fucking splendid.

"It just happened," Miles said frankly. "Come back over here, and it'll happen again." This was more the reaction he'd been expecting after the first kiss, and for it to happen now, after the mind-exploding second kiss, was unexpected and frustrating.

Evan shook his head emphatically. "This is the worst idea in the history of ideas. You don't even like me. I don't know why you decided to flirt with me, but apparently I can only take so much before I fold."

"I do like you," Miles said, even though it sounded stupid.

Evan shot him a look that said loud and clear that he definitely thought it sounded stupid. "Okay," he said, clearly not convinced. "But it's still not happening again. This is a major distraction that we don't need. And I don't really like you either. Or your face." His expression grew downright challenging.

The problem was that Miles didn't believe him at all. The other problem was that Evan still believed he'd meant that email.

"Fine," Miles said, unconcerned. Evan might be talking big right now, but Miles knew what it felt like when someone wanted him, and Evan wanted him. Miles just had to wait until Evan was done fighting with himself. It wouldn't matter how long it took, because Miles knew he was going to get what they both wanted.

CHAPTER EIGHT

NOT EVEN FIVE MINUTES after the kiss, the kitchen was overrun by Lucy and Steph and Chloe, Lucy's crew of prep assistants. Evan tried not to think what they would've thought if they'd come in just a tiny bit earlier and caught him kissing Miles.

Or Miles kissing him.

Evan still wasn't sure exactly how it had happened, only that it had happened at all, and if he was being very honest with himself, the world had shook and the floor had rocked and when he'd opened his eyes again, nothing was the same. It was the first kiss he'd always dreamt he'd get from Miles, and he'd let himself be persuaded into it because he'd imagined it would be like the first time.

It hadn't been anything like the first time. It had been dreamy and wonderful and perfect.

It couldn't happen again, but Evan could already tell from the determined glint in Miles' eyes that he wanted it to. That he believed it was only a matter of time before Evan gave in and let it happen again.

Miles thought he knew Evan, but all he'd seen was the professional surface he'd spent years cultivating. He didn't know anything about the steel inside that had been forged through even more shitty years making the best of bad situations.

And he'd seen enough in those situations that he wasn't going to let himself be swayed into a situation where he liked Miles and Miles just thought it was convenient and easy and a simple way to convince Evan to go along with whatever he suggested.

Evan was never going to be the guy who fell for that and then let it drag on. It was necessary for Miles to understand that now.

He scrolled through his email, pretending like he was actually working, while he listened to Lucy and her minions divide up the remaining *pain au chocolat* and exclaim all over the place about how talented he was, how innovative, how flawless his execution was.

Evan could see the remaining half of his abandoned *pain au chocolat* on the other counter, and he had a visceral memory of how much he'd really hated Miles when he'd taken that first bite. He'd hated that everything Miles had said was true, and he'd tried to hate that smug look as Miles watched him discover all his truths.

The final, and worst, truth being that he didn't hate Miles at all.

It was just ironic that Lucy and the assistants were so excited about Miles' talents, when Miles had only been tangentially involved. They wouldn't be squeeing all over the damn place if they'd discover Evan had made the *pain au chocolat* they were currently ingesting.

"Someday," Lucy was saying, "I want to take you to this little bakery down the street. The *choux* are a revelation. And I want to pick your brain as you figure out how they do it."

Evan tried not to grind his teeth together as Miles talked with Lucy. He shouldn't have been jealous. He and Miles weren't exactly friends, and Miles was a decent enough human being that Evan couldn't deny him workplace friends. Even if they weren't him.

"Are we done?" he asked as he stood, gathering his papers, notebook and laptop. "I have a meeting." He didn't have a meeting, and if Lucy went and looked at his schedule later, she'd know he'd manufactured a reason to escape.

Miles glanced over, and Evan steeled himself against the silent apology in his gaze. "Yeah, of course, if you've got to split, I guess I'll see you tomorrow."

It wasn't his proudest moment, but later as he collapsed on his couch, feet and brain and heart hurting, he realized what he'd done. He'd given Miles all the advantages, all the power, all because he'd run away.

What he should do was get up, and go right over to where Miles was probably in his apartment, cooking something delicious, and take some of that power back. His heart and something deeper, a fault line that ran right through the core of him, quaked at the thought. He could *do* something. It was a huge risk, the sort of unimaginable risk that Evan couldn't have conceptualized even a few months ago. But the promotion, even as uncertain as it was, had begun to give him the sort of solid foundation he'd always craved.

And once life had become less of a rat race towards one goal or another, always something necessary and vitally important, Evan had become unbearably aware of all the couples that surrounded him. And the contentment their happy relationships gave them.

He'd seen Reed grow confident and happier the longer he was with Jordan. He'd watched Nick worry and stew and pray as his husband, Colin, had figured out where he wanted to play football next. He'd seen one of Lucy's assistants blossom as she fell in love with her girlfriend.

Love was something Evan had only vaguely heard about, because any kind of love was constantly in short supply in the homes he'd grown up in. There were always more important priorities.

But he'd fulfilled those priorities and they weren't yelling at him anymore. He was clothed and fed and had a solid roof over his head. He had money in the bank. He wasn't living a terrified hand-to-mouth existence anymore. He could afford to be exploratory, even if the possibility scared the shit out of him.

But even the fear wasn't enough to stop him. Even the promise he'd made to himself only an hour earlier that he wouldn't let Miles kiss him again.

That was the thing. He wasn't going to let Miles do anything. He was going to be the one doing the kissing this time. The thought was fucking terrifying, but Evan had never let fear stop him.

"This is probably a mistake," he told himself as he got to his feet and went to look for shoes. "This is almost definitely a mistake."

Yet he still found the shoes, shoved his feet in them and still tromped one door down the hall.

Miles answered on the third knock, looking very surprised to see Evan on the other side of his doorway.

"Sorry about earlier," Evan said in a rush because suddenly he didn't know what to say. He didn't know how to go from the awkward realization he was standing on Miles' doorstep to kissing him like he wanted to. His lack of any experience besides just sort of falling into bed with people had never seemed daunting. It was now.

He didn't have a clue how to seduce someone. It seemed to come naturally to Miles, because when he wasn't pissing Evan off, he was trying to charm him—usually successfully. Evan didn't do that; Evan *couldn't* do that.

Miles lifted an eyebrow. "Are you apologizing *again* for kissing me back? I didn't think you had a bad time on the second try." He was holding a whisk in one hand, and he had flour on his shirt.

"I'm sorry," Evan said because all he could do apparently was apologize. And even he knew that apologies usually weren't preludes to anything sexy. "I interrupted you . . . cooking something."

Miles pushed the door further open, and just shrugged. "Is it an interruption if you do it regularly enough? Besides, I'm making dinner, you might as well come in if you haven't eaten."

Evan had been in too much of a hurry to escape the office and his inconvenient, annoying jealousy to grab food on his way home, and his fridge was empty except for three bottles of fancy mustard and half a bottle of sauvignon blanc. His stomach rumbled as he stepped into the apartment and he smelled something buttery baking.

"You eat too much butter," Evan said as he toed his shoes off near the front mat.

"At least butter's natural. It isn't processed shit," Miles called from the kitchen.

This apartment was basically the same as his own, except for the kitchen, which Evan could acknowledge was drastically different.

Not the layout. Not the countertops, not the appliances. Just the flour dusting the countertops, and something delicious sautéing on the stove, and the general appearance of a room being used.

Evan mostly used his to unbox takeout containers and to reheat the leftovers the next day.

"You want some wine?" Miles asked, gesturing to the bottle on the counter. "I've actually been to this winery, so I can vouch that it's pretty good."

Evan had just graduated from buying the very cheap wine at the grocery store, the wine that was a whisper above the box wine and the huge jugs of white zinfandel. He'd never actually been to a winery; in fact his only trip to Napa had been the six hour round-trip he'd made to collect Miles.

It wasn't like he didn't want to expand his horizons—Reed was always coaching him to do just that—but horizon-expanding took money and, until recently, he'd never been in any position to indulge.

He poured himself a glass of the cabernet sauvignon and sniffed it, carefully swirling the glass like Reed had taught him the first time he'd taken him to a nice restaurant for dinner.

"It is pretty good," Evan admitted. Even to his relatively uncultured palate. And it might give him the liquid courage to close the few feet of distance Miles was giving him.

"I know the sommelier who's in charge there," Miles said, and his voice grew grittier as he stirred the pan on the stove and then pulled it off the heat.

Evan almost asked if it was an ex-boyfriend but Miles seemed like he was going to tell him even if he didn't really want to know about all the people Miles had kissed before him. Especially not when Evan was planning on doing more kissing.

"You know Wyatt?" Miles asked, shaking the sautéed veggies in the pan and carefully stirring them into the bowl on the counter. "My old roommate?"

Evan barely remembered anything about his trip to Napa, except the lighter fluid stench coming off Miles and the guilt in his eyes. But he nodded anyway, even though all he had was an impression of a big guy, built like a linebacker with sun-bleached hair.

"Yeah, it's Wyatt's ex. Good sommelier. Terrible boyfriend." He hesitated as he pulled a partially baked pie crust from the oven, which explained the deliciously buttery smell in the apartment. "Got us some great wine though. Not that this one is spectacular, but he was connected, you know?"

Evan had learned really fast that some people—okay, *most* people—didn't want to know about how he wasn't connected at all. Or about his shitty childhood. Or about how he'd clawed his way up the ladder to success. He'd been on a handful of very terrible dates where he'd been at least partially honest when asked, and afterwards, he'd figured out that when people asked, they weren't asking because they actually wanted to know the truth.

Miles poured the contents of the bowl into the crust and sprinkled some sort of cheese over the top.

"What are you making?" Evan asked, because changing the subject seemed like the best plan he could come up with at such short notice.

"Veggie quiche with some really good fontina I picked up at the farmer's market," Miles said, like everyone came home from a trying day and whipped together a gourmet meal.

Sometimes it felt like too much for Evan to dial the number to the local Chinese restaurant.

Miles must have caught Evan's eye roll because he smirked. "Are you going to tease me now about the good fontina from the farmer's market?" He was leaning over the counter, eyes sparkling under the lights, looking too delicious for words, even with the flour dusting his t-shirt. *Especially* with the flour dusting his t-shirt.

"It just was such a cliché. You're like a walking chef cliché ninety-four point six percent of the time."

He didn't look concerned about Evan's accusation, though, and Evan couldn't help but be a little surprised. Two weeks ago, that comment would have gotten Evan a sour lemon expression and some biting remark back.

"Why are you being so nice?" Evan wanted to know. He wanted to know even more, like what Miles wanted from him, but he thought he'd start small. Simple.

"To you? Especially when you seem to enjoy making fun of me?" Miles shrugged, clearly unconcerned by the sudden shift in their relationship. "I'm not sure. Why does it matter?"

"It matters because it matters."

"Some things don't require you to overthink them. Just like some pastries shouldn't rise too much. Or that a dessert can be too sweet, but can never have too much chocolate."

"Life advice from Miles Costa. You should change career paths." Evan knew he got bitchy when he got defensive. "*Finding Your Best Self by Miles.*"

Evan ignored the twinge of hurt in Miles' eyes.

"Hey, I never promised I was some sort of expert. I sort of fall into most things," he said, voice still easy, "and when I got out of my own way, this seemed pretty obvious."

"I can't do that. I don't do that." Evan hesitated, confessions teetering on the edge of his tongue, but he held them back. "If something isn't going to work out, if something looks like it's going to fail, I make sure it doesn't." He didn't want this to fail, but he also didn't know how to make it a success.

Show me how, he wanted to beg Miles, but his pride would have stung far too much to ever admit that out loud.

"You know," Miles said casually, "that explains a lot about you. About how you are with your job."

Evan turned away, twisting the stem of his wine glass. "I thought I was the luckiest person in the world when I got a paid internship at *Five Points* my senior year of college. It was the best opportunity I was ever going to get, and I jumped at it."

"And you worked your ass off," Miles finished. When Evan glanced up, he was smiling ruefully.

"What?" Miles asked with amusement. "Don't tell me you've changed that much."

Evan flushed and nodded. "I haven't. I did everything they asked me to do. And it wasn't glamorous stuff, we didn't do any videos back then. Not like now. The culinary department didn't even exist. Most of the staff writers had assistants. I was an assistant to the assistants. And that makes it sound even better than it was."

"How did you end up working for Reed?" Miles asked. "He's never struck me as the sort who would get a new job and demand an assistant."

"Oh god, no," Evan breathed out. "That didn't even become official right away. I had started helping out here and there on the *Dream Team* set, this was right before I graduated from college, and I really wanted to transition from a paid internship to a full-time paid position. And I thought if I made myself an expert, the guy you went to for everything related to that show, I might *make* myself a job."

"So you helped Reed when he came on."

Evan leaned over the counter, wondering how, in a week, he and Miles had gone from hating each other to reluctantly working together, to conspiratorially trading work stories and sharing a bottle of wine as Miles cooked.

For the very first time he let himself think, *I want more. I want this all the time.*

"You and Reed have more in common than you realize," Evan confessed.

"We're both brilliant chefs?" Miles' incredulous look left Evan feeling warm inside. Too warm. He took a gulp of wine before belatedly realizing that was not going to help at all.

"Other than that," Evan said. "When he started, he was fucking lost. Jordan helped, of course, especially with his *Dream Team* producing duties. But the rest of it? I found myself doing a lot of stuff he asked me to help him with."

Miles leaned over the stove, pulling the oven door open a crack to check his quiche. Evan tried to ignore the way his t-shirt rode up his back, exposing a tempting slice of bare skin.

He failed. He wanted to reach over and touch that skin. He wanted to know what it tasted like under his tongue.

"So how long did you officially work as Reed's assistant?"

Evan hesitated. "Are we really having the conversation we should have had the first day you showed up? Right *now*?"

"You just knocked on my door. We're having a nice glass of wine. I kissed you today and we both liked it." Miles shrugged unrepentantly. "It makes sense to start over, as much as we can."

Evan couldn't believe his nerve, but Miles did seem to do that: float through life, unconcerned and not heavily bogged down by regrets or complicated situations. He was a surface person; Evan was desperate for roots. They were probably not the most obvious match, and Evan knew that, but sometimes fate was crazy like that. You wanted the wrong person, even if you knew he was the wrong person.

And then, suddenly, like a light flashing on, it didn't even matter.

Evan reached over and grabbed the hem of Miles' t-shirt and jerked him closer. "Then let's start over," he said, and kissed him.

It probably wasn't the best line ever. It wasn't even the most successful line, but that didn't matter because Miles' mouth was on his. Pleasure roared through Evan like a freight train. He hadn't even realized how much he'd wanted until he could just take, so he did.

He fisted his hand in the hair that he'd been watching and wanting for eight months, and it was just as soft and necessary as Evan had imagined it would be. It also proved handy to use as a directional force because Miles went just where Evan wanted him, sliding right back against the counter, his mouth a hot brand against Evan's.

It turned out that seduction was easy when you just took what you wanted. Evan took Miles' mouth, his hair, and then his body as his other hand slid right down his back, fingers testing and touching every lean inch of muscle the way his eyes had for the last week.

It was also easy when you didn't think, when you let the fire of desire consume everything—every fear, every worry, every quietly murmured doubt.

Evan flipped up the hem of Miles' t-shirt, and slid his hand right up the skin of his back.

It felt even more incredible than he'd imagined, and then Miles moaned, something wild and free and unhinged, like he was torn apart by Evan kissing him, by Evan pursuing him.

It wasn't like Evan didn't think he was worth wanting; it was more complicated than that. And Evan didn't want to do complicated right now. He'd done complicated his whole damn life, and right now a really cute boy was kissing him and beginning to sort of grind against his thigh, his hard cock definitely mirroring Evan's own.

It was so easy to just say, *fuck it*.

When Evan broke the kiss with a gasp, Miles' lips were red and wet, the same color as the raspberry strawberry tarts he'd made that had started everything. And it was so easy to tangle his fingers deeper into Miles' curls. Evan had barely even begun to push when Miles tore the floor right out from under Evan and sunk to his knees.

Yeah, Evan definitely wanted that, but he'd also never conceptualized that it was a thing that could actually happen.

He watched as Miles unbuckled his belt with legitimately trembling fingers. Something Evan had always been sure only happened in overwrought porn. But his own fingers didn't feel so steady either, so it could definitely happen, especially when the moment felt like this and you were so close to the edge you could tumble right off with only a gentle nudge.

There was no time to worry. No time to second-guess. Miles already had his cock out, pleasure spiking as he stroked it expertly with those long, slender fingers that Evan had already been fantasizing about for months.

Then Miles lowered his mouth, and Evan stopped thinking at all. There was only a fuzzy haze of bliss blanketing everything, and for the first time in what felt like forever, Evan just let himself feel it. Up until the moment his cock slipped out of Miles' mouth and he realized that Miles was babbling helplessly as his fingers reached back and gripped Evan tight by the ass, each of his ten fingers branding him.

"God, your ass in these pants," he was mumbling, "I love it so damn much."

And like the worst nightmare in the world, a single, blinding flash.

I really hate your face.

Evan tried to push it aside. He worked really hard, so hard in fact, that he felt himself grow the opposite. And then the flare of embarrassment as he couldn't help but flash back to every single damning word of that email. All those disparaging, drunk, stupid words.

He wrenched his body away, his softening dick falling from Miles' worshipful fingers.

Evan couldn't look down, couldn't see Miles' face as he realized everything was wrong.

His fingers were still trembling stupidly as he stuffed himself back in his briefs and zipped his fly. His belt buckle was hopeless and he just left it dangling uselessly.

"What's going on?" Miles asked softly. Carefully. Like he was afraid he'd spook a wild animal.

And it was Evan who was the wild animal; the wild card who'd just lost his mind and let Miles blow him and then lost the whole train because he couldn't forget—not really, not when it counted—that Miles didn't really like him.

Evan remembered too many homes he'd lived in, where the kids' faces would change the moment he walked in the room. And then how they'd suck up later that night, begging for Evan to do their homework for them.

He remembered every single time he'd gone to bed with that sick feeling in his stomach. Needed for something but never really liked. Never respected. Always used.

It turned out that it didn't feel different even if he was the one doing the using.

"I can't do this," Evan said, and to his own shock, his voice was steady. Rock steady. Like his belt wasn't dangling undone, and Miles wasn't still on his knees in his kitchen.

"It just . . ." Miles said, and then hesitated. And yeah, Evan didn't know what to say either. How else did you address the elephant in the room that the guy you were blowing suddenly and inexplicably lost his hard-on?

"It happened," Evan said with a hard edge, and forced himself to turn back and meet Miles' eyes straight on. To take in his position and remember that it was Evan who had put him there. "It's not going to happen again."

"You're the one who showed up on my doorstep!" Miles exclaimed, pulling himself upright.

"Yes, well, I wanted to check in with you before tomorrow. And now that I have, I'll be going," Evan said. He picked up his wine glass, letting the rest of the alcohol slide down his throat. It didn't help. He set the glass on the counter with a decisive click.

"Wait," Miles said. "Don't go. You haven't even had dinner yet."

"That's your dinner, not mine," Evan said. It hurt, realizing that it was probably never going to be his dinner. But the short-term pain was easier than the long term; he'd learned that the hard way.

"Why are you being like this?" Miles asked, and yeah, he was definitely annoyed.

"I'm being this way because we cleared the air, we had a nice glass of wine together, and now you want more out of me. But it's not going to happen. This wasn't some sort of impromptu date."

"You can't ignore this," Miles protested. "You wanted it too. I know you did." He didn't even have to say, *I had your dick in my mouth and it was hard and you wanted it. You wanted to come.*

"But I am ignoring it," Evan said, pulling the door open, "I'm exercising my right not to deal with this."

Evan shouldn't have been surprised that Miles followed him right out the door, socks and all. Really, he should have just kept going and not stopped, therefore tipping Miles off to the fact they lived next door to each other. A fact Evan had been very determined to keep to himself.

"What are you doing?" Miles stood, shock on his features as Evan pulled out his keys and proceeded to unlock his door.

"Going home," Evan shot over with a challenging look.

"You live next door," he stated incredulously.

"*Five Points* owns this building. Reed got me a good deal when I was looking for a new place."

"Just like my 'good deal,'" Miles said wonderingly. "I wondered why it seemed so convenient."

Evan rolled his eyes. "You should read your lease a lot more carefully. This place is rented to you as long as you're an employee of *Five Points*."

Miles didn't look phased for a moment, and Evan figured that was because he'd never been desperate and on the edge of homeless. If it ever happened to him, he'd learn to read his leases.

Tapping his foot impatiently, Evan asked, "Are we done here?"

It was so sudden, Evan would tell himself that was why he didn't see it coming. Except that Miles uttered some stupid line first about, "one more thing," and that should have been all the warning Evan needed that he was going to take another three steps, cup Evan's chin in one beautiful hand, and kiss him again.

Later, Evan would also tell himself that the reason he didn't stop it right away was because he was so surprised, but how could that really be true after what had just happened?

So if Evan fell into the kiss, let his head be tipped back against his door, let his mouth be nearly ransacked by Miles' mouth, let himself wonder if that was his slightly salty taste, then that was his own damn fault.

Then Miles broke the kiss way too soon, leaving Evan wanting more and again and *everything*, but it was all useless, and Miles' lips, wet and red, superseded anything else.

"You weren't supposed to do that again," Evan said unsteadily, because the blood had left his brain again and taken a fast route to his cock. He shifted his hips away from Miles, because even though he'd probably already felt his hard-on, Evan didn't need him to gloat about it. Yes, it was back. No, this still wasn't happening.

Miles placed a finger right on his damp lips to shut him up. "I know what you're about to say," he said, "and I'm just going to stop you there, before you say it."

Evan glared, but Miles didn't move. "Besides," Miles said, with a cute little shrug that Evan wanted to hate, but didn't, "we both know everything you were about to say was some bullshit you're trying to believe and that I don't believe at all."

Evan backed up a step, and then another, even though this was *his* doorway. Miles' hand fell to his side, and he was free to insist that Miles was the one who was full of bullshit, but for the first time in a long time, he didn't know how to refute something so blindingly obvious.

"Don't ever do that again." Evan crossed his arms over his chest—because, *defiant body language* and also it kept Miles at arm's length while Evan tried to figure out what to do with him.

"Kiss you?" Miles raised an eyebrow. "Blow you? I'm happy to do both again."

"Shut me up," Evan corrected. "Besides, I'm hardly the one who needs to stop talking. Or *typing*."

Evan's bomb hit Miles just the way he'd expected it too. Hard. And it left a trail of guilt and shame in its wake. It should have made Evan feel better, but it turned out that he didn't like seeing Miles look like a kicked puppy. The aggressively charming, certain-of-his-own-charisma Miles was a lot more fun. Evan licked his lips, and tried not to think about why that might be.

"I should really . . . apologize for that," Miles mumbled.

"For what?" Evan asked, loudly and clearly. "I'm sorry, I didn't quite get that."

"I was an asshole. I wrote some asshole things. None of which I really meant, by the way. And I'm sorry."

Evan shot him a level stare. "Five point seven points for execution, three point eight points for technique. And don't even get me started on sincerity."

"What?" Miles exclaimed, a little of his fight coming back. "I totally meant that. I *am* sorry."

"And yet it took you days to apologize." Evan paused. "Now that we've established that I'm good enough to blow, but not good enough to apologize to, I'm going in my apartment now. Move."

Miles conceded the doorway with a shambling, ashamed motion that made Evan feel even guiltier. And it wasn't his responsibility to feel guilty! He wasn't the one who'd written that email and then not apologized for it. Anything he wanted to ding Miles for, he should be free and clear to ding away.

It didn't matter that he'd spent the last week convincing himself that the email meant nothing and that he hadn't cared that Miles had sent it, because it was clearly all bullshit.

It mattered. Miles mattered.

Desire was fine and good when everyone had a good time and got their rocks off. But sometimes desire was slippery, and you couldn't get a handle on it.

It shouldn't have been a big deal. Miles had given Evan half a blowjob. He'd been enjoying himself so much he'd ached with it. Had been tempted, with Evan's dick in his mouth, to slide his hand down the front of his pants and hump his own palm.

It was tempting to do it now. Miles still didn't know what had stopped him after he'd gone back to his own apartment, and he'd spent the rest of the night sulking. He didn't know what was stopping him now.

Maybe because what he wanted was something he couldn't have, and the idea of settling for his own hand felt paltry in comparison.

If he couldn't have Evan, maybe at least he could think about him. Miles imagined that tight rounded ass naked, spread out for him on his bed. Evan, glancing back, desire written all over his face, pleading for Miles to touch him.

No. Miles shredded that fantasy, unhappy with it as he palmed himself through his boxer briefs. He was already hard—had barely gone soft since he'd been on his knees in the kitchen—and there was a damp spot in the cotton.

It would be so easy to get off. He just needed the right image. The perfect image. Miles rolled through them, one after another. Evan bending over, Evan on all fours, Evan on his knees, Evan with a cruel smile on his face as his fist wrapped around Miles' dick.

Pleasure arched through him as Miles shoved his underwear aside and gripped himself. That was what he wanted. He didn't want Evan on his knees for him. He wanted Evan owning up to every bit of his own power and control. He wanted Evan completely in control and completely under Miles' spell.

It was rougher than Miles usually liked, but that added to the swirl of fantasy in his own head. Evan, smiling with a hint of teeth as he worked him over good, thumb swiping over the head and making Miles moan.

Miles was making himself moan, but suddenly that didn't matter. It was Evan doing it. Evan was in charge. Evan was wringing this pleasure out of his body. Only Evan.

He couldn't even enjoy the hot burst of pleasure from his orgasm because he was already panicking about what it meant.

He wanted Evan, but Evan was pissed off. Evan might even hate him a little. And he might have a legitimate reason. Miles groaned and grabbed a handful of tissues from the bedside table. He should feel more relaxed now, his problem taken care of, but instead he felt edgier than ever.

What could he say to Evan so he would forgive him? Was it even possible or was Miles chasing after a pipe dream? Was he going to be resigned to forever fantasizing about Evan in his bed and never actually having him?

Evan didn't hesitate when he got back inside his apartment. He immediately headed for the shower and sanity. Stripping his clothes off, he turned the water on as hot as he could stand.

He ducked his head under the spray and hissed as the water beat down over his forehead.

Evan had known it was a mistake a long time ago to start thinking about Miles while jacking off. He'd always been afraid it would make things weird between them if and when Miles came to work at *Five Points*. It turned out that, ironically, Evan thinking about him while orgasming was hardly the weirdest part of their relationship.

He gave himself a tentative pump, and yeah, he was still hard, and still definitely into at least *thinking* about Miles while getting off.

Maybe he wasn't ready yet for Miles to actually be involved, but it was still so easy to just let his mind drift and settle on an image of them together.

Him bent over the kitchen counter, Miles sliding into him slowly, just thick enough to make him ache and feel it the next day. His hand caressing his back, letting him know how much he cared, even as his cock made sure Evan knew just how much he wanted him. Evan's hand sped up on his own dick, rough and careless, as he chased the pleasure he imagined Miles could give him.

It was over too soon, but Evan knew he'd been too worked up to last. He could still feel the ghost of Miles' mouth around him, and how wet and warm it had been. And that last thought was all it took to blow his load against the tile wall. He let out a groan, and wondered, just for a second, if Miles could hear. If Miles would know what he was doing.

If Miles was maybe doing the same thing.

Chapter Nine

Evan was pissed. Miles had (very) belatedly realized this last night, and had spent the morning realizing just how pissed he was.

The thing about Evan was that he wasn't like anyone else Miles knew. Nobody else could have been that angry and just hid it all, so completely, even the person he was angry at didn't know. Nobody else could have kissed him, and been as hard as he was, lost to the pleasure Miles was giving him, and feel the anger he did.

Miles felt incredibly stupid that he hadn't seen it before, but then he reminded himself that Evan must have worked hard to conceal it. It wasn't like Miles was incredibly oblivious. The truth was that Evan hadn't wanted him to know, and then suddenly he was practically shouting about how it had been too many days with too few apologies.

A tiny voice whispered in the back of Miles' head that Evan must be high maintenance, which was why he was so hot and so available, and yet so damn difficult, but Miles didn't think that was really it. There was something else going on, and Miles was determined to figure out what it was.

Even if Evan ended up right, and nothing else ended up happening between them, he still wanted to know. Which was a state of mind that Miles wasn't used to. He was used to not really caring too much about anything that wasn't in the kitchen. Now the joke was on him, because his life had been in a state of chaos ever since he'd met Evan, and he still couldn't walk away.

It would have been way easier, Miles reflected miserably, skulking behind Evan as he pushed the cart through the restaurant supply store.

"I can practically hear you back there pouting," Evan announced as he examined the list Miles had complied, and compared it to the display of whisks before them.

It was a sad state of affairs that they could be in his personal heaven, and Miles could barely even motivate himself to look at the tempting array of culinary tools in front of him.

"Are you going to let me pick out whisks?" Evan demanded when Miles didn't answer. "Or are you going to do your job?"

Last night, when he'd pulled the quiche out of the oven, he'd stared at it, realizing that he didn't want to eat it alone, even though when he'd decided to make it, he'd never even dreamt that Evan would show up at his door.

That was the problem with Evan. He burst in, and when he left, nothing was the same. There was an Evan-sized hole in the life that Miles had always considered very satisfactory.

It wasn't fair, but it was the bed he had made, and now he had to deal with it. Miles reached over to the whisks and grabbed a handful without even really looking at them, tossing them into the cart.

Evan shook his head and did that cute little half eye roll that usually meant he wanted to do some big production of an eye roll, but decided it wasn't worth the energy.

"When we're making . . . Twinkies or dongs, or dings, or whatever the hell you bake," Evan said snidely, "and you need the *right* whisk for the job, I'm going to remind you of this moment, and how it's all your fault."

"Believe me, I'm sure I won't need that reminder," Miles retorted fervently. "Probably because you'll never let me forget it."

"Only you," Evan said, pushing the cart forward with purpose, "would be annoyed I was pissed you didn't apologize after insulting me."

Miles wanted to find the even keel of the last few days—when they'd compromised and even found a way to work together—but it was completely lost. Maybe it was the kissing. Maybe it had been the almost blowjob. Maybe it was the anger simmering right under the peaceful surface. But it wasn't going to go back to how it had been only yesterday. That much was obvious.

It wasn't right, but he silently blamed Evan. Maybe if he hadn't kept his fucking mouth shut that he was angry then Miles would have apologized right away and prevented all this.

"Do we need anything else?" Miles asked, and gave himself a gold star, because at least he was making an attempt to converse politely.

Evan leveled him an incredulous look. "It's *your* list."

"Yeah, but it's in *your* hands," Miles retorted.

To Miles' surprise, Evan did actually look down and review the list. "I think we've got it all. Oh no, wait, we need silicone molds still."

"Joy," Miles muttered under his breath, even though silicone molds were usually something he really enjoyed.

If Evan ignored that comment, and instead pushed the cart over to the right aisle, then Miles told himself they were definitely better off.

Fifteen minutes later, they were checked out and just about done packing the bags into Evan's small compact.

"I have a lunch meeting," Evan announced when they both got in the car, "but after, we can head over to your place and work all afternoon. That good with you?"

Miles bit back a snide comment that he didn't really have a choice. He'd thought when he left the restaurant industry, his schedule would stop being dictated by someone else. It turned out that wasn't the case.

But instead of bitching, he nodded. There was some recipe research he could do while he waited for Evan. He'd planned on doing it last night, but after Evan left, he'd been in too much of a bad mood to do much of anything, including eat a slice of the quiche he'd been so excited over.

"Good." Evan sounded pleased with himself that he was back in control. Miles didn't like it, but he also didn't know what to do about it.

They stopped by Miles' apartment and unpacked the bags of supplies. Maybe Evan didn't want to fight anymore either, because by the time they made it to the *Five Points* office, the biting tension of earlier had been replaced by a frosty silence.

Miles wasn't sure it was an improvement, but he also didn't know how to fix it. So he kept his head down and when Evan grabbed his laptop from the cubicle next door, Miles acted like he wasn't even there.

When Lucy found him an hour later, he was pretending to do recipe research, but instead knew he was just staring broodingly at the laptop screen.

"You look down," she said, and the kindness in her voice was so welcome, he couldn't help but turn towards it.

"Rough few days," Miles admitted.

"We're heading over to the good coffee place, you want to come with?"

Lucy hadn't ever invited him to accompany her and her kitchen minions before, but it was a no-brainer for Miles to say yes. First, he loved the good coffee place. It was better in every way compared to the Starbucks downstairs. Second, Lucy had worked at *Five Points* since the inception of the culinary department. Almost as long as Evan. Maybe she knew something about why he was so damn prickly.

Maybe he should have asked Evan himself, but Miles figured he had already tried that last night, and while it had worked for a little while, Evan had eventually clammed up and then he'd run away.

"Oh yeah, I could definitely use a pick-me-up," Miles said and shut his laptop.

While they were waiting for the elevator to take them down to the ground floor, Lucy looked over with a compassionate smile on her face. "Evan running you ragged?" she asked, tucking a lock of short honey-blond hair behind one ear.

Evan had told him once that Reed had hired Lucy a few years ago, when he'd struggled to handle both the kitchen management duties and the producing aspects of his job. Miles had been surprised to learn that even with her efficiency and obvious skill set, she didn't have any formal culinary training.

"It's tough reconciling two visions for one show," Miles said as they stepped on the elevator together.

Lucy gave him a sympathetic grimace. "I can only imagine. Evan is pretty driven and usually very sure that his vision is the right one."

"Yeah," Miles said awkwardly. He wanted to ask, but he also didn't want to go on record as *asking*. "I didn't realize the extent of it until last night. I didn't know he'd started at *Five Points* as an intern."

"Oh yeah," Lucy said as they stepped off. Her two assistants, Steph and Chloe, were waiting outside the building. Steph hadn't even taken her work apron off, and it was dotted with bright swatches of some sort of red berry mixture. "He surprised everyone, but I don't think he ever surprised himself. He always knew he'd get the producing job. The rest of us just came on board a little later."

"Are you talking about Evan?" Steph piped up.

Chloe was lagging behind, typing something frantically on her phone. "Her girlfriend," Lucy whispered with a cute little smirk as she nudged her shoulder against Miles'. "They're practically inseparable and very adorable."

"Yeah," Miles said, at the same time that Lucy said, "He's feeling a little overwhelmed by Steamroller Evan."

"Steamroller Evan?" Miles' eyebrows raised and he hoped—*prayed*—that he wasn't breaking any sort of unspoken professional conduct to gossip about his producer outside of the office. But he was desperate for any sort of insider information he could use to convince Evan they were both on the same side. And also, that Miles *didn't* dislike him, no matter what that email might have made Evan believe.

"Shhhhh," Chloe said, proving that while she'd been texting, she'd also been listening to the conversation. "You know he hates it when you call him that."

"I don't care," Steph said stubbornly, "if you get in his way, and you won't get out of it, he'll absolutely steamroll you."

Three sets of eyes turned towards Miles as they entered the coffee shop, and he threw up his hands. "Ladies, let me get some caffeine first."

Unfortunately he didn't get much of a reprieve, as there was actually nobody in line.

When he ordered a muffin with his coffee, Lucy leaned over and whispered in his ear, "Don't get the banana walnut, get the white chocolate cranberry. Trust me."

He was picking at the wrapper, waiting for his cappuccino when Chloe and Steph came up to him. "So," Chloe said, "is he as hard to work with as I'm imagining?"

"It's not that hard," Miles said, which was sort of a lie, but he also wasn't going to throw Evan under the bus with the kitchen staff when they already called him Steamroller Evan. "It's actually nice to work with someone who has a passion for the details, for making sure that you're as successful as you can be." And that *was* true, and Miles had not even realized it was until this moment until he'd had to find something good to say.

"You can't tell me that him wanting to always be right is easy," Steph piped in.

They had him there. "No," Miles admitted. "It isn't always easy."

"You know why he has to be right. He's always trying to prove that him getting hired full time wasn't some fluke," Chloe said.

Miles frowned. "Why would it be? He got an internship and got offered a job because he worked hard."

Lucy approached, carrying a paper pastry bag. "He didn't tell you?"

It felt like everyone knew something that Miles didn't, and he was suddenly, blindingly sure that what everyone knew that he didn't was something vital.

"I don't know what he hasn't told me," Miles said flatly. He shouldn't feel embarrassed that Evan hadn't confided anything about his job history, even though they were supposed to be working closely together, but he was.

"It's okay," Chloe said, laying a sympathetic hand on his arm. "He's just so private. I'm not surprised he didn't tell you."

"What, that he's an axe murderer? That he's secretly hoarding chicken nuggets in his apartment?" Miles retorted.

"I'm just surprised he mentioned the internship and didn't tell you that it's an internship exclusively for foster kids who've been able to attend college," Lucy said softly.

"Foster kids?" Miles couldn't believe that Evan wouldn't have told him that he'd been a foster child, but it made sense that he hadn't. When had Miles ever been receptive to that sort of confession? Before or after he'd told him he hated his face?

"He tries to pretend that he didn't get the internship because of that," Steph said. "I guess because he's ashamed of it or whatever."

"Steph," Lucy admonished softly, "we've talked about this. Whatever reasons why Evan doesn't want to talk about his past are his own." She turned to Miles. "But I did think you should know, since I didn't think he'd tell you himself."

"I appreciate it," Miles said. He'd rather have heard it from Evan himself, but he had a feeling that would have been a long time coming—or not at all. And this felt like the big break that he'd been waiting for; the mysterious information that Evan had been holding back that Miles had desperately needed to understand how and why he ticked.

"I know it doesn't seem like it," Lucy said apologetically, "but I *do* encourage those two," she gestured to where Steph and Chloe were picking up their coffee, "not to gossip about everyone. Especially Evan. He doesn't like it, and frankly, neither do I."

"It hasn't been easy, working with him," Miles said, finally breaking down and admitting the truth. "We've been struggling."

"He's a great person, funny and smart and irreverent, but you do have to break through his shell."

Miles didn't want to tell Lucy that mostly what he'd done since arriving at *Five Points* was do things to reinforce Evan's shell. For example, that email had given it pretty much bulletproof coating, and he was still trying to figure out how to de-militarize it.

"I'm working on it," was all he could say. He didn't want to admit that a lot of the struggle was his own fundamental misunderstanding of the situation on day one, and how he'd acted like an unprofessional ass since then. He was trying to change, to start over, but he was beginning to think there was no way to do that—all he could do was try to move forward and be better.

And then Miles went and got really stupid. "But you don't have to sell him to me," he said, not even recognizing that conspiratorial edge to his low voice, "I really like him. Even if he can be tough to work with sometimes."

Unfortunately, Lucy understood exactly what he'd meant. Miles almost wished she was a little less sharp on the uptake. "I thought you might," she admitted. "When we walked in yesterday, I could feel . . . undercurrents."

No matter what Lucy might say about gossip, he knew it happened. It happened everywhere, at every workplace. It had even happened at Terroir, despite Bastian Aquino's notoriously hardcore anti-gossip policy. And nothing got people talking quite like a juicy workplace romance.

Evan was definitely going to kill him.

So much for starting over and trying to be better every day.

"Ah, well, you know. Adversarial relationships and all," Miles tried to joke, but the look Lucy shot him made it very clear she understood exactly what was going on and no amount of denial or *just kidding!* was going to convince her otherwise.

"We picked up your coffee!" Chloe said to Miles as she and Steph walked back to where he and Lucy were standing. "We're all ready to go."

"Oh good," Miles said, glancing at his watch and realizing he was about to be five minutes late to meet his *adversarial relationship*, "because I'm about to be late."

✦✦✦✦✦✦ ✦✦✦✦✦✦

"You're late," Evan said, head bent towards his screen, fingers not missing a beat as he typed furiously.

"I know, I'm sorry, I thought I'd grab a coffee." Miles slid into the chair next to Evan, but Evan still didn't look up.

123

"Oh, thanks for bringing me one too," Evan said levelly, even though he had to know that Miles only had one cup in his hands.

"I . . . uh . . . didn't know you wanted one?" Miles said sheepishly. He'd made it back into the building two minutes late, and then had raced to Evan's cubicle, only to not find him there. He'd made the rounds, until one of the writers stopped him and said Evan was in the conference room, still working after the meeting had ended.

Why hadn't it occurred to Miles to bring him coffee? He liked the good coffee place as much as anyone else. It was probably because instead of actively trying to charm anyone in particular, Miles just fell into bed with willing people and had never wanted someone who didn't want him back—or wanted him but fought it. Miles knew he was going to have to learn to be more aware and less selfish if he was ever going to convince Evan to consider dating him. A great almost-blowjob wasn't going to cut it. Not with Evan.

Sex was probably off the table now, even though Miles knew Evan wanted it. Miles wasn't familiar with the sort of self-denial Evan practiced; if he wanted someone and the feeling was mutual, sex happened. It was an easy way to live, and an easy way to get off. Everything about Evan was complicated, but Miles wanted him anyway. Inexplicably.

"I'm sorry I didn't bring you coffee," Miles said when Evan remained silent, typing away, the staccato of the keys all the response he probably deserved.

"It's okay." Evan paused. "I wouldn't expect you to be looking out for other people. Me, especially."

And yeah, that was galling. Especially galling when Miles had spent the last half an hour discovering that nobody had probably ever really looked out for Evan before. It probably wouldn't take an extraordinary amount of effort to make him feel special and considered. And Miles *still* couldn't figure out how to meet even the lowest of expectations.

"I'm sorry, I'm . . . I know it isn't an excuse, but I was with Lucy, and Chloe and Steph and . . ." Miles hesitated, trying to find the best way to say, *sorry, we were gossiping about you and they told me you were a foster kid and I wish you had told me yourself.*

All Miles knew was that was definitely not the way to break the news.

"And they told you all about me, I'm sure." Evan's voice was still painfully level. It was like he'd hidden every emotion behind some very high, very thick wall, and Miles, who thought maybe he'd been making at least a little bit of progress, struggled not to feel disheartened.

"Yeah, that was something they mentioned. And when they did, I couldn't help but wish you'd told me yourself. Just last night we were talking about how you started here, and you didn't mention it."

Evan's head snapped up, and Miles recoiled at the fire blazing in his dark eyes. "Why? So you could figure out how I worked? How to manipulate me better? I'm sorry, but that's personal information and I don't just share it with anyone."

"I'm not just anyone," Miles insisted. He could feel himself stepping onto unsure, potentially dangerous ground, but he was so tired of Evan retreating. This time he wasn't going to let him; he was going to chase after him.

"Right. I must have missed the memo where you were anything more than the talent I'm supposed to be producing," Evan said, and Miles realized his voice wasn't cold, it was hot with anger. And maybe that wasn't the best emotion for him to be expressing, but it was something, and Miles was so sick of beating against that cold wall.

"We kissed, I had my mouth on your dick!" Miles couldn't help but exclaim.

"Yeah, that turned out so well," Evan retorted.

Miles shot to his feet, frustration spreading through him. He knew he needed to keep his temper in check, because letting it run wild hadn't gotten him anywhere. But Evan pushed every single button of his like he owned them. "It's not like I forced you to kiss me. That was your choice. You did that, and you can't take it back."

"I keep telling you I am!" Evan's voice was rising, and now he'd stood and Miles had a sudden déjà vu of their argument in the break room before he'd gone running off to Napa.

"Your words sort of lose their effect when your hand was in my hair and your dick was literally in my mouth," Miles snarled.

"Good thing all I have to do with that is remember that email you wrote to me, and I'm as soft as I've ever been," Evan said bitterly.

"What email?"

Miles whipped his head towards the doorway and the new voice. Reed Ryan was standing in the entrance to the conference room, arms crossed across his chest, and he looked confused and determined and also definitely a little pissed off.

"Now look at what you've done," Evan hissed. "Can't keep your mouth shut for five seconds put together."

Miles couldn't believe Evan was blaming *him*; after all, Evan had been the one to bring up the email this time.

"What email?" Reed demanded when neither Miles nor Evan answered the question.

He turned towards Evan. "I knew things weren't going well, but I didn't know you'd reached the point of sending each other nasty emails or yelling at each other in the conference room."

"It's not . . . I mean, it's sort of . . ." Evan paused, trying to compose himself. "I was handling it."

"By not telling me," Reed said sternly.

"It's my fault, sir," Miles spoke up. He didn't think he'd called anyone but Bastian Aquino *sir* in his whole career, but right now, Reed was almost as scary as his ex-boss.

Reed frowned, his expression morphing between annoyance and overwhelming frustration. "I don't remember saying it wasn't your fault." His gaze fell back on Evan. "What I don't get is why you would keep it a secret, Evan."

Miles could hear Evan grinding his teeth from a few feet away. "I told you, I was handling it. I dealt with it. *Was* dealing with it."

Reed's expression softened, even as Evan forged ahead, and Miles realized as he listened to one excuse after another that he'd never heard Evan caught up in indecisive rambling before. He'd always known what to say before this moment.

"I was pretty sure it didn't mean anything, and we were getting past it—I thought I was getting past it—and I am, I know it didn't mean anything. I know Miles didn't mean it. He was drunk and stupid and well, really, really stupid. You know when someone says something mean and you know they aren't saying it because they believe it, but because they don't know what else to say? That's how it felt. It was all there between the lines. And the grammar mistakes. And the spelling errors."

Evan only stopped because Reed held up a single hand. "Can I read this email before I decide it was nothing?"

"No," Miles and Evan both answered at the same time.

Reed looked surprised. Miles thought he really shouldn't have been.

"It's private," Evan said stubbornly.

"Like Evan said, I was drunk and really stupid. Incurably stupid. And I said some stuff that I'm not proud of, but I also said some stuff . . . it is sort of private," Miles added, under no delusion that his stupid drunk words could still remain between him and Evan.

Reed Ryan was going to find out that he really hated Evan's face, and really loved his ass in the tight khakis he wore. Basically, Miles was going to have to move back to Napa because he was never going to get over the shame of it. Every time he saw Reed—his *boss* and also, the ex-owner of Garnet and a culinary god—Miles was going to have a nightmare flashback to his stupid drunk words.

Miles thought he'd explored all the humiliation he possibly could when Evan had read that email. Unfortunately, there were still embarrassing depths to which he could plunge.

"I want to read it. Now." Reed's tone brooked no disagreement, but Evan still opened his mouth to keep arguing. Miles elbowed him hard in the side.

"Give it up," he hissed under his breath. "No point."

"I deleted it," Evan said anyway.

"All this time you were so *subtly* blackmailing me with it. That god-awful marketing meeting. Compromising! Joan of Arc Julia Child! And you fucking *deleted* it?" The outraged words leapt out of Miles' mouth before he could stop them.

Evan turned towards him, shock written all over his features. "Are you insane?" he hissed.

Reed only shook his head. In disgust or frustration, it was hard to tell.

"You." Reed pointed at Miles. "You still have it. You sent it after all. I want you to forward it to me, and then join me in my office in ten minutes." He turned and walked out, leaving no room for arguments, and Miles at a loss for words.

"Go delete it right now. I don't know how, just do it," Evan hissed.

"I really think we've made this bed and we have to lie in it," Miles said, realizing a little too late that he shouldn't be using phrases that had the word *bed* in them. At least he hadn't said they'd made their kitchen counter and now they had to lie on it.

Evan threw up his hands in frustration. "Do you really want your *boss* to read that email? Really? I thought you had an ounce of self-preservation. Because I definitely do not want *my* boss to read that email."

"Trust me, I don't. But I'm not showing up in his office telling him I just deleted it. That would be worse than him reading it."

Evan shot him a look. "Are you sure about that?"

Miles' resolve crumbled a little. "Not entirely."

"Then go delete it. This is your fault. Therefore, it's your job to fix it."

"What if it can't be fixed?" Miles said, because he couldn't help but think that. Maybe he'd fucked up this situation beyond solving.

Evan rounded on him, as fierce and angry as he'd ever been. "*Everything* can be fixed."

Miles didn't think he could agree, but he also felt sick and every second he and Evan kept fighting over this made him feel worse. It was impossible not to see Evan's words through the frame of the knowledge he'd just learned about how he'd grown up alone and unwanted.

The one thing he knew was that he wasn't going to delete the email. Would it be humiliation heaped upon embarrassment for Reed Ryan to read it? Absolutely. But there was a sort of poetic justice to the automatic cringe that Miles felt every time he thought about it. He shouldn't have written it, and he definitely shouldn't have ever sent it. He should have apologized the morning Evan had showed up in Napa to drag his hungover ass home. Everything that came after this was payback for all those mistakes.

⁂

Evan knew the moment he walked into Reed's office that Miles hadn't done as requested and deleted the email. Reed's face said it all. Evan knew he should've watched Miles delete it, instead of escaping to the bathroom to try to compose himself for the lecture to come.

Because even if Miles had deleted it, Evan knew they were both in for a lecture the likes of which he'd never seen. Reed had a fierce temper, and even if he'd never seen it, he'd heard terrifying stories about it. Until this clusterfuck of a situation, Evan had been more than a model employee—he could even say he'd been Reed's best employee. There'd never been a single excuse for Reed to unleash his infamous temper.

Until now.

"Evan, sit down." Reed's voice was deadly calm, but Evan could also see the awkwardness in his expression. Yeah, he'd definitely read all about how Miles hated his face, and how much he appreciated the tight khakis Evan favored.

Evan did what he was instructed, because in the bathroom he'd come to mostly the same conclusion as Miles: it was pointless to keep fighting this. It was going to happen.

"I've read this email," Reed said, still very calm. Too calm, as far as Evan was concerned. "I'm not very happy about it."

"I'm sorry, I can't apologize enough," Miles cut in, but Reed shot him a single, deadly look and he shut up fast. Evan wished he could recreate that look and get those same kinds of results. But it turned out that Miles had more self-preservation than Evan had ever imagined he did.

"Do you know why I hired you?" Reed asked.

"Because I was good?" Miles said.

Evan barely held back a bitter chuckle. Miles had no idea how good he was. Or how fucked.

Reed leaned forward on the desk, his muscular forearms distracting but the look in his dark eyes was intense enough it was tough to even look at his arms. "I hired you because I believed you were a professional. That you'd started *Pastry by Miles* even though you were working at Terroir because you wanted more. That you were willing to work your ass off and sacrifice whatever it took to make sure you got more. That's why I promoted Evan specifically to produce your show. Because he's always, ever since he started here, done exactly that—gone after *more*. And I thought this drive would unite you, but all it's done is divide you. And that's a damn fucking shame."

Evan swallowed hard. He'd thought the same thing, once. He still wanted to believe it was possible, that they weren't doomed to fail, but the further they got down this angry, bitter, vindictive road, the more out of reach success felt.

Part of this was his own fault. But fault seemed so petty right now, when everything they'd built individually was threatening to fall around them.

"Apologies don't seem adequate, but that's all I have. And a promise to do better. To be better. To work with Evan better." Miles certainly sounded earnest, and Evan realized that was part of his charm. You genuinely wanted to believe him, even when you knew he would probably fail to deliver. That was definitely Evan's fault; he kept believing and kept letting himself be seduced into certainty, when nothing was certain.

"That's something." Reed, on the other hand, did not sound particularly convinced. He was a hard guy to win over, though, which was something Evan had always liked about him. And *still* liked about him, even though that particular trait was probably going to be enough to torpedo Evan's continued employment at *Five Points*.

"Evan?" Reed continued. "Do you have anything to say?"

What did you even say when you'd been saying too much from the first moment? Evan didn't know.

"I'm sorry, I should have told you about it earlier," Evan said. "But I think we can still make this work." That was mostly a lie, but Evan had always been a great liar. He didn't like lying to Reed, because he'd always respected him so much, but some things were more vital than honesty.

Evan had just clawed his way up to this point. He'd worked his ass off. He wasn't going to lose everything now over a little dishonesty.

"What I want to see," Reed said, "is a test. Proof of you two actually working together towards something. I want evidence. I want something I can watch and I can see how it's going to work if *Five Points* moves ahead and buys into this show for a season of episodes. Right now, I can't see that happening. But if you prove to me that you can, then you'll get my full support."

"You want a screen test?" Evan asked and he couldn't help but sound dubious. Miles was not ready for a screen test. *Evan* was not ready for a screen test.

"I want proof." Reed sounded solidly convinced. He was probably not going to be convinced by whatever footage they could cobble together.

Evan felt the death knell of all his hopes. He and Reed had agreed when Miles signed that screen tests wouldn't be necessary because he already had on-camera experience and his rapport with the camera was fantastic.

"Okay," Miles said, and he sounded so sure and so casually okay with the challenge that Reed had presented to them, Evan felt a little sick. Didn't he know what they were getting themselves into? Didn't he care about the amount of work he'd just committed himself to? "You'll get your proof. I promise."

Chapter Ten

"Are you insane?" Evan hissed at Miles as they walked down the hall from Reed's office. It didn't even feel like the first time he'd asked this exact same question this exact same way in nearly the same spot.

And didn't that just say it all?

Miles shot him a look like maybe Evan was the crazy one, but there was no way that was the case. "Maybe we shouldn't do this here," he said softly.

He had a good point, but Evan wasn't feeling magnanimous enough to admit it. Instead, he pointed towards the big double doors that led to the elevator bay. Wordlessly, Miles followed Evan to their cubicles, and they packed up their laptops. Evan also grabbed his big folder of filming notes, and they decamped from the office, walking the few scant blocks to the apartment building they shared.

Miles unlocked his door, and the first thing he said, when they were finally alone, was, "Are you hungry? I've got lots of leftover quiche from last night."

Evan decided the question he'd asked earlier applied even in locations that weren't the hallway outside of Reed's office.

"Food? That's what you want to talk about right now?" Evan's voice was inching upwards, both in volume and in pitch. It was a testament to how upset he was that he didn't even try to stop the inevitable.

They'd been on the cusp of a huge blowout in the conference room, and Reed had merely interrupted them. Maybe if they finished the fight, they could buckle down and finally get some work done.

But Miles shot Evan an incredulous look, and after setting his laptop on the kitchen counter, walked right over to the fridge and opened the door.

"Okay," Evan admitted, which was not easy for him to do. "I guess we do need to talk about food. Not whatever happened in here last night. Not your fuckups. Not my hang-ups. We need to figure out how to convince Reed."

Miles flipped the oven on and slid the pie plate, suspiciously full, into the oven.

Maybe Miles hadn't been able to eat either, after Evan had left. Evan had ended up with a liquid dinner, comprised of whatever remaining wine he had left in his apartment, followed by a shot of vodka from his freezer, and a restless, mostly sleepless night, punctuated by sudden and annoying bouts of accidentally turning himself on by dwelling on what had nearly happened.

"It's not going to be that hard," Miles said.

Evan didn't even know what to say. "You did hear him, right? He wasn't lying. He will absolutely need to be convinced. And I know Reed; that isn't going to be easy."

"No, it won't be easy. But he picked me for a reason, and he picked you for a reason. Those reasons haven't changed. We just need to figure out how to make those reasons work together a little better." Miles' gaze slid to the counter. "You know him better than I do. You know how this all works better than I do. So tell me what to do."

"You're really giving me control over this whole thing." Evan couldn't believe after all these weeks of fighting and clawing each other, Miles was just going to hand the power over without a single word of argument.

But Miles shrugged. "I can't go back to Napa a failure. I can't go back to restaurants if this doesn't work out. So it needs to work out."

Evan didn't need another word to convince him. "Okay," he said, flipping open his big folder stuffed full of notes. "Let's start."

"Food first," Miles said. "I've had too much caffeine followed by too much adrenaline. I'm all shaky."

"Fine." The food smelled good, almost better than it had last night, so Evan wasn't going to exactly complain if Miles wanted to feed him.

"Also," Miles said, fidgeting with the frayed edge of a kitchen towel. "I need to apologize. Really apologize," he continued when Evan opened his mouth to say that an apology wasn't necessary. "I was an asshole. I was insensitive. I was thoughtless. And I'm beginning to realize that some of those things aren't new. For that, I'm sorry. I'm going to be respectful from now on. The professional I promise you I can be."

"Apology accepted." Evan figured if they dealt with this, then maybe they could move on. And maybe he should take advantage of Miles' sudden contrition to set up some ground rules.

"But if you're really serious," he continued, "let's write down some ground rules." He opened his notebook to a blank page. "Rule number one, I think is pretty self-explanatory. No kissing."

Miles opened his mouth and then snapped it shut again. Evan was unpleasantly reminded of everything he could do with that mouth, before he pushed those thoughts right out of his mind. Remembering kissing Miles and Miles kissing him was not going to get them a full season pickup.

"Rule number two. No sex."

Miles didn't even react to that.

"Rule number three. No arguments," Miles added.

Evan lifted an eyebrow. "No arguing? You must really have had a change of heart in Reed's office."

"Not just Reed's office," Miles admitted. "I went to grab coffee with Lucy and when she told me about the circumstances surrounding your internship, I realized just how insensitive I've been, when this means everything to you. It means everything to me too. And I can stop arguing if it means we can save everything we've worked for."

Evan felt everything go hot and then cold inside him. Ice cold. Like an ice floe in Antarctica. It hadn't come as a surprise that Lucy had told Miles about his past. She had probably been trying to help, because rumors were flying fast and thick in the office that Miles and Evan weren't getting along. Lucy must have believed that she could assist by cluing Miles in, because normally she didn't encourage gossip.

Evan was still monumentally pissed off that she'd opened her big fat mouth, and he was definitely going to tell her that when he saw her next. They'd known each other and worked together for years now, and he expected better from her. Not for her to sell him and his secrets out to Miles.

"It's nothing," Evan said coldly. "It's less than nothing. Forget what she told you. It's not important."

"It *is* important," Miles argued, heat flashing in his eyes, frustration and admiration and galling sympathy. "I think . . ."

Evan ripped off the notebook page and stomped over to the fridge. He hung it on the fridge with one of the silly magnets Miles must have brought. This one was a brightly colored neon lobster. "Rule number three," he stated, pointing to the rule he'd written in his neat handwriting.

Miles' dark eyebrows slanted with annoyance and everything he was holding back, but he remained silent, letting the quiet grow until the beep of the oven timer interrupted his pouting and Evan's cold shoulder.

"Eat," was all Miles said, as he slid a wedge of quiche over on a plate, a fork balanced on the edge. "You've got to keep your energy up, and you look tired."

Evan wanted to retort something spiteful, but he buried the spike of heat under the cold wall of ice surrounding him, and merely looked pointedly over at the list on the fridge.

Miles didn't reply, merely walked over to the fridge and scrawled something under the third rule. "Rule number four," he announced, "sarcastic retorts are banned."

"Fine by me," Evan said, even though he felt a pulse of disappointment at losing the banter he'd actually enjoyed trading with Miles.

It didn't matter, anyway. Only one thing mattered now. Not fucking this up again.

"First," he said, between big bites of quiche he didn't really taste, "I want you to go through the cookie recipe again. That's what we'll do for the test. It's the easiest recipe on the list."

There was a mutinous jut to Miles' jaw but he nodded, and Evan watched as he began to assemble his ingredients.

He was right. He had to be right. There was no more room for error.

Miles watched as Evan ate his quiche and didn't even taste it, then pushed it aside only half-finished. He pressed his lips together and told himself that it didn't matter if this felt all kinds of wrong; it was what Evan wanted.

Or at least what he'd told himself he wanted, though that was a distinction that even Miles could acknowledge didn't matter anymore.

"I made notes last time we baked these cookies," Evan said.

As always, Miles' gut reaction was to correct, to snark just so Evan could snark back. A stupid petty correction that he could use to flirt with the other man. But this time, he kept his mouth shut, even though technically, *they* hadn't baked anything. Miles had baked these cookies by himself, and Evan had just watched—and also, if Miles was being really honest, drove him insane. With sexual frustration. With desire. With need.

"I bet there isn't time for me to teach you how to make them," Miles said, and sue him, he sounded regretful because he really was. The best afternoon he'd spent in forever had been the one when he'd taught Evan how to make *pain au chocolat.*

That was the afternoon when Miles had discovered that maybe teaching other people how to bake might not be too terrible.

Evan leveled him an annoyed look, frosted cold at the edges. "Both of us know that wasn't a serious offer. I'm not here to learn how to cook, and you're not here to teach me."

He was right, but the truth still stung.

Miles turned back to the counter where he'd been assembling his *mise en place* to make sure he had everything he needed.

"We need to finalize the recipe today," Evan announced. "So no crazy experimentation, please."

It was only all those hard years of being shit on by head chefs in kitchens that kept him even-keeled and calm when he nodded. "I'm going to do a quarter dark chocolate, and three quarters semi-sweet," he said. "That should balance out the bitterness nicely. And I'm swapping white sugar for brown."

Evan's sharp nod of acknowledgement shouldn't have hurt, but it did.

It didn't matter, though. Miles wasn't going to be the one responsible for killing off Evan's chances at a successful production of this show. He'd worked hard enough for it, and it wasn't fair for him to lose his shot because Miles was a careless jerk who couldn't keep his fingers under control when he got drunk.

The afternoon passed by achingly slow. Evan didn't question every decision Miles made, he only wanted solid, unchanging ones. And every question was polite, painstakingly professional and about zero degrees.

Miles hated every minute of it. In his fantasies, he might have dreamed about an afternoon just baking and hanging out in his place, and it was glorious. The reality was so much different and so much worse.

Third batch pulled out of the oven, Miles tested a cookie and gave a shrug when Evan asked if this was finally the final recipe.

"You can't tell me you don't know," Evan said, and for the first time, his frustration felt warmer. Hotter. Like Evan was just on edge as Miles, he'd just buried it under so much ice that it took time to melt and show through.

"They taste good." Miles shrugged again, because if Evan didn't get it now, he probably never would. Miles had sworn that Evan was close to understanding what drove him, but maybe after everything, it was safer to assume Evan didn't give a shit. "They taste really good, even, but perfection can't be rushed."

"Perfection," Evan said through clenched lips, "is not what we're aiming for here. We're aiming for good enough."

It felt like something inside Miles died a little with Evan's words. He had to turn back to the cooling rack, fussing uselessly with the warm cookies, so Evan wouldn't see his devastated expression.

"I didn't work so hard to become a chef so I could skate by on good enough," Miles said softly.

"Well, this certainly isn't what *I* worked so hard for either," Evan snapped. "We're all settling here."

It shouldn't have hurt more, but somehow it did. It burned, in a way that none of Evan's other snarky retorts had ever hurt before. Miles turned from the stove and wrenched open the refrigerator and pulled out a bottle of pinot blanc that he'd been saving for a special occasion.

He opened it with quick, efficient movements, and for a brief second, considered not even bothering with a wine glass, just dumping it into his empty water glass, but that felt wrong. Disrespectful of the wine and the effort the winemakers had put into crafting it. So he walked across the kitchen, grabbed a glass, and poured the wine.

"Really?" Evan snapped. "You're drinking? Don't you think alcohol has gotten us into enough trouble?"

"You want a glass?" Miles asked, because even though he *had* sent the email while drunk, it wasn't like Evan hadn't also used the excuse of a glass of good cabernet sauvignon to do something crazy. "Or are you afraid you'll kiss me again?"

Evan's lips compressed together, and he looked angry. The angriest he'd looked since the afternoon had started. "I told you," he said stiffly, "that won't be repeated. It doesn't matter what I drink."

"Then you should try a glass of this. It's special," Miles said, giving the glass a fancy little twirl and watching the golden liquid swirl around the crystal.

Evan made a face, but still went to get a glass from the cupboard, and poured himself a scant quarter of a glass. "What," he retorted when Miles shot him a questioning look. "One of us has to stay sober."

"I can bake drunk, sober, it doesn't matter. You're the one who needs something to loosen up," Miles said, even though he knew what he was risking by saying it out loud.

"I like who I am sober just fine," Evan said, but he didn't even *sound* convincing.

But it didn't matter. Miles had promised he would abide by the three rules—now four rules—hanging on the fridge. Drinking wasn't technically on the list, though it would inevitably lead to breaking one, or all of them probably, but it might also make Evan more bearable to be around during this exercise in torture.

Miles took another bite of cookie, and suddenly it didn't matter so much. It didn't feel like life or death if the batter had another eighth of a teaspoon of salt, or he slightly changed the proportions of dark to semi-sweet chocolate or if he substituted more white sugar for the brown. "Final recipe," he said, and tried to ignore Evan's triumphant expression.

He was supposed to be giving Evan what he wanted, right? All of this done exactly the way he wanted it. But Miles felt hollow. Uninspired. More like quitting today than he'd felt since this whole thing started.

All it took to squash that particular bug was the thought of Evan's face if he gave up and let *Pastry by Miles* fall apart.

Evan's fingers flew across the keyboard, as sure as they'd ever been. And something about Evan's certainty helped Miles believe at least a little bit that they were doing the right thing, taking the right path.

"There, recipe submitted to testing." Evan glanced up. "That's Lucy's minions, in case you didn't know."

"I didn't realize they were going to be testing the screen test recipe." Maybe if Miles had, he would've made another batch, tried another hunch. He didn't want to talk big with his impressive resume, and then fall pathetically short.

"It isn't a requirement," Evan said, "but I thought it would seem pretty dumb to pass the screen test, but not have the recipe tested. Besides, Reed knows when faced with a challenge, I like to go above and beyond. He'll probably expect this, on some subconscious level."

Miles grabbed a plate from the cupboard, slid two cookies onto it, and pushed it Evan's direction. He ignored it, which was a doubly unpleasant reminder: *one*, he didn't like sweets, and *two,* that it didn't matter to him how the cookie actually tasted.

"What's next?" Miles asked, draining the glass of wine. If he had to stand here for another minute and watch Evan type furiously on his laptop, he was going to go out of his mind.

"Remember the wing-wang?" Evan said absently.

"The *what*?" Miles asked.

Evan's eyes shot up to Miles' face. "The Ding Dong, or whatever it was that you called it."

"I remember it. I didn't think we were going that direction."

"We're not. We're going to practice filming, and because we have no equipment, we're going to have to be resourceful. Now where's that ficus you used last time? It'll be steadier than my hands and we're going to want to take this footage apart to make sure you're perfect. It'll be that much harder with the camera jerking all around."

Miles shook his head incredulously and went to grab the ficus from his bedroom. As he dragged it to the kitchen, he realized that Evan had helped furnish this apartment. He'd known exactly where the ficus was and just didn't want to talk about Miles' bedroom. Or *go* into Miles' bedroom.

He didn't think anyone had ever wanted him so much yet spent so much time and energy avoiding the subject of sex. It was a fascinating dichotomy that should have frustrated him enough to kill any interest Miles felt, but instead, it was doing the opposite. This quirk of Evan's made Miles hunt like a detective for any clues, verbal or otherwise, that gave away just how much he wanted. And each discovery was sweeter than if it had been freely admitted.

Miles didn't want to think about what this said about his emotional hang-ups.

Evan had already pulled the duct tape from the supply closet it was stashed in, and he pulled out a GoPro camera from his laptop bag.

"Where'd that come from?" Miles asked as he pulled the ficus into place opposite the big kitchen island.

"The extreme sports department," Evan said.

Miles frowned. "I thought it was just that one guy, and you said he'd been dropped too many times on his head."

"He has." Evan paused, checking the angle of the camera. "He won't even realize I've borrowed this."

The problem was Miles couldn't help but grudgingly admire Evan's determination to get shit done. He was pretty sure they had that in common. That much Reed was dead right on.

If only they could figure out how to align their priorities and stop fighting each other, they could run the world.

"Get behind the island," Evan ordered. "I want to check the angle of the camera."

Miles did as ordered, as Evan made a few minute adjustments.

"Now what?" Miles asked.

"Now, you make those cookies again." Evan paused and Miles wondered if he could make that other set of adjustments he'd wanted to, and if Evan would even notice. "And you make them *exactly* the same. No creative wanderings."

"Just make the cookies?" Miles leaned on the counter. He knew from how many editing hours he'd spent on *Pastry by Miles* videos that he had a not-insignificant charm factor when he stood like this. Evan didn't even blink, he just went right back to his laptop, moving it so he was aligned right behind the camera. Seeing everything it saw.

Maybe, he couldn't help but think, *I'm losing my touch*.

Something he'd considered ever since he'd walked into the *Five Points* offices and hadn't been able to see eye to eye with the cute producer.

"Make the damn cookies, Miles." Evan's voice was cold and hard as steel.

So he made the damn cookies. Again.

Evan knew what the problem was going to be before they even reviewed the footage. Miles was a natural behind a camera, usually relaxed and jovial, even self-deprecating when the situation called for it. His appeal had been one of the more persuasive arguments that had sold Reed on him when Evan had first shown him *Pastry by Miles* videos.

The other persuasive argument had been that they wouldn't need to spend weeks or months getting Miles comfortable in front of the camera. He wouldn't need a single ounce of training because he'd already given himself the best training regimen he could—tons and tons of experience.

But that was before, and this was after—though before and after what, specifically, Evan didn't want to think about—now everything had suddenly changed.

Miles was stiff and awkward on the first video. He spent a lot of time second-guessing both his words and his actions. Even worse, he kept directing hesitant, almost questioning glances at the camera, like he was asking Evan if he was doing the right thing.

This was not the *Pastry by Miles* superstar that Evan had been ready to finish molding.

Evan was at a complete loss. He didn't even want to look at Miles, currently elbow-deep in sudsy water, washing dishes, because then Miles might know how bad things were, and that would make them even worse. He was self-conscious now, but he wasn't aware of it yet. As soon as he became aware of it, it would be even more pointed.

"Was it that bad?" Miles asked, from over at his spot at the sink.

Evan didn't know how he could've given it away, but he was pretty certain that Miles hadn't even looked over at him the whole time he'd been watching the video, and he certainly hadn't admitted anything out loud.

"I don't know what you mean," Evan lied.

"You're totally silent over there. Which means you're usually plotting some sort of world takeover bid. Or how to tell me that all my other episodes were a fluke."

Evan had been definitely worried about the screen test before, because he and Miles saw eye to eye on so little, but when they'd come back to Miles' place, he'd suddenly become an acquiescent stranger. Evan had begun to think that maybe they could pull this off after all, mostly resting on Miles' natural charisma in front of the camera.

And now even that had deserted them.

"They weren't flukes," Evan said, but he wasn't even convincing himself.

The tense line of Miles' back as he scrubbed cookie sheets was proof enough that Evan definitely wasn't convincing him.

"It's been a long week," Evan said. "You're tired. I'm tired. This is a lot of stress. A few more practice run-throughs and the kinks will work themselves out."

Later that night, Evan lay awake in bed, promising to himself that he'd told Miles the truth. He'd been so vigilant when he'd picked the talent he wanted to produce for the first time. He'd followed what felt like hundreds of food bloggers. He'd done research for months. He'd narrowed and winnowed and made at least a dozen pro-and-con lists. He'd kept coming back to *Pastry by Miles* for a reason, and that reason had to be more than how cute Miles was when he smiled, eyes crinkling and so damn bright. It had to be more than when Evan had seen him for the very first time, he'd felt it deep down, right in the gut. More than just that he'd sworn to himself that one day he'd find a way to meet Miles Costa.

It had to be more because Evan had staked everything on his career, and he'd staked his career on Miles. But lying awake, sleepless as the hours ticked by, Evan couldn't help but wonder if he had been wrong this whole time.

The next day, Evan worked both of them like the devil, like a man terrified he was going to waste a single moment of time.

Thirteen times, Miles thought sluggishly as he leaned against the counter, not even caring if it was his good side or he was laid out seductively. He didn't think he could bring himself to stand up.

Despite what Evan had promised to him the day before, and that Miles had sworn to himself that he'd deliver if it killed him, the kinks had not worked themselves out.

Miles got more comfortable, and he'd developed a decent patter as he prepared the cookies, but there was no spontaneity, no life. No *zing*. He knew he felt annoyed and stifled at the man who stared coldly and calculatingly at the camera as he performed. Even when he worked his ass off to forget Evan's existence, Miles couldn't find the spark that had come as natural to him as breathing from the first *Pastry by Miles* video he'd recorded.

Even the stupid Ding Dong video he'd filmed to get back at Evan on their second day was better than the thirteenth run-through of the chocolate peanut butter cookies.

"Maybe we should use the Ding Dong video," Miles said. "I bet you some people would even find it funny."

Evan's expression said it all. He didn't find it funny and couldn't comprehend of anyone who would. And that, Miles thought, was the root of the problem. Evan couldn't unclench for five seconds and fucking *relax*, and his goddamn tenseness had caused Miles to lose his center.

He couldn't get it back, couldn't seem to re-discover it, and even though there was a smooth delivery to the performance (probably because he'd run through it thirteen times), even Miles wasn't delusional enough to believe a rehearsed demeanor would be enough to win Reed over.

"This," Evan said coldly, refusing to rise to Miles' bait, "is the video we're doing."

For better or worse, Evan was determined to stick to his plan, even as he saw it all going down the crapper. Miles didn't know whether to be angry at Evan for his ridiculous stubborn streak or to feel guilty for letting him down.

Maybe he felt both at the same damn time.

"Just so you know, if you tell me to do it again," Miles said, and he knew he sounded as tired as he felt, "I'm going to tell you to fuck off."

Evan looked up. He might be overly stubborn and too determined to stick to the path that wasn't working, but Miles could tell from the hint of despair in his dark eyes that he knew the score.

"No point," he said shortly.

Miles raised an eyebrow.

"Reed just texted me," Evan said by way of explanation, "we'll film the test tomorrow during one of the *Dream Team* filming breaks. Ten a.m."

It was so tempting to lean over, reach into the freezer and grab the bottle of Belvedere that Miles had found the other day. At the time he'd been impressed with the taste of whoever stocked the apartment, but then he'd remembered it was Evan.

It was always fucking Evan.

But they were screwed enough, he was probably going to move his ass back to Napa and beg for his job back. This was no time to be indulging in bad habits and screwing himself over worse. Besides, he'd learned the hard way that sometimes getting drunk only made everything worse.

He didn't even want to imagine what might have happened if he hadn't thrown a hissy fit, drank all that faux Kahlua and typed out an email that he'd never even meant to send.

He definitely wouldn't be standing here, contemplating the end of *Pastry by Miles* and wondering how much groveling he would have to do to get another job.

"You want a drink?" Evan asked and Miles looked up in surprise, wondering how he'd managed to read his mind yet again.

"No? Why do you ask?"

Evan shrugged. "Alcohol seems to be your crutch when things don't go your way."

It wasn't fair but it was true. That didn't mean it stung any less. "Things aren't exactly going your way either."

"Everything will be fine tomorrow," Evan said, but Miles didn't even bother arguing. They both knew the truth of what would probably happen during the test tomorrow. Some things were painfully inevitable, and they'd been on this crash course from the very first moment. "We should both get some rest. We'll cab over in the morning to the studio."

Evan's casual dismissal of Miles and everything they'd shared definitely stung. It might be self-preservation for Evan, but Miles didn't want to live without regrets and he didn't want to pretend that he was okay with this. Even with Evan's cold shoulder of the last two days, he still wanted him. He still wanted the possibility of hope for the future, even if that was at least a little delusional.

It was that thought that gave him the energy to push himself off the counter. He walked over to where Evan was sitting, head buried in his laptop, fingers typing away like it was some kind of barrier that protected him from anything real.

"I'll be out of your hair in a moment," Evan said, not even looking up.

Miles stood there, not exactly patient, but waiting because he was saving his pushiness for something that mattered. "You're not in my hair. I don't want you to go."

Evan still didn't look up. "You just said you didn't want to go through it again."

Miles shoved his hands in his pockets so he wouldn't just reach out and take, mussing up Evan's perfectly styled hair, his still-crisp shirt collar, the omnipresent bow tie. Today's was a leafy green.

"I don't."

Something in Miles' voice must have gotten through to Evan, because finally, he glanced up. There was apprehension in his buttery-brown eyes. Something like fear, even if he tried to hide it. Miles still saw it because Miles was looking for it.

"We talked about this." Evan spit it out, and his eyes flickered for a single brief moment to where the list was still hanging from the fridge.

No kissing.

No sex.

No fighting.

No sarcastic retorts.

Of course Miles had started ignoring number four almost immediately. It had been a natural reflex to try to get a reaction out of the suddenly icy Evan. But he hadn't tried the other three. He'd worked hard to not argue, to not fight back. It had been even harder to resist pushing Evan on the other rules.

He'd been as good as he could possibly be; he was done with it.

"We did," Miles admitted.

"Then what do you want?" Evan asked, even more defensively than he'd been the last two miserable days.

When Miles had walked over here, crossing the invisible line between kitchen and camera, between chef and producer, he hadn't understood that this was a watershed moment. It was crystal clear now.

Some things were so simple they didn't need explanations.

"You."

Evan's jaw dropped. "You really don't," he argued. "Not after everything."

"That's the thing, I want you more after everything. Even after how shitty all these rehearsals have been. Even if I have to go back to Napa and grovel. None of that feels like it matters now."

Evan shot to his feet, hands shutting his laptop, reaching for his bag. Not the reaction Miles had been hoping for. Everyone always said that if you laid it all on the line, if you were honest and straightforward about what you wanted, you got it.

Everyone were fucking liars. Miles couldn't hide his disappointment or the pain he felt as he watched Evan try to escape.

"What if I had never sent you that email?" he demanded. He was so tempted to just show Evan how much he wanted him, but he knew that wouldn't work. Evan had to *know* he wanted it too, even if they both knew he did. He had to acknowledge it to himself, and to Miles. And shoving everything he'd brought into his bag so he could escape was the exact opposite of that.

Evan looked up. Maybe it would've helped that Miles saw the same echo of frustration and pain in his eyes, but it didn't. It made it worse. Like this was their chance, and they were just passing it by.

At least Miles was fucking putting his ass out there. Evan was just running away.

"It doesn't matter. Because you did. And you can't change that." Evan's voice was hard, so hard it sounded like it might crack at any moment.

"I'm sorry I sent it," Miles said, and he knew he sounded desperate. He *was* desperate. "I've never been sorrier about anything in my whole life." He meant it. All of it. And it meant nothing.

"Me too," Evan said, and then he was walking out of the kitchen and Miles heard the front door shut behind him.

This time it didn't feel like a bad idea to reach for the bottle of vodka in the freezer and take a gulp, feeling it burn all the way down his throat.

Chapter Eleven

Evan didn't know who he was angrier at; Miles for making him want to believe him, or himself for nearly doing it.

He couldn't sleep. Since he'd left Miles' place, he felt like he'd been half a rationalization away from going back. To telling Miles that he wanted him too, screw how much he might regret it later.

But then he'd probably regret it either way, he thought, as he restlessly switched sides, staring at the bright neon-green numbers of the clock on his bedside table. He'd regret sleeping with Miles, and he'd definitely regret *not* sleeping with him.

The question was which regret was larger and more life-ruining in the grand scheme of things.

It turned out that the answer was shockingly simple; Evan wanted Miles. He'd tried very hard to fight against it, he'd actively attempted to stifle it, to pretend it didn't exist, and part of the exhaustion of the last few days was how much energy it took to deny such an obvious truth.

He was up and out of bed before he'd even thought it through—probably because if he let himself, he wouldn't have gone anywhere anytime soon, and he was done overthinking. It was easy enough to slip on a pair of shoes and scoot down the hallway to Miles' door.

The difficult part was standing in front of Miles' door, waiting for him to open it. It took every ounce of Evan's self-possession to knock, then knock again, and then knock *again*, the whole time praying that Miles hadn't taken Evan's rejection and gone looking someplace else.

After the third prolonged knock, the only thing keeping him rooted in place at Miles' doorstep was a stubborn belief that he couldn't have come all this way, through all this shit, and then at the end, Miles had given up on Evan before Evan could give up on himself.

Finally, the door opened. Miles didn't look happy to see him, in fact, he looked pissed off.

Evan couldn't really blame him for that.

An apology was right there, but at the last second, his dick just took over, and said what he'd been so reluctant to acknowledge: "I want you, I do."

A frown creased Miles' handsome features. "Now? You're going to get me up in the middle of the night, and tell me that *now* you've finally decided you want me?"

Evan hadn't considered that this wouldn't be easy. That Miles would expect some sort of groveling after all the overtures that Evan had rejected.

"Yes." Evan usually didn't *do* groveling. Pride was a hard-won possession, and he wasn't about to give it up, even for Miles.

Miles must have realized this, because after a long, heart-stopping moment, he pulled the door the rest of the way open, and Evan didn't move because he couldn't.

The reason why it had taken Miles so long to come to the door was because he'd already started without Evan. Probably because he'd never imagined that Evan would show up, interested in the bulge he was packing in those tight black briefs.

That was where he had been very wrong; Evan was more than interested. He licked his lips, mouth suddenly dry, and looked his fill. Miles' solid, slim chest, the tenseness in his biceps, the sweat beaded around his hairline, the mussed curls, how his fingers kept clenching and unclenching. The tautness of his abs as he held himself still and refused to cover up.

Evan approved because he shouldn't ever. He was gorgeous, a barely contained storm in that laid-back body.

"I didn't think you'd come back," Miles said, voice calm but with a tense edge.

Evan wasn't going to argue when there were so many better things he could be doing with his mouth.

Urgency propelled him forward, through the doorway, almost falling against Miles. Before he could, Miles reached out and caught him. Evan lifted his head towards his, and a long, eternal stare passed between them. Miles' eyes were smoky in the dim light, and Evan couldn't help but wonder if his own were darker. Intense. If everything he felt was reflected in them. The desperation. The desire. How hopeless he was against the two together; hopeless against Miles.

Evan could feel just how much Miles wanted him, hard against his stomach, pushing against the thin fabric covering his crotch, but Miles didn't move.

It was hard enough to take the first step here, it should feel easier to take the last. It wasn't. But nobody had ever considered Evan a coward, and he wouldn't act cowardly now.

Lifting his head, Evan fitted his mouth against Miles', and their lips moved against each other for a moment, uncoordinated and unsure, but then everything slid into place.

Evan had spent his entire life avoiding fantasy. He was practical and prosaic—all by necessity. But now, he had a sudden thought that this kiss wasn't just a physical manifestation of a deeply physical need, but that it was locking them together, two out-of-sync tumblers clicking uselessly, until one perfect moment when they clicked.

He almost wanted Miles to ask him if he was going to leave again, just so he could tell him that he wasn't, that he couldn't. But Miles seemed very uninterested in any more talking, hands moving down Evan's chest, only breaking apart to pull his shirt off, to pant unevenly into the damp skin of his neck.

It helped that Evan knew exactly where the bedroom was, and so exactly where to steer them, Evan shedding his shoes, then his sweatpants as they stumbled down the hallway, lips fused together.

When they reached the bed, Evan shoved Miles onto the edge, and placed a very possessive hand against the cock throbbing in his briefs.

Miles groaned into his mouth. Something insensible. Something very much like begging.

And Evan was perfectly happy to give him exactly what he wanted. He pulled the fabric down, watching as Miles' cock sprung from its confines, landing wetly against his abs.

Evan knew many people considered sucking cock to be a demeaning activity, like dropping to your knees somehow made you subservient, but he'd always gotten a power rush from it. Miles' shocked, pleased expression rushed through him as he lowered himself, flicking his tongue just briefly against the reddened head.

"Please," Miles said, and he sounded wrecked.

Probably Evan always felt a power rush because he liked making a big production out of a blowjob. Liked to tease. Liked to drive the man above him to barely wrung-out pleas. Some people wrote symphonies, some painted art, some sculpted out of clay and marble. Evan really liked to give a perfect blowjob.

He took his time about it now, wondering how far he could drive Miles with little teasing licks, fingers digging purposefully into the meat of his thighs, a counterpoint to the delicacy of what his mouth was doing to his cock.

Miles quickly fell to a litany of nonsense and moans. He seemed to understand that Evan didn't want his hands on him, and he kept them fisted in the comforter, knuckles white as he clenched the cotton.

But he must have gotten close before Evan even arrived, because it was too soon and he'd already reached a fevered point of begging. Evan tongued the slit, tasted the rush of salt, and knew he must be close, even though he'd barely given him anything to sink his teeth into.

As far as Evan was concerned, what made him really good at sucking cock wasn't a preplanned attack, but the ability to improvise in the middle. So he abandoned the delicate teasing abruptly, mouth sliding down Miles' cock, sucking with all the force he dared.

Miles' yelp was very rewarding and so was the flood of come on his tongue. He swallowed, taking his time about cleaning up every inch of Miles' prick as it softened in his mouth.

Finally Miles pushed him off, and there was only the sound of heavy breathing in the dim room. Evan suddenly was acutely aware of his own arousal, pressing against his thigh, sticky and hot.

"Give me a second," Miles breathed out, voice unsteady, "you might have killed me."

"But what a way to go," Evan said, feeling very satisfied—but not nearly as satisfied as he could be.

"If you'd believe it, you were doing the exact same thing in my head when you knocked on my door."

Evan raised an eyebrow. "Okay," Miles corrected with a silly little grin that shouldn't have made both Evan's heart and dick flex, but it did, anyway, "not quite the exact same thing. I don't have the same perverse imagination you apparently do."

"I'm about to get a lot more perverse," Evan threatened, the thrum of blood in his cock becoming more and more insistent.

"I've got you," Miles said, and the hand he extended to lift him up was gentle and so was his voice.

His hand however, was the right amount of rough friction that Evan didn't even know he needed as Miles fisted around his length and pumped him hard and reckless. Evan might have been ashamed at how quickly it ended, but then he had a feeling they both knew he hadn't only been teasing Miles.

Miles wiped his hand on the sheet and rolled over in the bed. Evan hesitated on the edge, not sure if he should stay or go. All of his hookups had always been only sex. Once orgasms were had, it was over, and Evan usually left, because he never liked letting strangers into his personal space. He'd spent too many years doing that.

But Miles was looking at him expectantly, like he expected Evan to roll over and go to sleep.

Evan almost said no. He almost said he was tired and he was going to walk the few yards back to his own place, and go to sleep in his own bed. But then he remembered the way their mouths had fit together, the eerie sensation of two people locking into each other, and though he wasn't sure he wanted to stay, he didn't really want to leave either.

So he lay on the bed in the warm spot Miles had vacated and watched as Miles reached over and flicked the light off. "Night," he said, and hated how uncertain he sounded.

"Night," Miles returned, all lazy satisfaction, like he'd gotten everything he'd wanted.

They both had; that much was clearly obvious from the way they'd both gone up in flames from the first moment they'd touched. Evan knew he should be feeling more resolved. But tomorrow's screen test still loomed over them, and there was too much ambiguity about the future for him to relax.

He rolled over and willed sleep to overtake him. It still didn't come. Even when Miles fell into a gentle patter of snores, too quiet to be annoying, and also too quiet to drown out his uneasy brain.

He told himself that he was making the right decision when he silently slid out of bed and locked Miles' door behind him with the key he still had on his ring. It was just a night of sleep, and in the grand scheme of things, it really shouldn't mean anything.

Was it fair of Miles to be pissed that he'd woken this morning and Evan had already been gone? Probably. Was it surprising that he'd opened his eyes to nothing but empty sheets? Not really.

Evan, even after admitting he wanted Miles and thoroughly acting on this desire, was still skittish. Still unsure. Never really convinced that Miles really wanted him, despite all the words and actions that proved otherwise.

A younger, more selfish Miles might have gotten frustrated with Evan before this, but Miles took pride in the fact that he wanted the other man *because* of how difficult he was to convince, not in spite of it. There was a careful hesitancy in Evan that Miles loved—because when he finally felt secure enough to let go, you knew you'd won him over, heart, body and soul.

And that was the end goal that Miles was really gunning for.

Now they only had to make it through this screen test and hope that it would be enough to convince Reed, because anything else they could fix later.

Miles just needed this *one* thing to fall their way.

They'd arrived on set to the expected chaos of a show that was just getting underway for the first day of filming. Reed was there, and his boyfriend, Jordan, who wrote the script for *Dream Team*. Quentin Maxwell and Landon Patton, the talent, were running late, which didn't seem to surprise anyone.

"That's why they told us we could do our screen test today," Evan murmured into Miles' ear, and with the hot breath brushing his skin, he had to remind himself that Evan wasn't going to do that hot little nibbling thing he'd done last night.

"Because things are already chaotic?" Miles asked.

"Because they won't be likely to get much done today at all. Landon and Quen can be . . . tough to wrangle."

"So it's not just me, then?" Miles glanced over at Evan, grinning. Evan was not grinning. That was another thing Miles wanted desperately—for Evan to *relax*.

But asking Evan to relax in the middle of chaos, during one of the most important days of his career, was useless. It wasn't ever going to happen.

"That was never our problem. Or *your* problem," Evan said.

Maybe another day Miles would have asked Evan to detail exactly what his problem was, but the memories from last night—what could be if they could learn to work together instead of against each other—were too fresh. The last thing he wanted to do was dredge up all the shit from the previous weeks.

They hadn't really resolved it, and it still lay there, stagnant and sour, between them. Maybe Evan thought they could move on without dealing with it but Miles knew they couldn't.

Even if Miles cared about Evan enough to let it go—and despite how stupid it was, he was edging closer to that place—Evan would never let it go. Miles didn't think he even wanted to.

"Are you ready?" Evan asked, jerking Miles out of the melancholy fog that he'd felt from the moment he'd woken up and realized he was alone.

"I was born ready," he said, putting on a confident front that he didn't really feel anymore. Before he'd come here, *Pastry by Miles* always made him feel freer, an endless opportunity stretched out in front of him. Now thinking of what could happen to his show, all he felt was apprehension.

It was hard to face that at least half of that was his fault, but he forced himself to.

Without that email, Reed wouldn't have demanded a screen test, and he wouldn't have spent the last two days unsuccessfully recording himself baking peanut butter chocolate cookies.

The cookies had been fantastic; his performance had been anything but.

Before, it had only ever been him. Then it had been easy to think it was just him and Evan, for better and worse. And now there was a huge crowd of people, and even though Miles had never cared before, suddenly what they thought mattered.

He swallowed hard, and unsuccessfully ignored the sudden tightness in his chest.

"Just remember that it just needs to be good enough," Evan said.

The hardest part of the last two days was watching the hopeful light in Evan's eyes go out as he figured out that Miles couldn't perform on command. And hearing his words now only proved that even Evan wasn't sure he could do it.

"Okay," Miles said, shoving his suddenly damp hands into his pockets, wondering if anyone would notice if he ran away and hid in the bathroom.

He didn't even have a green room because this wasn't even his show.

"You're going to be fine," Evan said. He placed a reassuring hand on Miles' back, high enough to be professional. Stupidly, Miles wished that he'd move it lower, make what had happened last night official and public. But that wasn't Evan's style. It wasn't even Miles' style. At least it hadn't been before he'd met Evan. Evan made him want all sorts of things he'd always avoided, and the painful irony was that he was the least likely to get them because it *was* Evan.

"Fine," Miles parroted back, tongue thick and uncooperative. He couldn't remember the last time he'd even been nervous but he was undeniably nervous now.

Evan checked his smartwatch. "Time for makeup," he said, and with his hand still on Miles' back, steered him over to the makeup station.

Miles had never worn makeup for *Pastry by Miles* before, and he forced himself to remember that they were trying to up the production quality for the new version.

It didn't help.

He sat down in front of the mirror and watched as the nice lady put a new, strange face on him.

The bathroom had never looked more appealing. Miles didn't even think about his little dinky kitchen in Napa because if he did, he wasn't sure he could keep it together.

❧❧❧❧❧ ❧❧❧❧❧

Would Miles be better if I had stayed?

The question echoed through Evan's brain for the hundredth time since they'd gotten to the *Dream Team* set.

Miles had been nervous and tense from the moment Evan had met him at the set, and instead of relaxing with Evan's hand on him, he'd only grown edgier.

Evan stood behind the central camera operator and crossed his arms over his chest, careful to keep the frown off his face, but feeling it reverberate through him.

Miles was standing in the kitchen, the place he always looked confident and sure, but he looked nothing like he usually did.

He looked like an apprehensive wreck, and it was taking every ounce of Evan's self-control to not walk up there and do something—*anything*—to calm him down.

Evan knew he should have stayed. He never should have left, never should have given Miles a reason to doubt that he liked him, that he cared about him, and Evan had been monumentally stupid enough to do it the day before the most important ten minutes of both their careers.

That was exactly why Evan almost never let himself do what he really craved. Because they were usually really bad ideas, and only made things worse, not better. Last night had been great. He couldn't even think about it without a little frisson of invisible pleasure, but it hadn't been worth throwing everything else away.

The director called for quiet. Miles forced out a painful little half smile, and then the worst ten minutes of Evan's life began.

He knew right away that Miles' performance this time was even worse than some of the recordings they'd done over the last two days. He'd worried about those, had been afraid that he was too stiff, so he'd pushed and pressed and hoped that they could make some improvements before this moment came.

Now Evan wished he'd just kept his fucking mouth shut, because he would have loved to have those performances be *this* performance.

"And now, uh, you put these in the oven for ten minutes," Miles said, and slid the cookie sheet into the oven. Wooden. Dry. None of the playful, laughing charm that had won over so many people who didn't care about pastry at all.

Evan had counted himself in that group, from the very beginning, and this hurt more than he ever could have imagined it would. Because it wasn't only his failure, it was the failure of a persona that Miles had believed in. A persona that he'd believed himself to be.

Evan wished he could take it all back, and leave Miles alone. Leave him to his bad production values, and poor lighting, and the single swipe of raspberry puree on one cheekbone. *Perfection.*

"Cut," the director yelled, and it blessedly, thankfully, ended.

"What just happened?"

Evan turned and Reed was standing there. Evan's stomach plummeted.

"He was nervous, uh, a little tense, I think," Evan said, and because there was nothing else he could do, pushed. "I have a lot of rehearsal footage that you should see. It's a lot better." Not by much, but it *was* better.

Reed raised an eyebrow. "You rehearsed? How much?"

"The last two days," Evan said, even though he was sure that Reed already knew the answer. Evan was unfailingly predictable.

"What I wanted to see," Reed said reluctantly, "was a meshing together of your two viewpoints. The organization and production value that you bring to the table, but the spontaneity and charm of who Miles is in the kitchen. Your point of view completely overwhelmed his. You rehearsed him way too much. He knew what he was going to say before he even said it. There was nothing here from *Pastry by Miles*. It was more *Pastry by Evan*."

It was one thing to know it, it was another to have his boss pronounce it. Evan wanted to sink through the floor and die, especially when he saw Miles approaching behind Reed, clearly hearing every word he was saying. The worried crinkle between his dark brows told Evan everything he needed to know. Miles was half a step out the door, half a step away from going back to Napa and resuming a life that he'd already outgrown.

And Evan, for the first time in his life, confronted a problem that he didn't know how to fix.

"We can do better," Evan said, because he didn't know what else *to* say. He believed they could; he had no idea how to go about doing it, but they couldn't be so good together sometimes without some potential for success.

Reed just shook his head. "I don't want *better*. I want what you had." He turned and pinned Miles with a single look. "Just because you want in his pants doesn't mean you should just nod your head and smile whenever he tells you to do something. He's not infallible. And neither are you." He threw up his hands. "For the love of god, take a long weekend and figure out how to work together."

"Uh," Evan said. Because he couldn't take a long weekend and not know what that meant for his future. Was he fired? Was *Pastry by Miles* as a *Five Points* property over before it had even begun?

"Get out of here," Reed said sternly, and his expression very clearly stated arguments wouldn't be tolerated. "I don't want to hear you did one minute of work. Go somewhere. Clear your heads. And come back here and we'll figure out this mess you two have made."

It was bad, but Evan supposed he was grateful it wasn't as bad as it could have been.

Miles looked like a thundercloud come to life as Reed walked off to supervise the finalization of the set for *Dream Team*.

"I'm sorry," Evan said, because everything else felt painfully inadequate.

"Yeah, you should be. The real question is what you're actually sorry for."

Evan swallowed hard. "I don't know what you mean."

"That's your whole damn problem," Miles said. "And we're going to fix it."

Which is how, two hours later, Evan found himself in another rental car, heading towards Northern California.

"You can't run away every time things get ugly," Evan said, because he didn't like where this was going. He knew what had happened the last time Miles had decided to go back to Napa, and they were on thin enough ice as it was.

"That," Miles pointed out, "is your other problem. You think I'm running away. I'm not. I'm blowing off steam. You've never blown off steam in your life. You're about to self-combust from all the steam building inside you. You put way too much pressure on yourself. Take too much on. We're going up to Napa to help you learn to let stuff go."

"Shouldn't we be working on how to fix the show?" Evan insisted. "We're half-fired at this moment in time. Blowing off work to drink and party doesn't seem like the best plan."

"Reed already told you that you're not working. And even if he didn't, I wouldn't let you. We've rehearsed enough. We need to learn to work together, and that's never going to happen if you can't fucking relax."

"So you're going to . . . teach me to relax?" Evan didn't know what to make of this plan. Actually, scratch that. He knew what he thought of it and it wasn't anything good. It was a terrible plan, probably going to result in them being totally, one hundred percent fired.

"Yes."

"I can relax," Evan insisted.

"And yet I have seen zero evidence of you actually relaxing," Miles said. "We tried things your way, and they failed spectacularly. You wound us both up so tight that I could barely breathe. I don't even know how you survive wound this tight. So we're going to do things my way."

"But . . ." Evan tried to point out, but Miles just interrupted him.

"No arguments. No circular logical shit. You're going to fucking relax if it kills me."

"It might, because I'll probably end up murdering you," Evan said, and he couldn't help how grumpy he sounded. He was *fine*. He didn't need to relax; relaxation never got anyone anywhere.

"Yeah," Miles drawled, his hand on the wheel relaxed as he smiled, skin crinkling near his eyes, "you can fuck me to death."

Evan harrumphed.

"Seriously, it might be fun. You might actually enjoy yourself for a minute."

"Are you going to keep bringing up sex just to remind me what happened last night?" Evan demanded. "Because trust me, I do not need a reminder."

Miles glanced over, and he was still smiling. Like the further north they drove, the further he unwound. Even Evan baiting the shit out of him didn't make a dent. "I don't know, I think *I* do. A little refresher, we could even say."

Evan snorted, because he just couldn't help himself. "Is that how you get guys in your bed? You never stop harassing them?" It wasn't hard to swallow the question of why Miles wouldn't stop harassing *him*. After all, he'd left Miles alone in bed, and fucked up his career.

He wasn't sure which Miles should be more pissed off about, but Evan knew he would never be big enough to let it go. But instead of biting his head off, Miles was driving them to Napa, relaxed and smiling, like last night had been perfect.

"When it's perfect, yeah, I'm not going to let that go. Let *you* go." Miles smirked.

And it sort of had been perfect, at least before Evan went and overthought everything. Before Evan remembered what the next morning would bring.

Somehow they'd both survived the morning, though Evan had a feeling that had more to do with Reed probably not wanting to deal with them than actually catching a break.

Still. They were still here. Still together. Evan felt the invisible belt holding him together loosen a single notch.

"It was pretty great," he admitted, and Miles' smile grew at least ten degrees brighter.

"See, that wasn't so hard, was it?" Miles teased.

"I don't know," Evan said, barely managing to keep a straight face. He was *not* going to grin at Miles like a lovesick loon. Except he sort of was. Miles was making him begin to believe in fate. "It might be pretty hard later."

Chapter Twelve

It was a long drive to Napa, almost six hours from the studio, but Evan felt like he spent most of it half-hard, blood simmering in anticipation of what they might do when they finally got to the hotel Miles had booked.

Miles seemed like he wanted it too, just as much as Evan did. The looks he'd been shooting Evan's direction were hardly subtle, and his comments were even less so. And every so often he'd put his hands on Evan, casually, in the middle of a conversation, like it didn't mean anything at all.

But it meant a lot. It meant that Miles worked him up and then carefully made sure he never really calmed down.

Instead of pulling into the hotel parking lot, they sailed right past, and Evan tried not to look too frantic as he opened his phone to verify the reservation. "This was the place," he said, trying to sound calm and not panicked. *Relaxed.*

He'd never considered himself particularly sex-obsessed before, but he craved Miles powerfully now that he'd actually allowed himself to.

"What?" Miles asked, as laid-back as ever. Evan wanted to strangle him and also shove his dick down his throat. He really hated how desperate Miles had made him—just by being himself.

"That was our hotel," Evan got out in a strangled voice. "We just passed it!"

"Oh yeah," Miles said. "It was. Good eye."

"What are you doing!" Evan didn't even recognize his own voice.

"Don't worry," Miles said, leaning over and resting a warm palm conveniently on Evan's thigh. Evan sucked in a breath. "We'll get there soon enough. I made us a wine tasting reservation first. A few of them, actually."

"A few?" Evan squeaked.

Miles shot him a soft, scorching smile. "A few, yeah. Is that a problem?"

If Miles thought Evan was going to be the first to break down and demand sex, he was crazy.

"No," Evan said, pulling himself back together only because he'd done it his whole life. "I'm good."

It was a complete and total lie, and Miles' expression made it clear he knew just how untruthful Evan was being.

"Yeah, you are," Miles said, and his voice was a slick caress across Evan's skin.

He was going to kill him by the time they made it back to the hotel. Or maybe he'd do as Miles had suggested and just fuck him to death.

"This," the sommelier said, "is our unoaked chardonnay." He poured a little of the golden liquid into each of their glasses. Evan shifted uncomfortably on his wooden stool.

He'd always believed wine tasting would be fun. Anything involving alcohol was *supposed* to be, right? But from the moment they'd driven up the winding road to the huge, imposing winery, with its expensive fixtures and obvious antiques, to being shown into the private tasting room, Evan had been on edge.

And not even the fun sort of edge that Miles had honed during the drive up.

This was the edge where Evan never knew what he was supposed to do, how he was supposed to act, what he was supposed to say. All accompanied by the fear and horror of choosing wrong and revealing himself as a fraud.

He might look the part of a young, successful adult, but it still felt like an act and like he might be exposed at any moment.

Reed had wondered once why Evan always made sure he was meticulously prepared and so extensively researched. *This* was why.

But Miles had dragged him up to these wineries before he could look into their dress codes, their wine lists, their tasting room etiquettes.

Evan didn't know how Miles could look so calm when he had no clue what he was supposed to say about the stupid wine.

Usually he looked up reviews, and formed an opinion before he even tasted it, because it helped create a good frame of reference. Evan knew he was wine-ignorant and even as he took a sip now, letting the liquid swell in his mouth, he was lost.

Miles didn't help at all, just tasted, expression thoughtful and frustratingly blank.

"What do you think?" the sommelier asked.

Miles had introduced him as Nate, one of his roommates' ex-boyfriends, and he looked the part of a professional sommelier—polished and urbane, his shoes probably costing more than Evan's whole outfit.

He'd only longingly glanced at the beautifully burnished cognac leather loafers a few times before they'd sat down.

The test had come and Evan had known there was no way he could pass. He didn't drink boxed wine, but he definitely bought wine under ten dollars. Sometimes even under seven dollars. He didn't have a rarified or educated palate.

Even though Miles claimed not to know much either, Miles still knew more because he'd worked at Terroir, and he'd lived in Napa.

"It's got a surprisingly buttery finish," Miles said, saving him even though he couldn't know how tense Evan had become at being asked to provide an opinion on the wine. "I thought you said it wasn't oaked."

"It's not," Nate sniffed.

"Could've fooled me," Miles said, downing the rest of the glass.

Nate scowled. "Amazing, you're still an asshole."

But Miles just smiled back, all charming congeniality. "And you're still a fucking snob. But you pour good wine, which is why we're here. So do your job, and pour us some more wine."

It shouldn't have been sexy hearing Miles tell off the sommelier, but it was an unexpected turn-on. Evan squirmed in his chair, torn between annoyance and fondness. He shouldn't want or like Miles as much as he did, but that ship had already sailed and there was absolutely nothing Evan could do about it now.

"This," Nate said, shooting a snooty glare from his brown eyes, "is an oaked chardonnay."

Evan glanced at the tasting card resting between them on the gleaming wood bar top. There was only one chardonnay listed—the one they'd just finished. He might not know anything about wine, but he did know how to read, so he spoke up.

"Which chardonnay is this one again? I don't see it listed."

Nate glared harder, but Miles' gaze met Evan's across their glasses, and they shared a conspiratorial, secret look that made Evan's stomach somersault.

"Costa, what would your old roommates say if they knew you were dating?" The sommelier lifted a glossy brown eyebrow, flawlessly groomed.

"We're not dating," Evan corrected frostily, and briefly considered explaining they were just fucking. But not enough for Evan's peace of mind.

"He's my producer," Miles said, completely breaking protocol by reaching over and pouring some more of the first chardonnay in his glass. "And that second chardonnay is disgusting. Don't pour that again."

He looked over at Evan, and the warmth in his expression made Evan wonder if he'd lied earlier. Were they dating? Was this a date? Was this whole weekend a date? Weren't you supposed to go on a lot of silly, short dates before you took someone on a weekend getaway?

It was stupid to even think it. They didn't even like each other, and they couldn't stop fighting for five minutes put together. But the times they weren't fighting? Evan lived for those moments. For the soft, sweet Miles who made him want to be soft and sweet too. Miles, who made him believe that he *could* be, even though he'd assumed for so long that he was hopeless. Too shut off, too closed, too much of a workaholic.

Miles made him want things he couldn't define.

"And to answer your question, we're going to a late dinner at the house tonight, so maybe you can call up Wyatt and ask him what he thinks."

Nate stiffened, and Evan would have had to be a lot more obtuse to miss the flash of hurt in his eyes. It was gone almost instantly, but it had been unmistakable.

"This," Nate said coldly after they'd drained their glasses, "is one of our library cabernet sauvignons. I hope your palate will appreciate it."

It was rich and complex, an enigmatic combination of the light and the dark. And Evan said so, out loud, before he could stop himself.

Nate merely looked constipated, but Miles smiled encouragingly. "It is good," he said. "Surprisingly dark, smooth finish, but light and drinkable. I like it." He downed the glass. "And you already know my palate won't appreciate it."

"True," Nate said. "But you," and he pointed to Evan, "actually have some potential, unlike that idiot sitting next to you."

Evan was almost stupid enough to protest, because of course he didn't have any potential. He drank cheap wine. He didn't really care too much what it tasted like—in fact, he ignored what it tasted like, because for so long, he couldn't afford anything better, and drinking wine at all had felt like a luxury, like he was better than he really was. But all that did was force him to remember who he was and where he'd come from. If Nate the snooty sommelier said his palate had potential, then it *did*.

Miles' smile was supportive. "Don't give him too many ideas, he'll be talking about cigar smoke and mahogany next." His hand reached out and rested on Evan's knee. It was big and warm and delicate and it made Evan shiver. He wanted to drag Miles away and damn the wine tasting to hell.

How Miles ever thought he was going to relax while winding him tighter than he'd ever been, Evan wasn't sure.

Nate poured a merlot next, which was apparently the winery's newest release. This time he looked to Evan for his impressions, barely glancing at Miles.

Emboldened by the compliment to his palate and the wine he'd already drunk, Evan felt marginally more comfortable offering his opinion. "It's spicy and burns a little, but a good burn," he said cautiously.

"You really shouldn't bring him over to that hellhole," Nate said as they were getting ready to go. They hadn't bought any wine, but when they were getting ready to go, Nate had pushed over a bottle in a brown paper bag. "For tonight," was all he said, and Miles had frowned. Evan was pretty sure the frown had something to do with Nate's ex-boyfriend, Wyatt. Miles' friend.

"It's not a hellhole. I lived there for two years," Miles said.

Evan figured he was allowed an opinion because he'd actually been there. "It's not even close to a hellhole," he defended. He didn't add that he'd seen actual hellholes growing up, and the run-down, worn house Miles had lived in couldn't even begin to compete.

Nate only shook his head. "You know where to find me if you get sick of them."

"What did he mean?" Evan asked as they walked to the car. He told himself he wasn't jealous, that Nate wasn't propositioning Miles if he got bored later. He was mostly lying.

"Nate works at a late-night wine bar too, pouring. Pays for his expensive shoes," was all Miles said as they got into the car.

"You don't like him," Evan stated, somewhat to his own surprise. "You really, really don't like him."

"Gee, what gave me away?" Miles asked with a lopsided grin in Evan's direction.

"I mean . . . you don't talk to me that way. I thought that's how you talked to people you didn't like." Evan had a fleeting thought that maybe this conversation shouldn't be happening now, after he'd had a few glasses of wine. Miles had pleaded required sobriety for driving, but Nate had poured most of the winery library for Evan.

At the time it had seemed like an excellent learning opportunity; a way to expand and refine his palate. Only now did Evan realize drinking so much wine had been a mistake. He was definitely tipsy, and even worse, he kept saying all sorts of things to Miles that he shouldn't.

Was this what being relaxed felt like? No. It was definitely what being drunk felt like. "That's because I don't dislike you."

"But, you definitely seem to. I mean, you *said* you did."

"I also said I thought you had a hot ass. Does that seem like something I'd say to someone I didn't like?"

"No." He *did* have a hot ass. It was hardly the first time he'd been informed of this fact, but none of those other times had made his face burn and his cock harden. In fact, all those other times, he'd varied between mildly and extremely creeped out.

"You're cute when you've been drinking," Miles announced.

"I'm not drunk," Evan said. Total lie. The way Miles grinned meant he knew just how drunk Evan was, and just how much he was lying.

"And yet you're still not relaxed."

Evan frowned. It seemed *very* obvious the best way to relax him. And because he'd apparently lost his brain-to-mouth filter, he said it. Out loud. "I know exactly how you can relax me."

Miles turned into a parking lot and pulled into a space. Evan glanced up at the sign above the rows of little wooden stalls. "What is this?" he bit off. This wasn't the sort of relaxing he wanted to sign up for. The wine tasting had actually been pretty fun; whatever this was, Evan already knew he wouldn't like it. Why? It was *cooking*.

"I thought you might want to come to the farmer's market with me," Miles said, so reasonably that Evan felt a tiny bit ashamed for snapping.

But only a tiny bit. After all, it felt like Miles had been pressing for weeks for them to have sex, so it shouldn't have been so difficult to get him to do it again. Especially when it had been so good the first time. Even better than he could have predicted.

"Is the farmer's market supposed to relax me?" Evan snapped.

"I thought watching me cook turned you on?" Miles glanced over, and there was so much heat in his gray eyes it was a miracle he didn't melt right onto the seat. Oh wait, that was Evan, who wasn't only feeling warm and loose from the wine he'd drunk.

"I don't think I remember saying that," Evan said. He should be a lot more ashamed at getting caught out, but this was *Miles,* and he'd probably read all the comments on his videos a few dozen times. And everyone thought Miles cooking was a turn-on, because it *was.*

It was those long fingers and the way he caressed every goddamn ingredient.

"Are you coming?" Miles said, eyes glittering with unrepentant amusement.

"*No.*" Evan gave a frustrated grunt. "Not even close."

"Come on," Miles persuaded, "it'll be fun."

"Fine, but if you fondle the raspberries again, I'm done," Evan said.

⁂

It was a hell of a lot sweeter than Miles had ever imagined it would be to see Evan so obviously needy for sex. And not just sex in general—sex with *Miles.*

Only part of it was that he'd never really had someone turn him down so many times and fight so hard against a mutual attraction. Most of it was that it was just Evan. Miles was beginning to realize he adored everything about him. From the way he'd stared enviously at Nate's stupidly expensive loafers, bought with too many long nights at the wine bar, to Evan's frustration that they hadn't immediately fallen into bed again, to his extraordinarily pleased expression when he'd been told he had a decent palate.

He was adorable, if you paid attention. Even if you didn't, Miles realized, but then he'd spent too long trying to ignore him. Even when Evan made himself difficult to ignore.

"Can you please explain what it is you're doing?" Evan asked, eyes obscured by a pair of aviator sunglasses he'd slipped on.

"As directed, I am not fondling the raspberries," Miles said.

Evan took a step closer, reaching up on his tiptoes to murmur into Miles' ear. "Then how come you're rolling them between your fingertips?"

Had he been? Given an inch, Miles was figuring out that he was desperate to go the mile. Consciously or even subconsciously. "Maybe because I want you as badly as you want me?"

"You're doing that annoying thing again, where you answer a question with a question," Evan hissed after Miles dropped the container of raspberries into the basket he was carrying.

"You love it when I do that," Miles insisted.

Evan sniffed. "No. I definitely do not."

"Sorry?" Miles asked, shooting Evan a lopsided smile. That smile had charmed legions during his single life, but all it did was emphasize Evan's frown.

"I don't get it," Evan said as they walked away from the fruit stand. "If you want me as much as I want you, how come we're not at the hotel right now?"

Miles shoved his own sunglasses on top of his head as he leaned down to examine some zucchini. Maybe he'd make a zucchini and squash ratatouille. Xander had a secret obsession with Italian food and would appreciate it. "Because," he said patiently, "we're at the farmer's market, buying supplies to make dinner. Also, because you're drunk and I don't want to do something you might regret."

A frustrated groan came out of Evan's mouth. "You're the one who took me wine tasting!"

Miles turned away from the zucchini, decided this needed his full attention. He couldn't get distracted by squash or Xander's *tendre* for rustic Italian. "I took you wine tasting because you like wine, and I thought you might have fun. Even though that jerk Nate was the sommelier."

"But . . ." Evan tried to say but Miles placed the produce basket on the ground, and wrapped his arms around Evan's narrow waist. Evan resisted a little, but eventually gave in, letting Miles pull him closer.

"No buts," Miles said seriously. "I do want you. I can't wait to take you back to the hotel, but this is also a break for you. A break you really need. And as far as I'm concerned, that's more important than getting a quickie at the hotel. *You're* more important than a quickie at the hotel."

Evan's eyes grew wide. Like he genuinely didn't believe he was more than a convenient fuck. Which, as far as Miles was concerned, was a bunch of bullshit. Yeah, he'd sent that email. Yeah, they fought and bickered like cats and dogs, but when had he ever made Evan feel like he didn't like him? Like he wasn't important? He'd been trying since he first realized to show Evan that he cared. Even more than he was ready to admit to.

"Oh." Evan seemed shocked and speechless. But maybe still not totally convinced.

So instead of letting Evan go and picking up the produce basket, ready to resume his shopping, Miles decided there was no time better than the present to do a little additional convincing.

It wasn't so easy for Miles to say the words yet—even in his own mind, he tripped uncoordinatedly over them—so he showed Evan just how much he was wanted. He kissed him, pouring in all the skill he'd learned and all the passion he felt for the other man, his tongue slipping between Evan's still-stiff lips, giving everyone at the farmer's market a nice show.

It took a long second for Evan to respond, but when he did, he threw himself into the kiss, tongue rasping against Miles', hands wandering down his back, landing pretty firmly on his own ass.

There were dim cheers somewhere over to his left, but all Miles could feel was Evan's mouth moving insistently against his own, his body pressed against his, his erection poking into his hip. And it hit him, like a ton of zucchini, that this was what he had really wanted, almost from the beginning.

Evan was what he had wanted. He had just been so slow—*way too fucking slow*—to see it.

Miles lifted his head and looked down into Evan's light brown sugar eyes. "You really . . . you really do want me," Evan breathed out unsteadily. Miles' own pulse was racing a hundred miles a second, and he didn't quite trust his own voice so he nodded.

And while Evan didn't say why he'd doubted, Miles thought as they resumed their casual stroll through the farmer's market that it weighed heavily between them. He ached for the young Evan, who had been convinced he wasn't worth anything, and that nothing had ever happened to change his mind.

Chapter Thirteen

"What are you making?" Evan asked, peering around Miles' shoulder as he sautéed the squash for the ratatouille he was making. "Something with a god-awful amount of zucchini, which I don't even like."

Miles glanced over at him, and even though he was still talking way too much and he'd taken his phone away from him twice now, Evan did seem a little more relaxed than he'd been in LA. Of course that might also be all the wine he'd drunk.

"You don't like zucchini?" He remembered Evan telling him he didn't like sweets, and then the way he'd devoured the peanut butter chocolate chunk cookie and then the *pain au chocolat*. Evan might think he didn't like something, but judgement should be held until he'd tried Miles' version.

He told Evan this, and his nose crinkled. "You're such an egotistical asshole," Evan said and Miles could only shrug.

"I'm a chef," he said, as an explanation. "And I'm making ratatouille, or a version of ratatouille. Xander loves rustic Italian, though he will almost never admit to it."

"Xander, huh?" Evan said, and he wasn't even the tiniest bit subtle about the green in his voice. "You've never asked me what I liked."

"You told me you didn't like sweets. I thought it was my duty first to change your mind on that score, and then we'd go from there."

"Your cookies were passable," Evan said, leaning against the opposite counter, sipping his wine. The wine that Nate had given him. Miles had already crumpled up the bag with its distinctive markings and buried it in the trash. Wyatt didn't need to backslide into that black hole of a relationship again, no matter how much wine Nate gave them. "The croissants weren't really yours, they were mine, so I can freely admit to loving those, even if they were a pain in the ass."

Miles pulled the zucchini off the stove. "So what do you like to eat then?"

"Pizza. Kung pao chicken. Tacos." Evan met Miles' surprised expression with a semi-belligerent glare. "What, I don't cook. So I order in or I go out."

"You need to learn how to cook," Miles said with a sad shake of his head.

"And I suppose you're just the guy to teach me?" Evan asked, leaning back into Miles' space. This time Evan kissed him, something quick and hot and almost brutal.

Miles pulled away, nearly gasping. "I'm a pastry chef. I know just enough about savory ingredients to get by. But," he added, dropping another quick kiss on Evan's cheek, "I'll be damned if anyone else teaches you."

"You two are disgusting."

Miles glanced up and Xander was standing in the doorway, holding a loaf of bread, the wrapper indicating their favorite bakery in Napa.

"And your heart is two sizes too small," Miles retorted. "I'll pick sappy and disgusting over lonely and miserable any day."

"I don't think we met before," Evan inserted, and though Miles couldn't figure out why, the casualness in his voice was replaced by a sharp edge. "I mean, we probably did, but I don't think we were properly introduced. I'm Evan Patterson."

Xander clearly had no qualms about looking Evan up and down because he did, freely. Miles ground his teeth and turned back to the tomato sauce he'd been simmering on the stove.

He didn't even put the bread down so he could shake Evan's outstretched hand. "And I'm Xander. Resident grinch."

Evan shoved the hand back in his pocket and took half a step closer to where Miles was starting to prep the ratatouille.

"What's this?" Xander said, sniffing appreciatively as he approached Miles' other side, resting a hand on his back. "You made ratatouille. For me?"

"Someday you're going to admit your obnoxiously refined palate loves Italian," Miles said.

"But not today," Xander said, sounding as smug as he ever had. Evan sniffed disapprovingly.

"I've never understood that," Evan said. "Someone makes you a meal, you should be grateful, not worried about how sophisticated it makes you look."

Miles felt Xander bristle next to him. "That's the difference going to culinary school makes," Miles said with a deprecating laugh. "It makes us all feel very important. Like we're culinary gods." He hoped that would be enough for Evan to let it go, and for Xander to back down and not engage. Because if Evan and Xander ever got into it, there probably wouldn't be anything left but rubble in his kitchen.

"I enjoy common food," Xander said, and Miles couldn't help but roll his eyes at his word choice.

"Yeah," he retorted, forgetting all about his vow to avert the fight and keep the kitchen intact, "'cause you're culinary royalty. I forgot."

"Like, In n' Out," Xander said defensively. "They use such fresh ingredients, and their cooking techniques aren't that shitty."

Evan glared at him. "Right, because McDonald's or Burger King is too basic for you."

"Yes, they are. If I want a burger, at least I want to eat a *good* burger, not some over-processed, greasy shit on a bun."

Miles could feel the waves of rage pouring off Evan, but even as he held a hand out to steady him—covered with tomato sauce and all—Evan snapped back. "Sometimes that's all people can *afford*."

And suddenly, Miles understood. People would never admit it, especially someone like Xander who had lived a solid middle-class life and had gone to culinary school right out of his parents' house, but good home cooking cost money. You needed equipment, you needed fresh produce and quality protein. None of that came cheap.

Miles had taken a class in culinary school on food sustainability, and he couldn't believe it when the instructor had informed them that eating out on cheap junk food was often much cheaper than cooking healthy meals at home.

And of course, Evan, living in a foster home and then living hand-to-mouth on his own, wouldn't have been able to afford to learn to cook. The guilt was sudden and sweeping, making him nearly nauseous.

"Xander, do me a favor," Miles said, words casual, his voice anything but, "shut the fuck up."

Evan knew he was supposed to be finding some magical well of relaxation in Napa, and up until now, even he could admit he was having a good time.

Separated from the antagonism that had dogged them from the first day, spending time with Miles was just as fantastic as Evan had hoped it might be, back at the beginning.

But spending time with Miles was not the same as spending time with Miles' old roommates, in particular the abrasive, argumentative one who was currently hanging off Miles like he wasn't going to let him go again.

The only romantic relationship Miles had ever described any of them having was Wyatt and his sommelier ex-boyfriend. He'd never said he'd been romantically or sexually involved with any of them, but it was hard not to believe this was lying by omission when Xander was putting his hands all over him.

Maybe that was why Xander was so bitter and unpleasant? Evan didn't want to think if things with him and Miles didn't turn out—which, he couldn't help but admit dispiritedly, was seeming more and more likely by the day—he would end up like Xander. Sad. Disillusioned. Resembling a rabid dog anytime someone talked to him.

"What?" Xander said, flinging his hands in the air, like he was innocent of all charges, which . . . had he *listened* to himself in the last five minutes? Evan didn't think so.

"You're an asshole," Miles said with a scowl.

This pronouncement didn't seem to phase Xander, who was probably called this on a daily basis. He sure deserved the title a lot more than Nate, Wyatt's ex, and *he* hadn't been particularly pleasant either.

Of course, Evan had partially incited the argument. He'd meant to keep his damn mouth shut, because he never brought up his old existence if he could help it, *especially* around people like Xander and Miles. But Xander had been so smug and obnoxious, Evan hadn't been able to help it.

"I'm going to go take a shower," Xander said. "I smell like lamb from all those chops I butchered during prep."

After he'd left the room, Evan busied himself with his wine glass, filling it again even though it had still been a quarter full. He couldn't look in Miles' direction. He'd been the one to insist he never wanted to talk about his childhood, and then he had blurted something like that out. The guilt on Miles' face had been unmistakable and the last thing Evan wanted was pity. Especially from Miles.

Evan had always imagined that falling in love felt wonderful, like rose petals and rainbows and kittens with balls of yarn. But all he felt was vaguely sick, like he might chuck up all the wine he'd drunk this afternoon.

"I'm sorry he's so . . ." Miles said helplessly. "So . . . Xander. I know he can be cruel, I should have warned you."

To Evan's horror, he felt sudden and unexpected tears in the corner of his eyes. Xander had been cruel, though it hadn't been premeditated. People said shitty things to Evan all the time and didn't realize just how shitty they were, because Evan avoided sharing any details of his past if he could help it.

Even Miles had only found out because Lucy liked to interfere.

It was stupid but Evan wished that he could have told him on his own, the way he wanted. He didn't know how long it would have taken him to finally tell the whole story, but Evan had a feeling it would have been good for him.

"You can't save me from everything," Evan said, trying to hide his sniff. "I'm plenty tough."

Miles' arms snaked around Evan's shoulders and pulled him close, his face tucking into Evan's neck. "I know, believe me I know. But that doesn't mean I like it when you get hurt. You deserve better. You've always deserved better."

"You didn't know me back then," Evan said because it was easier to argue petty details than it was to accept that statement. He kept waiting for Miles to force him to turn around and look him in the eye. To see the tear streaks on his cheeks. But Miles seemed to understand that this was a step too far, and to Evan's surprise, didn't push.

"I can't believe you've changed so much," Miles said softly. "I bet I would have loved the younger you just as much."

Evan's breath snagged. Had he just . . .? No, it wasn't possible. It was just a phrase. Miles didn't really mean it. He couldn't.

"Ha," Evan laughed unsteadily. "You know me well."

"I keep wanting to know you better," Miles said.

Somehow it was easier to say without having to look Miles in the eye. "Before you even came to LA, I wanted that." Miles' fingers tightened on Evan's shirt, the tips digging into his skin.

"How did we get so mixed up?" Miles asked, and Evan wasn't even sure he wanted an answer.

"We're both stubborn," seemed the most obvious answer. "But I think we're learning to compromise." He wanted to hope, out loud, that it wouldn't be too late, but they both knew better. They'd wasted their last chance, and the best hope they would have was for some part of the concept to be salvaged and for them both not to be fired.

It wasn't much of a hope, but it was something. Maybe they wouldn't end up separated by six hours on I-5. Maybe out of the disaster of the last few weeks, something good could still grow.

Evan turned and before Miles could say anything, kissed him hard. Saying everything he couldn't say out loud. It was incomprehensible that each kiss could be better than the last, but it was like they were slowing learning each other. They'd been so out of sync before, but that was changing.

It would be stupid and pointless to say that he wished it had happened sooner, but Evan still burned with it.

"Okay, you two are cute."

Miles broke away, and another one of the roommates was standing in the entrance of the kitchen. The young one, Evan thought with a resigned sigh. At least he'd been nicer than Xander. Not that that was particularly difficult.

"And I think your tomato sauce is burning," Kian added, crossing to the fridge and pulling out a bottle of water. He glanced over at the pot. "You're making Italian."

"Ratatouille," Miles said, returning to his pots and pans like Evan hadn't just almost poured his heart out. But if Evan looked close, he could see a tiny tremble in Miles' hands, and he couldn't remember ever seeing them anything but perfectly steady.

"So, you're dating now?" Kian asked, and Evan couldn't help but notice his casual look sharpened and also that he directed his question to Evan, not Miles.

He'd regretted telling Nate that they weren't dating from the moment the words had left his mouth, and the look in Miles' eyes when he'd said them.

"Yes," Evan said, and the world didn't stop spinning and the floor stayed shockingly level.

Miles turned around and the joy in his smile was worth how terrifying that had been.

"I guess we are," Miles said.

"I'm glad," Kian said. Evan had a feeling that Xander wouldn't be quite so glad.

"What's this?" the man in question said, entering the kitchen again, dark hair damp and eyes narrowed. "You're dating now?"

Evan lifted his chin. He really hoped Xander wouldn't continue being an asshole to him, but if he did, then he would deal with it. It wasn't like Xander was the first jerk he'd ever been confronted with. He wasn't entirely sure still what Miles had meant when he'd said he loved him, but suddenly he didn't care if Xander didn't like him.

It wouldn't mean that Miles liked him any less.

"We are," Evan said.

"That's stupid," Xander said, shaking his head. Like they were the first people to ever work together and date.

"It's sort of a tradition at *Five Points*. Unofficially of course. But you know about Quentin Maxwell and Landon Patton of course. And our boss, Reed, he's been dating Jordan Christensen for a few years now."

Xander's eyes darkened. "Aren't you all so fucking cute?" he sneered.

Evan realized with a jolt that Xander wasn't just an asshole; he was jealous.

Whether he was jealous of whoever Miles was with or just jealous in general, it was hard to say but if Evan had to guess, it was probably a combination. After all, he wasn't exactly going to find the love of his life walking around acting like a jerk.

Of course there were some guys who liked that, but Evan couldn't believe that would lead to a lasting, loving relationship.

"Yes, I'm sure it must be hard to hear about so many happy couples," Evan retorted.

Xander glared and he left the kitchen without a single word. Like Evan had just discovered his biggest secret. Or worst-kept secret, as far as he was concerned. Was it possible that Miles really didn't know how Xander felt?

Should Evan tell him? Or if he found out, would he drop Evan like a hot potato and run back to his ex-roommate? Evan squirmed internally; he didn't want to be selfish, but it had not been easy to get to this place. Was it wrong of him to not want to jeopardize it now that they'd figured some stuff out?

"Xander can be . . ."

"Xander," Kian piped up. He was cute and eager, like a golden retriever puppy. And thankfully, Evan got zero vibes from him that he was interested in Miles.

"I know it sounds hard to believe," Miles said, "but really, he does grow on you."

"Like a bad mold?" Evan said, raising an eyebrow. He glanced over to where Miles was meticulously arranging the squash and zucchini in an intricate swirling pattern over the bed of tomato sauce.

Kian laughed, and Miles huffed, fingers hesitating as he placed the last few vegetables into the dish. It didn't look like dinner, it looked like a work of art.

"Do you always make stuff that looks perfect?" Evan asked, which was a stupid question he already knew the answer to. He just didn't want to talk about Xander anymore, because his obvious feelings made Evan feel disloyal.

"I think he's incapable of making stuff that doesn't look flawless," Kian said. "But he almost never makes dinner. That's usually Wyatt or Xander."

"And Xander is still pissed at me for leaving, so we'd probably get paté foam or something equally odd, and Wyatt is . . ." Miles glanced up, questioning gaze directed at Kian. "Where is Wyatt?"

Kian shrugged. "He was right behind us. He came in with us. My guess is he's holed up in his room, skyping with his nana."

"They had to move her to a home last year," Miles explained as he slid the dish into the oven. "Wyatt is very close to her, and it's hard on him."

Evan wanted to ask who "they" were, because growing up with no family of his own had always made him morbidly curious about other people's. But before he could figure out how to politely phrase the question, Kian answered it.

"His dad left him and his brothers when they were very young, and then his mom died five years ago. Breast cancer complications. So it's just his two brothers and his nana."

"To be honest," Miles said, "I've never liked his brothers."

"They're weird jocks," Kian said. "I don't like them either."

"I don't think they contribute enough to help pay Nana's expenses," Miles said. "And they're weird jocks, besides."

Miles shot Evan a quick searching look, before returning to the stove, but Evan didn't volunteer anything. Maybe if he and Miles had been alone. Maybe if he had felt ready to share. But they weren't and he didn't. Not nearly. So he said nothing.

"Do I smell Italian?" Wyatt thankfully entered the kitchen a moment or two after they'd just finished talking about him. Not that he seemed like the sort of guy who would mind. He was tall, with wide linebacker shoulders, lots of tousled blond hair, and a laid-back, grounded attitude that Evan had immediately liked even though they'd only met briefly.

He was still trying to figure out why on earth these three great guys tolerated Xander's annoying attitude.

"Dinner will be ready in twenty," Miles said. "I'm gonna prep the bread, if you want to set the table?"

Wyatt raised an eyebrow at Kian, as he poured himself a glass of wine from the bottle on the counter. The bottle that happened to be the one Nate had given them. But he didn't turn an eyelash at the label, or ask where they'd gotten it.

Clearly, on Wyatt's side that relationship was over.

"Fine," Kian grumbled. Evan had a feeling that as the youngest, he ended up doing a lot of stuff that the others didn't want to.

"I saw Xander march out of here with a particularly virulent frown on his face. What is he bent out of shape about now?" Wyatt asked.

"That he's a miserable old man," Miles said.

"Well, that isn't new," Wyatt observed.

"I don't think he took the news that Miles and I are dating very well," Evan inserted, because he was curious to see how Wyatt would react to this. Would he guess that Xander was jealous? Was Evan really the first person to figure this out? That didn't seem possible, but Wyatt's expression still remained confused.

"Someday," Wyatt said, "he's going to meet someone he actually cares about, and it's going to hurt like a bitch when his heart grows a few sizes."

"Maybe it's permanently stunted," Kian answered cheerfully. "That wouldn't surprise me at all."

"But really, congrats. You seem like you'll be good for each other," Wyatt said, raising his glass. "It's high time Miles stopped playing it casual and breaking hearts right and left. I'll go get Xander, he shouldn't sit in his room and pout all night."

"He's going to if he wants to," Miles said.

"But he shouldn't," Wyatt replied firmly, setting his wine glass at one of the places of the big kitchen table Kian had set. And that convinced Evan once and for all that Wyatt was one of the good guys.

After he'd left the kitchen in search of Xander, Evan moved closer to Miles, bumping their shoulders together. "What happened with Nate and Wyatt?" he hissed under his breath. Curiosity was probably going to be the death of him.

Miles just shrugged though. "You met Nate, he's insufferable."

"But Wyatt dated him in the first place," Evan insisted.

"Yeah, I think Nate wasn't very happy he wouldn't get serious and introduce him to his family. To his brothers and his nana, rather."

"Yeah," Kian said, wandering over. "His brothers suspect he's gay, but his nana has no idea. She's sort of old-school Irish Catholic and I don't think he believes she'd understand."

The only nice thing about being a foster kid with no family of which to speak of was that when he'd come out, there hadn't really been anyone who cared or objected. Evan knew that it was definitely not that simple for everyone.

"I remember when I told my high school girlfriend I thought I was gay," Miles said, "and she just laughed and told me, 'of course you are.'"

"Yeah, not everyone is as understanding as your family, Miles," Kian said, and Evan, who wasn't the world's biggest toucher generally, surprisingly wanted to hug the apprehension out of his eyes.

"It's never easy," Evan said, even though it had been relatively cut and dried for him. He'd already been in a fairly open foster care situation with so many kids, the guardians hadn't really cared as long as you stayed out of trouble. Being gay hadn't ranked anywhere with getting arrested or burning the house down, so they'd just shrugged and moved on.

"What isn't easy?" Xander stood in the doorway, Wyatt following close behind him. "Dinner wasn't easy? If that was the case I could have helped you out, Costa."

Miles rolled his eyes. "Dinner was no big deal. Come sit down before I decide to punch you in the face."

But Xander did as he was told, and slumped into the seat at the head of the table, not surprising Evan at all.

The ratatouille was fragrant with oregano, basil and garlic; the zucchini and squash tender under the crusty lid of parmesan, the base soft with a zesty tomato sauce.

There was silence for a few minutes as everyone ate, sopping up the sauce with the garlic bread Miles had prepared.

"So where did you guys go today?" Kian asked.

Evan remembered how they'd crumpled the paper bag from the winery and buried it so Wyatt wouldn't see it.

"Uh," he said.

"A few wineries," Miles inserted and then very casually changed the subject. "I thought we'd do a picnic lunch up by the castle tomorrow. It's supposed to be a nice day. Wyatt, did you take care of that thing I asked you for?"

Wyatt nodded, mouth full of ratatouille. "It'll be under your name."

"Great, thanks." Miles smiled over at Evan, who was trying to decide if licking his plate clean would be rude.

"That was pretty good," Xander said. "Maybe if your video thing fails, you can go become a line cook at Olive Garden."

"Next time, I'm going to force you to make yourself Italian food. And it probably won't be as good as mine." Miles' voice still sounded kind, but he grimaced as he sipped his wine.

"What did you put in the sauce?" Wyatt asked. "There's an earthiness in it . . ."

"Evan," Miles said, leaning over, breath brushing his neck, which reminded him that it was only his stomach that was satisfied. "Wyatt's nose and taste buds are legendary. He can usually figure out what's in anything."

"But you asked?" Evan said, crinkling his own nose.

Wyatt shrugged. "People don't generally like it when I list their recipe out for them."

"You mean, *Xander* doesn't like it," Kian said, laughing.

"I think it's a wild mushroom, maybe? And red wine? A chianti?" Wyatt guessed.

"You're half right. Dried mushrooms reconstituted in some tempranillo."

"Damn it, that was the earthiness." Wyatt tipped his glass to Miles. "Well, kudos for fooling me."

Evan hadn't really realized how much Miles was giving up by leaving Terroir and his three roommates. Yeah, he'd taken a chance on a crossroads career move, but there had been reasons for him to stay in Napa. And a lot of those reasons were sitting at the table with them.

"How did you all meet?" Evan asked. He was sort of completely desperate to go to the hotel and remind Miles just who he was dating. And this time he'd only had half a glass of wine.

"Wyatt and Miles met in culinary school. Xander went to school in New York City and we met at Terroir. And I moved in last year, after I graduated, and got Chef Aquino's internship," Kian said.

"You mean, Chef Aquino's hard labor," Xander said.

"It's not that bad," Kian protested. "It's a really prestigious position."

Evan saw the concern Xander was voicing reflected in Miles' eyes. So Xander wasn't off-base or even overreacting.

"That's what they tell you to force you to take all the shit he dishes out," Wyatt pointed out quietly.

"I've got an early morning," Kian said, abruptly getting to his feet. "And I'm sure Evan and Miles have something important to do."

"You shouldn't push him," Xander said under his breath after Kian had left the room.

"Yeah, if I don't, then he keeps letting Aquino ride him. And I don't like that either," Wyatt said.

"It's gotten worse since I left," Miles stated rather than questioned.

"I swear to god, he's *obsessed* with him. Kian with Aquino, I mean. And, I don't know, maybe the other way around. It's weird. They're weirdly co-dependent on each other. I don't get it."

"I'll put out some feelers in LA," Miles said, getting to this feet. "Maybe we can convince him to leave. Take a job in LA."

"Kian ever leaving Terroir and Bastian Aquino? Yeah, good luck with that," Xander said bitterly.

Chapter Fourteen

Evan was quiet when they got into the car. Miles couldn't help but wonder if he'd pushed him too far, or if he was tired after such a long day. Maybe he should have given him what they both wanted, when they'd first gotten to Napa. He'd undoubtedly been eager then, and even though there'd been flashes of it through the day—some white hot in their intensity—Miles sensed now that he was deep in thought.

And not about Miles naked.

"You okay?" he asked.

Evan glanced up, his toffee eyes unexpectedly bright in the dim car. They slid down Miles' body, and Miles thought maybe he'd been overthinking earlier. Maybe nothing had changed.

"Xander really cares about Kian," was all Evan said, which really surprised Miles.

Evan wanted to talk about Xander?

Miles figured they'd been lucky to get out of the house without Evan punching Xander in the face. Why he wanted to discuss him now, Miles had no clue.

"Despite his best efforts tonight, he's not a jerk. I mean, he *is*, but not deep down. He's just . . . disgruntled. And yes, he cares about Kian. We all do. He's like our little brother."

Evan made a humming noise, clearly considering what Miles had said. They passed by a streetlight, illuminating Evan's flawless profile—elegant cheekbones, delicate nose, rosebud lips, proud chin—and Miles realized with a jolt that he had removed his bow tie sometime after they'd gotten into the car for the trip to the hotel.

"Eyes forward," Evan said, and he was clearly trying to pretend disinterest at the sudden, ravenous heat in Miles' face, but even he couldn't quite pull it off.

"No fair," Miles whined. Out of the corner of his eye, he saw Evan flick open one button of his shirt, and then another. And then another. Miles was pathetic and that was all it took to make him hard anymore—the chance to see Evan's bare skin.

"You made me wait all day," Evan said. "It's plenty fair."

"Cruel," Miles breathed out. Except that they both knew he liked it. Evan probably thought he'd get to control what happened when they got to the hotel, like he had the other two times they'd had sex, but Miles, while typically fairly laid-back and open in bed, was more than ready to assert himself.

And then Evan opened his mouth again. "I think Xander is in love with you."

Miles almost swerved off the road. "No. No way. That's just . . . that's not possible."

He took a quick, necessary peek to check the expression on Evan's face. He seemed concerned but not perturbed.

"Would it make a difference if he was?" Evan asked, and there was a raw honesty in his voice that Miles had never heard before. Sometimes it was tough for Miles to even figure out how much Evan contained and held back behind the wall he'd erected between himself and the world, but hearing him now, Miles realized just how much Evan cared about him.

How much he didn't want Miles to love Xander.

"No. Not a bit."

He chanced another glance over at Evan. He was smiling now, just a little one, around the corners of his mouth, but it was enough. "You really mean that."

"I mean, have you *met* Xander?" Miles asked.

"He's disgruntled and bitter and a little grumpy, but he's good-looking. And passionate. Those are two things I think you'd enjoy."

"*You're* what I enjoy," Miles vowed.

"I certainly hope so." The smug self-satisfaction in his voice was all Miles needed to hear to know Evan was okay.

"I can show you. Soon," Miles said, and saw Evan flick another button open. "Soon," he repeated, the word practically a vow.

Miles had never imagined that he would be making vows of any kind. He'd never imagined he was the sort of man who craved permanence that way, but Evan had changed everything.

"You'd better." Evan sounded just as impatient as Miles felt.

"Another mile," Miles said, pushing down harder on the gas. His driver's ed teacher would have been appalled at his driving. Probably also at his life choices, but Miles didn't really give a fuck anymore.

He whipped into the hotel parking lot. "I'll be back with the key," Miles said, reaching over, and leaving a brief but scorching kiss on Evan's mouth that promised everything he meant to do to him tonight.

Even though the desk clerk seemed to be efficient, he wasn't nearly fast enough for Miles. He pushed over his credit card across the counter and barely managed to refrain from tapping his foot on the marble floor.

Finally, he was given the room key, and he skidded out of the foyer to where he'd parked. Evan was already out of the car, leaning against the passenger side, impatient expression on his face.

And then, suddenly and unexpectedly, Evan let the ever-present wall fall and it was just the real Evan and him.

Usually he had to coax Evan out of his shell, and it felt so good to just press him against the car and not feel him hesitate before he kissed Miles back.

Instead Evan threw himself into it, and for Miles, it almost felt like the first kiss. Their first real kiss. The first time Evan kissed him and didn't think he was making a mistake, didn't wonder halfway through if it was the wrong thing to do.

He believed it was right and Miles was right, and Miles found that he had never believed more in the idea of the two of them against the world.

"Evan," Miles said, lips still hovering above Evan's. They were damp and shiny under the streetlamp and Miles almost gave in to the need coursing through him and said screw the words.

But Miles couldn't imagine that Evan had often gotten actions *or* words, so the words were important.

"Why are you stopping?" Evan said. Even with the emotional wall down, Evan was still completely himself. And Miles found himself enjoying the directness.

"Because we're still, unfortunately, outside. And I want to make love to you. Not against my car in a parking lot."

Evan's gaze was steady and warm. He didn't flinch, didn't cower, and didn't try to stop Miles. Didn't try to take control and make sure that Miles was too lost in pleasure to notice that Evan was still holding him at arm's length.

"Okay."

It was so hard to resist the urge to push, to rush, to devour Evan, but Miles held back by the skin of his teeth as they walked to the room. He'd even reached out and grasped Evan's hand, and Evan had let him.

Finally, they were in the room, the door was closing behind them, and Miles was free to do what he'd been longing to do all damn day.

He led Evan to the bed and kissed him, slow, but definitely not gentle. Miles poured every ounce of desire and love into the kiss, hands grasping Evan tightly around the waist, and then tugging out the shirt he'd tucked into his jeans.

"No khakis today, huh?" Miles murmured as his lips coasted down Evan's neck, pausing to nibble on his earlobe. "Taking a break in driving me insane?"

There was a definite catch in Evan's throat as Miles plucked open more buttons, his lips moving downwards across his exposed collarbones. They were so delicate, a delicious incongruity with his strength. Miles would be lying if he said that didn't really turn him on.

"I wasn't sure you could handle the khakis," Evan said.

"You're not wrong," Miles admitted ruefully.

"I almost wished I'd worn them," Evan admitted as Miles finished unbuttoning his shirt, and pushed it off his shoulders. Miles' mouth covered a firm pec muscle, then nibbled not very gently on his nipple. Evan gasped.

"Because I deserved it?"

"No," Evan said on another gasp as Miles' mouth moved to the other nipple. "Because I was jealous."

The idea was ludicrous but Miles didn't laugh because *one*, he had his tongue on Evan's glorious bare skin, pale and smooth and taut with the perfect amount of muscle, and *two*, this was Xander they were talking about. He couldn't even conceive of ditching Evan for Xander.

Miles' hands unbuckled Evan's belt. His cock was hard and there was an unmistakable wet patch on his boxer briefs. Just as Miles hoped, Evan gasped even louder, and suddenly he hoped, despite what he'd experienced so far, that Evan was loud and expressive in bed.

It was hard to imagine any interaction between them being devoid of a power struggle, but unlike the frustration that had dogged them before, Miles was definitely turned on by it.

"Maybe," he gasped himself, undone by Evan bucking firmly into his palm, "we just should have been fucking from the beginning."

Evan's look as Miles pushed him back onto the bed, and rid him of the rest of his clothes, was hot. Intimate. Everything Miles had really wanted, even back then, and had never expected to get.

"Maybe we should just fuck now," Evan said, purring as he flipped over and pushed himself up, sending a spike of unrestrained lust through Miles.

Miles was still fully clothed and despite Evan's wandering hands, hadn't really been touched since they'd left the house. He was still suddenly in very grave danger of coming in his pants.

"I . . . I . . ." Miles stammered, undone by the sight in front of him. Evan was glorious naked, the most beautiful man Miles had ever seen. He couldn't have even fantasized about how good he would look like this. "I was going to take it slow."

Evan's glance over his shoulder was scorching. "Not after this whole day, you're not."

Some things, Miles realized, were inevitable and not worth fighting.

He grabbed the lube and a condom from his bag and shed his clothes so quickly, he was almost afraid he lost a few buttons.

But instead of immediately prepping Evan to take him, Miles leaned onto the bed and covered Evan's body with his own, skin to skin. Letting him feel how hard he was, how wet at the tip, just from touching Evan and seeing him naked.

"You're so gorgeous," he whispered into Evan's ear as he kissed his neck. "So fucking glorious."

"I know," Evan said, so smug that Miles couldn't help but love him even more. "Now stop fucking around and fuck me."

Miles would have been very stupid to argue at that point.

His hands smoothed over the curve of the ass he'd been watching and worshipping for so many weeks. Evan made a low groan as Miles carefully circled his hole with a wet finger.

"Stop teasing," Evan groaned as his body clutched around the digit Miles slid into him. "Goddamn it, Miles."

"If you're still talking," Miles said with a grin, "I'm not doing it right."

"Exactly," Evan wrenched out, as Miles pulled his finger out, only to slide two back in.

Evan felt so incredible, tight and hot, around his fingers, his body greedily clutching to them as Miles finger fucked him. He had a sudden, horrifying thought that he wouldn't be able to make it good. Make it last.

"Slow down a little," Miles panted, which was embarrassing because he wasn't even the one being fucked.

Evan pushed his body right back on Miles' fingers at that particular demand. "*No.*"

Taking a deep breath, Miles knew they'd waited long enough. He knew he could please his man. Felt it in his bones. It was time to show him just how much he cared about him.

He made short work of the condom, and slid his fingers around Evan's cock, circling it firmly as he began to push his dick into Evan. Pleasure short-circuited his brain, fierce and electric. He could only swear as he bottomed out, gripping Evan's hip and his cock.

"Move," Evan hissed and so Miles pushed back his own pleasure and focused on the man in front of him. The man he loved.

Maybe Evan couldn't accept the words yet, but he could accept this.

Miles set as powerful of a rhythm as he dared, his gasps echoing Evan's as he thrust. It was almost too much as Evan started to push back, to demand more, greedy and perfect, his cock thrusting into Evan's curled hand, his ass taking everything Miles was giving and demanding more.

Evan let out a long, drawn-out moan, louder than Miles had even dreamt, and came into his hand. Miles barely had a moment to enjoy the clench of his body before he fell off the cliff too, fingers digging into Evan's skin as he orgasmed.

For a half moment, Miles didn't move. It was impossible, but he still wanted to stay like this forever. He'd never felt closer to Evan.

"Here," Evan said in a small, hesitant voice, reaching over and handing his underwear to Miles, so he could clean up.

The very last thing Miles wanted was for Evan to decide this had also been a mistake. So he carefully pulled out, and smoothed a reassuring hand down Evan's back.

"I'll be right back," he promised.

Evan was sitting on the edge of the bed when he returned, and he wordlessly took the warm, damp cloth Miles handed him.

"Thank you," he said. "But I think I might just take a shower. Is that okay?"

Miles wasn't going to stop him. He might have wanted to join him, but he also wasn't sure he could keep standing another moment. The bed was calling to him. "Sure, of course. I'm just going to lie down."

"Yeah, it's been a long day," Evan echoed.

<hr>

The shower went on and on, and Miles lay in bed, wondering if everything really was okay. Was Evan going to come back to bed emotionally restrained again? Was he going to say, with his actions and not his words, that they'd made another mistake?

Miles squeezed his eyes shut and prayed that wouldn't happen. He'd never really been in love before, but he was pretty sure being in love alone sucked. He didn't want to know what that felt like.

Finally the shower shut off, and Miles watched as Evan came out of the bathroom, towel around his waist.

"This is a nice place," he said as he rummaged in his bag. "The water pressure is excellent."

Was this what they'd been reduced to? Talking about water pressure? Miles dreaded what subject Evan would bring up next; whatever it was probably making very clear to Miles that he needed space.

But instead, Evan climbed in bed after pulling on a pair of clean briefs, and to Miles' shock, laid his head on his bare chest.

They were quiet for a while, Miles trying to absorb what was happening, Evan probably trying not to freak out.

Finally Evan spoke, in a quiet voice, just as hesitant as he'd been after sex. "Is this okay?"

"More than okay. I love it," Miles said. *I love you.*

Evan took a deep, unsteady breath, and said, "I'm not good at this."

"It's okay. I'm not sure I am either," Miles confessed.

"You're better than you think," Evan said wryly.

"It matters to me that you know I care about you," Miles said carefully.

A sigh. "I know," Evan said.

"This is probably the wrong time," he continued. "But I should tell you, so I'm going to." He took another deep breath. "My parents died when I was two. I don't really remember them. I lived in ten foster homes. The last one, I was there for three years. I moved out when I turned eighteen. I didn't look back."

Miles' fingers gripped Evan's damp skin. "I'm glad you told me."

"I'm not good at letting other people control me," Evan said, and the unspoken end of that sentence was, *because too many people controlled me before.*

"I'm not going to control you," Miles promised. "And if I ever do, feel free to slap me."

"I'm going to hold you to that," Evan said, his voice was growing drowsy. Miles realized that this was all part of letting down his emotional guard, and that staying the night was part of it. That trusting Miles enough to touch him like this was another. They had come so far from those first distrustful days, and Miles could only hope that when they returned to LA, he could convince Reed of that.

Chapter Fifteen

Miles had never understood why people committed themselves and their hearts by falling in love. It had always seemed like a very risky proposition with a lot to lose and very little to gain.

But somehow, the morning was better when he and Evan woke up together, both smiling bashfully, and the sun brighter as they sat on the hill by the *Castello di Amorosa* and nibbled at meat and cheese that Miles had spent too much money for at Dean & Deluca.

Even the champagne was more effervescent on his tongue as they did a tasting at Domaine Carneros.

He'd gone to bed almost certain that Evan would wake up and the emotional wall blocking Miles out would be back in place, but to his own surprise, he'd watched the whole day as Evan worked to keep it down.

Miles could tell that it didn't come naturally, but his heart was nearly bursting at how hard Evan was trying to make things work between them. They would probably never be able to avoid a power struggle—even for a laid-back guy, Miles had difficulty relinquishing control, which he knew was a bad habit he'd picked up in the restaurant kitchens he'd worked in—but there could be spice in a little day-to-day friction.

The most important thing was that Evan understood that Miles was in this for the duration. He was done cutting and running; he was done pretending anything other than this partnership had been life-altering.

But even through the great afternoon, Miles had wondered in the back of his mind about what Evan had insisted last night.

There was no way that Xander felt that way about him and he'd somehow missed it. Miles knew he wasn't the most observant person in the world, especially about relationships, but surely Xander couldn't have liked him *that* way without Miles realizing. They'd lived and worked together for years.

It was impossible.

And yet Miles couldn't dismiss it completely. Not because he was at all tempted to ditch Evan for Xander—but because it didn't feel right to come up here and flaunt his new relationship, all while his friend was hurting.

He needed to know. So he kissed Evan goodbye at the hotel, told him to take a long soak in the tub, said he'd be back before they needed to leave for dinner, and headed to Terroir to confront Xander before the dinner service started.

"What are you doing here? Aren't you supposed to be blinding the whole Valley with your annoying PDA?" Xander sneered as he added finishing touches to the sauces at his station.

He had a magic touch with sauces that even Bastian Aquino didn't have—not that the head chef ever would have admitted that. But Xander had been doing the sauces very early on in his tenure at Terroir and that only could mean one thing.

"Come in the dining room in a few hours, and I'm sure we could oblige you," Miles said. He wasn't technically supposed to be in the kitchens since he didn't work here anymore, but he'd left on good terms, and he didn't think anyone would kick him out. Maybe.

He shoved his hands in his black pants. "Why are you so angry?" he asked Xander point blank, because he needed to make this quick before anyone saw him, and also because he was sick of fucking around. Love had definitely shown him how vital it was to value what was really important.

"Nature? Habit? Preference?" Xander paused. "Take your pick, and then get out of this kitchen. You don't work here anymore."

"Here's the thing, Xander, you're not mad at everyone like you're mad at me. And it's new, since I left. So what's the deal? You're angry I moved on and left Napa? Left Terroir?"

Xander's aborted, angry hand movements told Miles only part of the story. He needed to know *why* Xander was so pissed.

"You've always been free to do whatever the fuck you wanted," Xander said.

"It was all me, you know that right? I was bored as fuck here, you know that, I know you do." Miles didn't like how defensive he sounded but maybe he was feeling guiltier than he liked over Xander's anger.

Xander's feelings weren't entirely his problem, but maybe they were a little his fault.

"Not everything is about you." Xander's knife flew over a bundle of chives. Then basil. Then Italian parsley. He was just about finished with the sauces, and then the dinner service would begin. Xander was an asshole, but he was a punctual asshole.

In five minutes, the line would be crowded with chefs. Miles tried not to panic and threw his Hail Mary pass. "Evan said that you were in love with me, and that's why you were angry I left."

Xander's eyes flew to his, shocked and belligerent. But he didn't deny it. "Evan is a nosy bastard. That might seem cute now, but you'll get sick of it. You can't take high maintenance and he's the King of High Maintenance Land."

"Are you?"

Xander slapped his knife down on his cutting board, sifting tiny circles of chives onto the floor. "Why does it matter?"

Miles was torn between strangling him and hugging him. "It matters."

"I wasn't in love with you, you egotistical bastard. Did I think . . . maybe? Maybe once or twice? Sure." Xander furiously stirred the mustard sauce he'd made his own since starting at Terroir. Miles had seen him make it a thousand times since they'd met, and it occurred to him suddenly that he wouldn't ever see him make it again.

And even though leaving this place had felt easy and like the right thing to do, emotion suddenly strangled him.

"Life is about change, Xander," Miles said softly, when he thought he could speak without embarrassing himself. "And we would have been a flaming disaster. You know that too."

"And?" Xander snapped. "It's not like you and Prince Charming have had an easy go of it so far."

"No, but we're getting there." He paused. "Xander, please. Don't hate me. In six months or six years, you're going to realize that you're done here too, and you'll leave."

"Maybe." Xander's testy tone had faded a little. Not much, but enough to give Miles hope.

"I know you're not going to be happy making Bastian Aquino's sauces for him your entire career. You're too talented for that, and you know it."

"I do." Xander stirred basil into another saucepan, and Miles realized with a pang that he didn't even know this sauce. It had been invented since he'd been gone. And that hurt more than he could have dreamt.

"Moving on is hard, but it's worth it. There's a whole life you can experience when you open your eyes."

"Don't worry, I'm not going to be up here, pining after your sorry ass." But Xander flashed a bright, quicksilver smile and it was enough that Miles knew he'd done the right thing coming here and talking to him.

"I wouldn't expect you to," Miles retorted fondly. "It's not that good of an ass."

Xander chuckled. "Get out of here before Aquino sees you and does something terrible."

"Throws me out?" Miles asked.

"No, forces you back into an apron."

❧❧❧ ❧❧❧

"Did you go talk to Xander?" Evan asked, forcing his voice to remain light and casual. He shouldn't care if Miles had gone to talk to his friend; it had been the right thing to do to clear the air. It had just been impossible for Evan to think of the conversation without the very slightest waver of concern.

Miles and Xander had known each other for years. Xander was a great chef, talented and intense, probably the sort of person that Miles had always imagined he'd end up with.

He definitely couldn't have foretold that he'd end up falling for someone like Evan.

Even Evan, who'd secretly been harboring a little crush after spending so many hours watching *Pastry by Miles*, couldn't have predicted it. It still felt very new and like a significant bump could derail it.

Of course, if the last three weeks hadn't stopped it from happening, then he should consider their relationship inevitable.

"I talked to him, yeah. Everything's good," Miles said, sitting on the bed next to Evan, resting a hand on his knee casually like it didn't still cause fireworks to explode under Evan's skin. He was never going to get used to touching so casually; each touch still felt momentous and important.

Evan told himself that it was in Miles' nature to share less and his own to be inquisitive. He still couldn't help himself from asking, "Did he admit to it?"

"Not exactly. But I think he'll be okay."

Evan felt like a terrible person for not caring if Xander would be okay. Of course Miles did; Evan still felt too threatened to be so selfless.

"What are we doing for dinner?" Evan asked brightly, changing the subject. The last thing Miles needed was to find out that he felt unsure still, *especially* unsure about Xander. Especially because Miles himself had given Evan zero reasons to be concerned.

It wasn't Miles' fault that Evan was, and would probably be for some time to come, a neurotic, insecure mess.

"I want to take you somewhere special," Miles said, his soulful gaze making Evan's heartbeat skip.

"You know," he giggled a little self-consciously, "I never imagined you were such a romantic."

Miles smiled. "Oh, yeah, you did. You dreamed about it."

This was so completely accurate Evan blushed.

"Does that mean you're going to let me spoil you?" Miles asked.

"Spoiled how?" Evan told himself firmly not to be apprehensive because wasn't that what every lonely, miserable boy of twelve that nobody gave two shits about dreamed about? Someone making an effort? Someone trying to impress them even if it wasn't particularly hard?

Why then was it so hard for Evan to accept?

If Evan had ever been able to open up to a therapist—and he had *tried* but therapists wanted you to talk about yourself and he never could—he was sure they would have been able to tell him why. As it was, Evan had his suspicions.

"I'm going to take you to the best restaurant in Napa," Miles said.

Evan had a sudden, horrified thought that he knew exactly what Miles meant. "You're taking me to Terroir."

Miles blushed. "I did say the best restaurant in Napa."

"I'm not sure your ego is going to fit through the doorway," Evan teased. It was easier to poke fun than to face what Miles was trying to do.

He couldn't think about it without his hand trembling, so he reached over and gripped Miles' hand hard.

"You're gonna love it," Miles promised, eyes soft, like he knew exactly what had Evan reaching for him like a lifeline.

It would have been so natural for Evan to just say back, "I love *you*," because he was pretty damn sure he did. Miles had hardly made a secret of his own feelings, but they still felt so inexplicable to Evan.

Evan kissed him instead, hard and hot, both a promise for later and as a replacement for everything he couldn't say. *Yet*, he swore to himself, but even Evan didn't have a clue when he'd be able to.

If Evan had imagined that they might be treated any differently because Miles had worked at Terroir, he was incredibly wrong.

From what he could see, the same excruciatingly perfect service was given to every guest as they checked in at the gracious patio that served as the open-air waiting room. Vines dripping with grapes wrapped around the wood beams, arcing over their heads as they waited for their table to be ready.

"Would you like a glass of wine?" Miles asked.

If going to wine tastings had been intimidating, it was nothing compared to standing at the entrance to the throne room of American dining. Did he want a glass of wine? Evan thought he *needed* one if he was going to make it through without breaking into a sweat or declaring loudly that he wasn't worthy.

"Sure," Evan said.

Miles was only at the bar for a second, and of course, he got the best service, because the bartender's eyes lit up when they spotted him. He returned with two flutes of sparkling wine.

"Cheers," he said, tapping Evan's glass with his own. "To the best weekend I've ever spent."

"You mean, the part where we weren't being insulted by your old room-mates?" Evan teased, enjoying the light that heated in Miles' eyes. He knew exactly which parts those were. Making love in the hotel room. Feeding each other bits of fresh bread in the meadow this morning, making out in the grass and not feeling the tiniest bit ashamed if anyone saw.

"I mean the part where I got to meet the relaxed you," Miles said.

Evan froze. How could he have forgotten Reed's admonishment as they left?

"Though," Miles continued thoughtfully, "I really like all the parts of you. Even the part that shoots daggers out of his eyes at me."

"You like that part?" Evan asked incredulously.

Miles' gaze took on a conspiratorial glint. "I love that part. It's sexy as hell knowing you want to kick my ass and that you will if I take a step out of line."

Something unwound in Evan at Miles' words. There had been a tiny kernel of doubt that had wondered if he would have to be on his best behavior from now on. If he would have to be the sweet, relaxed Evan all the time. Because there was no chance in hell of that happening.

"Don't worry," Miles said casually, "you know I love you."

Evan was torn between the eye-dagger-shooting thing or just dumping his champagne all over Miles' sharp black button-down, but then the designer-clad hostess approached, telling them their table was ready.

Their table wasn't on the patio, which from the reading Evan had done was considered a prime spot, but it was still near a huge bank of windows that overlooked the valley.

"I couldn't get the patio," Miles apologized after they sat down. "It was too late of notice. And even I don't have that sort of power."

"I'm impressed you got a table at all," Evan said. He wasn't disappointed they weren't on the patio. How could he be when he was here at all? The most any of his pseudo-dates had ever done was bring over Chinese or pizza before a hookup.

Miles had brought him to Terroir. The place he'd once described as the finest restaurant in America. The only Michelin-starred restaurant in California.

"Can you blame me for trying to impress you?" Miles said, reaching over and brushing his hand over Evan's knuckles.

Evan hid behind the menu, most of which was incomprehensible to him. He didn't know what half the words meant, and he didn't think he could really get away with googling them on his phone.

"Uh, yes," Evan said. "I was impressed by you before we even met."

"But then I made a shitty impression," Miles grinned charmingly, "so I'm just making up for lost time."

"Well, if that's the way you're going to play it, then figure out what I should be trying," Evan said, smiling back and feeling lighter than he had in forever. Maybe ever.

This must be what relaxing felt like. Or maybe it was love. It was fabulous either way, and he felt as light as the bubbles in his champagne flute. If anyone, especially Xander, tried to take this away from him, they were going to find out just how hardcore Evan Patterson could be.

"Yes, sir," Miles said smartly, and Evan couldn't help it, he burst into laughter.

Suddenly he was very sure it was going to be one of the greatest meals of his life, and that had nothing to do with the food.

***

Evan was really damn sure it wasn't just the food when Bastian Aquino showed up at the table between the main course and dessert.

"Miles Costa," Chef Aquino said, a self-satisfied edge to his voice, like he'd believed that Miles really couldn't stay away and that belief was now justified.

He was a powerful man, with short dark hair just beginning to silver at the edges, intensely dark eyes, and a pair of serious biceps bulging under his immaculate black chef's jacket.

Evan was struck a little dumb. It wasn't his finest moment, but pictures didn't do Bastian Aquino justice. He looked like he could snap his neck just as easily as he could a chicken's. Evan swallowed hard when Aquino turned his attention to Miles' dining companion.

Him.

"You're the individual who lured Miles away from my kitchen with promises he'd be famous," Aquino said, a crease forming between his brows.

Evan decided he might as well own it; if Aquino killed him in the middle of his restaurant, then at least he'd die a happy man. "Yes, I did."

Miles blustered across from him, a frown on his face. "That's not exactly true," he said.

Evan smiled. "Maybe next season when Miles is on the Cooking Channel, we can invite you to guest star with him."

Aquino clearly didn't like that at all. "Food doesn't need fame," he said. "Was the food up to the standard?" he questioned, directing it to Miles.

Evan supposed he should be a little offended, but then Miles was the professional between them. What would Evan know, besides that everything had been delectable and incredible?

"Your lamb was a little overcooked," Miles said, laughing. Evan thought that if Aquino killed both of them, Miles would go out happy too. A month ago, that might not have meant much to Evan, but it meant everything tonight.

Bastian Aquino practically growled. "I forgot, you're just a pastry chef." Then he smiled, and it was like the sunrise over the desert. Evan was surprised at how handsome he was when he wasn't wordlessly threatening people's lives.

"Dessert is still to come," Miles said with a lot of satisfaction. "Tell René that he'd better send his best."

Aquino gave a sharp nod. He turned to Evan. "He is happy. Thank you for giving him what he needed."

When Bastian Aquino left, just as abruptly as he'd arrived, Miles giggled. It might have more to do with the thrill of love than the wine they'd drunk tonight or even the fantastic food—no matter what Miles said about the lamb.

"What exactly is it you're giving me that I need?" Miles asked with a quiet snort, probably thinking Evan was going to say something dirty and inappropriate. And ninety-nine percent of the time, Evan probably would have. It wasn't like his wall was coming down; instead, it felt like he was welcoming Miles inside.

Evan hoped the truth of it was in his eyes when he replied, "Everything I can."

Later that night, lying in bed with Evan drowsing against his chest, the TV turned on low, a text came through on his phone.

Leaning over, he must have shifted Evan too much when he reached over to grab it, because he made a sleepy, annoyed noise.

"Sorry," Miles said. "It's Gina."

"Gina?" Evan asked, and Miles felt like a shitty brother, or maybe just a shitty person. How had he not texted her lately? How had he not told Evan about Gina?

"Gina is my younger sister," he said. "We're close. Well, we used to be, I mean we still are, she's just in her freshman year of college in Berkeley and we've both been a little busy."

Evan propped himself up on an elbow, hair mussed, eyes glowing in the dim light of the room. He stopped Miles' heart, because only in his wildest dreams had he imagined he'd get to see the other man like this.

"Is she okay?" he asked.

Miles didn't know what had given it away. The late hour, maybe? Or his own worried expression?

The text had said: **You're in Napa and no text?**

Miles had felt guilty enough that he hadn't told Evan about Gina; now he was feeling doubly guilty.

A second text came in before Miles could even reply to the first. **If I keep guilt-tripping you, will you let me meet him? Brunch. Noon.**

"Xander," Miles growled. He was *really* regretting introducing Gina to Xander. There was always another shoe to drop with him. He'd assumed things were good between them after their conversation today, but then he'd gone and texted Gina and told her all about Evan.

"What did he do now?" Evan didn't seem particularly concerned, which was good, because he had nothing to be jealous of.

"Interfered," Miles said reluctantly. Was he ready for Gina to meet Evan? Was *Evan* ready to meet Gina?

"Isn't that what he's best at?" Evan wondered.

"My sister wants us to stop by Berkeley so she can meet you tomorrow," Miles said. "I'm guessing she got a whole series of texts from Xander after he got off work."

Evan's arm was still across Miles' bare chest, so he couldn't help but feel him tense.

"Is that okay?" Miles asked gently. It seemed so unfair that he could have this whole incredible, infuriating, *real* relationship with his sister, and Evan had nobody.

"Are you asking if I'm ready to meet your sister or if I'm okay that I don't have a sister?" Evan questioned.

Miles flushed. It was a good thing that they'd both been lowering their shields, but he hadn't realized he was so easy for Evan to read.

"It's okay," Evan continued with a little smile. "Lots of people don't have sisters, I just happened to be one of them. I'd love to meet her, if you're good with it."

They'd acknowledged to each other and to several others that they were dating now, but it was definitely something more for Evan to meet his family. Miles' heart had made the commitment already, there was no going back from that, but now he had to make sure his head was on the same page.

"I'm good with it," he decided. As if there had been any other decision he could make. Evan would torture him slowly and Gina would help Evan finish him off.

He was in this now, and the truth was, he *wanted* to be.

"Then I guess we're going to lunch with your sister," Evan said. He seemed calm enough. "I'm glad I brought another bow tie."

"Someday," Miles said, cradling him in his arms, and then suddenly rolling him underneath his body, hovering above him. He let his hips drop, flush and hard, against Evan's. "I'm going to tie you up with those fucking bow ties."

Evan's gaze was bright and challenging. Miles couldn't get enough of it. "I'd love to see you try," he said.

And how was Miles supposed to ignore a dare like that?

Evan didn't think he was nervous—at least not precisely nervous. Apprehensive was probably the better term. It wasn't like he could do research to help him feel more comfortable; Gina was a person, not a location or a task or an activity. Any research he did should be restricted to brunch, conducted by actually *talking to* her.

He'd never had to go to brunch with a sibling of a boyfriend before. He wasn't sure he'd ever really had a boyfriend before, definitely not in the sense that he and the other guy had actually agreed that's what they were. He'd had half-assed relationships, he guessed, if that was what it meant when you drifted together, spent time together, slept together sometimes, and eventually drifted apart.

But nobody had ever wanted him to meet their family before. And it wasn't like Evan had any family for them to meet. None of the handful of guys in college had even known he was a foster kid; it definitely wasn't something he'd ever talked about.

But Miles knew, and he didn't care. It certainly seemed like he more worried about Evan's feelings than if Gina approved.

"She's going to love you," Miles said as they pulled into the restaurant parking lot. His smile was sweet and reassuring.

"I'm not worried about that. People usually like me." Evan shot Miles a coolly sardonic look. "You're the only one who didn't, and that turned out okay."

Miles laughed. "I did too like you."

"You had a very strange way of showing it," Evan retorted as they got out of the car.

Miles caught Evan's arm as they walked towards the entrance. "You should . . . um . . . definitely stay quiet about that part of it," he murmured. "Especially to Gina."

Evan might not have had any blood-related siblings, but he knew exactly how this worked. "So she can't give you any shit about it, right?" He grinned. "I don't think so."

"You're so cruel," Miles groaned in exaggeration. "I'm not sure this was a good idea."

But then a high-pitched voice yelped Miles' name, and Evan had the luck to see Miles' face the moment a tall, slender girl with long, curly dark hair piled on top of her head, came into view.

Evan had already figured out that Gina meant a lot to Miles, but seeing the joy on his face, then watching them wrap each other up in a tight, prolonged hug, made it crystal clear.

The first thing Gina did when Miles released her was turn towards Evan.

"Hello," she said in a friendly, conspiring voice. "You must be Evan." She extended a hand and Evan shook it immediately. She turned to her brother. "You didn't tell me how *cute* he is!"

Miles flushed, and Evan was greatly amused at his discomfort. "But," Gina continued with a quick, clever grin, "I shouldn't be surprised at all. I know what this one is like. But you, you I'm definitely looking forward to getting to know better."

Gina tucked her arm in his without prompting, and the stacked turquoise bracelets on her arm rattled.

"I'm hoping so," Evan said, and to his own complete surprise, he really meant it.

Miles threw his hands up in the air and made noises about going to get them a table.

"First, you need to tell me if he ever apologized to you," Gina said.

Evan was more than a little shocked that she knew so much. "No. Yes. Not exactly precisely when he should have."

Gina's expression was grave, belying the flushed excitement on her cheeks. "He's sort of an oblivious asshole, sometimes. But I guess I don't need to tell you that."

Evan laughed. "No, no, you don't. I know what I'm getting with him."

"Good." She leaned closer, bracelets clanking again. "Xander told me he took you to Terroir last night. Was it amazing?"

"It was terrifying, intimidating and incredible," Evan said.

"Miles tried to take me there once and I told him, over his dead body," Gina said. "I'm much more comfortable grabbing a burger."

"Don't worry," Miles said dryly, "I'm sure you can get a burger here."

"It's breakfast, Miles," Gina replied, all deadpan voice and sparkling eyes, "that means bacon and eggs and something sinful, like a cinnamon roll or a Danish as big as my head."

Miles ruffled her hair affectionately. "I'll have to send you a box of goodies. We've got tons of extras in my freezer. Some of them actually edible."

"Don't believe him," Evan inserted. "All of the ones he saved are definitely edible. More than."

"Oh, I like you," Gina said. "A lot, I think. You're going to be *great* for him."

Evan looked steadily over at Miles, who was still beaming at his sister. "I'm sure as hell going to try."

Reaching over, Gina squeezed his hand. "I wouldn't expect anything less."

Evan was sort of glad when this was the moment the hostess called Miles' name to let them know their table was ready. He was a little mistier in the eyes than he felt comfortable being, especially with someone he didn't know, even if that someone was Miles' sister.

"And I'll have the pineapple upside down pancakes," Evan said to the wait-ress who was taking their order. "And a side of bacon. Extra crispy, please."

"I'll have all this right out," the waitress said, stuffing her pad back in her apron, and moving on to the next table.

Evan only knew something was wrong by the strangled, stifled noise Miles made.

It hit him all at once. So long, being so careful, so cautious, never visibly enjoying any of the cookies he'd been making, or the *macarons*, or even the incredible dessert last night at Terroir.

No, all it took to screw him up was Gina beaming at him like an idiot, casually accepting, like he was going to be around for a long time. Like he was going to be a member of their family.

Miles made the sound again.

"What's wrong with him?" Gina asked, taking a sip of coffee.

"I think he just discovered that I like sweets," Evan said evenly.

Gina looked confused. Miles looked murderous.

"Explain," Gina said, looking rapidly more interested by the second.

But before Evan could open his mouth, Miles had cut in. And he sounded pretty pissed, but not cruel, or cold, or truly angry, which was better than Evan could have hoped for. After all, there had only been a limited amount of time he could keep this secret while dating an extremely talented pastry chef.

"The second day Evan and I worked together, he told me that he did not like sweet things. No desserts. No cookies. No pastries. Nothing. And he," Miles said, mouth twitching, like it was difficult for him to keep a straight, annoyed face, "kept up this charade until this moment."

"I was a little distracted today," Evan added, by way of explanation.

"You didn't even break over the dessert course last night at Terroir," Miles said incredulously. And that *had* been difficult, but truthfully, the toughest times had always been whenever he was eating something that Miles had made. There was something about taking what Miles had made with his own two hands and then putting it into his mouth that always made the taste even more exquisite.

Even the batches of peanut butter chocolate chunk cookies that hadn't quite turned out had nearly made Evan moan once or twice.

"You were right," was all Evan said. "They should have used thyme, not rosemary, in the white chocolate lemon mousse pyramids. But you *were* right about the gold; they certainly looked impressive enough."

Gina was giggling so hard she nearly choked.

"You guys . . . you are . . . *perfect* . . . for each other," she managed to get out in between hysterical chuckles.

"You're not mad?" Evan asked, lifting an eyebrow.

Miles just shrugged. "If I remember correctly, that was the morning after I filmed myself baking Ding Dongs. Anything you said that day is just payback for the video. Besides," he lowered his voice, "I definitely plan to get you back, at the soonest possible opportunity."

"Gross," Gina exclaimed, but she was smiling so big, her smile took over her face. And Evan couldn't help but smile right along with her.

Chapter Sixteen

As shitty as leaving LA had been, it was worse going back.

It was like the fury of a rainstorm after the weatherman warned you to bring your umbrella. Expected, completely inevitable, and very shitty.

"I can't believe you're not worried," Evan said to Miles as they walked into the lobby of *Five Points*. They weren't holding hands, but Miles liked to think just about everyone could see the growing attachment between them.

"It's pointless," Miles said. "Has anyone ever convinced Reed Ryan to do something he doesn't want to do?" Besides—and he wasn't quite ready for Evan to find out about this yet—he'd played the last card he could think of, and if that didn't work, maybe it was right for *Pastry by Miles* to die off.

"When I was really lonely last year, sometimes I pictured Jordan doing lots of stuff he didn't want . . . at least initially," Evan said.

Miles burst out laughing. "Of course you did."

"Have you seen them?" Evan demanded, laughing with Miles. "I mean, that's a lot of hotness to contain in one relationship."

Of course, that was the moment they ran into Reed, in the corridor outside their adjoining cubicles.

He raised an eyebrow. Reed was one of those men who could say a speech and never open his mouth. He definitely looked like he was talking now, even though he hadn't said a single word.

"Who's a lot of hotness to contain in one relationship?"

Miles thought Evan was pretty damn brave, but it seemed telling his maybe soon-to-be ex-boss he'd fantasized about him and his boyfriend was where he drew the line. If that was the case, then Evan was even smarter than he'd imagined.

"Miles and me," Evan said, chin jutting out, like he was half-expecting his boss to disapprove.

But Reed's frown rearranged into a big smile. "Then the long weekend was good for you," he said. His eyes took on a darker, amused glint. "You certainly seem more relaxed, Evan."

"We're working on it," Miles inserted, because he could see this conversation going all sorts of inappropriate places. And Evan, who had seemed so formal and wedded to professionalism when they'd first met, could be shockingly dirty when he was in a good mood. And thanks to Miles, he was definitely in a very good mood.

"I'm glad to hear it," Reed said, sounding genuinely pleased. Miles found himself praying to whatever god was looking down on them that maybe that was enough to save *Pastry by Miles* and Evan's job. They could manage if Miles at least saved his show, and Evan saved his job. They had each other. Miles felt certain of that, even if the rest of the world felt unpleasantly uncertain right now.

"Miles," Reed said, turning to him, thoughtful look on his face. "Come see me after you get settled in. I think we need to talk."

The moment Reed was out of earshot, Evan shoved Miles into his cubicle, excitement and terror warring on his face. "Is this it?" he whisper-yelled. Which, for Evan, was mostly yelling and very little whispering. "Is he going to cancel your contract?"

Miles had a very good idea what Reed wanted to talk about, and it was only tangential to his contract. "No clue," he said. He didn't like lying to Evan, even if it was a lie of omission, but he wasn't entirely sure Evan would be happy about this development. Even if it meant his job was saved.

Evan was one of those sticklers who he imagined might care more about how his job was saved, not just that it had been saved. Miles really hoped that he was wrong in this scenario, but they were still getting to know each other, now that Evan had actually started to let him in.

Reed was leaning back in his big leather chair when Miles walked in.

"Close the door," Reed said, and he still sounded thoughtful but not angry. Not angry was good.

Miles shut the door, sure that Evan had just gone into a paroxysm of curiosity and tension as he hid around the corner, desperately hoping that he'd be able to overhear their conversation.

Reed knew Evan better than he realized.

"You sent me this video," Reed said, rotating his gigantic monitor so Miles could see the screen. Not that Miles needed to; he knew exactly which video Reed was talking about.

"I thought you might want to see that our rehearsals provided some great footage," Miles said.

Reed chuckled. "You making a Ding Dong *was* solid gold footage. But," and he paused, that thoughtful look returning, "I don't think you made this during rehearsals. And not with Evan."

It had been a long shot for Miles to convince Reed that they had made this video together. It was funny and clever and a little subversive, which was everything that Miles was, and everything Evan mostly wasn't. At least the side of Evan that he tended to present at work. Miles had discovered in the last few days that he could definitely unbend if he wanted, if his mood was right, and he was surrounded by people he trusted.

But Reed probably didn't know that.

Reed frowned. And Miles realized that he *didn't* know that. Evan had never trusted Reed—his beloved boss, the person Miles might have guessed he was closest to in his whole life—enough to show that side of himself. He'd trusted only Miles. That revelation only made Miles more determined to convince Reed that they'd made this clip together.

"Evan was there. We made it together," he said. He'd heard once that the most effective lies were the simplest. He didn't know if that was even true, but he was willing to give just about anything a shot at this point.

Reed made a frustrated sound, but he still didn't look angry. "I know you're not telling me the truth." He hesitated. "The question is why. Are you worried I'm going to tear up your contract? Are you worried I'm going to send you back to Napa?"

"No," Miles said, and realized, belatedly, that he meant it. Suddenly the worst thing wasn't that *Pastry by Miles* might end, or that he'd be forced to beg for his old job back.

He'd known he loved Evan, he just hadn't realized how incredibly necessary he was to his life. It wasn't a great time to have this realization, but it certainly provided him a hell of a lot of motivation to pull this off.

"Then what is it?" Reed demanded. A meaty fist landed on the solid wood desk with a heavy thump. Reed's cooking had always been considered bold, bombastic and straightforward. Sort of like the man. Miles just hadn't seen a lot of evidence of it until now.

"Of course I don't want to get fired. Of course I want to convince you to green light a season of *Pastry by Miles*. Of course I want you to keep the team intact."

"I know you're trying to save him," Reed said. "And you're not alone in that. I've been trying to help him since I first met him, years ago. He's come a long way from that skinny, terrified, overly proud college kid. But that doesn't mean he's right for this show."

"I do love him. But that isn't why I'm doing this. I'm doing this because he's the best fit for the show. For me."

"What if I told you that it was either the show or him?" Reed asked, and that thoughtful look that had reassured Miles at first now only terrified him. He didn't know what it meant, and the unknown could be a bad place.

"Then I'd say it was an honor to meet you, I'd pack up my cubicle and I'd drive back to Napa today," Miles said.

"You really would," Reed observed, clearly a little mystified.

"I won't do this without Evan. Period."

"What if I promised he wasn't fired, that he'd be reassigned to a different department? Would that make a difference?" Reed asked.

Miles wiped his sweaty, trembling hands on his jeans. "No."

Reed tilted his head, intense eyes cataloging Miles minutely. Then, suddenly he nodded sharply. "Okay, then. Go get Evan. He's probably loitering in the break room, hoping that he can hear some of this conversation. It doesn't feel fair to leave him out of it."

Sure enough, Evan was there, pacing with a cup of coffee in his hand. "What's going on?" he hissed.

"Reed wants to talk to both of us," Miles said, and gestured towards Reed's office. "Let's go."

This time Reed didn't ask him to close the door.

"Here's your official shooting schedule," Reed said, almost before their butts were in chairs. He slid a piece of paper across the desk. "But only if you promise me the Ding Dong video stays. It's too funny to cut."

Miles could feel Evan's happy confusion radiating out of him, even as he said all the right things: about how they wouldn't let him down, about how they'd commit themselves to making the best show possible, how happy he was that Reed had reconsidered.

It was inevitable that as soon as Reed dismissed them, Evan would drag him into the break room. It was probably inevitable that Reed had popped his head out of his office and was listening to the whole conversation. It was definitely inevitable that the entire office had tuned in and was listening to their conversation.

"What is Reed talking about, Miles?" Evan demanded. "Did you really send him that stupid Ding Dong video?"

"Yes," Miles said. It was hard to meet Evan's disbelieving eyes, but he did it. He'd sent it; he had to own up to it. "I told him that we'd recorded it during rehearsals last week. He needed to know that we could do this. Together."

"You lied," Evan stated, and started to pace again.

"Technically," Miles said. "But I know we can produce content like this together. High production value, that's what you bring to the table. And I can bring the creative flair. I know everything we've done for *Pastry by Miles* has been a hot mess so far, but all each disaster has convinced me of is that we're meant to do this together. I don't *want* to do it without you."

"You sent it to Reed without telling me," Evan said, whirling around, voice and face unbearably hard. Miles could sense the wall going back up, and he wanted to beg, to plead, to fall to his knees. But with Evan, those things would fall on deaf ears. That much he'd discovered about the man in front of him.

"I saved the show. I saved your job. I saved our future, working together. Why are you mad?" Miles asked in exasperation. "Because I didn't tell you ahead of time? Because I lied to your precious Reed? Don't worry, he knows I lied. He knows and he doesn't care."

"I'm mad because you felt you needed to charge in to save me. I can save myself. I don't need your help with that," Evan said coldly.

"That's what people in love do," Miles said, leashing in his temper as close as possible. He needed Evan to realize what he'd been trying to do, not escalate this argument until both of them were so mad neither of them were listening. That was the mistake he'd always made before. He wasn't going to do it again.

Evan looked incredulous.

Miles retrenched and tried to explain again. "I want to be by your side for a long time. Long enough that there's going to be times when I need you. And times you need me. Nobody can be strong and perfect all the time. This time, maybe I helped you. Next time, I'm gonna expect you to be there for me. Hell, that's something you've already done. I sent that incredibly stupid drunk email, and you didn't instantly forward it to Reed. You had my back. The way I had yours today."

"Reed might have fired you for lying to him," Evan said.

"He might have. I was willing to take that risk."

"Why?" Evan asked, even though he had to know why. Reed had instantly known why.

"Because I love you," Miles said, rolling his eyes. "And you know that's why I did it. You know I love you. And you love me too."

"I . . . I . . . I don't know about that," Evan said, sounding unsure for the first time since he'd dragged Miles into the break room.

"Bullshit. You love me, and I love you." Miles reached and pulled Evan to him. The tension in his body cut like a cord, dissipating almost instantly.

"I might love you a little," Evan admitted into Miles' shoulder.

"What? What was that again?" Miles said loudly, teasingly.

Evan's head lifted from his shoulder, looking at him straight on. "I love you, you jerk." And he kissed him.

EPILOGUE

"Today, we're going to be making one of my favorite things," Miles said, leaning on the counter, staring at the camera like they were best friends and not a man and a machine, "a dong."

There was a ripple of laughter through the assembled staff. Wyatt Blake found himself joining in even though the line wasn't new to him. It might have been Miles' delivery or it might have been who he was delivering it to—regardless, the opening line was just as funny and just as effective as it had been the first time Wyatt had heard it.

Evan leaned against the end of the counter, hip popped, white shirt immaculate, bow tie flawlessly tied. He grimaced comically at his boyfriend's words, and Wyatt would never have guessed that this whole exchange was scripted, except that he'd seen it developed and then rehearsed.

"A *Ding* Dong," Evan corrected crisply. "It's a pastry, which is something I would guess you know about. A chocolate cake to be precise, filled with cream. Don't tell me you need *me* to educate you about a dessert."

Miles raised an eyebrow at the last part, and another round of laughter circulated through the crowd.

"You like cream-filled desserts, huh?" Miles asked Evan, who rolled his eyes.

"Bake, you idiot," Evan retorted. There was a thread of annoyance in his tone, and the ever-present eye rolls, but he still looked enamored. Probably because he was. Wyatt might have doubted it—couldn't help but doubt after what the two of them had done to each other—but he couldn't anymore. Not after Miles insisted he come to the first few days of filming for moral support, and Wyatt had seen firsthand how much they cared about each other.

Wyatt was still surprised that Miles had asked him and not Xander, but then he'd been so angry lately, he probably would have been shitty moral support. And Bastian Aquino never would have given Kian the day off.

That was probably why Miles had sent him a ticket and asked—more like pleaded—for Wyatt to fly down to LA. Wyatt had been happy to do it, because Miles was a friend, and selfishly because Wyatt needed a break of his own.

Miles followed Evan's command, with a single amused glance shot over to the other side of the kitchen, and started to assemble the dry ingredients for the chocolate cake portion of the recipe. The original concept of *Pastry by Miles* had always been Miles baking, and Miles still did bake, but now he was also peppered with questions by his producer, who instead of standing behind the camera, stood in front of it.

The concept was new and fresh and it worked like gangbusters. Miles had told Wyatt that they'd initially come up with the idea in a meeting where Reed Ryan had slammed his hand down on the table, interrupting one of Miles and Evan's many debates, and said, "You're going to think I'm crazy, but you have to film this. You two are *insane*."

It definitely wasn't like other cooking shows, but it also worked.

Because Miles was Miles, and he could sift flour in his sleep, he kept talking.

"Right now we're sifting because we don't want lumps in our dry ingredients. Or stuff that doesn't belong."

Evan was still watching, eyes narrowed, from the other end of the counter. He had a bunch of papers spread out in front of him, and it was clear he was still in charge of the episode. He was just doing it in full view of the camera, as ballsy as he'd ever been.

"I don't believe you've ever actually *found* something that didn't belong in the flour," Evan drawled. Wyatt didn't remember this particular dialogue, but Miles didn't miss a beat.

"Sand, grit, a marble, I think I even found a condom once," Miles said, flashing a charming smile to the camera, like *can you believe this guy?* "Don't worry though, it wasn't used."

"I'd be a lot more worried if you were finding used condoms in your flour," Evan said.

"Jealous?" The smile Miles shot down the length of the counter could have impregnated anyone within a few paces, regardless of gender.

Evan just laughed. "Of the guys who stuck their condoms in your flour, hoping to get your attention? No. Not even a little."

Wyatt realized with a bright, blinding flash why Miles hadn't invited Xander. How had he found out? Wyatt had been so certain that Miles hadn't realized Xander had that impossible crush.

But he must have, and that was why he hadn't invited Xander. On the other hand, Wyatt thought a little bitterly, he was safe because he didn't have a crush on anyone.

After the way his relationship with Nate had ended, Wyatt had been happy enough for awhile to stay unattached and single, but watching Miles and Evan flirt with each other would make anyone long for even a fraction of what they'd found together.

It wasn't just that he was sick of cleaning artichokes and prepping lamb chops and being held to a painfully exacting standard every second he was at work, he was bored and lonely. He'd thought that getting away for a few days and going down to LA to see Miles would help, but all being here did was throw into sharp focus what was missing in his own life.

"They're hilarious, aren't they?" Wyatt looked up, and Reed Ryan was standing there, grinning like a loon. Or like someone who'd just won the lottery. And he probably had, from an online cooking show perspective.

Miles had just begun to slowly whisk in the wet ingredients to the dry, and he was waggling his eyebrows, making more and more outrageous comments, aiming for some unknown reaction from Evan.

"It shouldn't work, but it does," Wyatt admitted.

"I knew they could work it out," Reed said. "I had a few dark moments. Once or twice I thought they might kill each other before working it out, but I was happy to be wrong about that."

Wyatt had no interest in such a combative relationship, but there was an invisible, undefinable thread between them, shining with love and respect and affection. It shouldn't hurt to see it, it should be something to admire, not something to be envious of, but Wyatt found he couldn't really help himself. Nate had been his only serious boyfriend, and they definitely hadn't had that.

"Now, I have the Cooking Channel sniffing around my set," Reed said, voice smug with satisfaction. "And the sort of buzz about our new show that I couldn't manufacture no matter what draw our marketing team comes up with."

Wyatt reminded himself firmly that he had come here to be a support to Miles, not to eat his heart out with jealousy over what he'd found, professionally and personally. He *wasn't* Xander.

"They're both very lucky," Wyatt said, and no matter how much he tried to regulate his voice, it still came out sadly wry.

Reed put a reassuring hand on his shoulder—Wyatt thought that next time he saw Xander, there was now something else he could lord over him—and said, "I know how talented you are. The possibilities are endless. Maybe it's time to leave the nest and explore them."

"With you?" Wyatt wondered if maybe this invite had also been a way to get him down to LA for a job interview. With Reed Ryan. Xander was going to *die*.

"Not necessarily," Reed said. "But I know about a few open positions in the area. I like to keep my ear to the ground. Would you be interested?"

Would he be interested? Wyatt didn't even know. All he knew was that he was suddenly and inexplicably sick of his own life. He was tired of trying to make ends meet, of struggling to keep his nana in the home, and having nothing left over for anything else. Sick of being told what to do.

"I'd be willing to listen," Wyatt said.

"Then we'll be in touch," Reed said, squeezing his shoulder again, then disappearing, merging into a group of people who all seemed to want to ask him a dozen questions.

Back on set, Miles was carefully pouring his cake batter into molds.

"Now," he said, "we can finally get onto the cream-filling part of the dessert."

"Your favorite part," Evan inserted.

Miles' expression turned hot and sweet. "Yeah, you don't enjoy it at all," he retorted, but his voice was so intimate it was impossible not to picture them pressed up together, instead of being separated by six feet of countertop.

"Cut," Alex, the director, called.

"What?" Miles asked, and Evan shot him a darker look.

"Dressing room," Evan said briskly, and Miles let himself be led off to their green room.

"What did we talk about before I agreed to do this?" Evan asked as soon as the door was firmly closed behind them. It was bad enough they were airing out their personal shit for the world to see; he was not willing to do it with three-quarters of their co-workers listening in.

"That there was a line," Miles said, expression growing concerned. "Did I cross the line?"

Evan honestly wasn't sure if Miles had crossed the line or if he'd crossed it on his own, but suddenly, he'd felt hot and cold all over, freaked out by how public this all was. Their relationship, and how they'd learned to make it work, completely exposed to everyone.

It was weird that throwing the doors open would make him feel closed-in, but it was happening anyway and he couldn't help it.

"I'm not sure. Maybe I did, without thinking. However it happened, it happened. I freaked out. And Alex must have noticed."

"You did have a weird expression on your face," Miles said. He reached out and pulled Evan close to him. Evan rested his head on Miles' shoulder. He shouldn't feel less exposed now, with Miles wrapped around him, but he inexplicably always did. "I'm sorry," he continued, his voice a warm murmur.

"This isn't easy for me," Evan murmured back. "I'm the one who's sorry for freaking out all the time."

"You didn't get into this expecting to be in front of the camera," Miles soothed, "I don't blame you for freaking out about it."

"But I agreed to it," Evan argued. "I agreed, and I knew exactly what I was agreeing to."

"You agreed because you were thinking with your producer hat," Miles said, a tiny bit amused.

"I knew it would be great TV," Evan admitted.

"You're amazing, you know," Miles whispered into his temple. "I love you so much. Even when you freak out. Especially when you freak out."

"At least you didn't come over and start kissing me," Evan said prosaically.

"I wanted to," Miles said.

Evan closed his eyes. "I wanted you to." He hesitated. "This is harder than I thought it would be."

"We can always stop," Miles insisted. "I told Reed this might not work out, and he's okay with whatever. You know that. You probably know that better than me."

"I don't mean . . . being in front of the camera is too hard. I mean not crossing the line is harder than I thought it would be. I look over at you, and I want to say what I would usually say, I want to do what I would usually do. And it sucks to hold back."

Miles' fingers flinched; Evan felt it through the cotton of his button-up, all the way to his skin. He shivered in response.

"How about you do whatever you feel comfortable with, and we'll just figure out the rest," Miles suggested.

Their relationship was so new, Evan was still figuring out how Miles knew the perfect thing to say to make him feel better.

"How do you do that?" Evan asked.

"Do what?" Miles ran a reassuring hand down Evan's back.

"Always say what I need to hear."

"I know you," Miles said seriously. "I love you. I expect the two are somewhat related."

Evan rolled his eyes, even though Miles couldn't see them. "I can't believe I didn't know right away what a sap you are. I love it. I love *you*."

"It's only you that brings it out," Miles admitted. "You know that."

"Thank you for being patient and you know . . . generally amazing," Evan said, waving a hand, shockingly unable to verbalize everything Miles was for him. Which did make sense because he'd discovered that love could be very difficult to pin down specifically.

"I told you once, we're going to be what each other needs. A strong relationship doesn't always have two strong people in it. I'm good taking my turn now, and you can take yours later." He paused. "Like during all the marketing and publicity."

Evan laughed damply. "I'll keep that in mind."

"You do that," Miles said, sounding very content, like he never wanted to move.

Someone rapped on the door. Evan was pretty sure it was Reed. "Time's up," the voice said. Yes, it was definitely Reed.

"You ready to go back?" Miles asked.

Evan knew they didn't have much of a choice, because he was both the producer and the star. He knew they had a strict schedule to keep. "As long as you're next to me. As long as we do this together."

"Always," Miles said.

THE ARGUMENT

A BITE ME SHORT STORY

"HEY BOSS, YOU WANTED to see me?" Evan said, sticking his head into Reed's office doorway.

"How many times do I have to tell you not to call me that," Reed said, smiling as he gave an absent gesture, almost all of his attention focused on the laptop screen in front of him.

"Another few hundred probably," Evan said, taking a seat in one of the chairs in front of Reed's desk. They weren't really boss and employee anymore—not since Cooking Channel had agreed to partner with Evan and Miles for the second season of their show. Technically, they both still worked for Five Points, had offices here, and even used their kitchen, but it was only a matter of time before all of that changed.

Once the second season aired on Cooking Channel, Evan knew that their lives wouldn't be the same again. Before Miles had shown up in the Five Points offices, finally having that badge of unqualified success would've been everything Evan ever wanted. He'd worked insanely hard for it, and knew that nobody deserved it more, but Miles had changed things. *Some* things, but not everything. While falling in love had slightly changed his priorities, it hadn't changed who he was, deep down. And that person was both freaking ecstatic and a little tiny bit nostalgic that in a few months, he couldn't call Reed 'boss' anymore.

"What's going on?" Evan asked, gently prompting him because Reed's attention had gotten re-sucked into whatever he'd been doing.

"Oh, *oh*, yeah, sorry," Reed apologized. He shut his laptop and scrubbed a hand across his face. He had several days' worth of beard growth and looked .. . stressed.

Evan worried about him, because Evan cared about him—but also because Evan was great at worrying. It was one of his most underrated skills.

"It's all good," Evan said, and this time discovered that he really *was* worried, because Reed looked stressed, and as far as Evan knew, there wasn't any actual reason why he should be.

"I just . . .I'm worried about you." Reed eyed him like he was afraid he'd jump up and start running around, raving like a lunatic.

"You're worried about *me*?" Evan questioned. "Did something happen with Cooking Channel?" *If it did, we'll just go bigger and badder and go after Food Network.*

"No, no, of course not," Reed said, and Evan let out the breath he hadn't realized he'd been holding. "I'd have told you first thing. Actually, you'd have probably told *me*."

"That's true," Evan said and felt additionally reassured that both he *and* Reed knew that Evan would be their first phone call if something had gone awry. "Then what is it?" he asked, genuinely mystified. "We're fine. We're better than fine, actually."

Reed sighed. "That's the thing. You're . . .you and Miles . . .you're just . . .you're *getting along*."

"We're getting along?" Evan repeated.

"Yes," Reed said with an emphatic nod. Like this explained everything.

"That's . . ." Evan cleared his throat. "That's what happens when you . . .*you know* . . .fall in love."

"Yes, and no," Reed said. "Some people, yes. You and Miles, no. You've always bickered. Obviously, some points were worse than others. Like when Miles wrote you that email . . ."

"I know about the email," Evan interrupted because he really did not want to talk about it ever again, especially with his boss. Even if his boss was no longer quite his boss anymore.

"What I mean," Reed said with a heavy sigh, "is that you don't change because you fall in love. You both had very distinct opinions when you started working together. And you had those, all the way from the moment Miles walked in the door, through the prep for the first season, *through* the filming of the first season. And then you got the Cooking Channel deal and you just . . .stopped."

Evan digested this. Reed was right about one thing—both he and Miles had very distinctive opinions. They'd never shied away from sharing them, even if that led to some bickering and yes, occasionally even a fight or two. They both liked being right—Evan because he was almost always right, and Miles because he was a chef and chefs were notorious for their egos. No matter what Miles claimed about being laid back or low-key or whatever, he was totally a chef, and totally sure that his way was not only the right way, it was the only way.

"I don't think we stopped," Evan said, even as he tried to cast his mind back over the last two or so months, since they'd gotten the Cooking Channel deal, and he couldn't remember one single fight or even a single time when they'd butted heads over . . .*anything*.

Could Reed actually be right about them? Had they started agreeing on everything?

Evan couldn't believe it, but his memory couldn't lie, could it?

Had he started agreeing with Miles because he was so crazy-in-love with him he didn't *want* to disagree anymore? Had Miles? Evan didn't know which of them had started this disastrous turn of events—or if it had been *both* of them.

"It's okay," Reed said awkwardly. "You're going to figure it out."

"Yeah," Evan said, a little dazed. "Yeah, I think you might be right."

"Nothing a good talk won't fix," Reed said with certainty. "Nobody's ever doubted how you feel about each other, even when you argue. Actually," he added, tilting his head as he considered this, "I think the fact that you bicker with each other, that you both have stayed true to who you are, is the most convincing part of your relationship."

Great, and now that was gone. Evan felt panic streak through him.

"If anyone can fix this, it's you two," Reed finished with a bright smile. Clearly having no comprehension of the uncertainty he'd just sowed.

"Right," Evan said. "Totally."

❧❦❧ ❦❧❦

Evan found Miles in the prep kitchen, painstakingly whipping some kind of creamy substance by hand. His biceps bulged under his slightly too-tight t-shirt, and Evan took a second to appreciate the view. Then he shook himself out of it because maybe this was the problem—maybe he was just too much in love with Miles and his annoyingly buff arms and his sweet smile whenever he saw Evan, and his devastating confidence in the kitchen. Maybe all of those things, plus everything else Miles loved about him, had sucked away every bit of Evan's certainty that *he* knew what was best.

"Hey," Miles said, most of his attention still absorbed by the cream, but he shot Miles one of those smiles that always made Miles' knees weak. It had been a problem from the very first moment they'd met, and then it had gotten *worse*.

Love was funny like that. You didn't just fall in love and call it good. You fell in love over and over again, every single day.

"Hey," Evan replied.

"I didn't know you were coming in today," Miles said. That had been the plan this morning anyway, when Miles had crawled out of bed, despite Evan promising all kinds of fun if he'd stayed.

Evan knew how much Miles *cared* about things like pretty much every kind of dessert—it was one of the many arguments they'd had, how much Miles wanted to be "true to his pastry roots"—and so he knew what it meant when Miles glanced over again, attention clearly divided by whatever he was making and Evan.

It would be flattering but it hit Evan that not only was Reed probably right, this might be unfixable. Miles, despite his insistence on pastry chef-level devotion, wanted to give Evan what he wanted. Evan, despite all his closely held individuality and principles, wanted to give Miles what *he* wanted.

"I was . . ." Evan hesitated. "But then Reed texted me and said he wanted to see me, and I thought . . ." He'd *thought* it would be fun and actually downright wonderful to surprise Miles at the office kitchen, as he tried to plan season 2's shows.

"You thought what?" Miles *put down* the whisk and maybe he didn't actually come over and touch Evan, but it was clear he wanted to. Despite Evan's clear and ironclad rules about PDA at the office.

Evan freaked out.

"I thought . . ." His mind whirled.

"Is everything okay? You look . . .*worried*." Miles broke the rules just about as easily as he ever had, reaching out and intertwining Evan's much smaller hand with his bigger, knife and burn scarred one.

And even though it was more evidence that they had changed—that *he* had changed—Evan discovered he felt calmer just having Miles right there. That had definitely not always been the case.

"I'm fine. Reed just wanted to talk about Cooking Channel," Evan said.

"Oh." With one final heart-stuttering caress, Miles let go of Evan's hand and picked up his whisk again, returning to the contents of his enormous metal bowl. "I thought something was actually wrong." Despite being fanatical about the pastry side of the show, Miles couldn't really give a shit about the production side of *Pastry by Miles*. He'd smartly left almost all the negotiations with Cooking Channel to Evan, and had only made a handful of stipulations, all of them revolving around creative control.

Evan knew that, which was why he'd picked it as a subject to divert Miles' attention from his momentary freak out.

"I trust you," Miles said, starting to whisk his cream again. "You'll make sure we don't lose our integrity."

What about what makes us us? Miles wondered. *How do I make sure we don't lose that?*

"We've already signed the contract, there's no chance of that," Evan said. Their celebration had lasted an entire weekend, and even though he strained his mind to remember, he couldn't identify a single time they'd argued during the entire seventy-two hours. It had just been all blissful, filled with love and pleasure and a realization that they'd formed an unshakeable trust in their partnership.

It should've been a good memory—a fucking *fantastic* memory—but now all it did was fill Evan with fear. Had learning to truly trust each other meant that they'd learned not to care about things they'd always cared about before? Would it mean that when they started filming season two, that snarky repartee that the audiences loved about them would be gone?

Would they no longer be #couplegoals on Instagram?

Maybe if Evan had worked a little less hard for his success, he wouldn't care.

"I'm going to finish this up," Miles said, "and then I'm headed home." To the apartment they shared. That had become official not even two months back. *Another* celebration had followed Miles turning in the set of keys to his own separate apartment. When Miles had put his spatulas in the drawers and his whisks in the crock on the countertop, he'd told Evan that he'd felt like he was home. Not because of this semi-shitty LA apartment, but because *Evan* was there.

"Okay," Evan said.

He didn't want to lose all those picture-perfect moments. The ones that warmed him backwards and helped him to forget so many years of loneliness. But he needed to figure out how to co-exist with all the memories *and* remind both of them they used to be sweet mixed with just the right amount of salty.

The good thing was that Evan wasn't a quitter, and he would make it happen. Somehow, some *way*.

"You'll be there?" Miles questioned, looking at him again, instead of what was in his bowl. Maybe Evan hadn't quite put his concerns to rest like he'd thought.

"Yeah, yeah, I'll . . ." Evan paused, still trying to formulate a plan that might have a chance in hell of working, "I'll make dinner."

Miles looked suspicious. Evan almost never cooked, for good reason. When your boyfriend had worked at a Michelin-starred restaurant, even as a pastry chef, there was no reason to try, as he could still cook circles around Evan—whose best talent was still ordering takeout.

"You won't order from that Indian place again, right? I think it gave me really bad gas last time," Miles said. Obviously he had concluded that the most effort Evan would be going to would be dialing the phone.

"I remember," Evan said with a glower. "If you think you suffered the most there, you're *wrong*. It was me, definitely me. Besides, I think I'll cook."

Miles still looked dubious, but he nodded. "Okay. I went to the market yesterday, so there's lots of stuff to choose from."

Miles went to the market nearly every day. He'd gotten into the habit of doing a lot of recipe work at home, which Evan usually enjoyed, especially now that his love of sweets was no longer a big secret.

"Sure," Evan said, faking confidence. He had no fucking clue what to do with a whole fridge-full of fresh ingredients, but he'd never been a quitter, and he wasn't going to start now.

Maybe if Miles came in during dinner prep, it would remind both of them just how much they weren't alike.

"And I'll be home in a bit," Miles added. "In case you need help."

"No help needed, but thanks," Evan said brazenly, even though he absolutely knew better.

He, one hundred and ten percent, absolutely fucking needed Miles' help.

Looking at the fridge did not improve the situation. Miles had been right; he'd been to the market in the last day or so, it was totally stocked, not only with butter, cream, and all kinds of fruit—the fresh component to Miles' regular recipe testing—but several paper-wrapped packages from the butcher, and a whole crisper drawer full of veggies. He'd even been to their favorite cheese shop, just down the street, and there were several tantalizing plastic-wrapped hunks of cheese. Along with some of the preserved meats that Miles had picked up, Evan could have probably cobbled together a cheese plate, piled up the fresh figs that he'd spotted on the top shelf of the fridge. It would've been a great, quick dinner, one they'd had lots of times because arranging pre-made food and ordering in were Evan's two culinary talents.

But, this time he'd specifically said he was *making* dinner, because the one *guaranteed* way Miles would step in, and probably shove his foot in his mouth by saying something critical.

Normally, this wouldn't be something he'd ever invite, which was why he'd almost strictly stuck to ordering in when it was his turn to figure out dinner. But today was an exception because Evan *needed* to know if they'd really become *that couple.*

So, instead of giving up when inspiration did not strike, Evan pulled a packet of boneless, skinless chicken breasts out of the fridge, and then a random assortment of vegetables from the crisper drawer. He could make a stir fry, couldn't he? Any idiot could make a stir fry, which was why when he'd bothered to date pre-Miles that had felt like the ubiquitous meal that anyone felt they could attempt to impress a potential boyfriend.

"You can do this," Evan told himself firmly. "It's chopping. And then cooking. That's so easy, it's embarrassing."

Evan was halfway through the pile of vegetables on the counter when Miles walked in. Initially, he hadn't been thinking clearly, and he'd been chopping them into small, even chunks, just like he knew Miles was particular about—and then he'd remembered that he wasn't supposed to be making Miles happy tonight. The opposite, actually. So he'd started chopping far more haphazardly, leaving some pieces much larger than others.

"Hey," Miles said, coming over to brush a kiss over Evan's mouth. He glanced down, taking in the knife in Evan's hand, and the piles of vegetables—most of them not chopped very neatly. *Say something critical*, Evan thought very hard in his direction, *tell me I'm screwing up dinner. Tell me you'll just take care of it. Say it so I can say something back.* But other than a faint purse of his lips, Miles kept his mouth shut.

Frustrating, maybe, but not the end of the world.

"I'm making stir fry," Evan said cheerfully. Not cheerful enough that Miles might get suspicious that he was up to something—but he definitely didn't feel quite this enthusiastic about stir fry. The real question was, *did anyone*?

"Oh, that's nice," Miles said. Clearly he didn't think so. He looked a little constipated, like Evan had just given him not *bad* news exactly, but an unpleasant variation.

"I think so," Evan said, beaming.

Come on, tell me what you really think. Tell me that a foot nearer the stove is a foot too close.

"And we're having . . .eggplant? In the stir fry?" Miles looked down at the little eggplants—that's what those were!—that he was chopping up inelegantly into large, uneven chunks.

"Don't you like eggplant?" Evan asked.

Miles rolled his eyes, propping his hip on the opposite side of the counter. Not interfering, not yet, but close enough that he could, if things got dire. And Evan intended for them to get *really* dire.

"I do," Miles said, "which you *know*. And I told you I was saving those to make some roasted eggplant pizzas this weekend. You know, when we were going to have Reed and Jordan over?"

Evan actually hadn't remembered that. But then sometimes when Miles got talking about food and recipes, he did zone out just a little tiny bit. Not enough that Miles might notice, but enough that his eyes wouldn't glaze over.

"Oh," Evan said. Then suddenly smiled, gesturing towards the pile of eggplant chunks. "Should I save these then? We could put them in a Tupperware and you can just roast them later?"

Miles looked at the eggplant dubiously. "That wasn't how I was going to prepare them," he said carefully. Way too carefully. This right here was why he and Miles had lost their edge; they were too fucking careful around each other now. Love made you do crazy things, like not want to insult your lover's chopping skills, even though they were *terrible*.

Six months ago, Miles wouldn't have even hesitated, and then Evan would have said something snarky back, and they'd have ended up having hot, wild sex on the kitchen floor.

Now, he thought a little resentfully, *they'd probably wait until they went to bed, like two perfectly normal, perfectly adjusted people.*

"How were you going to prepare them?" Evan questioned. He would really have to push Miles; that much was becoming painfully clear.

But he didn't really want to, and that, just as much as Miles' obvious reluctance to call Evan out on his poor knife skills, told the story of their relationship. They were *happy.* Happy getting along, happy loving each other, happy having sex after they got to bed, instead of on this cold, uncomfortable tile.

For a moment, Evan was almost tempted to leave it, but then he remembered Reed's concerned look, the worry in his eyes. What if they lost what made them special? What had made them so interesting and so attractive to the Cooking Channel?

"I was going to thinly slice them, then salt roast them," Miles said, and he couldn't quite meet Evan's eyes.

"Oh," Evan said. He didn't know what salt roasting even was.

Miles threw his hands up in the air, and Evan thought, *finally, this is it. I'm going to get a cutting remark shot in my direction any moment now.* But instead, Miles opened his mouth, then shut it again, and then finally said, "I'll just get some more Friday, it's fine."

"It's not fine!" Evan suddenly yelled. "Nothing is fine!"

Miles looked at him. "It's not?"

"You need to get mad at me!" Evan knew how unhinged he sounded.

"What?" Miles asked, mystified. "Why would I do that?"

"You always used to! We bickered all the time. We fought *constantly.*"

Miles looked even more confused. "That's what you want? Us fighting all the time?"

Evan set down his knife, despairing. "Yes. No. I don't know."

"This...this is what Reed wanted to talk to you about, wasn't it?" Miles said, reaching for Evan and pulling him into his arms. It felt fucking awesome, like it always did. Miles was like the boyfriend version of a warm, cuddly blanket. It was the exact opposite of what they were supposed to be doing, but Evan discovered he didn't have the self-control to pull away. Not when it felt so good.

"Yes," Evan said in a small voice, burying his face into Miles' shoulder. "He wanted to make sure everything was okay, because we're *getting along*. How fucked up is that?"

"Fucked up that we're getting along? Or fucked up that he's worried that we are?" Miles wondered and Evan had a feeling he didn't really want an answer. Because there really wasn't one.

"What if we can't turn it on for the cameras?" Evan asked quietly.

"I…I kinda like the idea that we don't have to be that way all the time," Miles said, his tone equally soft. "Don't you? Or did you like that? The bickering and the snarking at each other? We do it sometimes, still, just…it's nice to not have to do it all the time. I think …" He took a deep breath. "I think I actually love you too much to do it all the time."

Evan let out a heavy sigh. "Me too, I think. I . . .do you really think we can do it on set, the way we always used to?"

Miles shrugged. "Do you still *think* all that crap you used to say to me? Because I still have it flash through my mind sometimes, I just don't really want to say it anymore. Because most of the time you dish it back, because you're *you*, but then once in a while, I'd go too far, and you'd get this hurt look in your eyes, and *god*, I hated that."

"You really are a romantic," Evan said, smiling. "Seriously. A huge cheesy sap."

Miles just smiled back, like this was greatest thing Evan could have accused him of being. "Yeah, so?"

"I think I like it, too," Evan admitted.

"Imagine that," Miles said, pulling him close again, resting his chin on top of Evan's head. "I think we're gonna be okay. We're still us. We haven't really changed, we just fell in love. That happens, you know."

"I was here, I didn't exactly miss it," Evan retorted, and then for a second, froze, then started to grin. "I think you might be right."

"Wait a second, I want to get that recorded for posterity," Miles said with a faux-serious tone. "I might not even hear that ever again. I might be right? *Oh my god*."

"Hey, shut up," Evan said, slapping him lightly on the chest. "You're the worst."

"Am I?" Miles said, glancing down at him, his eyes darkening. "Maybe you really should shut me up."

He dropped to his knees, and Evan found his cock hardening like it'd been trained to, whenever Miles' admittedly fantastic mouth was anywhere near. He remembered all the times they'd done this—so many, they felt infinite—and also the very first time, when the attempt had ended in disaster.

"There you go," Miles coaxed, nuzzling Evan's hardening cock with his nose, as he reached up for the button and fly on Miles' jeans. He'd actually started wearing *jeans* now, at least on days they didn't have business meetings, which Miles claimed turned him on more than anything else.

Evan let Miles pull down his jeans, and then his briefs, and then everything went hot and red, Miles' mouth closing over him and sucking hard.

"Fuck," Evan breathed out, fingers curling over the edge of the counter as Miles continued to work him, the pleasure sparking through him in hard, desperate spurts. "You're so fucking good at this."

And he'd learned that too, since that first terrible blowjob that Miles had given him. The one he hadn't even managed to stay hard doing. He'd learned that Miles liked to be praised, liked to be told he was doing good, and Evan had discovered that nothing turned *him* on more than being the one who was doing the praising. Maybe that was another reason they'd lost their edge. It was too good to tell each other how great they were; so much better than making up stupid shit about how much they weren't.

Miles sucked and twisted hard, his mouth working Evan so perfectly that he knew he was getting close.

"Touch yourself," Evan begged, because there was maybe nothing hotter in the universe than watching how much pleasuring Evan pleasured Miles.

It felt like an impossibility that he'd never, ever get used to. That this brilliant, gorgeous, insane man would fall in love with him, and want to be his partner. Would choose it a hundred times a day, even when Evan was being difficult, even when he was being a brat. He'd still drop to his knees for Evan, would make him feel good in a thousand unique ways. It was a push and a pull that Evan had never believed he'd have, that he wasn't even quite sure he deserved.

But that didn't matter right now. What mattered, more than anything, was the flood of pleasure overwhelming him as he thought, *we could do this, forever, and it'd never be enough*. Evan barely got a single look at Miles reaching into his own open fly, frantically rubbing himself before Evan flew off the edge, pulsing over and over into Miles' mouth.

He slumped against the counter, eyes barely open as he heard Miles moan and follow right behind him.

"We've got to stop doing this," Miles said after a long moment, carefully pulling himself upright. He went over to the sink and rinsed his hands. "Do you really want dinner?"

Evan thought for a long moment. Dinner? What was dinner?

"I thought so," Miles said, and with no other warning, scooped him up and carried him to the bedroom they shared.

A long time later, as they lay in bed together naked, Miles said softly, his voice barely registering, "I don't really miss it."

Evan nestled closer, tighter, loving every bit of Miles' warmth. At some point they'd have to get out of bed and find something to eat for dinner. Not the chopped eggplant, probably. "Miss what?" he asked.

"Miss fighting," Miles said with a resigned sigh, "but if you really think we need to . . .I think we're cute no matter what, but you're the producer here. You're the expert."

"I never wanted to fight with you," Evan admitted. "I actually hoped that we'd be friends."

"Friends?"

"That was the most I was hoping for," Evan said wryly. "The rest was beyond my expectations."

"Ah." Miles didn't say anything else, and Evan wondered if he'd fucked up by admitting that.

"What I mean . . .is I don't mind telling you when you're being a stupid shit. But we don't have to fight just to fight," Evan continued awkwardly. "I . . .I don't want to do that. I'm so happy with you, I don't think we can really do that anymore."

Miles' arm tightened over him. "I hoped you'd say that."

"You did?"

"I mean. . .I wasn't *thinking* about it, or spending much time thinking about it. But I trust you. I know you've got my back, and that you wouldn't do anything that pissed me off, not on purpose. Maybe on accident . . ." Miles trailed off. "I guess what I'm saying is that I trust you. I know you won't screw me over. So my first reaction is just . . .let you do your thing, and I'll do mine."

Evan chuckled. "Imagine if we'd discovered that six months ago."

"If we had, we might not be here right now," Miles said. "It turned out that thing I loved to hate about you was that I . . .love you?"

"You're an idiot," Evan said, but he heard just how warm and soft he sounded. As gooey as the cinnamon rolls that Miles liked to bake them on lazy Saturday mornings.

"Never going to stop being that," Miles said, and that felt just right to Evan.

Catch Me

BETH BOLDEN

Chapter One

Wyatt couldn't take his eyes off him. Not his face, with those dark eyes and those cheekbones. Not his hands, cradling the single glass with its inch of golden liquid. Definitely not the way his arm muscles rippled under his tan skin. Considering how many guys were packed into this bar, including the mostly naked ones dancing on the stage, that the man had caught and held Wyatt's attention was an undeniable accomplishment.

Under any other circumstance, Wyatt would have opened with that line when he approached him. But that wasn't happening tonight, or any other night.

He was definitely cute though, with smile wrinkles around his dark eyes, and close-cropped brown hair. The loose, graceful way he held himself made Wyatt believe that he had a very decent set of muscles under his t-shirt and jeans. None of that explained why Wyatt couldn't look away. Maybe it was that the man didn't smile as much as he should. Only occasionally his very white teeth would flash, a contrast to his tanned skin, but it never felt like the smile reached his eyes.

Maybe it was the way he had so easily garnered every other person's interest in the bar.

Maybe it was because he was Ryan Flores, and the first "out" professional baseball player in the history of the game. He'd come out a few years before, right before the draft, and after spending a year or so in the minors, had broken out in a huge way during a Dodgers' playoff run. So what might have become only a footnote in the history of Major League Baseball instead got a whole paragraph.

It was a Thursday night, and Wyatt had come to Temple, one of the most famous gay bars in West Hollywood, hoping for a few beers, a chill night, and some well-deserved ogling of the gorgeous dancers. One of them had always reminded him of his ex, Nate, and now that Nate's memory had faded to a pleasant afterglow rather than acute bitterness, Wyatt had thought he might appreciate the similarity a little more.

Wyatt had not expected to run into the Los Angeles Dodgers' hottest property, and it was making his previously desired chill evening not very chill at all. But everyone always said he was adaptive, and this was basically true, so Wyatt had decided that people-watching worked too, especially when the people-watching was so god damned excellent.

Person-watching, mainly.

It was unexpectedly entertaining to watch groups of interested guys approach Ryan's VIP area, be ushered inside, and then promptly ushered back out five minutes later. He'd watched close to fifty guys try to flirt with Ryan Flores, and while there had been some vaguely flirtatious behavior in return, it was clear nobody was getting anywhere with him fast. Wyatt, who also wanted Ryan to smile more, understood both their desire and their frustration.

There was too much hesitation and assessment in Ryan's eyes, and not enough pure enjoyment.

It was a problem. It wasn't Wyatt's problem though; he had enough of those. He didn't need to add yet another to the pile.

"Want another?" The cute bartender with the white fluffy angel wings sauntered up and gave Wyatt another inviting look. They'd been offhandedly chatting whenever the bartender had a free second, and on another night, when Wyatt's attention wasn't so laser-focused on another man, he might have stuck around past closing and given the angel a ride home. Maybe another kind of ride, too.

He was absolutely hot—ripped abs paired with those wet-dream angel wings and dark eyeliner emphasizing his killer baby-blue eyes. There was a glint in them that promised he'd be very good—or maybe if Wyatt was lucky, very bad.

It wasn't his fault he looked too much like Kian, one of Wyatt's roommates back in Napa. Since Wyatt felt very brotherly towards Kian, it was not a comparison the bartender would have appreciated. Not with the way he kept eyeing Wyatt.

"No, thanks," Wyatt said. It would only be his third; he was definitely sober enough to get home, but he didn't feel like drinking. He didn't know you could feel too sober to get drunk.

Definitely too sober for this crowd, anyway.

"I don't think I've seen you here before," the angel said, undeterred by Wyatt's refusal.

"I'm visiting for a few days," Wyatt said shortly. It was insanity, but he didn't want to flirt with the hot angel bartender. He didn't really want to flirt with anyone.

Lie.

The person he wanted to flirt with was acting like he was holding auditions for his next boyfriend, and Wyatt, while generally optimistic about his chances with guys, was sure he wouldn't qualify.

Broke. A line chef at a prestigious restaurant, but *only* a line chef. Painfully single. Even more painfully, still mostly in the closet.

"You know, he's never been here before either," the angel said, gesturing up to where Ryan was holding court. His voice was bitter around the edges. "You sure you're not here to see him? You've been staring at him all night."

"Pretty sure," Wyatt said.

The angel made a face, which contorted his pretty features. Wyatt had a feeling he didn't often fail to pick someone up when he made the effort. But it wasn't the bartender that Wyatt wanted to make smile more.

"You're cute and all," the angel said, a sharp glint in his blue eyes, "but I don't think you'd stand a chance with him."

Wyatt shrugged. "Not trying to," he said. It was clearly past his time to go, if he'd succeeded in pissing off the hot bartender.

It just happened that the moment he was ready to leave was also the same moment Ryan decided to venture past the velvet rope of his private section.

His security flanked him as he made his way onto the dance floor, just as Wyatt was trying to wade his way around the edges. Some idiot designer had decided that the dance floor should be between the bar and the exit, and while undeniably keeping everyone going longer, it also made leaving annoying.

Wyatt heard a wave of interested noise wash over the dance floor, and through the customers milling around the bar. Everyone turned Ryan's direction. Not because he was the cutest guy there, or the most ripped, or the most unclothed, or anything obvious like that. It must be because he was rich and famous, Wyatt assumed. A real VIP at Temple on a Thursday night.

Even though he'd spent all night looking, Wyatt deliberately turned his head away from the dance floor. He didn't want to know who had captured Ryan Flores' attention enough to risk leaving his cushy, secure prison.

He couldn't possibly be jealous over a guy he'd never even talked to. And yet.

The crowd was sweaty and close, the music thumping loudly in his ears as he skirted the edges of the mass of dancing bodies as best as he could. His ass got groped three times, and Wyatt was pretty sure at least two of those were deliberate. He kept his eyes on the big double doors of the exit, not meeting anyone's eyes. He didn't want to get drawn in; what he needed was some air.

Finally he broke through to the other side, but the crowd on this side near the door was even pushier, shoving him back and forth a lot more aggressively. Wyatt wasn't a small guy—he was almost six foot, and had the long lean build of someone who worked hard for a living and liked surfing and rock climbing in his spare time—but he was getting jostled definitely more than he was used to.

The first sign something was wrong was that the bouncer at the door looked at him weirdly. But Wyatt didn't look back behind him, even though in retrospect, he really should have.

Wyatt burst through the open door and skirting the line to get in—on a *Thursday*, no less, he thought incredulously—and headed toward the next block, resting against a brick wall to catch his breath.

"I think this is when I should ask you where we're going."

Wyatt glanced up and nearly fell over.

Ryan Flores was standing in front of him, arms hanging loosely at his sides, an expectant look on his face, and the hint of a smile. Like Wyatt's shocked expression was very amusing.

"What are you doing here?" Wyatt demanded. Suddenly a lot of things made sense. Like why it had been so difficult to reach the door. Why guys had started shoving. Pushing. Trying to get to something behind him. Why he had felt like he was swimming upstream against some very determined fish. Why the bouncer had looked at him so oddly. Because it probably hadn't looked like Ryan was going with him, but *following* him.

Ryan smiled now, crooked and far more inviting up close than Wyatt had anticipated. "I thought you might know the answer to that. After all, you were staring at me for at least two hours."

"Three," Wyatt answered without thinking.

These things happened to other guys, maybe, but they didn't happen to him. Wyatt shoved his hands in the pockets of his jeans. Better to have them out of the way, better not to let himself start taking things—or *touching* things—before he figured out what the hell was going on.

"There you go," Ryan said matter-of-factly.

"I still don't understand," Wyatt said cautiously. He glanced around Ryan now, afraid they'd been followed by the crowd, but surprisingly, nobody had wandered over or was really paying any attention to them. It turned out that removed from the VIP trappings identifying him as someone important, Ryan looked like a normal guy.

Ryan smiled again, bigger this time, and it did devastating things to Wyatt's chest region. He had been right about wanting him to smile more, but it was far more treacherous than he could have ever imagined. He reminded himself that Ryan was a problem that he didn't need, but the argument wasn't exactly persuasive.

"You rescued me from the crowd. What a mob scene," Ryan said. He was a terrible actor, like he wasn't even trying. There was a conspiratorial glimmer in his dark eyes, and Wyatt wanted to just swallow the lame story and take him up on everything he was offering.

What would be the danger in that? Wyatt swallowed hard.

"At least," Ryan continued, "you could be a gentleman and offer to take me home. Especially after I followed you out here." He arched an eyebrow, and Wyatt wanted to be pinned underneath him, skin to skin, muscles clenched, the next time he did that.

"I could do that." Wyatt didn't even recognize the sound of his own voice. It wasn't like he didn't hook up occasionally. There was a decent gay community in Napa, and San Francisco was only a few hours away if he wanted something even more anonymous. But he'd never hooked up with anyone famous or anyone he'd helplessly stared at from across the bar for three hours.

"I brought my bike," Wyatt added. "I hope that's okay."

Ryan grinned. He'd smiled more in the last two minutes than Wyatt remembered from the last three hours. That couldn't have something to do with him, could it? "You wanna take me for a ride . . ." Ryan hesitated.

"Wyatt," he said, flushing, embarrassed that he hadn't introduced himself earlier. "I'm Wyatt." Flustered, he extended his hand, reminding him of the last job interview he'd gone on. Which was *stupid*, because this wasn't anything like that.

But Ryan took it anyway. His hand was big and ridged with callouses—similar to Wyatt's own knife-scarred digits, but just different enough to be exciting. Electricity flowed, making his fingers tingle, and he gripped Ryan's hand harder. Ryan's eyes crinkled with amusement.

"I'm Ryan."

"I know," Wyatt said stupidly. They weren't even shaking hands anymore, but holding them, and Wyatt wanted to hold more. He wanted to hold it *all*.

He wanted to know what those callouses felt like, deep inside him. He wanted to know if Ryan laughed in bed. He wanted to know if that tan went everywhere, or if there was paler, softer skin in places that the public didn't see.

Wyatt ignored the voice that said he couldn't have those things, and gripped Ryan's hand harder. He could be a different person, at least for tonight.

"Take me home," Ryan said quietly, earnestly, and Wyatt knew he was asking for something else completely.

He fully intended to take Ryan up on every single damn thing he was offering.

His motorcycle was around the corner, and when Wyatt tugged Ryan the right direction, to his surprise, Ryan held onto his hand. Refused to let go.

Wyatt told his ramshackle closet to fuck off, and they held hands the handful of blocks to where his bike was parked.

His hand was damp with nerves and the sharp pings of excitement flooding through his veins. His mind was swamped with a hundred fantasies, a thousand things he was dying to do with Ryan. But Wyatt knew he was only going to get a few hours. Maybe. If he was really fucking lucky. So he settled for the one that kept pushing itself to the forefront, and let out a shaky breath as Ryan settled behind him on his bike and wrapped his arms around Wyatt's waist.

His grip was tight, and Wyatt let his own hand drift down, fingertips grazing the muscular forearm resting against his t-shirt. He swore he felt goose bumps, and told himself to focus, before he killed them both.

Ryan hadn't told him where he lived, and that was fine by Wyatt, because he had no intention of taking him home just yet. He'd grown up in the LA area, before going to culinary school in New York, and the first thing he'd done when coming back to the west coast was re-acquaint himself with all the best biking roads around Mulholland and the Santa Monica mountains. He took them now, opening up the throttle, feeling the wind rush through his hair, Ryan's arms a steady, exhilarating pressure, never letting Wyatt forget what was at the end of this drive.

Well, not *quite* the end of the drive.

He took them to his favorite lookout, the one he'd come to as a teenager on his old shitty Indian, when he'd needed to get away from his brothers.

He wasn't running away from his brothers now, and he had a split second of nerves as he pulled into the dirt turnoff. Ryan's hands tensed around him, and then relaxed again. Wyatt parked his bike, and twisted in the seat, still ready to offer an apology, when calloused palms reached up, cradled his cheeks, his chin. Then Ryan's mouth was on his, and it was scorching with determination and purpose, tongue almost immediately in Wyatt's mouth, and he could only think, *I've got to feel those lips and that tongue on my dick before the night is out.*

It would be okay—he could be fine with only hooking up with Ryan for one night. He had to be. Because he couldn't imagine Ryan meant anything else. He was a broke line chef, not even a *sous*, who was still hiding from his grandmother.

There wasn't a lot that Wyatt could be proud of, but Ryan wanted him, and he intended to make good on it. Ryan climbed off the bike and Wyatt swung his legs around, leaning back against it, cradling Ryan between his legs.

His hands searched under Ryan's t-shirt, encountering tight, warm skin, only the tiniest bit chilled from their ride, and all those muscles he'd imagined he would find. Rippling abs, a pec that fit flawlessly into his hand. A tiny pebbled nipple that made Ryan groan into his mouth when Wyatt flicked it experimentally.

As far as Wyatt was concerned, Ryan went for his belt buckle too soon. Yeah, he was definitely hard, and he imagined Ryan would be too, if he followed the soft trail of hair down his chest, through the cut muscles of his abdomen. But he didn't want it to end so fast. He wanted more than just a quick, blazingly hot hand job. Even if they were on his bike and the road was just over there and anyone could drive by.

There was only a dim streetlight a few hundred yards away, but Wyatt could still see the dark intensity of Ryan's gaze as he pulled back. "You don't want to?" Ryan questioned, and there was definite disappointment in his voice.

Wyatt's voice was rough. "I've spent the whole night imagining this. Of course I want to."

"Then how do you want it?" Ryan gave Wyatt an experimental stroke through his jeans and his boxers, and he groaned. Yeah, he wanted those graceful and calloused hands all over his dick, but he also wanted his swollen lips wrapped around his cock. He wanted Ryan to bend him over the leather seat and open him wide to the cool night air, his thumbs brushing the inside of his cheeks and the furl of his hole. He wanted to fuck Ryan until they were both crying with it.

He wanted too much, and he'd experienced enough of life to know you never got everything you wanted. It was always better to temper your expectations. The problem was Wyatt couldn't do that tonight.

Not with Ryan.

He was still a stranger, but it didn't matter. Every time Ryan touched him, he went out of his mind. Every time Ryan smiled, it was the sweetest, most satisfying moment Wyatt had experienced in months. Maybe even in years.

But Wyatt knew he couldn't say any of that to Ryan. Not when he was clearly just looking for a quick hookup, so he kissed him instead. He wasn't stupid enough to believe that a kiss could make Ryan understand, but without the words, it was all he had.

He couldn't whisper it, and he couldn't scream it from the top of the tallest building in LA. His mouth, his hands, his body. That's what he had left.

Wyatt knew Ryan couldn't understand, but it was easy to imagine he had, because the kiss morphed from a solid wall of heat to something softer, something less driving and more meandering. A kiss that meant that they could take their time, even if they were on the side of the road.

Ryan followed Wyatt's lead and his fingers drifted up his abs, to his chest, touching everything under his t-shirt that he could reach.

Between kisses, Ryan murmured, "Are you sure you aren't a pro athlete?" He paused. "You're built like a fucking wall."

Wyatt took that as the compliment it was. "I'm actually a chef," he admitted.

Ryan laughed a little into the corner of Wyatt's mouth. His lips felt two sizes too big, and achingly sensitive, but he couldn't stop kissing Ryan. Couldn't get enough of the wondrous drugging feeling that took him over whenever their lips touched. Like everything, even if it all felt like it was going to shit, would be okay.

His dick was a solid, throbbing reminder that he was horny as hell, and just groping every inch of Ryan he could wasn't going to be enough. Or vice versa.

Finally, before Wyatt could say, *maybe I've finally had enough*, Ryan exhaled with a sharp, ragged breath and begged. "Can I, please?" he murmured into a particularly sensitive spot just behind Wyatt's ear. And because Wyatt didn't give a shit what Ryan wanted to do—he wanted whatever Ryan wanted—he simply nodded.

Ryan's hands went back to his jeans, unbuttoning and unzipping them, gently and carefully so that they didn't send the bike toppling over.

Not for the first time, Wyatt wondered if maybe he should have let the fantasy go, but then Ryan gestured for Wyatt to prop himself up against the bike, and lowered his mouth to the wet patch on his boxers.

His fingers dug into the leather seat, trying to steady himself, to control himself, as Ryan flicked out his tongue, tasting the wet of his pre-come on the cotton. When Ryan groaned, Wyatt had to echo him. It was so damn good already, and he'd barely touched him.

"Please," Wyatt whimpered, because even if he was dying to, there was no way he was going to last. And if all he got was some teasing, he would cry. He wanted Ryan's mouth on him, those sinfully full lips taking in his cock.

"Please what?" Ryan asked, fingers trailing up his bare thigh, tugging down his boxers finally. He knew what Wyatt wanted, he just wanted to make him crazy with need.

"Please . . . your god damn mouth," Wyatt ground out.

The moment Ryan's tongue curled around the head and then he sucked, Wyatt knew he was a dead man and the last five minutes of his life were going to be fucking brilliant.

"Knew you'd be good at this," Wyatt grunted, trying to be gentle as he reached down and cradled Ryan's head.

Then Ryan slid the rough pad on his finger to the back of his balls and pleasure exploded, whiting out his vision, making it almost impossible to avoid pressing Ryan's head down, begging him to take in more, to give him more.

There was only a split second before Wyatt knew he couldn't contain the building pressure anymore, and curled his hands possessively around Ryan's face, feeling the shape of his dick against Ryan's cheek, and it was all over.

The orgasm was like a roaring wave, overtaking him, emptying him out of everything—except this endless need to do it again, and again, and *again*.

"Sorry," Wyatt breathed out after he was able to speak again. "I'm so sorry." He'd been sort of rude, coming with almost no warning, assuming that Ryan would swallow.

But Ryan's expression as he stood was anything but pissed off. In fact, he looked smug as hell as he reached for Wyatt's hand, and placed it against his crotch. It was wet, and Wyatt stared at Ryan as he realized what had happened.

"You shouldn't be sorry," Ryan said. "Clearly I thought it was pretty damn hot."

The only problem with that was that now Wyatt wasn't going to get to take Ryan apart with his mouth, and his tongue and his fingers, or his cock. It didn't feel fair, and it left him feeling sort of hollow, now that this otherworldly encounter was drawing to an end.

"Well, uh, I just . . ." Wyatt didn't know what to say. His brain still felt sluggish after the orgasm of the millennium.

"It's okay," Ryan said, giving his thigh a reassuring squeeze. "I was staring at you too. And doing my own share of fantasizing. It was sort of inevitable."

"If you say so." Even though he'd had plenty of guys tell him how hot he was, Wyatt always had trouble accepting it. Especially now, from someone like Ryan. He could have had anyone he wanted, and he'd picked Wyatt.

"I do," Ryan said, and leaned over, kissing him again. Wyatt tasted himself on Ryan's tongue, and told himself that even if this was just a passing, quick thing to the other man, he wasn't going to forget. He would remember the rippled smoothness of skin over muscle, the strangled gasp Ryan had made when he'd pinched his nipple, the taste of his come on Ryan's tongue.

Finally, it was time for the inevitable. "I guess I'd better get you home," Wyatt said. "I promised I would."

"You strike me as the kind of guy who tries to keep his promises," Ryan said casually.

Wyatt thought he was, unless you were counting the many lies he'd told his own family about who he was. He nodded.

"Then, I guess there's nothing else for you to do," Ryan said, shooting Wyatt another one of those dimpled grins. It hurt that he seemed so casual about it, like none of this really mattered. And, Wyatt reminded himself, it probably didn't. Not to Ryan.

That was okay. Wyatt would have to be okay with it.

Ryan told Wyatt his address, and he punched it into his phone, quickly flicking through the map to make sure he knew the route. Wyatt only realized as they were near their destination, making their way up the coast, towards Santa Monica, that even though he'd had his phone out, Ryan hadn't given him his phone number.

It was hard to enjoy that last five minutes of Ryan wrapped around him, the cool night air whistling past them, because that *hurt*. It shouldn't have, because Ryan had never made him a single promise, or made a single assumption, but it still god damned ached.

But Wyatt didn't want to be *that guy*, the one who overshared and overstayed and didn't know when to quit, so he just smiled, and then smiled more, as Ryan got off the bike in front of the big double-gated entrance to his mansion.

"Thanks for the ride," Ryan said, and leaned over, brushing a single kiss across Wyatt's cheek. Somehow, that meant more than some torrid, heated kiss, but it still hurt more than Wyatt could have guessed when Ryan turned to go.

"See you around," Wyatt said stupidly, because he didn't know what else to say. He'd had hookups before, but none of them had ever felt like this.

It had never felt like someone had carved his heart out of his chest and had taken it with them when they left.

Ryan turned, and flashed Wyatt one last smile. "Yeah," he said, clearly amused by Wyatt's choice of parting remark, "I'll see you around."

Chapter Two

It was not ideal, but Wyatt went to his interview on a handful of hours of sleep and a melancholy edge to his mood. He was generally pretty easy-going, with a sunny, optimistic disposition. Becoming the leader of the family and being forced to put his beloved Nana in a memory care facility he couldn't really afford had changed him. He knew he'd gotten quieter and more withdrawn, a heap of serious problems he couldn't solve weighing him down.

Miles, his best friend, had told him last week that he was growing up. But Wyatt didn't think so. He was the same as always, he just needed something to take the edge off. Last night, Ryan had provided a much-needed distraction, a temporary lessening of the pressure he was living with, but it hadn't been enough.

In fact, coming to terms with the fact that Ryan was so temporary was part of what caused his latest bad mood. Even the thought that he could be making more money after today wasn't much of a consolation. "It's for a private chef position," was all Reed Ryan, the connection that had gotten Wyatt his interview, had said. Reed's description didn't exactly excite Wyatt. He didn't really want to stay at Terroir, and continue to get verbally abused by his boss, Bastian Aquino, for shitty pay, but he also didn't want to get paid to babysit and make peanut butter sandwiches with no crusts for a spoiled Beverly Hills family.

The fact that he badly needed the money was the only reason he showed up at all.

He was shown into the conference room in the trendy LA office building, and was just about to sit down at one end of the shining expanse of glass when a man entered the room, proving to Wyatt everything he'd assumed about this client.

The suit alone probably cost more than a year at Nana's facility, and Wyatt couldn't even begin to price out the watch. It was clearly expensive, real diamonds shining on the face, and the man wore it carelessly, like he had a dozen more. He probably did, Wyatt thought darkly. His face was scrunched tight and there was something untrustworthy about it, a slyness in the eyes that Wyatt couldn't miss. Wyatt didn't know if he could work for this man, even if the money was good.

"Hi, I'm Eric Talbot," the man said, extending a hand, which Wyatt shook firmly. He looked him in the eye, and tried to do everything else he remembered from that long-ago high school class in interview skills. Of course he'd had interviews after culinary school—for the jobs he'd gotten at other restaurants, and then at Terroir, but they were never like normal interviews. Nobody cared if you could communicate worth a damn in a restaurant; they only cared if you could cook.

"Wyatt Blake."

Eric settled down on one of the ultra-modern sculpted chairs, metal and clear acrylic married together in a tortured formation. Wyatt followed suit and waited a long, expectant moment for the interview to start.

"I'm sorry, we're waiting for the client," Eric said. "He's usually really punctual, but he texted me to say that traffic was brutal today."

This guy who looked like he could buy and sell Wyatt's whole family wasn't even the client? The client was even *richer*? Wyatt briefly considered telling him to just forget the whole thing, because this had been a huge mistake. He was meant to be in a restaurant kitchen. He was meant to wow patrons with his dazzling culinary skills. He wasn't meant to make peanut butter and jelly sandwiches and grilled chicken breasts with steamed vegetables on the side. Yet, he couldn't help but be relieved Eric Talbot wouldn't be his boss.

In the end, the only thing that kept Wyatt's butt in his seat were the bills that kept piling up. This job would be worth it, if Wyatt could keep them paid and at bay. The stress alone felt like it was slowly crushing him. Even making peanut butter and jelly sandwiches would be a decent exchange for a loosening of the noose around his neck.

"The client?" Wyatt asked. Reed had given him next to no information about this interview, other than date and time, and even Wyatt thought that was odd.

Weren't you supposed to do research and go prepared to these sorts of things? How could he research someone he didn't know?

"My client, actually," Eric Talbot said with a friendly grin that made him look marginally less like a bloodthirsty piranha. "I manage . . ."

Eric didn't get the rest of the sentence out before the door opened and Wyatt damned everything to hell and back.

This morning Ryan Flores was dressed in jeans and a sky-blue polo shirt, looking as fucking cute as he had the night before. Wyatt would have picked him up a hundred times out of a hundred, and there was no way it was a coincidence that Ryan had picked him up first and then just happened to be interviewing him today. Ryan didn't even look surprised that Wyatt was here, asking to join his staff. Wyatt tried to let that sink in. Ryan hadn't just been out of his league, he was in a different universe. *And* he was a liar. Somehow the former felt worse than the latter.

"Hi, I'm so sorry I'm late. I'm Ryan." Ryan extended his hand towards Wyatt, clearly having decided that he was going to play this like they had never met before, like they'd never hooked up, like he'd never pursued Wyatt at all. Like Wyatt hadn't wasted three hours of his life and a hookup with the hot angel bartender, staring at Ryan like he was something important and worthwhile.

"Wyatt." He stood, held out his hand to shake. He couldn't help but think about the night before, when he'd deliberately not shared his last name. And now it felt stupid and foolish, because Ryan must have known it the whole time. "Wyatt Blake."

It was impossible to avoid touching Ryan, but Wyatt kept the handshake brief, nothing like the intimate meeting of fingers and palms that they'd experienced the night before. Still, even the echo of it rocketed through Wyatt, and as he sat down, he slipped his hand under the table, clenching it painfully around his knee. He didn't want to be affected by Ryan's touch. Or the knowledge that Ryan had known they'd meet again this morning.

His words from the night before reverberated through Wyatt's brain. *Yeah, I'll see you around.*

The joke was definitely on Wyatt.

"Your resume is certainly impressive," Eric said, kicking off the interview portion. There was nothing Wyatt wanted more than to stop him right in his tracks, and walk out. Because whatever this was, he wasn't sure he wanted a part of it. But the starting salary kept him in the chair. Maybe it would be better to work for Ryan than to work for a spoiled family. It was theoretically possible, he surmised, and he should at least listen to the pitch.

"If I'm reading this correctly," Ryan said, glancing down at the copy of the resume that Eric had slid across the table to him, "you took a position demotion and a pay cut to work at Terroir."

"I did." At the time, with Nana not yet feeling the effects of her Alzheimer's, it had been a no-brainer. He'd saved on expenses by moving in with Miles and his other roommate, Xander, and it had been worth the demotion from *sous chef* to line cook, to work at Terroir, one of the most celebrated restaurants in the United States, and the only restaurant in California to have the difficult-to-obtain Michelin stars.

Ryan leaned back in his chair, so casual, like he hadn't been on his knees less than twelve hours ago. "Can you explain your thought process behind that decision?"

"It does look like an odd choice," Wyatt admitted. He wasn't happy about defending his decisions, but he would do it. "Even with the demotion, working at Terroir transformed my resume. It's one of the best restaurants in America. Working there proved that I could cook in one of the most demanding, exacting kitchens in the world."

Ryan tapped a pen on the glass conference table. "But now, you're leaving."

"I've worked there almost two years. It's time to move on." Wyatt didn't want to bring up the pressing financial situation that was forcing this change, but he had a feeling that Ryan and Eric had already dug up that information. Eric in particular didn't seem like the kind of guy who would leave anything to chance—and he wouldn't waste his time or his client's.

So even if Ryan was choosing to grill him, Wyatt had a feeling the job was essentially his. If he wanted it.

The million-dollar question of the day.

"This job requires someone who can manage themselves successfully. You mentioned that Terroir was demanding and exacting. I've heard Bastian Aquino can be a tough boss. Do you think you can successfully transition to working without supervision?" Eric asked.

Wyatt almost laughed. "Oh, definitely. In fact, it would be pretty welcome," he admitted wryly.

"You've never been head of a kitchen before," Ryan inserted.

"Sure, I have," Wyatt said. "My own kitchen. Is yours going to be so different?"

Ryan inclined his head, a hint of a smile on his face. "No. Actually, it shouldn't be."

"Can I ask why you even need a personal chef?" Wyatt asked. He figured it was fair that he interview Ryan—especially considering he'd obscured his motives last night—even as Ryan was interviewing him.

"I'm going to be doing more entertaining. It feels like I'm always sending out for food. It would be nice to not worry about it anymore. There would be nutrition guidelines provided by my trainer that you'd have to follow."

"Not a problem. I can easily integrate those into meal plans," Wyatt said.

"Do you have any more questions, Ryan?" Eric asked.

Ryan shook his head, and that basically ended the strangest interview of Wyatt's career. He couldn't imagine that Ryan wouldn't want to taste his food if he was going to be cooking for him every day. But then, he'd never worked for someone who integrated blowjobs into his interview prep before.

Ryan's behavior should be a turnoff—and it *was*—but it also left Wyatt curious. Even if Eric left, he didn't know if he could ask Ryan what had been the goal last night. He didn't know if he could bring up last night at all. Even before running into Ryan this morning, it had felt too raw to talk about.

"Here's the compensation package." Eric slid a single sheet of paper across the conference table. The starting salary listed had an extra digit than his current salary at Terroir. It was a no-brainer, even as his brain tried to talk him out of it.

He didn't know Ryan's intentions. His motives. Would he want to keep sleeping with Wyatt? Was this some sort of combined private chef/rent-boy position? Wyatt knew he should request to speak to Ryan in private and ask those questions, but instead he kept his mouth shut and nodded.

"When can you start?" Eric asked, like he had known if he threw money at Wyatt, he'd agree. And he, Wyatt thought bitterly, had been exactly right. He could totally be bought.

"I'll give my two weeks tomorrow," Wyatt said, clearing the bitterness out of his throat, "but I fully expect Aquino to kick me out immediately. He doesn't like it when staff leaves. So I'll be able to start in a few days."

"The job includes free rent at the ADU on the back of Ryan's house," Eric said. "I don't suppose you mind us running a background check. Standard procedure for anyone granted access to the property." Another paper slid across the glass, along with a pen, and Wyatt scribbled his name without even reading the verbiage. He didn't have anything to hide—unless the tryst he'd had with Ryan counted, and maybe it didn't.

After all, Ryan was out of the closet. He could do whatever the fuck he wanted, including hook up with some random guy he met at Temple.

"Great," Eric said. "I'll also make sure to issue you a credit card for food purchases, and for any equipment purchases for the kitchen. Anything over $500 requires Ryan's approval. But it's pretty well-stocked already."

Wyatt took that with a grain of salt. Well-stocked had different meanings to a professional chef than it did a sports agent who probably hadn't been in a kitchen in years.

Ryan waved a hand, and gave Wyatt an intimate smile that made his stomach clench. "Don't worry about it. You can get whatever you need."

Eric shot his client a hard look. "We talked about this."

"Yeah, we did," Ryan retorted. "And I made my decision." If Eric wondered why Ryan would trust someone he'd only met for five minutes, he didn't question it.

Eric rolled his eyes but didn't say another word, simply got to his feet, indicating the interview was over. If it had even been an interview at all. "Nicole at the front will have the paperwork for you to fill out," he said. "I expect you'll let us know when you can officially start." He held out his hand, and Wyatt stood to shake it again, and before he realized what was about to happen, he was alone again with Ryan.

Wyatt tensed. He didn't want to have this conversation. Could he escape still? Claim he had to get back to Napa? Claim he had a desperate need to fill out paperwork?

Shoving his hands in his pockets, Ryan shot Wyatt an endearing smile. He looked more nervous now than he had picking up Wyatt last night. How was that even possible?

"I hope this is all okay," Ryan said.

Wyatt was annoyed by how endeared he was. You wanted to manipulate him? Fine, just don't pretend like you hadn't. "I wouldn't have agreed if it wasn't okay."

Ryan's smile brightened, and Wyatt was frustratingly reminded of his own expressed desire to get him to smile more. He would be in a serious position to do that, if he chose to, now. But he was feeling backed into a corner, and the thought didn't fill him with any anticipation.

"I'm glad you did."

"I'm sure you are," Wyatt said, and some of his frustration leaked into his voice. He wasn't nearly as good at fronting as Ryan was. And that just annoyed him even more.

"I want us to be friends," Ryan said.

Wyatt stared at him blankly. Seriously, *friends?* "You just hired me. I'm your employee."

Ryan shrugged, like this was hardly a barrier to friendship. "Then you're going to be around all the time. It'll be great."

"Great," Wyatt echoed. "Yeah. Definitely."

"You can always text Eric when you're going to be coming back to LA," Ryan said, "or you can always just text me. That would probably be easier. Eric is terrible at passing on messages."

It was impossible not to remember how fucking much Wyatt had wanted Ryan's number last night. How disillusioned he'd been when Ryan had not even brought it up. And now he was offering it, willingly. Wyatt, who knew just how much he and his bank account needed this job, was still struck by a petty desire to shred the contract he'd just signed.

He did not need this bullshit in his life.

Of course that didn't stop him from agreeing, and whipping out his phone to type Ryan's number in it. It didn't stop him from texting Ryan back, so that he'd have his number in his phone, and it didn't stop him from smiling despite all the irritation swirling inside him when he left Ryan to finish signing the paperwork that would tie them together.

"You're going to need to find a new roommate," Wyatt said that night to Xander and Kian when he walked in the house, to watch them vegging out on the worn couch, watching re-runs of *Iron Chef*. The dubbed English originals. Not the execrable US remake.

He loved Alton Brown, but seriously he should have stuck to *Good Eats*.

"We already found one," Kian said, barely even looking up from the TV. Someone was butchering an enormous swordfish, and he was staring intently at the process. Probably because Aquino had decided he was going to cut down all his own fish now, and Kian was desperately studying up.

"I didn't even know when I left yesterday that I'd get the job," Wyatt said, still annoyed. The six-hour drive back to Napa hadn't helped clear his head. He'd spent the whole time trying to forget the feel of his hands on the leather seat as Ryan had taken him apart with his mouth. Or the feeling of Ryan's mouth, period.

It hadn't worked.

"Of course you were going to get the job," Xander inserted with irritation. "Did you expect us to sit back and not try to find someone new when you were gonna bail?"

This was typical Xander. Usually Wyatt could brush off his abrasive comments, but he was a little tender today. "Who is it?"

"It's uh . . . I think it's going to be good. For us. I mean. Not for you. Probably." Kian stuttered awkwardly every other word and couldn't look Wyatt in the eye. It made it very obvious who he was talking about.

"There's not going to be enough room in the closet for all his shoes. Or his wine," Wyatt said.

"How did you know it was Nate?" Xander demanded. "Did he text you to ask if it was okay?"

Wyatt had blocked Nate's phone number the week after they'd broken up, so *no*, but there was a limited number of people who Xander would willingly live with, and the main thing they all had in common was that they brought something to the relationship. Nate was a sommelier who worked for one of Napa's larger wineries, and so had connections as well as access to pretty decent wine on a regular basis.

"I thought he was living with that new guy of his . . . Rabe? Rake? Rage? I can't remember." Wyatt had known he was over Nate when he had heard about him moving in with the new guy and hadn't even blinked twice.

"Rafe," Kian said. "And they broke up. I guess Nate found him in bed with someone when he came home unexpectedly."

Wyatt raised an eyebrow. "Someone?"

"His boss," Xander added. "Phillippa Winchester."

"That must have been a shock," Wyatt said. He was basically relieved that both Kian and Xander were more into the hot gossip that Nate's new boyfriend was hooking up with his female boss, and that he didn't have to discuss anything to do with his new job or *his* new boss.

Or that they had also hooked up.

"He was so angry, he stormed right out. Spent the afternoon drinking cosmos on the patio at Terroir. I had to practically pour him into the car and then drop his drunk ass off." Xander did not sound pleased about this. "But the silver lining is that we have a third roommate again."

"You're going to hate living with him. You hated him when we were dating." Wyatt was very happy he was not going to be around to witness any of the shit Nate and Xander were going to give each other.

"Probably." Xander sounded resigned to this. "Beggars can't be choosers."

"Just don't hook up with him," Wyatt warned, even when he knew his warning would be ignored.

Not that Xander would actually hook up with him. No. He would let Nate work for it, and then turn him down, because Xander was a dick that way and also didn't like to hook up with anyone too close to home.

At least that was what Xander had always claimed whenever Wyatt and Miles went out in Napa and tried to convince him to come with them. But then maybe he just liked being celibate. Who knew.

"Like I would ever stoop that low." Xander smirked. "So what are you moving to LA for? Chasing fame and ass like Miles?"

Wyatt scoffed. "Like I care about that." He really didn't want to talk about his new job in LA—or who he was going to be working for. But Xander seemed determined to weasel it out of him.

"No," Xander said contemplatively. "But you're chasing something."

Stability, Wyatt thought, *and Ryan Flores.*

He'd gone to LA seeking the first, but never imagining he'd find the second.

"The interview was for a position as a private chef, for a high-profile athlete," Wyatt finally admitted.

"Who?" Kian asked, finally tearing his attention away from the fish butchering on *Iron Chef*.

"He doesn't want to tell us," Xander said, voice sneering just the tiniest bit.

"It's Ryan Flores, okay?" Wyatt snapped. He must really be torn up if Xander was managing to push his buttons. Usually he was able to steer clear of his friend and roommate's bad moods. But today, he'd drove right into the middle of one, and masochistically, he hadn't just walked away.

He did feel responsible for leaving them without a third roommate to split costs with, and forcing Xander to either accept a stranger or offer Wyatt's room to Nate.

"Oh, he's that cute baseball player," Kian said.

Xander said nothing, just stared moodily at the screen.

"It's a good job," Wyatt said. "He's going to be a good boss, I think."

"A lot different than Chef Aquino, that's for sure," Kian said, that worshipfulness edge appearing in his voice on cue, like it did every single damn time he talked about their illustrious boss and the owner of Terroir.

"Sometimes I think you like it when the Bastard tortures you," Xander said. And Wyatt was selfishly glad that Xander's bad mood had transferred from him to Kian. And he loved Kian. Kian was the sweetest of puppy dogs, and definitely did not deserve Xander's frustration.

Except that he totally enjoyed it when Bastian Aquino tortured him. And Wyatt knew that fact worried the hell out of both him and Xander.

"Don't call him that," Kian said automatically, and that was Wyatt's cue to check out. Go back to his room, and throw his shit in a duffel bag, donate the furniture to Nate who had picked out most of it anyway, and call it a night. He didn't have any doubts that he wouldn't make it through the dinner service tomorrow.

He probably wouldn't make it through giving his notice unscathed. Bastian Aquino's nickname was the Bastard for a reason.

"I'm going to pack," Wyatt announced to his friends, who were now glowering at each other. He didn't need any problems to add to his teetering pile, but he felt personally responsible for the fact that Kian and Xander were going to bicker all the time without him to intervene or distract, and Nate sure as hell wouldn't help out. He wasn't completely self-centered, but he was pretty damn close to it.

"Do you think Chef Aquino will let you work the two weeks?" Kian asked, even though they all knew the answer. Chef Aquino never let anyone finish their two weeks, except Miles, who had gone to professionally film his video blog series, *Pastry by Miles*. And the only reason Miles had gotten an exemption was because Aquino never cut his nose off to spite his face.

If Miles made it onto the Cooking Channel or some shit, which he and his boyfriend and producer, Evan, were always chattering about, then Aquino was going to want a piece of that action, and he was going to want to say that he'd groomed Miles and then kindly wished him on his way.

Wyatt was abandoning Terroir for a private chef job. Basically, for *money*, and Aquino, who despite having plenty of money of his own, hated that.

It should have bothered him. It should have made him even a little sad. But Wyatt found he couldn't wait to leave and head south.

To stability, and to Ryan.

Wyatt had known tying up all his loose ends in Napa would be easy. For someone who loved stability, he lived a surprisingly simple existence. His belongings—clothes, laptop, books, knives, his sous-vide—they all fit in two duffels and a handful of boxes. His furniture he donated to Xander and Kian to keep for Nate. If he knew Nate at all, he would refuse to argue with Rage or Rake or whatever the fuck he was called to get any of his own furniture back. All Nate really cared about was his clothes and his shoes and his fucking wine, anyway.

He typed out probably the shortest letter in the history of the world, giving his notice. One line, and it probably wasn't even a complete sentence. But he didn't believe Aquino would even waste time reading it, and he certainly wasn't going to reminisce fondly over the job he was leaving.

Someday, Wyatt let himself think, *someday*, I'm going to have a job where I respect people and they respect me back, and maybe I even get to call the shots. A job where I get to make the big decisions and when people love the food, it'll be because of me.

He wasn't naïve enough to think the job with Ryan was going to be like that. He was technically free of the Bastard's iron fist, but he was really only changing one controlling boss for another, slightly less controlling one. There were still going to be rules. Cook this meal, prep this week of lunches, make this protein shake every morning, follow all these dietary guidelines. Would a little bit more freedom really feel life-changing?

Wyatt didn't think so. The only life-changing part of this was the stupendous starting salary. *That* would change his life, and alleviate much of his stress.

With that thought on his mind, Wyatt drove his bike over to the memory care facility he'd moved his nana to a few months earlier.

She had gone reluctantly, and even Wyatt could acknowledge that she might not have needed the amount of care they could provide just yet, but he was terrified of getting a phone call in the middle of the night that she'd wandered away from her house or set something on fire because she'd forgotten she was using the stove.

It was a Friday afternoon, when Wyatt was usually at work, so it was great to be able to surprise her.

She was sitting by the window in her room, book upside down in her lap, eyes drifting across the gardens behind the home. The beautiful grounds had been one of the main reasons why Wyatt had picked this place for her—even if he couldn't really afford to. He'd desperately wanted to give her something beautiful, even as her life progressed further into the dark.

"Nana," he said softly, jerking her from her daydreams. She glanced up, blue eyes still bright even at her age, and the recognition in them was immediate.

Every time he came, he dreaded the first moment, the first time she might not recognize him. So far it hadn't happened, but the possibility was always there, twisting his stomach into knots.

"Wyatt," she exclaimed, getting to her feet, the book sliding to the floor with a thud. She glanced down in surprise, his gaze tracking her own, and he saw the astonishment in it.

She'd forgotten the book was on her lap. It could be the sort of momentary memory lapse everyone experienced—or it could be her disease progressing. Wyatt's stomach twisted again, but instead of letting the worry show, he smiled wide, crossing the room and wrapping her slight form in a big hug.

To him, as a boy, as a teenager, and even as a grown man, she'd always been larger than life. It was hard to feel her bony limbs under his hands as he led her to the small sofa that faced her TV.

"I didn't expect you today," Beatrice Blake said, her eyes shining like Wyatt had done something amazing, even though he still felt he wasn't doing enough.

"Had the day off," Wyatt said. He tangled his fingers in hers and held tight. Tight to anchor her to this world, and not lose her to the next. "For an interview in Los Angeles, actually."

Her smile dimmed a little, worry clouding her gaze. He'd told her a million times not to worry about the money after he'd taken over her finances, but she did anyway. "What's this new job? It can't possibly be better than Terroir."

"It's way better than Terroir," Wyatt said, and found that he wasn't even lying to her, though he had been prepared to. "It's for a really nice baseball player. He needs a private chef. It'll be a great opportunity to run my own kitchen."

Her pride in him radiated out of her sweet, barely wrinkled face. She'd never have admitted it to anyone, but she'd always been a little vain. And Wyatt liked to slip her the face cream she loved so much, and had always used religiously, even though it was expensive.

"He's a baseball player?" Bea asked.

"He plays for the Dodgers," Wyatt confirmed. "I think it's going to be a great opportunity."

"But you're moving." Her face fell a little. He already knew what she was thinking; she might not see him very much. Wyatt reminded himself to send his brothers a guilt text, trying to get them over here to see her more often, so she wouldn't be lonely.

"I'm going to be up here at least once a week, though," Wyatt insisted. "The nice thing about working for Ryan is that he's going to be on the road a lot, and I won't always be needed in LA."

"I'm just happy you're doing something for you," Nana said, a fierce edge to her voice. She might look delicate, with her spun sugar white hair in a cloud around her worn, pale face, but her blue eyes were still bright and she still wanted the very best for him. Would *fight* for the very best for him. Which was why he'd never told her about the shit that went down regularly at Terroir, or that he was taking this new job for the money, so she'd be properly taken care of.

"Tell me about what you've done this week," Wyatt said. He didn't want to lie to her. He *would*, but he didn't want to.

"It's so nice here, Wyatt," she said. "They have such nice people. And we do fun things. They take me to Mass every week. There's an art instructor once a week and we're working on a painting. I didn't think I had an artistic bone in my body, but it looks okay."

"You'll have to show it to me when it's done," he said.

She blushed. "I don't know about that. It's not exactly fine art."

"I don't care," Wyatt vowed. "I still want to see it."

"Your brothers came to see me, a few days ago," Bea said.

Something in her voice worried Wyatt. He trusted his brothers because he knew they weren't bad, trusted that they loved Nana too, but they could be careless. Selfish. "Was it good to see them?"

"Tony has a new girlfriend." Tony *always* had a new girlfriend. Wyatt barely refrained from rolling his eyes. "And Marco, I guess he got fired." That also didn't come as a surprise. Marco liked to drink more on work nights than was appropriate and probably had called in one too many days at the auto shop he worked at. "But, he tells me," Bea continued, "that he thinks he can convince the owner to rehire him."

Wyatt did roll his eyes this time, and she tapped him firmly on the shoulder. "I saw that, Wyatt."

"If they wouldn't be *so* predictable," Wyatt said.

"They're your brothers," Bea said, switching into Nana Lecture Mode, "and someday, they're going to be all the family you have left. You take care of family. Blakes always take care of family."

Something he'd been hearing his whole life. "I remember."

"When they were here, Tony and Marco didn't even say anything about you having an interview."

Wyatt hadn't told them. Hadn't much seen the point. He and his brothers were so different, and the two of them so similar, that he'd felt so many times like the outsider to their partnership. It made it hard to call or text. Especially now, that he was the only one who'd taken on the burden of Nana's care.

It *wasn't* a burden, Wyatt mentally corrected. He was grateful and privileged that he could. If only it didn't hang on his shoulders so heavily sometimes.

"I just found out about it, had to beg Chef Aquino for two days off and rush down to LA."

"And you're sure about this?" she asked, looking intently at him. "I don't want you to be unhappy."

"It's going to be good, I promise. Better for me, better for you." That was all he could say before the tears clogged his throat. He cleared it, hoping that she wasn't so aware that she'd somehow missed the flash of emotion.

"I brought you something," he said, reaching for the bag he'd brought in, hoping he could distract her. "Miles made them for you."

"Macarons?" she asked excitedly. Who would have ever thought his dear nana, Irish and traditionalist to the core, would love French pastries? Miles, that's who. And who packed her a box every time he knew Wyatt was going to see her.

"Lemon almond and raspberry chocolate," Wyatt said. "And some other strange flavors he wouldn't tell me, so I'm not taking responsibility for Miles' weird flavor combinations."

"He's a dear," Nana said, opening the box with excitement in her voice. She glanced up at him conspiratorially. "Do you think it would be wrong of me not to share these?"

"I think you should keep them if you want to," Wyatt said.

"But, Wyatt," she said earnestly. "God is always watching."

Wyatt sure hoped God hadn't been watching last night when he'd been with Ryan.

Every time she brought up God or religion, that was usually his cue to leave. It wasn't like he didn't want to tell her that he was gay. Or that he thought she'd shun him or be disgusted by him. Her beliefs were part of who she was. She'd been raised that way, and spent her whole life going to Mass. She was one of the strongest, most loyal people he'd ever met. Wyatt knew she loved him, unconditionally. But fear was irrational and he couldn't banish it and he couldn't bear to push her away from him by telling the truth.

Especially not now.

"I have to get ready to go into work, Nana," he said, rising to his feet. "Enjoy the macarons and your art class this week." He dropped a quick kiss on a papery thin cheek and felt his stomach twist again.

"Take care of yourself, darling," Bea said as he turned to leave.

If Bea had had any idea what was in store for Wyatt, she might have worried.

Which was exactly why Wyatt hadn't told her.

Bastian Aquino, AKA the Bastard, and the owner of the only Michelin-starred restaurant in California, stared down at the paper Wyatt had placed in front of him. His resignation letter.

"What is this?" Chef Aquino demanded. "What is this bullshit?" He snatched up the letter and looked ready to shred it to pieces. Wyatt wouldn't have been surprised. He'd seen it happen before and not just with paper. With homemade pasta. With fresh lettuce leaves. With a lamb chop lollipop he'd decimated, only the bone remaining. Never mind the gleaming white porcelain dishes. They routinely ended up chipped and mangled in the trash, their contents spilled across the walls of the kitchen, shards sprinkled across the floors.

It was a rare service when the Bastard didn't break *something*.

"My resignation," Wyatt said, making sure to keep his voice toneless, edgeless. Praying he wouldn't upset Aquino more than he had to.

"What, is working for the best restaurant in the world not good enough for you anymore?" Aquino sneered. "Do you fancy yourself somehow better than *my* kitchen? Feel like your shitty grillwork might be good enough to make it someplace else?"

Wyatt had a fantastic, intuitive touch with meat, especially on the grill. It was not easy, but still doable, to push that insult away and leave it behind him.

Mostly because he was going to be leaving this place and this asshole behind. Probably very shortly.

"Did someone even hire your sloppy ass?" Bastian demanded.

"Yep." Wyatt had absolutely zero intention of telling him who it was. There was a single, heart-stopping moment where they just stared at each other, Bastian's nostrils flaring with his terrible temper.

"Well fine," Bastian roared, sweeping a big hand across his desk, sending the resignation letter flying, along with cookbooks, recipe cards, a whole mug of pencils and pens, and his wireless keyboard.

The resulting clutter brought Kian to the doorway, which Wyatt had been hoping to avoid, yet also knew was inevitable.

"Get out," Bastian growled, and because Wyatt was smart, he did what he was told.

He should have spared a single sympathetic glance for Kian, who was about to head into the lion's den and be eaten alive, all because of Wyatt's defection, but he didn't. He wasn't that good of a person, apparently.

Chapter Three

"Do you think he figured it out?" Ryan's best friend in the whole world sipped her chai latte and eyed him with a keen blue stare that could sniff out a lie no matter how good it was.

Ryan was a terrible liar, and after being friends for three years, he'd learned it was always better to tell Tabitha King the truth.

"Do I think he figured out that it was weird I happened to pick him up the night before the interview? Yeah, he's not an idiot. He figured out something was up. I guess I should have told him it wasn't planned. I recognized him from the photo they'd sent with his resume, and well," Ryan shrugged, "he was so cute in person and suddenly it made sense. Two birds, one stone. A chef *and* a boyfriend."

Ryan pleated the empty sugar packet next to his coffee cup and wished that he'd texted Tabitha like he'd planned and canceled their coffee date. He was feeling weirdly guilty over his hookup with Wyatt, even though it had been unexpectedly spectacular, and he didn't want to rehash all his ugly emotions with her.

The first problem was that he'd chickened out at the last moment and went anyway, and the second problem was Tabitha was the universal expert at rehashing ugly emotions.

"You *like* him," Tabitha stated, looking very delighted at this turn of events. Ryan was not delighted at all. He was regretting the whole damn thing, even while acknowledging that it was the right thing to do under the circumstances. And all that conflict was making him feel queasy. The three sugars he'd thoughtlessly poured into his coffee weren't helping. He pushed the cup aside, wishing he could get something else to wash away the overly sweet taste lingering on his tongue. But Tabitha already knew something was up, and also that he really didn't want to talk about it.

"I thought that was the point," he pointed wryly.

"I still think you should have picked one of those randos you like hooking up with."

Ryan was glad he'd stopped drinking his coffee because he might have choked. He'd known Tabitha for three years now; he should long be used to her frank way of speaking, but she still managed to surprise the hell out of him once in awhile.

"First off, they're not *randos*, and second," Ryan paused with exaggerated faux affront, "I don't *like* hooking up with them."

"You don't like it?" Tabitha raised a flawlessly groomed blonde eyebrow. "That must be rather odd. I had this notion that sex was generally an enjoyable act."

"It is." Ryan ground his teeth together. "You know what I mean. I don't *enjoy* it because they're random guys, but a relationship just isn't for me."

Tabitha rolled her eyes. "Just because *one* relationship turned sour doesn't mean that every relationship will."

"It didn't turn sour. It became too damn boring," Ryan said.

"And yet, a relationship is exactly what you are hoping to achieve," Tabitha said, setting her latte down with a pointed click on the marble tabletop. "How do you propose to stay un-bored with Wyatt?"

"It's not going to be a real relationship," Ryan said. "You know that."

"It's real enough that you like him. It's real enough that you hired him to cook you egg white omelets every morning and grill your chicken every night. He's going to practically live in your backyard. That seems pretty damn real to me."

"I'm attracted to him. The sex was fantastic. If it's not serious and it's not real, I can't imagine why the sex wouldn't stay fantastic. And once in awhile, he'll come with me and we'll hold hands and get papped We'll host dinner parties and post sappy Instagram pics. And that'll fix all my problems."

"Sappy Instagram posts and holding hands in public once in awhile aren't going to solve everything," Tabitha said, sounding faintly exasperated. "*You* know that," she echoed him. Her eyes flitted to the coffee cup he'd bought and hadn't drank.

His stomach was still churning with all the sugar he didn't usually drink, but he still picked up his cup and took a healthy gulp, meeting Tabitha's eyes with a challenging glance of his own. "It'll fix enough," Ryan said. "The rest, I can fix on my own."

Tabitha let out an exasperated sigh. "I can't believe Eric fucking Talbot convinced you that you had to do this."

"You just don't like him," Ryan said. Which was true. Tabitha had hated his agent since day one—before Ryan and Tabitha had even met the first time, she'd hated Eric Talbot. But Ryan couldn't deny that the guy had done a very good, very aggressive job as his agent. He'd known that was what he needed, considering that even before the draft, Ryan had planned on coming out of the closet.

To his credit, Eric had not flinched once when told this, and had proceeded to make deals and eke every dollar out of Ryan's promo deals, despite that he was going to be the first professional baseball player to be out.

So when Eric said that Ryan had a problem with the new general manager of the Dodgers, and that he might choose not to sign Ryan to a new contract, Ryan couldn't help but believe him. No matter what Tabitha said.

"I hate him," Tabitha said, draining the final drops of her latte and setting the cup decisively on the table. "So when are you going to tell Mr. Blake that you've hired him as more than your personal chef?"

"I don't know," Ryan confessed. Eric had wanted to offer both jobs at the same time, and let Wyatt take his pick, but Ryan had vetoed that because after their hookup the night before, he wanted Wyatt. And Ryan knew Wyatt wouldn't agree right away.

But if Ryan could work a little charm on him? Convince him it was necessary? Seduce him with another few rounds of really good sex? Ryan's chances looked better.

"You're not going to tell him right away." Tabitha crossed her arms across her chest and looked even more pissed than when Ryan had brought up Eric Talbot.

"How can I and get him to say yes?"

Tabitha stood abruptly, and Ryan scrambled after her, as she gathered her purse and headed to the door of the café.

"Where are you going?" Ryan asked, even though he already knew.

"To go yell at your tiny-dick agent," Tabitha said between clenched teeth, turning in the direction of her car, heels clicking determinedly on the sidewalk.

"If you don't think I don't see his ugly fingers all over this, then I'm a lot blinder than you were counting on. You're *better* than this, Ryan."

Despite already convincing Wyatt to take the chef job—or maybe because of it—Ryan's day was already shitty. He did not want to spend the next two hours separating his best friend and his agent in order to prevent them from kicking the shit out of each other.

Tabitha had never explicitly told him all the unsavory things she'd had to do in her career as a sports journalist, but he'd heard enough to know she'd crawled through mud and shit and blood. And not all metaphorically either. Men she hadn't liked had touched her and they'd believed they deserved that privilege.

There was an underside to professional athletics that was dark and seedy as hell. Ryan had always prided himself on avoiding it, but he knew he was sinking into the mud with this fake relationship.

But the same panic that he felt every time he thought about being traded or his contract expiring streaked through him. Shouldn't he do everything he could to prevent either possibility?

"I'm not saying don't do it," Tabitha said softer, empathy in her eyes as she reached out to squeeze his arm. "I'm saying how you go about it is the difference between sliding into the shit and rising above it. You're a riser."

Ryan raised an eyebrow and they both burst out laughing. "I'm going to text Cal and tell him you told me I was a riser," he said and Tabitha made a face, but she was still smiling.

"Like my boyfriend would actually believe I saw your dick," Tabitha retorted, rolling her eyes.

"I'm telling him anyway."

Tabitha sighed. "I'm telling you—be honest. Lay it all out on the line. Give him the option to stay your chef. I wouldn't complain if there was something edible in your fridge."

"I'll tell him in a few days. Give him time to settle in." Ryan shoved his hands into the pockets of his jeans. If he said more, if he said he was also panicking at the thought of Wyatt turning him down, Tabitha would know he *really* liked him. And she was suspicious enough as it was. He didn't need to give her any more reasons to deploy her well-meaning interference.

"Just . . . soon." Tabitha's eyes had softened, but they sharpened abruptly back into knife points. "And don't let that fucktard convince you to do anything else."

The fucktard was waiting in the driveway, having an intense conversation in his car over his Bluetooth.

It wasn't like Ryan *denied* Eric was a fucktard, but he was Ryan's fucktard, with Ryan's leash tied really tightly around his neck. Ryan reminded himself firmly of this fact as he got out of his own car, and walked over to where Eric had parked.

Eric hung up with a barked order and Ryan braced himself for an argument, because basically everything with Eric ended up an argument. Sometimes Ryan thought Eric argued because he didn't even know how to do anything else.

"I got a text from your new guy," Eric said. "As expected, Aquino threw him out when he gave his notice, so he'll be here sometime tomorrow. Probably afternoon-ish. Do you want me to be here, to go over the rest of the expectations?"

Rest of the expectations. What a nice, polite way of saying Ryan would expect him to pretend to be his boyfriend and definitely not pretend to fuck him on a regular basis. And how unlike Eric to shy away from putting it bluntly.

"Don't bother. I'll tell him myself."

"You're not changing your mind, are you?" Eric demanded.

"No. But I want to give him an out, if he's not okay with it."

"You said you two hooked up, and it was good. Why wouldn't he want to?"

"Why wouldn't he want to play my boyfriend? I don't know, maybe he just doesn't want to. Not everyone is incredibly mercenary like you," Ryan said with an eye roll as punctuation. "Anyway, if he doesn't want to, he can stay on like he planned, as my personal chef, and we'll find someone else for the boyfriend."

"Who else?" Eric said impatiently, drumming his hands on the fire engine red hood of his Maserati. "Do you even have someone in mind?"

"Not at this time."

"I have things lined up . . ." Eric started in, voice growing more intense by the second, and Ryan didn't want to hear it, because he already knew it and also because Eric really was a fucktard.

"We'll cross that bridge when we come to it," Ryan interrupted with a harsh edge to his voice. "*If* Wyatt says no."

"So when are you going to ask him?" Eric snapped.

"Soon," Ryan said. Reminded himself again that Eric worked for *him*, and whatever he wanted to do, however he wanted to proceed, everything was ultimately up to him. Eric couldn't make decisions for Ryan, he could only advise.

Eric digested this, and even though he clearly wanted to demand a specific date, probably even a specific time, if Ryan knew Eric at all, he didn't. Definitely a good thing because Eric would have gone postal if he'd discovered Ryan intended to wait a few days. At least until Wyatt got settled in, and wasn't a total stranger.

Ryan didn't expect Wyatt to trust him so quickly, but he at least needed to show Wyatt that he wasn't a manipulative jerk. Tabitha had been right about that; like she was right about so many things.

"I also have the details of the new Adidas shoot," Eric said, following Ryan as he keyed in the garage code and ducked through the opening door.

"You could have emailed it over," Ryan said, annoyed that Eric hadn't taken a hint and *left*. He walked into the kitchen, and grabbed a water bottle from the fridge. He didn't offer Eric one and pointedly drank deeply as Eric leaned over the island counter and went over the main points of the new Adidas commercial shoot Ryan was doing soon.

"I asked them to try to downplay some of the more LGBT-friendly symbols," Eric said. "It's a contract year. I want them to emphasize that you're an athlete. A pro athlete."

Ryan made a face. "I wish you hadn't told them that. We can emphasize I'm an athlete some other way. You can get me another one of those *Men's Health* covers or something. I love that Adidas is ready and willing to embrace that I'm gay. That was why we signed with them instead of Nike."

"You can definitely do better than *Men's Health*," Eric scoffed, clearly changing the subject, which annoyed Ryan even more. "I think we can get *Sports Illustrated,* maybe even for their Opening Day special issue."

"You really think you can convince *Sports Illustrated* to pick me, instead of any of the other dozens of high-profile baseball players?" Ryan was not convinced. He had had a good year last year, and he'd made his mark in the playoffs the year before that. He'd already been a household name because he'd come out before the draft, but he was definitely beginning to be recognized for his baseball skills. As far as he was concerned, it had taken too long, though Eric kept telling him he was doing even better than the ten-year plan.

Eric was a fucktard, but he also had a ten-year plan for Ryan, which made hating him difficult. The ten-year plan also made deliberately circumventing Eric's ideas pretty stupid. Ryan usually tried to follow them, but this was a subject he was definitely willing to draw a line about.

"It's not decided yet, of course," Eric said, "but I feel good about your chances."

"I don't care. Call Adidas back," Ryan said with clipped tones.

Ryan saw Eric hold himself back for a second time in the last fifteen minutes, and that was basically a record, so it was probably better to end this conversation now, before Eric lost his temper and so did Ryan. They'd been working together for over three years now, and he'd learned that everything was just smoother if he could bring Eric around to his way of thinking without having to yell at him.

"You're sure?" Eric asked skeptically.

"Was I sure three years ago when I sat in your office for the first time and said I wanted to come out before the draft?" Ryan demanded. His temper was definitely fraying at the edges. He squished the plastic bottle in his hands and it made a satisfyingly loud crackling noise.

To his credit, Eric looked him straight in the eye. "You told me you had balls enough for both of us. I'd never had a client who questioned my balls before."

"There you go," Ryan said, tossing the bottle in the recycling bin. "Find them and call Adidas back."

Eric sighed. "Alright. I'll email you after I do."

He left without much of a goodbye, but that was fine by Ryan because he knew they were both on the edge, and the one thing he'd always sort of liked—at least *respected*—about Eric was that he knew when to quit.

Ryan flopped down on the couch in his media room and picked up the remote, even though he really didn't want to watch TV. Whenever he was this keyed up, all temper and fizzy emotions shook up with nowhere to go, he usually opened Grindr and found a hookup. Worked off his extra energy the good, old-fashioned way.

But he couldn't do that now. He was going to be in a relationship shortly—even if it was a fake one—and the only rule that Eric had laid down, with no exceptions, was that Ryan's hooking up days were over.

"Too many stories, too many rumors," was what Eric had said bluntly. "The GM doesn't like it. And if the GM doesn't like it, he doesn't like you, and then he has the ammunition not to re-sign you. And that's the last thing we want to cultivate in a contract year."

It was why they had landed on the idea of a fake relationship in the first place. The GM wanted to see Ryan steady and dedicated, on and *off* the field, because in his small, homophobic mind, being gay meant being a flighty party boy. And then Ryan had been dumb enough to give him the evidence to believe he was right.

The boyfriend was supposed to prove the opposite. But it also meant that Ryan had to walk the walk. Ryan didn't want to, but he wanted to stay in LA and play baseball more.

He couldn't help but wish Wyatt had gotten here today, instead of in a few days. Wyatt would have known what to do with all his excess energy.

Ryan flipped his phone over, the generic action movie on the TV all but forgotten. The little app icon for Grindr tempted him for half a second, but Eric had done a good job convincing him the temptation wouldn't be worth the risk. So he clicked on another icon instead.

Sorry that Aquino kicked you out, he typed out right under Wyatt's single "Hi" that he'd sent so that Ryan would have his number.

Ryan couldn't help but wonder, as he stared at the text screen, if Wyatt hadn't been annoyed at being deceived, that he might have sent something different. Something playful. Something flirtatious. Maybe even something sexy.

A ding from his phone made Ryan jump.

It wasn't exactly a surprise, Wyatt texted back. **Aquino has a temper. And he hates it when people leave.**

After the interview, Ryan had actually done a little research on Bastian Aquino, Wyatt's old boss. And after reading a handful of articles, he'd been surprised that anyone could tolerate such a dickwad for any amount of time, no matter how good the job was.

Don't worry. No plate smashing here. Unless you convince me to throw a Greek-themed party! ;) Ryan texted.

He half-expected Wyatt to brush him off because he was still pissed off that Ryan had kept the interview a secret. Ryan still didn't know why he hadn't told the truth. He'd meant to when he'd followed Wyatt outside, and then Wyatt had looked at him, awestruck that Ryan had followed *him*, and Ryan hadn't been able to confess that he'd sought him out because he looked exactly like the guy he was supposed to interview the next morning.

But, **Like it a little wild, huh** was the *very* unexpected text that Ryan got back as a response.

Wyatt had only a tiny inkling of how wild Ryan could get, but he had every intention of enlightening him.

I went off with you on your bike, didn't I? Ryan reminded him.

You did. The response came through almost instantly, like before Wyatt had put his phone away between texts, but now had kept it out, intent on talking to Ryan. And then he sent another text before Ryan could even come up with something else to say. **I really enjoyed having you behind me.**

Ryan stared at the screen. Usually it was a no-brainer that guys flirted with him. It was always overt and typically very blatant. He definitely wasn't used to trying to read between the lines. The last thing he wanted to do was guess wrong with Wyatt and scare him off.

After he typed and discarded half a dozen responses, Ryan settled on something equally as ambiguous. **I'll be happy to get behind you anytime you want.**

Wyatt clearly wasn't agonizing over Ryan's meaning the same way, because the next text came through too fast. **I got that impression. :)**

What the hell, Ryan thought. He'd done this so many times, it should have felt old and used up, but with Wyatt it was exciting again, got his blood pumping and the adrenaline fizzy in his veins like he was fourteen and it was the first time all over again. **No, you got the impression I'd get on my knees anytime I want.**

What about whenever I want? Wyatt shot back.

Ryan glanced down and wasn't surprised to see he was half-hard in his jeans. **I was pretty damn clear**, he texted.

And then . . . *nothing.* An excruciatingly long ten minutes went by without a single text. Ryan checked, then double-checked his coverage. Restarted his phone. Even wandered into the front of the house because the Wi-Fi was always stronger there.

Still nothing.

Ryan couldn't believe it, they'd had a really good, nearly sexy banter going, and the unfortunately short memories of their one encounter were already flashing through his mind in three-dimensions and full-technicolor. The sharp dig of the gravel into his knees. The clean, musky taste of Wyatt's dick, and the weight of it on his tongue. Ryan pressed the heel of his hand against his own interested dick. It didn't want to wait and entice Wyatt into repeating the past. It wanted more. It wanted everything, and it wasn't usually inclined to settle, even though Ryan was pretty sure he wouldn't need to.

Just not tonight.

Tonight, Wyatt was clearly going to leave him hanging and unsatisfied, which Ryan was man enough to admit he probably deserved. Not that he'd left Wyatt hanging the other night—he'd definitely been fully, if not completely, satisfied then.

But not entirely, Ryan thought, as he remembered the way Wyatt's face had fallen when he realized that Ryan had no intention of exchanging phone numbers with him.

No, Wyatt had definitely wanted more. He'd wanted more the next morning too, but Ryan had fucked that up by not being honest enough.

Not a mistake that Ryan or his dick were going to make again. As soon as Wyatt got here and settled in a little, he was going to find out what Ryan needed—and also what Ryan wanted—from him.

He never took a chance of being the last one interested, much preferring to cut and run and move onto something better, something more exciting, when a hookup ran its natural course. But tonight, he texted Wyatt again.

Ryan told himself it was the veneer of professionalism that he was trying to maintain because he was technically Wyatt's boss now. Not that he'd exactly been professional the first time they'd met.

I'll be around during the day tomorrow and probably the evening too. Hope to see you.

Ryan realized as he finished typing that it wasn't only his dick that felt that way. He wanted to get to know Wyatt; he wanted to talk to him again. He wanted to convince him to take a chance on Ryan's wild plan most of all, because that meant he wouldn't have to do it with a stranger he didn't even like.

He wanted it to be Wyatt. He just needed Wyatt to want it too.

Wyatt looked at his phone and slipped it back in his pocket. Two texts unanswered now.

"You realize we threw this party for you, right?" Xander said, his voice cutting right through the grind of the guitars in the music that someone—not someone with taste, but *someone*—had put on the playlist.

Wyatt looked up at the crowded rental he was moving out of in the morning, and realized he couldn't identify more than a handful of guys he'd worked with in the Terroir kitchen.

"I don't even know half these people," Wyatt half-yelled. He knew he didn't have a voice like Xander's, that could cut through so much ambient noise, and he was usually glad about that fact.

Xander scanned over the crowd with a critical eye. "I think a lot of these are Nate's friends."

They weren't Nate's friends. If they'd been Nate's friends, Wyatt would have known them. He considered pointing this out, but Xander was in a mood—frankly had been in a mood since Miles had moved to LA—and so he didn't. Certainly Wyatt leaving and having Nate take over his part of the lease weren't helping.

If Xander wanted to throw a stupid house party, buy too much booze, and invite too many people none of them knew, then Wyatt certainly wasn't going to tell him he wasn't going to regret it in the morning.

"I haven't seen Kian yet," Wyatt said, because changing the subject was a far safer approach.

Xander's lips compressed. "I'm sure the Bastard had some sort of ridiculous project for him that kept him late again."

"While I'm in LA, I'm going to look for a different job for him," Wyatt said, even though he'd already told Xander what his plans were. Still, they both knew it was going to be in vain. There was no way Kian would leave Aquino.

Wyatt didn't want to say it was love because he'd always believed that love needed generosity and respect and admiration to grow and flourish, but maybe he was wrong.

Not about Bastian suddenly becoming generous, respectful or admiring, but about any of those being required for Kian to fall in love with him.

It was a depressing thought, and Wyatt forced his mind back to the party, because even though he was saying goodbye, this was supposed to be a somewhat happy occasion. A celebration of the potential of the future.

The truth was all Wyatt wanted to do was pull his phone back up, despite Xander's face-melting glare, and text with Ryan. He was clever and cute and just a little aggressive. Aggressive wasn't something Wyatt thought he'd want after Nate, but on Ryan it felt more natural, more an extension of a well-meaning personality than a way to go about domineering everyone and everything.

And Nate had absolutely, definitely done that.

Of course Nate also hadn't lied about his intentions either, which was something Wyatt was still confused and a little upset about. Why not tell him? Why keep it a secret?

That mystery was all caught up in his own conflicted feelings towards Ryan. He still felt everything he had the first night they'd met. He'd never stopped. He was pretty sure that stopping was totally out of the cards now that he was going to be working for Ryan and literally living in his backyard. Cooking his meals. Taking care of him. All actions that Wyatt *knew* would develop his feelings even if he tried to hold them back.

But Ryan seemed interested too, despite the mysterious intentions, and that was something Wyatt was increasingly having to come to terms with. Would he let him? Would Ryan be the guy? Wyatt had always known, in the corners of his mind, that there would be a guy that would make him *want* to come out to Nana. That there would be a guy that he'd be dying to introduce to her, and not just as a "good friend."

It seemed insane that Ryan could be the guy. It also seemed insane that Ryan was interested, but that was an undeniable fact. Wyatt felt the sharp edges of his phone through his pocket, and finally pulled it back out.

Xander had decamped to the doorway, where he was interrogating Kian. Wyatt glanced down at his screen and before he could change his mind—or chicken out—typed a response to Ryan.

I'm leaving my friends and my job and the city I've lived in for years. The only definite thing I know about the future is that I'm going to see you tomorrow.

Chapter Four

"HI." WYATT SHIFTED AWKWARDLY from one foot to the other and tried not to feel like he'd fucked up already by knocking on the front door instead of doing something silly like going to the back of the house.

But mostly he tried the hardest not to stare, because he had definitely not anticipated Ryan opening the door only wearing a pair of low-slung athletic shorts and a thin sheen of sweat on his bare, muscled torso.

"Hi back," Ryan said, smiling so brightly it dismissed all of Wyatt's concerns. "Is that all you came with?" he asked, glancing at the duffel bag at Wyatt's feet.

"I have a few more boxes that are shipping down here next week," Wyatt admitted. "Other than that, yeah. I like to travel light."

"Live light too," Ryan said, and there was definitely an approving light in his dark eyes. "So do I. Come see the house."

Wyatt wasn't sure if he and Ryan had different definitions of "living light," because Ryan definitely had more than a duffel bag and a handful of boxes to his name. The house wasn't as big as it looked from the street and the gate that protected the driveway from the main road. But everything was clean and simple—lots of modern lines tempered by a worn-in homey quality that Wyatt appreciated.

"Living room," Ryan said, as Wyatt trailed behind him, trying really hard not to admire the firm roundness of his ass in those clingy shorts. "Dining room, you probably sort of care about that," he said absently. "And here's the one room you definitely care about." Ryan made some cute flourish with his hands and they stepped into the kitchen.

It wasn't a huge space but it had been well-designed, with a big island for prep, and good, professional-grade appliances. But if he was being honest, if there was one thing that could distract him from high quality appliances, it was a cute boy leaning against them. "Is there a pantry?" Wyatt asked, when he realized he'd been staring—and not even at the kitchen.

He felt the exact same magnetic pull to Ryan that he had that night. He hadn't really expected it to diminish but he also hadn't expected it to be blazing stronger than ever. Especially when they still hadn't addressed any of the growing baggage between them. Attraction didn't magically make any of that shit disappear, but it sure made it easier to ignore.

"Oh, yeah, of course," Ryan said. He walked past Wyatt, and Wyatt got one whiff of him. No cologne, but something earthy, like sunshine and dirt and grass. Wyatt wanted to know what his sweat tasted like on his tongue, what it felt like against his palms. But he kept his hands and his tongue to himself. Whatever was going to happen with them, there was no point in rushing in before they'd even talked about it.

There was a big pantry, with lots of empty shelves that Wyatt would enjoy filling. "This looks really great, actually."

Ryan shot him a lopsided, very charming smile. He probably even knew how charming it was, and it still didn't diminish the sheer wattage of it. "Are you just saying that? You can be honest with me, you know. Like I said last night, I promise no thrown dishes or hissy fits when my meat isn't precisely the right temperature."

Wyatt leaned back against the counter and shoved his hands in his pockets. Better to keep them where they needed to be, and not against Ryan's damp skin. "I wouldn't lie to you."

Ryan flushed, and looked ashamed. That had been Wyatt's original intention—to remind him that out of the two of them, Ryan had been the only one who'd lied. Despite that, Wyatt couldn't help but feel embarrassed that he'd brought it up first.

"I'm sorry, I should have told you," Ryan said. "About the interview, that is. I kept meaning to that night, and then I thought if I did, you'd really just take me home. Would you have?"

Wyatt was pretty sure Ryan already knew the answer to that question. So he deliberately skirted around it. "I don't want to be a joke or a toy to play with. Especially now that you're my boss."

"It's not like that, I promise." Ryan sounded and looked very earnest. Trustworthy, even. But Wyatt still wasn't sure that wasn't his attraction to him annoyingly surfacing and interfering again.

"Look," Ryan continued, "it'll stay separate. The professional stuff, the *you're my boss* stuff, and the personal stuff. And for the record, I don't really consider myself your boss."

"You pay my salary?" Wyatt pointed out, a little incredulously.

"Well," Ryan smiled, "technically that's Eric. And yeah, he's my agent, but it gives some separation, right?"

Wyatt wasn't sure he entirely agreed, but the attraction was still flaring up, brightly and almost painfully. He'd come here, hadn't he? He'd given up his job at Terroir, and packed his bags, and drove here, intending to work for Ryan Flores. And, if he was being really honest with himself, a good part of that was because he'd wanted more. More money *and* more time with Ryan. Was it so wrong that he might get both in the same position?

"Okay," Wyatt said, hoping that he wouldn't regret his agreement later. Hoping that even if he did regret it, that there would be some spectacular memories to make it worth it in the end.

"I guess that means I should show you the ADU," Ryan said.

"ADU?" Wyatt asked as he followed Ryan out of the kitchen, through the back door, and out to the lawn. There was a cute little cottage set a ways back from the main house, surrounded by flowering bushes and a palm tree.

"Attached dwelling unit," Ryan said, opening the door and leading Wyatt inside. "Eric said I should have it built when I remodeled the house, in case I wanted someone to stay with me but wanted to make sure we each had our privacy."

Wyatt was briefly tempted to tell Ryan that he wasn't sure he needed the privacy. He'd much rather be right in Ryan's pocket. He'd never considered his first instinct reckless before, but he knew he was acting reckless now.

"Eric seems like a good agent, that way," Wyatt said instead. Even though he'd done a very good impression of a human being encasing a blood-thirsty piranha the only time they'd ever met.

"Oh, he's an asshole," Ryan chuckled. "But he's my asshole. So it works out. Anyway, this is all yours. No kitchen, other than this little sink, mini fridge and microwave, but feel free to come use the one in the house at any time. I really mean that."

There was a tiny living room with a flat screen TV and a comfy-looking couch. A separate bedroom with a queen bed and dresser—even a miniature walk-in closet. A bathroom, with a clever closet enclosing a small washer and dryer unit, finished out the cottage.

It was everything Wyatt needed, barring the kitchen, which was just a few steps away.

What he wanted was standing in the kitchenette, examining the contents of the mini fridge.

"I told Gabriela to stock this," Ryan said, pointing out the empty shelves. "I'll have to talk to her."

"I can stock it, it's not a big deal." Wyatt was already a little embarrassed at the ridiculous salary that Ryan was paying him, never mind that he was dying to get into his pants *again*. He didn't need Ryan to pay for his groceries.

"Gabriela does the housekeeping, and runs the odd errand but she doesn't live here," Ryan said. "I don't really have a personal assistant. If I need help, Eric will usually loan me his. Nicole is intimidatingly efficient so I try to avoid it if I can."

"So it's just . . . me and you." Wyatt tried not to make that sound like an invitation, but he was acutely aware of Ryan's bare chest and the big fluffy bed in the next room. It was impossible not to think of what they could do in it. After all, it had been so good when it was just Wyatt's bike and a swath of gravel. The bed opened up endless possibilities that had Wyatt's head swimming and his cock half-erect in his jeans.

"Yep." Ryan smiled brightly. He seemed just as happy about this turn of events as Wyatt.

Wyatt wanted to reach over and pull Ryan against him, their first kiss and its incendiary intensity in sharp, perfect detail in his mind. The second, he knew, would be even better. The third might outdo every kiss he'd ever experienced before.

It was one of the reasons why he hadn't kissed Ryan yet. He didn't want this to be a casual, hookup sort of thing. He wanted to show Ryan that he wanted more. More than just a quick afternoon in bed together. Or a quick ride up in the Hills followed by a convenient blowjob.

And everything tempered by the sobering realization that Ryan was his *boss*. He'd never wanted to blow his boss before.

"We should talk about expectations," Wyatt said, dropping his duffel on the floor and digging out a worn pad from the side. He'd written a list of questions he'd needed to ask last night, after ducking out on his own farewell party.

"Expectations? You feed me when I want food. That's about it," Ryan said, and even though Wyatt didn't like the tiny crease forming Ryan's brows, he forged on.

This was stuff he needed to know to do his *job*. And for what Ryan was paying him, he couldn't shirk his responsibilities or his duties, all because he was desperate to get into his boss' pants.

"Expectations sounds more formal than I was intending," Wyatt confessed. "I just have a long list of questions, basically."

"Questions?" Ryan frowned. "We'll deal with that tomorrow. Tonight's your first night in LA. It's nice out; let's go for a drive. And this time we'll take *my* bike."

"Oh, uh, okay, sure." His first day at Terroir, Bastian Aquino definitely hadn't invited him out. Or issued the invitation with quite that fiery glint in his eye either. Ryan definitely looked like he was up to something. Wyatt might still be unsure, but he didn't think he had the willpower to turn this man down.

"I'll take a quick shower, and then we'll head out," Ryan said. "Feel free to settle in."

Settle in while Ryan was in the shower? Naked and dripping wet and only half a house away? Wyatt felt his temperature spike at the thought.

"I think I'm going to take a quick inventory in the kitchen," Wyatt said, because that felt so much safer than fantasizing about joining Ryan in the shower.

Wyatt was headfirst in a cupboard, cataloging mixing bowls, when he felt a warm hand rest on his back.

"Find everything you needed?" Ryan asked when Wyatt straightened. The athletic shorts had been swapped for a pair of jeans tight enough they made his heart thump harder. He'd done something cute and swoopy to his hair, and he smelled delectable, like spicy vanilla. Wyatt's mouth watered, and he was suddenly, painfully aware of his own faded jeans and old t-shirt.

He hadn't dressed to go out. Or to impress a cute guy, even though he'd known Ryan would probably be here. He'd dressed to drive six hours on his bike, and hadn't put anymore thought into it. Maybe he should have, instead of spending the last twenty minutes digging through Ryan's kitchen drawers and cupboards.

"You have the basics," Wyatt said, trailing after Ryan as they headed towards the garage. "I'm probably going to have to pick up some stuff."

Ryan seemed completely unconcerned by this, and Wyatt felt an awkward, embarrassed pulse at the acute financial gap between them. Ryan had enough money he didn't have to keep track, while Wyatt scraped by, even now with the increased salary.

That feeling when Ryan opened the garage door, a light shining down on a Range Rover, a Bentley, and a Tesla. And a really sweet street bike that had clearly been modified for speed, and then painted a flat, sexy matte black. In a pair of leathers, Ryan would look like fucking Batman.

It made Wyatt's serviceable bike look like garbage in comparison. And even though Ryan never seemed to compare, Wyatt couldn't help doing it.

Ryan passed by the cars without a second glance and pulled a sleek black helmet from a cubby on the wall. He extended the helmet Wyatt's direction. "You up for it?" he asked, that sly challenge back in his eyes.

It wasn't a question of what Wyatt was up for, but if the night would end without Wyatt getting everything he was up for.

He grabbed the helmet, and slid it on, watching as Ryan picked up another one, and did the same.

Ryan was maybe only an inch shorter, with slightly narrower shoulders, but it felt just as good to climb on the bike behind him as it had to feel Ryan's arms wrapped around him. It gave him hope that Ryan might echo his own versatile preferences.

Sliding his own hands around Ryan's waist, he let one drift down and feel the flexing muscle of his thigh as he pulled the bike out of the garage. Ryan's glance backwards was bright and challenging.

It shouldn't have surprised Wyatt that Ryan liked to go fast; after all, he'd seen the collection of cars, even though he only had a vague idea of what they were capable of. Wyatt knew more about motorcycles, and had definitely known this was custom and tuned for speed, but he still wasn't expecting the way Ryan floored it when they pulled onto the freeway.

The acceleration pushed Ryan's body more firmly into the cradle of Wyatt's, and he knew there was no way Ryan was going to miss how hard he was, cock aching in his jeans. He wanted everything they'd had last time they'd been on a bike like this, and so much more.

But while Ryan seemed to be in a hurry to get somewhere—weaving in and out of the traffic on the freeway, expertly maneuvering the bike even with the extra weight on it—he didn't seem to be in any hurry to go somewhere specific. They hit Highway 1, and even the early evening traffic didn't seem to phase Ryan.

The sun was setting, the sky ablaze with color as they headed further up the coast, and to his surprise, Ryan did finally pull off the road, but not towards an abandoned parking lot, but to a busy taqueria with a nearly full parking lot.

He stopped the bike with a spray of gravel, and pulled off his helmet, grinning like a loon. Wyatt reluctantly removed his hands from Ryan's waist, and took off his own helmet.

"And I thought I drove fast," Wyatt teased, pushing his hair back.

Ryan winced. "I might like speed a little too much."

"The adrenaline can be addictive," Wyatt acknowledged.

"Yeah," Ryan admitted. "You been here before?" he asked, gesturing to the building behind them.

The last thing Wyatt had expected was for Ryan to take him to a restaurant. But here they were. Wyatt shook his head, wondering if he should ask Ryan what the hell he was thinking.

"I haven't. I'm assuming I'm off the clock," Wyatt said, because he couldn't just *let* it go, not the way Ryan did. Probably because Ryan had all the advantages here, and almost certainly kept forgetting that Wyatt didn't have any.

"Of course you are." Ryan grinned recklessly. "Though maybe the apprentice has something to teach the master?"

"Master of what?" Wyatt scoffed. "You definitely know how to handle yourself on that bike."

"Master of good food, *duh*," Ryan said, slinging his helmet under his arm. "This place makes the best tacos in Southern California. Pretty good view, too."

Wyatt didn't even pretend to look out at Malibu, spread out underneath them. "Yeah, I really like it."

Ryan flushed. "You wanted to ask me some questions. I figured it might be good to grab some food."

"I'm not complaining. If you want to feed me, I'm not going to stop you," he teased back. If Ryan was going to act like this was a date, then he wasn't going to stop him from doing that either. In fact, he could definitely hold his own, if that's what this was.

Not everything had to be so black and white—either professionally or personally. Weren't the best things a gray-hued combination of both? Wyatt reminded himself of his good friend Miles and his boyfriend, Evan, who worked and loved and fought together, sometimes all at once.

If they could do it, then Wyatt could too, especially if it was Ryan he was doing it with.

There was a lengthy line at the little shack, and a lot of the picnic tables were already full of people enjoying their tacos. Wyatt half-expected someone to recognize Ryan, but everyone ignored them.

"I keep expecting everyone here to mow me down to get to you," Wyatt half-joked. "Am I going to end up being part-chef, part-bodyguard?"

Ryan shot him an incredulous look as they settled in the back of the line. "Please, I'm definitely not that famous. If Eric ever tried to saddle me with a bodyguard, I'd laugh in his face. Or something worse, like question his manhood or his net worth."

"You don't ever get people who recognize you?" Wyatt had known who Ryan was instantly, but then he'd been touched and undeniably impacted three years ago when Ryan had come out of the closet. Also he'd definitely thought he was hot back then. That feeling hadn't changed three years later, when he'd found him at Temple and had spent too many hours staring at him.

"I'm a baseball player, not a celebrity." Ryan rolled his eyes. "Every once in a while, yeah, I get someone who wants a selfie or an autograph, but it doesn't really happen all that often. Eric probably wishes it happened more. He's always wanting me to sign more deals to raise my public profile, but like I said, I'm a baseball player, not a fucking influencer, or whatever they call those assholes who take impossible Instagram pictures. If I'm going to take pictures it's going to be of all the sick places I visit."

"You like to travel?" Wyatt asked. He kept trying to ignore how much like a first date this felt like, but it kept cropping up. But the truth was, however it felt, he wanted to get to know Ryan.

"Confession," Ryan said, leaning closer, and nudging his shoulder against Wyatt's, "it's one of my favorite parts of being a baseball player. We don't get a lot of time in cities, sometimes, but every place just *feels* different, you know? And it's an experience to be in every single one."

Wyatt wished he *did* know, but he didn't. He'd worked his ass off getting through culinary school, had spent some time in Chicago, then Portland, and then had gotten the job at Terroir, and had jumped at the chance to come back to California. But his truth was that he'd barely ever left California since he was born, and even though he felt a little wistful at the thought of exploring the world and all the culinary delights it had to offer, he'd never really felt the lack of travel.

"I haven't really traveled much," Wyatt confessed. "Not much opportunity."

Ryan's smile was bright and infectious. "Maybe we can change that."

Wyatt didn't really understand how he could do that; it wasn't like Wyatt was going to go with Ryan on road trips as his personal chef. And that was the whole issue, wasn't it? Ryan had never defined his job role, and Wyatt had a feeling that wouldn't change. Ryan wasn't really a *definer*. He liked the adrenaline rush of making it up as he went.

"We'd better figure out our order," Wyatt suggested, gesturing towards the menu. "What do you usually get?"

Ryan rattled off half a dozen types of tacos, and added, with a lopsided grin, "And definitely beer. I wasn't supposed to drink during the season so I definitely want a beer with my tacos."

"Let's get a bucket then," Wyatt suggested. "We can share. And I definitely want to try those authentic shrimp tacos. And the *al pastor*."

When they were about to get to the register, Ryan shooed him away, with directions to find a table. Wyatt decided that he didn't care if Ryan bought him some tacos and a beer. It was fine. It didn't mean this was a date. It didn't mean anything, necessarily. It was a guy welcoming his new employee. Except it hadn't felt precisely professional when they'd been pressed together on his bike earlier, and it wouldn't feel that way on the way home either. Especially with Wyatt desperate for Ryan to pull over for every dark corner.

Ryan ventured over to the table Wyatt had found with his very capable hands filled with plates and the bucket of beers dangling from one finger.

It shouldn't have reminded Wyatt of the other night, but pretty much everything reminded Wyatt of the other night. The way Ryan walked, the way he smiled—brighter now, and more spontaneously—the way he bit his lip or wet it with his tongue, and definitely his strong, calloused hands.

"Food," Ryan crowed with excitement, sliding the paper plates across the table. "And beer!"

"Do you think there's anyone on the planet who doesn't like tacos?" Wyatt asked, digging a chip into the salsa verde, heat prickling his tongue as the jalapeños hit his taste buds. "Tacos are god's food."

"Tacos are amazing," Ryan agreed.

"What else do you like to eat?" Wyatt asked, squeezing a lime over his shrimp tacos.

Ryan glanced up, attention distracted from the food in front of him. "Is this part of the interrogation? Should I find my handcuffs?"

Wyatt thought Ryan would be sufficiently pleased at how his heartbeat picked up at the mention of his handcuffs. "No," he scoffed wryly. "I promise, it'll be fine. Just a few questions. I definitely find that food is a personal thing. Besides, I want to prevent you from tossing your meal at me, and keep your broken-plate rule intact."

"It's not going to be hard," Ryan said. "I'm really laid-back about food. Most of the time, I don't really care, honestly. Just put it in front of me, and I'll eat it."

Wyatt was skeptical but maybe that was from a history of working at the most exacting restaurant in America. "Okay, tell me this. When it's just you, what do you eat? Start with breakfast."

"A banana? An orange? Sometimes a mango or a papaya if I can get my hands on it. I like to buy those pre-boiled eggs from the store for protein. Maybe a frozen turkey sausage or two, if I'm feeling like making the effort."

Wyatt had seen Ryan's kitchen and how pristine it was. He had a feeling Ryan very infrequently "made the effort."

"I'm surprised you didn't mention any protein shakes," Wyatt said, swallowing a big bite of fantastic fresh and spicy shrimp. He'd done a little research, and the shakes seemed to be the ubiquitous item that most athletes imbibed.

Ryan's grin was too cute, all lopsided and embarrassed. "Those go without saying. I like to put low-fat peanut butter in mine."

"Smooth or chunky?"

Ryan choked on his beer. "Oh, smooth." An unholy glint lit his dark eyes. "Very smooth."

Wyatt had to swallow hard, even though he wasn't even eating at that moment. "Noted."

"But you're not writing anything down?" Ryan teased.

"I have a feeling I won't have any trouble remembering any of this. So far, it's not exactly complicated. What about lunch or dinner?"

"Eric is going to be really happy that I hired someone who takes his job so seriously," Ryan said. "I don't really care, honestly. Feed me something. Whatever you feel you want to make. October and November, I don't worry too much about what I'm eating, though towards Thanksgiving, I'm going to have to watch it a little, because I have an Adidas commercial shoot. And knowing Eric, who's arranging the whole thing, they'll have me mostly naked."

Wyatt's cheeks heated at the thought of all that bare skin. Except he wasn't picturing it on an Adidas set, he was picturing it in his bed, with Ryan raising his eyebrow the same he had the night they'd met. Daring Wyatt to do everything he wanted.

Maybe a pair of those handcuffs of Ryan's thrown in for good measure.

He was all quicksilver heat, hot and swift but possibly not lasting. Considering that Wyatt already wanted more, he wasn't sure he could settle for what Ryan might give him.

Who am I kidding? Wyatt asked himself. He was going to take anything Ryan would give him, love every second, and then somehow deal with it when it ended.

Maybe if he did a really great job, Ryan might keep him on after, no matter how wretched that would feel. It wasn't something to look forward to, but Wyatt needed the money.

"Everything okay?" Ryan asked, pulling Wyatt out of his depressing thoughts. Thinking about flings ending before they even began, worrying about fallout and finances.

Wyatt grimaced. "Sorry, just got distracted."

"I must not be entertaining you enough," Ryan insisted, and suddenly, there was his foot, his boot nudging Wyatt's. And even through two layers of leather, the impact blasted through him. It wasn't the first time Ryan had touched him since he'd arrived, but this wasn't just a simple touch. It had a purpose and intent.

I'm going to touch you a lot more tonight.

"I don't have any complaints so far," Wyatt said, a little teasing edge to his voice.

"You'd tell me if you did, right?" Ryan asked.

Wyatt toyed with a chip, crumbling it onto his empty plate. "Why wouldn't I?"

The truth was Wyatt was curious why Ryan had suddenly decided he needed a private chef when he didn't even have a personal assistant, but that wasn't exactly a *complaint*. Besides, Wyatt had a feeling he'd discover the truth eventually, even if he wasn't entirely sure he wanted to hear it.

The secrecy alone should turn him off, but he was in too deep. It was that blasted attraction, rearing its head again.

"You would," Ryan confirmed. "I'm just . . . maybe *you're* not being entertaining enough."

Wyatt rolled his eyes. "That's something you're going to have to get used to, unfortunately. I'm pretty boring."

"You like to cook, but what else do you do for fun?"

"In high school, I surfed," Wyatt said. "I've been wanting to get back to it."

"I know a lot of good spots. Maybe we can go together sometime," Ryan said. "I don't get to go during the season much, so I need to get all this in before spring training starts. So, cooking, surfing. And your bike. What else makes Wyatt Blake tick?"

If Wyatt hadn't already acknowledged this felt like a first date, he definitely would have thought it now. "The first thing I try to do if I have any free time is see my nana. We're really close."

"Cooking, surfing, your motorcycle, and Nana's boy." Ryan sounded approving, and he was smiling. "Never mind that sound you make when you lose control. How is a guy like you single?"

Wyatt didn't want to talk about it. He definitely didn't want to talk about it with Ryan, who had taken the chance to come out at the most impactful moment in his career.

"You finished?" he asked, getting to his feet. His voice sounded rough, a little of his desperation leaking into it. Desperation to avoid the question. Desperation to get Ryan naked underneath him, on top of him—whichever, Wyatt didn't even care.

Ryan's dark eyes were knowing as they stared up at him. "With the food, yeah. With you, not quite."

"Then let's go," Wyatt said.

He never would have dreamed of voicing that sort of demand to his old boss, but it was becoming very clear that his old job and his new job were fundamentally different. Ryan kept saying he was nothing like Bastian Aquino, and maybe it was time to hold him to that. Ryan had also claimed they could keep their professional and personal lives separate, and had driven that point home by taking him out to dinner tonight. So, he was off the clock, right?

Wyatt scooped up the empty plates and tossed them in the trash on his way to the parking lot, hoping that Ryan was trailing after him.

He could hear footsteps behind him, and it was all the confirmation he needed to drop his helmet on the seat, and wrap one hand around Ryan's waist and pull him close. "This what you had in mind?" he demanded, right before he kissed him.

He hadn't been able to forget how intensely Ryan had kissed him the other night, and even though at the time he'd believed he'd given as good as he got, it was impossible not to catalogue every missed moment.

This time Wyatt wasn't going to miss a thing.

His mouth covered Ryan's, his arm pulling him tight against him, and he let him know explicitly, with his lips and his tongue, just how much he'd wanted him the last few days. That he hadn't stopped wanting him, that he'd wanted him even before he'd dropped him off at his front gate.

All Ryan's teasing had done was push him to a point of desperation—a point of no return. He didn't care if it was over tomorrow morning or next week or next year. He just wanted as much of Ryan as he could get, in whatever time they had.

Ryan broke away, panting, but Wyatt didn't let up. His lips only shifted to his neck, feeling the pulse point there racing. Ryan definitely wanted him just as much. His cock was a hard, burning pressure against Wyatt's thigh, and he kept shifting a little, like he was just as desperate to take the strain off. But Wyatt wasn't going to let him go that easily.

"You didn't even let me finish my beer," Ryan said, and his voice was breathless.

"I'll buy you another one," Wyatt said, between kisses against the soft skin just behind Ryan's ear. Soft and sensitive, if the way Ryan kept squirming was any indication.

"I'm going to hold you to that," Ryan laughed, and it was still breathless. "How am I supposed to drive home like this?"

"Like I've been," Wyatt said, pushing his thigh right against Ryan's cock. "Like I've been wanting and suffering."

"Suffering?" Ryan's voice went higher. "That does sound serious."

Wyatt made sure that all his desire was in his eyes as he looked straight at him. "Oh, it is."

"Maybe we should . . . uh . . . try to help you out, then?" Ryan questioned.

"I'm a pretty relaxed guy," Wyatt admitted. "Until you drive me crazy."

Ryan laughed, and it was the exact laugh that Wyatt had been dying to hear since the first moment he'd seen him sitting and bored at Temple. "I guess I *have* been entertaining you, then."

"You have no idea," Wyatt muttered.

Ryan licked his lips, and Wyatt felt a pulse of *something* at the sudden nervous hesitation in Ryan's eyes. "Why don't you show me?"

They needed to make it back to his house in one piece though, so Ryan deliberately didn't think about it.

He didn't think about Wyatt's hands on him, clasped tightly around his waist, his thighs and stomach pressed firmly against his body.

He didn't think about how insistently and passionately Wyatt had expressed what he wanted. He definitely didn't think about the kiss they'd shared in the taqueria parking lot, or he probably would have said *fuck it*, pulled off the road, and let Wyatt demolish him in public with not a single damn ounce of shame.

But it would be worth the wait. Ryan believed that, and believed that the adrenaline spiking through his blood at the possessive curl of Wyatt's fingers into his leather jacket were going to mean fantastic things.

Wyatt had passively let him take over last time, barely issuing a single protest when Ryan had sunk to his knees in the gravel. He'd hoped that it wouldn't be like that every time, that Wyatt might appeal to the adventurous side of him that craved something different.

And Wyatt, without even having a clue, had done exactly that, yanking back the power between them in one smooth move.

Ryan pulled into the garage, and flipped off the engine. Wyatt didn't move immediately, but stayed where he was, pressing even closer into him, until Ryan didn't know where his legs ended and Wyatt's began. His fingers dug beneath his t-shirt, but instead of the rough touch he'd expected, his fingertips were featherlight on his abs, stroking all the skin they could reach, then meandering up to circle a nipple.

The visor in his helmet was fogging over, and Ryan felt lightheaded with desire, all the blood in his body rushing south. He moved restlessly against the leather seat, but Wyatt's hands were suddenly clamped around him, holding him immobile in place.

Ryan's hands clenched around his helmet, and he yanked it off. "Don't move," Wyatt said, and to Ryan's surprise, somehow he'd pulled his own off, even though it felt like his hands, those dynamite hands, had never left his body.

"Why not?" Ryan demanded, a little petulantly. If they weren't going to move off the bike, they could have taken care of this raging inferno of desire thirty minutes ago.

"Because I have too many plans for you to get off so easily," Wyatt said softly in a gravelly voice that Ryan was going to be using to get himself off for probably the next fifty years. He'd known Wyatt had a sexy voice, had experienced it on their last late-night drive, and felt the visceral impact of it during the interview. Had wanted to call him half a dozen times until Wyatt had showed up here this afternoon.

And now hearing it ordering hell and promising heaven was almost too much for Ryan.

"I'll be good," he swore, too far gone to care how shaky his voice was.

"You'd better be," Wyatt said. "Drop your helmet."

Ryan did as instructed, not even caring as the heavy plastic clattered onto the garage floor. Normally he took good care of his equipment, but right now, he didn't give a damn.

He felt the loss of Wyatt sliding off the bike, his back and ass suddenly cool without the heat of Wyatt pressed against him. "Get off the bike," Wyatt continued.

Ryan had strong knees. Non-surgically impacted knees. He still felt them shake as he dismounted.

"Good," Wyatt said from behind him. It was dim in the garage with only the emergency night light on, and he could only feel him, not see him.

"I told you I'd be good," Ryan said.

"Remains to be seen," Wyatt said. "Take me to your bedroom."

He hadn't said a word about hands, and normally Ryan wouldn't have, but he reached out and grasped Wyatt's hand. He'd asked Ryan to lead, and so Ryan was going to lead. Plus it felt good to finally be touching Wyatt back. Not nearly as much as he wanted to, but the strong clasp of his hand in Wyatt's was still a flood of sensation.

He led Wyatt through his dark house, not turning on a single light, to the master bedroom. He kicked his boots off and Wyatt followed suit. He'd deliberately omitted this part of the house in his tour earlier, imagining that they'd have sex in Wyatt's little cottage. He rarely ever invited anyone to his own bed—it always felt too personal for a hookup—but Ryan found he wanted it to be personal. He felt a little shaky with nerves, at how this whole evening had developed, even though he'd been subtly pushing Wyatt to see how far he could be pushed.

He hadn't really imagined what it would be like when Wyatt pushed back.

Wyatt hadn't issued any other instructions when they reached the bedroom, so Ryan sat on the edge of the bed, and just watched him. Wyatt flipped a bedside lamp on, barely even fumbling for the switch. "I want to see you," was all the explanation he gave. The light glinted on his blond hair, shadowing his cheekbones, and full lips.

"Then see me," Ryan said, pulling off his jacket, and then his shirt, dropping the clothes where they fell.

Wyatt took a step into the V of Ryan's legs, and kissed him again, so much like he'd kissed him in the parking lot, like he was starving and Ryan was a meal he couldn't wait to devour.

His tongue was hot and insistent in Ryan's mouth, pushing his head back, until they both fell back onto the bed together. Ryan pulled up on Wyatt's shirt, dragging it over his head. "Too many clothes," he panted into Wyatt's mouth. He blindly rutted right onto Wyatt's crotch, feeling he was just as hard as Ryan was.

Ryan trailed his hands down Wyatt's chest, his abs, his waist. He wasn't an athlete, but like he'd said their first hookup, he was powerful. Strong. Built like a linebacker, almost. Wide shoulders, narrow waist, strong arms, thighs Ryan could have wept over.

"You want me to take your clothes off?" Wyatt asked, raising an eyebrow.

"You take them, or I'll take them," Ryan said, a little aware at how close to begging he was.

"That's an easy decision, then," Wyatt said, and he unbuttoned Ryan's jeans and lowered the zipper, making quick work of them, leaving him in his boxer briefs.

"I'm taking my time with you tonight," Wyatt announced after Ryan had reached up to kiss him again, derailing any more clothing removal.

"Whatever you want, just *get on with it*," Ryan panted. Wyatt cupped his hard bulge, Ryan's head falling back against the pillow. "Yeah, just like that."

"Don't want anything else, just my hand?" Wyatt teased, an unholy light in his light-blue eyes. "I'm a little disappointed."

"I want it all," Ryan panted as Wyatt pulled his briefs down. "I want you to fuck me."

The smug look on Wyatt's face was such a turn-on, Ryan had to bite his own lip.

"I was hoping you'd want that," Wyatt said.

Wyatt didn't know that Ryan almost never asked for it. That even for someone who liked the adrenaline rush of a risky thrill, he almost never trusted anyone to do it. Never trusted anyone to take care of it. But he trusted Wyatt, which was crazy because he was still practically a stranger.

A stranger that Ryan had lied to and persuaded to practically move into his house. He shoved that thought away. "What are you waiting for? Lube and condoms, in the drawer," he panted, eyes glued to the thick bulge in Wyatt's jeans as he perched on the bed.

Ryan was afraid Wyatt would hesitate, and his hesitation would impact Ryan's certainty, but he opened the drawer and pulled out the required items, but still didn't finish shedding his own clothes. From the flex of his abs as he positioned himself between Ryan's legs, it was clear how turned on he was, but he didn't make a move to take his pants off.

Ryan squirmed as Wyatt trailed a finger up his hard, aching cock. Like earlier, when Ryan was expecting a rougher, more intense touch, he only got a delicate, exploratory one. Like Wyatt was trying to catalog him and every single one of his reactions.

"More," he straight-up begged now. "Give me more."

Wyatt's eyes darkened. "I'll give you more," he vowed, this time his finger trailing back down, past Ryan's balls, circling his hole.

Ryan thought he might have to beg again for something more than that light, exploratory touch. But like Wyatt had presented at the interview, he was a genius with his hands. Admittedly, he'd promised he was great with his hands in the *kitchen*, but he could have also sold them as genius in bed too, because it was the most mind-blowing prep of Ryan's life.

By the time Wyatt had worked a second finger alongside the first, he had found his prostate and was wringing moans Ryan would have been embarrassed about if it didn't feel so good. He was desperate for more, desperate to come, desperate to feel something more lasting than just the ephemeral brush of Wyatt's fingertips against his spot.

He knew Wyatt could give him more, and was just holding back. "I can take it, I promise," Ryan begged, too aware of the tears forming at the corners of his eyes. "God, give it to me, *please.*"

Wyatt didn't budge, didn't go any faster than the inexorable, painfully good teasing of the past few minutes. "If you come now, can you come later?" he asked, his voice soft, but hard at the edges. The same desperation that Ryan was dying from.

He pushed harder, even though he wasn't sure he could. Wyatt's fingers felt like magic, his cock probably would feel even better. "Sure, yes, just . . . please fuck me."

"One more finger," Wyatt coaxed, and slid a third in with the other two, but still just barely grazed against the spot that kept Ryan swearing a blue streak.

"God damnit," Ryan yelled. He'd never been happier for the advice of the contractor in charge of his remodel who had suggested better soundproof insulation.

The contractor had probably been thinking about loud movies or wild parties. Except Ryan was taking advantage by having loud and very close to wild sex, if Wyatt fucking Blake would ever fucking get on with it.

"I'm good, I'm good," Ryan babbled. "I promise." He'd known Wyatt was going to be good in bed, but nothing had prepared him for the reality.

"Not quite," Wyatt said, and leaned down, and took Ryan's cock in one long suck right at the same time he suddenly pressed against the spot he'd barely been dancing around all night. Ryan barely had a second to screech before he was coming so hard he saw white spots at the edges of his vision, pleasure coursing through him like a gigantic wave.

"You promised," Wyatt reminded him, suddenly leaving him empty of fingers and, wiping his mouth on the back of his other hand. And that was all the warning Ryan got before he lined up and slid right in.

Ryan didn't even remember when he'd taken his pants off, and suddenly full of a really great cock, he realized he didn't care. Wyatt could be a fucking pants magician, and everything was still great.

Wyatt pulled back and thrust, *hard,* and everything wasn't just great, it was fucking fantastic. A little sensitive, a little raw, a little too much but still exactly what he wanted.

After the first few strokes, Wyatt pulled out and flipped him over, and Ryan went, like the limp raggedy doll Wyatt had turned him into. And then holding his head against the bed, one hand against his neck, the other at his hip, proceeded to fuck him into oblivion.

Ryan would be embarrassed at the sounds he was making, but Wyatt was grunting plenty too, spouting lots of sappy gibberish that Ryan would wish later that he could remember.

But all he remembered later was the feel of Wyatt's cock pounding into him, dismantling him from the inside out. And just when he thought it was all too much, and he was about to beg for something—not for him to stop, not for him to keep going, but some unknown action that he didn't even know—Wyatt wrapped a hand around his cock, gave him a few strokes, and Ryan managed to come all over himself for the second time that night.

He barely registered Wyatt's following bellow, or how his fingers clamped down hard on his neck. It took him a long moment to even remember his own name.

"You are a maniac," Ryan said, as Wyatt came back to bed from disposing the condom. He had found a washcloth and had wet it. The water was even warm, Ryan marveled as he took it and wiped down.

"You seemed to like it okay," Wyatt said with a blush and a self-deprecating shrug that made it even sexier. He wasn't naturally that intense; Ryan just brought it out of him. They brought it out of each other.

"It was some of the best sex I've ever had. If not *the best* sex," Ryan admitted. His brain-to-mouth filter was gone, obliterated by two fantastic, world-destroying orgasms.

Wyatt blushed again, and then shocked the hell out of Ryan for about the millionth time that night by leaning over and giving him a sweet, affectionate kiss. "You're welcome," he said when he pulled away.

"I believe," Ryan said, reaching for his boxer briefs, even though moving seemed very overrated, "that you owe me a beer. And there's some in the fridge, with our name on them."

Wyatt didn't seem to know what to do with his hands without being able to shove them in his pants pockets. Ryan wasn't surprised to see him reach for his jeans, like he needed the comfort they provided. "I could go for a beer."

Maybe a beer would give Ryan the liquid courage he'd need tell Wyatt that he wanted him to be his fake boyfriend, with all the real benefits they'd just enjoyed.

But he knew, as he slipped down the hall towards the kitchen, shirtless with jeans hanging at his hips, that he wouldn't ask tonight. Maybe he'd find his courage tomorrow. Because he suddenly wasn't sure that Wyatt was going to settle for a *fake* relationship, even with the real benefits.

Chapter Five

Wyatt woke up the first day on the job in a bed that wasn't his.

Naked.

With his boss.

It was either the best first day or the worst; it was too early to say for sure.

The one thing he definitely knew was that he was hungry. His stomach was growling so loudly it was miraculous that Ryan hadn't woken up from its insistent grumbling. But, as he slipped out of the bed, Wyatt thought that it was probably better that they didn't do the whole "waking up together" thing.

It was probably going to be awkward enough, because they'd had fantastic, mind-blowing sex, had a few beers out by Ryan's fire pit in the backyard, and then had headed back inside for round number two.

Wyatt didn't exactly remember passing out in Ryan's bed, but he was pretty sure that Ryan hadn't exactly invited him. Of course, he *was* sure that Ryan was slurring with pleasure at that point, so it wasn't like Wyatt had fooled him.

Still, this would be better, Wyatt thought as he grabbed his clothes and headed towards *his* part of the house. Less awkwardness. Less questions. He'd have breakfast ready—he'd already checked, there were rudimentary supplies already in the fridge—and then he'd disappear after, and do some actual work by spending Ryan's money on groceries and more equipment.

No matter how relaxed Ryan was with him, Wyatt had no intention of shirking any of his duties. He might be doing a whole lot more than he'd been hired to do, but he was at least going to fulfill the rest of his responsibilities.

He grabbed a quick shower, appreciating the much-improved water pressure over the semi-shitty house he'd shared with Xander and Kian.

By the time he was back in the main house, letting himself in the back door, the house was still completely silent.

As far as Wyatt was concerned, that was fine by him. Ryan could sleep in if he wanted to, after all he was the boss and the professional athlete.

Wyatt raided the veggie drawer of the fridge, chopping up kale and spinach, red onion and mushrooms for a quick egg white frittata. It would have been better with a little goat cheese, but Wyatt thought, digging into his own portion, it wasn't half-bad. It was the first meal that Wyatt was preparing for Ryan, and even though he was having all sorts of un-professional feelings, he still wanted Ryan to think hiring him had been the right decision.

Breakfast finished, the dishes washed up, Wyatt went back to his cottage and grabbed his pad. Started meal plans for the week. Made an equipment list. Drank three glasses of water. Peed. And glanced at his phone, because Ryan couldn't *still* be sleeping, could he?

He'd only had two beers to Wyatt's three, and he certainly hadn't seemed drunk. A tiny bit tipsy maybe, but he'd been so adorable and then so unbearably sexy that Wyatt hadn't really worried.

He was worried now. It was past ten, and that seemed like an excessive amount of sleep even for a professional athlete during the off-season. Despite his brain screaming at him that this was a bad idea, Wyatt crept back down the hallway towards the master bedroom. He'd told himself firmly as he'd exited it this morning that he would not be taking advantage or invading Ryan's private spaces unless he was invited.

There had to be some sort of line, and Wyatt would maintain it because he was still a professional, god damnit.

Wyatt stopped short in the doorway, which was wide open. The bed, with its fluffy navy and white comforter, was empty.

"Ryan?" Wyatt called out. "I made breakfast, if you're hungry?" He was probably just in the shower or the bathroom. But the entire suite was dead quiet. Too quiet.

A growing uncertainty mounting in his stomach, Wyatt crossed the living room again and went to the garage. Flipping on the light, the bottom dropped right out of it.

The Tesla, which Ryan had told him last night he usually took in the city, was gone.

Ryan had left while Wyatt had been in the shower. And Wyatt remembered distinctly Ryan telling him last night that he hadn't had any plans for the next day. Had even hinted that he wanted to go shopping with Wyatt. But now, he wasn't even here. He'd left, without saying goodbye. Without a single god damn word.

Wyatt walked back to the kitchen in a daze, and stared at the covered plate he'd made for Ryan. His first gut reaction was to shove it all in the trash bin, but he'd seen too many documentaries and read too many articles about food waste to do so, even if he was fucking pissed. So he dug out a Tupperware container and shoved it in the fridge instead.

He couldn't explain what had happened between last night, which had been very clearly enjoyable on both their sides, and this morning. Had Ryan been pissed that he'd left the bed? Should he have left a note? Wyatt didn't know. He liked Ryan so much, but this was already messy as hell, and it had just started. How were they going to make it through with their professional and personal relationships intact?

Fuck, he didn't even know if they had either one, anymore. And it was the first god damned day.

Wyatt slammed the back door even though nobody was in the house to hear it. Grabbed the keys he'd just found and his worn leather jacket, and took off. If Ryan wanted to remind him to do his job, he'd fucking do it. If he stayed and stewed, he'd end up saying something he'd regret.

Like what a total jerk Ryan Flores had ended up being.

"I cannot believe you just *left*." Tabitha stared at him, eyes wide and disbelieving, arms crossed over a ratty UCLA sweatshirt, her mouth a thin, angry line.

Ryan really couldn't believe he'd just left either. Though, if he was getting technical about it, he hadn't left first. Of course, if he was getting technical, Wyatt hadn't really left. He couldn't leave. He lived at Ryan's house now, basically.

And Ryan had even known what Wyatt was doing. Probably some noble, professional thing—getting out of a nice warm bed to cook his bed partner, and technically his boss, breakfast. Ryan could even imagine that thought going through Wyatt's head. Wanting to stay, but feeling obligated to do what he'd been hired for.

It was why Ryan put extra time in the batting cages, why he still ran drills during the off-season. Why he'd even agreed to all of this in the first place. Because playing baseball was important, and being a professional was important. But understanding it, and facing it were apparently two different things, because Ryan had not faced it very well this morning.

Frankly, he'd not faced it at all. He'd lain awake, listening to the back door shut, and had known, deep down, that he couldn't lie to Wyatt anymore about the job. Not after last night.

Feeling raw, discombobulated, and more than a little scared, he'd run to the one place he'd never be turned away. Even when he acted like a total ass.

"Didn't I tell you that we were having breakfast this morning, darling?" he asked Tabitha, pasting on a sweet, rather saccharine smile that wasn't fooling anyone—Tabitha *or* her boyfriend.

Cal made a grumpy sound as he shoveled in toast smeared with mango jelly. He was elbow-deep in his iPad, looking at plans for his next remodel.

"Ryan," Tabitha said, her patience clearly at an end. "It is time for you to be honest with him. Completely, one hundred percent honest."

Cal said something that suspiciously might have been, "and not in our house." Which was sort of fair. It was early on a weekday and just because they both worked from home didn't mean that Ryan could just dump his problems at their doorstep.

"He is *not* going to say yes, if I ask him." Tabitha's expression softened, and Ryan had a feeling it was because of the raw fear in his eyes. He didn't know when it had become imperative that Wyatt not just be his personal chef, but that line had been crossed and there was no going back.

"I should really just call up Eric and tell him to forget the whole thing," Ryan said. Even though that sounded like both the best and the worst thing to do. Of course, not getting into a fake relationship with someone because you were scared was bad enough. How terrible was not getting into a real relationship because of good old-fashioned fear?

"And what, you're going to tell Wyatt you want to give a real relationship a shot, instead of a fake one?" Tabitha demanded.

That was exactly the problem. Ryan already knew he wasn't cut out for a "real" relationship. The fake version was probably the best he had to offer Wyatt, no matter how much he wanted to give more.

"I thought that you'd love the idea of me canning the whole fake-relationship bit," Ryan said. "You've hated it from the beginning. Of course I was never certain if you hated it because it was Eric's idea or if you just hated it."

"I hate the dishonesty of it," Tabitha said bluntly. She turned back towards the stove, babysitting the eggs in the pan. It was weird seeing Tabitha in her kitchen; it was even weirder seeing her attempt to cook.

"I'm learning," she'd said defensively when he'd nearly fallen over in shock to see her wielding a spatula and a frying pan earlier.

"You made your living being dishonest," Ryan pointed out.

Tabitha's eyes flashed, and for a single, heart-stopping moment he was sure she was going to dump the runny eggs in his lap and whack him on the head with the frying pan.

"Which is exactly why I don't want you to be dishonest. If you're going to do this—and even I can admit to the benefits—you should be honest about it. Go back to your house and tell Wyatt everything." Tabitha took a deep breath. "I lied all the time, for good reasons and for bad ones, and that's why I'm telling you that you don't want to go down that road."

"What if I'm sure he'll say no?" Ryan asked, and he hated how agonized he sounded.

"What if he says no?" Tabitha asked with an arched eyebrow. "Frankly I think more people should say no to you."

The long and short of it was that by the time Ryan slunk back to his house late morning, he was in a shitty mood. Tabitha thought he should experience people saying no to him? Well, she was going to get her wish today.

Ryan wasn't even surprised to find his house empty of Wyatt, and was even less surprised when he knocked on the addition and was met with silence and a locked door.

He knew he deserved the silence, whether Wyatt was in there or not. Ignoring him or not.

Ryan returned to the house and took a shower, taking a long time with the hot water, wishing that it could wash all his guilt away—and his feelings too, if he was being completely honest. He didn't want to like Wyatt. It had seemed so convenient at first, being so attracted to him, and genuinely wanting to know him better. But now that was backfiring because he wanted him around, he wanted *more*, and the casualty of being honest probably meant that Ryan was going to miss out on all that.

He walked back into the kitchen, half-considering another beer or maybe even something stronger, even though it was barely one in the afternoon, and nearly shrieked with surprise to see Wyatt there, unpacking a whole bunch of bags on the island.

Wyatt glanced up, eyes a stormy blue, a crease between his brows, and Ryan nearly ran back to the safety of his bedroom.

"I see you're back," Wyatt said frostily. And yeah, if Ryan thought he was going to dance around the topic, he'd been wrong. Wyatt was uncomfortably direct.

And honest.

"Yeah," Ryan admitted.

Wyatt was still staring directly at him, and Ryan shifted uncomfortably. "I see you went shopping."

"Yeah, I found the credit card and the keys on the counter." Wyatt didn't ask if it had been okay to use them; he'd just done it. "I took the Range Rover. I figured it would be better for errands."

"You can take whatever car you want, just not . . ."

Wyatt didn't even let him finish the sentence. "Just not the Tesla. Yeah, I figured that out real quick."

"You're angry," Ryan stated. Tabitha was whispering in his ear. His conscience was magnifying her whisper until it was as loud as a scream. *Be honest,* she kept repeating. "I guess it wasn't very nice of me to sneak out."

Wyatt looked away, finally breaking eye contact just when Ryan actually wanted it. "It's your house. I certainly don't have any right to be angry about what you do in it or where you go when you're not in it."

His conscience's shriek magnified to a cascading cacophony. "I don't do this very often, to be honest. And I'm not very good at it."

"Hiring a personal chef or hooking up?" Wyatt asked wryly. "Because I'm not sure which we're arguing about here." He still wasn't looking at him. He was taking those little annoying tags off the bottom of a bunch of kitchen equipment that Ryan didn't recognize. Pots and pans and some kind of whisk.

"No, I know how to hook up," Ryan said with a humorless chuckle. "The morning after. And I knew you'd be here, I definitely knew that before I started anything with you. I just didn't expect . . ."

"For it to be so awkward?" Wyatt's voice had thawed a fraction.

"Yeah, I guess you could say that."

"Well, it wasn't exactly non-awkward for me either," Wyatt said. "You're technically my boss."

"Not really," Ryan reminded him. "We talked about this. Personal and professional staying separate."

"Does it feel separate now?" Wyatt demanded. "I was handling it, I really was. And then I came to get you for breakfast and you were fucking *gone*, and you hadn't even done me the professional courtesy of telling me you didn't want me to cook for you this morning."

He glanced up now, and his eyes were blazing, a hot brilliant blue that made Ryan's chest ache. Wyatt was going to say no. He was going to say no, and Ryan couldn't do a thing to stop it. But the longer he went on without asking, the worse the ache got.

"I haven't been entirely honest with you," Ryan finally admitted.

Wyatt's expression didn't change an iota. "Imagine that," he said bitterly.

When Ryan stared at him in surprise—he'd never imagined that Wyatt would figure it out so quickly—Wyatt continued. "Yeah, I know you don't need a private chef. You don't even know what to do with me. So what am I really here for, some kind of stud escort service? You don't get enough dick on Grindr anymore? Want someone a little more dependable, with the added benefit that I can whip up some food when you get hungry for something other than cock?"

Tabitha had been right; he should have been honest from the beginning. If Wyatt said no, it was going to be because he'd lied to him from the first moment they'd met. Apparently dishonesty was a terrible foundation for a relationship, even a fake one.

"Not exactly, but you're sort of on the right track," Ryan said and watched as Wyatt's expression hardened. "Not just the sex stuff. I need . . . help with getting my contract renewed."

"How the fuck am I supposed to help you with that?" Wyatt interrupted.

"Please," Ryan asked, far too aware that he was pleading with him. "Please, let me get this out, and if you want to hate me, if you want to say no, then you can. You can keep the job being my chef. We'll figure out how to make it work. I'll be professional, we'll work out a job description and everything. I swear."

Wyatt didn't say a word, just stared defiantly at the kitchen supplies spread across the kitchen island. Ryan took a deep breath and continued. "The new general manager of the Dodgers, he's the one responsible for basically deciding whether to extend my contract or let me try the open market someplace else. I really don't want to leave LA. My family is here. I like it here. I want to keep playing for the Dodgers, but if the status quo doesn't change, the GM probably won't choose to extend me. He's not . . . precisely homophobic, but he has some fucking wrong ways of thinking. Like he thinks I'm some sort of flighty gay party boy. He wants someone who's serious, who takes baseball seriously, who isn't going to party and fuck every cute boy who crosses his path."

"How on earth am *I* going to help you reverse that impression?"

Wyatt's incredulity wasn't exactly misplaced. After all, they'd met at Temple. Ryan had undeniably picked him up, and then they'd hooked up. Twice.

"I need to have a steady, normal relationship. He needs to feel like I've settled down."

Wyatt's incredulity bubble exploded. "You *were* shopping for a boyfriend."

"A fake one, yeah. But even if the sappy feelings part isn't legit, I don't want some stranger. I want someone I would actually like. That I could like. And I like you."

A dark look passed across Wyatt's face. Ryan pressed on because he couldn't stop now. "The sex was great. Fantastic, even. We could have fun."

"So, we'd just pretend to be together, and keep having sex. Like . . . an added benefit?" Wyatt's apparent disbelief echoed Tabitha's when he'd first suggested the idea, and Ryan didn't like his deep, subterranean worry that they'd both been right. This *was* stupid.

Would it have been better to just hope that his relationship with Wyatt had turned out? That he could hold down a real boyfriend without becoming bored or boring him? But then if it didn't work out, Ryan would be right back to square one.

No, they needed parameters and guidelines and a set timeline. It was better to establish right away in cold blood that they weren't going to fall in love. It was just great sex and Wyatt helping Ryan out of a bad situation. Simple mutual benefits and nothing messy.

"This is insane," Wyatt said.

"It's all planned out," Ryan said. "You were initially just part of the set-up—Eric had decided that I needed a personal chef to round out the 'settled down' vibe we were trying to portray—and then I recognized you from the photo they sent me with your resume. I met you, and I realized that I didn't want to fake date some wannabe actor. I wanted to fake date you."

The expression on Wyatt's face was terrible.

"That's all this ever was? You wanting to convince me to fake date you?"

"No, no, no, I *never* lied. I mean I omitted some stuff. But I never lied. I like you. Last night was awesome. I hope we have a hundred more nights just like it, a *thousand*." Even as he scrambled, Ryan had a sick feeling that he wasn't going to be able to convince Wyatt.

Ryan told himself the nauseous roll of his stomach at the thought was just because Wyatt was going to quit and go back to Napa, out of Ryan's life before whatever they had together ran its natural course. It always sucked when you saw the potential of something good and it ended before it ever began.

"I can't do this," Wyatt said and there was an ugly finality in his voice.

"What if it's just like last night, just a few additional and totally harmless pap shots added to the mix?" Ryan begged.

Wyatt's eyes were two hard blue stones. Opaque and closed off. From what, Ryan didn't know. He hadn't gotten to know him well enough to figure him out yet, and that shouldn't have hurt but it *did*. "I can't flounce around with you, fake holding hands for the paps." He took an unsteady breath that Ryan could hear from across the kitchen. "I'm not out. Not to my family. And I'm not going to let them find out like this."

Ryan had come up with a thousand reasons why Wyatt might tell him no. It had never occurred to him that Wyatt wasn't out, and that's why he would turn Ryan's proposal down. His sexuality felt like such a natural extension of who he was, his personality open and relaxed.

Besides, that wasn't an excuse that Ryan could ever talk his way around. He knew exactly what coming out before the draft had cost him. Not just in dollars and cents, not even with how good Eric had turned out to be.

It had taken balls of steel to come out the first time to his family and then something even greater to do the same with his friends. And then something even more momentous to do it with the world watching.

He couldn't ask Wyatt to take that step if he hadn't chosen to do it before now.

"I'm so god damned sorry," Ryan said, and he was. He was sorry he hadn't realized. He was sorry that Wyatt was in a situation where he didn't feel like he could. He was sorry for himself, that he was going to have to find some stranger to fill a void that Ryan hadn't even realized existed until he'd met Wyatt.

"It's not your fault," Wyatt said. "I'm sorry I can't help you out. It's bullshit you have to endure that sort of double fucking standard. It's not fair."

"It's not," Ryan admitted. He wasn't going to say out loud that it wasn't fair either that Wyatt couldn't be honest with his family. There was a lot of fucked-up shit in the world, and there was a lot of progress to be made with erasing homophobia. Especially the latent biases of people like the Dodgers' GM.

"It's just my nana," Wyatt said, and he sounded wrecked. "She's not intolerant. She's not mean or rude or nasty. She just . . . she's just so religious. Always going to Mass. We've never talked about it, and sometimes I swear she knows, and I never have to say it out loud. But then she asks me when I'm going to bring a girl around and give her grandchildren, and *fuck*, I'm sorry. This isn't the baggage you wanted to get into."

"I don't care. I'm here to listen." Ryan walked over to the barstool opposite Wyatt. "Anything you want to talk about."

Wyatt looked surprised, which *killed* Ryan. Did he really believe that Ryan was some sort of insensitive asshole? "Why would you even want to listen? You took the hardest road you could and you *changed the fucking world.*" Wyatt flushed red, and Ryan began to realize that he was actually ashamed.

Ashamed that Ryan had come out of the closet and in such a public way, and he hadn't come out to his own family yet.

And that was the biggest bunch of bullshit yet.

"I'm not some sort of saint or god or good fucking person because I came out," Ryan said. "It doesn't make me any better than you. Any braver. Any stronger."

Wyatt's fingers clenched on the edge of the marble countertop, his knuckles going pale.

"It's different for everybody," Ryan added.

"I want to tell her," Wyatt said. "She's . . . she's . . ." And Ryan watched as his eyes glimmered with moisture suddenly. "She's not well. She's in a home. A mental care home."

"Oh god. I'm sorry." Ryan didn't think he could even express how sorry he was. At least not with words. He slid off the barstool and wrapped his body around Wyatt's tightly. "I'm so sorry," he murmured into the cotton covering his back.

"I want to tell her. I just . . . can't. What if the last thing she remembers of me is that I'm going to hell?" Wyatt choked out a sob and Ryan hung on tighter.

"I don't know her. But you love her, so I can't imagine she would think that."

Suddenly Wyatt shucked Ryan's grip and he got a single glimpse of wetness shining on Wyatt's cheek before he was across the kitchen, the back door slamming behind him.

Ryan looked at the brand-new kitchen equipment strewn across the island counter. "Fuck," he said succinctly, and pulled out his phone because he was going to have to tell Eric.

CHAPTER SIX

ONLY THE THOUGHT THAT he was a god damn professional got Wyatt out of bed at four, where he'd spent the afternoon wallowing in self-imposed and Ryan-imposed misery.

Wyatt didn't exactly blame Ryan for the truth, and it wasn't his fault Wyatt was miserable, but so many of the reasons still originated with him.

He wanted to date Ryan *for real*, not as a front to convince his general manager that he was a reliable person. Not because Eric had decided Ryan should date someone. Not because Ryan figured they were at least sexually compatible so fake dating for the foreseeable future wouldn't be *so* terrible.

Though that reason had at least made some fucking sense.

It had brought Wyatt so high that Ryan had picked *him* and then brought him lower than he'd ever been to have to turn him down. Frankly, he didn't give a shit what his brothers thought of him; if they needed a year or two or ten to cool off, whatever. But his grandmother . . . she had always made him pause. Especially now, because the last thing he wanted was to lose whatever time he had left with her.

Wouldn't it be better to just keep his mouth shut and have her drift away from reality with her nice, innocuous, pleasant, loving memories of Wyatt?

He looked in the mirror in the bathroom and wished his eyes didn't look red still. Curse of having blue eyes; if you cried, there was no way to hide it. He wet a washcloth with cold water and tried anyway.

After a minute of dabbing and trying to take away the remaining puffiness under his eyes, he felt a little more normal. He normally couldn't give a shit, but he didn't want Ryan to know he'd spent the afternoon crying.

It would be so easy to walk back into Ryan's house and tell him that he'd changed his mind. And so hard, Wyatt reminded his reflection. If he told the truth, then his nana might have a different view of him for the last bit of her coherent life, but at least she would have the *right* view.

Tossing the washcloth into the sink, Wyatt wiped his face, gave a quick damp swipe to his hair, and hoped that nobody would be in the kitchen. He wanted to prep dinner in silence.

Before he even opened the door to the house, Wyatt knew he wouldn't get any silence. Music echoed through a few open windows and grew much louder as he stepped inside.

A beautiful blonde woman was sitting on a barstool, sipping a glass filled with clear liquid and a lime slice. Her blue eyes latched onto him instantly, and Wyatt froze.

"Hello, you must be Wyatt," she said. Her tone was brisk and straightforward. She extended a hand and he walked closer to shake it.

"I'm Tabitha. Ryan's best friend," she continued, and even though he'd known forever he was gay, he couldn't help but be struck a little dumb by how crazy gorgeous she was. Flawless features, bright hair curling around her face, and those eyes. Never mind the excessive confidence she exuded. She'd belong wherever she chose to be.

"I'm not sure where he got to," Tabitha said because Wyatt still hadn't found his voice. "We spent the last few hours figuring out where to put everything. I'm sure you'll want to re-arrange but it gave him something to do, and it kept him out of your hair, which . . . you're welcome."

Wyatt stiffened. Had Ryan told this woman all his secrets? The reason why he'd turned Ryan's proposal down?

"Don't worry," she said. "He didn't tell me why. Just that it was a really good reason, and I had to keep him occupied so he wouldn't get selfish and try to convince you anyway."

Wyatt shoved his hands in the pockets of his jeans and fervently wished he didn't feel obligated to be a professional so he could escape back to his quiet little cottage. He didn't want to be interrogated by this woman, no matter how beautiful she was. Because that's exactly what this was—a very friendly, commiserating interrogation.

"Ryan doesn't have a selfish bone in his body," he said.

Tabitha laughed. Not the Disney Princess bell laugh he'd expected, but something a little darker, a little edgier. It sounded real, and it made him like her more, even if he didn't want to.

"I've heard a lot about you," Tabitha said speculatively, and Wyatt wasn't surprised at all. This woman, as friendly as her expression was, could pry secrets out of James Bond.

"I'm sure you have," Wyatt said wryly, turning towards the fridge. If he had to give up his quiet time, at least he could do what he'd been hired for.

"Oh, are you going to cook something?" Tabitha asked when he opened the fridge and started pulling out ingredients without even looking at them. "My sister is a really fantastic chef, but that's not the only way we're different. And Ryan isn't hopeless, he just doesn't bother. I'm glad you're going to bother for him."

Wyatt was afraid too many emotions were too close to the surface, but he turned back anyway. "I'd do a lot more than bother."

Tabitha sighed and tapped a nail, blood red and dangerous, against the side of her glass. He was beginning to suspect it contained more than just water. "I figured as much. We're going to have to figure out what to do about that, that's for sure."

"I bother because I'm paid to," Wyatt tried to claim, but they both knew the truth and her eyes turned sympathetic.

He half-expected her to call his bluff, but she didn't. Merely took another drink from her glass. It made him like her more.

Of course Ryan would have a brilliant, yet terrifying friend like Tabitha.

"How did you meet?" Wyatt asked because it got her off his case, and also because he genuinely wanted to know.

"I wrote his coming out story," Tabitha said breezily. "Among other things. We met three years ago when he was just a snarky kid from Stanford."

"What about you?" Wyatt asked.

"What about me?"

Wyatt took the corn over to the sink to begin shucking and cleaning the cobs. "You said Ryan was a snarky kid from Stanford. What about you?" He glanced back, and was a little surprised to see her soft expression.

"When we met, I didn't have friends. Not like Ryan. He was my first." She hesitated. "I know you don't want me to pry, it's written all over your face, but I have to say I understand why he likes you so much. You've got this calm, zen thing that would be very appealing for him."

"Zen thing?" Wyatt asked with a low chuckle. When he'd come into this kitchen ten minutes ago, he hadn't felt less like laughing. He'd wanted nothing more than to turn around and go back to where he'd came from when he'd spotted Tabitha. But there was something about her blunt honesty coupled with the empathy in her eyes that helped.

It was very clear why the snarky kid from Stanford had wanted to be her friend. Wyatt found himself feeling the exact same way.

"All centered and shit." Tabitha waved her hand in the air. "Don't tell me you do yoga."

"I'm actually more of a surfer, to be honest," he admitted.

Tabitha groaned. "Of course you are."

"Is that a problem?" Wyatt asked over his shoulder as he continued to clean the corn from its husks with a soft brush. He was thinking a fresh corn salsa with the fresh-caught shrimp he'd picked up this morning. Maybe even add some polenta. He had the time. It was nice to be able to cook in this relaxed environment, chatting with Tabitha, and not worrying about being screamed at or pleasing a never-ending parade of particular diners paying a fortune for their dinner.

"No, you're just disgustingly perfect." He could hear the roll of her eyes in her voice.

"Hardly," Wyatt retorted. "I could give you a load of reasons why I'm not perfect."

"Oh, I'm glad I got back for this," Ryan said. Wyatt's head whipped around, and yeah, he was definitely there, standing in the doorway. Wyatt felt a little like he'd gotten caught with his hand in the cookie jar, but he was exactly where he was supposed to be.

Tabitha had just happened to be here, and he was making normal, friendly conversation with her, like anyone might.

"I got fresh supplies," Ryan said, pulling out a bottle of Grey Goose from the paper bag he was holding.

"Should have gotten tequila," Wyatt said, forcing his voice to stay even and normal. "I'm making barbecued shrimp. Great with a margarita."

"I probably have some somewhere," Ryan said. "But Tabby was determined to drink all my vodka."

"I was trying to make you feel better," Tabitha said with dignity. "And I've been telling you for years not to call me that."

"Someday," Ryan said, slinging an arm around his friend, "you're going to realize that every time you say that, it makes me more determined than ever to call you that." His affectionate gaze was completely platonic, but Wyatt couldn't help it; he burned with jealousy anyway.

Even if they couldn't be a thing—fake or real or anything else in between—he still wanted to be Ryan's friend. Not just his employee. And Wyatt was terrified that turning down his proposal had left him his job, but had demolished everything else.

He couldn't imagine how much it would burn when Ryan moved on and found someone new to pretend to date, and fuck for real.

No matter how much he needed this job or how much he didn't want to leave, Wyatt wasn't sure he could stick around and watch that.

"You are an asshole," Tabitha said. "Even though you went and bought me more vodka."

"Yeah, I'm still trying to figure out how you coming over and drinking all my booze was supposed to make me feel better." Ryan was smiling, but Wyatt thought he could see the bad mood lurking behind his dark eyes. Present, but concealed. Just like his own.

It shouldn't have made Wyatt feel any better, but it did, a little. If Ryan felt bad, at least that meant he'd cared. He'd really wanted it to be Wyatt, and Wyatt still felt incredulous that Ryan had cared so much. It shouldn't have mattered. Wyatt should have been pissed as hell that he'd concealed his motives, but there had been genuine understanding in his eyes when Wyatt had told him why he couldn't accept.

"It's a secret talent of mine," Tabitha said. She turned to Wyatt. "Don't you feel better, too?"

"I'm fine," Wyatt said stiffly, even though they all knew it was a lie. Nobody knew it more than Ryan.

"Then it's time for me to get out of your hair," Tabitha said, gracefully sliding off the barstool. Even though Wyatt was beginning to suspect she'd drank quite a bit of Ryan's vodka.

"Wyatt's making dinner, you can't leave yet," Ryan said. They all knew what he really meant was, *you can't leave me alone with Wyatt.*

Tabitha reached over and patted him on the cheek. "I'm sure I'll be back."

Wyatt threw a towel over his shoulder. "I'm holding you to that."

She batted her eyes exaggeratedly and it didn't even make her look ridiculous, only more beautiful. "It isn't every day that I get to enjoy the efforts of a Michelin-starred chef," she said.

He wasn't really Michelin-starred. That had been his boss, Bastian Aquino, but he didn't correct her, only smiled.

"I'll call you an Uber," Ryan said, "you are so damn drunk."

"Don't worry, I already texted Calvin, he'll be here in a minute."

Ryan rolled his eyes. "Next time I'm not calling you."

Tabitha's expression was dead serious. "Of course you will. That's why we're friends." She tugged Ryan into a quick, tight hug.

Wyatt turned back to his corn in the sink. He didn't want to cry again, but he felt close and he didn't even know why.

He heard Tabitha depart, her sandals clattering on the wood floor of the hallway, and scrubbed harder on the corn cob in his hand. He wanted Ryan to come back to the kitchen, but at the same time he dreaded it.

"You're making shrimp. With some sort of corn thing."

Wyatt turned and Ryan was definitely back, framed in the doorway again. This time he came in, and sat right down at the barstool Tabitha had been occupying until a few minutes ago.

"I'm making shrimp with a corn salsa," Wyatt confirmed. "I hope that's okay."

"I told you. Anything you want to do is fine by me."

"What about foods you don't like?"

Ryan shot Wyatt a teasing, chastising look. "Starting the interrogation back up, I see."

"It's not an interrogation. And yeah, we got a little . . . derailed before." Wyatt willed himself not to flush, but the reminder was all he needed to go hot and then cold all over. He didn't know how they could still work together after the sex they'd had. Maybe that was the real question he should be asking, not what Ryan's least-favorite foods were.

"It was all—okay, *mostly*—your fault. Though it wasn't like I was complaining that you decided to get a little unprofessional."

Wyatt stiffened. And not in the good way. "I wasn't . . . I mean . . . I'm . . ."

Ryan held up a hand, and his smile was a little sad. Too much like he'd looked that first night at Temple. "If you apologize for having sex with me, *great sex*, mind you, I'm going to be offended."

"I won't, then," Wyatt said, even attempting a smile of his own. But he wasn't sure he'd been any more successful than Ryan.

Imagine being so torn up that you couldn't be in a fake relationship with someone. Wyatt figured it was pretty damn clear that he was willing to take just about anything Ryan could offer him.

"Foods I don't like . . . olives. This is an olive-free house."

"Olive oil?" Wyatt asked.

"Does it taste like olives?" Ryan asked archly.

"It'd better not," Wyatt said. He placed the cleaned cobs in a deep bowl and started slicing off corn kernels.

"I'm olive oil neutral then," Ryan said.

"What else?" Wyatt asked.

"Beets. Pickles—except maybe in a Cuban sandwich."

"Good call," Wyatt said approvingly. "There's nothing like a really good Cuban."

"Can you make one?"

Wyatt pulled tomatoes out of the wire basket he'd bought today. At least Tabitha and Ryan had known where to put these. He'd searched for the garlic for five minutes, only to find it in the produce drawer of the fridge.

He guessed Tabitha wasn't kidding that she and Ryan didn't spend much time in the kitchen.

"A Cuban? Um, yes. Definitely."

"Can I make requests? Is that allowed?"

Wyatt let his knife slice rhythmically through the tomato. It steadied him, even when he wanted to fly out of his own skin. Or fuck Ryan again. "You're the boss. What's allowed is up to you."

"What would I have been if you'd said yes this afternoon?" Ryan asked, voice soft.

Wyatt's knife hesitated. The ripe tomato, like his heart, bruised a little under the pressure of the knife. "The guy you were dating, I guess. Bonus: he cooks, too."

It was hard not to hear the hurt edge to Ryan's voice, and it was impossible to deny that he'd been eager before. Ryan had wanted this. Real or not real. And Wyatt could only assume it might have become real. Maybe.

"And now I'm your boss again," Ryan said, and he sounded frustrated.

"You made it clear this fake boyfriend was something you needed. I'm assuming you're planning on hooking up with him, whoever he is."

"That was the plan." Ryan wasn't even hiding his regret.

"So you're my boss, and hopefully, maybe we can figure out how to be friends." Wyatt already knew it wasn't going to be enough; but it was better than nothing.

"Is that what you want?" Ryan asked cautiously.

The chopped tomato got dumped unceremoniously into the bowl with the corn. Wyatt tackled a red onion next, chopping it a bit more forcefully than was entirely necessary. "It's not what I want," he said. "But it's reality."

"We can be friends," Ryan said. There was an understandable lack of enthusiasm—which Wyatt totally got. There was a decided lack of getting naked in being "just friends."

But the alternative was worse. It meant losing moments like this, and even though they'd only just met, Wyatt already knew Ryan was important. Truthfully, he'd known from the first moment, and every successive moment since convinced him he'd been right. Not for the first time, Wyatt thought that maybe even a fake relationship with Ryan might be worth jeopardizing what he'd spent so many years protecting.

Wyatt pushed the thought away, along with all the negative ones. They would make this work; they would figure something out. He hadn't missed how Ryan looked at him, too. "I asked Tabitha how you met, and she told me that you were a snotty kid from Stanford."

Ryan laughed, and like he'd hoped, the mood lightened. "I know it's tough to believe."

Wyatt finished with the onions and moved onto the bundle of cilantro by the cutting board. "Actually, not really."

In the middle of stealing a tomato chunk from the bowl between them, Ryan made an outraged noise and instead of popping it in his mouth, tossed it with deadly accuracy at Wyatt's face.

Ryan wasn't a professional baseball player—a *shortstop*, even—for nothing. The tomato landed with a plop against its target: Wyatt's cheek.

Wyatt had a vision of the walls of this kitchen spattered with red tomato juice and the floors peppered with corn kernels as Ryan pushed him up against the island, devouring him like he was all the food he needed.

"Shit. I think I promised you I wouldn't throw anything." Ryan sounded unsure, like he wasn't sure if Wyatt was pissed or not.

"It's not a plate. It's not a knife or a pot full of hot water." He looked up and shot him a quick grin. "I think I'll live from a tiny tomato." To illustrate his point, he flipped it into his open mouth.

"Imagine my relief you're going to survive," Ryan said with a laugh.

"So you were a snotty kid from Stanford and Tabitha wrote your coming out profile." Wyatt kept coming back to his friendship with Tabitha because it not only seemed fascinating from the outside, she seemed to be one of the most important people in his life.

"Did she tell you that?" Ryan asked curiously.

"Yes, but she didn't have to. I thought back to a few years ago and realized where I'd seen her before. On ESPN, giving an interview, right after the story broke."

"She's got a memorable face," Ryan said.

Wyatt rolled his eyes.

"Okay, she's generally pretty memorable," Ryan admitted.

"And nice," Wyatt added.

It was Ryan's turn to roll his eyes. "Not even close. Tabitha is a lot of things; beautiful, smart . . . unsurprisingly deadly, but she's not really *nice*."

"I think the honesty is nice." It had also been unexpected to find Ryan, a professional athlete, so close to someone who would unapologetically call him out on his own bullshit.

"She keeps me grounded. Keeps me honest. Keeps me real. Sometimes," Ryan hesitated, "sometimes it's easy to get lost. And she's always found me."

"That's what my nana has always been for me," Wyatt volunteered. He didn't want to revisit their earlier conversation; he *definitely* did not want to discuss his reluctance to come out of the closet, but Ryan still needed to understand why the reluctance was there. How vital to his life his grandmother was. "My mom died when I was a teenager, and my dad was never really around much. So she's really all I have."

"My mom is great and all," Ryan said, propping his elbows on the counter and leaning on them. His dark eyes were contemplative. "But it's my aunt I'm closest to. She could probably go toe-to-toe with you in the kitchen and might even come out on top."

"Not a professional?" Wyatt asked.

"Just a home cook, but the Puerto Rican food she makes is to die for. Better than any restaurant, here or back home."

At Wyatt's curious look, Ryan continued. "I go back. Work with some charities. I was born here, but I can't forget where I came from. I might be a good baseball player but I'd be a shitty person if I did that."

"Is she in the area?" Wyatt asked, and Ryan nodded. "Maybe she'd be willing to teach me sometime. I'd love to learn to cook some Puerto Rican specialties."

Ryan looked surprised, which Wyatt shouldn't have let get to him, but it did anyway. "Really?"

"Of course. And not just for your benefit either. For my own."

"Yeah, I'll talk to her. Maybe arrange something next week."

"Maybe she can even teach *you* something," Wyatt added slyly.

"How do you know she hasn't already?" Ryan asked with a hint of amusement in his eyes. "Maybe I'm fantastic."

Wyatt couldn't have denied it even if he wanted to; Ryan *was* fantastic. Just not in the kitchen. He held out the big chef's knife he'd been using to clean and chop the cilantro. "Come here and show me then."

The way Ryan eyed the knife was proof enough, but Wyatt was genuinely curious how much Ryan knew. He ignored the spark of electricity that pulsed through him when Ryan took the knife and their fingers brushed.

A micro-second, and he was stupidly breathless.

"What is this?" Ryan asked, frown creasing his brows. "Some sort of weed?"

Wyatt sighed. "It's official, you are *not* fantastic. It's cilantro."

"Oh, that goes in guacamole, right?"

"And about a thousand other things."

"What am I supposed to do with it?" Ryan played lost, hefting the knife up and posing like he was at the plate.

"Are you really going to pretend like you don't know how to chop so I'll conveniently come closer and show you?"

Ryan batted his eyelashes. "Would it work?"

Too well, Wyatt thought, but before he said it out loud, he remembered that they were supposed to be working on being friends.

Shoving his crotch against Ryan's incredible ass was not a proposition that would ever lead to platonic friendship.

"Sorry," Ryan said awkwardly into the silence that had descended between them. "It's sort of my natural inclination to flirt outrageously with the hottest guy in the room."

"Or the *only* guy in the room," Wyatt pointed out wryly.

Ryan didn't need to say that he'd gone after him that night at Temple, and he definitely hadn't been the only guy in the room then. He only shot Wyatt a significant look that said it for him.

"I need to check in with Eric. How long until dinner?"

As much as Wyatt wanted Ryan to stay in the kitchen and keep flirting outrageously, it was definitely better for him to put some distance between them.

It was only the first day of them attempting friendship, and Wyatt had a feeling it wasn't going to get easier—and it was already god damned hard.

"Half an hour or so?" Wyatt said, quickly calculating the remaining tasks he had to do.

"Perfect." And then he disappeared, pulling his phone out of his pocket, and leaving Wyatt to dinner and his increasing dilemma. "And you're going to eat with me. None of this upstairs, downstairs bullshit. We're friends, remember?"

Despite how terrible this day had ended up becoming, Wyatt couldn't help but smile.

⁂

"That was fucking incredible," Ryan said, leaning back on the sofa, and rubbing his flat stomach. Wyatt remembered the flex of his abs as he'd nibbled his way down them just the night before.

The night before they'd been unabashedly making out on this couch. Now they were sitting a healthy distance apart, and Ryan had put on a nature documentary without even asking Wyatt what he wanted to watch.

Wyatt had gotten the memo though; they needed to put some metaphoric and actual space between them, before they both forgot that this couldn't go anywhere.

He knew he should be relieved that Ryan had stopped trying to seduce him; he wasn't.

"Thanks," Wyatt said. "I was a little concerned that you wouldn't like my food after you hired me."

Ryan rolled his eyes. "You're one of the best chefs in the world. What is there to worry about?"

Wyatt might not have the stone-cold arrogance that some chefs had, but he'd always believed, deep down, that people should eat and enjoy what he served.

It was more complicated to address Ryan, because from the beginning he had never been just another diner to Wyatt. Not even just another boss.

It was probably a symptom of Ryan giving him a blowjob before Wyatt had ever imagined he could work for him. Or maybe it was because the first night they'd met, before they'd ever spoken, Wyatt hadn't been able to look away from his face.

"Want to make sure you're satisfied," Wyatt pointed out. And then flushed when he belatedly realized how that sounded.

Ryan chuckled humorlessly. "My stomach certainly is."

Wyatt didn't know what to say, so he said the wrong thing. It was a lifelong habit; one he regularly cursed. This was absolutely no exception. "So what happens now? You find some other guy to pretend to date?"

Ryan's face closed off instantly. "Basically, yeah," he said.

"Is that what you were calling Eric about?" Wyatt knew he was pushing; it wasn't fair to either of them, but despite all his best intentions and his resolve, he wanted to know if the offer was still open.

Could he still change his mind?

Could he still drive up to Napa and confess all to Nana?

Ryan would probably even come with him, if he asked. All he would have to do was kneel in front of her chair, feel her blue-eyed benediction on his face, and tell her the truth.

It would be wonderful, but it might also be horrible.

She might never forgive him for lying. She might not ever forgive him for who he was.

Something of his indecision must have flashed across his face because Ryan stood abruptly. "We had a lot to talk about." He barely paused as he walked out of the room, plate in hand. "That was great, thanks. I've got some . . . stuff to do."

Wyatt was barely to the kitchen when he heard the garage door open and the throaty purr of the Tesla engine as it pulled out of the driveway.

It was only when he was elbow-deep in hot soapy water, washing the dishes from dinner, that he realized that Ryan had avoided the question, and then not answered it at all.

CHAPTER SEVEN

Ryan knew he should have told Eric during their phone call that he'd asked Wyatt and Wyatt had turned down everything that didn't involve a kitchen, but Ryan was still aching over the whole conversation. Especially over the noticeable conflict and pain in Wyatt's voice when he'd turned Ryan down.

He hadn't wanted to say no, that much was obvious. But Ryan understood that sometimes coming out was difficult, and sometimes it was impossible.

That acknowledgement didn't stop him from lying in bed the next morning, staring at the ceiling, wishing that Wyatt's situation was different. Maybe it was a little selfish, because that might mean *Ryan's* situation would be different, but he reminded himself that there was no harm in wishing for things that would benefit everyone.

Just like there was no harm in a little flirting, as long as he didn't fall in too deep and hurt them both all over again.

It was also better, Ryan decided, for him to stay in his room and indulge in his melancholy mood than try to use Wyatt to improve it.

Wyatt also wanted to know when Ryan was going to start bringing around a cute boy to play his boyfriend, and probably play with other things, and he couldn't blame him for that. It was probably going to hurt like hell.

What Ryan couldn't acknowledge to him, was that it wasn't just going to hurt Wyatt. Ryan didn't want to play house with someone else. Not when who he really wanted was on the sidelines, watching.

And that was why he hadn't told Eric. Eric would have had a backup there that afternoon, probably all trendy haircut and tight pants and gym abs.

It was funny, Ryan thought as he shifted in his bed, realizing he was going to have to change his sheets because they still smelled like Wyatt and what they'd done the other night, because those things would have easily been enough to attract him only a few weeks ago.

He hadn't been picky about his hookups, but those had usually been things he wanted. And if he was lucky, he might even find them all in the same guy. But then he'd met Wyatt and suddenly he wanted something else: muscular forearms from knife work and constantly lifting heavy pans; blond hair half-messy from the wind; the intriguing hints of vulnerability that Wyatt revealed because he wasn't trying to be sexy or mysterious all the damn time.

Tabitha had been so right about what she'd whispered into his ear yesterday afternoon; he'd gotten in too deep and now he was fucked.

He could call up Eric today and tell him the whole thing was off. There had been no guarantees it would even change the GM's mind about Ryan. But Eric had unbelievable instincts when it came to contract negotiation and there was a very good chance he was right.

Telling Eric it was off was as good as acknowledging that he was willing to leave this city, his friends and his family behind. And while it was shitty that his fake boyfriend couldn't be Wyatt, this was his *life*. Even for someone who generally lived by the seat of his pants, there had to be weight to this decision.

"Fuck," Ryan told the ceiling. "Fuck all of this."

The ceiling didn't reply, which was probably better in the end.

He thought about calling Tabby and whining to her but he'd already unloaded on her *twice* yesterday, and he couldn't in good conscience do it again the next day. But he still couldn't bring himself to call Eric and tell him the truth.

Glancing out the partly open window showed a beautiful blue sky beckoned and Ryan decided that if he wanted to keep pouting, then he might as well spend time with someone who wouldn't get annoyed with him.

Or something.

He was in board shorts and a tank top, grabbing his phone and the keys to the Range Rover before he could change his mind. It was easy enough to pull his surfboard off the wall and maneuver it to the rack on top of the Range Rover.

Opening the garage door with the fob inside the Rover, Ryan realized belatedly he'd forgotten a towel and his wetsuit. Detouring back into the house, he grabbed the missing items and then stepped back into the garage with just enough time to see Wyatt coming around the corner, fresh from a run.

He was only wearing shorts, leaving his chest bare, and even though Ryan had already spent an entire evening exploring it, awareness and memory simmered in his gut, reminding him of what he couldn't have.

What he *shouldn't* have.

"Hey," Wyatt said, pulling a t-shirt from the back of his shorts and wiping his face. Ryan knew what he looked like after runs, and he never looked that god damned excellent. "Heading out?"

Ryan didn't think. That was typically his problem, and he usually knew enough about his flaws to combat them, or at least temper them with good judgement. The problem was he'd been daydreaming about Wyatt all morning, annoyed and caught in the memory of a few nights ago. And here Wyatt was, all glorious invitation.

"Yeah, I'm heading to the beach." Ryan didn't even hesitate. Just went for it. "You said you like to surf, you should come with me."

Wyatt looked regretful. "No board."

Ryan decided his brain-to-mouth filter must have died during his angsting this morning. Or maybe during the last time Wyatt had taken him apart with his mouth and those calloused fingers "I've got a spare."

Wyatt's expression moved from regret to confusion. Ryan wasn't sure he could blame him. "Are you sure?"

He was not sure at all. In fact, Ryan had no idea what the hell he thought he was doing. But he nodded anyway. "Yeah, come with me."

By the time they had gathered a second set of equipment, and were headed down the freeway towards Huntington Beach, Ryan had mentally justified that his offer fell under his agreement to be "friends." Friends totally went surfing together, right?

"I always went to Venice," Wyatt said when he saw the direction Ryan had taken the Range Rover. "It'll be fun to try somewhere new."

"How long has it been?"

"At least a few years," Wyatt admitted. "I'm sure I'll be total shit now. Last time I was in the water, I was three inches shorter and fifty pounds lighter. Before culinary school," he added as an explanation.

"I didn't realize culinary school was the same as boot camp," Ryan teased.

Yeah, they were supposed to be friends, but just Wyatt's voice was a hot lick of awareness right up his spine. When he felt that way, it was impossible not to flirt a little, and hope that Wyatt would flirt back.

"You wouldn't," Wyatt said, leaning back in his seat, the wind from the open window fluffing his blond hair.

"Professional cooking can be tough, and you need to be prepared," he continued. "There's often twelve- to fourteen-hour days. Long hours bending and lifting, all in a brutally hot kitchen. Not everyone can hack it. Culinary school isn't just about teaching techniques and flavors; it's about weeding out the ones without the stamina or the drive."

"So, culinary school is the educational equivalent of the Hunger Games."

Wyatt laughed. "You could say that."

Ryan glanced over and while he could imagine Wyatt a little shorter, it was hard to imagine him without his solid build or all that firm muscle.

"If it's so tough, why did you stick it out?" Ryan asked.

"It was what I wanted to do," Wyatt admitted. "I didn't care how hard it was. I sort of enjoyed how hard it was. I felt like I went in one person and came out another."

Ryan had a pretty good idea of what fifty pounds of muscle might look like on a frame the size of Wyatt's. "You *did*."

Wyatt shifted in his seat. Closer to Ryan, who didn't miss the movement. His hands clenched tighter on the steering wheel. "I don't think important things should be easy. I'm sure you worked your ass off."

"Yes, and no." Wyatt made surviving culinary school and his subsequent years in important kitchens sound like something noble. Ryan didn't want to talk about five-tool players, or how scouts evaluated them. He'd never been ashamed at how easily baseball had come to him. It was tough to imagine taking advantage of a situation when he'd had so much handed to him because of a set of natural skills, but he felt oddly shamed admitting it to Wyatt.

He drummed his fingers on the steering wheel. It wasn't shameful. It was okay to want *more*, and okay to take it. It wasn't like he'd wrested it from more-deserving hands. He'd wrested it with his own. "I've wanted to travel my entire life," Ryan admitted. "I never could see myself staying in LA."

"But you're actively trying to stay in LA," Wyatt asked with a perplexed expression on his face.

"I'm trying to stay playing for the Dodgers because my family is here," Ryan corrected. "I like baseball because the game can be great, and also because it gets me out of here on a regular basis."

Wyatt looked surprised.

"What, did you expect some paean to baseball the sport? How I love the smell of the grass and the dirt under my fingernails, and the brightness of the sun during a day game and the lights during a night game?"

"Maybe?" Wyatt said meekly.

"I do enjoy that stuff," Ryan said. "But someone said, you're a great baseball player, you could make a lot of money doing it, and travel at the same time, mostly on someone else's dime. So I said yes."

Ryan cut a quick slanted look towards Wyatt, who merely looked thoughtful and not judgmental. He hadn't really expected otherwise, but Ryan also didn't go out of his way to make this particular confession.

"You took a risk when you came out, then."

"Not really," Ryan admitted wryly. "I made sure any risk I had was mitigated. Well, technically, Eric made sure any risk I had was mitigated. He's good for that."

Bringing Eric up was the thing that hardened the look in Wyatt's eyes. Ryan told himself he shouldn't be shocked, because Eric Talbot was undoubtedly a garbage dumpster, but he also didn't think Eric had done anything to Wyatt to deserve that sort of reaction.

"And he also thinks you need to make yourself into some paragon of stability to keep your job?" Wyatt questioned. Ah, that was it. Like Tabitha, Wyatt had obviously decided that the fake-boyfriend idea was total shit. And frankly, Ryan himself had thought this same thing on and off over the last few months, so it wasn't like he blamed Wyatt.

"Sort of. And I'd get signed by someone else, probably for more money, if I wanted. So it's not exactly about keeping my job. It's about keeping LA my home base."

"For your family."

"Partly, yeah. And because I like it here. I like leaving it, but I also like coming back. If I was in Minnesota or Illinois or somewhere else, I might not feel that way."

"Minnesota would suck for sure, especially if you like surfing," Wyatt said, the corner of his lips quirking into a grin. "But you'd like Chicago."

"Not in the middle of winter," Ryan pointed out.

"Point. I was only there from March to September."

"You lived in Chicago?" Ryan asked.

"For a few months. Restaurant folded right after I got an interview at a great restaurant in Portland, so the timing was good."

"Shame you never got to experience one of those fabled Chicago winters," Ryan said.

Wyatt mock-shuddered. "I'll take California, thank you very much."

And he was the epitome of the California boy, Ryan thought as he watched Wyatt carrying his board towards the sand. Blond hair bright under the sun, the tall lanky build, all that tanned skin rippling with muscle.

Ryan hadn't thought there was a place he could look better than naked in his bed, but he was surprised to discover that he'd been wrong.

There was something in the quicksilver of Wyatt's smile as he turned to make sure Ryan was still following him. It made Ryan want more from him than just the admittedly mind-blowing sex they had had, which was something he'd thought he'd left behind years ago.

He thought about texting Tabitha and telling her she might be right, but she was already insufferable enough. Besides, if he didn't tell her, he didn't put it into words and the truth, while eye-opening, was also fucking terrifying.

"You coming?" Wyatt turned back fully this time, gracing Ryan not only with a quick glimpse of his bright smile, but his entire self. He looked worried, and Ryan wondered how long he'd been spacing out. Not something he usually did—*and* he'd already spent the morning doing it.

"Sorry," Ryan apologized. "I was distracted by such a fantastic view."

"I've always loved Huntington Beach," Wyatt replied.

Ryan snorted. "Not the view I was talking about."

Wyatt didn't say anything but the look on his face was enough for Ryan to know that comment wouldn't always go un-remarked upon. Eventually they would have to address the sexual tension simmering away between them. Eventually they would have to *do* something about it. And that day was one Ryan eagerly awaited and dreaded in equal parts.

"We gonna surf?" Wyatt asked as they set up their little camp over by one of the piers.

Ryan had tossed the wax over to Wyatt a few minutes before, and had been fidgeting with his tow strap since. He'd wanted to come out here and let the sun and the sand and the waves exorcise his bad mood, but now he wasn't sure he even wanted to go in the water.

He wanted to sit on the sand and look at the sunlight on Wyatt's hair, and ask him to tell him more about culinary school and Chicago and Terroir. Even about that nutjob Aquino.

Ryan was not used to wanting to pick social interaction over the adrenaline rush. It was weird, and he wasn't sure he liked it.

"We're here, aren't we?" Ryan asked, shooting Wyatt a disbelieving look, even though all the hesitation had been on his end. He wasn't ready to admit to anyone—never mind Wyatt—that he'd been contemplating something so out of character. "Last in the water buys burgers on the way home."

❧❧❧❧❧ ❧❧❧❧❧

Wyatt shouldn't have been surprised but Ryan was an exceptional surfer. Great technique, perfect form, textbook pop-up, the sort of rock-steady balance that he'd always craved.

It was hard not to watch him and to focus on the upcoming waves, bobbing in the surf, waiting for the one that he might not embarrass himself on too badly. There weren't a lot of surfers here today—it was later in the day than the hardcore bunch liked—but there was a good variety of skill on display. Still, it had been a long time since Wyatt had been on a board, and it was fucking hard not to feel a little pressed when Ryan was putting on a show rare for an amateur.

Ryan finished his run, coasting into the beach with the finesse of a seal sliding through the water, and immediately glanced back, like he wanted to make sure Wyatt was okay. Or maybe check him out again, it was hard to say.

That speculative, hot look of Ryan's took the decision right out of Wyatt's hands. It was going to have to be the next wave. If he waited here for the perfect wave, he'd be waiting all day. One of his old friends from high school had once told him, "if you wait for the perfect wave to ride, you'll never ride any."

He hopped on his board, fingers gripping the fiberglass and got ready. It wasn't exactly like riding a bicycle, but his instincts, long unused, still took over. His pop-up was a little shaky but Wyatt swore under his breath, dug his toes into the board and willed himself to stay upright.

He did a quick cut against the wave, gaining speed, and managed not to wipe out as he moved towards the beach.

When he popped out of the water, Ryan was waiting for him, smirk on his face.

"Not too shabby," he said as Wyatt shook the water out of his hair.

"Yeah," Wyatt scoffed. "Compared to Mr. Amateur Pro."

He was pretty sure Ryan blushed, though it was impossible to tell under the heat of the sun. "I'm not good enough to be a pro."

Wyatt gave him a grin. "Not quite."

"I get out a lot," Ryan admitted as Wyatt adjusted his tow strap, and they prepared to go out again. "It helps clear my head. I'm technically not supposed to be out here during the season—they're always afraid I'll get hurt or be too tired or strain something—but it helps. So I keep coming."

No, he wasn't quite good enough to go pro, Wyatt thought, watching Ryan. He tried too many risky things; nearly falling off his board despite his iron balance and his great technique. He craved the challenge, Wyatt realized, as he watched him try the same trick three or four times despite no successful attempts. He craved the rush he'd get the first time he got it right.

And when he did get it right, his smile was brilliant enough that even through the spray of the salt, it was unmistakable.

When Wyatt came back in after that run, Ryan had retreated to the camp they'd set up, and was toweling his head off.

"That was pretty sick," Wyatt said and collapsed on the sand. Surfing for an hour after a lengthy jog probably hadn't been his best idea ever, and he was definitely going to be feeling it tomorrow, but this afternoon had been worth it. Both the chance to get back into the ocean, and the chance to spend more time with Ryan—even if it ended up hurting more.

"I've been trying to land that right for ages," Ryan said, smile still sparkling. On anyone else, the look might have edged towards smug, but on Ryan it just looked like pure joy at finally accomplishing something he'd been working on for a long time. "Maybe you're my lucky charm."

Wyatt doubted that. "The waves were just with you today."

"Naw," Ryan said, leaning in just enough to nudge his elbow gently into Wyatt's rib cage. If he came any closer, they'd be embracing. And Wyatt wanted it, he wanted it badly, but he also froze, because even though he typically didn't worry while out in public, Ryan was famous. People watched him. People looked at him. People *wrote* about him. And while he certainly didn't expect his nana to be reading Ryan Flores fan sites, you never knew.

Ryan must have caught the panic on his face because he eased back. He must be confused, because hadn't Wyatt made out with him in a public parking lot?

And he *had*. Wyatt hadn't been thinking though. He'd only been feeling, and it had been so sweet after so long being so careful.

Look where that had gotten him.

⁂

Their burgers were sitting between them on the console, perfuming the air with grease and cheese, and Ryan was sucking away happily on his chocolate shake, when Wyatt glanced at his phone and realized the time.

"Oh crap, I didn't realize how late it was," Wyatt said. "Would you mind if I called my nana? She goes to dinner early and I don't want to miss her."

Wyatt thought he saw Ryan tense out of the corner of his eye. But that was silly, why would calling his nana upset Ryan?

He was already dialing when the answer hit him abruptly. His nana was obstinately the reason why he couldn't be with Ryan the way they both wanted; even if it wasn't her fault, he could still blame her.

"Hello?" Bea Blake's voice was tiny and faraway even though Wyatt knew the connection at the memory care facility was excellent. It was one reason why he'd chosen the carrier he had.

"Nana!" he said, trying to push away all the concern he was feeling over having the conversation in front of Ryan.

"Nana?" Her voice was questioning everything, even though she'd only said two words.

"You're Nana," Wyatt said fondly.

But instead of her bright, clear laugh, there was a puzzled, drawn-out silence.

"Who is Nana?" she repeated, clearly confused, and Wyatt's stomach tumbled to his flip-flops.

"You're Nana. I'm Wyatt," he said slowly, clearly. Maybe it was just the bad connection. Maybe she just couldn't hear him properly, and had gotten confused as a result.

"Wyatt?" she questioned. "Wyatt?"

If it was possible, his stomach sunk even lower. He tried to contain his panic, because he didn't want Ryan to hear, and he didn't want her to worry even more. It was something he'd read in the research books he'd checked out of the library when she'd first been diagnosed.

Don't panic. They'll hear the panic and panic themselves.

But it was too late, he heard it in his voice, no matter how he tried to contain it. "Wyatt is me. I'm Wyatt. I'm your grandson."

"Wyatt . . ." There was still that thread of uncertainty in her voice. Uncertainty that he'd been dreading hearing forever.

He remembered reading once that for patients suffering from memory lapses, just voices could sometimes be tougher than a voice and a face put together.

The rationalization didn't help extinguish his panic any.

"Yes, Wyatt. Your grandson. Wyatt."

She took a deep, shaky sigh. "Wyatt." And this time there was some semblance of normalcy in her voice as she said it. As she'd begun to place him. "You're Wyatt."

He closed his eyes, tightening his jaw, desperate not to cry. Not over this. Not in front of Ryan.

A hand reached over and lightly touched his bare knee. A reassuring touch. Even though he'd seen Ryan's uneasiness with Wyatt checking in with Nana, he was still giving Wyatt what little support he could.

It might have been small, only a light touch, but it meant everything.

"Nana," he repeated, voice breaking a little. The first time this had happened and he hadn't even been in front of her. And once it happened, it would keep happening, an inexorable tide that nothing and nobody could stop. Not even Wyatt, not even if he pushed it back with both hands and all his strength.

"I'm here, I'm here." She sounded flustered. "I'm sorry, I just got a little confused."

"It's fine," he soothed, even though it was anything but. She didn't need to know about that, or how his heart was breaking. "I just wanted to call and see how you were doing."

"I'm good. How about you, darling boy? You settle into your big fancy new job okay?"

She was back. The lapse had only lasted a minute, but it had left an indelible impression on Wyatt. He wasn't sure he would ever forget this moment. The grease in the air, the five pressure points of Ryan's hand on his knee, the sweaty grip on his phone.

He talked aimlessly for five minutes and then told Nana he had to go. He couldn't pretend like nothing had happened.

When he finally hung up, there was silence in the car.

Finally, Ryan broke it. "Was that the first time she didn't recognize your voice?"

Wyatt wasn't sure he could speak, so he just nodded.

"I'm sorry." Ryan sounded legitimately sorry, even though it was Wyatt who wanted to apologize for ruining a beautiful afternoon with this tragedy.

"Don't be. Please," Wyatt managed to say. "Please don't."

"We don't have to talk about it. But if you ever need to go see her, you just say the word," Ryan said.

"Okay. I . . . I appreciate it."

Wyatt knew he should be more grateful for Ryan's support and for his flexibility, but all he felt was a growing rage at fate and how it was trying to take yet another beloved member of his family. First his dad had left, then his mom had died, and now the one person he still felt close to was going to forget who he even was.

He clamped his hand over Ryan's, and as Wyatt gripped his hand, it struck him, suddenly and catastrophically, that the man Bea Blake would be forgetting wasn't even the *real* Wyatt.

"I texted my aunt this morning," Ryan said, clearly making good on his promise to change the subject. But Wyatt's fingers didn't let up on Ryan's for even a moment. "Would Friday afternoon work for you?"

Swallowing all the emotions back, Wyatt held on even harder. "Don't you have something important or fun to be doing besides going to your aunt's house and watching her teach me how to cook?"

Ryan laughed unexpectedly. "Obviously you've never met my *titi* Flor before, because she definitely won't let me just watch."

"I can't wait to meet her," Wyatt said, and discovered that he wasn't even lying. He wanted to meet the woman who could make Ryan laugh like that.

Ryan pulled into the driveway, the gate shutting behind them. "Do you think you could eat?" he asked, even though the bag of burgers was still sitting between them—a special detour to In-N-Out, and Ryan had whipped out his credit card despite the challenge he'd given earlier.

Wyatt still felt vaguely nauseous, but he'd only had a few eggs and some turkey sausage this morning before his run, and he'd worked up a real appetite surfing.

"Yeah, of course," Wyatt said. How had Ryan even known he'd gotten nauseous? Had it been written all over his face? He pushed the embarrassment away. If there was ever a situation to feel sick over, it was this one.

"We could even watch some TV," Ryan suggested.

Even though Wyatt had long come to terms with the fact that Ryan was nothing like his old boss, it still felt weird that Ryan was seeking him out all the time. Either because he actually wanted to be friends, or because . . . Wyatt didn't even know how to finish that thought. Because Ryan had explicitly and clearly expressed interest in a *fake* boyfriend, someone to convince the GM that he was dependable. And if fake boyfriend had been ruled out, real boyfriend was definitely not in the cards.

"Sure, but if you turn on another of those godawful nature documentaries, I might have to pass."

But then there was the way Ryan lit up at Wyatt's teasing, defying explanation. "What about *Star Talk*?"

"With Neil deGrasse Tyson?" Wyatt opened his car door. "I thought you were a stupid athlete."

"Well, this stupid athlete went to Stanford, and attempts to combat that stereotype by arming himself with knowledge," Ryan said flippantly, but his voice was warm and comforting and certain. And Wyatt realized then that Ryan didn't want him to agonize and obsess alone.

He thought about thanking him but going back to his cottage, but then Ryan was in the house, leaving Wyatt behind in the garage, and he was babbling about Twitter and flat earth conspiracists, and instead of dwelling, Wyatt let his words wash over him, taking all the ugliness with them.

Wyatt might not know what the hell they were doing, but they were friends. And that was going to have to be enough—at least for now.

CHAPTER EIGHT

OVER THE NEXT FEW days, Wyatt worked hard to create some kind of routine for his work and his friendship with Ryan. He didn't want the other man to feel obligated to hang out with him, or eat with him, or even talk to him, but Ryan always sought him out.

"Are you trying to push me away?" Ryan asked one evening when in determination that he should get a choice, Wyatt had set a single place setting in the cavernous dining room.

Ryan had showed up in the kitchen, where Wyatt was eating at the island, with his plate and silverware and had shot him a half-hearted glare. "Do you not like eating with me?"

It had been difficult not to flush. The problem wasn't that Wyatt didn't like hanging out with him, it was that he was increasingly loving it, and he'd really liked it to begin with.

"If I want space, I'll take it," was all Ryan had said about it before setting his plate down right next to Wyatt's.

They hadn't gone surfing again, and Wyatt hadn't invited himself to use Ryan's home gym. And Ryan hadn't pushed there either, which was probably smart. The truth was getting half-naked and sweaty together was a terrible combination if they wanted to keep things platonic.

The attraction was there. The possibility for it to deepen wasn't far behind. And at least half the time, Wyatt imagined saying *fuck it*, and pinning Ryan to the nearest convenient surface.

The wall. The kitchen counter. Ryan's bed. Wyatt's bed. In his wilder daydreams, Ryan's bike again. His imagination definitely wasn't doing him any favors. He'd go to bed, and lie awake in bed, running through memories, real and otherwise, and put off jerking off as long as possible until he was burning up and there was no other way to relieve the pressure of wanting Ryan.

And every time, even as he wrapped his hand around his cock and gave himself an experimental stroke, Wyatt knew that it wouldn't help because in the end, it wasn't what he really needed.

What he needed was the god damn real thing; on top of him, under him, pressed against him. Wyatt was discovering he wasn't particularly picky except it had to be Ryan Flores.

Wyatt wasn't naïve enough to believe it might be the same for Ryan, but there was more than one morning when he swore he caught the sharpened edge of sexual frustration in Ryan's eyes. He recognized it because he saw the exact same fucking thing in his bathroom mirror each morning.

"You ready to go?" Wyatt looked up, and Ryan was standing there, board shorts and a loose tank, one nipple almost poking out the armhole.

He'd dressed in jeans and a polo shirt that he'd dug out from the back of his meager closet, because he was going to see the aunt of the guy he liked, and old habits died hard.

Now Wyatt was wondering if he was criminally overdressed.

Ryan raised an eyebrow. "You know, I have lots of money but my family rarely lets me give it to them. My *titi* won't even let me buy her an air conditioner."

Okay, so he was definitely overdressed. But changing would mean admitting why he'd pulled these clothes out in the first place, and even though Wyatt thought Ryan probably knew, admitting it was a whole different story.

"It's okay," Wyatt dismissed, "I worked in hot kitchens my whole career."

"Don't tell me the Bastard didn't give you guys even a measly fan?" Wyatt had made the mistake a few days ago of referring to Bastian Aquino by his hated nickname, and Ryan had been unexpectedly delighted and had been looking for ways to bring him up so he could use it.

Wyatt shouldn't find it adorable, but that ship had definitely sailed.

Maybe he should stop trying to fight it, and instead figure out how to embrace it—no matter how impossible the situation felt.

"I shouldn't have told you Aquino's secret nickname," Wyatt admitted.

But Ryan just kept grinning in delight as they headed down the garage steps. Ryan opened the door of the Tesla, and Wyatt followed suit, sliding into the sleek car.

"If I ever meet him, I might have to accidentally slip one or two 'Bastards' in," he said as they backed out of the driveway.

"If you ever met him, you wouldn't even dream of it."

Ryan raised a dark eyebrow and the hot, insolent look in his eyes swamped Wyatt with desire. "I don't know if you've noticed, but I like living on the edge."

He'd definitely noticed. It had been a little hard to miss, and Wyatt, who considered himself laid-back but grudgingly cautious, found it strangely appealing.

At first he'd thought it was only Ryan's looks that had attracted him, but Wyatt was beginning to realize it wasn't just his exterior that attracted him—it was the whole package.

"You drive too fast," Wyatt pointed out as they screamed onto the freeway, the Tesla handling like a dream, even as he refused to glance over and check the speedometer. "Don't tell me you're aspiring to be a professional race car driver too."

The other night, Ryan had told him that in high school, before he'd gotten the big scholarship to play baseball at Stanford, he'd briefly considered surfing for a living. "Becoming a professional beach bum," Wyatt had teased, but it made sense. Ryan craved adventure, craved waking up and not knowing exactly where he was. Craved the liquid lighter fluid of adrenaline running through his veins.

"Maybe," Ryan said with a dimpled, slanted grin.

"All things considered, baseball must feel pretty sedate for you," Wyatt pointed out.

"Oh come on. You're not one of those idiots who think baseball is slow and boring, are you?" Ryan gave a self-conscious snort of laughter. "You totally are."

"I'm sure playing the game is a hell of a lot different than watching it," Wyatt retorted.

"This should have been my first question in the interview: do you think baseball is a boring lesser version of golf? Or curling?"

"Curling is fantastic," Wyatt argued. "Have you ever seen those Swedish guys?"

"Yes." Ryan's lip curled. "And I'm going to remember you voted baseball under curling because of the hot Swedes."

"You're very hot too," Wyatt said because he should be loyal *and* honest. Or something like that.

Ryan cut over three lanes, taking the exit ramp going at least seventy miles per hour. Wyatt didn't flinch, because he'd learned that if he flinched, Ryan would drive even faster.

"You're also a maniac," Wyatt mumbled under his breath.

"I heard that," Ryan announced cheerfully.

"Tell me about your *titi*," Wyatt suggested.

"Flor? She's been here . . . fifteen years? Twenty? We'll have to ask her. She came over with my mom."

It was on the tip of his tongue to ask about Ryan's mom, because even though he'd mentioned his aunt half a dozen times, his mother hadn't ever come up. But Wyatt didn't, because he knew how much it could hurt when someone thoughtlessly asked about his—and it had been eight years since she'd died.

Some wounds didn't heal, they just scabbed over.

"She basically raised me," Ryan continued, essentially but not completely answering the question that Wyatt hadn't asked. "She's probably my favorite person in the whole world."

The wound created by his nana not remembering him hadn't even had time to scab over yet, and it throbbed at Ryan's words.

"She and my two cousins run a cleaning business. Rich people's houses, all that bullshit. But she's good at it, and loves her clients and they love her. Someday, she wants to open a restaurant. I keep telling her I'll loan her the money, even charge interest, but she won't take a penny."

Wyatt thought of his nana, and one of the lesser lies that he'd told her recently: that the sale of her little bungalow in a Sacramento suburb would pay for her extended care in the memory care facility.

It wasn't the most painful lie he'd ever told her—that was still ongoing and likely to remain so—but it had been entirely necessary. She'd never accept Wyatt paying for her care.

"Anonymous donation?" Wyatt asked, even though they both knew it was useless because they both had tough-as-nails, independent female relatives. They were so easy to love, but almost impossible to help.

The wound ached again when Wyatt remembered that Bea Blake was no longer as independent as she'd once prided herself on being.

Ryan rolled his eyes. "If only that would work."

"You'll figure out something, eventually. You don't strike me as the kind of guy who just gives up."

"When you meet her," Ryan confessed, "you'll realize that she'll never let me. I just funnel as many nice, rich people as I can find her way, and that's how I make sure her dream comes true."

"You're a good person," Wyatt murmured.

"Not really. But at least I make an attempt," Ryan said flippantly. He pulled over next to a small house, painted bright yellow. "So, here we are."

Wyatt hadn't been nervous, but when faced with the prospect of getting out of the car, he realized he was really nervous. It wasn't so surprising that he wanted Ryan's *titi* to like him, and not because he wanted everyone to generally like him. Considering how compartmentalized Ryan typically kept his hookups, Wyatt wondered if he'd taken the job as Ryan's fake boyfriend if he would have ever met her at all.

"Just make sure you don't mention Eric," Ryan warned as they walked up the concrete path to the house. The grass on either side was neatly trimmed and there was a profusion of tropical flowers on either side of the front door.

"Eric?" Wyatt asked blankly.

"My agent. Flor hates him. She thinks he's a weasel."

The door opened and a shorter woman with dark hair pulled back in a ponytail and equally dark, intense eyes stepped out. There was a wide smile on her face, and a few laugh lines around her eyes and bracketing her lips. She looked warm and friendly and the way she immediately pulled Ryan into a big hug and then said loudly, "He *is* a weasel," made Wyatt want her to like him even more.

"No arguments from this corner," Wyatt said, extending his hand. "Thank you for inviting me into your home. I'm Wyatt Blake."

Flor let go of Ryan and gave Wyatt a quick, but very thorough look up and then down. If he'd thought Tabitha's examination had been tough, it had nothing on Flor's.

She reached out like she was going to shake his hand, but then pulled him into a hug. Wyatt got a fleeting impression of coconut and roasted pork and sunshine.

"You are ready to cook, yes?" she asked, leading them into the house. "Ryan told me you are very good."

The house was scrupulously neat, with warm wood floors and framed retro tourism posters dotting the walls. A navy-blue couch sat across from a flat screen television, with sunny orange and yellow pillows brightening its surface.

Wyatt had never felt particularly unsure about his qualifications before, but faced with Flor's fierce gaze, he wavered and Ryan ended up answering her instead.

"Yes, I told you," Ryan said. "He's a chef."

"Well, lucky you came in time. I'm making the *sofrito* first."

The kitchen was tiny, with just barely enough room for the three of them. But something incredibly delicious was already simmering on the stove, warming up the room. Ryan shot him a smug look, and Wyatt couldn't help but wish that he'd taken Ryan's advice and dressed down.

"*Sofrito*?" Wyatt asked, fully expecting that he would get incredulous looks from both Ryan and Flor.

"Oh, you didn't tell me he knew *nothing*." Flor directed this comment to Ryan.

But Ryan only laughed. "*Titi,* I told you he was a chef. He doesn't know anything about Puerto Rican food."

Flor turned to Wyatt. "*Sofrito* is . . . the most important thing in Puerto Rican food. It creates the important flavor. I usually make mine every few weeks and then freeze it."

Wyatt took in the counter full of peppers, huge bags of herbs, onions, garlic. "I can help chop," he offered.

Flor wordlessly handed him a knife. "Not perfect," she said once he began to break down the peppers. "We're going to blend it all."

But Wyatt hadn't learned knife skills in culinary school for nothing, and then honed them in one of the most exacting kitchens in the world. He knew what to do with a knife in his hand, even with Flor glancing over at him to check in every minute or so.

After he'd broken down the peppers and onions and had started mincing the garlic, Flor turned to Ryan, who despite what he'd claimed earlier, was just lounging against the kitchen counter, browsing through his phone.

"*Hijo,* he's very good with his hands." Her knowing look in his direction had him blushing and Ryan sputtering. He'd been right then, Flor had not met many—or *any*—of Ryan's boyfriends. If he'd even had one. That was still unclear and Wyatt wasn't sure it was even right to ask him.

"It's why I hired him," Ryan said.

"You didn't even give me a real interview," Wyatt pointed out. "We sat at a table and you half-heartedly asked me a few questions."

"True," Ryan admitted and Wyatt didn't miss Flor rolling her eyes.

"You're going to end up broke," she said.

"Been doing good so far," Ryan argued. "I have a huge shoot coming up for Adidas. I think I told you about that."

But Flor didn't seem to be deterred, even as she pulled out a big Vitamix blender. "You trust too many people, who want to take all of your money."

Wyatt wasn't sure he agreed. Yeah, Ryan was generous. He paid him a great salary and had insisted more than once on picking up the bill for things. Had given Wyatt a credit card to charge supplies and groceries. But more than one offhand comment he'd made had made it clear that he monitored it fairly closely. He wasn't tight-fisted by any means, but he certainly wasn't running through cash the way Flor made it sound.

"You'll have to forgive my *titi*," Ryan said. "She thinks anyone who gives a gift over a hundred bucks is careless with their finances."

Flor glared at him. "If you had told me how much this blender cost, I never would have taken it."

Ryan's eyes were guileless. "You could have given it back after you found out."

"Hardly. It saves me so much time and energy, it's cost-effective to use it," she sniffed.

Wyatt found himself chuckling into his garlic while still missing his nana so much it was hard to take a breath. He'd wanted to call her again, but frankly he was afraid to, terrified that he would dial her number and a stranger would answer again.

He knew it was something he might have to get used to—not *might*, he corrected bitterly, he *would*—but he wasn't ready. He needed more time, except that the disease wasn't exactly clued into his timetable, or anyone else's either.

"So what have you been feeding my nephew?" Flor directed this question Wyatt's direction, her bickering with Ryan over the blender concluded—at least for now.

"I've been to the farmer's market three times since I got here. So lots of fresh veggies. Salmon. Chicken. I made burgers the other night with roasted mushrooms."

Flor made a *tsking* noise as she began to load his chopped vegetables into the blender pitcher. "He takes terrible care of himself on his own. I thought this was a bad idea, but I've changed my mind."

Wyatt had a feeling that this was unusual, so he gave her a grateful nod. "It's very different from what I'm used to, but I agree. It's been good."

The toughest part had probably been being around Ryan and not being able to do what he wanted to him, with him, against him, *etcetera*, but second toughest had been all the unexpected free time he'd found himself with. He didn't know what to do with himself when he wasn't working fourteen hours a day, falling into bed, and then getting up to do it all over again.

"And you're used to what? Very long days?" Flor shot her nephew a knowing look. "I don't think you're keeping him busy enough."

"I'm only one man," Ryan complained. "I can only eat so much."

"*Sofrito* isn't cooked, then?" Wyatt asked. He'd looked up the rudiments of Puerto Rican cooking before this day, and he'd seen many recipes claiming to be authentic, but most of them cooked the pepper and herb mix down first.

Ryan groaned. "Don't get her started."

Flor shot him a glare. "Each cook does it differently. This is my way, at least for this dish."

"We're making *pasteles*," Ryan supplied. "Usually served on holidays or special occasions. Very fancy. And sort of my aunt's specialty."

"Not *sort of*," Flor corrected. "*Hijo*, come here and do something besides hold up that counter. Chop up the pork for me." She gestured to where she'd set up another plastic cutting board. A huge hunk of pork shoulder sat on it, waiting to be broken down. Wyatt's fingers itched, because he would much rather be doing that more delicate, more skilled work, than mincing another fifty cloves of garlic.

Also, despite Flor asking him to do it, Wyatt wasn't sure Ryan knew how. He'd acted very uneasy every time Wyatt had asked him to help with anything in the kitchen.

"Very fine," Flor reminded Ryan as he picked up the knife. "You know how it should be."

Ryan rolled his eyes. "*Sí*, I know."

And to Wyatt's surprise, Ryan very competently wielded the knife and began to break down the shoulder into more manageable pieces. It wasn't precisely how Wyatt would have done it, but he'd been trained in professional kitchens, and he was certain that Flor had taught Ryan.

In fact, now that Wyatt was seeing Ryan chop up the pork, he realized that Flor had been more concerned about *his* knife skills—for ingredients that were eventually going to be blended. Wyatt didn't know whether to laugh or be offended.

"Professional skills," Flor said, following Wyatt's gaze to where Ryan was working. "I only trust what I know."

Wyatt laughed. "And you taught him."

Flor broke into a huge smile. "Exactly." She turned towards Ryan. "I think I like this one. You don't let me meet many—or *any*—of your men, *hijo*, but I still like this one. Don't scare him away."

Ryan flushed red, knife pausing in the middle of a cut. "He's not *my* man, *titi*."

Throwing up her hands, Flor retreated back to the blender, and hit the power button. She didn't seem very convinced, and Wyatt was torn between embarrassment and pure satisfaction.

He'd totally dawdled through the rest of the garlic, because he'd been listening to Flor and Ryan chatter and then watching Ryan chop up the pork. So he was unexpectedly surprised when he heard a voice over his shoulder.

"You're looking awfully smug at that garlic clove," Ryan murmured near his ear. Only long practice helped Wyatt keep his rhythm and not let his knife falter.

"I don't know why I'd be staring smugly at garlic," Wyatt said.

"Okay, so you were staring at my ass at least fifty percent of the time," Ryan said, and Wyatt looked up at him to see smiling, little dimple and all.

"I think I wouldn't be staring smugly at your ass if I was getting it," Wyatt groused. Hopefully quiet enough that Flor wouldn't hear.

"True," Ryan admitted.

Wyatt wanted to ask again, *when am I going to come home to find another man in the house, the one who gets to play your boyfriend?* But Flor was right there, and Ryan had shut down the last time he'd asked. So he didn't, even though he could taste the question on his tongue.

"I'm going to smell like garlic for a month," Wyatt said, changing the subject for self-preservation reasons. "Reminds me of when I first started at Terroir, and Aquino put me on garlic duty for contradicting him once."

Ryan sighed deeply. "You're only convincing me more that I have to go up to Napa and kick the Bastard's ass. Soon."

"Language," Flor piped up from the other side of the kitchen. "I know I raised you better than that."

"That's his name," Ryan protested.

Flor raised an eyebrow. "Okay, it's his nickname, but it seems like a god damned accurate one," Ryan added.

"Bastian Aquino can be . . . well . . ." Wyatt hesitated. "He can be a bit of a jerk, sometimes. Even though Terroir was supposed to be such a great place to work, I don't miss it at all."

"When I first came here," Flor said, raising her voice to be heard over the Vitamix, "I work for company cleaning houses. They pay me a good wage. But the supervisor was awful. I quit, and started my own company. Less money, more happiness." She hesitated. "But Ryan wouldn't let you come work for him without paying you more." She sounded fond but exasperated.

"Don't worry, I'm not breaking the bank," Wyatt said. "And it's crazy how long I suffered at Terroir, just because it was *Terroir*, and a thousand chefs would have committed murder for my spot. Somehow that was supposed to make me like it more, I guess, but I didn't. Leaving was hard, I only wish I'd done it sooner."

Wyatt finished the garlic and passed it over to Flor who was still magically concocting the *sofrito*, mixing and matching ingredients and tasting each batch after she blended it. Once she determined a batch was perfect, she'd pour it into ice trays, and they went into the freezer.

"Tomorrow," she said, "I'll pop them out and stick them in freezer bags. And then they're good as long as they last, whenever I cook."

"I might do that with fresh herbs," Wyatt mused. "It's a brilliant idea."

"Not brilliant," she retorted. "Common sense."

"Amazing how the two things are often the same thing," Ryan said.

"Time for the pork," Flor announced. The skillet she produced was massive. Wyatt probably could have sat in it and paddled it out into the Pacific Ocean. "*Hijo*, will you grate the *yautia* and the bananas for the filling?"

Ryan groaned, but didn't hesitate to pull out the necessary bowl and grater, and begin what looked like an arduous job.

"I thought you said your *titi* wasn't going to make you work," Wyatt teased.

"I would never say that," Ryan loyally protested when Flor shot him a look from where she was beginning to load the pork into the hot pan.

"I hope you help Wyatt too," Flor said. "He's not your slave."

Ryan laughed. "No. Unfortunately."

"I have everything under control, usually," Wyatt inserted. He hadn't ever felt comfortable asking Ryan to help prepare meals because that was what Ryan was *technically* paying him for. Even when Ryan hung around the kitchen, which he did most days, having a beer or a bottle of water as he watched Wyatt prepare food.

"Also he's way out of my skill level," Ryan said. "He's playing dumb now, making sure not to overpromise and underdeliver, but he's got serious talent."

"Maybe he could teach you to take care of yourself better," Flor said, her voice going steely. "You eat out too much."

Teaching Ryan how to cook sounded like heaven and hell, all wrapped up in one delicious package. But Wyatt couldn't tell Ryan's aunt that he wasn't sure how much more time he could spend with him before giving in and dragging them both back to the bedroom.

Frankly, they might not even make it that far. The living room had a really nice soft carpet that had been figuring in Wyatt's imagination a lot lately.

"I do fine," Ryan argued. "You worry too much."

But Wyatt chimed in before Flor could. "That's her job," he said. "Just like yours is to hit a baseball really, really far."

"I do more than that," Ryan said. "I also run around in a circle and catch balls sometimes." The slanted, teasing look he shot Wyatt was almost more than he could bear. His fingers clenched around the edge of the counter.

Flor must have been at least partially aware of the undercurrents running through the kitchen because she waved Wyatt over and proceeded to distract him by giving him a long list of ingredients to be added to the browning pork. He was a food nerd, so it was an effective move.

"I'll send you the recipe later," Flor said when Wyatt was trying to remember everything they'd added. "We want it to be nice and cooked down. So we'll let it simmer a little, while Ryan finishes up the masa. Do you need the achiote oil yet?" She directed the question to Ryan, not even glancing his direction as she turned the pork mixture with a wooden spoon.

"Soon," Ryan said.

"When he was little he'd always beg to have *pasteles*," Flor confided in Wyatt. "But I told him he'd have to make the masa, and that usually cured his craving."

"It's a thankless job," Ryan pointed out loudly.

"But you've got a nice pair of muscles to get it done fast," Flor said.

And Wyatt couldn't exactly complain when he craned his neck to see Ryan straining against the old-fashioned box grater, biceps bulging. It was definitely a view worth turning around for.

The smug look Ryan shot him made it crystal clear he knew just how sizzling hot he was, and that he'd let Wyatt look and then keep looking any time he wanted.

He didn't know if the sudden heat in the kitchen was from the hot stove or the tiny sluggish fan pumping warm air lazily around the small room, or Ryan sweating over the grater—but Wyatt knew his polo was sticking to him in damp patches, and there was sweat beading along his hairline.

But from the way Ryan kept gazing at him, all smolder and no stop sign, it was clear he didn't mind. Maybe he even liked it.

If they'd been alone, maybe Wyatt would've stripped his shirt off and even though his abs weren't quite the caliber of Ryan's, let him look his fill anyway.

Except there was a reason they'd stayed mostly fully clothed around each other. They were dry matches desperate to burn, and all they craved was a single flame to set them alight.

But he couldn't set them on fire, because it might burn too hot, and then they'd both be caught in the backdraft.

"Earth to Wyatt," Flor interrupted his increasingly distracted thinking.

"Sorry," Wyatt said, turning his attention back to Flor. "I got distracted."

Her smirk told him that she knew exactly why he'd been so out of it, but she didn't say anymore about it, for which he thanked all the kitchen gods.

"Are you ready to finish the filling?" Flor asked and Wyatt nodded.

Flor moved it off the heat, and they each gave it a taste. Wyatt was impressed by the complexity of the flavor, even though she'd added a fraction of the ingredients they'd used at Terroir and some of the other restaurants he'd worked at.

"Do you think it needs more oregano?" Flor asked him, and the sly light in her eyes informed him this was a test. He'd always been an achiever, and he was desperate to pass.

"He doesn't know if it needs more oregano," Ryan inserted, but Wyatt ignored him, and closed his eyes, rolling the flavor across his tongue, tasting each separate ingredient. Savoring each component, and how they became more than the sum of their parts.

"No," Wyatt finally answered. "But it does need more pepper. And a dash of red pepper, if you have it."

"Cayenne," Flor confirmed, and in her hand was the jar of bright red powder. "Agreed."

"You're pretty good," Flor said, after both peppers had been added, and the filling was off the stove, cooling. "Not many people could have figured out what was missing without knowing what it was supposed to taste like."

Wyatt shrugged. "Some people have a nose for smells. Some people are good at figuring out flavors. I happen to have a combination of both. I can usually tell what's in any particular dish by smell. Definitely by taste. Makes it pretty easy to tell what's missing."

"Seriously?" Ryan asked. "You can really do that?"

"It came in very handy, especially at Terroir. If you think your aunt is terrifying, Bastian Aquino's tests were legendary."

"And you always passed," Ryan stated, with a quick grin. "I bet you did."

"He stumped me once or twice." A lie. Bastian Aquino had never stumped him, even though he'd worked hard at it. He'd called Wyatt a freak, even in his hearing, and even implied once or twice when he was particularly nasty that all Wyatt's skill revolved around something he'd been born with, not developed.

But Ryan was glowing, he was basking in it, and Wyatt already knew what lay that direction: disaster. They couldn't go down that road again, and then end it before it ever began. If that happened, he'd end up halfway to heartbroken, and then he'd have to quit.

Wyatt needed this job. He also needed Ryan, but he was figuring out how to justify only tiny nibbles. Hanging out, being buddies, that was enough to keep his hunger at bay.

If he had another real taste . . . all bets were off.

"Finally ready for the oil," Ryan said. He was sweating too, his forehead damp. Wyatt wanted to press his lips against his skin, taste the salt and the unique taste that was Ryan.

Thank god *Titi* Flor was right there. She was an excellent dissuading tactic.

Wyatt watched as Ryan finished the *masa*, mixing in the achiote oil for color, flavor, and to bring the grated fruit together to form a thick dough.

"Finally time to stuff the leaves," Flor announced. She set up three stations and for the next half an hour, they worked like crazy, layering in *masa* and pork filling, and then bundling it together in the banana leaf, a perfect packet of tastiness.

"How do we cook these?" Wyatt asked Flor.

"Boil for an hour or so," she said. "Salted water. They also freeze beautifully, which I'll be doing with about half these."

"Really?" Ryan pouted. "I promise to take those off your hands."

"Even *you* do not need a hundred *pasteles*," Flor said sternly. "Besides, you have a very competent chef in your employ who will make them any time you ask."

"You really think so?" Ryan asked, shooting Wyatt a speculative look from under his thick, dark lashes. Wyatt felt pinned. Exposed.

"I'm not sure they would ever measure up to your *titi*'s," Wyatt said quickly.

"Maybe I want to see what you can do with them," Ryan insisted.

"They're a lot of work," Wyatt protested, even though it was weak. He'd been making complicated meals all week because he was bored and also because he wanted to give Ryan something, a little return for everything Ryan had offered so selflessly.

"Like you wouldn't do anything he asked when he bats his lashes," Flor scoffed, putting an end to the question once and for all.

Wyatt turned back to his stack of banana leaves, cheeks burning with heat and embarrassment. Was he so obvious? He thought he had his feelings at least partially under wraps.

"Well, he's not alone in that," Ryan said quietly, and Flor made an approving noise.

✢✢✢✢✢ ✢✢✢✢✢

Wyatt and Ryan climbed back in the Tesla an hour later, fifty *pasteles* richer, with a load of unspoken, raw emotion boiling between them.

Flor had seen them off with a tight hug each. "You take care of him," she'd murmured to Wyatt under her breath during his. "He cares more than he lets on."

The problem was that Ryan already seemed to care, so if he cared even more, felt even deeper, Wyatt was afraid of what the future held for them.

He couldn't give Ryan what he wanted—what they both wanted—but they were both drowning here, and there were no good ideas left to hold onto.

"Thank you for bringing me today," Wyatt said, because trying to re-establish their friendship seemed like the safest bet.

Ryan merged onto the freeway, driving far slower than he had on the way to Flor's house. Wyatt wasn't sure if it was because he didn't want their bubble to end or if he was afraid of being alone with him.

Maybe a combination of both.

"Of course, I said I would." Ryan's voice was carefully neutral, and even though Wyatt *knew* he wasn't alone in feeling this way, it hit him hard that Ryan felt equally helpless.

A minute of silence passed between them, but it didn't seem to deflate the tension, only ratchet it higher.

Wyatt knew he had to do something to give them some space, before they made a mistake and did something they couldn't take back. "I thought tomorrow I'd head up to Napa, see my nana."

"Shouldn't be an issue," Ryan said, still so painfully neutral. Wyatt didn't know what he'd expected. Ryan to beg him to stay? To ask to go with him? Neither one was really an option, but sometimes, Wyatt realized, you wanted the impossible.

"I can make you breakfast before I leave . . ."

"No need," Ryan interrupted, finally sounding impatient. "I have a breakfast meeting with Eric tomorrow."

Wyatt knew without asking that the purpose was to discuss the faux relationship that Ryan should have already started.

Maybe when he got back from Napa, Ryan would have already found someone else. It would still be crushing, but at least it would be crushing without a single speck of hope to be found. It was the hope that was the worst; the tantalizing possibility if only Wyatt could decide the burden he'd been carrying forever suddenly weighed too much.

"I really hope you find what you need," Wyatt said quietly. He didn't say that he hoped Ryan would find what he wanted, because he was beginning to figure out that couldn't happen.

Ryan didn't respond, only gripped the steering wheel so hard his knuckles turned white, and Wyatt knew the conversation was over, and maybe even their budding friendship.

He'd have to see when he came back from Napa and surveyed the damage. He sighed; he wasn't looking forward to it.

When Ryan pulled the car into the garage, making an offhand comment about going for a jog, Wyatt did what he always did when life got too hard—he retreated to the kitchen.

It was still Ryan's kitchen, in Ryan's house, but Wyatt had a feeling that he wouldn't be disturbed.

He put the *pasteles,* carefully wrapped, into the freezer, and went to his cottage to change. Since it was still warm, he opted just for a pair of shorts, and when he got back into the main house, he opened the windows in the kitchen and turned the music up.

Moving his hips to the upbeat guitar, he pulled out ingredients for a savory goat cheese torta with roasted red peppers and a lot of garlic. He wasn't going to be kissing anyone, and if he got a perverse pleasure out of making sure that Ryan wouldn't be either, who could blame him?

He carefully lined the springform pan with plastic wrap, and then got to beating the cream cheese with the goat cheese. Frankly, he realized as he worked the whisk through the cold bricks, he should have let the ingredients get to room temperature before tackling them—his pastry chef friend Miles would be appalled at him trying to get a smooth, incorporated mixture from cold cream cheese and goat cheese, but it also gave his arm a good workout and Wyatt was in a mood where he wanted it to burn a little.

It took a few long minutes, then he added the heavy cream and started thinking about the herbs he wanted to add. The garlic was roasting in the oven still, and would be for another ten minutes. He'd add that last, to give it a little chance to cool.

Dill, he thought, pulling the leafy herb from the produce drawer in the fridge. He also had some great basil, and he added some parsley for good measure, chopping everything up finely, and mixing it into the bowl.

While he was waiting for the garlic to finish, he roasted his peppers, charring them on the gas stove, and then wrapping them in plastic so he could easily peel the skins off.

Finally he was ready to assemble everything, layering in long, thin strips of roasted red pepper in the springform pan with alternating layers of the cream cheese mixture.

Finishing wrapping it up, he stuck it in the fridge to chill, even though he already knew he wasn't ready to relax.

He whipped up a quick curry yogurt marinade and stuck it on the chicken breasts for dinner. With salad and rice, that would be a perfect dinner for him and Ryan—if he even decided to join him.

It was hard to say if the driving beat of the music was keeping him going, or all the heat in Ryan's eyes as he'd stared at him all afternoon. But the reason didn't matter, Wyatt theorized. He was still hot and worked up and frankly about to go out of his skin with desire.

He was just whipping up a batch of parmesan crackers to eat the goat cheese-cake with when Ryan walked into the kitchen.

He'd also opted not to wear anything other than shorts, riding low on his narrow hips, and Wyatt's hand clenched on the handle of the cheese grater. He remembered exactly what Ryan's skin had tasted like right there, at his obliques, where the skin went from tan to something paler. He wasn't ever going to forget the salty-sweet tang of his sweat.

Here he was, driving himself up the wall with all this food they didn't need, because he couldn't forget.

Ryan hadn't forgotten either. That much was obvious.

"You're here," he said stupidly. Like Wyatt would be anywhere else.

"I'm here," Wyatt retorted testily. "I'm your private chef, remember?"

"You're hard to forget," Ryan said, a wry edge to his voice.

That was the damning part of all this. Neither of them could figure out how to get past their attraction—if that's all it was. Wyatt had his doubts at this point.

"Yeah, well it's no walk in the park for me either," Wyatt said, attacking the Parmigiano-Reggiano like it had personally insulted him.

"Really?" Ryan sounded surprised and Wyatt looked up to find that he'd come around the kitchen island and was now seriously encroaching in his personal space bubble.

It was a mistake. They both knew it. But this thing had been bubbling away all afternoon like a good Sunday meat sauce, and Wyatt was running out of ways to tell his body *no*.

Besides, he thought with resignation, they hadn't eaten the roasted garlic goat cheese yet.

Wyatt set the cheese grater down decisively. "Really," he repeated.

The earthy scent of the cheese was still floating in the air as he reached out for Ryan at the same moment Ryan reached for him. His skin was damp under Wyatt's hands, and he wanted to taste it still, to reacquaint himself with the flavor, but he was too desperate for Ryan's mouth.

Later, he told himself. Even though they both knew there wasn't going to be a later. There was just going to be this desperate, electric, sweaty kiss.

Ryan's fingers dug past the waistband of his shorts and pulled him hard, until they were crowded up together. His mouth was devouring Wyatt's, like he couldn't stop, like he wouldn't stop.

It sucked that Wyatt was going to have to be the reasonable one when the last thing he wanted was to push Ryan away.

Somehow, he did it.

"We can't do this," he gasped into the space between them. Just a moment before they'd been a moment away from taking this even further. His dick protested that it wasn't going to be happening after all.

His heart was protesting too, but Wyatt was already in trouble enough, so he ignored both of them.

"I know." Ryan sounded wrecked. Wyatt couldn't see his expression because he couldn't look at him right now. If he looked, he'd do more that he regretted.

"I'm going to Napa tomorrow," Wyatt reminded him. *Go find someone else.*

Ryan didn't say anything; he just turned and walked out of the kitchen.

Wyatt had a feeling that he wouldn't see him back for dinner.

CHAPTER NINE

WHEN RYAN HEARD THE engine of Wyatt's motorcycle revving to take off, and the gate closing behind him, he sighed in relief and leaned against the dresser in his room.

He was supposed to be getting ready for his meeting with Eric this morning, but he'd been fighting the compulsion to exit the house, walk across the yard, and knock on Wyatt's door. Tell him not to go. Tell him to bring Ryan with him.

Beg him to change his mind, even though that was the very last thing Ryan should ever ask him to do.

He should feel relief that he was on his own again—he'd always felt like he was the best version of himself free and unencumbered—but the house already felt empty because he knew if he walked into the kitchen, there wouldn't be a familiar pair of blue eyes or that smile.

Ryan took the bike, hoping the speed and adrenaline would dispel the frustration bubbling away inside of him. By the time he made it to the café, he felt a little better but still edgy.

"You look like someone shot your dog," Eric said when Ryan sat down at the table.

"What the hell, man," Ryan said, now even more annoyed. "Why would you even say that?" He could usually handle Eric's usual lack of tact and incredibly blunt delivery. He could even appreciate it at points.

He was not appreciating it now.

"Because you look pissed off," Eric said.

Ryan sighed and leaned back in the chair, stretching out his legs from the ride in, crossing his feet at the ankles. "You're an asshole."

"I'm an asshole because I said it looks like someone shot your dog or I'm an asshole because I'm forcing you to give up on Dream Chef and find someone else to be your fake boyfriend?"

"Both." Ryan scowled.

"But mostly the latter," Eric deduced. He wouldn't be as good of an agent if he wasn't brilliant at reading people. Or probably as much of an asshole. The realization was a cold comfort, and Ryan realized that for the first time, the possibility of being traded or waived by the Dodgers didn't fill him with the worst dread.

It was Wyatt getting on his bike and going back to Napa, never to be seen again.

Ryan pushed the thought away, rationalizing that the only reason that he felt this way was because Wyatt had left this morning. *But he's coming back*, he told himself firmly.

"Fine. Whatever. Yes."

"Dream Chef is no doubt very dreamy," Eric said dryly. "I heard you took him surfing. I also heard you took him to Flor's house."

"You heard?" Ryan raised an eyebrow, feeling dangerously on the edge of getting *very* pissed. "I thought we talked about this. I don't like being followed."

Eric usually backed down when he heard that tone of voice, but this time he didn't. "You should be happy it was me and not some random photographer."

"I'm not important enough for the paparazzi to stake out," Ryan argued.

"As soon as they scent the possibility that you've found someone, they're going to want to know who it is. And those pictures will be very valuable."

"I thought we were going to organize that so I didn't have to worry about being stalked by the paps?" Ryan said.

"We are. But you have to have a significant other to take that romantic walk on the beach at Malibu. Or however we decide to do it. You have to have *someone*."

Ryan's stomach cramped at the idea that it wasn't going to be Wyatt. He put it down to low blood sugar. Being hangry always made him crabby as hell.

"Can we order? I'm starving."

"Sure, whatever, yes." Eric raised his hand and the waitress came rushing over. She was blonde and pretty, and Ryan wondered vaguely if she was his latest affair.

They ordered. Ryan ordered too much food, everything on the menu that wasn't something Wyatt had made him already. He didn't want a direct comparison; he honestly wasn't sure he could handle it. It was already fucking difficult to push the thought of Wyatt away just so he could keep it together. He didn't need Eric watching him cry into his cereal bowl.

"I found a great guy for you," Eric said as soon as the waitress left. "You're gonna love him."

Ryan knew he was pouting. He knew it was unattractive. He didn't give a shit. "I don't wanna love him. That's not the point."

"Okay, he'll be easy to tolerate." Eric pulled a picture out of his briefcase and slid it over. The guy was very cute, just as advertised. Blond twink material; bright green eyes and an infectious smile. Ryan tried to dredge up even a fraction of interest and failed.

"What's his name?" Ryan said, because he needed to say *something*. Eric was clearly eager and they needed to get this done.

"Matt."

Ryan tried to imagine dating, fake or otherwise, Matt. He failed. "He's an actor?"

"He'll do whatever. He's very flexible."

Ryan shot Eric a dirty, dark look.

"I meant for the role," Eric clarified, but the look on his face told Ryan the whole story. He'd meant exactly what Ryan had thought he had. And maybe a few months ago, he *might* have wanted to hook up with Matt. The point of finding someone Ryan liked was to pave the way for that possibility, that eventuality.

But Ryan didn't want to hook up with Matt, no matter how flexible he was.

"I've got nudes too," Eric said, patting his briefcase. "Just in case you want to see."

"Jesus," Ryan exhaled. "You're a fucking menace."

"He offered them. He really wants the job."

Ryan was disgusted and did nothing to hide it. "He *needs* the job, you mean." He'd lived in LA almost his entire life, he knew exactly how many desperate, out-of-work actors there were, and what a lot of them would do for the money to stay, or even for a good word in the ear of the right people.

It wasn't surprising to Ryan that Eric would use that particular disadvantage to *his* advantage. Which had been one of the reasons Ryan hadn't wanted to use an actor for this.

Eric waved a hand. "They all do. It's not really a surprise."

Wyatt had needed a job, no matter what story his pride had told, and Ryan had given him one. He wanted to give Matt one for similar but very different reasons. Except even Ryan knew he couldn't employ the whole world.

"Just meet him," Eric cajoled. "One date."

Ryan didn't say a word. Just glared.

"Okay not a date. A meeting. A business meeting. Very straightforward, to the point."

"And we'll pay him for his time," Ryan said with a sharp nod. "Generously." It wasn't much, but it was what Ryan could do.

Eric frowned. "Two days. Saturday night, I'll send him to your house."

Ryan didn't really want Matt in his house. He was a stranger. Of course Wyatt had been a stranger too, though that had only felt true for a few short minutes. Maybe Ryan just needed to give Matt a chance.

"Fine."

"You know," Eric said, leaning back in his chair, looking smugly self-satisfied that he'd convinced Ryan to give Matt a chance, "you could always just fuck Wyatt on the down low if you want him so bad. Fake date Matt, and fuck Wyatt. It would work out okay."

Ryan was disgusted but even more disgusted with himself because that thought had definitely crossed his mind more than once. Except that he didn't want to *only* fuck Wyatt. They were friends. There were other undercurrents that Ryan couldn't quite explain. But while he definitely wanted to fuck him, that wasn't it.

"Thank you for the personal advice," Ryan said stiffly. "I'll take it under advisement."

The food came then, which Ryan was infinitely grateful for. He could eat and ignore Eric for the rest of the meeting.

Eric droned on as Ryan shoveled eggs and sausage into his mouth. "What about Adidas?" was the only question he inserted.

"Adidas?" Eric questioned, having the nerve to look peeved that his soliloquy was interrupted.

"Yeah, what about their direction? Did you convince them to keep the focus more LGBT-friendly?"

Eric pulled out his phone and scrolled until he found what he was looking for, and slid it across the table.

It was a mockup, with another random person standing in for Ryan. He was staring right through the screen, eyes piercing, and he was naked except for a pair of low-slung black athletic shorts and a pair of black Adidas shoes with the details picked out in a rainbow of colors. The baseball bat he was holding was the only movement in an otherwise static ad, holding it diagonally across his body, like it was just about to spring into action.

It was eye-catching and arresting and Ryan loved it.

"I don't know what you told them, but this is dynamite," Ryan enthused, something other than annoyed for the first time since he'd sat down.

"It looks good," Eric admitted. "They didn't have the bat at first, and it lacked something. Even they liked the idea of adding it."

"What about *Sports Illustrated*?" Ryan asked.

Eric chortled. "When they get a look at the preview for this ad, they're going to be falling all over themselves to do a cover shoot for Opening Day. Trust me. You're going to be the new Colin O'Connor."

It was a comparison that Ryan had experienced from the moment he'd very publicly come out of the closet right before the draft. It was one he respected and appreciated, but frankly, he was done being the next version of O'Connor. He was ready to differentiate himself and be the best version of Ryan Flores. This Adidas ad might be the first step in that direction.

"We talked about this," Ryan warned.

"I know, I know. We did. But *this*," Eric said, voice growing harsher around the edges as he pushed Matt's picture back in front of Ryan's plate, "is how we get you to the place you want to be."

"I already told you I'd meet with him," Ryan said, leaning back and crossing his arms across his chest. "You don't have to convince me."

"To *meet* with him? No. I don't. But to give up your fantasy of Dream Chef, *yes, I do.*"

"Don't call him that." Ryan sighed. He ended up wanting to punch Eric in the face at some point during every meeting, but he was doing a great job of being infuriating today.

"It fits." Eric paused, and peeling a few twenties off the roll of cash he kept in his pocket, tossed them onto the table. "I have another meeting in a few. Are you done?"

Ryan was definitely done, though he was pretty sure that Eric was talking about the food still left on his plate. "Yeah," he said. He hadn't really been hungry after all. Or maybe he'd only been hungry for Wyatt's food.

If that was the case, then he was officially pathetic.

"You're wasting away," Eric said as he got up from the table. "Stop mooning after Dream Chef and get your mojo back."

"Saying shit like that is why you're getting a divorce," Ryan called out towards Eric's back, but he didn't turn around. It wasn't even true; Eric was in the middle of a horribly acrimonious divorce because he was a royal asshole.

He'd neatly maneuvered him into a corner where he couldn't help but seriously consider the possibility of fake dating Matt, no matter how much he didn't want to.

The problem, Ryan sighed, shoving his sunglasses back on his face, was that left him in a worse mood than he'd been in to begin with.

Wyatt had called his brothers and had told them to meet him at Nana's home that afternoon. Of course when he pulled into the lot, three minutes before the agreed upon time, they hadn't arrived yet.

It wasn't so much a surprise as it was a continual disappointment.

He checked his phone, cleared the handful of emails, and even though he didn't see any new texts, lingered over his conversation with Ryan anyway.

It felt stupid to text him that he'd arrived in Napa safely, because that wasn't something Ryan had asked of him. They were barely friends, clearly muddling through on that end, and anything else they could've been, Wyatt had shut down.

That didn't change the fundamental desire he felt to talk to him, even to send a short text telling him he'd arrived okay.

It was a problem, and one they were going to have to try to address when Wyatt got back to LA, because clearly it wasn't going away and it certainly wasn't getting any easier.

Wyatt checked in at the front desk, clipped the guest badge to his pocket, and went straight to his nana's room, hoping that he'd catch her in it. He hadn't told her he was coming because he hadn't known what to say to her after the incident over the phone the other day, and then the longer he'd gone without calling her had made him feel even worse.

Finally, it had just made sense to make the drive and try to find an equilibrium in person. He wasn't proud of it but he rationalized that her not recognizing his voice or his name had thrown him considerably and that she really did love surprises.

He found her in the same spot he'd left her at, only a few weeks before—sitting on her comfortable chair, a book in her lap, staring out the window at the garden.

"Nana," he said softly, and this time when she turned towards him, she didn't jerk and the book didn't fall. But her eyes were his worst nightmare come to life—completely, totally blank.

She didn't know him anymore.

Something nasty in his gut was clawing, desperate to get out, and he only held it together because he'd read that it was important not to upset the loved one when they didn't remember.

"Hello," Bea said quietly. She didn't ask his name, but she didn't have to. He saw the lack of recognition plain all over her face. He was a stranger to her, and he'd only left two weeks ago.

He should have been up here *every single damn week*, like he'd originally planned on doing. He'd not come last weekend because he'd told himself it felt wrong to leave Ryan when he'd just started the new job. But the truth cut a lot closer to the bone; he'd not wanted to leave because it was *Ryan*, and he was crazy about him, even if there was no fucking hope to be had.

"Hello," Wyatt parroted back, hands useless at his sides. He kept fucking waiting for the recognition to flash on her face, for her to realize he was her grandson, that she *loved* him. For her to throw her arms around him and proclaim how much she missed him, and how terrible her new painting was, but that she wanted him to see it anyway.

He'd even take her reciting the plot to the new romance novel she was reading this week.

"Wy, you're here," Tony's voice echoed from the doorway, but he felt growing horror as the recognition *did* begin to dawn on her, but it wasn't for him. It was for his brother.

"Tony, you came today," she exclaimed, rising to her feet and giving Tony the hug Wyatt craved.

It was even worse when she turned to him, and that little crease of uncertainty formed between her white brows when she looked at Wyatt.

"It's Wyatt, Nan, you know him. Your grandson." Tony's voice was patient, and he hadn't just had the legs cut out from under him, so he could still speak. But then it was Tony, Tony could give anyone a run for their money in the speaking department. It was probably why he went through girlfriends like candy bars.

"Wyatt," she said in a puzzled voice.

He saw the moment the fog lifted but even though he felt an incredible relief when she pulled him in for a tight hug, gripping him for far longer than she'd done with Tony, it was a bittersweet moment.

He'd known this was coming someday. He hadn't prepared for it, because he didn't think you really could prepare for the day when the woman who loved you and practically raised you didn't know who you were.

"Oh, I'm so glad you're here, Wyatt," Nana said in a soft voice. She didn't mention the lack of recognition earlier, and that was consistent too with what he'd read about her condition. "How is the new job in LA?" she asked, drawing him over to the couch, sitting down next to him.

He kept her tiny, gnarled hand curled in his. When Tony gave him a look, Wyatt glared at him. Tony could care about all that fake-machismo shit; Wyatt was going to spend time with his grandmother while he still could. Besides, Tony knew Wyatt had never given a crap about all that anyway.

And suddenly, people knowing that wasn't as terrifying as it had been only a few hours earlier. Wyatt had always heard people talk about life-changing events that drastically altered your priorities but he'd never experienced it for himself. Before today, he'd always assumed they over-dramatized the situation in the re-telling, but now Wyatt realized they hadn't. It really happened, and it was happening to him.

"It's good, it's real good," he told her. He didn't tell her that every day was an exercise in frustration. "I like my boss a lot. He's really nice. A friend, almost."

"She said you were cooking for some hotshot ball player," Tony inserted.

Wyatt looked over at his brother. His hair was cropped close, one of his tattoos poking out of his t-shirt sleeve. He looked good, better than he'd seen him in awhile. If the new girlfriend was the cause for this, then Wyatt found he might actually approve for once. "Yeah, I am." He hesitated, usually never wanting to test Tony's comfort level with anything but straight white men, but *fuck it all*. "Ryan Flores."

But there was only approval and excitement on Tony's face, and it occurred to Wyatt that even as he'd been working his ass off in Bastian Aquino's kitchen and so many others and learning a bushel of life lessons, Tony might have been growing up too. It was a strange thought, his brother acting like an adult, and it set Wyatt's world even more off-kilter.

"No shit? That's pretty cool. He's a great player. Got a bright future. Might actually get the Dodgers a ring one of these days. You're his private chef, Nan said?"

No mention of Ryan's homosexuality. No mention that he was Puerto Rican. Wyatt let out a breath. "Yeah, I'm cooking for him."

"Speaking of jobs," Nana interrupted firmly. "Where is Marco?"

"Actually working today," Tony said, turning his full-charm smile onto his grandmother. "Imagine that."

"Imagine that," Wyatt repeated back wryly.

Nana elbowed him hard in the side. "I know Marco can be difficult sometimes, but he's still your brother, and he tries."

"When it's convenient for him," Wyatt said under his breath, ribs still smarting.

"I'm cooking in the kitchen over at the Napa Tavern," Tony said. "You know the place?"

Wyatt did know the place and nodded. It was several steps above some of the shitholes Tony had worked at in the past and served good burgers. It wasn't Terroir, but then Tony had gotten kicked out of culinary school for rarely going to class, and then mouthing off when he actually went, so Terroir was way out of his league.

Stupidly, Tony had seemingly resented Wyatt's climb up the ladder of success, while never really attempting it himself. Wyatt had never understood why. Tony had lots of talent, though little taught skill, but everything he'd squandered, he'd squandered himself.

"You need to take me there sometime, Tony," Nana said kindly.

Tony and Wyatt exchanged dubious looks. The Tavern was not a place that Nana would enjoy. "We'll take you to Terroir next time they do Sunday brunch, how about that?" Wyatt asked. He could probably get Aquino to part with passes. *Probably.*

Or maybe he could convince Kian to get them on the guest list.

"Maybe Tony's new friend could join us," Nana offered.

"Yeah, I heard you had a new girlfriend," Wyatt said dutifully, because Tony was his brother and not a total waste of space. And even though she would probably be done with him in six months tops, Wyatt still felt obligated to show a vague interest.

But to Wyatt's surprise, Tony flushed. "Uh, yeah. About that . . ." He hesitated, and Wyatt didn't understand what was going on. Tony was always eager to talk about his latest hookup.

"Tony's girlfriend isn't a girlfriend, I guess," Nana said softly. "I misunderstood the last time we spoke, Wyatt."

Wyatt could not understand what was happening right now.

Tony, who had been part and parcel with Marco over the years. Not rampantly homophobic, but exuding all sorts of bullshit toxic masculinity? Who had bullied Wyatt for hitting or running like a girl? *Tony* was not straight?

"Nana," Tony hissed, but he looked pleased. Like he was happy it was finally out of the bag. "You were supposed to let me tell him."

"Oh, yes, I suppose I should have. I'm sorry, Tony."

Wyatt could only sit there in shock as his brother came out to him.

Not once in his life had he *ever* been envious of either of his brothers. Not a single fucking time. And now, he was green through and through with jealousy. Because Tony had found his nerve and his balls and his bravery before Wyatt had. He should be happy for him, proud of him, but the truth was that he was fucking envious.

"I'm just happy you're happy," Wyatt could only say woodenly.

"I am," Tony said, and for the first time, Wyatt could see that he was. And not only happy, but *free*.

The jealousy billowing in him grew exponentially.

"Let's go see my new painting, boys," Nana said, and they both stood, following her like she'd bidden them.

"I hope that everything's okay between us," Tony whispered, leaning towards Wyatt.

Wyatt could only stare back at him incredulously. He *must* know. "You know it is. You know I'm gay." He'd never explicitly told either of his brothers, but he'd always figured they must have some idea. The complete lack of girlfriends had probably tipped them off.

"Yeah, of course. I know." The sympathy in Tony's eyes was galling and it shouldn't have been. Wyatt should have been over the moon for him right now. "I just figured. She might not be around, at least as herself, for much longer." Tony shrugged. "I didn't want her memories of me to be a lie, and the more I thought about it, the righter it seemed. To tell her the truth. To tell other people the truth."

Nana brought them to the art studio at the home, and Wyatt stood in front of Nana's new painting, making all the appropriate noises, saying all the right things, but internally he was reeling.

Why hadn't he thought about this situation with Nana like Tony had? Why had he seen the situation through shades of fear, instead of trusting the woman who had raised him and loved him? Why had he doubted her inherent ability to love him unconditionally? He loved *her* unconditionally. He'd accepted everything that she was dealing with, and had done everything in his meager power to make sure she was protected and safe and taken care of.

Why had he assumed that she would feel any less towards him?

When he and Tony finally exited the home, Wyatt felt like he'd been wading through fog for the better part of the two hours he'd spend with her.

"You look thrown, man," Tony said, clapping him hard on the shoulder as they paused near Wyatt's bike. "Were you going to tell her first or?" He hesitated, like he'd been waiting for Wyatt to come out first, like Wyatt had that right in the family.

It was still too new for Wyatt to trust Tony, to confide in him. No matter what sexuality he was. "I don't know what you're talking about."

"Yes, you do," Tony said evenly. "I'm just figuring my shit out, and for awhile, I figured it was your turn first. You've been waiting a long time. New job. I figure you must be hooking up with Flores, that's why you left Terroir."

Wyatt rolled his eyes. Trust Tony to be so close, yet so far, from the truth. "I'm not hooking up with Flores." *Present tense.* "I left Terroir because the Bastard pays pennies on the dollar. I needed the money to help pay for Nana's care."

Tony had the nerve to look ashamed. "I'm sorry about that. I think in a month or two, I can start contributing too. And I'll harass Marco. He always seems to have money, though god knows I don't want to know where he gets it from."

"I don't know if I want Marco's blood money," Wyatt snarked. Was Tony even joking? Wyatt wasn't sure he wanted to know either.

"I'll just tell him to send you the legitimately earned dollars," Tony teased, sliding his sunglasses back on his face. "I've got to run, but don't be a stranger." They hugged, quick and tight, and Wyatt tried to remember the last time they'd even touched, never mind embraced. When they were kids, probably. And that made more sense now than it had ever made back then. Poor Tony, hiding for so long. It ached, that knowledge, but Wyatt still couldn't seem to assuage the jealousy.

Tony's old Mustang was parked next to Wyatt's bike. The paint looked better, and when Tony slid into it and started it, it didn't rumble like it was about to explode in fifteen seconds.

It was hard to realign his world again, but Wyatt realized as he climbed onto his bike that Tony was actually getting his shit together.

For the first time ever, maybe it was time for Wyatt to follow in his big brother's footsteps.

Chapter Ten

"I CAN'T BELIEVE TONY is gay," Xander said, setting his glass down on the old picnic table they'd scrounged up and set up outside on the cracked concrete patio two summers ago.

It was a balmy fall evening in Napa, and even though it was late when Xander and Kian had gotten off work, they'd obviously sensed Wyatt was troubled, and had brought out a six-pack to join him. Or to prevent him from brooding further.

"Maybe you should hook up with him," Kian inserted slyly, and something in his tone made Wyatt sad. Melancholy and missing the old, too-innocent boy who never would have suggested that. Or teased Xander with the knowledge that he didn't hook up with anyone. Clearly Nate living here was not good for him.

"With Wyatt's older, bad-boy brother? No, thanks. I don't have that much of a masochistic streak," Xander said after taking a long gulp of beer. "What about you?" he suggested, turning the tables back on Kian. "You're about the age where making a bad romantic decision feels right."

Except they both knew that Kian was already making a bad romantic decision, and instead of it being open and then closed, it was ongoing. Never-ending, until it finally, irrevocably ended.

"Yeah, no, thanks. Gross." Kian shuddered. "No offense, Wyatt."

"None taken," Wyatt said wryly, glad he was here, and glad that his friends could distract him from brooding over this afternoon's reveal.

"Are you going to tell her then?" Xander asked. He was a huge advocate for bluntness, in just ripping the Band-Aid right off. In his mind, it might hurt, but then you knew exactly where you stood. He'd been telling Wyatt to tell his nana for years now. Wyatt was not entirely pleased that Xander had turned out to be one hundred percent right.

He also fully expected Xander to exploit that, but he hadn't so far. Maybe he was waiting until it smarted less.

"I think so, yeah." Wyatt thought about telling them about Ryan, and about Ryan's offer that he could now accept without fear.

Would Ryan still want him? Was Wyatt okay accepting his offer when he really wanted so much more?

Before, not being Ryan's fake boyfriend had seemed like the worst thing that could happen, and now that possibilities were opening up, it seemed even more devastating that he might be able to go through the motions, but could never have what he really wanted for real.

"You could have done it years ago. I told you that she wasn't going to reject you," Xander said. So much for waiting until it stung a little less.

Wyatt tipped his beer bottle at his friend. "Thank you, friend, for always being brutally honest and for never wasting an opportunity to say *I told you so.*"

"Those are Xander's four favorite words in the English language," Kian said. He sounded edgy and resentful. Wyatt could only imagine what kind of shit Xander was giving him over Bastian. Or what kind of shit Aquino was giving him.

"All I'm saying is that it's not going to end well for you," Xander said tiredly. "I don't want you to get hurt."

"You don't know that," Kian said stubbornly. Wyatt felt like he'd just been dropped into the hundredth iteration of this particular argument. Maybe the thousandth.

"He's not a good guy. He's an asshole," Xander argued. "You *know* this." And suddenly, understandably, they were talking about the Bastard.

"You're an asshole too, and I don't want you to be alone. Just because people are tough doesn't mean they don't deserve love, and doesn't mean they're incapable of returning it."

Kian, Wyatt realized, was wading in even deeper. He was going to try to "rescue" Bastian Aquino from his lonely, miserable, angry existence.

Yeah, that was going to end *really* well.

Maybe it was selfish, but Wyatt was sort of relieved that they'd at least forgotten about his own problems, and were back to focusing on their own.

"I can't talk to you about this," Xander said in mounting frustration. He got up from the table, beer bottle empty. "I worked fourteen hours today. Will probably work sixteen tomorrow. I'm going to bed. It was good to see you, Wy, don't be a stranger. And for god's sake, go tell your nana you're gay."

The door to the house slammed behind him as punctuation.

"He's gotten so grumpy," Kian said, picking at the label on his bottle.

"I think he's worried about you," Wyatt said, and it wasn't even a lie.

"Don't be ridiculous," Kian said.

"You're in love with Aquino, and he's right. If he ever returns those feelings, he's still going to eat you whole, chew you up, and then spit you out. And coming from someone who's had a fraction of that happen to them before, it's not fun. It's not something to look forward to."

Kian's voice was quiet. "What if you believed that no matter how much it hurt, it would still be worth it?"

He knew, Wyatt realized. He knew that it was going to end, and he was never going to get a happy ending with Bastian Aquino, and he didn't even care. He loved him that much. So much for this being some sort of puppy-love crush that Kian would eventually get over.

And, Wyatt realized, as Kian patted him on the shoulder on his way inside, it even made some kind of twisted sense.

It would absolutely hurt like hell whenever the professional relationship between him and Ryan ended. It would hurt if it ended and nothing ever happened between them again. It wouldn't hurt worse if he got another taste of something more personal. At least if it ended then, he would have gotten something good out of it.

He would have been able to love Ryan for the time he was able, up close and personal, instead of staring in the window, wishing for something he couldn't have.

❦ ❦

"Hi," Wyatt said, placing his drivers license on the front desk corner with a decisive click, "I'm here to visit Bea Blake. And I don't know if he's available, but I'd like to talk to the doctor in charge of her case."

"Dr. Martinez? I'm not sure if he's in today," the front desk attendant said sympathetically. "But you can speak to the nurse on call?"

354

"That would be fine," Wyatt said with a certainty he didn't feel. He'd spent most of the night sitting outside at the rickety old picnic table, downing beer after beer, trying to drown out the fear that kept insisting he was making a mistake.

Finding out Tony had told Nana and she hadn't thrown him out, or told him he was going to hell, or that he wasn't lovable anymore—even though he was Tony—should have swept all Wyatt's insecurities clean. But it turned out that it wasn't as easy as deciding to do it and doing it.

Fear still held him back, still whispered things in his ear. It didn't matter if his head knew they weren't true, his heart still felt the echo of them.

"I'll go get the nurse," the young lady said with a smile. "Do you want to wait in the lobby?"

Wyatt wiped his damp palms on his jeans. He'd hoped for a quick, five-minute conversation, and then he could go find Nana and finally tell her the truth. But he'd also promised himself he'd talk to someone on her case about her memory loss patches recently. He needed to know what to expect. Online research was only getting him so far.

"Sure."

"There's coffee if you'd like some," she said, gesturing to the carafe set up in the lobby. "Help yourself."

The last thing he needed was more coffee, and he'd had the coffee here before and knew it was awful. He wished he'd asked to talk to the doctor on the way out, and then he wouldn't be spending more time waiting. Waiting until visiting hours today started had been hard enough.

The dark evil sludge that came out of the coffee carafe was the same as he'd remembered it, but optimistically he thought that at least it must be strong. He stirred in a sugar packet, looked askance at the fake cups of creamer, and grimaced when he took his first sip.

Still, it had wasted at least two minutes. Two minutes was good.

Two minutes he didn't have to think about what Nana might look like when he finally told her the truth.

He'd wanted to text Ryan since last night, since he'd made up his mind, and it might have been easier to focus on the good things that would probably happen after he took this step. But he hadn't known what to say to him. After all, he'd already unequivocally told him no, with no hope that he might change his mind.

Ryan had probably already moved on to someone else. And considering how fixated he was on a fake boyfriend, how could Wyatt possibly hope to win him as a real one?

"Mr. Blake?" He turned, and a woman, mid-thirties, with blonde hair and kind eyes was standing at the entrance to the lobby. "They said you wanted to talk about your grandmother's case?"

"Yes, I did," he said, thankful that he hadn't had to wait long.

"She's in her art class now," she said. "I'll walk you down there and we can talk. I'm Gretchen, by the way."

He shook the hand she offered. Noticed it was trembling a little. Hoped that she'd put it down to the caffeine in the noxious liquid they passed for coffee.

"I've recently moved away for work," he said. "I can't get here as much as I'd like to. I know consistency and routine are really important for her mental state. But I can only get here maybe once a week. I'm still calling regularly though. And last week, she didn't recognize my voice or my name right away." His voice broke on the last few words, and he gritted his teeth, knowing that couldn't be explained by the terrible coffee and hoping that he wouldn't actually burst into tears in the middle of the lobby.

She took his elbow and steered him down one of the wide hallways. "I've consulted extensively with Dr. Martinez about your grandmother's case," she said. "I'm sorry to say, that's not a huge surprise. She's going to have lapses."

"I didn't think they'd come so quickly."

"Alzheimer's is a disease we still don't know very much about. There's going to be accelerated periods and then periods when her condition stabilizes. Moving here and uprooting her from her home probably sent her in a bit of an accelerated period, but it should stabilize. I'm assuming she does eventually recognize you."

"It's usually only a minute or so. She recognized my brother Tony right away."

"That's good," she said, even though it wasn't.

He wanted to tell her how unfair it was that Tony would be the one she'd remember. That he'd quit his prestigious job so he could earn more money to take care of her. That she was the only person in his life that he knew he couldn't lose; which meant, of course, that she was the one he was bound to lose.

"It's not good. None of this is good," he practically growled. It was instantly embarrassing, and that wasn't just because her face fell.

"Of course it's not good," she hastily corrected. "I don't mean that. I'm sorry for sounding callous or insensitive."

"You're not . . . I'm just . . . on edge," he said. Which was the best way to phrase it. He took another gulp of the devil coffee, even though there was no way it could help.

"I've spent some time with Mrs. Blake," she said, "and I promise you, she's who she was before. The disease hasn't progressed enough to erode the foundation of who she is. You have a lot of time before that happens. The best advice I can give you is to take advantage before that happens. Too many people I see wish that they'd spent more time, or called more, or made more happy times with their loved ones."

"That won't be a mistake I'll be making," Wyatt vowed. He'd figure out a regular visit schedule and call every day. It didn't even matter if there wasn't anything to say. Just hearing her voice would be enough.

But most of all, he was going to begin this new routine by telling her the truth.

They stopped in front of a classroom with the door open. Wyatt could smell paint and thinner wafting out. "She's right in there," Gretchen said with a smile. "You want to get her?"

❦

"Wyatt, not that I'm not glad to see you, but that was my painting class." Bea Blake didn't look very happy as he took her arm and led her out one of the big double doors to the garden. The same garden she was always looking at.

Maybe it wasn't enough to stare at the grounds out the window.

Also maybe he wouldn't cry if he told her in a semi-public place.

"I'm going back down to LA right after this," he said, leading them to a secluded corner of the garden, and sitting down on the bench there. "But I wanted to see you before I left."

Her face softened. "I can catch up later," she promised. "I'm glad you came by."

Good, because he already had enough guilt saved up to last a long while. He didn't need to add delaying her completing her painting onto his already heavy conscience.

"I wanted to tell you something, actually." He took a deep breath. For a second, he thought about bringing up Tony, but reconsidered. This needed to be just about him.

Bea reached out and took his hand in hers. "You know you could tell me anything, darling boy, and I'd love you regardless."

It wasn't as if she had ever said anything different. She'd been variations on the same theme for his entire life, but between losing both his parents, and never being close to his brothers, he'd always been too afraid to believe that she wouldn't just abandon him too. No matter what she said.

But for the very first time, he found the echo of truth ringing in her words. She meant it, and she trusted him to trust *her*.

"Nana, I'm gay." He'd thought of so many lead-ins. So many excuses. So many ways to word it over the years. He'd tasted the words on his tongue more times than he could even count. So when it came down to it, maybe it was better to keep it simple. Straightforward. The bare bones of truth.

Bea's face didn't change, her smile just softened another degree. "Oh darling, I know. It's okay. I love you no matter what."

"What? You *knew*? Who told you?" Wyatt shouldn't be panicking because he'd actually managed to tell her the truth, and nothing had changed. But he was. How had she known? And how long had she known?

He'd been torturing himself for how many years for *no good fucking reason*.

"Nobody had to tell me. I have eyes," she retorted tartly. "I know you. I love you. Also, you've never had a girlfriend. It wasn't hard to put two and two together."

"Oh." The wind out of his sails, he crumpled against her, like he was still that eight-year-old kid, whose dad had just left, abandoning his mom and his two brothers. Like he was thirteen and his mom had just passed.

"It's alright," she soothed, her hand combing his hair back from his forehead. "Everything is alright."

And for the first time in a very long time, Wyatt believed her.

❧❧❧❧❧ ❧❧❧❧❧

"Thanks for coming over," Ryan said tightly, awkward as he sat across from Matt on the uncomfortable living room couch he never sat on. Why was he sitting on it now?

Because he couldn't imagine welcoming Matt into the kitchen. That was Wyatt's domain now, and Ryan wasn't going to betray him like that. He didn't want him in any part of the house he'd shared with Wyatt, and that had only left the living room.

Not that he had any intentions of hooking up with Matt. He was definitely as cute as his pictures had promised—bright, hopeful green eyes and short spiky blond hair. There had been more than one moment when Ryan had caught him checking him out.

It should have made Ryan want to lead him right back to the bedroom. Or the couch. Or any convenient horizontal surface. But instead they'd ended up in the uncomfortable, stuffy living room that he never used—for good reason.

"Are you okay?" Matt asked. "You don't seem all that happy I'm here."

"It's not you," Ryan insisted, feeling guilt swamp him. He was being an asshole, and for what? Because Matt's green eyes weren't blue, and he didn't like to surf?

It wasn't Matt's fault that he wasn't Wyatt.

"Seriously," he continued. "I'm sorry. I . . . I don't really want to do this. But I need to."

Matt's expression was sympathetic. "I get it."

Besides, if he couldn't have Wyatt, why did it matter who played his fake boyfriend?

"Let's get out of here," Ryan said with a grimace at their surroundings. Coming in here had been a bad idea. "Grab a beer and go outside to the fire pit. Try to get to know each other. We're going to be spending some time together and we can't keep acting like strangers."

Matt raised an eyebrow, getting to his feet. "Are you sure?"

He wasn't sure at all. But he had to move past this, because something kept tugging him back and Ryan didn't like anything holding him in, or holding him back. "Yeah, I am."

"Well, I'll be honest I need this job, so I'm going to stop being a selfless good guy and asking you if you're okay with it."

Ryan barked out a laugh and led him into the kitchen. "I guess being an actor in LA isn't all that easy."

Matt nodded vehemently, leaning against the island and launching into a long, over-dramatic story about some audition he'd just been on. Ryan tried to ignore the voice in the back of his head that said this was like every bad first date he'd been on, and listen to Matt's story.

Frankly, this was one of the reasons he'd stopped going on first dates.

Ryan pulled a pair of beers from the fridge and ignored the other voice that reminded him this was Wyatt's favorite brand.

Matt paused when Ryan handed him the bottle. "Are you even listening to me?" he demanded.

Ryan froze. "I'm sorry?"

Matt set the bottle on the counter with a decisive click. "You said you wanted to get to know me. You said you were doing this. And hey, I'm an actor. I can work with almost nothing. But you can't get far enough away from me and you're barely paying attention to anything I say. Honestly, usually I don't have to work this hard to make a guy interested in me."

"I'm sorry," Ryan repeated, and he *was*, but not that sorry. "It's not you, it's me." He imagined how much Eric was going to drive him crazy over this. How painful his grating, obnoxious whining would be. He imagined Wyatt coming back and Ryan dropping to his knees and *begging* him to reconsider. He imagined leaving Flor and LA and everything he loved. He imagined terrible winters in Ohio or Wisconsin or the death trap of the Trop.

But nothing seemed quite as terrible as doing this.

"Seriously?" Matt demanded, and the worst thing was that Ryan even sympathized with him. "What is with you? It's not like we're going to declare our eternal love or register at Macy's or adopt a kid. We're going to hold hands and I'm going to go to your games and wear your jersey and be cute in the wives' section. We don't even have to hook up if you don't want to, though I wouldn't exactly mind."

Alarm bells were clanging in his head. It wasn't like he *wanted* to do any of those things. Not even with Wyatt—though it was scary as fuck that doing them with him didn't sound all that bad—but he didn't want to hook up with this cute guy.

He couldn't have gotten it up right now if he was being paid or he was being jacked full of Viagra.

Of course that was the moment the back door to the kitchen opened and a pair of blue eyes narrowed, taking in the scene in front of him.

Ryan. And a young, cute guy. Beers in front of them. *Wyatt's* favorite brand, even.

"You're back," Ryan said, fifty percent excited, fifty percent panicked.

Matt's sympathetic look at Ryan was galling, and definitely deserved. He was totally fucked over this guy, and if even Matt could tell with about ten seconds of evidence, then it was probably extremely obvious.

"I'm back," Wyatt said slowly. His hand was still on the doorknob, and he hadn't taken a single step into the kitchen.

"This is Matt," Ryan said, because Flor had drilled good manners into him. "This is my private chef. And friend. Wyatt."

"I'm going to be Ryan's fake boyfriend," Matt said, piping up, and fucking him over big-time. Even though Ryan had literally been about to tell him that *no*, he wasn't about to be his fake boyfriend. Ryan had been about to say that if he couldn't have Wyatt, he didn't want anyone, no matter how insane that sounded.

It *was* insane; Wyatt would never believe it. And from the doubting, incredulous expression on his face now, Ryan wondered if he could even keep him in his life after this clusterfuck.

"No, you're not," Ryan insisted desperately.

Matt crossed his arms and raised his eyebrows.

Wyatt wasn't reacting at all, though. He still had that deadened expression on his face, completely shut down, like this was his worst nightmare and he couldn't quite process it.

Ryan totally understood that mind frame; he was smack in the middle of it right now.

"I need to talk to you," Ryan said, directing his desperation in the right direction this time.

Wyatt crossed his arms over his chest, mimicking Matt. He didn't really have a right to be upset. Jealous, maybe, but Ryan found he didn't give a shit right now what was deserved and what wasn't.

Ryan wasn't going to beg in front of that little snot Matt, so he did the next best thing. He walked towards the doorway, stopped right in front of Wyatt, and waited for him to give in.

"Fine," Wyatt said, breaking after half a minute of tense silence. He backed up and Ryan followed him out to his little cottage. Wyatt had left the door open behind him, but Ryan shut it decisively. He didn't even care if Matt decided to help himself to whatever in the house. If Matt robbed him blind, it still wouldn't matter.

"I'm sorry about that," Ryan said.

But Wyatt only shrugged. "You said you were going to do it. You had to find someone else. I didn't really expect to come home and find him in the kitchen, but it's your house."

Ryan opened his mouth to say that it *was* his house, but that it didn't matter because in the end, Matt wasn't going to be his fake boyfriend. Not now, not in a day or a week or in a hundred years. Except Wyatt kept talking.

"The thing is," he continued, beginning to pace back in forth in the tiny living room, "I realized something in Napa this weekend. And I came home because I wanted to tell you that I'd changed my mind. So seeing him in there threw me. I didn't like it."

Ryan gaped. "You didn't like it?"

"I fucking hated it, okay?" Wyatt turned and there was something fierce and hot in his blue eyes. They latched right onto Ryan's face and he felt like he was burning under the heat of that gaze. "If you need a fake boyfriend, I want it to be me."

He stalked right up to where Ryan was standing mute and disbelieving. "Tell me it can be me."

Ryan did the only thing that made any sense in this fucked-up situation: he placed his hands on Wyatt's chest, and kissed him.

He didn't react, just stayed frozen in place. Ryan pulled back a fraction. "Please," Wyatt begged, voice cracking, "please tell me that this means yes."

Ryan laughed, and it felt like the weight of the decision lifted with each exhale. "Yes. Yes. Yes."

"Oh thank god," Wyatt breathed out, and his hands reached out, grasping Ryan's waist. "Because I missed this too much."

I missed you too. The thought was instant, but Ryan was prevented from saying it because Wyatt pulled him even closer, until they were flush against each other, and kissed him.

It was everything like their first kiss—the sudden burst of heat and electricity that had flared between them from the first moment—but even though the intensity was just as fierce, it felt calmer, mellower. Much more certain. As if Wyatt had finally realized that this wouldn't be their last kiss, but the first in a long chain of them.

"Fuck it," Ryan breathed into Wyatt's mouth, every nerve ending in his body lighting the way they never could for Matt. He dropped his hand to the growing bulge in Wyatt's jeans, because now that he was allowed, that he was allowing himself, he didn't want to waste another second doing something other than touching Wyatt every way he'd dreamt about.

"Right now?" Wyatt murmured wryly. "But there's that guy in your kitchen." It wasn't like Matt was stopping Wyatt either, because his hands were already at the waist of Ryan's shorts, hooking into the elastic and pulling them down.

"You want to wait any longer?" Ryan asked, breathless because Wyatt's big capable hands were already curling around his dick, and he hadn't been completely hard before, but he definitely was now.

It was like Wyatt knew he needed it a little rough, because his callouses were sliding along his length and his thumb was curling around the head of his cock and it felt so good, he could only pant into Wyatt's neck.

"I'm done waiting," Wyatt said, sounding so final that Ryan quivered at the implications. This was supposed to be them agreeing to be *fake* boyfriends. But it felt real, like it was so much more than just playacting in front of a camera.

But then, there wasn't a camera here now, was there? And they were both so into each other that nothing, including Matt stealing all his worldly possessions, would have torn him away from Wyatt.

Wyatt twisted especially hard, and Ryan groaned. "I said," Wyatt repeated with a grin, "that I was done waiting."

"Oh. Right." Ryan scrambled for the button and the fly on Wyatt's jeans, and tugged them down, along with his boxer briefs. Wyatt's cock was just as perfect as Ryan had remembered (and fantasized about). He'd been wanting this for weeks now, and now that he was finally going to get it again, he wasn't going to half-ass it.

Ryan matched Wyatt's pumping rhythm, slow and a little rough, because he'd figured out that was how Wyatt must like it. And sure enough, his head lolled back, eyes glazing over, as Ryan worked his hand over his dick.

"Tonight," Wyatt panted, "we're going to do this again. Slower. Better."

Ryan definitely remembered how it had been last time. Not exactly slow, but a steady, inexorable burn of pleasure that had left him hazy for hours after. And if that happened again, Ryan definitely wasn't going to complain. But that wasn't what he was in the mood for.

"Oh, yeah, it's gonna be better," Ryan promised. "Slow. Definitely." Gasped as Wyatt's hand tugged him just right. He was going to lose it, because it had been too long without those hands on him. "But it's gonna be you at my mercy."

Wyatt's sly expression, agreeing to all that and more was what did it for Ryan, and he came with a low cry, orgasming over Wyatt's hand.

"Shit," Wyatt groaned, and followed right after Ryan.

Laughing, Ryan steered them over to the kitchenette and with a free hand grabbed some paper towels. They cleaned up, but he couldn't quite meet Wyatt's eyes. This was just supposed to be about them hooking up, but because of how much they'd wanted each other it had somehow felt like more.

Ryan wasn't sure how he felt about that.

He did know he had to go see what Matt was doing in his kitchen, though.

"Are you just going to kick that guy out?" Wyatt asked as he zipped his jeans up.

Ryan raised an eyebrow. "Well he's definitely not staying."

"He doesn't seem like a bad guy."

Only Wyatt would find his rival nice.

"You talked to him for about thirty seconds and said less than ten words," Ryan pointed out.

"But you talked to him longer. He couldn't be all that bad," Wyatt said.

"Except," Ryan said, opening the door to head back to the house, "I only have one opening for a fake boyfriend, and that is currently filled."

To Ryan's surprise, Matt was still sitting in the kitchen, sipping on a beer, scrolling through his phone.

When they walked in, he looked up. "Ah, must have been a pretty good conversation," Matt said.

"It was okay," Ryan said nonchalantly.

Next to him, Wyatt tried—and failed—to stifle his laughter.

"I guess this means I didn't get the job," Matt observed, and Ryan felt a pulse of guilt at how bummed he sounded.

But before Ryan could tell him that he was sorry and that Eric would be in touch for the payment for this evening's "work," Wyatt was leaning over on the counter by him. "I know, it probably sounded really cushy," he said sympathetically. He glanced back at Ryan, but now he was smirking, and Ryan knew that expression promised bad things. "Hanging out with a cute guy, holding hands, going to free dinners and events and sitting in the wives' section at the Dodgers' stadium. But trust me, you dodged a bullet here."

"What?" Ryan squeaked out in surprise.

Matt's eyes had gone sly and calculating. "How so?"

Wyatt gestured to where Ryan was standing, but didn't take his eyes off Matt. "He's a spoiled brat of epic proportions. Expects you to wait on him, hand and foot. Expects you to tell him all the time how gorgeous he is, like the mirror isn't telling him the truth. And in bed? All taking and no giving. Trust me. You really ended up with the better part of this bargain."

Matt's eyes narrowed. "How do you know all this?"

"Duh. I'm his real boyfriend," Wyatt said. "Or maybe his sex slave. We haven't really put a label on it yet."

"I'm not really big on labels, *honey*," Ryan said, coming over, and slinging an arm roughly around Wyatt's shoulders. "Isn't that true?"

Wyatt barely lost a beat. "*And* he won't actually define your role, which means that he can decide it's whatever the fuck he needs *right now*."

Matt took another gulp of his beer. "If you're trying to make me feel better, it's not working."

Wyatt looked very surprised, and Ryan was very amused. He clearly had no idea what a terrible liar he was. "Why?"

"Because you're a really shitty liar, so I'd guess that whatever you're telling me is exactly the opposite of how he really is." Matt paused. "*Plus*, he hasn't exactly kicked you out of the house for saying all that, *and* he looks like he wants to drag you back to wherever you just went for round two. So I call bullshit."

Wyatt shrugged. "It was worth a try."

"I can do better than that," Ryan offered. "I'll find you another job. It won't be free dinners or holding hands or wearing my jersey in the wives' section, but I can see what I can do."

"Really?"

Ryan sighed at Matt's disbelieving tone. "Like I said, this was all me. Nothing to do with you. I'm sure you would have been a fantastic fake boyfriend, but there's someone a little more my style."

Matt raised an eyebrow. "I'm really not stupid, guys."

"What do you mean?" Wyatt asked.

"I mean, there *is* no fake-boyfriend position. You're clearly Ryan's *real* boyfriend," Matt said, slipping off the barstool. "Thanks for the entertainment and the spank bank material for later, but my Uber is here."

Ryan and Wyatt stood there, more than a little shocked, as Matt went out the back door with a single jaunty hand wave that just as easily could have been a middle finger.

"I don't think he likes us very much," was what Wyatt said after a silent moment.

Ryan was relieved that Wyatt was pointedly ignoring Matt's final comment about how they looked like they were really together. Wyatt had *just* agreed to play Ryan's boyfriend. He didn't need to have issues already with either of them believing it was more real than it actually was.

"He wasn't so bad," Ryan teased, turning in Wyatt's embrace. "Now maybe I should drag you back where we came from and do what Matt suggested and have round two."

Ryan swore he saw something flicker in Wyatt's eyes. Was it unease? Fear? Something else? But then Wyatt leaned down and kissed him, quick and fierce, and Ryan decided it was nothing. Nothing worth worrying over, anyway. Not when Wyatt's mouth was on his and his hands were all over his body. Everything that had been so close but so far these last few weeks.

He wasn't the type to deprive himself when he found something he really wanted, and he wasn't about to start now.

Chapter Eleven

Before he even opened his eyes, Wyatt knew the bed he'd been sleeping in wasn't his.

He knew this bed, though. Knew the mattress, the sheets, the particular natural scent of its regular occupant. Knew the occupant, intimately.

It was hard to forget the last time he'd woken up in this bed. He'd gone to make breakfast and had only figured out too late that Ryan had bailed. Escaped. Disappeared.

Wyatt reached out hesitantly, brushing the skin of Ryan's arm. His rhythmic breathing didn't change. Lying there, close enough to touch Ryan, he figured he had two choices.

One, get up and go start breakfast, like he'd done the last time. Hope that things would go differently and that Ryan wouldn't leave.

Two, wake Ryan up himself, and guarantee that he wouldn't leave because he didn't *want* to.

It wasn't even a choice. Door number one never had a chance. And maybe, Wyatt thought, pushing the sheet down his naked body, that wasn't fair, but he'd been trying to play fair up until now, and that hadn't gotten him anywhere.

Maybe it was time to play unfair.

Ryan's breathing barely changed as Wyatt rolled over, and then nestled himself in the blankets kicked to Ryan's feet.

His dick was still soft, but as Wyatt ran a tentative finger up the underside of his balls, he had a feeling that wouldn't last long.

Wyatt had just wrapped his tongue around the head, and started sucking when he felt Ryan tense.

"I thought you were a dream," Ryan said, voice soft and rough, as he reached down to cradle Wyatt's head with his palm, running his fingers through his hair.

Wyatt traced a pattern on Ryan's hardening cock with his tongue. "A good dream, I hope."

He shouldn't have worried, but some things were hard to shake, and Ryan literally running away after their first—or second, but who was counting?—night together was one of those. Maybe it would have been easier if they were something more than employee and employer, or convenience with added benefits.

But Ryan had made his feelings very clear, and Wyatt, having just gotten at least part of what he wanted, wasn't about to look a gift horse in the mouth.

Speaking of gift horses and mouths, he lapped at the head of his, sucking off a little bit of pre-come.

"It had real potential," Ryan observed sleepily.

Wyatt took that as a request to continue, so he did, trying to lose himself in Ryan's taste and scent and the feel of his hardness against his tongue, in his mouth. And he did, swallowing his come with the glow of satisfaction on a job well done.

Almost.

Even when Ryan wrapped his big calloused hand around Wyatt's dick, pumping him until he felt woozy from pleasure, he couldn't quite forget that this was all supposed to mean nothing.

He'd never been good with hookups, he reasoned as he wandered back to his place for a quick shower before making breakfast. He just had to adjust to this new normal. Having Ryan was definitely better than not having him at all. That much was true.

"You're quiet this morning," Ryan said, pushing his toast around his plate, trying to sop up the rest of his over easy eggs. He looked up, grinning. "I figured earlier it was because you had my dick in your mouth but now you don't have any excuses."

"Maybe I'm tired," Wyatt said, trying to match Ryan's sly, teasing tone. "Someone kept me up most of the night."

It had been so good it was hardly anything to complain about. But last night Wyatt had felt lost to the pleasure of finally getting what he'd craved so badly, and this morning he felt like he couldn't drown out the voice in the back of his head that kept whispering, *what's next?*

"And maybe," he added, Ryan looking up, surprised at his serious tone, "I'm curious what happens next."

"What happens next? Now that we're faux-happily-ever-after poster children?"

Wyatt nodded and told himself firmly that the word shouldn't sting. It was just a word. It didn't *mean* anything, and Ryan didn't mean anything cruel by it. It was the truth, plain and simple. He had agreed to be Ryan's fake boyfriend, not his real one. Ryan couldn't be held responsible for the feelings Wyatt couldn't seem to help.

"Oh, I guess I should call Eric. I'm sure he's been blowing my phone up with a bazillion messages after Matt left here last night."

"Is there some sort of plan?" Wyatt didn't even care what it was. But maybe if he knew, if he prepared himself in advance, it would be easier to deal with.

"Lots of plans, to be honest," Ryan said. "Dozens, probably. Eric likes contingency plans. I think the last one he had involving you, and not someone else, was hosting a dinner party here. Something super couple-y, with lots of social media posts from the people invited. Way to generate some news buzz before we confirmed it."

Wyatt cleared his throat. "We should do a barbecue instead of a dinner party. Something a little more casual."

Ryan brightened at the idea. "That's a good idea, actually. I knew you'd be great at this."

Great at being a fake boyfriend. Wyatt internally raised his hand in a mini, half-hearted fist pump of triumph.

"Let me call Eric, and I'll run the idea by him. Maybe in a day or two? How long do you need to plan something like that?"

"Plan it?"

Ryan laughed. "Like the food, silly. I'll take care of the rest. Or Eric will. Or actually Eric's assistant."

"The food's the easiest part," Wyatt said with an eye roll as punctuation. "Promise, I can handle it. How many people?"

"Maybe ten? Fifteen? Tabitha and her boyfriend. Flor. Her kids. A few teammates if they're in town. Eric, of course."

"You're going to invite Eric?" Wyatt was still on the fence about Ryan's agent. He wasn't sure which side he was on, or if he even acknowledged there were sides. Or if he just played everyone, maneuvering everyone exactly where he wanted them, like pieces on a chess board.

"Of course. He's got to orchestrate this whole thing, right?" Ryan laughed, and the carefree edge to it hurt. Unintentionally of course.

You need to get yourself together.

This was what he had agreed to. This was the new normal. It was time to get his head and his heart on the same page, onto the same plan.

"Right, *duh*," Wyatt said.

"But you liked Tabitha, right? And Flor?" Ryan sounded a little concerned, as if Wyatt might not like his friends or his family, which was ridiculous. Because what fake boyfriend required their approval?

"Of course I did," Wyatt teased. "They're hella intimidating, but strangely, unexpectedly, nice."

Ryan beamed. "I think they'd take that as a high form of praise."

"Well, I meant it." Wyatt shoved his hands in his pockets. "So barbecue for fifteen. I can do that in my sleep."

"That's because you're brilliant." Ryan hopped off the barstool, slid his empty plate into the sink, and kissed Wyatt's cheek. "I'm gonna go call Eric."

"How about . . ." Wyatt hesitated, and then decided to just go for it. "Would it be okay if I invited some friends too?"

"I didn't even know you knew anyone in LA. I'd love to meet your friends," Ryan said, and sounded so god damned sincere, Wyatt wasn't even sure he was acting. And maybe he wasn't. Maybe that was the attitude Wyatt should take. It was all real, until it wasn't.

"They've been super busy filming, but I bet I could drag them away for an evening," Wyatt said. "You probably don't watch any of the *Five Points* culinary shows, but they star in *Pastry by Miles.*"

Ryan rolled his eyes. "Tabitha works for *Five Points*. Not in the culinary department, because that would be an epic fucking disaster, but yeah, I do. Once in awhile. I heard about that new show. Heard it's good."

"Yeah, I worked at Terroir with Miles Costa. He and his boyfriend, Evan, produce the show and star in it."

"Well, I'm dying to meet them," Ryan declared. "Invite them!"

It was easy to suggest inviting Miles and Evan to the barbecue. It was another to actually do it.

"Did you drown in the Pacific?" Miles asked when he picked up the phone.

Like Miles hadn't been so overwhelmed with filming the second season of *Pastry by Miles*, practically on top of finishing the first season, that he hadn't bothered to keep in touch either.

"No," Wyatt said testily, flicking through recipes on the iPad he'd set up on a cookbook stand. "I've been busy." That was actually a lie, but Miles didn't need to know that.

"Actually, Xander told me that you're barely working at this private chef gig. Lots of time to experiment in the kitchen, time off to go surfing, all those extended naps in the afternoons." Miles made the fairly innocent word *nap* sound as dirty as it could.

"That is . . . almost completely a lie," Wyatt protested. He hadn't been whiling away the afternoons by having wild sex with Ryan every day, though if the opportunity had come up, he wouldn't have said no.

"Xander doesn't lie," Miles retorted. "That's his whole problem."

It was definitely *one* of Xander's problems; he was painfully, bitterly honest. Wyatt wouldn't say he was lacking in tact, more like it was completely absent from his vocabulary.

But Wyatt didn't want to talk about Xander. Of course he didn't really want to talk about himself either, so changed the subject. "How's season two going?"

"Going to be a wild success, of course. Even better than season one. Cooking Channel has been making overtures about season three but I need to get Evan away from the studio before he forgets where we live."

"You should get away like . . . tomorrow night, for example," Wyatt offered.

"Tomorrow night? I was thinking more like a three-week trip to Fiji. One of those huts overlooking the water. No Wi-Fi, no laptop, no cellphones. Definitely no clothes."

"That too," Wyatt said, leaning against the kitchen counter. "But circling back to tomorrow night, Ryan and I are hosting a barbecue at his place, and you and Evan should definitely come."

"You and Ryan?" Miles sounded suspicious, like he had a feeling where this was going, and really, honestly, he didn't have a fucking clue.

"Ryan needs to give the impression that he's settled and responsible to his team, so I've agreed to act as his . . . partner socially," Wyatt improvised. It didn't sound much better than saying the phrase, *fake boyfriend*, and Miles was going to figure it out in ten seconds flat, but it made *him* feel better.

"You're going to be his fake boyfriend," Miles said flatly. "And this barbecue is what, your coming out party?"

Miles had always been too smart for his own good.

"Yes," was all Wyatt could say.

"We'll be there," Miles said with absolute finality, shocking the hell out of him. Wyatt had at least expected him to have to consult Evan and their mutual schedule together.

"Really?"

"You like the guy, right?" Miles asked.

"Uh, yeah, I guess. I mean, I don't guess. I do. I do like him."

"And you're sleeping together." Miles didn't even phrase this as a question.

"How did you know?"

"Because," Miles said impatiently, "that's what always happens in these scenarios."

"It's not what you think," Wyatt protested.

"I don't think anything," Miles said gently. "Only that you'll probably put yourself out there and then get crushed to shit by the hot football player."

"Baseball. He plays baseball."

Miles' silence in response was telling. So he'd nailed it on the head. It wasn't necessarily going to end that way, there were lots of ways it *could* end. That was definitely the way Wyatt kept imagining though, and dreading.

"We'll be there," Miles finally repeated. "What time? Text me the address. Actually," he paused. "Text Evan the address. He can add it to the schedule."

"Sure."

"Xander said he seemed nice."

Wyatt nearly dropped the phone. "Xander hasn't even met him yet!"

"I'm sure he did some sort of creepy digging. YouTube binge-watching all his interviews or whatever."

"He means well," Wyatt said. "He's really worried about Kian. I'm surprised he made the time from his schedule of worrying about Kian to worry about me."

Miles sighed. "When we first met him, I didn't expect that he would end up so fiercely protective."

Wyatt couldn't help but be reminded of something Kian had said the other night. That just because he was an asshole didn't mean he wasn't deserving of love.

"Someday," Wyatt promised, "we need to figure his shit out."

Miles laughed. "Maybe when we don't have enough shit of our own."

"There," Wyatt said, "I just texted Evan the address, and now he's going to find you in approximately five point three seconds and demand to know what's going on."

"Probably." Miles sounded happy about it. "Hey, you don't need me to bring anything? Some sort of dessert?"

Miles was an incredibly talented pastry chef, and Wyatt probably should have taken him up on the offer. It wouldn't be any trouble for him, even as busy as he was, and trouble and the effort for Wyatt would be far more substantial. But there was some stubborn part of him that wanted to make this dinner all himself. Also, it would definitely keep him involved and busy enough that he wouldn't have the time to worry about what might happen at it.

"Nah, I'm good," Wyatt said.

"Your loss," Miles retorted. "We'll see you tomorrow."

Ryan walked back into the kitchen five minutes after he'd hung up with Miles.

"Everyone on my side is confirmed. Eric is *thrilled*," Ryan said, making an expressive face of distaste.

"I bet he is," Wyatt said. "Miles said he and Evan could come too."

"Eric practically fell over himself at how excited he was that you knew the stars of *Pastry by Miles*. He likes the connection and they're popular on social media. He thinks it'll be a great fit."

Wyatt had thought it would be a great fit because Miles and Evan were his friends. But apparently genuine friendship wasn't all that was required these days.

"I'm sure he's disappointed that you ended up with the slightly less famous chef from Terroir," Wyatt said wryly.

Ryan surprised him by coming up next to him, and wrapping an arm around his waist, leaning in to brush a quick kiss across his lips. "But I'm not disappointed, and that's all that matters," he said seriously.

"Say that after I've attempted to make a dessert," Wyatt joked weakly. He felt even less comfortable with how demonstrative and affectionate Ryan was now. Like the last barrier had been lifted and he could act however he wanted—and what he wanted was to act like Wyatt was his boyfriend.

Just go with it, don't fight it, he reminded himself.

And in this scenario it meant acting like he'd just gotten what he wanted too: Ryan as *his* boyfriend.

"I'm sure it's going to be great," Ryan said loyally. "And I'm happy to help with whatever you need."

Wyatt turned slightly, pulling Ryan fully into his arms. "What if what I need is a very dirty nap?"

Tugging on his hand, Ryan smiled slyly. "Then let's go take a nap."

The next day it was tough not to regret spending hours "napping" in Ryan's bed. He'd had a big list of stuff to do, including shopping and prep, and instead he'd let himself be talked into a few hours of sex alternated by actual sleeping, followed by ordering pizza in and making out on the couch.

Frankly, it hadn't even required much convincing on Ryan's part, but Wyatt was slowly, but surely, getting to a better place with that.

Acting like they were just together with no weird *faux* bullshit had been the answer to all of Wyatt's questions about what he should do. The strangest—and the best—thing was that Ryan didn't ever hesitate, or pull back, or question anything Wyatt was doing.

It was all good. Great, really. Except that how great it had been yesterday meant that he was now at the grocery store at six in the morning, shopping for the barbecue.

"You really made me come grocery shopping," Ryan whined, slouching against the cart, a hoody pulled over his head, eyes sleepy. "At *six* a.m."

"Didn't you tell me once that Colin O'Connor does his own grocery shopping?" Wyatt asked.

Ryan sighed. "I did tell you that, didn't I?"

"He probably doesn't go this early," Wyatt suggested.

"I was going to say that if you'd ever met O'Connor, you'd know he probably does. But why would you have met Colin O'Connor?"

Wyatt elbowed him in the ribs. "Unfair. True, but unfair."

"I mean, he's okay. Everyone always wants us to be great friends, I guess because we're both gay and athletes and out of the closet. But that's not really much basis for a friendship, is it?"

Wyatt piled a handful of watermelons into the cart that Ryan was half-heartedly pushing. "You have a point."

"He's nice and all. But we're not friends."

"Yeah," Wyatt teased, "you seem really happy about that."

This time Wyatt caught an elbow to the ribs. "If he wanted to be friends, it's not like I'd turn him down, but he's so serious and settled down. I heard he and his husband were adopting. Or doing in vitro or something. That's not really my scene."

Wyatt could see that. "I think people who believe you're friends are probably assuming that you two have experienced situations that nobody else has."

"You're saying he's punched out a homophobic asshole on his team?" Ryan sounded so hopeful, it was hard not to be endeared even further. And Wyatt was already *very* endeared. He kept expecting to reach the ceiling on endeared, only to discover that it kept going up and up and *up*.

"He might have. That seems like the sort of thing he'd do," Wyatt said. "And if you want me to be impressed at your prowess and convictions, I sure am."

Ryan scoffed. "If I was trying to impress you, I'd do this." And he pressed Wyatt against the cart in the middle of the produce section, hands pulling up Wyatt's t-shirt and settling, cold and certain against his stomach. Wyatt was just about to protest, but Ryan kissed him instead, swallowing all his words.

There wasn't anyone to see; nobody to photograph them. But Ryan did it anyway, so Wyatt decided when they finally broke apart that spontaneous kissing was definitely allowed. He was going to be taking a lot of advantage of that ability.

"Where are we on the list?" Ryan asked breathlessly, digging for it in his pocket. "You got watermelons. Did you get strawberries or mangos?"

"I think there's also pineapple and avocado," Wyatt said, pulling the cart towards the fruit displays because Ryan had given up on pushing it. He was whipped because that fact didn't even annoy him.

"Double strawberries," Ryan pointed out as Wyatt began to sort through the plastic containers. "Whatever that means."

"It means that I need strawberries for the salsa and for dessert."

"You know, you didn't have to do this. We could have just gotten the dinner catered."

Wyatt was still absorbed in picking strawberries. "I'm going to pretend you didn't say that. I'm a *professional*, I can handle a little dinner party. Also, isn't this why you hired me? Because I don't think you hired me to make your smoothie or grill your chicken at night. Or give you a morning blowjob."

"You're very handy," Ryan said in lieu of an apology. "I'm spoiled rotten, I know."

Wyatt began loading pineapples in the cart, then moved onto mangos. "You absolutely are."

"You love it," Ryan teased, and Wyatt had to hold the answer back, because damnit, he did. He kept creeping closer to that revelation, and every minute they spent together like this, he sped up. Soon enough it was going to be inevitable that he didn't just love that Ryan was spoiled rotten, but every damn thing about him.

"Where to next?" Ryan asked, shoving the pen behind his ear. "I think you got all the produce and the fruit."

"You're a good grocery shopping partner," Wyatt pointed out as they headed towards the butcher. "I'm impressed."

Ryan preened. "You're never going to regret agreeing to be with me."

He wasn't wrong; even if it all went wrong, and Wyatt ended up with a broken, demolished heart, he didn't think he'd regret it.

❧ ☙

"Hiding out?"

Wyatt glanced up and saw Tabitha lingering in the kitchen doorway. He was putting the final touches on the main course of the barbecue—tri-tip steaks that he was planning on grilling and slicing thin.

All the cold salads were prepped and in the fridge. He'd set up the appetizer buffet in the backyard, and put Ryan in charge of drinks. Everything was coming together, and he was feeling calm and collected, until Ryan's best friend decided to drop by the kitchen to check in.

He knew he wasn't intimidated by Tabitha because of her beauty. It was probably because it felt like she saw right through him, past his skin and his rib cage, to the frantically beating heart underneath. The traitorous heart who was just about ready to topple head over heels in love with Ryan.

"I'm finishing up prep," he said. "I'm not just here as the eye candy hanging off Ryan's arm."

Tabitha walked in, setting her glass on the counter with a click. "You're not even here as eye candy."

"Tell Eric, who's already been through here, telling me to change my shirt, fix my hair, get ready for a hundred pictures that I'm apparently going to have to take tonight. All demonstrating just how hot Ryan's new boyfriend is."

Wyatt had told himself not to let Eric get to him, but it seemed to be a losing battle.

"Eric's an asshole," Tabitha said.

"That's what everyone keeps saying," Wyatt said crossly, "and yet we all still have to deal with him."

"Someday, Ryan will get fed up, and he'll dump him. For someone with an actual shred of empathy. But Eric makes him lots of money so that probably won't happen for awhile."

Tabitha didn't need to point out that Wyatt would likely be long gone by that point.

"Are you here to take a selfie with me?" Wyatt finished rubbing the dry seasoning mix onto the meat, and then transferred it to the tray.

"Actually," she said, "I'm here to ask if you need any help. Which seems a little ridiculous, I'll admit, but my mother always tried to drill manners into me. Even if it was mostly unsuccessful."

"Actually, you can help me," Wyatt said. "Grab that salt, I need to season the meat and I don't want to wash my hands again."

"You're going to let me do something this important?" Tabitha asked skeptically, while still coming around the corner of the island and picking up the salt shaker.

"It's just salt. You seem very intelligent. I'm sure you can manage," he teased.

"How much?" she asked, shooting him a grateful look. He didn't imagine that many people upon meeting her for the first time noticed her intelligence first.

"Just shake it liberally all over," he said. "And then the pepper grinder next."

She did as directed, as he rubbed in the seasonings further. "Would it be patronizing to tell you that you did a good job?"

Tabitha shook her head. "I like praise, and you're good at it."

"Praise?" Wyatt questioned, as he walked over to the sink, scrubbing his hands under the spray.

"Yes, and putting people at ease," she said. "That's one of the reasons Ryan likes you."

He turned, grabbing a paper towel to dry his hands off. "You mean that's why Ryan picked me."

"No," she insisted with a sharp shake of her head, "that's not what I said. That's why he *likes* you."

Before she could elaborate, Ryan burst in. "The grill's ready, I think."

"Good," Wyatt said, hefting the tray.

"Miles and Evan just got here," Ryan said, trailing after him, Tabitha bringing up the rear. "I love them already, though I was surprised at how uptight Evan is."

"Everyone is, after they meet Miles," Wyatt said.

"Miles and Evan?" Tabitha questioned. "From *Pastry by Miles*?"

"Yeah, they're friends of mine. Miles and I worked together. Lived together too, for awhile."

She let out a heavy sigh and shot a glare at her best friend. "And you didn't tell me they were here? I've been *dying* to meet them!" She elbowed her way between Wyatt and Ryan, escaping out the back door first.

"Are you ready for this?" Ryan asked quietly as they paused on the threshold. To Wyatt's surprise, he didn't sound ready; he sounded apprehensive.

Wyatt looked out over at the crowd milling around the backyard. It had definitely looked more intimidating in his mind. But he wanted to reassure Ryan, so he leaned over, brushing a quick kiss over Ryan's mouth. "Never readier."

Wyatt headed straight to the grill; he needed to get the meat on so all these guests could get fed. He was glad, as he used the tongs to position it just so on the metal grid, that he'd planned for far more people, because there were definitely more than that in the backyard.

Probably more like twenty-five or thirty, if he was being honest.

"So this is the LA life, huh?" Miles asked from behind him.

Wyatt turned, and pulled him into a quick hug. "I'd like to remind you that you moved to LA before I ever thought about it."

Evan was next to him, and got hugged too, because Wyatt was happy and feeling generous. "I'm so glad you guys are here," he said.

"I can't believe you're dating Ryan Flores," Evan said.

"I told you, babe," Miles said, voice dropping in volume, "he's not *really* dating Ryan Flores."

Evan waved a dismissive hand. "Isn't that all a matter of semantics?"

Technically, Wyatt didn't think that Eric would think of it that way—and probably not Ryan either, no matter how affectionate he liked to be in bed. And outside of it. And in grocery stores.

"It's a good move for you," Miles said, clearly trying to sound positive. Except that while he'd never been a Debbie Downer like Xander, he'd never exactly been the cheerleader type either.

"The private chef job was a good move," Wyatt corrected. "This is probably stupid, but I'm doing it anyway."

Miles shrugged, and it was clear from his expression that he agreed with Wyatt. "As long as you're happy."

"I'd be happier with a drink," Wyatt admitted. "Make sure the tri-tip doesn't spontaneously combust while I grab one."

Miles nodded, but eyed the grill with trepidation. He was a pastry chef, and happiest—and most comfortable—around desserts. He could deal with some savory preparations, but barbecue was definitely beyond his skill level.

Meanwhile Wyatt headed towards the makeshift bar that Ryan had set up in the shade. There were metal bins full of ice and bottles of beer, as well as a few bottles of various white wines.

He grabbed a beer from the bin and was just looking around for a bottle opener, when Tabitha showed up, a handsome blond man in tow.

"Wyatt, I'd like you to meet my boyfriend, Calvin."

Wyatt reached out and shook his hand. He had frankly appraising blue eyes and a firm grip. The fact that Tabitha's expression and voice softened as she talked about him made him like Calvin already.

"Cal," he said in a friendly voice. "Call me Cal. If you do, I'll keep pretending that I don't already know all about you."

Wyatt raised an eyebrow. He finally located the bottle opener and popped the top off. Taking a long drink, he realized mid-sip that meant Ryan had been talking about him.

"What do I have to do to get the details?" he asked with a grin.

Cal laughed and Tabitha snickered. "You're going to feed me homemade tri-tip with the fixings," he said. "And I'm sure Tabitha told you she can't cook. I'm grateful enough that I'll tell you anything you want to know."

"Calvin," Tabitha admonished in a low voice.

"What?" he asked innocently. "Should I not tell him how crazy we know Ryan is for him?"

"We could," she said primly, "but *that* is none of our business."

It wasn't, but Wyatt couldn't help but wonder if it was true. And then, if it *was* true, why Ryan kept insisting that their relationship had to be pretend.

"How about you tell me why Ryan is so scared of relationships that he has to hire a boyfriend who'd be perfectly happy to date him for real?" Wyatt asked, wondering if he was giving too much away, then deciding he didn't give a crap.

Tabitha definitely had seen through him, and he wouldn't be shocked if Calvin weren't right there behind her.

"That," Cal said, "is unfortunately beyond my pay grade. You're going to have to ask Ryan about that."

Tabitha muttered something that suspiciously sounded like, *"but he won't tell you."*

It wasn't like Wyatt had necessarily expected Ryan's friends to sell him out, even to a guy who was crazy about him. But he did learn one thing; that there was definitely some reason why Ryan would opt for something pretend instead of something real.

"I've got to go check on the meat," he said, "but it was great to meet you." They shook hands again, and Wyatt was off to the grill again, but Eric waylaid him in the middle of the yard.

"There you are," he said, putting his arm around him, like Wyatt had seen him do with Ryan more than once. Ryan hadn't seemed to have much compunction in just shrugging him off, like a pesky fly, but Wyatt knew he should tread a little more carefully. After all, while Ryan signed the checks for both Wyatt's jobs, Eric cut them.

He didn't know if he should feel more or less bothered thinking of Eric as his boss, instead of Ryan.

"I need to check on the food," Wyatt protested, even as Eric steered him towards a pocket of people underneath one of the big trees. The group included Ryan, and Wyatt shouldn't have felt a twinge of nerves, but he did. This was it, then, the very first time he met strangers and got introduced as Ryan's new boyfriend.

"What you need is to mingle, and meet your boyfriend's friends," Eric said pointedly, hitting Wyatt's suspicions right on the head.

Wyatt felt his palm dampen against the beer bottle in his hand, but he lifted his chin. "Hey, babe," he said, directing his comment at Ryan.

"Look who I found, hiding out," Eric said, laughing obnoxiously. "I told him he needed to join the party."

Wyatt's dislike of the man grew exponentially. He hadn't been *hiding*; he was in charge of the food for this party so if he disappeared to take care of something, he shouldn't need an excuse. And now he was being forced to present one.

"This your new guy?" a gorgeous African-American guy with dreads and kind eyes asked.

On cue, Ryan walked over to Wyatt, and finally Eric let him go—probably only because it was Ryan's turn to take over. Except that Ryan didn't eagerly walk over, excited to introduce his new boyfriend to his friends. He practically dragged his feet and his whole persona exuded reluctance.

"Yeah, this is Wyatt."

Wyatt couldn't explain it. Ryan had kissed him in the middle of the grocery store. He'd hardly been private about it. Never mind that this was all his idea. Wyatt was only playing the part that he'd been asked to play.

Ryan leaned and gave him a quick, perfunctory kiss that didn't resemble anything like one he'd given Wyatt before the party. Wyatt told himself that he was thinking too much; if Ryan was a little apprehensive over this whole charade, that was fine. It wasn't like Wyatt himself hadn't had a few anxious moments. This was a big deal, and the very first time. It would get better, and Ryan would seem less stiff and less like he wanted to be somewhere else—or with someone else.

"Picture," Eric demanded, and while Wyatt wanted to refuse, he didn't.

It was easy enough for him to wrap his arms around Ryan and press a loud kiss to his cheek as the camera clicked, because he wasn't playing a role. Ryan let him, even leaning in a little, and the soft look in his eyes as Wyatt pulled away made him think that maybe he'd imagined the whole thing.

"Hi, I'm Andrew," the handsome man said, reaching out to shake his hand, acting like this was all normal. "I'm happy that Ryan's finally met someone. Where *did* you meet, if you don't mind me asking?"

"Temple, actually," Ryan said quickly. "Can you believe it?"

If Andrew looked a little more disbelieving now, it wasn't like Wyatt could blame him. Nobody ever met a boyfriend at Temple. Found hookups, yeah, but long-term happy relationships, rarely.

"You should go with me sometime," Ryan added.

This time Andrew looked at him weirdly. "You're still going to Temple? By yourself?"

Of course he wouldn't be. You went to Temple alone or with a group of friends to find a hookup. And Ryan didn't need a hookup if he had a boyfriend at home.

"We like to dance," Wyatt covered for Ryan, who was just standing there, silent.

"Then maybe I will," Andrew said. He seemed nice and very friendly, and Wyatt thought they might be friends, except that he had a feeling Ryan wouldn't be on board with that plan.

He couldn't say why, exactly, though the reason probably lay with the guarded look in Ryan's eyes.

"I've got to go check on the food," Wyatt said, excusing himself. "But it was great to meet you."

❧❧❧❧❧ ❧❧❧❧❧

Wyatt rarely checked his social media accounts and rarely posted on them. That hadn't stopped Eric's "communications manager" from vetting all of them, even though he had nothing to hide. He'd been reminded by Eric three times tonight that he would be expected to start posting, beginning with tonight and for the foreseeable future.

So when he checked the tri-tip, he took a pic of the grill, and posted to Instagram. He was still a chef, and food had always figured so prominently in his posts before. He figured it would be good to keep things normal.

He did notice that several people had taken pics of him, and tagged him in them. One of the posters was Andrew, who was apparently a third baseman for the Dodgers. Andrew, who Wyatt was about sixty-five percent sure was gay and still in the closet, had tagged him in the picture of him and Ryan, and called them the "cutest couple I know #relationshipgoals."

They weren't relationship goals. They could barely speak to each other out here in the yard, though everything had felt perfectly fine before they'd walked out here. Wyatt fought back the inclination to announce that the party was over, and drag Ryan back in the house, where everything made sense.

"Hey."

Wyatt glanced up and Ryan was standing there, an apology in his eyes.

"Everything okay?" Wyatt asked, keeping his voice light and casual. They were still figuring this fake relationship out, and balancing it with their private lives. That was hard. They wouldn't get it right instantly.

"That was weird back there," Ryan confessed. "I knew we were going to do it, I just didn't think it through."

"It's okay, I think everyone assumed it was normal," Wyatt said.

"Yeah," Ryan grinned, "because you're a stealth ninja and you slipped that line in about liking to dance. I thought I'd blown it big-time."

So Ryan wasn't really apologizing—or *not* apologizing—for his general standoffish behavior, but for accidentally inviting Andrew to Temple without Wyatt.

Still, he was here and he was sorry. Even if he hadn't said it explicitly.

"A ninja, huh?" Wyatt grinned. "I love the sound of that."

Ryan leaned in and kissed him, this time nothing perfunctory or quick. He even slipped in a little tongue, wrapping his arm firmly around Wyatt's waist. It was easy to forgive him when he kissed like that—like Wyatt was his whole world and this wasn't a charade at all.

"Food's almost done?" Ryan asked, stroking a hand up and down his back. "Smells awesome."

"Yeah, could you go grab the cold salads? You might need an extra pair of hands. Then we can get ready to slice this in a few minutes."

Ryan nodded, and took off, collecting Cal to help.

It was so easy to forget the early uncomfortableness in the low-key excitement of the party as the food was served, everyone gathering family style around a big table Ryan had set up outside in the yard.

He took about twenty selfies, and from his constantly vibrating phone in his back pocket, assumed most of them had been posted and he'd been tagged.

The party started slowing down a few hours later, even though Ryan had lit the fire pit.

Wyatt had gravitated towards it, lounging against a bench seat, with a beer dangling in his hand. He felt so mellow, like nothing could disturb his much-won peace. A few people had stopped by to chat, including Tabitha and Andrew. When Ryan slid in next to him, his arm going around his shoulders, Wyatt assumed the party was mostly over.

"It went well, don't you think?" Ryan asked. He sounded just about as relaxed as Wyatt felt, and he couldn't help but be relieved at that. He'd worried that Ryan would stay uptight, but that hadn't happened. He'd relaxed into the role, and even though he didn't act exactly as he did when they were alone, it was close enough that Wyatt wasn't going to angst about it.

"I think it went great," Wyatt said honestly.

"Eric said a few outlets have already picked it up. They all think you're very cute and that we're very cute together."

"Well, that doesn't feel too far from the truth," Wyatt said smugly.

"Even TMZ posted," Ryan said.

"Who's TMZ?"

Ryan laughed. "I think we did forget one thing tonight, though." He held up his phone. "We didn't take a selfie together to cement our very cute couple-ship."

"I took about a thousand selfies," Wyatt protested.

"So, what's one more?" Ryan pointed out.

Which is how they ended up with a very cute picture on Ryan's Instagram—the palms and twinkly lights of the backyard in the background, with the glow of the fire pit reflected in their faces, pressed closely together.

"I'm going to caption this #bestnightever," Ryan announced.

"You don't think that's a bit of an exaggeration?" Wyatt asked lazily. He was dreaming about bed. Ryan's or his—he wasn't sure he cared at the moment. It had been a long day.

"I don't, actually." Ryan's voice sounded serious, devoid of any teasing edge, and Wyatt thought that he might actually be telling the truth.

Chapter Twelve

"How do you feel about going up to Napa this weekend?"

Ryan looked up from where he was checking his email. Wyatt's head was still mostly in the fridge, as he put together a quick lunch for them.

"I feel good about it," Ryan said. "No plans here. Did you have something in mind?"

"This weekend is one of Bastian Aquino's famous invite-only brunches at Terroir. I promised my nana I'd take her, and Tony, my brother, is going too. I could add you to the list, if you wanted."

"Does this mean I can finally meet the Bastard?"

Wyatt laughed as he began to spread pesto on one side of the bread. "I'm not sure I want you meeting him if you're going to call him by his infamous nickname. He's killed people for less. But yes, he does generally make a pass through the dining room to take his allotment of praise."

"Excellent, I'd love to come and meet your nana. Plus, I have an idea for something else we can do in Napa." Ryan had a feeling Wyatt wasn't going to like it as much as he was; Wyatt didn't have the same craving for adrenaline that Ryan had.

But Wyatt kept piling sliced turkey and cheese on the sandwiches like he wasn't concerned. Of course Ryan had discovered that when Wyatt was cooking, even if it was as simple as building some paninis, he was usually absorbed in his task.

"Napa Skydive is up there," Ryan threw out casually, leaning back, and taking a long drink of his iced tea. "I thought we could give it a try."

The shocked, apprehensive look in Wyatt's eyes was priceless as he looked up at him.

"Oh, it'll be fun," Ryan teased. "You're gonna love it."

"I'm not an adrenaline junkie like you," Wyatt protested.

"Yeah, you play it downright safe when we surf," Ryan teased. Like just this morning Wyatt hadn't been attempting tricks that Ryan wouldn't even try. "I'll tell that to the gigantic bruise you're probably going to be sporting tomorrow."

"I already told you," Wyatt said as he slid the sandwiches into the pan, and weighed them down with another big heavy skillet, "I did that on purpose. So you'd kiss every inch of it."

Ryan couldn't help but laugh. Hanging out with Wyatt was fun and always so unexpected. If he'd known that hanging out with your hookups was like this, he would've been tempted to do it before. But then, he had a feeling there weren't many Wyatt Blakes out there in the world.

If he'd ever run across someone like him before, Ryan wanted to believe that he'd have realized it right away, the exact same way he had this time, and done whatever he could not to lose him.

The adjustment to being together, even if it was fake, had seemed pretty smooth, despite his sudden anxiousness the night of the party, and so much of that had been because of Wyatt. He was calm and collected, and endlessly supportive. He made doing this easy, and every hour they spent together further convinced him of the truth he'd known from the first moment they'd met: he could only have this fake relationship if it was with Wyatt. He couldn't have done it with anybody else.

"I guess if you come to brunch with my nana and my brother and endure not calling Aquino the Bastard to his face, I could skydive. Besides, isn't that super safe now? And don't they hook you up to the instructor?"

"Luckily for you," Ryan said, "I've got enough hours to be considered an instructor. We can get hooked together."

Wyatt's response was a smoky, hot look shot from his cool, blue eyes. "How did you guess that's my favorite position?"

Ryan snorted. "It wasn't very difficult, considering how often it occurs."

"Are you complaining?" Wyatt slid the sandwich onto a plate and pushed it in front of Ryan. "Because I sure as hell am not."

Ryan definitely wasn't. He'd unapologetically had a lot of sex and lots of it had been good, some of it had been great, and a little had even been extraordinary, which is why he'd expected some of his sexual obsession with Wyatt to wane as the novelty faded. But there was something addictive about him, and whenever Wyatt offhandedly mentioned how much he enjoyed them together, Ryan couldn't help but be a tiny bit embarrassed at how much he agreed.

With how much experience he had, Ryan wasn't the one who was supposed to be so into it, but he'd definitely passed casual bystander by a while ago. It wasn't that it hadn't *ever* happened, but it was definitely unusual.

He took a bite of the sandwich, and nearly moaned. It was perfect—the bread, the meat, the cheese, with the herb notes in the pesto. "I'd ask how you keep doing this," Ryan said, "but you'd just tell me you're a professional. Even when you're only making a sandwich."

Wyatt smiled, looking very pleased with himself. "It's never *just* a sandwich," he said. And Ryan was pretty sure that the end of the sentence was *when it's for you*, and he didn't know how he felt about that.

Except that wasn't even true. He knew. He liked it. He loved it. That was probably selfish but Ryan couldn't help himself.

"Should we take the Tesla or maybe the Maserati? Or the Ducati?"

Wyatt shrugged, in the middle of his own sandwich.

"I have an even better idea," Ryan said. Wyatt didn't like it when he, in his words, "threw his money around," but he decided he'd be okay taking that risk. "You take care of getting Bastian Aquino to let us into this fancy brunch, and I'll take care of the transportation and the hotel. Okay?"

Wyatt looked suspicious but nodded in agreement.

It was still worth it four days later when, instead of staying on I-5 to drive up to Napa, Ryan pulled off the freeway, and pulled up to the private terminal at LAX.

"I thought I told you I didn't like you throwing your money around," Wyatt said, frustrated edge to his voice, as they embarked onto the small private plane. "We could've driven."

"And wasted six hours on the road, when this way, we can check in to the hotel early, get a massage, spend some time in the sauna, and have sex before we have to meet your brother Tony for dinner."

"You are incorrigible," Wyatt said, finally cracking a smile as they settled into their plush leather seats. "I'm not sure whether to encourage or discourage you."

"I think you should wait until we get to the hotel before deciding," Ryan teased.

Wyatt rolled his eyes and settled back in for takeoff. "I told you we could stay with the guys. They have some extra room, since both Miles and I moved out."

"I am not staying with your ex," Ryan stated. He'd known that from the first moment Wyatt had confessed that his ex-boyfriend had ended up moving in with his old roommates. He kept telling himself it wasn't a jealousy thing, but when he couldn't come up with an alternative explanation, he'd been forced to conclude it turned out he *was* the jealous type, at least when it came to Wyatt.

Of course he hadn't been able to admit that to Wyatt, so he'd used some bullshit privacy excuse that he was pretty sure was horribly transparent. But Wyatt was such a good guy, he'd let it go gracefully and not made it an issue.

But it also meant that Ryan could check them into his favorite hotel and Wyatt couldn't complain about the price.

"I'm not arguing about staying with Kian, Xander, and Nate, but I recognize that expression," Wyatt grumbled. "It usually means you're up to something."

"I'm totally up to something," Ryan agreed cheerfully. "But you're gonna like it."

"Does this have something to do with the massage, sauna, and sex you mentioned earlier?" Wyatt couldn't quite hide the eagerness in his voice.

"You're just gonna have to wait and see." Ryan mimed zipping his lips shut, and tossing the key over his shoulder.

"Gentlemen," the stewardess said, entering the main cabin, "we're just about ready to take off. Would you like something to drink before we do?"

"Mimosas?" Ryan asked. Wyatt rolled his eyes but nodded in agreement.

"Are we celebrating something?" she asked when she returned to the cabin with two crystal flutes.

"Us," Ryan said, shooting her his most charming smile. "I think that's something worth celebrating."

She laughed. "I'd agree. Now please keep your seatbelts fastened. It's a quick, short flight and the pilot probably won't turn off the seatbelt sign. But you can press this little button," she indicated a discreet call button by Ryan's seat, "if you need anything during the flight."

"Cheers," Ryan said, tipping his glass Wyatt's direction. He rolled his eyes again, but toasted back.

"I'll admit," Wyatt said a few minutes after takeoff, "this is better than driving."

"I'm glad you approve," Ryan teased.

"I worked at Terroir, which is pretty much synonymous with wealth and excess, but we didn't get to experience any of it."

"That doesn't seem fair," Ryan said, but he wasn't very surprised. Wyatt had let slip a few days ago how much money he'd been making before working for him, and it had been appallingly low, considering how many hours Wyatt had worked, and how tough his job had been.

"Bring it up with the Bastard," Wyatt said with a resigned sigh. "Actually, I shouldn't say that, because you might."

"Wyatt," Ryan asked seriously. "Your nana is coming with us to brunch, right?"

"I told you she was."

"I'd never do anything to embarrass you in front of her. I promise."

Wyatt downed the rest of his mimosa. "But we should tell her about our relationship."

"You don't want to lie to her," Ryan guessed.

"I don't."

"Then we don't." It didn't matter that Eric had asked him to post some photos of their trip and the brunch. To show their "deepening" relationship, he'd said, because Wyatt wouldn't introduce him to his grandmother unless Ryan was important.

But then, Ryan had a feeling that Wyatt hadn't asked him to come with him this weekend to perpetrate their fake-relationship agenda. He'd wanted Ryan to meet his nana because it was important to him.

"Are you sure?"

"Don't tell me you asked me to come because you imagined a whole bunch of cute staged Instagram photos," Ryan said.

"I thought you should meet her while she still might remember you," Wyatt said and Ryan could hear the pain in his voice.

"Then that's what we'll do."

Ryan closed his eyes and leaned back in the chair and wondered if Wyatt realized he'd just revealed how much he cared. If he knew Wyatt at all, he probably didn't care. He'd volunteer it if Ryan asked.

The problem was Ryan wasn't sure if he wanted to ask.

A little over an hour later, they landed in Napa, and Ryan led Wyatt to the car he'd rented and asked to be left near the private terminal.

He was happy to see they'd even gotten exactly what he'd requested—a Tesla Model X, which he'd been dying to test drive for awhile now.

"You're awfully spoiled, I hope you realize this," Wyatt said, as he loaded their bags into the back.

"I was thinking about trading in the Range Rover. Combining a trip with a test drive was efficient." Ryan checked his phone for the time, typing in the address of the hotel in the mapping app. "We made great time. Even with the traffic on a Saturday, we should have just enough time until we meet your brother."

Twenty minutes later, they pulled up to the hotel. As soon as Ryan was out of the car, the valet was at the door, taking his keys. He didn't always expect to be recognized, but it was a nice perk when he was and he got great service as a result.

"I'm internally rolling my eyes," Wyatt hissed in his ear as they walked up to the front desk.

"Why just internally?" Ryan teased.

Wyatt flushed. "I don't want to embarrass you by looking uncomfortable with all this."

Ryan assumed by "all this," Wyatt meant the expansive lobby with its shining wood floors and soaring vaulted ceiling, the metal and glass modern chandeliers echoing the design of a wine bottle.

Maybe he meant the way the manager recognized him and pulled him aside, checking him in ahead of the rest of the line waiting for service. Or that he showed them to the suite personally.

"I didn't realize you came here so often," Wyatt said as he dropped his bag on the sofa.

"Flor likes to go wine tasting," Ryan said with a shrug. "And I like to give her trips because she can't argue with those."

Wyatt raised an eyebrow.

"Okay," Ryan corrected, "she argues about them *less*."

"I don't blame her," Wyatt admitted. "I don't want you to think you *have* to do any of this. It's nice, and I appreciate it, but I don't need it."

Ryan wondered if Matt would have expected all this, part and parcel with his position as Ryan's public boyfriend. He wouldn't have blamed him for expecting the private jet, the luxury suite, the couples' massage booked in fifteen minutes.

In some ways, Wyatt was the perfect fake boyfriend, but in others, the role didn't sit right at all. Ryan was just now beginning to figure out the reasons why that was—or else he would have, if he'd allowed himself to think about it. Instead, he shoved the logic aside, and settled his hip on the edge of the couch.

"Noted," he said, feigning a pout. "Now come over here and kiss me. We've got a few minutes until our massage and I'm feeling neglected."

Wyatt laughed, but Wyatt came, and his lips on Ryan's were the last piece of the puzzle he needed to shove the rest of those annoying thoughts aside.

Introducing his boyfriend to Tony was blowing Wyatt's mind for several distinct reasons.

One, Tony was accepting of aforementioned boyfriend.

Two, Tony had mentioned his own boyfriend several times since they'd arrived an hour earlier.

Three, Tony was definitely flirting with Ryan.

Wyatt didn't feel comfortable bringing Nana to Tony's new gig at the Napa Tavern, but it was exactly the sort of place he wanted to bring Ryan. Laid-back and chill, with great food and an extensive draft beer list. He might be recognized, but none of the people in the bar would give two shits.

Tomorrow was going to be enough of a clusterfuck, Wyatt didn't want to make a public production of the night before.

"Wyatt, you didn't tell me your brother was this cute," Ryan said, eyeing Tony up and down. It was still weird enough watching Tony flush and look undeniably pleased. It was even weirder that Ryan was the one causing the reaction.

"When we talked about my family, I didn't really think it mattered how cute my brother was," Wyatt retorted fondly.

Ryan was two and a half beers in, and for someone who didn't drink much, it was enough to make him a little tipsy and a lot more daring than usual.

Anyone else might feel threatened, but Wyatt was feeling especially chill from the massage/sauna/sex combination that Ryan had arranged for the afternoon. It turned out it was difficult to feel threatened when the sex they'd had was so spectacular.

Ryan made a face. "I sort of expected you to get all hot. Jealous and protective and all that."

"Wyatt's never been like that," Tony answered for him. "He's always gone with the flow."

Maybe that was true. Maybe it was also true that Wyatt had never felt like he'd had something to lose before.

"Are we really going to talk about going with the flow?" Wyatt teased. "You've flowed around plenty."

Tony's grin was wolfish. He set his elbows on the table, his tattooed forearms on full display and leaned forward, dark eyes sly. "Guilty as charged."

"I also did not expect for you to have a bad boy as a brother," Ryan said.

"He's not bad," Wyatt said, rolling his eyes, before Tony could even tee off on that particularly juicy bit of bait. "He just wants everyone to think so. He's always just been a mouthy, snotty asshole."

"Also guilty," Tony said with a laugh.

"I've definitely had a thing for bad boys," Ryan mused, pausing to drink his beer. "Sorry, but my current tastes are running more towards Cali beach boys." He reached out and touched Wyatt's neck, his hand warm against his hairline. "I've got to piss, be right back."

Tony barely waited until Ryan had cleared the table.

"I thought you said you weren't really together," Tony demanded, his expression going from playful to serious. "You said it was just an image thing." And Wyatt *had* told Tony that, when he'd called to make the plans for this weekend, but the fake-boyfriend thing had still been so new that Wyatt hadn't expected Ryan to be so touchy-feely even when they weren't trying to pretend anything.

"We're not," Wyatt said.

"Could've fooled me, and just about everyone else in this place," Tony muttered.

"It's . . . complicated," Wyatt said, which was an expression he normally hated. The fact that he didn't even hate it now spoke volumes.

"You like him," Tony stated, like he fully expected Wyatt to argue with him. Wyatt wasn't sure what he'd have to gain from that. His like was pretty fucking obvious, there wasn't much point in denying it.

"Yeah, I do."

"You need to figure your shit out. You've always had your shit together. A lot better than me, that's for sure. It doesn't feel right to watch you playing free and easy with this guy, not when you obviously like him."

"It's still developing," Wyatt defended. "We're figuring it out." Technically a lie, but Wyatt was scrambling still, trying to acclimate himself to this bizarre new world where Tony felt able and obligated to give him advice on his love life.

"You and Nate, that was doomed to fail because he loved you more than you loved him."

Wyatt rolled his eyes. "Why am I not surprised you knew about that and pretended not to?"

"Because we live in the same town and you weren't exactly subtle?" Tony shrugged. "I've got to get back to the kitchen, but I just wanted to say, don't let the opposite happen here. He's obviously having fun, but it's more than that for you."

"Thank you, Captain Obvious," Wyatt hissed through gritted teeth as Ryan emerged from the bathroom and made his way back to the table.

"Hey, it was great to meet you," Tony said, standing as Ryan approached the table. "I've got to get back to the kitchen. I'll send some food out for you guys."

Ryan grinned, and Wyatt realized that somehow in the last hour, between all the flirting and the beers, Ryan had become friends with his brother. "You too, and thanks for that. We'll see you tomorrow."

They didn't hug as Tony departed, but it was a near thing. Wyatt set his forehead against the table and considered banging it against the wood.

"What is your deal? I thought you'd like that I liked him," Ryan questioned, downing the rest of his beer.

"I did. I do. I'm just . . . acclimating," Wyatt protested.

"Is it weird?"

"I'm almost thirty years old, and my brother just met my first boyfriend. And I've found out that not only has he known basically this whole time that I was gay, but that he's bisexual. And very curious. So to answer your question: yes, it's weird."

Ryan rubbed a reassuring hand across Wyatt's shoulders. "Should I tell you about the time Flor walked in on me giving our next-door neighbor a blowjob?"

Wyatt let his head fall back against the table. "God, no. Definitely not."

Ryan was Ryan and didn't listen to Wyatt's half-hearted denial. "He was so hot, and liked to wash his car. Like, *every* weekend. And since it was LA, and usually at least eighty, he never wore a shirt. I spent three summers on the front porch, tongue on the ground, desperate for a chance to show him that I wasn't a little punk teenager anymore."

Wyatt wanted to stick his fingers in his ears and yell *la la la la la la* until the story stopped, but the only person possibly more stubborn than himself was Ryan. There was no way he wasn't going to hear this story, eventually. It might as well be now, when he was already two beers in.

"Anyway, the summer I turned eighteen, he finally invited me over to help him wax."

"Him?" Wyatt nearly yelped.

"No, no," Ryan laughed, "but that would have been a great pickup line. He invited me over to wax his *car*."

"You went, obviously," Wyatt said.

"Obviously," Ryan teased. "How else was I supposed to get my mouth on his cock?"

"I can't think of any other way." And somehow, Wyatt was smiling again, and the world didn't feel quite so weird anymore.

"Right, it was brilliant. So we ended up in my house."

"Wait," Wyatt interrupted. "I thought you were waxing *his* car?"

"We were, I had to invite him for a soda. I didn't want him to get heatstroke, right?"

"You're such a good Samaritan," Wyatt said sarcastically. "Was the blowjob to make sure his pipes didn't get clogged?"

"Actually," Ryan said thoughtfully, "we were in the kitchen, and suddenly he dropped his jeans. Said that he knew I'd been waiting for it."

"You had," Wyatt pointed out. "You said you'd been flirting with him for years."

"It was everything I'd been fantasizing about, but then Flor walked in, and yeah . . . not the ending I'd anticipated. She dragged him out by his ear, and he moved six months later."

Wyatt chuckled. "Am I supposed to feel sorry for him or for you in this story?"

"Him, obviously. You know how good my blowjobs are and his got interrupted mid-suck."

Wyatt snorted his beer as he laughed helplessly. "Just don't tell my nana that story."

Ryan's expression was angelic as he said, "Oh, I've got lots of others." He turned, so he was straddling the bench, and put his hands on Wyatt's shoulder. "Do we have to let your brother feed us?"

"Did you telling me about giving the hot guy next door head *then* being caught by Flor turn you on?"

Ryan shrugged, eyes so bright, the curve of his lip giving away that he was trying hard not to grin. "Maybe? No shame." His hands slid down Wyatt's chest, and found their target—the waist of Wyatt's jeans, tucking his fingers under, and tugging him closer. "Let's go," he murmured. "We can always order room service later. I've got a pressing . . . issue that we need to discuss."

Wyatt leaned in, his lips almost brushing Ryan's. His eyes had darkened so much it was tough to see the pupils in the dim room. "Is there a fire?"

Ryan lost the fight, and grinned wide, lighting up like a neon sign. "In my pants? Yes. Absolutely." Wyatt felt his heart thump arrhythmically in his chest, and wondered if this was what really falling for someone felt like. Uneven and uncertain and all-consuming. He didn't know what he'd been doing before meeting Ryan. Maybe just marking time until this moment?

This moment right here, right now, his brain and his heart and his dick screamed at him, and it was the easiest decision in the world to grin right back and say, as serious as he could, "That sounds serious, we should go take care of that situation."

"I don't think you've ever driven faster," Ryan said, sounding breathless and approving as Wyatt pushed him back up against the door.

"Like that, huh?" Wyatt asked, nudging his neck to the side so he could kiss his way down to it, and then back up to the sensitive spot on his ear.

He'd been spending the last week cataloging every especially sensitive spot on Ryan's body and felt he had a bit more to explore tonight.

"You driving fast or you exploiting my ears?" Ryan teased.

"Yes," Wyatt said.

"Watching you drive fast was one of the sexiest things I've ever seen," Ryan confessed, and the truth in his tone made Wyatt's traitorous heart beat even faster. Did Ryan know statements like that affected him? Did he care? Was that why he made them?

The questions distracted Wyatt for a split second, and that was all it took for his back to be the one flat against the door.

"This is much, much better. More my style," Ryan purred as he lifted Wyatt's t-shirt off and slid a hand down the center of his chest, pausing right over the button of his jeans. "I love it when you're at my mercy."

"Am I?" Wyatt questioned. "Or are you at mine?"

Ryan's fingers hesitated on the button he was working open, and he glanced up from his crouched position. "Because I want this so badly?" He ghosted his palm against Wyatt's erection and he hissed through his teeth at the sudden pleasure.

"Yeah, I want it too," Wyatt admitted. "Did you think I didn't?"

"Doing this to you," Ryan said, his voice low and gravelly, as he popped the button and pulled Wyatt's jeans and boxer briefs down, "reminds me of the night we met."

For Wyatt, it was a reminder that he'd been falling from the first time he'd glanced up from the bar and seen Ryan across the dance floor, in the VIP section. Roped off. Exclusive. Unobtainable. Until suddenly, they were on Wyatt's bike, flying across the Hollywood Hills and none of those things were true.

"Doing this to you," Ryan continued, tongue slicking across Wyatt's abs between hissed words, "reminds me that I wanted to the first second I ever saw you."

It was the echo of Wyatt's thoughts, and that was too much. Wyatt's fists flexed against the wood of the door, and he wanted to drag Ryan up by his hair, and crush his mouth to his. Tell him everything he felt, that it was so much more than sexual desire. That it had always been more than just a hookup. That he'd been a fucking light in the midst of the darkness that Wyatt had been trudging through for too damn long.

But that was edging far too close to the other feelings spilling over and they weren't really together. Not the way Wyatt was desperate for them to be.

Ryan's tongue teased against the head of his leaking cock, and Wyatt pushed away everything else but the way it felt. Hot and silky, wrapping around him as perfect as it had the very first time they'd done this. When Wyatt hadn't realized that it could feel like this.

"God damnit," he gritted out as Ryan sucked him down. "You're too god damn good."

Ryan's glance up was half-angelic, half-devilish tease. Wyatt loved it all; the way he loved all of him.

"You want it like this?" Ryan asked, cock slipping out of his mouth, his lips red and swollen and perfect.

Wyatt was undone and could only nod, watching as Ryan began to expertly work him over, everything blending together in a red-hot wave of bliss, so much more intense than it had ever been before.

When he finally let go, shooting down Ryan's throat, they both hesitated for a long moment after, and Wyatt could hear himself panting in the quiet of the room.

Or maybe that was Ryan.

"Give me a sec," Wyatt said, every nerve ending feeling raw and over-exposed.

"You can fuck me later," Ryan said, and he sounded equally breathless, even though Wyatt knew he hadn't lasted long enough for Ryan to have made a real effort.

Wyatt slid down the door, and landed in an awkward heap next to Ryan. "Whatever you want," he said, and knew it was true no matter how you sliced it. Whatever Ryan wanted; that was what Wyatt was going to do.

It probably had something to do with falling in love with him.

CHAPTER THIRTEEN

"Oh, Wyatt, you didn't tell me how cute he was," Bea said as Tony helped her out of the car. "He's adorable."

"And now he also has a much bigger head. I'm not sure how we're going to fit through the front door," Wyatt teased as he and Ryan walked up to meet her.

"I'm Ryan, Mrs. Blake," Ryan said, reaching out to clasp her hand in his. He leaned down and brushed a quick kiss across her cheek. "It's so nice to finally meet you."

"You as well, dear boy." Nana beamed up at him. "You're much cuter than you are on TV."

Wyatt didn't know his grandmother even watched baseball. Tony, who was just finishing with the valet, gave him a distracted shrug that meant he didn't know either.

"I didn't know you followed the Dodgers," Ryan said, sounding surprised and pleased, before Wyatt could even ask her what she was talking about.

"I didn't, not before now," she said, tucking her arm into Ryan's proffered one. "But they replay games all the time on MLB Network. Who knew?"

Wyatt fell back, next to Tony and watched them walk up the steps into the big patio that surrounded Terroir on all sides. There were a number of people milling around, holding glasses of champagne and coffee cups, all chattering away, looking superior because they'd managed to score an invite to the most exclusive brunch in Napa.

He, Tony, and Ryan barely looked like they belonged—Tony least of all with his close-shaved head and tattoos peeking out of his short-sleeve button-down.

His nana, with her sweet smile, and brightly printed floral day dress, looked like she never belonged anywhere else, and it filled his heart with a bittersweet joy that he was able to give her this, even as her memory began to fail. She might not remember today's details exactly, but hopefully she'd remember that she had grandsons that loved her very much.

"I'll go grab us some drinks," Wyatt said as Ryan made sure to get them close to the trellis, where the front gave some shade from the sun.

"I'll help," Tony said.

As they approached the outdoor bar to order, Tony leaned in and asked, "You okay leaving your boyfriend with Nana? She might grill him."

"And find out what?" Wyatt asked with exasperation. "That he's an awesome guy? I hope so. I've never gotten to introduce her to someone I really cared about before, and you know what? I'm glad I could with Ryan."

But Tony just shook his head, a look on his face that made Wyatt's stomach wrench. "I heard some stuff," he said. "After you left, I heard from a guy in the kitchen that knows someone else who used to hook up with him all the time."

"*Used to*," Wyatt emphasized. Did he like thinking about Ryan's history of various hookups? Not particularly, but he hardly expected him to be a saint before they'd even met. Sex was amazing; it was a perfectly natural reaction to want to have it if you could.

"I'm just saying," Tony hissed as the person in front of them picked up their drink and departed from the bar. "You need to think about this."

"I'm done thinking," Wyatt said, and turned to the bartender. "Nico, it's so good to see you."

"You too, Wy," he said, "what can I get you?"

"Two mimosas, a coffee with cream, no sugar, and a Bloody Mary."

"You catch sight of the big boss yet?" Nico asked as he began to prepare the drinks. "Or should I ask, has the big boss seen you yet?"

"Thankfully, no." Wyatt wasn't under any impression that Aquino felt any less betrayed now than he had before. Just because Kian had worked his magic and gotten his hands on the brunch tickets didn't mean Wyatt was forgiven for the ultimate betrayal: leaving Terroir behind.

"Better keep it that way," Nico said, placing the drinks on the bar. "He's on the warpath today."

This was nothing new, but the extra heads-up was nice, and Wyatt was reminded of how much he'd always liked Nico.

"Thanks," he said, throwing some bills on the bar, tipping generously and happy that now he could, after leaving Terroir and going to work for Ryan.

"I think it was Nico," Tony said under his breath as they picked up the drinks and made their way to where Ryan and Nana were sitting in the shade. "Conner said it was some bartender at Terroir that he'd been hooking up with."

"Nico isn't even gay," Wyatt protested. "I don't know why we're even talking about this still."

"Because, baby bro, I don't want to see you hurt. And you really like this guy."

"And this guy really likes me," Wyatt said defensively. After all, Ryan had made it clear that if he couldn't have Wyatt, he hadn't wanted to have anyone. As his *fake* boyfriend, sure, but that must mean something?

Wyatt wanted it to mean something so badly.

"Here's your mimosa," Wyatt said, and he knew he sounded short as he handed Ryan his glass, but Tony was reminding him that only a short while ago, they hadn't gotten along.

"Thanks," Ryan said, beaming up at him, making Wyatt feel guilty. "We've just been chatting about my new ad campaign for Adidas."

"He says he might even be on the cover of some magazine," Nana said, smile bright as she looked up at Wyatt. "He's definitely cute enough."

"And now his head is definitely not going to fit through the front door," Wyatt teased. He hadn't explicitly told Nana what he and Ryan were—he hadn't wanted to lie to her, and Ryan had been surprisingly okay with that—but she'd clearly connected the dots anyway.

A man approached their group, and Wyatt tensed. Had Aquino found out he was here and sent security to boot them out? But no, the man was dressed in a pair of preppy khakis and a blue chambray button-down and had a combination of nerves and eagerness in his dark eyes.

"Ryan Flores?" the man asked, gesturing with the phone in his hand. "I was wondering if I could take a pic with you."

This had happened to them before when they were out. Once when they were surfing, once when they were grabbing food. It wasn't a big deal, and Ryan dealt with it like it wasn't, giving the fan a selfie and a smile both times.

But this time, Wyatt caught a flicker of annoyance on his face before he quickly covered it.

"Sure," he said, rising to his feet and going over to where the guy was standing, anticipating the selfie request.

"Actually," the man hedged, "a selfie would be great, but what about a pic with your boyfriend? You guys are so cute. I follow your Insta, and my husband laughs, but I swear I can never decide if I want to *be* you or hire you to come cook for us."

The hesitation on Ryan's face was distinct this time, and he didn't cover it up. Wyatt told himself it didn't matter, but it was hard to convince himself. After all, what was so different about taking a picture here, when they took pictures together on a regular basis and posted them—just so everyone, like the man in front of them, would think exactly what he thought?

"Uh, I think he'd probably prefer his privacy today," Ryan said awkwardly. "Selfie instead?"

They took the selfie and though the man thanked him and wished him luck in the upcoming season, Wyatt got the distinct impression that nobody had come out of that encounter happy. Not Ryan, whose smile had dimmed considerably, not the fan, who seemed pretty disappointed, and definitely not Wyatt, who now couldn't help but wonder why Ryan had turned him down.

Thankfully, Tony had kept Nana distracted, so Wyatt didn't have to answer any questions right now about why that man had believed he and Ryan were together. He'd had an answer ready, but he felt a little too raw to explain anything right now.

"I'm going to go check on the seating time," Wyatt said, and wasn't even embarrassed it looked like he was escaping because he *was*.

Callie, the hostess, had a permanent smile etched on her face, but the smile deepened a little as Wyatt approached her. "Oh, Wyatt, it's so good to see you," she said. "We've missed you around here."

"You're a gem. Do you have any idea when the seating is going to begin? I've got my nana here, and she's not great in the sun."

"And your boyfriend too, if I hear the rumors right," Callie said with a sly wink. "Ryan Flores, what a great catch."

It was exactly the impression they were explicitly and implicitly trying to give, but Wyatt still felt himself shy away from the implication. "Yeah," he said, neither confirming nor denying anything. "Any idea on the time?"

"Five minutes," she said. "And I don't know if anyone told you but the Bastard is on fire today. Steer clear."

Wyatt hadn't been too worried before because Kian *had* managed to get the tickets, and they were unequivocally in his name. He knew Aquino often reviewed the guest list himself, so if there'd been an issue, Wyatt had always expected Kian to call him and cancel the tickets.

But now, he wasn't sure. Not when the Bastard was in apparently a very bad mood.

When he returned to the waiting trio, there was unexpectedly two others that had joined their party.

"I'm sorry," Ryan said, not sounding very sorry at all, "but I'm not taking pictures today."

Wyatt's heart clenched. How many times had they been out and Ryan had agreed to pictures? At least half a dozen times. He'd never denied fans before, not when Wyatt was present, and suddenly Wyatt couldn't help but wonder if this had something to do with him?

Was Ryan avoiding a situation like the request he'd denied earlier? Wyatt wasn't sure he could feel worse, and yet his stomach kept falling. But he plastered a smile on his face and sank to the bench next to Nana.

"Only a few minutes to go," Wyatt promised, reaching over and holding her hand. "You're going to love it."

"It's a beautiful place," she said, her eyes sparkling. "But then I'd never expect anything else from you. You've only ever kept your eye on the biggest prize, determined to win it." Her gaze strayed over to Ryan, and Wyatt had a feeling he knew what she was really referring to.

"Being the best, working for the best, that's always been important to me," Wyatt agreed. "But some things are just as important. Like being able to spend time with you." He didn't add that making more money was important, so that she could stay in the home she was at and be well cared for. But it meant something to him, that he was able to give that to her. More than the worthless prestige of Terroir had ever brought him, anyway.

"You're a good grandson," Nana said, her tender expression putting to rest forever his worries that she wouldn't care about him because he was gay. He'd made a mistake by not telling her before, but maybe she'd been a convenient excuse because *he* wasn't ready to finish telling the world yet.

The truth was, he'd never appreciated how much Nate had pushed him, but he was beginning to wonder if that was because he'd never really loved Nate. Because now he wished Ryan would push a little harder.

"Let's go have a fabulous brunch," Wyatt said, helping her to her feet. "I see people starting to go in."

Tony and Ryan trailed behind them as they headed towards the front door. Wyatt had a single moment of unease when he handed the tickets to a woman he didn't recognize manning the entrance. But she checked his party off the list, and then Callie led them to their table. It wasn't the best table, off in the corner, away from the main dining room, but Wyatt could care less. The food would taste just as good here, and this way he might avoid seeing Aquino.

"Tell me about the menu," Nana asked as they sat down.

"Chef Aquino doesn't typically like menus," Wyatt explained, "but he knows he couldn't get away without a menu during regular dining hours. People like to know what they're eating and have some input into what it is. But during Chef's bi-annual brunches, he serves whatever he feels like. Usually three or four courses, with pastries."

"It's a stupid affectation," Tony said.

"Yet it's packed," Wyatt said wryly. "I guess when you're as famous as Chef Aquino, you don't care how egotistical it looks."

"Or you do it *because* it looks egotistical," Tony said under his breath as the waiter approached their table. He was new, because Wyatt didn't recognize him either. One month out of this place, and already he didn't recognize all the staff. Of course turnover was to be expected when the boss was often referred to as the Bastard.

"I don't think he cares much about what people think," Wyatt said.

"Actually," Ryan inserted. "I'd disagree. He probably cares too much."

Wyatt had never thought of it that way before, and maybe it didn't make him like his ex-boss any more, but it did help shed some light on his personality.

"I had a coach like that once," Ryan said with a shrug. "It's so important what people think of them, they're willing to bulldoze everyone and everything to look good. Sound familiar?"

Wyatt had to nod.

"Is there any way we could see Kian and Xander while we're here?" Nana asked. "I know they're working, but maybe they have a break and could come say hi?"

"Never going to happen. I'm sorry, Nana. Chef Aquino is the only kitchen employee allowed on the dining room floor. But maybe we can steal them away after brunch is over. I'll see." Wyatt didn't think it was likely, and also didn't want to attempt it because doing so would mean getting into the kitchen. Putting himself straight in the crosshairs of the Bastard was definitely a bad idea, but he didn't want to tell Nana no. He also didn't want to have to explain that despite being back in the Terroir dining room, he was definitely not allowed back in the kitchens.

The waiter returned with their drink refills, and as he was distributing glasses, looked over at Ryan in a way that was not very casual. Wyatt resisted the urge to nudge his chair closer, because jealousy was stupid, and also they weren't really together anyway.

"I'm sorry, but you're Ryan Flores, aren't you?" the waiter asked as he set Ryan's mimosa in front of him.

If Wyatt had needed other proof that the waiter was new, here it was. Being fired for this was the very least thing Aquino would do. Waitstaff were given very strict instructions not to call attention to celebrity visitors to Terroir. Asking if he was Ryan Flores was breaking every one of those rules.

"I am," he confirmed.

"I'm such a big Dodgers fan," the waiter gushed, and Wyatt told himself that this was cute, it was adorable, it was anything but annoying, but he couldn't quite pull it off. "I lived here as a kid, and just came back a few months ago."

Which explained why he was breaking the cardinal rule of the Terroir dining room and also why he wasn't acting chill like most LA fans did.

"Great," Ryan said, and sounded just as annoyed as Wyatt felt.

"I'll have your first course up shortly. It's a lavender chamomile honey yogurt with fresh berry compote," he said.

"Chamomile," Tony said in disgust as the waiter departed. Wyatt found what he hoped was his brother's foot under the table and kicked.

"What?" Tony demanded. "Is Aquino trying to put us to sleep?"

"It's so interesting to me that chefs these days find inspiration everywhere," Nana said loyally. "Imagine using lavender in food. I used to grow lavender in my garden."

"You're not a fan of these unique inspirations?" Ryan asked Tony.

"I prefer simple food, prepared really well," Tony said. "Farm to table is well and good. But it needs to be something the diner recognizes. I like the way the Tavern does it."

Wyatt bit his tongue and did not remind Tony that the reason he'd ended up on this "simple is better" path was because he'd been booted out of culinary school and had never had an opportunity to cook at a restaurant with a reputation for complexity like Terroir.

"What do you think, Wyatt?" Nana asked him.

"I think there's room for both points of view, and both types of food prepa-ration. Some people aren't going to want lavender in their food, and that's fine, and then there are some diners who want to try something that nobody else has made before."

"I've always wanted to try a more mobile approach to dining," Tony said. "I love the food cart concept, where you can change the menu up at will, and always try something different. I think people are a lot more apt to try something if it comes from a food truck with a cute name, and in something recognizable, like a taco shell or a burger bun."

"That's . . . actually really interesting," Wyatt said. "I'd love to work in that sort of framework."

He knew he wouldn't be Ryan's personal chef forever. After all, despite taking the job and keeping it, they both knew Ryan didn't really need one. Eventually he'd have to move on, and maybe the idea was one to tuck away for a rainy day. He couldn't really imagine working with his brother, but Tony had clearly matured and changed. Maybe it was time to put all that past history aside and give something a try.

"Your first course," the waiter said with a flourish, setting down bowls of yogurt, beautifully arranged with a floral pattern of bright-red berry sauce traced across the surface.

Nana's face said it all; that coming here to this had been worth the risk of Aquino's wrath and worth Ryan's uncomfortable fan encounters.

"Oh, Wyatt, this is so beautiful," she exclaimed. "I'm not sure I can even eat it, it's so pretty."

⁂

The brunch passed with Bea raving over each and every dish, her smile grow-ing brighter with every moment that passed. Even Wyatt managed to re-lax—though he wasn't sure if that was because Aquino didn't make his way into the dining room or because Ryan had relaxed, too. In any case, no other fans approached them, and even their waiter toned down his interest which Wyatt sensed Ryan was grateful for.

As the meal drew to a close, and he pulled out his wallet to pay the bill, Wyatt checked his phone. To his shock there were three texts from Xander. Xander wasn't much of a texter, even on his best day, and he, like the rest of the kitchen staff, always put his phone into the storage lockers during a shift. Three texts during Terroir's famous brunch service was the equivalent of a 911 call, complete with SWAT team and Life Flight.

Just as Wyatt expected, when he opened the texts, they were supremely unhelpful—cryptic one-word messages like "emergency," and "help," and the last one, "this is bad."

Wyatt felt himself tense. If Xander thought something was bad, then it was very bad. But how bad could it be, he reasoned. The food coming out of the kitchens was as flawless as ever, and none of the waiters looked worried or harassed. If something bad had gone down in the kitchens, then it was at least somewhat contained.

The thought didn't really set Wyatt's mind at ease. He texted back, "I'll be at the back door in five," and hoped that Xander still had his phone on him so he'd see the message.

"I need to check on something," he told Nana, Tony, and Ryan. "I'll be right back."

"Are you going to see Xander and Kian, dear?" Nana asked, oblivious to the undercurrents of Wyatt's worry.

"Something like that," he told her, rising to his feet.

"Make sure to pass on how wonderful the meal was," she insisted. Ryan's eyes were questioning across the table, but Wyatt gave a quick shake of his head to indicate that he didn't need to accompany him.

Exiting the front door, Wyatt made his way around the side of the building, down to the employee parking and entrance.

Xander was leaning against the wall next to the door, eyes closed. He was still in his whites, with one of his trademark chili pepper head-wraps on.

"What's going on?" Wyatt demanded.

Xander's eyes opened and Wyatt realized how weary he looked. There was no shift you took at Terroir where you didn't feel exhausted by the end, but this was an emotional weariness and a clear concern that got Wyatt's stomach churning.

"Kian," Xander said simply.

"Callie and Nico both warned me he was in a mood today," Wyatt said. "I hoped that it didn't have anything to do with Kian."

"Do you remember when someone sent overcooked branzino to the gover-nor?"

Wyatt remembered. They'd all walked on eggshells for at least a week, everyone terrified to provoke Aquino into another angry explosion. His ears had rung for at least a day from the blistering lecture they'd all been given, even though at best they'd all been tangentially involved in the branzino incident. The culprit, of course, had been summarily fired, after a rant that promised he'd never again work in food service in California.

As far as Wyatt knew, that had held, and the guy wasn't even able to get a job at McDonald's, working the fryer.

"It would be hard to forget."

"This was . . . minor in comparison. Except," Xander said, taking a shuddering breath, "it was all on Kian. The Bastard found out he'd gotten you tickets. I guess he felt it was a betrayal."

Wyatt was speechless. He'd expected Kian to get a minor lecture for the infraction, if it could even be termed that. He'd never imagined that Kian would bear the brunt of Aquino's temper.

"It wouldn't have been so bad," Xander continued, "except that Kian didn't just stand there and take it. He dished it right back. I guess that's maybe why it didn't touch the rest of us. Chef was too busy trying to contain Kian, and then too busy weeping in his arms about how Kian doesn't care about him after all."

"What?" That seemed both improbable and impossible. Chef didn't have personal feelings. Everything was directed to and from the professional side. It was never a personal betrayal—only a professional one, and according to Aquino, that was always worse.

Wyatt didn't personally agree, but then he'd never had the balls to tell him that before. Kian apparently had.

"Kian started to let him have it, telling him he was being unreasonable and mean, and it was all so true and so pointed, and I couldn't help but think he'd been listening to both of us too long. Mostly me, because it was all there in the delivery, which probably could have given industrial-grade acid a run for its money. But Aquino didn't take that lying down, so he started screaming back. Then suddenly . . . Kian said one sentence, and he stopped yelling, so we couldn't hear it. But Aquino shut right up, and we all heard him beg Kian not to leave."

"I don't understand," Wyatt said. "He begged him not to leave? *Bastian Aquino* begged him not to leave?"

"Exactly," Xander said. "Worst day ever."

"I'm failing to see how this is bad for Kian. It clearly means he's got a hold on Aquino, and frankly it's terrifying, but maybe Kian can handle it."

"Kian can't handle it," Xander growled. He started pacing back and forth. "All this means is that they've got a terrible hold on each other. If Aquino had yelled at him and then fired him, then he would've been hurt, devastated probably, but he would've gotten over it eventually. Found a new job, fallen in love with someone more appropriate. But all this proves is that Aquino feels the same, and if Kian figures this out, he's never going to get out while he still can."

Wyatt hadn't thought of it that way before. But then he remembered what Kian had said the other night, about it being worth it, no matter the cost.

"I don't think he's going to get out. No matter what, he's not going to," Wyatt said slowly. "I think it's time to let it go, Xander."

Xander threw up his hands in frustration. "Would you have stopped that chef from overcooking his branzino and saved his career if you'd been able to?"

"Of course I would have," Wyatt said, crossing his arms over his chest. "You know I would have. But this is different. This is personal, not professional, and they're already halfway in it. You can't stop it now. All you can do is support him, now, and if it goes bad."

"Not if, *when*," Xander predicted darkly.

Wyatt knew better than to ask why Xander was so convinced it was going to end badly. He wouldn't get an answer. Not a real one, anyway. Xander kept all those feelings locked up tight—except for the little that escaped when he worried about someone he cared about.

"That's all we can do," Wyatt repeated.

The door next to them opened, and Xander jumped, which proved how worked up he was. But it was just one of the bartenders from upstairs. Nico, in fact.

Wyatt was the one who froze when he saw who it was. "Oh, Wyatt," he said. "I think they're about finished upstairs."

"I know, I was just checking in with Xander," Wyatt said.

"I've got to go back in," Xander muttered, and shouldered his way through the door without even saying goodbye. Which was to be expected in Xander World, even when he wasn't in a bad mood. And he was in a terrible mood.

"So," Nico said slyly, not leaving, and filling Wyatt with foreboding. He remembered what Tony had said about him, and wished that he could forget. "I heard you're here with Ryan Flores."

"Yeah," Wyatt said, hoping that a short answer would keep Nico from continuing the conversation. But Nico wanted to talk, and nothing was going to stop him.

"And that you're living with him."

"I'm his personal chef," Wyatt inserted.

"Yeah." Nico sounded like he hadn't bought that for a second. "I know all about his arrangements."

"I'm not stupid enough to think I'm the first guy he's been with," Wyatt defended.

"Possibly," Nico said. "But he's never gonna stay with one guy. He's not built that way. He likes it all kinds of ways, with all kinds of guys. Likes to keep it exciting."

That sounded like Ryan, the adrenaline junkie, and even though Wyatt had always loved that part of his personality, suddenly he wasn't entirely sure.

"There's no crime in enjoying sex," Wyatt said shortly.

But Nico was determined to torpedo everything—or do *something*, Wyatt still wasn't sure. Was he jealous? Was he hoping that if he got Wyatt to leave, his hookups with Ryan might continue? Wyatt didn't know. All he knew was that Nico kept fucking talking and wouldn't stop.

"Just . . . lower your expectations," Nico counseled. "Actually, scratch that. Obliterate your expectations. Because he's never going to let you have any."

That *didn't* sound like the Ryan that Wyatt had come to know. At least most of the time. He couldn't help but think of the few awkward instances that Wyatt had desperately tried to write off as growing pains with a new very public relationship.

But maybe it was more. Wyatt cursed Nico for getting into his head, when that was the very thing that he'd clearly set out to do.

"I'll take that under consideration," Wyatt said. "And I've got to go. Thanks for the advice, I guess."

"You've been quiet," Ryan said.

"Yeah, I can't imagine why," Wyatt grumbled. "I'm only preparing to throw myself out of an airplane."

"But you're going to be with me," Ryan said, as the plane taxied towards the runway. "It's all gonna be good."

"I guess I should be happy you settle for skydiving and aren't into BASE jumping," Wyatt said. The truth was Nico's confessions had him worked up far more than the possibility of launching himself out of an airplane with only a parachute to stand between him and death.

"Oh, I've tried that too," Ryan said. "But I like myself in one solid piece, thank you very much, and management didn't like it when they found out. I guess it made them think I was a bad investment. They aren't exactly wild about the skydiving either, to be honest. Or my collection of fast cars. They called Eric in and yelled at him for half an hour over the Maserati I bought at the end of the season."

"Gee, I can't imagine why."

"I know it's stupid, but it's an addiction," Ryan said, with a helpless little shrug that Wyatt found adorable, even when he didn't want to.

It wasn't Ryan's fault that Nico existed. It wasn't Ryan's fault that Nico had decided to give him unsolicited advice. It definitely wasn't Ryan's fault that Wyatt had listened despite all his intentions not to. But despite all those things that Wyatt knew to be true, it was impossible not to feel a little frustrated. Maybe even a little angry.

If Ryan hadn't been so awkward about their relationship today, Wyatt knew he wouldn't have listened to Nico. How was it that Ryan could be perfectly normal and perfect boyfriend material except when he was trying to prove he was Wyatt's boyfriend?

It made no sense, and Wyatt liked things to make sense. The culinary arts were full of irrefutable facts, and there was a comforting certainty in the kitchen. At first, when Ryan had been so determined that his boyfriend had to be Wyatt, it had been easy to believe that he'd meant more than just a random guy he'd picked to play a lover.

Now, Wyatt couldn't be sure. And yet, he was allowing himself to be strapped to him anyway, doubt be damned.

"What other crazy things have you done?" Wyatt asked, because hearing how many ways Ryan had conspired to kill himself was somehow easier than wallowing in his own confusion.

"Besides BASE jumping? Last year I was trying to get my wingsuit certification, but I got busy and had to let it go. I actually like it better than BASE jumping, because it's a longer flight, more like flying."

"Is it just shit in the air?" Wyatt asked.

The airplane engine revved up and they started down the runway. "I love this part, so maybe it *is* just shit in the air?" Ryan said.

"Taking off?"

"It's the anticipation in the air," Ryan said with relish. "Knowing I'm going to choose to jump out of this plane."

Wyatt shook his head. "I think I'll stick with surfing."

"Have you gone deep-sea diving? That's pretty wild, too. Totally different vibe, but still gets the blood pumping."

"Do you swim with sharks too?" Wyatt asked sarcastically.

"Once," Ryan said with a grin. Wyatt regretted asking.

"Don't worry, I'll try to contain your life-threatening activities to waking me up in the morning and this skydive," Ryan said, and Wyatt wanted to find him as endearing as he had only this morning. It wasn't that he loved him any less, it was that he doubted him more. Right about now he wished he could push Nico out of the plane.

"I appreciate that," Wyatt retorted dryly. "Now go over the steps again, please."

"Again?"

"I'm a chef, I like to be prepared," Wyatt said.

"Okay, it's gonna be great, I promise. When we get close to altitude, I'll hook us together. You'll be attached to my front." Ryan paused, and Wyatt realized that he was waiting for him to make a sexual joke. "Okay, maybe not your favorite place to be after all," he teased. "Anyway, when we reach altitude, we'll inch our way to the door, and then I'll push us off."

"I can't believe I let you talk me into this," Wyatt said. The plane was flying higher and higher, and it was impossible not to look out the window and see the fields of Napa getting smaller and smaller beneath them.

"It'll be about a minute of free fall," Ryan continued, "and then I'll pull the parachute."

"And there's a backup, right?"

"Of course there is," Ryan retorted. "I told you not to worry. This is safe. I mean, not *safe*, because we are jumping out of a plane, but as safe as that gets. You remember the landing I told you about?"

"Yeah," Wyatt said. They'd practiced it a few times on land. Speaking of land, he was really wishing he was back on it. He eyed the toy-sized trees with trepidation.

"We're about to altitude," the pilot said over the intercom. "We'll open the door shortly."

"Just take a breath," Ryan counseled as he began to hook them together. "Maybe a few breaths. It's gonna be great."

"If you say that one more time," Wyatt hissed.

The door opened, and Ryan didn't have another chance to say it again, because suddenly they were at the edge of the plane, and then they weren't in the plane at all.

The wind rushed past Wyatt's ears as they free-fell in the deep-blue sky. He could feel Ryan's excitement even though he couldn't see his face. As for himself? It wasn't . . . terrible he decided as they continued to fall, the ground rushing closer and closer.

It was even sort of a pleasant rush. Kind of like when Ryan had climbed on the back of his bike. When he climbed on the back of Ryan's. A feeling of putting yourself in someone else's hands with the hope that you'd be safe.

After today, Wyatt didn't know for sure if he was still safe in Ryan's hands. But he loved him enough that he couldn't just pull away. His whole body jolted suddenly, and he realized that Ryan had pulled the parachute.

After a few minutes of coasting to the ground, they landed, legs getting a bit tangled, and they fell to a heap on the ground before Ryan could unclip them. Wyatt pulled his helmet off and took one deep breath, and then another. He didn't think he'd get his breath back so quickly.

Ryan finally unclipped them, and Wyatt did the only thing he'd wanted since they'd jumped out of an airplane—he leaned down, yanked his helmet off, and kissed him. Ryan tasted like air and sky and fresh air, and his breath was coming in short, breathless pants as he pulled back.

"You loved it, didn't you?" Ryan grinned, eyes glittering from the adrenaline rush. "I knew you would."

I love you.

Wyatt shrugged, faking nonchalance, and Ryan stared at him for a moment, then tackled him to the ground, hovering above him for a split second before covering Wyatt's mouth with his own.

Chapter Fourteen

"This is a really big deal," Eric said, reaching out to smooth down the collar of Wyatt's shirt.

Ryan had to stop himself from pushing Eric's hands away, and doing it himself. He wasn't sure if Wyatt's eye roll was more to do with Eric stating the obvious or Eric invading his personal space.

"Believe me, I'm aware," Wyatt retorted dryly, at the same time, shucking the hand off his collar with a shrug of his shoulder.

So, maybe both.

Ryan wished that Eric hadn't decided that he needed to show up to give them a last-minute pep talk on their first public outing, because he had a few much more fun ideas to give everyone the indelible impression he and Wyatt were definitely together.

But apparently showing up with their hair and clothes messed up, looking like they'd just fucked on the car didn't give the impression Eric was looking for.

Ryan maintained it still would've been a lot more fun than the lecture they were currently receiving.

"I don't want you to spend the whole evening together," Eric continued, even though Ryan knew he was barely paying any attention and Wyatt had clearly tuned him out altogether. "Constantly hanging on each other gives the idea that you're insecure in your relationship.

"The car will be here any minute. I just spoke to the event concierge at Temple, she's going to make sure you guys have a great time, and will let you know when there's something you need to participate in." He paused, and

Ryan thought for one miraculous second that Eric was done talking, but then he kept going. "It goes without saying that you need to both be on your best behavior tonight. Have a few drinks, but don't get drunk. No crazy antics. No semi-public sexual exploits."

"Awwww, there goes everything I wanted to do," Ryan teased and to his disappointment, Wyatt's expression didn't change. Instead of the melting smile that he'd grown to expect, Wyatt looked stiff and nervous. Withdrawn, almost, which had been the norm since they got back from Napa a week ago. There'd been a few times when Ryan had really been able to get him to relax, and laugh with him like he had at the beginning—usually after a few beers or a really intense workout—and he still approached sex with a fierce intensity that Ryan definitely enjoyed.

More than once, he'd considered asking Wyatt what was wrong, but in his head, that conversation fell exclusively into the "relationship" category, and since he couldn't go there, he avoided it.

Eric shook his head, amused despite his own lecture, and went to go see if the car had arrived yet, finally leaving them alone. Maybe Ryan couldn't ask Wyatt what was wrong, but he could make sure this was still something he wanted to do. It was hard to doubt that Ryan was still something he wanted, because the sex was so raw and consuming, but maybe it wouldn't hurt to ask.

"Is this still okay?" Ryan asked, turning towards the other man. Wyatt looked up, surprise in his expression.

"Why wouldn't it be?"

Ryan might be a baseball player, but he wasn't dumb. Even he knew that answering a question with a question was a great way to deflect.

"You just seem quiet, that's all," Ryan observed. It occurred to him suddenly that he'd made this exact same comment before they'd gone skydiving.

Ryan didn't think he was getting bored; the very nature of their relationship was designed so he *wouldn't*, so he *couldn't* get bored, but maybe Ryan had miscalculated?

Maybe even though they weren't technically in a relationship, they were doing too many relationship-like things—like going to Napa, spending time with Flor and Wyatt's nana and his brother, going to brunch, now this couples outing to Temple.

Boredom was something that wasn't allowed to happen. Ryan couldn't let him pull away, and not only because of the fake relationship that Wyatt had committed to, but because the more Wyatt retreated, the more attached Ryan realized he'd become.

He needed to fix this, because whatever this was, because it definitely had morphed into something more than Ryan had ever anticipated or expected.

"It's gonna be great," Ryan said, feeling stupid because he kept saying that and he wasn't sure that Wyatt believed him anymore.

But Wyatt smiled this time, and pulled him close, and brushed a brief kiss across his lips. "It will," Wyatt agreed, "I'm just disappointed we couldn't take the bike. Re-enact the night we met."

"Maybe tomorrow," Ryan said, hating the hope that bloomed through his system. All he wanted was to get back to how good they were together. The fantastic sex they were having should have been enough—it had always been enough before—but now he wasn't sure. They were missing something else; Wyatt was holding it back, and even though Ryan didn't know what it was, he craved it anyway.

"The car's here," Eric announced in the foyer.

Ryan slipped his hand into Wyatt's, and gave him a bright smile. "Let's do this," he said.

The concierge, Anne-Marie, met them at the private back entrance of the club. Eric had decided, in his fake-relationship wisdom, that it would be better for the photographers to get them on the way out of the club, instead of heading in.

Ryan didn't know why this was, but he'd learned to save his energy to argue with Eric on the major points, not the minor ones.

"Around midnight, we'll bring you up to the stage, as you're our VIP hosts for the evening," Anne-Marie said, as they walked into the back of the dim club.

"What are we supposed to do?" Wyatt asked.

"On stage?" Anne-Marie questioned as she tucked a strand of bright-red hair behind her ear. "Whatever you like. Dance. Kiss. Each other? The dancers?" She waved a hand. "You two are so cute, I'm sure you'll come up with something."

Wyatt raised an eyebrow, like this wasn't something they heard all the damn time. Like it wasn't something they had *planned*.

"I mean, your Insta pictures are so gorgeous, like some sort of fairy tale," Anne-Marie said. "And obviously, yeah, you set them up to look that way, but there's a truth in them that you don't see very often. I can tell you're both very fond of each other."

She turned to them. "I'll escort you to the VIP booth now, if that's okay?"

Ryan was officially pathetic. He wanted to beg her to tell him more about how they cared about each other, even while he argued with himself that caring about each other had never been the point of this. They were only supposed to *seem* authentic, while having great sex, but something had gotten crossed along the way.

"Sure, yeah, that'll be great," Ryan said when Wyatt stayed quiet.

The VIP area was the exact same one that Ryan had occupied the night he'd gone looking for a fake boyfriend and had found his personal chef instead.

He wanted to ask Anne-Marie if that was something Eric had arranged, but decided against it because it exposed too much of his nostalgia and stupid feelings in front of Wyatt.

"I'll see that the waiter brings over your bottle service," Anne-Marie said, as they settled on the plush velvet couch. Wyatt looked way more comfortable than Ryan felt, but he tried to copy the other man's relaxed posture. The reason, Ryan realized as Anne-Marie left, was because he'd never been here with another man before. Definitely not with one that he was pretending he was in a relationship with.

Definitely not one that he apparently had stronger feelings for.

When you fell in love with someone, Ryan reasoned as the waiter approached, you were supposed to feel excited and happy, not greet the discovery with dread. Except that was all he could feel, as he envisioned Wyatt growing bored, just as his ex had described, and then having zero choice but to seek excitement somewhere else. In someone else's bed.

"Welcome to Temple," the waiter said, and for the first time Ryan looked up at the man. He was dressed in a pair of tight black leather pants, riding low on his hips, his rippling obliques exposed, and a pair of black feathery wings. His light-blue eyes were rimmed with black, making them pop even more. He looked like a just-debauched fallen angel, which was just the sort of fantasy theater that Temple liked to indulge in.

There was no excuse except that the guy was objectively hot, there was undeniably interest in his baby blue eyes, and Ryan was both miserable and desperate.

"I feel like I must have died and gone to heaven," he teased the waiter.

The waiter perched a hip on the edge of the couch, leaning in closer, and Ryan didn't have to be looking at Wyatt to imagine his expression. "I'll tell you a secret," the angel murmured low, so Ryan had to scoot even closer to hear, "I got kicked out of heaven."

Ryan heard Wyatt's incredulous scoffing noise behind him, and yes, it was silly and ridiculous and over-the-top dramatic, but the guy was gorgeous and no doubt this was a very common fantasy.

"Were you very, very bad?" Wyatt asked from over Ryan's shoulder, in a faux-serious voice. "I bet you were super naughty."

The angel rolled his eyes, but his voice kept that faux-conspiratorial tone that had pulled Ryan into the fantasy from the first moment. "I discovered being bad is a lot more fun than being good."

Ryan sympathized; he'd discovered this same thing himself, at sixteen. And at eighteen. And at twenty-one. And again, at twenty-five, when he'd been unable to stay away from Wyatt Blake.

It was a lesson he kept re-learning. Maybe it was a lesson he could re-learn tonight.

"That's definitely a lesson we don't need to be taught." Wyatt sounded amused and vaguely interested and Ryan leaned back, tucking himself against Wyatt's side. It wasn't a shock when Wyatt's arm curled around him. Protectively, Ryan told himself. Wyatt was jealous. Normally, Ryan hated dealing with jealous guys, but he'd take jealousy over boredom, especially if it was Wyatt.

"I'll stay close," the waiter said. "Just in case you need anything. Or need a refresher course."

"We'll take a few beers, too," Ryan said, because he remembered Eric's warning, and he might as well try to keep to one of his admonitions.

To Ryan's surprise though, Wyatt bypassed the beers, and went to the bottles of liquor, pouring a few fingers of vodka into a glass, splashing in a little juice and nothing else.

"I thought he was flirting with you, at first," Wyatt said, mouth drifting towards Ryan's ear so he could hear him over the music, which was increasing in volume by the minute, "but actually I think he was flirting with both of us."

Wyatt again proved how observant he was.

"I think so too," Ryan said, sneaking in a little ear nibble as he turned to talk in Wyatt's ear.

Wyatt shrugged. "He's cute but the whole act is too much for me."

Wyatt was always so damn straight forward, it wasn't a surprise that the act was too theatrical for him. Ryan didn't even like it all that much, but he intended to use it.

"I don't know, cute goes a long way," Ryan said, smiling up at him. "Let's go dance."

Wyatt threw the rest of his vodka back, and Ryan set his beer down. Wyatt caught up Ryan's hand and they walked down the set of stairs to where the rest of the club was partying. Ryan intended to keep to the edges—after all, they needed to be seen, and not just because they were the VIP guests for the evening—but Wyatt took them deeper into the crowd. Ryan should have protested but he just followed.

"You didn't dance last time you were here," Wyatt observed, lips right against his as his hips ground into Ryan's.

"You weren't dancing," Ryan retorted, hands gripping his shoulders firmly, and Wyatt just smirked back.

Wyatt had a natural rhythm that Ryan had already observed from their surfing sessions, and he was a decent dancer, though frankly most of what they were doing was pseudo-dry humping anyway. The crowd and the feeling of Wyatt's hips grinding into his, hands a possessive brand on his back, creeping down towards his ass, raised his temperature quick, and after only a few songs, he felt damp all over. There was sweat slicked at Wyatt's temple, and Ryan wanted to lick it up.

As one song changed to another, Ryan tugged Wyatt towards their VIP area, and he followed easily.

It was a little easier to talk when they were away from the pounding bass emanating from the speakers. Wyatt leaned down. "I think we should tell the angel that you've been very bad indeed." Ryan could tell from their close proximity that Wyatt was hard in his jeans. He wanted to tell him, screw this, and let's go home and screw me, but the voice in the back of his head whispered that he couldn't let this go. He couldn't let Wyatt become complacent and bored and end up in someone like the angel's bed, only without Ryan.

Wyatt threw back another shot of vodka, this time with no juice, and Ryan opened the bottle of tequila with a quick wrench of his fingers. He'd just taken a shot and was sucking on a slice of lime when the angel waiter approached again.

"Need anything?" he asked. "Maybe some help with your shots?"

Wyatt's eyes were blank as Ryan looked at the waiter.

"Sure, sounds like fun," Ryan said carelessly. He couldn't look at Wyatt as the guy reclined on the table, like a tempting buffet, and poured a shot of vodka right into his abs.

There was no backing out now, he could hear the whoops from the crowd, which meant they'd been spotted, and he couldn't push him away.

Besides, he told himself as he leaned down, slurping the tequila off the guy's skin, it was the least boring thing he'd done in ages.

The slice of lime was waiting for him in the angel's mouth and he took it with his own, lingering for a long second. Ryan knew it was all part of the act and the fantasy the club provided, but there was undeniable interest flashing in his light-blue eyes. He wanted Ryan, and he'd probably even take Wyatt too, if that's what it took.

"Can I get you anything else?" the angel asked huskily, partially sitting up. The tequila left his bare chest shiny and Ryan could see exactly where his tongue had been in the flashing lights.

And that was the real question. How far was Ryan willing to take this? How far was *Wyatt* willing to take this?

Anne-Marie chose this particular moment to return. Ryan was pretty sure it wasn't even midnight on the nose, but certainly she'd been observing the activities with everyone else, and had decided the best time to drag them to the main stage was when the entire club was already watching.

"Time to go," she said.

Ryan decided that she must have seen a lot of shit in her tenure because she barely batted an eyelash at what they'd been up to.

Before they went, Ryan turned back to the waiter. "Your name," he asked. "And a dance when we get back."

He could feel Wyatt tense next to him. "With both of us," Ryan clarified, making sure that his intentions were clear.

"Alex," he said, as he began to pile empty glasses on the tray. "And I'll be around when you're done."

That was exactly what Wyatt was afraid of—that Alex would be there when they got back to the VIP area, and Wyatt would have to decide where he stood on the subject that Ryan had spent the whole evening hinting at.

It could have been worse, Wyatt thought as he climbed the stairs, trying to look calm and not nervous because he was about to get in front of about a thousand people, not because Ryan kept trying to set them up a threesome. Ryan could have dragged Alex up there to the stage with them and forced the decision in front of the entire club.

They got to the stage, and the DJ announced them. Wyatt kept a firm grip around Ryan's hips, feeling zero compunction about pulling him a little rough towards him. Ryan leaned over and played it up, kissing him noisily on the cheek and then moving to his lips.

If this was happening, it was happening on *his* terms. Wyatt yanked Ryan even closer and made it even showier, playing to the crowd by dipping him low, and pouring all his frustration into the kiss. The noisy crowd faded away, giving way to a low roaring in his ears. He opened his eyes as the kiss finally ended, and Ryan was staring at him, an inscrutable expression on his face.

The DJ said more nonsense that Wyatt didn't understand even though they were practically on top of one of the speakers, and then finally Anne-Marie led them down the stairs and off the stage.

But it wasn't a solution, because they were still under the crowd's microscope and Alex was waiting, an impatient look of excitement plain on his features, for them to collect him and give him the dance he'd been promised.

Maybe under different circumstances, Wyatt might have enjoyed dancing with him. Would have definitely entertained the threesome idea, but right now, it didn't feel right. Not now. Not under these tenuous circumstances. Not when Wyatt felt five seconds away from grabbing Ryan back and keeping him all to himself.

The uncertainty was breeding jealousy and envy in him, and Wyatt didn't like it, but he didn't know how to exorcise it either.

Wyatt grabbed Ryan's hand just before they were about to head up to the VIP area. "Wait," he said loud enough that he could be heard even over the pounding bass of the music. "Wait. We need to talk."

Ryan turned back to him, pulled his hand back and crossed his arms over his chest. "Are you okay with this?"

The question was a challenge and it was stark black and white, with none of the shades of gray Wyatt knew were important. At least to him.

"We need to talk," he repeated. Even though there was no possible way to talk in here. Not with the music and the strobe lights, and Alex practically hovering over Ryan's shoulder.

He wasn't stupid enough to think they'd get away with it again, but Wyatt decided he was going to try anyway. He pulled Ryan's hand back, and led him the same way he'd gone the first night they met, winding through the crowd and right out the front door, leading him past the bouncers and the eager partiers waiting to get in, down the street, and into the mouth of the alley they'd first spoken in a month ago.

Every second, Wyatt expected Ryan to pull away, to go back to the club, to go back to Alex. And that, Wyatt realized as quiet finally surrounded them, was a microcosm of the whole problem.

He didn't trust Ryan not to break his heart. He didn't trust Ryan to pull the parachute if things got hairy.

"What are we doing here?" Wyatt asked, the question spilling out before he could stop it. If Ryan's earlier question had been a challenge, this was a demand.

"Drinking, partying? Eventually getting photographed and introducing all the housewives in the grocery store checkout line to our relationship?"

"I don't want a cute answer," Wyatt said. "I want the truth."

"Keeping it fun. Keeping it exciting." Ryan's voice sounded brittle. Wyatt's first instinct was to claim bullshit on that too, but he was beginning to think Ryan was actually telling the truth.

"Why can't we have a drink and dance some and make out in the car on the way home, and have undeniably spectacular sex when we do? Isn't that exciting enough for you?"

Ryan hugged himself and Wyatt wasn't sure it was because of the temperature, which seemed mild enough, even for November.

"It's *always* going to get boring. That's what *always* happens."

"Bullshit," Wyatt retorted. "I jumped out of a fucking plane for you. If you want exciting, I'm going to give it to you, because I care about you. But I'm done playing games."

"I don't . . . I don't understand." Another lie. Wyatt found his normally moderate temper beginning to spike. The one thing he hated was being lied to, and Ryan was doing it a lot, and not just tonight.

"Sure, that guy in there is hot, I'm not going to deny it, but we don't need him. Do you need him?"

"I . . . you don't want to go home with him?" Ryan sounded incredulous. When Ryan had been the one flirting with him all night, not Wyatt.

"I want to go home with *you*," Wyatt bit out.

"I'm not dumb," Ryan sneered. "I don't believe that you'll want that forever. You'll get bored, you'll start looking, and someday you're going to wish we took him home. And instead of the three of us, it'll just be the two of you."

"Tell me *you* don't need that guy," Wyatt said again. "Tell me you just want that guy, and we'll figure this out. Because it's not about what I want. It's about what you want."

The look in Ryan's eyes was pure stubbornness. "I want to have fun. I never want to be bored. Never again."

It shouldn't have hurt so much because he'd anticipated it, but it burned like hell anyway. "And I'd bore you, eventually," Wyatt said quietly. "I get it. Thank you for being so clear."

He turned to go, because he couldn't stand there any longer and try to figure out which stupidity coming out of Ryan's mouth were lies and which was the truth. But Ryan caught his arm. For a split second, Wyatt's heart rose, because maybe now he would finally get the answers he wanted. Maybe he could finally break through this barrier that Ryan had insisted on erecting.

"Where are you going?" Ryan demanded. "We're supposed to get photographed together."

The hope hit the barrier straight on and crashed and burned. Because to Ryan, the games were all that mattered. He hadn't even listened when Wyatt had tried to lay his heart on the line for him.

All he could do was shrug. "Go get the fucking angel to do it with you. I'm done." And he walked out of the alley alone.

❦

Ryan was still unsteady when he walked back into the club. The moment Wyatt had walked away, he'd wanted to run after him, and beg him not to give up on him.

But he'd been really fucking clear, hadn't he? He'd laid out the details of the arrangement and had never given Wyatt any expectation that he would change the rules. And now that Wyatt wasn't getting what he thought he wanted out of the deal, he was done?

Fuck that. Fuck him.

His temper had boiled over after that, leaving him raw and shaky, and clenching his hands over and over again, wishing for a bat to hold onto. To ground him. To beat against the most convenient stationary object.

It wasn't supposed to go this way, and it definitely wasn't supposed to end like this.

He went back to Temple because he didn't know what else to do. Marching back up to his VIP section, he unscrewed the lid off the tequila and took a shot from the bottle. He was buying it after all, he could do whatever the fuck he wanted to with it.

"You okay?"

Ryan looked up and the angelic waiter was standing there, looking confused. Well, that made two of them. "Not really," he admitted. He took another long swig of tequila and wiped his mouth with the back of his hand.

There was part of him that really wanted to take the angel home anyway. Keep Wyatt up all night with the sounds of their fucking. Make it crystal clear that whatever Wyatt thought Ryan felt, he was wrong.

The truth was, he didn't know if Wyatt was wrong. Maybe Ryan was wrong. Maybe whatever they'd been doing was bound to crash and burn at some point. Nothing simple ever stayed simple, and even Ryan could acknowledge they'd crossed over into complicated awhile ago.

"You want a drink?" he asked Alex, extending the bottle towards him. "I probably shouldn't be drinking alone."

"Can't, sorry, I'm working, and I'll get fired if they catch it on the cameras," Alex said apologetically.

Ryan took another long drink from the bottle, large enough for both of them. It suddenly occurred to him that while the interest in Alex's eyes might have been genuine, he'd probably been paid to flirt outrageously with them.

It wasn't so much different than Wyatt, who he was paying to be his boyfriend and to cook cute, couple-y meals that he could post to his Instagram. But even then he knew it was a lie, because even though he'd been paying Wyatt since day one, money had never been part of what existed between them.

"Was that your boyfriend who left?" Alex asked, perching just on the end of the couch.

"Yes. No. I don't know," Ryan admitted. His total ignorance of the realities of the situation made him want to drink more. But he didn't, because he'd learned a long time ago that getting drunk never really helped. Tomorrow morning he would wake up hungover and miserable and still fucking clueless.

Alex shrugged. It was clear he thought Ryan should go figure that situation out before trying to make threesomes with hot Temple waiters happen. And the galling part was that he was absolutely fucking right.

"I don't suppose I can give you a ride back to my place," Ryan said, even though he didn't even want to. He wasn't even sure anymore if *Alex* wanted to, but this situation was already so monumentally messed up, surely fucking it up more couldn't make it worse.

"You're cute. You're rich. You're famous. Normally, sure. But not tonight. Not when it's not even me you're thinking about."

"We can just not think at all," Ryan said, sounding a little desperate. The last thing he wanted to do was go home alone, and sit in his empty house, imagining the conversation if he went and knocked on Wyatt's door.

Nothing good, that was for fucking sure. But the thought would tempt him all night.

The look Alex shot him was pitying. "You can't turn that off," he said, and got up to leave.

Ryan ended up alone on the couch in his VIP section, sipping his tequila, and trying to figure out how to text Eric that the photos tonight were off.

He'd composed version fifty-three of the message when instead, Eric texted him.

Why am I not hearing rapturous reports of your cute coupledom? Eric said.

Slight snag, Ryan texted back before he could lose his nerve. The tequila also helped with that. **Photos tonight off.**

He sent another text to call the car, and then turned his phone off, gripping the neck of the bottle of tequila.

Maybe waking up hungover would at least fuzzy up some of the extraneous feelings he was never supposed to have in the first place.

Chapter Fifteen

"Are you going to tell me what the fuck happened last night?"

Ryan came awake slowly and painfully, aware at first only of a bright, hideous light shining in his eyes and an annoyed voice looming over him.

"What are you doing here?" he groaned, turning over, trying to take his sheets with him. The empty tequila bottle thumped to the floor from the bed.

Not his greatest plan, taking the bottle to bed. But Alex wouldn't come, even if Ryan had wanted him anyway, and Wyatt . . . Ryan pushed the thought of him from his head, because that pain was even worse than the ache in his head.

"You are certifiably insane," Eric retorted. "What the fuck happened? All I'm hearing last night is rumors you're cheating on Wyatt, there are reports of you flirting with some waiter with angel wings on, and then you cancel the pictures?"

Ryan groaned again.

"Do you need me to go remind him that he signed a contract? That he is *legally obligated* to be your boyfriend until we tell him otherwise? Because I can do that."

It was funny how everything seemed bad, until Eric waded into the middle of it and things suddenly became catastrophically terrible.

"Please do not do that," Ryan said, all too aware he was begging. "And for the love of god, turn the fucking light off."

"Did you have a fight?" Eric demanded. "Where is he?"

"In the cottage, I don't know. I didn't have a GPS tracker put on him."

"He didn't answer the door, and I realized I don't have a key," Eric said impatiently.

"A situation I'm incredibly jealous of right now," Ryan moaned into the pillow. "Just leave me alone."

"No," Eric said. "We need to fix this problem you created last night. And fix it quick. The rumors are flying fast and loose, and I need something concrete to combat them. Do I need to remind you why we came up with this plan in the first place? This is not making you look great."

"It's not my fault," Ryan said. He didn't know if he was lying or not. Only that he wanted to make Eric stop.

"You're the one with the high profile," Eric countered. "So automatically, everything is your fault."

"You're fired."

Eric ignored that which was probably better for everyone. "Tonight you're going to go out to dinner, and there are going to be photographers and you're going to sit in the most public table in the whole fucking restaurant, and you are going to be the cutest couple LA has ever fucking seen. I don't care if you hate each other right now, you're going to put all that aside and *fix this*."

It sounded hideous. The Temple thing had been so much more their speed, with the added bonus of a cute twist that it was the place they'd met. A twist that Eric had made sure all the gossip columnists knew about. And now that was all ruined because Wyatt had decided that Ryan's determination to never give him a reason to cheat was stupid.

If anything, Ryan reasoned despite his pounding headache, that proved just how much he cared. Ryan had been about to propose that threesome for *Wyatt*. A completely selfless act if there ever was one.

The problem was, he wasn't sure if it was the tacky taste of tequila poisoning his mouth or the bright light shining in through the window, it no longer made quite as much sense as it had the night before.

"Fine, we'll go to the dinner," Ryan said. He could admit he'd been at least partially wrong. He could go knock on Wyatt's door and grovel, apologize for the stupid threesome idea, hope they could go back to where they'd been, and beg him to go to dinner.

He could do that.

He groaned into the pillow again.

Maybe.

"I think you need more of an intervention than I have the patience to give," Eric said. And the worst part of that was Ryan knew exactly who he meant instead, and that was even worse than Eric.

And when something was even worse than Eric, it was a very serious problem.

"You look incredibly shitty," Tabitha said when he opened the door.

It wasn't entirely fair. He'd at least managed to drag himself out of bed, and into the shower, knowing she'd be coming and would expect brushed teeth and no tequila body odor at a bare minimum.

"I feel incredibly shitty," Ryan retorted, shutting the door behind her.

"I should have known you'd fuck it up with him," Tabitha muttered to herself as she made her way through the foyer and down the hall towards the kitchen.

Ryan stopped in the doorway when he realized where she was headed.

"Oh, don't be ridiculous," she chided him. "He's not even here. He's hiding too, I'm sure. Probably angry at you, and I'm sure it's mostly, if not completely, deserved."

"You're my best friend, you're supposed to take my side," Ryan said petulantly, sliding onto one of the barstools and setting his aching head gently against the marble countertop.

"That's not what best friends do," Tabitha said briskly, opening the fridge. "They give you the unvarnished, ugly truth and help you deal with it. Thus, why I am here."

"You're here because Eric bribed you with the newest Gucci bag," Ryan said. "I heard him on the phone."

"I would have come anyway, darling. I didn't want to waste a chance to get something out of that asshole." She placed an ice pack against his forehead. "Wyatt's not here so you might as well tell me everything that happened."

"I don't want to talk about it," Ryan said, his voice muffled by the countertop.

"But you should, and you're going to. Otherwise how are you going to tell Wyatt that you have to go to dinner tonight?"

"Eric told you about that too, I assume," Ryan groaned.

"If you are going to enact this charade," Tabitha said, far more kindly than he probably deserved, "you need to actually put the effort in. It's not all cute Instagram photos and rumors of you surfing together. You dropped the fly ball last night, and threw an interception, to mix metaphors. Time to fix it and show all those fans of yours that you're actually very happy together."

"I'm not sure it can be fixed," he admitted. The look on Wyatt's face had been blank and devoid of anything, like he'd shut down and then shut it all away. Maybe Ryan couldn't get it back. Maybe Wyatt didn't want him to.

"I'm certain there will be some groveling involved," Tabitha pointed out sternly, pulling out the barstool next to him and settling in. "Now, from the top please. I need to know how bad it is before we pick the appropriate groveling method."

"He's been . . . quiet since Napa," Ryan said. "I thought maybe he'd changed his mind about us. The sex was still so good, though, so maybe it was nothing. Maybe I misjudged."

"Did you ask him if he'd changed his mind?"

Ryan shook his head and almost instantly regretted it. "No," he murmured.

"And did you ask him what was wrong?"

"No." Ryan hesitated. "I was afraid it would feel too . . . boyfriend-y. That it would open up what we had to even more complexities. And I wanted to keep it simple."

Ryan didn't even have to look at Tabitha to know the look she was giving him was galling.

"It was stupid, okay? I should have asked. I wanted to ask."

"That isn't why I'm annoyed with you, and definitely not why he's annoyed with you," Tabitha said. "So, he was quiet, and you didn't ask, and then you went to Temple, and decided to pick up a waiter dressed like an angel? I'm not following that logic."

"I thought he was bored, okay? I thought he was bored of . . ." Ryan paused, because he didn't want to say *me* and he definitely didn't want to say *our relationship*. That was the whole problem. He'd gone into this very deliberately trying to avoid a relationship, but they'd ended up there anyway.

"Bored? Let me tell you, Wyatt Blake does not strike me as the kind of guy who sticks around when he's bored."

"Exactly," Ryan said miserably.

"You thought he'd get bored and leave you? Really?" Tabitha's incredulous voice didn't help. "Wyatt is crazy about you."

"It sounds stupid but I had an ex, well, you knew him actually. David. He cheated on me, at the end. And he told me that he'd been driven to do it because he was bored. You know how much that relationship ending hurt me, and since that point I've made sure to never let things get that far. Ever."

"David cheated on you? That miserable small-dicked bastard," Tabitha muttered. "You never told me."

"It was fucking embarrassing," Ryan admitted.

"I just can't believe he had the balls to use that excuse and then you actually *believed* it," Tabitha said.

"How was I supposed to know? I was bored too! I didn't get why everyone was so hot to be in a relationship, because I was just as bored as he was."

"Darling," Tabitha said carefully, "I think that was because *he* was boring and you were not right for each other. Not everyone with a little hiccup in their relationship adds excitement via cheating."

"I know that, of course I know that," Ryan retorted.

"So that was what you were trying to do last night? Add in excitement so that Wyatt wouldn't cheat on you and leave you because he was bored?"

"It sounds so stupid when you say it."

"Well," Tabitha hedged.

"He didn't understand," Ryan said. "He just said he wanted to stop playing games and kept demanding to know if I was enough for him."

"Oh dear," Tabitha said. "What did you tell him?"

"That I didn't want him to get bored! I wasn't thinking about me, I could go on like this for . . . I don't know, a long time probably. I'm not bored."

Ryan realized what he'd said just as he said it.

"Oh fuck," he groaned. "I'm in love with him, aren't I?"

Tabitha put a reassuring arm around his shoulders. "It's not that bad, I promise."

"I was so worried he'd leave me that I actually drove him away." Ryan slammed a fist on the counter. "I'm a fucking idiot."

"I'm pretty sure he's in love with you too, so maybe tone down the *woe is me* inevitability that he's gone for good," Tabitha said. "You can still fix this."

"If I agree to make it official, probably," Ryan admitted.

"You just admitted that you're in love with him. Isn't that something you want?"

"What if it happens again?" Ryan asked seriously. "What if he cheats on me? What if he leaves? David, I didn't love him at all, I don't think, and that was so humiliating. I don't think I could survive it, if it happened with Wyatt."

"Darling," Tabitha said softly, "you can't go into a relationship expecting it to end. You have to believe in each other and trust each other. Trust that Wyatt isn't going to use some bullshit excuse to cheat on you. And that if you get worried he will, or that he's not happy with you, communication is key. You'd be surprised what people can figure out when they actually talk to each other."

"You think I should do this," Ryan stated. He couldn't even believe that after being *so* clear upfront, he'd gone and done the exact thing he'd warned Wyatt not to do.

"I think it's worth a shot. You two clearly care about each other. I want you to be happy, and I think you were really happy with him."

"I was." Ryan hesitated. "I am."

"Then you should go for it," Tabitha said, giving him an extra encouraging squeeze.

"What if he turns me down?" Ryan asked, because the fear of that eventuality was terrifying, squeezing the breath out of his lungs.

"Do I think you're going to say, *let's get together for real*, and he falls all over you? No. It's not that simple. Love isn't that simple."

"Groveling, then," Ryan said.

"There will probably be some groveling involved," Tabitha hedged.

"Do I get on my knees or . . ."

Tabitha held up a hand. "And that's where I step out. Whatever you two do in the bedroom or any other room of the house is between you."

"No, I meant, how should I grovel? Begging? Promises? Gifts?"

"I think," Tabitha said slowly, "that's going to depend on two factors. One, who Wyatt is as a person. And two, how pissed off he is at you."

"And you think he's really pissed off." It was unreal that while facing that particular fact, which was something he'd suspected since Wyatt had walked out of the alley, something in his chest started to ache even worse than his head.

"I think that Wyatt is an honorable guy, who keeps his promises, and that he's in love with you. He wouldn't ditch you last night if he wasn't really pissed off." Tabitha stared at him frankly, and Ryan realized there was actually something that she was insinuating but not actually saying. Which was the scariest thing of all, because Tabitha was renowned for telling the unapologetic truth. If she was trying to cushion this, then it must be really bad.

"Oh god," Ryan said, a spike of panic rising through him. He'd thought the worst it could be was groveling, maybe even begging Wyatt to forgive him. And then in the twenty or so minutes since he'd come to terms with his own feelings, he'd seen them in a sort of nebulous, happy-ever-after future.

But what if Wyatt didn't come back? What if Wyatt came back and didn't forgive him?

It could be so much worse.

"You might as well just lay it on me," Ryan said bluntly. "I know you're holding back, and it doesn't suit you. I'm already down; I'm not sure it's going to get much worse."

"He's pissed, he's embarrassed, his pride is in shambles because during your first night out as an official couple, you were all over some waiter dressed in a trashy Halloween costume. But the worst of it is that you definitely hurt him a lot."

The ache in Ryan's chest intensified. "I don't suppose me explaining I was incredibly stupid and never meant to will fix that?"

Tabitha's look was soft and sympathetic. "We can sure hope it will. Or else I'll be back here in a few hours with ice cream and more tequila."

⁂

"I have a great idea. We should hire an assassin," Evan said excitedly.

Wyatt looked up from his hot fudge brownie sundae in surprise.

"He really doesn't mean that, I swear," Miles said.

"Doesn't he?" Wyatt said dully. He shoved the hot fudge around in his bowl and didn't put the spoon in his mouth. He'd been sitting here for half an hour, watching Miles' famous caramel crunch ice cream melt in a puddle of hot fudge, barely able to stick a spoonful in his mouth.

He must really look awful because Miles usually took exception to his friends not eating the desserts he made for them, but he hadn't said a word.

"I'm not sure I do," Evan revised. "It sounded really badass, though. At one point I thought about hiring an assassin to kill you, Miles, when we first started working together."

Wyatt was not as surprised by this as he should have been. Evan and Miles, while rapturously in love now, had not always gotten along. And Evan was all for finding unusual solutions to problems, thus the assassin.

"True love," Miles announced proudly. "That's really true love right there. You were willing to pay someone a lot more money to get rid of me."

Evan rolled his eyes but they were still so fond that Wyatt's heart ached. Just yesterday it felt like he and Ryan had been on the same path as Miles and Evan. Instead they'd been heading in the opposite trajectory. Instead of hating each other at first like his friends, they'd immediately connected. That first night had been magical, and Wyatt had been so sure that *this* was the guy. He was still pretty sure he still felt the same way, under all the anger and the humiliation and the hurt, but he couldn't believe anymore that Ryan was the right guy.

The right guy wouldn't want to keep pretending when the reality was better than any fantasy.

Still, he'd come here to Evan and Miles' place early this morning and after plying him with a gourmet breakfast he had barely been able to choke down, they'd sat him down in front of bad reality television for two hours. Then Miles had made him the sundae, proclaiming that brownies and caramel crunch ice cream topped with hot fudge could cure any problem. At the very least distract from one.

Wyatt was marginally distracted, but he didn't really feel any better. Miles would try to keep him here, and away from Ryan, but Wyatt was beginning to think he should go home, and try to figure out how they were going to proceed. Would Wyatt stay his personal chef? Would the fake relationship be on? Could he even get out of that contract he'd stupidly signed, all hopeful and optimistic only a few weeks ago?

Knowing Ryan's shark of an agent, getting out of it was probably going to be a nightmare. But on the upside, Ryan could probably hire the waiter to take his place pretty easily.

"You don't have to go back there, you know. We can go get your stuff. And you can stay with us for awhile." Like Wyatt didn't know Miles and Evan had marathon sex sessions complete with noises he'd really prefer never to hear. "I can even put out feelers for a new job. There's so many more opportunities in LA. With your resume, you'll get something fast."

He probably would, Wyatt reasoned. Miles wasn't even lying. But despite everything, he wasn't really sure he was ready to quit his current job just yet.

Wyatt didn't think he was nearly as stubborn as some people—like say, *Xander*—but once on a path, it was hard to shove him off of it. And he'd fallen in love with Ryan pretty irrevocably. It was probably going to take more than an angel to change his mind.

"I'm tired," Wyatt finally said. "I'm going home to try to get some sleep."

He'd gone home from Temple the night before, and had lain awake in bed all night, fully expecting that he would hear Ryan come home from the club with company. He'd tortured himself for hours, preparing his heart for what he might hear or see the next day. But he wasn't sure that Ryan had come home at all, or else he'd come home and been too quiet for Wyatt to hear.

Removing himself from the house and going to Miles' had seemed like such a good plan, but now he wasn't sure that being around Miles and Evan was helping him at all, no matter how sympathetic they were.

Or how many assassins Evan was willing to hire.

Miles opened his mouth and Wyatt held up a hand. "I know, I don't have to. I need to."

"Well, make sure to text me, tell me how it goes," Miles said quietly. Evan had faded into the living room, leaving the two friends alone in the kitchen. "I know how rotten you must feel if you can't even work up an appetite for my caramel crunch ice cream and homemade hot fudge."

"You even made brownies without walnuts," Wyatt said ruefully. "I'm sorry I couldn't enjoy them."

"I'll wrap them up," Miles said, beginning to do just that. "You can snack yourself into a chocolate coma later."

"Thank you," Wyatt said. And to his embarrassment, he was near tears. Again.

Miles walked over, handing him the container full of brownies, and wrapped him in a big hug. "You're a great guy," he said. "Either Ryan realizes he needs to do better by you, or you'll find a guy who will. You deserve that."

Wyatt left, saying a quick goodbye and drove his bike home to Ryan's house.

Wyatt was not ashamed that when he reached the gate, he kicked off the power on his bike and walked it in. Ryan wouldn't even know he'd come back. Of course that was assuming he'd noticed he was gone in the first place or that he even gave a shit.

He collapsed in his bed, and as he snuggled into the pillow, couldn't help but be grateful that they'd been sharing Ryan's bed. His sheets were thankfully completely Ryan-free.

He fell asleep hoping that Ryan was suffering a little because, unlike his own, his bed wasn't a Wyatt-free zone.

Ryan took a deep, steadying breath and braced himself for the difficult conversation to come. He knocked twice, trying for soft but determined. If you could even interpret that from a knock.

Nothing.

Wyatt was either ignoring him or he wasn't home. Normally, Ryan would have been fine giving him the space he wanted, but after last night's relationship debut had not gone as planned, Eric was chomping at the bit to get things back on track.

He'd given Ryan stern orders that they would go to dinner tonight and they would at least pretend to be the most loved-up couple in LA.

That meant that knocking again wasn't an option, it was a requirement.

He did it, a little louder this time. More authoritarian.

Still nothing.

The third set of knocks were more door *thumps*, and they must have done the trick because the door swung open, revealing a sleepy-looking Wyatt, shoving a hand through his hair.

His expression went from confused to angry to hurt. And it was the last that made Ryan's heart ache. It hadn't been very hard to figure out that was what was hurting so much in the vicinity of his chest. Even Tabitha hadn't had to tell him.

"What are you doing here?" Wyatt demanded.

Ryan discarded the immediate and obvious explanation that this was his property and attached to his house. "I wanted to apologize," he said.

"Not interested," Wyatt said, and tried to slam the door shut, but Ryan got his foot and calf in before he could. Usually Wyatt had incredible reflexes, even more deft than Ryan's, but he'd clearly just woken up.

"I was an asshole last night. Rude and thoughtless and cruel. I genuinely am very sorry," Ryan said.

Wyatt had taken a step back away from Ryan's entry into the house and took another. And then another. Ryan shut the door behind him. His neighbors didn't need to hear this and send the scoop to TMZ.

Wyatt didn't look convinced, so Ryan tried again.

"You're right, I was playing games. And I'm done."

"Done how?" Wyatt asked.

"You were right about so much," Ryan said, desperately latching onto the tiny opening that Wyatt had just given him. "About how the boredom thing was about me, and not about you. I should have told you I wasn't going to get bored, and should have listened when you said you wouldn't either."

Wyatt sighed. "Listen, I don't really give a shit that you're not going to get bored in a fake relationship. Or by hooking up with me, or whatever. I don't care."

"What if it wasn't just a fake relationship? What if we weren't just hooking up?" The Ryan of six months ago would have been aghast at the direction this conversation had taken, but frankly the Ryan of six months ago had been a tool.

Wyatt hadn't just made him a better person; Wyatt made him *want* to be a better person.

"You want to be together? For real?" Wyatt sounded very skeptical, and Ryan honestly could not blame him. He sat down on the couch, leaving Wyatt hovering around the TV. He'd read once that if you wanted someone to believe you, you needed to be absolutely sure of your own actions. Sitting down on the couch like he belonged there seemed the most affirmative action that Ryan could take at the moment.

"I do," Ryan said.

There was a flash of hope in Wyatt's eyes as he sat down on the chair opposite and leaned over, his elbows resting on his knees. "I want to believe that," Wyatt said. But then his face hardened. "I'm just not sure I can."

Ryan figured this was the best time to lay all his cards on the table. Tabitha had warned him as she was leaving that going to dinner tonight in an attempt to fulfill the original agreement was going to fuck with Wyatt's ability to forgive. Ryan's apology would just look like he was manipulating Wyatt to get what he needed from him.

"You need to nip that right in the bud," Tabitha had cautioned. "Tell him right away and be as honest as you can. Tell him your hands are tied with this. Otherwise he'll have every reason to believe you're lying."

"There's something else," Ryan added. "Last night . . . I don't even need to tell you that last night I monumentally fucked up. Not just with you, though that's the part that possibly has the worst and most lasting consequences. I also fucked up our agreement. I fucked up the impression I was trying to give people. I was trying to look like someone responsible and trustworthy, someone who cared about you, and instead I made it look like the opposite."

"Believe me, I was there. We don't have to rehash it," Wyatt said dryly.

"What I'm trying to say is that Eric has set up a redo. For tonight."

Wyatt stared at him incredulously, then jumped up and started pacing between the living room and the kitchen. "Are you fucking kidding me? That's why you're here? That's why you're apologizing? Because you need me to go play nice with you in front of some fucking photographer?"

"No. I'm here because I'm sorry. But yes, we do need to do that."

Wyatt looked straight at him, a challenging look in his eyes. "How can I ever believe you if you make me go do this tonight?"

"I don't know," Ryan said and it was the most wretched truth he'd ever told. "I really wish I could figure it out, because this is killing me."

"It didn't seem to be killing you last night," Wyatt said, and there was a cruel edge to his tone that Ryan told himself that he absolutely deserved.

"I know. I was . . . I guess I should tell you why I acted that way. I probably should have started with that. When I first got drafted by the Dodgers, I had a boyfriend. And he was a little older, and exciting, and I loved that. I thought I loved him. And then one day, I came home early, and he was fucking some guy in our bed. I kicked him out, of course, but not before he told me that he'd had to do it because we'd gotten too boring. We'd stayed in and ordered pizza and watched Netflix and he'd gotten *bored*. I realized then that I'd been bored too. After that, I swore that I'd only do hookups. Because that would never happen in a hookup."

"Because you'd never stay long enough for anyone to get bored," Wyatt said slowly. "I want to say that's really stupid of you, to believe something a cheating asshole tells you, but you thought you loved him. And he echoed something you were feeling too."

Ryan nodded miserably. "Tabitha said we were both wrong for each other, and that if it's right, it doesn't matter if you're boring together, because you never get bored."

"I don't know, I could go for boring sometimes," Wyatt said ruefully.

"I just want you to know why I would do something like last night," Ryan said. "I was confused, things between us had gotten so complicated and you'd gone sort of quiet, and I thought, completely stupidly, that you were bored."

"I wasn't bored," Wyatt admitted. His eyes looked so blue from across the room, boring into Ryan. "I was falling in love with you and afraid that you didn't feel that way about me."

"Oh." Ryan had said plenty of times how stupid he'd been, but this really drove the point home. If he'd only *asked*, instead of assuming that Wyatt pulling away was a bad thing. "You said, *was*."

Wyatt shrugged. "That's not something that changes. I'm just not sure I trust you. Those are two separate things."

"Because of the dinner tonight."

"Because of the dinner tonight," Wyatt repeated. "Because of a hundred other things that I shouldn't question but I am anyway." He sounded upset and conflicted, and Ryan probably should have felt more sympathy for him, but he was also doing a little happy dance internally that he sounded conflicted at all. Wyatt could have just kicked him out, but he'd listened, and they were trying to figure things out. Of all the ways this could have gone, it certainly hadn't gone the worst.

"I really am sorry, but I can't get us out of the dinner. Believe me, if I could, I would. I would do it, if it helped you trust me again," Ryan said. He knew he was begging; he'd always assumed it would feel worse. More demeaning, maybe. But it felt right. Like putting everything on the line for someone he loved.

"That's okay," Wyatt said, and for the first time, there was a hint of a smile on the corner of his mouth. "I could think of worse ways to spend an evening than being wined and dined by a cute guy."

"You'll go?"

"I didn't think I had much of a choice," Wyatt said wryly. "Not if I don't want to get sued by Eric."

"Threats and blackmail are really more his style," Ryan said. "But yes."

"You need to get a new agent," Wyatt said.

"Sadly, you are not the first person to tell me that." Ryan took a deep breath, and asked the question that really worried him. "What are we going to do about going forward? After tonight?"

Wyatt sighed. "I care about you. I care about what I started building here. I don't want to leave, even if I'm mad at you, even if you've embarrassed me. So I won't. But I don't think we can go back to where we were right away. I need time. I need to figure out if I can trust you again."

"Okay." Ryan was feeling cautiously optimistic. Wyatt had agreed to go to dinner. Wyatt wasn't leaving. Wyatt was willing to wait and see if he could give Ryan another chance.

Best-case scenario, considering how catastrophically he'd torpedoed things the night before.

He'd considered more than once if he should tell Wyatt he loved him too—because now the other man had told him twice he felt the same. Once in anger and now again, while they were trying to resolve things. But Ryan hadn't wanted to tell him as an apology. He wanted it to be a moment of celebration and happiness. Something bigger and brighter. Special. Just like Wyatt was to him.

So the three little words would have to wait but he had another ace up his sleeve. Tabitha had suggested presents, and though people usually gave apology roses or apology chocolates, Ryan was betting on his apology gift being a hell of a lot more successful than that. He'd wanted something concrete that could say so much better than he could two important things: *one*, that he knew he'd messed up and *two*, that he was willing to put the work in to fix it. But the present wasn't going to be delivered until late tonight, or early tomorrow, no matter how much he'd pleaded, so Ryan would have to wait.

And waiting was really not his strong suit.

Chapter Sixteen

Ryan didn't know what to do with himself. In his own house.

This was why he'd avoided dating for so long; it always turned him into an unsure neurotic who was always afraid every decision was the wrong one and would doom the relationship before it even got off the ground.

The one good thing, he thought as he loitered in the hallway between the living room and the kitchen, waiting for Wyatt to appear for their dinner date, was that he'd already done the fucking up and probably couldn't mess the relationship up any worse.

He heard the back door open and close and Ryan sauntered a few casual steps to the right so he could see Wyatt walk in and through the kitchen. He was wearing dark jeans and a light-blue button-up nearly the shade of his eyes. His face was still shadowed, faint circles under his eyes, but he'd lost that pinched, angry, hurt look from earlier, and Ryan was relieved. He didn't think he could sit through a whole dinner, seeing that look while knowing it was all his fault.

"You look great," Ryan said enthusiastically. Tabitha had told him how important it was he take every opportunity to show Wyatt how much he meant to him. But that had probably been too much enthusiasm, deployed too quickly.

Wyatt looked taken aback. "Okay. Thanks, I guess?"

Definitely too enthusiastically.

Honesty and the communication were the key, Ryan reminded himself. "That . . . came out wrong. I don't know how to do this—not the right way anyway. I've only had one boyfriend, and it didn't end well. So I'm almost definitely going to mess up again." Admitting to failure in advance was not easy, but he did it anyway because it was *true*.

"I don't want a perfect boyfriend, I want a real one," Wyatt told him, voice soft and pleading. "I want *you*."

"I want you too," Ryan said, and he couldn't help the ache that spiraled through him at just how much. "Exactly as you are. And you do look good. That wasn't . . . I wasn't lying. I just haven't always said what was on my mind, how much I care about you, and I'm trying to fix that. Trying to be better, for you."

"I want the Ryan I've spent the last month with," Wyatt said, walking over and pulling Ryan into an unexpected hug. "Not some other version of you. Not someone who's trying to be someone they're not. When I said I want you, that's exactly what I meant."

Ryan ordered himself not to get too comfortable, and not to turn Wyatt's innocent embrace into something else. To just enjoy it, and not grab hold too tight, afraid that this would be his last chance. Wyatt wasn't going anywhere. He was sticking around and letting Ryan prove that he was telling the truth.

He let him go reluctantly. "We should go, our reservations are soon." And because he hadn't asked last time, he asked this time. "Are you okay doing this?"

Wyatt shrugged. "Do I wish we didn't have to do this tonight? Yeah. But I understand the reasons why we need to."

"I'm sorry," Ryan automatically apologized as they moved towards the garage. "That's my fault."

"You can stop apologizing," Wyatt pointed out wryly.

"Sorry," Ryan said and grimaced. "I told you I'd be bad at this."

"Just relax," he coaxed, reaching out to give Ryan's shoulder a quick squeeze.

Ryan moved through the garage and opened the passenger door of the Maserati. He'd had it washed and detailed this afternoon until the midnight-blue paint gleamed in the dusk light.

"What's this?" Wyatt asked, stopping short. "We're taking the Maserati?"

"You want a real boyfriend, and this real boyfriend intends to give you the best he can," Ryan admitted.

"Also, because it looks pretty damn cool in the pictures," Wyatt said, sliding in. Ryan snorted as he closed the door.

"You're not wrong," Ryan admitted as he got in the driver's side. "I'll admit about ten percent of the decision was how killer we're going to look pulling up in it."

Wyatt rolled his eyes as Ryan pulled out of the driveway.

"Where are we going?"

"Some place in Malibu that's apparently *the* new restaurant," Ryan said. "I thought you'd enjoy it. I made sure Eric got us a good table."

"A public table, you mean," Wyatt retorted, and there was the faintest edge of bitterness to his voice. And Ryan couldn't help but think that he also wished they hadn't had to do this so soon after their fight. They both would have benefited from some time. Even if it was hard. Even if it hurt. Throwing them in together so fast had left a lot of issues unresolved.

Fear bubbled up inside him, but he didn't have an outlet for it, so he pushed his foot down on the accelerator, feeling the engine roar to life.

"Yes, a public table," Ryan said. "You know why we have to sit at a public table. And I'd apologize, but you just told me I've apologized enough already."

Wyatt didn't say anything, just looked out the passenger window as Calabasas passed by. Ryan turned onto a windier road, but didn't slow down. Pressed down harder on the accelerator, actually. When he'd bought this car, the salesman had promised second-to-none acceleration and handling, and he'd never had a chance to take it out like he should have after it had been delivered.

What was the point of owning a car like this if you didn't test its limits a little?

"I wish you wouldn't drive so fast," Wyatt said to the window, and yeah, he was definitely still annoyed.

Instead of slowing down, Ryan took the next turn at seventy. It was a stupid thing to do. Stupid and reckless, and a remnant of a time when he hadn't cared what sort of attention he got, even if it was negative. He'd thought he'd left that attention-seeking behind in high school, but the fear kept creeping up.

He didn't like Wyatt ignoring him. Even if it was Wyatt trying to avoid an argument.

"God damnit, Ryan," Wyatt ground out as the car flew around another curve in the road, tires squealing.

"What? Is this too fast for you?" Ryan teased darkly as he stepped on the accelerator in the flat, jumping up to triple digits as easily as breathing. Reveling in the attention he was getting again.

"I don't care if you're hooked on adrenaline, but this is stupid and reckless," Wyatt ground out.

Ryan glanced over at Wyatt, and registered how pissed off he looked. But it was a split second too long, especially when he was going over a hundred miles per hour. Especially when the next turn was a lot tighter than he remembered.

He jerked the wheel reflexively, and knew a moment too late that he'd miscalculated. He'd forgotten about the damp road. It had rained early this morning, just enough to bring out the oil on the road, but not enough to wash it away. The tires tried to grip but failed, and before Ryan could even yell out a warning, or brace himself against the roof, the car was flipping, his stomach heaving as they rolled down the road in a cacophony of metal scraping against asphalt.

They finally slid to a halt, and the first thing Ryan did was frantically look over at Wyatt, who was slumped against the leather seat, eyes closed. He unbuckled, and immediately started checking him for injuries, heart beating a thousand miles per hour. Faster than he'd ever driven. Faster than he'd ever drive again.

"Oh god, oh god, oh god," he chanted under his breath as he realized Wyatt's arm was crooked at an awkward angle. And when his hands reached up to set his head at a better angle, they came away wet and red.

He smeared blood everywhere as he dug his phone out of his pocket and dialed 911. All over his phone and his shirt and the leather interior of the car. Streaks of rusty red everywhere.

The operator answered immediately, asking him the emergency and taking down the information as Ryan spit it out, voice shaky.

"Are you hurt?" the operator asked.

"No, I'm fine, I'm fine. But my boyfriend, he's not fine. I think his arm is broken, and he's knocked out. I think he hit his head against the window. Oh god, what if he's dead?" It had never occurred to Ryan to check his breathing, but now he did, pressing his fingers against the artery in his neck to feel the blood beating there.

The pulse was faint but it was there, sluggishly beating against his fingertips. "We need an ambulance *now*," Ryan demanded. Fear was making him nauseous. Wyatt still hadn't moved. His face was pale and unresponsive.

"Don't move him out of the car," the operator ordered. "The ambulance will be there shortly. Maybe keep talking to him, see if you can wake him up. And if he does, keep him calm."

Ryan set the phone down and did his best to cradle Wyatt's head so it wouldn't flop. "I'm so fucking sorry," he whispered to him. "And I'm going to damn well apologize for this because it's my fault again. Showing off, trying to get your attention. I just . . . I'm so afraid you won't see me otherwise. That you won't stay. That you'll find someone else, someone who doesn't have any problems. Someone who doesn't do stupid shit like drive too fast and end up hurting you."

Wyatt's fingers quivered against Ryan's, and he took that as the right sign and kept going.

"I love you," he said. And it felt like such a waste to say it now, when he could have said it fifteen minutes ago, when they were both fine. Angry, but fine. When Wyatt might have been more receptive to hearing it. When they weren't lying in a heap of mangled metal and plastic, and Wyatt's blood wasn't all over Ryan's hands.

"I love you," he repeated again, heart in his throat, "please don't fucking leave me. Not like this."

⁂

"Let me get this straight," Eric said, his voice a hardened mask, no doubt hiding apoplectic anger. He hadn't been still since arriving at the hospital five minutes earlier, pacing in the hallway with Ryan outside of Wyatt's room. "Instead of going out tonight and fixing *last night,* you took Wyatt out to dinner. But you never made it to the restaurant because you crashed your Maserati and now Wyatt has a broken arm and a concussion."

Ryan hadn't thought it was possible for the events of the evening to sound any worse, but somehow they did, recited through Eric's clenched teeth.

"That sounds about right," he said morosely.

"You told me you want this," Eric said. "You begged me to find a way to fix your management's opinion that you're reckless and careless with your personal safety. I told you I'd help you, and I've been fucking *trying.*"

Nobody liked Eric much, Ryan included, but it was hard to deny that he'd been trying, despite all the ways Ryan fucked up.

Eric threw his hands up in frustration. "I can't help you if you won't help yourself," he continued.

"It was a mistake. A mistake that won't happen again. I was . . . messed up over Wyatt."

"And just like that, you're *not* messed up over Wyatt?" Eric asked in disbelief. "To be honest, he's messed you up since the first night you met him. I don't think crashing your Maserati is going to help with that."

"It's not, it's not. I've been messed up because I was fighting how much I cared about him, but I'm not fighting it anymore. This is where I'm meant to be."

"In a hospital," Eric muttered under his breath. "Standing vigil over your injured boyfriend."

Ryan couldn't help but admit he wasn't always the world's quickest learner, but he'd learned now. He'd felt how easily it all could end. How silly it felt to keep fighting something when it felt so natural. He didn't know how he could have let it go on so long. He'd been a fucking moron, and maybe he could get out of this without paying the heaviest price. He leaned against the wall and wished Wyatt would wake up so he would know if he'd ever forgive him for almost killing both of them.

"I called you because you always told me to call if you things got . . . rough."

"It got rough alright. I'll clean this up because that's my job," Eric said. "But no more bullshit. It doesn't suit you."

"Agreed," Ryan said miserably.

Eric turned to go, but held back for a split second. He reached out, and for a grade A asshole, he had a pretty convincing sympathy face. "You're a good kid, Flores. Don't let the system change you."

Then he was gone, walking down the corridor with purpose, no doubt to start handing out non-disclosure agreements like party favors.

Ryan heard a very familiar shriek and looked up to see Flor walking fast and determined towards him, fury in her eyes.

He closed his own in supplication. This night had already been so long, and was growing longer.

⁂

Wyatt's arm really hurt. His head too. He didn't want to open his eyes because he was pretty sure that would hurt just as badly, but he needed to know who was saying those words. It was a voice he recognized. He was sure of it. He just couldn't place it right now because his brain was so fuzzy. He didn't even know why he was hurting.

"We could charge you for reckless driving," he heard someone say. Not a voice he recognized. It was harsh at the edges, and clearly pissed off. "And even though there weren't any other vehicles involved in the accident, your passenger could file charges since he ended up in the hospital."

Accident. He had vague flashes of screaming metal and a surge of fear and then nothing. A voice in the darkness, reaching out to him. Begging for him to wake up.

Wyatt strained, anxious to hear the other voice in the conversation, hoping that it was the man who had been so desperate for him to be alright.

The man who loved him.

But the voice who responded wasn't his at all. "Officer," the accented voice said insistently, "it was just an accident. The road was slick. You said so. And Ryan, he's sorry. He's learned his lesson."

"To the tune of a wrecked Maserati?" the same official voice retorted dryly. "I'm sure he has. But I will need to check in with Mr. Blake and make sure that he doesn't want to file charges."

"When he's awake, you can speak to him if you like," the accented voice continued. "Right, Ryan?"

Ryan. That sounded familiar. Was Ryan the man who'd professed his love in the car?

Wyatt, struggling through the fog in his brain, thought that might be the same man.

"I . . . Ryan . . ." he forced in a harsh whisper. His mouth was so dry and tasted smoky and metallic. The echo of blood and pain.

He hadn't managed to open his eyes yet, but the moment he spoke, there was a person at the bed next to him, cradling his hand in his two hands. They were big palms, creased with callouses. Capable hands, hands he could be safe with, despite his presence in a hospital bed that seemed to prove otherwise.

"Wyatt, are you awake?"

That was the voice. This was the man.

He finally opened his eyes and a thousand memories came rushing back at the sight of his face. Dark eyes, pleading and terrified, stared back at him. Blood spatter on his white button-down shirt.

They were supposed to be on a date. At a restaurant. At a public place. Getting their pictures taken. He'd been angry; *so* angry, but that felt so far away now.

"I'm sorry," Wyatt said, and Ryan laughed wetly, wiping his face with a blood-splattered hand.

"If I'm not allowed to apologize again, neither are you," he said, leaning down so Wyatt could catch the words.

"My arm hurts," Wyatt said matter-of-factly. He didn't want to look over and see why it was immobilized. Did he even still have it? Was the pain just a phantom reminder of the limb he'd used to have?

"It's broken, but it was a clean break. The doctor thinks it'll heal quick and you'll be back in the ocean with me soon," Ryan promised. "And you have a mild concussion, from a contusion on the back of your head."

"The blood?" Wyatt asked, lifting his good hand, and gesturing to the bright red all of Ryan's shirt.

"It's yours," Ryan said wryly. "I only have a few minor scratches. A bruise or two. I'll be fine."

And then it hit Wyatt head-on. Ryan had been the driver of the car. The rest came rushing back: Ryan driving way too fast. Wyatt demanding he slow down and Ryan not listening. Hitting the slick spot.

"Eric is gonna kill you," Wyatt said. "If I don't first."

"You're upset," Ryan suggested hesitantly.

"What the fuck were you thinking?" Wyatt demanded, even though the tone of his own voice made his heart hurt worse.

Ryan shoved his hands into his pockets. "I'm not sure we should be talking about this now," he said hesitantly, voice wavering. Wyatt had seen Ryan Flores in a lot of moods, but never like this. Never diminished, scared, *guilty*.

Wyatt looked around, taking in Flor hovering in the doorway, blocking the police officer he'd heard earlier. "Can we have the room, please?" he asked, and Flor nodded immediately, shutting the door behind her a moment later.

Leaving him and Ryan alone.

"If you want to call it off, you can," Ryan said nervously.

"I don't want to call it off." Wyatt's head kept aching and Ryan's behavior was somehow making it ache worse. "I want to figure this shit out, once and for all." He paused, collecting his thoughts, the shards of memory that kept fitting back in place, one at a time. "You told me you loved me."

"I do, I do love you. I was . . . so scared you'd leave. Scared you were only sticking around because you said you would. Maybe because you didn't want to get sued." Ryan laughed, self-consciously and without much humor. "You told me you'd stick around because you wanted to learn to trust me again. But you were angry in the car, and I was afraid it was all ending again, and I . . . got desperate."

Wyatt took a deep breath, trying to keep his temper because the closer he got to the edge, the more he hurt. And he didn't want to have any more to blame Ryan for. "I love you, you fucking idiot. I'm not going anywhere."

Hope flared in Ryan's eyes. "How can you even say that after . . ."

"After you wrecked your Maserati and almost killed us?" It was Wyatt's turn to chuckle at the irony. "God only knows. Maybe because I know how much fear can control you. It controlled me for so long, how can I blame you for falling victim to it?"

"I didn't think about it that way," Ryan said and the stiffness in his back was softening a little, bringing him closer to Wyatt's side.

It was all instinct to reach out and take Ryan's hand, curl it in his own, despite the ache in his bones. Ryan gripped it fiercely, like a lifeline.

"We don't have to know everything right now. We don't have to figure everything out right now," Wyatt said. "That's all I meant earlier. Honestly . . . I couldn't leave. Not now. Not before. I . . ." Maybe he should have felt ashamed as the tears clogged this throat and made it difficult to speak, but it had been an emotionally trying forty-eight hours, and he was reaching the end of his rope.

"I love you," Ryan said, finishing his own sentence. "I meant it earlier. I'm not . . . going to do this right. I promise. But I promise you that I will be there to figure it out afterwards. Every single time."

There wasn't complete peace and acceptance in Ryan's dark eyes as he gazed down at Wyatt, but there was more. The fear was receding, and Wyatt felt it leaking out his own mind, along with the anger.

On cue, there was a brisk knock at the door. Ryan raised his head and reluctantly let go of Wyatt's hand to answer it.

It was the police officer. Of course.

"I need to take his statement," he said gruffly. "Now that he's awake."

Ryan looked over at Wyatt, who inclined his head in agreement.

The police officer walked in, and took up a spot at the end of Wyatt's hospital bed. Ryan resumed his previous spot, and grasped Wyatt's hand like he'd never let it go again.

"Mr. Blake," the officer said, "could you please tell me what you remember about the accident?"

"Do we have to do this right now?" Wyatt asked, even though he already knew the answer.

"Yes," the officer said, unrelenting.

So Wyatt quickly and efficiently rehashed what he remembered from the accident. They'd been driving fast, maybe, he relented, but not outrageously fast. The road had definitely been slick. They'd flipped a couple of times. He didn't remember much else.

"And what about charges, Mr. Blake?" the officer asked expectantly.

"Charges?" he asked blankly. "Why would I want to file charges?"

"Mr. Flores' reckless driving endangered your life," he reminded Wyatt.

"Mr. Flores," Wyatt pointed out, voice as clear and strong as he could make it, "despite some lapses in judgment, is *mine*." Ryan's fingers spasmed against his. Flor reached out a reassuring hand towards Ryan, but he brushed it away. "I'm not pressing charges against him."

"Are you sure?" Ryan asked, but his voice was so hopeful. So full of love that Wyatt could almost block out the pain in his head.

"I'm definitely sure," Wyatt retorted dryly, tugging his hand and bringing Ryan closer. Close enough to kiss. Maybe he shouldn't have been, but he was.

The nurse outside must have heard the commotion, because she bustled in then, giving him some ice chips for his dry mouth, and talking about discharge papers after he saw the doctor again.

"I called Miles," Ryan admitted. "I left a voicemail. I think he was filming or something."

"Why did you call Miles?" Wyatt questioned.

"I wasn't sure . . . wasn't sure you wanted to be in the same car as me again. Not so soon, anyway," Ryan said, voice halting.

"Do you think I didn't mean it?" Wyatt asked.

"I know you do," Ryan said, his voice growing stronger again. "But I didn't know that then, and I wasn't ever going to presume your feelings for you again. But," he added, a wry grin blooming on his face, "I should probably call Miles and let him know his services are no longer required. And that you're not dead."

"Does this mean we can finally go home?" Wyatt said, in relief.

"I think the doctor needs to discharge you still," Ryan said.

Wyatt knew the look he shot his boyfriend was unfair. He did it anyway. He hated these hospital sheets—they were scratchy, and he had a feeling they'd frown at Ryan climbing into bed with him. And he definitely needed to feel Ryan against him very soon.

Ryan reached out and carefully pulled him against his side, hugging him close. "You want me to go get the doctor and get it over with," he stated, amusement bright in his voice.

"I do," Wyatt admitted. "Let's go home."

Ryan reached out and intertwined their hands together, and helped him sit upright in the bed. "Let's go home," he agreed easily, giving his hand a final squeeze before he turned away to go take care of the rest of the paperwork.

Ryan drove like Wyatt's nana the whole way home. Wyatt, a little tired and loopy from the pain pills, didn't tease him about it. He figured there was lots of time for that later. And just that thought was miraculous. Instead of an enforced ending, and a time limit, there was endless time extending before them, the possibilities never-ending and boundless.

The gate opened and Ryan carefully drove the rental Prius into the driveway. Right next to a looming black mass that hadn't been there when they'd left in the Maserati earlier in the evening.

"What's this?" Wyatt asked as Ryan came around to help him out of the car. He was a little unsteady on his feet, and the doctor hadn't wanted his arm jostled the first few days. Of course, that was the excuse Ryan had latched onto to practically never let go of him. Wyatt was definitely not going to tease him about that, because he was enjoying it too much.

It all felt like a dream come true, a hope and a wish coalesced into reality.

A fake boyfriend evolving into a real one.

Ryan helped him out of the car and they walked a few feet to the left of the big mass, just enough so that with the lights of the house, Wyatt could make out the faded writing on the stainless steel side.

"Tacos," Wyatt recited, realization dawning. "It's an old food truck."

"It's yours," Ryan said. "I love you being my personal chef. I hope you never stop. But I'm not selfish enough to want to keep you all to myself. You need to spread your wings. Experiment somewhere other than our kitchen."

Wyatt was speechless, staring at the stainless steel shell.

"It needs a lot of work," Ryan rambled on, "but I'm going to help you. It can be our project. Maybe even Tony will want to help. I got the impression he might, and you and your brother could use something to bring you together."

"You bought this for me," Wyatt said incredulously.

"I was trying to grovel. Might have gone over better if I hadn't wrecked the Maserati first. Oh, well. Anyway, in the morning, you can look in it. It's basically a wreck. I wanted to buy you a brand-new one, but Tabitha said that was overdoing it."

"She would be right," Wyatt said. "This is still too much."

"Trust me, you haven't seen the interior. It needs a *lot* of work. You might think it's not enough in the light of day."

"I don't think so," Wyatt said, and turned towards Ryan. "I thought you were afraid of me leaving. But you just gave me the ability to leave."

"I was, I *am*. But someone told me once that letting love in means you need to accept what you're afraid of." Ryan's voice was wry. "I told you before I'm not going to be good at this. But I'm going to try, every single day. Today, this is me trying."

Wyatt raised his good hand to Ryan's face, cradling his jaw. "I love you. I'm not going anywhere. Even if you try and fail. Even when I fail. We're in this together."

"Together," Ryan echoed, and leaned in and kissed him.

EPILOGUE

THE FOOD TRUCK SHONE bright silver under the merciless LA sun. "What A Catch" was painted in a handwritten green script along the side of the truck, the letters nearly reaching the top of Wyatt's head as he stood in front and critically eyed the setup.

"I still don't think the menu is big enough. The letters are still hard to read from a medium distance," Wyatt said, raising his voice so Tony could hear him from inside.

"We sell enough tacos to buy a new chalkboard today, you can have it," Tony shouted back at him, the rhythmic chopping sound of his knife against the butcher block countertops they'd installed last week nearly drowning out his voice, and the Foo Fighters playing on the Bluetooth speaker.

The Foos were more Tony's scene than Wyatt's—he liked his food prep music a little chiller—but in this brand-new joint venture between the brothers, compromise had quickly become one of the most vital ingredients.

Wyatt rolled his eyes even though Tony couldn't see him. "We're not selling any tacos today, dipshit."

Tony popped his head out the back door. His hair had grown out a little in the six months since they'd started rehabbing this truck, but it was still cut close to his skull, and a few more tattoos decorated his forearms. The two most important were also the smallest: a bright pink, yellow, and blue pansexual flag and a tiny, red, split heart. Tony had opened up much more about the former than the latter. He still wouldn't talk about the first guy to break his heart—the first *person* to break his heart, if Wyatt was being specific, because Tony had always been the one to do the heart-breaking—but Wyatt hoped he would soon. Tony was clearly hurting, no matter what sort of jovial front he put on.

"That's right," Tony snarked right back. "We're *giving* them away to your boyfriend."

"My boyfriend's team," Wyatt corrected. "And I think catering a charity event of the Los Angeles Dodgers our first time out is a really great achievement."

"I'll say this," Tony said casually, and Wyatt almost missed the hint of pride in his voice, "you don't like to start small."

Wyatt didn't have to ask who Tony was proud of. It was definitely both of them. Probably because they'd managed to do it together, without killing each other. A real achievement that had never been a sure thing, and had been touch-and-go more than once.

The truth was, Wyatt didn't like taking charity from Ryan. They'd begun their relationship—the fake one at least—with inequality, and Wyatt had spent the last eight months trying to figure out the right balance between them.

"He offered to pay for them," Wyatt pointed out. He had, and Wyatt had turned him down flat. Ryan had already done enough getting them the gig and an opportunity to iron out the kinks that went with opening a restaurant, even if it was on wheels.

Especially if it was on wheels.

"Where is he, anyway? I thought he was getting here early to help us set up?"

"I think he had a last-minute meeting come up," Wyatt said. "I'll come in and help you finish prep. It's not like he could've helped with that anyway."

Wyatt followed Tony into the small cabin of the food truck. It was a tight fit with the two of them, but at least he didn't have to stoop. He'd paid a lot more than he should have to get the roof raised just enough that neither of them had to stoop.

They fell into their regular rhythm which until eight months ago, Wyatt never would have guessed even existed. He'd believed he and Tony were so different for so long that figuring they were more alike than he'd ever imagined had turned his world topsy-turvy.

As soon as he'd regained his equilibrium, he'd realized just how much he *liked* his brother.

Ryan had looked very smug when Wyatt had admitted this one night.

"I knew you would. Or that you did? I'm not sure which is right," Ryan admitted. "Sometimes it takes a shakeup to see what's right in front of you."

"A shakeup in the form of a wrecked Maserati?" Wyatt had teased.

Ryan hit him hard in the shoulder. It stung, offsetting the pleasurable afterglow from the sex they'd just had.

"I told you that wasn't going to get old," Wyatt teased again.

"I thought real dating would mean more sappy, cheesy fluff, and less tormenting me," Ryan said mournfully.

"But the tormenting is so fun," Wyatt said with a chuckle.

Wyatt could still feel the warmth of Ryan's smile as he'd gazed lovingly at him, even months later.

"Hey, you sappy idiot," Tony called over, "did you get the pulled pork on to heat?"

Wyatt awkwardly pointed an elbow at where the big hotel pans were warming in a water bath. "I might be sappy but I'm not an idiot," he retorted.

"You and Ryan disgust me," Tony said, shaking his head. "You were just thinking about him, I could tell you were. You get this incredibly fond look on your face, like you're staring at him and he's not even fucking there."

"I spend a lot of time imagining his face instead of actually seeing it," Wyatt argued.

"Even the long distance hasn't dimmed your honeymoon period." Tony lifted up a big cardboard box of butter lettuce and with a few efficient movements began breaking each head into individual leaves.

"And it's not going to," Wyatt said. "Not even now that Ryan's signed his new contract and he's going to be playing for the Dodgers for years to come."

Wyatt wanted to tell his brother he was just jealous, but he didn't because he *was* and that was the whole problem. Not of Ryan, specifically, but of the forever happiness that Wyatt had found with him.

Frankly they were so blissfully in love, it was a miracle the world wasn't jealous. Instead, the world ate it up with a spoon. Without even trying, Wyatt had somehow become *the* chef in LA to follow on Instagram, and when he'd worn Ryan's jersey to Opening Day, the picture had gone viral.

It would have been so easy to lose their way with all the publicity and the attention, and with the shaky beginning of their relationship, Wyatt should have been more worried. But Ryan had never once given him cause to worry.

For someone who'd claimed he didn't want a relationship because all relationships became boring eventually, Ryan had fully and completely embraced their coupledom.

And when, late one night while binge-watching a show on Netflix, Ryan had leaned over and said, "I think I'm bored now," Wyatt had never been happier.

It was the only time since the accident that he'd ever brought it up, and the last time too.

"Hey, you guys in there?"

Wyatt turned around, and Ryan had just pulled up next to the food truck, driving a white Range Rover. He'd stuck his head out the open window, and Wyatt put down the knife and emerged just as he climbed out.

"You're late," Tony grumped, though his tone didn't have any heat in it.

"I know, but I was running an important errand. Picking someone up from the airport, actually," Ryan said, going to the passenger door and opening it. To Wyatt's shock, the snowy-white hair of his nana emerged, shining in the sun.

"You brought Nana," Wyatt said, dumbfounded.

Ryan's smile was warm as he carefully helped Bea out of the back of the SUV. "I did. She deserved to be here, to watch her boys open their brand-new food truck."

"Wyatt," Bea exclaimed, walking towards the truck and intercepting Tony, giving him a hug, "it looks even better than the pictures. And, Tony, I'm so proud of you."

Wyatt climbed down, and wrapped her in a long hug after his brother released her. "I'm so glad you came," he whispered into her shoulder, glancing up to see Ryan staring at them, a soft look in his dark eyes. "Ryan always has the best surprises."

"That's because he's lovely, darling," Nana whispered to him. "You marry that boy, you hear me?"

Wyatt surreptitiously wiped the moisture out of his eyes before Tony could see and make fun of him. "I'm sure going to try."

"It's beautiful, *hijo*. You didn't tell me how shiny it is." Wyatt finally let go of Bea, and met *Titi* Flor's loving stare.

"Wyatt, you have much to be proud of," she said, reaching him and wrapping him in a big, warm hug.

Wyatt's gaze locked with Ryan's. He looked only a little embarrassed. "I figured it would be good for Nana to have someone to look after her," he said, "and Flor wasn't going to be left at home today."

"You should all be here today," Wyatt said, throat suddenly tight with emotion. "Tony and I couldn't have done it without you."

"You could have," Ryan said, his voice a vow, "but we're happy we could be here to share it with you."

Flor led Bea off to one of the decorated picnic tables, chattering the whole way, the older lady smiling and offering her own opinion right back.

"Those two could run the world if they set their mind to it," Ryan said fondly, as Wyatt wrapped an arm around his waist.

"It was a great surprise," Wyatt said seriously, "thank you for making sure she was here."

"You want to make the most of the time you have left with her, and whatever you want is what I want," Ryan said, reaching over to cup Wyatt's cheek in his palm. "I love you."

It wasn't the right time, or the right place, or like anything that Wyatt had started vaguely planning in his head. But suddenly the thought was there, stark and bright and so right it overpowered everything else.

"Marry me," Wyatt choked out. Ryan's eyes grew wide. "Not today, not now. Just someday. Promise me, we'll do it before she can't remember."

Wyatt remembered all too well those dark times before he'd met Ryan when he'd been determined that the last memory his nana had of him would be a lie. Now he wanted to shine as much light and beauty and truth onto her last days as he could.

And what was lighter or more beautiful or more full of honesty than a wedding?

"Damn you," Ryan laughed, the love in his eyes swamping Wyatt, "just had to steal my thunder."

"You were going to propose?" They hadn't even talked about it, but Wyatt couldn't say he was surprised. Ryan, once he had figured out that Wyatt was what he wanted, had been the best boyfriend. Not a perfect one, but he'd kept his promise and was a real one.

"Someday," Ryan said with a bright grin.

"I think that's a yes," Wyatt said, pulling him in even tighter.

His only answer was to put his hand in Wyatt's, and kiss him hot and fierce—for forever.

THE TRAINEE

A CATCH ME SHORT STORY

"ARE YOU FUCKING KIDDING me?" Alex barked, staring at his boss, Marcella, like she'd just grown a third head. Or just saddled him with a brand new trainee on his first shift during Halloween, one of the most insane nights of the year at Temple.

Alex wished she'd just grown a third head instead. That might have been easier to deal with.

"You're a pro, this isn't a big deal," Marcella insisted, tucking a long strand of hair behind an ear. She was on the shorter side, and deceptively sweet looking for someone who ran one of the hottest gay clubs in West Hollywood and did do with unflinching resolve and an iron fist.

He'd long learned that arguing with Marcella was pointless and only ended up an exercise in frustration. Before he'd gotten on her good side, he'd discovered how shitty it felt to be on her bad side.

Of course, having Marcella trust him wasn't much better, because now she'd handpicked Alex to take a newbie under his wing on Halloween.

"Does he even have any serving experience?" Alex asked, leaning back against the narrow hallway to the employee locker room.

"He's really cute," Marcella said, which was totally a non-answer. The sort of non-answer she was (in) famous for.

"That's a no," Alex said with a sigh.

Her eyes flashed, and he remembered, unpleasantly, what it had been like when she didn't like him. "Maybe you shouldn't have scared the last three newbies away. Then you wouldn't have to train one tonight."

It hadn't been entirely Alex's fault. They'd been stupid and slow and further proof that a pretty face didn't mean that you had a brain underneath it. And yes, he'd even fired the last one himself—he'd found him giving a blowjob to a customer in the VIP restroom.

Alex might have even let that slide, but it had meant he'd been dealing with a full and busy VIP section all on his own, and that had just pissed him off. You wanted to get down with some of the customers? Then do so on your own fucking time.

"I can't keep finding pretty gay boys who want to work here," Marcella complained, which was completely untrue. Alex was sure there was a metaphorical queue down to Tijuana because Temple was well-known and as waiting jobs went, it definitely paid well. Also, there was the bonus that a hookup was always easy to find; Alex hadn't been on Grindr in months.

"I'll take care of him," Alex ground out between clenched teeth. He knew what Marcella was really saying. She wasn't happy that she had to keep producing candidates for Alex to fire or who quit after only one of Alex's withering stares.

It didn't matter that if a guy couldn't handle Alex, there was no fucking way he was going to be able to work at Temple. As far as Marcella was concerned, that wasn't her fucking problem.

"Excellent." Marcella didn't even look surprised, because she wasn't. Alex could probably work somewhere else, he knew that much, but he liked this job, and he wanted to keep it. "He's in the front, filling out paperwork, and I'll send him back when he's done."

Alex turned towards the grimy mirror, covered with years of who knew what substances, and slipped on the leather harness his wings clipped to. Temple was a paean to most everything churches didn't stand for—specifically lust and intoxication—and also took advantage by adopting religious imagery and subverting it. The stained glass and hardwood pews decorating the interior were just the beginning. The wait staff and dancers were usually also decked out in costumes, which meant that Halloween wasn't really that different for the employees. He checked his eyeliner and used his thumb to wipe away a nonexistent smudge under a startling blue eye.

He knew he looked good; he couldn't look anything else and work here. Could he do without the constant stream of sexual offers and groping hands? Of course. But he also got great tips, especially with working the VIP lounge like he had been the last year. Also, most celebs knew better than to feel up the staff; that shit gone around fast, and for so much of Hollywood, queer was still a bad word.

"Are you Alex?"

Alex glanced up, and gave an inward groan.

The boy in the doorway—*man*, he reminded himself, because Marcella was adamant about only hiring over twenty one—was so green he was practically glowing with it.

He was definitely just over the age limit, and seemed perfectly designed to fit the twink label. Small and slight, but with surprisingly developed abs and biceps, his blond hair carelessly swept across his forehead. Wary green eyes studied Alex, while all he could imagine was how well this kid was going to go over here.

Alex was going to spend the whole shift trying to keep the newbie from getting lured into the bathrooms.

"I'm Alex," he said shortly. He reached out, and they shook, the kid's hand surprisingly firm, and even though Alex could tell he was nervous and apprehensive, he also looked determined. Something that had been in short supply with the other newbies he'd tried to train over the last month.

"Matt," the kid said. "I brought my costume. Where should I change?"

"Costume?" Alex raised an eyebrow. Hadn't Marcella told him that Temple provided its own costumes?

"It's Halloween!" Matt said, sounding far too excited for someone who must have left his trick or treating years behind him. Right?

Alex barely held back a snort of laughter. "Everyday is Halloween here." And then because Marcella had basically insisted he tread lightly around this one, continued. "Show me what you've got." Maybe Matt had something good, and that's why he'd brought it. For example, after a few months of work, Alex had invested in his own leather harness to hold up his wings, after he'd gotten sick of the cheap canvas crap that Temple had.

Matt pulled a huge bright yellow coat out of the duffel bag at his feet and then a wide brimmed hat, followed by the crowning achievement, an enormous pair of boots that looked like they'd absolutely dwarf him.

"What's this?" Alex asked, even though he already knew.

"My costume!" Matt's excitement was undiminished despite Alex's frown. It boded well for his ability to not storm out when shot a chastising look during service, but maybe it only proved just how naïve he was.

"You're a . . .firefighter?"

"It's a classic," Matt said. "That's what the rental store said anyway."

"It would be. But this is Temple, and people come here for something a little. . .different," Alex said, trying to explain gently. But he was no good at gentle, which was why he was a shitty person to be training anybody. Especially someone with those woodland hill eyes straight out of a Disney DVD.

Alex went over to the costume wardrobe, sized up Matt with a quick head to toe sweep, and pulled out the first thing in approximately his size.

"What is that?" Matt asked, eyeing the fabric, or lack of, dubiously.

"It's a priest robe," he told him, pushing the costume Matt's direction. "Try it on."

Matt did not look convinced. "It doesn't close in the front?"

It was difficult to refrain from a bitter chuckle, but Alex did it by sheer strength of will, and also a weird little pulse of sympathy for the sweet kid in front of him who was about to get chewed up and spit out by a system he clearly wasn't familiar with.

"It doesn't close in the front," Alex confirmed. "So you're going to wear this." He reached into the wardrobe again, grabbed a pair of gold lamé briefs, and tossed them Matt's direction.

He caught the briefs and stared at them like they were about to bite him. Glancing back up, his voice took on a beseeching edge. Like Alex could somehow save him from this, even though this was exactly what he had signed up for. "But I'm an actor," he said, like this explained and validated every single one of his concerns.

Alex sighed heavily. "Then act like you god damn like it," he said with finality. "Go get changed. We have a lot to go over before the doors open."

Matt did not know what he'd been expecting, exactly, when he'd agreed to take a job as a waiter in the VIP section at Temple. His agent hadn't been thrilled about the offer, but with nobody biting after so many auditions, Matt needed a job. At least this one meant he might meet people from Hollywood with connections. Working at the Coffee Bean wasn't going to get him anywhere, but this might.

Still, he couldn't stop staring at the gold briefs in his hands with trepidation. This was not what he'd expected, but then that wasn't Alex's fault. It also definitely wasn't Alex's fault that he was both incredibly hot and incredibly daunting, with his perfectly styled dark hair swept back from his gorgeous face, and those intimidating light blue eyes, flawlessly lined with black, staring at him fiercely.

Staring at him like he expected Matt to fail. Staring at him like he expected that Matt wouldn't make it even ten seconds in a club like Temple.

It was the same damn thing he'd experienced in his small Midwestern home-town. Sweet, hopeless Matt, with his acting dreams, and that unfortunate proclivity for men.

Well, he'd sort of shown them. He'd made it to LA. He'd found lots of other men who didn't think he was weird at all. He just hadn't quite nailed that acting thing yet. The closest he'd gotten so far was potentially starring as Ryan Flores' fake boyfriend. And that hadn't even happened because Ryan had been so obviously in love with someone else and had shown him the door before Matt could get the job.

He'd loved watching the Dodgers play before this but whenever he saw Ryan now, he got an ugly twinge that was probably jealousy. Not jealousy of his real boyfriend, but jealousy that Ryan had a job he didn't only love, but that also paid him tons of cash.

Still, it was hard to resent someone who sent you box tickets. Even if Matt had to sell the tickets to pay for rent, the gesture had meant something. Of course he would have rather had the job instead.

He changed without saying a word. Alex had disappeared, wings swishing through the doorway with a practiced little half-turn, like he'd been born wearing them. And he seemed so at-ease with the idea, maybe he had.

He was definitely not born to be a priest, Matt thought to himself, staring at the mirror as he shrugged on the robe. The black-banded collar still went tightly around his neck, practically choking him, while the robe swished open freely to reveal his entirely bare body, leaving only his dick covered by gold lamé. He couldn't help but wish that his Iowan tormentors could see him now. They'd probably keel over dead.

"You look good."

Matt glanced up to see Alex back in the doorway. His eyes narrowed as he gave Matt another head to toe perusal, this time more leisurely. Yet it didn't really feel personal, like Alex was complimenting him, or the many hours Matt spent in the crappy gym at his apartment complex, but more like Alex was sizing him up for how other people might think of him.

It was stupid and completely counterproductive to doing this job and learning everything he could from his trainer, but Matt had a sudden and desperate urge to make Alex's brisk professionalism waver, if only for a moment. He wanted to affect him not as a peddler of hot male flesh, but as a man.

Alex stared at him steadily, and Matt met his gaze, staring right back. He had a feeling not many other employees or even club-goers were able to do that, because Alex softened a little. Not much, but enough.

"Yeah, you're going to do just fine," he said. "Just smile and give that little doe-eyed look every time anyone needs something. They'll forget they don't have their drink, because they'll want your number instead."

I want you to want my number, Matt thought, even though he knew how dumb that sounded. It didn't matter that he hadn't said it out loud, he still flinched.

"Don't worry, they won't bite," Alex said, reaching out to pat him on the arm. He hesitated, grinning a little. The smile made him look far more attainable than the brooding stare ever could. "Probably."

Matt knew he was cute, not hot, but he pasted on the best seductive look in his acting toolkit. After all there weren't many who could look at Alex in all his winged glory and not at least try to get his attention.

"So how does this work?" Matt asked, trying to sound confident when he didn't feel confident at all. They emerged from the back of the club onto the main floor, with the VIP section to the right, two main bars flanking either side, and the dance floor with its pulsating lights and stage for the dancer right in the center.

"We're VIP waitstaff," Alex said as they walked into the roped off section. "That means everyone you serve is probably going to get bottle service."

"Bottle service?" Matt had never felt so far from Iowa.

Alex, who'd seemed more sympathetic in the last five minutes, actually honest-to-god flinched. "You don't know what bottle service is? How did you even get this job?"

It would definitely suck to get this job and then lose it before he even collected a single tip.

"I told Marcella I was an actor," Matt said, which he had a feeling wasn't why he'd gotten the job. He'd worn the tightest lowest-necked white t-shirt he had, one of the few that had lasted through his bulk-up once he'd gotten to LA and realized that it didn't matter how convincingly he could cry on camera. If he didn't have any muscles of which to speak of, he wasn't even going to make it to the audition phase of a role.

The shirt had been tight and Marcella had looked him over much the same as Alex had done—head to toe, like a slab of meat instead of a person. Of course Matt wanted to be a person, but if slabs of meat got a regular paycheck, he could be fine with that too.

Alex sighed. "I'm sure that's the resume point that persuaded her," he said, not sounding at all convinced that Matt's fledgling acting career meant jack shit to Marcella.

"Bottle service?" Matt prompted again, because he didn't want Alex to go down the path towards, *why do you even have this job?* He wanted Alex to stick firmly in the, *how do I train him?* category.

"Bottle service," Alex confirmed. "VIPs will pay up the ass for a bottle of alcohol, usually several. And they'll get mixers and ice, which we'll stash in these drawers built into the tables." He pointed to the discreet drawers under the table surface. "We have an unofficial tab guideline for VIP tables. If your table looks like they aren't going to drop 5k, you need to get them out of there."

Matt had been in Los Angeles for almost a year now. He knew because it was impossible to not know how extravagantly some people lived in this city, but he still had to do a mental adjustment to wrap his head around dropping five thousand dollars just for booze.

"How do I get them out?" Matt asked.

"Flex and ask nicely. And if that doesn't work, call security."

"Right," Matt muttered. He had a feeling he was going to be calling security every time.

"It doesn't happen very often," Alex added. "Especially on nights like tonight. I just wanted to warn you because Marcella will have your head if the VIP tables don't pay out."

Matt wanted to believe the way Alex's unnaturally light eyes lingered on his exposed abs, making his skin prickle, and the concern in his voice meant he might care a little what happened to him. But maybe Alex just didn't want to train another newbie.

"She seems . . .tough." That was the nicest description Matt could come up with.

Alex nodded. "But she'll have your back." He hesitated. "And I will too. Let's go over the shot specials."

"Aren't I a waiter though? Not a bartender?" Matt asked as they walked towards one of the huge bars flanking the dance floor.

They stopped at one of the computer terminals. "You'll be anything you need to be, especially on busy nights like tonight." He sighed. "Let me guess, you're more used to men buying drinks for you than pouring them for yourself."

Matt couldn't help himself; he laughed. "No. No. Not at all, actually. Wait," he asked. "are you saying that because you think I'm hot?"

Alex rolled his eyes. "We work here. We're all hot." But there was an uncomfortably honest glint in his light eyes. Like he'd been caught and he hadn't really wanted to be.

"Right, okay. Well, I'm not actually a big drinker. I'm a depressing drunk and so I don't tend to have more than one or two at a time."

To Matt's surprise, this news was not met with more eyerolls or disbelieving looks. Alex just carried on like Matt hadn't confided in him, explaining the point of sale system, how to swipe his employee card. How to order drinks. How to run tabs. How to cash out tabs.

"There shouldn't be any crazy money situations happening in VIP," Alex said as a way of finishing up. "Most people who come here know what it costs and are prepared to pay for it. But I'll be around if you run into trouble."

"I appreciate that." Matt flashed him his friendliest smile. "I'll probably end up taking advantage of that."

"It's why I'm here," Alex pointed out wryly. "I wouldn't be much of a trainer otherwise."

Matt remembered how, before he'd gone to find Alex in the back, Marcella had warned him that he'd scared off the last three new trainees. And that he shouldn't let Alex "intimidate him" with his glowering or his generally bad temper.

It had been impossible not to brace himself for the worst, but while Alex seemed passingly frustrated with his lack of experience, he wasn't mean or cruel like Marcella had hinted at.

Still, he wasn't going to risk Alex's anger by repeating any part of that conversation now.

"You're a great trainer," Matt said with enthusiasm, and Alex nearly chuckled. Matt could almost see him holding back. "I guess how good you are remains to be seen."

"No, you're just . . .precious," Alex said, and while that might not have been a compliment it was hard not to take it as one.

At least that was what Matt told himself as Alex moved them behind the bar and showed him where all the different bottles and mixers were kept. He even pointed out the book with the plastic coated pages that detailed all the drink recipes he could ever need to make.

Right after they finished at the bar, the music increased in volume, and Matt was grateful he'd ducked out on that concert last week due to lack of funds. Not that his hearing was probably to continue to stay excellent—not with the pounding bass reverberating through him.

"You feel ready?" Alex asked, touching his robed arm to get his attention.

Matt didn't feel ready for anything except Alex touching him again. And maybe someplace else than the polyester fabric he was currently wearing. Still, he nodded. He needed this job. Visions of red stamped final notice envelopes piled on his kitchen counter told him that he was as ready as he would ever be.

"Looks like we've got our first table," Alex said. The bar was steadily filling, and they watched as a group was led past the velvet rope into the VIP section.

"What are they wearing?" Matt asked, squinting to see through the dark room and the strobing lights.

Alex tilted his head, and a smile curled up the edges of his lips. "Sexy Avengers?"

Iron Man was wearing a pair of red leather pants, a helmet, and a glowing light glued to the middle of his bare chest. Thor was in a big blond wig and jeans. Following the theme, he carried a big hammer but wasn't wearing a shirt either. Another man was painted head to toe in green body paint. Hulk, Matt realized.

"Do you think they know?" Matt leaned in closer, so Alex could hear him better. Or at least that was what he told himself. He caught a strong whiff of Alex—woods and pine and something lighter, something sweeter. Matt told his mouth to stop watering and that he wasn't going to be getting it on Alex's skin or any other part of Alex anytime soon.

"That they look stupid?" Alex chuckled, the first laugh Matt had gotten out of him. "Trust me, that's nothing." He glanced over at Matt's half-a-robe and gold lamé briefs and Matt had to smile back in agreement.

"Point taken," Matt said. "Let's go see if these heroes are thirsty."

"They always are," Alex said, and they walked towards the VIP section.

The problem wasn't that Matt was new or clueless or didn't even really drink.

No, the biggest problem was that Matt was nice and had kind eyes and really fantastic abs. Matt was incredibly distracting, and not because Alex was having to bail him out constantly.

Like Alex had anticipated after meeting him and spending half an hour with him, Matt took to waiting tables in VIP like a duck to water. Most of the time Alex thought Marcella was full of shit, but she'd been absolutely right about this guy.

He had a totally different vibe than Alex's smoldering, sexy glower. He was sweet and almost innocently flirtatious, chattering genuinely to everyone he met, and the guys in VIP, who all loved attention thus why they were dumping lots of money to be the center of attention, ate it up.

Alex had given Matt the Sexy Avengers table, and had kept half an eye on him the whole time. His own table, full of half-hearted ninjas with cheap black masks and fake plastic nunchucks and swords, weren't very much work, because they were a quiet, somewhat understated bunch. He was pretty sure they were a bunch of music execs from Columbia, and a year and a half ago, he would have shit himself and tried to pass them a demo tape. But tonight, he just accepted their crappy costumes and that they were all involved in their phones.

The upside was they definitely drank a lot, and Alex could appreciate that. While he was on the way to grab another bottle of Grey Goose, he ran into Matt at the POS computer.

"Everything okay?" he asked. The crowd was surging and the music had gotten impossibly even louder, but Matt was still smiling and it didn't even look fake. Either Matt was a really great actor, or he was actually enjoying this job.

"Oh yeah," Matt said, smiling over at him as he punched buttons confidently. Alex observed out of the corner of his eye and to his own surprise, they were all right.

Alex lifted an eyebrow. "The guys at my table are super nice," he confided. "But you're right, they all want my number."

A man would have to be committed for life or dead not to want this magical ray of sly sunshine in his life. Alex resolutely pushed that thought aside. He might pick men up at Temple, but he'd never slept with a fellow employee. You didn't shit where you ate, that much he knew. And Matt, Matt would never believe in just a hookup anyway. You could read it in his eyes and his face. He wanted sex, sure, but he also wanted to fall in love. He wanted cohabitation and to adopt a puppy or a kid someday. And Alex, who was supposed to want those things too, but had gotten jaded and bitter somewhere along that road, didn't want to be responsible for turning Matt into himself.

"We didn't cover that," Alex said carefully, his eyes glued to a patch of exposed skin that had a distinct greenish tint to it. Like he'd been rubbing up against the Hulk. Alex told himself that the flare of jealousy wasn't jealousy at all. It was professional concern.

The problem was it wasn't even a good lie.

"Cover what?" Matt asked in surprise.

"Hookups," Alex said bluntly.

Matt's eyes grew a little bigger.

"You're free to do whatever you want, after hours. Get as many numbers as you want," Alex said, and he knew he sounded like a harsh asshole, but there was that flare again, and he didn't want to call it what it was. Plain, old-fashioned jealousy. "Just don't bring any of that baggage here."

Matt stared up at him. "What if I don't want any numbers?"

Alex realized he must be gaping a little because Matt laughed self-consciously. "They're hot, yeah, and connected, and I guess I should. But I'm just not really interested."

Alex found his voice. "Then don't let them pressure you. Remember, security isn't just here to protect the patrons, it's here for us too."

Laughing, Matt held up his robed arm, and must have flexed because his abs tightened in a way that Alex absolutely did not find distracting. "I remember. Just flex, right?"

Matt's laugh echoed in his ears as he departed back to the VIP section, and Alex faced the computer, trying to remember what it was he'd even come over here for.

It took a good thirty seconds to remember, and by the time he made it back to the VIP section with the bottle of alcohol, the ninjas were restless. One of them had removed his mask and shot Alex a lazy glare.

"Where have you been?" he asked.

Alex had dealt with a multitude of shitty customers over the years. He'd learned to swallow his annoyance and his anger and deal with it. "It's a busy night," he offered non committedly as he set the bottle on the middle of the table and began refreshing drinks.

"Yeah, you were busy alright," one of the other ninjas snickered with a drunken belligerence. Again, nothing that Alex wasn't used to, but it was still a struggle to not react. "Busy flirting with the cute blond priest."

"You should ask him to leave the Avengers to their hero antics and come over here," another ninja chimed in. Alex's hand tightened on the bottle of Goose he was pouring. "You're hot but not any fun."

"I got you your vodka, didn't I?" Alex snapped finally. "And I wasn't flirting. I was training. He's new."

"Doesn't look new to me," the first ninja pointed out slyly. And damn him, Alex couldn't help but glance over to the Sexy Avengers table, where Matt was clearly laughing at something that Iron Man had just shown him on his phone. He looked relaxed and happy and not overwhelmed or overworked like Alex remembered being, having to socialize and have a good time with a bunch of strangers.

The truth was, Alex didn't know what he was more jealous of, the easy way Matt had fit in at Temple, or the way Iron Man was resting his hand casually across his back.

He had zero intention of asking Matt to hang out with the ninjas, who were drunk and getting drunker by the minute, if the way they were sucking down the new bottle of Grey Goose was any indication. But he went over to the Avengers table anyway, because no matter how fantastic Matt looked like he was doing, he'd made a promise to check on him.

Matt was still preoccupied by his conversation with Iron Man, and didn't hear Alex walk up.

"I didn't even know there were Iowa memes," Matt confided with a bright, excited voice. "I'm definitely going to follow that site as soon as I go on break."

"It's a little bit of home, even if I'd rather die than go back," Iron Man said, grinning. He'd taken off his helmet and he was handsome, with dark wavy hair and a jawline that could cut steel. Or iron, Alex thought humorlessly.

"Oh," Matt said turning around, "I didn't know you'd come over." There was an apology in his eyes, like he'd been caught doing something he shouldn't be.

"Just wanted to check in and see how you were doing," Alex said, trying for casual and not quite hitting it.

"Oh, I'm good. These guys are great," Matt said, beaming.

"There'll be a few more tables that'll show up right before the big costume contest," Alex pointed out. He wasn't trying to say that Matt had been slacking; it was clear he hadn't been. The drawers all looked full as various Avengers opened and closed them, fixing drinks. And there were several bottles of alcohol on the table. There wouldn't be a concern about the Avengers hitting the table minimum.

"That's fine," Matt said calmly. "Rick and I were just sharing some Midwestern memes. You know, can you parallel park a tractor?"

Any other night of the year—any other *person*—and Alex would have shook his head regretfully, no. He always pretended he didn't know anything about trailers or farms or harvests, but there must have been a Halloween spell in the air because the truth spilled out before he could stop it.

"Born in bred in rural Ohio, myself," Alex said wryly. "So yes, I do know about that."

It only hit Alex after he turned to leave what they had in common; and what they should never have in common.

He reached out and grabbed Matt's arm, closing it around the cheap fabric of the robe. He could feel the muscles underneath tense. And Alex couldn't help but wonder if Matt outwardly enjoying the Avengers touchy-feely flirtation was actually just an act.

Maybe Matt was a better actor than he'd believed. And if that was true, then they definitely needed to talk.

"Need you for a minute," Alex said, surprising himself with how rough his voice sounded.

"Sure," Matt said.

Alex took him back to the backroom, gesturing quickly to one of the other waiters to keep an eye out in the VIP. It was better they take their break now anyway, before it got closer to the big 1 AM costume contest. Typically they wouldn't take their breaks together, but with only two tables full right now, it would be fine.

"What's going on?" Matt asked, the confident smile slipping only when he thought he'd done something wrong.

"You're from Iowa?" Alex asked.

"Yeah, and you're from Ohio." Matt's smile came back, brighter than ever, like he'd just discovered the jackpot—something they had in common. And they did have something in common. Something that Alex wished to god they didn't.

"That's exactly the problem. You came to LA to be an actor and what, ditch all the mud and tractors and ignorance behind? Get some sun? Make it big?"

Matt nodded.

Alex grimaced. "I did too. I came here to be a musician. I believed my voice and my songs were too good for me not to make it. But you know what happened?"

Matt didn't speak. Didn't move.

"What happened," Alex growled out, "is that life got in the fucking way. *Reality* got in the fucking way. I learned that I was good but there's always someone around who's great. There's a million people in this town who all want something better, and there's never enough stardust to go around."

"I don't understand what this has to do with me," Matt said. There was a pucker, the very beginning of a frown forming between his blond brows, and it was the first time all night that he hadn't looked happy. And that was Alex's fault. He should stop now, while he was still ahead, but instead he plowed on recklessly.

"Because you're working here! You're a natural. Not quite the same style as me, but give it a year or two, and the shine will be a little more manufactured and you'll stop going to auditions, you'll stop calling your agent, you'll live and die by the tips here, and you'll be perfectly okay getting numbers for hookups."

Matt's gaze turned a little more calculating. "So basically what you're saying is that you don't want me to become you."

He ran his hand through his hair, not even caring if it looked like shit. Who was he even trying to impress anyway? The fucking ninjas? Thor? The Hulk?

"I'm saying you can't work here and not get stuck. Not when you could be as good at it as me. Just. . .just don't do it."

"I need this job," Matt said steadily. "And just because working here made you give up on your dreams doesn't mean that I'm going to give up on mine."

Alex stared at him. The light in the locker room was pathetic at best, a few rickety fluorescent bulbs illuminating everything a sickly green hue. But Matt shone, his blond hair glittering in the terrible light, nearly too good to be true. A mirror of everything that Alex had been, and a mirror of everything Alex had lost.

"I wanted to work here," Matt continued, "because important people come here. People who could help me in my career. I'm not here to drink on the downlow and hook up when I'm bored. I'm here because I want more and Temple is a stepping stone to that."

It was almost laughable. "I thought that too, at one point," Alex said. He'd long since stopped trying to pass off his demo recordings, and instead took the tips and phone numbers instead. Case in point: the ninjas back in VIP now. Even if Alex was still bringing his demo tapes to work, he wouldn't even have dreamt of trying to get them interested in his music.

Matt reached out for him, hands slipping up past the leather harness of his wings, to his neck. His hands were delicate but strong. Certain and sure, Alex thought with a tinge of despair.

"I want to hear you sing sometime," Matt said softly, and before Alex could warn him off, tell him this was the worst idea anyone had ever had, leaned in and kissed him.

If Alex had allowed himself to notice earlier, he would have thought how soft and pillowy Matt's lips looked, and how much he might want to do more than just look at them. Experiencing them was even better, his blood sluggishly pounding sticky sweet through his veins as he stood there still and let Matt kiss him.

If he kissed Matt back, he'd want to do more than just kiss him. He'd want to slide his hand down those hard-earned abs and feel his hardening dick in its gold lamé wrapping. He'd want to show Matt just how naughty angels could be.

Finally Matt pulled away. His lips were red and wet and Alex couldn't help it. He swallowed hard, his hands flexing at his sides. Matt's hand still cupped the side of his neck, warm and reassuring. "I just wanted you to know that I don't think you're a failure." He said it quietly, like he was afraid it would spook Alex.

Alex was not used to anyone being afraid of his darker feelings. He wasn't used to sharing them at all, or letting potential partners know they even existed.

What he should do now, before Matt walked away, was to tell him that he was a terrible choice for a hookup, but especially for a boyfriend. He should tell him that he didn't fuck with co-workers, that he had made it his personal mission to never shit where he ate. And yet, he didn't say any of those things. Couldn't quite his mouth to work properly. Maybe because he could still feel Alex's mouth on his own.

"I'll see you back out there," Matt continued when Alex still said nothing.

Alex was going to pretend like nothing had happened.

Matt wanted to be an actor for a reason, and that was because he was good at it, so he employed a few of the skills he'd learned in school and buried the frustration and rejection so far down nobody, even Iron Man, who was scary perceptive, could see it.

He'd noticed Matt's mood when he'd returned to the VIP section after kissing Alex.

"You hooking up with him?" Sexy Tony Stark had asked, leering a little.

"It's not like that," Matt had answered shortly. But it could be, he knew it could be, and it could be so much more than just a casual hookup in a backroom when they were both horny. He'd felt the pain in Alex's voice when he'd talked about giving up and seen the hope flash when Matt had insisted that he never would.

He hadn't been lying. He wanted to hear Alex sing. He wanted to see the genuine smile he tried to hide away in favor of that mysterious brooding smirk.

"But you want it to be," Hulk chimed in.

"He's hot," Matt said, like that was all Alex brought to the table, and even he could tell he was lying. So much for being a good actor.

"And there's that mystery that floats around him like a cloud," Thor pointed out. "That's not attractive at all."

"Okay, I'm intrigued," Matt admitted. "But I really don't think he's interested. I think he just has some sort of weird savior complex." He forced himself to smile and not think about the kiss that Alex hadn't really returned. "Are you guys ready for the costume contest?"

Everyone nodded, and after making sure Iron Man's arc reactor was firmly glued to his chest, Matt left the table to make rounds at the other two tables he'd been assigned after coming back from break.

He saw Alex out of the corner of his eye, pouring drinks and looking even more morose, while still managing to look even hotter. It was pure magic. Annoying, but still magical.

Serving the rest of his tables, he pasted on a happy, charming smile which hadn't felt so fake earlier, and got everyone pumped up for the costume contest that would be starting shortly, encouraging even some of the shyer clubgoers to get involved.

He'd thought his Sexy Avengers were pretty lame earlier, but they kept claiming they had a secret weapon that would guarantee a win.

"Where's your secret weapon?" Matt asked as he slid by the Avengers table, shoveling ice into fresh glasses, refilling drinks from the bottles on the table.

"Should be along soon," Iron Man said. "He had to work late."

"On Halloween?" Matt ignored that he was working on Halloween. He and Alex and everyone else in this club, from the DJ to the dancers writhing on the stage to the overworked bartenders.

It was something Matt was going to have to get used to if he kept working here. If he could keep working side by side with Alex, and not think about the way he hadn't kissed him back. He shook his head a little to clear it. He and Alex had only known each other for a couple of hours, he knew he already should have forgotten about it.

But there was the look in those gorgeous eyes as the emotional wall shutting out the world had flickered and then come down, even if only for a split second. That look wasn't going to leave Matt anytime soon. Not with all the potential it had held.

The music faded from an insistent thump to only a mild pounding, and the DJ announced the costume contest was going to start in five minutes. Everyone participating needed to report to the side of the dance floor.

Matt wasn't sure what to expect, and tensed, ready to go see to the rest of his tables, but instead there was a mass exodus from the VIP section. As he stood at the edge, watching the long queue form, he felt the presence behind him.

"Should've warned you," Alex said, his voice deep in Matt's ear, "costume contest is always fucking lit."

"I hope their secret weapon shows up, otherwise the Sexy Avengers are screwed," Matt said before he could bite the words back. He didn't want to start any more unnecessary conversations with Alex. If he was going to keep working here, and god knew he needed the cash the job was going to bring in, they were going to keep things strictly professional between them.

The last thing he needed was cute inside jokes about how bad the Sexy Avengers' costumes were and how desperately they needed their as-yet-unnamed "secret weapon."

"You mean the Sexavengers?" Alex teased.

"That's terrible," Matt complained, but he was still smiling. Damn him.

"About as good as their costumes, I'd say."

Matt huffed, refusing to laugh, but finding it more and more difficult.

"Listen," Alex said, moving closer until Matt could feel his body heat through the cheap polyester fabric of his ugly priest robe, "about earlier. . ."

"Not necessary," Matt interrupted. "I get it. It was a bad idea."

Whatever Alex had been about to say next—Matt was certain he was about to agree with him—faded in the loud screams that signaled the beginning of the costume contest.

Instead of continuing with a pointless conversation, they stood and watched the parade of skimpily-clad, imaginatively-costumed men prance across the stage

"The Sexavengers are screwed," Matt huffed out. He couldn't believe he was still using Alex's dumb nickname, but it was far too apt not to use.

"They're hot, though," Alex rumbled deeply next to him. "They've got that going for them." He hesitated. "Are you going to give the Hulk your number? Or Iron Man?"

Matt turned, with what he was sure was a gaping look of astonishment on his face. "Are you fucking kidding me?"

"What?" Alex retorted defensively. "You're going to give one of them your number. You've been flirting with them all night."

"I've been working. I was flirting with you."

"So you're not going to give one of them your number?" Alex asked, and Matt thought he heard hope in his voice.

Matt rolled his eyes. "No." He was just about to add that he had kissed him in the back, and ask him if he actually remembered that moment in time when a blood-curdling shriek went through the crowd.

"Oh my god," a voice screeched out, "I can't believe you almost started without me."

The crowd parted and the Sexavengers paused at the back of the stage. A tall, very leggy man wearing a black vinyl catsuit stopped at the front and in one swift movement launched himself onto the platform.

Alex started laughing. "Their secret weapon," he said.

"Oh my god," Matt gasped out as Black Widow reached out, teetering only a tiny bit in his high heeled boots, and high-fived Iron Man.

"The Avengers!" the DJ yelled to the crowd, who responded by screaming even louder as the foursome strode down the runway, playing up their characters the whole way.

"They're totally going to win," Alex pointed out, still chuckling. "I hope they still give you a decent tip."

"What?" Matt demanded. Alex's gaze was a little too sympathetic for his tastes. He liked the mysterious loner vibe he gave out—he'd like it a lot better though, if Alex would expand his repertoire to include loner plus partner.

"Didn't I tell you the prize for the costume contest?" Alex asked. "It's getting your bar tab comped."

⁂

Alex had to give Matt credit for a lot things.

For not relying too heavily on Alex on a busy night when usually anything could and *did* happen—the Sexavengers winning the costume contest with their secret weapon, Black Widow, definitely hadn't been on his radar.

For casually and gently turning down about a dozen requests for his number, including Iron Man *and* the Hulk. One of the ninjas—the least sullen one, even—had asked for Alex's, and he'd given out a fake one. Alex wasn't sure what that said about him, and what that said about Matt.

But most importantly, for not even saying a word as he'd handed the celebrating Sexavengers a bill that came up to exactly zero dollars. He'd held his head high, and on a night when he probably would have made some serious change in tips, probably only got what little cash the guys had carried on them. And considering the brevity of their costumes, that was almost definitely not much.

Alex glanced over to where Matt was scrubbing out one of the ice drawers with a ferocity that definitely translated to a frustration of some kind. Maybe someone braver could have asked him which kind of frustration he was feeling, but Alex had long since made his peace with his lack of bravery.

He'd quit trying to make music his life's work, hadn't he?

Even with the bright lights exposing the worn edges and stained floors of the club, Matt still looked as bright as a brand new penny. Alex gazed at his blond head and knew he should go over and apologize.

What was he even sorry for? For jerking him around? For flirting despite his own ironclad rules at work? For not kissing him back? For worrying about him even though he barely knew him?

For wanting to know him so much better?

The last reason settled into him, into his bones and his veins and his head. Into his heart. Because Alex knew that was what he really wanted. He wanted to know Matt so much better.

"I'm sorry."

Matt glanced up, and there was a definite frown creasing his handsome features. He'd taken off the hideous priest robe and was wearing an old t-shirt and worn athletic shorts. Alex didn't know if he'd taken off those gold briefs, but there was definitely a part of him that hoped not.

"For being a shitty trainer? Yeah, no worries. I got the memo coming in."

Yeah, definitely some of that frustration etched on Matt's face was directly Alex's fault.

"I was a great trainer," Alex said quietly. "At least I tried. Patience isn't my strong suit. But you didn't need it. You were great tonight."

"Then what are you sorry for?" Matt demanded. "For rejecting me? For not kissing me back and then asking me who's number I was getting tonight? For being so god damned worried that I was going to turn into you?"

Alex's hands clenched into tight fists. He almost wished he hadn't taken the wings off; when he wore them, he felt stronger and more powerful. Invincible, almost, like a different person. Maybe that was why he'd gotten so caught up with working here, and forgotten how much he wanted to make it as a musician. That was difficult and hard and too real. Working here and donning his angel persona every night was an escape when the rejections in reality kept piling up.

In Temple, with his wings in place, nobody ever rejected him.

Well, *one* person, but the last person Alex was going to talk to about Ryan Flores was Matt.

"I misjudged you, from the very beginning," Alex said softly.

"Same," Matt ground out, and then re-commenced scrubbing, like this conversation and Alex's admittedly poor apology weren't worth his time or attention.

And maybe they weren't, but Alex had been giving up for a long time now, and he wasn't willing to do it anymore. Not with Matt. Not with a lot of things, if the way he was feeling was right.

"I should have kissed you back," Alex said. "I wanted to."

"But you didn't," Matt retorted.

"If you'd come over here, we could try it again, see if it goes differently this time."

Alex might have guessed Matt was unaffected by his offer, because he kept scrubbing away. The ice drawer in that VIP table had probably never been cleaner in its entire existence. But his back tensed, the muscles clearly outlined in threadbare cotton.

"I know you still want to," Alex added, a little arrogantly. He might not be wearing the wings, but the knowledge of who he was in them still simmered beneath his skin.

Matt glanced up warily. "And if I do? How's that going to end? With a quick hookup in the backroom that we pretend doesn't exist in the light of day and every night after this one?"

Alex got tired of waiting for Matt to come to him, so he moved closer and crouched down, so his blue eyes could meet Matt's straight on. "I can't promise what's going to happen tomorrow. I can't promise anything, except that I want to try. You make me want to try, and nothing has made me want to in a long time."

He reached out and cupped Matt's cheek. "I shouldn't, because we don't really know each other yet, but I like you. And I think you like me."

"Everyone likes you," Matt scoffed.

"Everyone's intimidated by me. Everyone creams themselves over those stupid wings and the eyeliner and the way I act like they're all beneath me. I want to give you more than that."

Matt raised an eyebrow. Alex had no idea that he was going to be so difficult to win over, but somehow that was another bonus in his favor. He was simply unimpressed by all the shit people usually cared about.

"You want to give me your dick," Matt said flatly.

"Have you seen yourself? Of course, I want to give you my dick," Alex said, rising and starting to pace back and forth. "But I'm telling you that I want more than that. If celibacy is what will convince you, I'm fully prepared to never give you my dick."

Matt's gaze flicked from the ice bin to Alex's eyes and then lingered at his crotch. "I don't think that's going to be necessary."

Alex laughed. He couldn't help himself. "I was sort of hoping it wasn't."

Matt stood and came closer. Much closer. Close enough that Alex could see the gleam of success in those sky blue eyes. "Then what are you waiting for?"

Nothing, it turned out. Alex leaned in and kissed him, the exact way he'd wanted to earlier tonight. He wasn't going to lose his nerve and his chance again.

***--

Thirteen months later

"Oh god, yeah, just like that baby," Alex mindlessly crooned as his hands slipped around his boyfriend's head, fingers digging into his blond hair to the scalp beneath.

Matt, otherwise known as Alex's boyfriend, must have been listening though, because he kept going, taking his dick in his mouth even further, the pleasure whiting out Alex's vision.

His fingers tightened and they'd been together long enough—over a year now, which Alex couldn't quite believe, still—that Matt knew he was about to come, and doubled his efforts, sucking hard and squeezing his balls just the way he liked.

Alex came with a shout, emptying his load down Matt's throat. He rose to his feet, wiping his mouth, a irrepressible grin on his face. "I remember a time when you were willing never to give me your dick," he teased, wrapping his arms around Alex's shoulders and rubbing his own hard dick a little against Alex's tensed thigh.

"I'm not sure I really meant that," Alex confessed.

Matt laughed, and like always, he couldn't help but feel thankful that nothing, not even ten months working at Temple or thirteen months dating Alex or finally getting a job on an exciting new TV pilot, had been able to dim Matt's brightness.

"I knew that," Matt said, rubbing a little more insistently. "You know what else I know?"

"That we need to leave in five minutes?"

"Yes," Matt said.

"Come here," Alex said, even though Matt was already practically humping him. He laid his palm right over his dick and Matt was so worked up from blowing him, he came with only a few additional rubs.

"Thanks," Matt sighed happily, leaning his head against Alex's chest, right where his heart beat. Before Matt, there were days and weeks and even months where Alex had forgotten he even had a heart. But Matt reminded him every single day, and if that was all he brought to Alex's life, he'd still be fucking grateful.

The thing was Matt brought so much life and laughter and brightness, not just love, that Alex sometimes felt like he was overflowing with it. So much so that it had started to leak out in little bits of lyrics, and then melodies and then actual songs. And now, tonight, he was set to go perform all those songs for a club full of music executives who, if his agent were to be believed, were all desperate to sign him to a record deal.

"You need to go change now," Alex said ruefully, dropping a kiss on his hair.

"Yeah, but you were so wound up before, you would've gotten to the stage and squawked. Now you won't." Matt sounded very satisfied with himself and he should. He was probably a hundred percent right.

As Matt walked back to their bedroom to change his pants, Alex couldn't help but feel that all of this—the happiness and the light and the hope for the future—that was in his life now was all because Matt had told him once, "I want to hear you sing someday."

THE INVITATION

A CATCH ME SHORT STORY

"Oh my god," Tony said, sticking his head in the doorway of the food truck. "Did you see who's here?"

Wyatt hadn't seen who was here, because he'd been working his ass off in this tiny, stuffy kitchen of their food truck, prepping for the event they'd be hosting in . . .he checked his watch . . .approximately twenty minutes.

"No," Wyatt retorted testily, "because I've been in *here*, trying to get all the prep done."

"Oh," Tony said, clearly unconcerned. But then that was sort of Tony's mantra. "But seriously, you won't believe who's here."

"Should I guess?"

But Tony obviously didn't want Wyatt to guess—what he really wanted was to unveil the news with as much pomp and drama as possible. Basically, Tony being Tony.

"*Colin O'Connor* and his *husband*," Tony hissed with delight.

Wyatt rolled his eyes. Tony had just moved down from Napa about two months ago, to help Wyatt get the food truck up and running. While he seemed to technically comprehend that Wyatt's boyfriend was a professional baseball player and actually kind of famous, the truth was, he always seemed surprised when celebrities showed up. Even though they almost always came at Ryan's invitation.

"Yeah," Wyatt said. Admittedly, those two popping up *was* unexpected. Ryan definitely wouldn't have invited them. In fact, Wyatt remembered Ryan bitching about how boring and stodgy they must be, only a couple of months before.

He's so serious and settled down, Ryan had said about Colin, like that was the worst possible thing that could happen to someone. Ironically, one of Ryan's favorite things these days was for Wyatt to make dinner and afterward, to cuddle on the couch.

Of course, Wyatt wasn't going to be dumb enough to point out Ryan's newfound domestic tendencies, because the person most benefiting from them was *him*.

"Have you met them before?" Tony asked excitedly. "Has Ryan?"

"I think they sort of tangentially know each other." That was probably true enough. No reason to tell Tony a bunch of stuff he would almost certainly unload when faced with a celebrity of Colin O'Connor's stature. And Colin definitely didn't need to be told to his face that Ryan thought he was dull and tedious.

"He's *hot*," Tony said, climbing into the truck and picking up the knife. He'd left fifteen minutes earlier to write up the menu board and apparently had been star-struck enough by Colin and his husband for a job that normally took only a few minutes to stretch to fifteen.

"Which one?" Because while yeah, Colin *was* hot—that *Sports Illustrated* cover had been mind-numbingly sexy—he'd always been more attracted to dark-haired guys. Like Colin's husband, Nick. Or like his own boyfriend, Ryan.

"I mean, they're both hot as hell," Tony said, "but have you *seen* Colin O'Connor in person? It's like being blinded by the fucking sun."

"He's married, you remember," Wyatt reminded his brother.

He also reminded *himself* that it was good and wonderful and fantastic that Tony had discovered his sexuality, all the while hoping he wouldn't have to extricate Tony after he propositioned Colin and his husband for a threesome.

"Yeah," Tony said with a happy sigh. "It's too bad they didn't go into porn."

"It's too bad who didn't go into porn?"

Wyatt looked over and Ryan was standing in the doorway of their food truck, a perplexed frown on his face.

"You don't want to know," Wyatt said.

"Actually," Ryan said, leaning on the doorframe and grinning evilly, "I kind of do."

"You really don't," Wyatt said. "Besides, I don't have time to tell you, because Tony's discovered an epic boner for Colin O'Connor and his husband and abandoned me to all this prep work."

"Nick's hot," Ryan said, moving into the trailer, which was officially over-full now. "Let me guess, that's who should have gone into porn."

"It'd have been convenient *and* a money-maker," Tony said.

Wyatt rolled his eyes. His brother was incorrigible on the best of days, and then recently Ryan had made everything worse by *encouraging* him.

"I mean, that *Sports Illustrated*?" Ryan said. "We all got off on that forever."

"Late to the party, but I'm totally there with you right now," Tony agreed.

"Can we work now? Or is that asking too much?" Wyatt complained. "We have twenty minutes left to *feed* Colin O'Connor and his husband, and about a hundred other people, and it's going to be tight."

"That's what he said!" Tony crowed, and Ryan actually *laughed*.

❦ ❦

But it turned out that Tony wasn't really that wrong. When the meal was served, and Wyatt was finally pulled from the truck to do his chef-ly rotation around the long tables, he came face to face with Colin and forgot his own name.

"Hey, I know you," Colin said, switching the remnants of his meal from one hand to the other, and holding his hand out to shake. "You're the chef. Ryan's boyfriend. Wyatt, right?"

"That's me," Wyatt said lamely, shaking his offered hand, and also, *horribly*, discovering that the *Sports Illustrated* cover hadn't done him justice. Not at all. Wyatt wondered dimly, with the part of his mind that hadn't been blown out by the supernova of hotness that was Colin O'Connor, why he hadn't done porn. Football had probably paid a lot better, though with a face like that, who wanted to keep it covered up with a helmet all the time?

"Lunch was fantastic." Colin kept talking, like everyone who met him didn't have routinely X-rated fantasies about him. Even people who had partners they were perfectly, completely, utterly happy with.

"Thank you," Wyatt said, and as if on cue, Tony appeared next to him.

"Hi," Tony said, extending his own hand, "I'm Tony Blake. Wyatt's brother."

"Another chef!" Colin seemed positively thrilled by this news. "I guess it runs in the family."

"What runs in the family?" A slight, dark-haired man wearing what must be a furiously expensive pair of silver aviator sunglasses appeared next to Colin.

"Oh, honey," Colin said, wrapping a gloriously muscled arm around his husband's shoulders. Wyatt wondered if it would be really bad manners to ask him to take his shirt off. Just for comparison with that *Sports Illustrated* cover. "This is Wyatt and Tony. They're brothers, and they made lunch for us today."

Nick eyed him up and down. Even behind the mirrored sunglasses, it was clear it was both a leisurely and a complete perusal. "Oh?"

"Wyatt is Ryan Flores' boyfriend, you know," Colin said.

"Yeah," Nick said. Wyatt had a feeling there wasn't much he didn't know.

"You know, Ryan and I are always getting compared, but I don't think I've ever exchanged more than a word or two with the man," Colin said, gesturing around like this was impossible. Like he couldn't quite believe it. "Is he here? He must be, I'll have to find him and say hi." And he departed then, apparently not only to throw his trash away but to find Wyatt's boyfriend.

"Really?" Tony said skeptically.

Wyatt nearly slapped a hand over his brother's mouth, before he word-vomited all over the sidewalk, but of course he didn't. And of course Tony kept going.

Why? Because it was Tony, and he'd apparently been put on this earth to make his younger brother's life hell.

"Is that so surprising?" Nick asked casually.

Wyatt would have to be an idiot to think that anything this Nick guy did was casual. He was an actual piranha in a really attractive form. Not quite as attractive as his husband's, but *still* definitely not unattractive. Not at all. But then, because Tony apparently *was* an idiot, he answered.

"Well, they're not really alike, you know?" Tony said. "Ryan's young and wild and well, you know, my bro's taming him a little, but can you ever tame a beast like Ryan?"

Nick raised an eyebrow.

"Well, can you?" Tony repeated. "And no offense, you're both smoking hot, but you know, also fucking domestic? And who wants that?"

Wyatt wanted to drop through the floor and *die*.

"Lots of people," Nick said smoothly.

"Apparently," Tony grumbled.

"Not ever you," Wyatt retorted, getting his voice back. "I'm sorry about my brother, honestly," he said, shooting Tony a glare. "He's . . .we don't take him out in public very often."

Nick did the unimaginable then. He actually straight up *grinned*. Like he was absolutely fucking delighted.

"I bet not," Nick said, then he did something even more insane. He pushed his sunglasses back and smirked. "Do you ever get a chance to have a night out without him tagging along?"

"Uh," Wyatt hesitated, and Tony jabbed him in the side with a sharp, pointy elbow. "Uh sure, I guess."

"Because we wanted to invite you and Ryan to our house in Malibu," Nick said.

Tony straight up *squeaked* next to him, and Wyatt's brain whirled. Yeah, he totally wanted to go see Nick and Colin's amazeballs house in Malibu.

"That'd be great."

Nick grinned again, dropping his sunglasses back in place. "I think you'll find out that we're not nearly as 'boring' as you'd imagine. I'll drop you an email, Wyatt. Nice to meet you both."

As he walked away, Tony started spluttering, and Wyatt was so shocked he couldn't move.

"Oh my god," Tony said, "I think he just propositioned you and Ryan. For an *orgy*."

"No way," Wyatt. "There was *no way* that he did that. He was just inviting us to see their house, to hang out a little."

"You should go, and then *film it*," Tony exhaled in a rush. "And then I could watch it!"

Wyatt turned on his brother, kind of outraged. Also kind of turned on. But he couldn't exactly admit that, could he? "Even if it actually was an invite to an orgy, which it *wasn't*, you want to watch me having sex? I'm your *brother*."

"I'd just watch them, and well, maybe Ryan a little bit." Tony's eyes grew big as Wyatt's expression turned murderous. "I mean, he *is* totally hot, and that's a sign of . . . I don't know . . .*honor*, or pride, or something that you got a hot boyfriend."

Was it really? Wyatt didn't know what to think anymore.

"Are you going to tell Ryan about this?" Tony asked, as they walked back to the food truck.

"Of course I am," Wyatt retorted.

"Well, I *hope* you would, but you know, it might be a really good surprise too. Like *woooo, happy birthday, you just won an orgy with Colin O'Connor and his hot, snarky husband.*"

"It's not his birthday, not anytime soon," Wyatt said. Then clenched his teeth. "Besides, for the final time, it wasn't an invite to have group sex with them. It was just a casual invitation."

Tony threw up his hands. "You know what I mean."

"Then yes, I am going to tell him. Oh my god, surprise him with a Colin O'Connor orgy. I can't believe you," Wyatt said.

"You're obviously going," Tony said.

"I don't know," Wyatt said. "It depends on the date but I'll probably try to make it work. For *dinner*. Not for an *orgy*."

Tony held out his hand for a high five, but Wyatt just rolled his eyes.

"Grow up," Wyatt said, but Tony just laughed.

Clearly that was never happening.

❧❧❧❧❧ ❧❧❧❧❧

"So, explain what this is to me again," Ryan said a week later when they were in the town car that picked them up to take them to Colin and Nick's Malibu estate. "We're going to have an orgy . . .?"

"Have you been listening to Tony?" Wyatt demanded.

"Uh," Ryan said.

"We are *not* going to have an orgy," Wyatt said. "We're having dinner. That's all."

"Are you sure?" Ryan asked.

And he *had* been, because it wasn't like Nick had used the words "orgy" or "group sex" at all, but then how could someone like him do that and keep it secret? He'd have to be circumspect about it. And suddenly Wyatt was sweating, unsure that maybe they just *had* been invited to an orgy.

"Uh," Wyatt hesitated.

"What did he say?" Ryan asked with growing curiosity.

"I. . ." Wyatt didn't even remember what the words anymore. Only the impression they'd left. All that sly humor in Nick's dark eyes. The meaty biceps exposed by Colin's skintight t-shirt.

But it was too late to remember anyway, because they were pulling up to a massive wrought-iron gate that put even Ryan's to shame.

"I guess they take their security really seriously," Ryan muttered under his breath.

"The man owns a *private island*," Wyatt hissed. "Also, if we were regularly inviting people over for foursomes, wouldn't you want a lot of security?"

Ryan looked at him, sudden anxiety blossoming over his face. "Is that really what you think this is?"

"No, no, it's definitely dinner. Just dinner . . we've both clearly spent too much time with Tony lately."

"Right." Ryan didn't look very convinced.

"Who knows what's going to happen," Wyatt said with a shrug as they pulled through the gate and up the drive. The car stopped, and the driver opened the door for them. "Whatever does, we're fine."

"This is a terrible idea, why are we doing this?" Ryan hissed. "What if Tony was right, and it's not just dinner?"

Wyatt shot him a look and then reached out for his hand and gripped it firmly. "Does it matter? We're young and attractive and *exciting*."

Ryan shot him a look. "Who are you trying to convince? We're spending more evenings cuddling on the couch than out at Temple these days."

Wyatt honestly wasn't sure. Maybe he was trying to convince *himself*?

But before either of them could chicken out the rest of the way, the massive hardwood front door swung open and Colin and Nick were standing there.

"Hey," Nick said, waving them up the stairs. "How was the drive over?"

"Uneventful," Ryan said, shaking hands with Colin and Nick again.

"Come see the house," Colin said. Anyone who sounded that excited about real estate probably wasn't into group sex, but then Wyatt could still hear his brother's sly voice as they walked into the massive foyer. *He could be into real estate* and *porn. They're not mutually exclusive interests, baby bro.*

The house *was* enormous, and as they walked through it, Colin excitedly pointing out different architecture features, Wyatt slowly began to relax. Anyone who took them on this kind of specific tour of the house and grounds was definitely not interested in having an orgy any time soon.

Wyatt let out the breath he hadn't quite known he was holding as they ended up in the enormous backyard, and then as Ryan walked up next to him, he heard his boyfriend exhale in a long *whoosh* as they both took in the incredible view of the Pacific Ocean.

"Imagine having the money for this," Ryan said, even though he was a millionaire many, many times.

The pool went right up to the edge of the fortified cliff, giving the impression that you could just swim right out into the ocean, even though it was several hundred feet down.

"It's pretty fucking amazing, isn't it?" Nick said, walking up to them. "Colin's just letting the chef know that we're about ready to eat."

"Yeah," Wyatt said. Ryan's house was really nice—the entire neighborhood was full of multimillion dollar homes. But this compound sitting on a piece of priceless property, with an incomparable view? That was a whole different ballgame. Literally.

"You guys have a chef?" Ryan asked.

Nick rolled his eyes. "Didn't you hire Wyatt to be *your* chef?"

"Yeah, but . . ." Ryan flushed. "That was different."

"Probably because you didn't ever intend for me to be your *actual* chef," Wyatt teased.

Ryan grinned. "That's true," he admitted. "You were too cute to resist, lookin' all serious in that CV photo you sent."

"Dinner's ready," Colin said as he approached their group. "I thought we'd eat out on the lanai."

"Look at you, all formal," Nick jabbed him as they walked over to where the table was set. "Can you really call it a lanai if we're not in Hawaii?"

"Our designer calls it a lanai," Colin said stubbornly.

"Who's your designer?" Ryan asked, so eager that Wyatt already knew they'd be going home, maybe not with a couple of satisfying orgasms under their belt, but at least the name of Colin's designer, who would probably transform their backyard into something magical and also charge a fortune to do it.

Colin launched into a rhapsodic description of the designer and the miracles he could create, though frankly, Wyatt thought he'd have to be pretty basic to not be capable of doing something fantastic with the raw material that Colin and Nick had given him with this place.

"Hey," Nick said, leaning over as the first course was laid in front of them. "Between us, how is Ryan's team treating you?"

Wyatt looked at Nick. Those silver aviators were back on his face, but the rest of his expression seemed kind. Concerned, actually. But it wasn't like Wyatt could just forget that Nick still worked in the news media. It'd be a real good scoop if he could say, *Ryan Flores' boyfriend is unhappy with how pushy the Dodgers are.*

"Ehhhhh," Wyatt said, not wanting to lie, but also not wanting to be completely honest either. He didn't know Nick well enough for that, couldn't hope to trust him that much yet. "I think it'll be okay. They're just . . .you know . . .excited that they have a new couple they can send to all these LGBT-friendly events."

Nick nodded. The concern on his face hadn't really gone away. "Just don't let them push you too hard," he said, forking a slice of tomato in his salad.

"I'm trying not to," Wyatt admitted, and that *was* honest.

"Good." Nick sounded satisfied that he'd at least gotten him to concede that. "Colin still has a few years left in his contract so I try to keep some professional distance because with my job, it can be a conflict of interest. But you don't have that kind of good excuse."

Wyatt nodded, understanding and maybe more than a little jealous that Nick had such a great reason to not get too involved. Already the Dodgers were pushing for more appearances. He'd claimed he was busy with the food truck, but truthfully, Tony was handling more and more of those responsibilities.

Something else that Wyatt hadn't expected when he'd accepted Nick and Colin's invitation—the reminder he wasn't sure what he really wanted to do with his life, still.

As they finished their dinner, the sun had just begun to set and the intense painful blue of just a few minutes ago had already faded to intense shades of scarlet and purple and orange. "We should take a dip," Colin said. "What do you guys think?"

Wyatt thought of finally getting to verify that Colin O'Connor was as blindingly hot as he'd been on that *Sports Illustrated* cover, and also couldn't help but wonder if he'd be able to sneak a picture or two for Tony. "Yeah, that sounds great," he said. "But I'm afraid we don't have any trunks with us?"

Nick's glance was wicked. "Do you really need some?"

Colin's glare at his husband was swift, and he flushed, bright red spreading up from underneath his collar, up his neck and headed towards his cheeks. "We have some they could borrow," he spluttered. "They don't have to be *naked*."

"But it'd be fun, wouldn't it?" Ryan inserted, and Wyatt felt his hand, under the table, squeeze his knee reassuringly.

Was Wyatt willing to get naked in front of Colin and Nick? They'd be in the pool, wouldn't they? And it wasn't like he had anything to be ashamed of. He was fit—maybe not quite as fit as Colin, but then who was?

Maybe, Wyatt thought speculatively, his own, very hot, boyfriend.

"Sure," Wyatt said, and ordered his cock not to stir in his shorts, though he was feeling it already.

Without a single word, Colin stood and peeled off his shirt.

And suddenly, it was a hell of a lot harder to ignore the way his nerves were tingling with the beginnings of arousal. Colin was definitely as hot and ripped as the cover they'd all spent their teen years stealing and using as jackoff material.

"Show off," Nick drawled, but his expression was full of love and so much affection it seemed to simply radiate out of him.

"Yeah, but you love it," Colin retorted with a grin. "You wanna join me?"

"I think I'd rather watch the show," Nick said slyly. "Come on, then, show me. I'm waiting."

Colin tipped his head bashfully, but proceeded to strip off his shorts, leaving him only in a pair of incredibly tight bright blue briefs. Wyatt swallowed hard. This was somehow even better than the *Sports Illustrated*, and yeah, staying soft would be fucking impossible, especially when Colin shot his husband a hot look, that promised all kinds of additional naughtiness, and reached for the waistband of his briefs, beginning to tug them down.

Wyatt glanced away, turning his attention to his own boyfriend. The show didn't feel like it was meant for them, but more for Nick, and he felt both incredibly turned on and painfully awkward watching it. He heard Colin hit the water and felt a wave of relief rush through him. It wasn't like Colin O'Connor wasn't just over there, totally naked, but at least he was mostly covered by the water now.

Ryan met his eyes with a fiery glance of his own. "Let's go," he said, and stood too, shedding his shirt and his jeans as he went, and Wyatt was pretty sure he wasn't the only one watching the delectable curves of Ryan's ass, hidden just under his own tight briefs as he sauntered over towards the pool. He glanced back, like he wanted to make sure Wyatt was still watching. And *fuck,* like Wyatt could ever look away from him. He was glorious, all lean, chiseled muscle wrapping up the sweetest, funniest guy that Wyatt had ever met. The most loyal, and the most lovable. How had he gotten so goddamn lucky?

He knew a lot of people thought he was just with Ryan because he was rich and a professional baseball player, but Wyatt would've loved him if he was penniless.

"We're pretty fucking lucky, aren't we?" Nick echoed his own feelings.

Wyatt looked up at the other man in surprise. He hadn't heard him get up, but he was already shirtless, his jeans unbuttoned and partially unzipped. Tony had been right; he was hardly a slouch in the looks department either, and from the predatory way Colin was staring at him from across the pool, where he and Ryan were circling each other, his husband definitely thought he was hot as hell.

"The luckiest," Wyatt agreed, finally standing.

"A lot of people think I'm here for this shit," Nick said, waving his hand over the backyard and the sunset view, and it *was* incredible, "but I'm here for the guy, and only the guy, honestly."

It was impossible to see them together and think any differently. Wyatt knew that Ryan had once said they were boring, but Wyatt was seeing a different side of them now—and a vision that he hoped that one day he and Ryan could emulate. Utter, complete, everlasting devotion.

"We'd better not let them get started without us," Nick said, shucking his jeans the rest of the way, and Wyatt followed suit, pushing away the pulse of shame he felt at his half-hard dick when he saw that Nick was hardly soft either.

They were an attractive group; it was to be expected. Right?

Finally naked, Wyatt dove into the deep end of the pool, the water cool and refreshing on his skin. When he reached the surface, pushing his hair out of his eyes, Ryan was right there, dark lashes spiky with water, the incendiary look in his eyes making it clear just how much *he'd* enjoyed the show.

"This is nice," Nick said, floating over to where Colin was stretched out on the far side of the pool. Colin immediately wrapped a hand around him and tugged him closer, so close that Wyatt had to wonder how tangled they were, under the protective camouflage the water offered.

Just as he thought it, Ryan's hand snaked down, underneath the water, and circled his own dick. Wyatt spluttered, and Ryan's expression turned calculating. "You okay there, honey?" he asked sweetly. Innocently. When he was *nothing* of the kind.

"Fine," Wyatt said, letting Ryan lead him to the wall that overlooked the Pacific. "Just . . . really, really fine."

"You sure are," Ryan said.

Colin laughed.

"See?" Nick said. "No swimsuits required."

Maybe it wasn't quite the orgy that Tony had envisioned, but it was *something*, and Wyatt knew that Ryan was never, ever going to accuse these two of being boring again.

He pushed away the thought of his brother, as Ryan's fingers teasingly circled his cock, not exactly jerking him off, but not really letting him get soft either.

"I'm glad we came," Wyatt said, and discovered that despite all his nerves of what these two might expect, he really meant it. Not many others knew what it was like to be in a couple with someone who was rich and famous and used their considerable physical gifts to earn their living.

"We've had our eye on you guys for a while," Colin admitted and then flushed again. It was cute how awkward he was. "Not like *that*," he hastily added, which caused his husband to laugh.

"Then like what," Nick asked innocently. Wyatt had a feeling that particular trait was as much a part of his personality as it was Ryan's. Which was basically not at all.

"You know, they're like us, a little," Colin tried to explain.

"Yeah," Nick agreed, nodding thoughtfully. And it was a little bit like looking in a mirror, gazing over at the other side of the pool, one guy with dark hair cuddling with a blond one.

Wyatt felt Ryan's muscles bunch under his fingertips as he stroked the damp skin on his back. They were both feeling hot and trying to tamp it down, and it was *hard*.

Literally.

"You should come to a game sometime," Nick said. "We have this private island out near Miami. You could stay with us."

"That'd be fun," Ryan said. "Have you ever thought of trying to play for a different team? Maybe one a little closer to LA? I mean, you own all this." He gestured. It was crazy, thinking they owned this in California, but also had a compound in Florida, where Colin worked.

"Maybe someday," Colin said thoughtfully. "Not sure I'll play forever."

"There's always the Riptide," Wyatt said, referring to the Los Angeles NFL expansion team that was only a few years old.

"Yeah, they've got a great quarterback though," Colin said with a grin. "Have you ever met Heath Harris?"

Ryan shook his head.

"He keeps to himself a lot," Nick said. "Nice guy though. Great football player."

"Yeah," Colin said, a little bit sulkily. Like he didn't like his husband calling anyone else great but him. It might have been ridiculous, but the love between them shone so bright, like a golden thread that stretched from one heart to another.

"Stop it," Nick said, amused as he smacked Colin lightly on the arm. "You're my favorite QB, and you know it."

"Am I your favorite baseball player?" Ryan asked, turning towards Wyatt, an impossibly sexy grin on his face. Wyatt rolled his eyes. Like it was even a question.

"From the moment you gave that interview," Wyatt admitted, and that was actually the truth.

"See," Colin whispered, his voice still carrying across the pool, "they *are* like us!"

Nick laughed, a low and sexy growl, and out of the corner of Wyatt's eye, he saw Colin reach for him, kissing him hard and long.

Wyatt turned to Ryan and decided that he'd waited long enough to kiss him too, so leaned down, capturing his mouth with his own.

The sunset faded slowly from view as they alternately floated through the pool, exchanging casual small talk, until finally Colin said, "I'm going to go grab some towels." He lifted himself out of the pool, the muscles in his arms bunching as he did it, and Nick watched, entranced. And frankly, Wyatt was pretty distracted by the sight himself.

"I'm gonna help," Nick said, following suit, and Ryan and Wyatt watched as they went into the house, still dripping water.

Ryan turned to him. "They're totally going to have sex," he whispered intensely.

It was the exact same thought Wyatt had, and his cock began to fill again, just at the thought. Tony had said they'd make pretty hot porn, and he was *right*.

Wyatt reached for Ryan, pulling him close, and Ryan wrapped his legs around his waist, their mouths meeting again in a hot clash that told the entire story: they both thought it was pretty damn hot that Nick and Colin had escaped to have sex.

"Oh my god," Ryan said, suddenly wrenching his lips off Wyatt's. "Oh my god," he repeated again.

"What?" Wyatt said, and Ryan turned them slightly, and used his elbow to slightly point towards the house.

"*Look.*"

The house was a sprawling entity, spreading out across almost the entire front of the backyard, most of the rooms with windows no doubt installed to take advantage of the ocean view.

It seemed impossible to believe that Nick and Colin had forgotten that those same windows would have a good view the other direction, but they must have, because Nick had Colin pinned to a wall, a window giving both Wyatt and Ryan a pretty damn clear view of what they were doing.

"Oh fuck," Wyatt exhaled sharply.

"How . . .do they not know we can see them?" Ryan asked. It felt wrong to watch, but also impossible to look away.

Colin was against the wall, Nick leaning into him, their mouths fused together as they kissed endlessly, and yeah that was definitely Nick's hand wrapped around Colin's cock and it was jerking him off hard and fast as Colin's head tipped backwards, hitting the wall.

"We should . . ." Ryan said but couldn't quite finish his sentence.

"Take advantage of this," Wyatt said. He crowded Ryan against the wall, his hands reaching for Ryan's rapidly hardening dick.

"In their pool?" Ryan said, his tone a little scandalized.

"They can afford to have it cleaned," Wyatt reasoned. "Besides you think they don't do this all the time?"

"Good point," Ryan said and leaning in, kissed him, heat flaring between them as Wyatt began to pump Ryan's cock just the way he knew his boyfriend loved. Hard and tight, just on the other side of pain, because nothing got Ryan going like a little adrenaline.

"What about you," Ryan panted into Wyatt's mouth. "I wanna . . ."

"I'll be fine," Wyatt ground out. But the truth was, he'd been on the edge all evening, and seeing Ryan fall apart like this, in his hands, and having seen Nick do the same to Colin? He had a feeling it wasn't going to take long for Ryan to pull him over the edge with him, and just as he expected, Ryan's fingers wrapped around his own cock, giving it an experimental pull.

He was right; it definitely didn't take long. It felt like white lot lava was pouring through him and he couldn't quite catch his breath as they frantically kissed and jerked each other off.

Ryan came first, his teeth digging into the meat of Wyatt's shoulder as he tried not to make any noise, shuddering through his orgasm. Wyatt followed, feeling that incredible surge of pleasure intertwined with love that he never failed to feel when they were this close.

They only had a second to come down from the high, and then Nick was there, a towel wrapped around his own waist, holding a pile of fluffy white towels, and setting them on one of the low chaise lounges that surrounded the pool.

"Have fun?" he asked, his eyes twinkling mischievously, even as his expression remained casual.

"Oh yeah," Wyatt said in a deadpan voice. "*Loads.*"

❦

"So," Tony asked the next morning as they were working on prep in the food truck, "how was Colin and Nick's house? Everything you'd hoped it'd be?"

They'd ended up compromising on Muse today, the music pumping out of the Bluetooth speaker just loud enough that Tony had to raise his voice to be heard.

Wyatt's hands were steady as he cut into the pineapple on his cutting board. "Yeah," he said, "it was fun." But his mind still went blurry and hot at the thought of what they'd done. How much he'd actually enjoyed it, even though maybe it was a little bit wrong.

"I'm so jealous," Tony said with a hard exhale of regret.

"I can tell you though," Wyatt added with a grin, "that he definitely puts the *Sports Illustrated* to shame."

"What!" Tony exclaimed. "What! You have to tell me more, you can't just leave it like that, that's so unfair."

"I don't kiss and tell," Wyatt said. "I guess you'll just have to use your imagination."

"It's a good thing I've got a great one," Tony muttered. "Won't kiss and tell . . .you're the worst."

"Good thing Ryan thinks I'm the best," Wyatt said, and knew deep down in his bones that someday, they would have that incredible devotion that Colin and Nick shared. It was only a matter of time.

And he knew, too, that it wasn't going to be even remotely close to boring.

Read Colin & Nick's story, *The Rainbow Clause*, on Amazon, Kindle Unlimited, and Audible.

Savor Me

BETH BOLDEN

Chapter One

Wʜᴀᴛ ᴛʜᴇ ꜰᴜᴄᴋ.

Xander Bridges slammed on his brakes half a second before he remembered it was storming, the rain coming down in unrelenting sheets, and the road resembling a creek more than it did an actual swath of asphalt.

It would have been really fucking difficult to make him forget it was raining—the water coming down from the sky had been relentless for his entire drive home from another long day at Terroir, the Michelin-starred restaurant where he worked insane shifts as a *sous chef*. But the sight before him made him forget nearly everything.

To the left, there was a vineyard, which was not the surprising part of the view. There were vineyards everywhere you looked in the Napa Valley, some better, some worse, some merely mediocre. Xander *knew* that the vineyard he was looking at now wasn't any of those. It was one of the first vineyards that had ever been planted by the Hess family, and therefore one of the first vineyards ever planted in Napa. It wasn't just good or great or anything else on that spectrum; essentially, it was priceless.

And there was a man out there, battered by the sheets of rain, yanking up the vines with his bare hands.

It wasn't even close to the smart thing to do. Xander hit the brakes anyway, and skidded along the edge of the road, finally coming to a stop right next to the embankment.

He sat there for a moment, heart thumping with the surge of adrenaline. From the skid he'd taken or the man, who was still ripping up the vines, it was hard to say.

If Wyatt or Miles, his best friends, had been here, they would have told him to keep his ass in the car and drive away. No good could come from him walking into the torrential downpour and confronting someone who was clearly insane. But Wyatt and Miles weren't here—they had moved to LA, leaving Xander behind—and he was riding a rough-edged *fuck it* mindset these days.

The only smart thing he did was to leave his phone in the console, charging, and to pull off the zip-up sweatshirt he'd thrown over the undershirt he generally wore under his chef whites.

It was wet, sure, but it wasn't cold, and he didn't need to be bogged down by extra soaking wet fabric.

He knew it was going to be miserable, but the first blast of moisture to the face still made him gasp as the rain ran down his face. Slamming the car door shut, he struggled through the mud of the embankment, finally making it to the edge of the vineyard. He climbed over the short, pointless wire fence, and started walking toward the man destroying hundreds of thousands of dollars of vines. Maybe even millions.

The man hadn't seen him yet, even though Xander stopped in front of him, only a few yards away. He was completely intent on the vines, hacking away at them with his bare fists, tearing and pulling and grasping, caught up in a rage that Xander recognized, deep down. He'd never acted on it though, had only internalized it, and had developed a finely honed sarcasm to express it safely.

The man wasn't internalizing jack shit.

It occurred to Xander that despite not wanting to ruin his phone, he shouldn't have left it in the car. Now he was completely at this man's mercy, and he didn't seem particularly stable, with a side dish of barely leashed control.

He shouldn't be here. Shouldn't be interfering. But he was here now, increasingly soaked, and so he spoke up.

"What the fuck?" Xander asked.

The man looked up, rain pouring down his face. His hair was dark and cropped close to his head, his face a pale swath under all that water, his eyes a surprisingly light bluish-green. They stared right through Xander, as he held himself motionless.

It was something to behold; all that muscular power being held still. And Xander knew just what was hiding under his soaked flannel shirt because it clung to every inch of him. His jeans, too. Xander shouldn't even be thinking it, but those were definitely the finest thighs he'd ever had the privilege of not seeing.

At least if he died, he'd have a real good view at the end.

"What are you doing here?" the man growled. "You're trespassing."

"And you're basically ripping up money," Xander challenged right back. He really should have called the cops, instead of deciding to confront this guy by himself. What he was doing *was* a crime, wasn't it?

A segment of vine still hanging from the man's hand dropped to the mud with a solid *plop*. "They're mine, I can do whatever I want with them."

"Including being stupid?" Xander asked. Really the only stupid person here was him, but it was in his nature to keep pushing and not let things go. It was how he'd ended up *sous* at Terroir, and also how he'd ended up in this vineyard, past midnight, in the middle of a gigantic storm. It was probably how he was going to end up murdered, he thought darkly.

The empty fist opened and then clenched tightly again. "You don't know what you're talking about."

This was undeniably true. "So why don't you tell me," Xander suggested. Not like they were in the middle of a storm. Instead like they had just met at a local bar, and Xander, completely unlike himself, had approached the built and rugged man everyone kept eyeing nervously and offered to buy him a drink.

There was shock radiating out of those light eyes. Like the last thing he expected Xander to do was to ask. To *care*.

As far as Xander was concerned, that was his ultimate curse. He always, always, *always* cared too much, no matter how much he tried to hide it under layers of sarcasm and bitterness.

"You really want me to tell you." His voice was cautious and a little gentle now, nothing like the fierce growl from only a few minutes ago. As if Xander had managed to calm him despite himself.

"I'm here, aren't I?" Xander spread his arms, the rain continuing to come down around them.

"Hell if I know why," the man grumbled. "Let's get out of the rain first." He jabbed a finger quick and sharp toward a ranch-style house that sat a few hundred yards away.

Xander hesitated, and the man must have sensed it. He extended a muddy, grimy, *bloody* hand. "I'm Damon Hess."

Damon *Hess*. Well, now it was official. Xander felt stupid as shit. Damon probably owned these vines—or his family did. And why he was out here, in the middle of the night, ripping them to shreds, really wasn't any of Xander's business.

Yet when he shook his hand, palm sliding wetly against Damon's, Xander couldn't miss a loneliness he recognized peeking out from behind the wall in his eyes.

Maybe the man really needed someone to talk to, and that was why he'd resorted to the worst-case scenario of pulling up the god damned vines. God knew, Xander hadn't been able to talk his friend Kian out of making an enormous mistake, but maybe he could be an ear for Damon.

"Xander Bridges," Xander said. "Sure, why not. Let's go talk."

The walk to the house was both short and also an eternity. His pants were soaked through, the sodden fabric slapping against his legs, rain dripping down his chest in big, fat rivulets. He couldn't wait to stop getting poured on, and find a towel. Karma, Xander supposed, for going after Damon, even though there was a god damn storm swirling around them.

It was his whole fucking problem, encapsulated into one single decision. He always thought he could be good for people, could *fix* them, but the truth was, he was just as much of a disaster, if not more of one. His meddling typically made things worse, and at the end, he was always left holding the shit end of the stick.

Damon threw open the back door of the house, glancing back at Xander. Luckily, it was the laundry room, and it was covered in a functional linoleum that they probably couldn't ruin. Probably. Xander stayed on the concrete stoop, pretty sure his shoes and pants were both headed to the trash bin.

"I'll go grab some towels," Damon said. He leaned over, fingers fumbling with the muddy laces of his boots. And Xander, who was a terrible human being, couldn't help but check his ass out.

He felt only a single pulse of guilt; it was a pretty fantastic ass, though not quite as fantastic as Damon's thighs. But then, those were clearly a work of art, deserving of all sorts of worship that Xander would never get to perform.

Damon finally got his boots untied and toed them off. He was only gone a moment, which made sense because it wasn't that big of a house. It certainly wasn't the kind of simple, homey residence that he'd expect a Hess to own, never mind live in. It felt more like a caretaker's house, or a vineyard worker's house.

When he re-appeared, he was toweling off his head, color back in his cheeks, and Xander nearly took a step back, right back into the mud. Damon, who had looked pretty attractive in the middle of a rainstorm, was crazy hot. Sort of loner, intense hot, with that farmer thing going on. He unbuttoned his plaid shirt and dumped it straight into the open washing machine.

Turning toward Xander, Damon extended a towel. "Feel free to use the washer, if you'd like," he said, and the gruff sort of edge was back in his voice. Like he'd invited Xander here on a whim, and now he was rethinking the whole thing.

Well, that made two of them. But Xander was curious now, too. Why would a Hess live here? Why would a Hess tear up his own vines? Never mind *those* vines?

He wiped his face off, and without a second thought pulled his white tank over his head. He was in decent shape, and despite his own inability to stop checking Damon out, there was very little chance Damon was actually interested in men.

Xander dropped the wet cloth into the washing machine and tried not to look as Damon dumped his own white undershirt in. He was definitely ripped. His muscles practically had muscles. He was tall and big, and since it wasn't that big of a room he took it over.

Damon didn't look over at him as he wrapped the towel around his middle and shed his jeans, the fabric landing with a sodden plop on the floor. Xander copied his movements, shoved the wet pants into the machine, and Damon got it started.

It wasn't until the mechanical whir of the washing machine began that he looked up at Damon again. "Want some coffee?" he asked.

"We've got an hour or so to kill," Xander said wryly. "Sure."

He followed Damon through the house, and it was exactly as he'd imagined. The furniture was worn, and the house was lived in. There were books scattered throughout, a worn blanket tossed thoughtlessly across the back of the leather sofa.

The kitchen was small, but very neat and very clean. Which, considering Xander's profession, was an essential requirement.

A stainless steel espresso machine gleamed on the counter, and a glance at the brand told Xander that it was worth probably more than all the furniture in the house combined.

Damon fired it up, looking like he knew exactly what he was doing. "Espresso okay?" he asked.

"I'll take a cappuccino if you can manage it," Xander said.

Damon gave a rough laugh, and leaned over, grabbing a carton of milk from the fridge, all while holding his towel firmly around his waist.

Xander slipped onto one of the barstools that overlooked the kitchen. "Why don't you tell me what you were doing out there?"

"You're a chef," Damon said, not answering Xander's question.

"I am." Xander wondered what had given him away, then remembered he'd still been wearing half his chef uniform. At least before the distinctive checkered pants had gotten soaked and muddy and had taken a trip to Damon's washing machine.

"A good one?" Damon's voice was deep and rumbling, like a boulder rolling down a hill. Xander liked how he could feel it deep in his chest. If he was being really honest, he liked it a little too much.

"Yes," Xander said shortly. He'd left his jacket with Terroir's emblem embroidered on the pocket in the car, and it seemed like that was for the best. Xander had no intention of sharing that he worked for one of the best restaurants in the world.

"So you're connected," Damon said. He turned back, holding out a solid white enamel mug in one hand, the other still keeping his towel up. Xander wanted to ask him what he was packing in his boxer briefs that had him so protective, but a lot of people didn't understand or appreciate his sense of humor, and Damon was still very much an unknown entity.

Xander took the coffee and took a sip. It was excellent, which either said something about the person who'd made it, or at least about the investment Damon had made in the machine.

"What does that even mean?" Xander questioned. Damon turned back to the espresso machine to make his own cup. "Why does it even matter?"

"I don't want this getting out," Damon said quietly. "People in Napa talk."

"Yeah, it's a surprisingly small community," Xander agreed. The wine and restaurant businesses were particularly intertwined, which was probably why Damon had questioned what kind of chef he was. Definitely good that he hadn't mentioned he worked at Terroir. "I'll keep my mouth shut, but I have to tell you, people are going to notice that you're ripping up your vines. Especially those particular vines."

"You know what they are?" Damon questioned. He'd finished making his own coffee, and from Xander's vantage point, it looked dark and thick as mud.

"I've lived here a long time. I know a lot about this area."

"It's inevitable people will notice the vines are gone. I just don't want them knowing *why*." Damon's jaw tightened and his eyes looked particularly bleak, so light and clear in his tanned face.

"I'm not going to go blabbing around, if that's what you're asking," Xander retorted.

"But you're the kind of guy who pulls over at midnight, and goes tromping out into a muddy vineyard in the middle of a storm to ask me why," Damon said.

"Like I said, I know those vineyards," Xander said, setting his coffee on the countertop with a decisive click. "I don't think I need to tell *you* what they represent."

Damon looked away, his fingers tightening on his own coffee cup. "No, you do not." He hesitated for a long moment, and if Xander's clothes hadn't been in the wash currently, he would have left. There was no point in trying to talk to someone who didn't want to talk. It was like trying to milk solid fucking stone.

Xander didn't know which annoyed him more; this difficulty or Kian, who would actually listen to everything Xander said, and respond all the way up until the point where he flatly refused to change anything he was doing.

"I'm an alcoholic," Damon said finally.

"Wow, that sucks. For a Hess, especially," Xander said. He was definitely surprised, at least at first, but when the confession sunk in properly, he realized it wasn't all that shocking. Damon looked like he'd cornered the market in loner-ism. He was hiding out here, except that the property was surrounded by the very thing he was trying to battle.

In fact, there were miles and miles of it, caging him in entirely. Suddenly, it wasn't a shock that Damon had tried to tear down his vineyard with his bare hands—it was amazing that he hadn't devastated all the vineyards in the Napa Valley.

"For a Hess, yeah. It's definitely not convenient for my family." Damon's voice was bitter. "I'd actually moved away, was doing better, away from all . . . *this*. But then my grandfather died, and they all wanted me to come home so desperately, I guess he thought leaving me one of the original properties was supposed to be an enticement."

"And it wasn't," Xander said.

"It's a fucking jail sentence," Damon gritted out. "I've been sober four years, and this is a test I don't want to fail. But I don't know how to pass either."

"Put that way, I can't blame you for destroying those vines. Have you thought about selling?"

Damon looked mildly shocked. "Selling this property? To who? This has been Hess land as long as there have been Hesses in California. Besides," he added wryly, "one of the stipulations of the will was I had to keep it for at least ten years."

"Does it have to be a vineyard?" Xander asked. His family had always been supportive of him. It hadn't mattered if he wanted to be a chef or if he was gay. They hadn't ever cared, had always loved him no matter what. It was hard hearing about someone who seemed decent who hadn't had that unconditional support system surrounding him.

Damon shrugged. "I don't give a fuck what it is, as long as it's not a vineyard."

"This is still wonderfully fertile land," Xander said. "Why don't you grow something else?"

Damon leaned against the back counter, and Xander had a really difficult time not staring at his bare chest. A dark trail of hair that started just under his belly button disappeared into the towel, accentuating the ripples of his abs. He looked like he worked for a living—or maybe *worked out* for a living.

And even though Xander had sworn off crushes on men who were almost definitely straight long ago, he wanted to lay his palm across the bulk of Damon's pectoral muscle and feel his heart beating underneath.

Xander told himself that he wasn't staring, that he wasn't obvious, but Damon was big in such a small space, and it was nearly impossible to look anywhere else.

A loud *buzz* from the washing machine interrupted the sudden silence, and Damon shot Xander a tiny, lopsided smile. The first smile he'd given Xander since they'd met. It wasn't much but Xander had a feeling that he didn't really have a lot of reasons to smile these days.

"That's the cycle finishing," Damon said apologetically. "I'll go throw the wet things in the dryer, and you'll be on your way in about twenty minutes."

"Twenty minutes?" Xander asked, surprised—and if he was being very honest, disappointed—at the length of time he'd be required to stay here.

"Whether I like it or not, this is still a working farm. If you'd ever worked a farm, you know how vital laundry is," Damon said, as he walked back toward the laundry room. Xander trailed him, not wanting to let him out of his sight. And that was definitely a problem.

"You've been tending the vines?"

Damon threw the clean clothes into the dryer and pressed the start button. He'd used the edges of the towel to tie some sort of complicated, very secure-looking knot around his waist. That towel wasn't going anywhere, no matter how much Xander wished it would. "There's not exactly anybody else."

"Your whole family?" Xander pointed out. Damon looked up swiftly, his light eyes going darker. "I'm sorry," Xander said hurriedly. "I have a terrible habit of being uncomfortably honest."

Damon's eyes went softer as they walked back to the kitchen. Xander resumed his position on the barstool, and to his surprise, Damon picked up his coffee from the kitchen and sat right down next to him. "I bet that doesn't make you very popular sometimes."

This was true, but Xander didn't want to talk about it. Which, he supposed, was pretty hypocritical of him. After all, he'd tromped across a muddy vineyard to demand Damon tell him why he was destroying his vineyard.

"Sometimes," Xander answered vaguely.

"So," Damon said, "what do you think I should plant instead of grapes?"

He hadn't been intending on telling Damon where he worked, but then Damon probably hadn't intended on telling Xander he was an alcoholic, so Xander figured he owed him. "I work at a restaurant named Terroir." He saw the moment the name registered and how familiar Damon was with it. But Xander forged on, anyway. "We source everything we can from local farmers and suppliers. This would be great ground to grow vegetables."

"I didn't know Bastian Aquino was a proponent of the farm-to-table movement," Damon offered wryly.

"Chef Aquino does what is most convenient for Chef Aquino," Xander admitted. "And it makes him look good to try to source stuff locally."

"Yeah, that sounds like him," Damon said casually.

"You've met Chef Aquino?" Xander asked, which was *stupid*, because he was a Hess. The Hess family didn't run the Valley exactly, because there were too many big wine families for anyone to have a monopoly, but they were definitely one of the more important players.

"A couple of times, before I moved away," Damon said. "You must have skin like steel to work for him."

"Yeah, something like that." This was hardly the first time someone had pointed out that Bastian Aquino was an asshole, and it was definitely not going to be the last. "There's a reason he's affectionately known as the Bastard."

"Have you ever thought about leaving?" Damon asked.

Had he ever thought about leaving?

It was tough to consider leaving, when everyone else kept leaving *him*. First, Miles, to his big cooking show career in Los Angeles, and then Wyatt, as a private chef to professional baseball player Ryan Flores.

Only Kian was left out of their original foursome of friends and roommates, and Xander wasn't sure that these days Kian would even consider them close anymore.

That was the problem with trying to give people advice; when they wouldn't listen and you started sounding like a broken, desperate record, your friendship generally suffered.

"I hadn't. I became *sous chef* six months ago, and it's better with some power in the kitchen." This was a terrible lie, but Damon, who had plenty of demons of his own, didn't need a rundown of Xander's.

Especially considering that up until tonight, he'd even been tending the vines he'd eventually be driven to tear down. It must have been a bad night, and Xander was glad he'd intruded if only because Damon had clearly needed a distraction.

"You seem very capable, so I'm not surprised Bastian would promote you," Damon said.

"You've never seen me in a kitchen," Xander pointed out.

Damon flushed, and Xander had a heart-stopping moment where he thought he might be flirting with him. But that wasn't possible.

Because even if by some miracle Damon was interested in guys, he probably wouldn't be interested in Xander. He was a *Hess*. He owned some of the most valuable land in California. He was undoubtedly rich, with a handsome trust fund. Add to that his incredibly good looks, all of which added up to the fact that Xander needed to get out of here before he began thinking there could be some nebulous possibility here, with Damon.

"I'm going to go check the dryer," Xander said, sliding off the barstool before he could get any more wild ideas.

Damon didn't say anything, just stared down into his empty coffee mug.

Maybe he knew Xander was running away, but he definitely didn't know why, and as far as Xander was concerned, that was what mattered.

The clothes in the dryer were still a tiny bit damp, but he pulled them out anyway, tugging his pants on, and pulling on his tank top. He dumped the towel into the washing machine, and walked back out toward the kitchen.

Damon was washing out Xander's mug in the sink.

"Thank you, for coming to talk to me tonight," Damon said before Xander could say goodbye. "I was having a really bad night. Worst night in awhile, if I'm being honest. And you showed up, even though you didn't have to, and kept me company."

It ached that Damon thought Xander had done it for selfless reasons. And there *were* selfless reasons, but selfish ones too. Like the way the muscles in Damon's back bunched as he dried out the mug.

"You're welcome," Xander said quietly. He knew he should ask if he should stay, if Damon would like his phone number if he ever had a bad night again, because it didn't seem like Damon had a lot of people he could talk to. But he didn't do either of those things. Self-preservation, he told himself. "Actually, I should be going. I have an early morning tomorrow."

"Of course you do." Xander told himself that it was okay, that everything was fine, because there was a dark thread of amusement in Damon's deep voice. If he was amused, he couldn't still be struggling so much.

"Thanks for the coffee, and the washing machine, and for not calling the cops on me," Xander said in a rush. He couldn't quite look at Damon's bare back anymore, and Damon hadn't turned around to face him either.

This was better all around, Xander told himself.

"See you around," Damon said.

Then there was nothing left to do except go the way he came, opening the back door to only a weak sprinkle. Xander said a blessing, shoved his feet back in his muddy sneakers, and closed the door behind him.

Chapter Two

One year later

Xander took the same route to work that he'd been taking for the last year.

He and Kian shared a car sometimes, when Chef Aquino didn't need him ridiculously early in the day, and once Kian had asked why he'd changed his route.

Xander couldn't tell him that he wasn't willing to drive by Damon Hess' vineyard and see him on his land again. It wouldn't have mattered what he was doing, Xander still would have pulled over and demanded to know if the spark he'd felt that night was one-sided.

And if it wasn't, he wanted to know what they were going to do about it.

He didn't drive by, because he already knew it was a mistake to do anything about it. That's why he didn't even give himself the option.

It was sort of a lonely existence—home to work and then back home again. He argued with Kian about his ill-advised crush on their boss. Argued with Nate, their other roommate, about everything he could think of, and entertained himself by rebuffing every sexual offer he made. Nate entertained himself by continuing to make them.

There were some days when Xander would give anything to drive by the vineyard. Some days, ignoring the basic curiosity took all his self-control. Had Damon torn up the rest of the vines? Planted a garden? Sold the property? In the year since that night, Xander had imagined three hundred and sixty-five different possibilities.

Some good, some bad, some made up of plain normal life, but all full of a tantalizing possibility that Xander couldn't seem to forget.

He knew he was romanticizing a single encounter that hadn't even lasted an hour. But when the alternative was resenting the happiness his friends had found in LA, and worrying about Kian's future, most nights Damon looked really damn good. Maybe even better than he had for real.

The memory took on an elastic quality, like it wasn't quite real, and Xander exploited that, tugging it and turning it and manipulating it just a little. A second longer where he'd lingered, staring into Damon's eyes. An undeniable interest in those eyes, instead of the more ambiguous truth.

When his job sucked, like today, it was comforting to pull the memory out, and relive his encounter with Damon the way he wished it would've happened.

"Bridges, what the *fuck* are you doing?"

Xander jerked himself out of the memory and instantly re-focused on the monotonous work in front of him. Naturally it was impossible to tell what was so terrible about his prep work on the eggplants—but that was par for the course with Chef Aquino. Every basic action was a disaster waiting to happen, and inevitably a disaster in his own paranoid mind.

Aquino yelled because he was a notorious sadist who apparently got his rocks off by torturing everyone within hearing distance.

Especially anyone who worked for him.

"Those aren't thin enough," Chef bellowed. His arms were crossed across his broad chest, chef jacket rolled to his elbows, exposing his forearms. They were objectively nice-looking forearms but Xander would have rather crawled into a pit of fire ants naked than find his boss attractive.

Besides, Kian had the market cornered on that kind of insanity.

"I'm using the mandolin," Xander said slowly. Enunciating. Chef was not stupid, but sometimes he threw a hissy fit about the same stuff that he insisted they do every single damn night.

Apparently today was one of those times. To illustrate, Xander pointed to the metal slicer in front of him, clearly set on an eighth of an inch, because preciseness was the cornerstone of every kitchen, and the foundation of Terroir.

"Is that set correctly?" Chef demanded. Xander barely refrained from rolling his eyes, because it was *clearly* set on the correct setting.

Instead of saying anything, Xander leaned over, checked the setting, and exaggeratedly set it a click higher, then returned the dial back to an eighth of an inch.

"All better," he said in a fake relieved voice. It wasn't that convincing, because 1) Xander was not that good of an actor, and 2) he put in zero effort.

Chef's eyes narrowed, like he wanted to call Xander on his attitude in front of the entire kitchen, who was currently watching their exchange with a held breath. It was the beginning of prep. If someone pissed Chef off now, they were in for another eight hours of hell. But he turned away abruptly instead of arguing, and stomped off into his office, calling for Kian as he walked off.

It wasn't something Xander was proud of, but he was relieved that Kian was going to have to deal with the Bastard's passive-aggressive pouting now instead of him.

After all, Kian was the one who acted like he was in love with that monster.

Damon Hess almost never gave a shit. Not anymore, not after he'd been forcibly dragged, demons kicking and screaming, back to the Napa Valley. Today, though, today mattered. Which was why he had given about half a shit, and had made sure his boots weren't muddy, and his jeans didn't have any particularly awful stains or patches.

"Do you have a reservation, sir?" The Terroir hostess was as polished and elegant as the rest of the surroundings. Just casual enough, with her colorful scarf elegantly arranged over her classic little black dress, a pair of designer flats on her feet. There was always a reminder that under all the unstructured relaxation, this was one of the finest dining establishments in America.

"No," Damon said.

"I'm sorry," she said, and she might have been a budding actress, because she sounded genuinely apologetic. "We don't have any tables available."

She did, but she didn't know that he knew that. He also really didn't want to act like his father, walking into places, demanding everything he wanted, just because he was a Hess.

Unfortunately she wasn't leaving him much choice, continuing to stare at him with that pleasant rejection smile on her face.

Damon sighed, considered leaning conspiratorially over the hostess stand, but it looked pretty flimsy, and it wouldn't help his case to destroy the furniture.

"My father is meeting me here," he lied. "I'm sure he's going to be really disappointed that we couldn't get a table at Bastian's restaurant."

She did two double takes. One, at the father comment. The second, that he called Chef Aquino, *Bastian*. Not many people did that and lived to talk about it.

Damon figured that he could have really been an asshole and called him the Bastard, but he still wanted a table, and that might have been a step too far for the hostess.

"And your father is?" she asked, directly yet delicately.

"Nathan Hess." Damon would have rather ingested rocks than used that name, but he also really needed a table, and she'd left him no choice.

Her shoulders straightened. "Of course, right this way, sir."

The *sir* was back, too, despite his too-casual jeans, and Damon hated it because he knew why she was saying it.

He was shown to a table near the floor-to-ceiling windows, allowing diners to look out on the incredible vistas of the Napa Valley, but near the corner, which guaranteed privacy. Damon had only come here with his father a handful of times, but it was enough to remember that this was his regular table.

The hostess waited for him to seat himself, draping the napkin across his lap with an elegant flick of her wrist. "I'm sorry, again, sir. I didn't recognize you. We didn't realize you'd come home."

Damon hadn't realized he'd come home either, so they had that in common. Maybe because home had never felt like a place to him, but a person, and then that had gone to hell. "Of course," he said. "Not an issue."

He was barely settled—pointedly ignoring the temptation of the wine book sitting so innocently in its cognac leather binding—when the waiter arrived to introduce himself.

"Mr. Hess, it's so good to see you, sir," the waiter said. He was Bastian's perfect combination of urbane formality. "I hear Mr. Hess will be joining us."

"He may be running late," Damon said, and the waiter didn't bat an eyelash. Likely he didn't give a shit, as long as he got a good tip. Which Damon fully intended to leave him.

"May I fetch you a glass of wine while you wait?" the waiter asked. He'd told himself to expect the question, because he was a Hess and because this was Napa, so it was easy enough to turn aside.

"I'll have iced tea, unsweetened," Damon said. "And I'd like to speak to a *sous chef* in your kitchen. Xander Bridges."

Damon fully expected to see the panic lights flashing in the waiter's eyes, and he didn't disappoint. One of the tenets of Terroir was that you *never* saw any kitchen staff on the dining room floor, with the illustrious exception of Bastian Aquino himself. That was because Bastian was an egotistical maniac who couldn't bear anyone else taking credit for his creations.

Even though everyone in here knew that Bastian wasn't actually cooking their food.

"I'm not sure that's possible, sir," the waiter said. He had begun to sweat at his temples, and Damon might have felt sorry for him, but this was important.

Damon had learned from a very young age from observing his grandfather and his father that the most effective way to get people to do what you wanted was to keep repeating the request, over and over, without embellishment or explanation, until you simply wore people down.

"I know," Damon said. "But I'd still like to see Xander Bridges." He didn't raise his voice, but made sure he sounded confident and firm.

He actually sounded like his father, which he would have hated and avoided at all costs except that these were extenuating circumstances.

"I'm . . ." The waiter paused, hesitating. "It's really not done, to bring kitchen staff to the dining room."

"If my father was sitting here," Damon said, still staying pleasant, because it wasn't the waiter's fault that Bastian was crazy, "would you tell him that it wasn't done? Or would you go to the kitchen and bring Xander Bridges up here?"

The waiter was definitely sweating now. "Uh," he said, all eloquence momentarily evaporated.

"Listen," Damon said, leaning closer to the waiter and lowering his voice. "I know it's a huge no-no, to do what I'm asking. But I *need* you to go get Xander Bridges."

"It's important?" the waiter hedged.

"I wouldn't ask if it wasn't really important," Damon promised him.

"Okay, I'll see what I can do," he said.

"Thank you," Damon said, and resolved to give him a *very* large tip. And a job, if everything turned out according to plan.

The waiter was back in five minutes. Damon had looked perfunctorily through the menu, and thought, as he gazed at the listed dishes, that Bastian had used to be more innovative.

This didn't feel *tired* exactly, but it lacked the excitement of previous years. Or maybe Damon had just changed, and wanted something wilder, a little less controlled.

"Are you ready to order, sir?" the waiter asked.

Damon knew he wouldn't be staying long; what he really wanted was to grab a burger at the Napa Tavern, but he felt obligated to order something besides the iced tea.

"I'll take the burrata appetizer," Damon said, handing the menu to the waiter. "And what about my request?"

"I'm working on it," he promised, glancing around pointedly at the other diners. "It *is* the middle of the dining hour, and Mr. Bridges is the *sous* in the kitchen."

Damon had come on a Tuesday, deliberately late, for that exact reason. It was almost the end of service. It should be easy for Xander to duck out and see him for five minutes. There was even a better chance Bastian Aquino wouldn't notice Xander breaking the rules.

He wasn't the world's best planner, but he'd been thinking about this for a long time—just over a year, actually—and while he'd initially thought about catching Xander in the staff parking lot after he was finished for the night, he'd eventually decided that this way carried more weight.

It made him look serious, and it should, because Damon was incredibly serious.

"I'll be happy to wait," Damon said.

The waiter beamed. "Very good."

He returned ten minutes later with the appetizer, and Damon was just digging into the soft, creamy cheese with a toast point when Xander slid into the chair opposite his.

"What are you doing?" Xander hissed. He'd taken off his chef jacket, and had thrown on a navy blue sweatshirt. As disguises went, it wasn't great, but it was probably enough.

"I needed to talk to you," Damon said.

Xander's eyebrows nearly hit his hairline. "It's important," Damon tacked on. "Sorry?"

"You practically gave Nico a heart attack," Xander said. "He doesn't usually wait tables, he's subbing tonight, and demanding a kitchen staff member come into the dining room didn't make his night any easier."

"I'm sorry," Damon repeated. "But I really needed to talk to you."

"So, talk." Xander drummed his fingers impatiently on the tablecloth.

"I'd ask if you remember me, but you obviously do."

"Despite what you probably think, I don't go charging onto other people's property every day, demanding they tell me what they're doing," Xander hissed.

"I didn't think so," Damon said, and he grinned in spite of himself. Xander looked good; of course, he'd looked good that night too. If he was being honest, that night in general and Xander specifically had figured in more than one of his dreams. And his fantasies.

"I ripped up the rest of the vines," Damon continued. "And I'm growing a vegetable garden." *Just like you said.*

Damon hadn't exactly gotten up bright and early the next morning to do it, but it had been close. As soon as Xander had said what he should do, everything, which had felt muddy for so long, had suddenly become crystal clear.

"If you're here to become a supplier for Terroir, you're asking the wrong person," Xander said.

"I don't want to supply Terroir," Damon said. "I want to supply my own restaurant."

"You're opening a restaurant?" Xander asked. This time he looked truly surprised.

"I am." Damon leaned across the table, eyes intent on Xander's dark ones. "And I want you to run it."

Xander froze, looking shell-shocked for a single moment, then leaned back and gave out a bark of laughter. "You want me to run your restaurant."

"I want you to be my head chef," Damon said stubbornly. It had felt for the longest time that this was the only deal breaker in the new plan that had taken over his life. He had to have Xander. No matter how crazy it sounded.

"I have a job," Xander said slowly.

"Aren't you sick of being yelled at?" Damon offered. "I don't know if you've noticed, but I'm not exactly the yelling type. Or the extreme control freak type."

"I noticed." Xander's tone was dry.

"Of course, I'll pay you more than you make here. And you'll get total autonomy over the menu. Input into the design of the space. I want a partner, not a slave."

"You've been practicing this pitch," Xander observed.

"This is important to me," Damon admitted. His mouth felt dry at just *how* important and he took a long drink of his iced tea. "It would be dumb of me to leave it all to chance."

"Aren't you worried I'll say no?"

All the time. Constantly. "It's a good job. Freedom, when you haven't had any for a long time. An opportunity to express your point of view as a chef. And even though I might have been shit at growing grapes, I'm good with the earth. My garden is thriving. Anything I don't have, we'll get from some friends of mine."

"You're really serious," Xander said. "You're really here, offering me a job. After a year."

So he did remember. He'd paid attention, and noticed that Damon had never sought him out. And he hadn't only because Damon hadn't been ready to find him again.

"I am," Damon said steadily.

"Let me think about it," Xander said. He hesitated. "Can I come by and see the garden?"

"I was going to offer, but I was afraid it might hold . . . bad memories still." Damon could hear the wryness in his voice. It was ironic that the man he'd met on one of the worst nights of his life might possibly be the tool in his salvation.

"Not at all. Can I come by tonight? After work? I'll be here only an hour or so longer."

"Sure, of course. You remember where it is?" Damon asked, almost not believing how well this conversation had gone. There had been no interruptions by screaming egotistical head chefs, and Xander seemed to be genuinely considering his proposal.

"I could hardly forget," Xander said, his voice low and serious. It did something to the pit of Damon's stomach. The same thing that he'd felt that night, a year ago. Before, he'd only felt it with women; Xander was the first man.

And like he'd known then, he understood that it was a complication. It wasn't that being attracted to a man bothered him, it was that being attracted to Xander bothered him.

Because the one thing he knew better than anything else was that they could never get involved because Xander deserved better than a shell of a man still desperately trying to find his way. Tearing up the vines had helped. The garden had helped. Building something concrete and unassociated with alcohol would help. But he was under no illusions that he would ever be ready to risk someone else's heart.

Especially not someone like Xander.

It was hardly possible for Damon's land to feel more chaotic than it had the first time he'd been there. The land was dark still, but there was a sweet peacefulness to it now, Xander thought as he wandered between the aisles of leafy greens. Damon's pain wasn't overflowing out of it anymore.

"I can't believe you listened to me," Xander admitted, looking up at Damon, who was still watching him warily from the head of the garden.

"Why shouldn't I listen to you?" Damon questioned.

"I don't know—maybe because I was a completely unknown person, bursting into your vineyard in the middle of the night?"

Damon laughed, low and a little wry. It sent an all too familiar spike of heat through him. For weeks—for *months*—after that night, Xander had thought about him and worried. Had wished more than once that he was less of a coward and could be Damon's friend without worrying about wanting more. He could with countless other men, but he was undeniably attracted to Damon, and knew he was eventually going to want more than just friendship.

Now Damon had come back into his life, and this time it was *him* who wanted more.

A business partner. A head chef. And unspoken between them, a *friend*.

Could Xander be those things and not turn into the worst version of himself? The angry, bitter version of himself who couldn't resign himself to not getting everything he wanted?

He didn't know. But he also knew this wasn't an opportunity that came around every day.

"What did your family say?" Xander asked.

Damon just shrugged, big body a dark outline against a darker sky. No, it wasn't really Xander's business what his family thought of him ripping up seventy-year-old vines. What mattered was that they wouldn't show up to interfere, leaving Xander without a job after burning down the bridge he'd spent years building.

Bastian Aquino was not exactly the "forgive and forget" type. If he left Terroir, he was *leaving* Terroir. There would be no going back. Even if Damon's restaurant never made it off the ground.

Was he ready to take that step?

It came as a total surprise that he was. When he'd been promoted to *sous chef* over a year ago, it had been an exciting change, with more responsibility. Only a little, of course, because the kitchen was Chef Aquino's and he never let anybody forget it.

"I'd like to build something," Xander said. "Here. With you."

It should have scared him more that all the parts felt equally important. He did want to build something. He wanted to do it here, in the place where so much of Napa had begun and evolved, now ripe for a new chapter. And he wanted to do it with a man he barely knew.

Despite the episode with the vines and the storm, Damon felt strong and sturdy. Unshakeable. Just the right person that Xander could batter with his own bred-in mistrust.

Damon didn't just look surprised he'd agreed; he looked elated. That was a god damn genuine smile he was wearing on his handsome face.

"Really?" he asked, excitement seeping into that rough-and-tumble voice.

"This is a good start. I like it." Xander leaned down, and picked up a clump of dark brown dirt. It crumbled between his fingers, fertile and rich. God knew his advice wasn't always great—or taken into consideration—but he'd been right about this. From the look of the plants, he'd been dead right. This was a fantastic place for a vegetable garden.

"When should we start?" Damon asked, like he wasn't really in charge. And maybe, Xander thought with astonishment, he didn't think he was. After what felt like a lifetime of bending and scraping and obeying every order, equality and freedom felt like such a heady thing.

But Xander wouldn't be Xander if he didn't test things. "Aren't you the boss? Don't you have a plan?" he asked lightly.

Damon gave a deep bark of laughter. Xander felt it to his bones. He wanted to put his hands all over the man and feel it as he laughed. "I do. But we're supposed to be partners? When do *you* want to start?"

There was nothing for Xander to do then, but be as honest as Damon was being. "As soon as possible."

Smiling, Damon nodded. "Okay. Do you want to discuss your salary or benefits or anything?"

That was the last thing Xander wanted to do but he wasn't stupid. "You said you'd pay me more than Bastian."

"I will." Steady. Confident. *Sure.* "How much do you make now?"

Xander rattled off a number. He was pretty sure it was correct. To be honest, as long as he had money in the bank to pay rent, he didn't worry about money.

"Twenty percent more now, and then consider it doubled when we open," Damon said calmly.

Xander might be *laissez-faire* about money, but that was not an insignificant amount. "Are *you* sure?"

"I'm a Hess, aren't I? We should do something with my god damn trust fund, and paying your salary seems as good a use as any," Damon said.

It was hard for even Xander to argue with that.

This time when Xander left, they exchanged phone numbers, Xander promising to be back in a couple of days, after his time at Terroir was finished. Damon mentioned a contract, Xander agreed to read and sign it, which normally would have felt foolish to him, but this was Damon. He was like a rock. Unshakeable, even with the addiction. Probably even more so, because of it.

Even though Xander had misjudged people before, he knew he wasn't misjudging now.

When he turned to go to his car, he glanced back, and saw Damon standing there, watching him go. A darker outline in the dark of the night. And it felt right to have his eyes on him still.

So right that Xander gave himself a blistering lecture when he got into his car.

"You will not fall in love with him," he sternly told his reflection in the rearview mirror. "You will not fall for another straight boy who won't love you back. You won't pine or yearn or otherwise ruin your life panting after someone you can't have, like Kian. You *won't*."

God knew if the lecture would stick, but at least Xander knew where the lines were drawn.

"Where did you go last night?" Kian asked as he julienned about a hundred thousand carrots, his knife flashing as it flew through the orange flesh.

Chef Aquino must be in a bad mood. He hadn't forced Kian to prep vegetables for the side sauté they served with some of their main dishes in ages. It was an annoyingly menial job, even though Kian was really good at it.

Probably because he'd been stuck doing it so many times.

"Why are you doing that?" Xander asked, gesturing with a whisk at Kian's mound of carrots instead of answering his question. He still wasn't sure how to break the news. Or if he even should. Was Kian still on his side, still *his* friend, or had he permanently defected to the Aquino camp?

"Steve, one of the new kitchen assistants, quit unexpectedly today."

"Do you even have to add the *unexpectedly* part?" Xander wondered out loud. "It seems a little unnecessary these days."

The meaner Chef got, the faster his new employees departed. And that only wrenched him tighter, leading them all in a vicious cycle. Some days it felt like Kian was the only one who could talk him down.

"We needed him to prep these today," Kian said, not even bothering to answer Xander's question.

"So you're doing it instead." Xander was prepping the sauces, which was his main job every day, along with soup of the day. That, a delicate creamy *vichyssoise*, was already simmering away on the stove in a gigantic pot.

"Someone has to do it, and that's part of my job. To fill in, wherever I'm needed. That's part of the cross-training Chef promised I'd get."

Xander rolled his eyes as he peeled shallots. Three years in, and there was still that note of hero worship in Kian's voice whenever he talked about Bastian Aquino. These days, it was accompanied by a healthy dose of unrequited pining.

That worried Xander enough, but at least it was still unrequited. The day it changed, Xander was going to have to punch the Bastard in the face for taking advantage of a subordinate. For taking advantage of *Kian*. Xander wasn't looking forward to it.

"Oh yeah, you've gotten a really well-rounded education," Xander drawled. "A great opportunity to grow a thicker skin."

Kian's knife didn't even pause. It still flew through the carrot at breakneck speed, each julienned slice perfectly sized. But his voice got harder around the edges. "I don't know why you keep doing this. If you're not happy here, if you don't enjoy working for Chef Aquino, then *leave*. I don't need you to stay here just to protect me. I'm a grown man. I can take care of myself."

"Yeah, that's exactly what I'm worried about," Xander muttered. Kian looked up. "And maybe I will," he said louder. "Maybe that's where I was last night. Maybe someone offered me a really good job."

Kian's eyes went wide. "Did they really? Who is it? Are you leaving?"

"Shhhhhh," Xander snapped. "I'm . . . I haven't told anyone else. Especially Chef."

"Maybe don't do it today. You know, with Steve and all." Kian's tone went wry. He might defend Chef Aquino to the ends of the earth, because he was not very secretly in love with him, but he was also a realist.

Steve hadn't even been around long enough for Xander to remember his name.

"I'll tell him in a few days," Xander said. "We're still finalizing the details." Damon had texted this morning, promising a copy of the contract in his email in a few days. And Xander, while giving his word, was still not stupid enough to quit his job until he'd made sure that everything Damon promised was also in writing.

"Who is it?" Kian whisper-demanded.

"It's a Hess," Xander said, and sue him, he definitely sounded a little smug. "They want to open a farm-to-table restaurant and they approached me for the head chef position."

Kian's already big eyes grew wider. "*Head* chef?" And Xander did understand his surprise. The Hess family was big in Napa, and if they were really going to open a restaurant under the familial auspices, they'd bring in someone well-known to head the kitchen.

They definitely would not be hiring Xander, who had never been head chef before, and who was definitely not well-known.

But Damon Hess wasn't his family, with none of their high-profile obligations, which had opened the door wide for Xander.

Xander thought about telling Kian but he was going to be worked up enough already, being the last of their friend quartet to still work at Terroir—and everyone and their mother knew he wouldn't be leaving anytime soon—so he kept quiet about that important detail.

"Head chef," Xander confirmed.

"Wow." Kian's knife still worked away, reducing the pile of carrots from stupendous to merely numerous.

"Don't you have zucchini to do after that?" Xander asked. He finished chopping his shallots for the wine butter sauce they served with rockfish, and moved onto garlic.

"And the red peppers," Kian said. "Also I think Chef said he wanted to add turnips today too. Said he got some in fresh. What kind of menu are you thinking of?" As he asked, his knife flew through the last of the carrots.

"I got offered the job last night," Xander retorted. "I haven't signed the contract. How could I have decided on a menu yet?"

Except that he had. He'd spent the last few years of his time in Terroir getting through the worst of Chef Aquino and his temper by clinging to his food imagination. What might he do with this rockfish, if he served it? A sweet corn gastrique, maybe?

Definitely not this tired shallot butter wine reduction that he could make in his sleep.

"You're going to take it, aren't you." Kian said it flatly; a statement, not even a question. Like leaving Terroir was some kind of unspeakable crime.

Xander slammed his knife down onto the board. "Of course I'm going to take it. We're not all like you, in thrall to the Bastard. You wouldn't take another job even if the French Laundry came calling."

"I don't want to work for Thomas Keller," Kian retorted stiffly.

"That's exactly the point I'm trying to make." Somewhere Xander had lost the steam of his temper, and all that was left was regret. Regret that he'd never been able to save Kian from wasting his abilities and all his blood and sweat and tears, sacrificing them to a man who didn't care.

The color rose on Kian's pale cheeks. Pale, despite living in California. Probably because he never left this god damned kitchen.

"You're pissed off that I won't listen to your fucking advice," Kian spat out. His knife had finally stopped, and it trembled, the shining steel flickering under the lights of the kitchen. "Well, not everyone is you, Xander, and you don't know what's right for everyone. Maybe if you did, you could tell yourself, and you wouldn't be so god damned bitter all the time."

If Chef was around, he wouldn't tolerate this argument, never mind a friendly discussion. Work was for work, as he liked to say. It was not social hour. But he wasn't around, probably dealing with the fallout of Steve's departure, and Xander discovered that despite usually not giving a shit, he *really* didn't give a shit today.

He still hadn't picked up his knife. Instead, he leaned over, and flipped the gas off the stove. The shallots that were slowly sautéing in a puddle of melted butter would slowly grow cold and congeal without their heat source.

"What are you doing?" Kian demanded. His flush rose brighter.

"Leaving," Xander said calmly. "You can tell Chef Aquino I'm done."

Kian stared at him wordlessly. No doubt shocked silent.

"You could come with me," Xander said. "You *should* come with me."

"You should at least give your two-week notice," Kian insisted. "It's only fair."

"Why? So Chef Aquino can scream at me and belittle me and act like he's better off without me when I know the truth? That I should have been promoted to *chef de cuisine* forever ago, but that Aquino pretends he doesn't need one, so he doesn't have to? Yeah, no, thanks. I'm done."

He picked up his knife, slid it into the cloth wrap, next to all his other knifes, and rolled it up. He didn't look back as he walked out, but he knew Kian was staring at him the whole way.

There should be guilt at how he was leaving Kian to deal with the Bastard, but wasn't that what Kian wanted anyway? To *deal* with him, all the fucking time?

Instead of guilt, all Xander felt was delicious, intoxicating freedom as he left Terroir behind with one gigantic middle finger to all the shit he'd put up with for far too long.

Chapter Three

"So the rumors are true. You *did* destroy this vineyard."

Damon looked up from his position on his knees in the dirt, where he was carefully weeding around his cabbages.

Bastian Aquino stood tall and arrogant, eyes covered with silver aviators, arms crossed across his chest, his mouth compressed into a tight line.

Damon didn't say a word, didn't move an inch. Sometimes it was good to remember he was a Hess. Not always, but sometimes.

"You tore up all these vines and then stole my *sous chef*," Bastian continued. "I'm still trying to figure out what I ever did to you."

Like most egotistical assholes, Bastian would naturally make Xander's defection about him.

"Nothing," Damon said, finally rising to his feet. It didn't matter to him what position he occupied—he already knew that power had nothing to do with being on your knees, but Bastian clearly hadn't. The only way to face him was to don the trappings of an authority he'd long rejected.

Sort of the way he'd done to trick his way into Terroir.

"I know you lied to get into my dining room," Bastian continued, the edge of his voice cruelly patronizing. "I know you weren't meeting your father. He never would have asked a server to bring a member of the kitchen staff to a table. He never would have ordered a single appetizer and an iced tea and then left."

Nathan Hess wouldn't have. He would have never dreamed of speaking to a staff member unless he needed something. He would have ordered a full meal, several bottles of wine, and then spent the next several hours enjoying what he considered the just fruits of his labor.

"Is your problem with the single appetizer or the iced tea?" Damon asked mildly. He wasn't going to fight with Bastian Aquino about his father. Xander—that was a slightly different story.

Bastian ripped the sunglasses from his face and took a few strides, stopping short of where the garden began, eyes narrowing at the muddy knees of Damon's jeans.

He couldn't help but wonder the last time Bastian had gotten his hands—or anything else—dirty.

"*My problem*," Bastian snarled, "is that you fucking poached my best chef."

"If Xander is your best chef, then you can't be surprised that he left. Isn't that what good chefs are supposed to do? Spread their wings? Develop their own point of view? I thought that was supposed to be something you wanted. The pedigree of a whole stable of famous culinary offspring."

"Generally that's the idea," Bastian said. It looked like it hurt to admit it.

"Then why are you here?" Damon asked, turning away from the man in front of him. He'd already wasted enough breath on Bastian Aquino; he was never going to understand why everyone left him.

"I came to tell you to back off, and that when Xander rethinks his behavior, you're going to encourage him to stay at Terroir."

Damon glanced over from his position by the cabbages. When he'd woken up this morning to Xander's text that he'd walked out in the middle of prep for the night's dinner service, he'd half-dreamed that Xander might show up bright and early in the garden. It turned out Bastian Aquino was not a pleasant substitution for what Damon really wanted.

"He doesn't need to stay at Terroir. He shouldn't stay at Terroir. He doesn't *want* to stay at Terroir." Damon made sure his voice stayed calm, but it was firm. Implacable. His demons were a hell of a lot tougher than Bastian Aquino, and he faced them down every damn day.

"He will if I offer to make him *chef de cuisine*," Bastian said smugly.

Damon didn't know exactly what that particular position entailed, but by the way the chef was referring to it, it was illustrious and there might be some circumstance under which Xander would take it.

He still didn't know Xander well enough to be sure, but he'd gotten an indelible impression of him from just the few times they'd met. Damon knew Xander was loyal and hardworking, and would never walk out on a job just because he got annoyed with something.

The annoyance would have to be long-occurring, far-reaching, and far more serious.

"I think if Xander wanted to keep working at Terroir, then he wouldn't have left," Damon said simply. "I don't think it matters what position you want to dangle in front of him, he's done with you. He's done being treated like a toy you can win back with a prize, after you've mistreated it. Xander deserves to work for—*with*, actually—someone on his side. And that's never going to be you."

"You seem very sure about that," Bastian retorted wryly, a corner of his mouth twitching upwards.

"I am," Damon said. And he was.

"You think you can be that *partner*," Bastian sneered, shoving his sunglasses and covering up his smug, handsome face. "A Hess who isn't even a Hess. A Hess who ripped up his own vineyard."

Better than the drop-dead drunk Hess, Damon desperately wanted to say, but Bastian Aquino had already spent too much time poisoning the place where he'd begun to find peace.

"Get off my land," he said, beginning to rise to his feet again, because if push came to shove, he would literally throw him off of it, if he had to. Bastian Aquino wasn't a small man, but Damon was bigger. And Damon owned a wealth of determination that Aquino couldn't even begin to touch.

But to Damon's surprise, Bastian actually did as he was told, turned and stomped off, and left him wondering what the hell had just happened.

Xander woke to someone pounding on his bedroom door. He opened one eye, saw the mostly empty bottle of cabernet that he'd stolen from Nate the night before on his nightstand, and promptly closed it again. Rolling over, he groaned.

The pounding continued and intensified.

"Xander, I know you're in there," the voice outside the door insisted. It was Kian. It could only be Kian. Though, Xander theorized, it could also be Nate, pissed that he'd nicked one of his better bottles of wine. But Nate knew he'd taken it, and had even offered to drink it with him.

But Xander had been celebrating and hadn't felt like entertaining himself by turning down Nate's sexual offers.

"You're wrong," he croaked, "Xander isn't here."

Kian finally got sick of pounding on the door and opened it. He didn't look amused.

"I need to talk to you," he said, leaning against the doorjamb and doing his best Bastian Aquino impression, which was not very good, because Kian was a marshmallow and couldn't pull off asshole even with extensive training.

"So talk," Xander said, rolling over and burying his face in the pillow. "Clearly nothing is stopping you."

"You walked out last night," Kian began, but Xander interrupted him before he could get the rest out.

"I quit," Xander corrected grimly. "I didn't just walk out. I fucking *quit*. Just in case that wasn't clear."

Kian glared. "Believe me, it was."

"Okay then," Xander said.

"What I keep trying to tell you is that you don't have to. Leave, that is. Chef is here . . . and he wants to talk to you."

There wasn't much Kian could say to get his undivided attention right now. Not with rancid red wine on his tongue and the insistent throbbing in his temples. "Chef is here?" He couldn't help it, he gawked a little. "In *our* house?"

"Yes," Kian said primly.

"What the fuck."

"I suggest," Kian said, his tone of voice much more insistent than a suggestion, "you get cleaned up and get out here before he gets tired of waiting and leaves."

But would that be all that bad, in the scheme of things? Xander wasn't sure. He did know that the last thing he expected was for the Bastard to show up at their house, prepared to beg him to come back to his old job.

He knew what it was like when people quit Terroir. There was usually screaming and yelling and almost always missiles of some sort. When Wyatt had left, Bastian had cleared his whole desk—keyboard, laptop, paperwork, several glasses—with a single sweep of his arm.

As far as Xander knew, there had never been a counteroffer.

And maybe there wasn't one. It was entirely possible that instead of coming here to win him back, Aquino had come here to kill him. But Xander was fairly sure that he wouldn't commit murder in front of Kian—or make him clean up the mess.

Even if he wasn't going to take whatever offer Aquino had come here to make, Xander figured it was probably worth hearing. His curiosity demanded at least that much.

He threw the covers back and staggered upright. Kian glared. "Hurry up," he said, before closing the door behind him. No doubt he was freaking out that their boss—*his* boss, Xander corrected—and the unrequited love of his life was sitting in their living room, probably trying to assess the dubious provenance of their couch.

Dressing was as simple as throwing on a pair of athletic shorts and a shirt that was probably clean. *Mostly* clean, Xander decided as he sniffed it. Good enough. He stopped by the bathroom, brushed his teeth, vaguely tried to neaten his bedhead, and called it good enough again.

As he predicted, Bastian was on the couch in the living room, with Kian hovering within reaching distance, looking an uneasy mixture of anxious and elated.

"Xander," Bastian said to him. He sounded just as arrogant as always, but there was the tiniest bit of contrition layered over it. An apology without the actual words.

Meaningless, basically.

Xander crossed his arms over his chest and didn't sit down. "What do you want?"

"You quit last night."

"I did," Xander said steadily.

"You're not even going to give me the benefit of a two-week notice?" Like there was ever a real two-week notice at Terroir without some benefit to Bastian.

"No."

"Or an opportunity to counter what Damon Hess offered you?"

Xander glanced over at Kian, who had the nerve to look ashamed. "Not much is a secret, is it?" Xander said bitterly.

"Kian is worried about you. Worried you're throwing your career away on someone who can't properly support you. You know, he isn't even really a winemaker. He's not a restauranteur. He's playing at growing a garden. But he's not even a Hess—not like you think."

Xander regarded Bastian steadily. "He's exactly what I think he is."

"So there's nothing I can offer you that might make you change your mind?" Bastian looked sneakier than usual, and considering that Xander had never trusted him on a normal day, this was worrisome. "What if I made you my *chef de cuisine*?"

"You mean the job I've deserved for six months?" Xander demanded. "The one you should already have offered me?"

"I can't apologize for that, Xander," Bastian cut in smoothly. And no, he wouldn't, the bastard. He never apologized for anything.

"I think I'll take my chances with the 'not real' Hess," Xander said, using finger quotes. Kian, out of his field of vision, gave a stricken gasp. He probably couldn't imagine anyone turning down Bastian.

But Xander was sick of his shit, sick of the backhanded manipulations, the hissy fits, and was definitely not interested in continuing to work for someone who didn't feel it was necessary to treat him right until he actually walked out.

"You really mean that." Bastian sounded like he couldn't even believe it. "Hess said you'd say that, but I couldn't believe it. Couldn't believe you'd turn down *chef de cuisine* to work for a part-time gardener whose restaurant is currently a ramshackle shed without a real kitchen."

It had clearly been too long since Aquino had worked in someone else's kitchen, because the idea of creating his own space, shaping his own legacy, sounded incredibly appealing to Xander. Even if it meant a shit ton of work. Even if it meant working in a ramshackle shed without a real kitchen.

It was only after Xander had worked through *that* thought that he had another one.

Damon had talked to Aquino? He'd told him that he'd turn down the promotion?

Xander frowned. "You went and talked to Damon?"

Bastian stood and began pacing in the tiny empty space of their living room. Xander could practically feel Kian's anxiety begin to spike. "He *poached* you. In my own fucking restaurant! What else was I supposed to do?"

Xander crossed his arms across his chest and gave his ex-boss a glare that sang with finality. "Fucking ask *me* if I wanted the job. Not my new partner. Not my friend and my roommate. *Me*. That's your whole problem. That's why I left. You have to control everything, and it fucking sucks." And apparently he really wanted to flush everything down the toilet because the word vomit kept coming. "And that one," he said, pointing in Kian's direction, "is too nice to ever say anything to your face, but you're a psychotic megalomaniac who desperately needs to be checked."

Aquino's expression shuttered hard and fast. He gave Xander one last bitter, angry look and turned and marched away.

"You're an idiot," Kian hissed. "Are you really going to let some guy tell Chef Aquino what you want to do?"

Xander rolled his eyes. "Are we really going to do this? You and me, *really*?"

"I don't know what you mean," Kian said stiffly. He was still glancing over at the door every ten seconds, like Aquino was going to march back through it, throw him over his shoulder and take him with him—and Kian was going to *let* him.

"I mean, are you *really* going to get bent out of shape over my new partner telling Aquino to take a hike when I was going to do that anyway? When you would follow Aquino to the depths of any hell he concocted, just because he asked you to, just because you're too in love with him to ever tell him no?"

Kian opened his mouth and then shut it again. "No," he finally said shortly. "No, I guess we're not."

"Okay then," Xander retorted, the testy edge to his voice growing sharper. "I'm going to go back to bed, contemplate my brief joblessness, and you can go running after Aquino, because I know you're dying to."

Kian looked like he was desperate to argue, but they both knew it would be a lie. Turning, Xander walked back down the hall to his bedroom and tried to ignore it when he heard the door shut behind Kian and the engine turning over on Bastian's Audi R8.

Picking up his phone from the table, he sent Damon a quick text. **The Bastard was just here, I'm assuming you had to deal with him too. We'll talk later tonight. I'll be there around five.**

He lay back down, stared at the ceiling and tried to banish the thought that he'd just made a life-altering mistake. Things would be different, Xander told himself, but they could be *good* different. At the very least, he wouldn't be making the same mistakes over and over again.

Then he remembered how his blood had spiked every single damn time he looked at Damon, and *yes,* maybe he was about to make a mistake, but at least this was a familiar mistake.

"What's all this?" Damon asked when he opened the door.

"Dinner," Xander said, hefting one of the grocery bags a little higher on his hip. "I got the impression last time I was here that you were good with that espresso machine but that you don't use your stove that much."

Damon grinned, unexpectedly fierce and bright, and it nearly knocked Xander right back. "Guilty as charged," he admitted, opening the door wider to let Xander come into the house.

It looked much the same as it had that night, a year ago. A little cleaner, perhaps, like Damon had gotten that text and had decided to neaten up in anticipation of Xander coming over.

This is not a date, Xander reminded himself.

He'd had to remind himself of this more than once when he'd been at the grocery store picking up food for tonight. First he'd agonized at the meat counter. When you brought a filet for dinner, what did it *mean*? What about salmon? Shrimp?

Love, marriage, or maybe even eternal devotion? A white picket fence?

Xander had to stop himself before he asked the butcher if the different cuts had deep, secret meanings, like flowers. There was no cut of meat that communicated: "this is just a friendly work dinner, but if you wanted it to be more, I could be convinced. And by the way, do you like men?"

"I decided," Xander told Damon as they walked through the living room toward the kitchen, "that it would be completely stupid for you to hire me if I'd never even cooked for you before."

Damon shrugged, one side of his mouth quirking up a little. It had the side effect of making his bottom lip look very bitable.

Xander set his groceries on the kitchen counter and began to unpack them like they held the secret to world peace. He was attracted to Damon and it was a problem, but their partnership didn't have to be defined by his inconvenient attraction.

"I think I'd like to see you explore what you're interested in," Damon said quietly as he settled in one of the barstools. The same one Xander had occupied a year ago. Xander told himself that meant nothing. After all, there were only three barstools to pick from. Maybe that one was secretly the most comfortable and Xander had just gotten lucky.

It did something to the base of his stomach to think that Damon didn't care; that he just wanted to give Xander the freedom and the space to do what *he* wanted. It had been a very long time since anyone had thought highly enough of him to do that, and Xander told himself not to be fooled into thinking that's what this was.

"You really don't care?" Xander asked in disbelief.

He'd never hired a chef before. Maybe when you hired one, you just naturally assumed you were getting *their* point of view, not your own.

"My point of view is the garden," Damon said. "As long as you use as much of it as you can, I'm good."

And Xander had taken at least that much away from their previous conversations about the restaurant, so he'd bought lots of vegetables, which he spread out across the counter now.

"Someday," he told Damon, "all this will be from your garden."

Damon set his elbows on the counter, forearms rippling with muscle, because even though he was wearing another plaid shirt, of course he'd rolled up the sleeves. But his intent couldn't be to drive Xander crazy; it was just probably more comfortable. Maybe those crazy gorgeous forearms didn't even fit properly into shirts.

Xander swallowed hard and looked away. "I figured I'd make a quick pasta with roasted garlic and sautéed vegetables. I got a nice salmon filet too."

"Salmon's good. I like salmon," Damon said.

It was weird cooking in someone else's kitchen, and it was even weirder doing it with Damon watching him so intently.

All of Damon's pans were hung up on a nice suspended rack in front of the front counter. They weren't the best pans he'd ever worked with, but they were fine for his purposes tonight. He picked one and set it on the stove. After breaking down the head of garlic, he set a few cloves in to roast, and cleared the marble counter to make his fresh pasta.

"So Aquino came to see you," Xander said. He'd figured out quickly that Damon wasn't a big talker, unless you asked him a direct question and expected an answer. And not only was the purpose of tonight's dinner to make sure his cooking didn't disgust his new partner, it was also important to get to know each other better. After all, Xander had come here with every intention of signing the contract, and he knew there was due diligence he needed to exercise first.

"Yeah, this morning. I knew he was a jerk, but wow," Damon muttered darkly.

"And he told you about the job he wanted to offer me," Xander said. He wasn't mad exactly . . . but maybe he was. Maybe he would have taken the *chef de cuisine* position—Damon didn't know him well enough to know either way.

The last thing he wanted was a partner who thought he knew best and would speak for Xander. Of course, Xander didn't really think Damon was like that, but the worry was still there, hidden in the back of his mind.

After all, Xander wouldn't be Xander if he wasn't always expecting the other shoe to drop.

"Yeah," Damon said, and then he laughed self-consciously. "He told you that I said you'd turn it down, didn't he?"

Xander had wondered if Aquino was trying to play them against each other, hoping he'd come out on top if their partnership fell apart before it ever began, but it was extra annoying to discover that he'd been right.

"He did," Xander confirmed.

"I did say that I thought you'd walked out for good reasons that had nothing to do with me. I didn't think you'd take the job back, unless they were extraordinary circumstances."

"It wasn't even extraordinary circumstances that made me walk out," Xander said wryly. He cracked a few eggs in the center of the flour he'd formed into a loose pyramid shape on the marble. "More the straw that broke the camel's back. He pulled one of his stupid ego stunts and I suddenly thought, what the fuck am I still doing here, catering to this asshole?"

Damon nodded. "I didn't mean to speak for you, I just wanted him off my land with his smug attitude, if I'm being honest."

Xander waved a flour-dusted hand. "It's fine, really. He *is* a smug asshole, it's undeniable. He was even smugger when he came by my house today. It felt good to tell him to get the fuck out.

"But," he continued, "I don't want to get things off on the wrong foot. I just left a restaurant where nothing I said mattered. One of the reasons your offer looked so appealing was my opinion counting. And I want it to count."

Damon didn't say a word, just slid a sheaf of papers across the eating counter, until they were precariously balanced over where Xander was mixing his pasta dough.

"It's all there," he said. "You get full say over the menu. Kitchen design. Collaborative input over the design and direction of the dining room and the restaurant itself. I want us to be partners. Don't let Aquino get in the way of that."

"I don't want to," Xander said. "I want this to work out."

The intensity of Damon's gaze told Xander that he was telling the truth. Xander still wasn't sure *why*—specifically why Damon had picked him to be head chef, but maybe that wasn't important. Not nearly as important anyway as having full control over the kitchen spelled out in the contract.

All the rest they could figure out later.

"I don't have a pasta machine," Damon said apologetically just as Xander whipped out a long wooden rolling pin that he'd had forever and that worked beautifully on pasta.

"I guess you don't need one," Damon added, a self-conscious smile on his face.

"I'm adaptable, and I like doing things by hand," Xander said as he steadily rolled out the dough. "This whole process is relaxing for me."

"Is that why you started cooking?"

"I'm not sure why I started," Xander admitted. "Probably because my mom was always teaching in the late afternoons and someone had to make dinner."

"Your mom was a teacher?"

Xander told himself the real interest he was hearing in Damon's voice didn't mean anything. He wasn't sure he entirely believed it.

"Piano," Xander said. He shifted the sheet of dough on the counter, making sure it wouldn't stick. He looked up at Damon. "Pizza wheel?"

"Second drawer to the left of the stove," Damon answered right away, and Xander had to admire a man who was organized enough to know where all his tools were.

"I eat frozen pizzas a lot," he admitted when Xander pulled it out of the drawer.

"Not anymore you don't," Xander retorted. He paused, pizza wheel above the dough, and really thought about Damon's question from earlier. "I guess I started cooking because I had to. I kept going because I was good at it. But I'm ready to figure out again why I still want to."

"I hope you can." Damon looked down at his hands. From where he was standing, Xander could see the nicks and cuts and the sheen of dirt that he couldn't get off no matter how much he washed. They were the hands of someone who worked with them for a living.

Xander began to cut the dough into long, thin strips, demonstrating his own confidence in his hands. Not many people made pasta with only hand tools—but Xander liked the rustic quality it gave the pasta. He also liked relying entirely on himself to get the job done.

"That's amazing," Damon said, sounding awed as Xander, with a few clever flips of his fingers, curled the pasta into several little nests, dotting the countertop. "You're totally going to throw away my frozen pizzas."

"You want pizza, at least let me make it for you," Xander insisted. He ignored the thrill that resounded deep at the idea of feeding Damon for every meal.

He wasn't Damon's personal chef, but maybe he wanted to be. Maybe he wanted to be everything Damon needed.

Definitely everything he wanted.

He pulled out his chef's knife and began decimating the pile of zucchini and squash that he'd bought at the store, and maybe his chopping motion was a little more emphatic than it needed to be, but who could blame him?

It didn't matter that he'd gone down this road before, and it had been epically disastrous. Clearly he hadn't learned, because it didn't feel like falling for Damon was a matter of *if*, more a matter of *when*.

Finishing up with the vegetables, and moving onto the salmon, Xander looked up, surprised at the quiet. Damon wasn't a big talker, but they'd been having a decent conversation, he was taken aback to see that the other man had disappeared.

The seasoning on the salmon was simple—just a squeeze of lemon, a sprig of dill, and some salt and pepper. Despite claiming he didn't cook, Xander noticed that his pepper grinder was high quality, and the salt was the brand Xander himself recommended.

Damon might not cook for himself, but he knew his way around a kitchen. Xander wondered why he'd stopped. He knew it didn't always make sense to go to the trouble just for yourself, but Damon, despite his solitary demeanor, maybe hadn't always been alone.

"Table's set," Damon said, and Xander turned back from the stove, surprised to hear his voice. He'd gotten lost in the quiet, and in the rhythm of prep and cooking.

The salmon sizzled on the stove behind him. "Where are we eating?" Xander asked. "I've got about five more minutes here. The pasta just needs to cook, and then tossed with the vegetable medley."

"Outside," Damon said, gesturing. "I figured we should eat our first meal together as partners in the garden. Found an old table, dragged it out. It's not perfect, but it'll work."

"That's . . ." *Pretty fucking romantic*, Xander didn't want to say. "That's really nice," he rephrased, mentally wincing at how lame that sounded.

A few minutes later he was carrying plates outside, following where Damon had gone through the sliding glass door to the garden. Sure enough, there was a flagstone patio with an old wooden table set with silverware and glasses, and *god damnit*, he'd lit candles and there were several strings of clear Christmas lights crisscrossing the patio, augmenting the mood lighting.

This is not a date, Xander reminded himself for the hundredth time.

Maybe it wasn't him that needed reminding though. *But did Damon even like men?* Xander wondered. He didn't really give off a gay vibe, though Xander had felt some sort of interest directed toward him more than once.

And now there was this.

"I hope iced tea is okay," Damon said. "I brew it myself."

Normally Xander would have begged a nice white or a rosé from Nate to complement the meal, but obviously he wasn't going to drink in front of someone who was a professed alcoholic. Not unless Damon made it explicitly clear that it was okay. And from Damon's offer of tea, Xander took that the opposite was actually true.

It was okay, it was fine. Xander didn't *need* a glass of wine with a meal. It just would have settled the sudden fluttering of the butterflies at the base of his stomach as he set the plates down on the table and slid into a chair.

He watched, trying to be casual and not like he was internally freaking out, as Damon lit the candles, and slid the lighter into his pocket.

"This looks great. Thank you for coming over and cooking," Damon said, and his warm smile made Xander wonder just how lonely he'd been since coming back to Napa.

"It was no trouble. Plus, I figure it's a semi-decent audition." *More* than semi-decent, if Xander was being honest. He cut into his salmon, and was definitely pleased by the slight pinkish tone of the inside. It was *perfect*.

Eat your fucking heart out, Bastian Aquino.

"You don't need to audition," Damon scoffed.

"Because I worked at Terroir?" Xander said, taking a sip of tea. It was well-brewed, with the faintest hint of mint on the tongue. Not too sweet, either. And was that basil in the aftertaste? Xander remembered the perfect cappuccino from that night a year ago, and now this tea, clearly crafted with love and skill. An undeniable skill.

Damon inclined his head, twirling pasta on his fork.

That was a non-answer, but Xander wondered if he'd get anything more straightforward out of the man. He was quiet, so much of him buried far under the surface—and he was dying to go digging.

"Obviously, you grew up here," Xander said. "But you mentioned you left for awhile."

The corner of Damon's full mouth quirked up. Like he knew that Xander was digging and *why*. Maybe he did, but then if he knew, why had he set this table with candles?

"I did leave. It turns out that living in Napa sucks for an alcoholic." He took a deep breath. "I left after my divorce. Not only was Napa too small for me and the vines, it was too small for me and Rachel."

It shouldn't have hurt. It was hardly an official statement of his sexuality. Lots of men married women and liked men. Lots of men liked both. It was hardly the end of hope, but the salmon in Xander's mouth turned to ash.

"I didn't know you were divorced," Xander said stupidly, like Damon was an open book, when actually the opposite was true. The truth was, he didn't know what else to say without exposing his own interest in Damon. He'd known it was a bad idea from the first moment, and here was nearly the confirmation he needed to believe it.

"I don't exactly go around talking about it," Damon said with a quiet, wry amusement.

"Right, no, of course not." Xander hesitated. "I've never been married."

"I know," Damon said, and the amusement was a little more pronounced now.

Xander raised an eyebrow.

"You and your friends, all Terroir employees, all living in that rental house. You're not exactly low-key, not in this small town. Lots of people are willing to talk if you ask."

So Damon knew he was gay, *and* he'd asked about him. Xander knew what he'd probably heard: gay orgies and all other sorts of sordid rumors. None of which were actually true, because nobody who worked fourteen-hour days on average, six days a week, had the energy to hold orgies.

"And what did they say?" Xander asked, more than a little bitterly. He couldn't help it. He felt dumb and played, because he'd gotten distracted by an incredible pair of forearms and some soulful gazes.

"That you're hardworking. That you all barely sleep. That you run that restaurant for Bastian Aquino. That you're good guys who work for a shitty boss."

Not what Xander had been expecting him to say.

"That was all I listened to," Damon continued and the kindness in his voice was both galling and a balm to all that bitterness flooding him.

"You could have come and asked me directly. Might have avoided some of the more . . . colorful stories," Xander pointed out.

"I didn't want to approach you before I was ready." Damon ducked his head, flush on his cheeks, almost like he was bashful about this confession. "I sought you out when I was ready. That night we met, I wasn't ready. Not even close. I'm still not as rock steady as I want to be, but the garden helps and this project has kept me going. Even more, I want to be the kind of partner you deserve."

"You are," Xander said, and he knew how god damn earnest he sounded. Like the kid he'd been right out of high school, desperate to prove to everyone how genuine he was. He hadn't been that kid for a long time, but he felt the echo of him tonight, sitting across from Damon.

"We'll see." Damon's smile was wry. "Sorry to be such a downer, on such a great night."

"This is important stuff we should be talking about," Xander said, even though part of him desperately wanted to laugh off this whole conversation. Probably because it struck so deep, and Xander was used to keeping that softer side of himself barricaded with jaded sarcasm. But jaded sarcasm just didn't feel right, at least not at this moment.

Definitely not when Damon was beginning to open himself up.

Chapter Four

Hands down, it was one of the best meals Damon had ever eaten. Even though he'd watched Xander prep it with his own two hands, it was a marvel that he'd done it with *only* those hands. It was a far better meal than any he'd ever had at Terroir, and that was prepared by an entire staff and countless pieces of expensive equipment.

Xander had come to his house with a bag of groceries and a knife, borrowed a pan and a pizza cutter, and had made an astoundingly delicious meal. It was talent and drive, all wrapped up in one package.

A *cute* package.

Damon had been telling himself not to notice—or if he was going to notice, then he should just ignore the attraction. But sitting across from Xander, staring at him in the candlelight, it was much harder than he'd imagined. Especially when he looked relaxed and much more at peace than he had that night a year ago.

At first he'd been too worked up himself to notice the anxiousness that Xander wore like a cloak. Or a very difficult-to-scale wall complete with archers equipped with fiery arrows and soldiers pouring boiling oil.

But tonight his guard had fallen a little, and despite everything, Damon wanted desperately to believe it was more than just quitting a job he'd really hated.

Damon wanted to believe the smile on Xander's face had something to do with him.

"Thank you," Damon said. "If that was an audition, you nailed it."

"I know." He was a little smug, and it was more than a little adorable. The way his nose scrunched up, the eye crinkles, the expressive look in his dark brown eyes.

Damon had imagined he might be in danger, hanging around Xander all the time, especially considering the impression he'd made on him in such a short time, but this was Trouble with a capital *t*.

"You'd better watch yourself. Not sure your head's gonna fit back through the back door," Damon teased.

"You wanted a chef," Xander said, spreading his arms. "You got one."

"They're sort of thick on the ground in Napa," Damon softly insisted, "but it turns out I'm particular."

"Imagine that, a Hess particular." The sarcasm in Xander's voice cut through the dreamy romantic quality of the candlelight and let in a little of the real world. Specifically his family.

He couldn't exactly tell Xander he didn't ever want to talk about his family. After all, this land was their legacy, and his trust fund was making the restaurant a reality. Truth was, he *really* didn't want to talk about them, and it felt like Xander brought them up as some sort of defense mechanism. Damon still didn't understand why, and this was definitely not the first time it had happened.

"What's your deal with the Hesses?" Damon asked. Might as well be honest, at least before Xander walked back in the house and signed the contract that would tie them together for the near future. Of course, that also meant the question had barely made it out of his mouth.

Something ugly churned deep in his stomach, exactly the opposite reaction he should have had after that incredible meal.

What if he changes his mind?

"Nothing," Xander said, but his chin was jutting out again, and his fingers were drumming anxiously against the wood tabletop. It sure didn't look like nothing.

There was a definite voice in his head, begging him to leave it, to make sure he didn't drive Xander away with his insistent questioning. After all, Xander wasn't signing with Hess Vineyards, he was signing with Damon, who stayed as far away from his family as possible.

But Damon's last name was still Hess, and it wasn't going to change.

"Really?" Damon asked.

Xander sighed. "I said it was nothing, and it is. It's stupid."

"I don't want it to interfere," Damon offered. "Not with what we're about to build."

"It won't. I promise. I know you're not your family. And to be honest, that's what it is. I've had a few run-ins with Hess employees. But you're not like them."

The thing Damon had discovered before coming back to Napa, and definitely after returning to the Valley, was that he could run as far and as hard as he could, but his family was still his family. Time and distance couldn't alter his blood, no matter how much he wished otherwise.

"Okay, that's fair." Damon stood, and brushed off his jeans. His best pair, without any mud or holes. Terroir hadn't even gotten that much from him. He leaned over to snuff out the candle, and the scent of beeswax filled his nostrils.

"If you don't mind, I'm going to go read through the contract," Xander said.

"Sure. I'll just clean up." Xander looked like he was about to protest, but Damon held up a hand. "I'm no good in the kitchen, but I can use a sink and a dishwasher."

"If you insist, I'm not going to stop you," Xander conceded with a smile. He'd relaxed again, and Damon found himself hoping that Xander let whatever issue he had with his family go for good this time.

He gathered up the rest of the dishes, and when he let himself in the sliding back door, Xander was at the counter, absorbed in the printed pages of the contract.

"Dry reading?" Damon asked as he flipped on the sink, filling it with hot soapy water.

It was obvious that Xander was a professional cook, because even though he had used a number of pans and utensils to prepare the meal, they were all neatly piled next to the sink, and the counter and stove had all been carefully wiped down.

"It could be more interesting," Xander admitted. "Do you mind if I take this with me?"

"Sure, but if you'd like I can email you an electronic copy to take to a lawyer," Damon said steadily. It was the right thing to do, but his heart had wanted Xander to sign tonight. Before he could figure out that Damon wasn't as good of a bet as he appeared.

"That would be nice, but I'm not taking it to a lawyer. I just want a copy for myself."

Xander had gotten a real nice sear on the salmon filets, and the pan needed to be soaked. Filling it with hot water, Damon set it aside. "I don't want you to look back on this conversation and wish you'd done things differently," he said.

"It's a straightforward contract, and anyway, I trust you."

Damon glanced over, and was surprised to see in Xander's expression that he really meant it. "I know we just met," Xander rambled, "I know we also met under . . . extraordinary circumstances. But I choose to believe that we can make something extraordinary with those circumstances."

It was inevitable that it would happen one day. Damon had known since he was twelve that he was attracted to both sexes. But he'd met his ex-wife so young, there had never been an opportunity to explore that attraction with men.

Until now.

He kept his trembling hands submerged in the sink, holding like a lifeline onto the pot he was scrubbing. He didn't want Xander to see how affected he was—and he definitely wasn't ready to approach Xander yet. If he was ever going to feel ready.

Also just because Xander was gay didn't mean he was interested in Damon. After all, Xander knew he was a recovering alcoholic, and Damon had always imagined that not many people would ever choose to take that sort of burden on in a romantic partner.

Still, the possibility existing at all, even in a nebulous future, made Damon swallow hard.

"That's a lot of trust to give," Damon said, voice raw. He didn't have to add, *to someone who you personally witnessed falling apart only a year ago.*

Xander shot him a quicksilver grin, and went back to reading the contract.

He finished washing and drying the dishes, putting them away, but Damon felt shaken to the core by Xander's words, and his own reaction to them.

Whether Xander acknowledged it or not, he was taking a chance, and there was definitely a part of Damon that didn't feel worthy of it, especially when he heard Xander scrawling his signature on the contract, the pen scratching across the paper.

"There," Xander said with finality. "All it needs is your signature."

He could have slid it over the counter. Damon's hands were still a little damp, but he could have leaned over the prep counter and signed.

Instead, Xander left it next to him. *Right* next to him. Like he was inviting Damon into his personal bubble.

Damon hesitated, almost definitely for a second too long, because Xander chuckled, low and a little rough, and it did all sorts of things to Damon's stomach.

The truth was, Xander had a supernatural effect on Damon's stomach. He fed it incredible food while giving it the sort of nervous, hungry butterflies Damon hadn't felt since he was a teenager.

"Come on, I don't bite," Xander said, flashing another one of those bright smiles. "Hard."

There was nothing else to do but walk out of the kitchen to where Xander was sitting, until their shoulders were brushing up against each other.

It was the closest they'd ever been. Damon could feel the warmth of Xander's skin through the cotton of his t-shirt, and his fingers trembled so hard he had to clench them tightly together.

Xander *had* to know he was prodding the bear, but he offered the pen up anyway, dangling it in front of Damon's face. "You ready to sign?" he asked.

It was blatant flirting—even Damon knew what it was, and he was clueless about most romantic behavior.

He plucked the pen out of Xander's hand, gave himself a pat on the back for not succumbing to his *very* base desire and signed the contract, right above where Xander had.

"It's settled then," Xander said. Damon took a step back, back out of Xander's space. No matter how much he wanted to stay, wanted to see what else Xander might invite, this was a slippery slope and Damon wasn't sure he was ready to tackle it yet.

Honestly he wasn't sure he would ever be ready and he wasn't willing to subject Xander to the same thing he'd already done to the rest of his friends and family, but mostly his ex-wife.

"You want to see the restaurant?" Damon asked.

Xander raised an eyebrow. "Maybe instead of auditioning, I should have been looking at the space."

It was difficult for Damon not to flush bright red. Xander might not have seen the evidence under his farmer's tan, but its existence flustered him regardless. He *should* have shown Xander the restaurant first thing.

"It's not much," Damon warned as they walked out the back door and he took Xander through the edges of the garden. "There's a lot of work to be done."

It was difficult to see Xander's face in the growing dusk, but Damon glanced over anyway—an instinctual reaction he was finding it tougher and tougher to resist. For so long he'd stood out in the fields with just himself and the vegetables for company, and imagined what Xander might say to him. It was surreal to have him actually here, and Damon had to keep reminding himself that he was in fact real and not a figment of his imagination.

Damon brought them to the old barrel house on the property, long abandoned by the Hess family. Even as this vineyard had remained a jewel in the crown of their legacy, wine production had been brought into the twenty-first century by his father, increasing capacity and ensuring consistency of quality. Places like this one had faded away, some remaining ramshackle buildings on the Hess properties, others torn down to make way for more vines.

When he'd inherited this property, Damon had fully expected that this barrel house would have gone the way of so many others, but to his surprise, it had still stood. Weathered and not in the best of conditions, but still existing, a testament to a time long gone.

"This is the restaurant," Xander stated, and when Damon glanced over, he was gaping. And not in a good way. "This is a *shack*."

"I told you it needed some work," he retorted defensively. "Think of it like a blank canvas. We can do whatever we want with it. And the history . . ." Even if it wasn't history that Damon always appreciated, it remained important, and it was important to Damon for Xander to recognize that.

This was what was left of his legacy, and the only part of it he still felt comfortable embracing.

Xander took a deep breath. "A blank canvas, falling apart around our ears."

"It's not going to be falling apart. When I left Napa, I did construction for awhile." Damon was all too aware of how defensive—and desperate—he sounded. "I can fix it."

Xander's expression was incredulous. "You worked in construction?"

It was unsaid hanging between them. *But you're a Hess. Your family practically runs this valley. You have a huge trust fund.*

All of that was true. And for a while, none of it had mattered to Damon, and it was all he could do to get away and do something, *anything*, else. Working with his hands had been soothing somehow. Creating something with his own two hands. Building something, instead of tearing it down.

But that was stuff he barely even felt comfortable sharing with his sponsor still. He couldn't tell Xander. No matter how attracted to him he was, he was still almost a stranger. They'd agreed tentatively to trust each other, but that didn't mean sharing every personal feeling.

"I enjoyed it," Damon retorted shortly. "Anyway, it's going to come in handy, because now I can help fix the building. Our restaurant."

"Do you have a name yet? I noticed there wasn't a clause in the contract providing me approval or denial on the restaurant name."

"The Barrel House." Damon told himself Xander's opinion of the name meant little, but maybe it would also help him to understand the complex association Damon had with his own history.

Xander was quiet for a long moment. He tilted his head, eyes skimming the building from top to bottom again, taking in every broken board, every sagging eave. It still had good lines, and Damon knew he could bring them out again. "It suits the building." He hesitated. "It suits *you*."

He would have to be in a lot more denial to think he hadn't been waiting with bated breath for Xander's opinion. "I think so," Damon said quietly. It was a relief to imagine that at least Xander might be beginning to understand.

"Can we go inside?" Xander asked. "Without being in mortal danger, anyway?"

"Of course. It's all superficial damage. Easily fixed. *Restored*. That's what I plan to do with it anyway. It's not going to be fancy or polished, but it's going to be what it was before."

Damon led the way into the house, opening the door on hinges he'd kept continually oiled in the last year. He'd spent a lot of time in this building, making plans.

"Kitchen would go over there," Damon said. "I want it to be open. Want diners to see their food being prepared."

"Glass panels," Xander said. "Floor to ceiling."

Damon had never considered glass walls. At first he might have rejected the idea as far too Terroir-like for their restaurant, but the more he thought about it, the more he liked the idea of the high end merged with the more rustic originality of the building.

"That could be really cool," Damon said. He had his phone out of his pocket, and was making notations. People he would need to call.

"Tables over here, then," Xander continued, waving an arm. "Hostess stand here. Refinished wood. A little glass for contrast. Simple, classic earth tones."

"No barrels," Damon said.

Xander looked over, and there was a concerned wrinkle between his dark brows. "Barrels?"

"It's called the Barrel House, but I don't want any barrels in here. I want the history but not the strong association with the winery," Damon insisted.

Xander's face softened. "I understand."

He probably thought he did; most people who didn't struggle with something as basic as a drink menu sitting innocuously on a table on a restaurant thought they knew what it would be like. They didn't.

Alcohol, especially here in Napa, was *everywhere*.

"I don't want to serve it. No wine. No beer. No booze."

Damon told himself that Xander couldn't possibly be surprised; after all, he'd *just* said he didn't want old wine barrels decorating their restaurant which was named after them. How could he want alcohol on their menu?

"But this is a restaurant in Napa," Xander said slowly. The wrinkle had reappeared as quickly as it had disappeared the first time. "People would expect they can get a glass of wine with dinner."

"No." It didn't make sense to add any additional arguments, because this wasn't an argument Damon intended to have. It was his one line in the sand. Still, he braced himself for an explosion out of Xander.

Instead, Xander did something he did not expect. He reached over and wrapped him in a tight, not-very-quick hug. He lingered, his hands, insanely capable and talented, lingering over Damon's shoulders. And when he finally moved away, Damon wanted to grab him back and tell him never to stop.

"It'll be a challenge," Xander said, and his voice was very matter-of-fact, nothing like the sudden tenderness of the hug he'd just given Damon. "And nobody can say that I'm not up for a challenge."

"You seem very sure of all of this, no matter how many obstacles I keep throwing your way," Damon said incredulously. He'd planned on confessing this particular wrinkle at some later date. Not the first night. Definitely not the night they'd signed the contract, when it would be so easy for Xander to walk back to the house and rip it up.

But it had felt wrong *not* to tell Xander. Not exactly a lie, but something akin to it.

"I'm a very determined person. And I'm determined to make this work," Xander said.

"Something we have in common," Damon pointed out.

"So . . ." Xander hesitated. "Where do we begin here?"

There were old broken-down barrels, fragments of the wooden racks that had used to hold them, and other random crap scattered around the enormous room. "Clean this up first," Damon said. "I'm planning on starting tomorrow."

"I suppose since I don't have any other plans, I'll be here," Xander said wryly.

In his head, it was a simple answer. *Yes.* This was never something Damon had wanted to build alone; he'd always wanted a partner. And simply, he needed the help. But something else entirely came out of his mouth.

"If you want. You're not obligated to help. Not with this part of the process."

Damon didn't imagine the incredulous look Xander shot his way. Damon felt like shooting an even stronger look at himself. Why did he keep self-sabotaging this way? If Xander was less *Xander*—less determined, less stubborn, less committed—then he would have been out of here, running as fast as his legs would carry him.

"I'll be here anyway," was all Xander said. "What time?"

"Eight. Is that too early?"

"You remember that my boss used to be Bastian Aquino, right? That guy that showed up here today, in all his manipulative *fuck you* glory? Eight is nothing."

"Even when you were working an evening shift?'

Xander gave a short laugh. "Like that ever mattered to him."

"Well, it matters to me." Damon meant it. He just hoped, even with all the stupid shit he'd said tonight, that Xander believed him.

Xander patted him on the arm. It was a far cry from both his earlier embrace and the ambiguous invitation into his personal space. Damon fought the instinct to reach out and grab his hand back.

"If I'm going to be back here at eight, I'd better get home," Xander said. "I'll see you tomorrow."

It wasn't a date, but as Damon watched Xander walk out to his car, he realized that he felt gypped that he hadn't gotten a goodnight kiss.

"You're home at a weird time," Nate said when Xander walked into the kitchen to get a glass of water.

Nate was leaning against the far counter, a glass of rich red wine dangling from his fingers.

Xander switched directions and grabbed a glass from the cupboard and poured himself a few inches of wine from the bottle on the counter. It was Nate's wine, which meant it was really good wine. Also, his stomach was still jittery from butterflies and water wasn't going to settle them enough for him to sleep.

"I can't believe you missed the hot gossip. I quit last night." Xander took a sip of wine, glancing over at the bottle. "This is good."

"Don't sound so surprised," Nate grumbled.

Xander shouldn't have been surprised. Nate was a certified sommelier, and worked at one of the more prestigious wine tasting rooms in the county. He also moonlighted at a smaller, very exclusive late night wine bar. He was also his friend Wyatt's ex-boyfriend, and certifiably obnoxious. His access to very good wine was one of the only reasons Xander had agreed to let him move in as his and Kian's other roommate.

Also, it was a little flattering and more than a little entertaining when Nate would hit on him. Xander had never been tempted to give in to more, but quitting had him feeling freer than he had in a long time.

And it was undeniable that Damon, with his soft, hesitant, but fiery looks under his lashes as he'd eaten Xander's food had set him on fire. He was worked up with no place to go, except to his own bedroom with his own hand, and nothing about that sounded particularly appealing.

Frankly Nate, despite his model features and slim build, had never appealed to him either, but maybe . . . *maybe.*

"So you finally left Terroir. I guess it was only a matter of time," Nate said, taking another long drink of wine. "I bet Kian's freaking out."

"Kian is mad as fuck," Xander said.

Nate laughed. "Where is he, anyway? He's not home yet either."

"Feeling lonely?" Xander said, and he knew he was baiting Nate. It wasn't right. It wasn't good. But somehow it felt satisfying.

"Are we going to do this again?" Nate questioned.

"Do what?"

"You taunt me into flirting with you, then shut me down. What are you, frigid? A virgin?"

"Neither," Xander said. He finished his wine and sauntered back close to where Nate was standing, and picked the bottle up off the counter. "Do you mind if I finish this?"

"Nothing I say would probably stop you," Nate grumbled.

"True," Xander said. He finished filling his glass and tilted it toward Nate. "Cheers. What should we toast to?"

Nate rolled his eyes. "I want to believe this sudden *friendliness* is you turning over a new leaf, but you never do anything without about ten ulterior motives."

"I do not," Xander retorted. "You're . . . my roommate. We can share a glass of wine and toast to something pleasant. It wouldn't kill you."

"It wouldn't kill you," Nate said, voice very steady as he gazed right into Xander's eyes. His eyes were a nice innocuous brown. Perfectly nice, if you liked brown eyes. Xander usually didn't have an opinion, but maybe he should. Maybe instead of throwing his heart away to someone who—per usual—did not appreciate it, he should give someone a try who could actually be interested in him.

He never would have picked Nate for that option, but Nate was also convenient.

Setting his wine on the counter, Xander gave a nod. "You're right; it won't kill me."

He leaned in, telegraphing his intentions a mile away, and brushed his lips against Nate's.

Xander wanted to believe that he had every intention of giving this . . . experiment . . . a real shot at success. But the instant his lips touched Nate's, he instantly knew it was a failure. Nate wasn't who he wanted. He already knew who he wanted; he'd been desperately trying to get him out of his mind for a year now, and Damon was still as firmly as entrenched as ever.

All tonight's "business meeting" had done was make Xander want Damon even more. And this experiment? It was a hot fucking mess.

"Well," Nate said, after Xander had pulled away. The truth must have been written all over his face because it was clear Nate knew. "That could've gone better."

"It could have," Xander admitted with a sigh. He leaned back against the counter and picked up his wine again. "That was a terrible idea."

"Kissing me when you're actually thinking about someone else? Yeah, I could have told you that."

Xander digested this. "How did you know I was thinking about someone else?"

"You had that *gung-ho, I'm going to do this despite everything I really want* sort of thing written all over you. Also, you've never been even the slightest bit interested in kissing me before tonight. You let me flirt with you because you're bored."

It was not a particularly flattering list of reasons. Even Xander could admit that. "I'm sorry," he said. "And I'm sorry I keep drinking your wine."

"It's okay," Nate said, and he actually sounded like he meant it. "It's better than drinking alone. After all, your ex-boyfriend didn't end up hooking up with a rich baseball player and then falling in love with him."

"I don't have an ex-boyfriend," Xander said, and the wine must have loosened his tongue because he normally never would have admitted that. Especially to Nate.

"Really?" Nate didn't sound all that surprised. "I guess that makes sense. You keep falling for the wrong guys. So is this new one going to end up like Miles?"

"I wasn't in love with Miles," Xander said stiffly. "He was my friend."

"Right, okay, you just keep telling yourself that," Nate said. "So, this new guy?"

Xander sighed. Swirled his wine in his glass. "Almost definitely straight."

"Almost definitely? Sounds like there's some room for movement there."

"He looks like he's interested, sometimes. There's something between us, for sure. But he was married to a woman."

Nate smacked him hard across the arm. "So he could be bisexual or pansexual or maybe he didn't even *know* he liked men. Lots of gay men marry women at some point in their lives."

Xander raised an eyebrow. "All I'm saying," Nate continued, "is that you keep falling for these guys and then never doing anything about it. Almost like you're scared they're going to like you back."

"I am not scared."

But Nate's gaze was gallingly truthful. Like he could see right into all of Xander's soft, mushy bits inside and knew what was really going on: that he was scared shitless a good portion of the time. Especially when it came to relationships.

"Then give this guy a chance to open up his horizons. You deserve that, at least." Nate drained his wine, and tipped his empty glass jauntily toward Xander. "Cheers. To new beginnings."

Chapter Five

The alarm went off at 7 a.m., and instead of getting up like he always did, Xander hit the snooze button once, and then twice.

There was part of him that was excited to go to Damon's, and help jumpstart the beginning of his new career. There was another part of him that felt absolute dread.

Dread *and* guilt.

It had been so stupid to kiss Nate last night. Stupid, petty, and childish. The ultimate move when you were holding so tightly to your blinders that you couldn't see even a fraction of the truth in yourself. But just because Xander knew why he'd done it, that didn't magically erase any of the guilt.

Of course, he should feel the most embarrassed over facing Nate, but the thought of running into him in the kitchen, sleepy-eyed and grumpy, pouring himself a cup of coffee, didn't keep him in the bedroom. It didn't matter that Damon would never find out what he'd done. *Xander* knew, and that was bad enough.

Finally, when he couldn't possibly avoid it anymore, he got out of bed and slunk down the hall to take a fast shower. He threw on jeans and an old t-shirt he liked to jog in, and because he had at least an inkling of the sort of work they'd be doing today, tied on a pair of work boots that he hadn't worn in years. Not a lot of call for construction work for a chef. But Xander's stepdad was a general contractor, and had always believed in having a pair of good work boots handy.

His stepdad would love Damon, and his determination to build something out of nothing. Especially out of the ashes. But that didn't matter, Xander reminded himself, Frank was never going to meet Damon. At least not in the context of him approving and becoming friendly with him—becoming part of the family.

Xander could hear Frank's no-nonsense voice in his head now: *You can't let the past define your future, kid. You've got to give it a fresh chance.*

It sounded way too much like Nate's, *you keep falling for these guys and doing nothing about it.*

He grabbed two pieces of brioche bread, and slathered on some of the apple butter Wyatt had sent them in his last care package—like Xander and Kian, who were both chefs, were somehow starving without him feeding them. Frankly, Wyatt was probably bored, sitting around the mansion he lived in with his professional baseball player boyfriend. Making apple butter for Xander and Kian was probably keeping him from climbing the walls.

The time on the clock in his car was 8:03 when he pulled into Damon's gravel driveway.

"Cappuccino?" Damon asked distractedly when he opened the door. His hair was still damp and he was wearing another one of those damn flannel shirts, already turned up to the elbow, exposing way too much muscular forearm for just after eight in the morning. Xander felt dizzy with it.

A little forearm skin was enough to make him fluttery. If he ever saw Damon naked, he'd probably keel over dead.

"I'm not going to turn down your coffee, pretty much ever," Xander said, following him to the kitchen. In the morning light, away from the dusk and the dark of the night before, the atmosphere felt slightly less charged. But the electrical zing when Damon handed Xander his cup and their fingers brushed for a split second was still there. It was just fresher and more innocent in the morning than it had been the evening before. Full of more serious possibilities than a fling, or a single night that Damon would probably regret.

The fact that he was even considering serious or possibilities at all were enough to have Xander turning toward the back sliding door, staring out at the blue sky over the garden. Better to look there than straight at the person he had trouble looking away from.

Better to stave off the inevitable and eventual feelings as long as possible.

"You ready to get started?" Damon asked. He had his own cup of coffee, thick and rich and dark—Xander could smell it even though he stood a few feet away. It made him want to crowd into Damon's space, take the cup from his hand, and taste all that richness right off his tongue.

Yeah, kissing Nate had definitely not made him forget about wanting to kiss Damon. He looked down at his watch. It was seven minutes after eight. He'd been in Damon's presence for four minutes, and he'd already felt it again.

What he should really do was bring up Damon's ex-wife again, and pry a little, no matter how incredibly rude it would be. Maybe then he'd find some unassailable evidence that Damon was straight and his heart would stop wishing for shit it couldn't ever have.

But even Xander, who had a reputation for being blunt as fuck, couldn't figure out a way to bring up Damon's ex-wife without torturing them both. So instead he nodded, and said, "Sure, let's get started while we still have the day."

"My granddad used to say that all the time," Damon admitted as they trudged through the morning dew toward the barrel house.

"Funny, that's a favorite saying of my stepdad, Frank," Xander said.

"Let me guess, he thinks it's awesome to get up early," Damon said. "It's still dark out and he's chomping at the bit to get going."

Xander shared a commiserating smile. "Basically."

"God, *morning people*," Damon said with a bright, blinding grin.

And Xander, who might have lumped himself in with that group until this morning, when guilt had weighed him down so much he'd had trouble getting his ass out of bed, simply nodded. Just to see that smile again.

"You're not a morning person but you're up this morning. Eager to get started?"

Damon unlocked the door to the barrel house, clipping the keys to his belt. "I've already started. I've been up early every morning since I started the garden. I've found it's a lot easier to work in the mornings."

"I guess I didn't think of it that way," Xander admitted. Damon had already been committed to this project for a year. Because without a garden, there would be no garden-to-table restaurant.

"It's okay, I get it. This building is the beginning for you. First," Damon said, gesturing around at all the broken-down crap piled in the corners, "we've got to get all this out of here."

Xander sighed. "I was afraid of that."

"Afraid to get your hands dirty?" Damon asked, shooting him a quick, slanted look. Xander felt it along his skin, in the blood in his veins. It was difficult to see this project and this partnership as a mistake that was only going to lead to a broken heart, but when he stood here, on this land, looking at the walls of this old, still majestic building, it was impossible to see himself anywhere else.

Some things, Xander decided, were inevitable, and some fates unavoidable.

And this was his. It had been crystal clear the moment he'd kissed Nate, but the truth was, he'd known it for a lot longer than that. He'd known it, deep down, the first moment he'd seen Damon's figure through the pouring rain. Why else feel so compelled to stop?

"No," Xander said. A lot more than his hands were going to get dirty on this project.

Some of the debris had to be broken down into smaller pieces of wood. Damon produced a pair of gloves for himself, and then surprisingly, a pair for Xander that fit him perfectly.

Xander flushed as he pulled them on, trying not to think that Damon had sized up his hands, and then gone and bought gloves to fit.

Damon must have seen, because he explained, sounding nearly the most self-conscious that Xander had ever heard him. "Your hands . . . you might put them through hell," Damon said. "But I'm not going to let you get a splinter on my watch."

"You realize I get worse than a splinter all the time," Xander had responded, and hiding the fondness in his tone had been impossible. Maybe they couldn't ever be *in* love, but Damon clearly cared what happened to him.

"Burns, cuts, scratches, right?" Damon asked and Xander nodded.

"Don't care," he concluded. "No splinters, not if I can help it."

They'd gotten to work then, Xander trying to focus on the pile he was breaking down and lugging outside to the spot Damon had designated. It was harder than he'd imagined it would be. Not the work—that was easy. The wood was old and soft. Easily broken down so it could be carried outside in armfuls. No, the problem was Damon, and the flex of his biceps as he used a crowbar to pry the metal ring off some old wine barrels. The problem was the little grunt he let out when he pried each one off.

Xander tried not to think about how Damon might sound as he fucked, that little grunt louder as he bottomed out every time. He totally failed.

"Something really interesting in that wall?" Damon asked, totally catching Xander in the middle of a really good, really explicit fantasy. The other problem was that it had been so long since he'd had sex, and it didn't look like that streak was getting any shorter, considering how the kissing experiment with Nate had gone.

Xander blushed bright red. The wall in question was the wall right behind Damon. "Uh no, just . . . thinking of a new dish."

"What is it?" Damon asked, because *of course*.

"Uh, uh, it's . . ." Xander was usually a lot quicker, even with a lie, but not much of his blood was in his brain at the moment.

"Sounds really good," Damon said solemnly.

Xander resembled the color of the radishes Damon was growing outside. "Really good," he managed to agree.

Damon laughed. "Whatever it is, I think I want some."

The culmination of all of Xander's problems: Damon probably didn't want any, and probably wasn't ever going to want any.

"Yeah, yeah," Xander grumbled, turning back to his own pile and getting back to work before his inconvenient erection could be any more obvious.

The work wasn't particularly hard, but it was time-consuming. There was a lot of crap tucked into the corners of the barrel house. Xander was pretty certain it hadn't been cleaned out after it had stopped being used. They'd just kept everything in here, a mausoleum to the old-fashioned method of winemaking. Over time, it had rotted and broken down and then finally fallen apart.

"I'm hungry," Damon said after a few hours of work. "I'll go grab us some sandwiches from the corner market."

Xander considered protesting, and saying he'd make lunch instead, but his arms and legs were streaked with dirt and grime. He'd have to shower to feel ready to enter a kitchen. And he knew the "corner market" was actually a pretty high-end country store that catered to tourists who wanted a picnic to take with them on their wine tasting tours.

"Sure."

"Any preference?" Damon said, removing his gloves and setting them on one of the barrels in a long line he was breaking down.

"Anything that looks good. I'm not picky."

Damon looked surprised.

"Don't look so shocked," Xander teased. "We're not all Gordon Ramsay."

"Gordon Ramsey isn't picky," Damon protested. "He wants to eat food that's edible that wasn't prepared in a kitchen that looks like a garbage dump. He doesn't want food poisoning. Can you really call that picky?"

Xander burst out laughing. "Are you in the Gordon Ramsay fan club?"

"I actually watch a lot of bad reality television," Damon admitted in a quiet voice, like he was almost ashamed to admit it, but not enough to change the subject. "Gordon is pretty cool."

Xander raised an eyebrow. "He is?"

"He's good to kids. He tries to help people that don't always know how to help themselves," Damon defended.

"He also yells a lot, which, as you can imagine, I'm not a fan of," Xander said. "That was all I knew about him."

"You should watch *Kitchen Nightmares* sometime," Damon said. "I have pretty much the whole show saved on my DVR."

"Do you watch *Real Housewives* too?" Xander asked in a teasing voice. "Orange County or Atlanta?"

"I used to, but I got into food shows in the last year or so," Damon said, and he sounded self-conscious again. "*Chopped* and *Food Network Star* and *Holiday Baking Championship*. Even watched *Kitchen Wars* on-demand."

Xander definitely did not ask if the sudden interest in food was because Damon had decided to open a restaurant or if it was meeting him. "I keep trying to get my friend Miles on *Holiday Baking Championship*. He'd do so great. Right now he hosts a show on *Five Points*. But he could do a lot bigger things, if he wanted."

"You're friends with Miles Costa?" Damon asked. Undeniably starstruck. "I never miss his show." He hesitated. "Duh, of course, he worked at Terroir with you."

"He was one of my roommates, before he left for LA," Xander explained.

"I'm going to need to meet him sometime," Damon said. "Okay, I'm off to the corner market."

It was only after Damon walked away that Xander realized they'd had an extensive conversation about bad reality TV. And it wasn't like he didn't have those conversations with straight guys sometimes, but wow, he could still feel the echo of it, the same as he'd had with Kian or Nate or any of his other gay friends.

Instead of asking about *Real Housewives*, he should have asked about *RuPaul's Drag Race* instead.

This particular fact wouldn't have told Xander what he wanted to know, but it might have given him a clearer idea if he even had a chance.

Fifteen minutes later, Damon returned with a plastic bag full of sandwiches.

"What is all this?" Xander asked as he dug through the bag. "There must be six sandwiches in here."

"I wasn't sure what you wanted. Bonus points: anything we don't eat today, I can have for dinner."

Xander glanced up. "You eat cold sandwiches from the corner deli for dinner?"

"Long days," Damon said, and he sounded almost apologetic. "I don't have the energy or the inclination most days to make a dinner for one."

Xander tried to remember the last time he'd made a meal for just himself. Even in the mornings when he and Kian were rushing to get to Terroir and Nate was headed to the winery, he'd often make a big scramble with whatever was left in the fridge.

And at Terroir, there was the big meal they all shared before the dinner service started.

In fact, Xander couldn't even remember the last time he'd truly eaten a meal alone. Suddenly it made a lot of sense why loneliness seemed to emanate from Damon. Every single time Xander had been over to his house, there'd been zero evidence of any other visitor.

It made Xander's heart hurt for him. Divorced, estranged from his family, and dealing with the sort of demons that haunted men, Damon needed a friend, badly.

A little voice deep inside Xander told him that Damon needed a partner—and not just in his business ventures. Xander just wasn't sure that was him. Even if Damon was genuinely interested, Xander had never even had a boyfriend before. And if Nate was to be believed, that was because Xander couldn't put himself out there enough to make it happen. If he couldn't even convince a guy to date him, how could he be the sort of rock that Damon might need?

"It's pretty sad, isn't it?" Damon scoffed, and there wasn't even bitterness in his voice. Simply resignation.

"It's not, it's really not. Not sad anyway. I was thinking that I couldn't remember the last time I ate alone. You don't do it much in my world. You tend to eat in packs. Either at our house or at the restaurant."

"That sounds really . . . nice." Damon sounded plain wistful now.

"You need to come over to our place," Xander said, picking at the label of the roast beef and Havarti he'd selected. "It's not fancy, but we can make a mean meal." And, unspoken was the fact that Damon wouldn't be alone.

"You don't have to do that," Damon said, picking out a turkey with cranberry cream cheese. Xander's second choice. Damon, whether he realized it or not, had good taste.

After all, he'd picked Xander to be his head chef, hadn't he?

"I want to," Xander insisted.

"I guess you're going to have to do a lot of recipe testing," Damon suggested hesitantly. "I guess you have to feed the possibilities to someone."

"Exactly," Xander said, shooting Damon a quick grin.

"I'm going to go wash my hands," Xander said. "I'm gross."

He stood, leaving the wrapped sandwich on the wine barrel that was serving as their impromptu table.

"You're dirty, not gross," Damon corrected, and this time when he smiled, even his dimples came out. Xander got the briefest, most tantalizing peek of what a younger Damon, less lonely and less tormented, might have been like. And even though he was already hooked, it felt like that single moment was enough to reel him right in.

"House is unlocked," Damon continued when Xander hesitated. Torn between going to wash his hands and telling Damon very firmly that he could not say that sort of thing to him because he might get ideas and he already had enough of those swirling around his head.

"Great," Xander said shortly, and turned toward the house.

He washed his hands quickly and efficiently, forcing away any and all of his curiosity to poke and prod around Damon's very clean hall bathroom. Xander didn't even think Damon used it, but the temptation was stronger than it should have been.

Clearly, Xander wanted to know more about him, but he wasn't sure Damon would open up if he asked.

He returned to the barrel house, to find that Damon had waited for him to start eating. Xander didn't point that out, but it was hard not to feel, *again*, that

Damon was that real deal he'd kept telling himself he was waiting for. Someone kind and thoughtful. Someone who put Xander first.

They ate their lunch and then continued working, mostly in silence, which was something Xander was fine with. Unnecessary chattering was heavily frowned upon at Terroir, and at pretty much every other restaurant he'd ever worked at, so he'd long ago killed that need inside him to fill up emptiness with words.

Xander figured that if Damon had something important to say, he'd say it, and assumed that Damon understood the opposite was also true.

Four rolled around, and Xander looked up as he wiped a dirty forearm across a forehead that was damp with sweat.

"You about finished?" Damon asked.

"Yeah, I just have the remains of this pile."

"I just broke down the last wine barrel. I think . . ." Damon let out a short, almost incredulous laugh. "I think we might almost be done lugging out all the shit in here."

"A miracle," Xander said dryly. He'd known this would be hot, heavy, unpleasant work. He wouldn't have been caught dead doing it, if this wasn't going to be partly his place too. And, Xander figured, he had done far worse things with a far worse view, all in the name of culinary advancement.

"As soon as we're cleared for burning, I'll have a big bonfire with this pile," Damon said.

"A bonfire?" Despite his own best intentions, that sounded fun. And maybe even a little romantic.

"Maybe tomorrow night. Maybe the night after. You wanna come and hang out, watch it all burn?"

Xander wondered if Damon realized he'd been leading him into the invitation. If he'd wanted to invite him anyway. But in the end, it didn't matter, because he'd been asked, and he was definitely not going to turn it down. "Sure. Sounds like fun."

"I have a schedule," Damon said next. "Next on it is refinishing the floors, which I plan on doing next week. You want to help with that too?"

Xander knew, from his stepdad's work in construction, that refinishing floors was back-breaking, unpleasant and messy. He still nodded.

"I'll let you know about the bonfire," Damon said. "But in the meantime, I'll be tending the garden. Thinking about clearing some more land, maybe put in an orchard. It won't be ready right away, maybe not even for a few years, but eventually, we'll have fruit."

An orchard. Xander shaded his eyes and looked the way Damon was pointing, far in the distance. Yeah, he could see apple trees there. "Can you text me a list of vegetables that you'll be ready to harvest for the restaurant opening?" Xander asked. "I'm going to spend the time in recipe development."

"Yeah, sure. And I almost forgot." Damon dug in his back pocket and pulled out his wallet. Handed a plastic card to Xander. When he took it, it was still warm from his body. Xander curled his fingers around it, the edges biting into his palm. "That's a debit card to the bank account I've set up for the restaurant. Feel free to charge any purchases to the account. There's plenty of money in it."

Xander remembered Bastian Aquino demanding a receipt for some strawberries he'd been asked to pick up at the farm stand. He remembered his honesty over the dollar amount being questioned without one. And here Damon was, just handing him the key to a whole bank account.

This must be what being trusted felt like.

The next day, Damon felt stupid that he hadn't invited Xander to see what a day in the garden was like. He didn't need his help, but he'd discovered that even though it had taken months to get used to the silence, it only took a few evenings and a day together to remember how much it sucked.

It took him the entire morning to go through the garden, checking plants, pulling encroaching weeds, spraying everything with his homemade bug repellent that he'd invented after too many evenings scouring the internet for something non-chemical and organic.

Then Damon looked over at the big pile of wood and garbage that he and Xander had spent the last day dragging out of the barrel house. Really, he needed another day to sort through it, and get the bonfire ready. He didn't want to wait another day, but there was no point of having the fire if he couldn't do it properly. Also, the forecast called for some rain tonight, and if he tarped the pile, the surrounding ground would be damp enough that the burning restriction for the county would probably lift.

He worked the rest of the afternoon, sweating through his shirt and sorting out the garbage he'd have to take to the dump. By five, he was halfway through, and felt good about confirming the bonfire tomorrow night. Maybe he should even get marshmallows and graham crackers at the store, make it a s'mores party.

Grabbing his phone from his counter, he shed his filthy clothes right into the washing machine and texted Xander on the way to a much-needed shower.

He typed in: **Bonfire + s'mores tomorrow night?** and hit the send button.

It was a difficult decision between a cold shower and a hot one, but the boiling temps, barely counteracted by the old air conditioner in this house, made the decision for him.

He'd soothe his aching muscles by swallowing a few painkillers with dinner. There was a time when he'd have wanted to drink a beer or two or six to drown out the pain. And that had always been the problem with him and alcohol. There was no safe middle ground of a handful of beers. There was only no beer or a whole six-pack and then whatever other booze he could scrounge up in the house.

Cold water sluiced over his overheated skin and he leaned back against the tile wall and tried to think of nothing, because the alternative was thinking of Xander, and Damon knew he'd already crossed too many lines thinking of Xander.

He didn't need to cross this one. But he couldn't seem to stop his own hand, as it drifted down his chest, his stomach and settled low at his groin, wrapping around his half-hard cock. The water was cool and refreshing and his dick hadn't seemed to get the memo that he wasn't supposed to be thinking about this.

He'd tried thinking of Rachel. He'd tried thinking of other women. The hot checker at the grocery store who always gave him appreciative looks whenever he bought food. But none of them did it for him anymore. His body knew what he wanted, and it wasn't so much a shock that it was a man, as it was a surprise that it was Xander.

Since realizing and acknowledging he was bisexual in junior high, he'd never gotten a chance to try anything with a guy. Rachel had asked him once how he could even know, if he'd never even kissed a guy. He'd asked her how she knew she liked guys before she'd kissed him, when they were fourteen and snuck into one of the big winery parties his family threw.

She'd responded that she'd just *known*, and before he could even point out the double standard, she'd laughed, a little self-consciously and pointed it out herself.

That was the first and only conversation they'd ever had about it, but when she'd left him, she'd told him that someday he'd meet someone who wouldn't mind wrestling with his demons.

The *someone* had reminded him that now that he and Rachel were over, and when he finally got clean, there was always the chance that when he found himself attracted to someone again, that person wouldn't necessarily be a woman.

And now it had happened, and it was definitely not a woman.

Damon gave his cock a half-hearted tug. His body was definitely all-in, interest piqued like it hadn't in years, but his mind was still freaking out. Not over the fact that Xander was a man, though that was a little intimidating considering how little experience he had, but over the chance that he could fuck it all up again.

Rachel had been bad enough, and she'd gotten away before he'd truly been able to ruin her life. But what if he ruined Xander's? He wanted Xander to be part of his personal life, but he was already part of his professional one. What if he couldn't keep it together? What if the Barrel House pushed him back into old and destructive habits? Damon still wasn't certain he trusted himself.

He definitely didn't trust himself enough to drag someone else into his hot mess.

The problem was his body was hearing, but not really listening, to the arguments his brain kept setting out. It knew exactly what it wanted—a firm mouth, stubble scraping against his cheek as they kissed; a muscular shoulder he could brace his hands against. But mostly he wanted those scarred, talented hands, so delicate but so tough, wrapped around his cock right now.

Damon had a lot of self-control these days. He'd spent years developing and cultivating it. Which was the only reason he'd managed to keep his thoughts of Xander PG-rated until now. But after spending some quality time with the man, his control washed away like a dirt road in a flash flood.

He tipped his face back, felt the water wash over him in a cool rush, and stroked himself with certainty this time. An embarrassingly short time later, he was watching the result wash down the drain.

"Damn," Damon said to himself.

A quick wash later, he got out of the shower, wrapped a towel around his waist, and because he apparently couldn't help himself at all, checked his phone.

There was already a text from Xander. *Three* texts from Xander, in fact.

Damon groaned out loud. He was so fucked. Especially if Xander was as drawn to Damon as Damon was to him.

We're on.

S'mores sound really good. I'll bring homemade marshmallows.

Don't argue. They're so much better than the ones at the store. Will prove it tomorrow night.

Damon wasn't going to argue, and if he had, he only intended to put up a token protest. He was more than ready to let Xander prove the marshmallows, and just about anything else, tomorrow night.

Chapter Six

"What the fuck are you doing?"

Xander glanced up from the candy thermometer he was carefully monitoring to see Kian standing in the doorway. It was four in the afternoon on a Thursday, and Kian wasn't at Terroir.

There must have been a disruption in the Force, or maybe the Bastard finally grew a single heart molecule.

"I could ask you the same question," Xander retorted steadily. He and Kian hadn't seen each other since their fight almost a week ago, and every time he thought about the way Kian had sided with Aquino, something in his stomach burned.

He would've sworn it was indigestion, but after dealing with it for a few days and swearing off all spicy food, it remained, persistent and annoying. Making him, who was completely the innocent and wronged party in this scenario, feel *guilty*. It wasn't right, and Xander wasn't happy about it.

"I cut myself pretty badly, had to go to the ER," Kian said. "Chef told me to take the night off."

This time Xander really looked at his friend, and it turned out the large, white bandage on his hand was tough to miss. If you were looking for it, anyway.

"Are you okay?" he found himself asking, because no matter how pissed off he felt, Kian was still somebody he cared about.

"Twelve stitches," Kian said nonchalantly and even for a chef, who regularly cut themselves, that was bad.

"Actually, twenty-four," Kian added. "They had to stitch the inner too."

Xander kept his eyes glued to the candy thermometer and the hot sugar boiling away, but he said, "Must've been deep then."

"I could see the tendon," Kian said. "It's that damn Japanese mandolin."

Even for an experienced chef, the Japanese mandolin with its wickedly sharp and completely unprotected blade had scared the shit out of Xander. He'd always worn the special Kevlar gloves with it, no matter how much Aquino baited him by calling him a pussy.

He was fine being a pussy, as long as he was a pussy who wasn't missing any fingers.

"You weren't wearing the gloves, were you," Xander said. He didn't really need to ask. There was no way Kian would wear them, not if he was trying to impress Aquino. Even if Aquino never would have used it without them.

Actually, as far as Xander was concerned, Aquino hired people so he didn't *have* to use the Japanese mandolin. Talk about pussy moves.

"Of course I wasn't wearing the gloves," Kian said. "They slow you down big-time."

Xander raised an eyebrow. "And a bisected finger doesn't?"

Kian shrugged, like the injury wasn't a big deal. The truth was, they'd probably given him some good pain meds, the kind of meds that made you not care about a single damn thing. When Kian woke up in the morning, and *felt* the twenty-four stitches, it was definitely going to be a slightly bigger deal.

"You didn't tell me what *you* were doing," Kian said, wandering over, smelling like a hospital and also like eggplant, which made sense, because Terroir had a dish of paper-thin eggplant slices roasted, and then layered together with whipped goat cheese and fresh herbs. It was delectable, and also dangerous.

"Making marshmallows," Xander said.

"Isn't this normally Miles' sort of thing?" Kian asked, referring to their friend who was a famous pastry chef. "Is that Hess guy making you work pastry too?"

"Yes, and no," Xander retorted.

"Then why the marshmallows?" It seemed that Kian on pain meds was also an inquisitive Kian.

"Because I wanted to expand my culinary repertoire," Xander explained, not very patiently. "And I'm going over to Damon's tonight. We're building a bonfire of all the crap we lugged out of the building that's eventually going to be the restaurant. And I thought s'mores with homemade marshmallows would be fun."

"Fun." Kian tested the word, rolling it around in his mouth like a savory treat. Like he couldn't quite remember what it tasted like. And frankly, working himself to death for Bastian Aquino probably meant that he didn't.

Of course Kian was also clearly masochistic and maybe working for Aquino qualified as fun.

"Yeah, fun. Do you even remember what that is?"

"Very funny," Kian scoffed. "You're such a fucking comedian. You should quit your job . . . oh wait, you already did."

"For a *better* one," Xander retorted. Normally he didn't stay so patient, and Kian had probably expected that the result of his baiting would be another argument. Clearly, he was spoiling for one. But Xander didn't *want* to fight. The sick feeling in the bottom of his stomach had made that clear enough.

"If you weren't injured," he continued, voice still mild, with only a hint of bite to it, "you could bloom that gelatin for me."

"Or if I knew what that was. I'm not a pastry chef," Kian said sulkily.

"You know what gelatin is." Xander rolled his eyes and pointed to the small glass measuring cup. "Just pour the packet into that cup of water and stir it a bit. It'll get thick."

The rising temperature on the candy thermometer stole his attention away and when he looked back, Kian had reverted to regular form, pouring in and stirring the gelatin conscientiously. Maybe even a little too conscientiously, considering the relative simplicity of the task and the focus Kian was giving it.

"Once it's bloomed," Xander said, "pour it in that big stainless steel bowl there."

"Really going to miss Miles' professional stand mixer, aren't you?" Kian asked, eyeing the small-ish hand mixer Miles had left them, all the while making pointed comments that they wouldn't even need that because baking was foreign to them.

Xander was totally going to send him pics of these killer marshmallows when they were done. He could do pastry, he just chose not to.

"I think it'll be fine," Xander said confidently.

Kian gave him a dubious look. "You won't mind if I stand over here? I already had twenty-four stitches today, I don't need any third-degree burns on top of that."

"Nobody's going back to the emergency room." The candy thermometer hit the right temperature and he pulled it off the heat, re-adjusting his oven mitt on his hand. "Now or never," he said to Kian or maybe to himself.

Carefully, he poured the boiling hot sugar into the bowl, re-dissolving the gelatin, and switched from the oven mitt to the hand mixer.

"See?" he said, switching on the mixer, carefully keeping the beaters submerged in the hot mixture. "No big deal."

Kian nodded, but still stayed on the other side of the kitchen, which considering he'd already had to go to the hospital today, was probably safer.

A few minutes later, even with his hand-mixer handicap Xander had beautiful snowy white mounds of marshmallow.

Kian even looked impressed as Xander poured it into the prepared pan, dusted liberally with cornstarch and powdered sugar. "And now they just set up?" he asked.

"Yeah, for a few hours. Then just cut into squares."

"If I knew this was so easy, maybe I would have tried it before now." Kian had a sweet tooth and a somewhat disparaging opinion of pastry chefs, their friend Miles withstanding, which didn't make much sense.

"No, you wouldn't have," Xander said, laughing. But that feeling in the pit of his stomach had finally began to recede, and Kian had softened during their time together in the kitchen. It could be just the pain medication he was on, but Xander didn't think so. Kian was wound so tight because Bastian was wound so tight. They were each other's mirrors and as a result, each other's worst nightmare.

"Come with me tonight," Xander offered suddenly. "Like I said, it'll be fun."

He probably should have asked Damon before inviting anyone over to his house, but he had a feeling that the man would probably enjoy meeting Kian. Maybe he should even invite Nate. He wasn't sure he was working tonight.

"Are you sure? You don't want to be alone with Mr. Wine Big Shot?" Kian questioned.

Xander definitely wanted to be alone with Damon, which meant he absolutely shouldn't be.

The hesitation was enough to tell Kian everything he needed to know, especially because he knew too much about Xander's romantic history. "You've got another unrequited crush, don't you?" He sighed.

"It might not be unrequited," Xander defended. Even if it wasn't, it was still a bad idea.

"He's probably straight. Did he tell you he wasn't straight?"

Trust Kian to figure out the crux of the issue immediately, like an arrow straight to the heart. "He was married to a woman before," Xander admitted.

Kian's sympathetic expression was like death. Xander could feel the bell tolling for all his hopes, even as he tried to remind himself Damon had looked interested more than once—or at least *intrigued*. "That doesn't mean he's straight," Kian rallied.

"Doesn't mean he's not." Xander knew how bitter he sounded. "Just like old times, right?"

"Miles wasn't straight," Kian said. "Not that him being gay really helped."

"Not exactly." He hadn't been in love with their friend, but he'd crushed on him forever, always hoping for more, and assuming it wouldn't happen. And in the end, of course it hadn't. Miles had only ever seen him as his friend, and then had proceeded to move to Los Angeles for work and fall in love with his producer.

And that was all well and good for them, living in their happy LA bubble of love and success, but where had it left Xander?

Alone. Like always.

"I think you should try, Xander," Kian said. "I know the chances of him reciprocating are small, but you can't just keep letting these chances to find somebody pass you by. Sometime you're going to have to take a leap of faith."

That sounded like vintage Kian, all hope and sweetness and light. Before Bastian had gotten his talons into him.

It also sounded unpleasantly like what Nate had just told him the other night.

Xander rolled his eyes. "If I tell you I'm considering it, would you leave me alone?"

"Yes and no." Kian grinned. "I want to meet him. So instead of giving you some time alone, I'm going with you. I can do reconnaissance."

"Reconnaissance?"

"You know," Kian said impatiently, sounding higher by the second, or maybe just more manic, "reconnaissance to find out if he's interested in guys."

"Oh god," Xander said. "No, you will not. You absolutely will not."

Kian grinned wildly. "Oh, but it'll be fun!"

Of course, the marshmallows were not amazing or incredible or even the tiniest bit transcendental.

Kian peered over the side of the pan and poked at the goopy mess with an offset spatula. "What's wrong with them?"

"I don't know," Xander snapped. "God, Kian, it's like you expect me to be Miles or something."

"They *were* supposed to set up, right?" Kian asked.

"Of course they were." Xander grabbed for his phone. "I'm calling Miles."

"I'm going to go take a shower," Kian announced lazily.

"Wrap your hand!" Xander called after him after dialing. He hoped that Miles wasn't filming today, but it felt like Miles filmed a lot of days now.

"Wrap my hand?" Miles answered, voice puzzled. "Did I hurt my hand?"

"Oh, that was for Kian," Xander said. "He cut his finger pretty badly today. Twenty-four-stitches badly."

"That explains why he's not at Terroir right now," Miles said. "And I know you're not there because you quit, you smug bastard. I'm still wondering why all I got was a text message to our group chat."

"Because you're a busy and important man and I like to respect your time?" Xander asked meekly.

Miles laughed. "No. I get it. The days after I quit all I wanted to do was sleep and constantly fist pump because the torture was finally over."

"You barely spent any time with the Bastard," Xander pointed out.

"And yet, my job still sucked." Miles paused. "So what's the emergency?"

"How did you know?"

"You always text. You never call. Wyatt's the actual phone-conversation friend in our group. You just send terse texts."

"They're not terse, they're to the point," Xander grumbled.

"What's the emergency?" Miles repeated. "Apparently we're going to some fancy LA restaurant tonight and I need to look presentable. Evan's picking out shirts and I'm going to end up in one that's mandarin orange if I'm not careful."

Awhile ago, Xander would have been unavoidably jealous of the casual affection and undeniable love in Miles' voice as he talked about his boyfriend and producing partner. Now, all Xander felt was relief that he'd never actually done anything about his crush on Miles. They were so much better as friends.

"I was making marshmallows and they didn't set up."

"You were . . . what?" Miles questioned. "Marshmallows? You're not the pastry chef at this new restaurant, are you? Because I'm guessing that's not going to work very well for anyone."

Xander paced across the kitchen, not even bothering to glance over at his sad pan of marshmallows. "No. I'm not insane. I'm going to a bonfire tonight, it's a new work thing, and I wanted to bring something fun. S'mores always seem fun."

"Fun? Xander Bridges looking for something fun? You've got a crush."

"Why do you have to make that sound so accusatory?" Xander objected. "What if I do have a crush? Why is that a problem?"

A year ago, he might have believed that Miles was jealous, but he knew better now. Miles was afraid he'd end up miserable and alone.

Sometimes Xander was worried about that too. Then he'd met Damon and then met him again a year later, and during the last week, that particular fear didn't feel so pressing.

"It's not a problem. It's cute. You're making marshmallows for a crush. Who is it? You said it was a work thing? Oh," Miles said, realization clearly dawning, "it's the Hess guy, isn't it? Your new partner?"

"Did Kian tell you?"

"It was a lucky guess," Miles said, but he was a terrible liar. Kian had totally texted him.

"So how do I fix them?"

"What happened to them?"

"They didn't set up. They're just . . . mush."

"Sounds like you didn't whip the sugar enough with the gelatin," Miles speculated. "Especially if you're using that pathetic little hand mixer I left you instead of my professional stand mixer."

"Kian totally texted you," Xander retorted, a little outraged and a little touched.

"Kian cares about you," Miles argued. "Kian is worried you're going to do the same thing with Damon as you did with all those other guys. You can't just stand back on the sidelines forever, even if it means you're protecting yourself."

"Did Kian write that out for you?" Xander asked bitterly. "If I call Wyatt will I get a similar but different version of the same lecture?"

"Kian cares about you," Miles repeated, a lot more gently this time. "And he's right."

"I don't even know if he likes men. Or if he does, if he likes me."

"Believe it or not," Miles reminded him dryly, "you're fairly likable. Plus you'll never know if you do nothing. Relationships require a certain amount of *fuck it* to work. That means giving up control. And I know you're not good at that."

Xander leaned back against the counter. "I'm not."

"If you called up Wyatt you'd probably get a similar version of this speech because he knows that just as well as I do," Miles said. "You've got to take a chance."

Xander was quiet for a long moment. "Sometimes I think I like unobtainable people because that means I never have to do that."

That was what his crush on Miles had really been about. Someone safe he could like from a romantic distance, even as they'd become closer friends. An excuse to never actually do anything. An easy way to protect his heart.

"There's nothing to be gained without the potential of loss," Miles said.

"How did you get so damn smart?"

"It's not me. It's all Evan." Miles' voice grew a bit hushed, almost reverent. And Xander *was* jealous then—jealous because he'd never talked about anyone that way before, and all he wanted was the chance. He wanted it, and he definitely wanted it with Damon. Maybe even more than he was afraid.

"So I need to whip the marshmallows more."

"I think so," Miles said. "Let me know how they turn out. I'm going to do an orange-shirt intervention."

"Good luck," Xander said and hung up.

They both knew he was going to end up wearing the orange shirt and liking it.

"So what did Miles say?" Kian asked as they walked to the car a few hours later.

Xander rolled his eyes. "You already know what he said. You can rest easy, knowing you called your ringer in and he gave his best effort."

"The real question is," Kian said, "was he successful?"

"I guess you'll have to see," Xander said, but he was grinning, a little effervescent from the realization that he had every intention of letting his walls down. Maybe not tonight, necessarily, but soon.

"Are you telling me reconnaissance is no longer required?" Kian asked archly. "Because I was definitely looking forward to asking Damon all sorts of uncomfortable questions like, *do you like cock? And how do you feel about dick?*"

"Don't you dare," Xander said. His heart accelerated at the thought that Kian could and might and that Damon could say yes. And then he would have zero excuses left.

"I won't need to, if you do your part," Kian said, but he sounded so satisfied there was no question that he had already known how Xander would decide. Maybe he'd even known before Xander did.

Xander was still trying to figure out how people with the most troubled love lives were often the ones who saw other people's the most clearly when they pulled up to Damon's house.

Then he saw Damon's face, smiling as he walked over to the car, and Xander realized knowing why was irrelevant. The only thing that mattered—just like the first awful batch of marshmallows buried in the trash at home and the second, perfect batch, bagged in the back seat of the car—was the result.

Chapter Seven

Damon had been telling himself all afternoon not to get his hopes up but he was still inevitably crushed when Xander texted him about five to say he was coming over in a few hours and that he was bringing his friend and roommate, Kian.

Of course, he'd responded in the affirmative, confirming that Xander was free to bring whoever he wished, but Damon couldn't help but think that Xander was bringing a friend to make sure the atmosphere didn't feel too date-like.

Damon reminded himself that the dinner they'd shared the other night had felt plenty date-like and Xander had barely batted an eyelash, but then, besides practically inviting him to sit on his lap to sign the contract, he'd not exactly made any overtures either.

This would all be a little easier—and a little harder, too—if Xander wasn't interested in him.

But then Xander's car pulled up to the house, and he stepped out. His grin was wide, and it took a second, but Damon realized that smile was for *him*.

It wasn't for Kian, who must be the guy getting out of the passenger side of the car. Or food. Or a job offer. Or the Barrel House. It was for *Damon*.

Xander slung an arm around his shoulders, pulling him into a half hug. "Wait until you taste these marshmallows I made," he said. "I think pastry might be my second calling. Maybe we won't even need to hire a pastry chef."

Damon snorted, soft and amused, both from Xander's clear affection and also from his ego. "If you want to work yourself to death, that's on you."

"It's ambition. Just ambition," Xander said, laughing. "By the way, this is my friend, Kian. Kian, this is my new partner, Damon Hess."

As he shook Kian's hand, there was definitely a part of him that liked Xander's introduction. Partner sounded so much better than boss. Probably to Xander too, after so long under Bastian Aquino's thumb.

Kian was a few inches shorter than Xander, and had that look like he was just coming into his adult muscles. Still slender and a bit slight, with a mop of blond hair and a pair of baby blue eyes.

Damon nearly made the crack about Aquino out loud, but then he remembered that Xander had mentioned the other day that his friend had an unfortunate crush on the man.

He hadn't been lying. It was definitely unfortunate. Bastian looked like he could eat Kian for lunch and then spit him back out again for dinner.

"So you still work at Terroir?" Damon asked, as they headed back toward where he'd set up the wood and debris for the bonfire.

"I do," Kian said, and shooting Xander sort of a half-hearted glare. "But I got the night off."

"What he means to tell you," Xander said conspiratorially, "is that he nearly chopped his finger off with a Japanese mandolin."

Damon glanced down at Kian's hand, and sure enough, it was wrapped in a thick white bandage. He'd been so busy staring at Xander, appreciating the tan of his skin against his white t-shirt, that he'd barely spared Kian a glance.

"That sounds . . . dangerous," Damon said.

They stopped in front of the enormous pile they were about to set on fire.

"This also looks dangerous," Xander said, with a gleam in his eye that Damon *knew* meant both terrible and wonderful things.

"You say that with such relish," Kian complained. "You're going to make Damon think you're a sort of pyro creep."

Damon definitely did not think Xander was a pyro creep. Far from it, in fact. But the problem was to explain this without sounding like he had a real serious crush. Which he definitely did.

"Uh, um," Damon hesitated.

"See?" Kian said triumphantly, and Xander frowned.

"No," Damon said firmly. "Definitely not a creep. Nothing like a creep." If anything was creepy, it was probably his own smile as he gazed longingly over at Xander, trying to communicate just how wrong Kian was.

The frown disappeared, which wasn't all Damon wanted, but he'd take it. "So where are these fantastic marshmallows?" Damon asked, trying to change the subject and very aware that he was doing so clunkily.

Xander pulled a Tupperware container out of the paper bag he was carrying. "Right here. I thought it wouldn't do to get too gourmet, and stopped by the store for regular old graham crackers and Hershey's milk chocolate bars to go with them."

"Should have gone for the Valrhona," Kian muttered.

"Don't mind him," Xander said, leaning closer to Damon, his shoulder brushing Damon's arm and making his heart skitter like a teenager again, "his pain meds are wearing off, and he can't take any more until tomorrow morning."

"Should he be here? With his injury?" Damon asked in a low voice, hopefully out of Kian's hearing. He was also hoping his question looked like friendly concern and not annoyance that Kian was crashing their non-date.

"Socializing is good for him." Xander tipped his head up toward Damon's, grinning, and his stomach fluttered. "He's never able to leave that damn restaurant."

"Is socializing good for you too?" Damon asked. He kept his tone even, but it didn't matter how it sounded, the question still sounded flirtatious.

But Xander just nodded, and didn't move away. "I'm not . . . I'm not always good at it," he confessed. "Maybe you can help me practice."

Damon remembered very well the last person who'd asked him for help "practicing" in this area—he'd eventually married her. If Kian hadn't been standing only a few feet away, maybe he even would have thrown rational thought to the wind, and kissed Xander. All in the name of practice, of course.

Maybe it was better that Kian was here. It kept Damon from doing anything he couldn't take back tomorrow.

"I'm not either," Damon admitted. "Maybe we can practice together?" It was hard to even say it without blushing, and he wasn't sure he quite managed it.

If the way Xander glanced over at his friend, and then back to Damon, and then down to Damon's lips, not even being very subtle about it, was any indication, then he thought he'd just been given the green light.

Of course there was still the problem of Kian. He'd walked over to the other side of the big pile of debris, but he was still present.

"Are you two going to stop flirting so we can burn this down?" Kian asked.

Yep. Definitely still present.

Xander blushed a really cute shade of red, but he didn't deny it. And neither did Damon, which he hoped Xander noticed.

"Yeah, let's get this fire started," Damon said, and blushed himself at the double entendre he'd accidentally used. Kian laughed, and when Damon found the courage to glance over at Xander, he was smiling too. He figured that the nervous determination on Xander's face was probably reflected in his own.

"How can I help?" Xander asked.

"Um, you could find some sticks to toast the marshmallows," Damon suggested. "I'm going to go grab the matches from the house."

<hr>

"Well," Kian said as Xander pulled some long sticks from the pile in front of them, "he sure seems interested from where I'm standing. No reconnaissance required."

"Shhh," Xander hissed at his friend. "He's going to hear you."

"And know he's interested? Yeah, I think he knows that already."

Xander yanked a stick out, examined and then threw it back in. "It's not that simple. We're business partners. Technically he pays my salary. This restaurant is something we both need. I don't want to fuck that up."

"You don't know it will," Kian said, his tone at odds with the optimism of his words. "Now you're just making excuses."

"I don't know it won't," Xander countered. "I'm just trying to be cautious here and make a good decision."

"Are you? Or are you just afraid of something good happening?"

Xander finally found a pair of sticks he liked, and set them aside. "Something good *is* happening. We're opening a restaurant. I'm going to be head chef of my own place, finally. I don't have to get yelled at anymore. If anyone's yelling, it's going to be me. That feels pretty damn good."

Kian opened his mouth, probably to argue that Bastian was a wonderful person under all his verbal abuse, but Xander didn't want to hear it. "I don't care," was all he said. "I know you and I are always going to disagree on this, but he's a shithead."

"Who's a shithead?"

Damon had come back with the matches, and once he spotted Xander's sticks, pulled a pocket knife out, and opened it, passing it to him handle-first. Like the credit card from a few days ago, the metal of the knife was also warm from his body heat. It was old too, well-used, with nicks and scratches. Xander absently rubbed the warm steel with his thumb as he started to trim the sticks and whittle the ends to a point.

"Aquino is a shithead," Xander said shortly.

"No argument from me," Damon said cautiously. Like he knew, even without being told, that this was a delicate subject between the two of them. "You got that okay?" he asked, gesturing to the sticks Xander was prepping.

Just as he asked, the knife slipped, and poked him right in the thumb. Like all of Damon's equipment, it was well-used but also well taken care of and the edge was sharp. Blood welled from the tiny wound. Xander stuck it in his mouth and sucked it. "I *was* fine," he teased. "You just had to go and ask."

Damon was by his side in a second, a hand on his back—warm and heavy and reassuring. "Sorry. It's sharp."

"It's fine, I'll live," Xander said with a chuckle. "At least it doesn't need twenty-four stitches."

Still, Damon reached over and eased the knife from Xander's grip. "I'll just finish these up real quick," he said apologetically. Like he'd fucked up by keeping his knife sharp and lending it to Xander.

The sticks were almost ready anyway, and it only took Damon a few more expertly aimed swipes of the knife to finish them off.

"I'll start the fire now," Damon said, handing the sticks over to Xander and pocketing the knife.

From the way he lit the fire, Xander could tell he'd done it before. Knew exactly where to get the kindling set and in only a few minutes, there was a roaring bonfire in their midst, chasing away the evening chill in the air.

Xander dug out the container of marshmallows and stuck two on the end of the sticks, handed one to Kian.

"They look delicious," Damon said when he wandered back over. He reached down and popped one from the container at Xander's feet into his mouth. "Taste delicious too," he said through a mouthful of marshmallow.

"I proved it to you. What do I get in return?" he teased, all too aware that Damon was standing close, much nearer than he needed to, only a few inches away, their shoulders practically touching. He leaned in closer.

"Anything you want," Damon said quietly, eyes flicking to Xander's, and then over to where Kian was standing, prepping his own s'mores. Xander felt a single brush on his hand and glanced down to see Damon extending a finger to graze the back of his hand.

It felt more tremendous and shattering than a hundred other, far more intimate touches.

"I'm not good at this," Xander repeated from earlier.

Damon smiled, a bittersweet story written in his eyes Xander hoped he might hear one day. "Me either. But I'm running out of reasons why we shouldn't try anyway."

"Me too." Xander kept his voice low, hoping that Kian, who was pointedly turned away from them, nearly around the other side of the bonfire, wouldn't hear them. It had been the right thing to do to bring Kian, considering their recent problems, but he also regretted bringing him along. Anticipation filled him, all too aware that something was going to happen between him and Damon, but not entirely sure when.

Xander reached back and looped their fingers together. He hoped Damon understood. Felt it when he saw Damon's quiet, satisfied smile. Sometimes Xander felt like he'd made a career out of falling for the wrong men; never before had he started anything with anybody feeling like it wasn't going to eventually end in disaster. But this felt fated. Like he'd come here in the middle of a rainstorm not because he needed to stop Damon, but because he'd needed to meet him instead.

"Let's make some s'mores," he said after a minute. "We can't let Kian have all the fun."

He reluctantly detached their fingers and held the stick with the marshmallow closer to the flames.

"Can you get the chocolate and the graham crackers ready?" Xander asked distractedly, trying to rotate the stick so the marshmallow didn't spontaneously burst into flames. The fire was hot, and burning even hotter every second. "This is going to go pretty quick."

When he glanced back, Damon was there, the requested items already unpackaged and waiting. "Oh," Xander said.

"I have made s'mores before," Damon said, amused. "I might not be your culinary equal, but I can help."

Was it any wonder that Xander, despite all the reasons to be afraid of this, and to approach it more carefully, more cautiously, kept wanting to throw all his worries to the wind and make Damon his?

Xander carefully deposited his marshmallow on the upturned chocolate and cracker and left Damon happily munching away as he went to go check on Kian.

"Didn't Nate say he wasn't working tonight?" Xander asked his friend, hoping he wouldn't immediately understand what he was *really* asking.

"You mean, can't Nate come get me so you can make out with sexy farmer over there?" Kian asked archly.

"No, yes, um, I mean . . ." Xander stumbled. He and Kian might not have been as close as they once were, and he wasn't quite as familiar with this more pointed Kian. Kian with all his soft edges beginning to harden and sharpen. Xander wasn't sure he liked it, but he definitely knew who was to blame for it.

"I took care of it," Kian said.

"You took care of it?" Xander questioned.

"He should be here in a few minutes," was all Kian would say.

"You didn't ask Nate?"

Kian turned to face him. He didn't look happy. "Nate told me what you did. That wasn't cool, Xander."

"I thought maybe . . . I don't know. I thought maybe I should be trying the easy way for once, not just fruitlessly pursuing the hard way."

"Nate is a person, he's not an experiment," Kian argued. "And it doesn't really look fruitless from over here."

"I didn't . . . I wasn't sure. I didn't know." They were all bad excuses, and Xander already knew he was going to have to make a groveling apology to Nate at some point, but he hadn't known he was going to be called out by Kian for not doing it yet.

"Not all of us are good at this," Xander continued after taking a short, clearing breath. "I'm trying." He took another breath, trying to say the right thing for once. "I think what I'm trying to say is that not all of us are as sure as you."

Kian looked surprised. It made sense, because Xander had surprised even himself. "What, no more warnings?" He looked up, like he saw something in the distance and gave a little wave.

Must be the person Kian had called to pick him up.

Then the person walked closer, and his shadowy form cleared into the recognizable bulk of Bastian Aquino.

"He texted me to check on how I was doing after service," Kian said, and Xander knew the defensive tone he was using was all his own fault. Was Bastian the right person for Kian? Maybe it was only for Kian to say. "I told him he could come and check on me in person. We'll get out of your hair in a minute."

"No warnings," Xander answered Kian's earlier question with certainty. "You're an adult. You know what you're doing."

Kian sighed. "Not really. But maybe. Maybe soon."

Damon watched as Bastian and Kian left. Xander walked over, a partially eaten s'more in his hand.

"Was that Aquino?" he asked, even though he already knew the answer. Somehow being alone with Xander had been easier with the added protection of Kian's presence. Now they were alone and his nerves were flaring. Did he have the right to do this? Even with the warning to Xander that he was bad at this? Still, Xander couldn't say that he hadn't been as upfront and honest as he could be. He knew Damon was an alcoholic. Sober and recovering, but still an alcoholic. Rachel hadn't known when they'd started dating, but that was high school and even Damon hadn't known what the future held.

"Yeah." Xander stared out at the retreating figures, and Damon had a feeling more than just their burgeoning relationship was on his mind.

"You okay?"

Xander finished his s'more and nodded. "I keep trying to save him from a big mistake with Aquino but maybe it's not a mistake. Maybe I'm wrong. Who's to say I'm right?"

"Probably everyone else who knows Aquino?" Damon suggested. It occurred to him that if Xander's friends knew about his alcoholism, and what had happened with Rachel, they might be warning Xander off him. The same way Xander had warned Kian off Bastian Aquino.

"The truth is," Damon continued with a heavy sigh. "None of us have a perfect track record with relationships. All we can do is make the effort to do better."

Xander's dark eyes were very serious. "Is that what you want?"

Damon wanted all sorts of things. He wanted to be good, to be a better man—both for himself and for Xander—and he also wanted to be very, very bad.

He reached out and took Xander's whole hand this time, lacing their fingers together. Maybe this was supposed to be hard, but he'd known since Rachel walked out that eventually he'd date again, and it might not be a woman. Wrapping his head around dating again was really the tough part, not the fact that Xander was male. "I want you."

Damon didn't know how Xander could still look surprised, but he did. It was a happy sort of surprise, like winning a lottery you hadn't entered, but Damon had to ask.

"You look . . ."

"Surprised?" Xander answered wryly. "Well, you *did* say you were married before. To a woman."

It had never occurred to Damon before that this could be a problem. He'd heard vague rumblings of the gay community underappreciating bisexuality, but he never would have pegged Xander with that sort of prejudice.

"Is that a problem?"

"No, no, of course not," Xander reassured him, gripping his hand tighter, and tugging him closer. He slid a hand around Damon's waist, and it felt so good that he had to hold back the pleasurable shudder. It had been so long since anybody had touched him. But it wasn't just that; it was Xander. Only Xander. "I hoped. I hoped even though I've been let down before. The truth is, I couldn't help myself."

"I didn't think I was very subtle," Damon said with a wry laugh.

"I told you I wasn't good at this. I'm . . . it's hard for me to open up for people. But I want to try."

"And I want you to," Damon said. Resting his hand on Xander's shoulder, and pulling him into an embrace felt as natural as breathing.

He'd thought about it before, but now he knew for sure. If Xander tipped his head back just a fraction, their lips would meet.

Damon had just about gathered enough courage. He knew Xander wanted this. He knew *he* wanted this. But then Xander spoke again.

"Did you know this would happen when you came to Terroir?" he asked softly.

"I didn't know. But I sure hoped," Damon admitted. "I knew the way I felt—the way I *could* feel—and I hoped you felt a little of what I did."

Xander's eyes were so soft. Damon admitted that he didn't know him that well, but he'd never seen Xander look at anything—or anyone—like that before. It was incredibly humbling, and more than a little enthralling, that it was him on the receiving end of that look.

"I looked for you for months," Xander said. "I wanted to do this. Even back then. Even if it seemed like a terrible idea."

He moved so slow that it felt an eternity before Xander's lips met Damon's. So slow that he would have lots of time to change his mind. He had a feeling that was Xander's whole plan. And that was before Xander even knew this was his first kiss with a man.

Damon didn't think of how different it felt because it was a man, only that it was different because it was Xander. It was slow and sweet and gentle, just the softest brush of his lips over Damon's. Once, then twice, and then he held a little longer the third time.

"Was that your first kiss with a man?" Xander asked, a shy grin on his mouth. Damon couldn't wait to kiss it again. He hadn't realized how much he'd missed just kissing, and he had a lot of lost time to make up for.

"Yes. And I'm glad it was with you."

"I have to say," Xander said, "I keep expecting you to freak out but you seem fairly calm about all this."

"Freak out because I'm interested in a guy? I've known I was bisexual since I was in junior high. I just met my ex-wife young and never really had a chance to experiment. Even if experimenting was my type of thing."

"It's not?" The question was coy and a little flirtatious. Damon knew this was an important conversation—but he also wanted to know why they were still talking when they could be kissing.

"You. You're my type of thing. I don't need to sleep with a bunch of people to know what I like."

Xander seemed really pleased at this answer. "So I don't need to ask if you're sure?"

"Have I seemed not sure during any of this?" Damon asked archly.

He pondered this for a moment and then answered. "No. Actually no. You're good."

Damon grinned. "Let me prove to you just how good I am."

It turned out that it was both very much the same and also very different kissing Xander than it had been kissing Rachel. Then Xander shifted his mouth to a different angle, slanting it much more purposefully against Damon's, and his mind dissolved into perfectly white static. His hands gripped Xander's shoulders, sliding down his sides to grasp his hips and pull him closer.

Kissing was good. Kissing was great. Making out was fantastic. Xander tasted like spun sugar, and his tongue was clever, twisting Damon into knots of pleasure, his cock hard against the zipper of his jeans. He didn't even know he wanted to be touched until Xander did, sliding a palm against it and laughing into Damon's mouth as it twitched in surprise and in an overload of feeling.

Damon broke the kiss, panting embarrassingly, wanting to devour Xander all over again when he saw how red and wet his mouth looked in the remnants of the fire.

It felt like there were two roads. One led to easy, uncomplicated pleasure, and maybe a more complicated journey to figuring out what they wanted from each other. It would be so easy to take that road now, to take Xander's hand and lead him back to the house. To even lead him to the barrel house, which was so much closer, and to let them both take the quick, easy pleasure that they both clearly wanted.

Or they could wait. They could take the road slower. Make it deeper. Make it feel more meaningful when Xander finally came to his bed.

Damon already knew he was going to be happier and also way more disappointed by the choice he was going to suggest. And also that that particular path was probably going to lead to blue balls tonight and more nights in the future.

"Can we take this slow?" he asked, and hearing it out loud, he remembered all too well the awkward teenager he'd been and laughed.

But Xander didn't look embarrassed or disappointed. He looked like he was happy to do whatever made Damon happy. "Sure, of course. I'm happy to go at your pace. This is all new to you."

Damon tugged him close again, making sure he could feel how much he wanted him—though Xander had to know, it was important that he didn't think this had anything to do with him.

"I'm going to enjoy having you show me everything. Every single thing you want," Damon whispered in his ear, pressing a single kiss against his neck. He tasted like smoky sugar, and Damon was never going to eat a marshmallow again without getting hard.

And if he kept Xander around, and Xander kept making him marshmallows, then that might work out well for both of them.

Chapter Eight

It was an unexpectedly hot day for fall in Northern California, and the Barrel House didn't have air-conditioning yet. Xander wiped off his forehead as surreptitiously as he could, hoping that Damon hadn't seen him sweat.

It was silly and childish, but he knew he was walking on eggshells around him. A few kisses, a few promises, and he was a lovesick teenager, terrified of saying or doing the wrong thing.

He knew he was supposed to trust Damon more, but deliberately opening himself up to anybody was new for him. It had been hard enough to make the initial decision to do so, and then he'd realized it was a continuing choice every day.

Each day when he woke up, he chose Damon and all the risk he came with instead of protecting his soft, vulnerable heart. Right now the decision was hard, but ultimately lopsided. Damon won out every single time, no doubt about it. Xander wasn't naïve enough to believe that would always be the case.

"Are you okay?" Damon asked. Xander jerked in surprise. He'd been so sure that Damon was absorbed in listening to the contractor talk about the plans for the restaurant remodel, which were currently spread over the temporary job site office—a pair of sawhorses and an old door Damon had taken off the hinges.

"Fine, I'm fine," Xander said.

Damon smiled. "Sorry, it's boring."

"Just a whole different language," Xander said apologetically. "If we're talking menus, I'm here with bells on."

When Damon had mentioned he was meeting the contractor today, and had offered for Xander to join them, he'd thought it was a good idea.

Okay, he'd actually thought it was a chance to see Damon again after they'd both been busy over the last few days. What he'd been hoping for was more making out and less mind-numbing, nitty-gritty construction details.

David, the contractor, grinned. "I'd be happy to come back to discuss menus. I really admire the work you did at Terroir."

David was shorter than Damon, and all compact muscle, but they were in almost a similar uniform of jeans, work boots, and a plaid shirt. Damon's was autumnal orange tones and David's was red and blue. Still, he had a nice smile, and seemed to know what he was doing. Plus, Damon had known him for a long time, and Xander trusted Damon's judgement on this sort of thing.

Now, menus? That was a whole different ballgame.

"Maybe you'd just like to come back for the tasting sessions," Xander offered. "Once the kitchen is in."

"Yeah, the kitchen," David said, like Xander's words had reminded him of something else to discuss. "Do you have a list of kitchen equipment that you need?"

There was not going to be a large amount of space in the Barrel House kitchen. Not like the gigantic Terroir kitchens that housed every wet dream professional kitchen appliance Bastian Aquino could get his hands on, times two.

Xander was going to need to be careful and conservative, and only put in exactly what he needed.

He'd been working with his hand-drawn kitchen diagrams and appliance dimensions for a few days now, in anticipation of this request, and he still hadn't finalized everything.

"I'm still working on it," he admitted. "The space is tricky."

"I told you that you could have more space, if you needed it," Damon inserted, looking worried.

Xander might have a crush but he was still determined to make this restaurant a success. "And take away from table space? No way. I can manage."

"We might be able to build a small addition in the back for the refrigerated units," David said, pulling out a pencil from a pocket and beginning to sketch directly on the plans. "That would give you a little more work room in the kitchen itself."

Xander leaned over the table, looking at David's scribbles, and tried not to jump out of his skin when Damon placed a steadying hand on his back as he leaned in too.

Tried not to internally freak out when Damon kept his hand there after they were upright again. That was definitely something not "just partners" would do, and if David didn't know they were involved—or getting involved—before, he probably knew now. But he didn't even act like he'd noticed.

"It might add a little more to the budget," David said. "And we'll have to alter the permits, but I think I can charm their way through. They're not much different than the originals."

Damon waved a hand, completely dismissing the extra expense as they walked outside—like somehow he'd known Xander was hot and a little miserable. "I don't want Xander in a cramped kitchen. He's an artist. He needs space to work his magic."

Xander was in the middle of basking in this sweet compliment when he noticed Damon's face change abruptly. His mouth compressed into a grim line, and his eyes hardened unmistakably.

He looked up and followed Damon's sightline to an older man getting out of a silver Mercedes sedan. He had dark hair, touched with a little silver at the temples, and could be Damon's twin, if not for the additional lines around his eyes and mouth.

This must be Damon's father. The famous patriarch of the Hess family.

Damon, who'd had zero issue putting his hands on Xander in front of their contractor, dropped his hand from Xander's back like it had suddenly caught fire.

He didn't want to listen, but as the older man strode toward them, it was impossible not to hear the tiny, niggling voice that the last few days had just begun to silence.

This is just a phase. Damon doesn't really want you. It's just convenient. This isn't for real.

Xander tried silencing the annoying voice by reminding himself that while Damon might be comfortable with bisexuality, that didn't mean he was out to his father.

"David," Damon said, reaching out to shake the contractor's hand, "thanks for meeting with us today. Will you get me a new quote with the changes? Go ahead and start the revised permitting process though. I know it takes a long time to push through and we're in a rush."

Xander hadn't really thought about whether they were in a hurry or not—though he understood that a business' purpose was to make money and all they were doing now was spending it. They couldn't begin to recoup that loss until the restaurant opened.

Still, it was strange that Damon hadn't said anything to him about opening quickly. Or about his dad not knowing about his bisexuality.

"I'll send it over tomorrow," David said, shaking Damon's hand briskly and then moving onto Xander's.

When David started to walk toward the driveway, Damon's father had just reached them.

"Xander," Damon said, his voice mechanical and nearly unrecognizable. "I'll talk to you later."

Xander wasn't stupid. He knew he was being dismissed. It was inevitable that despite understanding the generic reason why, it would still sting. What really bothered him was that he didn't *really* know why. Couldn't he stand here and be a business partner? Wasn't that still his most important function in Damon's life? Why couldn't he meet Damon's father under that circumstance? Damon's sexuality didn't even need to come into the picture.

He'd grown up a lot since high school, since that terrible, awful crush that had decimated his heart when he'd finally realized that he was always going to be Dustin's ugly secret. He'd had years to separate himself from that pain, years to build a wall to prevent him from ever feeling that pain again. And now, today, Xander realized as he turned and walked away that he hadn't just let Damon wiggle under the fence. He'd torn down a part and practically invited him to waltz inside.

Even as he came up with a half dozen very practical, very logical reasons why Damon might not want to introduce him to his father, Xander couldn't help but think this was why he'd stopped letting people in.

Because they inevitably disappointed you, and worse.

Damon watched as Xander walked away. He knew he wasn't happy with Damon's decision to summarily dismiss him, and he couldn't blame him. But he couldn't let his father dig his poisonous claws into Xander. He'd never done anything to deserve that sort of pain. Damon was used to it; he'd been dealing with its side effects his entire damn life.

"Not going to say hello to your father?" Nathan asked. Passive-aggressive had always been his favorite language, and clearly nothing had changed, despite Damon avoiding him as best he could the last year and a half since he'd moved back to Napa.

"I have nothing to say to you," Damon said shortly.

"But you so politely dismissed your friends so we could talk," Nathan pointed out. "It would be a shame not to take advantage."

"Lots of people think you're important and that your opinion matters. Go talk to them."

"Maybe," Nathan threw out, "I want to see the wreck of our family's oldest vineyard. Are there even any grapes left, Damon, or did you destroy them all?"

This old argument again. Nathan had, of course, come to see him after that night a year ago, livid that he would dare to destroy something so precious. Damon could only retort that maybe his father should care that the vines had been destroying *him*.

Nathan had just shaken his head, disappointed and hurt, which was so much worse than his cutting anger, because it came with a healthy dose of guilt and that had always been tougher for Damon to shake. "Always such a drama queen," he'd said.

Yes, Damon was definitely being overdramatic with his alcoholism. According to his father, alcohol was the golden calf that had always been so good to their family, and anyone who rejected it was rejecting the Hess name.

The day Damon went to rehab, his father had texted him to remind him that alcohol was "always a choice." Like he'd ever had a choice in being an alcoholic.

"There's still some left," Damon said. "Though they won't be around for much longer. Should go check them out before I burn those too. Gonna plant a really nice orchard. Apples, I think."

Nathan's lip curled into a disgusted sneer. He still managed to look handsome, because that was another of the Hess family gifts—or curses. All depending on your angle.

"What are you even doing here?" Damon demanded. "You're not here to see my garden or my land. If you're just here to remind me what a terrible Hess I am, you've succeeded. Now, leave."

Crossing his arms across his chest, Nathan actually had the nerve to look concerned. "I played a round of golf with Walter last week. He mentioned to me how happy he was that you were investing your trust in the family business."

"It's my trust," Damon argued. "I can do whatever the hell I want to with it."

"Including throwing it away on a pipe dream? Starting a restaurant? In that old shack?"

"Why does it matter to you?" Damon was struggling. It wasn't like his horrible, overachieving, critical father was the only reason why he'd become an alcoholic—but he sure hadn't helped.

"It matters," Nathan enunciated each word carefully and slowly, like Damon was an idiot who needed help understanding, "because when you burn through your trust starting a business in a field you have no experience in, in a highly competitive market like Napa, with one of Aquino's rejects, you'll be back on my doorstep, begging to join us again."

"I wouldn't beg, and I certainly wouldn't beg you," Damon said. "I'm capable of working. I've done it before. I can do it again. I know manual labor isn't something your highly privileged brain comprehends, but I'm good at it."

That was the whole root of this disconnect with his father. He didn't *get* Damon, and had long since given up trying.

"You're a Hess," Nathan said. "You're not meant to be working the fields. You're meant to own them."

Damon wanted to tell his father that he could do both, that he was enjoying doing both now. But it had always been useless to argue with Nathan Hess, and nothing had changed in years.

"Thank you for the unsolicited advice." Damon paused. "Now since you're so eager for me to exercise my rights as a land *owner*, get the fuck off my land."

Nathan threw his hands up, his expression making it perfectly clear that he hadn't wanted to come here and argue, but that he'd done it because he'd felt obligated. Not out of fatherly love or familial concern, but fear of financial waste.

Damon watched him walk away and told himself that he'd reconciled himself to a shitty father years ago. But if that was true, why did every encounter feel like razor blades slashing at his composure, at his sense of self? When would he *finally* feel like he wasn't obligated to fulfill the duties of being a Hess? He'd left the family. He'd left the business. He kept to himself, and did his own thing.

The money and the land still tied him to them though, and if it had been any other land, and money from anyone else but his grandfather, he might have rejected both. But his grandfather had *cared* about this land, about what it had meant. Had felt an obligation and a responsibility that far eclipsed his father's *noblesse oblige* bullshit. And when Damon walked it, early in the morning, the sun creeping over the hills, he remembered the only person in his family who hadn't been a total waste of his time.

He'd come here and taken back his land first for his grandfather, and then he'd discovered, especially after that horrible night, a purpose of his own.

John Hess would have been proud of him—no matter what he'd done to the vines. If Damon closed his eyes, he could almost hear his deep, gritty voice. *It's your land*, he'd have said, *you can do whatever the hell you want with it. They're just vines.*

Damon shoved his hands in his pockets, because the urge was strong to call Xander, because he couldn't have a conversation with a ghost. Xander might be one of the few who'd understand besides his grandfather. But their relationship was so new, so fresh, so tentative, and he didn't want to crush it with all his personal baggage. Xander didn't need to hear all of that, definitely not yet, no matter how much Damon wanted to tell him.

He knew some of what Damon struggled with, but he definitely didn't need to know the whole of it. Rachel, who'd practically known him his whole life, had gotten sick of it and left. That had hurt badly, but he'd persevered, and he'd even felt cautiously optimistic about his chances with Xander.

His father showing up had re-opened old wounds, reminding Damon of their existence when he'd been trying so hard to pretend he wasn't fucked up.

That being a Hess carried with it a whole load of ridiculous expectations and that it was bad enough being born into it. Anyone sane didn't *choose* it.

After being dismissed by Damon, Xander went to the grocery store, randomly wandering the aisles, picking up vegetables, and then putting them down again. He finally managed to fill half a cart with ingredients he thought he could use to work on recipes for the restaurant. He went back home, put the food away, and went on a grueling, punishing run.

The truth was Xander really wanted to be pissed, but after exhausting himself, all he felt was empty and directionless. Instead of cooking anything, he grabbed carrots and a tub of hummus and plopped down on the couch.

It was easy enough to feel certain of Damon and Damon's feelings when they were together, but it turned out it was also easy enough for doubt to creep in. No matter how much Xander wanted to trust him completely, he didn't know him completely. *Couldn't* know him completely, not yet anyway.

He stewed all night as he sat on the couch, laptop in hand, as he researched some recipes he wanted to try for the restaurant. He was sure he'd enjoy the quiet, but it turned out the quiet was actually way too quiet—especially when he was upset and wanted someone to vent to. He never thought he'd miss the ambient noise of Nate and Kian being in the house, but it turned out he did.

He almost texted his friend Wyatt, but remembered that this was one of the nights he and his brother ran their food truck near Venice Beach, so he'd be way too busy to listen to or comment on Xander's bad mood.

Calling Miles again was out of the question, as was calling Kian.

Xander impatiently tapped his fingers on the laptop keyboard. Everything he was thinking now was total crap, and he hated how much sense that made. For him, food came from a place of care and love. He cooked because he wanted to share with someone. And right now, what he wanted was to share with Damon.

He glanced at his phone, sitting so innocently on the coffee table. Wouldn't it be better if he found out now that this was normal behavior for Damon? Wouldn't it be better to know now if Damon wasn't worth the trust he wanted so badly to place in him?

The truth, no matter how painful, was always better than a lie. And if Xander was lying to himself, then he needed to know.

He could've just texted—Damon had always answered texts quickly, even quickly enough for Xander's natural impatience—but he dialed his number instead.

Xander's heart thumped in his chest, loud enough that he could hear it even over Alton Brown's muted voice on the TV. He didn't have to wait in suspense very long; Damon picked up on the second ring.

Like he'd been waiting too, trying to decide whether he should call Xander.

Xander pushed that thought aside. He was doing it again: his hopeful heart making up the best possible scenario for him to believe, instead of the truth.

He needed the truth.

"Xander," Damon said breathlessly. Exactly as breathless as Xander felt.

He'd considered playing all his cards close to his chest, acting like everything was okay, and waiting for Damon to say something about earlier this afternoon. But when faced with Damon's voice, Xander discovered that was total bullshit.

He wasn't the kind of guy who prevaricated. He wasn't the person who let shit go for a half-hearted explanation. He'd done it when he was much younger, and after that flaming disaster of a relationship, he'd sworn to himself that he wouldn't let himself be manipulated again. After that, he'd always been straight, to the point of making guys uncomfortable. It was why he'd stopped seeking relationships. He wanted a level of honesty that nobody was quite prepared to give. The initial shock of his attraction to Damon and discovering that it was mutual had thrown him off-balance enough that he'd forgotten who he was. Who he'd become, out of necessity.

"What the hell was with that today?" Xander demanded.

Silence.

Damon didn't know the truth-seeking missile that had been Xander. He'd met him briefly that one night, a year ago, but even then the shock of attraction had melted his rough edges away almost immediately.

Damon didn't know the guy that Miles and Wyatt and Kian did. And it was time he did.

"That was my father," Damon said. "You didn't want to meet him."

"You're right," Xander admitted, and he didn't want to be an asshole, though he knew he got mistaken for one sometimes, "I didn't want to meet him. But I also didn't want to be shoved aside like some sort of toy you're ashamed of."

More silence.

This might be the end of their relationship, personal *and* professional, if Damon didn't understand what Xander was trying to say. He tried again, a little less abrasive this time. Miles had told him for years that wanting honesty didn't necessarily mean being a dick, and Xander had never felt that particular piece of advice had much merit. But he did now.

"You could have explained that to me," Xander added. "Instead of just telling me to leave, like David. You hired him."

"I hired you," Damon said, sounding perplexed, and it was only the confusion in his voice that prevented Xander from exploding into a rage of flames.

Yes, he had technically hired Xander. *Yes,* he was paying him a salary. But they were partners, Damon had made that clear, and they were trying to be even more.

Reducing him to a mere underling hired to be at his convenience smacked of everything that Xander had joyfully left behind at Terroir. He'd done that because he'd believed that Damon would be a far better boss than Bastian Aquino had ever been.

"Can you just . . . let me in?" Damon asked.

Xander nearly dropped the phone. "You're here?" He ran a hand through his hair, messy after a quick shower, and left to dry however it wanted. He glanced down at his old pair of jogging shorts he'd shrugged on. He looked like hell, but maybe that was okay.

Honesty, right? In all things. Including his appearance.

"I wanted to say I was sorry," Damon said, and he did genuinely sound apologetic. "I wasn't expecting . . ."

It was clear what Damon hadn't been expecting. He hadn't been expecting Xander to come at him like a runaway freight train on fire with rage—justified or not.

Xander set his laptop aside, and went to the front door, opening it. Damon stood on the front porch, phone to his ear and a pizza box in his hands. His mouth twisted in a wry, apologetic smile. "You are here."

"I said I was," Damon said. "I'm not going to lie to you."

Damon couldn't possibly know about the fears lurking in the back of Xander's brain, and buried deep, like unexploded mines, in his heart. He still set them to rest. He extended the pizza box. "I thought you might be hungry, and my mother said never to go to someone's house empty-handed."

Popping open the box, Xander took in the scent of fresh dough, tomatoes and grease. "Pepperoni and mushroom?"

Damon shrugged, and looked embarrassed. "Is it terribly self-serving of me to admit that it's *my* favorite?"

Xander just stared at him.

"I thought if you didn't want it, I might as well get something I would eat," Damon said. He stopped, glancing around. "Are you just going to leave me on the porch, rambling about pizza?"

Xander had considered it. It might be an excessive punishment for Damon's crime but he was still mad—or afraid, he'd lost track of what each felt like. "I don't know," he said slowly.

"You don't know." Damon looked like he wanted to grab the pizza back and go back to his car and stress eat the whole thing. Xander understood the impulse all too well.

"I need to tell you something about me first," Xander said, shifting his feet. It was one thing to preach honesty, and to demand it at every turn, but it turned out it was totally different to demand your own honesty when it came to someone you cared about.

"I don't date because I'm not good at it. I need . . . a measure of transparency that most people aren't willing to give," Xander admitted. "I can be a real asshole about it."

"And you don't think I can give it?" Damon asked. Calculatingly, a bit harder than Xander expected.

"I don't know . . . I thought you could. I wanted you to be able to. I wouldn't have started this otherwise. But this afternoon . . ."

"Made you doubt," Damon finished for him. Which was good because Xander hadn't been exactly sure what this afternoon had made him feel.

But he knew the truth, and he wondered if he would ever have the courage to say it out loud. Or if Damon would just say it for him.

This afternoon had made him feel vulnerable again, and he'd sworn that he'd never feel that again. Taking down that wall that separated him from the rest of the world had initially felt good and right, especially when it was Damon he was letting in. But he'd been caught up in the rightness of it, the first initial swoon of realizing that his crush was mutual.

Damon was going to screw things up, he'd admitted that much to Xander before they'd even kissed. And *anyone* would and could. Nobody was perfect.

Xander pushed down the natural fear that bubbled up inside him. "A little, yeah."

"I'm sorry," Damon said, sounding genuinely contrite. "I'm sorry I made you doubt. My dad . . . he fucks me up bad. I can't say he's the reason I'm an alcoholic, but if one person was actually at fault, he would be. I didn't want you to be poisoned by his shit, or watch me as I tried to avoid it."

And looking back, Xander could see that. He'd seen the fear in Damon's eyes, the reluctance as his father had walked toward them.

He understood trying to protect people you cared about from terrible things. He'd been trying to protect Kian for what felt like forever.

This wasn't all that different.

Xander turned and walked into the house, gesturing for Damon to follow him.

He settled back down on the couch, and Damon wavered, unsure, in the doorway to the living room. "Come sit," Xander said, patting the spot next to him, "let's eat our feelings."

Damon walked over, a grateful look in his eyes as he sat down.

They'd each unapologetically devoured two pieces when Xander spoke. "Was it bad today?"

Sighing, Damon leaned back on the couch, crossing his hands across his stomach. He looked younger and more vulnerable than Xander had ever seen him. "Yes."

"Why did you come back to Napa, if he was so awful?" Xander couldn't help but ask. "You could've stayed away? Don't get me wrong, I'm selfishly happy you're here, but wouldn't you have been better off someplace else?"

"My grandfather left me that land when he died about a year and a half ago," Damon said softly. "And I loved him. I wanted to make him proud. I wanted to prove to him that I could be more than just a guy who loved booze."

"You can, you *are*," Xander argued, suddenly feeling irrationally and fiercely angry that anybody could shit on their own family like this—especially for a disease that nobody could prevent. "You're doing an incredible thing. Brave and important."

Damon shot Xander a lazy, soft glance. "I know. Doesn't make it very easy."

"Easy things aren't worth doing," Xander scoffed, and then grinned. "Besides, I'm here, I can help."

His glance slid away, and Xander felt the pizza, greasy and heavy, settling nauseously in his stomach. "You can, you have. But I take more than I give. Today was a good example of that."

"We both have . . . baggage," Xander pointed out. "But I know we can work through this. I want to work through this. I called you even though I was angry with you. But I still called. And you weren't sure if I'd open the door, but you came here anyway."

Damon reached up and cradled the side of Xander's face with his palm. "I want better for you than to have to deal with my baggage."

Xander had had a feeling this was where this conversation was going, and there was no way he was going to let Damon push him away selflessly when he'd already faced his own demons and told them off. "No way. You don't get to make that choice."

"You sure about that?"

"You try to take my personal autonomy away, I'll kick your ass," Xander said.

Damon burst out laughing, and Xander patted himself on the back for lightening his mood. "I'd like to see you try."

"Admittedly, it would probably end up being a lot more homoerotic, and would almost definitely devolve into sex, but the point remains. This is my decision, and I'm not going anywhere."

Damon raised an eyebrow. "Homoerotic? Think I can get a demonstration?"

Leaning closer, Xander kissed him firmly on the mouth. He tasted like spicy tomatoes and the earthy musk of mushrooms. Normally he might not like it, but he loved it now. He deepened the kiss a little, Damon's other hand reaching up to pull him closer. It was good, soft but hot, a reaffirmation of everything they'd both admitted they felt. But before it could get too hot, Xander pulled back.

Damon's bottom lip jutted out, and he pouted. "We're still taking things slowly?"

Xander had to nod. He was Damon's first time with a guy. He didn't want to rush him, no matter if he wanted to rush himself. There was too much at stake here—Xander's heart for one, the restaurant for another.

"Fine," Damon grumbled. "It's probably the right call, but for the record, it sucks."

Xander plopped back against the couch. "Yes, it does. And not even in the good way."

Chapter Nine

Xander was fussing with a ravioli filling—simple but essential that it be absolutely perfect—when his phone rang.

He picked it up gingerly with flour-dusted fingertips and set it between his shoulder and ear as he continued to stir some caramelized onions on the stove.

"What's up?" he asked Damon.

His heart still accelerated a little whenever Damon called him or texted him or otherwise acknowledged his existence. At first Xander had been embarrassed by it, but then he'd caught Damon's fingers trembling the other night as they'd sat on the couch, watching a movie. Damon's cheeks had flushed bright red, and all Xander could do was confess his own crush symptoms.

They were still taking it slow, because Xander was still irrationally worried that Damon might change his mind, and also because neither of them really knew how to just *date* someone. Damon had been married forever, and other than few meaningless hookups, Xander had been celibate and alone. They were still figuring it all out, and they had a mostly unspoken agreement that sex complicated a brand-new relationship that was already complicated enough.

"Good news," Damon said. There was the sound of wind on his side of the line, like he was driving with the window open. Which made sense, because they were having a surprisingly hot spell. Xander was personally sweating his ass off in his un-air-conditioned kitchen.

"Did the permits come through?" Xander asked, continuing to stir his onions. He was looking for a jam-like texture, after the onions had started to really break down and grow caramel in color. The result was not quite there, but he was regretting deciding that today was the day he was going to perfect his ravioli recipe.

"Yeah, they're in. David's starting construction tomorrow. And good news, the HVAC people are going to be in pretty soon, installing the new air-conditioning."

"If the building wasn't going to be a mess of dust and dirt, I would seriously consider packing up and moving recipe testing there," Xander complained. "It's hot as hell in here, and for some reason I thought it'd be a great idea to hunch over a stove all day."

"The ravioli recipe?" Damon sounded sympathetic.

Xander hummed in agreement, reaching down to grab a taste with a fingertip. Close, but not quite. He plucked his bottle of balsamic vinegar from the counter and added a splash, tasted again, and then splashed in some more.

"It needs pepper," Damon said, his teasing tone light and happy. So far from the wounded despondency of a few days ago when his father had visited him. Xander wanted to believe he had something to do with Damon's attitude bouncing back, but it was easy to doubt himself. Too easy.

"You think everything needs pepper," Xander scoffed. "If you tell me this dish needs pepper, I'm going to throttle you."

"Okay, no pepper. Does that mean we aren't having the waiters come to your table with a pepper grinder for your salad?"

Xander made a wounded noise over the phone. "You're physically hurting me. Of course not. Like I would ever make a dish that needs to be liberally coated with fresh ground pepper! That's only for food that has no flavor and they're trying to hide it by ruining your taste buds up front."

"Huh." Damon sounded thoughtful. "I never thought of it that way before."

"That's why you hired me," Xander said, and this time he could say it without even a hiccup, had been practicing saying it and acknowledging it for the last few days. Damon *had* hired him. He was technically Damon's employee. Yes, he was also more—they both believed that—but he couldn't let himself forget that one fundamental fact. He'd started this by pretending facts weren't facts, and that wasn't going to get either of them anywhere. If he was going to commit to this relationship, he wasn't going to let himself forget who he was, or where he'd been. Honesty—and *self-honesty*—was vital.

"It's true," Damon said casually.

"What else are you doing today?" Xander asked, finally pulling the onions off the heat. They looked perfect, and after taking another taste, also had perfect flavor.

"Weeding. Watering, at least after the sun goes down." He sounded as eager for it as Xander felt.

Just as Xander was thinking of how much he'd pay for a dunking that wasn't just a cold shower, Damon suggested, "You could come over, if you wanted. I'll have the sprinklers out. We could run through them like kids. It's not much but it's something."

Xander wiped the sweat from his forehead. Imagined Damon in a white tank, soaked through, outlining every one of his incredible muscles. It was not a tough decision to make.

"Count me in."

"Dusk is about nine," Damon said. "I can't water until then."

"I'll be over then." Xander paused. "I can bring over some of these ravioli. You can try them, but there's one important condition."

"I can't say it needs pepper?"

Xander laughed. "That *and* you don't complain that they're hot. Or warm. Unfortunately they're not meant to be eaten cold."

"You could make a cold ravioli salad," Damon suggested.

Xander couldn't help it—he laughed again. "Pasta salad? With ravioli?"

"That's weird, isn't it?"

"It's . . . different. But different could be good." Xander had an idea, and then three more, just in the quick pause before Damon answered. They weren't really high-end ideas, but every time he had that thought, Xander shoved the snooty voice of Bastian Aquino right out of his head, and did whatever the fuck he wanted.

So far that had seemed to work well for him. Whether that would work once the Barrel House opened and critics showed up, that remained to be seen. But nothing was more freeing than forcing himself not to care what other people thought.

"I like different," Damon said loyally. "Especially your different."

It was taking time, but Xander was finally beginning to believe he deserved that hushed, reverent note in Damon's voice.

"Yours is pretty great too," Xander admitted.

Silence stretched between them, full of things that Xander knew neither of them had the nerve to say just yet. *I miss you. I'm craving you. I want you so badly it hurts.*

Xander was left wondering how long this self-enforced celibacy could continue lasting. Probably not much further, if he was being honest with himself.

"I'll see you tonight?" Damon finally said.

"Yeah, of course. About nine," Xander said, repeating himself because he wanted to linger on the phone, just to hear Damon's voice, even though what he really needed was to finish up the ravioli, get out of this boiling hot kitchen, and take a very cold shower—and not just because it was a hundred degrees outside.

"See you then," Damon said, and finally clicked off.

Xander sighed as he set the phone back on the counter. It was now liberally smeared with flour, like just about every other surface in the kitchen, including his arms and probably his face.

Turning his attention back to the caramelized onions, he tested them with his fingertips, making sure they'd cooled down enough to incorporate them into the rest of his mixture, but they weren't nearly ready yet.

He picked up the pan and hauled it over to the fridge, stuck it on a shelf and stood there for a good minute just letting the cool air billow over him.

"You'd better be paying a higher fraction of the electric bill this month," Nate said from behind him.

Xander didn't budge or even turn around. He still felt a shaft of embarrassment deep inside at how he'd treated his friend. Using him while he'd only ever wanted to kiss Damon. "It's hot as balls."

"And somehow you're still in this kitchen, sweating them off." Nate sounded amused, and it helped break the ice between them. Xander relaxed a fraction, and once he did, found it was easier to let the embarrassment go.

"I have work to do," Xander retorted.

"What, working in the kitchen is work? I thought your new career was all about working Damon Hess?"

"That would be nice, but it's not in the job description," Xander said. He'd do it. He *wanted* to do it. Was slowly dying that he hadn't yet. He was no stranger to celibacy but waiting for Damon to be ready to take things up a notch was giving him an epic case of blue balls.

"Yet."

Xander turned around, bringing out his pan of onions, and this time when he touched them with a finger, they were cool enough. He shut the fridge and walked back over to the prep counter.

"What is that supposed to mean?" he asked.

"That means that Nathan Hess is talking. About you and his son."

"Fuck," Xander swore. "I don't like that guy. I wish he'd leave Damon alone." *And me*, Xander thought.

Nate raised an eyebrow. "It doesn't sound like nothing's going on," he pointed out.

"We're taking things slow," Xander said, hoping that he wouldn't regret confiding in Nate. He had a real ear for good gossip, and this was sweet stuff. Nathan Hess' son hooking up with his new employee and an ex-Terroir chef? It had all the trademarks of a real juicy rumor.

"I can't believe you're not climbing that like a tree," Nate offered.

"Me either," Xander muttered. "Wait, how do you even know it's Damon Hess? And what he looks like?"

"Kian told me. And after your aborted little experiment, I looked him up," Nate pointed out, reaching in the bowl of filling and pulling out a bite before Xander could smack his hand. "But you don't need me to tell you he's hot."

Xander definitely did not.

"He's also technically your boss," Nate continued. Xander was beginning to remember why they hadn't ever really been friends. Why he had disliked Nate the moment Wyatt had brought him home the first time. "I bet you don't feel hypocritical at all, especially after the way you've been trying to get Kian to stop panting over Aquino."

Xander gritted his teeth. "I don't feel that way, no. Bastian Aquino is an asshole who emotionally manipulates people. Especially his employees. Damon couldn't do that even if he wanted to. He doesn't have it in him."

"His father is Nathan Hess." Nate's expression was incredulous. "You clearly know a little of what he's like. I know Damon doesn't like him much, but I'd worry, if I were you."

"Well, it's a good thing you aren't," Xander said. "If I save you some leftovers will you leave me alone to finish this in peace?"

"The truth hurts, sometimes, doesn't it?"

"You sound like a smarmy Bond villain," Xander pointed out. "If I give you some ravioli, will that serve as an apology for how I used you terribly?"

Nate chuckled. "It might, if it was a real apology?"

"Just so we're clear, I'm not apologizing for the kiss. I'm apologizing for . . ." Xander tried to find a reason that made sense that *wasn't* about the kiss, and his sluggish brain wouldn't respond.

"The kiss." Nate rolled his eyes. "Yeah, I get it. Apology accepted."

The first thing Damon smelled when he stepped outside was the rich scent of the earth after baking all afternoon in the hot sun.

It was one of his favorite scents, especially when the land he was smelling was his own.

His father might show up and issue threats, but this land was still Damon's, and as far as he was concerned, it was going to stay his as long as he was in one piece.

He dragged the hose and sprinklers over to the first set of plants. A more professional garden might have in-bed sprinklers, and there were some nights when Damon wished he had them, but he'd also discovered there was a soothing peace to each night's work, tending his garden in the dusk.

If the restaurant failed, yes, he might have to work another job to pay the property taxes on it—the property taxes Damon's grandfather had ensured would always be paid by gifting him a trust upon his death. Grandpa might not be very happy that Damon was spending all that nice, safe property tax money on a restaurant, but he'd also always wanted Damon to fulfill his dreams.

He might be back to construction again, but Damon had made his peace with that possibility. If the worst came to pass, and the Barrel House wasn't a success, the only thing that worried him was Xander.

Xander was depending on him—and on himself—to carve out a niche for now and for a long time to come. Damon was going to do everything he could to make that dream a reality.

"You haven't started yet."

Damon glanced up and Xander was standing there, fists on his hips, dressed in a white tank top and a pair of running shorts. There was a lot of firm, tanned, muscled skin on display, and Damon swallowed hard. He knew what he wanted; he just wanted Xander to trust that he wanted it. To stop questioning whether he'd change his mind.

He wasn't going to. He'd known embarrassingly early in their high school courtship that he was going to marry Rachel. And he'd known from the first moment they'd met that Xander was going to be important to him.

Damon definitely wasn't ready for Xander to know just how important yet. Here Xander was, terrified that Damon was going to get cold feet about having a guy for a partner, when in reality, Damon was afraid he was going to move too fast or demonstrate too much commitment.

It was an ironic situation that might have been funnier if it was a little cooler outside and he didn't want Xander quite so much.

Stop thinking so much, he told himself, and before he could question his own decision, stripped off his worn t-shirt, and couldn't help but watch as Xander's eyes grew big. Damon knew he looked good; he'd started working out in earnest after rehab because he'd always liked to drink in the evenings and if his arms were too tired to even pick up a bottle, then there was a little less temptation.

"Are you okay?" Xander asked carefully.

Instead of answering, Damon turned the hose on him instead of on his carrots.

As the cold water hit him, Xander yelped, throwing his hands up. "I take it back, I take it back," Xander said, moving out of the way to try to dodge the spray after that first, frozen moment. Damon might have been worried, but he was laughing so hard it was hard for him to avoid the stream of water from the hose.

"I thought you were hot," Damon teased.

Xander slipped on a patch of muddy ground, and nearly lost his balance, but his recovery was excellent. He moved with the grace of an athlete—or a dancer—and Damon never wanted to stop watching.

He only realized too late that Xander wasn't just trying to move out of the way of the water. He was actively moving toward where Damon had plugged in one of his sprinklers. He leaned down for a second, his wet running shorts plastered to his ass like a second skin, and Damon lost track of what it was he was supposed to be avoiding. That incredible butt, toned and shapely and essentially begging for Damon to do terrible, wonderful things to it?

A cold spray of water to the face from the hose Xander had unhooked from the sprinkler had him gasping, but his thoughts hadn't gotten any cleaner.

"You're playing dirty," Damon gasped through another burst of water to the face. He wasn't going to tell Xander this, but it felt damn good after sweating all day.

Xander's eyes narrowed, a bright smile blooming across his handsome face. "You love it," he shot back.

He really did, and he never wanted Xander to stop. He loved every sneaky part of him, every achingly blunt part of his personality. Damon wanted it all, if only Xander would let him.

Damon turned the hose on himself, water cascading over his head. "I love *this*," he teased. "But you could lean over again. Could use another firsthand bit of evidence to prove how much I love it."

Following suit with his own, Xander turned his hose on himself, drenching every inch in water. His tank clung to every lean, muscular curve of his body, and Damon wanted to drop to his knees in the mud and *beg*.

I want to prove myself but I want to prove it to you first. Please let me touch you.

"Yeah," Damon ground out, voice gruff and low, his erection growing despite the cold water he was pouring over himself, "yeah, I love that."

Xander's eyes sparkled with impudence as he sidled closer, letting Damon get a good look. He placed a cool palm on Damon's bare chest, right where his heart beat hard and fast. "I love it too," he said.

The hose dropped to the ground as Damon reached out and gripped Xander by his hips, dragging him those last few inches until they were plastered together.

"Is this what you want?" Damon demanded. "Tell me if it's not because I can't . . . I can't. I'm not going to change my mind. I promise."

Xander stared at him, mouth open, for a long moment. He must have felt Damon's hard-on through his paper-thin shorts and Damon's jeans—completely soaked and plastered to his thighs.

"You promise," Xander stuttered back.

"I promise I'm not going to change my mind," Damon vowed. "Because I don't know about you, but I'm feeling pretty damn gay right now."

Laughing, Xander ran his hands down Damon's chest, tracing the trail of dark hair that led to his fly. "You know what? Me too."

Damon decided that was all the agreement he needed, and bent his head down, kissing Xander fiercely. Refusing to hold back anymore, he kissed him with all the desire that had been building inside him without a single outlet. He hadn't wanted to scare him away with all he was feeling, but the time for that had passed. Xander had claimed he wanted honesty, so Damon was going to give him all the honesty he could handle.

Breaking the kiss, Xander panted into Damon's neck, his breath hot against his skin. "Do you mean to tell me that we could have been doing that this whole time?"

Damon shrugged, feeling a little bashful about how much he wanted Xander—but not ashamed. He'd gotten over that in high school. He knew what he'd like, even if he'd never indulged in it before.

"I feel stupid," Xander said, cradling his palms across Damon's cheeks, stroking his beard, his neck, his ears, each pass of his fingers a graceful arc. His hands finally curled around Damon's neck, thumbs rubbing the top of his spine.

Damon thought he looked like he wanted to say more, and decided that while they certainly hadn't finished talking things through—not by a long shot—he was done talking for the night.

"Come on," he said gruffly, reaching up and curling his hand around Xander's bicep, tugging his hands away. "Let's go inside."

It felt like déjà vu, walking to the back door of the house, soaking wet, clumsily untying his boots while balancing against the doorjamb. But before, he hadn't done it with a throbbing erection and he hadn't dreamed about putting his hands all over the man next to him. Yet.

If he'd been thinking straight a year ago, he might have pushed Xander impatiently against the washing machine, but he fixed that mistake by doing exactly what he'd been dreaming of. Xander laughed brightly in between hot, unrelenting kisses, as he tried to shed his soaked tank top.

Then suddenly they were pressed together, damp skin to damp skin, nothing separating them, not even an excuse for why they should stop.

Damon half-expected Xander to produce one, but instead, his fingers trailed downwards, pausing at the top of his fly. He sucked in a hard breath, and Xander tucked in a fingertip, just stroking the skin of his lower abs.

"Please," Damon whispered, as he touched his forehead briefly to Xander's.

He flipped them, forcing Damon against the washing machine with a show of strength that somehow made him even harder. Xander opened the button with a flick of his fingers, and trailed them down his fly, fingers teasing and stroking along his hard length.

He'd always known Xander was good with his hands. Damon had always watched them in the habit of regular tasks—chopping and whisking and mixing—but now he watched Xander's hands with a whole different fascination as he tugged down his jeans partway and then his boxer briefs. Then those hands, so capable and so beautiful, wrapped around his cock, thumb reaching up to give a teasing little swipe to the damp head.

"God," Damon uttered in a gravelly voice, his eyelids slipping shut so he could enjoy the pleasure already spinning through him, "just like that."

Except that Xander didn't do it "just like that." He stopped moving his hand and his fingers completely, trapping Damon's length in his hot, wet palm.

"Look at me," Xander demanded, voice strained. Damon had imagined lots of times—more times than he should ever admit to—what Xander's sex voice might sound like. He'd imagined it in his ear, as Xander pleaded for Damon to give him more, to give him everything. And every single time Damon had done it. At least in his mind.

"What?" Damon asked stupidly, opening his eyes.

Xander rewarded him with an experimental twist of his fingers. "That's better," he crooned. "I want you to watch me. I want you to watch me jerk you off."

"Better. Yes. Now." Damon felt like he was beyond words as he glanced down, and took in the full image of Xander's hand wrapped around him. Then he glimpsed Xander's face. Lips tight with concentration, eyes teasing and burning with the exact same desire Damon felt.

"Feels good, huh?" Xander said, giving another stroke, a tiny bit faster this time.

Damon didn't even need to answer, the expression of bliss on his face probably gave him away. Or maybe his own hands, white-knuckled on the edge of the dryer.

Still, he'd learned his lesson. He kept his eyes open and watched as Xander slowly and inexorably pushed him toward the edge, one tantalizing stroke at a time.

"You like it like this?" Xander asked, even though it was probably very clear how much Damon liked it. "Or harder, and faster, like this?" He sped up, his hand motion making his bicep flex, and Damon bit back an oath.

"You keep that up," Damon gritted out, "and it's going to be over really soon."

"That would really be a shame," Xander crooned, glancing down at his hands. "You've got a beautiful cock."

Xander's words were fizzing in his veins, each syllable a tiny bubble of pleasure exploding.

"What?" Xander continued, expression going sly, his hand slowing down infinitesimally. "You like it when I talk dirty? You want to hear how many ways I want this cock? I want you to hold me down and fuck me so hard I cry. I want my mouth on it. I want to suck you until you come, and then I want to keep you in my mouth until you can't help but get hard again."

It was too much. Damon tried to hold on, but it had been a long, lonely time for him the last few years, and the visuals of Xander's words and the rough edge of his voice as he told Damon all his fantasies was too much for him to handle.

He tensed, and then exploded, Xander stroking him through it with a very satisfied grin on his face. Just like he was the cat who'd finally gotten all the cream he wanted.

"Fuck," Damon groaned as Xander lifted his hand and gave his finger an experimental lick. "You're going to kill me."

"Oh, but the trip is going to be fantastic," Xander said with a sharp, feral grin. "Return the favor?"

Damon opened his mouth to agree, but to also remind Xander that he'd never done this before.

"It's okay," he soothed, edges softening as he guessed at Damon's insecurity. "You've jerked yourself off before, right?"

Damon had practically worn off his skin jerking off thinking of Xander in the last few weeks. He nodded slowly.

"Then you're fine," Xander said. "Just do what you think you'd like."

"What about what you like?" Damon asked.

"We'll figure it out," Xander promised. "Now *please* do something before I get tired of waiting and do it myself."

That was something Damon really wanted to see—but *someday*. Not today. Today he wanted to give Xander at least a little taste of the pleasure he'd just received.

He cautiously reached down, loosening the tie on Xander's shorts. He knew he wasn't as graceful about it as Xander, and it was definitely more awkward than it looked to push down Xander's wet, clingy shorts. He should be thankful he hadn't been wearing jeans, like Damon was.

Xander was wearing tight black briefs with little chili peppers dotted all over them. Damon knew he must be staring, both at the cute underwear that totally personified him, but also at the pretty impressive hard-on.

Blushing, Xander gave a little aborted shrug as Damon reached out and stroked him once through the damp cotton. "I like fun underwear," he admitted, and Damon thought this was a facet of Xander that he could get used to. Really, really fast.

"I like them," Damon admitted. "They're sexy as hell."

"I hoped you might think so," Xander said, and blushed again. Harder this time.

With minimum difficulty, Damon managed to push them down, letting them fall to the floor with Xander's running shorts, his cock springing up fully hard and definitely ready to go.

Damon wrapped his hand around it gently, and it was him that swore, not Xander. It felt so different from touching himself—so much better than he'd imagined. He'd always been a giver, and he knew from the first feel of Xander's cock that he was going to want to give all the time.

"Ahhh," Xander exhaled as Damon began to pump him slowly. "Don't have to be so gentle."

Damon knew his smile grew wicked. "Like it rough, do you?"

Xander panted. "Maybe."

Damon had already decided that he was down for giving Xander whatever he wanted. Both inside and outside the bedroom—or as this case might be, inside the laundry room. So he jerked him harder, sliding his thumb around the wet head, gathering pre-come to help ease his way a little better.

Xander was right; he did know what to do. His other hand gripped Xander's hip, and held him tight and fast as he gave him what he'd asked for. A little rough, with no quarter. Xander came with Damon's name on his breath and a wide-eyed incredulous look, like he'd just been smacked by a freight train.

"Wow," he exhaled shakily. "Wow."

"Good for a first time?" Damon asked self-consciously. He didn't feel quite as confident as Xander about tasting the stripes of come on his fingers, but he wanted to. Maybe next time. Maybe next time he might even feel confident enough to offer a blowjob.

Licking his lips, Xander smiled bright. "Uh, yeah. Definitely no complaints." He paused. "Did you know I wanted you for the first time in this room, a year ago?"

Damon laughed. "What if I told you that I wanted you before that?"

"Even looking like a drowned rat?"

Reaching up with his clean hand, Damon stroked Xander's cheek. "Even in the pouring rain, standing in a mud pit, you had so much passion and fire in your eyes. I wanted some of that fight for myself. I wanted you to share it with me." He hesitated. "And you did. You *do*, every day. Thank you."

Xander's laugh was shaky, unsure. Even more unsure than he'd been about to get Damon's first hand job. "You're welcome."

Damon reached down, picked up his t-shirt, wiped his hand. Pulled Xander's hand into his own, and wiped it too. He didn't know the etiquette for these kinds of things—not yet anyway—but he knew he always wanted to do the right thing.

From Xander's damp eyes that he guessed had nothing to do with the sprinkler fight they'd had, Damon hoped he'd managed it, despite the lack of experience.

Chapter Ten

The next morning, Xander was in the kitchen, taking advantage of the cool morning by baking a few practice batches of focaccia, when Kian wandered in.

"How's your hand?" Xander asked. He hadn't seen Kian much the last few days, and while he could still see a bandage, it was of the Band-Aid variety and covered in tiny My Little Ponies.

"Better," Kian grumbled, pouring himself a cup of coffee. "But still annoying. I hate having to wear gloves at work."

"It's the worst," Xander agreed, whipping off the damp cloth covering his dough and testing its rise with a fingertip. "I'm thinking about doing a rosemary and sun-dried tomato topping for this focaccia. Thoughts?"

Kian dumped sugar in his coffee and pursed his lips as he thought about it. "You're serving focaccia? I thought you weren't doing an Italian bent."

Xander had spent the last two weeks telling himself he wasn't trying to turn the Barrel House into an Italian restaurant, or even a restaurant with Italian influences. He'd tested a lot of recipes in the last weeks, but the ones that always ended up being the best were inspired by some of Xander's favorite rustic Italian food.

This morning, lying in bed, desperately trying to tamp down his rising feelings for Damon, Xander had wondered why he was fighting his own natural inclinations so hard? Did he want to make his life harder? More complicated?

He liked cooking Italian food. He liked Damon. Why did he spend so much effort trying to deny himself things he liked?

Xander had a feeling he could go to years of therapy and never quite understand that particular idiosyncrasy.

"Things change," Xander told Kian. The Kian of last year, even, would have probably left it at that. But this new Kian, the one who seemed to be actively pursuing Bastian instead of waiting in the shadows, hoarding the little scraps of attention the chef would throw him, was a Kian that Xander didn't really understand.

Somehow his good friend had grown up and Xander knew it wasn't fair to say he liked the other version better—but he'd *understood* that version better. Xander liked what he could reason and quantify, and Kian wasn't one of those things anymore.

"I knew you'd do it," Kian muttered. "It was inevitable. Just like you hooking up with Damon."

"How do you know we're hooking up?"

Kian laughed. "You look about a hundred times more relaxed this morning than you looked a week ago. You've got the *Xander got some* dreamy expression down pat."

Xander really wanted to tell him that in all the years they'd known each other—three at his last count—Kian couldn't know this was his post-sex expression because he'd been celibate the whole time. But telling Kian that would open him up for all sorts of questions that Xander did not want to answer. Most importantly, why he had decided that Damon was different, even though Damon still represented a lot of things that scared the shit out of him.

He couldn't answer the question himself, so he could hardly explain it to Kian.

"Okay, that's fair," was all Xander said.

"But to answer your question, I like the idea of the sun-dried tomatoes. But what about sort of a sun-dried tomato pesto on top? The topping is really the best part of focaccia, so why skimp? Coat that bitch."

It was a really good idea, which didn't surprise Xander at all because Kian had been a special chef even back in culinary school. It wasn't exactly a mystery why Aquino had taken one look at his naïve, sunny disposition and boundless talent and had coveted all those things for himself.

"You can dedicate your first Michelin star to me," was all Kian said breezily. Like receiving one was inevitable, but Xander didn't really have the heart to tell him that the Barrel House, at least in the iteration that he and Damon were creating now, wasn't the type of place that Michelin sought out.

It was the kind of place you took a first date if you wanted good food and not a lot of pretension, or a good spot to soak up a long day of wine tasting.

Xander was good with that, but he hadn't found a way to tell Kian that it was not Terroir-lite. It wasn't because he was ashamed of what he and Damon were creating, more that he couldn't find an explanation *why* he was okay with it. He'd known as early as culinary school that he was meant for bigger, brighter things. It had taken an association with the bigger and brighter to realize those things weren't always in line with what kind of food he wanted to serve people.

Sometimes it was really about the image and not the food, and Xander was done with that sort of subterfuge. But Kian wasn't. He was still guzzling the Kool-Aid as fast as Bastian Aquino could mix it up.

"Knock, knock," a voice said, as the front door opened. "I heard you were baking this morning and decided I needed a coffee refill and something more substantial than a banana."

Damon walked into the kitchen, and Xander went hot and cold all over remembering the things they'd done—not exactly groundbreaking—and what he'd said—groundbreaking for him, and if Damon's reaction had been anything to go by, him as well.

But they'd both enjoyed it, Damon especially hadn't been able to stop marveling at how much he'd loved it. He hadn't specifically said the part where Xander let all his inner raunchy fantasies out, but his meaning had been clear enough.

"Good morning," Xander said, because that was the only G-rated thing in his brain right now.

"Good morning," Damon replied, leaning down and giving him a kiss that wasn't brief by any means.

If Kian hadn't known they were hooking up before, he definitely knew now, and Xander was torn between wanting to tell him how amazing it was, to finally find someone he wanted to trust, and warning him that Bastian wouldn't be this kind or understanding or giving.

But Xander had forced himself to quit his Kian-must-be-saved quest, and that meant sticking to it.

Kian made a low whistling noise as Damon's lips left Xander's. Xander let his eyes open when Damon was still close, and the heat in his greenish-blue gaze nearly singed his eyebrows. Yes, they were going to need a repeat of last night, but this time, Xander was going to be aware he was doing it, and he wasn't going to half-ass it like an afterthought.

"Did you sleep well?" Damon asked lowly. By the time Xander had finally driven home last night it was late and he'd been floating along on a river of endorphins. He'd known he'd sleep like a baby, and had mentioned that much to Damon as they were saying goodbye.

He *hadn't* said just how much he wanted to stay, and just fall asleep on Damon's couch, pressed up close against him. He definitely hadn't said how much he really, secretly, wanted Damon to invite him to his bed.

Those things could all still happen, Xander had reminded himself. They were still new at this, and still figuring things out. Someday, Xander wouldn't have to pry himself off the couch and head back to his own separate, very lonely bed.

"Like a baby," Xander said, pasting a bright smile on. Once he was wearing it, he discovered it didn't feel forced.

"I didn't want you to go last night," Damon confessed softly, echoing exactly what Xander had been thinking.

"Funny," Xander said, ignoring Kian's fake vomiting sounds, "I didn't want to either."

"Next time," Damon promised, and it felt like a vow.

A vow that Xander was absolutely going to hold him to.

"I actually came by to show you something," Damon said, leaning his hip against the kitchen counter, cozying right back into Xander's personal space.

"This sounds like the beginning of a really bad porn," Kian announced loudly, "and that means it's my cue to leave."

"I don't know, I thought it sounded like a pretty good porn," Xander defended with a raised eyebrow. "I think we'd enjoy it anyway."

Damon's hand curled possessively around Xander's hip. "I think you're probably right."

They stood there for a single moment, staring at each other. Xander was absolutely thinking about last night, and the way Damon was looking back, there was no way he wasn't thinking about the same damn thing.

"Are you thinking what I'm thinking?" Xander asked, his lowered voice barely a gasp. He felt breathless and lightheaded, his cock thickening beneath his sweatpants.

Damon flushed. "It was so good, it's hard to think of anything else."

"So you don't regret it?" Xander teased. He had to do something to break this moment, or they were going to end up on the kitchen floor, making out and probably coming in their pants. Which . . . might not be a terrible thing, he realized, except that Kian was definitely home, and Nate probably was too.

He didn't want to do anything with Damon if they had an audience. Especially if he was going to try out more of the talk he'd used the night before.

"I told you last night. I don't regret a thing." Damon sounded amused, but reluctantly did let go of Xander's hip.

"Good." Xander stuck out his tongue and swiveled away, grabbing a bowl, and headed toward the deck, where he kept his herb planters. There he gathered rosemary, basil, parsley, and oregano. Damon watched from the sliding glass door.

"I can grow those for you," Damon offered.

"I sure hope so," Xander said as he tossed the bundles on his massive wooden cutting board and began to mince them.

"Can you text me the varieties you like?" Damon asked. "I *did* actually swing by to show you something. I've got a meeting in town in about twenty." He made a face. "As much as I'd like to stay."

"Oh, right." Xander had forgotten about the reason why Damon had supposedly stopped by. He'd secretly hoped there hadn't really been an excuse at all, and the thing Damon wanted to show him was actually his dick. Again.

Damon pulled his phone out of his pocket, and flipped through a few screens. "Here," he said, extending it toward Xander. "I got the first drafts on the logo for the restaurant."

Glancing over, Xander looked through the different choices the graphic designer had provided. "That one," he said, pointing with a flour-dusted finger. It was a combination of a swirly, elegant font and rough-looking letters that seemed inspired by the wood that the Barrel House was named for.

"I like that one too." Damon stared at the screen. "But I think I have a few notes for Carol. I'll email them over and as soon as she sends me the final, I'll text it to you."

Since the night Damon had come to Terroir, determined to woo Xander into working for him, he hadn't known how this was supposed to work. How their professional and personal relationships—both so new and so different from anything either of them had experienced before—could co-exist.

This morning, for the very first time, Xander glimpsed a future that looked very much like today had. And to Xander, it was one of the best things he'd ever seen. Instead of feeling dread that they might fuck one or both of their relationships up, he could see it working. One of the facets of their partnership encouraging and nurturing the other and vice versa.

This might not end in a fiery disaster; this could really *work*. Nobody was more surprised than Xander, who tried hard to keep both a level head and also a realistic, pragmatic view of the future. He rarely let himself get carried away, but he threw both arms around Damon, smudging his plaid shirt with flour and leaving the scent of herbs behind.

"It's just a logo," Damon said, laughing.

But it wasn't just a logo. It was the combination of both their visions, it was their two selves melding and merging and becoming more powerful together than they were individually.

"Sorry," Xander said, but he was laughing too. "I got a bit carried away." He brushed as much of the flour off as he could, but they were both smiling. As good as last night had been, it felt like this morning was even better.

Wasn't the morning after supposed to be awkward and difficult? Maybe they were running on a high of sexual endorphins and potential professional success and maybe they were eventually going to come back to earth, but Xander didn't want to think about that.

So he didn't. He brushed a kiss over Damon's cheek, fingers still lingering on the waist of Damon's jeans, and sending him off with a bright smile and a promise he'd bring some of the focaccia over tomorrow morning.

***

"I can't stop looking at you this morning," Xander said. He'd had the thought the moment he'd climbed out of the car, dawn rising over the Napa Valley hills, and Damon's dark hair and eyes matching the muted colors of the plaid he wore today. "You're gorgeous."

Damon looked up and smiled, only a little self-consciously. "I am?"

Xander nodded emphatically. He didn't always say this sort of thing—he was far more likely to spit out, bluntly and clearly, all the things he didn't like, than to let anything pass his lips that was overly demonstrative.

He was still afraid of falling harder, of being the one left holding what was left of their relationship after Damon moved on. *If* Damon moved on, Xander told himself firmly. There were zero indications he had any intention of doing that, but it was still hard for Xander to trust completely.

So he usually kept comments like, *I can't stop looking at you this morning*, to himself, but the few he'd let out recently had produced such a beautiful effect on Damon that he'd started *wanting* to relax his own self-imposed rules.

And really, it was silly to let a little fear get in the way of Damon's gorgeous blush whenever Xander complimented him.

"You don't look so bad yourself," Damon said, pulling Xander in and planting a firm kiss on his mouth. "But I always think you're handsome."

Xander usually got the *you're so cute* moniker, so being told he was handsome was surprisingly electrifying. Or maybe that was just the hot look in Damon's eyes as he said it, his gaze sweeping down Xander's white t-shirt and black running shorts.

"You don't have to suck up," Xander teased. "I brought treats."

Damon looked just about as excited to taste the focaccia samples as he had to see Xander pull into the driveway.

"Should we go in the house?" Damon asked, glancing around. He'd been checking on some of the plants, as he did most mornings before David arrived to work on the Barrel House building. They were starting refinishing the flooring soon, and Damon had complained at length at what a nasty, dirty, smelly job it was.

"It's so nice out here," Xander pointed out.

"My hands are dirty." Damon lifted his palms and they were streaked with mud.

"That's okay. I'll feed you and you can tell me what you and David have planned for today."

"We're going to expand the front door, add in a few more windows and add the back door," Damon said, eyes glued to the container in Xander's hands as he popped the lid open.

Immediately the air smelled of fresh baked bread, herbs, citrus, and garlic—and not just the morning dew over the freshly tilled earth.

"I have three kinds for you to try," Xander said. He picked up a piece and held it toward Damon's lips.

"Lemon basil," Xander said, as Damon took a quick, neat bite.

"Mmmm," Damon hummed as he chewed. "That's really, really good."

"I know," Xander said, and he couldn't help but sound smug. He'd already sampled these all himself. In fact, these were the second and third versions of his original idea—or Kian's original idea. He'd perfected them since then, and he'd been hard-pressed to keep himself, Kian, and Nate out of the Tupperware container long enough for Damon to try them.

"What's the next one?" Damon asked.

"Sun-dried tomato with rosemary and orange zest."

Damon made a face. "Orange zest?"

"Trust me," Xander said, as he pulled the piece out of the container and held it up toward Damon's mouth.

He chewed longer on this piece, his thoughts clearly whirring as he let each unique taste roll off his tongue.

"That was . . . incredibly interesting and shockingly good," Damon finally pronounced. "I wasn't sure about the orange zest, but it . . . worked?"

"Unusual flavor combos aren't usually my sort of thing," Xander confessed. "But that came to me in a dream when I was napping yesterday, and it totally worked. To my own surprise."

"You weren't surprised," Damon scoffed. "You're brilliant and you know it."

Xander grinned. "True." He pulled the last piece out of the container. "Last one. Garlic herb. A more generic combination. Safe maybe, but still delicious."

Damon chewed this piece just as thoughtfully as the last two.

"Is it weird," he asked in a conspiratorial tone, like maybe Bastian Aquino was watching this whole taste test go down from outside the fence, "that I liked the orange and sun-dried tomato one best?"

"No, not at all. It's really good." Xander was still surprised that Damon had picked it. It was definitely a little outside the box, and he hadn't been sure if Damon's palate would like it or hate it.

"We'll do a rotating focaccia," Xander continued. "So we'll have options for the less adventurous. But the sun-dried tomato-orange will be featured every day."

"So you've decided to go with the rustic Italian spin on farm-to-table?" Damon asked.

Xander sighed.

"I love the idea, I really do. Mostly because it's what you love, and I'm a firm believer that you should always do what you love."

"It's not that simple."

"It's exactly that simple," Damon argued. "I'm not asking you to be Mario Batali, I'm telling you to cook the food you love—because that love is *always* reflected in the finished product. A happy chef is usually a successful chef. And I want both."

Mario *fucking* Batali. Xander tried to grasp at the peace and contentment he'd felt just a few minutes ago, watching the sunrise gleam on Damon's dark hair and admiring how strong and capable he looked in one of his ubiquitous plaid shirts with the sleeves rolled up.

"I'm definitely not going to be Mario Batali. I don't want to be *that guy* that started an Italian restaurant."

"Why not?" Damon still sounded mystified, and Xander wasn't sure he was even capable of explaining.

"Because in high-end restaurants, you typically can't point to one single inspiration or culture."

"And high-end matters to you?" Damon asked. Even though Xander told himself he was imagining things, he could hear the hurt edge in his voice.

And *yeah*, he hadn't been intending to be a high-end establishment trying for Michelin stars. Definitely nothing like Terroir. But he didn't want to be laughed at either, and despite being completely confident in his own abilities, somehow this was the one tender spot in his ego.

"What other people think of our restaurant matters," Xander snapped.

"Impressing people is good, even if we're not going for Michelin stars." Damon seemed to mentally digest this. "I'm sorry. I guess I thought we'd be impressing people with our great food. No matter what country inspired it."

Panic clawed up from the bottom of Xander's stomach, where he felt slightly sick. Like he'd eaten too much focaccia with too much olive oil over the last twenty-four hours.

"That's not it. No. Don't be sorry." Xander reached out and grasped Damon's bare forearms, his fingers curling around them. His skin was warm even though the sun had barely come up. "I'm the one who's sorry. This is . . . this is all me. My insecurity. I'm going to it figure out."

"I wish you'd let me help," Damon said softly.

"I wish you could," Xander said with reluctance. "But this is something I've got to come to terms with."

"I was going to suggest we could take a little trip—maybe a bit of research thrown in," Damon said ruefully. "We need to go to San Francisco to pick out the major equipment you need. I thought we could stay at the family townhouse while we're there. Do a little fine dining. Get away while David refinishes the floors."

Xander raised an eyebrow. "While David refinishes the floors?"

"That's all you got from that?" Damon scoffed. "That David is going to be stuck refinishing the floors by himself?"

"No . . ." Xander drew out, trying to hide his smile as long as possible. The fight didn't last longer than a few seconds. The grin bloomed across his face. "It actually sounds incredible. You have a family townhouse in San Francisco? You want me to pick out equipment? When can we leave?"

Damon laughed, and pulled him the rest of the way into his arms, hugging him close. "You're adorable."

"Seriously, when are we leaving?" Xander asked. "I've got lists to put together."

"Lists?"

"Restaurants we have to go to. Food suppliers I want to visit. Equipment I need. Clothes I'll have to pack."

"Few days?" Damon hesitated. "I promised David some sort of help, and I have to find the help first before we escape."

"I suppose I can wait that long," Xander told him with an exaggerated sigh. He rose to his tiptoes and kissed Damon on the cheek. "I'll let you get to that. I've got more recipes to test today. A variation on scampi. I bought the store out of bay scallops."

Watching Xander walk back to his car, Damon wondered how much the scallops had cost, but as soon as he had the thought, he dismissed it. It didn't matter. He had the money, and he wanted to give Xander whatever he needed to be successful—whether that was a crate of bay scallops, high-end equipment or a confidence boost.

The San Francisco trip was sort of unnecessary and entirely unplanned, but Damon knew what it felt like when the unique pressure of the expectations Napa held started to creep in. He was seeing it in Xander right now. But it was a good time to get away—Damon would be happy to hire someone to help David finish the floors, and he hadn't really had time to spoil Xander yet.

Taking him to the city and staying in the condo would be a chance to do that.

Which left Damon one last action to take. It just happened to be something he really didn't want to do. He dialed the number reluctantly, but with determination.

"Hi, Nancy," he said when his father's secretary answered the phone. "It's Damon. Can I talk to him?"

Damon wasn't sure who was more surprised that he was calling—him or Nancy. If it wasn't for Xander, and that haunted look in his eyes, he wouldn't be making this call at all.

"Sure, of course," Nancy said, fumbling a bit. "Let me transfer you in."

A click, a single dial, and then his father's rich voice answering, "Nathan Hess."

So Nancy hadn't told him who was calling. Damon took a single deep breath. "It's me."

"Damon!" Nathan sounded surprised. And pleased. Never a good combination. "I wasn't expecting your call."

"I need a favor," Damon managed to say.

"Of course. What do you need? Wine for the new restaurant? You should really go through our distributor, but I don't think anyone would be surprised if I sold to you directly. You're a Hess, after all."

Yes. He was a Hess, and he was always going to be a Hess. Damon gritted his teeth. "No. I'm going to the city for a few days. I need to use the condo."

"Oh." His disappointment was clear. "Naturally. I'll have Nancy email you the codes. It's not in use currently."

"I thought as much," Damon said stiffly. "And it seemed silly to stay in a hotel when it was empty."

"Right. Naturally."

"Thank you," Damon said, and this was even harder than asking for the favor in the first place. "I'll look for the email."

"I'll tell Nancy to send it right over."

"Bye." As Damon clicked off the call, he realized that he and his father, who had never really known how to talk to each other, had spent that entire conversation talking about other people.

For a brief moment, he wondered if he should have told his father that Xander was coming with him, but no, that was a terrible idea. Nathan knew abstractly about his son's sexuality, but had never actually been confronted by it. Damon didn't know what he would say—or do—if he was confronted by it now.

Better, much much better, to play it safe when it came to Xander.

Chapter Eleven

"Fucking hell," Xander said, pushing his sunglasses up and staring at the townhouse through the windshield of Damon's car. "This is yours?"

"Well, it's not *mine*," Damon pointed out, more than a little subconsciously. How had he forgotten how Xander initially had reacted to the fact that he was a Hess? Was it so wrong he wanted to show Xander some of the nicer perks of being part of the family? "Technically, it's my father's."

Xander's gaze swiveled over to him only for a split second. Then it was right back to the white stucco edifice with its lake blue shutters. "You're going to inherit it one day, though."

He really wasn't sure that was true. Yes, he was his father's only child, but after what he'd done with his grandfather's legacy, Damon really wasn't certain he was even still in the will. But that touched on all sorts of issues that 1) Damon did not want to discuss right now and 2) Damon did not want to discuss ever. Even with Xander. *Especially* with Xander, if he was being truly honest with himself.

So he changed the subject.

"If you think the outside is gorgeous, wait until you see the inside," Damon said, turning off his Jeep and opening the driver's door. "I usually hate houses designed by interior decorators, but the one my dad hired really did a good job. It doesn't feel look a showpiece, more like a real home."

The sad part was that Damon had partially grown up in this house and while it might have *looked* like a real home, it had never really felt like one.

But that was another thing he didn't need to tell Xander. Damon knew from personal experience that the poor-little-rich-boy act got old for everyone after awhile, if it didn't start out that way.

"What's the kitchen like?" Xander asked, and this time his voice was eager, not hidden behind shock or dismissal. "Wait, no. Don't tell me. I want to be surprised."

Damon pulled their bags from the trunk and shut the hatch. "Well, let's go inside," he teased. "I don't want to keep you waiting."

Following him up the stairs, Damon repeated the entry code his father's assistant had sent over and Xander carefully typed it in.

"What happens if I enter this wrong?" Xander asked in a hushed, almost reverent tone. "Will there be cops? Firemen? Will they arrest me?"

"If the cops are hot, they can definitely put me in handcuffs," Damon joked as Xander swung the door open. No alarms went off. "But the truth is, yeah, my father pays for a security system for this place, but I just asked him for the code so I know it's good."

The entry was a narrow, arched passageway they passed through, emerging into an open rotunda, complete with a circular staircase, edged with a gleaming curved wood banister.

"Hooooly shit," Xander exhaled. He seemed transfixed by the handblown glass chandelier at the top of the rotunda. Then he turned back toward Damon, his eyes narrowing. "You just asked him for the code? I thought you sort of grew up here."

Damon sort of had, which had been part of his explanation when Xander had asked questions about it on their drive from Napa.

"As you might have guessed," Damon finally admitted wryly, "we haven't been close in some time. Well, more like *ever*, but yes, I did used to spend a lot of time here. My dad is a workaholic and the city was where he did a lot of his work. He came, so I came too."

"Where was your mom?" Xander asked.

"Traveling back then, doing marketing and publicity for the winery. She didn't want to hire it out because she thought she could do it better herself. Then, dead from a stroke." Damon knew people believed that if you sped through bad news like it was rote and routine, then it made the terrible shit less terrible.

Damon didn't believe that worked at all.

"God, I'm sorry," Xander said, voice low. "I . . . I realized we didn't know much about each other. Our families, that is."

"And now you just realized why I don't talk about them?" Damon laughed without humor. "Sorry."

"Why don't you give me the full tour?" Xander asked, turning on a determined and brightly sunny smile. Damon appreciated the effort, but he wanted to tell him that if it had ever been that easy to leave his family and their demons behind, he wouldn't have ended up so dependent on the bottle.

"This way is the living room," Damon said, reaching out and taking Xander's hand. The touch of his skin wasn't quite enough to dismiss his bad mood, but it helped. The sweet wry look Xander shot him helped too. That Damon had epic plans to fully corrupt every single room of this damn townhouse really helped.

Maybe they could start in the living room.

"Wow," Xander said, turning toward the big picture window that looked out on the San Francisco marina. "This view just doesn't quit."

"When this townhouse came up for sale, my father bought it sight unseen," Damon said. He'd told himself he wouldn't mention any other Hesses for the rest of the trip, but being back in this place made it impossible. The memories—good and bad and every other shade in between—were hiding in the corners like ghosts. "He told the realtor to make the offer based on the address alone. When she asked him if he wanted to see the pictures, he told her that if he didn't like it, he'd tear it down and build something else."

Xander squeezed his hand. "It must have sucked growing up with someone who thought he could buy anything."

When he'd thought of, and told, that story, Damon hadn't been thinking of that bad habit of Nathan's. He'd only been thinking it was one of the few stories he could think of that he found vaguely amusing.

But that had always been Nathan Hess' problem. He'd worked hard and believed that every interaction was transactional. And Damon had never had anything his father had valued enough to trade with.

"Yeah," Damon said shortly, regretting that he'd told the story. He'd always believed Xander was an intuitive person who was better at reading people than you'd expect someone who'd locked themselves away in a kitchen for a career could. From the first moment, staring at each other in the pouring rain, Damon had felt like Xander knew him.

Now it felt like he saw right through him, and Damon wasn't sure if he liked it or if it scared the ever-living shit out of him. There were dark corners and cobwebs he didn't want anyone—especially someone he could love—to see.

There was a Casset hanging above the fireplace, the only color shining bright on a simple white wall. Xander let go of his hand and went closer, eyes taking in every brushstroke. He didn't ask if it was real—and Damon was grateful because then he didn't have to answer.

They went through the dining room, with a spiky modern chandelier that Damon didn't recognize. It looked like a trendy piece of destructive art. Perfect for murder in the middle of a dinner party.

Damon imagined what his father would look like with the spikes buried in his chest, and then abruptly swept the image away. He didn't want his father dead; he wanted his father to have never existed at all.

The kitchen, which was a major part of why they'd come to the townhouse and not some random hotel in San Francisco, elicited a large enough gasp from Xander that Damon believed coming here was worth it.

The space was cavernous, bordering on nearly obscene, with acres of shining wood floors and rows of lake blue cabinets that perfectly matched the shutters outside. The blue was beautiful outside, but it was startling inside a kitchen, and even more startling was the fact that all the high-end professional appliances had been custom ordered in the exact same shade of blue.

Nathan had once told Damon that the color was the same tone as his mother's eyes, but he'd always believed that was more of his father's bullshit. Now he looked and he wasn't quite sure.

"I know we're going out to dinner a lot," Xander said, fingers a death grip on Damon's hand, "but I've got to cook in here. Please. Just one night."

"Anything you want to do," Damon said. "It's all up to you."

Xander reluctantly let Damon guide him out of the kitchen and upstairs. There were a series of bedrooms, each more luxe than the last, but culminating in the master with its textured blue walls and *chinoserie* hand-painted ceiling.

"This color," Xander stated hesitantly, turning around the massive room, "it's used a lot in this house."

"The blue?" Damon repeated stupidly.

Xander's frank look was a clear direction to cut the bullshit. But Damon wanted the bullshit; it was a lot easier to stomach than the truth.

"It was my mom's favorite color," Damon said softly. Which was one hundred percent true, no Nathan Hess bullshit needed to embellish it.

"It also looks a little like your eyes," Xander replied.

It was impossible to miss the flash of guilt on Xander's face, and no matter how painful some of this felt—dredging up so many old wounds that Damon kept hoping had healed finally—he'd come here for a reason. He'd wanted to share the best of his family with him, and he wanted to try to tell him some of what he'd come from. The good and the bad and the horrendous.

Xander was the kind of guy who wouldn't take some of him. He'd want it all, when he figured out that's where the two of them were headed, and Damon would have to give him as much as he demanded.

Some of it wasn't going to feel good or cathartic. Some of it was just going to suck.

"Don't feel bad," Damon said, reaching out and pulling Xander flush against him. Xander's head tucked under his chin, and a hand stroked up and down his back.

"I don't feel bad," Xander said in a muffled voice. "I want to fucking kill them for not giving a shit about you."

Damon managed to laugh through the lump in his throat. "Thank you."

"Is it . . . would it be okay if we stayed in here?" Xander asked with hesitancy.

Damon hadn't had any intention of doing so, even though it had never really felt like his parents' room, but he found himself nodding anyway. He'd never imagined that some things were better with the right person beside you, and just having Xander here helped. It hurt too, but Damon was beginning to believe it was the sort of catharsis he needed to grow. Even after therapy, he'd dragged all this baggage around with him—every inch of this house and the others he'd grown up in—but it was impossible to really move past it without ever looking at it.

"Are you sure?"

Damon sighed. "I don't talk about this stuff, because part of how I've been sober is by pretending it didn't happen. But it happened, and I can't keep ignoring it forever."

Reaching up, Xander's hands cupped his cheeks, staring right into his eyes. "If you didn't ever want to talk about it, that's your prerogative. I don't know everything you've been through, but figuring out how to stay sober makes you the bravest person I know. So yeah, you can ignore it as long as you fucking want to."

It was impossible not to laugh at Xander's indignant tone. He wasn't going to let anyone judge Damon—even himself.

Damon pulled him close, hugging him tight. "You're so great. How did I get this lucky?" he murmured into Xander's shoulder. He wasn't sure he wanted him to hear how he felt just yet, but it was also impossible not to say anything.

The honesty in Xander's dark eyes was stark and bright. "I think that all the time."

"You want to go to the Wharf? Stop by Ghirardelli?" Damon asked after a long moment where they just held each other. He'd never expected to have anyone again, not with his emotional baggage and his alcoholism, and Xander was so miraculous, he just wanted to bask in him. But they'd come to the city for a reason. "Tomorrow we've got some appointments to look at equipment."

Xander slid away, right out of Damon's grip. They weren't perfect. Sometimes he still pulled away when Damon held him too tight. Another reason why he hadn't confessed all his feelings yet.

"Appointments?" Xander lifted an eyebrow questioningly.

"The family name has a reputation people see coming from a long way off. I might not be my father, but being a Hess carries weight."

"Right." Xander, while really enjoying this house, didn't seem to know how to accept that there were a lot of different facets of being a Hess. This house was definitely a benefit, but the expectations and strings attached could be a real bitch.

"The Wharf sounds great," Xander said after a long pause. "We could swing by Boudin for lunch."

Xander didn't know why he'd suggested such a godawful tourist trap for lunch, but he'd sort of been feeling out this new Damon who'd emerged since they had arrived in San Francisco.

He was a Hess no matter where he was geographically, but standing in that elegant, insanely expensive townhouse, looking like he belonged even with his worn blue button-up and jeans, still bits of mud on the heel of his boots, had thrown Xander for a loop. He wanted the Damon he knew back—this newer, richer, darker Damon wasn't someone he quite recognized and he definitely didn't know how to deal with him.

It was even harder to convince himself that this Damon would happily publicly date someone like Xander. Someone who up until a few weeks ago had gotten his hands dirty on the regular in a kitchen. Someone who worked for an hourly wage.

Damon acted like it didn't matter, but it mattered. At least to Xander. In his experience, only rich people thought money didn't matter.

"Wow, it's packed in here," Damon said in a dismayed voice as he surveyed the packed Boudin café.

"It's right by the Wharf," Xander scoffed. "What were you expecting?"

"I don't know," Damon said, as they shuffled in the available next few feet, adding themselves to the winding line that went up to the bank of order stations. "It's been years since I've been here."

"Packed, but good bread," Xander said. "Ready to carb load?"

Damon grinned, a spark of the man Xander had started falling for emerging. "Would I ever turn a good carb down?"

Xander had never seen him hesitate over anything he ate, but he also worked hard, and there were lots of instances where Damon mentioned hitting the weights. And Xander had definitely seen evidence that he didn't need to worry about carbs. Not with Damon's flat, muscular stomach, and rippling biceps and thighs. A spike of arousal echoed through Xander as he thought of what they were probably going to do in that gigantic raft of a bed later tonight.

He'd wanted them to go slow at first, but now that they'd started, Xander had discovered he wasn't just hungry, he was starving.

"I'm going to get the chowder bread bowl *and* the roast beef sandwich," Xander announced, making his position on carbs very clear.

Damon nodded, and as they finally got up to the ordering counter, he listed off a similar order, and after Xander ordered, whipped out his credit card.

When Xander shot him a look, Damon shrugged and mouthed, "tax deduction," in his direction.

Xander didn't think the IRS was going to necessarily approve of a tax-deductible trip in which they hopefully took advantage of that incredible townhouse to have sex on every single surface available. But he guessed if they produced enough receipts for the restaurant it wouldn't matter.

Besides, a Hess would have a skilled and aggressive accountant on their payroll, Xander told himself as he went to find a table.

He finally located one in the faraway corner of the busy café, and they ate quickly without much conversation.

"You want to do the Wharf or Ghirardelli?" Damon asked as they walked back outside.

"You pick," Xander said. He was full from lunch, but he could always make room for chocolate.

"I haven't ever really done all this tourist stuff," Damon confessed. "My father would have hated it."

"Wharf it is," Xander said. It hadn't escaped his notice that Damon had mentioned his father more in the last twelve hours than he had during the whole time they'd known each other. He considered bringing it up, but he also didn't want to push Damon. He was trying to open up, and he didn't need to be pried open, all his bloody, dark insides spilling out. He'd tell Xander when he was ready.

Damon reached out and gripped his hand, nearly stopping Xander in his tracks and definitely vetoing any questions about his dad. "Is this okay?" he asked, a little self-consciously.

"Of course it's okay," Xander said. He didn't ask if it was okay for Damon, because he'd been the one to reach out. But then Xander had made it very damn clear that he wasn't into dating someone who he couldn't take out in public.

He'd done that once before, and gotten burned, and he wasn't into repeating the experience. Especially not with someone he could really care about like Damon.

"I know we're not the most traditional of couples," Damon said, and he still sounded nervous. His palm was warm and a little damp. Nerves? Xander wasn't sure. "But I think this is nice sometimes."

Xander spent a lot of time trying to pretend he didn't need this sort of wooing—hand-holding, extravagant trips to the city, fancy dinners, expensive kitchen equipment—but that was a total lie. He liked it. He liked the certainty it gave him that he was who Damon wanted.

"I like it," he admitted to Damon.

"So I shouldn't stop?" he teased back. "You're not gonna get sick of me?"

Never. But that was too soon to say, much too serious much too soon. "I'll make sure to let you know if I do," Xander retorted lightly.

But he felt all sorts of light and bright as they walked down along the bay to the Wharf.

He bought an ugly nautical-themed magnet, claiming he was going to stick it on one of the industrial-sized fridges they were buying this weekend. Even when Damon let go of his hand in one of the more crowded touristy stores, his hand lingered on the small of his back, leading him without being asshole-ish or obtrusive about it.

And Xander couldn't help it. He kept seeing the future, laid out before them like a beautifully varied Persian carpet, dotted with milestones and the good and a little bit of the bad, but with love woven through it consistently and constantly. The more he imagined it, the more real it became, and the harder he continued to fall.

By the time they returned to the townhouse, a little sunburned and stuffed full of Ghirardelli's ice cream sundaes, Xander was searching for some balance. Something to prevent the other shoe from dropping quite so hard.

It made perfect sense to drop their bags in the master bedroom, and for Xander to tackle Damon, somewhat successfully, to the bed.

"What are you doing?" Damon asked with a laugh as Xander settled over his big, muscular thighs. Thighs he definitely intended to get between very, very soon. Like *right now* soon.

"What," Xander said, dipping down to plant a kiss on Damon's lips, "do," he repeated the action, feeling Damon smile under his mouth, "you think I'm doing?"

"I have a few theories," Damon drawled as Xander propped himself back up with a palm to his lover's chest.

"Oh?" Xander used that hand to start popping open the buttons on Damon's shirt, slowly revealing the worn, thin white tank that he was wearing underneath. "Jesus," he exclaimed in a hushed tone, reverently stroking up and down the fabric that left very little to the imagination. Shirtless Damon was a revelation—there was no question of that—but with the dips and shadows outlined in the tight, nearly transparent cotton, he left Xander's mouth dry.

"Like what you see?" Damon's lips quirked up at the expression on Xander's face. Though it probably wasn't just at how turned on he definitely looked. Xander experimentally rocked his denim-clad cock against Damon's taut, flat abdomen, and felt his muscles flex in response.

"You know I do," Xander retorted, and there was heat, but it lacked his normal teasing edge. He was done teasing—both Damon and himself.

"Come up here and kiss me," Damon pleaded, and it was impossible to deny him. Xander leaned out full length on Damon's broad chest and kissed him. They'd both been thinking about this for days, and the kiss turned wild almost instantly, Xander's tongue slipping inside Damon's mouth, curling around his lover's.

Damon's hands clamped over his hips, and ground Xander and his cock into his stomach in a slow rhythmic motion that left him seeing stars. "Stop," Xander finally had to say, tearing his mouth from Damon's. "If you keep this up this is going to be over way too quick."

"So? We have all night. I made dinner reservations, but I'd much rather stay here, with you."

"No argument here," Xander said, still gasping a little as Damon's hands continued tormenting him.

"What do you want?" Damon asked then, a hint of hesitancy in his tone. He tried to act like this wasn't all new to him, but it was. Xander didn't always like taking the upper hand, but while Damon was still figuring sex with guys out, he was perfectly happy to lead the way. He shimmied down Damon's body, dislodging his hands as he settled between his thighs. His fingers opened the button of his jeans and slid the zipper down.

"I want this," Xander said, sliding his jeans down and ghosting his palm over Damon's cock. "Are you going to let me have it?"

Damon's pupils were blown wide, his expression wavering between ecstatic and disbelieving. He nodded, swallowing hard, his Adam's apple bobbing.

Xander took that as a green light, slid his jeans off the rest of the way, followed by his socks and then his boxer briefs. "I'm going to suck your cock now," he said, remembering how he'd promised himself that he'd continue the dirty talk that Damon had enjoyed so much last time. It was a little more difficult to do that with his mouth full of dick, but he could do his best.

His eyes grew bigger, tracking every movement of Xander's without blinking.

He was fully hard, curving a little toward his stomach, the tip damp with pre-come. Xander leaned down and licked up the underside, tongue curling around the tip.

"Holy fuck," Damon exhaled.

Xander was under no illusions that this was the first blowjob Damon had ever received, but he was determined it would be one of the best ones.

He gave his cock a shallow suck and let go with a *pop*. "You have a really gorgeous cock," Xander said, hand reaching up to stroke the length experimentally. "I've been wanting to do this for a long time."

Damon gave a short, humorless bark of laughter, and the thigh muscles under Xander twitched. "What was stopping you?"

It was clear it was a theoretical question, and Xander just smiled. "Nothing stopping me now."

Damon's hand reached down, cupping the back of his head, and Xander let his mouth be guided right back to his dick. Xander figured that was Damon's way of saying there was enough time to do all sorts of dirty talk later, and that he wanted Xander's mouth to be doing something other than talking.

Xander got the hint, and went to work, bobbing his mouth up and down in earnest, hand resting low to cup Damon's balls. He must have been doing a good job, because Damon kept groaning like he was killing him, and way too soon, he tugged hard on Xander's hair. He glanced up and Damon was sweating, breaths coming in short pants.

"I'm too close," Damon said. Xander gave his cock a little flick of his tongue, and watched his head fall back to the bed, and he groaned loudly again.

It was just a few more strokes to finish him off, Xander letting his come pump onto his tongue. He swallowed and crawled up Damon's chest. For a split second he forgot that Damon hadn't done this before, and started to lean down so they could kiss.

Then he remembered, realizing that Damon might not be comfortable tasting his own come in Xander's mouth. He hesitated, nearly pulling back, but Damon's big hand returned to the back of his head and pulled him in the rest of the way.

They kissed for long minutes, Xander rocking almost subconsciously against Damon's stomach, pleasure spiking through his veins. If the kissing bothered him, Damon didn't show it once, instead he dove in, hands wrapping around Xander's waist, sliding down toward his ass.

Finally Xander pulled up, knowing he needed some sort of relief. Just the thought of Damon's hand wrapping around him again made him almost come in his pants.

"Can I try that too?" Damon asked, surprising the hell out of Xander.

"If you want to," Xander said, trying to be casual. "It's not required."

"I want to," Damon said stubbornly. "I'm not going to be very good, prob-ably, but I still want to try it."

Xander gave a short laugh. "Truthfully, it's hard to give a bad blowjob."

Rolling them over, Damon pulled off his tank, the way his abs flexed leaving Xander a little short of breath. He reached out, stroking them. "You're so gorgeous."

Damon smiled. "If you think so, I'm not going to argue. But you . . ." he was just finishing pulling off the rest of Xander's clothes, "are so fucking hot."

Leaning back on the headboard, Xander grinned. "Do your worst."

Damon hesitated, just staring at Xander's cock. There wasn't much blood in his brain at the moment, which was probably why Xander had forgotten how he'd dirty-talked/coached him through the hand job the other night.

He could definitely do that again. It was hot as fuck, and they'd both enjoyed it.

"Lick the tip," Xander said, and his eyes fluttered close as the pleasure radi-ated through him. "Yeah, just like that. Fuck, that feels good."

Damon did it again, curling his mouth around the head, just the way Xander had. He didn't know whether to be pleased or annoyed that Damon had been coherent enough to take mental notes. But it felt so damn good, any annoyance he did feel faded almost immediately.

"Slide it in your mouth," Xander directed. "Just as much as you feel com-fortable. Use your hand for the rest." It shouldn't have felt so good and so hot to have Damon doing exactly what he was telling him to do—somehow the anticipation should have been less, since he knew what would happen—but somehow the pleasure doubled, tripled, multiplied beyond anything Xander had ever experienced before.

Damon was undeniably cautious as he took Xander's cock in his mouth, curling his tongue right around the underside, and Xander's vision whited out.

How could he have been disappointed in Damon not lasting longer, if he was liable to come much faster?

"God damn," Xander exhaled slowly. "Do it again."

Damon hadn't even needed the direction, because he already was, taking Xander further, taking him down so good that it was hard to imagine that he hadn't done this before.

Xander felt his orgasm building. He made the mistake to glance down to check on Damon, but all that did was give him the ball-busting image of Damon sucking his cock, blissful expression on his face, like this was all he had ever wanted. And suddenly the oncoming orgasm wasn't just a possibility but a certainty, roaring down the line like an out-of-control freight train.

"Damon," Xander was barely able to squawk out to warn him. But Damon kept his mouth on his cock, clearly determined to duplicate Xander's actions.

And then Xander couldn't think at all, because the orgasm was blasting through him, the pleasure digging in with claws.

When he finally opened his eyes again, Damon was wiping his mouth, but he was smiling so brightly that Xander's heart gave an agonized beat in his chest.

How could he keep reminding himself that eventually Damon would tire of his interlude when he seemed so god damned happy to be doing it? It was hard bordering on impossible.

Chapter Twelve

It was almost impossible to not feel smug after Damon settled back on the bed next to Xander. He hadn't made any moves to put clothes on, and if he wanted to sit here naked with Damon, he certainly wasn't going to do anything to dissuade him—like put his own clothes back on.

The smugness probably came from the fact that Xander kept sighing happily and murmuring at how good it had been. Damon was under no illusions that he had any blowjob skills. Yes, he'd taken one for the team and watched quite a bit of porn to try to get a better idea of what he was doing, but there was nothing for learning like practical experience, and before today, he hadn't had any.

Still, Xander wasn't exactly complaining.

"If you liked it," Damon offered, trying and failing to keep a cocky edge out of his voice, "I'm happy to try it again."

Xander raised his eyebrow, shooting him a dubious glance. Damon adored that questioning look of his—like he was trying to front by pretending he wasn't one thousand percent on board with that idea, and it was Damon's job to break down his pseudo-skepticism. And Damon *really* enjoyed digging his way right behind the façade to find the truth beneath. There was something very satisfying about proving to both of them that Xander was equally vulnerable.

"Soon," Damon added with a grin. "Real soon."

"Or we could try something else," Xander offered slyly.

Damon felt his stomach tighten with something hot and nervy. He had a feeling he knew what Xander was suggesting, and it wasn't that he wasn't interested. He definitely was—but it felt like Xander had shot him straight to the heart with adrenaline. He was maybe a little too interested.

He'd definitely watched too much porn this week, fantasizing the whole time that the men on screen were him and Xander.

Xander placed the palm of his hand on Damon's chest, probably feeling just how fast his heart was suddenly racing. "Just to be clear," he added, "I want you to fuck me."

As if the first adrenaline shot hadn't been enough, Xander gave him another. "Yeah? Is that what you want?" Damon wasn't a young guy anymore, but he could already feel himself getting hard. Like he'd been granted his number one fantasy, and his cock was going to make sure it didn't let him down.

Glancing down, Xander smiled so smugly that he grew harder with just the look. Clearly it wasn't just *his* fantasy.

"Yeah, and it's what *you* want too," Xander pointed out. He reached down, and gave Damon's cock an experimental little stroke.

"Well, I was the one to suggest we stay in bed instead of going to dinner," Damon said. But it was impossible to pretend he wasn't dying for it. It felt like all his previous orgasm had done was take the very edge off his hunger, and afterwards, he still felt insatiable.

Xander grinned at him knowingly as he stroked a little harder, making Damon moan. "I'll be right back," he said.

He scrambled off the bed, went over to his bag on the dresser, and pulled out a tube and a whole string of condoms. Damon gave himself a very firm warning that he wasn't going to come early; he was going to make sure they both fully enjoyed this.

Giving him a very frank stare, Xander set the lube and condoms on the bedside table. "I think it's going to be easier if you let me take the lead here."

Like Damon hadn't been letting him take the lead every single time so far. But he nodded anyway, because his practical experience wasn't just lacking, it was literally nothing.

Xander settled back on the bed, but this time closer to the edge and within easy reach of the supplies. "Why don't you come over here and kiss me first?" he asked, and as Damon scooted over, he was definitely gratified to see that Xander was already half-hard too. He wanted this just as badly as Damon did.

This time, Damon didn't hold back, he leaned over and kissed Xander greedily, taking his mouth the same way he intended to take his body. When Xander reached over and began to stroke his dick again, Damon followed suit, mimicking his actions. It only took a minute or two, and they were both breathless.

"Stay right there," Xander said, his voice low and gravelly, shooting another dose of arousal through Damon's body. "Don't move."

Damon had no intention of disobeying.

Grabbing the tube, Xander wet his fingers, and rising to his knees, slipped his fingers behind himself. "Watch me," he demanded.

"Oh fuck," Damon swore, once he realized what he was doing. "Fuck, fuck, fuck."

"If I blow you," Xander asked, his voice even deeper, "are you going to come?"

Damon shook his head sharply, reins tight on his self-control as he did what Xander asked and watched him prep himself.

"Good," Xander said, groaning a bit on the end of the word. He leaned forward and there was no teasing this time, he just slid Damon's cock into his mouth. He moaned around it, and the vibrations shot right through Damon's veins, lighting him on fire. Gripping the sheets with his fists, he reminded himself that they were both going to enjoy this and he had to control himself to make sure that happened.

But it was too hard to watch and not surrender, his eyes flickering shut of their own accord. Xander must have glanced up and seen because almost immediately his warm, wet mouth was gone, and his other hand was gripping the base of Damon's cock tightly.

"Don't come," he warned. "And open your god damned eyes."

Damon did, and swore as he watched Xander moving up and down on his own fingers. "I'm almost ready," Xander said. "Are you ready?"

Damon thought he could have prepared for this for a hundred years, and he never would have been ready, but he nodded anyway.

He was definitely not ready for Xander to pull his fingers from his body and climb over him again, grabbing a condom on his way, ripping the wrapper viciously and eagerly with his teeth. He positioned Damon's cock where he was wet and ready, sliding that hand up and down a few times after he'd sheathed Damon's dick with the condom.

Like he wasn't already rock hard and eager to go, Damon thought desperately as he tried to hang onto the last shreds of his restraint.

"Don't you fucking move," Xander warned, and suddenly he was sliding down very slowly, hands braced on Damon's chest.

It was different than fucking a woman—somehow tighter and hotter—and Damon let out a long exhale as he forced himself to stay perfectly still. The last thing he wanted to do was hurt Xander, but it was tough to ignore every instinct of his body.

"Fuck," Xander moaned. "You're so god damned big."

Damon got the impression this was both a good thing and a bad thing, but he wasn't about to apologize, because he couldn't even figure out how to voice anything, let alone an apology when it felt so incredible. He could only hope that it would feel that good for Xander after he adjusted.

Finally, Xander settled his thighs on top of Damon's and froze there for a moment, his wide eyes staring right into Damon's.

"You haven't moved," Xander said, face relaxing a bit.

"You told me not to," Damon panted.

Xander's hands curled into Damon's chest, each fingernail leaving a divot. Damon couldn't complain because the pain grounded him, and helped him regain a grip on his urge to move.

"That doesn't mean you wouldn't," Xander said, and Damon couldn't help but think he was far too coherent right now. Damon was one big bundle of exposed nerves, all blind instinct and emotion, and he needed Xander to be in the exact same place.

But then he finally moved, shifting up and then sliding back down, and from the way his face crumpled, Damon realized that his coherency of even a moment ago had been one big act.

"Does that feel good?" Damon asked, remembering how much Xander had liked the talking before. It didn't come as naturally to Damon but he didn't mind making an effort. Especially not if Xander enjoyed it as much as he had.

"Fuck yes," Xander swore. "I can feel you everywhere."

"That's right," Damon encouraged him. "Take what you want, baby."

Xander moaned again, and the sound echoed right through Damon, tapping right into the source of his pleasure and magnifying it even more. He sped up and Damon bit down on his tongue, tasting the blood in his mouth as he tried to hold on, wanting Xander to enjoy this as much as he was.

"Touch me," Xander gasped. Damon didn't need any further instruction, he reached up and wrapped his hand around Xander's leaking cock, and twisted it in his grip, repeating the motion with the same rhythm Xander was using to ride him.

It only took a few more pulls of his cock, and Xander let out a strangled scream, tensing up and throbbing tightly around Damon's dick. He hadn't expected that—had never felt anything so good in his entire life—and as Xander began to paint his chest with stripes of his come, Damon couldn't hold on any longer.

Xander woke up alone, stomach grumbling and heart wondering why the other half of the bed was empty.

They'd ordered a pizza late, devouring it like they were starving, and then had fallen back into bed, talking and giggling until late.

He couldn't quite remember falling asleep but he was pretty sure he'd had Damon wrapped around him when he had.

Getting up, he went to the bathroom, and smiled wide when he saw a note propped up on the tile vanity counter. *Went to grab coffee and breakfast,* it read, with a big *D* scrawled across the bottom. He did his business, and decided that if Damon was going to bring him breakfast in bed, he'd better do his part to make that happen. He settled back into the nest of sheets and leaned back against the headboard, feeling lighter and freer than he could ever remember feeling before. As far as he was concerned, the other shoe wasn't going to drop. As far as he was concerned, after last night, the shoe didn't even exist.

It was a really fucking amazing feeling.

It was only then that he heard the voice echoing through the townhouse, coming from down the stairs. And it wasn't Damon, because Damon didn't have a voice that feminine. Xander grabbed the sheets and pulled them up further. He didn't know where his briefs had gone last night, and he wasn't about to get rid of his cotton shield to go find them either. The voice came closer.

"Damon? Are you here?"

Whoever she was, she must have the access code, because he heard her make a confused noise and then start up the staircase.

For a split second, his heart beating wildly, Xander considered hiding. Maybe in the massive walk-in closet? No, it was totally empty, and if she even stuck her head in, she'd see him—and his bare ass—in a second.

"Damnit," Xander swore under his breath. Every option he desperately flipped through seemed worse than the last. Which was, of course, to let her come into this room and catch him here, minus Damon and with the lube on the side table and a whole string of condoms on the floor, it wasn't going to be a state secret what they'd been doing all night.

Stupidly, he flattened his hair, trying to arrange it into something that looked less like they'd been fucking all night, though he knew that ship had already sailed. He yanked up the sheet practically to his chin, and that was all he had time to do before a young woman poked her head into the master bedroom.

She saw him instantly, and he wasn't sure who went redder.

"I'm sorry," she said. It wasn't much of a consolation, but she sounded at least a fraction as humiliated as he felt. "I didn't know . . . I thought Damon was here."

Xander smiled wryly. "He was. He went to get breakfast."

"Oh." She hesitated, and he knew that was when she took in the long strip of condoms on the floor. He'd loved bringing them, and pulling them out to Damon's obvious delight. The whole night had been so perfect, and now it was crashing down around his ears. "*Oh.*"

He watched her try to regroup. She was pretty, with light brown hair curling around her shoulders, and kind eyes.

"I guess, um, I guess I'll wait downstairs for Damon."

Xander said *fuck it* and scooted out of bed, trailing bedsheet as he went. "Let me get some clothes on." He paused. "How did you even get in here?"

Burying her head in her hands, she definitely looked as embarrassed as he felt. Maybe even more. "I'm Rachel. Damon's ex-wife. His father told me he was in town for a few days, and gave me the entry code. It never . . . I never imagined that he would bring someone."

The woman's humiliation was beginning to make more and more sense. This was Damon's wife. Xander froze, and couldn't help but wonder if she had even known if he was bisexual. Xander wanted to believe she had, because Damon didn't seem like the type to keep that kind of secret from someone he loved, but then Xander kept waiting for Damon to make their relationship public, and that hadn't happened yet.

"I'm his new head chef," Xander said flatly. "I'll see you downstairs." He definitely wasn't going to drop his bedsheet in front of her now that he knew who she was.

She turned and fled. Though he'd had hope that she would just leave, the embarrassment overwhelming her, after he found his clothes and ventured downstairs, he found her in the empty kitchen, leaning over the counter.

"I'm so sorry," she said again. "I should have known Nathan wouldn't have good intentions."

"He didn't know," Xander said flatly. "Damon didn't tell him he was bringing me." His hands reached out and he gripped the edge of the marble tightly. Like maybe he could keep himself from falling apart. The last person he wanted to do that in front of was Damon's ex-wife.

"So you're the chef for Damon's new restaurant?" she asked, clearly trying to change the subject, and he might have appreciated that, but he couldn't find it in himself to appreciate anything about her. It wasn't fair and it wasn't right, and he knew absolutely fucking nothing about her, but he *hated* her.

"I am," he said shortly.

"And you're . . ." she hesitated, "you're involved with Damon."

"I am," he repeated. "We're together."

That seemed to throw her a little, but she recovered quickly enough that it was obvious she'd known that Damon was interested in both men and women.

"I'm happy he has someone," she said, surprising the hell out of Xander. He'd half-expected a jealous tantrum, but instead she looked pleased. It shouldn't have really surprised him because she had such kind eyes, but he wasn't doing his best thinking right now. She reached out with a hand. "I'm Rachel. It's really nice to meet you."

The petty, nasty part of Xander did not want to shake her hand or introduce himself. But if Damon came home and found them in a catfight in his kitchen, it wasn't exactly going to reflect well.

He shook her hand briefly. "I'm Xander Bridges."

Rachel gave him an appraising look and Xander fought not to squirm at her careful perusal. He began to wish he'd taken time to put something on other than an old pair of running shorts and a loose tank. "You're the chef who just left Terroir, aren't you?"

Damon had barely mentioned his ex, only a few times in passing, and frankly that had been a few times too many for Xander so he'd never asked about her. His confusion must have showed, because she laughed.

"I'm a restaurant consultant, here in San Francisco," she explained. "You're now the third person to leave Aquino in the last eight months. Word starts to get around."

"People leave all the time," Xander defended.

"Yeah, but not someone with your skill level, and not when he promised you *chef de cuisine*, and you left anyway. Now it makes sense. You wanted to be in charge of your own restaurant." She paused. "*And* I suppose working for Damon seemed like a pretty good gig. He's a good guy."

It was petty and stupid jealousy, but Xander didn't want to listen to his ex-wife talk about how great Damon was. He already knew, thank you very much.

"It does make sense why he'd come to the townhouse," she continued. "He wouldn't come here at all when we were married, and when Nathan called me to say he was staying here, I was a little shocked. That's really why I stopped by. I wanted to make sure he was okay and not like . . . punishing himself somehow by coming back here."

Curiosity overcame his reservations about talking to Rachel. "He wouldn't come here *at all*?"

"I don't know what he's told you," Rachel said, her voice dropping, "but Damon has a really difficult relationship with his father."

"He's told me," Xander said dryly. "It would be tough to miss if you were paying attention. And I am."

Rachel smiled. "I really meant it, you know? I *am* glad he has someone and he's happy. We were good for a little while, but we were two kids struggling with something we didn't understand."

"His drinking?" Xander guessed.

"I wanted to help him so badly," she said with a heavy sigh, "but I didn't know what the hell I was doing. He needed an adult, a support system, and I was so young, I couldn't be what he needed. I hoped for so long that it wouldn't mean that he didn't date again." She smiled wryly. "It was selfish, but I didn't want that on my conscience."

"I do think he worries about it sometimes," Xander admitted. "Not because of you. But because he's afraid he's not worth the risk."

"And you obviously know that's bullshit."

"Obviously," Xander retorted.

"Do you mind if I wait for him?" she asked. "I haven't seen him in so long, and it would be good, to see him happy." Her smile had a bittersweet edge, and

Xander realized that their marriage hadn't been a particularly happy one. Why was he jealous of it? It hit him like a lightning bolt that his jealousy wasn't about Rachel or Damon—it was his own past rearing its ugly head. He wanted so badly for Damon to admit to the people around them that they were together. If he did that, maybe Xander could finally stop worrying that it wouldn't ever happen.

"Of course not." He gave her a lopsided grin. "It's only awkward if we make it awkward, right?"

She laughed. "I knew he was bisexual, just in case you weren't sure."

"I figured you must have. You were more surprised that there was someone in his bed than the fact that it was a man. Do you think . . ." Xander hesitated. "Would you imagine he'd have trouble telling anyone?"

She shook her head emphatically. "He made zero secret of it when we were together. We'd check out hot guys together, honestly. I really wouldn't worry about it."

But her words only made him actually worry more. The niggling fear in the back of his head expanded with her confession. If he had no issue with it, and had been unapologetic about it years ago, why would he continue to hold back? Was he ashamed of Xander? Was the problem not that Xander was a man, but that Xander was *Xander*?

That didn't seem possible after last night but with the cold light of day and Rachel's admission, it was hard to trust any other explanation. But before he could question Rachel further, he heard the front door open and then close.

Xander stepped into the foyer, the soaring ceiling above them. Damon was carrying a paper bag and a coffee carrier with a few cups in it.

"You're up," Damon said, sounding disappointed. "I was hoping to surprise you."

Xander took a few steps closer, until Damon could hear him with a low murmur. "Rachel is here. In the kitchen."

Damon couldn't look more surprised than if he'd told him Bastian Aquino had just asked them for a threesome. "What?"

Xander just shrugged. "I guess your dad told her you were here."

"Shit," Damon hissed. "Was it as bad as I think it was?"

"No. I mean, *yes*, but we're both adults, and she doesn't seem too jealous."

"She wouldn't be," Damon admitted wryly. "She remarried a year and a half ago."

Xander hadn't bothered checking out her ring finger, but it made sense, considering everything Rachel had said this morning. She hadn't come here to get Damon back, or to even see if he was interested. She'd come here to do exactly what she said; to make sure he was okay.

"Do you want me to tell her to leave?" Xander asked. "You don't have to talk to her."

"Nonsense," Damon said firmly. "We're friends, sort of."

It shouldn't bother him for Damon to walk into the kitchen without a second thought, leaving Xander behind, but it sort of did. He wanted answers to all the questions swirling through his head, and he wanted to sit Damon down and force him to explain. But the truth was, Xander just wasn't brave enough to hear the truth—if it was what he suspected.

Still, he put a brave face on, and followed Damon into the kitchen. He shouldn't have flinched when he saw Damon hugging her, but he couldn't quite help it.

It wasn't jealousy exactly; it was something more like envy that he'd had zero issue standing up in front of all his friends and family and marrying Rachel. They weren't ready for that by a mile, not even close, but Xander suddenly wasn't sure that if they made it that far in their relationship that Damon would do the same with him.

And that *hurt*.

"It's so good to see you," Damon said. "You look good."

"So do you," she retorted, giving him a little smack to the shoulder. "*Happy*."

Damon flushed, like he'd been caught in some sort of secret. "I am."

"And you're starting a restaurant. You should have called me."

"I wanted to do it on my own," Damon said dryly. "And I have someone with plenty of experience." He glanced back, right at Xander, and smiled broadly. "No offense to your skills, Rach, but it'd be overkill."

"Understood. But I'd better get an invite to opening night," she insisted.

Damon glanced back again, like he was making sure it was okay with Xander. And Xander wasn't stupid; he knew his envy or jealousy or whatever the fuck it was, wasn't attractive.

He nodded, adding, "Of course."

Her face lit up. "Oh, that's so great. I can't wait."

"We're actually here to scope out equipment and furniture," Damon said, glancing down at his watch. "And we'd actually better be going. We have appointments starting in an hour."

Xander took that as his cue to leave. He reached out, took Rachel's hand, and he could say, almost without a lie, "It was really good to meet you."

She beamed, like she totally agreed, and it made his statement even less a lie. "Ditto."

Xander was in the shower when Damon came in to bathroom, leaning a hip against the vanity counter. "Thank you for not freaking out when she showed up," he said.

"It's fine," Xander said. It wasn't quite fine, but he didn't know how to tell Damon the things that were bothering him without word vomiting it all up.

"I love that you're so chill," Damon said earnestly.

Personally, Xander didn't think he was chill at all, but he was willing to agree with Damon. "It's no problem. She's nice."

"We were young and stupid when we got married," Damon said, which was basically a version of what Rachel had told him earlier. "I think she was relieved when we got a divorce. She met someone more her style and married him not long after."

"It sounds like you're both happier now," Xander offered cautiously.

"Definitely." Damon's smile made it clear that was true. If only his smile could banish all Xander's new worries.

"We have a couple of restaurant supply stores to hit," Damon said, "and then dinner tonight at Michael Mina. Is that okay?"

"It sounds great," Xander said, flipping the water off, and he realized that despite this whole debacle, he meant it.

CHAPTER THIRTEEN

IT WAS TOUGH TO wrap his head around it, but Damon was about to open a restaurant, and after coming back to Napa, the reality of it hit hard. During their San Francisco trip, they'd ordered the restaurant equipment Xander had picked out, and had purchased the rest of the tables, chairs, and other miscellaneous furniture they'd need for the dining room.

As an extra bonus, he'd taken Xander to Michael Mina, where they'd definitely enjoyed the food, but more than that, Damon had loved the glint of determination that had emerged in his lover and head chef's eye. Xander might have felt like his rustic Italian food couldn't find a place in high-end dining, but after eating Michelin-starred Michael Mina's rustic Greek food, he'd been converted.

It could be done, and it could be done well—and Damon knew Xander was just the person to do it.

David had texted him to let him know the refinished floors were done, and that both the new addition for the kitchen and the bathrooms were now roughed in. He gave the project another few weeks, and after reading his text, Damon had sat down heavily. It wasn't hard to feel overwhelmed. Opening a restaurant involved so many decisions, and a to-do list that was frighteningly long.

Still, as the week post-San Francisco ticked by, he and Xander were able to cross off a good portion of it.

The logo was finalized and Damon ordered the signage, and tonight, Xander was cooking him the rest of the dishes he'd yet to taste. If everything was delicious as Damon knew it would be, the menu would be finalized too. Of course, it was seasonal, so the menu development wouldn't ever truly be finished, but getting that first one locked in was vital.

"I'm nervous," Xander said as Damon sat at the dining room table in Xander's rental house, watching as he wrung his hands.

"You shouldn't be," Damon reasoned.

Xander shot him a glare. Damon found it sexier than he probably should have. That was the problem since they'd started sleeping together; everything Xander did, conscious and unconscious, seemed to turn him on. He'd been celibate a long time, and he'd forgotten what it was like to be completely, head over heels attracted to someone.

He lifted his fork and tried to ignore the clanging voice in his head that told him that he wasn't just head over heels attracted—he was head over heels *in love.*

He'd felt it before they went to San Francisco, but afterwards, there was no pulling back or rescaling the cliff. Jumping off it had felt as natural as breathing, and it was undeniable, even if he wasn't even close to being ready to admit it to Xander. Though that probably had more to do with Xander than Damon's own feelings.

"You take me to Michael Mina," Xander said, starting to pace, "and then you came back and expect me to be *satisfied* with mediocrity. I can't be. I *won't* be."

"Your food isn't mediocre." Damon had discovered in the last few weeks that his boyfriend—because that fact was also undeniable even if they hadn't exactly discussed the label itself—had a secret dramatic side that only emerged when he was stressed.

Xander was absolutely, one hundred percent stressed right now. He threw his hands up and muttered. Probably something unpleasant about Damon's father in Italian. Again, probably way sexier than it should have been.

Whenever Xander got a little worked up, it was so easy to distract him by kissing him or touching him or offering a convenient method to work off his extra energy. But tonight, they *had* to finalize the menu; Damon had promised to send it to the printers in the morning. They couldn't get distracted with sex, no matter how much Damon might want to.

"It sure feels that way right now," Xander grumbled.

"Well, why don't you serve me some of it, and I'll give you my honest opinion. I promise."

Xander raised an eyebrow and shot him a very dubious look. "You promise to be honest?"

Like Damon hadn't been honest, as honest as he could be anyway, for their entire partnership and relationship. Besides, if they could make it through his ex-wife showing up while Xander was still lounging around in bed, a whole chain of condoms on the floor, they could make it through anything.

Though Rachel, after Xander had gone upstairs, had smacked him in the shoulder then given him a high five. "He's nice and really cute and a real catch," she'd murmured to him while she was hugging him goodbye. "Don't let him go."

He hadn't exactly let Rachel go, but in the end, it boiled down to that. How could he have asked her to stick around when the love between them had slowly been suffocating, strangled by Damon's demons?

Still, he agreed with her. There was no way he was ever letting Xander go, even when it still sort of felt like he was getting away with the better end of the deal.

Stressed-out drama queen episodes and all.

Damon rose up out of his chair at the dining room table and crossed toward the kitchen, stopping right in front of Xander. "You," he said, reaching out and taking his hands in his own, "are special. Talented. But even more than that, I know you can do this because you used to do this every single damn night. Bastian might have been the seed of Terroir, but by the time you came around, he was just a supervisor. You and the rest of the kitchen staff earned him his stars every year. I know you can do this because you've already done it."

Xander stared at Damon like the thought had never occurred to him.

"How many nights did you turn out his tired dishes, reinventing them without ever changing the recipe? Making sure they were flawless? And how many nights," Damon demanded, "did you stand there and wish you could make something else? Something *better*?"

Xander glanced away, like he didn't want Damon to see the look in his eyes. The truth of what Damon was forcibly revealing to him.

"Every night," he finally murmured. "I thought it every single fucking night."

"This is your time," Damon said, squeezing his hands. "This is your chance to do just that. I know you're not going to blow it because there's never been anybody less inclined to blow things."

A laugh bubbled out of Xander's throat, and Damon gave himself a mental pat on the back. He looked marginally calmer than he had a few moments ago, and he was laughing, relaxing a second at a time.

"I'd say I'm pretty inclined to blow things," Xander pointed out with an amused voice.

Damon pulled him into a quick, tight hug, then lingered because each day they grew closer, and each day, he was less inclined to let him go.

"Hold that thought," Damon said when he finally did. "Now, are you going to feed me or not?"

There was a new resolve in Xander's expression and Damon wanted to believe that he'd helped put it there—but truthfully, Xander had a stockpile of steely reserve and all Damon had done was show him where it was.

Returning to his chair, he watched as Xander cooked the halibut, gently lifting it out of the pan with a thin metal spatula, arranging it on the prepared plate just so. He walked over and placed it in front of Damon.

"Halibut with lemon and a fresh tomato gastrique," Xander said.

Damon lifted his fork. "Are you not eating?"

Xander let out a rueful laugh. "I've eaten this about ten times in the last five days. I think I'm good."

The halibut was buttery on his tongue, with just the sour, yet impossibly sweet, tang of the lemon. The burst of tomato and fresh mint finished off the bite. It was glorious, and while Damon knew his expression said it all, he couldn't help but add a single word. "Wow," he said. "Just . . . wow."

"It's simple but it's a perfect simplicity," Xander said and he sounded justifiably smug.

It should have occurred to Damon long before this. After all, he'd sought out Xander in the first place, determined to make him his partner in the restaurant and any other way he was willing to be. Still, somehow the realization took Damon entirely by surprise.

Maybe it was the stray thought that he wanted to see that smug expression of Xander's for years. For forever, if he had his way. He'd never tire of seeing the man he loved acknowledge just how brilliant and talented he was.

Because he did love him. Had started falling in love with him a long time ago, maybe even that night a year ago, and he'd simply never stopped falling. Until now, when his heart fell right at Xander's feet. And Xander just stood there, smiling away, thinking that this was all about a perfect piece of halibut, when the truth was it was so much more.

"You really like it," Xander stated, not even questioning it. Knowing it. *Believing* it.

"I love it," Damon said honestly.

"I thought you might."

Damon reached up a hand. He might not be ready yet to tell Xander—he still wasn't a hundred percent sure he was even doing the right thing, involving Xander in his life, burdening him with his problems—but he could show him.

He grasped Xander's hand in his and tugged him down, pulling him down to sit in his lap. "You really need to try this," he said.

Xander made a face, but he was also smiling and looking undeniably pleased. As well as settling right into Damon's lap like it was a throne made just for him. And as far as Damon was concerned, *it was.*

"I suppose you could tempt me with a bite," Xander said.

Loading up the perfect bite on his fork, with a little bit of everything, Damon guided it gently to Xander's lips. He chewed and swallowed, a pensive expression on his face. "It is pretty good," he admitted, the smugness melting into a boyish, bashful pleasure at the taste.

Damon fell hard again. He had a feeling he would be falling many times a day for as long as his relationship with Xander continued. Possibly even after it ended. There was a terrifyingly beautiful complexity within this man—his certainty and his honesty tempered with his sweetness and his kindness and his loyalty. The way he'd look right before he sucked Damon's cock, combined with this look right here.

"I am so glad you came into my vineyard a year ago," Damon whispered. He wasn't sure if he even wanted Xander to hear him, but he also couldn't swallow the words back anymore. They just spilled right out. "And I'm so glad I went looking for you again."

"I am too," Xander replied with a grin, laying a big smacking kiss on Damon's cheek before hopping off his lap. "I hope you're hungry because I have two more dishes I want you to try."

Damon watched him go. It was impossible not to look at him with the overly romanticized goggles of someone in love, but they still felt tempered—and maybe even tainted—with too much reality.

If the restaurant wasn't a success. If their partnership didn't work out. If he relapsed and lost his fight with sobriety.

There were so many potential pitfalls between them it was impossible to just throw everything to the wind and trust it would work out. But at the same time, he knew he'd come too far, both personally and professionally, to let Xander go now.

"Are you coming to the interviews tomorrow?" Xander asked as he threw some thinly sliced carrots into a sauté pan.

"Interviews?" Damon, lost in thought, couldn't remember what was happening tomorrow.

"Remember, I'm picking staff tomorrow," Xander said patiently. "Well, not *picking* per se, because I already know who I want to work with. It's sort of a formality but I still want you there to meet them."

"Oh, right. Yeah, I think I can make it." Damon didn't even bother to check his calendar; if Xander wanted him there, he'd make sure he was available.

"David texted me to tell me the equipment was all hooked up too," Xander said excitedly. "I'm going to have everyone cook a recipe. Maybe I'll have them try the halibut."

Damon didn't mention that he'd had a long walk through the restaurant with David just this afternoon, going over a thousand tiny details, and when David had told him the kitchen hookups were all done, he'd been the one to encourage him to tell Xander.

David had looked at him strangely, and asked if maybe Xander wouldn't want to hear it from Damon himself. Even though he'd known David forever, and he *knew* David wouldn't give two shits about Damon being involved with Xander personally, he'd still shied away from the implication. Tried to act like it was all just professional between them.

It wasn't shame or guilt or his inability to claim his own sexuality. He just didn't want Xander's life and career torpedoed by association with someone like Damon. Someone who was still a ticking time bomb.

Damon knew it was all Xander's choice. He was a grown man, with an intelligent and analytical mind, who could make his own informed decisions. But Xander had only ever seen the sober and controlled Damon; he'd never met drunk Damon. Never experienced any of drunk Damon's terrible choices.

It wasn't like Damon was going to go out and get drunk to prove a point, simply to show Xander what *could* happen if he lost control, but Damon couldn't seem to get his lingering concern to dissipate completely.

"I can't wait for tomorrow," Xander said, happily babbling away, a complete one-eighty from Damon's darker thoughts.

He dragged himself back to the present, forced himself to sit here, in this moment, with the man he loved who was cooking food they'd soon be serving to their patrons. It was a crowning achievement, and he should enjoy it.

"It's going to be great," Damon enthused. "I can't wait either." It wasn't faking it, he reasoned with himself, it was re-focusing himself into the place he needed to be. The place he *should* be.

"This is the full menu," Xander said, distributing a single sheet to each potential staff member that stood around him in a loose semicircle. "We'll be creating seasonal menus and specials based on what's fresh and in season. The majority of the vegetables will be coming straight from the garden outside the door."

Billy, the ex-Terroir line cook who had grown up in the last two years, and who Xander really wanted to be *sous*, raised a tentative hand. "Can I see the wine list?" he asked. Xander knew he had ambitions to be a chef/sommelier, and in Napa that wasn't even that unusual. But he had a feeling that Damon's no-alcohol policy might dissuade Billy from taking this job. Xander just hoped that Billy could see the other benefits of working here.

"There isn't a wine list." Xander met Billy's eyes like he held a fraction of Damon's conviction but the truth was he liked wine. He liked drinking it, he liked the taste, and he'd liked the way he used to unwind after a long day with a glass. He wouldn't go as far as to say he *missed* it, but he sort of did. But he'd known the score when he took this job with Damon, and he'd known it was non-negotiable. That hadn't stopped Xander from wondering if he should bring it up about half a dozen times. A Napa restaurant that didn't serve wine was an aberration, and while sometimes unusual things stood out, Xander was afraid Damon's policy would sink them before they could even begin changing people's minds.

"No wine list?" Billy sounded disbelieving. "The restaurant is called the Barrel House."

"It's called that because of the history of this building. Damon Hess feels the name is representative of the heritage of this land, while he's recreated it in a new image."

"You mean he tore out all those vines." Billy's voice was flat.

"Yes."

"So you won't be serving any alcohol," Susie, who he really wanted to steal from the French Laundry, piped up. "Seriously?"

Xander didn't like all these questions. He also didn't like that all these questions echoed so many of the concerns he'd had about this. He knew Damon's feelings, but maybe he should bring it up anyway. It was worth a try; Damon was a reasonable and logical person who wanted this place to be a success.

"Let's move onto the first dish," Xander said, hating that he was actively copying one of Bastian's voices—the one he used when he didn't want a single voice of dissent. He didn't like the feeling that Damon had put him in this position.

No. What he really hated was that he hadn't even considered the position existed before now. Usually Xander was thinking a dozen steps ahead, and his feelings for Damon had blinded him to reality.

But he'd also hated it when they went to Michael Mina, and the glorious wine list—one of the very best in the Bay Area—went untouched on the side of the table. He'd told himself that he didn't resent Damon for this one rule and that he didn't need booze to be happy—both of which were true, but it also turned out that he couldn't keep everything as black and white as that.

Xander knew he was beginning to slip into a gray area, and he wasn't sure there was nothing he could do about it.

Damon chose that moment to poke his head into the kitchen. Xander held back the frown. He'd told Damon to be here ten minutes ago, so he could meet everyone, but he'd been surprisingly late.

"This is Damon Hess, the owner," Xander said, introducing Damon, who only gave a brief, distracted wave while mostly looking down at his phone.

That was bullshit because this was *his* staff, too. Xander reached out a hand and possessively wrapped it right around a plaid-covered bicep. "Damon is responsible for the incredible garden you see outside. He also has real plans to make improvements. Even an orchard, at some point."

"I definitely have the land and the space," Damon responded, still distracted and now wiggling right out of Xander's grasp and walking over to stand in the corner.

It was definitely weird, and Xander couldn't figure it out.

He stood there, surrounded by the men and women he'd asked to come to the new restaurant for an interview and "audition" and Damon couldn't seem more distant or fidgety.

Had they taken things too far in San Francisco a week ago? Were they moving too fast? Was Xander alone in falling in love? He didn't know, but the thought scared the shit out of him.

Xander tried not to consider the possibility that seeing Rachel again had shaken Damon. He'd insisted he'd moved past her and that their relationship hadn't been healthy on either side, but the niggling thought remained in the back of Xander's uncooperative brain.

He went through the motions of describing how the sauce was made, and then demonstrated how to construct the plating. Terroir had been famous for its beautiful plating, and Xander had always enjoyed the intricacies of making each dish a work of art.

"Now we sauté the halibut," Xander said, and while he heated the pan, couldn't help but wish that Damon was a little more consistent. Sometimes Damon was incredibly supportive and attentive, like last night, when he'd never been sweeter, but then sometimes he was also like he was today. Distant. Removed. Cold.

Xander didn't understand how those two halves could belong to the same damn person.

"We add the butter near the end of the cooking," he continued, hands moving on autopilot, like he'd done this dozens of times, which he actually had.

He'd been so excited to share this part of the process with Damon; introducing him to the small, hand-picked kitchen team he'd assembled, and part of Xander was definitely peeved that he was acting like he wasn't involved with this at all. Damon's money was paying for these people, at least at the beginning, just like it had paid for the renovation of this building and the glass and the tables and chairs in the dining room and the high-end gas stove he was currently sautéing on.

It had even paid for this pan and the spatula in his hand.

He'd also been counting on Damon to help Xander make a strong case for why the staff should leave their current employment and take a chance on a Napa-area restaurant that didn't serve wine. Xander decided right then that he was done letting him skate by.

"When I made this dish the other night for Damon," Xander said, "he nearly fell to his knees and begged me for more." He shot a sharp look in Damon's direction, and when he looked up, he definitely looked skewered. His dark brows furrowed and he didn't look too pleased either.

"I'd like everyone to try the recipe," Xander finally said, after he lifted out the fish and deposited it on the already prepared plate. Fish last, as it was the crowning piece, and also because the halibut's cooking time was both short and incredibly precise.

He turned to Damon and placing an insistent hand on his bicep, practically dragged him out of the kitchen and into the dining room where nobody could hear them.

"What is your deal today?" he demanded.

Damon shrugged, which was even worse. "Sorry, I guess I'm just distracted. Didn't sleep well."

Xander had slept next to him, and knew he'd slept just fine, so that was just bullshit. He was about to say so when Damon continued.

"Do you think you should be so . . . friendly in front of our employees?" Damon finally asked, dropping his voice down until even Xander could barely hear him.

"Friendly?" Xander crossed his arms over his chest.

"You were practically caressing my arm when you were introducing me to them," Damon said.

Xander couldn't believe it. Actually, *scratch that*. He could. He could totally believe it because it had happened to him once before, and he had sworn to himself—an ironclad promise he'd never had any intention of breaking no matter how soulful Damon's dark eyes were or how ripped his arms or how when he looked at Xander it felt like he was seeing (and loving) his whole complete self—that it would absolutely never happen again.

And now, it was happening again. "You don't want *your* employees to know we're dating." He said it flatly, without emotion, like somehow that could contain the sudden hurricane whipping up inside him.

"No. *No.*" Damon said it clearly. "I don't want . . . I guess I want to make sure we stay professional."

"Explain," Xander said. He was holding himself back from judgement—barely.

"We want to maintain high standards, we want to have a professional work environment, right? I think that starts with us. If you're going to be flirting with me, talking about me on my knees begging for you, that doesn't exactly scream professional. You worked for Bastian Aquino. I know you want something different than Terroir. Maybe Aquino wasn't alluding to his sex life, but he was a shitty boss. I want to be something better, and I want that for you too."

Xander took a deep breath, and let it out slowly. Trying to calm himself down. "So if I told everyone in there that we were dating but we're going to be keeping that part of our lives at home, you wouldn't care?"

"I told you," Damon said, patiently. "I don't care if people know if we're together. I care if it affects the Barrel House. We've both put a lot into this. Let's make it a success."

Xander wanted to believe him. He really did. He *almost* did, but not quite. There was still that voice whispering in the back of his mind that this was just like Dustin had been. Dustin had been full of excuses too, and in the beginning some of them had been good ones. Convincing enough that Xander had agreed easily to let the matter of their relationship being public slide.

And, he added, further trying to silence that voice, it wasn't like Damon wasn't willing for people to know. He just didn't want it encroaching in the workplace. He didn't want it affecting the restaurant he'd poured all his money and his dreams into. Xander couldn't blame him for that.

He nearly retorted that if Damon wanted to make the Barrel House a success, then he should hire a sommelier and have them pick a wine selection, but he held back. That wasn't this fight. This was a whole different fight.

"Okay," Xander said, cautiously. "But you should know why I'm concerned." He hesitated. He had never intended to tell Damon about his high school boyfriend, and how he'd left him. *Left* wasn't even the right term. Dustin had drifted away further and further, no matter how tightly Xander had tried to hold onto him, no matter how desperately he tried to convince Dustin to come out.

"Tell me," Damon encouraged, and that helped. It always seemed just as Xander was about to get truly fed up, Damon managed to dig himself out of the hole.

"My boyfriend in high school. He wanted all the convenience of a boyfriend. In secret. I couldn't get him to be honest about me. I just made myself a promise after going through that heartbreak that I wouldn't let it ever happen again."

"And you're afraid it's going to happen again," Damon answered.

"Maybe a little, yes."

Damon pressed a swift kiss to Xander's lips. "I'll take out an ad in the paper and tell every single person I meet. I'm not ashamed of you. I'm not ashamed you're a guy. I just want to keep it professional here."

Xander already knew he was going to make the conscious decision to trust Damon. After all, Damon had given him no reason to doubt him before this.

Sure, he hadn't told his father about bringing Xander to San Francisco, but based on the comments Rachel had made, Damon didn't typically share anything with his father.

All he needed to really reassure him was to remember those few days in the city. Damon had been so attentive and wonderful. *Loving*, Xander could even say. And now this.

That was the kicker, here, Xander thought ruefully. He loved Damon, and he wanted Damon to love him back. Wanted it so much that he was even willing to believe him despite his own ugly history.

He leaned in to brush a kiss across Damon's cheek. "The rest will have to wait 'til we get home," Xander said cheekily, purposefully trying to lighten the mood. "I'd better get back in there before they destroy something."

Damon raised an eyebrow. "Is that a possibility?"

Xander laughed. It felt like the unsettled ground they'd been walking across for the last day or two had solidified. Everything was fine, they were going to be fine.

"God, I hope not," Xander confided. "Else I should have hired other people."

"Can you spare one more moment?" Damon asked, sounding so hopeful that it was hard for Xander to deny him, so he nodded his agreement. It would be good to test the new staff's focus and dedication. Damon *was* right about that; he did not want to be another Bastian Aquino, micromanaging everyone within an inch of their lives.

"Come with me," Damon hissed with a naughty grin, and grabbed his hand, dragging him off toward the nearly finished bathrooms David had just put in.

He pulled Xander inside one of them, and locked the door behind him. "What are you doing?" Xander asked, mystified.

"This," Damon said. He crowded Xander against the door and, without any warning, leaned in and kissed him hard and fast, one hand reaching up to cup his cheek and the other slid down toward his hip, gripping it tightly.

It took Xander a single moment to catch up. For someone who didn't like PDA at work, Damon was pretty amenable to sneaking off to the bathrooms to make out. But then Damon changed the angle on the kiss and it went from merely passionate to straight-up dirty, and Xander was reminded of how busy they'd been and how much he wanted another marathon night of sex.

"That," Damon said, breaking away breathless, "was an apology. I'm so sorry. I was an ass. It won't happen again. Especially now that I know how much it hurt you."

"It's okay," Xander said, curling his hands into his pants so he wouldn't reach out and run his fingers up Damon's obvious hard-on. "I know you're not an asshole."

"We good?"

This time Xander felt confident in his answer when he nodded. "We're good."

"I'd tell you good luck," Damon said, "but I know you don't need it. You've got this." He looked like he believed one hundred and ten percent in what he was saying. And someone who looked like that might finally love Xander the way he'd been waiting for.

Xander put a hand over Damon's heart, just resting it there. He was silent a long moment. Maybe he shouldn't say it. He'd known it was true for a long time, but maybe it was too soon. Maybe it would scare Damon away. But, he reasoned, Damon should know. Maybe Damon even *needed* to know. Xander thought he'd been pretty clear that he wasn't in this to fuck around, but maybe he needed to be even clearer.

"I love you, you know," he said, and he got the words out with only a tiny waver of uncertainty. And nobody could blame him for that.

"I know," Damon said, a smile breaking over his face like a particularly spectacular sunrise. "I love you too."

Xander grinned back giddily, his heart beating madly in his chest, matching Damon's beat for beat. "I should get back."

"You should," Damon said. But he didn't move either.

"It seems like neither of us is pretty good at this professional-at-work thing," Damon added after a long moment. He was still smiling.

"It's okay, I forgive you," Xander said with another brief kiss to Damon's cheek. "I'll see you tonight." He reached around, unlocked the door and slipped out, feeling like a new man as he headed back into the kitchen.

Damon *did* love him, he hadn't been imagining that. And someone who loved him the way Damon seemed to wouldn't fuck this up, Xander reasoned. He just wouldn't.

Chapter Fourteen

"I heard a crazy rumor today," Kian said, walking into the kitchen. Xander almost did a double take, but then remembered that today was Kian's one day off every two weeks.

"That you didn't actually have to work?" Xander asked, not looking up from the focaccia dough he was kneading.

"It's actually a two-parter," Kian said, pulling out the orange juice carton from the fridge and a glass from the cupboard. "One, you've decided to become a baker. Two, you're not serving booze at your new place."

Xander punched the rising dough down a bit harder than he probably needed to. "It's not a rumor," he said.

It was Kian's turn for the double take. In fact, Xander was pretty certain he almost spit his juice out. "Billy was actually telling the truth?"

"He was." Xander punched the dough down again as he remembered Billy's email response to the job offer he'd sent. It had been polite enough, but there'd been a whiff of incredulity between the lines, like he couldn't believe Xander was going along with this. Still, he'd agreed to take the position—but only if Xander was able to talk Damon into serving a limited wine menu. Billy even volunteered to help create the list himself.

"I know you care about him," Kian said, "but that doesn't mean you have to go along with every crazy scheme he comes up with."

Xander knew Kian wasn't talking about Billy.

"That's rich, coming from you," he nearly sneered.

"I think it's worth at least having the conversation. I know Hess has money but you want to be at least commercially viable, you know? How long can his trust hold out if he's paying to keep you afloat?"

Xander knew. He kneaded the dough instead of answering, each turn and punch down more vicious than the last. He was never going to be able to bake this—the waste of flour and oil and yeast serving Xander's frustration instead of his stomach—but it felt good to use to hands.

"Being involved should make it easier to talk," Kian continued.

"Supposedly, yet I don't see you doing it," he pointed out darkly.

Kian crossed his arms over his chest, his juice long forgotten. "I don't see why you keep dragging me into this. We're talking about you and Hess. Or *I'm* trying, at any rate."

"There's nothing to talk about. Damon has a . . . difficult history with alcohol. He doesn't want it around. He doesn't want to serve it."

Kian's face did soften a little. He reached out and put a hand on Xander's shoulder, and he slumped at the touch. "You still need to talk to him. This is your life, too."

"I had two ideas," Xander said after a long silence. "I thought about making a menu of non-alcoholic cocktails to divide the focus from alcohol."

"That's good. And what's the second?"

"Donate profits from any alcoholic sales to a substance abuse charity." Xander stared at the dough. He'd been awake most of the night thinking about the quandary, and he, just like Kian, had known he needed to talk to Damon about it. It was at least worth a conversation.

"So you *are* going to talk to him," Kian said.

"It's the only logical thing to do." Xander had just been trying to come up with something else to do instead, and had come up with exactly nothing.

"He coming over tonight?" Kian asked, and Xander nodded.

"I'll make myself scarce then." Kian put an arm around his shoulders and pulled him into a quick hug. "You're doing the right thing."

After Kian disappeared, Xander dumped his overworked focaccia dough in the trash and after cleaning out the bowl, started re-assembling a new batch with fresh ingredients.

The truth was Xander didn't know if bringing it up with Damon *was* the right thing. Why did they have to serve booze anyway? People could get booze anywhere. Why did they have to get a drink with their dinner at the Barrel House?

Logically, Xander knew they didn't. But people were creatures of habit and expectation, and at higher-end restaurants in the Napa Valley, there was always wine.

Maybe someday they could flout the trend, and do whatever the fuck they wanted, but you had to establish yourself before you broke the rules. Especially when you were expecting customers to help pay for your continued existence.

He spent the rest of the afternoon lost in the familiar and reassuring rhythm of baking. Even though preview night was in two days and the opening was the day after that, none of this would keep. At least it wouldn't be as fresh as Xander demanded it be.

Xander collapsed on his bed after a quick shower, hair dripping onto his bare chest. He shouldn't feel so worried about this conversation. He and Damon loved each other, and Kian was right; this was exactly the sort of thing they should be able to talk about with that level of emotional commitment. But Damon had always shied away from discussing his alcoholism, like somehow it tainted him and therefore Xander by comparison. Instead he locked it away, behind walls that he hadn't let Xander see behind yet.

"Now, that's a sight I could get used to."

He glanced up and saw Damon in the doorway, smirk on his face. Seeing Damon and knowing they loved each other was still a rush that Xander wasn't quite used to. He grabbed the towel around his waist and started to stand up, but Damon took the few steps to the bed and put a hand on his shoulder, holding him in place.

"Stay," Damon said quietly. His dark eyes were intent on Xander, filled with longing and lust and need and desperation and a thousand different shades in between.

Xander raised an eyebrow, questioning Damon's request, and was rewarded with another flash of bone-melting desire in his lover's gaze. For some reason, Damon adored it when Xander challenged him in bed; it was guaranteed to stoke Damon's blood so much hotter and this time wasn't an exception.

"Brat," Damon said, affection and hunger layered equally together in his voice as he lowered himself to his knees in front of Xander. He licked his lips in anticipation and that alone would have turned Xander's knees to jelly even if he wasn't already sitting down.

Damon peeled back the towel, not in any huge hurry, which definitely meant that he was going to tease and take his time.

"Suck my cock," Xander said, surprising even himself at how breathy his voice was. "I know you want to."

Laying a reverent hand on Xander's bare thigh, Damon leaned in, breath warm on his skin.

"Fucking tease," Xander swore impatiently as Damon's tongue reached out and licked right up the underside of his cock.

"You love it." Damon's voice was rough and wild, and his hands clamped around his thighs, dragging them open wider.

For someone with zero practical experience when they'd started dating, Damon had taken to blowjobs like a fish discovering how to swim for the first time. He was gentle yet demanding, both of Xander and of himself. Like he desperately wanted to prove to both of them that he wanted it—that he wanted *Xander*.

"You love this too," Damon said, one of his hands sliding higher, cupping around his quivering thigh, curling downward, brushing his balls and then lower. He gave Xander's hole a brief touch, then another. His fingers were damp, maybe even wet, though Xander couldn't remember seeing any lube when Damon came in.

Maybe he was a magician. Frankly, with the way his fingers and his mouth were teasing him, quick little tantalizing touches that seemed to drive him higher and higher until he was mindless with how much he wanted Damon's cock inside him, that made sense. Because nobody had ever made him feel this way before—out of control and yet completely grounded with how much Xander trusted him.

It took too long for Damon to even slide a whole finger inside him, and like he sensed Xander's desperation, he didn't make him wait nearly as long for the second. By then, the towel was gone, Damon's shirt was off, his biceps bunching and flexing as he slowly fucked Xander thoroughly with his fingers. The first time they'd done this, Damon had been more hesitant, but now he knew Xander, and he knew what he liked.

"Good?" Damon asked, voice nearly a growl as he practically slid Xander across the bed with his thrusts. "You want more?"

Xander knew he said words. He knew they were probably something pleading, but he wasn't entirely sure of what he was saying. Sweat dripped into his hair, into his eyes as he held onto the edge of the mattress, moaning as Damon finally began to slide his cock inside him.

"Tell me how it feels," Damon insisted, a hand smoothing down Xander's back, burying itself in his hair. He wasn't rough though. Every touch felt touched with love, with adoration. "Tell me," he repeated when Xander uttered some sort of complete gibberish.

"Big. Full. Close," Xander gasped. "So close."

Damon draped his big body over Xander's and began to work his hips in and out, in the same driving insistent rhythm he'd fucked him with his fingers. "Yeah, I'm close. I'm in you, and you're in me," he murmured into Xander's damp hair. "God, I love you."

"So much," Xander managed to say as he wrapped a hand around his own cock, getting in one long stroke before his orgasm roared through him. Damon gave one last deep thrust before throwing back his head and groaning in pleasure.

They slumped to the bed together, the sheets and blankets shoved to one side. "I like being able to reduce you to single-syllable words," Damon finally said drowsily, stroking up and down Xander's back. "Makes me feel like I'm giving you exactly what you need. Not just what you want."

Xander sighed, the buzz of pleasurable contentment warring with his anxiousness of earlier. The sex had helped take him out of his head a bit, but the residual worry hadn't dissipated. He knew they still needed to talk.

After Damon slipped out and grabbed a cloth, cleaning them both off, he came back to bed, resuming his earlier position, a gentle hand on Xander's back. It was easier, Xander discovered, to ask if he wasn't looking at him. So he gathered his courage and leapt.

"I want you to talk to me about everything," Xander said quietly. "I love you, and sometimes I think you want to save me from the bad stuff. The stuff you've been through. I want to know. I want to help you bear it."

The hand stroking his back hesitated for a split second, then continued its lulling rhythm. "I don't tell you because it's ugly. And you don't need that ugliness touching you," Damon said. Xander didn't miss the undercurrent of iron beneath his words. He didn't want to share, and somehow Xander was going to have to convince him.

"It's not ugly. It can't be when it's *you*. All it does is prove to me how brave and strong you are," Xander argued. At first it had seemed easier not to look in Damon's eyes when he asked these questions, but now it suddenly seemed impossible to say any of this if he *wasn't*. He turned over and immediately saw the doubt clouding Damon's expression. "I love you. No matter what."

Damon rolled to his back and sighed heavily. "People are telling you that you're stupid for hitching yourself to a guy who won't even serve alcohol at his restaurant, right?"

It was not fun getting caught, but Xander reached out anyway, grasping his upper arm, then sliding his hand toward where his heart beat steadily in his chest. "It's not stupid. But I still want to talk about it."

"It was inevitable." Damon sounded close to tears, like he'd been dreading this moment for their whole relationship and now it was finally happening.

Xander reached up and cupped his cheek, tilting his head down so Damon could see his face. "We can't pretend like it doesn't exist. I wish we could, too, but that's not real life. I want this love to be real, and to be real, it has to exist in the real world."

This time Damon didn't look away and Xander recognized the look brewing in his eyes as resolve.

"I don't remember when I started drinking," Damon said quietly. "I . . . I always did. Always. I remember holidays, Christmas or Thanksgiving or probably even the Fourth of fucking July, my dad leaning over and letting me sip from his glass. Usually it was wine. Sometimes it was a beer. Occasionally a glass of whiskey or a gin and tonic. I got used to it, I liked it. I liked the way it made me feel when I got older, and it felt so *normal*, like it was something I'd been around forever, like it was a part of the family."

He took a deep breath, pausing, and Xander laid a hand on his bicep, squeezing gently. "It was a part of your family because of who your family is," he replied gently.

"I know alcohol isn't evil. I know some people, *lots* of people enjoy it and it doesn't ruin their lives. They don't start using it because it's a better parent than their father or because their mom is never around. I know that. Logically, I do get it." Damon's fists flexed once, then again. "But sometimes, some things aren't logical."

Xander didn't know what to say, other than a desperate need to apologize. For the shitty childhood Damon had experienced? Because occasionally Xander wanted to enjoy a glass of wine? Because he wanted to serve alcohol at the Barrel House?

Because while Xander now understood Damon's relationship with alcohol better, he still selfishly wanted to serve it.

"It's the point of the thing," Damon admitted. "It's not that I don't see a lot of value in any argument you might make, but when I ripped those vines up, I knew exactly what I was doing, exactly what I was throwing away, exactly what those vines were worth—I was doing it because I was done with alcohol completely. I was sober, had been sober for years, but it still haunted me."

Xander looked at the man he loved frankly. "Do you really believe that ripping up those vines meant you aren't ever going to want a drink again?"

Looking away, Damon shook his head slightly.

"I'm not the person who has to tell you what to believe, and what to discard. I'm not you, and I can't make decisions about what's important and what has meaning. But the physical manifestation is gone; it's still here, inside you, and it's going to be there until the day you die." Xander pressed his palm to Damon's chest, right where his heart beat. "Even if you never take another drink, it's going to be part of you. I can accept that—I want to accept all of you—but can you?"

Damon turned further away, and Xander's heart ached. Maybe he shouldn't have been so honest; but he couldn't be in this relationship and be any other way. He'd always prized truth and he couldn't become another person for Damon. No matter how much it fucking hurt.

"I don't know," Damon mumbled, turning his face into his arm. Xander thought if he lifted it away he might find damp skin. "I don't think I know anything."

"You know lots of things. You've conquered your demons. But locking them away doesn't mean they *go* away." He slid off the bed and went around to the other side, crouching by where Damon's face lay against his arm. And as he'd imagined, Damon's eyes were red and wet. "Let me ask you something. If we serve wine, let's say, at the Barrel House, are you going to want to have a drink any more than you normally want one?"

Damon shook his head emphatically.

"If you ever feel that's true," Xander said with quiet determination, "then this isn't a conversation. It's a decision, solid and final. But I don't think you're really tempted anymore."

"I hate it. I'm envious of it. I'm jealous as hell of anyone who can just have one glass of wine with dinner and call it good," Damon finally admitted.

"The final decision is yours," Xander said. "I'll respect whatever you decide. It's your restaurant, it's your land, it was even your idea. And it's your disease. I'm willing to do whatever you want. Would I like to serve wine at the restaurant? Yes, because sometimes I like to have a glass of wine with dinner, and I know other people do too—especially people who come to Napa. But I'll abide by your decision and we don't ever have to talk about it again."

Xander kept his word. He let Damon have some time alone in his room as he showered again, and when he was done, he went into the living room and flipped on the TV.

Damon heard him calling for Chinese, putting in an order for sweet and sour pork and Damon's regular order, Kung Pao chicken, and some fried rice and potstickers. He heard the delivery guy at the door, and heard the door shut again, even smelt the spicy aroma of dinner in the air, but he didn't come out of the bedroom.

He considered leaving and going back to his lonely house. It had always been lonely, since his grandfather had died and left it to him and he'd moved back to Napa, but ever since he'd met Xander, being alone there had grown claws. Now, he found it nearly unbearable.

Sometimes he wondered if he'd decided on building a restaurant because that meant he'd always be surrounded by lots of people on his land.

Maybe that was what this was really about; not the booze at all.

No, Damon thought grimly, it was really always about the booze. He was a Hess, living in Napa; that much was inescapable. He'd left here briefly but he still came back home. He belonged here, whether he wanted to be here or not, whether he resented that fact or not.

Xander was a great believer in the truth, and Damon knew, as he dragged himself upright and wiped his eyes, that he meant everything he'd just said. But that didn't mean he didn't mean what he *hadn't* said—and what Xander hadn't said was that he didn't think the restaurant could be a success without serving wine.

What it boiled down to was that he didn't think the restaurant could be successful with Damon involved. Because Damon and wine did not mix, no matter how Xander tried to justify his opinion. An alcoholic shouldn't be around alcohol, that much seemed pretty obvious, at least to Damon.

Rachel was happening again. Exactly what had prevented Damon from even dreaming about love was happening again.

Damon gingerly leveraged himself up and walked to the bathroom, shutting the door with a quiet click and staring at himself in the mirror. Red eyes, tight mouth, hopeless expression. He recognized the man in the mirror a little too well.

As devastating as the divorce had been, Damon knew he loved Xander more completely and more fully—more *maturely*—than he'd ever loved Rachel. They'd been kids; he was a man now and so was Xander. Losing him was going to destroy Damon all over again, except it was going to be much worse this time around, because Damon wasn't going to be able to run away to lick his wounds.

Xander was going to be right there, right in front of him, every day, and it was going to hurt like hell. It was a good thing, then, Damon thought darkly, that he wasn't a stranger to pain.

He dressed and went into the living room. Xander had an old episode of *Kitchen Wars* on, Landon Patton and Quentin Maxwell bantering over a lazy Susan contraption, berries flying everywhere, and every molecule in Damon's body ached at the normalcy he was never going to be able to have.

Xander flipped the sound off, and looked up at Damon, concern written all over his face. "Are you okay?" he asked. "I . . . I . . . maybe I shouldn't have made you talk about it."

"No. No, I'm glad you did." He took a deep breath. "You're right. What you said is right. We should serve wine."

"You think we should serve wine?" Xander asked cautiously.

"No, I really don't. But what I want doesn't really matter. It hasn't mattered in a long time. Ever, probably." Damon sighed. "Eat your dinner. You have training tomorrow and you need your strength. I'm going home."

Xander raised his eyebrow and it didn't do anything for Damon. Nothing like what it normally did. He felt beaten and numb instead. Like he'd fought his battles all over again, but this time he'd lost.

He loved Xander. He was talented and smart and bright and deserved a restaurant that would showcase him to his best advantage; a jewel in the proper setting. Damon knew, with his issues and his darkness, that he couldn't really be a part of that. Not really. Xander would figure it out sooner or later, the same way Damon just had.

Xander belonged to the shiny, bright world of people who could have a glass of wine with dinner or a beer on a warm afternoon and it didn't mean anything.

People who didn't have a difficult and complex reaction to a drink menu on a patio table. Damon had known this from the very beginning, he'd understood it was fundamentally true almost from the first moment, but he'd tried to push the inevitability aside, and then he'd straight-up begun living in a fantasy world where it didn't exist at all.

Earlier tonight, Xander said he wanted a real love. This was a real love, in a real world.

He got up and put his arms around Damon, pressing a kiss to his cheek. "I'll talk to you tomorrow, okay?"

Not talking wasn't going to happen. Breaking up wasn't going to happen. Not with the restaurant opening on the horizon, only a few days away. The best Damon could do was to pull gradually away until Xander realized the same thing he just had. They were better off as friends and business partners.

"Yeah, of course," Damon said, ignoring the lump in his throat.

"Night. I love you." Xander pressed another kiss in, deeper, firmer this time. Like he could permanently brand his lips there. Damon wanted to tell him that it didn't matter, he was going to feel his mouth against his skin forever—there was no erasing it now.

"I love you too," Damon said, and meant it just as much, if not more, tonight, than he ever had.

Xander just didn't realize that those three little words also meant goodbye.

❧❧❧ ❧❧❧

The second the door closed behind Damon and he heard his car start up in the driveway, Xander dialed his phone in a blind panic.

"Wyatt," he said desperately, "I think I just really fucked things up."

"What did you do?" Wyatt asked. "Did you over-whip the marshmallows again?"

"Have you been talking to Miles again?" Xander demanded.

"Of course I talk to Miles. We live in the same freaking city," Wyatt drawled. "Stop changing the subject. What's got you sounding so panicked?"

"I told Damon we should serve wine at the Barrel House."

Wyatt was silent for a long moment. "Didn't you tell me last month that he was a recovering alcoholic?"

"Yes," Xander said miserably. "He is."

Xander didn't know what he'd been thinking—actually, scratch that, he knew *exactly* what he'd been thinking. He'd been thinking with his ego, hyper-aware of what people were saying about him, worried that nobody would give the restaurant a chance because of the lack of booze.

He'd let his fear get in the way of . . . Xander hesitated, unsure how much he'd really fucked up, then realized he'd let his fear jeopardize *everything*. The restaurant. His relationship with Damon. His future and Damon's future, seemingly so bright only a few days ago, suddenly dimmed because he'd been dumb enough to listen to Billy and Kian. And his own fucking ego.

"Listen, opening a restaurant is a crazy thing to do. It's absolute insanity before it happens. People say stuff all the time when they're stressed. Chalk it up to that and move on."

The last time they'd talked, Xander had given Wyatt a very vague idea that he and Damon were just sort of screwing around, nothing serious. Why had he done that, when Wyatt was going to find out the very first time he saw him and Damon together? Especially when that particular event was going to be happening shortly with the restaurant opening?

Plain and simple, Xander hadn't wanted to be the new Kian. Involved with his boss and his partner, potentially screwing up his own future.

The worst part of this whole thing was that he hadn't even needed Wyatt or Miles to warn him. He'd done it all on his own, with zero help from anyone else.

"I don't think he's going to move on that easily," Xander admitted.

"Why not?" Wyatt sounded distracted and he suddenly heard the roar of a crowd in the background. Flipping to ESPN, Xander sat down heavily and watched as Wyatt's boyfriend Ryan hit a solid stand-up double in front of a packed Dodger Stadium.

"You're at Ryan's game, aren't you?" Xander asked flatly.

"Yes, but as I'm discovering, the baseball season is 162 games long. I think I can talk to you for five minutes to keep you off the cliff *and* be a supportive partner.

"You really care about him, don't you?" Wyatt persisted when Xander didn't respond.

Xander was quiet still, but Wyatt could be damn stubborn when he wanted to be and he wasn't letting him off the hook now.

"I love him, okay?" Xander finally said, voice cracking. "I really love him, and I fucked it all up."

"You're going to apologize, and he's going to forgive you. It's gonna be fine." Wyatt's voice was almost drowned out by more crowd noise. "I'm sorry, I really do have to go now. But I'm coming up tomorrow, and I'm bringing Miles with me."

Xander almost told Wyatt not to bring Miles, because somehow it was worse that Miles was going to be front and center to him totally screwing up his life. Wyatt was chill; Wyatt also always understood. Miles was a little pricklier.

But he didn't, because in the process of epically fucking up, he'd realized just how much he needed his friends here. Even Kian, who he kept trying to be pissed at. Maybe if Kian hadn't brought up the rumors and his concerns hadn't so closely echoed Xander's own. That was bullshit though, and Xander knew it. It wasn't Kian's fault he'd selfishly mouthed off, suggesting that his recovering boyfriend serve booze at their restaurant. That was all on Xander, and he wasn't being pessimistic when he knew he'd be paying for it.

Chapter Fifteen

Xander woke up to a text message from Miles the next morning, demonstrating very clearly that yes, he and Wyatt definitely talked. **Apologize**, was all it said, and Xander wished it was just that easy.

There was nothing on his phone from Damon, which was unusual even with how busy they'd gotten with the preview night tomorrow and the real opening the day after that. Damon still got up early to tend the gardens, though he'd been talking about hiring some gardeners to help him out, and he liked to send something Xander would wake up to.

Sometimes it was silly like, **you know, you were drooling all over my chest last night while you were sleeping** or sometimes a picture of the sunrise. Lately he'd been sending simple, **I love you**s.

It was difficult to not read something into the fact that Damon not only hadn't sent that particular message, but that he hadn't sent anything at all.

His heart was aching and his stomach was in his shoes, but Xander was still a god damned professional, and he dragged himself into his chef whites, pulling back his hair with one of his favorite chili pepper bandanas and drove to Damon's.

He didn't even bother detouring toward the house. Instead, he met with one of his food distributors, set up a delivery schedule, and received orders from his other distributors. After everything was meticulously labeled and put away, his new employees started showing up.

Billy shot him a little smirk, and Xander gave him a cold stare, daring him to ask if he'd brought the wine issue up with Damon. But Billy must have been smarter than he assumed, because he didn't say a word. Maybe the fight was written all over his face. Xander didn't know, and he wasn't sure he *wanted* to.

The morning was devoted to organizing the kitchen, putting all the tools and equipment away and establishing the processes by which Xander expected every single member of his team to do their jobs. This might not be Terroir, but he'd learned there that organization was next to cleanliness and godliness.

Noon rolled around without Damon showing up at the restaurant, and Xander let everyone take a break. He ran down to the corner store and grabbed two sandwiches and some bottled water, walking into the back door of Damon's house without even a knock.

Xander set the food on the counter, the quietness of the house unsettling him. He wasn't even sure Damon was here, and after a thorough check of the rooms, realized that he'd been right. Damon wasn't even around today, the first full day of training and only a day before the preview night.

The Barrel House was ready: the dining room stood pristine, the furniture arranged, the plates stacked in the kitchen waiting to be filled, the massive refrigerators already beginning to fill up. The crates of vegetables from the garden had been sitting on one of the stainless steel counters this morning, like Damon had left them early and then departed, not even bothering to wait for Xander.

The concern that a simple apology might not be enough began to swell inside of him. He pulled his phone out and sat down heavily at one of the barstools, staring at the screen. But instead of dialing Damon's number, he called Miles.

"When are you guys going to be here?" he asked before Miles could even ask if he'd apologized.

He would have—he *wanted* to—but Damon wasn't here to apologize to. And Xander couldn't help the bad feeling lingering that Damon had arranged it that way on purpose.

"Soon," Miles promised. "We're about two hours away." He paused, and Xander gave him full brownie points for waiting more than twenty seconds before asking. "Did you apologize?"

"I haven't been able to," Xander said. "I wanted to. I came to his house, with lunch as a peace offering, and he's not even here."

It was obvious from the whispered consultation that Wyatt and Miles were having in the car that neither of them believed this boded well for Xander. The knowledge he'd really, truly, *epically* fucked this up, continued to gnaw at him.

"Did you call him?" Miles asked.

"Yeah," Wyatt chimed in, Miles clearly having put him on speakerphone, "you should call him. It's only two days until opening. He's probably running a thousand errands."

Except Xander had seen Damon's ever-evolving to-do list for the opening, and he'd whittled it down to just a few items. They'd worked it together, crossing off item after item, and that had helped make it a lot more doable. Not for the first time, Xander regretted forgetting, even for a split second, that they were always better together, working as a united front.

"Okay, I'll call him," Xander said, and not really because Miles and Wyatt thought he should. He knew he should.

"Okay, we'll see you tonight," Miles said, and Wyatt chimed in, adding his goodbye.

Xander hung up and stared at the screen, working up the courage to dial Damon's number. It probably should have been tougher, but then Xander imagined life without him, a life where they were professional partners and nothing else, and his fingers flew across the screen.

Damon answered on the final ring. "Hey," he said, sounding distracted. "Everything okay?"

"I'm in your house, eating a sandwich, and you're not here." Xander wasn't going to buy that faux casual tone of his. Everything wasn't okay, and no matter what Damon pretended, he couldn't believe otherwise.

"I had stuff to do today," Damon said. "Besides, I thought you'd have your hands full with training. How's it going?"

"I do, and it's going well. But I wanted to talk to you."

It must have been clear from Xander's voice what he wanted to talk about because Damon went silent.

"I didn't want to do it over the phone, but you're not here." He knew he was supposed to be apologizing, but frustration still leaked into his tone.

"If this is about the conversation from last night, we've both said enough, don't you think?" Damon asked snidely, and it cut Xander to the bone.

"No . . . yes . . . I mean, I wanted to apologize."

Damon sighed heavily on the other line, and Xander felt his unease begin to ratchet into a full-blown panic.

"You were being honest, why would you need to apologize?"

Xander didn't miss that Damon had answered all his questions with questions of his own.

He gritted his teeth. He'd fucked up; he'd not imagined that apologizing and forcing Damon to hear it and accept it would be easy, but this was turning out to be far trickier. "I was insensitive and tone-deaf. It's your restaurant, and you told me straight off how you were planning to run it. It's not fair that I come tromping in at the last moment and demand you change your mind."

"You were right; if I want to be commercially viable, I'm going to have to make some changes."

Xander didn't want Damon to accept what he'd said as legitimate. He didn't want him to be quietly, mildly agreeing to his argument; he wanted him to be pissed as hell. As pissed as Xander was at himself.

"You shouldn't make any changes, not because of what I said," Xander argued.

"But you just made the case last night," Damon said, and he sounded perplexed. "It was a good argument."

"It was not," Xander retorted. "It was insensitive and insecure and cruel. Not to mention quite a bit selfish. I love you. We are going to make this work no matter what we serve. That much I'm confident about."

"Okay," Damon said, but it was absolutely clear that he wasn't agreeing with anything. Xander's fingers tightened over his phone, and even though he might be grumpy and tactless sometimes, he didn't generally have a temper. It was flaring now, and he was struck with a sudden inexplicable desire to demand Damon's location, storm over to where he was, and express his feelings. Strongly.

The worst part was that he knew he was still attempting to apologize.

"I don't think you get it," Xander said, barely hanging onto the reins of his anger, "I fucked up. Badly. I said a lot of shit that I shouldn't have, and you going and accepting it is not good. It's not okay. It's not what I want, at all."

"It's what you asked for, Xander," Damon said quietly. "I've got to go. I'll see you later."

Later, Xander realized after, he'd said *later*. Not tonight, not tomorrow, not the day after. Not in the kitchen during the preview or during their triumphant opening. Non-specific, so Xander wouldn't know if he could depend on him, or wouldn't know for sure if he turned around one day if he'd see his quiet, steady smile.

The phone left his hand before he could even help himself. It shattered into about a hundred pieces against Damon's hardwood floors—reclaimed wood, Damon had told him once—and at the time all Xander had wanted was to reclaim *him*. He still wanted that, he'd have to be dead not to want it, but right now, all he wanted was to burst into tears and imagine that after his crying jag ended, everything was going to be okay.

But he couldn't help but wonder that nothing was going to be okay again.

"You broke your phone," Wyatt said, edge of his mouth quirking up, like he was really trying to tamp down a smile. It wasn't funny, but maybe in a thousand years, after this restaurant opened successfully, and Damon had forgiven him, Xander thought he might find it amusing too.

But right now, he wanted to punch Wyatt in his perfect face.

"I broke my phone," Xander muttered back.

"I'm guessing that apology didn't go so well," Miles said gently.

Miles never did anything gently, especially when it came to Xander, and that was another blow to his aching heart and his rapidly fading belief that this might all fix itself.

"He wasn't even mad!" Xander yelled. It was pretty ironic that the only one mad here was him, when Damon deserved to be really pissed over what he'd said.

That was the worst realization of all; Damon wasn't angry because he believed what Xander had said was the truth. Had probably worried about it for awhile, had carried that concern in the back of his head, and then Xander had gone and given it to him on a silver platter.

Xander resumed pacing back and forth in the living room, ignoring that Miles and Wyatt were exchanging looks of concern.

"Did he say he'd be back for tomorrow?" Wyatt asked. Tomorrow was the preview, and while everything was set, it was something that Damon should be there for. *Deserved* to be there for. This was his restaurant and had been his dream long before Xander was even involved.

"No," Xander muttered, stopping in front of the sofa and collapsing on it, the old springs squeaking. "No, he was deliberately vague."

Xander ignored more concerned looks. He didn't need them to be worried; he was worried enough for all of them, a constant gnawing at the base of his stomach.

He stared at his hands as the silence dragged out. Wyatt and Miles didn't even know what to say, because what *was* there to say? They'd both miraculously ended up with healthy and happy relationships, but of course, that wasn't in the cards for Xander. Of course he was going to fuck it up. That was inevitable. He should have held onto that bone-deep pessimism he'd cultivated for so long, but instead he'd let it get swept away by Damon's magnetism and the mind-blowing happiness Xander felt whenever he was around.

A wine glass was set down on the coffee table in front of him with a click. Xander glanced up and saw Miles standing there, a glass of his own, filled with ruby red liquid, in his hand.

"Really?" Xander demanded. "You really think this is the best time to have a drink?"

Miles shrugged. "Have you had a drink since you met him?"

Xander remembered one; the night he'd been wild to kiss Damon, and had come home and had kissed Nate instead, believing that he could convince his mind and his heart and his body that anyone would do.

"See, that's not really healthy either," Miles said firmly. "You can't stop being who you are for him. I know you probably could have been more diplomatic with what you said the other night, that much I will agree with completely, because subtlety has never been your strong suit, but you had a point."

Reaching out, Xander picked up the glass. Stared at it. It was a beautiful color, clearly one of Nate's better bottles that Miles had just stolen.

"Booze isn't a crutch for you," Wyatt agreed quietly. "You need to be able to enjoy a glass if you want to. You can't change for him, and he can't change for you. Yeah, you might be better and stronger together than you are apart, but you still need to be yourselves."

Xander took a sip. He had been a little carried away by Damon's dream and his ambition and his entire self; it had been hard not to since so much of those things were reflected in Xander himself. But he had resented a little his self-imposed sobriety. He'd never asked, but then Damon had never clarified either, and back then, when they were still figuring their relationship out, Xander hadn't wanted to give him any reason to walk away.

The wine was rich and dark on his tongue. This was definitely one of Nate's better bottles. "This is good," he said. "Nate is going to kill you."

Miles waved a hand, clearly unconcerned. "That guy is weak. I could take him in my sleep."

Wyatt chuckled, almost definitely amused because at one time, a very long time ago, Nate had been his boyfriend.

"This is what we're going to do," Miles said, and he suddenly sounded like he *could* take Nate, or just about anyone else for that matter. "We're going to go get you a new phone. We're going to get some more wine. We're going to go over tomorrow's arrangements. And the preview *will* kick ass, I promise."

It was impossible not to voice the secret, dreaded fear that was lodged in the base of his throat and in his stomach, and weighing down all his limbs. "What if he doesn't show?"

"Then he's a fucking idiot," Wyatt said, reaching over to give Xander a reassuring shoulder squeeze. "I know it's not the same, but we're going to be there, and we're going to get through this. I promise."

Xander didn't sleep.

Lying awake, it was impossible not to notice that the cotton of the sheets still smelled like Damon. It had only been a few days, but it felt like an eternity.

His new phone sat on the nightstand charging, its silence damning Xander to another sleepless night, taunting him endlessly. Finally, he picked it up and stared at it. Found the number he'd dug up this afternoon when Miles and Wyatt had left him alone for five minutes and he'd realized that Damon wasn't going to answer or reply to any of his voicemails or texts.

It was late—after midnight—but Xander hoped she would forgive him for calling, but he didn't know where else to turn and he just couldn't take it anymore. The phone rang twice, then three times, and just when he thought she wasn't going to pick up, a breathless female voice answered.

"Who is this?" she asked, sounding annoyed.

"It's Xander. Xander Bridges. We met once . . ." He trailed off. Suddenly what had seemed like such a good idea, felt like a terrible mistake. He shouldn't be calling Rachel. She wasn't involved with Damon anymore. She didn't know him anymore; that was why people got divorced, right? They'd lost sight of who the other person in the marriage was.

"We did," Rachel confirmed, her tone hushed, but no longer angry. "Is everything okay?"

Xander's throat constricted. He pushed the tears back. "No."

She was quiet for a long moment.

"I wouldn't call you," he finally said, "I wouldn't do it unless I knew what else to do."

She laughed, a little wry and a little wet around the edges. Like she was crying too. "He's not an easy person. He likes to run when he's afraid."

"He won't listen to me," Xander admitted.

"And you think he'll listen to me?" Rachel asked.

"It was the last thing I thought I could try," Xander said. "The preview is tomorrow. Well, today, actually, and I can't . . . I don't *want* to do it alone. I wasn't supposed to be alone."

"I can come," Rachel said. "And I can call him, if you want me to. But it's not going to make a bit of difference."

"Can you just . . . tell him, for me? He's not answering my calls anymore. Won't talk to me, anymore."

"Once, he disappeared for a week straight. We'd been married for three months," Rachel said. "He did come back, but he wasn't the same. He carries his demons with him, and they're always trying to get to him. Sometimes they win." She sounded resigned to it, but Xander wasn't. He wanted to fight, fight *with* Damon, if only he would let him. Let him *in*.

"I'll call him," Rachel said finally. "I'll let you know if I get ahold of him. Try to get some sleep. You're going to need it for tomorrow."

Xander didn't want to tell her that it was going to be impossible, but in the end, he must have finally fallen asleep in the early morning, because the next thing he remembered, he was opening his eyes up and listening to a hushed argument happening right outside his bedroom door.

It was painful dragging himself out of bed, but he did it because the only thing Miles and Wyatt had to argue about was *him*, and he wasn't going to let them discuss him when he wasn't even present.

Sure enough, when he wrenched his bedroom door open, Wyatt and Miles were caught red-handed, their conversation stuttering to an abrupt, awkward halt.

"What's going on?" Xander demanded.

They both looked at him, both attempting innocence, and neither one pulling it off. Finally Wyatt sighed and said, "For the record, I think this is a bad idea."

"What's a bad idea?" Xander really hoped that they hadn't heard him call Rachel.

"Come on," Miles said reassuringly, reaching out and taking his hand. "Let's go have some coffee and I'll show you."

In the kitchen, Wyatt poured him a mug of coffee, adding in half a spoon of sugar, just the way he liked. He took a sip. If Wyatt thought coffee was enough to distract him, he was sorely mistaken. "What did you want to show me?"

Miles moved away from the opposite counter, revealing a plain white box tied with white ribbon. "It was sitting on the front porch this morning," he explained. "There's a tag. It's for you. It's from Damon."

Xander hesitated, his grip tightening on the mug. The truth was, he wanted to throw that too, but when they'd taken him to get a new phone, Wyatt had pulled him aside and made him promise he'd stop throwing things. "I know you're pissed, I know you're confused, and you have every right to be," he'd said, "but you can't let that turn you into Bastian. Because I know that's the last thing you want."

He didn't want to end up like Bastian; sad and lonely and isolated, too emotionally scarred and too much of an asshole to even see something good right in front of him. He didn't want to be a jackass, he didn't want to make his employees worry that one day he'd snap and toss a plate at their head.

He didn't want to be that guy or that boss or that friend; he'd always aspired to be better than that. But with the fallout from Damon disappearing, Xander was beginning to realize just how slippery the slope into becoming that man was. A few more doses of distrust and bitterness, Xander knew, and he and Bastian might practically be clones.

He didn't want that, but he also didn't know what to do with all this anger boiling away inside him. He kept trying to keep the noxious steam inside him—absorb the fumes and not let it spread to everyone else—but it was tough.

The truth was there was a part of Xander that was dying to act out, to spread it far and wide until everyone was just as poisoned as he was.

"You don't have to open it," Wyatt said, reaching over and gripping his elbow. "We can just leave it here, we can put it away in a closet, and you don't have to face it until you're ready."

But Xander shrugged. "I'm not ever going to be ready to face it. And whatever's in that box, it can't be worse than going to the restaurant today and not seeing him, knowing he's not going to show up."

It should have hurt worse to undo the ribbon, feel the silk slide under his fingertips as he set it aside and opened the lid. Maybe he was just numb; frozen so he didn't have to feel all the pain slipping through him like water.

Under the lid was tissue paper, which he pulled aside to reveal a pristine white chef's coat. Above the left breast pocket was the embroidered Barrel House logo, and underneath it, his name, and "Executive Chef." Xander traced his finger across the blue threads, remembering nights in a room this exact same color.

Was it better or worse that Damon remembered? Xander didn't know, all he knew anymore was that it hurt and he just wanted the agony to end.

"You've worked a long time for that title," Wyatt said softly.

"I'm sure he ordered this weeks ago," Xander said, even though that didn't help at all. "He just wanted to make sure I had it." That was all he could surmise, because there was no note, no last-minute expression of good luck, no promise that he would be there tonight, ready to watch Xander's triumph.

"It's going to be okay," Miles said, and even he didn't sound convinced that it would be anymore.

You're not going to cry, Xander told himself sternly, reaching inside and finding that steel that had always seen him through the worst of Bastian's days back at Terroir. *You're not going to let anyone see*, he promised himself, *you're going to walk in proud and head high, and nobody is going to know you're dying inside.*

By the time he was out of the shower and they were getting ready to head into the restaurant, Xander couldn't decide which was worse: that Damon believed the worst about himself or that he had decided it was okay for this day, which was supposed to be one of the best of Xander's life, to devolve into an agonizing exercise in emotional containment.

He was a bomb, waiting to go off, and maybe if he just kept going, putting one foot in front of the other, not thinking, not remembering, not *wishing*, he might not explode. Even for Xander, there were a lot of *maybes* and *mights* in that sentence.

"I knew I would find you here."

Damon glanced up in surprise. Nobody else knew he liked to come here, way up on the hills of Mount Veeder, only accessible by a dirt road, and never used except for once a year by the land surveyors hired by Hess.

Someday, his father would develop this land. But not now, not until all other options were exhausted, because it was a trek.

And today, Rachel had made the trek up here.

"Xander must have called you," he said morosely, staring at his feet, picking at a loose thread on the hem of his jeans.

"He did. He didn't know what else to do, because you just ghosted on him." There was definitely a reprimand in his ex-wife's voice. "I thought I told you not to fuck it up."

She sat down beside him, put a hand on his knee. "What are you doing here?" she asked. "You're supposed to be down in the Valley, helping him. Being there for him. Running your new restaurant, not up here, pretending like you're not good enough for any of those things."

"It's not pretending," he insisted roughly.

"I told him that you're always fighting your own self, and sometimes you win. You need to figure out how to lose." Rachel's voice was soft, but he couldn't look at her.

"I let you down. I *left* you. I fucking abandoned you for booze. I don't think that's winning."

She laughed, shocking him enough that he glanced up at her. There was a wry expression on her face and tears in her eyes. "You never left me. We left each other because we weren't happy. Did the alcohol help? Of course not. But you can't take all the blame for the disintegration of our marriage, Damon. It was already over. It was nearly over before it even began. And now you've met someone you can really love, who loves you back—loves you so much he's willing to throw his own pride to the wind just to help you. *Fix this*."

Damon stared out over the Valley. The cause of so much of his pain, and now the cause of so much of his hope. "I can't."

Rachel sat up, and dusted off her legs. Blocked the harsh rays of the sun as she stared down at him. "Then you don't deserve him."

It was a sentiment that Damon had spent the last two days trying to believe, but with Rachel's pronouncement, he had to admit it didn't sound quite right.

He still didn't believe that. At least not enough to stay away entirely.

After arriving at the restaurant and the initial painful realization that *no*, Damon was not here, Xander discovered there was so much to do, it was impossible to think of anything but the task in front of him, and the fifty million tasks left to do. That helped; not quite enough, but it was enough to make him functional.

He thought about calling Rachel again and asking if she'd gotten anywhere, but the gaping hole left by Damon's continued absence answered every question he would have asked her.

Xander started the team prepping. Miles assisted Monica, the part-time pastry chef, not even saying a word about how menial the tasks were, just chipping in and wordlessly assisting, and when Monica looked over at him like she wanted to say something about Evan or his show, he'd simply shook his head.

He wasn't Miles of *Pastry by Miles* today, he was Xander's friend. It helped shore up Xander's defenses a little, and when Wyatt wordlessly volunteered to manage the front of the house—a job that Damon had given himself—it helped a little more.

At five, Xander went into his tiny private office, tucked behind the kitchen, something he'd claimed not to need when he and Damon had first discussed the remodel, and Damon had insisted on anyway. He pulled off his old stained jacket, and just stared at the new bright white one sitting on his desk.

It fit perfectly, and Xander didn't want to know *how* Damon had known, even though he already knew how. Too many nights with Damon's mouth and hands skating across his shoulders and chest and stomach, becoming intimately familiar with every ridge and curve of him.

The door opened before Xander could dwell any further, saving him from a headlong tumble into misery. He did up the buttons as Wyatt looked at him steadily.

"It's time," he said and all Xander could do was nod wordlessly. It was a good thing his staff, while not yet completely familiar in his recipes, were already impeccably trained and knew every single responsibility. He didn't need to say a word and he probably wasn't going to be able to.

He just had to get through the next four hours.

Wyatt pulled him into a quick, tight hug and whispered into his ear, "We can do this. *You* can do this."

One hour down, and Miles had gone out to assist Wyatt with seating. He reported back that diners were cleaning their plates, all with joyful smiles on their faces. One of the new wait staff reported offhandedly to Xander, while he was standing at the pass-through, inspecting plates bound for tables, that diners were having difficulty even selecting their meal for the night, because "everything sounded amazing."

So far there hadn't been any complaints regarding alcohol, or if there was, Miles and Wyatt were keeping him perfectly, completely isolated from it, and he'd never been more grateful. If even one person walked up to him and demanded a glass of wine, Xander was probably, almost certainly, going to punch them in the face.

Two hours down, a plate came back to the kitchen for the first time. Xander stared at it, the perfect presentation slightly jumbled, and finally looked up wordlessly at the waiter.

"Too much red pepper flakes," he said apologetically. "Could she get it remade with less? She's particularly sensitive to spice."

Xander wanted to retort that if she was sensitive to spice, she shouldn't order something with *pomodoro* in the title, but he took the plate, dumped it in the garbage, sent it down to Chris, his dishwasher, and began to remake the food himself.

Hour three, the kitchen and the dining room were humming along so seamlessly that Xander took a piece of focaccia and a glass of water to his office and tried to force something down.

It didn't work.

He should be the happiest man on the planet right now. His restaurant was a success. People were happily buying his food and claiming they couldn't wait to return. But it all felt empty without Damon here.

Four hours into the preview, they were winding down. Miles came into the kitchen and told him he should hire Monica, the pastry chef, full time, and that he needed another line chef because they were going to end up being busy. Xander made a note on his to-do list and tried to give his friend a genuine smile, but instead it felt fake and plastic. Like someone else was happy and smiling for him. There just wasn't any joy inside of him, and there definitely wasn't enough for a real smile. Miles hugged him and told him he'd stay the rest of the week.

Hour five, and as the staff cleaned and Miles and Wyatt bickered over the tally for the evening and closed out the register, Xander went outside to try to clear his head.

It felt like a fog had overtaken him, the price of having to go through this all while feeling abject despair and abandonment.

He was just leaning against the back of the building, gulping in air and trying to clear his mind, when he spotted a dark figure in the distance, standing in between the rows of vegetables.

Heart thumping painfully, he pushed away from the building and started walking toward him. He knew who it was; he never could have left him alone for this night. After all, this had always been *Damon's* idea, first and foremost. He'd even been the one to convince Xander that the plan had merit. He never could have left him alone tonight.

He started jogging, then he ran, breath coming in harsh pants as he reached the man he loved.

Damon looked over at him, almost in surprise. Almost as if he hadn't expected to get caught or if he had expected it, that Xander wouldn't have even come over.

And fuck that, Xander was in love with him. He'd said some stupid shit, sure, and he'd not understood entirely where Damon was coming from, but he still loved him, and he still wanted this. If he was being honest with himself, he wanted it even more than he had before, because now he knew what it was like to do it without Damon.

"You got it," Damon said first, before Xander could even figure out where to start. What to say first. Should he hug him? Kiss him? Punch him? He didn't know, but in the end it didn't matter.

"I got what?" Xander demanded incredulously.

"Your jacket," Damon said, reaching out like he was going to touch the embroidery right over his heart, but then his hand jerked back, like he hadn't ever intended to touch him. "You needed it, and I couldn't let you go without. Not tonight."

"Then you should have brought it to me yourself," Xander said. He was trying to stay calm, but it was really fucking difficult.

"I couldn't. You know that. I . . . I never should have done this." Damon said this with a small shake of his head, like he couldn't believe he'd ever imagined he could, and that just added more fuel to Xander's anger.

"We *were* doing this!" he yelled. "As far as I was concerned, two nights ago, it was actively happening. I know I fucked up, I know I wasn't as understanding as I needed to be. But I can be better. We can fix this. You can't just walk away and not let me fix it."

Damon's eyes were sad in the moonlight as he stared at him. "I knew after I divorced Rachel that involving myself with anyone ever again was a huge risk. I'm a burden, Xander, and I don't need you to say it for me to know it's true."

"You have baggage. You're an alcoholic. I know. I get that. I don't think less of you, and I don't think you're going to destroy me if you are. You didn't even destroy Rachel. She's moved on, she's happy, she's got a husband and a job and a life. Your demons aren't going to torpedo anyone—even *you*." Xander felt desperate, like his chance was slipping away. He wasn't sure if Damon would believe him, now or ever. He certainly didn't *look* like he believed him.

"They run deep," Damon said with regret in his eyes and his voice. "Sometimes I don't even know how deep they run."

"Then we'll figure it out together," Xander said, and he knew he was pleading. He wasn't even above begging. "Just don't vanish. Don't shut me out." He hesitated, anger swelling again when he thought of what he'd endured today. "Don't fucking take what was supposed to be the best day of my life and make it impossible to get through. I can't do this again. This is not what was supposed to happen."

"It's what needs to happen," Damon said gently, and when Xander tried to reach over, to touch him, to remind him of what they'd shared, of what they'd been through already, he pulled away.

"You can't do this," Xander said blankly. "You can't do this."

"I know it doesn't seem that way now, but this is better for everyone. Including you."

Xander snapped. "You're fucking right it doesn't seem that way. You don't get to make these choices! You don't get to decide that you're too fucked up to be with me. You're the best man I've ever met. The strongest, the bravest, but right now you're acting like a fucking coward and it isn't a good look."

"You're right, it's not. But then you've always been right about a lot of things," Damon said, and Xander wasn't stupid, he knew what a goodbye sounded like.

"Wait," he said when Damon started to turn to walk away. "You can't do this. We're supposed to be a team. We're supposed to do this together."

"It's your restaurant now. You run it. You're going to make it shine. I have faith."

Xander didn't want to tell him he didn't have faith in himself. He didn't want to tell him that running it alone hadn't been what Damon promised. But it was too late to say anything he didn't want to say, because Damon was walking away, and it seemed that even apologies weren't enough to save this.

Alone, in the middle of the garden where they'd first met over a year ago, Xander finally started to cry.

Chapter Sixteen

Damon sat in the car, eyes on the lights of the restaurant and on the solitary figure in the dark field, and cried. There were a hundred things he was thinking, but one particular frustration stood out above all the rest.

Why? Why him?

One of the first things he'd demanded after showing up in rehab was *why*. Why did he rely so heavily on alcohol? Why did having one drink make him want ten more? Why did life only exist in technicolor when he had a drink in his hand?

Grant, his sober coach, had looked at him frankly during one of their first sessions and had told him that there wasn't an answer to any of his questions, and that Damon was going to have to find a path to sobriety a different way.

That had pissed him off, and subsequently, he'd spent the last four years pissed off that he didn't know *why*. He'd gotten sober anyway, with determination and with Grant's support, but the whole time the questions had burned away inside him.

The questions were why he'd been out in the pouring rain, ripping up the vines in the first place. The questions were why, after Rachel, he'd been determined to stay single so that he wouldn't ruin any other lives besides his own.

For a little while, falling in love with Xander had brought happiness and joy and hope to his life, wrenching it from his boring black-and-white existence, and transporting it into technicolor reality for the first time since rehab.

It had been hard enough to find his way to sobriety and leave all that brightness behind when booze had been responsible, but love was a lot tougher to turn his back on. What he wanted was something he had no right to demand, but he couldn't seem to stop himself.

Xander didn't even know why Damon had walked away; it wasn't because he "fucked up" and said some stuff he wanted to take back. It was because the stuff he'd said brought all Damon's fears into the forefront.

There was a part of him that wanted to go see his father and demand an explanation, or maybe even apology. But he'd covered that after rehab. Nathan Hess took zero responsibility and had zero fucks to give that his son was an alcoholic. No amount of ranting or threats or tears were going to change his mind. Damon had stopped looking for answers from his father a long time ago because there were never any to find.

He glanced down at the phone in his hand and realized his fingers were trembling. He couldn't remember the last time he'd seen them shake like this—then it hit him. The last time, he'd wanted a drink so badly he could nearly taste the wine pooling on his tongue. Or the beer. Or the whiskey. He hadn't particularly cared what it was, only that it promised oblivion from feeling like this.

He couldn't pinpoint the time or the day, or even the month. It had become part of him, a background haze that he could ignore now because he wanted to be better more than he wanted the emptiness alcohol brought. But today?

Today and the fight with Xander had just reminded him of how easy it was.

Damon knew what he had to do. He called the person who had seen him at his worst and had still never judged him.

"It's been a long time, Damon," Grant answered, only letting it ring twice. "Is everything okay?"

Right after the two months Damon had spent in rehab, he and Grant had talked every day—sometimes multiple times a day. He'd supported Damon going to collect his vineyard inheritance when nobody else did. Grant's phone calls and texts and emails had gotten Damon through a lot of bleak nights, but in the year since first meeting Xander, they'd dwindled, especially as Damon became more confident in his sobriety.

By the time he hired Xander, he and Grant were only exchanging emails once or twice a month. And before, that was perfectly okay. Damon was fine, he didn't need Grant's help. The last email from Grant had mentioned that sometimes there were other, uncovered issues that stemmed from alcoholism, and he'd encouraged Damon to find a regular therapist.

Damon had thought Grant was full of shit until now. But clearly he had issues, or else why would he have left the man he loved to deal with the restaurant opening by himself? Why else would he have walked away tonight, even though it had hurt like hell to do it?

"No," Damon answered truthfully. "No, it's not okay. I'm not okay."

"Are you drinking?" Grant asked, his voice careful. "Do I need to come get you?"

"I'm sober." He took a deep breath. "In love. But sober. I just don't know how to deal with it. Sobriety I know, love is a complete fucking mystery."

Damon felt Grant's knowing smile over the phone line. "We talked about this. What happened with Rachel wasn't entirely your fault. Marrying so young, you'd already begun to drift apart by the time you started drinking more heavily."

"I know," Damon said, but he wasn't sure he really believed his own words.

"It doesn't matter if you have an addiction, Damon. You still deserve good things. Like finding someone to love."

Damon's voice was barely above a whisper. "How do I believe that?"

"Probably a lot of therapy, but I'll get you started since you called me first. Does this person love you back?"

Damon thought of Xander's destroyed face as he'd walked away. "I think so, yeah."

"Do you think they're a smart person? Intelligent? Thoughtful? Do you think they value their own happiness?"

"Of course I do," Damon snapped. He never would have fallen in love with Xander otherwise.

"Do you think they'd fall in love with someone who wasn't worthy of their love?"

"I know what you're doing." Damon knew the leash on his temper was short tonight; it was almost definitely because it had nearly killed him to walk away from Xander. Staying away completely had been impossible. He'd come because he couldn't be anywhere else. He'd stood in the garden for hours, watching the lights and the customers pour in, and then pour back out, happy and grinning, full from Xander's creations. Anger and envy had surged inside him, nearly bringing him to his knees, but what had actually done it was Xander showing up. Yes, he'd come here, but he'd never actually expected Xander to catch him.

"Then you know what I'm going to say," Grant said, always so painfully reasonable. "If the person you love sees something worthwhile and worth loving in you, then it must exist. You don't have to believe me. You just need to believe in them."

"I do," Damon whispered. He'd believed in Xander from the first moment they'd ever met, rain dripping relentlessly through his dark hair.

"Then you have your answer. You just have to *choose* to believe it."

"You make it sound so easy."

"It is that easy. You can do this, I have faith that you can. Now, tomorrow morning call one of the therapists I sent you."

"I almost called my dad, and I'm so glad I didn't," Damon confessed. "I'm glad I called you instead."

"I'm glad too," Grant said. "He's a waste of your time. You're never going to get a worthwhile answer out of him. You already know that. But this person you love, that's a different story. They deserve better; they deserve your best." He hesitated. "And don't tell me you're not capable of your best because you're an addict. We both know that's not true."

For the first time in days, Damon felt a spark of what Grant was describing.

"Yeah," he said. "Yeah, you're probably right."

Grant laughed. "I'm totally right. Now go fix this."

"I'm going to," Damon said. "There's just something I need to do first."

The security code to the vault was unchanged. Damon supposed he should be surprised, because of the hundreds of dollars of wine stored here, but his father was a creature of habit, and also egotistically believed that nobody would ever dare steal from him.

He looked up at the camera in the corner, and gave his father, who would be watching the security footage hours from now, a one-finger salute.

Nathan was damn lucky that the only thing Damon intended to steal from him was some alone time.

Pulling the door open, hearing the hiss of the pressure release, Damon stepped into the vault, and let the particular smell of wine barrels and dust wash over him. Even though he'd wondered if it might, it didn't make him desperate to pull a bottle from the shelf and drain it dry.

Maybe he was never going to get answers from Nathan Hess. Maybe he was never going to get answers at all, but he could still let go of his poisonous anger—and all the frustration that Nathan was never going to apologize. Not for being a shitty father, not for giving him booze at such a young age, not for making it seem like a perfectly normal part of every single day.

He walked around the vault, pulling out a bottle here, examining the label of another. The wooden racks didn't just hold the cream of the Hess collection, but also housed Nathan's personal wine collection. Even though Damon had been out of this lifestyle for years now, he could still recognize and appreciate the value of some of the bottles he was looking at.

An idea was beginning to form in his head. He didn't know initially why he'd come here—it had seemed like a good plan to go back to the beginning, and this had always felt like the start of it all. He'd been watching his father come in here for years, ever since he was a little boy, to pick out a bottle for a special occasion or even for a normal Tuesday night. He knew this place like the back of his hand. And maybe he'd been wondering if coming here, to the beginning of his own obsession with alcohol, would make it tougher to resist the draw of the oblivion so close at hand.

But all he felt was a vague disgust. He didn't want to be that man anymore, holding onto old, ancient baggage, with all its anger and its hostility and its uncertainty. He knew he wasn't going to drink anymore; Xander had been right about that.

"I don't want a drink," Damon said out loud, feeling a little lame, but also hoping that his father had installed sound with the sophisticated security system. "I really could give a damn if these are worth thousands."

He thought coming here would absolve him of all the guilt and the frustration, but all it showed him was that he'd absolved himself of it a long time ago, he just hadn't realized it. He'd already moved on; he just hadn't caught up with the fulfilling, happy life he was already living.

If he hadn't conquered the thrall of his addiction, he never could have dreamt of starting something of his own. He never would have built a new future for himself. And he sure as fuck wouldn't have fallen head over heels for Xander.

There were only two things he needed to do now before he went to Xander.

The first would have to wait until morning, but the second he could take care of right now. He looked right up at the other camera, smiled broadly, gave his father the second middle finger of the night and sauntered off.

"There's a lot of stuff about last night that we can celebrate," Miles pointed out, pouring another cup of coffee. They were sitting on the outdoor porch of one of their favorite brunch places, conducting a complete rundown of last night's preview success.

Xander knew they were trying to cheer him up, but it wasn't exactly working. Not after the way Damon had turned and walked away last night. The very worst was Xander knew how much it had hurt him, and he'd known just how much it was hurting Xander. And he'd done it anyway. Xander didn't know whether to be pissed as hell at Damon for attempting to ruin them, or leaving him on what was supposed to be the greatest night of his life—or for Damon believing that he didn't deserve Xander's love and support.

"You're not even listening to me," Miles said with a frown.

"I can't imagine why," Xander retorted back.

"We're just trying to . . . cheer you up," Wyatt said with one of his more optimistic, sunny smiles plastered to his face. "And if that fails, then distract you."

Xander reached for his glass and took a big sip of his peach mimosa. "Then distract me."

"You should be hydrating," Miles said with a frown at his glass. "You drank a lot of wine last night."

Yes, he had. He hadn't only done it to forget; he'd also done it as sort of a petty *fuck you* to Damon. Except he'd woken up this morning with a bottomless pit in his stomach, the victory from last night long since faded.

Xander switched his champagne flute for the water glass, and glared over the rim at Miles.

"Well, if you really want to be distracted," Wyatt said. "We can talk about what didn't go well last night."

He switched his glare from Miles to Wyatt. "What?" Wyatt exclaimed. "You need to know, since you're the general manager now."

"Speaking of that," Miles said. "You need to hire a front of the house manager. As awesome as it is for Wyatt and me to be handling that side of things, if Damon's not coming back, you're going to need someone."

Xander took a deep breath. Was he ready to face the possibility that Damon might not ever come back to the Barrel House? Not really, but he wasn't sure he had a choice.

Except the idea of doing it alone, without Damon being that steady and certain force behind him, was a nightmare. Xander wanted to bury his head in his hands and wail that he couldn't do it. Instead he finished the rest of his mimosa and set the glass aside with a decisive click.

"Do you think we could cancel the reservations tonight?" he asked.

"What?" Wyatt and Miles bellowed at exactly the same moment.

"I know I said there was stuff to work on," Wyatt continued. "But it's small stuff. For a preview, last night went so smooth. There's no reason to cancel the reservations."

Xander set his elbows on the table and leaned forward. "There is, if I never intend to open. I'm not doing this alone. I didn't sign on to do this alone."

There was total silence at the table.

"Are you kidding?" Miles burst out finally. "You can't do this, not now! Not when you're so close!"

"Miles is right," Wyatt said seriously.

"I should record this," Xander said. "I don't think you've ever said Miles was right, *ever*."

"Well, he's right *now*," Wyatt countered. "You've worked so damn hard to get to this place. Just think of how many shitty shifts you endured to be offered head chef. How many times did Aquino yell at you? Throw a plate at you? Are you really going to give up after you've finally gotten out from under him?"

"This isn't me giving up," Xander tried to tell them.

"It sure as fuck looks like it," Miles pointed out.

Xander glared but neither of them backed down.

"I just can't believe you're willing to throw this opportunity away because Damon let you down," Wyatt said with a shake of his head.

"He didn't just let me down, he broke my fucking heart," Xander burst out.

"We know," Miles said, reaching over and squeezing Xander's hand. "And I wish he hadn't. I want to go find him and chop his balls off, and shove them down his throat. But this isn't about him, Xander. This is about *you*. You're the strongest person I've ever met. The most driven. The most determined. You shouldn't let one guy's shitty behavior change that."

"You quit before you've even started, and you've let him win," Wyatt added.

Xander's gaze narrowed. "You know, you're a real asshole."

"What, me?" Wyatt asked with a faux innocent tone and a hearty laugh.

"You know me too well," Xander retorted. "You know exactly what will get me to the Barrel House tonight."

Miles shrugged. "To get you there, we're willing to play dirty. You've sacrificed too much to just give up now, and we love you too much to let you."

"Don't make me cry," Xander drawled, but inside he was feeling all warm and fuzzy. Who made it through life without friends like Wyatt and Miles? He might even consider adding Kian to the list, even though sometimes he wanted to twist his neck in frustration.

"We'll be there tonight," Wyatt said. "And we'll be there as long as you need."

"Next Friday, we'll be here until next Friday," Miles inserted with a grin. "And then you either have to pay us or hire someone else."

"Fine," Xander grumbled. "Now let's hear about the issues that need cleared up for tonight."

"You're going to need another mimosa," Miles said and flagged the waitress down.

❧❧❧❧❧❧ ❧❧❧❧❧❧

"Chef," Miles said, his voice respectful, but his eyes glittering with amusement. "I need to talk to you for a minute."

Xander glanced up. They were two hours into dinner service, and even though there were a few moments where he wanted to set down his pan and walk right out, sticking his best chef's knife in Damon's door for good measure, things were going even smoother than they had during the preview.

But Miles didn't just look amused, Xander realized as they walked toward the back, to the long prep tables by the refrigerators. The problem with having a large glass wall in between the kitchen and the dining room was that everyone saw everything. Xander typically didn't have anything to hide, except when his heart was broken and Miles was making *that* face.

"Everything okay?" he asked, dreading the answer.

"Do you want the bad news or the really bad news?"

Xander raised an eyebrow. "Really bad news first."

Miles still didn't say anything. "Okay," Xander corrected testily, "I guess I'll take the bad news first."

"Bastian Aquino is here. He wants a table."

"I don't care about that asshole," Xander said. "If he's decided to lower himself by eating at my humble establishment, you might as well give him a damn table."

"Damon is also here," Miles said, before Xander could really prepare himself. He'd sort of expected what Miles was about to say, but maybe there wasn't anything he could do *to* prepare himself.

"I can't talk to him right now. We're in the middle of service," Xander complained.

"Which is what I told him," Miles soothed, reaching up to put a hand on Xander's shoulder.

"But he's not going to continue to take no for an answer and you don't want him to cause a scene," Xander finished wryly. "Fine, tell him I can give him thirty seconds."

"You want me to bring him back here?"

"He decides to bail," Xander said firmly, "and he comes to confront me in the middle of opening night, when Aquino just walked in? He can say whatever he's come to say in front of God and everybody. I'll be in the kitchen."

Miles looked mildly impressed. The hand on his shoulder squeezed reassuringly. "You've got this," was all he said before he walked back out toward the front of the restaurant.

Xander was focusing on the food at the pass-through, making sure every single plate was picture perfect before the waiter picked it up to take it to the table.

"Xander," Damon said roughly, and Xander's fingers hesitated on a lacy nest of microgreens decorating the top of his eggplant parmesan. He didn't look up; suddenly he wasn't sure he could. Why had he thought this was a good idea? That speech of Wyatt and Miles' from earlier this morning, when they'd talked up how brave and hardcore he was, that's why. Xander mentally cursed them both.

"You have fifteen seconds," Xander said, his voice thankfully steady, but he still didn't look up. He was painfully aware that the whole kitchen had slowed down and all his employees were focusing more on the confrontation in front of them than their own tasks. But could he really blame them? Hell, *he* certainly wasn't focusing on his own tasks right now.

"Miles said I'd have thirty," Damon said, and the flippant edge to his voice just pissed Xander off. He did not get to waltz in here, no matter how shitty the things Xander had said were, and make jokes.

Xander glanced up and he knew his expression was hard as steel. "You got docked fifteen seconds because it turns out you're not the good guy here. You're an asshole."

Damon's eyes were bloodshot and he looked tired. Something uncomfortable bloomed in Xander's stomach. Was Damon drinking again? Had their fight pushed him away from his sobriety? As pissed as Xander was, he didn't ever want that for him. He loved him—still, always, *forever*—no matter what Damon had done. Even if Damon was an asshole.

"No," Damon said wryly, answering the question Xander hadn't asked. "No, I'm not drinking again, even if I look like shit. Apparently not sleeping for multiple nights in a row does that to you."

"I'm still waiting," Xander inserted testily. "I've got a job to do, a job you fucking hired me for."

"I know, and I'll leave you alone after this, to do it and do it brilliantly. I saw Bastian come in when I did, please make sure you knock his fucking socks off."

"Well?" Xander asked again. "I'm still waiting."

"I just didn't want you to go through tonight without you knowing. I love you." Damon said the words clearly and loudly, definitely loud enough for every interested party in the dining room to hear.

It shouldn't have mattered, not after his behavior of the last few days, but Xander felt his eyes fill. For so long this was exactly what he'd wanted—someone to love him with zero shame or embarrassment, and he'd finally found that.

Except that Damon had still massively fucked up the last few days, and Xander wasn't ready just yet to accept such a bad non-apology.

"I know," Xander said calmly. "I know you do."

"And I need to apologize?" Damon guessed with a heavy sigh. "I know I do. We'll talk after dinner, and I'll apologize the right way. I just wanted you to know I love you before you do this."

"We'll see if it's the right sort of apology first," Xander challenged.

Damon's face broke into a bright grin. "Oh, it's gonna be good."

Xander's hands stilled on the microgreens. "It better fucking be."

Turning around, Damon sauntered out of the kitchen and to Xander's surprise, he saw him walk over to where Miles was greeting guests at the host stand. They exchanged a few words, and Miles *left*, like he intended to give Damon the job he'd so callously forfeited.

"Chef," Billy said, suddenly right next to him. "Chef?"

Xander's gaze snapped over to him. He was still replaying watching Damon greet guests in a snazzy, sharp sport coat and jeans, one of his nicer plaid shirts underneath, smiling and shaking hands like he felt a real sense of pride in the Barrel House.

The pride that Xander had been convinced after the last few days that he'd felt alone.

Maybe things weren't quite as they seemed.

"What?" Xander barked.

"Nothing," Billy stammered. "I just . . . didn't realize you were involved with the owner."

Xander rounded on him. Was it nice that Damon had made that particular confession in front of everyone, so there was zero confusion about where he stood? *Yes*, but he also had zero intention of letting his staff turn into a bunch of gossipy grannies on shift.

"Right now," Xander bit off, raising his voice so every single employee could hear him, including Chris who washed the dishes, "Bastian Aquino is sitting in our dining room. You might have heard of him. He's the head chef at Terroir, he has Michelin stars, he's my old boss, and he's affectionately known as the Bastard. Just in case you thought your distraction was going to slide for one millisecond. Now, let's get to work."

"Yes, Chef," they replied in chorus.

"Damn right you will," Xander said, and did something he hadn't in two full days—he smiled.

❧❧❧❧❧❧ ❧❧❧❧❧❧

It had been a really great night, Xander realized as he rolled his shoulders and cracked his neck, releasing all the tension from so many hours bent over stoves and plates. Tonight, Bastian had proved there were rare exceptions to his Bastard nickname by even sending compliments back to the chef. He'd also said that he could tell Miles was working on his desserts, and his regular pastry chef better be up to Miles' level, or the quality was going to suffer when he went back to his real job and his real life.

But Xander had been in such a good mood that he'd just laughed. Bastian wasn't saying anything he didn't already know, and if he hadn't offered *any* criticism, then Xander would have believed he'd been taken over by the pod people.

The kitchen had been scrubbed clean, and the staff had slowly been departing, even Billy high-fiving Xander on his way out. He had a feeling that Billy wasn't going to quit if they never put wine on the menu. He'd bought in, and even though the waitstaff had reported a few odd looks and comments with no wine list on the tables, he felt like Napa was slowly buying in too.

It wouldn't be easy, but they could build something with a lot of hard work and dedication.

They, Xander realized. He was still thinking about the Barrel House as a joint effort, something he and Damon shared together. To know that for sure going forward, he was going to have to leave the safety of his kitchen and go find him.

He was nervous and apprehensive about it. What if Damon's apology wasn't as kick-ass as he'd promised? What if after hearing it, Xander still felt angry and betrayed? How were they supposed to move forward if he couldn't forgive?

And Xander wanted to move forward and put these two days of hell behind them so badly he could nearly taste it. The only problem was he couldn't do that if he didn't let Damon make his apology first. Besides, there was another apology that Xander still felt honor bound to make.

Whether Damon's reaction was deserved or not, Xander still hadn't had the faith in him that he should have. He'd been selfish and callous, and he needed to make that right.

He walked into the dining room, the lights turned down low, and when he didn't see Damon anywhere, ventured outside. There were lights on in the distance, where Damon's house sat, so he wandered that direction.

When he crested the slight ridge that hid the house from the restaurant parking lot, Xander froze.

There were candles on the table sitting on Damon's patio, the same setup that he'd had the first night Xander had ever cooked for him. The night that Xander had long believed was their first date. But it wasn't just the candles that stopped him, it was the wine bottle sitting on the table, a single empty glass next to it, glittering in the candlelight.

"What are you doing?" Xander nearly yelled, panic overtaking him as he raced down the ridge toward the patio. "You can't drink. Not like this. Not for me. God, please don't do this."

But Damon just smiled. "Don't worry," he said as Xander skidded to a stop next to the table. "I'm not drinking. The wine isn't for me. It's for you."

Xander sat down opposite him with a huff. He looked at the label, recognizing it as one of the most prized Hess vintages. One of the vintages that had helped Nathan Hess rule Napa.

"Where did you even get this?" Xander said, picking it up and reading the label carefully.

"My dad's vault," Damon said casually.

Xander looked up suspiciously. "Is this your really good apology? A thousand-dollar bottle of wine?"

"It's part of it," Damon said. "I know you haven't been drinking around me. I know you enjoy wine, and I want you to know that while what you said probably could have used better delivery, it was all true. I don't really want to drink anymore, not really. I don't want to be that man anymore. I want to be better; you *make* me want to be better. The last thing I want to do is hold you back from things you like doing."

"I never said I enjoyed drinking wine," Xander said. Which was technically true.

Damon laughed. "You never had to, sweetheart. I knew. I saw your face at Michael Mina, when they took the wine list away, and I realized then that I was the one holding you back. Then you tried to convince me, with a very logical argument, by the way, that we should serve alcohol at the Barrel House. And that's when everything I believed, deep down, came back in spades. I never believed that as an alcoholic I deserved happiness and hope and all that. I thought I'd fucked up my life, and nobody should get dragged down with me. Nobody else deserved it."

Xander opened his mouth to say that was complete and total bullshit, but Damon beat him to it.

"I know, that's such asinine crap," Damon said wryly. "I can't believe I took that to heart for so damn long. But I did, and I'm still fighting against it. I also want you to know that it's not going to change overnight, no matter how much I want it to. But I'm going to start seeing a therapist, who's going to work with me on this stuff. I'm going to be better. I *want* to be better."

"Wow," Xander said softly. "This *is* a pretty good apology. Except that you haven't really apologized yet." He shot a quick grin at Damon. "But maybe I can have some wine first?"

Damon poured it without a single tremble in his fingers. Maybe Xander shouldn't have believed him, but he did. He understood how it was so easy to believe that you were worthless and didn't deserve someone to love who loved you back. He'd believed that too, for a long time, and instead of figuring out he was wrong, he'd gotten angry and bitter. That's when Damon had found him—or he'd found Damon.

Xander took a long sip. The aroma was glorious, the flavor unmatched as it slid across his tongue. "This is really good wine," he said. "Is your dad going to kill you?"

Shrugging, Damon didn't seem particularly concerned. "I'm sorry I didn't believe more in myself, and that I didn't believe more in you," he said seriously. "If you give me another chance, I swear you won't regret it."

"I believe you. I believe *in* you," Xander said, either the emotion or the wine making his voice hoarse. "I love you."

"I know," Damon said, and his smirk made Xander's heart soar. "Now come over here so I can kiss you."

Xander wanted to and even got up from his chair because damnit, he wanted to kiss Damon too. It had only been two days but it had felt like an eternity. But then he looked over at his glass. He'd been drinking. He didn't know what Damon's tolerances were or what the rules *really* were.

"Oh, get over here," Damon said with the brightest laugh. "I poured it for you, didn't I? Do you trust me?"

"Forever," Xander said, coming over and settling on Damon's broad thighs. He linked his hands around his neck, pulled him close and kissed him.

EPILOGUE

Twelve months later

"How are you feeling?"

Damon leaned back on his therapist's couch and discarded the initial, defensive response because that wasn't going to get him anywhere. He'd learned from his weekly sessions that the sarcasm he was picking up from Xander did him zero favors with Amy.

"I'm good," Damon said.

Amy's eyes narrowed. He liked her because she didn't take any of his bullshit, and always said exactly what she meant. "Tell me more," she said, tapping her pen insistently on the yellow pad resting on her lap.

It was one of his therapist's favorite sayings, and Damon narrowly avoided gritting his teeth together. "Well," he said, "tonight is the big celebration dinner. We've been open a year, and haven't managed to kill each other yet."

"And?" Amy asked.

"And my father is coming because I invited him." Damon frowned at a stain on the rug in front of him. "I'm trying to figure out if I regret that yet."

"Why don't you tell me why you invited him?" she suggested. If he didn't know better, he'd think she enjoyed watching him squirm a little under her microscope of honesty.

"You know why I invited him," Damon retorted. "We discussed it for weeks."

"Tell me like I don't already know. Tell me like I'm a stranger."

"I want him to see what Xander and I have built together, and I want him to meet my boyfriend."

"If he doesn't appreciate what you built, and doesn't like Xander, will the evening be a disaster?" she asked.

Damon's mouth twisted into a wry smile. "I try not to let him ruin anything anymore. I guess if he comes and is his normal asshole self, I won't be very surprised, but I also won't be disappointed."

Amy smiled. Damon still found it a little terrifying, but he'd learned to trust it over the last year. Learned to trust *her*. "Does that help answer your question?"

He was never sure whether he loved or hated that every time he wasn't sure about something, she'd ask a handful of questions and his answers would always guide him to his own conclusion.

Damon shook his head. "How do you do that?"

"Practice. Now what else is going on?"

"Xander and I are still talking about selling alcohol," Damon admitted. "Neither of us can make a decision that sticks. Every time I bring it up, saying I'm good with it, he tells me that we don't need it. And vice versa."

"It actually sounds like you've found your decision," Amy said.

"I . . . I . . . guess so?" He hesitated. Considering how long they'd been discussing it, it seemed like the final answer to the question would have been more obvious, but this *was* a subject filled with a lot of personal baggage, and they were both wary of that baggage. But then, if a year had gone by and they still weren't serving alcohol, Amy was probably right. That *was* the answer.

"I know so," Damon finally said with a lot more certainty.

Amy nodded approvingly. "You've come a long way from the first time we met."

The first time they'd met, Damon had been a tsunami of guilt and low self-esteem, endlessly grateful that Xander still loved him and was willing to accept his apology, but not entirely sure how to move forward with that, and to be better for both of them.

"I can feel the confidence radiating out of you," Amy pointed out. "It's a whole different vibe. But the real question is, how do *you* feel?"

"I don't know that I feel all that different," Damon admitted. "I feel less guilty. I feel less like I'm going to fuck Xander's life up. I still look at him sometimes and think *god, I'm lucky*, but there isn't that fear with it that someday he'll figure out he's too good for me."

Damon thought for a moment. "Now it just feels like we're good for each other."

"The first time I met him, I thought that too," Amy said. "And I think you knew it. You just had to discover it for yourself."

"You really like to do that, don't you?" Damon asked with a long-suffering tone of voice, even though he would readily acknowledge to just about anybody else how amazing Amy was and how much of a difference she'd made in his life.

She laughed. "You know it."

Their session length usually varied. Sometimes, if the subject was difficult or hard to talk about, they'd only talk for half an hour. Occasionally Damon couldn't shut up, and they'd chat away for the full hour. Today was a shorter session, which despite discussing Nathan briefly, hadn't been particularly difficult emotionally.

As Amy walked him to the door, she put a hand on his shoulder. "I think you should consider going to every other week, despite how much I enjoy our weekly sessions," she said.

Damon glanced up in surprise. "Really?"

"You're doing great," Amy said. "And don't say you're not fixed, because you know from rehab that fixed and better aren't the same thing."

"I know," Damon agreed seriously.

She pulled him into a quick hug. "Come back in a few weeks."

Damon didn't always leave therapy feeling like a load of crap, but today he felt light and happy and like over the last year, he'd finally found the road he needed to walk on—and the person he wanted to walk on it with.

"You're smiling," Xander said as soon as Damon walked into the Barrel House. "I thought you were seeing Amy this morning." He walked down from where he was laying place settings at the gigantic table that ran the whole length of the dining room. Setting a table wasn't normally something Xander's staff let him do, but he'd forbidden anyone from coming into work today, insisting that this dinner—the Barrel House's one-year anniversary and also a celebration of the restaurant's unbelievable success—was something he wanted to do himself. Or at least with Damon's help.

The dinner was also a temporary goodbye as the staff went on a three-week paid sabbatical while David oversaw an expansion of the dining room and added a pizza kitchen which included an enormous wood-fired oven Damon had shipped from Italy.

As for Xander, he had demanded a vacation, and he and Damon were headed to southern Italy for a heavy dose of sun and great food, with a lighter dose of work scoping out new suppliers.

"I was," Damon said, and grinned even harder.

Xander raised an eyebrow. "Usually she makes you think too hard and I need to give you a wide berth." That was one of the reasons he hadn't liked the idea of Damon going to therapy today, because the truth was, Xander couldn't do everything, and he needed Damon's help to pull this dinner off. And Damon stuck in his own head was not usually a great helper.

"Not today," Damon said, pulling Xander into a tight embrace, his hands smoothing down the shoulders of his white chef's jacket. "Today was different. She even thinks I can go to every other week instead of every week."

"Really?" Xander couldn't help the surprise in his voice. Some weeks, Damon made it sound like he was still slogging through the worst of his low self-worth and family-inherited baggage. He'd been seeming lighter, and the fact that he'd wanted Nathan to come to this dinner had definitely signaled important change. But Amy thinking he could reduce his therapy sessions was huge.

"You sound happy."

Xander smiled. "I'm so happy that you're happy."

"I was never *not* happy," Damon said seriously. "You've always made me happy. But now when I'm just standing still, even lost in my own head, I'm content."

"Your gray is lighter," Xander pointed out.

"Together we're sort of a light taupe," Damon teased, pulling him even closer. "Now kiss me before I change my mind and we throw everyone out and celebrate just the two of us."

Xander did as requested, pressing his lips to Damon's, and the electrical surge he felt every time they kissed hadn't ever gone away. Even though it had been over a year since the very first time.

"Wait," Xander said wrenching away breathlessly as Damon tried to deepen the kiss while he stepped them backwards, back toward the bathroom. The same bathroom that they'd first told each other they were in love, all those months ago. Damon still had a real nostalgia for that particular bathroom.

Xander had a feeling when he proposed, he was totally going to do it in that bathroom, and he wasn't even going to be disappointed.

"Wait what?" Damon asked innocently, even though the way his dick was poking Xander's hip made it very clear that he had zero virtuous intentions for their trip to the bathroom.

"Did you really want to celebrate with just the two of us?" Xander asked. From the moment a month ago that he'd concocted this plan to throw a celebration dinner, Damon had seemed a hundred and ten percent on board, but he was always partial to anything Xander suggested.

It might be because he was crazy in love with him.

"No way," Damon said. "I fucking lugged in this table from the rental company *and* assembled it. This thing is happening, even if I have to pull people in off the street."

Xander laughed, and the tiny niggling doubt floated away like a cloud in a particularly blue sky. The same place all his doubts, the big ones and the small ones and the medium-sized ones, had all been going for the last year. Just when he thought he couldn't trust or love or adore Damon more, he opened more of himself up to Xander, and he fell just a bit harder.

It might have been annoying if Xander wasn't so damn happy.

"Then we'd better get this table set and then start on dinner," Xander said, reluctantly disentangling himself from Damon's arms before he could make do on all his unspoken promises and actually drag them into the bathroom.

"I guess if we're inviting people to dinner, they're going to need plates and silverware and glasses, and something edible in those," Damon said, definitely sounding disappointed.

"We run a restaurant together. It's been open a year," Xander teased, "and I feel like you're finally learning something about the food business."

"It's only because I have the best teacher," Damon retorted with a broad grin.

Damon surveyed the scene before him: employees and friends and even family—Xander's parents and his own father, deep in discussion at the quieter side of the table—sparkling water bottles and wine bottles intermingled across the surface, and platters holding the remainder of the meal he and Xander had made together.

Surrounded by people he loved—and people he had even learned to tolerate, like his father—he felt an inescapable swelling of rightness. However difficult the path had been to get here, he was here now, and the tougher parts of his life fell into place, giving the greater ones perspective.

He stood, Xander catching his eye from where he was surrounded by Kian, Wyatt, and Miles. Ryan, Wyatt's brand-new husband, was lounging next to them, half-lidded eyes following his lover wherever he went. Evan was there too, making notes on the back of a menu as he talked to Nate. Learning more about wine? Thinking about ideas to incorporate into their hit show, *Pastry by Miles*?

Damon tapped his glass once, then again, gathering everyone's attention.

"The first thing I want to say is welcome, and thank you for coming," he said. He hadn't always loved public speaking—or even tolerated it—but a bonus side effect from his therapy sessions with Amy was that he felt more naturally confident in expressing how he felt and what he wanted.

He definitely knew exactly what he wanted now, and just how he was going to get it.

There was a smattering of applause and Xander kept giving him narrowed looks that all said *what the fuck are you doing?* No, they hadn't planned on making any speeches, and Damon had initially been wanting to do this when they were in Italy, but sometimes the right moment came along. Wasn't it worse if Damon just let it pass them by?

"The second thing I want to say is that the Barrel House wouldn't be what it is today if not for every single person in this room. Xander and I couldn't have done this without you. Billy and everyone in the kitchen, I know you were skeptical at first. Fuck, we were both skeptical at first, too. But what I really wanted was to focus on Xander's brilliance, and you guys made that possible. I can't thank you enough for that."

Xander rose then. "And, somehow without drinking, my boyfriend still manages to be cheesy and a little bit maudlin." He walked over to the head of the table where Damon was standing and slung an arm around his shoulders. "I think what he's trying to say is that he's grateful for everyone sticking with us, especially during the shaky beginning."

"Not so shaky!" Wyatt called out, and he was smiling like crazy.

Xander shot him a look, as always fiercely protective of Damon. Damon couldn't have been more endeared if he was trying.

"We also have to thank Miles and Evan for sneakily mentioning how great the Barrel House is on their show," Xander continued. "If you'd asked for permission to name drop, I would have said no. But luckily for us, you didn't ask."

Miles mimed giving him a fist bump across the length of the table.

Xander turned to Damon, eyes glowing, and he knew this was the moment.

"There's actually a third thing," Damon said, reaching into his pocket and pulling out a small box. "I was going to wait and do this in Italy, but I just discovered that I want to share this with everyone we love."

Among whoops, Damon dropped to one knee and opened the box, revealing a simple platinum band. "I love you, I've loved you from the moment you walked out in the rain and asked me what the fuck I was doing. It turns out what I was doing was waiting for you."

Silence fell as Xander stared down at him, not saying a word. He didn't look unhappy exactly, but he also wasn't saying yes. Or no. Or *let me think about this for a damn second*. Damon's heart skipped a beat, and then another. He didn't move, giving the love of his life a moment to figure out what he wanted to say.

This was Xander, so chances were he had a lot to say.

Finally, he spoke, and instead of heartfelt tears or smiles, all he said was, "Why aren't you proposing in the bathroom?"

There were a lot of things Damon could do in response to that question. But truthfully, there was only one; he roared with laughter.

"The bathroom?" he asked incredulously.

"You love that bathroom," Xander countered, a glimmer of a smile on his face, eyes soft and warm. There wasn't a question of him saying no, it was more the venue that Damon hadn't quite gotten right.

"If you want a proposal in the bathroom, we'll go in there right now."

"You've got it," Xander said, and held out a hand to Damon, helping him up.

They walked past all the incredulous faces, and shut the bathroom door behind them, muting the excited chatter.

"Well?" Xander asked, raising his eyebrow the way Damon adored. "You're not going to get down on one knee again?"

"This is a small bathroom," Damon complained.

"Hasn't ever stopped you before," Xander pointed out cheerfully.

Damon laughed again. "One of the many reasons I love you. You don't let me get away with any bullshit."

"One of the many reasons I love you—you totally give in to *all* my bullshit," Xander retorted, but there were tears in his eyes now, and he pressed Damon against the door, kissing him the way he intended to for the rest of their lives.

A minute later, Damon came up for air, and pinned Xander with a look he'd learned from the source. "So was that a yes?"

"What do you think?" Xander asked, holding up his hand and wiggling a finger, which suddenly seemed to be sporting a silver band. Damon glance down to the box, and discovered he'd been so distracted by their first engaged kiss that he hadn't even noticed Xander take the ring out.

"Yes," Damon said, and pulled him in for another, even deeper kiss—lasting forever or eternity, whichever felt the longest.

The Spa Day

a Savor Me short story

"You really need to relax," Damon said, in a tight, tense voice that made it clear that *nobody* would actually be doing any relaxing anytime soon.

"I don't think *any* of us will be doing any relaxing," Xander said rigidly. "Besides, isn't the worst way to get someone to calm down, to *tell them* to calm down?"

"Uh." Damon hesitated. "No?"

"It's just the Michelin reps," Xander said through clenched teeth as he eyed them through the large glass partition that separated the Barrel House kitchen from the dining room. "What could go wrong?"

"Nothing," Damon said loyally, and Xander could see him nearly reach out to wrap an arm around Xander's shoulders. Xander knew he'd have done it too, if they'd been home alone, or if the dining room had been empty. But they were at the restaurant and it was packed, and while Xander might not normally give two shits about showing PDA in front of their clientele—if they didn't like it, they could fuck off, as far as he was concerned—the Michelin guys might feel differently.

And right now, all that mattered was Barrel House maybe getting its first star. The fact that the Michelin inspectors were here was news enough. Xander had acted as if their coming was inevitable, but secretly he had worried, late at night when he couldn't sleep, when Damon was snoring away next to him, that all his certainty would dissolve into embarrassment if they *didn't* come. But they had. It was hard to recognize them if you didn't know what you were looking for, but they were creatures of habit because the idea was to judge each restaurant on as level a playing field as possible.

When they'd come in, Damon had spotted them right away, then after seating them—in the prime table no less; the Barnsdales were just going to have to make do with the *second* best table tonight—Damon had hurried over to where Xander had been plating in the kitchen, carefully watching as each plate cleared the pass-through.

"They're here," he'd said quietly. "I'll serve them myself."

Xander had looked up and felt everything inside him condense into one big knot of anxiety. "No," he'd said. "Let Mari do it. She's a good server. We don't want to give away we know it's them." *Besides,* Xander hadn't added, *you're a mediocre server at best.* He hadn't said it because he loved Damon, flaws and all, and it wasn't *his* fault he was a terrible waiter, because usually the most serving he ever did was filling in for the occasional sick day.

"Yeah, yeah," Damon had agreed, nodding mindlessly. "I'll take care of it."

Mari had done an exemplary job with taking their orders, and as Xander had examined their choices, he'd become more and more sure that this was them. The infamous Michelin inspectors, who could make or break a restaurant with a single sentence in their guide. Stars were what everyone wanted: one was really good for an up-and-coming restaurant like Barrel House; two was amazingly good, and they reserved three for chefs like Bastian Aquino who ran his ship so tightly even the tablecloths were afraid of creasing in his presence.

Xander knew the best they could probably hope for was one star, but even that was potentially incredible and also career-making. It was all he'd ever wanted since culinary school; to be the head chef in his own establishment, and to earn Michelin stars. He'd gotten so much more than he'd ever dreamt of. Not only did he have the restaurant, but he had the love of his life working right alongside him. It felt like a fantasy sometimes, a dream that went on just a little too long, just long enough you knew it couldn't quite be real.

He'd been excruciatingly careful with the order, not even letting anyone touch the food except himself. He couldn't have earned this star without his staff in the kitchen, or without Damon's endless support and love, but if this star was going to be his, he was going to be the one to earn it.

When the dishes finally went out, carried in Mari's capable hands, Xander leaned back against the counter and tried to take his first real deep breath since the inspectors had walked into the restaurant. But it felt impossible to breathe because they were eating now, and then Damon had joined him, suggesting to him that he actually *relax.*

Relax. Like that was going to be happening while the Michelin inspectors ate his food.

"Hey," Damon said, turning to him, wearing a huge, proud smile on his face. "We did it. They actually *came.* Even if we don't get a star, we still did that. And we did that together."

Xander looked over at him, and couldn't help his own grin. "Yeah, we did, didn't we?"

"Did you ever doubt it?" Damon asked, even though he knew Xander through and through and undoubtedly already knew the answer.

"That they'd come?" Still, they might have been together going on six months now, but he wasn't going to make it easy for Damon—and Xander knew Damon wouldn't have it any other way.

Damon nudged him. "That we'd do it at all. That we'd open, that we'd be full every night. That we'd open for lunches. That you'd be talking about adding weekend brunch. And yes, that the Michelin dudes would come."

Xander leaned into him, just a little. Maybe not enough that the Michelin inspectors would notice. "They're not *dudes,*" he said in a hushed, dramatic voice.

But Damon just beamed. "Everyone's a dude to me, you know that."

Xander did. It was reason number two million six hundred thirty-five thousand and twenty-four why he'd fallen in love with him in the first place. Damon didn't stand on ceremony; the only reason he even cared about Michelin or the stupid stars was because *Xander* cared, and Damon wanted only the best for the man he loved and the restaurant they'd built together.

"At least a little respect might be in order," Xander said. "They could make or break us."

"Nope," Damon said, sounding supremely confident. "No way. We've already made it. Our dining room is full. Our margin is decent. We haven't had any turnover. You're happy. I'm happy. That's making it, baby."

Xander thought about this for a long moment. Everything Damon said was true. They'd built this place and then filled it, and kept guests coming back time after time. And even better, they'd managed to find a work-life balance that worked for both their restaurant and for them.

Still, those Michelin stars were everything he'd ever dreamt of; it was hard to let that dream go, even when a better one might beckon.

"It is," Xander agreed. "But I still want the stars."

"Then you'll get them," Damon said, supremely confident, watching as the Michelin "dudes" dug into their food.

What nobody had ever told Xander was that the waiting for the new guide to come out, for the phone call that would make all his hard work and his sacrifices worth it, was the fucking worst.

It was months, and as the weeks dragged on, Xander found his anxiety ratcheting tighter and tighter. What if, after all of this tense waiting, the call never came? What if he'd been tested and hadn't measured up? Xander didn't know how he'd deal with that.

It was clear that Damon knew that Xander was struggling; he'd started giving him more space in the kitchen at the Barrel House, because even Xander knew that his temper was fraying.

And at home? Things were much the same, even though Xander could acknowledge that he'd gotten shorter and testier. He knew he wasn't laughing at Damon's dumb jokes. He wasn't flirting the way he liked to with his boyfriend. Their sex life had taken on a distinctly intense, angsty desperation that Xander couldn't seem to turn off.

He kept telling himself that if he got the phone call, then everything would be fine. But every day that the phone call didn't come, the worse it began to feel, until one day, Xander woke up and didn't even want to go into work. He wanted to pull the pillow back over his head and go back to sleep. Maybe if he ignored everything that was giving him so much hell, it might just go away.

But that wasn't the way life worked.

"Are you okay?" Damon asked cautiously as Xander stumbled, bleary-eyed, into their kitchen a few hours later. He'd already texted his sous chef that he wasn't coming in today, and the good news was that Xander had specifically hired someone who could manage well enough without him. It wasn't like Xander didn't take days off occasionally, but he usually did so for a reason. And he knew the only good explanation for this was that he couldn't face going into the restaurant and all those judging stares. Not for another day.

"I'm not sick, if that's what you're asking," Xander said morosely, opening the refrigerator door and then closing it again almost immediately. He didn't want to cook, he didn't want to sleep, it felt like he was going out of his skin with all this anxious energy.

"I know you aren't," Damon said carefully. "But there's more than just being physically sick."

Xander nearly accused him of calling him "mentally sick" but that was a step too far, even for Xander. He'd pushed Damon plenty of times, but never that far. He'd never wanted to before, and the fact that he'd been tempted was really evidence of how out of control he was.

"I'm a mess," Xander said, collapsing onto the living room couch. "A fucking wreck."

Damon left the kitchen and detoured into the living room, propping a hip on the edge of the couch. "Yeah, you kinda are. I think you need to figure out a way to relax."

Xander rolled his eyes. "I don't know if you've noticed, but the sex isn't helping. And I can't believe I'm actually admitting that."

"I know," Damon said wryly. "I figured that out, too, actually." Of course he had; Damon was way too astute to have missed it. "I'm not talking about sex. I have another idea, if you trust me?"

It wasn't even a question; there was nobody Xander trusted the way he trusted Damon. "Of course."

"Then I'll make a call. Put on some loose clothes and get ready to go. Your hair . . ." Damon waved in the direction of Xander's head, barely containing his smile.

"Yeah, yeah," Xander said, brushing it back from his forehead. "I'll fix it."

"Okay good." Damon leaned down and kissed him briefly. "I'll be right back."

❧❧❧❧❧ ❧❧❧❧❧

If he'd been in a different kind of mood—AKA a normal kind of mood—Xander might have tried to eavesdrop on Damon's conversation so he could figure out where they were going. He didn't really like surprises and Damon knew it, but there was a reason why Damon hadn't told him and Xander figured that was solely because he never would have agreed to whatever it was.

Massage? Acupuncture? Energy healing? Xander wasn't sure he believed in the relaxing properties of any of that, but he was willing to try just about anything.

When he finished dressing and taming his hair, he walked back out into the living room and Damon was waiting for him.

"All ready?" Damon asked.

"Am I going to hate this?" Xander asked plaintively.

"I don't know," Damon said, "I've never done it before, but I've heard good things. At the very least, I'm not asking you to do anything I wouldn't do with you."

"You're going to do it too?" Xander wasn't sure why he was so surprised. Damon had never been the kind of guy who shoved you in face-first without holding your hand and falling in with you. It was yet another reason why Xander loved him.

"Of course I am," Damon said with a quicksilver grin. "You ready to go?"

"I'm never going to be more ready," Xander muttered, and they walked out to Damon's truck.

The drive was not short, and at first that made Xander more anxious, causing him to tap his fingertips against his thigh impatiently, until Damon had shot him a look.

"Sorry," Xander said, "it just turns out I'm shitty at waiting for things."

Damon chuckled. "I know. It's been a little hard to miss. But we're almost there."

A minute later he turned the truck onto a side street, a discreet sign identifying the nondescript building making Xander's eyes grow wider. "We're doing a *mud bath*?"

"Yeah," Damon said, nodding enthusiastically. "It's supposed to be relaxing for both body and soul."

"Okay," Xander said. He wasn't sure how he felt about the idea of a mud bath, but he'd already told himself that he was willing to do whatever Damon suggested. At least this suggestion didn't involve needles?

The spa itself seemed relaxing as they walked in. Damon gave his name, which naturally got a double-take, since they were still in Sonoma County. Xander saw Damon make a little grimace at the note of deference in the receptionist's voice, and he knew that despite all the progress Damon had made over the years, he still disliked being a Hess.

"This way," she said, pointing towards a doorway. "We'll take you to the mud room first."

"The mud room?" Xander questioned under his breath. Remembering, even though this was the worst possible time, the first time he and Damon had ever met, and how they'd stripped down, soaked to the skin, in the little mud-slash-laundry room in Damon's house.

Xander had never imagined that they'd ever see each other after that night. He'd definitely never imagined that they'd end up partners and lovers and intertwined in so many different, unique and wonderful ways that he wasn't always sure where he left off and Damon began.

With anyone else it'd have been claustrophobic and a little *too* connected, maybe, but with Damon, it was just right.

The woman ushered them into a room entirely covered in tile, with a rank, rich smell coming out of the huge pits of mud set into the middle. "This is the mud room," she said, closing the door behind her. "It'll be the first step in your process today. First, you'll need to undress, and then carefully slide into the hot mud."

"It's hot?" Xander asked, eying the big pits dubiously. He really didn't want to get anywhere near them, but he would have to get a lot more than just *close*.

"Oh yes, it's very warm," she said, smiling. "It's got a set of heaters at the bottom of the pit, so it'll get warmer as you sink further down. But be careful to not touch the bottom with your feet, because it'll burn you. You'll want to use the concrete edge to swing your butt in and out of the mud, instead," she suggested.

"Right," Xander said, staring at the pit with concern. Burning hot mud. Okay then. Still, it could've been needles; that would've been way worse. Right?

Xander wasn't quite sure anymore.

"You'll want to stay submerged in the mud for twenty or so minutes," she continued. "There's a clock over here." She pointed to an inset clock, high on one wall. "And after, please shower back here." Part of the room had been separated by a thin, translucent shower curtain, and Xander saw showerheads behind it. "After you are free of all mud, we'll proceed to the mineral bath."

"Is that at least a little cleaner?" Xander muttered under his breath. The guide just smiled.

"I'll let you two get started," she said. "I'll be back in about thirty minutes."

When she closed the door behind her, Xander's gaze met Damon's. "Are you sure about this?" Xander asked.

"Honestly, no?" Damon said with a chuckle. "But we're doing it. At least the weirdness might help you forget for a little bit about . . .well, you know."

"I know," Xander said. Maybe Damon was right; maybe this would help him forget about his anxiety and stress for at least thirty minutes. Even that reprieve might be worth getting into a hot tub of mud.

"I guess we should get going," Damon said and began unbuttoning his plaid shirt.

Normally there was nothing Xander liked better than to watch his boyfriend undress, but usually there were much more pleasurable activities that followed the undressing.

Still, Xander pulled his own t-shirt over his head and pulled down his loose athletic shorts, stowing his clothes, including his shoes and socks, on one of the wooden benches against the wall. With trepidation, he approached the closest mud pit.

"Don't look so excited about it," Damon teased, as he headed towards his own. "Now how are we supposed to do this again?"

"I think we're supposed to sit on the edge and kind of . . .*swing* over?" Xander suggested. "Just don't touch the bottom. That much I got."

Xander watched as Damon did it, looking like a fucking piece of Roman statuary as he flexed his biceps, using his strength to plop his ass right into the mud.

"Ah!" he yelped, and Xander nearly came to his rescue—because that was what true love did, right?—but what stopped him? All this fucking mud.

"Is it okay?" Xander said, gingerly sitting on the side of his own pit. "Am I going to die?"

"No, but it's weird," Damon said. "She said it was hot, but I really didn't think about what hot mud would feel like."

"Let me guess," Xander said, taking a deep breath and beginning to scoot over, his ass hovering right over the oozing mass, "it feels way fucking strange."

"Just about," Damon said wryly as he slowly sank down into the mud, his body disappearing one little bit at a time as gravity did its job. "Just try it. It's . . .you'll get used to it."

"Fuck," Xander bit off as his ass touched the hot mud for the first time. "Fuckity fuck fuck," he yelled. "I'm not getting used to this!"

He looked over and Damon, the backstabber, was *laughing,* as his body mostly disappeared from sight, buried in the mud.

"God, I hate this," Xander said vehemently as his body began to sink too. "And it *smells.*"

"I think it's supposed to," Damon offered. "I think that's part of its benefits."

"The smell?" Xander said with disbelief. "How does that *help* you?"

"I honestly do not know," Damon admitted. "I'm . . .this whole thing is not what I expected."

"Seriously," Xander said. He found as he relaxed into the mud though that he felt buoyed and light, floating and suspended in its mass. "I want to fight anyone who said this would center my chi."

Damon laughed again, and Xander found himself laughing too, despite the mud surrounding him.

"I'm not sure it's supposed to center your chi," Damon said, still giggling.

"Well, it's fucking not working," Xander retorted, smacking a mud-covered hand on the concrete side of the tub, a big blob falling off his wrist and landing on the tile floor with a loud *splat.*

"Fuck, that sounded weird," Damon said, and he was laughing again.

"Are we just supposed to . . .sit here? Lay here?" Xander wasn't sure what exactly you called being submerged in mud.

"I guess," Damon said, shrugging, his shoulders moving under the mud.

"Okay, well, here goes nothing," he said, wiggling further down, gasping as his body hit a hotter pocket of mud. He leaned his neck back on the concrete headrest and tried to close his eyes, but frankly, after even thirty seconds, he already knew this wasn't the relaxing solution he'd hoped it would be. How could it possibly be?

"I don't know about you," Damon said, his bluish-green eyes dancing with amusement as he glanced over at Xander, "but I keep sinking."

"I think that's the mud's way of telling me I feed you too much," Xander said.

"Maybe," Damon said, chuckling. "Definitely possible. Besides, muscle weighs more than fat."

"It's like a fucking black hole of mud, sucking us to hell," Xander complained, because he, too, was now sinking further than he felt entirely comfortable with. He kept having to brace his forearms, more mud falling off him in unceremonious *plops* to prevent his entire body from sinking down further.

"I feel like that introduction didn't prepare me for this." Damon's forearms were braced on the edges too, and he was flexing in such a distracting way that suddenly Xander was disappointed there was about a thousand gallons of mud between them. They'd used to laugh through sex—drunk on happiness and love—before the Michelin inspectors had come, and he thought, *just maybe*, they could actually do it again.

"Yeah, she was pretty nonchalant about it," Xander agreed. "Hey, just spent twenty minutes of your life, trying not to drown in the boiling hot mud—*oh*, and make sure you don't touch the bottom of the pit either, because your feet might fry."

"Not exactly a recipe for relaxation," Damon agreed with a charmingly helpless smile. "I'm sorry this wasn't what I thought it might be."

"Don't be," Xander said and discovered he actually really meant the words. "This is more fun than I've had in ages."

"Really? Me too," Damon said.

"Imagine that." Xander let out a huffed laugh. "We needed to come to the *mud baths* of all places, to find something fun again."

"I don't think we'll have to go this far again," Damon said, his gaze a caress against Xander's mud-smeared cheek.

"Me either," Xander said, and suddenly he *did* feel relaxed. Terrified, too, of the boiling hot mud at the bottom of the pit, and also wondering how on earth he would ever get mud out of every crevice it had seeped into—but overall, this was what they'd needed. To get out of their own heads for a few hours. To remember a time when they'd laughed and loved and not given a single shit what anyone else thought.

"Do you think we can get out now?" Damon wondered.

"It hasn't been twenty minutes," Xander said, pointing to the clock, though he too was just about ready to get out of this pit.

"And?" Damon asked. "Do you really think you can get all this mud off in only ten minutes? Because I sure as hell don't."

"Good point," Xander said dryly. "I guess we can begin the . . .*de-mudding* now." He braced his hands on the concrete edge and tried to pull himself out of the mud. "Fuck!" he exclaimed. "This is a lot harder than it seemed."

"Ugh, yeah," Damon agreed, and when Xander glanced over, he could see that his boyfriend was struggling less, but he was still struggling to yank his body out of the mud. "This sucks." He finally pulled himself clear, and Xander couldn't help it; he burst into gales of laughter as Damon stood on wobbly legs and mud began to fall off him in huge blobs, dripping viscerally as he walked over to where Xander was still half-submerged in the pit.

"Need some help, babe?" Damon asked dryly. "Or maybe you'd like to stay in there a bit longer?"

"I'm good, thanks. Get me out of here," Xander said. He offered an arm up and between the two of them, pulling hard, they managed to extricate Xander from the sucking mud pit.

"This is just . . . truly gross," Xander said, walking naked to where the showers were. He could hear and *feel* himself shedding mud, each clump landing with one nasty sounding *plop*.

Damon flipped the other shower on. "I'm just trying to figure out how anyone could ever advertise this as a 'fun couples' experience," he said.

"What," Xander said flatly, beginning to wash away all the most obvious encrusted mud bits. "That's what they told you? *Seriously?*"

Damon nodded wryly. "Seriously."

"They're on crack," Xander burst out. "Like, actual *high-as-a-fucking-kite* crack."

Damon burst out laughing as he used his hands to slough off all the extra mud, the water finally beginning to run clean. At least clean*er*.

"But," Xander added, because he'd learned a long time ago that being honest with the man he loved was always the right route to take, "I *do* feel better, even though this wasn't anything like I expected it'd be."

"It wasn't for me, either," Damon admitted. "But I'm glad. We were both kinda . . . going out of our minds there."

"No," Xander admitted with a chuckle. "No, that was just me. Definitely *only* me, but I appreciate you trying to be nice about it."

Damon ducked his head under the water and finished rinsing off. Xander flipped off his water and then Damon's. Damon smiled as Xander leaned over and brushed a clean-ish kiss to his mouth. "I think we both kinda smell like . . ."

"Mud?" Damon supplied. "Yeah, we kinda do."

There were robes hanging on a hook near the door, and they slipped them on. They were cozy and comfortable, basically the opposite of the entire experience so far, but as they waited for the lady to take them to the next room, and Xander cuddled against Damon's bigger, bulkier frame, he thought that playing hooky from work had never felt so unexpectedly good.

The sound of a knock on the door resounded through the tile-lined room. "Oh good, I can't wait for what we get next," Damon said under his breath.

Xander elbowed him as he stood and walked towards the door. "You've already submerged yourself in mud, how bad could it be?"

"Hey," the woman said after Xander opened the door to her cheery, overly enthusiastic smile. "How was the mud bath?"

"Enlightening," Xander admitted.

"Oh, good!" she said, clearly taking the more positive connotation to his reply. "Let's go get you situated in the mineral baths. These are fun. A nice relaxing time."

"Sounds like it," Damon said, his face so straight as they followed her out of the tiled mud room and down the hall that Xander knew he was being sarcastic.

She showed them into another tiled room, but this one had a small circular tub in it, similar to a hot tub in style. "I'll let you soak in here for about half an hour," she said. "There's towels on that bench."

"What?" Damon said when she left, closing the door behind her, "no instructions on how to climb in and out? No heaters to avoid? No mud to wash off?"

"It actually *sounds* relaxing after the last room," Xander admitting, shedding his robe and climbing into the water, exhaling in happiness at the perfectly warm temperature and the cool fizzy bubbles that enveloped his body as he sank in.

"Oh, this is nice," Damon agreed as he floated next to him. Xander leaned over and rested his head on Damon's shoulder.

They were quiet for a moment until finally Damon said, "Do you want to talk about it?"

Xander had a very good idea of what the subject was, but he still played dumb. "Talk about what?"

Damon made a rumbling noise of frustration, and Xander decided that he'd been pushed far enough—both with his behavior in the last few weeks, and now the mud bath—so he took pity on his boyfriend. "No, but I guess we should."

"Yeah," Damon agreed. "We should."

Xander took a deep breath and floated deeper into the pool, letting the fizzy bubbles leech away his anxiety. "I'm afraid we won't get it and I'm afraid we will. I'm not sure what the future holds and . . .and it scares me."

"I know," Damon said, wrapping his arms around him. Xander followed suit by wrapping his legs around his boyfriend's waist. "But we're going to be fine.

Even if the restaurant closed tomorrow, even if we never get any stars, even if all our fields burned down, I know we'd deal with it together, and that's what matters to me."

"I know," Xander said, and he *knew* it, so why did he feel like he'd be a failure if he didn't win any stars?

"But I get this is a big deal to you, personally. Not everything is about our relationship," Damon said, and Xander let out the breath he hadn't quite realized he was holding.

"We're partners, though," Xander said, playing the devil's advocate, even though he just wanted desperately to take Damon's words at face value.

"Yeah, and you're the creative genius, which means this shit *matters*," Damon said. "And that's okay."

"Even when I become a neurotic mess?" Xander asked hopefully.

"Especially when you become a neurotic mess," Damon said, leaning over and pressing a kiss against Xander's bicep. "I love you. Michelin stars or no. But because I love you, I want you to have what you need."

"I love you too," Xander said, and he felt like he was breathing easier than he had in a month. "And if we don't win them this year, we will the next. We're just getting started, you know."

"I know," Damon said, certainty radiating out of his words.

And Xander wondered . . .it had only been six months since they'd gotten together, but Damon had been making statements like that, and he had to wonder if Damon was considering making their partnership a more permanent one.

"Hey," Damon said, when Xander fell quiet, "are you really okay?"

"I will be," Xander admitted. "Honestly, it's just the waiting. It's . . .it's hard."

"I know," Damon said, and it sounded like he was talking about something else entirely.

It turned out that Xander had to wait another three days. One morning, very early, when Damon had already left for the garden, and Xander was contemplating hitting snooze on his phone alarm one more time, even though it was a baking day at the restaurant, the phone rang, deciding for him.

"Hello?" Xander answered hesitantly. He didn't recognize the number.

"Hello, is this Xander Bridges?" the pleasant voice asked.

"Yes," Xander said.

This was it, he thought, *everything changes now.*

"I'm really pleased to be able to tell you that this year's Michelin Guide has awarded you with one star for your restaurant, Barrel House."

Xander felt hot and cold all at the same time, his heart palpitating with the excitement and the sudden realization of this lifelong dream. "Thank you," he managed to get out.

"It was our pleasure," the voice said. "Look for the guide coming soon. We'll send an advance copy."

"Of course, of course," Xander said, but he was already upright, racing through the house, phone loosely near his ear, searching for his shoes—because what he needed, more than anything else, was to find Damon *right now.*

Finally he located a pair of Damon's old galoshes by the back door—the ones he liked to wear when it had rained for three days straight and the garden was a mud pit.

He shoved his feet into them and launched himself out the back door, still making meaningless conversation with the woman on the phone.

Now she was reading him the entry and he heard words like "casual but elegant" and "exceptional rustic Italian-inspired" and "best focaccia" and even "non-alcoholic beverages." Everything he'd ever dreamt of her saying, but the truth was, it wasn't all him. He'd done it, of course, but he'd have never done it without the single most important person in his life: the man he loved.

"That sounds great," Xander said, breathing hard as he raced through the backyard towards where the garden started. Damon had the hose out, the water shooting out of it in wide swaths of crystalline droplets, floating through the air in a net of sparkles. He turned when he heard Xander's footsteps and for a single shared moment, they stared at each other, Xander's expression and the fact that he was out here at six in the morning wearing Damon's galoshes telling him everything he needed to know about what Michelin had decided.

"I have to go," Xander said and clicked his phone off, sliding it in his pocket and racing towards Damon.

They collided in a heap of arms and legs, but Damon was unbelievably solid—wide and strong and built like a fucking tree, something that could withstand even the hurricane that Xander was. He kept them upright and murmured as he hugged Xander tightly, "I knew you could do it, I *knew* you could."

Xander shut his eyes tightly, happiness cascading through him. "*We* did it," he corrected Damon firmly. "It was us. Together. Unstoppable. Always."

Damon's hands tightened around Xander's waist and he knew then it was only a matter of time. This was a partnership that neither of them would ever tire of or want out of. It was forever.

Indulge Me

BETH BOLDEN

CHAPTER ONE

"DID YOU HEAR WHO'S coming in today?"

Kian Reynolds barely glanced up from the reduction he was stirring on the enormous industrial stove. He'd let his sauce scorch in the last class because he'd let himself indulge in some of the gossipy chatter, and he wasn't going to make that mistake again. He wasn't here to make friends; he was here to learn to cook.

"It's Aquino. Bastian Aquino."

Kian's gaze drifted up for a split second before he could stop himself. "It's *Chef* Aquino," he corrected. "Isn't he the head chef at Terroir?" Mark, one of the mouthier guys in Kian's class, snorted. "Isn't he? Don't you know, Reynolds?"

What Kian knew was that almost every student at their culinary academy was desperate to get the internship Chef Aquino was offering to their graduating class. As for Kian, he had already set his sights a lot higher. Napa was all well and good—Terroir, Chef Aquino's restaurant, even had a few of the coveted Michelin stars. New York City was absolutely aspirational. Chicago and San Francisco were definitely the homes of great culinary minds. But Kian knew how good he was, and he was going to accept nothing less than an apprenticeship in London or Paris.

Graduation was only a month away, and he'd sent off his applications, and now all he had left was waiting for the replies—*and*, he added, stir this reduction and try to fend off some of the nastier gossip.

Kian had figured out very early in their three years of training that not many of his fellow students liked him. His mom claimed their dislike was based entirely in jealousy, and while Kian could definitely see that point of view, it didn't make him feel any better when the snide comments and sideways glares started.

"I know who Chef Aquino is," Kian finally said, keeping his voice steady and calm. It was hard to live in Napa and avoid Bastian Aquino's existence.

"Funny, considering you're the only student in our class who didn't apply for Terroir's internship," Mark sneered.

"You're not even supposed to know that," Kian said. "Recommendation letters are private."

"Hey!" Mark held up his hands in mock surrender. "Sue me, I overheard two chefs discussing how weird it was that such an . . . *exemplary* student didn't apply."

He's just jealous, Kian told himself, but it didn't really help take the sting out of Mark's words. Maybe he *was* dumb. Maybe he shouldn't have skipped every job opportunity on this continent in a fit of artistic superiority. Except he knew he had exceptional natural skill that the instructors here had taken the opportunity to hone. Over half the teachers had personally suggested some of the restaurants he'd applied to in Europe. He stirred his reduction, eyes focused on the velvety texture, waiting until it was precisely the right consistency. Was he being obnoxiously cocky if it was true?

"Maybe you're just worried you wouldn't be able to keep your hands to yourself. He might be old, but Aquino's still pretty damn hot."

Kian knew Mark was gay, and it was no big secret how attractive he thought Chef Aquino was. He'd also made no secret out of the fact that he'd wanted Kian to suck his dick, but Kian had put a very quick end to that possibility.

He wasn't going to tell his mom that, but Kian believed that *jealousy* probably accurately characterized both problems Mark had with him.

"If you want to follow Chef Aquino around like a puppy dog, picking up his laundry and picking up the dishes he breaks every service, why should I stand in your way?"

Kian wasn't proud of losing his temper, but after three years of listening to that asswipe Mark, sometimes it was hard to reel it in. Today was apparently one of those times. Still, he'd assiduously watched his reduction the whole time, unlike the last time when he'd very vaguely scorched it during another "discussion" with Mark. Plus, Mark was *still* speechless, which Kian was definitely going to count as a win.

"I'd like to think the job is a little more than just kissing my ass," a deep voice announced, and Kian glanced up from his reduction and nearly dropped his wooden spoon right into the pot.

It was Chef Bastian Aquino in the flesh, and he was so much *more* than Kian had ever imagined.

He'd gone to a very small combination junior and senior high school in southern Oregon. His town had less than two thousand people in it. Even Napa could be small, especially when you were like Kian and kept to a strict routine of school and then the tiny studio apartment he was renting. He hardly ever did anything, ostensibly to save money for Europe, but mostly because nobody ever invited him out.

The result of all work, no play was that Kian had never met anyone who walked into a room and sucked every bit of air out of it.

Chef Aquino was magnetic, his dark eyes intense and his features generous but delicate, like they'd been sculpted by a master. He wore a simple blue blazer and an old Rolling Stones t-shirt with his jeans and made them look like high fashion. Kian could barely tear his eyes off of him, but he had to know if he was alone in wanting to drop to his knees. When he glanced around, it turned out that he definitely was not the only one. Even Marta, who made no secret about being asexual, looked fairly shell-shocked.

The man in front of him exuded mastery. You'd trust him to roast the most perfect duck breast, and you'd trust him to take you to bed and demolish you in the best way. Kian gulped air, but his lungs still felt empty. Like Bastian Aquino had command over even the elements.

He sauntered forward, casually but clearly aware that he owned the room. Kian realized as he stopped in front of him that he was completely used to owning every room—and every *kitchen*—he stepped into.

"Nothing to say to that?" he asked, raising a single dark eyebrow. He had a faintly exotic accent in the corners of his voice, and Kian ordered his knees not to automatically buckle.

Knowing the chef expected an answer and almost definitely an apology, Kian opened his mouth and shut it again. His mind was one long, circling litany of *stupid, stupid, stupid,* and he couldn't seem to break out of it, or break free of Aquino's spell.

That's what it was, right? Kian thought desperately. A spell of some kind. Aquino was a culinary magician, who cast spells on anything and *anyone* he wanted.

"I'm sure it's a . . . lot of work," Kian finally managed to force out of his uncooperative mouth.

Chef Aquino nodded once, succinctly and surely. And Kian knew that he'd work you hard and long hours, and that he would be an insanely exacting boss—and that he'd adore every impossible moment.

Suddenly, he wasn't sure he couldn't go to Europe. Could he leave Napa and get a job in London or Paris, while knowing that a man like this existed? And that he could have worked for him?

Desperation forced another sentence out. "I'm sure you're looking for the best, the most dedicated student for your internship, Chef," he added. *And that's me*, he added wordlessly. *Maybe it should be me.*

Of course he'd had no clue what Bastian Aquino was like so he'd never applied for Terroir's internship. Michelin stars in America? He could remember saying scornfully to someone that they must be easier to earn here, anyway.

In this moment, with Bastian Aquino's eyes taking him apart molecule by molecule, he wanted to drop to his knees and plead forgiveness for that rash comment. Because of course, even though they'd never met before and Aquino had no clue who he was, somehow he *must* know Kian had said it.

"I bet you know who that'd be, wouldn't you?" Aquino didn't even seem interested in hearing who Kian thought it was; he'd clearly meant it patronizingly and that might have stung, except that he reached out and tapped Kian reassuringly on the shoulder.

The contact was electric. Kian felt like he'd just been plugged into the closest outlet and then switched on high, like one of those gigantic commercial mixers that whirled away, fast as lightning, no matter how thick or goopy the dough was in their bowls.

Even Aquino seemed to react, which Kian couldn't quite believe because *of course* it was only him that had experienced the live current between them. But Chef flinched and withdrew his hand quickly, the echo of the feeling reflected in his eyes.

"It would be me, Chef," Kian said quietly.

But Aquino turned away without saying a word and left the room with Chef Charles. Kian could only think that his shot had passed as quickly as it had begun. He could go to one of the instructors and beg to apply for the Terroir internship, but after all his disdain about any job opportunities in North America, he had a feeling that was going to be pointless. But they wouldn't understand that the concept of leaving for Europe while Mark or another one of those useless idiots became Bastian Aquino's personal intern was intolerable. It shouldn't have hurt. He'd only spent five minutes staring helplessly at the man, but somehow it meant more than that and Kian was left believing that he'd always regret not trying harder.

The smell of his reduction wafted up and hit his nose just as he realized that he'd neglected stirring it for the aforementioned five minutes.

Kian picked up his spoon and gave it an experimental stir. It was definitely dark brown in spots, nearly black in fact, and the undeniable scorched smell told him the whole story. He sighed; he was going to have to start from scratch on the three-hour process.

Mark walked over and peered into Kian's pot. He sniffed, his exaggerated grimace making him look even uglier than his personality did. "Forget about it again?" he asked. "Told you Bastian was hot."

"Chef Aquino," Kian said stiffly, dumping the contents of the pot into the garbage at the end of his station. "He's not some dudebro you're casual acquaintances with. He's a . . . he's a . . . a . . . " Kian struggled to put his feelings about Chef Aquino into words—especially words that Mark couldn't exploit later.

"He's dreamy? He's hot? You want to worship the ground he walks on?"

"This isn't *Grey's Anatomy* in the kitchen," Kian retorted, trying to hide that he'd had *all* those thoughts. "He's not Chef McDreamy."

"He could be," Mark speculated as Kian walked over to the pantry and picked out more ingredients for his reduction. Mushrooms, shallots, garlic, thyme—he dumped them all in his bin. "*You* want him to be, and you didn't even want to work for him."

It was annoying his face was so goddamned transparent. Chef Aquino had probably realized it as well, but then people probably obsessed about him all the time, so it wasn't like Kian was alone in feeling that way.

"I still can't believe you were the only one in our class who didn't apply for the Terroir internship," Mark continued, even though Kian was careful to give no sign that he was even still listening. His knife flashed over the mushrooms, decimating their flesh into tiny, even pieces.

"You're an ass," Marta added in, from her own station across the kitchen. "You act like you weren't panting just the same as Kian when Aquino walked in. He's got a way about him."

The understatement of the century, Kian thought. He slid his mushrooms into the pot, drizzled in a little olive oil and started chopping his shallot into miniscule pieces.

The challenge of today's class had been to create a reduction that tasted "meaty," except without any meat used. Every ingredient had to be vegetarian.

After the shallot, Kian went back to the pantry and grabbed a few carrots. He diced those finely and added them to the pot.

His burned reduction had been good, but *expected.* And something that had always set him apart from his other classmates was his willingness to use his instincts to create something unique.

Smoked paprika was his next unusual ingredient and as he returned from the pantry, Mark's eyes were unsurprisingly on both him and the glass jar in his hand.

"You didn't use that last time," Mark said.

"Maybe I decided that my reduction wasn't very good and needed to be improved." It was usually better not to engage Mark, but he'd been shaken by Chef Aquino and needed to get his bearings back. Even though he was undeniably thinking about the reduction challenge, because he still needed a good grade in this class before graduation, half if not *more* of his brain was still contemplating the Terroir internship.

Should he convince his instructors to throw his name into the ring at this late date? *Could* he? He could ask, of course, but he had a feeling that after he'd been so adamant about going to Europe, nobody was going to understand.

What could he say? *Now that I've met Chef Aquino, I don't think I can let him get away?*

Marta walked over to Kian's station. "He was something else, wasn't he?" she asked, leaning down and resting an elbow on the stainless steel countertop.

"Mark?" Kian didn't even look up.

Marta laughed. "Silly, you know I'm talking about Aquino. You guys had a moment there. I was afraid you were going to burst into flames for a second."

It happened; you just couldn't see it.

"He's just another chef," Kian said, and Marta shot him an indignant look. *Well*, Kian thought, *if Marta's caught too, at least I'm not alone.*

"And Terroir is just another restaurant?" she asked pointedly.

But they both knew he was wrong. Bastian Aquino wasn't just another chef and Terroir definitely wasn't just another restaurant. Marta left, back to her station to watch her reduction. Kian stirred the vegetables in his pot and shook in another bit of smoked paprika. Then pepper. Then the thyme. Then, feeling like he had to be adventurous or *fail*—like Chef Aquino was somehow still watching him, testing him—Kian went back to the pantry and returned with a jar of turmeric.

Mark was watching him intently but hadn't moved to copy him yet. Which was either a very good sign or a very bad one. Kian wasn't sure yet.

He added the turmeric and continued to stir. Twenty minutes in, he added red wine, let it reduce, and then added stock, using the edge of a wooden spoon to test the flavor as it developed.

It needed something else though, a missing flavor that he couldn't quite put his finger on, something that would add depth and interest. A *zing*. After a moment of consideration, he went back to the pantry—Mark gaping at him, Marta observing him with only a little less interest—and came back with a hunk of bittersweet, dark chocolate, cumin, and Mexican oregano.

He'd realized what he was really trying to create—a reduction that was actually more like a Mexican mole. Their instructor hadn't said anything about the reduction needing to be traditionally French, and if he wanted to set himself apart, the only way he could do it was by making unexpected and unusual choices. Creating food that others didn't expect.

When Chef Charles, their instructor, came around to taste their reductions, Kian's reduction hadn't been on the stove for nearly as long as the others or even as long as his first one had, but he stopped completely short as he tasted it.

"No meat?" he asked with a raised eyebrow as his spoon descended towards Kian's pot for another taste. None of the other students in their class had warranted a second taste. Again, Kian figured, that was either a very good sign or a very bad one.

Sometimes you died on the hill of your own creation, but you never reached the top unless you took a risk to get there.

"No meat," Kian confirmed.

"It's nearly . . . a mole," Charles said with astonishment. "But it's not, is it?"

That was the fine edge; they hadn't been asked to make a mole. They'd been asked to create a reduction. If Charles decided that he hadn't fulfilled the assignment, it wouldn't matter how good it was. He'd struggled with that, in their first month of school. Just because something was delicious didn't mean it met the requirements. Creative impulses, while important, needed to be tempered by the hierarchy of the kitchen. And he, Charles had told Kian repeatedly, was going to be at the very bottom after graduation. Not exactly washing dishes, but definitely not experimenting with the kitchen's recipes, either.

"It's not a mole," Kian said decisively. Sometimes, he'd discovered, confidence could be everything. That was why it stung even more that he'd been so awestruck by Chef Aquino. Eventually he'd recovered his natural confidence, but for those first few precious moments? He'd been lost. Figuratively. Literally. In every single way that mattered.

Mark had wandered over to see why it was taking Chef Charles so long to critique Kian's reduction. "It smells like a mole," he said, with a rotten egg look on his face. Like he already knew he'd been judged and found wanting.

"This is impressive work," Chef Charles finally pronounced. "Extra points for creativity and not going in the traditional direction of your classmates. I'm impressed by your ability to impart significant flavor in such unique ways."

"Thank you, Chef," Kian said.

He'd already been wavering on his decision, but Chef Charles' comments cemented his purpose. Tomorrow morning, before class began, he was going to ask to speak to him privately—and he was going to ask about the Terroir internship. Surely, the quality of work he was currently doing warranted a late entry into the internship sweepstakes?

It was a gamble, but the chance to work for Chef Aquino was worth any risk.

"I asked you to recommend your top three students," Bastian Aquino said, leaning back in the chair opposite Charles' desk. "Instead of three, I'm inundated with recommendation letters. Are you telling me that everyone in this graduating class is equally untalented?"

Charles shook his head, his full head of wavy, graying hair flopping over his eyes. Bastian had long been of the opinion that Charles was someone who fell into the category of "those who can't, *teach*." The hair was just another piece of evidence that he'd been right about him. Someone that sloppy couldn't ever belong in a truly disciplined kitchen.

"There are some very talented students," Charles said diplomatically. Another reason Bastian had never liked him; he wasn't really honest, he was fucking *diplomatic*. And he'd learned in a twenty-year culinary career that you couldn't ever be both.

Bastian cut right through his crap to the heart of the matter. "Who is the most talented? The one you'd most imagine fitting in at Terroir?"

Charles hesitated. Bastian, not usually the most patient person in the world, wanted to reach across the desk and squeeze his solid neck until the name fell out of his mouth. Three months ago, he'd decided he wanted an intern, so naturally had gone to the most prestigious academy of culinary arts with the intention of selecting their very best student.

It wasn't supposed to be this hard. Charles wasn't supposed to send him fifteen recommendation letters, all essentially the same. There was supposed to be someone who stood out. Someone who he instantly recognized as having the qualifications, the skill, and the talent to at least do what he told them to.

"There is one," Charles finally said. "Unfortunately, he didn't apply for your internship."

Bastian stared at him. "He what?"

Charles cleared his throat. "He didn't apply. Every single other student applied. But not this one."

Shoving his chair back, and running a quick hand through his hair, Bastian prowled back and forth in front of Charles' desk. "He *what*?"

"He didn't apply," he repeated, wincing. "He wants to go to Europe."

Just that fact alone convinced Bastian that this was the intern he needed. Someone who *knew* he was better than everyone else. That was the student Bastian wanted to hire.

"Let me talk to him," Bastian said. "I can persuade him."

"I'm really not sure you can. He's very determined. And I'm sure he'll receive job offers from the European restaurants he's applied to." Charles shrugged, like Bastian was just supposed to accept that he wasn't going to get the best student this graduating class offered. Clearly, he didn't know Bastian very well, if he believed that was going to happen.

Bastian didn't just expect the best—he demanded it. Out of the staff that surrounded him, out of the ingredients he cooked with, but most importantly, out of his own self.

He leaned forward, fists gripping the chair. "Let me talk to him."

Charles continued to hesitate. "That's not really our way here."

Holding his breath, Bastian tried to count to ten like his anger management counselor had told him to. He made it to four.

Not success, but progress, at least.

"You want me to continue to accept graduating students from this academy at Terroir?" Bastian demanded. "If you do, you will let me speak to this student. *Now.*"

"Now?" Charles looked confused.

"I'm here to finalize this decision. I don't care where he's at. Go get him *now.*"

"He's not even here yet," Charles stammered.

Bastian stared at him in stony silence, punctuated only by a knock on the door.

Rising to his feet, Charles shuffled over and opened it, exchanging a quick word with the person on the other side. Bastian, his patience in its death thralls, rolled his eyes. Finally, Charles opened the door wider, and Bastian saw the boy whom he had seen in the kitchen classroom yesterday. The one who'd gone out of his way to insult him, and in nearly the same breath, swore that he possessed the best set of qualifications.

"Kian, this is Chef Aquino," Charles said. "He is here to select an intern for his restaurant, Terroir."

Kian was so young. Had he been this young in culinary school? Bastian couldn't remember. But Kian was definitely young, and slight, his white chef's jacket nearly dwarfing his narrow shoulders and thin arms. Only an air of fierce determination and the look in his light blue eyes grabbed Bastian's attention. This was someone who knew what he wanted, and what he wanted was Bastian.

That wasn't very unusual. What *was* unusual was that, for the first time in a very long time, Bastian wanted back.

"Kian is our best student," Charles added. "He was the one we were just discussing."

Bastian prowled a bit closer to him and tried to ignore the feeling that he was a big bad wolf, after a particularly tasty bit of prey. He glanced up at Charles. "Not available? Not even here yet?" he asked with a raised eyebrow. "He seems to be here now."

Shrugging his shoulders, Charles gestured towards Kian, like *you wanted him, there he is, my work here is done.* Maybe that was why he'd ended up here, instead of working in a restaurant or even, God forbid, some hotel somewhere: a willingness to do the bare minimum and call it good.

Bastian eyed Kian resolutely. So he wanted to work in Europe, did he? Thought, just because he was the best in this small culinary school, in this even smaller graduating class, that he deserved better?

What he deserved was someone who was prepared to remind him every second of every shift that there was a higher ideal he was aspiring to. Someone who was willing to help him unlearn every bad habit instructors like Charles had instilled in him.

"So you want to go to Europe?" Bastian asked, and took in the momentary panic in Kian's eyes. Had Charles been wrong? It probably wouldn't be the first time, if he had been.

"I do. I *did*," Kian said.

"Willing to work seventy hours a week for peanuts?" Bastian paused, gaze focused on Kian's narrow, handsome face. "Willing to scrape plates for a year, just to get into the kitchen?"

He had no poker face whatsoever. Surprise, shock, denial flashed through his eyes in rapid succession. Charles, who still thought he was needed or useful, inserted a heavy sigh into the conversation.

"You're supposed to be preparing these students for what comes next, Charles," Bastian continued, barely wasting a breath. "Instead, you're filling their heads with dreams and *ideas*. Even if they take him, they won't let him near a stove. You know that. But it seems like *he* doesn't know that."

"*He* has a name," Kian inserted testily. "And *he* wants to know the truth. If I work for you, will I get into the kitchen? And not just to scrape plates?"

Bastian knew he was a bastard. Knew that sometimes his employees even risked life and limb to call him that behind his back. Occasionally a recently *ex*-employee would even be ballsy enough to call him the Bastard to his face. But he never felt like one, not when he was demanding what he knew he deserved out of his employees—which was the very best. But he felt like one now, with Kian, all nervous naivety, not even given the basic information on what to expect from instructors who should have known better.

It felt wrong to take advantage of that lack of knowledge, but still, Bastian didn't pause. He wanted the best; he needed it. And while Charles was a fucking moron, he'd identified Kian as the best. If he had to manipulate him and his overly obvious emotions, he'd do it.

"With Charles as your instructor, I'm surprised you weren't training to be a dishwasher," Bastian said cruelly.

"I'm here to be a chef. Not a dishwasher." Kian's lips were clamped tightly together, and there was a fierce determination in his eyes. And that, more than anything else, was what convinced Bastian that he was actually the best in his class. Nobody with that look would ever settle for second best.

"Then you want to work at Terroir," Bastian said, ladling on casual contempt thick and heavy. "But it seems that you didn't think so when you sent your applications in. I don't see one here with your name on it."

Shame bloomed across Kian's fair cheekbones. "Obviously, that was an unfortunate oversight . . ."

"Obviously," Bastian interrupted.

"I would very much like to work for you," Kian finally said, cheeks still flaming, but his chin held high, meeting Bastian's cold eyes dead on.

Bastian had already made his decision, had played Kian like a fiddle to make sure he agreed with him, but it was the obvious pride that convinced him it was the right one. When Bastian inevitably yelled at him—likely in the first five minutes of his first shift, if not even earlier—Kian would take it, and with a stiff upper lip, fix whatever he'd fucked up.

He was that type and that type was the sort that Bastian liked to hire.

At least that was what he told himself as he and Kian shook hands, and he departed the academy. It had nothing to do with the fact that just touching him made his cold, dead heart race again in his chest. He'd just gotten excited about winning, something he loved almost as much as he loved his mother. That was all. In three weeks, when Kian officially started as his intern at Terroir, he would be just like any other chef under him. Under him professionally, but never personally, because Bastian didn't do that. He'd only been tempted once before, and the way it had ended convinced him it couldn't ever happen again.

CHAPTER TWO

CHEF AQUINO SHOWING UP at Chef Charles' office, right when Kian had been determined to talk to him about the Terroir internship, had been kismet. Even more amazingly, Chef Aquino acted determined to win him over, revealing some important facts that *did* make Kian uneasy, because clearly he didn't know that Kian had already realized how stupid he'd been.

When the internship announcement had come out, Mark had been furious, and had threatened to tell everyone that the graduating student who'd won the internship had been the only student who hadn't applied for it. It hadn't been very hard to stop him. All Kian had to say was, "Do you really want to admit to *everyone* in the whole academy that you lost out on a prestigious position to someone who didn't even apply for it?"

As it turned out, Mark didn't want to advertise that particular fact, so he kept his usually noisy trap shut, and the other students, unsurprised that the top student in the class had won the top post-graduation position, moved on.

Chef Charles had pulled him aside the day before graduation, and in his office, showed him three letters from the European restaurants he'd applied to—two in Paris and one in London.

"They're yours, if you want them," Chef had said, but the kindness in his voice didn't convince Kian at all.

"If I want them?"

Chef Charles pushed them closer to Kian. "I'm sure they're acceptances." Kian was moderately sure, too, but instead of replying, he merely grabbed the envelopes and stuffed them into his apron pocket. He had no intention of fulfilling Chef's curiosity. Or anyone else's, ever again.

Didn't Chef remember what Chef Aquino had said when he was here? Didn't Chef remember that all his encouragement to reach for the stars, and to apply at these international bastions of gastronomy, had all been based on a lie?

Maybe not a bald-faced lie, but a lie of omission, at least. Kian had no intention of slaving away in the dish room for a year at any of those restaurants. He didn't intend to scrape plates until the head chef miraculously remembered his existence. His intention was to glean as much training and information as he could, and then move on, doing the same, until he was ready for his first executive chef position. In his notebook scrawled list of goals, he'd set the age at twenty-seven, but secretly, he felt he could accomplish everything even faster.

It was very simple: Chef Aquino wanted to teach, and Kian wanted to learn.

Then there was the attraction that Kian felt. But since he was utterly convinced it had to be one-sided, there was no point in even worrying about it. It wouldn't interfere because the concept of Chef Aquino being interested in him was like the moon deciding to come down to the earth one starry night. It just wasn't going to happen, and Kian told himself that was good, because it made something that could be very complicated, not very after all.

He'd open the envelopes later, when he was alone, Kian thought absently, and then promptly forgot about them completely because when he checked his email later that night, there was an email with his contract from Chef Aquino himself.

He'd start the day after graduation, and Kian could practically hear the sweet-sour tone of his voice as he read the email. "If that's too soon, that's too bad," the email read. "And if you wanted to indulge in the sort of bacchanalian exploits that most students wish to after a graduation ceremony, that's also too bad."

Kian didn't know what *bacchanalian* meant, but he did know that he wasn't interested in it. What he was interested in was working. Specifically for Chef Aquino.

He showed up at the Terroir side door, as directed, fifteen minutes early—he'd read *Kitchen Confidential* by Anthony Bourdain, of course, and while there was a lot of crap that he couldn't imagine being applicable to a three-Michelin-starred restaurant like Terroir, he'd taken to heart the emphasis Tony placed on not just being on time, but *early*. If Anthony Bourdain, the rock star rebel of the culinary world, could do it while he was on all the drugs he could get his hands on, then Kian could do it while he was clean and sober and well-rested.

A man wearing a bandana covered in chili peppers answered his hesitant knock. His face was bitter somehow, like Kian had just caught him sucking a slice of lemon, and he didn't say anything, just stared right at Kian.

"Well?" he finally said impatiently. "Was there something you wanted? To stare?"

"I'm Kian Reynolds. I'm here to work for Chef Aquino."

Kian felt, as the chili-bedecked man in front of him examined him from head to toe, carefully, like he was a dirt-crusted organic carrot or a particularly thorny hunk of ginger. "You're the Bastard's new intern?"

It wasn't easy, but Kian kept the same pleasant expression plastered to his face. He knew everything always showed, and he'd been so determined that this wouldn't happen today that he'd spent a lot of the night before practicing neutral expressions in his bathroom mirror.

But the man in front of him must be a lot more observant than Kian was capable of fooling because he laughed, suddenly and unexpectedly. It was a good laugh, a friendly laugh, even though it was tinged at the edges with the same bitterness that existed in the corners of his expression.

"Haven't you ever heard him called the Bastard before?" he asked curiously.

"No," Kian said stiffly, "and that's really inappropriate, considering he's the executive chef and your boss."

The man leaned closer. "Let me let you in on a little secret before you walk in here. If you don't find a way to keep a sense of humor about what an absolute asshole Bastian Aquino is, then you're going to lose your soul."

This seemed unnecessarily dramatic for a man who wore chili peppers on his head.

"Can you just please take me to Chef Aquino?" Kian begged. He knew the weird man in front of him had blown through all his carefully neutral expressions already and he didn't have any extra in reserve.

He gave Kian another one of those penetrating looks, before suddenly nodding sharply. "Yeah, sure."

Opening the door wider, he let Kian walk in, and as he stepped over the threshold, he had one of those full-body realizations that nothing was ever going to be the same again. He was a *chef* now and he was working for *Bastian Aquino* at *Terroir*. This was only the beginning and it was already awesome. He could go anywhere from here; only the sky was the limit.

The door opened into an employee locker room, narrow metal lockers lining the space. "Yours is somewhere," the man offhandedly tossed out. "Your whites will be in it. What did you say your name was again?"

"Kian," he said, glancing up and down the row for his name written on the piece of blue tape haphazardly stuck to each metal door.

"Oh, you're over here," he said, pointing to one, near the end. "I'm Xander, by the way. Xander Bridges. I'm the *saucier*, and I work the line during service."

"Oh," Kian said, feeling very impressed. He'd heard great things about Terroir's sauces, in particular, and this was the man who created them. Maybe it was okay that he liked to say rude things about Chef Aquino and wear weird headwraps, if he was that talented.

"I'll take you to Aquino now," Xander said. "Come with me."

They walked through the kitchen, which was so vast, it was hard for Kian to conceptualize. The "line" itself was wide and while not exactly spacious, had clearly been designed to maximize a chef's natural movements as he prepared dishes. The range was enormous, with at least twenty burners, several which were already occupied by huge pots, bubbling away even though it was not even eight in the morning.

"I also do the soup, sometimes," Xander said, the pride in his voice betraying how prestigious being asked to make the daily soup was. "Which is why I'm here so early."

They passed though the line, which was still quiet. There were several long stainless steel prep tables, right next to a whole line of commercial-grade walk-in fridges. "Veggies," Xander said, pointing to a door. "Dairy. Meat. Seafood. There's another larger one, on the other end of the building, for wine."

Chef Aquino's office was easily identifiable. It was glass-walled, and even though there were oatmeal-colored shades, they were all drawn up, leaving Chef to survey his entire domain at any time. Kian had a feeling he rarely drew the shades. There was a single desk, metal and glass, with a keyboard and an oversize computer monitor.

Xander rapped briefly on the glass next to the open door and Chef Aquino looked up, every one of his dark hairs in place, his immaculate white chef's jacket already buttoned up to the throat. He looked pristine and perfect, and when his dark-eyed gaze hit Kian, it felt like the first time all over again. Like an electric current crossed with a wooden beam hitting him straight in the temple. But a *good* sort of pain, the kind of pain you craved all the time.

"Chef," Xander said, somehow finding his respect, which Kian had a feeling was buried fairly deep, "this is Kian. He said he's starting today."

Kian had had three weeks to contemplate them meeting again, and what his first day might be like. He'd imagined Chef Aquino shaking his hand, leading him on a thorough tour; still contained but going out of his way to show Kian the way the Terroir kitchens worked, exactly.

What Kian got was that single quick, penetrating glance and then a brusque reply, after Chef had already returned his attention to the paper he was scribbling on. "Get him changed and then take him to the dish room."

At first, Kian was sure he'd misunderstood. Xander finally had to grip his shoulder and literally pull him away from the doorway. He knew he should say something, but he didn't know what that was. Hadn't Chef Aquino convinced him to come work for him by offering to teach him? Promised him work that wasn't the dish room? Yet that was exactly where he was telling Xander to send him.

He couldn't be as callously crass as Xander when it came to their boss, but he could still, politely, make sure that Chef remembered who he was, right? But Xander didn't even let him formulate the question, he just dragged him off.

"Wait, wait," he muttered as Xander kept his grip firm around his upper arm. "I need to remind Chef Aquino that I'm not here to be a dish washer. I'm supposed to be his new intern."

Xander gave a sharp bark of laughter. "Yeah, he knows." He dropped Kian's arm, finally, when they were back in the locker room. "Get changed."

But Kian was not going to change into anything until he understood exactly what had just happened. "I don't understand."

"Of course you don't. You're like . . . a baby. Or a puppy."

Kian bristled. "I'm twenty-one. I've just graduated from culinary school. I was the top of our class. Chef Aquino *handpicked* me to be his intern."

Xander just looked bitterly amused. "Like I said. A puppy. For the record, the intern job basically means you're the Bastard's bitch, at his beck and call. And what he wants you to do today is work in the dish room. So dish room it is. Do you speak Spanish?"

Kian had grown up in southern Oregon, which meant that he did, a little. As he slowly stripped down and changed into the whites in the locker, he informed Xander of that fact.

All Xander said was, "God, where did you learn to change? Your grandmother's house? Hurry it up. You need to get to the dish room and I have to get back to the fucking soup."

Trying to hurry, Kian was surprised to discover that the whites fit perfectly. He'd never sent his sizes to Chef Aquino, but somehow he must have known. He thought about asking Xander if that was normal, but even though he seemed to be a weird guy, probably used to odd questions, his impatience was beginning to show. Kian had begun his first day by seemingly pissing off Chef Aquino just by existing; he couldn't risk pissing off the one person who'd been relatively helpful.

When he was done, Xander showed him the dish room, an already bustling space filled with steam and a single man, who seemed to be in a hundred places at once.

"This is Jorge," Xander said. "He's from Honduras, and he doesn't speak a lot of English. Good luck."

Kian looked at Jorge, who didn't smile back at him. He had a sudden feeling that this was Chef Aquino's first line of defense at weeding out the self-important and the useless that passed through his kitchen. If that was true, then Kian wasn't going to fail. Not on his first day, but more importantly, not *ever*. He straightened his shoulders and held out his hand.

"I'm Kian. I think we're going to be working together today."

Jorge looked at his outstretched hand like it was an insect. He didn't make a single move to shake it. Instead, he gestured at the front of the line, where a bunch of dirty pots sat.

Unfortunately Kian understood all too well. What Jorge wanted was for him to scrape those pots, and then the towering set of plates next to it. How was there already so much to be cleaned? The restaurant wasn't supposed to open for hours.

But it didn't really matter *why*. All that mattered was that, until told otherwise, Jorge was his boss, and he'd better do what he said, or else he wouldn't ever see Bastian Aquino again.

Jorge held out a long, rubberized apron, and a scraping tool. Kian tried not to let his frustration show in his face, but he'd blown way past any neutrality he'd ever acquired, and Jorge just laughed, and it sounded way too much like Xander's.

Maybe Kian understood after all why they called him the Bastard behind his back.

Bastian was not used to feeling guilty, but the sickly feeling at the base of his stomach followed him around during the rest of the day. Manipulating employees into becoming the best version of themselves was routine; it was okay that they hated him for it. He got their most exemplary work, and eventually they got sick of him and left. But somehow the thought of Kian hating him filled Bastian with self-loathing.

It didn't matter that Bastian knew he was doing the right thing. It didn't matter that Kian was so green, the last place he needed to be was on the line, fucking everything up during a service. He needed to learn, and he needed to prove he was strong enough to dedicate himself to this emotionally and physically grueling work.

He still saw Kian's shocked and disappointed face every time he closed his eyes, and it was *annoying*. Bastian didn't like feeling this way; didn't like feeling responsible for another person. Kian was Kian's own keeper, and it was up to him to prove himself.

It was only the force of his convictions that kept Bastian out of the dish room. He got a brief glimpse of him, face already white and exhausted, at the employee meal before dinner service began. Bastian considered sending help to the dish room, but Jorge typically managed on his own, and probably enjoyed having someone to boss around.

Bastian always kept a very close eye on how things ran during service, and tonight, like every night, clean plates and dishes and bowls and empty sauté pans didn't seem to ever be in short supply.

He almost stopped by after the dinner service ended, but that would also be unusual, and he wasn't willing to single Kian out so quickly. The rest of the staff would figure things out soon enough, if Kian was able to stick it out, and burdening him with additional shit, on top of Bastian's usual shit, seemed unfair.

He left in his Mercedes right when the service ended, depending on the other chefs to finish cleaning the kitchen to his exacting standards. The drive was only a few miles, but tonight, that didn't feel long enough, so he kept driving. It was late, but he still found himself idling in the driveway of a house about ten minutes from Terroir.

He must have been sitting there long enough, because when he glanced up, a woman bundled in a lilac fuzzy robe, graying hair curling around her shoulders, was standing on the front walk, a small smile on her face.

"It's late," was all she said to him as he got out of the car, approaching her.

"Why aren't you sleeping?" Bastian asked. He'd somewhat expected to come here and find her asleep.

Bastian leaned in, giving her a hug, and brushing a quick kiss over each cheek.

"Because you weren't sleeping," his mother replied tartly, leading him around the back of the house to the sunroom that Bastian had had built for her a few years ago. "Is everything alright?"

"No. Yes." Bastian couldn't even make up his own damn mind as he settled down in one of the wide, comfortable chairs. He propped his clog-shod feet up on the coffee table, and his mother gave him a single, castigating glance, before he moved them.

"It's very unlike you to be unsure," she said.

She was right.

"I had a new employee start today," he said.

"You are *always* having new employees start," she said, her accent still faintly musical after all the time spent in America. "Maybe because you're an asshole."

"*Maman!*" Bastian exclaimed.

She just shrugged. "I hear the stories. People love to talk. So what was so special about this new employee? Did you finally decide to hire a *sous*?"

"I have a *sous*," Bastian argued tiredly.

"And yet he doesn't do what a normal *sous* would do, because you cannot bear to let anything go. So it isn't a *sous*. Who is it?"

"His name is Kian Reynolds. He just graduated from the CIA outpost here, in Napa."

"So he is very young," Celeste Aquino observed.

"Very young," Bastian confirmed, and even though his thirty-five years wasn't old, he felt like a dirty old man, thinking about a twenty-one-year-old this way.

"And you like him," she added slyly.

He shrugged, an echo of her own from a moment ago. "I don't *dislike* him."

"Ahhhh. *Quelle surprise,*" Celeste said sagely. "You are human after all."

"You birthed me," Bastian said with annoyance. "I think you'd know whether I was human or not."

"Eh," she said. "I wonder sometimes. You are more machine than man. But this boy, this Kian, he makes you want to be more man than machine. That's not a bad thing, darling. You can't stay alone forever."

Bastian shot to his feet. It was just like his mother to assume he and Kian would fall in love and spend a happily ever after together after he'd only said that he didn't dislike him. Such an auspicious start to a romance.

"He's my employee. My new intern. And he's young." Bastian paced back and forth. "I don't know what's going to happen. *Nothing* if I'm to stay his boss, and I want to because I think he could be very good. I want to teach him, more than anything, and it's hard to be patient enough to do that."

Celeste settled back in her chair and her knowing smile drove him wild. It was like she knew he was going to fail, before he even started, and nothing ever set him on a more determined path than people assuming he couldn't achieve the goals he set for himself.

"You," he said to his mother, "are even better at manipulating people than I am."

She shrugged, but the twinkle in her dark eyes gave her away completely. "I worry for you, sometimes," was all she said.

"Maybe you should worry for him, instead," he said darkly.

"Will you be able to sleep now? Should I make you some hot milk?"

Bastian growled. *Hot milk*, his ass. But his mother was not only used to his mercurial moods, in the beginning, he'd learned them from her—and maybe a little bit from his hot-tempered Spanish father.

"No hot milk then. Take your drive home," she said, getting to her feet and swirling her fuzzy robe around her like it was a Dior or a Gucci. "I need my beauty sleep."

He brushed another kiss across her cheek. "You're beautiful, always, *maman.*"

Slapping at his shoulder, she scoffed, but couldn't hide the pleased gleam in her eyes. "Goodnight, Bastian."

Despite talking to his mother, Bastian didn't feel any more settled when he finally reached his own house. Stripping down, he took a hot shower, intending for the water beating on his back to relax that tight muscle throbbing in his neck, but he still felt wound tight.

Maybe it wouldn't even be a problem. Maybe Kian, annoyed with the way Bastian had manipulated him into taking the internship, would quit after the first day. Plenty of prospective employees had. He wouldn't be the first, and Bastian was sure he wouldn't be the last. Lots of chefs, especially those who weren't fresh from school, took major offense to being asked to do dishes. But Bastian's typical trial for new chefs was rather well-known in the industry now, and most brand-new employees expected it.

But Kian clearly wasn't hearing industry gossip.

Maybe tomorrow he wouldn't show up, Bastian thought as he turned the shower controls off. If he didn't, and Bastian ever saw him again, maybe at the farmer's market or giving one of those lame culinary demonstrations at Dean & Deluca, Bastian could get him out of his system with a single night of hot, brainless fucking.

Rubbing himself down with a towel, he flopped down onto the bed and after switching off the light, attempted to switch off his brain.

It didn't work.

Instead it decided to show him, in graphic detail, what that night of hot, brainless fucking might be like, if Kian didn't show up for work the next day.

Kian would be slender but tough, all wrapped up in that milky skin, blue eyes flashing with determination. He'd want everything Bastian was willing to give him, and he'd love every second of it.

Groaning, Bastian rolled over. He couldn't jerk off to thoughts of Kian. Not if the possibility existed that he was going to have to stuff all those inconvenient and messy thoughts right back into their boxes. He knew from experience that if he slipped up, there'd be no hiding from his own desires.

You should have taken the god damned hot milk, Bastian thought, his temper spiking as he fisted his hands in the sheets. Anything not to touch himself.

What he should do was bring Kian into his office tomorrow and tell him that they'd both made a mistake, and that Terroir was the wrong place for Kian to further his ambition. It would be a lie, because Bastian already knew it was the perfect place, if Kian could be tough enough to stick it out. It wasn't like he hadn't lied to employees and suppliers and friends and ex-lovers thousands of times before; as long as he got what he wanted, it didn't matter. But something about lying to that clearly trusting face was abhorrent. Bastian didn't think he could do it.

What could he say instead? *I'm sorry, but I want you too badly for you to stay?* Yeah, that definitely wasn't going to work, because he'd seen the worship in Kian's eyes, and there was only one way that conversation could end.

There was only one option left, and that was to bury everything so deep, even he forgot he'd felt anything. He'd done it before, he could do it again. It was just a matter of determination over emotion, and despite what everyone believed, Bastian controlled every god damn emotion that escaped him. If he lost his temper, it was because he *chose* to lose his temper. There were only two emotions he'd always been helpless against: the enduring love for his mother, and its mirror, the hatred he'd always felt for his father.

Someday, he knew he was going to have to let that go; Celeste always told him that. But he *could* control what he felt for Kian.

And he believed that completely, at least until he showed up at Terroir, bone dry cappuccino in his travel mug, at the early hour of seven thirty. Nobody else would be around now, and he could get a head start on his inventory and ordering for the weekend.

Except that he wasn't alone after all. A bright cap of blond hair shone in the sun, as Kian tipped his head back, absorbing the early morning rays.

Bastian flinched, staring at the boy who hadn't yet seen him. Not only had he come back, but he'd come back *early*. As Kian's boss, this filled him with cautious optimism. As someone who was not-so-successfully trying to bury his attraction, it was the shittiest possible outcome.

"You're here early," Bastian said, making sure his voice was devoid of anything. Approval, disapproval, endless, rapacious lust. *Anything.*

Kian nearly jumped as his gaze flew to Bastian's face. "Oh, yeah. I always heard timeliness was important."

"Even in the dish room?" Bastian asked, raising an eyebrow. He typed in the code to open the back door and reminded himself to tell Xander or Wyatt to make sure Kian knew it. If he was going to show up earlier than everyone else, an insane proposition, he might as well know how to get in.

"Especially in the dish room," Kian said very seriously as they walked into the locker room. "Jorge and I have some new methods that we're looking to work into the current practices."

Bastian raised an eyebrow. Typically he didn't like anyone fucking with his restaurant, especially implementing anything new without his permission, but there was something so earnest about Kian, it was difficult to burst his bubble.

"You'll like them, I promise," Kian said, backtracking like he'd thought better of making changes without permission. "Would you like to hear about them?"

Bastian usually didn't give two shits what happened in his dish room as long as the dishes got washed. Jorge had worked for him forever and knew how to get things done. Maybe things could be improved, but having to listen to Kian's ideas was a bad idea when he'd actually slept and wasn't still fighting that pesky attraction. "Not particularly," he said casually. "Just don't fuck anything up."

"Of course not, Chef," Kian said, and goddamnit, those earnestly shining blue eyes just *killed him*.

He'd died enough last night, and right now, he couldn't take another moment, so he gave a sharp nod and departed the locker room, hoping to hole himself up in the office until he could forget everything he wasn't supposed to be remembering.

During family meal before the dinner service yesterday, one of the other chefs, a nice guy with surfer blond hair and blue eyes, had said to Kian, "Oh, so you're the new guy. Liking the dish room so far?"

Kian hadn't quite understood how he could know he'd been relegated there, but then the blond guy had laughed again. "Killed me too, for a couple of days, but what got me through it was knowing everyone's had to do it at one time or another."

As he'd cleaned up the dishes from the meal, Kian had turned this scrap of information over in his head, until he'd come to what seemed to be the right conclusion. Chef Aquino did this to *everyone* who started in the Terroir kitchens. Everyone had to put their time in, to prove they were willing to commit. Chef hadn't singled Kian out; this was the trial by soapsuds that he gave to everyone.

It sure made it a lot easier to trudge back to the dirty work he and Jorge had for the evening. It was hot, back-breaking work, but as they scraped, Kian began to think of some ways it could be less hot and maybe even less back-breaking.

At the end of the service, Xander had come in personally to check on him, which Kian felt sort of went against all that world-weary bitterness he carried with him all the time. And Kian, who didn't speak enough Spanish to communicate to Jorge what they could change to make the work easier on both of them, employed Xander as a temporary go-between slash translator.

Jorge—and Xander, as well—were skeptical of Kian's ideas. It seemed the way things had always been done at Terroir was the way things *always* had to be done at Terroir.

"My advice," Xander had said, when they were on their way out an hour later, "is if you really think this will work, just do it. Don't ask for permission. Ask for forgiveness later."

Wyatt, the blond chef, had frowned at his friend. "Aquino is going to chew him up and spit him out, once he discovers what he's done."

"Maybe," Xander said. "But maybe not."

It was a risk Kian felt he needed to take. He had to show Chef Aquino that he was different, that he was *better*. And Jorge, who had been employed at Terroir for years, seemed willing to go along with Kian's ideas, as long as they stayed Kian's ideas.

Kian had stayed up too late finalizing the plans, and then was up even earlier than the day before, determined to get a head start before the dishes began in earnest.

Of course, that was when he was dumb enough to not only run into Chef Aquino himself, squinting and vibrant in the early morning sun, smelling of freshly roasted espresso, but to accidentally confess his entire plan.

Still, Chef Aquino hadn't said *not* to do it. That was practically permission, right? Kian thought Xander might have agreed with him, if he'd been here already. But he wasn't, so he was on his own.

Sink or swim, Kian told himself, and he knew which one he needed to do. He rolled up the sleeves of his chef's jacket and got to work.

Chapter Three

Bastian had known Kian had something indefinably special from their first meeting. But he was sure of it, beyond a doubt, when early one morning—he'd had to set his alarm twenty minutes earlier to actually avoid running into him in the parking lot—he'd gone into the dish room and seen what Kian had changed.

It was a lot more efficient, so efficient, in fact, that Bastian felt a tiny pulse of shame for never trying to improve Jorge's situation. Jorge was a silent, diligent, reliable worker, and he wouldn't have ever considered changing anything because he was so grateful for the job Bastian had given him ages ago. But Kian wasn't just trying to prove his loyalty. For some reason, he was trying to prove that he deserved to be promoted from the dish room.

It wasn't like Bastian didn't have every intention of doing that. What was the point of going to all the trouble of hiring an intern if you kept him scraping plates? But he liked the hunger and the tenacity and the risk Kian had taken. It reminded him, if he was being very honest, of himself, a very long time ago.

That was both good and, frankly, sort of terrifying. Bastian knew what sort of hell he'd raised and how difficult he'd been in every kitchen he'd ever set foot in—including his own.

Definitely his own.

When Xander showed up, they consulted about the soup. He liked Xander, even though he didn't have a lot of respect for anyone else's culinary skill, including Bastian's own. There was a healthy ego brewing in that chili pepper-bedecked head of his, and someday, he wouldn't be content with making all the sauces and the soup three times a week.

Someday, Xander was going to demand more, probably *chef de cuisine* or a position as *sous* that wasn't essentially meaningless. Bastian was going to have to give it to him or lose him, and that stung. But Bastian knew it was the price of wanting to work with the best. Each of them were hungry and ambitious, and Xander was hardly an exception to this rule.

Someday, Xander would make a great head chef, but today was not that day, and to keep his ego somewhat in check, he shot down the first two of Xander's ideas for the soup, forcing him to dig deeper into his well of inspiration and find something that was really good. He looked about five seconds away from beating Bastian with the huge stainless steel soup ladle, but Bastian was fairly certain that he wouldn't resort to assault—at least not yet. At least not until Xander had gotten what he wanted out of his employment at Terroir.

"When Kian comes in later," Bastian said offhandedly, like this wasn't the reason he'd come over here in the first place, "tell him to come see me, first thing."

Bastian watched as Xander tamped down his temper, embers still flaring in his brown eyes. He knew Xander wanted to remind him that he was a chef, not a messenger boy, but Xander had a small dose of self-preservation, at least, and managed to keep his mouth shut. He gave Bastian a quick nod.

"Excellent," Bastian said. It was time to teach Kian more than just how to efficiently scrape a plate.

***

"Before you get started, he wants to talk to you," Xander hissed as Kian rounded the corner into the kitchen.

Xander already had a few splashes on his whites, which meant that he'd been elected to make the soup today. Usually that put Xander in a better mood, but he didn't look like he was in a particularly good one today.

"Everything okay?" Kian asked, a gut reaction. He'd rearranged the dish room, with Jorge's help, but he had yet to hear a peep from Chef Aquino about what they'd done.

He hadn't been fired either, which Kian was taking as a fairly positive sign.

"He just wants to see you," Xander said. "And watch out, he's in a mood."

"A mood?"

"A bad mood." Xander grimaced. "Though that's hardly unusual."

Since meeting him for the first time, Kian had become more than a little obsessed with his new boss. He'd read every magazine feature and restaurant review he could get his hands on. He listened to every story whispered during prep that he could hear from his own dishwashing station. He lingered over the family meal if talk turned to Bastard stories, of which there were many.

The thing was, Xander wasn't entirely wrong. Chef Aquino definitely had some bad moods. He was unbelievably sensitive to even a perceived insult, easily frustrated, quickly bored, and had a zero-tolerance policy for mistakes. But Kian wouldn't have said that he was always in a bad mood. His mood was mercurial, and he tended to react badly to stimulus—sometimes even if it was something good.

Kian had realized that what Chef needed was someone to be the first line of defense, to absorb whatever was going on before it could even reach Chef. And that, he was convinced, was the real reason Chef had hired an intern. Chef Aquino might not understand exactly why yet, but Kian believed that was why he was at Terroir.

The kitchen was comfortably staffed, and though there was always a lot of work to be done, Kian hadn't been able to identify one particular hole that needed filled—except protecting their commander-in-chief.

Chef would teach him everything he knew, and Kian would make Chef's life a little easier. He'd already decided it was a good trade-off.

He approached Bastian's office and, surprisingly, the blinds in Chef's office were lowered for the first time in the week since Kian had started at Terroir. His heart beat a little faster with the realization. Maybe he was going to be fired after all. But he'd also heard all the horror stories. Chef wouldn't care about privacy for something like a termination. He'd do it in the middle of service, right on the line. He didn't care about anyone else's pride; only his own.

Kian had been washing dishes at his house since he was seven years old and had done another healthy stint in the dish room during culinary academy. Chef wasn't trying to teach him how to wash dishes; he was trying to teach humility. Maybe his ego had been a little inflated after dominating so many of his classes. So instead of approaching the office like Xander might, like even he might have a week ago, Kian knocked hesitantly.

"Yes," Chef answered immediately, and Kian walked in. Chef gestured to the chair opposite the desk. It was made of a metal base and a hard plastic sculpted seat. It was unbelievably uncomfortable, which was the complete opposite of the modern leather office chair Chef was seated in. Kian had a feeling that particular disparity was completely on purpose. It occurred to him, not for the first time, that maybe Chef was actually a closet sadist.

"You wanted to see me?" Kian asked.

Chef was already dressed for service, but he hadn't buttoned the top few buttons of his coat, the lapels hanging open, revealing a tanned neck and even the hint of a collarbone. Kian tried to focus on the desk instead, but Chef's hands were there, clearly scarred and nicked, but strong and sure. His nails were trimmed short, and he tapped one on the glass desktop. Just the sight of those hands was enough to nearly send Kian into a fantasy spiral. But at the last moment, the point of no return, he jerked his focus back, trying to remember that Bastian Aquino wasn't just the sexiest man he'd ever seen, but also the most competent. And his boss.

Someone who, with one single word, could make sure that Kian was never hired to work in a kitchen ever again.

"I've spoken to Jorge," Chef said. "And I've looked at the changes you've made to the dish room." He tapped his fingers again, like he wasn't sure how he felt about either one.

But Kian wasn't fooled for a single moment. Chef knew exactly how he felt; he was just trying to draw out the moment so Kian would squirm, would insert something ill-advisable into the lengthening silence.

Kian might be very green, but he wasn't stupid. He stayed quiet and waited.

Chef nodded absently, but with approval. "To my utter shock, they were actually good changes." He paused again, and Kian curled his fingers around the plastic seat, fighting the urge to fidget. "Why did you make them?"

That was not a question that Kian had been expecting.

"Uh," he said, and saw the reaction instantly. Chef's dark brows slammed together, his lips curling patronizingly.

He doesn't like it when people don't know, Kian reminded himself. *He likes it when his staff is confident, but not overly confident.*

"I did it," Kian said, starting all over again, "because I saw inefficiencies, and I know how important efficiency is to you."

"And you didn't bring the suggestions to me because . . . ?"

Kian took a deep breath. He *knew* what Chef expected him to say. Knew and had to fight against his petty machinations being exposed for exactly what they were.

"I wanted to impress you," he admitted, "and I wasn't sure you'd give me the opportunity to do that if I didn't take matters into my own hands."

Chef hummed absently, fingers resuming their tapping. "*And* you wanted to get out of the dish room," he added.

"I'm here because I want to help you and because I want you to teach me. If for now that means I need to stay in the dish room and make it as good as it can be, then I'm willing to do that."

Kian was almost one hundred percent sure that this moment was the first time he'd ever surprised Chef Aquino. His eyes grew wide for an instant.

"You really mean that," he said, like he fully expected Kian to deny it. "You'd stay in the dish room if I told you to."

"If you think that what I need to learn is how to scrape plates better, it's not very flattering but you're the expert. I trust you."

Bastian leaned forward, his dark eyes mesmerizing as they searched Kian's face. "I think you really mean that."

It wasn't easy, but Kian held his ground. There was undeniably a part of him that wanted to crawl across the floor and *beg* to be let out of the wet, humid, torturous dish room and back into the kitchen, where he belonged.

That wasn't all he wanted to beg for. Before he could stop the thought in its tracks, he imagined crawling across the floor, to where Bastian sat, waiting for the head nod of permission, so he could feel those powerful thighs under his fingertips, and then raise up on his knees, mouth so close to the significant erection bulging in Bastian's white and black checked pants.

"Reynolds?" Chef questioned again, and Kian couldn't help it. He flamed bright red, making it unavoidably clear just what he'd been thinking about.

"I do mean it," he said, hating how his voice trembled a little, at the very end. And not because he'd been caught; but because the fantasy was so real, so visceral. The blinds were closed, and Chef was staring at him like he might not actually fire him if he tried it.

"Shadow Wyatt at the grill tonight," Chef ordered in clipped tones, and the heat of the earlier moment was doused by his sudden coldness.

Kian told himself that he shouldn't be disappointed, because whatever he'd just been fantasizing about was an impossibility, but it was tough not to be.

He wanted the learning and the knowledge Chef Aquino wanted to teach him, and he wanted the fantasies too. It was incredibly good for his sanity that he was going to have to settle for the former, but there was a part of him, deep inside, that yearned, anyway.

It had been a week since Bastian had pulled Kian from the dish room, but the conversation in his office haunted him still. He'd done his utmost to make sure that they were never alone after that, because the desire in those innocent blue eyes to be much less innocent was difficult to resist. And Bastian knew, as much of an asshole as he could be, there was no way he could ever fulfill any of the fantasies Kian was collecting.

Whatever passed between them was going to have to be strictly, completely, professional.

It stung, but Bastian had done much harder things, and it wasn't like a lack of sex was going to kill him. He'd already been mostly going without, because being a professional chef in charge of one of the most prestigious restaurants in the country meant excessively long hours and mind- and body-numbing exhaustion. Even one-night stands deserved better.

It was entirely Kian's fault that he'd thought about sex more in the last month than he'd thought about it in the previous six.

"What are we doing today?" Kian asked, all unvarnished eagerness.

"Do you know what the most vital part of Terroir is?" Bastian asked as they walked from his office towards the bank of large walk-in fridges.

"The line?" Kian asked, more hesitatingly than Bastian thought he normally allowed himself. He would have to be a lot stupider to not realize that Kian was trying to play the sort of chef—the sort of *person*—that Bastian normally admired. Confident but not overly cocky. Sure but always willing to be taught something new. Sometimes he wanted to tell Kian that you couldn't manipulate a manipulator. And, sometimes he wanted to shake him and demand to see the real Kian. Not the Kian that he thought Bastian wanted.

What scared him the most was that it was very possible that they were one in the same.

Bastian pushed all that away, deliberately distancing himself from those embarrassing, semi-hysterical, desperate thoughts. Just because he already knew he was screwed didn't mean he had to acknowledge it.

"Not the line," Bastian replied patiently. "The line can't prepare the fish special if the fish we receive is poor quality, or if the fish isn't available at all. The most vital part of this restaurant, and *any* restaurant, is inventory."

Kian looked a little disappointed, like he believed the most vital component of Terroir would be sexier. What Kian didn't know yet was that a properly stocked kitchen was the sexiest thing in the whole god damn universe.

"I take inventory every single morning," Bastian continued, yanking open the door to the dairy fridge. "I know you've been watching me in my office." He nearly wanted to grab those words back. They were dangerous, just as it was dangerous that Kian couldn't tear his eyes away from his boss, even when he was supposed to be doing something else. "What do you think I'm doing every morning?"

"Making phone calls?" There was an element of frustration in Kian's voice, like he didn't appreciate being asked questions that Bastian knew he didn't have the answers to.

"Calling our suppliers. Ordering. Verifying orders. Then when orders come in, I check every single one. I open every crate, every box. I examine every single piece of produce that comes into this restaurant. And if something isn't right, I make a phone call."

He held out a clipboard and a pen to Kian. "It's time you learned how to do this."

For a split second, Kian made a face, like he couldn't imagine anything less enjoyable than counting and making notations on a sheet of paper. Then his expression changed, like he'd needed to remind himself that everything Bastian asked him to do was important. It was the same look he'd worn when Bastian had banished him to the dish room.

It remained to be seen whether every experiment Bastian tried would turn out like the dish room, but he hoped, like he hadn't hoped in years. He expected all his employees to eventually let him down, some of them spectacularly, most of them by their commitment to mediocrity. Kian was the first who truly gave him hope. Bastian didn't know if the hope was what attracted him in the first place, or if it was what might deepen this attraction into something uncontainable.

If it hadn't been for the hope, he really would have fired Kian the first day, and then fucked him out of his system.

"I just count the boxes, and then write it down?"

"You do more than just count. You *inspect*. You know the menu. You know the specials. You should know the breakdown of plates that we serve every night. More meat on Fridays and Saturdays. Fish on Fridays. The reports that I put up every Monday? Study those. Memorize them. Without that knowledge, this task is impossible."

"Because otherwise I won't know how much fish is enough, and when we need to order more," Kian said, and Bastian felt the familiar flash of recognition resonate through him. He recognized so much of himself in the younger man in front of him. The eagerness, the barely leashed ego, the willingness to work as hard as it took to achieve goals. Those were familiar enough traits, but when reflected back, were apparently irresistible.

"Precisely," Bastian said, and followed Kian deeper into the dairy fridge. Cartons upon cartons of butter, stacked. Lesser stacks of gourmet European butters, purchased to finish certain dishes. Huge jugs of milk and cream. Rows upon rows of eggs.

"The sheet is laid out just like the fridge," Kian observed, his pen making miniscule tick marks alongside each ingredient.

"Did you believe that I'd make my life harder and not easier?" Bastian asked wryly.

Kian glanced up, blue eyes wide even in the dim light. "No, never," he said, and his voice was worshipful.

He didn't want to know what falling off that pedestal would feel like, because it was inevitable that it would hurt. A lot.

Other chefs who came to work at Terroir believed Bastian was the best, but nobody held any old-fashioned ideas about him. They called him the Bastard for a reason. The first time he threw plates, a little of the shine in Kian's eyes would dim. It wasn't going to stop him from throwing them, but it bolstered his resolve to keep his hands off his intern. Things were going to end up complicated enough without deepening that hero worship into something more intimate.

"I remember, always, that nothing is ever perfect," Bastian said gruffly. "That's what we aim for. But the best of us know it's unattainable."

But Kian's attention was already pulled into the inventory, counting wrapped hunks of butter, his fingers quickly flicking away the paper to test their firmness. With anyone else, Bastian might believe his thoroughness was because he was standing in the fridge, observing, but he knew that it wouldn't matter later. Kian knew the bar, and like Bastian himself, was constantly motivated to exceed it.

It wasn't a large space, and Bastian, to his own regret because kitchens tended to be cramped and small, was a large man. It was one of the reasons he'd built his kitchens at Terroir to be expansive and his line more spread out than others—too many years of trying to make himself impossibly smaller. But still, the fridges, while large, weren't designed for two. Even if one was as slender as Kian.

Kian turned to him, pointing to an item on the clipboard, and Bastian realized, a second too late, as he crowded closer, that there was no room behind him to back up. Kian, absorbed in the printout on the clipboard, didn't look up until it was too late, until they were nearly nestled together, right against the shelf holding about a hundred dozen cartons of eggs.

Kian's eyes widened in surprise and he fumbled the clipboard, nearly dropping it. He should have just let it fall, but Bastian reached out and his hand grasped Kian's shoulder.

They froze like that, Kian nearly bent towards him, their gazes locked, and Bastian couldn't help but think, *fuck, hell, shit, this is never going to work*. And Bastian, despite his temper, usually considered himself an optimist.

There was the shock reflected in those blue eyes, and then sparks of heat, lighting them both on fire. It would be so easy to just lean down and discover what that mouth tasted like. Like the bitter coffee Kian liked. Maybe a piece of chocolate that Miles, one of the pastry assistants, had slipped him during this morning's prep. Dark and dangerous, that's how Kian would taste, even though he looked like sunshine, his hair bright even in the dim light.

"Sorry," Kian mumbled, flushing, and objectively Bastian knew he should take his hand off his shoulder, and let him move away, to a respectable distance—at least a distance that didn't have their thighs pressed together, so he couldn't feel the heat of Kian's body next to his. He might be slender, but it was clear to him now that it wasn't just his determination that was strong, he had a body to back that up. His fingers spasmed over a surprisingly firm shoulder, and then slipped down to Kian's bicep.

Kian's eyes watched him the whole way, the wonder in that blue gaze leaving him more breathless than he'd ever admit to anyone. Bastian could only imagine what his own dark eyes looked like, pupils dilated, his fingers gripping Kian's arm like he couldn't bear to let him go.

It wasn't impossible—Bastian was renowned in the culinary world for his legendary determination—but it damn near felt like it.

"Don't be sorry," Bastian said, and immediately regretted it, because that was admitting something he couldn't take back.

It was admitting to something that could never, ever happen between them.

Bastian dropped his hand, and thankfully Kian took a step back, and then another.

"I was . . . I was going to ask why the mascarpone is on the shelf, but not listed here," Kian said, voice high and stunned. Like he couldn't believe what had just happened.

Bastian, unfortunately, could believe it. There'd been a reason he'd been avoiding being alone with Kian.

Unfortunately there was no way to truly train Kian and not end up alone occasionally. Maybe it was time to address the elephant in the room, make it clear that no matter what anyone's personal feelings were, this was professional, and this was *Kian's career*, which somehow had become more important to Bastian than his own need. And that was so momentous that Bastian refused to look any further into it.

"It would be good, wouldn't it?" Bastian asked, trying for casual, ending up nowhere near that tone. "Between us?"

Kian nearly dropped the clipboard again. He looked shocked, and Bastian reminded himself of American sensibilities. Maybe he should have framed the conversation in a subtler way—but then there was the risk that Kian wouldn't understand, and then they'd have to do this again.

"Excuse me?" Kian squeaked.

"It would be good between us," Bastian repeated, this time making sure it wasn't a question, but a statement. Of fact. Because it would be. Nobody was denying that. "It would, and it would happen more than once, and we'd enjoy ourselves. But it can't happen, because we're doing something more important. We're preparing you for a career that I know could be spectacular."

But Kian was still stuck on the first thing Bastian had said. "It would be good if we slept together?"

Bastian shot him a look that was trying very hard to be bored, but sex with Kian wouldn't ever be boring. He was insatiably curious. He would want to discover. He would turn Bastian's world upside down during the expedition, and probably ruin his own in the process.

"Don't you think so?" Bastian asked.

"Uh," Kian said, sounding truly unsure for the first time since his first day.

"This is . . ." Bastian gestured between them, "just an excess of hormones. It won't last. We have more important things to do."

Kian still looked shell-shocked, like Bastian confirming the attraction between them was mutual was enough to blow his mind.

"So you're saying," he finally spoke up, "that it might feel good now, but that it would waste this opportunity."

Bastian nodded sharply. "And be an impossible distraction. You have a future. It would be a crime to waste it."

"And . . . doing that, would be wasting it?" Kian sounded like he didn't quite believe Bastian, and that made sense. He was young. Romantic, no doubt. And Bastian was probably a romantic figure to him. All that hero worship.

"Trading a brilliant career for a few fleeting moments of pleasure?" Bastian didn't bother considering this. "It's not even a question. I just want to make that clear because this . . . hormone surge is going to happen, occasionally, between us. And I want to make sure that we're on the same page."

"Same page," Kian echoed. "Okay. Yes. Same page. I can do that."

"Good," Bastian said, and focused his attention on the clipboard. "Ah, yes, the mascarpone cheese. It's because it was a special request from the pastry chef, René. I'll have to add it to the inventory sheets. Just notate on the side for now."

Later, Bastian felt guilty for springing such an important conversation on Kian unprepared, but they'd needed to clear away any uncertainty and erase the distraction of *maybe, someday*, from the conversation completely. It had been the right thing to do, to bring it up and to pack the attraction away in a box with no lid.

Chapter Four

The echo of the conversation with Chef—*no,* Kian told himself firmly, *you want him, you can call him by his name, at least in your own head*—Bastian lasted for weeks.

It took Kian a long time to sift through the layers of it, even though Bastian had been very clear and extremely forthright. But first there'd been The Moment, which was how Kian thought of it in his head. The Moment had torn away all pretense, forcing Kian to admit that he wanted it all—he wanted everything Bastian had to teach him, and he wanted his hands and mouth all over him, too. The Moment had made it obvious that Bastian felt the same.

And just when the incredulous delight had filtered through him, shockingly sweet, Bastian had proceeded to explain that moments like The Moment would keep happening, but instead of focusing on them, they needed to focus on Kian's career.

Kian wasn't stupid. He didn't believe that Bastian could be a boss and a mentor *and* a boyfriend. Or even a friend with benefits.

Even the thought of Bastian as a friend with benefits made him hot and then cold all over. And it wasn't just the benefits part.

Bastian committed himself in everything he did. He loved and hated passionately, with commitment. They couldn't just casually fuck and then work together in the restaurant the next day, pretending nothing had ever happened.

As the weeks passed, and then a month, and then two, it wasn't like Kian disagreed with Bastian's assessment. It was fundamentally sound.

It still sucked.

It didn't mean that anything changed either. Most days, in fact, during the majority of them, the relationship between him and Bastian was strictly a professional one. Kian kept close, absorbing everything Bastian taught.

Not just Bastian either—one morning when he reported in, Bastian sent him over to Xander, to learn how to make sauces, and to shadow him on the sauté station during dinner service.

"Must think pretty damn highly of you," Xander muttered as he meticulously set up his *mise en place*.

Kian had already whipped out his little notebook and was making notations on how Xander liked things arranged. Every chef liked it slightly different, and while Xander wasn't quite as particular as Bastian, he still had very definite ideas of how his ingredients should be prepped and set up.

"I'm assuming you know all the mother sauces," Xander said and Kian nodded. That had been a whole semester's worth of classes at the culinary institute. He'd aced that particular course, but he'd learned in the few months since he'd graduated and started working at Terroir that anything he'd learned in school was almost completely useless.

In fact, Bastian had told him more than once to forget everything he'd been taught. The first time he'd said that to Kian, it had been a particularly frustrating and difficult day.

He'd gone back to his little studio apartment, beyond discouraged, which hardly set him apart from anyone else who worked at Terroir. Everyone had a bad day once in awhile, and almost always the reason for that was their illustrious head chef. But Kian believed that what set him apart was that he could shed the frustration and show up the next morning even more determined to learn everything he could from Bastian.

Everyone else slowly grew jaded and bitter, until they started using the Bastard nickname on a regular basis.

Xander was the leader of that particular faction at Terroir. Even though it should have made Kian like him less, he surprisingly didn't.

In spite of the nod, Xander led him through the preparation of each sauce and reduction meticulously, Kian making notes on each one.

When they finished, it was time for family dinner. "Hey," Xander said, pulling him aside before he could join the others at the long table, "Wyatt and Miles and I are getting a house together. There's a fourth bedroom. You interested?"

He actually was. He'd been looking around for a new place because his studio was decrepit and depressing, even though he barely spent any time in it. "Sure. Miles is a pastry assistant, right? The only one René likes?"

"Yeah. He's cool."

Kian agreed with that assessment. He often brought "experiments" in to family dinner, augmenting dinner with some truly delicious pastries and desserts. For that alone, he seemed like a good choice for a roommate.

"I'll send you the ad with the rent and info and stuff," Xander said, shoving his hands in his pockets. "But it's a good deal and a decent enough house, for the price."

"I'm in," Kian said firmly.

For a moment, Xander looked surprised, like he hadn't really expected Kian to agree. And that, Kian realized as they were getting ready for service, made sense because Xander was sort of prickly at the best of times and could be mean at the worst. He didn't make friends easily, but it seemed that he and Kian were actually becoming friends.

At least that was what it felt like until service started and Kian discovered just how unprepared he was to work the line at a high-end establishment like Terroir.

"Two duck, three chicken, four scallop," Bastian called out in a loud voice.

Xander's hands were moving like quicksilver, everywhere at once, checking all his sauté pans, and somehow, impossibly adding more to the stove, even though it felt like it had been full only a moment ago.

Up until now, Kian had been stuck on the simpler appetizers, assembling the salads, and dishing up the soup. He'd been small time and, tonight, he was getting a taste of the big leagues.

"Yes, Chef," Xander barked out, then turned to Kian. "Get those scallop pans going and don't fucking overcook them, not if your life is valuable to you in any way."

"Yes, Chef," Kian said, and tried to calm the trembling in his fingers as he set the pans on the stove and dug the ingredients for the scallop dish out of the refrigerated pull-out drawers underneath the gigantic stovetop.

He knew how to cook scallops, but it was incredibly intimidating to cook them for two of the harshest critics on the planet—Xander and then Bastian.

Still, as the routine tasks took over his hands, they helped. His movements became more certain, and he was fairly confident they were perfectly cooked when he carefully started plating them.

"Wait," Xander said, even though he wasn't even looking in Kian's direction. Did he have eyes in the back of his head somehow? "Those aren't caramelized enough. Chef likes a deep golden brown."

It was not easy to be told he'd screwed up even though he'd given it his very best attempt. "They're cooked through," he insisted stubbornly.

Xander held up his hands. "Your fate."

He'd been confident before, but now he uncertainly slid the plates to the pass-through, ready for the final garnishes and the inspection, which was Bastian's domain.

Bastian started to set a spray of pea greens gently on the top of one scallop when his tweezers paused in the middle of his delicate task. His brows slammed together and when he glanced up, his gaze eviscerated Kian.

"Are these done?" he demanded.

"They're done," Kian promised. Inside he was quaking.

"Caramelize the next batch a little more."

Kian wasn't going to point out that cooking scallops was difficult, but cooking scallops with a gloriously brown sear on them while making sure they were perfectly cooked *while* cooking about ten other things perfectly simultaneously was not easy to do. But he thought it.

After shift he brought this up to Xander while they were in the locker room. "How do you do that?" he asked, because he'd long since learned that there were myriad tricks of the trade that he hadn't learned at the institute, and Xander, if he was in a giving mood, sometimes felt like sharing one or two.

"You think it's impossible right?" Xander asked with a wry smile.

"I think it's really fucking hard," Kian admitted.

Xander's smile widened and deepened, and for the first time, Kian really believed they were becoming friends. Not just co-workers and potential roommates but *friends*.

"That's why they pay us the big bucks," Xander said, stretching his neck.

Kian frowned. "They don't pay us big bucks."

"Yes, well, I guess that's why the Bastard gets paid the big bucks, then. You'll figure it out. It's all about placement of the pan on the stove at different stages of cooking. I'll show you how I do it tomorrow. Right now if I think about scallops, I might vomit."

"Yeah, sure," Kian said. He didn't love how young and naïve he sounded. But that was the job, he figured. He was still learning. Still evolving. Still growing.

And if luck was on his side, that would keep happening, every night, until finally he woke up one day and he was a fantastic chef, ready to be promoted and ready to run his own kitchen.

A month later, he was actually able to sub for Xander, when he had the flu and could not actually stand, and the sauces Kian prepared, though not as subtly brilliant as Xander's, didn't make Chef throw the pans across the kitchen. He cooked pan after pan of scallops flawlessly, leaving Bastian to only raise a single eyebrow as the plates slid over to the pass-through. He took over daily inventory and was meticulous enough that even Bastian couldn't find a thing to complain about.

Slowly, he began shadowing every part of the restaurant, and after the Xander flu incident, Bastian actually encouraged it. It was good to have someone who could step in on a moment's notice and not fuck everything up. Kian was proud of that, and proud of the way he was helping Chef not be so overwhelmed with the incredible amount of daily work that just he was responsible for—never mind everyone else who worked at Terroir.

The days slipped by, eventful in the way that each one seemed very uneventful. Each and every one of them was long. The hours were brutal, but somehow living together helped. Even though Bastian had looked once over the reading glasses that had made their way into more than one of Kian's nightly fantasies, and suggested it was a terrible idea to live with people you worked with, it had been the right choice.

The days didn't seem quite so long when he could come home, flip on the TV, listen to Xander and Wyatt bitch about what shitty thing Chef had said to them tonight, and watch as Miles smiled slow and wide, distributing the pastries he'd snitched from the extras.

It was a good life, and Kian liked it. He might have loved it, if only those Moments could stop happening. They made him yearn for disasters.

Disasters like kissing in the fridges, blowjobs in Bastian's office, Bastian pushing him against one of the stainless steel prep counters late at night and fucking him mercilessly.

Considering that he already knew they'd be disasters, it was surprising that he couldn't push them out of his mind.

His friends teased him mercilessly, because of course they'd picked up on his crush. They didn't call it that, of course, because Kian knew they were secretly horrified since Bastian was their living nightmare. And it wasn't like he didn't say shitty things to Kian sometimes. It wasn't like he didn't make him come to Terroir earlier and stay later than anyone else. It wasn't that he hadn't ever thrown a pot or a dish at some mistake Kian had made. Those incidents happened often enough they weren't even out of the ordinary.

But he also got to see Bastian in a light they didn't.

On the last Sunday of every month, Bastian tested recipes, and from the very first time Kian joined him, it was something special they did together.

This wasn't the first time, but somehow, the miracle of creation never failed to excite him. And sometimes, if Kian was very lucky, Bastian would let down his guard a little, and Kian would catch him staring at him, as he went about his tasks. Something that Bastian would never do when others were around, because Kian knew he was terrified of anyone finding out that the Bastard had *feelings*, even if they were primarily sexual feelings.

"What about the butter?" Kian asked, holding the buttery, lemon-dill reduction out towards where Chef was bent over a plate, tweezers out as he settled the garnishes onto the plate.

They were trying out a new langoustine recipe, and Chef had asked Kian to put together a butter sauce for drizzling. Except that instead of drizzling it, Bastian had moved right onto the garnishes.

"Oh, shit, yeah," Bastian said, glancing up. "Maybe around the edge of the plate?"

When they'd first started working together on Sundays, Bastian definitely hadn't asked Kian's opinion. But slowly, as their time together progressed, he'd begun to ask a question here or there, until, in the last few months, the sessions had started to actually feel collaborative.

Kian looked at the plate Bastian had chosen and knew that sauce ringing the edge of the plate would be a messy proposition at best.

"Let me taste it first," Bastian demanded, and Kian passed over the pot. He dipped a spoon in, licked it clean, and let the flavor of the sauce linger on his palate. Chef tasted a hundred things, every single day, but the recurring thought of, *that should be me*, and the automatic denial was second nature to Kian by now.

"God damn, that's good," Bastian said fervently. "The little spice on the end, that's glorious."

"Thank you, Chef," Kian said formally, but he was smiling. Nothing ever felt better than a compliment from Bastian, mostly because compliments were so scarce, but also because you knew he *meant* them.

Unceremoniously he dumped the langoustine in the trash, sliding the plate down near the rest of their dirty dishes. Dishes Kian would probably end up washing, since Jorge wouldn't be in until later, and he'd have his hands full.

"That sauce needs to be the focal. Which means, a new plate." Bastian prowled over to the shelving unit that held his plate selections, and picked one, then another, and then a third.

They clattered as he deposited them on the counter in front of Kian. "You pick," he said.

This was new. Sometimes Bastian asked his opinion, but he'd never been given control of a decision before. And plate selection was huge. It determined plating and garnish and Bastian had told him a thousand times, those often determined the ultimate success of a dish. Food was visual before it ever hit the taste buds.

Kian examined each one carefully, envisioning in his mind the langoustine, the French beans, the sauce, the garnishes. Only one stood to him as the perfect choice. He glanced up at Bastian, who was watching intently.

"Go on," Bastian said, making a little shooing gesture with his hand, the other tucked up under his armpit. A fierce look of concentration fell over his face as he watched Kian plate the langoustine.

When Kian was finally done, and wiped the plate, Bastian spent a long time looking at it from every angle.

He'd poured the sauce into the bottom of the curved bowl, curled the langoustine in a loose spiral, positioned the beans upright, letting them fan out, and in a final touch, used the eyedropper to dot the surface of the yellowy cream sauce with basil oil.

"You've been paying attention," Bastian said finally.

Kian was almost offended. Was there anyone who assumed he *hadn't* been?

"All it needs," Bastian continued, "is one final touch." He abruptly turned on his heel and headed in the direction of the walk-in fridges. When he came back, he was holding something in his hands. Carefully he leaned down and nestled one of the miniature Anaheim peppers they'd just gotten into one of the langoustine folds.

"Visually, it's right," Bastian said, but he gave a sigh of frustration. "But if any idiot eats that, it'll overwhelm the shellfish and the sauce. What else do we have that's red?"

"What about a single slice of radish?" Kian suggested. "It's a nice vibrant red, but the flavor is fairly neutral."

"Let's try it," Bastian said, and Kian went back to the walk-in, grabbed a radish, then his fish deboning knife, very sharp and very flexible and carved a single, nearly paper-thin slice. The edges were bright red, and the starkness of the white was a good contrast to the yellow and green base. He swapped it for the pepper, and knew it was right when Bastian sighed again, but this time in satisfaction.

He reached over and clapped a hand on Kian's shoulder.

They didn't always touch. Touching always felt a little like Russian roulette, especially in the sacred confines of the Terroir kitchens. But once in a while—Kian was never sure if it was because he'd done something good enough to be rewarded or if Bastian was so impressed he couldn't help himself anymore—he'd reach out like this with a brief clasp of his shoulder.

This time, though, he lingered and Kian's heartbeat accelerated. He couldn't stop it and he couldn't slow it down.

He looked up to see Bastian looking at him, intently. There were a thousand dangerous things brewing in that dark gaze, and Kian trembled.

"You are so . . ." Bastian broke off and dropped his hand, his earlier frustration magnified.

For a moment, Kian considered bringing up the conversation that they didn't talk about. If Bastian was finding it so difficult to stay professional, maybe they could relax the rules a little.

Except that wouldn't work either. If one or both of them ever broke down and touched with more than just friendly, professional intent, the resulting wildfire would be all-consuming. There wouldn't just be a slight bending of the rules, the rules would be entirely incinerated.

There was nothing to say, nothing to be done, because Kian *still* believed Chef was right. He was learning so much, absorbing everything, and if they hadn't had that conversation so long ago, would these Sundays even be happening? Sundays where he'd even begun to establish his own point of view as a chef?

"I'm sorry," Bastian finally said. He sounded wretched—just like Kian felt. "I'd tell you to find another teacher, but I'm horribly territorial and I'd probably end up punching them in the face."

Kian laughed, because he wasn't going to cry. Not in front of Chef Aquino. Six months ago, he might have spent a week in wonderment, that Bastian cared enough about him to be territorial at all. But now, all he felt was a hazy sort of desperation.

How long could they continue like this? Kian's contract with Terroir had been for two years, initially, and he'd intended to stay at least that long, if not longer.

But later that night, as he lay awake in bed, every muscle in his body exhausted but sleep somehow still elusive, he wondered if he could possibly last two years like this.

Something inside him ached, and he was afraid it was his heart. It had been so much easier when he'd believed, like Bastian had hinted at, that their connection was just hormones. But after six months, Kian was afraid that wasn't all it was anymore. He didn't want just to protect Bastian anymore. He wanted to teach Bastian, the way Bastian was teaching him, how to handle the stuff that overwhelmed him. Instead of avoiding it, he wanted to be consumed by the fire between them; he wanted to pull Bastian in with him.

Bastian's own frustration with the arrangement had shown in his face today, but how were they supposed to stop? There was nothing to be done, Kian realized, except to keep going.

Keep learning, keep growing, and keep suffering.

Two months later, one of Miles' pastry videos went viral, and he packed up and moved to LA.

When he watched Miles make himself a drunken mess over his new producer, Kian told himself firmly this was exactly why Bastian had insisted they keep things professional between them. He didn't want to be Miles, and he didn't want to be Miles' new producer either. It was messy and embarrassing and it didn't even matter that they ended up happily together.

Kian told himself firmly that he was thrilled for them, and left it at that.

Four months after that, Wyatt, witnessing the money Miles had made in LA, let himself be lured down there too. He got a job as a private chef for a baseball player, and at this point, Kian was resigned that all his friends were going to abandon him.

As long as Xander stayed, he'd be okay.

Of course, Wyatt leaving meant that Wyatt had to resign from Terroir.

Unfortunately, Kian, who took care of almost all of Bastian's personnel issues now, as well as prepping and subbing as needed on the line during service, couldn't be the one to take Wyatt's resignation letter.

It was going to have to be Bastian, and Bastian wasn't going to be happy about it.

He loved firing people, but people leaving him? *Not good. Abort. Do not pass Go. Do not collect two hundred dollars.*

It would've been weird for Kian to be in the office when Wyatt submitted his resignation but he hovered outside, waiting for the moment when everything went sideways.

He heard murmured voices, and then Bastian's voice edging upwards. Wyatt was still too hard to hear, which meant that he was keeping his own temper, even as Bastian's sneering tone cut right through the glass walls of his office and echoed throughout the whole kitchen.

"Did someone even hire your sloppy ass?" Bastian demanded, and he said it loud enough, Kian could see heads rise across the kitchen. He sighed and leaned back against the wall. This was going just about as badly as he'd imagined it would. The worst part in Kian's opinion was that he knew Bastian didn't mean anything he'd just said. He was so angry because losing Wyatt, who was a fantastic chef with an intuitive touch for meat, was a blow. It didn't excuse the verbal abuse, but at least it helped explain it.

Kian was startled from his studied nonchalance when a crash resonated through the entire kitchen. Almost immediately Wyatt stormed out, his blue eyes narrow and his expression very pissed off. He didn't even acknowledge Kian, who raced past him to discover that *yes,* Bastian had swept the entire contents of his desk onto the floor.

He sighed, and leaned down to pick up a piece of coffee mug that was spinning at his feet.

"I can't believe that fucking bastard quit," Bastian said in a huff, but Kian had known him long enough to know it was all defensive posturing. *I can't believe he left me,* was what Kian heard.

"He needs the money. His grandmother is in a home," Kian said quietly. "And this private chef gig pays really well."

"Private chef," Bastian sneered. "So he's going to go grill plain, tough chicken for some socialite in LA?"

Being Bastian's intern and being friends with Wyatt and Xander was a fine line to walk. He often knew more than he felt comfortable saying to his boss—things that his friends told him in confidence. Like that Xander's new sauce recipe was almost directly lifted from a Tom Colicchio cookbook, or that Wyatt wasn't going to be cooking for a socialite at all, but the only "out" player in professional baseball.

Bastian definitely didn't need to know that there was definitely something going on between the baseball player and Wyatt.

"Probably," Kian said noncommittedly in his most soothing voice. He leaned down and picked up the keyboard, which was missing a few important keys. This was the fourth keyboard they'd been through in the last year, and Kian had started buying extras because he might still need to place online orders for supplies and ingredients the day that Bastian decided to throw a hissy fit. They couldn't run out of artichokes just because Kian didn't have a keyboard.

Kicking a pen, Bastian slumped down into his chair. The anger had passed now, and they'd moved on to guilt.

"I shouldn't have said those things. I just . . . saw red," Bastian said hopelessly.

Kian set the broken keyboard on the chair opposite the desk. He maneuvered around the random detritus on the floor and took a chance by moving closer to Bastian than he normally allowed himself. Even took the risk of placing his hands on Bastian's broad, muscular shoulders, emphasized by the cut of his white chef's coat.

Bastian stared at him, and something inside Kian trembled. They didn't often touch, because even a hand on a shoulder was dangerous, and Kian never initiated contact. But he did today, curling his fingers into the starched cotton of Bastian's jacket, holding him steady as his own pulse accelerated.

"Maybe next time, we can figure out a way for you to only see . . . orange," Kian suggested softly.

"I have a temper," Bastian snapped. "It's not going away." He jerked out of Kian's hands, and the moment broke, like an egg cracking against the edge of a bowl.

It would be nice if Bastian's temper mellowed, but Kian was not laboring under any false impression that it would. Bastian's temper was part of who he was; it was the product of the intense pressure he put on himself and on others to produce perfection every single day. It wasn't ideal, it wasn't always professional, but it wasn't going away.

Still, if Kian could figure out a way to convince him to take a second to *think* before he acted, then maybe the collateral damage would be less. At the very least, Kian would end up needing less keyboards.

Leaning down, Kian began to gather up pieces of the coffee cup and the pens and pencils scattered over the polished concrete floor. Out of the corner of his eye, he watched as Bastian began to pace in the small space, his arms crossed across his chest, like the physical movement might contain what kept trying to escape.

"I just . . . Wyatt . . . he's good," Bastian said, and Kian glanced up to see that he'd stopped pacing and was staring at him, crouched on the floor.

"I know he is," Kian said calmly.

"He knows it too," Bastian muttered, like that made up for the insults he'd just spit in Wyatt's direction.

"Yeah, he does. Which is partly why he's leaving."

Kian had gathered almost all the pens from the desk and was moving onto the paperclips sprinkled across the concrete.

"Here," Bastian said, and Kian looked up from the floor to see the mesh paperclip holder held at eye level. He'd crouched down next to Kian and was also picking up paperclips.

This was by no means the first time Bastian had cleared his desk in a fit of temper, but it was definitely the first time he'd helped Kian clean up the mess.

Kian tipped a handful of paperclips into the container. "Maybe I should get one with a sealed lid," he said, trying to use a bit of humor to distract him from the fact that Bastian was right there next to him, helping him. If he turned his head and leaned a little to the left he'd be pressed right against him.

It might not be an apology, but it was *something*.

Sighing, Bastian pushed back on his heels, observing the mess surrounding them with a cynical expression. "This life is hard."

"Really?" Kian retorted sarcastically. "I had no idea."

Bastian, who could be a sarcastic son of a bitch, ironically hated sarcasm in others, so he ignored Kian's statement. "And this," he gestured between them, "makes me tense."

Like on cue, Kian tensed himself. It was the first time Bastian had overtly referred to the non-relationship between them since that first conversation in the dairy walk-in. He'd come close that Sunday when they'd tested the new langoustine dish—a dish that had carved out a permanent place on the menu, which Kian was still unbearably proud of—but he'd never come out and said it directly.

"It's hard," Kian agreed softly. He didn't really believe that sexual frustration was making Bastian an edgier or more terrible boss than he'd been before. It was a convenient excuse, but Kian still understood what he really meant. There were definitely days, those occasional times when their hands would brush or he'd catch Bastian staring intently, possessively, at him, and he also wanted to throw something.

He'd been at Terroir a year now, and there was a part of him that had fiercely believed that after all this time, something would have happened to shift the status quo, even though they both believed that it was better that nothing ever happened between them.

But Bastian's determination to keep his hands off was forged from steel, and Kian couldn't deny the selflessness attracted him even more.

It grew harder, every day, every week, every month, and still neither of them flinched.

Maybe they never would. That possibility had seemed completely impossible a year ago, but maybe he'd been wrong. After all, it couldn't get much harder than this, could it?

"I'm sorry," Bastian said, so quietly that Kian nearly missed it.

Kian reached out again, and it was perilous, but he covered Bastian's big scarred hand with his own, smaller one. "Don't apologize," he insisted in a hard tone. "Don't you dare apologize."

Bastian's smile was wry. "Even for losing my temper?"

Kian's mom had told him once that when he fell in love, he needed to accept everything about the object of his affection. "You don't have to love everything," she'd said with a laugh, "you don't even have to like everything, but you need to accept who they are because you can't change them."

Kian couldn't believe it had taken him so long to realize, but *of course* he was in love with Bastian. Maybe it was because he'd been trying to keep those feelings locked away, covered with the convenient, much less serious, "hormones" label. But now that he'd realized, it was impossible to deny it was true.

And Bastian—who still shot him yearning looks, who was teaching him every single thing he knew, who seemed to delight in Kian stretching his culinary wings, who denied them the very thing they wanted because it would be better for Kian's future—he *must* love him too.

It should have been a joyous realization, but all it did was fill Kian with frustration.

What was he supposed to do about something he couldn't do anything about?

Nothing, he thought darkly, *I'm going to do nothing. Nothing has changed.*

Chapter Five

Nothing, Bastian reminded himself as he pulled into the valet parking station at the downtown San Francisco hotel, *you will do nothing*.

Kian was next to him, eyes wide as he took in the huge buildings and the crowds of people on the streets around them. He absorbed sights and sounds and flavors like a sponge, regurgitating them in the most unusual ways. Bastian had been sure that with time, his desire would fade, and they could settle into a more normal mentor-student relationship, but he discovered that he was more drawn to Kian than ever. Not just his body or his physical attributes, but his mind—and his heart. He was incomprehensibly loyal, and believed, even after being let down enough times to turn other people bitter, in the best of everyone.

There had been part of him who believed it was a mistake to take Kian on this short trip to the city for the culinary demonstration, but he needed an assistant, and Kian had become essential to him. So he'd booked them two separate rooms, even though the temptation burned in him.

Nobody at Terroir would know what happened this weekend. Nobody would ever know if they didn't use the second room—the only witnesses would be the two of them. But Bastian knew, just as he'd known a year and a half ago, that it still couldn't happen. He was still Kian's mentor, and what a student he was turning out to be.

He could comfortably sub at any station on the line, even somehow, inconceivably, pastry, and he had made Bastian's life both easier and fuller, more complete. When he came home, he didn't feel as alone as he had. Technically he still ate alone, showered alone, went to bed alone, but Kian was a ghost next to him, his faithful shadow, the memory of who he was keeping Bastian company always.

It was still hard, to work together every day, and keep the feelings in the tightly-lidded box. But other than a handful of slips when he'd admitted to Kian just how tough it was, he'd done it because it needed to be done. He'd known at the very beginning that Kian was going to be a special kind of chef, and in the last eighteen months, he'd fulfilled all that promise and more.

Bastian shouldn't feel dissatisfied—he'd accomplished exactly what he'd set out to do, which was keep his hands off Kian, and make sure he learned everything Bastian could teach—but the feeling followed him around anyway.

It reminded him, far too often, that he didn't *need* to be alone when he ate, when he showered, when he slept. That as gratifying as the shadow of Kian was, real flesh and blood would be exponentially more satisfying.

Shaking the thoughts away, Bastian got out of the car, tossing the keys to the approaching valet, and grabbed their bags from the trunk. Kian trailed a few steps behind as they walked into the lobby, eyes wide and growing wider, at the spectacularly massive Dale Chihuly glass chandelier, executed in metallic gold and a progression of bloody reds.

On the drive down, Kian had asked him if he did these sorts of demonstrations often. Bastian had nearly told him that he should already know this, because he'd been working for him for eighteen months already, and he hadn't left the restaurant once. Not a day off in eighteen months.

That's what the old Bastian would have said anyway—with a bark and a bite in his voice. But even though his employees ignored it, he knew he'd grown softer. Less frustrated with things like social niceties. More apt to answer questions about himself, especially when posed to him by Kian.

"No," he'd answered simply. "I hate doing them."

"Then why are you doing this one?" Kian had asked.

"A favor," was all Bastian had said, but he had a feeling that the favor would show himself soon enough and all Kian's questions would be answered.

It turned out the favor was hovering near the enormous carved mahogany desk that doubled as the hotel concierge.

"It is so good to see you, *mon cher*," Luc said, approaching Bastian with open arms.

"This is a surprise," Bastian muttered, managing to duck a little and avoid his embrace full-on, relegating him to a sort of half hug. He deliberately set the bags on the floor, also avoiding Luc attempting any cheek kisses.

He wasn't going to do that. Definitely not with Luc. And somehow, surprisingly, the thought of Kian witnessing it wrenched his stomach.

"They said you wouldn't come but I told them otherwise," Luc announced cheerfully. "Even the great Bastian Aquino can leave the enclave of Napa for a weekend."

There were many times Bastian had been tempted to punch Luc in the face, but none more than right now.

"I gave my word," Bastian ground out, "so naturally, I am here."

"Of course, of course," Luc said. "Shall I show you the setup now or . . ."

Bastian had known Luc would be here. He had fully expected that Luc would want to avoid him as much as Bastian wanted to avoid Luc. However that did not seem to be the case.

"We just arrived. Can we not check in to our rooms first?"

"We?" Luc pointedly looked around Bastian and then saw Kian, who was still transfixed by the Chihuly.

"My assistant and I," Bastian said stiffly.

"Your assistant?" Luc said slyly, looking Kian over from top to bottom.

Bastian had been wrong; this was the moment he wanted to punch Luc more than any other.

"My assistant," Bastian repeated, stressing the *assistant* part. But the knowing look in Luc's eyes was unmistakable.

It was evidence of how pathetic Bastian had become that he almost wished that Luc's sly insinuation was true.

"Well, I'll see you two in the ballroom in a little while. I want to make sure I remembered how you like your *mise* at your station."

When they were finally in the elevator, heading upstairs, Kian turned to Bastian. "Who was that?"

"An old friend," Bastian said, hoping that the closed-book tone of his voice would strongly suggest to Kian to leave it at that.

But one of the things he adored most about the man next to him was his insatiable curiosity. He didn't want to just try one thing with an ingredient, he wanted to cook it a hundred different ways, until he'd discovered the best possible way to prepare it.

He wasn't ever going to leave that tantalizing glimpse into Bastian's past alone.

"Someone you worked with?" Kian asked as Bastian handed him the keycard to his room. "He looked pretty young."

Not as young as you, Bastian thought to himself.

"Someone I mentored a few years back," Bastian said, "when I first opened Terroir."

"Oh," Kian said. "Someone like me."

Someone who is nothing like you.

But Bastian was stupid and said, "Sure." It wasn't accurate, not in any way that mattered, but he believed it might stop the questions, and that was really what he was after.

He never wanted to talk about Luc, and he definitely didn't want to talk about Luc with Kian.

"Oh," Kian said, and the slightly wounded edge in his voice made him immediately want to take it back, but he didn't, because what was he supposed to say? *I don't want to hurt your feelings? Nobody is really like you? Nobody ever, not for me?* Those were things a boyfriend would say, and Bastian wasn't Kian's boyfriend.

Saying them would only make everything worse, and their relationship already felt constantly fraught with the tension of doing absolutely fucking nothing.

"We'll go downstairs in an hour," Bastian said. "So get changed. We'll have to make sure my *mise* is how I like it." It was unspoken that Kian would have to fix it if it was wrong.

Kian nodded, and they both disappeared behind their respective doors. Bastian leaned back against his, head tipped back, eyes closed, wishing that he'd refused to repay Luc's favor by showing up today.

He should have brought Xander, not Kian, though he knew if he had, Xander's semi-abrasive self would have scared away everyone and Kian's wounded puppy dog eyes would have followed him around for a month.

He hadn't really been able to refuse Luc calling in his favor and taking Xander, or another one of the less experienced chefs had never been an option. It was fate that he was stuck here, only one wall away from what he desperately wanted, and he couldn't stop putting his own damn foot in his mouth.

For a moment, he nearly called his mother, but he'd tried very hard not to tell her anything else about Kian. Certainly, she knew something was going on with him, and almost certainly she had guessed it was Bastian's intern shadow, but somehow she'd refrained from pushing him.

Probably because she knew he was too much like his father in ways he didn't like, and as a result, didn't react well to being pushed.

He'd just showered this morning, but he took another one, because the idea of flipping on the television was abhorrent and he was not ready to work—his focus was far too fractured. But the long hot shower quieted his concerns, and he dressed meticulously in his chef whites, like a general donning his armor for battle.

He exited the hotel room, and found Kian waiting for him patiently in the hallway.

"Ready?" Bastian asked, and Kian nodded again, uncharacteristically quiet. Bastian recognized the mood though—before taking shifts at some of the newer-to-him stations on the line, he would often grow silent and introspective, as he prepared for the difficult task at hand. It was a technique that Bastian admired, so he let the silence draw out as they took the elevator downstairs.

The ballroom was filled with chairs, hundreds of them in neat, tidy rows, with a large stage at the front. Luc was standing on the raised platform, directing traffic. Other chefs would be giving demonstrations today, but everyone melted out of the way as Bastian and Kian approached.

"Ah, the illustrious Chef Aquino," Luc said, his voice grating on Bastian in ways that it never had before. Either he'd been protected by a healthy helping of hormones, or Luc had gotten more annoying in the intervening years since he'd left Terroir.

"Where is my *mise*?" Bastian demanded. Kian appeared next to him, no longer the subservient half a step back.

"Right here, Chef," Luc said, gesturing towards the setup in front of them.

Kian got to work immediately, and Bastian suddenly wished that he hadn't brought someone who was so meticulous, that it left nothing for him to do except be engaged in conversation by Luc.

"He is very thorough," Luc said.

Bastian shot him an incredulous look. "Did you forget the way I like things?"

"Oh no," Luc said, shooting Kian another head to toe, scorching look, "I couldn't forget what you like. Especially not when you keep reminding us all."

Bastian wasn't blind; he saw the way Kian's back tensed. He knew what all this talk was about.

"This is not the place, or the time."

He lowered his voice and with the hope Kian wouldn't hear, forced himself to step closer to Luc. His old protégé, his old lover. Someone he'd never really expected to see again. Someone he hadn't cared to see again. Because when he'd told Kian that his future was more important than a few fleeting moments of pleasure, he hadn't been speaking from a place of inexperience.

He'd already done this once, and he'd fucked it all up. He wasn't going to let Kian become another Luc—jaded, bitter, downright nasty with disappointment. It didn't matter that Luc didn't have a shred of the loyalty that Kian held dear.

It didn't matter because Bastian could never stand here and have Kian sneer at him the way Luc was. He could stand a lot of things—uncomfortably hot kitchens, cramped spaces, cooking with not enough prep and not enough help, sixteen-hour days, six days a week—but he couldn't stand that.

"If you brought me here," Bastian continued, in a low, brutal voice, "only to insult me, then I'd be happy to leave and have you perform the demonstration."

Luc gave a sharp nod and turned to check up on some other important task, leaving Bastian to stew.

"An old friend?" Bastian looked up to see that Kian had finished the double check of his *mise* and his eyes were burning with injustice. "You were friends with him?"

There was the undeniable question in his words. *Friends?* Kian was silently asking. *Or more?*

But Bastian was still not prepared to get into it, not right now, not when he was about to give a demonstration for approximately five hundred members of the culinary media.

"Friends," he replied shortly. He couldn't miss the way Kian's expression shuttered, but what else could he say? *I fucked up with him, a way I'm never going to fuck up with you?*

The demonstration was thankfully a rather easy dish, actually one of Kian's inventions, the langoustine with dill butter sauce. With ease, despite being in front of five hundred members of a press that would joyfully rip him to pieces, he removed the shell, and carefully sautéed the langoustine. Blanched the beans. Prepared the sauce. Did all of the above with as much grace and skill as he could.

Answered questions. Tried to even make a joke or two, which mostly didn't go over, as he wasn't renowned for his humor.

But that was okay, because he caught Kian's expression, where he stood at the side of the dais, and he was smiling. Luc was not, but Luc seemed to have developed a permanent scowl on his handsome face.

He finished the demonstration to generous applause, and even took a handful of questions, something he normally would not have done.

When it was finally over, he was incredibly relieved and had a headache probably induced from being too nice for too long. Definitely from tolerating Luc's sly looks and endless supply of semi-rude remarks.

Luc had always been too clever for his own good.

Bastian and Kian rode the elevator back upstairs in silence. Luc had extended an invitation to dinner, same as he had with all the other chefs that were in town, but he wouldn't have expected that Bastian would accept.

Instead, he really wanted to take another hot shower, and order in some mediocre room service he could complain to Kian about.

But Kian was young and vibrant and worked too hard, for too many long hours.

He turned to him. "You should go to dinner here. I'm tired. I'm going to order in and probably fall asleep early."

Kian frowned. "You want me to go to dinner with Luc?"

That was the very last thing Bastian wanted. "No, I meant, we're in a beautiful, vibrant city. You should see some of it. Expand your palate."

Maybe if Bastian wasn't feeling quite so stung over all of Luc's insinuations, he might have taken Kian himself, damn the headache. But there were too many people—*let's face it,* Bastian thought to himself, *all the people*—who would assume they were a couple. A much-older gentleman taking his young, delectable boyfriend out for a fancy dinner, all to spoil him.

Maybe another time their opinions might not matter, but they mattered tonight.

"You're not going?" Kian asked flatly.

He shook his head. "Headache."

They reached their floor, and in short order, their rooms. Kian pulled out his key but hesitated, looking at Bastian.

He'd just performed in front of a whole score of media, all willing to rip his head off, but it was the questions in Kian's eyes that terrified the fuck out of him. Bastian whipped out his keycard and escaped into the room before he could ask any of them.

The second shower didn't help nearly as much, as an uncharacteristic ball of guilt settled into the base of his stomach. What made it feel even worse was that he knew, if Kian texted one of his friends, Xander maybe, and accused him of being an unfeeling, abrupt asshole, they would all tell him that he shouldn't expect anything less. He was the Bastard, after all.

The guilt gnawed at him through his room service dinner, which ended up even more mediocre than he'd imagined, and that he just pushed halfheartedly around the plate.

He did drink the wine that accompanied the meal though, and settled back in the bed, television on low, and tried not to think at all.

A firm knock on the door knocked him right out of his unthinking reverie.

His first horrible thought was that it was Luc, here to gloat some more.

His second horrible thought was that it was Kian, here to ask all the questions he hadn't let him earlier.

A glimpse into the peephole confirmed that it was option number two. Kian stood there, nervously shifting from one foot to the other, with a very determined look on his face.

Bastian sighed. They could either do this now, or he was sure he'd be interrogated on the way home and might actually end up crashing and killing them in the process. This way, tonight, seemed marginally safer.

The alcohol he'd drunk burned in his veins as he opened the door, tempting him unbearably. This was just as he'd imagined it happening, wasn't it? The dim light of the hotel room. Kian coming over late at night. Sometimes it felt like there could only be one end to this story.

"Yes?" Bastian asked as Kian let the door close behind him.

"I asked you if Luc had been like me and you said *sure*."

Bastian propped a hip against the credenza. He crossed his arms across his t-shirt-clad chest and wished he was wearing something more substantial than a pair of striped pajama pants that his mother had bought him. "That's not a question."

Kian frowned. "You said we were the *same*, but that isn't true, is it?"

There was an unbearable temptation to tell the whole truth, but that felt incredibly dangerous. Too dangerous, especially in this room, with nobody the wiser to what actually happened in it.

"It's true," Bastian claimed. "He was my protégé. I didn't have an intern then, but he assisted me, when Terroir first opened."

Kian took a step closer, then another, and Bastian nearly stumbled backwards. He hadn't expected Kian to be this aggressive, but there'd been flashes of it lately. Kian touching *him*. Kian approaching *him*. And Bastian knew, with a flash of insight, that this status quo couldn't continue forever, because Kian was changing. He was growing up. He was finding his feet in this world. Sooner or later, he would demand more, and Bastian was not ready for that confrontation. Not even close.

"He wasn't *only* your protégé," Kian said, putting a hand on Bastian's chest. "You slept with him."

For a moment, Bastian considered denying it, but it was useless. Kian already knew the truth. "I did."

A very hard look crossed across Kian's face. "So all that . . . *crap* was because you'd done this before and it hadn't worked out very well for you."

"No . . ." Bastian tried to insert but Kian had been saving up this speech and he intended to unleash it—not even Bastian was going to be able to stop him.

"You pretended like it was *so hard* for you, like it didn't matter that I was *dying* for you," Kian ranted, fingers curling tightly into the fabric of his t-shirt, right above where his heart beat in double time. "You let me think, you let me believe, it was only me. But it wasn't. This is what you do. You do *this*."

"No," Bastian uselessly argued. *There's nobody like you. Definitely not Luc, that fucking disloyal asshole.*

"Why did you even do it? To prove you could? To make yourself feel better about Luc? Because I don't see that working out very well for you," Kian continued, voice growing higher and more hysterical. "I'm not his substitute, I'm not his stand-in, don't you understand? I won't be, I'm not."

Later, Bastian would think back to this moment and envy the solitary certainness of his brain function. He'd only wanted to do one thing—*prove Kian wrong*—no matter what the cost, and that made him do something incredibly stupid and incredibly dangerous.

And probably, Bastian would later think, incredibly inevitable.

He grabbed Kian's wrist and dragged him even closer, until they were hip to hip, chest to chest, and Kian was panting, wordless as they stared into each other's eyes.

This was more than inevitable. It had probably been foretold at the beginning of time—Bastian Aquino was going to meet someone who made him question every ounce of his determination, his resolve, his ego, and who was eventually going to tear his self-control to shreds.

He kissed Kian.

Kian instantaneously melted under him, leaning against his chest and pouring everything into the kiss, even as Bastian selfishly took it all back out. *Mine,* he gloated inwardly, *this is all for me.*

Bastian's hands slid up to his shoulders, to his head and he cradled it in his palms as he did the thing he'd told himself from the first moment that *he would not do.*

The kiss ended in a breathless whimper as Kian pulled back, his eyes as wide and shocked as Bastian had ever seen them. Like he'd just blown every circuit in Kian's body. And he probably had; personally, Bastian felt just as decimated. Like everything he knew about love and attraction and those fucking hormones he liked to blame everything on, was wrong.

"You shouldn't have done that," Kian said, harsh pants against Bastian's cheek.

"I know," Bastian said, and his voice was a surprisingly honest caress. "But I couldn't help it. You . . . you're not like him. You've never been like him. In the most rudimentary ways, yes, you have some similarity. But he is so different, and I was different than I am now, I was selfish and egotistical, and I took whatever I wanted, damn the cost."

Bastian removed his hands carefully and Kian took an unsteady step back. Hesitant, like he wasn't quite ready to let go yet.

Still, Kian was able to crack a little smile, and Bastian thanked God for that. "Selfish and egotistical . . . back then?"

Waving an impatient hand, Bastian had to hold back his own laughter. "You are . . . *god damn* . . . you're my downfall. You know that."

Kian didn't say anything, those blue eyes boring right into Bastian's soul. Like he could read him, and every single thing that was written there, good *and* bad, and somehow he accepted them all.

Nobody had ever done that for him before. Even his own mother sometimes despaired of all his less-than-stellar qualities.

"We're not doing this," Kian said very quietly, and very certainly. "Not like this."

Bastian was afraid to ask what that meant. But secretly, he was afraid he knew.

Not like this, maybe, but some other way, some other day. And Bastian wasn't sure he could turn him down, not after the taste he'd just had.

Chapter Six

The kiss. The Kiss, as Kian liked to think of it, should have changed something. Before, if you'd asked him what kissing Bastian would change—he unequivocally would have said, "everything."

Of course, he hadn't anticipated what Chef would do on their first day back from San Francisco. He'd called Xander into his office, and Kian had stared frustratingly at the closed blinds and wondered what was happening. There was very little that happened at Terroir anymore that he wasn't intimately familiar with, and Bastian doing this today, after The Kiss, and deliberately not telling him, hurt.

Ten minutes later, Chef announced to the kitchen that they finally had a *sous chef*, and that *sous chef* was Xander.

Kian, who did not typically feel Bastian's need to throw things, wanted to pelt his friend with every eggplant at his prep station, which was a very large pile.

It wasn't that Xander wouldn't make a fantastic *sous* or that he didn't deserve the position, because he definitely would and he definitely did. But the timing of the promotion was infuriating, and Kian knew exactly what he was meant to take away from it: that Bastian was in charge, and that Kian was still an intern or his assistant, or whatever they were calling his position these days.

He wasn't *sous*, and nothing was happening between them, as far as Bastian was concerned.

In spite of The Kiss. Maybe even because of The Kiss? Kian didn't know anymore.

He stayed angry for weeks, and Bastian gave him a wide berth, like he knew Kian's temper, which had never shown itself until now, was prodigious when aroused.

The worst was that he couldn't tell any of his friends about what had happened. Xander took his promotion in stride—more like he'd finally gotten what should have been his forever ago, rather than any sort of exuberant celebration at being promoted. How was Kian supposed to tell him, "by the way, I think Chef promoted you to *sous* because we kissed and he wanted to remind me that nothing else was ever going to happen between us"?

He couldn't. Not ever. At least not while keeping Xander's friendship, which had come to mean more and more to him since first Miles, and then Wyatt, had departed for the brighter lights of Los Angeles.

But as the days passed into weeks and then into months, Xander's promotion didn't change much in the Terroir kitchen. Chef only spent slightly less time on the line, and Xander, who wasn't exactly the greatest leader of men either, didn't seem particularly bothered by this.

Kian continued to sub in at various stations. He continued to be the sole assistant to Bastian during their test kitchen Sundays. He was afraid to ask if Bastian had offered the spot to Xander, and he'd just declined it—but he wanted to believe Chef hadn't wanted to give away his spot to anyone else. Besides, their collaborations were good, sometimes even great. They almost always ended up on the menu, at least as a seasonal special. And they *were* collaborations. They came up with the concepts and recipes together, always, and Bastian had even stopped asking Kian what he thought; he naturally assumed that Kian would offer his opinion when the right moment arrived.

Kian decided Xander not knowing about certain job perks was perfectly fine. He enjoyed them more than Xander ever would. Xander would see being stuck in the kitchen with Bastian on a day he'd normally have the morning and afternoon off, as hell on earth.

Of course, Xander wasn't in love with Bastian.

After they returned to Terroir from San Francisco, and Bastian promoted Xander to *sous*, the moments that made Kian's heart beat feaster and his breath catch happened further and further apart.

Kian knew his own feelings hadn't changed. Suspected that Bastian's hadn't either, but after being confronted with Luc, and almost making a monumental mistake, it made sense for him to pull back.

It sucked, and it frustrated the hell out of Kian, but he *still* wasn't sure pursuing a relationship between them would even be the right thing to do. So he let Bastian pull away, let him redefine their relationship more professionally, and tried very hard to be satisfied with that.

Everything hit the fan when Xander announced to Kian that he'd been offered a new job. Even though he saw evidence of Xander's resentment all the time—and it wasn't like he hadn't ever been angry at Bastian himself—Kian couldn't believe Xander was actually leaving Terroir.

"You're going to take that job, aren't you?" His voice sounded flat, resigned. Maybe three months ago, he would have still believed that with Xander out of the way, Kian might be promoted to *sous*. But lately, Kian had begun to realize that was never going to happen.

Kian was in the spot Bastian wanted him to be in—closest to him, yet so far away, at the very same time.

"Of course I'm going to take it." Xander slammed his knife down on the board. "We're not all like you, in thrall to the Bastard. You wouldn't take another job even if the French Laundry came calling."

First off, Thomas Keller would never try to poach him from Bastian. Second off, Kian couldn't imagine a life where he didn't see Bastian for at least twelve hours a day. It was unthinkable.

The annoying voice in his head, the one he'd been trying to ignore but that kept growing louder and louder during these last few months, told him, *if you left, you could finally figure out how to fall out of love with him.*

Kian didn't really want to fall out of love. There was a somewhat masochistic side of him that enjoyed loving Bastian, despite all the pain that came with it. Moving on would undoubtedly hurt even more, but maybe he'd feel less stagnant. Less like he was running and standing still simultaneously.

"I don't want to work for Thomas Keller," Kian insisted.

"That's exactly the point I'm trying to make," Xander retorted. His temper had cooled, and he just sounded regretful now. Still trying to save Kian, even when Kian didn't want to be saved.

The thing was, Kian hadn't come to Terroir looking for a knight in shining armor. He was capable of making his own decisions—good and bad—and even though Xander hated that he'd fallen in love with Bastian, that had been *his* choice. When Xander had opened the door that day, Kian had walked in wanting a teacher, which he'd gotten in Bastian, and maybe a friend, too. For a long time, Kian had believed he and Xander *were* friends, but now he suddenly wasn't so sure. Weren't friends supposed to be supportive, even when they believed you were making a mistake? But Xander, no matter what happened, or what Kian did or didn't say, couldn't leave this thing with Bastian alone. Even worse, he didn't know the half of it. He didn't even know about The Kiss.

"You're pissed off that I won't listen to your fucking advice," Kian spit out. He'd been chopping carrots for the vegetable medley. It was meaningless prep, especially for him, but he'd been assigned the task because that was what he *did*. He did the stuff there was nobody else for, and he was damn sick of Xander pretending that didn't mean anything.

He continued, barely taking a breath. "Not everyone is you, Xander, and you don't know what's right for everyone. Maybe if you did, you could tell yourself and you wouldn't be so god damned bitter all the time."

Instead of saying anything, Xander just reached over and turned the gas off on the stove where he was currently prepping sauces for the night's service.

"What are you doing?" Kian demanded.

Xander pulled the rug out from under him. "Leaving," he said. "You can tell the Bastard I'm done."

With that single sentence, Xander packed up his knives, pulled his coat from his locker, and despite Kian's incredulous expression, walked out.

He didn't know what he was supposed to tell Chef; *how* he was supposed to tell Chef. Xander and he had plenty of differences—it was difficult to *not* have differences considering how they both liked having the final word on everything—but he'd promoted Xander to *sous*. He'd trusted Xander to have his back.

Kian stood in the doorway of Bastian's office and couldn't help but remember the first time he'd ever stood here, terrified and unsure. That time, Xander had had *his* back, but he didn't anymore. And probably not ever again.

Anger and determination coalesced into a hard, knotty ball inside his stomach.

"What's going on?" Bastian asked absently, sorting through the stack of papers on his desk that Kian had left for him earlier. "Don't tell me Steve's come back to throw a fit."

Steve, one of the brand-new kitchen assistants, had walked out an hour into prep because he didn't feel like he was being treated with respect.

Kian had thought this was ridiculous because as a *newly hired kitchen assistant*, he didn't deserve any respect because he had yet to earn any. Bastian had grumbled, but because Steve's worth had been so minuscule, there hadn't been any tantrums. Kian had been assigned his prep work and that was that.

Xander's departure was going to be a whole different kettle of fish.

"Xander just left." Since coming to work for Bastian, Kian had done some reading on the side about how to deal with difficult personalities in the workplace. Most, if not all, espoused the technique of being direct, but never dramatic.

Bastian still hadn't looked up. "Is he sick? You can make the sauces for tonight. Did he at least finish the soup before he left?"

Kian walked further into the office and shut the door behind him, which mostly got his attention. "He's not sick."

"Not sick?" Bastian looked slightly pained, white lines bracketing his mouth, and that terrifying combination of fear and anger simmering in his eyes. "He quit, didn't he?" he asked flatly.

Kian could only nod.

"God damnit," Bastian bellowed. "Without even a fucking word to me. Did he think he could just walk out and it wouldn't haunt him forever?"

Kian considered telling him to not even bother. If the Hess family had decided on Xander, even Bastian Aquino wasn't going to get them to change their mind and give him back.

"I don't know what he was thinking," Kian said, and that was at least honest.

"How much of Steve's prep do you have left?" Bastian asked. "Maybe I should handle the sauces tonight."

"I've got about half my prep left and then I can finish the soup," Kian offered.

"We'll at least get a temp in to cover the prep tomorrow," Bastian said, rising from his chair and buttoning up his collar. Walking around his desk, he paused next to Kian. "You keep giving me strange looks."

"I keep expecting to have to clean your desk off the floor," Kian said, and he was only half joking.

Bastian sighed. "I saw orange, okay? I saw it, and I'm pissed. But I also think we can get him back."

There was no way Xander was going to come back to Terroir, no matter what Bastian enticed him with, but conceptualizing a plan was at least temporarily delaying Bastian's temper, and Kian wasn't going to spoil that.

"Where is he going?"

For a brief moment, Kian considered telling Bastian he didn't know. Maybe a month after The Kiss, he might have. Maybe even two months after. He'd been pissed for a long time, but now he was just resigned. "Hess. They're opening a farm-to-table restaurant."

"Huh, that's a surprise, I would have expected to hear rumblings," Bastian said, and started to walk past Kian, but at the last moment he stopped. He glanced around, like he was confirming nobody was watching, and then he lifted his hand to Kian's cheek briefly, the fingers brushing against it.

"I'm sorry," he said quietly. "I'm sorry I gave Xander the *sous* job, not when you deserved it."

Kian had been dying for this apology for six months, but even the tender, apologetic look Bastian swiftly shot him wasn't enough.

He wanted more. He wanted Xander's old job. He wanted more than just the fleeting touch of Bastian's fingers on his cheek. He wanted another kiss. He wanted even more than that.

It didn't matter that it was dangerous or that Bastian had said it was impossible. It didn't even matter that a part of Kian believed Bastian was right, because there was another part of him that was actively rebelling. That part wanted more and was not going to be placated with less.

"And you're still going to try to convince him to come back?" Kian said incredulously. He didn't need Xander back; they both knew it. Bastian could promote Kian and the kitchen would probably run *better*, not worse, without Xander.

But Bastian couldn't have looked more surprised than if Kian had been the one to walk out in the middle of prep.

"I don't think you understand," Bastian began, and Kian knew his mental gymnastics so well by this point that he knew exactly what he was going to say. *I don't apologize to anyone, and I'm apologizing to you. You're special, you're important, and you need to stay exactly where I've put you.*

Kian had liked that place, but even at the beginning, it hadn't quite felt like enough, and by now, two years in, Kian was tired of it and *bored*.

"I understand," Kian cut him off. "More than you realize."

Bastian's hand dropped to his side and he flexed it, like he was trying to forget the way Kian had felt under his fingertips. Even if he never forgot, it wouldn't be enough. Kian wanted to weasel his way under his skin, until there was nothing else between them. Until Kian didn't know where he stopped and Bastian began. He loved him. Why had he ever thought this sort of half relationship would ever be enough?

"I guess you do," Bastian said slowly.

"I need to check on the soup," Kian said and walked away.

He wanted to be shocked and incredulous that, in one breath, Bastian would tell him that Kian should have had the job that was Xander's , in the next, tell him he was getting Xander back. But the truth was, Kian wasn't, at all.

He'd known the person Bastian was for a long time now, and he'd loved him anyway. Believing that his mother's advice was solid, he'd loved the good and the bad parts of him, and that wasn't going to change, at least not anytime soon. But he was done tolerating Bastian's shit and he was done giving in.

Most of all, Kian was done being jealous of Luc for having things he never would.

⚘⚘⚘⚘⚘ ⚘⚘⚘⚘⚘

The service passed in a blur of Bastian yelling and far too much work. Kian went home and crashed, passing out on his bed diagonally, with his socks still on. He didn't know where Xander was, and he wasn't sure he even wanted to.

A loud, insistent series of knocks drove him from his warm blankets the next morning, until he finally gave in. He got up, not even bothering to throw a shirt on, and jerked the door open.

He'd half expected a one-night stand of Nate's—their new roommate—or maybe even some kids selling magazines or tubs of cookie dough.

It wasn't a one-night stand of Nate's or a kid. It was Bastian, his aviators and a grumpy look on his face.

"Took you long enough," Bastian grumbled. "Were you dead?"

It was too bad it hadn't been one of those kids. Kian really wanted some cookie dough right about now. He'd scoop it right from the tub, and eat it spoonful by spoonful, unbaked.

Breakfast of champions.

"No." Kian kept his voice neutral. "What are you doing here?"

"I need to talk to Xander," Bastian said, like he couldn't believe Kian had forgotten. He hadn't—not exactly, anyway—he'd just chosen to prioritize other things. Like making it through last night's hellish service and then sleeping.

"I haven't seen him."

"His car's outside," Bastian said impatiently. "Go get him. I'm sure he's sleeping off a hellacious *I just quit Terroir* bender."

Bastian was probably right, but there was something imperious in his tone today that Kian didn't like. He crossed his arms across his chest and let Bastian look at all the bare skin he had on display. Let him look and want. Maybe it would only be a fraction of how much Kian wanted, but that was better than nothing.

"Or I could go drag him out myself," Bastian said, raising an eyebrow.

Kian rolled his eyes. "Fine. Come in and wait in the living room." He held the door open and Bastian followed behind him. Kian couldn't see him but he had a feeling he was eyeing everything, from the mis-matched furniture they'd picked up at Goodwill and IKEA and on the side of the road, sometimes, to the winery posters that Nate had tacked all over the walls.

It wasn't much, it certainly wasn't the sleek, ultra-modern house that Bastian lived in on the top of Mount Veeder. But Bastian knew what he paid his chefs, and even with three of them in this house, they weren't buying multimillion-dollar houses anytime soon. Kian refused to feel ashamed, because he loved the house they lived in. It felt like *home*, not the house Bastian merely existed in between shifts.

"I'll go get Xander," he said shortly, and left Bastian in the living room, while he clearly debated whether to sit on the couch or not.

Fuck his snobbery, Kian thought wretchedly. There was a reason why, in all the many, *many* fantasies he'd had of Bastian, they'd never been at his own house. And today, that really pissed him off.

Tonight, he was going to imagine Bastian blowing him in their bathroom with the chipped tile. Fantasy Bastian's eyes would say everything, but his mouth would be full, wouldn't it?

Taking out his frustration—sexual and otherwise—on Xander's door, he pounded hard on the thin wood, and then even harder when Xander didn't open it.

"Xander, I know you're in there," he said loudly.

"You're wrong," a voice finally croaked on the other side of the door, "Xander isn't here."

Kian remembered that Xander's bedroom door didn't even have a lock, and bracing himself for whatever he might find, decided he was sick of waiting, and just opened it.

"I need to talk to you," he said.

"So talk," Xander said, rolling over in bed, his hair a mess, and his pallor pale, like he'd drunk too much last night. "Clearly nothing is stopping you."

"You walked out last night," Kian said.

"I quit," Xander interrupted him. "I didn't just walk out. I fucking quit. Just in case that wasn't clear."

It had been abundantly clear. Kian had never wanted to punch Xander in the face more than he did right now. And Xander could be annoying and frustrating and infuriating a good portion of the time.

"Believe me, it was clear."

"Okay then," Xander said, and rolled back over, leaving his back to Kian.

It was really difficult to say who Kian was more pissed off at—his friend or his boss. Maybe he should just sic them on each other and let them fight to the death.

"What I keep trying to tell you is that you don't have to. Leave, that is. Chef is here . . . and he wants to talk to you."

"Chef is here?" Xander finally sounded like he was paying attention, Kian thought with satisfaction. "In *our* house?"

"Yes."

"What the fuck," Xander said tiredly.

"I suggest," Kian retorted primly, "that you get cleaned up and get out here before he gets tired of waiting and leaves."

After a long moment, Xander finally listened and slid out of bed, staggering to stay upright.

Kian let the full force of his glare out. And he'd learned from the very best.

"Hurry up," Kian said, and shut the door behind him.

He marched back into the living room, not even a fraction less pissed than he'd been before. He didn't sit down, though Bastian had finally managed to do it, perching on the edge of the couch.

"Is he coming?" Bastian asked shortly.

It was like he didn't know Kian at all. How often had Kian failed to complete a task to his satisfaction? Kian couldn't even remember the last time that had happened. He *always* got his shit done. And constantly questioning if he could, if he was up to it, was really beginning to get to him. Let Bastian question everyone else, the rest of the kitchen that fucked up regularly and couldn't really be counted on. He was Kian, and he was different.

Xander finally emerged, looking slightly less like hell. "What do you want?" he barked at Bastian.

"You quit last night," Bastian said, and despite his own current feelings, Kian was grudgingly impressed at how even his voice sounded.

"I did." Xander also sounded surprisingly even-tempered.

Apparently the only one in this room who wanted to throw something was Kian.

"You're not even going to give me the benefit of a two-week notice?"

Kian barely refrained from rolling his eyes. There was never a two-week notice at Terroir. Only flaming tempers and Bastian's desk in pieces on the floor.

"No," Xander said, still steady.

"Or an opportunity to counter what Damon Hess offered you?"

Xander instantly looked over at Kian, who felt a tiny twinge of shame. Yeah, he'd sold Xander out, but Xander hadn't said where he was going was a secret. And *who* was Damon Hess anyway? That name didn't even sound familiar, and Kian thought he knew all the Hesses in town.

"Not much is a secret," Xander retorted bitterly, which wasn't fair at all. If he'd said it was a secret, Kian would have at least considered not divulging it.

"Kian is worried about you," Bastian said, which was completely untrue. Kian was worried about *himself*. "Worried you're throwing your career away on someone who can't properly support you. You know, he isn't even really a winemaker. He's not a restauranteur. He's playing at growing a garden. But he's not even a Hess—not like you think."

Suddenly, Xander's reticence to tell Kian more yesterday made sense. It wasn't the Hess *family* that was starting this restaurant. It was some far-flung edge of the family, not connected in the same ways at all.

Maybe Kian was more worried about Xander than he'd realized. What was he *thinking*?

"He's exactly what I think," Xander said.

"There's nothing I can offer you that might make you change your mind?" Bastian offered slyly, and Kian gritted his teeth. Here was the job offer that should have been *his*—the second one that Xander had been offered and he hadn't. The first had stung, this one *ached*.

"What," Bastian continued, "if I made you my *chef de cuisine*?"

The *sous chef* was typically the second-in-command of a kitchen, especially if the executive or head chef was on premises, and involved, like Bastian was. If the executive chef was distant, or less involved, there needed to be someone *in* the kitchen who was nominally in charge. And that was the *chef de cuisine*. Kian had never imagined that Bastian would consider taking that step back—or ceding the control of his kitchen to someone else.

To *Xander*.

Yes, it definitely ached, because in some far-flung future, when this inevitably happened, many years distant, Kian had always believed that position was his. Nobody else knew Terroir like he did. Nobody else deserved it like he did. Nobody else had worked as hard.

"You mean the job I've deserved for six months?" Xander demanded. "The one you already should have offered me?"

Xander was . . . wrong. There was no way around it. He was blind to what really happened at Terroir. Blind to anything but his rapidly expanding ego. Kian sighed inwardly.

"I can't apologize for that, Xander," Bastian cut in smoothly. And of course he wouldn't. He didn't apologize to anyone.

Except to you, Kian thought. *Twice.*

"I think I'll take my chances with the 'not real' Hess," Xander said.

"You really mean that," Bastian said, and he sounded surprised. Of course he'd probably believed that this offer would be the one thing that would sway Xander's mind. "Hess said you'd say that, but I couldn't believe it. Couldn't believe you'd turn down *chef de cuisine* to work for a part-time gardener whose restaurant is currently a ramshackle shed without a real kitchen."

Xander frowned. "You went and talked to Damon?"

Bastian stood and began to pace, which Kian knew was a bad sign. "He poached you. In my own fucking restaurant! What else was I supposed to do?"

To salvage his prodigious pride? Kian wasn't sure. At least he understood why Bastian had come here and why he'd offered Xander the job, even though he'd known he wouldn't take it. He'd had to do *something*, so he could feel in control again.

"Fucking *ask me* if I wanted the job. Not my new partner. Not my friend and roommate. *Me*. That's your whole problem. That's why I left. You have to control everything, and it fucking sucks." Kian froze. Xander was notoriously lacking in basic tact, but this was a lot, even for him.

And then it got worse. Xander pointed in Kian's direction. "And that one," he said, "is too nice to ever say anything to your face, but you're a psychotic megalomaniac who desperately needs to be checked."

It was too much. For Bastian's temper. For his ego. For his everything. Kian held his breath as Bastian shot Xander a death glare, and then marched right out of the house.

"You're an idiot," Kian said, which was all he could say. "Are you really going to let someone else, some guy you don't even know, tell Chef Aquino what you want to do?" This was completely unlike Xander, and while Kian was *still* undeniably pissed, that worried him. What was Xander's deal with this Hess person? Was it serious? Because Kian saw reflected back in Xander's eyes some of his own insanity—the determination to follow Bastian everywhere, no matter what happened, no matter what he said, no matter what he did. And that was so unlike Xander, it was sort of terrifying.

"Are we really going to do this? You and me, *really*?"

Kian desperately wanted to pretend that he didn't know what Xander meant. But unlike Xander in this moment, he wasn't stupid and he wasn't unaware of the mistakes he kept making. "I don't know what you mean," he retorted through stiff lips.

"I mean, are you really going to get bent out of shape over my new partner telling Aquino to take a hike when I was going to do that anyway? When you would follow Aquino to the depths of any hell he concocted, just because you're too in love with him to ever tell him no?"

It was such a painfully accurate assessment that Kian felt the wind knocked out of him. He'd done that. He'd done that for *two years*.

"No," he finally said. "No, I guess we're not."

"Okay then," Xander said and he finally sounded pissed. "I'm going back to bed, to contemplate my brief joblessness, and you can go running after Aquino because I know you're dying to."

Xander was right, but he was also wrong. Yes, Kian wanted to go after him, but not to apologize or try to placate him or any of the things that Xander assumed he'd do.

No, he wanted to read him the fucking riot act. *Chef de cuisine, really? Xander?*

Which was exactly what he said when he wrenched open the door of Bastian's car.

Bastian had the nerve to look a tiny bit ashamed. "Get in," he said. "Let's get a coffee."

Kian gave him a look, since he still hadn't put a shirt on, and he was currently in socks, but no shoes.

"We'll go through the drive-through," Bastian amended, leaning back and rubbing his temples. "I didn't sleep last night. I lose too many more good chefs and people are going to talk. They're already fucking talking."

"You care too much about what other people think," Kian said, which was true, but was also an unfortunate symptom of the restaurant business. Everyone had an opinion, and when those opinions were formed by important people, it could make or break a restaurant.

Bastian's glare was expected. He pulled out of their drive in a spray of gravel. "You know it matters."

Kian had heard this story before; too many good chefs would leave a restaurant, and there'd be blood in the water. For patrons, for other chefs, for *critics*.

They'd come in droves, hearing that Terroir's *sous* was gone, to see if the standard of the food had fallen at all.

Kian didn't need to tell Bastian that he would make sure with every fiber of his being that nothing would change, because Bastian was just as committed.

"How did you know it wasn't a Hess restaurant?" Kian asked, changing the subject.

"I know because I know," Bastian said, annoyingly. "Also, because Nathan Hess has been talking to *me* about taking over the bistro at their winery. I'd just about decided to tell him I was interested, but now there's this wrinkle."

"No Xander."

"No Xander," Bastian agreed. "He was an ass, but he was a reliable ass. I still like the bistro concept, I've been wanting to open a second location for awhile now, but I'm not sure I want it on Nathan Hess' property."

"Why not?" Kian asked as Bastian pulled the car into the parking lot of his favorite coffee shop.

Bastian pulled out his phone and dialed. "Yeah, it's me," he said when someone on the other end answered. "Two cappuccinos. Dry. No sugar. Double shots."

Of course this was Bastian's idea of a "drive-through."

"You're insufferable," Kian said as he rolled his eyes.

The smile Bastian shot him was cocky and so sure of himself it made Kian's knees weak. If he hadn't been sitting down, he would have wobbled. As it was, his nipples tightened even in the comfortable warmth of the car, and Bastian, who noticed everything, swept his gaze across his chest.

Kian blushed, and then flushed even redder when a young woman exited the coffee shop, bearing two cups of coffee. Bastian rolled down the window, took the cups, and gave her a twenty-dollar bill.

"Keep the change," he said.

The woman's eyes lingered over him, nearly completely undressed in the passenger seat of the car, and he wondered if he'd hear through the rumor mill next week that Bastian was driving his young hookups around.

It's not like that, but I wish it was, Kian couldn't help but think.

"Drink your coffee," Bastian said brusquely. "We have a long day."

Oh yeah. No Xander. No kitchen assistant.

"I called the temp agency, they're sending over someone, but I'm sure they'll be useless," Bastian grumbled.

"Is the Hess deal why you offered Xander *chef de cuisine*?" Kian asked between sips.

Bastian's expression was locked up so tightly Kian couldn't decipher it. "I offered him *chef de cuisine* because I knew he wouldn't take it."

It shouldn't have made sense, but in a strange, fucked-up sort of way, it did. Bastian had known it was useless, had known that Xander was done with Terroir, but he'd wanted to salvage his pride, to at least make an effort to win him back, even if it was a fool's errand.

"Someday," Kian said seriously, "your pride and your ego are going to get you into big trouble."

Bastian laughed—rich and full and hearty. Kian wanted to lean over and lick the tiny speck of milk foam off his upper lip.

"Someday, huh?" he asked.

"You've done okay for yourself so far," Kian said with a shrug.

"High praise, coming from you," Bastian retorted dryly.

"I learned my expectations from the best." Kian looked over at him. Bastian's hands were clenched on the wheel.

There was silence for a minute. Kian thought he could fill in what Bastian was going to say next. *We can't do this. This is dangerous. This is impossible.*

It was all of those things, and inevitable, too.

Bastian cleared his throat. "I should get you home. Like I said, it's going to be a long day."

It almost didn't matter that Bastian hadn't actually said those things, because he'd thought them, and Kian had known he'd thought them—that was *almost* enough.

"Yeah," he finally said. "I'll need to give the rundown to the new temp."

"Right, yes," Bastian agreed. He started the car and drove them in silence back to Kian's house.

Kian knew he should ask who was going to take over Xander's role as *sous chef.* He should remind Bastian what he'd said just yesterday—that it should have been Kian's job, all along. But he didn't ask, because, he realized as he got out of the car, he was afraid of what he'd do if Bastian said no.

Chapter Seven

"Chef!"

Bastian looked up from the soup he was stirring. Derek, the new kitchen assistant that Kian had been training, was standing in front of him with a panicked expression on his face.

"What is it?" Bastian asked. He halfheartedly wondered why Kian wasn't taking care of Derek, who liked to freak out over every little thing. Bastian would have fired him weeks ago, but Kian kept insisting he could cure him of his dramatic streak.

But Kian wasn't here, and he definitely wasn't controlling Derek's melodrama, which seemed to be more developed than ever.

Derek wrung his hands, and Bastian suddenly noticed the bright red streaks across his white apron. He didn't think they were prepping beets today, and the color was wrong, anyway. The only thing that was that color was . . .

Bastian dropped the ladle into the pot. He knew he should be fishing it out, but instead he tuned into what Derek was currently stammering about: ". . . and I told him he was going to need to get it stitched, there's blood *everywhere*, and I think Jorge fainted . . ."

"What." Bastian interrupted him flatly. "Who cut themselves?"

Derek had the nerve to look impatient, like Bastian should have been paying attention this whole time. "I told you. Kian cut himself on the Japanese mandolin."

"Oh fuck," Bastian said and skirted around Derek, walking back to the prep stations, where most of the commotion was centered.

Kian was in the middle of a crowd of white-coated chefs, and Bastian caught a glimpse of his pale face. Far too pale.

He knew Kian liked using the Japanese mandolin without gloves because he could get through the prep work faster that way—and he probably cared about speed more than safety because Bastian kept piling more and more shit onto his plate. His stomach lurched sickeningly.

"Get out of the way," he bellowed, and the crowd cleared nearly instantaneously, revealing a mess of bloody towels on the counter, with another, even bloodier, towel currently wrapped around Kian's hand.

"Chef," Kian said, and nobody else might have known him enough to hear the wobble in his voice, but Bastian heard it, because he felt like he lived and died by the various subtle inflections in Kian's voice.

"Let me see," he said, even though he hated to have Kian take pressure off the wound.

One glimpse was all Bastian needed.

Most of the time they didn't really miss Xander, but Bastian did today. Wished, maybe for the first time in his career, that everyone who left Terroir hadn't done so under terrible circumstances, because nobody else was taking care of Kian but him, and he didn't want to leave the restaurant now, two hours before service. But he would.

Pain and shock swam in Kian's big blue eyes, and Bastian knew only half a second before he collapsed, but it was enough that he was able to stagger forward and catch him.

Kian might have grown up in the last two years, but he was still too skinny, and Bastian was able to pick him up easily. He ignored the gaping stares of the rest of the chefs in the kitchen and hoped they wouldn't talk—even as he knew this would be the most discussed Bastard story in the history of Bastard stories.

"We're going to the ER," Bastian said in his most strident voice, even though everything inside him was collapsing into itself. "I'm going to make it back before service, but I need you to finish prep. Everything *must* be ready when I get back. Michel," he called out to the man who'd taken Wyatt's place at the grill, "please make sure the soup is ready. The ladle is probably still floating around in the pot."

Michel looked surprised. But Michel was still new, and hadn't figured out that Kian was what made this whole restaurant run the way it was supposed to.

Bastian didn't remember driving to the emergency room. He didn't remember Kian groaning as he picked him up, didn't remember carrying him through the doors, didn't remember yelling, didn't remember a nurse wheeling out a gurney—it only caught up to him when he sat down in the chair opposite Kian's bed.

He'd woken up after making it to the private room and was giving answers to the nurse for her intake paperwork.

When she finally finished up and said the doctor would be in shortly, Kian turned to Bastian. "You couldn't have sent me with someone else? What about prep? What if we're not back for service?"

"It's fine," Bastian soothed, even though soothing wasn't really in his repertoire. "Prep will be fine." He hoped. "And *I'll* be back for service, but you won't be. I'm going to drop you off at home. You're taking the night off."

Kian pouted, which shouldn't have been adorable, but was, somehow, anyway.

"It wasn't even that bad," Kian insisted, which they both knew was a lie. It had been bad. Bad enough that just thinking of it made Bastian's stomach roll nauseatingly.

"I push you too hard," Bastian muttered to himself, but Kian had heard him and he couldn't take the words back.

Like he hadn't been able to take the kiss back, no matter how much he wished he could. He'd done everything he could to push Kian away, to kill their chemistry, but instead of growing fainter, all it did was grow stronger.

In San Francisco, Kian had been angry because he'd believed Luc's existence meant that he wasn't special after all.

What Kian didn't know, and couldn't ever realize, was that Luc's very existence in Bastian's life was enough to make Kian special. Kian was everything Luc hadn't been: loyal, kind, funny, insanely self-sacrificing, but with enough ego that he respected his own skill. If he hadn't been only twenty-three years old, with a whole brilliant future stretching out in front of him, and also Bastian's student and employee, he'd have believed wholly and completely that Kian was the perfect man for him.

He'd believed that, surely, that sort of bizarrely romantic thinking must have died with the disappointment of Luc, but Kian made him remember exactly why he'd believed it in the first place.

"You push me exactly the right amount," Kian argued. Of course he'd say that. Bastian had brainwashed him into believing that he was the best, with the best judgement. And that definitely wasn't true. What had just happened proved that conclusively.

Celeste was going to be pissed at him. Even more pissed than when she'd discovered he had promoted Xander to *sous*.

"*Merde*," she'd said to Bastian that day. "You are stupider than anyone on the planet."

"I know," he'd said miserably as he sat on her porch during yet another sleepless night. It had been bad enough imagining what kissing Kian would be like, but the reality of it had blown his mind.

His mother would have been thrilled he'd finally stepped over his self-imposed line with Kian, but he couldn't endure her excitement when he couldn't ever do it again.

The doctor walked in then, jerking Bastian's attention back to Kian and his finger.

"It's deep," he finally pronounced, after an examination that had both Kian and Bastian gritting their teeth. Kian because it fucking hurt and Bastian because apparently he couldn't stand to see Kian in pain. "You'll definitely need stitches. Inner *and* outer. We'll give you something for the pain."

"Something strong," Bastian intervened, before Kian could open his mouth and insist he needed to be sharp enough for the evening's service.

Even if he was beginning to wonder differently, Bastian was in charge of both Kian and Terroir and his word was final.

"Something strong," the doctor agreed. "We'll do a local and have him take some pills too."

"Good." Bastian nodded.

"And you are?" the doctor asked, turning towards Bastian. "His boyfriend? Husband?"

Oh god. "His boss," Bastian finally managed to admit between clenched teeth.

"Ah," the doctor said. "And I'm assuming," he waved at Bastian's coat, "he won't be working tonight."

"Definitely not." Bastian shot Kian a look, who surprisingly, didn't argue. Probably because the doctor's examination had hurt a lot, and he knew the stitching would hurt worse.

It wasn't like Kian wasn't incredibly tough—he'd astounded Bastian continually with his mental and physical strength—but clearly he'd reached his limit.

And despite that he'd just told the doctor they weren't involved, Bastian reached out and grasped Kian's good hand with his own. Their palms slid together, Kian's smaller hand fitting into Bastian's much larger one. Glancing down at their hands, Kian smiled softly.

"I'm going to go grab the necessary supplies," the doctor said, and he closed the door behind him. If Bastian wasn't mistaken, he'd been smiling too.

Boss and so much more, Bastian wished he'd had the balls to say. But no matter how strong the pull towards the man in front of him was, he still wasn't convinced it was right to cross the line that he'd built and then reinforced. He'd done it for a reason, and that reason still felt valid, even more so when he looked back over the last two years and realized how accomplished Kian had become.

It should feel more vital than ever, to preserve that professional distance between them, but today made Bastian feel like it was more of a fool's errand than ever.

The doctor returned with the supplies and a nurse, and even though they gave him plenty of pain medication, Bastian still didn't let go of Kian's hand. Bastian could tell he was trying not to rely on him and not squeeze his hand too hard, but he kept tensing and then trying to relax.

Finally, Bastian murmured to him, "Go ahead. It hurts. It's scary. I'm here for you."

The doctor lifted his gaze a moment and shot their hands a single glance, but Bastian didn't care. His boy was in pain, and that was all that mattered.

Finally, it was over, and the doctor removed his gloves, tossing them into the trash can.

"The nurse will be back with your release paperwork," he said. "I'm assuming you'll be driving him home."

"Yes, of course," Bastian said.

"Good," he replied, and after giving Kian some final cleaning instructions, and when to expect the stitches to disintegrate, and what to do if they didn't, he left.

Kian's eyes had grown wide and dazed with the pain medication. He looked down at their hands.

"You didn't need to do this," he said. "It'll make you late for service."

It probably would. But in the last few hours, Bastian had discovered something more important than a service at Terroir. The realization was still blowing his mind.

"This is my fault," Bastian said brusquely, "so *yes*, I should be here."

"Not your fault," Kian said, still staring at their hands. Like he couldn't quite believe it was happening. "You tell us to use the protective gloves, and I don't."

"Yeah, because you're too busy to use them," Bastian said.

Kian smiled. "No, because I like to impress you."

It was almost impossible not to groan in frustration. "Yeah, exactly," Bastian insisted, the edge of his voice growing rough. "I let you do it. I like it when you try to impress me. I'm a terrible boss, and a terrible person."

"No," Kian said dreamily, "you're wonderful and I love you."

It wasn't as if Bastian didn't know. The way Kian looked at him, hot and possessive and adoring, when nobody else was watching made it difficult to deny. But it was one thing to wonder about it, far too late at night when Bastian should be sleeping, and it was another to hear Kian say it.

There were a million things he wanted to say. *I'm too old and too grumpy and too egotistical for you. I'd just ruin you. I'd ruin your future, which is going to be spectacular. I'll only slow you down.*

But most of all, *I love you too.*

But before he could make the choice, the nurse bustled in with the release paperwork, and when they made it to the car, it felt too late. And maybe, Bastian thought morosely, Kian hadn't meant it after all. He was hopped up on drugs. He probably wouldn't even remember this in a few hours.

Bastian *hoped* he wouldn't remember this in a few hours. They hadn't exactly been great at keeping the status quo—the kiss still loomed large, and he thought about it all the time—but Kian's confession might destroy the line forever.

The kitchen was nearly clean from the night's service—it hadn't been the smoothest dinner they'd ever served at Terroir, but it hadn't been a disaster either—when Bastian's phone rang.

He usually kept his phone in his office when he was on the line, but tonight he'd kept it in his pocket—just in case Kian needed him.

It had stayed quiet all service, but now Kian was calling him.

"What?" he asked quietly, ducking outside, hoping nobody was outside for their post-service cigarette. "Are you okay? Is everything okay?"

Kian laughed, and Bastian still heard the drugs in his voice. "I'm fine. I'm at Damon Hess' with Xander."

Bastian frowned. "You're *what?*"

"I'm at Damon Hess' with Xander," Kian repeated again, like it was no big deal. "But you need to come get me. I think they want to start making out and I'm sort of in the way."

Leaning against the building, Bastian looked up to the sky, wishing and despairing all at once.

"You didn't drive?" he asked, before he remembered that with the meds he was on, driving was a bad idea.

"Silly, Bastian, I can't drive. Xander drove." Bastian's heart skipped a beat. Kian had only ever called him Chef, or Chef Aquino to his face. He'd always imagined that Kian thought of him differently, maybe even by his first name, but hearing it was so much different than just imagining it.

"Give me twenty minutes," Bastian said. It was a monumentally terrible idea. Considering Kian's weakened brain-to-mouth filter and Bastian's own dangerously shaky line between what was right and what he really wanted—this felt like an even worse idea than San Francisco had been.

And San Francisco had been a certifiable disaster.

Still, twenty-four minutes later, Bastian pulled up to Damon's farm. He could see smoke and light coming from the property behind the small ranch-style house and debated whether he should get out of the car or if he should just text Kian to say he'd arrived.

But this was Damon Hess' property, and there was a part of Bastian that wanted to show both him and Xander exactly where Kian's loyalties lay. Just in case they had any insane thoughts about poaching him. Kian was *his*, and there was a barbaric, caveman-esque part of Bastian that wanted everyone to know it.

Even though everyone probably already did. They'd both attempted subtlety, but that wasn't really Kian's strong suit, and it definitely wasn't Bastian's.

He got out of the car, and stripped off his chef jacket, tossing it in the back seat, leaving him just in his white tank. He'd already swapped his working clogs for the sneakers he usually kept in his office.

Detouring around the house, he saw the beginnings of the garden as he had the last time he'd been here. It even looked as if Hess had ripped out even more priceless vines, the vineyards in the back looking thinner than they had before, in the dim light provided by the bonfire.

He could see Hess and Xander, standing close together, and to his own astonishment, he *was* surprised. He didn't generally expect romantic attachments in other people, probably because his own had been so few and far between. But it would help explain why Xander hadn't even been a little tempted by his counteroffer. He'd known Xander wouldn't take it when he'd offered it, but he hadn't expected Xander to be so sure, so quickly.

But he had, and Damon must be the reason. Bastian supposed he could see the attraction. He was good-looking, if a little brooding for his own tastes. Xander had never been particularly caught up in good-looking men before, but Bastian supposed that was what those people who believed in love at first sight were always nattering on about.

Sometimes you saw someone, and you connected with them despite everything.

Bastian approached the bonfire as he watched the light flickering off the delicate features of Kian's face. Two years in and he still couldn't explain it, couldn't quantify it. Couldn't fucking contain it. He knew the moment Kian saw him because his face lit up, like Bastian's arrival flicked on a lamp inside him.

Bastian was the least humble person he knew, but the way Kian looked at him sometimes was incredibly humbling. He knew he didn't deserve it and wasn't ever capable of deserving it—and Kian knew that, had been witness to so many moments that should have changed his mind, but he'd stayed steadfast and loyal and true, and Bastian couldn't deny it any longer, *in love.*

"You came," Kian said, approaching him, his voice still a little breathless.

"I said I would," Bastian said. "How's the finger?"

"It hurts." Kian made a face, and Bastian chuckled in spite of himself.

"I'm sure it does," he said sympathetically. "Let's get you home."

Kian glanced down at Bastian's hand, and then at his own, the one he hadn't tried to bisect today. He knew what Kian wanted, and the better part of him should have turned away, continued on to the car so Kian wouldn't have a chance.

But Bastian had never pretended to be an angel, and he stayed there, waiting as Kian reached out and took his hand in his own.

There was a million things Bastian could say. One of them definitely was, *I only did that because you were hurting and scared and it made us both feel better.* But he didn't, because even though the circumstances were different, the way Kian's hand curled into his own still made him feel better. Helped cleanse away a little of this wretched day.

Because he's still hurting, Bastian told himself as they walked back to his car, but even he didn't really believe the lie.

Kian had to let go when they reached the car, but as soon as they were back inside, Bastian took a deep breath and placed his hand on the center console, palm up. Eyes wide, Kian glanced at the offered hand, and then back up to Bastian's face.

It was the simplest of touches—it could even be construed as platonic, but there was nothing platonic about the thrill Bastian experienced whenever Kian touched him.

Kian smiled and tucked his hand right back into Bastian's own.

Bastian let out the breath he hadn't realized he was holding. "We should talk about this," he said carefully, even though the last thing he wanted to do was talk and potentially destroy the rest of the ramshackle hut currently trying to contain all his apprehension about this relationship.

Shooting him a very frank look, Kian shifted around in his seat. "If you're going to say that you regret today, that you regret taking me to the emergency room and that you regret holding my hand, even as you're doing it now, you might as well not bother."

"I meant about what you said earlier," Bastian said, and even though his voice was steady, he knew his pulse wasn't, and it was very possible that Kian could even feel how terrified he was in the sudden dampness of his palm.

"What I said earlier?" Kian asked, and even though he'd been so green and innocent when he'd started at Terroir—and in some ways, *still was*—Bastian knew when he was actually clueless and when he was just pretending. He could fool other people, maybe, but not Bastian. Never Bastian.

"You know what you said earlier." It was likely very obvious that he was trying to avoid actually saying the same words Kian had, but then Kian was also pretty damn transparent about his own memory.

"What was it?"

Bastian gnashed his teeth and pulled the car over onto the side of the road. He threw the car into park and turned his full attention onto Kian, who had the faintest smile on his lips.

"Is that it?" Bastian demanded. "You want me to say it?"

Shrugging, Kian glanced down at their intertwined hands again. And Bastian knew exactly the point he was trying to make.

"You can't be in love with me," Bastian said flatly, even though he knew he was, and that this was just plain foolish. "You shouldn't be."

"But I am," Kian said simply. "And I think you're in love with me too."

"We can't do this," Bastian said, and he knew just how desperate he sounded.

"We're already doing it." Kian's voice was gentle, coaxing. "We're doing it right now."

It hurt, maybe even worse than Kian's finger getting sliced up by the Japanese mandolin, but somehow Bastian managed to pull his fingers away from Kian's. Stopping the kiss in San Francisco should have hurt worse, but somehow he managed to feel more now than he had even then.

This is for Kian, Bastian reminded himself. *This is for Kian, even if it doesn't feel like it. Even if it feels like the worst thing on earth. You can do anything, for him.*

Kian stared at him incredulously. "Really? This is what you're going to do? Pretend you don't care about me?"

"I do care about you!" Bastian said, and the pain blooming inside of him made him sound so much angrier than he wanted, than he'd intended. "I'm doing this *because* I care!"

"Then why don't you care about what *I* want?" Kian demanded.

"You don't know what you really want! You don't know what you're giving away." Bastian knew it was a lie when he said it, and fully expected that Kian wouldn't believe it.

But from the way Kian's eyes shuttered, and he turned away, gaze determinedly focused on the dark landscape outside, he thought Bastian believed he was an idiot who didn't know anything and hadn't, in the last two years, thought through the downsides of their relationship at all.

Maybe, Bastian thought brokenly, *that's for the best.*

"Take me home," Kian said, and his voice had dropped about fifty degrees.

For a split second, Bastian wanted to take it back, to plead his forgiveness, but the words were already out there, and Kian already believed them.

It was too late for them, like it had been from the first moment.

⟡⟡⟡⟡⟡ ⟡⟡⟡⟡⟡

It seemed like the right thing to do after dropping Kian off was to drive right past the turnoff to his house and continue down the road to his mother's.

Celeste did not look particularly surprised to see him when she opened the door.

"Rough day?" she asked and handed him a warm mug. "Hot milk," she explained as they headed towards the back porch. "With a touch of brandy."

Bastian took a grateful swallow and nearly burned his tongue. "Ahhh," he exclaimed.

She made a sympathetic noise. "You were five minutes earlier than I thought you'd be."

That was odd, even for his mother. Bastian set the mug aside. "How did you even know I was coming?"

"I follow a few of your chefs on Instagram," Celeste said primly. "More than one of them posted the bloody towels. It wasn't hard to deduce who it was that hurt himself. And that you'd twist yourself into knots when it happened."

Bastian didn't know how to react to Celeste's confession she even *had* an Instagram, never mind that she was following some of his employees. She rolled her eyes at his surprise. "I follow you too, of course, but it's all advertisements for the restaurant. You need to figure out something more personal to put on there. Frankly," she said, making a disappointed *cluck*, "it's very boring, Bastian. I'm surprised you even have followers."

"Uh," Bastian stammered, not very eloquently.

"I even follow your young man. Kian. Very cute. Clever. I can see why you like him."

Even though the mug of milk was probably still close to boiling, Bastian reached for it anyway and took a long gulp. "He's not *my* young man, *maman*."

808

Her dark-eyed gaze was penetrating. Under it, he felt eight again, caught again sneaking sweets off the shelf at the corner market with his friends. Except this time the sweet was Kian.

"He could be," she said thoughtfully.

He greatly disliked the point she was trying to make and *hated* that she was right.

"No, no, *no*," he ground out. "He can't be. I'm his mentor. His boss. It would be inappropriate and an incredible distraction."

Raising an eyebrow, Celeste sipped her own milk. "And it is not now?"

It was something more destructive than mere distraction; she was absolutely right about that.

"Bastian," she continued, reaching out to place a soothing hand on his knee, "you can be so rigid sometimes, and I hate to say it, but that reminds me of your *papa*."

He couldn't help it; he grimaced.

"*Oui*," she said, "he wasn't a good man. He was mean and neglectful. Your intensity, your certainty you are always right, those you get from him. But that doesn't make you bad, not like he was."

"Maybe I'm not bad, but I'm certainly not good either," Bastian admitted darkly.

Celeste shrugged, lace ruffles on the sleeve of her nightgown fluttering in the midnight breeze. "You are human. Not bad, not good. But you have tried to do good, staying away from Kian."

"Hasn't done much good." Bastian took another gulp of milk, the brandy burning the way down his throat. He didn't feel like the way forward was any clearer, but like she always did, his *maman* still made him feel better. Or it could've just been the excellent brandy.

"When you came to me two years ago, on his very first day, I told myself, *Celeste, he will not last a month.* But I was wrong. You held back, because for the first time, you care more about someone else than you care about yourself. And that is why you are nothing like your *papa*."

"I want to believe that," Bastian said, his throat suddenly aching. "I want to be better."

"And this young man, he makes you better," Celeste insisted. "I know, I see it."

"So you think I should just . . . give up?" It was both the very best thought and the worst.

"Do I think you should just go to Kian and say, *I was wrong, let us be together?* No. No, you should not. Because you do not get to expect him to drop all *his* concerns and suddenly expect him to be at your beck and call. You know better than that, Bastian."

Was that what he'd expected? That when his desires finally overrode his apprehensions, he'd just crook a finger and Kian would come running, desperate for even the crumbs from his table?

Yes, *maybe*.

The truth hurt.

"See, you have much to talk to him about," Celeste said, sounding very final, as if she'd discovered his solution for him. When Bastian felt just the opposite, unmoored and unsure.

Bastian finished his milk. "I don't even know how to begin." *Especially after tonight*, Bastian thought, *he probably hates me after what I said.*

"That," Celeste said, smiling, "is up to you to figure out, Bastian, darling. I can't solve everything for you. How else would you learn?"

"I said . . . something to him tonight," Bastian confessed. "He's probably not very happy with me right now."

"Then apologize to him," Celeste said.

Bastian stared at his hands. "I guess I do owe him one."

"At least one, I'm sure."

"Actually," Bastian offered, "I think I've apologized to him more than I've ever apologized to anyone before. Except you."

To his horror, Celeste's eyes filled with tears. "Oh, Bastian," she said, rising and wrapping her slim arms around him. "You love him."

Of course he loved Kian. How could he not?

When Bastian woke up the next morning, he felt resolved. He was going to ask to see Kian first thing in his office and he was going to apologize. An apology with no strings attached and no expectations.

But of course, he'd been in love for the better part of two years, with no end in sight, so there were *some* inevitable expectations attached.

He still wasn't sure if he'd been wrong or if he'd been right, but Bastian was beginning to realize that it didn't matter anymore. They couldn't continue this prolonged dance of *not ever*. They'd probably even moved beyond *not now*. They needed to figure out how to move forward into *this might actually be happening*.

Bastian caught a glimpse of Kian's bright hair as he walked out of the locker room and started to hurry over to him, but Kian stopped him with a single, dead-eyed look. He looked awful, white and drawn, shadows under his eyes, like he hadn't slept, and it appeared that the very last person he wanted to talk to was Bastian.

He should have gone over and followed through on the apology. He *knew* that, but for the first time in a very long time, when faced with an uphill battle, he didn't batten down the hatches and keep attacking. He waved the white flag and he turned back around. *Tomorrow*, he told himself, even as he knew that if he didn't do it right now, there was no point in doing it at all.

When Kian came over to him finally, it was mid-morning, and for half a second, Bastian's heart beat a little faster.

"I need the daily assignments," Kian said, in a dry, utterly professional voice that Bastian had never suspected he even owned.

"Right, right, of course," Bastian said, wiping his hands on a towel. They were shaking, and he thrust the towel away awkwardly before snatching it right back. "Let me get them for you."

Maybe what he should have done right then was not just apologize but give Kian the job he deserved—Xander's old job, the *sous chef* job that had been his forever. But he didn't, and he didn't apologize, and as Kian turned and walked away, Bastian believed that this was the very worst.

He'd always believed before that he and Kian had been professional with each other, but professionalism devoid of Kian's sunny smile, the light that shone in his eyes, and those single, brief glances that were more like caresses—it was hell on earth and Bastian was never going to survive it.

Chapter Eight

Kian couldn't believe it. Even after everything that Damon had put Xander through, they'd ended up together. Instead of Xander sulking alone, ranging from furious to distraught that Damon had abandoned him during the opening of their restaurant, they were currently cuddled up together on the couch—like Kian didn't even exist.

Xander probably wouldn't be happy to hear that Kian was especially pissed off that of all the people in the world, *Xander* had ended up blissfully happy and blissfully in love. Prior to meeting Damon, Xander had been bitter and lonely and downright curmudgeonly. While Kian was happy for his best friend, it wasn't supposed to be *Xander* who'd found the love of his life—it was supposed to be Kian.

But then, Kian thought morosely as he tried to avoid watching the happy couple make out, *I've already found the love of my life.*

Every single fucking time Kian believed that he and Bastian had finally managed to find a way through their situation, instead of pointlessly and endlessly spinning their wheels in the exact same damn spot, Bastian would slam on the brakes.

It wasn't like Kian hadn't thought this through. He *had*. He'd spent the last two years, falling deeper and harder, and trying to ignore his feelings, but they weren't going away. The chance they would seemed slimmer than ever. He'd weighed the pros and the cons, and he'd decided that something needed to change. Anything had to be better than the place they were in now. But Bastian wouldn't even have a conversation about it. He said, *nope, it's not happening,* like he was the one who got all the say in their relationship.

As far as Kian was concerned, that was fucking bullshit.

Kian might be young and a little naïve, not as experienced in the culinary arts, but he knew what he wanted. He knew what it might cost, and he was willing to take that chance anyway.

He couldn't sit here anymore. As much as he liked them both, Xander and Damon were sickening together, and every second Kian did nothing, he got angrier.

And he was already really fucking angry.

You don't know what you want! You don't know what you're giving away.

Bastian's words from a month before kept echoing through his head—but he'd been so fucking wrong. Kian knew because Kian wasn't a fucking idiot. It was definitely a risk, but life was a risk, and why should they settle for this hopeless half relationship when they could have more? Possibly without sacrificing a goddamn thing?

Kian stood up suddenly.

"Where you going?" Xander asked lazily, and Kian tried to ignore that Damon was kissing a line up his neck. "You look sort of pissed off." He sounded surprised, like Kian couldn't possibly be pissed off.

Oh, Xander had no fucking clue how pissed off he could be.

"I *am* pissed off," Kian bit off. "And it's none of your fucking business where I'm going."

Xander would almost definitely try to stop him, if he knew, and so Kian wasn't going to tell him. This was something he needed to do for himself.

He grabbed his wallet and his keys and climbed into his tiny little used hatchback.

The drive to Bastian's house didn't take very long. He'd thought when he arrived there would be less anger and more nerves, but as he pulled into the circular driveway, he still felt pretty fucking pissed off.

He banged on the front door, and then again when Bastian didn't come to the door. It seemed unbelievable that he wouldn't be home, because where else could Bastian be?

Picking up another young, naïve kid because he steadfastly refused to touch Kian? He'd never believed that was even a remote possibility. First, it didn't even seem like something Bastian would do, and second, he'd never caught even the tiniest bit of gossip that Bastian was out in Napa, hooking up with random guys.

But where else would he be?

It was so late, the only thing open this late were some of the seedier bars on the outskirts of town. And while Kian had believed at the beginning that Bastian led this incredibly glamorous life, he'd long since learned that Bastian did exactly what all his chefs did: go to the restaurant early and leave late and go straight home after.

He pounded on the door again, not because he really thought Bastian was going to answer, but because he had to get some of this goddamn frustration out somehow.

Maybe Bastian was right after all, Kian thought despairingly, maybe there really was never a right time for them. He'd refused to believe it before—when you felt something this strongly, it needed to be for a reason—but fate was currently, very forcibly, reminding Kian of all the realities that he didn't want to face.

He nearly pulled out his phone and called Bastian. He imagined barking into the phone, demanding to know his whereabouts, the way Bastian did when any of his employees dared to be even five minutes late.

But before he could dial, he heard tires on the gravel turnoff to Bastian's house, then he saw lights.

A moment later, Bastian pulled up, parking his very fancy car right next to Kian's junker.

He got out, and even in the dim light, Kian could see he was frowning.

"What are you doing?" Bastian asked. "Is everything okay?"

It was Bastian's normal MO to ask a series of fast-paced questions. The practice tended to put the other person on edge, and immediately established in any personal encounter who was in charge.

Kian had recognized the technique after being subjected to it hundreds of times, and afterwards, he'd continued to let Bastian do it. Because at Terroir, he *was* in charge, and Kian was supposed to be learning from him.

But they weren't at Terroir now, and Kian had zero intention of letting Bastian just take over the way he always did.

He'd come here to flip the script, and he intended to follow through.

"Where were you?" he challenged right back.

Bastian looked gratifyingly surprised. "Where was I?"

Kian crossed his arms over his chest, and tried, despite his babyface, to look stern. "Where were you?"

"Uh," Bastian said, pausing on the top step. "I was visiting my mom."

Now Bastian wasn't the only one looking surprised. "Your mom lives here?" Kian asked.

"Yeah, a few miles up that way. Sometimes I visit her when I can't sleep."

That was the opening Kian had been waiting for—not Bastian talking about his mother, but Bastian admitting that he was struggling just as much as Kian was.

"You can't sleep?" Kian questioned as Bastian typed in the code to unlock the front door.

Bastian shot him an incredulous look.

"Me either," Kian admitted, because while he'd intended to control this conversation, honesty was also important. They walked into the foyer, and then into the living room.

Bastian's house was on the extreme end of the open-floor-plan concept. The kitchen sat to the left, with a long counter and barstools set neatly in a row. A long bank of windows, with the terrace that looked out across the valley, let in the only ambient light.

Kian assumed the bedroom lay to the right, but he'd never been in there before. Maybe tonight that would finally change.

"I came here tonight because I'm done not doing anything about it," Kian continued, walking over to the windows. He wondered if anyone could see in, and then decided he didn't give a fuck. If they wanted to watch, let them watch.

"What do you mean?" Bastian sounded guarded and uneasy. Not surprising, considering he was a control freak and Kian had just yanked all his control away.

"I'm done playing around," Kian said, turning around. "We've played around for two years."

Bastian gave a sharp bark of laughter. "Is that what we were doing? I thought I was teaching you to become a great chef."

"You were, you *have*, at least enough that I know what it takes to be one. And I intend to be one." Kian paused, gesturing between them. "What I'm talking about is a little more personal."

Bastian opened his mouth, no doubt to deny that anything personal between them existed, which was a huge fucking lie, and that set Kian's determination on fire.

He was going to keep denying this as long as he could. As long as Kian *let* him.

"Yeah," Kian interrupted. "About that." And he reached behind his head and tugged his t-shirt off. "I told you I'm done fucking around, and that means I'm done fucking around." He tossed the garment onto the arm of the couch.

Bastian laughed again, but it wasn't quite so bitter and it wasn't quite as controlled as before. "What do you think you're doing?"

Toeing off his shoes, Kian kept his gaze steady on Bastian. "You know what I'm doing."

It would have made this a hell of lot more dramatic if he'd been wearing more clothes, but he was wearing enough. He leaned down and tugged his socks off, first one and then the other. They landed next to his t-shirt.

Fists clenched at his side, Bastian looked torn—like he wasn't sure if he should demand Kian put his clothes back on, or join him, instead.

Kian knew exactly which way he wanted Bastian to fall.

He unbuttoned his jeans and then unzipped them, but didn't shuck them quite as quickly, just let them hang on his hip bones. Raising an eyebrow, he shot Bastian a very frank look.

"Are you going to join me?" Kian asked finally when Bastian just kept staring, like he was the angel and the devil, wrapped up in one altogether too-tempting package.

If Bastian continued to emphatically deny it, Kian wasn't sure what else he could do. Could he stand, for an extended period of time, naked in Bastian's living room until he made up his mind?

Fuck yes, he could.

Shoving away the last remnants of modesty, he shoved his jeans past his hips and let them fall to the floor. Bastian continued to stare; Kian wasn't sure he'd even blinked in the last few minutes.

"Are you really going to stand there and tell me you don't want this?" Kian challenged. He tucked a finger under his boxer briefs and saying a quick prayer—probably not to God, who wouldn't approve of this at all, but maybe the Devil instead, because he sure as fuck would—he pulled them down.

He stood there proudly and completely naked and let Bastian just *look*.

For a long, interminable second, Kian wasn't sure what was going to happen. Was he going to end up going back home, heart heavy and the worst case of raging blue balls that he'd ever experienced?

"I don't know why you're doing this," Bastian said and he sounded absolutely wretched. "Put your goddamn clothes back on."

"No," Kian said.

"Goddamn it, you're killing me." Bastian's voice had grown dark and deep, gravelly at the edges, and it seemed impossible, but Kian's cock grew even harder.

He'd never imagined he was much of an exhibitionist, but standing here, naked as the day he was born, and letting Bastian just *look* was an incredible turn-on. Of course, he'd rather if Bastian got his stubborn ass over here and finally touched him, but just this felt like *almost* enough.

"This is me saying to you, I've thought about it. I've considered the pros and the cons," Kian finally said, when the tension and the silence ratcheted even tighter between them. "This is me choosing you."

"Don't I get a say?" Bastian challenged.

Kian had to nod. "Of course you get a say, you can tell me to fuck off, and I'll go home. But I don't think you want to tell me to fuck off, Bastian."

When he said his name, Bastian closed his eyes, praying to someone—or something, maybe?

"No," Kian said tightly, "no, you don't get to close your eyes and not look when you turn me down."

"I'm not turning you down."

"No?" Kian raised an eyebrow and considered his next step. Bastian was so close to breaking—he could feel it, his self-control falling to pieces, but how to get it to crumble the rest of the way? "Then why are you still over there?"

Bastian laughed despairingly. "I don't fucking know."

In that moment, Kian knew. He knew what would break Bastian. Was he willing to play that dirty? *You've already shown up at his house in the middle of the night,* Kian reasoned, *and taken all your clothes off. What's a little further?*

He reached down, and hoping Bastian didn't see his fingers trembling, wrapped them around his cock. Pleasure rocketed through him. It wasn't like Bastian touching him, not exactly, but with his gaze on him, it was different and better than just doing this by himself, in his sad lonely room.

Bastian gasped sharply in the silence stewing between them. Rhythmically, he clenched and unclenched his fists, and Kian was so selfish—he wanted to know what those hands felt like instead of his own.

"I'm so fucking horny," Kian said, "and all I want is you. I don't want to go down to the Tavern and pick someone up. It wouldn't be enough. But if you won't help me, I guess I'll have to help myself."

Letting out a shaky breath, Bastian took a step closer, then another, until he was standing right in front of Kian. His eyes were so dark, Kian thought he could drown in the pupils. His breath was uneven, shaky even, and then Bastian dropped to his knees, and Kian couldn't breathe at all.

How many times had he imagined this? A dozen? A hundred? A thousand?

But Kian had never imagined that it might actually happen. If anything ever happened between them, Kian had always expected that he'd end up fulfilling somewhat of a subservient role, because those were the places they occupied in real life. But this wasn't reality, it was an aching fulfillment torn from the pages of a fantasy.

Kian's hand had frozen on his dick, and Bastian reached up slowly, his eyes never leaving Kian's. "This," he said, as his fingers slowly and carefully removed his own from his cock, "this isn't yours, this is mine. And I didn't say you could touch yourself."

He couldn't help it, he groaned as Bastian's calloused palm closed around him, pumping him so slowly, Kian wanted to cry.

"You came here, and you asked for it," Bastian growled. "You're goddamn gonna get it."

"Then what are you waiting for?" Kian demanded.

Bastian's hand slowed to a crawl, and it shouldn't have been so incandescently hot, to feel each and every ridge and scar and burn, sliding painfully slowly across his cock, but it was.

Still, he'd only dipped his toe into the fire, and it burned so good that he wanted more, he wanted to jump in and be consumed by it.

"More," he insisted. "Goddamn it, Bastian. Don't tease."

Bastian grinned wickedly, and it shot another pulse of heat through Kian. "What, like you teased me earlier?"

"Someone had to do it, or else we'd be stuck at the edge forever," Kian said, his voice so rough. The slow yet confident twist of Bastian's hand was driving him insane.

"Somehow," Bastian said, and he sounded way too cocky, way too sure of himself, "I always thought we'd go over the edge together."

Without another word, he leaned down and slid Kian's cock into his mouth, wrapping around him so tight, he had to bite his lip so he wouldn't yell.

"Oh, god," Kian moaned as Bastian proceeded to suck him so thoroughly, he wasn't sure he'd have any brain cells left when this finally ended.

And it was getting closer, faster, the pleasure spiraling out of control way too quickly. Kian tried to hang on, to prolong the dirty joy of seeing Bastian on the floor, sucking his cock. Nobody else, he knew, would ever see him like this. Fingertips pressed into his thighs and Kian panted, increasingly losing control.

Then Bastian's tongue twisted cleverly across the head and Kian did yell. "God fucking damnit, Bastian," he shrieked as he emptied down Bastian's throat.

For a long moment, neither of them moved. Kian was panting and so was Bastian. He wiped his mouth with the back of his hand and they stared at each other. Maybe Bastian couldn't believe he'd finally touched him; Kian knew *he* couldn't believe it had actually happened. Part of him wanted to reach down and pinch his bare arm, to make sure he wasn't dreaming.

Instead, he reached down and wrapped his fingers around Bastian's arm, tugging him up. *I always thought we'd go over the edge together*, Bastian had said. And even though he'd been obsessing over who had the control before, suddenly it felt important that they were standing as equals, together.

Bastian stared at him for a second, then curled into him, cradling his cheeks between his palms, and kissed him. Kian could taste himself, and even deeper still, the rich dark, cappuccino flavor that he remembered from San Francisco.

They kissed and kissed, like they were trying to make up for lost time, all those times that they'd desperately wanted to do this and hadn't. Bastian's jean-clad legs slid against Kian's bare ones, and he reached around, tugging off his own shirt. Kian gasped loudly into Bastian's mouth as their bare chests collided together. It felt even more intimate somehow, than when Bastian had been sucking his cock.

Kian reached down and thumbed open the button on Bastian's jeans, cupping his palm around his straining erection.

"Fuck," Bastian exhaled after he'd wrenched his mouth off Kian's. "Fuck, if you keep that up . . ."

Kian finished tugging down his jeans, and then shoved his underwear down too, Bastian's cock finally bobbing free of the constraining fabric. It was impressive, and even though Kian had just come, he felt a little frisson of desire just seeing it for the first time.

"Then come," Kian said, wrapping his hand around it. "I've teased you enough today."

Bastian's eyes stared back at him, wide and shocked, and he mumbled, "You can't tease me too much. Not you. Never you."

But he'd clearly been on edge, probably from the moment Kian had stripped his t-shirt off, and so Kian spit on his hand and fit it next to his other one, giving Bastian a steady and tight rhythm as he jerked him off.

It didn't take very long, but then Kian hadn't imagined it would, the very first time. They'd been torturing each other with some form or another of foreplay for the last two years. There was plenty of time to take their time and make it good—and not like this wasn't spectacular already. The novelty of the touch actually really felt like more than enough.

Bastian spilled into Kian's hand with a groan, his eyes fluttering shut. He didn't think he'd ever seen something as beautiful in his life as Bastian giving up control to him, letting Kian pleasure him.

They were going to have to do this all the damn time.

Kian grabbed for his t-shirt and wiped his hand off, and Bastian's cock. He was still staring at him, like he couldn't quite believe this was real, and not a dream he didn't want to wake up from.

"Yeah," Kian finally said, with a smile, "that really happened."

And then, unexpectedly, Bastian grinned too—and it was wide and bright and like nothing Kian had ever seen before. "Yeah," he said, and somehow his grin grew even wider, even brighter, nearly bright enough to blind Kian, "yeah, it really did."

"You sound surprised," Kian said.

"Well, you did just show up here in the middle of the night and take off your clothes." Bastian didn't sound mad, or even conflicted, he just sounded . . . happy. And Kian realized that he hadn't ever really heard him happy before. Not like this.

There was always a deep, contented exhaustion in his voice after a long, successful service. Sometimes Kian saw the joy of creating something unexpected and wonderful, during those test kitchen Sundays. But it had never been like this before.

"I don't regret doing this," Kian said seriously.

Bastian's grin turned conspiratorial, another look that Kian had never imagined he'd see on Bastian's face. "Neither do I." He looked skyward, like he was thanking God or maybe even the Devil. It was hard to say with Bastian. "I probably should, but I don't. I can't. It's been so long coming." He hesitated. "You want something to eat?"

Kian had never turned down food in his life, and definitely not food prepared by Bastian Aquino, in a post-sex haze.

"Sure," he said.

"And then we can do that again, but *better*," Bastian promised as they headed towards the kitchen.

Kian raised an eyebrow. "Better?"

"I mean, that was pretty fucking mind-blowing," Bastian said, "but I think we can do better, don't you?"

Kian had never been so eager to try in his whole life, so he nodded.

"Laundry's just down the hall," he said, "if you wanted to wash your shirt."

Bastian had moved towards the kitchen but hadn't made any move to put clothes on. He was just as powerfully built as Kian had always imagined, staring at him in his loose chef's whites. His thighs and arms looked like they could snap Kian in half, and he sort of wanted Bastian to try.

Kian gathered up his clothes and figured *what the hell*. He'd already stripped in front of him, what was staying naked a little longer?

And, he thought, as he headed down the hallway, it would definitely wrench the tension that still simmered between them a little tighter.

Bastian stood in front of his fridge, staring at the contents, but not really seeing them, as the cold air rushed over the cooling sweat on his body.

Normally, he'd be much more decisive, but the normal structure of his mind had just been entirely decimated by Kian.

The feel of his bare skin under his fingertips, Kian's hand stroking his cock, every single kiss, but most of all, the sheer bliss of giving in and not thinking at all.

At some point, they'd need to sit down and decide what all this meant for them, and definitely at some point, Bastian would need to reciprocate the three little words that Kian had said a few weeks before.

And, he added, he absolutely owed Kian an apology. Or ten.

But he was still enjoying not thinking, so instead, he let himself get lost in the contents of his fridge.

A few minutes passed, and Bastian heard Kian walk into the kitchen behind him.

"Cooking naked, while very sexy," Kian said, "isn't very safe." Bastian turned slightly as Kian tossed him a t-shirt and his pair of briefs.

He'd put his jeans back on, but he was shirtless, and for a second, Bastian wanted to forget all about the food, and instead trace the line of every muscle, every tendon, every inch of skin. He'd wanted this for so long, and it seemed insane to be *cooking* instead of touching, when all they'd done for two years was cook. But, he rationed, they needed to eat. They needed to carb load, probably, because now that Kian was in his bed, Bastian had no intention of leaving it for the next twelve hours.

Tomorrow was supposed to be one of their test kitchen Sundays, but there was no pressing reason not to postpone it until later. They could sleep in. Bastian could make them breakfast and they could even eat it in bed.

But all that energy was going to need to come from somewhere.

Pasta, maybe? Bastian considered, pulling on the clothes Kian had brought him. Rice? He could make a stir-fry. He had chicken, he had lots of vegetables.

The mushrooms in particular were calling to him, and as he plucked them from the shelf, he realized just how dull his normally sharp mental acuity was tonight. He'd make risotto, with roasted wild mushrooms. Carbs and comfort food, all in one.

Kian had settled at one of the barstools and watched as Bastian pulled out the mushrooms, an onion, garlic, butter, and a clear plastic container of stock from the freezer that he dumped into a pot to thaw.

"Risotto?" Kian questioned as Bastian fetched the arborio rice from the pantry. "Are we trying to carb load?"

Bastian peeled the onion and began to dice it finely. "Didn't you hear what I said?" he asked, a hint of a smile tugging at his lips. He couldn't stop smiling, it was obviously a symptom of the Kian disease that had completely overrun his immune system. "I said I thought we could do better. Better is going to require practice."

"And you're a perfectionist," Kian finished for him. His hair was rumpled, and Bastian's fingers itched. He wished he remembered exactly when he'd run them through the golden strands, the feel of them sliding through his fingers. It had all gone so quickly, once Kian had started taking his clothes off. Bastian's mind had just flipped off, and he'd switched right onto autopilot.

It was a shock he hadn't kissed him the first moment he'd seen him next to his front door, looking frustrated and cutely disgruntled.

"I'm a perfectionist," Bastian agreed. *I made you, didn't I?*

"I think," Kian mused, "that this is the very first time you've ever cooked for me."

Bastian was about to say that Terroir certainly counted, because Kian had eaten lots of things he'd cooked. Hundreds of dishes, probably.

Kian rolled his eyes. "And Terroir doesn't count. That was work. This isn't . . . work."

It was difficult not to notice that Kian didn't define what was going on, just that it wasn't solely professional anymore, and since Bastian was still reeling from their earlier encounter, he thought that was okay for now. They meant something to each other, they'd crossed over that strictly platonic line, and it was fine not to understand what that looked like or was defined as right away.

The one thing Bastian did know was that now that the line had been crossed, he wasn't nearly so restricted in what he could say.

"I wanted to, you know," Bastian said, glancing up. Kian's eyes on him were soft. "I'd lie awake at night and dream of inviting you here, of what I'd serve you, of what we'd do afterwards."

"What's that?" Kian asked, raising an eyebrow.

Bastian shot him a somewhat incredulous look. "Do you need it described to you? Because you didn't seem to need directions earlier."

"I meant," Kian corrected slowly, "what would you serve me?"

"Something simple. Something delicious. Something irresistible."

"Well yes." Kian sounded amused. "I already assumed it would be all those things."

In his mind, Bastian was pulling out the heavy-bottomed pot and setting it on the stove, melting a big fat pat of butter in it, and starting to sauté the onion and garlic. Instead, he was leaning against the counter, his knife forgotten on the cutting board, and staring at the man just across it. He couldn't see his own expression, but he knew it was sappy sweet. If anyone he knew at Terroir could see him right now, they wouldn't believe it.

He'd never acted this way with anyone in his whole life; and that made sense, because in his whole life, he'd never felt this way about anyone.

"I wanted to apologize to you, after we had that . . ." Bastian didn't know what to call it. He didn't want to call it an argument, because that assumed both sides had made their opinion and their feelings known. Instead he'd said something stupid and Kian had been justifiably and understandably pissed at him, and he'd shut him out.

"When you said I couldn't possibly know what I wanted?" Kian's stare challenged Bastian in every way, which was just one of the things he loved about him. That, on top of the apology he'd just given Kian, was definitely something he should also be saying, but he'd never told anyone but his mother that he loved them. Shouldn't the words be given a little more *gravitas* than tossed casually over a kitchen counter while Bastian cooked them dinner?

"I was trying to make you angry so that you'd stop trying to change my mind," Bastian admitted. He picked his knife back up and continued dicing his onion.

"Yeah, I figured that out. Just . . . not right away," Kian said. "I was pretty pissed off at you."

Bastian wanted to roll his eyes—how could Kian have ever believed that he really meant that—but then he remembered what Celeste had said to him. And it uncomfortably echoed what Kian had said to him before, after he'd started stripping all his clothes off.

Of course you get a say, you can tell me to fuck off.

They both knew Bastian was never going to tell Kian to fuck off.

He tossed the onion in, followed by the garlic, stirring around the aromatics with a wooden spoon. "You were within your rights to be pissed off," Bastian said apologetically.

"Does this make me the person you've apologized to most in your whole life?" Kian wondered.

Bastian laughed; he really couldn't help it. "Other than my mother, definitely," he said.

"Not to Luc?" Kian questioned so innocently, Bastian might have actually believed it if he hadn't witnessed just how annoyed Kian had been over his ex-lover.

"I never felt the need to apologize to Luc," Bastian said as he stirred in the rice, letting it toast in the butter, "because the only thing I ever did to him was make the mistake of sleeping with him.

"I meant it, you know. You're nothing like Luc," Bastian continued steadily, even though he was quaking inside. Kian had helped tear some of his walls down, but the foundations were so solidly well-established, it was going to take more than an incredible orgasm to demolish them entirely.

"I believed you," Kian said. "I believed you even more when we came back to Terroir and you promoted Xander."

It was hardly the worst decision Bastian had ever made—though it would probably make the top ten—but Kian kept bringing it up, like it *still* stung. Or maybe he was fishing for the job, still.

It was a risk, but Bastian had to ask, *had* to know. "Is that why you came here? To convince me to give you *sous chef*?"

Kian looked shocked, like he couldn't quite believe the question for a second, and Bastian braced for the worst, and opened his mouth to apologize but shut it again. Kian got up from the barstool, sauntered around the counter, casual but so purposeful, and crowded right into Bastian's space. Putting a hand on Bastian's shoulder, he pulled him in even closer, and kissed him.

It was still new enough, still fresh enough, that each and every kiss felt revelatory. He could do this now, it was allowed, and not only that fact blew his mind, but the passion Kian poured into the kiss finished off the rest of it.

Kian released him and Bastian nearly staggered backwards. He tried grabbing for Kian—because one of those kisses would never be enough—but he'd already gone back to his seat.

"That's why I'm here," Kian said steadily. "I'm not here to get a job. If I want a job, and I deserve a job, we'll talk about it. But it'll be separate from this, and preferably at the restaurant."

Bastian was speechless, and a little flabbergasted that Kian wasn't *more* speechless. "Why not here?" he asked and was embarrassingly aware of how stupid he sounded.

As he shrugged, Kian's tough exterior wavered enough that Bastian could see what the charade was costing him. "Because of *that*," Kian said firmly. "Here is for that, and a whole lot more, I hope, and the restaurant is for work. They need to stay separate."

"I'm glad you think so." And Bastian *was*. He didn't want to be the one to dictate the terms of their relationship, because he'd already done such a shitty job so far—and the perfectionist in him was more than a little humiliated by all that failure.

"Why didn't we do this a year ago?" he asked, checking the mushrooms that were roasting in the oven. Then he walked over to the wine fridge and selected a nice white, opening it with a few economical movements. He deglazed the pan and then pulled down two wine glasses, pouring them each a glass.

"We weren't ready," Kian said, swirling his wine like an expert with the sexiest twist of his fingers. There were a few very good reasons to actually finish dinner. *One,* he'd never actually stopped cooking to have sex before, and doing so now would set a dangerous precedent. *Two*, they were absolutely going to need the energy, and once they went to bed, Bastian had no intention of leaving it anytime soon.

"I was definitely ready," Bastian argued.

Kian rolled his eyes. "I'm not talking about your dick."

Bastian's hand, stirring another ladleful of broth into the risotto, stilled. "If you say that again, you're never going to eat this meal."

"What am I going to eat instead?" Kian asked slyly, the curl of his upper lip nearly irresistible. How had Bastian ever resisted him in the first place? He couldn't even remember; the memories of his willpower obliterated by Kian's skin and his cock and his hands. The naughty gleam in his blue eyes.

"*We*," Bastian argued, "are going to sit down and eat this risotto like civilized people, then we're going to go to bed." He paused. "And then we aren't going to be civilized at all. So behave yourself before I drag you off to the bedroom like a caveman with a particularly tasty carcass."

Kian leaned forward and licked his lips. "Is that a promise?"

CHAPTER NINE

AT TERROIR, A PROMISE was beyond solid, it was ironclad.

In Bastian's kitchen, it turned out that a promise was just as substantial, something that Kian had absolutely been counting on.

He'd long since recovered from his earlier orgasm, and while he might be younger than Bastian, Kian had definitely seen the outline of Bastian's hard cock in his briefs. All it had taken was one very hot kiss, and a little dirty talk, and he was more than ready to go.

Since Kian was too, there seemed very little point in finishing this food exercise.

"Is that a promise?" Kian asked, licking his lips as seductively as he could get away with. Truthfully, he didn't know what the limit even was; or even what they were really doing here. He'd set the most basic of boundaries: sex in this house, work at Terroir. That had felt like the most Bastian was able to tolerate. Kian could tell he was trying, but him pulling down even those boundaries had unmoored the man he loved.

Probably because Bastian fucking adored boundaries.

Bastian set the wooden spoon onto the counter next to the stove and flipped off the gas on the stove.

"Come over here, and see," Bastian challenged.

Kian loved that; they challenged each other like this, just the way they challenged each other in the kitchen. He'd never imagined meeting someone who could face him in every aspect of his life, and then he'd met Bastian and couldn't believe he'd ever find anyone else who fit that particular set of criteria so perfectly, and so effortlessly.

They were perfect for each other. Someday, Kian thought, as he took a lazy sip of wine, eyeing Bastian over the top of his glass, they would talk about that, but for now, this was enough.

This was more than enough.

"You drive me insane," Bastian ground out, and yeah, that was definitely mutual. His biceps bulged in his t-shirt as he clenched his fists around the edge of the marble countertop.

"You sound surprised by this," Kian pointed out. Had he really believed that all he had to do was ask once, and Kian would just fall to his knees?

Probably, yes. Frankly, it was taking a lot of self-control to not do just that. But Kian had come here, tonight, to make a point, and that point had a much wider significance than merely breaking down Bastian's argument against them hooking up.

If he crawled over there now, the very first time Bastian asked, it would only emphasize that Bastian was as in charge here as he was at Terroir, and that wasn't going to work. He couldn't have the upper hand everywhere; as much as Kian loved him, he knew Bastian would become insufferable.

"Surprised that you're secretly a fantastic sexual tease?" Bastian laughed with dry amusement. "It's a good sort of surprise."

No doubt Bastian had figured he was young and therefore inexperienced and couldn't really keep up. He was right about the first two, but Kian had zero intention of fulfilling the last prediction.

"Why don't you come *here*?" Kian said.

"No orders to crawl?"

"If I wanted you on your knees again, I would've asked for that." Kian continued to sip his wine, the alcohol brewing in his stomach alongside a very healthy dose of lust.

He never wanted Bastian to stop looking at him like that—like he was an angel and a god and a very naughty boy who needed to be spanked.

"How about on my feet?" Bastian asked, skirting around the corner, and tugging Kian's barstool so it swiveled around. Kian set his glass on the counter and was very aware his fingers were trembling. He smoothed the fabric down Bastian's shoulders, reveling in the fact that he was *allowed* to touch now, after so much time fighting down the inclination.

Bastian trailed fingers down his thigh to his calf and then lower, to his bare foot. He picked up and tucked Kian's leg around his waist. "I think," he said steadily, even as the heat in his eyes lit them both on fire, "it's time we go to the bedroom. What do you think?"

Kian moved his other leg to mirror the first, gasping as Bastian pulled him tight against him, their dicks, with too many layers of clothing in between, brushing together.

Later, he'd think with triumph that Bastian had *asked* him, not merely demanded or even assumed. He'd *asked*. It was hard to even think straight, not with Bastian looking at him with all that scorching purpose, but it was enough for Kian to tilt his head back and let himself be kissed again.

It was the first kiss Bastian had initiated since their first, and the heat from it scorched Kian, pulling him in so deep that he barely even noticed as Bastian tucked a hand under his ass and lifted him off the barstool.

He carried him all the way to the bedroom, and Kian got a fleeting impression of an impressive bank of floor-to-ceiling windows, covered with dark partly translucent black shades, and a huge bed with a plain navy quilt, before he was deposited on it.

"Do you know, I've never once stopped cooking to have sex?" Bastian asked, breathing heavily, but not, Kian didn't think, from carrying him. Probably from the kiss which had spun out and out until they were both breathless.

Kian wasn't surprised by his confession. "I guess you haven't had really good sex, then," Kian theorized.

Normally, Bastian would no doubt be offended by the suggestion that he was less than brilliant at everything he attempted. But tonight, he just sat back on his heels and contemplated this statement. "I think you might be right," Bastian finally admitted. "What about you?"

"I have a feeling it's about to happen," Kian said, reaching up and pulling back against him. "I want you to fuck me."

Bastian looked surprised. Kian supposed that made sense. He'd been taking charge of every aspect of this encounter, and now it looked like he was giving away control. Kian would have assumed Bastian had more of a progressive opinion of sexual politics, but obviously not.

"What," Kian said, "just because I want your cock in my ass, like I've been fantasizing about for two fucking years, that makes me the weak one? The subservient one?"

For a second, Bastian looked even more shocked. Then he slowly started to smile. "Goddamn it, you are fucking perfect," he said, leaning down and kissing him thoroughly. He broke away only to say, "I would be fucking privileged to fuck you."

"Then what are you waiting for?" Kian asked.

Bastian leaned back again and stripped off his shirt. Kian trembled inside at having so much of Bastian revealed to him. He was powerfully built, with wide shoulders, impressive arms, and a flat, lightly rippled stomach and a trail of dark hair disappearing into his black briefs.

It was Bastian's turn to smile cockily as Kian looked. "Like what you see?" he asked, running a hand lightly up Kian's jean-clad leg. "I think you do," he said, answering his own question as he cupped his cock in his palm. "I think you love it."

"I do," Kian moaned. "Fuck, you're so gorgeous."

"The first time I ever saw you," Bastian said, reaching up to unbutton Kian's jeans, then lowering his zipper, "I wanted to bend you right over the counter you were standing by. Just pull your pants down and tease you until you were begging me for it."

It was scary how similar Kian had felt. He'd gone home that first night and alternating between his determination for Bastian to teach him how to be a great chef had been a truly stupendous orgasm, as he imagined Bastian punishing him for his snarky comment.

Bastian tugged his jeans off, his slow, methodical movements deliberate. Kian bit his lip. "Is that what you want me to do now, beg you for it?"

"Would you?" Bastian asked, the dark edge to his voice sending a thrill right through him.

"Maybe." *Definitely.* Kian met his eyes in the dim room as Bastian pulled his boxer briefs off, still moving in that very slow, very deliberate manner, like there was no need to rush at all. They'd been waiting for two fucking years. That felt like a pretty good reason to Kian. His cock bobbed free, hard and aching.

"Maybe," Kian breathed out unsteadily, "maybe if you did something worth me begging."

Bastian rolled his eyes. "You hold that thought." He leaned over and opened a drawer behind Kian.

"What's that?" Kian asked, trying to see, but the room was too dark.

"You want me to fuck you raw?"

"Oh." Kian told himself that this was already the best sex he'd already had, that it was totally fine and he wasn't disappointed at all that Bastian had already moved past the really spectacular foreplay. But he sort of was. He'd expected better—or at least something different, with the teasing promises he'd been making and the deliberately slow way he'd stripped his clothes off.

"Too quick for you?" Bastian raised an eyebrow. "We'll see what you say when you're begging for my cock."

Kian gasped as Bastian's fingers glided down his thigh, barely brushing against his cock and then his balls, and then found his hole. But instead of immediately inserting a finger, he just stroked around the rim, little teasing touches that had Kian squirming within moments.

He leaned over and his breath barely ghosted over Kian's cock, which twitched against his belly, the wet head rubbing against his skin. "Did you want something?" Bastian asked, sounding very satisfied.

Something that Kian wasn't—at all. "*Yes,*" he demanded.

Bastian chuckled, a dark, warm sound, and Kian shivered.

Finally, he slid the tip of his finger inside as he licked a long stripe up Kian's cock. "Yeah," Bastian said as Kian moaned at the fleeting brush of pleasure, "you're definitely going to be begging for me."

Kian almost said something back—something like, *you wish*—but then Bastian's mouth was back on his dick and the finger was moving and pleasure crashed through him.

It went on and on and on: Bastian's mouth barely skimming along the length of his cock, his finger breaching him a little further on each thrust, only to retreat back a second later.

Kian's hands fisted in the sheets and he felt caught in a vise of pleasurable agony, and no matter how he moved, how he shifted, he couldn't escape the inexorable, slow burn of Bastian's hands and his mouth.

He wasn't even particularly against begging, but something about the playful glint in Bastian's eyes made him bite his lip and hold back the cries to do *more, please god, anything.*

"Nothing to say?" Bastian asked, as a second finger teased around the first. "Maybe you don't want this at all."

Kian moaned even though that wasn't really what Bastian wanted. He wanted to know just how desperate Kian was for it—which was frankly ridiculous because he'd been desperate for it for *years.* And all that had changed in that time was that he'd impossibly wanted it even more.

"Enough," he finally gritted out. "I fucking want it."

Bastian's grin lit up the room. "That wasn't really begging."

"Did you really think I would, if you challenged me?"

"Not really, but it was fun to try," Bastian said, his smile somehow growing even brighter. He slid the second finger in and leaned down, wrapping his tongue around the head of Kian's cock, sucking hard.

Spots dotted Kian's vision at the sudden onslaught of bliss sizzling through his veins.

"God, you're so good," Bastian grunted, almost to himself more than Kian. "So goddamn perfect."

"Fuck me already," Kian demanded.

"So bossy." But Bastian slid another finger in with his two and this time it wasn't just Kian who groaned.

A minute later, he slid his fingers out and Kian watched as he ripped open the condom with trembling fingers. And he thought, through a haze of satisfaction, that he'd done that. He'd made Bastian's fingers shake, he wanted him so goddamn much.

"Please," Kian wailed, finally breaking as Bastian's cock brushed his thigh, and then lower, then slipping in an inch.

Kian had only had penetrative sex with one other person, and it had been nothing to write home about. But then, the prep and the foreplay had been nothing like it was with Bastian. And Bastian was definitely in a whole other universe than the other guy.

It was a revelation to feel Bastian slide further and further inside him, until he didn't know where he ended and Bastian began. He slipped in farther and then froze, Bastian's fingers digging into his skin as Kian squirmed against the fullness.

"God, no, stop," Bastian begged, the sound practically wrenched out of him. "I can't . . ."

And it was so good to hear the desperation in his voice, Kian couldn't help it. He pushed back against Bastian's grip, until all of his cock was buried inside him.

"I can't," Bastian repeated, this time his voice a plea.

"Fuck me," Kian demanded. His hand slipped down to grasp his own cock, and they both moaned again.

Bastian was the worst at taking orders—he only gave them at Terroir—but he listened to Kian now, and started to move. Kian's fingers shakily circled his cock, tugging it carefully because he felt right on the edge, and he knew as soon as he came, Bastian was done for. They'd both needed this for so long, and their earlier orgasms had barely taken the edge off all that wanting.

His thrusts picked up speed and then he hit a spot inside that had Kian seeing not just stars but the whole goddamn galaxy. He was right on the precipice, he just needed a little more, and he wanted Bastian to be the one to give it to him.

"Kiss me," Kian commanded.

Bastian froze, like he was surprised by the sudden demand, and then his face softened. He leaned down, and the kiss was softer, and sweeter than Kian had expected. He'd braced for the hot rush of a sloppy, wet hungry kiss, something like what their bodies were already doing, but the tenderness of it unwound him until he was gasping into Bastian's mouth, come spurting between them, clenching around Bastian until he too, gasped and came.

For a long moment, neither of them moved, or spoke. Most of Bastian's weight was still back on his elbows, but Kian liked that he was covering him, enveloping him. He'd wondered forever what this might feel like, and now that he'd felt it, he didn't know what he'd do if he lost it.

Before, there was always that fleeting, niggling worry in the back of his mind—that he'd dreamt all those moments, a whole chain of them, that led up to this one. That San Francisco was the product of a tired, fantasizing mind. That he'd imagined all those hot, dirty looks. That the times he'd caught Bastian staring at his ass had been all a mistake.

He hadn't been wrong. It wasn't only him that had suffered in silence, wanting but never taking.

But now that they'd both taken—and no matter who'd taken the cock, Kian believed they'd definitely taken each other, Bastian's currently awestruck expression was evidence enough of that—what were they going to do?

It was easy enough to banter and flirt in Bastian's kitchen. But what about the Terroir kitchen? It was so easy to say, *oh that stays at home*, but could it? Was it even possible?

Kian felt a shiver of something real and concrete enter into the little golden bubble he'd been living in since Bastian had finally touched him for the first time.

How the fuck were they going to do this?

It was like the moment hit Bastian at the exact same time, because it was then that he retreated, carefully sliding out of Kian and purposefully looking away to dispose of the condom. He grabbed a tissue from the box on the beside table and wiped Kian and then his own torso. He disposed of that, and then there was nothing to do but look at each other and wonder.

What are we going to do?

Bastian sat down on the side of the bed and rested his elbows on his knees. He still hadn't looked at Kian.

There was a part of Kian that wanted to shamelessly beg now. *Don't say you regret it.*

Clearly he didn't, not really, anyway. You couldn't regret something you were such an enthusiastic participant in. But the chances of him saying it were too real for Kian to wait for the words.

Instead, he spoke first. "I thought you were going to make me dinner?" Kian asked.

Bastian's glance his direction was swift and amused. "Don't say you wish I'd done that instead."

"I don't," Kian said steadily. "But now I'm starving."

It wasn't really a solution, to get half dressed again and go back to the kitchen, but Kian knew that was the place *he* retreated to when he felt lost, and he had a hunch Bastian was the same.

"Then I'll make you dinner," Bastian said, reaching for his shirt and tugging it on. "Come, get dressed. I'm hungry too."

When Kian came back to the kitchen and resumed his spot on the barstool, Bastian had the gas on the stove back on, and he was poking at the mushrooms in the oven.

"Salvageable?" Kian asked.

"Not really," Bastian grumbled and grabbed the pan bare, not even bothering with a towel, and dumped out the contents into the trash. He looked up and then smiled, which surprised Kian because nothing bothered Bastian more than good food wasted. "But it was totally worth it."

"Of course it was." Like after waiting so long, the sex *wouldn't* be crazy hot. He'd known it had to be; he'd needed it to be. And it had still eclipsed even his wildest dreams.

"Get over here," Bastian grumbled. "You're completely capable of prepping these mushrooms while I try to salvage the risotto."

Kian thought it was the height of the fantasy to sit here, watching as Bastian made him dinner with his own hands, crafting the flavors just for the two of them. But it turned out that he'd been wrong.

The real fantasy? The fantasy that bled into real life until Kian didn't know where one ended and the other began?

It was standing hip to hip with Bastian in his kitchen, preparing dinner *with* him.

Maybe, Kian thought as he chopped the mushrooms into chunks, dropping them onto a fresh sheet pan, it was because this felt like something a couple might do together. Because his deepest, most closely held fantasy, the one he wasn't sure he'd ever be able to confess to Bastian was just that: living as an established couple. Fighting, loving, working—doing it all together.

They'd just taken the very first step towards that, but there were a hundred roadblocks and those were just the ones he'd thought of. In the end, it might not be possible, but Kian knew now that he could at least say he'd tried.

And tonight, that was enough.

Bastian finished the risotto, Kian pulled the mushrooms from the oven, and together, they plated.

Nothing fancy like at Terroir, but aesthetics were still important. They dished up the pale risotto in dark brown enameled bowls, Kian arranged the mushrooms over the top and then Bastian grabbed a bottle of basil oil, drizzling that over everything.

Kian picked up one of the bowls as Bastian grabbed spoons, hesitating over the silverware choice. "Forks maybe?" he asked.

"Bring both," Kian suggested, and hesitated, because he didn't know where to go. Were they eating in the kitchen? The living room? It was far too cold to eat on the table on the terrace. And Bastian was fairly fastidious—Kian couldn't imagine he'd ever want to eat in bed.

In the end, Bastian surprised him by balancing his bowl and the silverware in one hand, and gently placing the other on the small of Kian's back and leading him to the couch.

Kian played it safe and sat on one end, curling his bare legs underneath him.

Glancing over at Bastian, he was surprised to see a hurt flash through the other man's eyes.

"Do I smell bad or something?" Bastian asked.

Hardly. He smelled spicy and dark and wonderful, like bergamot and rosemary with the slightest hint of espresso and chocolate. Kian wanted to bury his nose into his neck and not move, but the last thing he wanted was to make Bastian uncomfortable with his clinginess.

He shook his head.

"Then why are you all the way over there?" Bastian asked.

Kian knew exactly how to sit, where to go, what to do, when they were at Terroir. He knew better than to ever touch Bastian, always leaving a buffer between them.

But this wasn't Terroir, so he slid a little closer. Bastian made a frustrated noise and reached out, crowding Kian against him with the arm he'd slung over the back of the couch. He reached up and stroked the back of Kian's head with his fingers, absently toying with the strands of his hair. "This is better, isn't it?"

Bastian had astonished him more than once tonight, but this was the biggest surprise of all. That Bastian Aquino, head chef of Terroir and not-so-affectionately known by his staff as the Bastard, was a cuddler.

"What?" Bastian questioned, a smile crinkling the corners of his eyes. "I wasn't allowed before."

"You didn't allow yourself," Kian grumbled, barely able to hide his own smile as he scooped up a bite of risotto and mushrooms.

"Still, I'm going to take advantage of it now," Bastian said, eating deftly with only one hand as he balanced the bowl in his lap. "If you don't have any objections."

Kian laughed because all of a sudden he felt a little teary and more than a little overemotional, and he absolutely was not going to bawl his eyes out on Bastian's couch over a little cuddling. "Just don't tell me tomorrow you've changed your mind."

Bastian's gaze was steady and soft. "You must not know me very well. I'm rather . . . intractable when I've set my mind to something."

"I might be familiar with that particular tendency," Kian said, sniffing.

"Eat your food," Bastian said. "Then we'll go to bed."

❧ ❧

It was after noon the next day when Kian let himself in the house with his key. He'd definitely hoped that Xander would already be gone, or might be at Damon's, but no, he was right there, at the kitchen table with his laptop and a huge mug of coffee.

"You're back," Xander said steadily, not looking up from what he was typing. "There's coffee on and I brought some bread from the restaurant."

Kian set his keys on the counter and grabbed a mug from the cupboard. He was definitely a little sore this morning, muscles used in places that felt like they'd only ever gotten occasional use. When he looked up from pouring his coffee, Xander was watching him.

"So, it finally happened," Xander said conversationally. Like he hadn't been arguing against it happening for the full two years they'd known each other. "Or maybe you just braided each other's hair and told ghost stories."

It really wasn't any of Xander's business but Xander was also his best friend. Kian hesitated.

"*Please*, like I would tell anyone," Xander added as he rolled his eyes.

"You're right," Kian conceded. "You're not exactly the person I'd go to for hot gossip. And for the record, no, we didn't braid each other's hair or tell ghost stories."

A smile flitted across Xander's features. "I didn't think so. Wouldn't have pegged Aquino as that type."

"And me?" Kian asked as he sat down next to his friend. He tried not to worry if Xander was going to see the fairly obvious marks on his neck or if he was going to mention them. It wasn't like he and Damon weren't always practically fucking on their couch, when they had an empty house of Damon's they could screw in.

"You're the type, but I can see that's not all you were up to," Xander said in a shockingly judgement-free tone. He tilted his head, as if to see the marks in a slightly better light. "Aquino is thorough, I guess."

Kian fought against the blush, but it rose across his cheeks anyway. "Very," he admitted.

This morning, as Kian had finally pulled on his clothes for the trip home, Bastian lazing on the bed, watching like a great big tabby, he'd said, "I think I got a little carried away last night."

There was so much to remember, that it had taken Kian a minute to remember that after eating, they'd ended up making out on the couch, Kian perched in Bastian's lap, mindlessly rubbing against each other as Bastian had kissed and bit up the sensitive tendon just behind his ear.

"It's fine," Kian had said, brushing away his concern. "I'll just make sure to wear my coat buttoned all the way up."

But from his own glance in the rearview mirror this morning and the buried astonishment in Xander's gaze as he looked at the marks, that probably wasn't going to cut it.

"As long as you're happy," Xander said.

Kian had not been expecting such full acceptance of his developing relationship with Bastian. "No more concerned lectures?"

Xander sighed and set his elbows on the edge of the table. "I know that sometimes I've been a shitty friend," he admitted, "but I was worried. I was afraid he'd take advantage, I was worried he'd use you up and throw you away, but none of that happened. Instead you fucking pined after each other for *years*. Those are feelings with power. Who am I to argue with that?"

"Yourself?" Kian asked, raising an eyebrow.

Xander laughed.

"Okay, that's fair," he said, then hesitated. "It's only because I'm a friend, and I care about you that I'm asking. You're okay? Everything is okay?"

"I'm good. Really good." He suddenly laughed. The realization that the last sixteen or so hours had actually happened was just now hitting him. "I can't believe that actually worked."

"What did you do?" Xander sounded amused now. "You sure seemed pissed off, heading off last night."

"I was. I was furious. Just . . . fucking tired of him getting to dictate the terms of what we were. So I showed up at his house and just started taking my clothes off."

Xander choked on his coffee. "You did *what*," he said when he finally managed to take a breath.

"He wasn't *listening*," Kian argued. "What else do you do with someone who won't listen to you?"

"Not take my damn clothes off," Xander said, still laughing.

"Hey, don't judge. It worked." Kian flushed. "Really, really well."

Xander shook his head. "Apparently. Just . . . be careful. Be honest with each other. I know Aquino isn't easy to deal with, but god knows you've figured out the right way to do it. And for the love of god, ask him for my job. You're already doing the work without getting the credit or the salary."

Kian really didn't want to confess that in the last two years, he'd gotten enough raises that he'd been making more as Bastian's special "intern" than the *sous chef* at Terroir. Bastian had made sure he knew his contributions to the restaurant were appropriately valued, even if he didn't always say it in words.

But then that was Bastian, and Xander was right, Kian had figured out the best way to deal with him.

As for the credit, it would be nice, but anyone who was already in the Terroir kitchen knew to listen to Kian when he asked for something. He got a wide berth, respect, and he realized, the chafing he'd begun to feel in the last few months hadn't been over his position in the restaurant—it had been the rut he and Bastian had fallen into.

Now that they'd resolved that, Kian thought maybe he wouldn't feel so stagnant. He was only twenty-three. He still had a lot to learn. He'd become *sous* eventually, and at some point, maybe he'd even leave Terroir. But for now, he didn't feel like rushing the process. He was content right where he was.

Chapter Ten

After his shower, Kian had tried various methods to hide the blooming bruises on his neck, but he finally gave up because the neck kerchief looked incredibly contrived, borrowing one of Xander's chili pepper bandanas didn't seem right, and the makeup called more attention to them than it hid.

He was just going to have to go in and hope everyone was too busy working to examine Kian's neck—and if they did, they wouldn't connect it to Chef's unexpectedly good mood.

Because that was exactly what Kian expected to walk into when he finally arrived at Terroir: Bastian not yelling and quite possibly spreading encouragement and good cheer wherever he went.

Of course when he walked in, what he heard was Bastian verbally destroying the hopes of the new young kitchen assistant.

"This is fucking garbage," Bastian yelled, the gravelly edge of it echoing in Kian's memories from the night before. "You want to just take the trash and dump it on a plate and serve it to our guests?"

"No, Chef. I'll fix it." Derek sounded a tiny bit teary, but also resolute, which was a fucking relief. Kian wasn't going to have to coax him out of the bathroom for service—at least not this time.

Kian forced himself to take his time putting his stuff in his locker, making sure his coat was fully buttoned, not that it would do much to hide the bruises on his neck, before walking out into the prep stations.

The last thing Kian had expected to be greeted with after the night before was a glare, but Bastian definitely glared. It was almost certainly residual from

Bastian's encounter with Derek, but no matter what little white lie he told himself, it still stung.

"You'd better fix it," Bastian growled, and then turned towards Kian. "I've started the soup, but you need to finish it, and you need to monitor the hell out of Derek's prep. He's a fucking mess."

Bastian was all business as they walked towards the massive bank of burners, where the gigantic pot of soup was bubbling away in the corner. "It's a take on a *posole*," he said. "You know how I like that to be finished."

"Yes, Chef," Kian said, and ignored the thrum of arousal he felt when he said the words. He remembered this morning, crawling down Bastian's body and sliding his cock into his mouth. Bastian's hot gaze on his face, on his mouth, as he'd sucked him off. It was hard to even believe that man even existed in the brisk, tough, blank-faced Bastian in front of him now. Kian wouldn't have believed it, but he'd experienced it.

Kian had been the one to say he wanted things to stay the same at Terroir, and there was definitely a part of him that was undeniably glad they had. Terroir was like a support system, always there, always morphing but still strong and stable underneath the culinary experimentation, and Bastian was absolutely an extension of his own restaurant.

But another part of him wanted to see just a sign, even the faintest hint of a smile, some sort of reassurance that everything that had happened wasn't just in Kian's head.

Maybe he'd dreamt the whole thing after all.

He'd believe it, except for the chain of bruises currently dotting his neck.

"When you're done with the soup, I'd like to see you in my office," Bastian said, surprising the hell out of Kian. "If you're not too busy managing Derek."

Kian didn't think he'd imagined the sudden thaw in Bastian's dark eyes. "I shouldn't be."

"Then, I'll see you in a bit," Bastian said, and walked back to his office.

Sighing, Kian went to check the soup and then to go find Derek, who had better not have retreated to the bathroom again.

The blinds were up on Bastian's glass walls when Kian approached his office, so he didn't think Bastian had asked to see him for anything non-Terroir related.

Last night had been a revelation, a reveal of all the soft, sexy inner parts of Bastian, but Kian knew, as surely as the sun setting and rising, that he wouldn't reveal any of that in the heart of his empire.

Kian didn't even want him to. Those parts were for Kian and Kian alone to enjoy.

He knocked on the glass and Bastian glanced up from his computer monitor.

"Oh, that was quick," Bastian said.

Kian fought back against the urge to apologize and explain that he had done everything to a quality level Bastian would approve of. He didn't need to apologize *or* explain. Bastian trusted him, he believed that, so instead of answering, he merely took the seat.

A year ago, he'd used the corporate credit card Bastian had given him to buy more comfortable chairs for the office, and Bastian had given him a look when he'd brought them in but he hadn't said a word. Kian figured that he was willing to sit here and take whatever shit came out of Bastian's mouth, but he didn't need to do that *and* be uncomfortable at the same damn time.

"Xander has been gone three months," Bastian said. "I think it's high time I promoted someone to *sous* chef, and I can't think of anyone more qualified or that deserves it more than you do."

Kian couldn't help himself. He gaped.

Of course, the moment Kian decided he was perfectly fine not being promoted to *sous*, Bastian decided that the time was finally right.

But Bastian wasn't even done. "But the more I thought about it," he continued, "I realized that if I want to partner with Nathan Hess, I'll be relying on you more and more. And that's why I want to offer you the *chef de cuisine* position."

Kian shot to his feet. "You want to do *what*?"

"Don't tell me you're surprised by this," Bastian said, leaning back in his chair and crossing his arms over his chest. "You've wanted this."

He wasn't going to apologize for being ambitious. Yes, he'd wanted it. Specifically he'd wanted Xander's job, the *sous* chef job, but only if he was qualified for it and Bastian believed that he'd earned it.

While he desperately wanted to find some sort of equal footing with Bastian, he wasn't stupid enough to believe that extended to culinary knowledge, experience, or Terroir.

"Of course I want the job," Kian said. "I'm just not sure I wanted it like this."

"Like how?" Bastian challenged.

Kian rolled his eyes. He wasn't going to say it, but they were both thinking it. Last night had been momentous. He didn't want Bastian to ruin it by making him think he'd gotten the job because he was good in bed, not good in the kitchen.

"I told you when Xander quit," Bastian added, his voice softening, "I told you that I should have promoted you instead."

He'd been so fed up—angry and frustrated—when Bastian had confessed that particular tidbit, but later he'd thought about it. And he wasn't sure he really agreed with Bastian, which was blowing his mind.

"I knew this kitchen better than Xander did, but he had five more years of experience than I did—that means he had more than *double* the experience I do. That's not insignificant," Kian pointed out.

Bastian made a frustrated sound. "Would it be too much to ask for you to just say, *thank you, Chef*, and take the goddamned job?"

Yes, it probably would, and if Bastian had only wanted a sycophant in his kitchen and in his bed, Kian wouldn't be here right now. He definitely wouldn't have been curled up with Bastian the night before. Bastian wanted someone to challenge him. Someone to call him out on his bullshit.

But he also really wanted this job. He'd wanted it before he'd even known what it was, and long before Bastian had ever offered it to Xander. If Bastian thought he was ready, maybe Kian should defer to him. After all, he was always claiming to know everything.

"I'll take it," Kian said after a long moment. "But I think your timing continues to suck."

First the Xander promotion right after they'd gotten back from San Francisco and now this. It was only two instances, but it felt like a pattern of their personal lives influencing the decisions Bastian was making in the restaurant. That didn't only feel wrong, it felt completely unlike the Bastian that Kian believed he knew.

Bastian laughed, and it broke up the tension that had built up between them. "I'll give you that," he said, and even though he didn't offer another apology in words, the tone was there, in his voice. "I'm not very good at this. I'm rather . . . inexperienced, if you'd believe it."

Not sexually, clearly, but with being in a relationship with someone he cared about? Kian could see that. "Just tell me this has nothing to do with last night."

Kian dropped his voice towards the end, as the door was still open. He didn't think anyone would eavesdrop, but this industry was also cutthroat and god knew what people would do to get ahead.

There were absolutely people in the world who might find out about last night and believe that Kian had only done it to get this promotion, and Bastian had let it happen because that was his right as Kian's superior.

Those people were fucked up, but they existed, and while Kian might be naïve, he wasn't *that* naïve.

"Of course it doesn't," Bastian said. "Do you really think I would promote you because of *that*?"

Kian shrugged, because the timing remained suspicious.

"I know . . . I know it looks like that," Bastian allowed. He looked reluctant to continue, but he did anyway, like this was worth enduring the discomfort of the remaining confession. "I have a bad habit of reacting poorly when I lose control. I lost control in San Francisco. I never meant for . . . *that* to happen. Not with you. I'd told you we couldn't, and I had fully intended to keep that promise, but you get under my skin, past my defenses, and what you said that night—it struck something inside me. I knew what Luc's presence made you feel, and I didn't want you to feel that anymore. But that didn't change anything about our situation. I still believed it shouldn't happen, but how could I tell you with words when words were clearly meaningless? Promoting Xander was a reminder to you, but mostly to myself, that even if I favored you, the hierarchy of the kitchen was still important. There were still vital reasons not to cross the line again. Yes, you have less experience than Xander did, but we work better together than he and I did, and that's essential in a *sous*. Which is why I told you that it should have been you instead, not him."

It wasn't an explanation that Kian had ever expected to hear. It didn't take the sting entirely away from that day—it had happened and nothing could change that, or the way he'd felt at the time—but hearing Bastian's reasons helped. He hadn't done it to be an asshole. He'd done it, like he'd done so much, because he had been trying to do what he believed was the right thing.

Kian nodded. "And today?"

"If I explain everything, am I going to lose my essential mystery?" Bastian wondered archly.

"If you explain everything, I might actually want to take this job, and then we can celebrate later. Properly." Kian grinned.

Bastian returned the smile, definitely lighter at the edges, and it was a forcible reminder that while Bastian's hair might be threaded with gray, he wasn't really old. He'd just shouldered an incalculable burden with an incredible amount of accompanying pressure at a too-young age.

"I'd hate to take away the possibility of a celebration," he said gravely. "Fine. I offered you the job today, not because of what happened last night, but because I realized I was holding you back. I was holding you with me. Not because I didn't think you were ready, but because I didn't want to let you go. That wasn't right. When our relationship changed, I realized that was what kept stopping me from giving you this job you deserved. And if you deserve *sous*, then there's no reason you can't be *chef de cuisine.* I'm not disappearing. I'm not going to turn into Emeril or Mario and be unavailable. But I do want to take this opportunity with Nathan Hess, and I need you to take charge of things if I do."

"Okay," Kian said, feeling unsteady and unmoored. *Chef de cuisine* at a Michelin-starred restaurant at twenty-three years of age. It was practically unheard of.

"I became *sous* when I was twenty-three," Bastian said. "And I know it was the making of me as a chef. I believe you can do this."

The steady look of unflinching belief in Bastian's eyes helped to steady Kian. He *did* believe in him; he wouldn't have given Kian this promotion otherwise. Not with his life's work, Terroir, hanging in the balance.

"Thank you, Chef," Kian said. "I intend to make you proud." He rose to his feet. "I need to check on the prep for the evening's service."

"Of course." Bastian stood too, and hesitated. It was so different from this morning when Kian had left Bastian's doorstep, and they'd kissed goodbye, their embrace turning heated as soon as their lips met. It was the only time they'd ever done that, but strangely, it felt odd not to repeat it now.

And from the way Bastian paused, the sudden nervous energy in his hands, Kian knew he felt the exact same way.

"I'll make the announcement at family dinner," Bastian said. Kian ducked his head in agreement, and then walked out the door before he did something monumentally stupid like try to kiss him.

After promoting Kian, it was readily apparent to Bastian that there was nobody even remotely suited in the kitchen to promote as *sous*—and Bastian wasn't cruel enough to expect him to succeed without the proper tools he'd need, and that included a trusted and competent second-in-command.

Two days after the promotion, a resume crossed his desk that caught his attention. A fellow student with Kian at the Academy. He'd worked at Michael Mina since graduation but was looking to move back to the Valley. Bastian checked the references, even spoke to Michael himself, and decided this was the best *congratulations, you're promoted* present he could find.

Other than giving Kian a truly spectacular blowjob the night before. Kian had claimed breathlessly that he'd never come so hard in his life, but then Bastian had bent him over the counter and fucked him like he'd wanted to do so long ago, the first time they'd ever met, and he'd come again, even harder the second time.

Bastian hadn't lied when he'd told Kian that he'd believed he could succeed. He *could*—he had all the tools, most of the skill, and definitely the drive required. Watching him as he directed the line during service, Bastian was struck again by how much Kian reminded him of himself at that age. Ferocious and determined to achieve that success only because he'd truly earned it.

But Terroir was a large establishment, with the capacity for large crowds, and Kian was going to need a *sous* chef he trusted. That wasn't an easy thing to find, but someone he already knew? Someone he'd gone to school with? That was a very good start.

The first sign of a problem came when the new hire walked in, and instead of looking pleased, Kian frowned.

"Mark?" he questioned. "What are you doing here?"

Bastian did not frequently rethink his decisions, but he couldn't help but feel, looking at Kian's displeased expression, that maybe he should have included Kian on the hiring process to find Kian's *sous* chef. Which felt appallingly obvious, once Bastian thought it.

Merde.

"I've been hired here," Mark said smoothly, looking over at Bastian. "I'm your new *sous.*"

Kian's eyebrows slammed together and the gaze he directed Bastian's direction was decidedly frosty. "I see," was all he said. "Welcome to Terroir."

Between getting Mark's orientation done, and getting him up to speed prior to service, there was no time for Bastian to pull Kian aside to try to explain.

The additional time was also helpful, because after watching him during the service, Bastian felt like Mark could actually be a decent addition to the team. He wasn't quite quick enough yet, but he was careful, and had clearly learned some good habits at Michael Mina. Maybe Kian would come around once he saw Mark's possibilities.

No, Bastian reminded himself resolutely, *he would come around*. Because Bastian had no intention of getting rid of Mark just because of a small personality conflict. He'd endured Xander's sneers for years, and even that godawful ridiculous nickname, and he'd done it because Xander was a fantastic chef, and he'd wanted him in his kitchen.

It was too suspicious to be continually taking the same car to and from the restaurant, so Kian and he had driven separately this time. *This is good*, Bastian thought as he drove home after service, *an extra ten minutes to get my head on straight.*

Bastian knew Kian had every intention of cornering him to discuss Mark. He'd been terse and brief all service, and he'd barely looked in Bastian's direction. None of those little quick glances that felt like a caress—something to connect them when they couldn't touch.

He pulled into the driveway, saw that Kian's little hatchback was already parked, and braced himself for the forthcoming and unavoidable argument.

It had been almost a week since Kian had shown up, determined not to be turned down, and it had been one of the best weeks of Bastian's life. Still, in the back of his mind, he'd been bracing for the moment when something happened to mar all that uninterrupted perfection. He'd known it was inevitable because they were both two very opinionated, driven individuals and Kian's new promotion, while not giving him equal footing with Bastian, gave him a decided step up from where he'd been before. From the way Kian had taken over in the kitchen, he knew it too, and no doubt he had every intention of exercising that newfound power now.

"What the hell, Bastian," Kian spit out from almost the second Bastian opened the car door and stepped out. He'd given Kian the keycode to the house a few days ago, but he'd chosen not to use it tonight, and instead had lain in wait for Bastian outside.

"I take it you don't approve of Mark as a choice of *sous*," Bastian said, and hated how tired he sounded. He knew everyone believed he enjoyed a fight, but he actually dreaded them. He dreaded their prelude, he dreaded the actual yelling, and he absolutely dreaded the aftermath.

He knew they would get through this, because Kian was a reasonable person who wanted the best for Terroir, just the same as Bastian did, but he was also unexpectedly stubborn, when allowed the freedom to be.

It was sexy as hell when they were flirting or during foreplay or even in the middle of sex. It was not sexy as hell now. Now, all it meant was a conversation that should have been easier, wasn't. Bastian knew he shouldn't, but he resented Kian for it.

"Of course I don't fucking approve," Kian spit out, words tumbling over themselves. "How could I possibly approve when you never asked me?"

"Is that the problem? That you were not consulted?" Bastian typed in the entry code to the front door himself and walked in. Kian shut the door behind him harder than he needed to. Forcing himself not to jump at the sudden bang that echoed through the house, Bastian set his keys and wallet on the counter and walked over to his wine rack. Picking out a nice pinot noir, he opened the bottle with careful, slow movements and poured himself a glass. Didn't pour one for Kian because he hadn't asked, and Bastian wasn't feeling particularly generous at the moment.

The whole time, Kian kept up a long monologue about why Bastian had fucked him over.

"There are a lot of problems with this. First, your fucking overbearing motives. You put me in charge of the kitchen, but then you keep interfering, you *hire new staff* without even asking, without even letting me interview them first. You always think you know what's best for everyone, like a chess master setting out his pieces, and it fucking pisses me off. And then, you had to hire *him*." Kian said the word like it was bitter and poisonous, and Bastian tuned back in. Maybe he would finally hear what the real issue behind Mark's hire was.

Other than that you did it without his permission and without even asking him, Bastian's guilty conscience proclaimed loudly and very clearly.

"What is your issue with Mark?" Bastian asked and was more than a little proud of how even his voice was. Some of what Kian had said stung, but it was also *true*, so he tried to let it go. "I know you went to school with him."

"He's a fucking suck-up, piece-of-shit, copycat asshole," Kian said bitterly. "Two years ago he wanted in my pants, probably to try to steal anything he could to get ahead of me. He would have, but he didn't even realize I was smarter than he was and could figure out what he wanted in a second flat. He's a snake, plain and simple, and I don't want him in my kitchen."

Bastian took a long sip of wine. "*My* kitchen," he corrected softly, firmly.

Kian flushed a bright shade of puce. He didn't say anything else.

"I'm sorry you don't like him," Bastian finally said. "I'm sorry you didn't get along before. I'm sorry he was shitty to you in school. I certainly hope that he thinks better of trying to get in your pants now—because he'll find that I do not like to share. But based on his performance tonight, I do think he could earn his place at Terroir. I want you to give him the chance to do that."

"Why?" Kian asked, and he sounded even angrier now than he had ranting about Mark.

"Because sometimes we don't personally like someone but they're good enough at what they do that we tolerate their shittiness as a person. And also because sometimes we're an idiot at eighteen, but we grow up," Bastian said. "He did good work. He has good references. Let's give him a chance."

Kian frowned. "He was just on good behavior tonight because you were there."

"And tomorrow, and during subsequent evenings, *you* will be there. As *chef de cuisine,* you are my representative. It's up to you to make sure he stays in line. If he doesn't, then you know what to do with him."

Kian's face grew harder around the edges than Bastian had ever seen it before. "Yes," he said shortly, "I take out the trash."

"Eventually, yes. *If* he proves that he can't handle Terroir." He tipped the wine in Kian's direction. "Would you like some?"

"I really want to hate you right now," Kian grumbled, and instead of answering, Bastian pulled out another glass and poured, generously. Kian had earned this wine today, though Bastian wasn't going to be the one to tell him that.

"But you don't," Bastian said, smiling.

Kian smiled, thawing a little. "I really don't, even when I do. How does that work?"

"God, I wish I knew," Bastian said, and reached for him. "I am sorry that I didn't consult you ahead of time. But I can't say that if I had, and you'd told me all that, I wouldn't have hired him anyway."

"Because he had good references and did well tonight?" Kian slipped out of his grasp, eyeing Bastian coolly over his glass of wine.

"Yes," Bastian said honestly. If he couldn't be honest, this relationship would never get off the ground. Just because they loved each other didn't mean that they could truly accept each other, and if Kian couldn't accept that he'd do anything for Terroir to succeed, then this wasn't going to work.

"So, that thing you said when you gave me this job," Kian said steadily, "you meant that."

"Did you want me to give you a free pass on Mark, and get to do whatever you wanted with him just because we're sleeping together?" Bastian questioned. "Because I had the impression that you wanted to keep Terroir at Terroir and sex at home."

"I do." Kian looked very unsure all of a sudden. "I was going to say, I wanted you to trust me, but then I realized that trust has to go both ways, doesn't it? You want me to trust you, here."

"While I'm trusting *you* with Terroir, which is the most precious thing in the world to me." *Almost the most precious,* Bastian mentally corrected. He still hadn't returned Kian's three little words from the emergency room, but then Kian had yet to say them while not on drugs. They were still figuring all of this out. It was too soon to tell Kian that he'd become just about as important to him as the restaurant and the career he'd built from scratch with blood and lots and lots of sweat.

"Oh," Kian said, and his eyes lit up, like he suddenly understood. "*Oh.*"

This time Kian was the one who moved closer to Bastian, reaching up and putting a hand on his neck, his shoulders. "Sweetheart, we're figuring this out. I don't know how the fuck to do this," Bastian confessed quietly. "I don't know how to love you and love my restaurant."

Well, maybe he *was* doing this right now.

Kian's mouth formed a small *o* of surprise. "You love me?"

"Did you ever doubt that I did?" Bastian stroked up and down Kian's arms, bare as he was wearing just a t-shirt he'd thrown on after service.

"Noooooo, not exactly," Kian hesitated. "Maybe a little bit. Tonight."

Bastian had felt the doubt, the coldness radiating from him, and maybe that was why he'd finally let those words slip out. His subconscious had known better than he did just how thin the ice they were walking on was.

"I wanted to make the words more special," Bastian confessed. "I always want to do right by you. Even when you think I'm fucking up, I'm still trying to do right by you. I didn't think there was anyone at Terroir who deserved to be your *sous* and I went looking for one. For you. Only for you. All for you."

Kian's lip trembled. "You love me that much?"

"More," Bastian chuckled, leaning down to brush a kiss on his lips. "So much more. If I loved you less, I could have resisted you. If I had loved you less, I wouldn't have ever hired you to begin with. Less is not really a problem here, trust me."

Kian melted into the kiss, and for a second, Bastian let himself be consumed by the fire that blazed between them. He was still shocked by how hot they always burned, and how quickly it always seemed to burn out of control.

But it was Kian who broke away, panting. "I do trust you. I do." He hesitated, and Bastian's heart became a manic thing, pumping away wildly as he watched Kian wet his bottom lip. "I meant what I said, when I told you in the hospital. I love you too. I've loved you for a long time."

Bastian's heart was still thumping hard as he pulled Kian flush against him. Somehow, he was still too far away, still not as close as Bastian needed him to be. "*Mon cher*, I've loved you for far too long," he murmured against Kian's lips, "I need a shower. Join me and let me show you how long."

CHAPTER ELEVEN

It wasn't that Kian didn't theoretically agree with Bastian's suggestion that he give Mark a try at *sous*. He'd made good points, and Kian was not only willing to approach his new position in charge of the kitchen at Terroir with logic, he *wanted* to.

Bastian finally telling him he loved him too certainly didn't hurt either.

When Kian walked into the Terroir kitchen the next day, flipping on lights as he went, he was determined to fulfill Bastian's belief in his potential. It started like so many days at Terroir, with Kian receiving shipments, logging them in, and making sure that the huge walk-in fridges were ruthlessly organized and that any item that was even slightly questionable had been disposed of.

Mark came in on time, which was really ten minutes early, and that filled Kian with additional optimism. He'd been notorious for barely ever making it to class on time, and Kian had hoped that Michael Mina had broken that particular bad habit.

"Johnson," Kian acknowledged his arrival as he walked in from the locker room. "Do you want to go over prep assignments?"

Mark nodded, but his face contorted into a frustrated little grimace. Kian told himself that this was normal, prep was hell, and frankly they had a very green kitchen assistant who also happened to be a drama queen. Mark would have picked that up right away, and also probably knew Kian was going to ask him to watch Derek closely—just as Bastian had asked Kian to do. It was exactly the kind of expression Xander might have made, but of course, he wouldn't have ever done it to Bastian's face, he would have waited until he was gone first.

Mark, Kian acknowledged, was still a little stupid, but a little stupid was better than a lot stupid. He could work with that.

"Derek, you need to watch him. I want to see a perfect dice. I know he's capable of it, he just gets lazy and sloppy, and that isn't how we do things here," Kian said as they hauled out crates of vegetables out of the walk-in.

"I'm surprised Aquino permitted it," Mark said. Kian told himself firmly to ignore the little twisty jab in his words.

"*Chef* Aquino," Kian said, emphasizing his title, "isn't the villain he's painted to be. He's tough, he has exacting standards, but he's willing to work with people to meet them. But Derek knows he's on borrowed time, so if he gets sloppy, you let me know and I'll deal with it."

Glancing at Kian up and then down again, Mark chuckled under his breath. And yes, Kian was a decidedly less intimidating figure than Bastian was, but that didn't matter. Kian had learned from the best. He could eviscerate anyone without lifting a finger.

"All of this?" Mark asked as Kian hauled the last of the eggplants out. "That's a lot of work."

"Terroir is a larger restaurant than Michael Mina," Kian said shortly. "You'd better get on it."

All in all, not the greatest start to their working career together, Kian considered as he grabbed his own veggies to start the daily soup special, but it also hadn't been the worst. Mark was suspicious and a little intractable, but Kian still believed he could win his respect. He had always been a good chef, but from Bastian's mentorship, he could run this restaurant exactly as it needed to be run.

He didn't intend to have quite as firm of a hand as Bastian had—he believed that he could get results without any of the yelling or the worst of the insults. But the way Kian got there mattered far less than the end result. He knew that was all Bastian cared about.

As Kian's knife flew through the carrots he was prepping for the soup, it was a habit to watch out of the corner of his eye for Bastian—forgetting that Bastian was meeting with Nathan Hess today, and wouldn't be in until much later. If at all, Bastian had added absently.

Kian wasn't dumb enough to take his tone at face value. This was, undeniably, a test. A test Kian intended to ace. Even without Mark, Kian knew he was still at a disadvantage. Bastian might have promoted him, but a part of Kian knew he wasn't really ready, and that meant he needed to work twice as hard to prove himself.

He took an hour and took his time on the soup, believing that the prep was underway by Mark. Kian had a feeling he wouldn't appreciate being checked on every ten minutes anyway. None of the work he was doing was particularly difficult, except maybe dealing with Derek, and Kian had left a detailed list of what needed done.

He also had a pretty solid idea of how long it should take to complete the list he'd compiled, so he was surprised—and not in a good way—when he detoured through the prep station to find that after an hour, Mark and Derek had barely made a dent in the crates of vegetables spread out over the counter. If he looked at the list, he would guess they'd barely completed a quarter of the prep, when they should really be more than halfway done.

And even worse, instead of working with purpose and speed, they were taking their sweet-ass time and gossiping like two old ladies.

"He came in with this whole *chain* of bruises down his neck. And I know there's no boyfriend," Derek said, completely fulfilling Kian's worst impression of him. "So who gave them to him? I'd like to know."

"You don't think it was Aquino, do you?" Mark said, and there was that sly tone that Kian remembered so well from their culinary academy days.

"Excuse me," Kian said in the firmest Bastian impression he could manage.

Mark didn't look the tiniest bit embarrassed at being caught gossiping about Kian *or* the illustrious head chef of Terroir. Derek, however, did Kian the favor of at least blushing at his sudden appearance.

"Why is this not all done, already?" Kian asked. "You should be a lot further along by now. We have a lot to do. There're stocks to get ready. Sauces to start. And you guys are still fucking prepping."

"Derek here was just giving me the big scoop," Mark said, and glanced right at Kian's neck. Thankfully in the last week, the bruises Bastian had kissed into his skin had already faded considerably. This morning he'd looked in the mirror and been a little disappointed to see them slowly disappear, but now he was undeniably glad. Mark *could not* find out that Bastian had been the one to leave them. Kian wasn't sure what he'd do with the knowledge, but it wouldn't be good; Kian knew that much.

"Derek's *job*," Kian emphasized, "is to help you with the prep work of the day, not gossip." He didn't reiterate what Mark's job was because Mark fucking knew what his job was. He was just pushing Kian, seeing what he could get away with, and he had to know, Kian *needed* him to believe, that Kian was going to push back.

But the way to earn Mark's respect wasn't to call him out in front of Derek. It was to show Mark that Kian was in charge, and that he wasn't going to tolerate any bullshit on shift.

"Just to make sure that's very clear," Kian continued, "Derek, I'd like you to go help Jorge in the dish room. I'll finish assisting Mark with prep."

Of course, Kian had other things to do, but with his presence to stifle any further laziness, he knew they could finish blowing through the rest of the list.

"Yeah," Mark said indulgently, after Derek had already departed, "maybe you could slice my eggplants for me. On the Japanese mandolin, right?"

Kian gritted his teeth. So he'd heard that story too, had he?

"Correct, and I'd be happy to," was all Kian said. Maybe if he didn't engage Mark, then eventually he'd lose interest in pursuing whatever story he'd concocted in his head.

Of course, it just so happened to be a *true* story, but Mark couldn't ever figure that out.

Kian whipped through the eggplants, being careful and also not putting the gloves on, because he didn't want to give Mark any more reasons to believe the story he'd heard was the truth. His finger had long since healed, leaving only a thin, nearly invisible scar.

The rest of the chefs piled in for the service, and Kian directed them as necessary—but they'd all been at Terroir long enough that they knew exactly what to do, and how to do it. And Kian, to his own surprise, realized that he'd been telling them what to do a lot longer than his official promotion. Maybe, Kian thought as they sat down to family dinner, Bastian was right. Maybe he did in fact deserve this position. But no matter how many times he told himself that, he still felt over his head.

He wished he could've confided in Bastian and talked it through with him—wasn't that what you did with a partner?—but the thought of admitting any weakness to Bastian was terrifying. He was relentless and inexorable. Weakness was denied until it didn't exist. Mistakes happened once and only once. Kian had become very good at sticking to Bastian's personal rules, but he'd never been this far out of his depth before.

Kian put himself on the pass-through, adding garnish and inspecting each plate as they left the kitchen, and assigned Mark to one of the three sauté stations on the enormous stove. Sauté was easily the most grueling station, other than the grill, but Wyatt's replacement was so good that Kian wasn't going to tempt fate by testing Mark there.

As he started calling out orders for starters, Kian watched Mark at his station. He was just learning the recipes, so it was not surprising that his movements weren't as confident or as innate. Or as quick, Kian thought as the starters went out, and more entrée orders poured in.

It was still early, and they were by no means at capacity yet, though Michelle, the front of house manager, had dropped by during family meal to grab a bite and to tell Kian they were totally booked up tonight. Which meant that as busy as it seemed now, this was still quiet compared to how many orders they were going to have in an hour.

"Keeping up?" Kian asked, keeping his tone light as he swung by Mark at his sauté station.

"Yes, Chef," Mark said in a strained voice.

He was only just keeping up, but that was still keeping up, so Kian let it go. And then Mark sent some scallops up to the pass that were definitely not quite done.

Overdone scallops were a criminal offense in the Terroir kitchen, usually causing Bastian to throw the plate, or worse, a whole stack of plates. Under-done, that was just a rookie mistake, but Mark and Kian had been working in professional kitchens for exactly the same time. Just as Kian was too experienced to make a rookie mistake—Mark should have been as well.

Kian dumped the dish in the trash can and set the plate onto the stainless steel counter with a click that resonated through the kitchen, despite that there was the normal loud chatter that accompanied every service.

"Chef?" Michel, Wyatt's replacement on the grill, asked, the expression on his face hopeful that the offender wasn't him, while he clearly believed that it wasn't.

"Are we trying to poison our guests?" Kian asked, raising his voice just enough to cut through the normal kitchen noise. "Are we trying to make them ill? Five hundred bucks for a night of food poisoning doesn't sound like a very good tradeoff."

Everyone stilled, and Kian continued. "Those scallops were raw, Johnson. Make them again and make them *right* this time."

"I plated the wrong pan," Mark said mulishly, pushing another towards Kian.

But it had been a good minute and a half since Kian had first spied the nearly raw scallops. Ninety additional seconds for a pan of perfectly cooked scallops would mean that this batch was now *overcooked*. He glanced down at the plate, not taking it, just looking. And he could tell, without even touching a single fingertip to them, that they would be tough and nearly inedible.

"You plated the wrong one again, Johnson," Kian said. "These are overdone. Start over."

Bastian would have been throwing things by now, and Kian told himself he was proud that his voice was steady, but still calm. Relentless, because perfection was a difficult journey yet a possible one. They were here at Terroir to achieve perfection. It didn't even matter that Kian loved Bastian and never wanted to serve a plate that wasn't perfect in his restaurant; he would have striven for that no matter what his personal feelings were.

But he knew, the hard realization lodging in his gut, that he could not let him down. Not now. Especially now.

"But, Chef," Mark dared to argue, "I have . . ." and he signaled to the six other pans he had on the stove in various states of cooking.

Kian knew the glint in his eyes was dangerous, and for the first time Mark seemed at least partially chastened. "Are you telling me that you are unable to handle your station?"

"No, Chef," Mark finally said.

"Then get me another plate of fucking scallops. And tomorrow, we'll have a one-on-one lesson on how to cook them properly so this doesn't ever happen again."

It was a lot for a chef like Mark to swallow; he had his ego, like they all did. But he'd also fucked up and knew it, and so he turned back to the stove and began another pan of scallops.

Michelle, watching the entire exchange, gave him a smile, just reassuring enough, but not patronizing. She'd worked for Bastian too long to ever do that.

Two minutes later he handed her the plate, after checking it carefully himself. The scallops were cooked perfectly. Kian couldn't have done any better himself.

And that, Kian told himself later, as the kitchen was being scrubbed down, and he was sitting in Bastian's office, feeling like half-an-imposter in the big leather chair behind the desk, was why he couldn't just give up on Mark. He *knew* better. He had potential. He had all the tools needed to succeed. Bastian was right. He just needed . . . fine tuning. Kian wasn't sure he was the right person for the job, but he'd made it through tonight, hadn't he?

He also hadn't yelled once, and that, too, felt like an accomplishment.

Mark poked his head in the open doorway. "Chef," he said, and the challenging note in his voice was not entirely gone, but it was diminished. Enough that Kian couldn't help but still feel optimistic about this working out.

"Is it done?" Kian asked.

Nodding, Mark didn't move. Kian waited for him to speak, because clearly something was on his mind.

"Michael Mina was a lot smaller," Mark said, repeating his excuse from the morning.

"And Terroir is not," Kian responded back smoothly. "You need to up your game. I expect your best effort tomorrow."

"Derek was right," Mark mumbled, as he turned, "you've turned into a copy of that bastard."

Clearly he hadn't meant for Kian to hear him, but he also hadn't really gone out of his way to muffle his voice enough. Kian's temper spiked, because not only wasn't he a copy of Bastian, it was the sort of comment that only a few weeks ago would have been something he'd have taken as a compliment.

And now, with the sneer of Mark's voice still ripe in the air, he couldn't anymore, and that really, *really* pissed him off.

When he heard another set of footsteps outside the door, he didn't even look up. "I'll be there in a moment to lock up," Kian bit out sharply. He wasn't in the mood to talk to Mark anymore today—and he wasn't stupid enough to think he could actually tell Bastian about what had happened.

"I already locked up."

Kian glanced up in surprise because that wasn't Mark's voice at all.

"It's still weird for me to see you in that chair," Bastian said softly. "Sorry, I didn't mean to surprise you."

It was undeniable that he was in a bad mood, and Kian's gut reaction was to demand to know why he was here. Was he here to check up on him after his first shift as *chef de cuisine* without Bastian there as support?

"You didn't." Kian sighed, and sat back. "It was just a long day."

Bastian sat down on one of the opposite chairs, and he was right, it *was* weird to see him like this, their normal roles reversed. "Michelle texted me and said it was a good service."

It was impossible not to hope that Michelle, who'd witnessed the entire scallop incident, hadn't told him that part of it. But whether Bastian knew about it or not, he didn't say another word.

"I thought you could use a hot bath and a little food," Bastian said. "And maybe a drive home."

He was really tired but he raised a questioning eyebrow anyway. "Do you think leaving my car here is a good idea?"

"I really don't give a fuck, you're worn out. Let me drive you back." Bastian stood, like Kian's agreement was a given.

Of course Bastian didn't give a fuck if Kian's car was seen here overnight. It wouldn't be his reputation that would be compromised. He'd probably get high fives and the subtle admiration of everyone for finding a cute young guy to fuck. The gossip would assume that Kian had slept his way to the top, instead of the truth—that he'd worked his ass off.

If Bastian couldn't think that through, then Kian wasn't going to help him along.

Finally, he seemed to get it when Kian didn't move. "You're afraid people are going to talk."

"People are already talking. People have been talking for two years." Kian paused. "I don't want to give them any evidence that they're right." He didn't want to mention that Derek—already on his last chance at Terroir—had been gossiping or how intently Mark had been listening, but he would if Bastian pressed him.

"How about we park your car on the other side of the building? Where we get the deliveries?" Bastian suggested. "Michel is scheduled to receive the few we're getting tomorrow, and he'll keep his mouth shut."

Kian would have agreed with him only yesterday but after catching Derek today, it was hard to trust anyone. Before today, he'd believed he had Derek's full support and his respect because he'd personally saved Derek's overdramatic ass more than once.

"I'm just going to follow you back," Kian said, standing up. Today's service had driven home the fact that he was in a far more precarious position than he'd believed, and he didn't want Bastian trying to convince him otherwise.

"If you insist," Bastian said as he followed him towards the locker room. "But you have the morning off, tomorrow, yes?"

Kian grabbed his coat and his bag. "You know I do."

He flipped on the after-hours lights, and they exited the restaurant into the cool night air, the already-locked door closing behind them.

"I made brunch reservations for us tomorrow," Bastian said as Kian stopped at his car door.

"You did what?"

Bastian shrugged, but his shoulders looked tight, and maybe he needed the hot bath as much as Kian did, after a long day dealing with Nathan Hess. Not anyone's favorite person.

"You said sex at home, work at Terroir, but . . ." Bastian hesitated, and Kian couldn't remember him ever looking so uneasy, so unsure of himself. "But I don't want our options to be only limited to that."

Kian supposed there were places they could go where they wouldn't necessarily be recognized, but he very much doubted that Bastian had made brunch reservations at one of them. He would have called up one of his many friends, who'd offhandedly mention the incident to another friend, or even worse, they'd been seen by someone who knew them.

Bastian shoved his hands into the pockets of his jeans, looking frustrated. "This isn't just fucking to me. I don't want to be your dirty secret."

"And you think I do?" Kian questioned. "You think that's how I think about this? After two years of waiting, and wishing that we could do something about how we felt, you think I'm only here for *sex*?"

There was a part of Kian, vocal but somewhat drowned out by the overwhelming exhaustion he felt, that told him they needed to talk about this when he wasn't already in such a bad mood.

The problem was that the conversation had already started and from the way Bastian's expression had tightened, Kian knew he wasn't just going to leave it.

"Listen," Kian said before Bastian could say something else—probably something he'd regret later—"I'm worn out, I had a fucking long day. I'd like to take you up on the food and hot bath idea, but I don't want to fight about this. Not now."

Bastian surprised the hell out of him by laughing. "Are you trying to avoid a fight?"

"Aren't you?"

"Yes. No. I don't really fucking know. I just know I don't want this to be a secret. Not forever, anyway." Bastian looked confused, and *sounded* confused, which probably confused him even more.

Kian reached up and slid a hand around Bastian's neck, tugging him down closer. Bastian leaned in, like he'd only been waiting for the invitation. "Not forever," he agreed. "But you *just* promoted me to *chef de cuisine* at twenty-three fucking years old. Let's give it a little time."

Sighing, Bastian leaned in, resting his forehead against Kian's. "You're right. I'll change the reservation. We'll go someplace else."

"Thank you," Kian murmured. "I know it sucks, I know this isn't . . . normal."

Bastian's grip tightened on Kian's hips. "I don't give a fuck what's normal. I love you. I just want to do right by you. Always."

Kian reached up and kissed him then. It was just a quick little brush of his lips against Bastian's, but that still felt like risking it. The parking lot was empty, but anyone driving by right now would see all the evidence they needed. "Let's go home," he said, reaching for his door handle. "Someone pretty amazing promised me a hot bath and some food, and I'm starving."

Bastian's smile was warm and sweet. "For the food or for something else?"

Kian risked another quick peck, this time to Bastian's cheek. "Can't I be hungry for both?"

"Go," Bastian said, chuckling with amusement, "before I decide that this parking lot is private enough for what I have in mind."

⚜

Kian didn't know if Bastian had deliberately lured him to his house with only a promise of a bath, but once he'd suggested it, Kian wanted it. They'd spent more than a few late nights tucked up together in Bastian's oversized tub and it was already a favorite spot of his.

"Food first or bath?" Bastian called out as Kian let himself in the front door of his house.

"Food," Kian said, walking into the kitchen. They tended to get distracted in the bath and he had a feeling that an orgasm would be enough to finish him off completely for the evening.

"I figured," Bastian said. He was sautéing some ingredients in a pan, and there was already a pot of water bubbling on the stove. "Pasta?"

"Works for me." Kian slid onto one of the barstools. "This doesn't really get old, you know."

Bastian looked up, and the boyish smile on his face made Kian's heart contract. "Me cooking for you? Why wouldn't I? You're the one who worked hard in the kitchen today. I only had the longest fucking meeting in the history of meetings."

"That bad, huh?" Kian asked.

"I knew Nathan Hess was difficult," Bastian admitted. "But he makes me look like a fucking saint, and that's a problem."

"What was the meeting about today?"

"We were supposed to be finalizing the contract, but instead he threw me and my lawyer for a loop. Demanded a percentage of profits as well as a monthly rent. Seemed to think I was doing him a favor, instead of the other way around."

"You know Xander's boyfriend is his son, right?" Kian said.

"I am well aware." Bastian's voice was testy as he added a pint of cherry tomatoes to the pan. "I am not going to ask *Xander* to intercede on my behalf."

Kian stole a tomato from the pan, quicker than Bastian could bat his fingers away with his metal tongs. "I didn't think he should," he said. "I'm just saying that maybe it would be easier to do this without Hess. Xander says he made Damon's life a living hell. Do you really want to make that your problem too?"

Whatever Bastian answered, it was clear how he felt from the expression on his face. He grunted noncommittally as he used his tongs to check the pasta.

"Get the plates," was all he actually said, which Kian thought made it rather obvious.

They were sitting side by side on the barstools, eating their late night pasta in silence, when Bastian brought it up again. "I'm hoping my lawyer can convince his lawyer that he's fucking insane," Bastian said but he didn't exactly sound confident. "If he thinks I'm paying a dime from my profits, he'd have to be."

"Why don't you just do this without him?" Kian asked. "You don't *need* him, not really."

"No," Bastian sighed, pushing the food around his plate. A bad sign all around, because like everything Bastian made, it was delicious. "But it would be easier. He already has the facility, the kitchen. It needs some updating, but that would only take a few weeks. Staff wouldn't be difficult. Menu wouldn't either. It's . . . a lot, honestly, building from the ground up. I was trying to avoid it. Maybe it's unavoidable."

There was a part of Kian—a part he'd been trying very hard to ignore these past weeks—that wanted to tell Bastian that this clearly wasn't the right time to do this, and that even if it meant a demotion, it was okay to give up the proposed partnership with Hess. It was the same voice that wouldn't stop whispering at him that he was ill-prepared and not experienced enough to run Terroir nearly by himself.

Kian ignored the voice. "Maybe it is," he said, trying to inject as much cheer into his voice as he could, despite his exhaustion.

"Let's take a bath," Bastian said. "It seems we both had trying days. I'd frankly like to forget mine as soon as possible."

That was the most direct reference Bastian had made to the scallop incident yet—nearly like he wished Kian would tell him, but despite that hunch, Kian had no intention of saying a word. Bastian had tasked him with running Terroir, had given him Mark, and despite Kian's concern, believed in him completely.

There was no way Kian was going to tell him that he was over his head and that Mark was a nightmare, possibly developing into something even worse. It just looked bad, he told himself as Bastian took care of the dishes and Kian walked to the bathroom, because he was so tired. Everything would be better in the morning.

He flipped on the hot water and plugged the drain, perching on the edge of the tub. He stripped off his t-shirt, toeing off his socks.

Bastian appeared in the doorway and pulled a small lighter out of his pocket, flicking it on and lighting the vanilla-scented candles scattered around the tub. They were new, Kian realized, and he hadn't even noticed, he was so god damned worn out.

"I told you," Bastian said quietly, placing his hands on Kian's bare shoulders, "I want to take care of you."

Kian had never been particularly interested in being taken care of before, but he was too tired to fight it.

He looked up, and nodded slowly. "Okay," he said.

"Then what are you waiting for?" Bastian asked, gesturing to the rapidly filling tub. "In you go."

"You're not joining me?" Kian frowned, slipping his jeans and then his underwear down over his hips, leaving them in a pile with the rest of his clothes.

"Sweetheart, you're dead on your feet. I've been there, so I know how you feel. Get in."

Kian did as he requested, sliding into the water, sighing at how perfect the temperature was—just a shade cooler than too hot to stand.

Reaching up, Bastian flipped the lights off, and then to Kian's surprise, Bastian turned back with a few little bottles and drizzled one in the water. The scent of chamomile and vanilla filled his nostrils and he sank back against the tub edge, his head tipping back. He could fall asleep right now, just like this.

"I'd say you work too hard, but . . . I'm still me," Bastian said, his voice a dark rumble.

"And I'm still me," Kian retorted with only a little heat, "and I wouldn't stop even if you asked me to."

"I don't want you to stop, I just want to make it a little easier when you do," Bastian murmured. He leaned against the tub deck, wetting a washcloth and reaching out for Kian's leg.

Never in a million years would Kian have imagined that Bastian would take such a subservient role, or would bend that everlastingly proud back to wash him, but he was doing it now, hands careful and firm on his skin.

It was inevitable, because Kian would have to be dead to not be aroused by the feeling of Bastian's hands on him. Lazy arousal unwound through him, the scent of the steam surrounding them lulling him to a dreamy state where even his cock thickening under the water wasn't something to be worried about.

He felt his blood quicken when finally Bastian closed his fingers around it, giving it a gentle but purposeful stroke. "Is this okay?" Bastian murmured, the dim light of the candles shadowing the stunning angles of his face.

Kian found he couldn't even reply, could only nod as Bastian continued to stroke his cock, fingers wringing the pleasure from him with a measured, even touch. His orgasm took him by surprise, but Bastian must have realized it was coming, because he was ready with the wet washcloth, and as the aftershocks faded, Kian slumped back against the lip of the tub.

"Feel any better? Bastian asked.

He was in a warm, cozy tunnel, so far away, so out of it, that he thought he'd answered, but maybe he didn't at all. Maybe he fell asleep in the tub, and maybe Bastian lifted him out, as gentle as he'd ever been with anything in his whole life, dried him off, and took him to bed.

Maybe, because in the morning, Kian still wasn't sure how he got underneath Bastian's soft, silky sheets.

Chapter Twelve

"When I said that we needed to go somewhere for brunch where we wouldn't be recognized, I wasn't anticipating *this*," Kian hissed under his breath as they settled into the booth, the vinyl squeaking underneath them.

"You told me it was important to you that nobody would see us together," Bastian said. "I can guarantee that this is the last place anyone would expect me to go for brunch."

Kian still looked disbelieving. "Okay," Bastian continued, drumming his fingers on the table, "I can be a little bit of a snob."

"A little?"

Bastian rolled his eyes. "I am not going to apologize for my high standards." He looked around, taking in the cheap fixtures, the tired, haggard waitresses, and the wailing baby three tables over. "But what's important to you is important to me."

"I just keep expecting you to run out of here, screaming," Kian teased. He reached over the table and grasped Bastian's hand in his own smaller one, his thumb rubbing one of his burn scars.

"We haven't even ordered yet," Bastian said, and figured this was as good a time as any to examine the laminated menu card the waitress had set in front of him only a few moments before. It was still damp from being wiped down—from what, Bastian wasn't sure he wanted to know.

"Unlike you, I've been here before. Many times," Kian said, not even bothering to glance at his own menu. "You don't seem surprised by this."

"You were in school. You were on an intern salary for the first six months. This place is cheap and open twenty-four hours. I might be a snob, but I'm not an idiot," Bastian said. He paused. "Fruit Loop pancakes? Cinnamon roll pancakes?"

Kian laughed. "Those will definitely be too sweet for you."

"How do you know I don't have a secret sweet tooth?" Bastian said, pouting a little. Maybe he had been interested in the cinnamon roll pancakes, if only because he was curious what they'd be like.

"You don't have a secret anything, not from me," Kian said, "though I admit that you're sweeter than I thought you'd be."

"What, you believed I'd be throwing plates at home? Yelling at the TV?"

Kian looked thoughtful as he stirred some of that awful fake creamer into his coffee. "Actually no. I just think you have a soft side that most people don't get to see."

It was hard, but Bastian ordered himself not to blush. He knew what this was really about—the bath he'd given Kian last night. At the time it had felt right, to take care of him like that, but he also had no intentions of discussing it.

"I think it's nice," Kian continued and Bastian gave him full bravery points for actually taking a sip of the sludge they called coffee here. "Don't get me wrong, I really like it."

"I'd be worried if you didn't." Bastian told himself not to get defensive, but it still lingered in the edges of his voice.

"Hey, hey," Kian said, reaching for his hand again. "I'm trying to say thank you, you surprised me, in a super nice way, and I'm doing a bad job of it."

"You'd had a really hard day, some of which was my fault. What was I supposed to do? Tell you to suck it up?"

Kian's smile was luminous. "You'd tell just about anyone else that."

"Exactly." Bastian sipped his ice water, and tried not to grimace at the metallic taste. "You're not like everyone else."

The waitress appeared at their table, breaking the moment. "Are you ready to order?" she asked.

"Yes," Kian answered, before Bastian could argue that he'd barely glanced at the menu. "We'll both have the grand slam breakfast. Scrambled eggs. Bacon, extra crispy. Hash browns, well done. Sourdough toast. Butter on the side."

Just when Bastian thought Kian was done surprising him, he'd go and do something like that. Anyone else ordering for him would have gotten a full-on Bastard glare, but Kian had said he'd been here lots of times—maybe he knew better. Bastian would give him the benefit of the doubt.

"And an order of the cinnamon roll pancakes," Bastian added smoothly.

When the waitress left, Kian shot him a look of disbelief. "They looked okay," Bastian defended.

"My advice at someplace like this is to keep it simple. It's hard for them to fuck up eggs and hash browns," Kian suggested. "But I guess you do have more of a sweet tooth than I thought."

"I usually indulge it with really good dark chocolate truffles," Bastian admitted with a wry smile, "and I will torture you sexually for hours if you admit it to anyone, but they looked pretty good in the picture."

Kian raised his eyebrow. "It's probably all marketing and a really good food stylist," Bastian said.

"Seems legit." He did not seem convinced. "But I'm definitely interested in this sexual torture thing."

"It isn't as fun as it sounds." Bastian tried to keep his voice serious, but instead the tone came out all growly sex. It wasn't his fault; in a moment of self-sacrifice aided by a healthy helping of guilt, he'd gotten Kian off but hadn't had any release himself. And this morning, there hadn't been time because he'd promised Kian brunch before his shift started.

"Yeah, I don't buy that for a moment," Kian said. "So, let's get this straight. The famous Bastian Aquino has a secret soft side and a secret dessert kink. I like it."

Bastian shrugged. "If I can't tell you those things, then who else?" Maybe Kian really hadn't believed that he'd never told anyone but his mother that he loved them before. Because Kian seemed more surprised than he'd ever expected.

"Let me guess, Luc doesn't know about either of those," Kian said.

There was nothing Bastian regretted more than ever letting Kian know about the existence of his ex. If Luc could even be considered that, because of course he hadn't known about either.

Luc had gotten the hard-as-nails Bastian who, at that stage of his life, had wanted to believe that his softer underbelly didn't exist at all. His father had died only a year or so before, launching Bastian into a desperate, overly ambitious race to out-work even his own entirely absent father.

That hadn't been Luc's fault, but he'd never had access to any of the softness Bastian hid like it was shameful. The only person he'd ever been tempted to uncover it for was sitting in front of him.

"Luc got the Terroir version of me, and not much else," Bastian admitted. "So I guess I do owe him something of an apology, after all."

"Or not," Kian said with a grin. "He was enough of an ass when we met. Decent payback."

"I doubt he would feel that way."

"Frankly, I don't give a shit how he feels," Kian said.

It was this hard, nearly bloodthirsty attitude hiding beside the sweet, kind smiles that had ultimately convinced Bastian that Kian could handle Terroir, including a *sous* chef who didn't really like him.

"How did Mark do last night?" Bastian asked. Michelle had texted him some updates, but he'd really been hoping that Kian would tell him his own version of events. He'd anticipated not even needing to ask, but Kian had been very close-lipped about service the night before.

"He was fine," Kian said in a closed-off voice, making it clear he had no interest in discussing Mark.

It was totally fine that Kian wasn't telling him, Bastian told himself. He wanted to handle it on his own; and technically he wasn't obligated to tell Bastian anything, since he'd handled the incident with the scallops himself.

Maybe with a few less broken plates than Bastian himself would have, but that was also okay. Kian wasn't his carbon copy; he might not need to throw things to get his point across.

"Michael Mina is a lot smaller of a restaurant," Bastian offered, despite Kian's clear directive that he didn't want to talk about Mark.

"I know that," Kian said shortly and Bastian swore inwardly, because why the fuck hadn't he just left it alone? Because it wasn't in his nature to leave things alone, he thought shortly, it was in his nature to pry.

It was in his nature to control everything; even the man he loved.

"He'll adjust," Bastian said, aware of just how lame and unlike himself he sounded. When he'd headed the kitchen at Terroir, adjustment was instantaneous, or bad things happened.

He knew Kian didn't feel that way; Derek was evidence enough of that. Bastian had allowed Kian to coax him along because he hadn't felt like dealing with yet another new employee, but any other time, he would have been long gone, likely in a shower of pottery shards.

Kian looked startled. "I wasn't anticipating him doing anything else," he said.

"Right, right, of course," Bastian said, and searched for another topic they could discuss that didn't have anything to do with Terroir. But Terroir had been their primary discussion point for so long that Bastian floundered.

The waitress arriving with their plates saved him.

The food didn't look . . . terrible. Bastian was willing to admit at least that.

The bacon seemed adequately crispy when he tapped it with the tines of his fork, and even the eggs seemed moderately fluffy. The hash browns looked like a deep-fried slab of potato, which was not something Bastian usually found appealing. The toast was dry and too pale, but Kian slid over the caddy of packaged jams anyway.

The pancakes were sitting at the edge of the table, the white ropes of frosting in danger of sliding unceremoniously off the top of the brown speckled pile.

"I'm currently thinking everyone who works for me should get a raise so nobody has to suffer through this," Bastian said.

"Oh, stop being such a snob," Kian said fondly, and Bastian was so glad he'd moved past the subject of Mark that he scooped up a pile of eggs onto his fork and took a bite.

Ignoring the slick of fake margarine, they actually had a decent flavor—they were definitely real eggs and not egg substitute which Bastian had been secretly afraid of.

"See, it's not going to kill you," Kian said, gesturing with his bacon. "It's just breakfast."

"This isn't really breakfast; it's breakfast-adjacent," Bastian sniffed, but he was eating the rest of his eggs, and even took a bite of bacon, letting the sharp saltiness linger on his palate.

Then he watched with horror as Kian reached for the bottle of ketchup the waitress had deposited on their table and proceeded to coat his hash browns in a thick layer of red goop.

"I don't think I know you at all," Bastian said, eyeing his plate dubiously.

"It's just ketchup, it's not poison," Kian said with a little giggle.

"We're going to have to agree to disagree on that," Bastian said with a shudder.

But Kian's gaze was fond as he met Bastian's frown. "You really are the worst, sometimes."

"I'm here and I'm actually eating this food," Bastian protested. He took another bite of eggs and bacon, and eyed the pancakes out of the corner of his eye again. If he tried them, he was going to save them for last, because the unrelenting sugar was going to be overwhelming.

"Under duress," Kian pointed out, waving his fork. "You've even managed to insult ketchup."

"I'm not sure what else I was supposed to do with it."

Kian shoveled a big bite of deep-fried potato into his mouth and smiled as he chewed. "Eat it," he said, once he'd swallowed. "Try it. I thought you were an adventurous cook."

He'd already finished his eggs. He only had a bite or two left of the bacon. He supposed that if he was going to try the hash browns he should prepare them as directed. "Fine," he said, reaching for the ketchup bottle, squeezing a very tiny amount on the edge of the slab. "How is that?"

Kian shook his head. "You need to be diner trained," he said with a laugh.

Bastian shot the offending bottle a withering glare. Any human would have run before this, but the bottle wasn't smart enough to figure out that it had ended up on the Bastard's shit list.

"I was trained at Le Cordon Bleu in Paris," Bastian argued. "What else would you suggest?"

Kian rolled his eyes. "In a *diner*. When you order hash browns you always get them well done and you always smother them in ketchup. It's the only way."

"*Merde*," Bastian muttered and squeezed out some more of the slop onto his plate. It was a really fucking good thing that nobody he knew would ever be caught dead in a place like this.

"There you go," Kian said, sounding very satisfied. "Now eat up, darling."

"I think you're enjoying this," Bastian grumbled.

"Oh, I am."

"I thought you loved me," Bastian argued. "Why would you want to torture me?"

"This was *your* idea," Kian said with a laugh. "And I do love you, even more, if you'd believe it."

"I think you're laughing at me," Bastian said as he continued to poke with his fork at the hash browns.

"You're just so damn cute," Kian pointed out. "Just eat the damn things."

"I feel like a Michelin inspector is going to pop out of this faux woodwork and revoke my stars," Bastian said, but he scooped up a healthy bite and finally put it in his mouth.

Initially, he was tempted to actually spit out the food in his mouth. Overcooked potato, somehow raw yet burned around the edges, smothered in that fake margarine, so slick and oily, Bastian nearly choked. And over the top of all of that, the bland acidity of the ketchup. Then he chewed again, and swallowed. Took another bite. Chewed that one and swallowed again.

Kian was outright laughing now.

"Trash!" he echoed Bastian's voice. "This is trash!"

Bastian glared but kept eating. He ate the whole slab in record time and shoved the plate away. "I think you've ruined me."

Kian's glance felt like a caress on his cheek. "Then we're ruined together. Exactly as it should be, as far as I'm concerned."

"I suppose I should put aside my snobbery and try these too," Bastian finally said with a sigh, pointing at the pancakes.

Kian just nodded, looking on with unabashed interest. "I've been waiting. Maybe you could even give Chef René a few helpful tips." Chef René had been trained in Paris under the masters of French pastry and even considered Christina Tosi, of Milk Bar fame, an imposter.

"If I told Chef René, he'd probably fall over dead," Bastian said with a rumbling laugh. Despite the oddness of the cuisine, this was one of the best mornings he had in a very long time. Definitely the most fun, because fun hadn't really been something in his vocabulary until he'd met Kian.

"He does eat a lot of butter," Kian replied very seriously, his eyes twinkling.

Bastian cut into the stack of pancakes, making sure to get some of the melting frosting onto the wedge of pancake on his fork. He put it in his mouth and promptly spat it back out, the first thing he'd been unable to stomach since they'd arrived.

"Oh my god," Kian said, and he was laughing so hard, he nearly fell out of the booth. "Were they that bad?"

"Worse," Bastian said with disdain, wiping his mouth with his napkin. "I feel violated."

"Well, I think that's our cue to leave," Kian said with a little hiccup. "I'll go pay the check?"

Bastian grabbed for the receipt the waitress had left but Kian was too quick. "I invited you here," he insisted, which was maybe something he shouldn't be bragging about right now.

"And I think this is something I can pay for," Kian said with a quick roll of his eyes. "I'll meet you outside at the car."

Even days later, Kian couldn't believe that Bastian had really taken him at his word and brought them to the one brunch restaurant he was sure they wouldn't be recognized.

Bastian's expression of wonder, followed by the one of ultimate disgust, had already been filed away in Kian's vault of special memories. They were still figuring out how a relationship worked between them, and he wasn't naïve enough to believe that a relationship fraught with as many difficulties as their own, was guaranteed to survive forever.

But if it ended, he'd still have all those memories to warm him later. There would be good, mixed in with the heartbreak, and that was what Kian was determined to take from this.

"Chef, that's smelling a little . . . burned," Mark offered, his voice for once somewhat deferential.

"It's supposed to be," Kian said, jiggling the sauté pan with a practiced movement.

"What are you working on?" his *sous* asked. They were nearly done with prep for the day, and Kian had ducked out of his official responsibilities a tiny bit early to work on a recipe he'd been toying with in his mind. Something that echoed the hash browns he and Bastian both unexpectedly loved.

"Spin on *tortilla Española*, with a little bit of a *patatas bravas* twist," Kian said, referring to the Spanish potato dishes. "Might be a possibility for a new vegetarian entrée."

"Yeah, like Aquino would ever let you put a dish on the menu," Mark muttered under his breath.

Kian was afraid of the day he'd finally decide it was okay to say his bullshit to his face. For a second, he considered informing Mark that Kian was either directly or partly responsible for about half the Terroir menu, but ultimately he decided it wasn't worth it.

The bare facts were unappealing to him; to Mark it didn't matter if he was wrong, he'd already formed his opinions and it was going to take a lot more than a single sentence to change his mind.

"For a French-inspired restaurant, you guys do some weird shit," Mark said, louder this time, so clearly Kian was meant to respond to this comment.

"Adapt or die," Kian said succinctly, which was one of Bastian's favorite sayings. He slid a thin metal spatula under his potato cake and lifted it slightly, checking its crispness.

"You're literally becoming his clone," Mark huffed. "I'd never have imagined you'd end up here, parroting him instead of developing your own point of view."

Kian rolled his eyes. "What do you call this? You *just* said we were doing some weird shit. How do you know that isn't my point of view?"

"Good point." Mark leaned against the edge of the stove. Kian belligerently hoped his coat would catch on fire.

"I like to filter unexpected dishes through a French perspective," was all Kian said. *None of this is going to change his mind*, Kian reminded himself, but it was hard. He didn't enjoy being disliked—though in reality, who really did? Maybe Bastian. Except that even that long-held belief was slowly fading away in the face of his sweeter, softer side.

Maybe Bastian didn't enjoy being disliked after all. Maybe he just tolerated it because that was the cost of running a restaurant like Terroir.

"Maybe you just want to filter *yourself* through Aquino's perspective," Mark said, waggling his eyebrows in a grotesque re-enactment of what he thought might be going on between them.

Kian barely held back a shudder. "You are fucking crazy," he said succinctly. "Bastian isn't a *filter*."

He only realized his mistake that would probably be his undoing when an unholy light lit up Mark's face.

"Oh, it's *Bastian* now, is it?" Mark said, his eyebrows working double time now. Kian glared. He hoped he'd get an eyebrow cramp—if that was even a thing, and Kian believed it *should* be.

One of the reasons why Kian had hated Mark so much at culinary academy was the way he could scent the blood in the water, and when he did, he'd pounce harder and faster. It wasn't like Kian hadn't learned to be tough during his two-plus-year stint at Terroir, but Mark was a different animal.

He had all the pieces. He probably wasn't going to put them together quite right, but in the end, that wasn't going to matter. The right way—*we've been in love with each other forever*—wasn't nearly as interesting as the story Mark would no doubt concoct.

"You're just jealous that we're friendly," Kian tried to deflect, but it was a bad excuse.

"Yeah, *real* friendly," Mark said, his sly insinuation unexpectedly painful. "I wondered how you managed to convince Aquino to make you *chef de cuisine* at twenty-fucking-three. Now I know. You did it on your knees."

"I did it on my two feet, *Chef*," Kian retorted tightly. "And this conversation is over."

It had only been a five-minute conversation, but it had eroded away any headway Kian had been making to establish himself from a position that Mark might, in some faraway, possible future, respect.

He'd wanted to believe that Kian was under-qualified and out of his depth, but before he'd only had gossip. Now he had ammunition to back it all up.

Dinner service was a tense disaster.

Kian gave himself a pep talk prior with a reminder that he didn't want to be the irrational asshole Bastian could be sometimes. He didn't want to yell or throw things or generally be a dick. The problem with that strategy was it assumed you already had your underlings' respect, and while Kian might have had *most* of the kitchen behind him, he didn't have it all.

He threw his first plate at 7:31 PM and instantly felt sick with guilt. Mark had deliberately goaded him into it by mishearing on purpose the orders and the instructions Kian was shouting out over the regular kitchen noise.

"I thought you said four scallops," Mark said, his tone genuinely apologetic, but Kian knew better. Mark didn't have bad hearing and he definitely wasn't stupid; he was trying to push Kian past his breaking point.

Unfortunately, he was succeeding.

"I said *five* scallops," Kian ground out, his voice rising despite every effort to prevent it. "Are you fucking deaf tonight?"

"Not at all, Chef," Mark said.

"Then get another fucking pan going," Kian yelled. "And apologize to everyone else because they have to figure out how to fucking hold the rest of the dish. Times *four*."

And when a minute later, Kian asked for the scallops, Mark shot him a bewildered look. "You already have the four up there. What do you mean?"

The tense air in the kitchen shattered when Kian swept the bare plate, no scallops to be found, off the counter and to the floor, where it exploded in a thousand tiny white shards of porcelain.

He'd always believed that it must have made Bastian feel better—after all, if it didn't, if you only felt *worse* afterwards, why the fuck would you continue to do it?

Kian couldn't answer that question, because he definitely didn't feel any better. Somehow he felt even fucking worse, and like he was slowly beginning to lose his grip on his self-control. He'd broken a plate today; what was next? Mark's nose?

When service finally ended, he hid out in Bastian's office again, burying his pounding head between his hands, and wondering how the hell everything could have devolved so quickly. The kitchen was a tense, fraying mess, and everyone was clearly affected. There'd been other issues tonight, at other stations—stations that Kian would have depended on a hundred percent before tonight—and at the head of everything, he felt like the very worst offender.

He couldn't tell Bastian how quickly everything had fallen apart. Bastian had trusted him with his restaurant and believed in him completely. How could he go to him, the man he loved and the man he respected more than any other, and confess that he'd fucked it all up?

He couldn't. He knew he couldn't.

Michel had been the one to approach him, not Mark, even when that was clearly outlined as Mark's job. "Kitchen's cleaned, boss," Michel said, voice gentle and quiet as he stood in the doorway.

It was the first time Michel had ever used that particular nickname, he'd always used the respectful and traditional "Chef" title with Kian, like he appreciated how difficult it was for Kian to fill the shoes Bastian had passed down.

Kian told himself it didn't mean anything, Michel still respected him, but the thought felt empty. *He* felt empty.

He'd thought being the boss would feel more like it had before, when he'd been doing a lot of the same things, but with Bastian's tacit permission. But it didn't, and now it was hard not to face the fact that a lot of the kitchen staff weren't as completely behind him as he'd thought.

Probably they'd thought the same thing Kian did—that he wasn't really qualified for this job, and maybe even knowing what they did about the close working relationship between him and Bastian, they'd made the exact same assumption Mark had.

"Thanks," was all he said shortly.

He knew Bastian would be waiting for him at his home, for their *food followed by sex* evening tradition, but Kian wasn't sure he could even face him tonight.

It was a cop-out, and Bastian would know that, but he texted him anyway, begging off. **Hard day today and I'm tired. Going home and passing out.**

To his surprise, when he drove home, Xander's car was in the driveway, and he was actually sitting on their beat-up couch in the living room when he walked in.

"You look like shit," Xander said. "Is that why you're not at Bastian's?"

Kian collapsed onto the couch and bit his lip as hard as he dared, praying the pain would keep the tears at bay.

He couldn't cry, and he definitely couldn't cry in front of Xander. His phone buzzed in his pocket and he ignored it. It was probably Bastian, and the very last person he wanted to talk to right now was him.

"You're home early," Kian said dully, eyes on the TV, even though he wasn't really watching it.

"Seriously, you don't have any clue when I get home," Xander pointed out. "You haven't been here in weeks. Not since you finally got into Bastian's pants."

Kian clamped his lips tighter together.

"Though, I know how hard being in a relationship is when you work crazy hours," Xander continued, like he didn't even realize Kian was right on the edge of breaking down. "You've got to make time while you can. But that doesn't explain why you're here, not there." He glanced over at Kian, and he realized his mistake. Xander knew.

"I threw a plate today," Kian said slowly. "Maybe Mark is right. Maybe I am becoming Bastian."

"I can't believe I'm saying this, but maybe the Bastard isn't all bad. He has a few redeemable qualities. Ones you have too. If you threw something today, it was because you were at the end of your rope. I know what that feels like." Xander paused. "Feel like talking about it?"

Did he want to talk about it? Kian wasn't really sure he did, but he thought he should.

"I feel like raiding Nate's good wine stash," Kian muttered.

Xander stood up and gestured towards the closet Nate, a sommelier and their fellow roommate, was always threatening to lock. "Pick your poison," he said.

Kian stood up too, and walked over to the closet, opening the door. He almost pulled out a pinot noir that he knew was really good, but the last time he'd drunk pinot had been with Bastian, and he didn't want to think about Bastian right now.

Instead he chose a cabernet and walked to the kitchen to grab the opener.

"So, what happened today?" Xander asked as Kian opened the bottle with a few quick, efficient movements.

They didn't really have wine glasses, so Kian pulled two mugs from the cabinet and poured a few healthy glugs of wine into each, handing one to Xander.

"Do you remember anything about a guy from culinary school who'd made my life a living hell?" Kian asked, figuring they were going to need to go back to the beginning.

"Yeah, Bart? Was that his name?"

Kian took a long gulp of wine. Nate was probably going to kill them for stealing this particular bottle, because the wine was full and rich on his tongue. "Mark, actually. Two weeks ago, Bastian hired him as my *sous*."

Xander looked stunned. "I'm sorry, I thought you just said *Bastian* hired your *sous*."

Kian shot him a wry look. "Don't worry, he's already apologized for that one."

"And he should still be apologizing," Xander said. "Jesus fucking Christ."

"Yeah, I'm not sure you're wrong." Kian looked down at the wine in his mug. "He's got control issues, which you know better than anyone."

"At first, I thought it would be gratifying and a little bit funny to watch Aquino's control issues go head-to-head with Damon's dad. Now I'm not so sure," Xander said, as he opened the patio door off the kitchen, and they stepped outside, settling down at the old, worn-out picnic table they'd dragged into their backyard one day.

"It's not gratifying or funny?" Kian asked.

"No, it's fucking insane and it makes me worry about you. What happens when this falls through, because we all know it will, and Bastian goes back to Terroir? You're demoted? Mark takes your job? I don't fucking know. I don't know how you're handling all this. I'd be a wreck."

"How do you know I'm not a wreck?" Kian asked quietly, staring out in the dark night.

"Are you?" Xander sounded startled.

"I don't know. Maybe. I should be able to handle Mark. I should. But he keeps getting under my skin, and I gave him some fucking good ammunition today."

Xander had always been the smartest guy Kian knew. He figured it out in under ten seconds. "Oh Jesus, he found out you and Bastian were sleeping together. You didn't tell him, did you?"

"Of course I didn't fucking tell him," Kian said bitterly. "I'm not an idiot. I told Bastian we needed to keep it quiet. I don't want anyone to know."

"Listen, everyone's favorite gossip subject has always been Bastian. That's not your fault. You slid into his orbit and *poof*, it happened. You got that job at a really young age. People are gonna talk about it."

"It's like Mark looks at me, and he *sees* me, the me inside that's quaking and afraid and fucking terrified. And he calls me on it. Constantly."

"Easy solution. Fire him and hire someone you actually like. Or promote Michel. I've always liked that guy."

"Bastian thinks he's too quiet. Too contained." Two things Bastian could never understand. "And I can't."

Xander scrubbed a hand over his stubble. "Fucking hell. He told you not to."

There was a part of Kian that didn't want to sell Bastian out to Xander. But Xander was his best friend, and Xander had always wanted the best for *him*. Not for Terroir, but for *him*. For all the talk of his soft side, Bastian hadn't done that, and Kian didn't believe he ever would. He needed to be okay with that, and aside from Mark, he *was*. But Mark was the wrinkle that was fucking everything up.

"If it helps," Kian muttered into his wine, "he made a few very good points."

"It doesn't." Xander sounded annoyed. "He's supposed to be creating an environment where you can succeed, not dragging you down by putting you in a bad spot."

"I don't think he sees it that way," Kian said with a heavy sigh.

"So what are you going to do?" Xander asked finally.

Kian tipped the rest of the liquid in his mug into his mouth. It helped, a little. "I don't know."

"I'm guessing you have no intention of telling him how tough Mark is making things."

"How can I? Xander, he told me he believes that I can do this. He trusts me, completely. How can I go to him and say, *I can't*? You know how Bastian would take that. It would ruin everything."

Kian couldn't actually bring himself to say it would not only ruin his future at Terroir, but their relationship. But he *knew* it would. Bastian might not exactly have him up on a pedestal but he *did*. He believed that Kian could do anything he set his mind to. He believed in his superiority over puny little insects like Mark. How could Kian say, *you were wrong* while preserving the things Bastian loved about him?

Plain and simple, he just couldn't.

"So you're going to go back tomorrow and just . . . keep throwing plates?" Xander asked skeptically. "And hope that eventually Mark gets sick of dodging them and quits?"

Kian couldn't tell him that he hadn't even thought that far ahead. "Yeah, sure," he said.

Xander laughed humorlessly. "You are so fucked. I . . . I wish there was something I could do. You know, right, that if you ever leave Terroir, you can always work for me?"

Truthfully, Kian had never even considered it. He'd never considered what would happen to make him leave Terroir—by choice or not.

"Yeah, of course. Thanks."

Xander stood up and put a reassuring hand on Kian's shoulder. "Just remember that, okay? I've got to go, Damon's picking me up."

Kian watched him go inside. He didn't move. Working for Xander wouldn't be that bad, he assumed. Xander would be a good boss. But he wasn't Bastian. Nobody was Bastian, except Bastian himself.

Chapter Thirteen

Kian would have told him if something was wrong.

Kian wouldn't lie to him by omission.

Kian still trusted him.

Bastian repeated these three things over and over as he paced through his kitchen. He wouldn't let himself look over at the dining room, where he'd actually set the table for their evening meal. Kian had really enjoyed the bath he'd had the other night, so Bastian had decided that putting out his nice dishes and buying a few additional candles wouldn't be too much.

But then Kian had texted and claimed to be too tired to come by. It was the first night he hadn't come over since their relationship had begun. Bastian's first instinct was to, of course, believe him. After all, he knew better than anyone how exhausting managing the reins of Terroir was, night after night—and he was used to doing it.

But after a few minutes, doubt had started to creep in. He'd texted Michelle, and asked her how the night had gone, something he'd really tried not to do. Everything he found out about Terroir, he wanted to find out from Kian.

The annoying niggling worry he was hiding something still bothered Bastian.

Michelle's reply hadn't reassured him. She'd been deliberately vague, giving no details, merely telling him everything was fine.

It immediately made Bastian believe that nothing was fine.

For five interminable minutes he resisted the urge to drive down to Terroir and make sure it was still standing.

He was lucky to have lasted five minutes, he told himself as he drove down the hill towards the restaurant. After he parked in his normal spot and got out of the car, he looked over the lot and it was quiet and empty, everything as it should be. He typed in his code at the door and walked inside.

He wasn't entirely sure what he'd been anticipating finding here. Stainless steel gleamed in the dim light of the emergency lights, and he ran a hand along one prep counter. It was weird, not knowing what had happened on it today, depending instead on little snippets of what other people told him. They weren't ever detailed enough for his comfort.

That, Bastian knew, was the main problem. He wanted to be here every night. He wanted to watch it all, his control freak side comforted by knowledge that nothing happened he wasn't aware of.

Taking over as *chef de cuisine* at the restaurant was a huge job—Bastian wasn't going to discount the enormous effort that Kian had put forth to reach that position and to maintain it. But sitting back and trying not to strangle Nathan Hess? Letting someone else, even someone else as beloved as Kian, step forward and run his restaurant? It felt impossible sometimes.

"Just because it's not easy doesn't mean it's not right," Bastian said out loud, the words echoing through the empty room.

But he'd been followed around by an unassailable belief that his chosen path was the right one for the last twenty years. Not once had he ever felt even a tiniest bit of uncertainty, and now he was plagued by it. Surely that meant something? But what it was, Bastian didn't know, and that was even worse.

Pulling his phone from his pocket, Bastian weighed it in his hand for a long moment. Finally, he dialed the number he'd selected.

His mother picked up on the fourth ring, just when he was afraid she'd gone to sleep already.

"Bastian," she exclaimed, "is everything alright?"

He didn't know what to say. Was everything alright? It sure didn't fucking feel like it.

"I just drove down to the restaurant in the middle of the night, to make sure it was still standing. And I resent Kian for knowing what happened tonight when I don't." Bastian figured this would answer the question much better than he could.

"You're there, at the restaurant now?" his mother asked.

"Yeah."

"Hang on for a few minutes," Celeste ordered. "I'm coming down there."

It was late, the roads were dark, and a little bit slick from the rain they'd had earlier in the Valley. He opened his mouth to tell her that she shouldn't, but she interrupted him.

"Bastian, I am still your mother," she said and hung up the phone.

Bastian went into his office, flipping on his computer but instead of doing any actual work, merely stared mindlessly at the screen, waiting for her to show up.

The knock on the back door came much sooner than he'd anticipated. Jumping up, he made his way to the door and opened it.

Celeste had a scarf tied around her head and made her leggings and wrap sweater look like high-end fashion, like she wasn't his mother at all but a retired model.

"Goodness," she said as he opened the door wider, "it is empty in here during off-hours."

Bastian frowned, and she placed a hand on his arm. "Let's go upstairs," she said. "I wouldn't turn down a nice nightcap, if you could find one."

They took one of the service elevators and he led Celeste to the bar, settling her in one of the high stools before ducking behind the bar.

"Any preference?" he asked.

"Something that will loosen your tongue," Celeste said primly.

"I called you, didn't I?" Bastian argued as he set out glasses, and pulled ingredients from one of the under-counter fridges.

"That means you know you *should* tell me what's bothering you, not that you actually will."

Deftly, Bastian peeled an orange, rubbing the edges of each glass with the oils. He dropped a piece of peel in, added a few dashes of bitters, and then poured in a measure of cognac into each glass. A brandied cherry completed each drink, and he placed one in front of Celeste, and the other at the place next to her.

"I'd be concerned your bartenders will be upset, as I'm sure they account for every orange, for every ounce of alcohol," Celeste offered as he sat down, "but it's difficult to imagine anyone being upset with you and actually daring to express it."

"You'll need to meet Kian," Bastian said ruefully. "As for the drinks, you're not wrong, but I'll leave them a note."

"The man you love," Celeste said. "Yes, I would very much like to meet him."

It was foolish but Bastian spluttered anyway. Of course he loved Kian, but he hadn't anticipated his mother calling him out on his feelings. Was he so obvious? Or maybe he was just obvious to her.

Celeste took a sip and hummed approvingly. "Very good," she said, "but then I would not expect any less. As for you being in love with Kian, of course you are. You gave him the most precious part of you."

He was quiet for a long moment. He took a drink, but the alcohol didn't help. "I see the best version of myself reflected in his eyes. But I don't *want* to be that version. I don't want it. I want to love him, but I don't want that." He was all too aware of how miserable he sounded. "I thought this deal with Hess would feel differently, like I was growing and changing and adapting. Learning how to let go. But I don't want to let go."

Her laugh startled him. "Oh, darling, you are your father's son."

It was impossible to hear that pronouncement and not tense from the very ends of his hair to the tips of his toes.

"He was an asshole, *vraiment*," Celeste continued, her words doing nothing to alleviate Bastian's edginess, "but some of the things that made me hate him, make me love you more. You're both stubborn to a fault, and feel intensely, both your likes and dislikes. You do nothing by half measures. That dedication is why we are sitting here now, at your beautiful restaurant."

"I know all that," Bastian said, though he hadn't quite come to terms with some of it. Anything remotely familiar to his father was abhorrent and to be rejected, always, no matter what his *maman* claimed.

"Of course you can't let go. The best version of yourself isn't a man who does, it's a man who *doesn't*."

That was a concept that had somehow never occurred to Bastian. "A man who *doesn't*?"

"You've convinced yourself that to be better, to be a partner worthy of your Kian, you need to let go." Celeste shook her head. "Your greatest asset is your ability to *never* let go. I would guess that is one of the reasons he loves you."

"I can't, I can't just come back here, and upset the structure," Bastian argued. "Kian would hate me for doing that. For dividing the loyalty he's trying to earn."

"Why would you being here divide his loyalty? Would he manage things differently than you? Give different direction?"

It wasn't difficult at all to shake his head. He'd trained Kian meticulously himself, and if Kian had ever given him a moment of concern about the direction of his management at Terroir, Bastian never would have promoted him in the first place. He trusted *Kian* implicitly, but he worried that the trust was not reciprocated.

"Then, why can you not be here during service?" Celeste asked simply. "You don't need to completely absent yourself. You've made yourself miserable, trying to deny something that is part of who you are."

"*Oui*, I am so stupid," Bastian murmured. Every inch of carpet, every ladle, every chair, every cocktail on the menu, bottle of wine in the cellar, onion in the storeroom—they were all an extension of who he was. He was nothing without Terroir and Terroir was nothing without him.

Celeste placed a hand on his arm. "You are a man. It is to be expected."

Bastian laughed, the tone rough with emotion. "You're too good to me."

"My lot in life," she said sweetly. "As is Kian's. He knows what you are, Bastian, better than anyone else. He worked for you for years. He knows what you are, what you need. He has never fought against that."

"Once," Bastian said ruefully. "Once, and he was right. Right while being wrong at the same time."

Celeste raised an eyebrow. "Do I wish to know what happened?"

This time Bastian's laugh felt less torn out of him, and more a product of genuine amusement. "No. No. Definitely not."

"You are a good son, and a good man. I hate to see you doubt that."

"I've done some . . . sometimes I'm not good. I can be cruel," Bastian admitted, finishing his drink in one gulp.

"Your chosen profession, that is cruel though, sometimes?"

"Sometimes," Bastian acknowledged. She wasn't wrong. The fine dining kitchen was a place of exacting standards, and sometimes a very thick skin was needed to deal with the cutthroat atmosphere and unrelenting perfectionism.

His own behavior wasn't always ideal, but Celeste did have a point. He knew he could be better, but she was right; his greatest advantage was that he never wanted to let go of anything.

It was why he hated it when employees left, even when there was a good reason for them to move on. It was why he'd refused to promote Kian, even when he deserved it. It was why staying home during service these last few weeks had nearly killed him—even though he'd been willing to try for Kian.

Clearly he'd been approaching this situation entirely the wrong way.

"Do you feel better?" Celeste asked.

Scrubbing a hand over his face, Bastian thought for a long minute. Truthfully, a little of the panic he'd been feeling had died the moment he'd walked into the kitchen. It wasn't all gone, but it had calmed considerably.

The only thing still bothering him was the text that Kian had sent him, and the niggling feeling that he was actually hiding something.

"Much," Bastian said. "Finish your drink and I'll drive you back home."

"But," Celeste tried to interrupt but Bastian shot her a hard, uncompromising look.

"Yes, you're my mother, but it's late, and I'm not letting you drive home without me. I'll send someone with your car tomorrow."

While he waited for his mother, he pulled out his phone and finally replied back to Kian's text. **I know you're tired, but I'd like to see you.**

Glancing back at the words, it was impossible to deny there wasn't an inherent demand in them, similar to how Bastian moved through life, expecting all barriers to melt away or be conquered. But he was reminded of his mother's words as they walked to his car.

He knows what you are, Bastian, better than anyone else.

After he dropped Celeste off at her home, giving her a quick kiss on her soft cheek, he checked his phone, and to his surprise, Kian had actually replied.

Out on the back deck was all he'd said, which Bastian assumed was an invitation of sorts.

The house was dark when he pulled up to it, and Bastian realized as he got out of the car that he'd barely ever been here. He was Kian's boyfriend and he'd made him come to him almost every time. Yes, he wanted to avoid Xander and their other roommate, who was apparently a sommelier, but even when he'd tried to make their relationship feel equal, inequalities kept cropping up.

Kian was sitting on the back porch, a mug in his hands. When Bastian approached, he didn't think he was being too paranoid to believe that Kian didn't look exactly thrilled to see him. Maybe he should have given Kian the space he'd clearly been wanting. But Bastian was so terrified that a night of space might lead to even more space, not less.

"I'm sorry," was the first thing he said when he sat down.

Kian looked surprised. "For what?"

Bastian drummed his fingers on the table. "For being myself?"

"I knew what I was getting into when I took my clothes off the first time," Kian laughed.

He leaned over, bumping shoulders with Kian, and glanced down into his mug. There were clearly dregs of wine in it. Bastian raised an eyebrow.

"It was a night," Kian finally confessed. "Nothing I can't handle. But a night nonetheless."

It was impossible not to wonder when Bastian's first instinct had shifted from tough-as-nails to apologetic. Because he'd nearly been about to apologize *again*, and that wasn't his fault. Not really. Well, he conceded, it might have been, because he'd been the one to hire Mark.

"Do you want to talk about it?" Bastian asked carefully. Not apologizing, necessarily, but trying to be supportive—the way a normal boyfriend might be. He wasn't ever going to be a normal boyfriend, but Kian was right. He'd known what he was getting into when he'd made his feelings clear.

"Honestly?" Kian asked wryly. "No, not really."

It was exactly what Bastian had feared. He tried not to react, but Kian knew him well, and could probably see how afraid he was.

"I already know you didn't burn the place down," he said, trying to make it lighthearted.

He must have failed because Kian looked startled. "You went to Terroir?"

"Not because of you. Because of me. I guess I was also having a bad night. Bad week, actually."

Kian frowned. "Do *you* want to talk about it?"

"It's not anything to do with you. I said you'd made me the happiest I'd ever been, and I meant it," Bastian said, reaching out and brushing a kiss across Kian's lips. "I love you. But letting go of the restaurant is hard for me. Impossible, actually."

"You make it sound like something really terrible," Kian said with amusement, "but I already knew that."

"That's why I went. I . . . missed it. I missed knowing everything that happened."

"I know I'd miss it so I can hardly blame you for missing it. You *created* it," Kian said simply.

"Would you be okay if I came by? Not to undermine your authority. Not to take away your decisions. To just . . . be there. Would that be okay?"

Kian laughed. "It's your god damned restaurant, Bastian."

"Yeah, but." Bastian took a deep breath. "I'm trying to keep things separate."

"You told me way back at the beginning this was going to be messy."

"I was right," Bastian said. "And I'd still do it, every time."

Kian stood up, a gleam in his eyes that always boded well for Bastian and offered a hand. "Do you want to go make things messier?"

Remembering his words from earlier, Bastian hesitated. "I thought you were tired."

"I think I'm getting a second wind," Kian said, grinning. "Come on, we've got an empty house. Let's use it."

Kian didn't know exactly what had driven him to his house tonight—but even though he couldn't identify what it was didn't mean that he couldn't understand it.

Even when he wasn't sure he could face Bastian, he'd still missed him, still craved his touch.

He reached out and took Bastian's hand, the rough scars from too many cuts and burns now so familiar to him. All it took was the feel of their palms sliding together, the nearly innocent gesture a reminder of the not-so-innocent nights they'd spent wrapped up in each other.

"You're sure there's nobody here?" Bastian asked as Kian pulled him through the sliding door.

"Xander and Nate both know we're together," Kian said, trying not to roll his eyes. Bastian wasn't all that concerned about keeping their relationship a secret, so Kian didn't get why he'd even care if they heard them. It wasn't like Kian hadn't had to lie awake some nights, listening to one or both of them have sex in their respective rooms.

"Yeah, I know," Bastian admitted. "You trust them, that's enough for me. But I wanted . . ." A look of uncertainty that Kian had never seen crossed Bastian's face. "I want you to fuck me."

Bastian had hinted once or twice that he shared Kian's versatile interest, but he'd never expressed a desire for Kian to fuck him before. It didn't surprise Kian that he wouldn't want anyone around if that was really what he wanted. Bastian would equate it with a loss of control, with the resulting vulnerability.

"Okay," Kian said, and squeezed Bastian's hand reassuringly. He knew better than anyone else how difficult typical and utterly normal relationship milestones were for him sometimes. He'd assumed they would come easier, once Bastian had insisted he take over Terroir, because Kian had always believed that the restaurant represented all of Bastian's control in one brick-and-mortar structure. But maybe that wasn't entirely true, because Kian had never seen the shadowy fear that he saw in Bastian's eyes tonight—or his clear need to relinquish control while he fought against it at the same time.

"I'm not good at this," Bastian murmured.

"At trusting someone else or being fucked?" Kian asked archly. "Because you keep saying that, and I keep not believing you."

Bastian cracked a tiny smile. "Are you going to lecture me again about sexual politics? Because I'm not going to lie, that was hot the last time you did it."

"Probably because I was half naked while I did," Kian said, and hated how all it took for his breath to catch was a few words. Bastian, for all his hang-ups and control issues and occasionally dickish behavior, was the key to every lock inside him.

"I can arrange that." He hesitated. "Where's your bedroom?"

It hit Kian then that this was only the second time Bastian had ever been in his house, and that they'd never even kissed inside it. Their entire relationship had played out in the starkly luxurious confines of Bastian's house. He'd never dried off after a shower with one of Kian's threadbare towels. He'd never seen his bare bones room, with its mattress that lay on the floor. He could have upgraded—he had some money saved—but it had never seemed important. He was barely ever home, and then he and Bastian had taken their relationship past mere pining, and then he'd never been home at all.

For all his vaunted internal boasting that their relationship was more equal than ever, it wasn't, was it?

"This way," Kian said, walking Bastian down the hall, opening the door to his bedroom. He wasn't worried it would be a mess; you'd have to live in a room for it to be a mess, but he'd barely even been in here the last few weeks.

"Save your breath," Kian said wryly, "there's no real compliment to be found, but that's okay."

Bastian raised an eyebrow. "It is?"

"This is just a place I sleep. And not even that, lately."

"But not tonight," Bastian said, reaching out and pulling Kian to him. "My house is a soulless box and I've never felt that as acutely as I did tonight."

Fuck it, Kian thought. "I don't care where we are, I just want to be with you," he admitted, and afraid of what Bastian might—or might not—say in return, kissed him.

They'd shared so many different kinds of kisses: undeniably passionate, sweet and tender, filthy and lustful. But none of them had ever felt like this one had, an echo of what Kian had just gone out on a limb to claim; kissing Bastian felt like coming home.

The kiss deepened and lengthened, drawing out like a golden thread that Kian didn't want to break. Maybe instead of fucking, they could just make out all night, their hands moving restlessly over each other, swallowing their mutual groans.

But Bastian had admitted to wanting something that he never had before, and Kian wouldn't be a very good lover if he selfishly ignored that. So he tugged Bastian closer to the bed, and finally pushed him down on it, climbing on top of him and fitting their mouths back together.

Even if he was trying to be generous, it was impossible not to take some plea- sure for himself, he thought as he rubbed his hardening cock against Bastian's thigh. It wasn't like he had a lot of experience to compare this to, but with Bastian, everything always felt like the first time, but *better*.

The novelty hadn't worn off, not in the least. If anything their desire for each other had only increased once they'd let it free of the restraints, and everything was *better* because they'd begun to learn each other.

Kian stripped off his t-shirt and wiggled out of his shorts without even climbing off Bastian. He hadn't realized he was so flexible, but it turned out that needing to be naked ASAP made all sorts of things possible that never had been before. Bastian lifted his head and pulled his own t-shirt off, leaving Kian rutting helplessly against Bastian's jean-clad crotch, with only his briefs as a barrier.

"Fuck," Bastian whined helplessly, "you feel so fucking good."

Kian already felt on the edge—the kissing and the touching felt goddamn perfect, it was impossible not to be—but to fulfill Bastian's request, he'd need to find some sort of self-control. And get on with it, because he knew his own wasn't nearly as ironclad as Bastian's.

Leaning over, he sorted through the crap in the drawer of his bedside table. Bastian's hands skated up his sides, fingers tickling the sensitive skin, and his mouth found a nipple, making Kian's concentration waver. He needed a condom and some lube, and he needed to stop trembling so he could find them and do this properly.

Bastian had always deserved his best, and that was never more true than this moment.

Finally, he managed to put his hands on what he needed, barely managing to shut the drawer, before Bastian had them flipped over, lips coasting down his chest and towards the straining cock in his briefs.

If Bastian put his mouth on him . . . it didn't matter how much Kian wanted to keep his composure, it would be completely gone. There was something insane, still, about seeing his cock between Bastian's lips, and the wicked way he used his tongue coupled with that mind-blowing sight always unwound him desperately fast.

He needed to stay focused. Kian reached down, his hand skimming over Bastian's skull, to the close-cropped dark hair, sprinkled with silver. The silver at his temples was still one of the sexiest things in the world to Kian. He squeezed his eyes shut—that was not something he needed to think about right now. Instead he inserted a reminder of how, the last time Nate had brought someone home, they'd sounded like a drunk rooster.

It helped, and he was able to regain focus, hands reaching down to tug on Bastian's shoulders. "Not now," he said even though there was definitely a part of him that wanted it—desperately.

It was too simplistic to say tonight was supposed to be about Bastian, because it felt like a lot of their nights had been about Bastian. But then, a lot of their nights had been about Kian too. They were a self-centered, mostly egotistical pair of chefs who believed they were more like gods than men. It wasn't a surprise that their sexual escapades often took on an indulgent, worshipful side.

Kian pushed Bastian onto his back, and quickly divested him of shoes, socks, and pants. His fingers trembled over his briefs, finally reaching up for the waistband to also pull them down.

"I want this," Bastian said, and though his voice was gruff and deep and he was in as much of a sexual thrall as Kian, he still wanted to reassure him.

That was the Bastian Kian knew and loved—the one that so many others had never been privileged enough to see. Once, Xander had told him that there must be more to the man, for Kian to be so wild about him, and Kian had merely said yes, that was true. Hadn't gone into detail and hadn't wanted to. What he experienced, what he saw that nobody else did, that was for him and his eyes alone. It might be selfish, but he wasn't going to share it.

"Then I'm going to give it to you," Kian said lowly, slicking up his fingers as Bastian spread his legs.

Bastian was tight and tense, and Kian took longer, certainly longer than Bastian would have liked, considering how he swore and begged, loosening him up. First just rubbing around the taint and his hole, not teasing exactly, but not giving him anything Bastian wanted either. Finally, he slid in a single finger, coaxing it in deeper, searching for the spot that would make Bastian swear even louder.

He'd promised Bastian they were alone, with the unspoken vow that nobody would hear him scream, and he had every intention of fulfilling it.

"Come on," Bastian begged in a high-pitched whine. "I'm not made of fucking glass."

He wasn't, but he was still precious, and Kian could tell that he hadn't done this in awhile. He wasn't going to rush him.

"Remember when you said you weren't sure you'd had good sex before," Kian said in a breathless rush.

"I hadn't." Bastian's eyes were dark and intense on his face. "I have now."

Kian slid in another finger next to the first, pushing them both up against his prostate. Bastian yelped, his entire body bowing in pleasure on the bed.

"It always will be, with me," Kian swore. "I wanna make it good for you, every time."

"You fucking blow my mind," Bastian said. "Every time." His voice shook, and Kian took advantage of his sudden relaxation to slide in a third finger, pumping them carefully but with purpose.

He'd wanted this for so long—figuratively and literally. He'd dreamt about being deep under Bastian's skin, so far in that Bastian didn't know he was even there, Kian was simply a part of who he was. An inseparable, impossibly necessary piece, and without him, Bastian would be like a clock without one of its gears.

With shaking hands, Kian opened the condom, and finally managed to slide it on, slicking himself up after. He took a deep breath, and felt, not for the first time this evening, that once they took this step, nothing would be the same after.

He was okay with that—much more than okay, if he was being honest with himself—but he needed Bastian to be, even though he'd been the one to ask for it.

"Please," Bastian finally said, as Kian smoothed a hand down his thigh. "*Please.*"

Kian pushed in slowly, steadily, inexorably. Bastian's cock jumped on his muscled stomach as Kian's cock slid home, Bastian's eyes never leaving Kian's.

He'd always known that being inside Bastian would be overwhelming, but it was so much more than he'd ever thought. Bottoming out finally, he thought joyfully, *I'm here now, I'm never leaving.*

"I wanted you like this. Forever." Bastian's voice was guttural and deep, wrecked with pleasure. He wrapped his hand around his cock, and Kian's hips stuttered as he clamped down around him.

Kian prayed he was close, because he didn't think he could last either. It was the most overwhelmingly intense experience he'd ever had in bed, and it didn't seem to end, just went on and on as he continued thrusting, pleasure sizzling through his nerve endings. He realized he was actually whimpering, as he desperately tried to hang on.

But Bastian seemed determined to wring his orgasm out of him, just the way he'd tried to wring every last ounce of determination out of him during their last two years at Terroir. He was stroking his own cock in earnest now, face contorted, and Kian dug his fingers into Bastian's hips, holding on for the ride.

Bastian tipped over the edge with an actual yell, splattering his chest with come, and Kian followed only a second later, as the contractions practically pulled the orgasm right out of him.

Kian slipped out and collapsed next to him, Bastian wrapping an arm around him, his expression sleepy and blissful.

"Thank you," he said.

Bastian rarely apologized—he'd already admitted to Kian that he was the only person he'd ever apologized to, barring his own mother—but an expression of gratitude? That was completely unheard of.

"You're welcome." Kian paused. "I do love you, you know."

Bastian's expression was relaxed as he rolled over, facing Kian. "I love you too. Even when I'm not good at this."

"I don't know if anybody is," Kian admitted.

"You seem to be." Bastian's tone was contemplative, like he hadn't figured out yet how that could be.

"I just hide it really well," Kian admitted. "Most of the time I have no idea what the fuck I'm doing. I just know I love you, and I start there. The rest? It is what it is."

"It is what it is," Bastian repeated, a wrinkle appearing in his dark brows, like he was trying to puzzle out what that really meant. But, Kian thought, it meant what he'd said it meant. You just had to figure it out, one step at a time, and he'd always hoped, they'd do that *together*.

Maybe that's what Bastian really coming over tonight was about, Kian thought as he finally sat up and went to the bathroom to grab them a damp towel to wipe down with. Maybe Bastian was finally figuring out that doing things together was better than struggling in vain alone.

He'd missed seeing him every night at Terroir, and even though the evenings after service were always wonderful, it was like losing an arm, the phantom feeling following you even though it was already gone.

Kian had been clear that he wanted a separation of their work and personal lives, but he hadn't ever said that he wanted Bastian to remove himself.

Maybe, he thought as he settled into Bastian's arms to finally go to sleep, Bastian had finally discovered he felt the same way.

CHAPTER FOURTEEN

MARK WAS DUMB, BUT he wasn't stupid. The next day during family dinner, Kian offhandedly mentioned to the staff that they might see Bastian a little more. "He's working on the menu for the new restaurant," Kian had said, even though Bastian hadn't been entirely clear about what he'd be doing. Still, the announcement bought Kian what he wanted, which was a reprieve from Mark on his bullshit.

He might push Kian when Bastian wasn't around, but the threat of him suddenly appearing made him take a step back.

A week passed, with Bastian dropping by nearly every day, usually during prep, almost always staying for family dinner. Most days he left when service began, though once or twice he'd actually retreated to his office, and when Kian walked by, it was obvious he was doing work on his computer.

The kitchen definitely ran better with more of Bastian's presence, which rankled Kian a little bit, even though he tried to tamp down the feelings of inadequacy. Bastian was a figure of monumental proportions, and he'd spent twenty years developing a fearsome reputation to augment it.

He had his Michelin stars, he had a temper, and he had an insane commitment to perfection that nobody, even Kian, could match. That, Kian kept telling himself, was *fine*. He was good. They were doing better than ever. Despite Bastian's clearly uncomfortable feelings about hanging around Xander, and to a lesser extent, Nate, he'd even made the effort to spend some time with Kian at his house.

Everything felt good, if not great, but Kian couldn't seem to shake the sensation of impending doom.

At first, he'd assumed it was because he felt guilty at hiding just how shitty Mark was from Bastian. Then, when Mark, no doubt terrified of Bastian and his inexorable retribution, had taken a step back from his normally shitty attitude, Kian justified that the problem had fixed itself and there was no need to confess that it had ever existed.

That wasn't entirely true, but it was true enough that Kian knew that couldn't be the issue that kept him up nights, long after Bastian had fallen asleep beside him.

Something was going to go wrong, and because of the pressure cooker nature of their jobs and their tempers, it was inevitably going to be a huge fucking mess.

Bastian continued to battle with Nathan Hess on every point of the contract they still hadn't signed. A week in, as Kian was preparing to leave for Terroir, Bastian leaned against the bathroom counter and said, "I'm not going to be in today. Hess and I have what should be the very last fucking meeting on this contract."

"Good," Kian said. The ongoing contract negotiations had obviously exhausted and annoyed Bastian, even though mostly he seemed to argue with his lawyer over conceding anything.

"Maybe if it actually goes well, we'll come to Terroir for dinner to celebrate."

Kian grinned. "Isn't it a little tactless to rub your perfection in the face of the man you've just defeated?"

"Is that what that is?" Bastian asked, but he was smiling too, the giddy, gleeful smile of a man who knew he had his opponent's number.

"Prevarication isn't your strong suit," Kian said seriously, reaching out and brushing some invisible lint off Bastian's shoulders. Today he was dressed not for the kitchen, but for business in a dark navy suit with crisp white shirt underneath, a few of the buttons popped open in deference to the more casual tone of Napa.

"No," Bastian admitted. "I see what I want and I take it."

For a second, Kian considered reminding him that out of the two of them, it had definitely been him who'd done the lion's share of the demanding. Demanding credit, demanding respect, and demanding Bastian in his bed. But Bastian looked so adorably smug and certain of Hess' upcoming defeat that Kian refrained.

"Good luck," he said reluctantly brushing a single kiss across Bastian's mouth. "Own his ass, please."

"Done." Bastian really was unbearably egotistical sometimes, but at least he'd never directed it at Kian before. Kian didn't know exactly why, but he imagined that Bastian knew better than to try.

Prep started out like most prep did, an interminable parade of mostly dull tasks, all to be completed with efficient speed and measured against exacting standards.

Derek had been doing better the last few weeks, and Kian took the risk to assign him some of the more complicated prep, working on the Japanese mandolin.

He looked very skeptical as Kian carefully explained how it worked, and what needed to be done with the crates of eggplants piled on the counter. "Isn't that what you cut yourself on?" he asked, eyeing the shining blade dubiously.

"I wasn't wearing the gloves. You're going to wear the gloves."

"Like a pussy," Mark inserted.

It was the most questionable thing that he'd said in days, long enough that Kian had almost begun to believe that the days of snarky, rude comments were over, and that he'd finally given up on questioning Kian's authority.

That had apparently been too good to hope for.

"Not like a pussy," Kian said between gritted teeth. "Like a smart, intelligent person who would like to keep all their fingers."

"I heard Aquino *carried* you to the ER," Mark said slyly.

Derek had the nerve to look guilty. So Mark hadn't been behaving after all—he'd just been going behind Kian's back to extract every bit of gossip that he could out of the rest of the staff.

He understood why the kitchen staff gossiped; their jobs were hard, if not actually impossible at points, and gossip helped alleviate some of that unrelenting pressure. And, it had been the moment of a lifetime to watch their notoriously hardheaded head chef lose his mind over an injury.

"I don't remember that, actually," Kian said.

"Yeah," Mark agreed, "because you fainted, like a *pussy*."

It was hard, but not impossible, to keep his voice level and calm. "I'm confused here, Mark. Who's the pussy here? First it's Derek, for using the gloves. But then it's me, for *not* using the gloves and cutting myself so badly I passed out."

Mark's glare was belligerent. It was clearly going to be one of *those* days, like somehow Mark had been in the bathroom this morning with him and Bastian and had heard Bastian wouldn't be around to witness his shitty behavior.

It was unbelievably annoying, but Kian refused to let him see how it was getting to him.

If he did, Mark would never let it go, and Kian would be forced to either fire him, or report him to Bastian—both of which meant that Bastian would find out that Kian hadn't been able to handle the problem himself.

Kian wasn't ready to accept that yet, but it felt like today, Mark wanted to keep pushing him.

"Put the gloves on," Kian directed to Derek. "Try the first eggplant, I want to make sure the settings are perfect."

Derek did as directed, while Kian continued to feel the heat of Mark's glare.

"There, that's good. Just keep your movement steady and you should be fine," Kian said.

"Is that what Bastian tells you?" Mark asked snidely.

The problem with Mark was that he wasn't dumb at all. He was annoyingly intelligent; usually smart enough to make sure that anything he said that was really offensive had another potential meaning.

Kian ignored him and continued to focus on Derek.

The other problem was that Mark seemed to have a knack for knowing just the moment when he'd pushed Kian too far and he always retreated. He had to know that if he pushed too hard and too far, Kian would just snap and fire him on the spot, no matter the consequences.

But he always made sure Kian wouldn't.

He did this time too, retreating after that last, infuriating comment back to his own station, and his own tasks.

After making sure Derek was all set, Kian stalked off, taking a five-minute breather in Bastian's office and then venturing out to start the soup.

But maybe he was actually the dumb one, because he'd expected that Mark would mostly leave it alone, at the most do something questionable during service, like forget every fucking ticket Kian called out to him.

And that definitely would have been shitty enough, but Kian would have dealt with it. Maybe he might have broken another plate, even though he still felt a sickening knot of guilt from the last one.

If Mark continued to fuck up the sauté station, all he'd do was make himself look incompetent and lazy. Somehow, he must have figured that out, because he didn't throttle it back and he didn't do anything during service.

Kian had made an extra batch of the curry carrot soup for family meal, which paired well with the big salad Derek threw together, and the flank steaks Michel grilled, slicing them thin, still nearly bloody in the middle.

It was a Saturday night, and the reservation list was completely booked, which meant it would be a difficult, stressful service. Too many tables, and not quite enough staff—not quite enough *competent* staff, Kian corrected—to deal with it.

He'd probably end up at sauté and leave Michelle to give a straightforward if rudimentary glance over the dishes before they went up to the dining room. She'd worked at Terroir for awhile, and he'd seen Bastian rely on her before, so Kian felt okay doing it.

Not great, just okay, but he couldn't dig Mark out of his mess of tickets and monitor the dishes at the same time. And if Bastian didn't like that, Kian thought with a sigh, trying to stretch out the kink in his neck as he sat down to dinner, then that was too goddamn bad, and he should have made sure Kian had the staff he needed to succeed.

He definitely wasn't counting Mark as a plus in that particular column.

Speak of the devil. Mark sat down next to him, a deceptively innocent look on his face. Of course Kian knew better, but he also couldn't physically force Mark to shut up. Well, he *could,* but that would be a Human Resources nightmare.

"Neck stiff?" he asked innocently.

Kian looked over at him, inherently suspicious. "Must have slept on it wrong."

Almost everyone was at the table, absorbed in the soup and the salad and Michel's excellent meat, paired with the good bread. "Or," Mark suggested slyly, "maybe you were too busy sucking Aquino's cock to worry about how bad your neck would feel in the morning."

You could hear a pin drop at the table. Almost everyone at it had been present, two months previous, when Kian had cut himself on the Japanese mandolin. They'd all witnessed Bastian losing his mind, the hottest gossip in ages. Even Kian had heard about it, because while he'd certainly not witnessed it, being passed the fuck out, the story had spread like wildfire. They'd seen Bastian pick Kian up bridal style and reject outright anyone else who attempted to help. They'd known Bastian had waited with Kian at the emergency room, and had driven him home afterwards, to the point of being late for a service. Something that had never actually happened before that particular day.

As Kian met each set of eyes at the table, he realized that they all knew. They knew and they'd all been talking about it, not only among themselves, but to Mark. Mark who would take this potentially salacious bit of gossip and turn it inside out, until it was the worst version of itself.

He'd make Kian look like a cock-sucking sycophant, who'd do whatever it took to get ahead. And Bastian? Bastian would be his normal asshole self, willing to take advantage of a much younger employee whom he was currently mentoring—to the point of demanding sexual favors for career favors.

Kian felt sick to his stomach. It wasn't like some of these people didn't respect him, but they'd clearly begun to form some other kind of opinion of him, and it wasn't good.

He stood up slowly. "Excuse me?"

Mark leaned back, indulgent and smug. "You heard me. Are you really going to deny it?"

It sounded so sordid when Kian thought about it, which was exactly why he'd wanted to keep it a secret. Nobody knew that they'd resisted doing a single thing about their feelings for over two years. Nobody knew that Bastian was a better person than they'd ever imagined. Nobody knew Kian would have rather quit than take this job because he was sleeping with the boss.

But none of that mattered, because it sure as hell didn't look like any of that.

"You are." Mark laughed incredulously. Kian clenched his fists and tried to remind himself what a nightmare it would be if he punched his own *sous*. "You're really going to stand there and try to pretend that the vaunted and much-worshipped pecking order at Terroir can't be undone as easily as Aquino undoes his pants at night?"

It was beyond stupid to engage. Even though it was a Saturday night, and they were going to be packed to the rafters with guests tonight, what he should do was fire Mark's traitorous ass and call Bastian in to help, screw closing his deal with Nathan Hess.

Unexpectedly, Kian felt so betrayed, and not only by the staff he'd been working with so many months—years, even, for some of them. No, the main betrayal was Bastian's. He'd saddled Kian with this *dick* and then manipulated the situation so Kian didn't feel like going to him for assistance was even an option. It was fucking unfair and even though Kian had claimed it would never happen, he felt a surge of something that felt a lot like hatred.

Which was why he did the opposite of what he knew he should do.

"It's not like that," he said, and instantly knew it was wrong. He'd not only confirmed Mark's version of the story, despite saying otherwise, and he'd gone on the defensive.

Mark, clearly sensing blood, pounced. "So you're saying it *is* happening. You're sleeping with Aquino."

There was nowhere to go, except right through the shit, and try not to slide off the edge in the process.

"I can't believe it," Michel said, and he didn't sound happy. *Michel,* who was someone Kian would have loved to have as his *sous.* But it would never happen now because there was a look of sheer disbelief on his face now—as if Kian had just betrayed everything he'd ever believed in.

"It's not like that," Kian repeated stubbornly, despite knowing that there was no way he could win from this position. He'd already admitted defeat.

"Oh, what's it like?" Mark asked creamily. "Do you really love each other?"

Kian looked around the table and knew nobody would believe him if he claimed that was true. They'd already made up their minds, and they weren't siding with him.

Somehow, he'd become the villain of the entire shitshow, which made no fucking sense to him at all. But if he was going to get labeled that way, he might as well go whole hog.

Kian had never punched anyone before, but with the adrenaline surging through his veins, it turned out it wasn't all that hard. His hand didn't even really hurt, he thought as he gazed at his scraped knuckles, at the speckles of blood, because of course once he'd hit Mark, he hadn't wanted to stop. The blood, and him collapsing onto the floor were finally enough for him to pull back, panting.

He stared down at the floor, at Mark's bloody, obnoxious face, and wished he could keep going until he was just a red smear on the floor. A burst tomato, strewn across the concrete.

Michel grabbed his arm and held him back, even though he'd already stopped. Mark was both taller and looked stronger, but that hadn't mattered.

Probably because the last thing he'd ever expected Kian to do was punch him in the nose.

"Holy shit," Michel whispered, and for a blissful second, Kian thought he only sounded so shocked because he too had been surprised that Kian could punch the daylights out of Mark.

But that wasn't why. Kian looked up and Bastian was standing at the pass-through, stunned expression on his face. Then his eyes hardened, and in his place was a man Kian didn't recognize.

That wasn't exactly true, though. He was familiar, like a blast from the past. This was the Bastian Kian had met that very first day, who hadn't given a shit. Who hadn't been in love with Kian. Who wanted to remind him who was boss, who was really in charge.

Fucking hell.

Bastian had been through a lot of bad, weird, and confusing situations in his twenty-plus years in the culinary industry. He had never once, not in all that time, ever come face-to-face with one and found himself speechless.

He was speechless now, rooted to the spot he'd stopped short at a minute before, when he'd listened to Kian give Mark all the ammunition he'd ever need, and then lose every single fucking ounce of control.

It wasn't like he didn't *also* want to punch Mark in the face, but he couldn't exactly do it after he was already on the floor, bleeding.

"My office *now*," he finally said, and didn't miss the swift, guilty look Kian shot in his direction. Or the wounded expression Mark pasted on after being helped to his feet, with a rag to staunch the blood currently gushing out of his nose.

Bastian stomped over to his office, yanking the door open and pulling down the blinds so forcefully the bottom edges all crashed to the floor.

Was this what Kian had been holding back from him? That Mark had been trying to convince the rest of the staff to join his mutiny? That he was heckling him during his shift?

Bastian had told him to suck it up, to deal with Mark not liking him, but this was something entirely different, and he hoped, feeling a surge of guilt himself, that Kian would have known to come to him about it.

But he hadn't, and now the Terroir kitchen had been witness to more than just broken plates.

Kian and then Mark slunk into his office, as Bastian stood at the doorway.

He looked out at the rest of the crew, who were understandably gaping at this turn of events. "Finish your meal and get prepped for service," Bastian snapped. "And stop fucking staring."

He closed the door behind him and didn't even bother sitting down in his chair. He stood, facing his *chef de cuisine* and his *sous chef*—the two members of the kitchen staff who should have been working out problems with the *rest* of the employees, not letting their petty fight poison his restaurant.

"What the fuck," he finally spit out. "What the ever-loving fuck is wrong with you two?"

Kian opened his mouth, like he wanted to explain, but then he shut it again, inexplicably. Considering his position at Terroir, it *was* his responsibility to explain what had happened—never mind that it had been his fist that had met Mark's face.

But instead of opening up, instead of offering any apologies or reasoning why he'd suddenly lost his fucking mind, he said nothing.

Bastian watched as Mark eyed Kian, trying to figure out if he was going to say anything, and when he didn't, he jumped in.

"Chef, it was just some harmless gossip that some people took a lot more seriously," Mark said, innocence dripping from his voice. Bastian guessed that he was referring to Kian, and maybe if he didn't know Kian as well as he did, believing him would have been easier.

The thing he didn't understand was Kian's continued silence.

"Kian?" Bastian finally asked and felt another surge of frustrated anger that he'd had to *ask*. Didn't the man have any sense of self-preservation? One of the two of them would have to go, and despite the blood currently smearing his knuckles, Bastian was almost certain that it shouldn't be Kian. But if he didn't fucking speak up and defend himself with his side of the story, how could Bastian keep him?

It felt like a betrayal, like suddenly Kian didn't care enough to bother fighting.

Don't you dare put me in this fucking spot, he thought. *I can't beg you. I won't.*

Kian shrugged, and Bastian might have believed he didn't care at all, except the devastation in his eyes.

Like he'd already been fired. Like Bastian had already given up on him. When Bastian had actually been fighting for him every step of the way, and the only one who'd given up was Kian.

"Mark," he said, "go pack your things. You're fired."

Frowning, Mark didn't move. Not very smart of him, because even though Kian was a good seventy pounds lighter and a few inches shorter, Kian had already taken him out tonight. And Kian had stopped after a handful of hits; Bastian wasn't sure he could, not with the toxic brew of fury and aggravation boiling inside him. During the best of times, he had a temper; this definitely wasn't the best anything.

"Excuse me, sir," Mark said, "I just don't think that's fair. I know you're . . . involved, and I shouldn't be dismissed just because you don't want to fire who you're sleeping with."

It was becoming clearer just how this asshole had managed to get deep enough under Kian's skin to drive him to bloody his nose. He was a *dick*, with somehow even less self-preservation than Kian. Bastian straightened his back and gave Mark the coldest glare in his entire arsenal.

"Get the fuck out of my sight," was all he said, but Bastian had a feeling it would be more than enough to demolish any bravery this asshole had left.

Mark blanched, but *still* didn't seem to get how badly he'd fucked up, because he asked, "What about a reference?"

It was impossible to miss the shock crossing over Kian's face. Bastian didn't even know if what he really felt was shock; shock felt too small, too insignificant.

"Let me make sure I understand you," Bastian said, voice silky smooth with rage. "I hire you to come and be Kian's *sous*, with the belief you will support him with the staff and in the operation of this top-tier restaurant. But instead of doing any of that, you've been lazy, slow, and too busy gossiping to do your job properly. Then, to top off your sniveling, pathetic little machinations, you think it's a good idea to cause mutiny among the rest of the staff, with some nasty, completely untrue gossip that Kian was promoted because he's good at sucking my dick. Did I get all that correct?"

Bastian couldn't meet Kian's eyes as Mark stared at him. It had been easy enough to put together, and for some goddamned unknown reason, Kian hadn't come to him. One word of this and Bastian would have been happy to fire Mark himself, and even call Michael Mina to tell him what a snake his former employee was. Not even a snake, Bastian corrected, a *worm*. Maybe even a disease on a worm.

"That's not . . ." Mark hesitated. "That's not entirely how it was."

"If I call Derek or Michel in here, what will they tell me?" *Since you*, Bastian thought pointedly at Kian, *won't fucking defend your own ass.*

"It just didn't seem . . . fair." Mark hesitated. "Sir."

Bastian rolled his eyes. "So it *is* true. Well get this, *life isn't fucking fair.* I can't believe that even after all of that shit, you have the nerve to ask me for a *reference.* Like I would ever lower myself to even speak your name ever again. And don't expect one from Michael Mina either, because he's going to be hearing about this little stunt. Hope you have enough money saved for a ticket far, far away, because you're never fucking working in California again, if I have anything to say about it."

Mark chose that particular moment to flee the office, and Bastian was left staring at his *chef de cuisine*, his lover, who'd betrayed him as much as he could be betrayed.

He walked around the desk, until he was right in front of Kian, who looked suddenly, visibly nervous. He should have been nervous a hell of a lot sooner, as far as Bastian was concerned. Maybe Kian thought he'd neutered him over the last few weeks, but Bastian was still in charge.

"Anything to say for yourself?"

Kian actually glared. "What, you wanted me to roll on him? Why should I even bother? You never wanted to hear the shit he did, you told me to put up with it. So I did."

"I sure didn't tell you to punch him in the face." A terrible realization was dawning on Bastian. He'd done this. He'd put Kian in charge of something he couldn't hope to control—he didn't have the experience or the will or the skills yet—and then he'd compounded the problem by hiring Mark.

Why had he been so blind? Was it really like Mark said? Had he promoted Kian because he was good at sucking cock? Or had it been because he loved him and wanted desperately to believe in a slightly different, slightly better version of Kian? A Kian that didn't exist quite yet?

Regardless, this experiment was over, and Bastian didn't know how to end it without ending everything else. His stomach twisted. Maybe losing Kian was inevitable. He'd always been too young, too vibrant, too goddamned sweet, and it was probably only time before he realized that he was too good for Bastian, who deep down, was just a mean old grump. But he'd believed he'd get more time first, more days, more weeks, that he could file away and pull out when he got too lonely to function.

"No, but you set me up to fail," Kian said, and he sounded really pissed. Bastian wasn't even sure he was wrong; but regardless of whose fault the catastrophe was, *it existed*, and Bastian had to fix it.

"I'm going to go upstairs, tell Nathan Hess that the deal is off, because I have shit to sort out of my own. You'll be my *sous*, if you feel like you can possibly control yourself going forward."

"And if I don't want to take the demotion?" Kian demanded. Bastian wanted to believe he didn't understand why he *wouldn't,* but he did. Kian wanted so desperately to feel like they were on equal footing, but the truth was, they were never going to be able to exist that way. The situation had been prepped ahead of time to never be equal.

"You either accept the demotion, or you're fired." Bastian told himself that he wouldn't take that awful step, but deep down, he knew better. Kian had his same pride, his same iron will, the same determination, the same inability to accept defeat.

Maman, you were wrong, Bastian thought bitterly as he saw the acceptance in Kian's eyes.

"You can't fire me," Kian announced, breaking the heart that Bastian had never even believed existed until they'd met, "because I quit."

"Fine." The word made Bastian ill, but what else could he say? He couldn't refuse to accept Kian leaving. He'd already ruined everything enough.

"I'll be by later to pick up my stuff from your house." The jut of Kian's chin was so prideful, Bastian knew he recognized it from his own reflection. *Don't do this*, he wanted to beg, to plead, *don't be the worst version of yourself. Don't be like me.* But he was Bastian Aquino, head chef of Terroir, and he didn't beg anyone for anything, ever. Even the man he loved.

"Is that really necessary?" he finally asked, even though he already knew the answer.

Kian laughed without humor. "Did you really believe that we could keep this separate? Lovers at home, professionals at Terroir? It was doomed to fail from the beginning, and I know you're not stupid. You warned me. You knew it would happen."

What could he say? He'd wanted so badly to believe otherwise? Wanted it so much that he'd believed he could *hope* it into reality?

"That's what I thought," Kian said bitterly, turning and leaving.

Bastian was left alone, again, inevitably, and this time he wondered, *what the fuck am I going to do now?*

Before, he'd always known. But Kian had demolished every structure he'd ever erected. He was a mess of crumbled rubble, all his walls demolished, his infrastructure blown to bits.

And still, if anyone asked him, which he hoped to God they wouldn't, he still believed it had been worth it.

He pushed away from the desk, and feeling every one of his years, marched out into the kitchen to save Terroir from certain disaster. It was what he'd always been the best at, and now it was all he had left.

Chapter Fifteen

Kian didn't start crying until he walked into the kitchen and saw the coffee mug Bastian had drunk out of just yesterday sitting in the sink.

It hit him then, like an inescapable blow to the head. He'd never pour Bastian another cup of coffee and tease him about liking it dark as mud. He'd never wake up tucked up next to him. He'd never kiss him again. He'd never smile at him over some boring prep at the restaurant. He'd never again set foot into the Terroir kitchen.

Because it wasn't just one blow; it was a thousand, big and small and every size in between, and every single one fucking hurt. Kian stood there and felt each one as they hit him, hard.

Nobody was home, and there was nobody to see him cry. Xander would be at the Barrel House, Nate was probably at the winery, where he worked in the tasting room. He'd have hours and hours before anyone came home to bother him, and that seemed like both the best and the worst thing to happen to him.

He could go to Bastian's house and get all the stuff he'd left there. He still had the code, and that way he'd avoid having to go over everything again with Bastian. But going to Bastian's would be even worse than spotting his mug in the sink.

He'd been spinning fantasies in his mind, imagining someday moving into Bastian's house and making it a real home, instead of the soulless box that Bastian had called it. He'd imagined a life they could share, where they gave and took in equal measures.

At the time, he'd wanted so desperately to believe that it was possible, but it wasn't. He'd been blinding himself to the realities of their situation. They'd never been even remotely equal. The only equality that had existed between them were advantages that Bastian had willingly ceded to him.

There shouldn't have been anything else but pain, but now there was the inevitable streak of humiliation winding its way through him. He'd been full of wishes and hope this whole time, but Bastian had only been pretending.

Kian stumbled into his bedroom, and lurched back, like he'd been burned by the lingering smell of Bastian in the air. It had been almost forty-eight hours since he'd been in here, but it didn't matter. The whole room would need to be aired out, every inch of fabric washed, the walls scrubbed, the carpet cleaned. Even then, he'd never be able to eradicate the memories—and Bastian had only spent a handful of nights here.

Hours before anyone would be home, so many useless hours spreading out in front of him. He needed to do something, keep busy. Keep himself from thinking; if he could keep his mind blank, he thought as he dried his eyes with the edge of his t-shirt, he might not break down.

He pulled off the sheets, stuffing them in the washing machine down the hall. Next, he went to his closet to find the other set he vaguely remembered having. Sorting through the random crap that accumulated, he accidentally nudged a cardboard box on one shelf, sending it careening to the floor, all its contents spilling out.

Kian groaned and righted the box. He didn't have the energy to deal with this today.

Except one of the items that had fallen out was his old Institute apron. As he crumpled up the fabric, planning to shove it right back where it came from, he heard the crinkle of paper.

Shit.

It had been two years since he'd even considered any of the overseas job applications he'd sent, or the letters he'd received as a response. He'd never even opened them, too blown away and excited by the possibility of working for Bastian Aquino at Terroir. He hadn't cared one way or the other if he'd been hired.

He'd shoved the responses away in a pocket of his apron and totally forgotten about them.

One by one, he pulled them out. Three in total. Still sealed. For the first time, Kian really faced what his sudden change of heart had cost him. He could be working and training in Europe right now, at restaurants far more prestigious than Terroir. Restaurants with decades of brilliance stretching behind them.

He'd given all that up because Bastian had walked into his class, and he'd gotten an instant hard-on.

Why hadn't anyone stopped him? Why hadn't anyone pulled him aside and insisted that working for someone solely because you had a personal and professional crush was a terrible idea? He hadn't told his mom why he'd changed his mind on Europe because he'd been sure she'd be upset. Later, he knew Xander and Wyatt had conspired to try to find him a job in LA, a misguided attempt to get him away from Bastian. By then it had been too late, he'd fallen in love and he'd refused to even discuss leaving.

But at the beginning? There'd been room then, even in the first, full-body flush of his infatuation. He might have listened to reason. He might have changed his mind.

He might not have wasted the last two years.

Right now, they felt like a waste. Yeah, he'd become *chef de cuisine*, but he no longer believed that Bastian had promoted him because he deserved it. Mark, as galling as it was, had been fucking right. He'd gotten the *chef de cuisine* job because he was sucking Bastian's cock.

What did it matter, Kian thought bitterly, if you lied to yourself because you knew better or because you hoped for better? It turned out the same in the end.

He should have taken one look at Luc and not been horribly, terribly envious; he should have taken one look at Luc and understood he was a cautionary tale. Bastian was like a hurricane. He swept into a life and then out of it and left no structures standing in his wake.

Kian fingered the wrinkled paper of the envelopes. There was a part of him that was dying to open them, dying to know what he'd chosen Bastian over. But there was another part of him that dreaded facing the truth, and that actively didn't want to know what he'd given up without a thought.

A voice in his head called him a coward, and Kian flinched because it sounded too much like Bastian. But then, he'd been an excellent mentor. He'd taught him never to be afraid of the truth.

That was ironic, Kian thought, and ripped one envelope open, and then another, and then the last.

They were all job offers. They'd all wanted to hire him.

A sob escaped his throat, and then another. He sank to his knees, crying over everything he'd lost today, and two years ago—before he'd even known better.

Kian sat there for a very long time. He stopped crying, eventually, but he still didn't move. The house grew dark and he stayed right where he was.

Eventually, he heard a car pull into the driveway, and assumed it would be Xander. It was late, but not quite late enough for Nate to come home.

Footsteps echoed down the hall, and before Kian could brace for it, the hall light turned on, leaving him flinching into the sudden brightness.

"What's going on?" Xander asked, kneeling down and taking in the situation. The sheet-less bed. The letters spread out on the floor in front of Kian.

"The inevitable," Kian said dully. He couldn't look at Xander. "I quit, and I guess we broke up."

"You guess?"

"At the beginning, we told ourselves that it would stay separate. Work at Terroir, personal at home. But it didn't, it couldn't. It was all tangled together, from the very beginning." Kian had never felt so bleak, so hopeless before.

"You didn't know any better, but the Bastard did," Xander growled, and Kian knew just how angry he was. He wanted to tell him that it wasn't just Bastian's fault; it was his own too. After all, he'd just punched Mark in the face and then refused to give any explanation at all. He'd lost control of the kitchen, and Bastian had been right to demote him.

But instead of explaining, Kian just shrugged. It hurt too much to try to explain, even if he knew what side Xander would inevitably be on.

"And all this?" Xander asked, pointing to the letters.

Kian glanced up, his eyes full of pain. "Did I ever tell you that at one point, I was going to Europe?"

Kian had been expecting the call all day, so it was easy enough to hit ignore half a dozen times.

When the unknown number started calling, Kian let it go to voicemail three times before he finally answered.

"Xander called you," Kian said in an edgy, annoyed voice.

"How did you even know it was me?" Wyatt asked, mystified.

"Xander has a method," Kian retorted. "He offered me another bottle of Nate's wine last night. I'm not sure he has any other comforting methods in his repertoire. He's run out, so he called you."

Wyatt sighed on the other end of the line. "This *is* Xander we're talking about. Not exactly the most comforting person in the world."

"Right." Kian knew he didn't sound convinced, and he found he didn't give a fuck. There was a huge number of things piling up that, in the last two days, he'd discovered that he didn't give a fuck about.

Everyone had always thought he was sweet and naïve and a little blind. The truth was, he'd just stupidly, optimistically, believed in the best in people, and in the world. And now he knew he'd been so fucking wrong, this whole damn time.

"Xander called me because he's worried about you," Wyatt soothed.

"I've got money saved, I'm good for my share of rent." Kian dipped his sponge back in the bucket of soapy water at his feet. He'd already finished airing out and cleaning every inch of his bedroom, and he'd moved on to the living room because doing nothing wasn't acceptable, and he didn't have anything else to do.

If he stopped, he'd think, and thinking was so wretched Kian was determined never to do it again.

"I don't think that was what he was worried about," Wyatt said wryly.

"I'm fine," Kian said, not giving a single shit that he didn't sound fine. "In a week or so I'll look for a new job."

He'd do it, because he was bored and there was only so much cleaning to do, even though the thought of another kitchen—a kitchen without Bastian at the head of it—made him sick to his stomach. He could do it because he was a goddamn professional. That was what Bastian had trained him to be, even though he'd failed at the end.

"I know Xander is desperate to hire you," Wyatt said.

"Did you call for any actual purpose or just to make yourself feel better?" Kian demanded, inexplicably furious all of a sudden. "Because you're not making *me* feel any better."

There was a long silence on the other end of the phone. Kian pinched off the disappointment that Wyatt didn't really care either and tossed it away. He didn't need that on top of everything else.

When Wyatt finally spoke again, it was slowly, like he was carefully picking every single word. "Xander told me about your European jobs. That you think you've wasted the last two years."

"I did," Kian retorted bitterly.

"Actually," Wyatt said and then hesitated. "I really don't think you did."

"You don't really believe that." The only reason Wyatt would say that would be to try to talk Kian out of feeling that way. And Kian wasn't dumb, not anymore. His eyes had been forcibly opened wide.

"I do. Do you love him?"

"I don't see why that matters." Kian swallowed back the unexpected tears lingering in the back of his throat. Suddenly it didn't matter if Wyatt *did* care about him, he just couldn't talk about this anymore.

"You might as well just tell me, because we all know you do." Wyatt sighed. "Does he love you?"

Kian nearly hung up the phone. It was only the impossible kindness in Wyatt's voice that kept him from doing it. "He said he did, but I'm not sure I believe him anymore."

"He must love you, because he gave you a job you weren't really qualified for, but that you wanted a lot. He didn't give it to you because you guys were fucking; he gave it to you because that's what you do with someone you love—you give them what they want, even if it isn't always good for them."

Kian hated the sob that escaped him. Even more than he hated that Wyatt was right. He'd been ill-prepared, even with all of Bastian's training, and he'd known that when it had been offered to him. He should have turned it down, but there'd been that irresistible glow of living up to the man on Bastian's pedestal.

That had turned out so well, too.

"I've fucked it all up," he cried. "I knew it was too soon, I knew it was a mistake. I should have told him."

"You can't go back and change the past," Wyatt said softly, "you can only change the future. So what are you going to do with it?"

"I guess . . ." Kian took a deep breath. "I guess I could contact these restaurants in Europe again. See if they'd consider hiring me still."

"Do you want to go to Europe?"

Truthfully Kian didn't know what he wanted. No—that wasn't true. He wanted things to not change, but Wyatt was right; he could only change the future, not the past.

"I don't know," Kian said. "Bastian said they'd have me doing dishes for a year."

"At least," Wyatt said with a chuckle, then his voice grew serious. "You didn't waste your time at Terroir. Bastian was a good mentor to you. He taught you an enormous amount, and you were already talented. It wasn't a waste, because you got to do more in two years than anyone in Europe would do in five."

"Swear to god?" Kian demanded.

"Swear to god." Wyatt laughed again. "Seriously, go work for Xander while you figure it out. You could do it in your sleep and it'll keep you occupied and sane. Somewhat, anyway. It *is* still Xander's restaurant."

Kian had considered that too. Working for Xander at the Barrel House might hurt the least, out of all the options available to him. Was that a pussy move? He wasn't sure anymore. Self-preservation, while not something that Bastian had ever encouraged or cultivated in himself, wasn't so bad.

"I'll think about it," Kian promised. "I'm not ready to be *chef de cuisine* and I'm done doing dishes. I'm not sure where I belong anymore."

"Somewhere in between. But I know you'll figure it out, you're the smartest guy I know," Wyatt said.

Kian scoffed. "That's bullshit. I went to my boss' house and *took my clothes off*."

There was silence on the other end of the line. So Xander hadn't told Wyatt *everything*.

"I reserve the right to take back that statement," Wyatt said. "Nobody ever said you didn't have balls, though. Wow."

"Love makes you do really stupid things," Kian pointed out and Wyatt agreed.

"You know you can text me anytime," Wyatt stated. "I have to go make sure Tony doesn't blow up our food truck. He's deep frying a turkey or . . . maybe a whole ham. Or something."

"Go save your truck," Kian said. "And yes, I do."

Wyatt was right, Kian realized after he'd set the phone down and had continued scrubbing the living room wall. He hadn't wasted the time. It helped alleviate some of the humiliating sting, but the yawning chasm of pain was still right there, hovering on the edge of Kian's consciousness. Not thinking he'd wasted his time wasn't the same as not missing Bastian so much he could barely breathe sometimes.

Maybe Wyatt was right about something else too. Working for Xander wouldn't be so bad; it would at least be better than continuing to scrub this wall.

Bastian didn't know how it happened, but his whole life had suddenly become a fucking disaster. Wyatt and Xander were long gone. Kian was gone. That worm Mark was gone. He was left with a bare bones staff, not nearly enough to run a restaurant the size of Terroir. Also spring and the tourists were coming and they'd be able to open up the patio in a few weeks. That meant even more tables to service, and not nearly enough people to service them.

He'd considered begging Kian to come back, not just because things were bad on the staffing front, but because every time he thought so much as his name, Bastian felt like throwing up. And since he thought about him all the damn time, that was a problem.

Terroir needed Bastian to be leading it, not hiding in the bathroom, curled inwards around his traitorous stomach. He never actually threw up, he just *wanted* to, constantly.

After the second day without Kian, Bastian finally assumed that this horrible feeling must be what a broken heart felt like and stopped going to the bathroom to hunch over the toilet in vain.

He was a master at ignoring things that might have bothered others: sickness, exhaustion, injuries, personal problems. He couldn't even remember the last time he'd actually *had* a personal problem, but he'd always assumed he could push those petty hurts away, like he did everything else.

But Kian wasn't a petty hurt, he was a gaping hole in Bastian's chest, a maelstrom of regret and guilt.

On the third day, his mother called, and he'd ignored it. She called again, and then again, and then again. Biting off a whole string of bad words, he left the prep station, hoping that Derek wouldn't fuck anything up in the five minutes he was gone.

He exited out the back door, and leaned on the brick wall, taking a deep breath of fresh air. He'd been working almost nonstop since Kian had walked out, and somehow, even though two years ago, Bastian had done everything without Kian, it turned out that he'd come to rely on him so much that now the burden felt too heavy to bear.

Not a realization that Bastian was particularly happy to come to.

"What is it, *maman*?" he asked when she picked up the phone on the second ring. "I'm very busy, the restaurant is swamped, and we've had some . . ." Bastian paused, he didn't want to tell her about Kian in the context of complaining they didn't have enough staff, but what else was there? He wasn't going to sit at her knee and cry into her lap. He'd never been that child, and he certainly wasn't that child now. "We've had some staffing problems."

It was foolish to hope she'd let it go at that vague statement, but he'd cross that bridge when they came to it. Yet another painful inevitability he'd need to face; admitting to his mother that he'd fucked up everything with the love of his life.

"Bastian," she staid sternly, "I am hearing the strangest rumors."

Sighing, Bastian scrubbed a hand over his face. He couldn't remember the last time he'd really slept. Probably before Kian had quit. "I wish you wouldn't listen to those."

"I went to Barrel House last night," she continued, like he hadn't said a word. "And for once the rumors were correct. Kian, he is not working for you anymore? He was working at Xander Bridges' restaurant? What has happened?"

It was inevitable that Kian would go to work for Xander. Bastian had theoretically prepared himself for that eventuality, but it stung so much more than he'd ever imagined it would. Salt on an open wound, sprinkled liberally.

"I really don't have time for this right now, *maman*," he said, trying with one last ditch effort to dodge the question.

"Bastian Pierre Aquino," Celeste said sternly. "Do I need to come down there and harass you until you tell me?"

Bastian laughed because otherwise he was going to cry, and he couldn't remember the last time he'd ever cried in front of someone. Frankly, before this week, he couldn't remember the last time he'd cried at all, but he'd passed that milestone the first night without Kian beside him.

It was shameful, but at least it was honest, Bastian thought bleakly. He deserved the misery; he'd fucked this whole thing up, and he didn't really blame Kian for quitting.

For leaving him too, maybe. But Kian was almost certainly right, their personal relationship would never have survived their professional one imploding.

That didn't mean Bastian had forgiven him for it, or himself.

"He quit," he finally admitted quietly, "probably because I drove him to it. I set him up in a position where he was doomed to fail." Deep ragged breath, to try to suppress the tears that threatened. He had yet to cry at Terroir and he was determined that it *would not* happen. "I don't even blame him for being pissed off at me. I was very stupid."

"Oh, Bastian," Celeste said softly. "I am so sorry. Will he not forgive you?"

Bastian thought of all the times he'd seen himself reflected in Kian. "I doubt it." He hadn't tried, because he didn't know what to say, and he definitely didn't know how to fix the situation. Kian would chafe as *sous*, that was something Bastian believed fully, and he wasn't ready to be *chef de cuisine*. What else was there?

"You haven't even tried," Celeste said with damning judgement in her voice. "Bastian."

"There is no way to fix this," Bastian swore. "If there was, I would have thought of it. I would have done it already. I'm dying here."

"I'm sure you are, my darling. Go back to work, and I will think on it."

"*Maman*," Bastian argued, because the last thing this fucked-up situation needed was interference. But she had already hung up, and checking his watch, there really wasn't time to call her back. Frankly, there hadn't really been time to talk to her in the first place. He took one last breath of fresh air, and then went back inside.

He had a lot of work to do.

Working for Xander was like slipping back into a familiar position that he recognized—but the edges didn't quite fit properly and they chafed. The kitchen was too small. The fact that the diners could see everything they were doing in the kitchen was weird, and Kian didn't like it. He didn't know how Xander stood it. He did understand why Xander had designed it that way; the chefs were held accountable for their behavior with so many eyes watching, and he could never lose his temper the way that Bastian did frequently.

The same devastating wave of pain swept over him the same as it did every time he thought of Bastian, but a week had gone by now. It didn't hurt any less, but he was starting to get used to it.

"Chicken special," Xander called out. "Three top."

Xander ran a good kitchen. The food was delicious and high quality but a little more relaxed than Terroir had been. It was a good fit for Kian, but he already knew this was temporary. He didn't really want to stay forever.

Xander kept telling him that eventually he'd feel differently, that when he finally got Bastian out of his system, he'd see how good it was to work for someone else.

He'd sounded so sure of this theory that Kian hadn't wanted to contradict him. But he was never going to get Bastian out of his system. Even when he hated him—and there had been one or two or ten moments of that—he still loved him. He didn't believe that was going to change anytime soon, no matter what Xander claimed.

One of the waiters approached the pass-through as Kian put on three sauté pans, starting the chicken.

"There is a lady that wanted to send compliments to the chef," he said, smile glimmering in the corners of his mouth.

Kian frowned. "She wants to send compliments to Xander, you mean."

"No," he said, shaking his head. "She was very specific about sending compliments to *you*. Kian Reynolds. She said you have a mutual acquaintance you both care about."

Kian's hand froze on one of the sauté pans. "How old was she?"

"Oh, maybe sixty? Beautiful. Distinguished."

It had to be Bastian's mother. The age was right. The description was right. "Did she speak with an accent?"

"Yeah," the waiter said. "How did you know? She's French."

Something everyone learned about Bastian Aquino at some point—his mother was French, his father Spanish. A conflagration of hot temperaments swirling inside him, fighting containment.

"Xander," Kian said, "come take over these pans."

Xander didn't look happy but he came over anyway. "You already took a break," he objected, but there was something to be said for working for your best friend.

"Yeah, and I'm sorry, but I need another. I just need . . . five minutes, if that's okay?"

Muttering under his breath, Xander didn't respond, but bumped Kian out of the way with a hip check.

"I'll be quick," Kian promised, and wiped his hands on a towel, unwinding his apron and hanging it on a hook before walking into the dining room.

Bastian's mother was everything he'd been told, and sitting alone at a corner table, a half-drunk glass of one of Xander's creative mocktails at her elbow.

"Hello," Kian said, and she looked up. He could see hints of Bastian in her face, her dark hair, streaked with gray.

"You are Kian," she said, clearly delighted, starting to stand up.

"No, no, please," he said, sliding into the chair opposite her. "I only have a minute. I just . . . I wanted to meet you."

"And I you. I am Celeste Aquino, but please call me Celeste," she said warmly, reaching out for his hands. "You are just as Bastian described to me."

Kian thought he'd been prepared, but he really wasn't. Bastian had described him to his mother? Sometimes it was easier for him to believe that Bastian had never really been serious, that Kian had imagined the way Bastian looked at him. But if he'd told his mother about him, then Kian hadn't misremembered anything. It had all been real, and that hurt worse than believing that Bastian had lied to him.

"Oh, darling, you are just as sad as he is." She frowned. "He is devastated without you."

Kian cleared his throat. "Sometimes things just don't work out. He told me that it wouldn't, the first month I worked for him. It shouldn't have been a surprise that it all fell apart."

"I would like you to come to my house, for tea. When are you free?" she asked, and for a second, Kian nearly turned her down. What point was there in making this harder than it already was? Sitting in Bastian's mother's house, wishing that he'd introduced them before everything had gone to hell? Forming a friendship with Celeste, even though there seemed to be little point to it?

It was a bad idea, but Kian was learning that even acknowledging that fact didn't always stop him. It sure hadn't stopped him with Bastian.

"Tomorrow," he said. "I have the afternoon off. Is that too soon?"

"No," she said, clearly delighted. "You will come tomorrow. One o'clock." She slid a piece of paper across the table. "My address."

Kian stared at the paper, realizing that she had come here tonight with the express purpose of talking to him, and not for a few minutes that he could steal from the kitchen. She wanted to get to know him and knew he wouldn't be able to do it during service.

His heart beat a little faster, even though he told himself firmly that he should not get his hopes up.

But it was too late, and hope was too addictive in the face of despair.

Chapter Sixteen

"Darling, come in," Celeste Aquino said, opening the door to Kian.

Bastian's mother's house wasn't the soulless modern box that his own was. It was painted French blue, with charming white shutters, and a proliferation of gardens surrounding it, from the start of the drive all the way up to the house.

"Thank you for inviting me," Kian said, hating how stiff and nervous he sounded. Since accepting the invitation the night before, the only thing that had stopped him from canceling was the fact that he didn't know her phone number. And he couldn't exactly call Bastian and ask *him*.

"Don't worry, he is not here. He is working, of course," she said, leading him through the interior of the house, which was laid out just as open as Bastian's own, but decorated in her own style. Celeste took him out onto the back terrace, and they sat at a table and chairs for two, set with delicate china and a center serving tray filled with petit fours and tea sandwiches.

"See, isn't this lovely?" Celeste asked and Kian nodded mutely. This shouldn't feel like a test, but it was. He'd never imagined meeting Bastian's mother without Bastian actually being present.

"It's a beautiful view," Kian added. "And your gardens are stunning."

Celeste poured tea into his cup. "This ground is so fertile, I enjoy it so much," she said. "When Bastian said he wanted me to come with him to California, of course I agreed, but I had no idea I would like it so much here."

She handed him the cup, and then offered him a choice of sandwiches. Like Bastian, she was clearly a perfectionist, because everything was elegant and beautifully prepared.

"I taught him to cook, you know," she said conspiratorially. "Though he will deny it now."

Kian took a bite of smoked salmon, chewed, and then swallowed. "Why would he?" He didn't add that she was hardly the type of mother that he could ever be ashamed of.

"You know Bastian," she said with a little airy wave of her hand. "No doubt he wants everyone to believe he came out of the womb knowing how to cook. He lets none of that show through his armor."

He'd let a little of it show, with Kian. But not much, and not, Kian had realized during the last week, enough for Kian to feel comfortable showing any of his own weakness. That was why he'd resisted telling him about Mark causing so much difficulty. Bastian's expectations of perfectionism were difficult to face, but even tougher because his own personal standards were so high. You could hardly blame someone for expecting too much when they expected even more out of themselves.

"No, he doesn't," Kian admitted softly.

"I know it's painful to talk about him," she said, kindness echoing through every syllable of her words. "If you really don't want to, I won't blame you, but I think it would help if I told you a little of his past. I'm assuming he has never told you, *non*?"

"I know what's on his Wikipedia page," Kian admitted wryly.

"It would be nice for these conversations to come up naturally, for him to tell you himself, in his own time, but I think, I *think* he will eventually come to you, and you knowing these things will help."

Kian knew he was staring incredulously at her. "Why would he come to me?"

She laughed. "Bastian, you know he does not let things go. He does not give up. He does not quit. He is searching for a solution to your professional problem, a place you will fit, a place you fit with him, and I know he will find one eventually. Because he is Bastian."

Kian knew him well too, obviously not as well as his mother knew him, but he wasn't so certain.

"I see you doubt," she said, leaning forward a little. "But that is alright. Still, I would like to tell you, if that is alright?"

"Yes," Kian agreed. "it's alright."

Celeste took her time, pouring more tea, popping a sugar cube into her own cup with a delicate pair of silver tongs, offering him another sandwich. Finally, she spoke. "Bastian's father, I assume he has not told you of him."

"No." Before, he hadn't really found that odd because they were still getting to know each other more personally than as just mentor and trainee, and Kian had believed they had all the time in the world to have those conversations. But then nothing had turned out the way he'd expected it to.

"He was . . . to put it mildly, a brute. Mean and cruel and rigid. Bastian has a terrible fear of being like him, while at the very same time, being very nearly like him."

"He isn't mean or cruel or rigid," Kian protested. "He's got a temper, yes, and he comes down on you if you mess up, but he's not, he's not really like that."

"*Vraiment*," Celeste agreed. "He is not. He has his father's drive for perfection, his commitment to excellence, his need to be the very best at what he begins. He is neither cruel nor mean—but he fights it, every single day." She took a sip of tea. "It is why he feels the need to control everything so completely. Even you."

Kian nodded slowly. Hearing about Bastian's father did help explain some of why he behaved the way he did.

"You love to work with him, yes?"

"I did," Kian said. He thought about what Xander had said, how he would eventually want to move on, to work for someone new, but he knew he never would. He was always going to want to be somehow adjacent to Bastian. They understood each other, on a very elemental level, in a way that few others did. Their creativity echoed in one another, one side complementing the other.

Celeste eyed him steadily across her teacup. "Why did you not take the *sous* position then?"

Why hadn't he? It wouldn't have been a great fit—he would have felt shamed and embarrassed and like a failure if he had. But it also would have meant they could have tried to work things out.

"It was embarrassing to fail. And to fail that way," Kian finally admitted.

"Ah," she said. "So, ego. The first day you met, Bastian came to me and said you were alike, and I thought, there is no way this is possible, you are too young, you are much sweeter than Bastian, but I see now I was wrong. You want your personal and professional relationships to feel equal."

"It's . . . I know it's impossible," Kian said.

"This is why he struggles. He wishes to find you a place where you feel respected and not still his trainee, but also a place you deserve." She winced. "It will not be easy."

Kian finished his tea. It was one thing to know that everything with Bastian was over, it was another to hear his mother say it, in that sad, regretful voice. He stood. "Thank you for the tea," he said, "but I really need to be going."

"Of course, your new job," Celeste said, her voice brightening. "And you will promise me to come by sometime, again?"

"Yes, I'll try," Kian promised as they walked through the house together.

As he went to open the door, she surprised him by placing her hand against it, keeping it only partially open. "You also must promise me that if he comes to you, and he tries to make it work, you'll remember what I told you."

Why this continued insistence Bastian would eventually contact him? It had been over a week since Kian had quit and there had been only silence. He didn't expect that would change, not at this point. Celeste had even admitted that the solution was difficult, if not impossible.

"I will, though I don't think he intends to contact me," Kian said wryly.

"He loves you," Celeste said. "He won't let you go, I know he won't."

As he walked back to his car, Kian wanted to believe her, because she so clearly believed her own words, but instead, there was only doubt.

Bastian had never really wanted to love him; he'd only done it because Kian had finally forced him to acknowledge it by coming to his home and taking all his clothes off. He'd set them on this path, and maybe Bastian resented that; maybe he wished that they'd continued on as they were, loving each other from afar, and never doing anything about it.

At least then, he'd still have Kian at Terroir.

It was a week later that the recruiter called.

Kian nearly told her to forget it, because he already had a job at Barrel House, but she kept insisting that the offer was lucrative and promising and that he would want to at least listen to it.

"I'm nobody," he'd said wryly into the phone, right before his shift started, "why would you even know to contact me?"

"Everyone knows about you," she said with certainty, "and you're who the client wants."

Kian was not convinced but he finally agreed to hear the proposal. She gave him an address of a little café outside of town, and said they would be using a back room, for privacy.

Frankly, he thought the whole thing smelled fishy, but when he told Xander, he'd just shrugged.

"So, someone wants to interview you," he said. "Word gets around. You dealt with the Bastard longer than most people. He personally trained you. You're young and fresh and hungry. It's not like I don't want to keep you here, but I get the feeling you don't intend to stay."

Xander wasn't wrong.

"I guess," Kian said dubiously.

"What's the worst that can happen?" Xander demanded. "It's a shitty job and you say no?"

Kian wasn't sure what he was afraid of, but instead of looking forward to the meeting with the recruiter, he dreaded it. He nearly called her twice to call it off, but then Wyatt had sent a text, wishing him good luck on the interview, and after that, it had seemed silly to cancel it.

Xander was right. All he had to do was say no if it was a job he wasn't interested in.

The café was one he'd been to before, though he'd never been ushered by the hostess with such deference to the back room, where a young woman with auburn hair and black-framed glasses was sitting at the end of the long table.

"Hello, I'm Lindsay Frost," she said, "and you must be Kian Reynolds."

"Yes," he said, reaching out to shake her hand. "It's nice to meet you."

"The honor is all mine. Wow, Terroir. What a way to start your career." She motioned towards the only other place at the table that had been set. He sat down, but still couldn't shake the feeling there was something going on that he didn't understand.

"I've been very lucky," Kian said.

"Bastian Aquino as your mentor? You sure have. And to be *chef de cuisine*, his appointed choice, at your age? Wow, I have a whole list of people who want to talk to you," she said with a laugh.

Kian knew going into this that he'd need to be honest. He'd need to tell the truth about what happened and how he'd quit Terroir. He took a deep breath and tried to find a way to confess that didn't make him look all bad.

"I only worked as *chef de cuisine* for a few weeks," he admitted. "But I was fully in charge of the kitchen for quite awhile before that."

She seemed completely unconcerned by his confession, and that made no sense. He wasn't crazy, because he knew that most of the time, interviewers wanted to know why you'd left a job abruptly, after only a few weeks. Especially one as prestigious as the one he'd quit.

"And now you're working at Barrel House?" she asked, consulting notes on a pad of paper in front of her.

"Xander Bridges is a friend," Kian said. "I'm not sure where I want to go next, and that seemed like as good of a place as any to spin my wheels while I figured it out."

"You've definitely been working with some exalted company," Lindsay said.

Kian wanted to say that none of them really seemed all that exalted, especially Xander, who still insisted on wearing that awful chili pepper headwrap, but that wasn't going to convince anyone to hire him.

"Can you tell me a little more about the job?" Kian asked.

"Oh yes, of course. Sorry. Just so excited to meet you." Lindsay glanced at her notes again. "It's a small restaurant, much smaller than Terroir, a little more casual than fine dining, but still high-end cuisine. Dinner only. Approximately fifty seats. A five-person staff. You'd be in charge of developing the menu, though it was suggested that some sort of rotating small plates menu would be preferred, and in charge of the kitchen and the staff."

On the surface, exactly the sort of position Kian was looking for. He hadn't been ready to be *chef de cuisine* at someplace like Terroir, with three hundred seats, and catering events, and twenty people to manage in the kitchen, but he could do something small. It would be a great learning experience. And small plates, he loved those, and could very easily develop a menu around that concept.

Still, something held him back.

"I'm assuming there's an owner or investor?" Kian asked. "When can I meet them?"

"Well, um," Lindsay hesitated, which was *so* weird. "Yes. There is. They're very busy, out of town a lot. Unfortunately they couldn't be at this meeting, but they gave me the power to offer you the contract, if you'd like to take a look at it. It's very generous."

More alarms pinged in Kian's head. They wanted to hire a head chef they'd never even met before? That seemed like a bizarre choice.

Still, Kian looked over the contract when Lindsay pushed it across the table. It was very generous. The salary was good. His decisions on menu and personnel were final, that was actually written into the contract. There was a business manager to oversee those choices, but if he wanted to do something, he could do it, immediately.

"Do they own other restaurants?" Kian wondered. The business manager position was odd, though maybe not so odd considering that the owner hadn't even bothered to meet with him today. But then if they hadn't, why was the business manager not here in their place?

"Oh yes," Lindsay said, and it seemed like she was going to continue but she shut her mouth abruptly.

Xander had told him that the worst that could happen today would be for Kian to turn down the job. Simple enough, to just say no, and there was a part of Kian that was tempted, even though there were a lot of factors that made it seem like a perfect job for him.

Tailor made in fact. Like the job had been designed with exactly his skill set and his experience in mind. It would be a little bit of a stretch, but nothing he couldn't handle.

"Could I meet the owner if I wanted to?" Kian asked.

Lindsay's eyes grew wider, like saucers, and that was when he knew. There was something going on, and he wanted to know what it was before he signed anything.

"He's not available," she finally stuttered out.

"He, huh?" Kian asked.

Suddenly, he knew who was behind this mysterious new restaurant, this mysterious new job. Of course getting Lindsay to admit that wasn't going to be easy, because of course, she was terrified of letting the secret out—and of him.

There was really only one person it could be.

"Who owns this restaurant?" Kian demanded.

Lindsay looked lost and decidedly out of her element, which jived with the rest of this charade, which hadn't been anything like any interview Kian had ever heard of before. Which meant she probably wasn't a recruiter, but only pretending to be one.

"I do."

Kian glanced up and Bastian was standing in the doorway. He had the nerve to look sheepish, but Kian's temper flared anyway. He knew he'd promised Celeste that he'd listen, that he'd consider what Bastian said when he came to him, but all he could think was, *why the fuck was all this necessary?*

"You own it," Kian said flatly. "No wonder. The job seems perfect for me, probably because it was *designed* for me."

Bastian shot Lindsay a single look and she fled, grabbing her purse and exiting the private room, shutting the door behind her.

Kian rolled his eyes. "You have it all figured out, don't you?" he accused. "You even hired some random person to try to recruit me, because you didn't want to recruit me yourself."

Bastian sat down and Kian flinched. It hurt, having him so close, and knowing he was so far away. Even further than he'd been this morning.

"Please," Bastian begged, and there were so few times Kian had ever heard that note in his voice that it was impossible not to at least listen. "Please, give this a chance. I've been tearing my hair out for the last two weeks, trying to find a way to do this with you, trying to find a way to work this out, and this is the only way I could find."

"You don't even *own* a restaurant of this description," Kian said, tossing the contract in front of him.

"Yes, I do." Bastian's voice was steadier now. Surer. "They broke ground today."

"What?"

"It's an expansion of Terroir, sort of. A more casual, friendlier version, right next door. The kitchens are being expanded." Bastian's gaze on him was warm, so warm. Warmer than he'd ever seen before. "We'll share initially, but we've shared before."

"But I'm still in charge." Kian still felt incredulous. "I'm in charge of my part of that kitchen."

Bastian nodded earnestly. "You'd be completely in charge of *your* kitchen. You'd call all the shots."

"But you'd still own it." Kian didn't know how that was going to make this slightly different version of what they'd already tried any better.

"Technically yes." Bastian sighed. "Your immediate boss would be my business manager. But yes, I'd still own it."

"And if I turned this down?" Kian demanded. "What would happen then?"

"I love you. Whether you work with me or not. I want you to be in my life. If you keep working at Barrel House, we'll figure out a way to make it work—if that's what you want." Bastian paused, like he was trying to come to terms with the possibility that Kian wouldn't, and it was *hard*.

Kian felt a pulse of satisfaction that this whole fucking situation didn't just feel impossible for him, that at least Bastian was right there in the trenches with him.

Did he want to keep working at Barrel House? Work with Xander and date Bastian? It would fix the professional and personal messiness that had caused their breakup the first time around, but Kian wasn't sure it would fix the gaping hole in his chest. He wanted to learn more from Bastian; he'd left and it had felt wrong, all the way, and he still didn't feel right.

Maybe Xander was right, and with time, the hole would heal and ache less. But Kian really didn't think so. He'd always believed that when the time came for him to move on from Terroir, he'd know—and while he'd still quit, none of it had felt right.

"I don't know what I want," Kian admitted softly. "I liked the sound of the job, and then I found out you were behind it the whole time . . . fixing everything without even giving me a chance to tell you what I wanted."

Bastian's eyes grew wide, and then wider. "I . . . I guess I did, didn't I?" He sounded so ashamed, and Kian couldn't help but feel a little guilty. Bastian had been trying, and that was what Kian had wanted, wasn't it? When his mother had promised Kian that he'd be in touch eventually, he hadn't believed it, even though he'd desperately wanted Bastian to make the effort.

To come to him. To *want* him. To tell him that he couldn't live without him.

"You did," Kian said, and tried to soften his voice. It wasn't entirely Bastian's fault, not after what Celeste had told him, that he wanted to control everything. It was his natural inclination, and right now, he was fighting it, all for Kian. What else could he really ask for?

"I'm sorry. It was my fault you failed, and all I wanted was to go back and fix it. But I couldn't. All I could do was try to make it better going forward, and that was what I focused on. Making it better. Making it work; making *us* work."

There were worse things, Kian realized, than a partner who tore themselves apart trying to fix a problem that had made you both miserable.

"This is always how it's going to be, isn't it?" he asked, even though he already knew the answer. "Neither of us have really changed. I'm still going to challenge you and you're still going to hate it."

"I don't hate it," Bastian claimed, even though Kian knew it was a lie.

"It makes you uncomfortable," Kian corrected. "I know it does."

Bastian actually squirmed in the chair, like he was uncomfortable now. "Not always."

"I'm not talking about when we're at your house or my house or in bed. I'm talking about when we're working. Because that's what we're talking about right now. How to fix our professional relationship."

Bastian's face fell, devastation filling his eyes, and Kian realized what he'd just said.

"No, no," he said quickly, reaching for Bastian, and cradling his big hands in his smaller ones. "No. I don't know what's going on between us, not professionally, but I know I love you, and I know that you love me. We *fit* together, which is why our personal relationship is so much easier to figure out."

"I'm not sure what you're saying."

"I'm saying you can't leave me, because I won't let you," Kian promised, squeezing his hands. "How does that sound?"

Bastian choked out a laugh that actually sounded a lot more like a sob. He hadn't said, because that wasn't Bastian's way, but Kian knew instinctively how much he'd been suffering. Being apart was like living without a limb, and on top of that, he'd been working nearly nonstop—while also trying to figure out a way to give Kian exactly what he wanted and needed.

"It's good. Good. I . . ." Bastian took a deep breath. "I missed you so fucking much."

Kian pulled him in for an embrace and felt Bastian's full-body shudder. "It's okay," he soothed. "We've got each other again."

When Bastian finally pulled away, his eyes were damp, and Kian's own weren't exactly dry either.

"I tried to control you," Bastian admitted after a long silence. "I tried to control the restaurant through you." His voice grew rougher. "I'm not a perfect man, Kian, as much as I want to believe otherwise. I make mistakes. I made a big one, but it wasn't *this*. I wouldn't change that for the world. I should have known we couldn't keep everything separate. It's too messy, and it's messy because it's real."

Kian raised an eyebrow. "And you think this will fix it?" He still wasn't convinced. He desperately wanted to go back to work for Bastian, he desperately wanted to take this job, but there was still a part of him that believed what Bastian had claimed two years ago.

They couldn't work together and have *this* too. It wouldn't ever work.

"I'm not expecting it to work out all the time," Bastian said, "but I know I have to try. I can't let you walk out again, not like before. That . . . it killed me. I thought the worst was when we kept our hands off each other, but that wasn't the worst. Not having you here, in my life, that was the worst."

"Neither of us has changed," Kian said slowly, "I don't know how this won't end in disaster, all over again. And if it does, I'm not sure I can handle it."

Bastian's eyes were intense on his. "I'm not a different man. I can't be a different man. I am the man I am, the good and the bad. But I'm more aware now. That's all I can be. And you've grown up. You're assertive and confident and challenge me in ways that I never expected."

"And you're okay with that?" There was no way to keep the disbelief from his voice. Bastian had claimed to try before and had failed utterly.

"I don't hate it as much as I thought I would," Bastian admitted. "I know we can't . . . we can't ever really be equals. Not really. I know that's what you wanted. I know that now. But I think this gives us the best chance to be more equal. Your best chance to grow, a little bit outside of my shadow."

Kian didn't say anything for a long moment. There was a part of this that felt too good to be true, too perfect almost, but this didn't feel like it had with the *chef de cuisine* job which he'd known wasn't right. This felt far more like the right sort of beginning.

There were so many paths open to him right now. He could keep working for Barrel House. He could find a job at another restaurant. He could take this job now, that Bastian was offering him.

The truth was, he knew what he wanted, but he was fucking terrified of losing Bastian again. Of losing everything he'd ever cared about.

"I'm afraid," Kian admitted, his voice cracking. He'd never let Bastian see any weakness, always afraid that it would mean Bastian's admiration and his respect and his love would die in the face of it. And maybe it would have, before, but Bastian *was* growing.

All Kian could do was trust that he was ready to see it. And if there wasn't any trust between them, how could they ever hope to have a personal *or* a professional relationship?

"I know," Bastian said very softly. "I am too. Absolutely fucking terrified."

And suddenly, shockingly, the way forward felt very clear. Kian knew what he should do, what was absolutely the right move for him, and it also happened to be exactly what he wanted.

He reached over and grabbed the pen that Lindsay had left on the table, and without a word, signed the contract, pushing it over towards Bastian after he was done.

Bastian grinned, so bright it nearly hurt. "You won't regret it, I swear," he promised, and Kian leaned forward, his mouth only an inch or so away from Bastian's.

"I probably will, at some point," Kian said thoughtfully, "but you're worth the risk."

Bastian's eyes were dark, deep wells, staring right into Kian's. "I am?" For the first time, the inherent cockiness in his tone was more subdued. And that, Kian realized, was his fear talking.

Fear of things falling apart, fear of the messiness overwhelming them, fear of failure, fear of not being enough, of Kian not loving him enough to stick out all the times when he wanted to quit because it was too hard.

Bastian probably felt that the fear he felt was an embarrassing weakness, something to push Kian away, but in the end all it did was convince Kian completely that they'd both do whatever it took to make this work.

"You're worth everything," Kian admitted and leaned forward that last inch to kiss him. It had been too long since the last time they'd kissed, and even though he knew now that they had all the time in the world, he didn't want to wait another second.

EPILOGUE

EIGHTEEN MONTHS LATER

"I think this is a very bad idea." Bastian wasn't perfect, would never be perfect, and still liked to construct all sorts of walls to keep his deeper feelings from the world. The only difference now was that at least when he constructed the walls, he built them with Kian inside.

Kian rolled his eyes. "It's going to be great. How could it not? It's a wedding."

"Your friends all hate me," Bastian said, and, unusually, sounded like he actually regretted this.

It was hard, but not impossible, to keep his chuckle hidden inside. It was just so unusual to see Bastian on such shaky ground, uncertain of how he'd be received. What Kian had discovered more and more over the months, as their personal relationship deepened and their professional relationship flourished, was that he'd always had these feelings, he just was total shit at expressing them. But now he'd started to, with Kian as the only witness.

"You didn't seem to mind them hating you when they all worked for you," Kian pointed out wryly.

Bastian thought about this for a long moment, then gave a sharp nod, his eyes following Kian from the closet to the suitcase on the bed, as he packed for their trip down to southern California.

Bastian had gotten home a little earlier, so he was already packed, and he kept eyeing his duffel, sitting on the floor by the bedroom door, with extreme trepidation.

"Did you do laundry this week?" Kian asked from the depths of the closet. The shelf holding his jeans was pretty bare. He'd meant to do some earlier, but

Cluster, the small plates bistro adjacent to Terroir, was in the middle of a menu overhaul, and he'd been too busy.

"Did I do laundry?" Bastian appeared in the doorway, arms crossed over his bare chest. "Do I ever do laundry?"

"Not if you can help it," Kian sighed.

"I have time to throw in a quick load now," Bastian offered.

Four years ago when Kian had walked into Terroir for the first time, he never would have dreamt that one day Bastian would be offering to do his laundry.

The problem was that even though he was a relentless perfectionist in the kitchen, it turned out that Bastian was fucking awful at chores like laundry. Last year, he'd even managed to turn an entire load of whites bright pink even though there had been nothing red to be found.

Socks regularly disappeared, stains didn't come out, and even though Bastian, who hated failure with the fire of a thousand suns, meticulously folded every item, somehow everything always came out wrinkled.

Kian shot him a loving look. It was sort of adorable how bad Bastian was at laundry. "I think I'm going to have to pass on that offer."

A frustrated noise escaped Bastian. "I was going to be careful."

When you were dating and living together with someone like Bastian Aquino, diplomacy was of the utmost importance. "I'm sure you were," Kian said, with the straightest face he could manage.

"I know it's mind-boggling that someone with Michelin stars is unable to do a load of laundry," Bastian said with a disgusted sigh. "God knows I know how pathetic I am."

"Hey," Kian said, reaching up and brushing a lingering kiss on his cheek, rough with stubble after a very long day, "if the worst thing you ever do is fuck up my clothes, I'm good with that. I'm just going to run a load myself. There's time before we leave tomorrow for it to dry."

Kian pulled a selection of jeans and shirts out of the hamper and then Bastian trailed after him as he went down the hall to start the washing machine.

"It wasn't that I didn't care that they hated me, before," Bastian said.

Oh, so they were back to the prior subject of conversation—that all of Kian's best friends didn't like him, their dislike long predating Kian and Bastian's relationship.

Kian shot him a look over his shoulder. He hadn't given a single fuck that they'd hated him. He'd been not-so-affectionately called the Bastard and he'd carried the insult of that nickname regally, like a fur cloak.

"Oh, really?" Kian asked, turning back to him after hitting the start button on the washer.

"I didn't *like* it," Bastian claimed.

Kian rolled his eyes as they returned to the bedroom so he could finish packing. "They don't hate you. It'll be fine."

Celeste had texted him this morning, telling him that she'd told Bastian the same thing. Apparently this was something he was really worried about.

"Listen," Kian continued, pushing Bastian down on the edge of the bed they shared, and climbing onto his lap. He'd grown another inch and had begun to fill out his lanky body a little, but Bastian would always be bigger than him—something Kian hoped would never stop being hot. "This is a really happy occasion that is actually *not about you*. Just relax and try to have a little fun. That's what you typically do at weddings."

Bastian glared. "I know what to do at a wedding."

"Oh?" Kian raised his eyebrow. "And how many of them have you taken off to go to in the last . . . let's say . . . ten years?"

"I've been a little busy." Despite his words, Bastian's grumpy expression was beginning to crack, and Kian could see the beginnings of a smile. And he could *feel* the beginnings of something else stirring under his crotch. This position turned Bastian on just as much as it did Kian.

"A little advice then," Kian murmured, leaning in a little until they were almost kissing. Nearly, but not close enough. "Smile. Laugh. Eat. Drink. Enjoy yourself."

Bastian's arms wound around his middle and pushed Kian down, brushing their growing erections together. "Are you going to be there?"

"Yeah, I am."

"Then it shouldn't be very hard for me to do any of those things," Bastian admitted.

Even though they'd been together a year and a half, Bastian being sappy and sweet still turned Kian's world upside down. It shouldn't have been unexpected by this point, but it always was, in the best possible way.

Kian leaned down and kissed him long and slow and filthy. "I love you," he whispered against his lips.

Bastian didn't answer but from the way he crawled up his body, Kian knew exactly what his answer was.

Bastian hated weddings.

If there'd been a way to avoid this one without hurting Kian's feelings or looking like a complete asshole, he would've done it. But considering that one of the grooms was a former employee of Terroir, and one of Kian's best friends, it was impossible. Add to those facts the other fact that both grooms were up-and-coming in the culinary scene, and this was *the* wedding.

That still didn't mean that Bastian had to like it.

"It's awful, isn't it?"

Bastian glanced up from where he'd been minutely examining his program, stuffed and uncomfortable in his suit, and saw a blonde woman, a rueful expression on her face wearing a turquoise dress with flowers strewn across it.

"You must be Kian's boyfriend," she said, settling in next to him. Bastian, who'd been actively trying to keep his expression neutral, frowned.

"I'm Tabitha King," she said, holding out her hand.

Bastian let his frown deepen, even though there was a strong possibility that Kian would see it and be disappointed in him. This was a *wedding*, and it was supposed to be filled with love and beauty and happiness, right?

Bastian was more intimately acquainted with those concepts than he'd ever been, but the visible outpouring still made him nervous.

"Do I know you?" he asked, shaking her hand briskly. She had a surprisingly firm handshake and a way of looking at you that stripped most pretense away.

"I'm Ryan's best friend," she said.

It took him a long moment to place who Ryan was, and then he remembered Kian mentioning that Wyatt, his old employee, had ended up dating Ryan Flores, the baseball player.

"But this isn't Wyatt's wedding," Bastian objected.

She tilted her head and the look in her blue eyes was as sharp as one of his Japanese steel knives. "Correct. I also work at Five Points, which is why I'm here."

"So you work with Miles and Evan, then," Bastian said, a little pleased that he'd finally managed to figure out the somewhat complex personal relationships. He'd never claim to be a very good boyfriend in that regard. His focus was too single-minded. It had expanded to include Kian, but not Kian's circle of friends, most of whom, unfortunately, were ex-employees and hated him.

Tabitha shrugged. "Not really, but they're two really nice guys."

It dawned on Bastian that not only was she clearly friendly with Wyatt, she would also be friendly with Miles. Therefore she knew exactly who he was, yet she'd still identified him as "Kian's boyfriend," and not as Bastian Aquino, head chef of Terroir.

"Miles used to work for me," Bastian admitted, even though technically Miles had worked for René, the head of pastry at Terroir.

"I know." Tabitha eyed him steadily.

Bastian sighed. "Then you know three quarters of the wedding party hates my guts."

"Thus making you the most interesting person at this wedding," Tabitha pointed out, "and why I'm over here talking to you, instead of sucking up to my boss."

"I'm flattered," Bastian said dryly.

"At least I'm not asking you when you're going to do this," she said, giving a general wave around the wedding preparations.

He adored Kian, and he was almost completely certain that Kian adored him, but this sort of event, with the proliferation of flowers and silky tents and strung lights and a full wedding party—not his type of thing at all.

"So you thought you'd come over here *not* to ask when we're getting married and also because I'm the most interesting yet most hated person at the wedding?"

She laughed. "Something like that. And because you were sitting alone, and I know what that's like."

When Kian had told him that Miles had asked him to be one of his attendants, it hadn't struck him right away that meant that he would be on his own, surrounded by people who either knew him personally and didn't like him or who had definitely heard the worst of the rumors about him.

He'd fully expected to have to sit through the ceremony by himself, even though Kian had insisted that he could sit with Damon and Ryan. He and Damon had come to an uneasy truce, but they weren't ever going to be friends, and after getting a glimpse of Ryan, in sunglasses and a very sharp suit, with a trail of fans following him around, Bastian had decided he wasn't going to go to the trouble to introduce himself.

"Well, thank you," Bastian said stiffly.

She laughed again. "I couldn't drag my husband to this—he hates weddings too—and he's working besides, so you're stuck with me. Though," she added speculatively, "you need to let me introduce you to Ryan after the ceremony."

It would be so easy to brush her off. It wasn't like Bastian hadn't been doing it his whole damn life, never letting a single person close.

He'd thought he could just let Kian in, and leave the rest of the world out, but the longer they dated, the more impossible that seemed.

This wedding was the prime example of that, and he was beginning to realize that loving Kian came with all this other stuff too—and other *people*, one of whom was sitting next to him right now.

"Sure, I'd like that," Bastian said, voice gruff and suddenly swamped with emotion because Kian had brought *life* with him when he'd let him in.

He'd brought people and joy and vitality and a messiness that Bastian didn't always like, but in the end, enjoyed nevertheless.

"I knew you'd come around," Tabitha said impudently. "You're really not as scary as your reputation promised."

Bastian opened his mouth, very willing to promise that he was as scary as it took, but then the music started—a goddamn string trio complete with harpist.

He leaned closer to her, and said under his breath, "I didn't realize that Miles was the string trio type."

Tabitha smothered a laugh. "You clearly haven't spent much time with Evan."

So apparently *Evan* was the string trio type in their relationship. Frankly, Bastian thought as the ceremony began, he wasn't sure he could picture Miles settling down with a string trio type. Even when Miles had been filming his pastry videos, he'd always been so casual and laid-back.

But then Evan and Miles approached the officiant, dressed similarly in gray suits, and their hands gripped tightly together. Evan's white shirt was buttoned up and topped off with a pale yellow bow tie. Miles had not only eschewed the bow tie, he'd left the top two buttons of his shirt unbuttoned.

And somehow, despite that clear outer difference illustrating their inner differences, they couldn't take their eyes off each other, the love radiating out of them so palpable, that Bastian had to wonder if he and Kian were so obvious.

They'd spent forever hiding their feelings, so maybe they weren't. Or maybe, like Michel had told him wryly and more than once, they'd always been shitty at hiding. Everyone had always known, but it had only been that worm Mark who had figured out a way to twist it, to make their feelings for each other so negative.

Right before he spoke, Bastian realized that he recognized the officiant. That was Reed Ryan, and somehow Evan and Miles had managed to drag him out of the kitchen, which was impressive.

"Ladies and gentlemen, family and friends, welcome," the officiant said, smiling wide. "I'm Reed Ryan, and I've had the pleasure and the pride of knowing Evan and Miles for several years now, and I was so touched when they asked me to officiate their wedding. Of course, I was also terrified because I'm the worst public speaker ever, so please bear with me."

The assembled friends and family laughed, but Bastian knew from the strain on Reed's face that he wasn't trying to lower expectations; this truly wasn't easy for him.

"Today," Reed continued, "we've all gathered here to witness the loving union between Evan and Miles. Every single one of you is here because you've all had a special part of their lives, and they've asked you not only to bear witness to their union, but to help create beautiful memories of this special day."

Bastian shifted uncomfortably in his chair. He didn't think he'd been asked to come to help create beautiful memories. He'd been asked because despite everyone's beliefs and against all the odds, he and Kian had created a lasting relationship together.

He knew how long Xander and Wyatt and to a lesser extent, Miles, had fought against Kian having feelings for him. Just because they'd finally accepted that Kian wasn't leaving Bastian anytime soon didn't mean they suddenly approved of whom he'd picked to be his partner.

And there was nothing like a wedding to drill that point home.

He wouldn't be particularly surprised if that was another reason why the woman next to him had chosen this particular seat.

Kian, standing in the front next to Xander and Wyatt, smiled at him, and even though he wasn't enjoying himself, Bastian couldn't help but smile back.

"First," Reed continued, "is there anybody who has an objection to this couple joining their lives together?"

It was difficult to imagine standing up where Evan and Miles were in a few years, but Bastian still made a mental note to make sure that particular sentence was erased from the ceremony, as he could imagine more than one person deciding that they definitely had an objection. Or ten.

Bastian couldn't imagine anyone objecting to Miles and Evan. So he was shocked, along with the rest of the audience, when Wyatt stepped forward, his blond hair shaggy and longer than it had ever been when he'd worked at Terroir.

"I do," Wyatt said, clearly and loudly, with a voice that carried. Several rows away, Bastian heard his boyfriend, Ryan, laugh out loud.

What was going on?

Reed must have anticipated this because he just smiled, and said, "What is your objection?"

"I object," Wyatt said, clearly trying for a serious tone, but failing because he kept smiling so brightly, "because you should be ridiculously in love to get married."

Miles laughed then, Evan's warm gaze never leaving his future husband's. As if there was *any* doubt they were ridiculously in love.

"If I am, how do you suggest I prove it?" Miles asked, his voice amused and curious.

"Maybe spirit him away to a tropical island and spoil him horribly?" Wyatt suggested. "Oh wait, you already did that. I guess," he said with a shrug, "it's inevitable, you *should* marry him."

"Thanks," Miles said dryly.

"Any other objections?" Reed asked, but Bastian had figured out there were going to be at least two others, the exact number of remaining attendants who had yet to speak.

"I have one," Xander said next.

"Of course you do," Evan said, loud enough for the audience to hear and chuckle along with the wedding party.

"I'm somewhat infamous for my objections," Xander continued, "so don't think I present this lightly. But I think two people who are getting married should spend more time together than you do. Be partners, in the truest sense of the word."

This time it was Evan who responded. "You mean, more than live together and work together? What sort of partnership would you suggest, Bridges?"

Xander's gaze was steady, and clearly not on the couple standing in front of Reed, but his fiancé, one row up from Bastian. "True partnership means you support each other through thick and thin, even when it's hard, and especially when it feels impossible. You need to have each other's backs, every single time, no matter the obstacle."

Miles' voice wasn't quite steady as he answered Xander. "I think we can do that, don't you?" he asked his husband-to-be in a hushed voice.

"I think with you next to me, we can do anything," Evan said.

"Then I withdraw my objection," Xander said, and the look he directed towards Damon was practically a caress.

"Let me guess," Reed said, "there's one more objection."

"Yeah, I've definitely got one," Kian said, and even though Bastian had been anticipating this, his heart started beating harder. A hand reached for his and gave it a little squeeze. It must have been Tabitha. Maybe she'd even been put next to him so he wouldn't do anything crazy like leap up in the middle of Evan and Miles' wedding and do something insane that would make everyone hate him even more, like proposing to Kian.

He wasn't sure anymore it was the proposing part everyone would hate him for. But interrupting Evan and Miles' wedding and making it all about him? That was a fairly good reason.

"What's your objection?" Reed asked.

Kian gazed right at him, and maybe Michel was right, Bastian thought in a haze, maybe they had always been terrible at hiding their feelings. "From my own relationship, I know just how important loyalty is. Without it, you might as well give up now, because you're never going to be able to stay together. True loyalty is protecting the person you love with every fiber of your being, but also knowing when to let them go and set them free. Supporting them, even if their choices aren't your own."

Miles' look at Evan was both dry and a little watery. "I can't imagine knowing anything about that."

"We've made it work, we'll make it work every day," Evan promised. "Because I love you."

"I guess," Kian said, his own glance an invisible caress against Bastian's cheek, "I don't have an objection after all."

The assembled guests all chuckled, and Reed said, "Then it's time for your vows."

Bastian reached over and gripped Tabitha's hand. "Thank you," he murmured to her.

Her smile back was brilliant. "Anytime."

And from the way Kian was looking at him, Bastian suddenly knew that it would only be a matter of time before they did this too. Maybe not with the string trio and the bow ties, but definitely surrounded by the people they cared about, who cared about them.

"After the ceremony, I also want to introduce you to my husband," she said quietly.

"You said he hadn't come?" Bastian questioned.

Tabitha rolled her eyes. "Like I would ever let him out of a wedding."

Watching Evan and Miles exchange rings, Bastian realized that Kian had known how uncomfortable he'd feel during the ceremony, having to sit alone, and that he wouldn't ever seek out Damon or Ryan. So he'd asked Tabitha, whom he probably knew through Ryan and Miles and Evan, to sit with him. To make sure that he felt relaxed and comfortable.

Love swirled all around him and all through him, lighting him up inside, and Bastian knew he could never go back to the lonely workaholic he'd been before Kian. Kian had changed his life, had opened him up *to* life—and love, and a thousand other things that he'd been missing before.

"And I want you to meet Kian," Bastian said, because he could no longer help playing along. "He's the love of my life."

THE WEDDING

AN INDULGE ME SHORT STORY

THE MAN IN FRONT of Bastian Aquino cowered, shoulders sinking inward, eyes falling downward, fingers trembling as he extended the check toward the world-famous chef.

Anyone witnessing the scene might have expected that the man had done something truly horrific—robbed someone, or even committed a murder. Perhaps participated in a severe maiming. Nothing else could possibly explain the way he hesitantly glanced up at Chef Aquino, somehow certain that he would be struck down, or at least verbally annihilated, for the crime he'd committed.

In Bastian Aquino's world, what the man had done might not be on par with a class one felony, but it was still catastrophically severe. One week before one of the most anticipated weddings the Napa Valley had ever seen—Bastian's *own* wedding to rising star chef Kian Reynolds—and the caterer that Bastian hired to cook for the reception had just quit.

"What do you mean, *quit*?" Bastian asked through clenched teeth. He couldn't believe this was happening to him. Once he and Kian had become engaged, it was a common prediction that he'd develop some kind of insane bridezilla tendencies, considering his regular behavior in the kitchens of Terroir. Except that everyone *could* concede that ever since Kian had come onto the scene, now Bastian's bark was nearly always sharper than his bite. Still, his reputation preceded him, because before Kian, that had definitely not been true.

Bastian knew what everyone thought of him; in fact, he'd done his own share of exaggerating his reputation because it suited him for new employees to be a little terrified of him. It meant much less yelling if they began their careers at Terroir properly scared of what sort of punishment Bastian could exact. But while he demanded complete commitment as well as absolute perfection, he knew he'd mellowed. Whether that was encroaching middle age, or his soon-to-be husband, Bastian wasn't sure he wanted to know which was truly to blame.

Still, he knew money had been passed back and forth, betting on how insanely controlling he'd be about the wedding. And sue him, he wanted a damn nice wedding. He had lots of . . . Bastian guessed you could call them *friends* . . . in the culinary industry in Napa and out of it. There was nothing wrong with wanting a beautiful event that not only celebrated the love he shared with Kian, but also cemented them as the first couple of Napa. That didn't seem like much to ask. And in the end, money smoothed the way like it usually did, and the planner they'd hired had taken care of *almost* all the headaches.

However, Bastian had insisted on hiring the caterer himself, after Kian had refused to let him cater their own wedding. "You'd be busy the whole event," Kian had objected the first time Bastian had suggested it. "Isn't the point of a wedding that the grooms are supposed at least *see* each other?"

"Fine," Bastian had grumbled, a little aware but not at all unhappy about the fact that he'd learned to give so much, especially when Kian asked. It felt like a perfectly reasonable tradeoff when in return he was lucky enough to receive Kian's love, unyielding support, eternal devotion—and his rather delicious body. Bastian was a smart man, and even a stupider man would never turn that away, though he had done his level best before they'd figured their shit out.

So, Bastian catering the wedding had been out, and he'd been forced to find a caterer that fit two particular criteria—*one,* they could produce food of extraordinary quality rivaling Bastian's own, and *two,* they were not one of Bastian's personal friends, because that was yet another promise that Kian had extracted from him. Their friends would be allowed to enjoy the wedding too, *no* exceptions.

But now this caterer—*no,* Bastian couldn't even consider him a caterer; *he was a spineless worm*—was cancelling on him only a week before the wedding.

Everything was a disaster.

Bastian stared at the worm in front of him and tried to think of an insult grandiose enough that it could express how unbelievably angry he was in this moment, but inspiration did not come.

"Get out," Bastian spit at him, and the man fled, no doubt anticipating dishes thrown at his head and worse. The check fluttered down to the ground and Bastian huffed in frustration.

With only seven days, how was he supposed to find a caterer who could meet both criteria? Obviously, Bastian realized, it would be impossible, no matter how much money he threw at the situation, and it would be a monumental waste of time to even try.

Incredibly annoyed that he had been reduced to *begging* for help from an ex-employee (and a *friend*, Kian would have added with a sly look on his face), Bastian leaned down, picked up the check and then stalked out to his car.

It was a short ride to the Barrel House, which was his old *sous'* new restaurant. "You can't keep calling it *new* when it's three years old," Kian would have inserted, but Kian wasn't here—*Dieu merci*, he had gone down to LA to spend some time with Wyatt and Miles before the wedding. He never would have gone if he'd known the catering would blow up; the truth was, it had been hard enough to persuade Kian to leave Napa with only seven days until the wedding.

"I can call the restaurant any damn thing I please," Bastian muttered as his Audi swung into the paved driveway of the Barrel House.

It was mid-afternoon and therefore the restaurant was closed, but Bastian banged on the door anyway. It took a moment, during which Bastian, who normally would never admit to fear, actually worried that Xander wouldn't answer the door, but finally a large man unlocked and opened it.

"What the fuck are you doing?" Damon asked, noticeably not opening the door any wider so that Bastian could actually come inside. They might be the partners of best friends, but it was not surprising that Bastian and Damon had never warmed to each other. After all, Damon had poached Xander for his restaurant, and that was not the sort of thing that Bastian forgave.

Still, it *had* been over three years. And Bastian *was* desperate. Maybe he could find it in himself to let go of that particular transgression.

"I'm . . .in a bit of a bind," Bastian confessed, trying out a humble smile that didn't do much to warm the cold expression on Damon's face. "More of a total disaster than a bind, actually. The caterer for the wedding just quit and . . ."

"And you thought you could just waltz over here and demand that Xander cater his best friend's wedding?" Damon did not sound amused.

Bastian put away any poor facsimile of meekness; if Damon thought he could out-bad ass Bastian Aquino, then he was more delusional than Bastian had believed.

"I thought I could come over and *ask*," Bastian insisted. "After all, like you said, I *am* marrying Xander's best friend."

"Despite all of Xander's best efforts to talk him out of it," Damon pointed out.

"*Oui*," Bastian growled.

"Wait," Damon suddenly backtracked, "the best caterer in the entire valley—he *quit* your wedding? Does he have a death wish?"

"Apparently," Bastian said through clenched teeth. "Now is Xander here or not?"

Reluctantly, Damon opened the door a crack wider. "He's in the kitchen."

"Excellent," Bastian said, and smacked the door, pushing it back until it hit Damon square in the chest. Damon was not a small man, he clearly spent a good portion of his time in the gym, and Bastian knew he spent the rest still personally tending to the enormous fields of vegetables that they served at the Barrel House. Bastian pushed again, and Damon still didn't move.

"*And*," Damon added, "if Xander says no, you can't throw a ridiculous amount of money at him, or threaten to destroy his reputation or this restaurant. You say okay and walk away."

Bastian glared. Was he really so unreasonable? He didn't think so. Besides, he rather *liked* the Barrel House—Kian liked to go on dates here and make faces at Xander through the enormous panels of glass that surrounded the kitchen—though he rather would have swallowed fiery hot coals before admitting to it.

"Of course," Bastian said. "If he says no, I'll just find someone else willing to cater the biggest, most important event Napa has ever seen."

Damon rolled his eyes, but he opened the door just wide enough to let Bastian through.

After Damon's rather uncomfortable greeting, Bastian, who'd believed thinking of Xander, with his entire kitchen staff to help, had been rather genius, was suddenly afraid he might say no.

But Xander didn't say no.

After Bastian finished telling him about the catastrophic development and making the proposal that Xander and his kitchen staff supplement Bastian's own army of Terroir employees for a joint catering effort, Xander said *nothing*, merely wiped his hands on a towel and sighed.

Bastian held his breath.

"Are you going to tell me next how every celebrity chef in California and beyond will be there?"

Bastian considered this. "Would it help convince you?"

Xander just sighed again and finally looked up at him. "Probably not."

"That's why I haven't said it," Bastian said, though honestly, he hadn't mentioned it because he hadn't *thought* of it—but Xander seemed to be genuinely considering the idea and he wasn't going to ruin it by admitting the truth.

"Do you care what the menu is?" Xander asked, and then before Bastian could say, *yes, of course he cared what the menu was*, seemed to reconsider. "That's an incredibly dumb question. Sorry, I'm tired. This is an insane idea, but yes, I'll do it."

"Really?" Bastian couldn't quite believe it.

"I get to dictate the menu, and you just smile and nod, okay?"

Bastian resigned himself to eating rustic Italian—Xander's particular culinary forte—at his wedding. It definitely wouldn't have been his first choice, but he wasn't sure there *were* any choices, not anymore. Not if he and Kian didn't want to starve at their own wedding.

⁂

"Hey babe," Kian's bright voice chirped out over the phone. Bastian was sitting on the back terrace they'd added to the house they'd shared last year, sipping a nice merlot to celebrate fixing the catering disaster before it could even become a disaster. At first Bastian had thought the new terrace might keep Kian from visiting his *maman* less frequently and cooking up plans with her that made

Bastian's life more difficult, but it turned out that though his *maman*'s terrace was a draw, it was Celeste herself that was the main attraction for Kian.

Still, they both really enjoyed sitting on their own terrace after a long, busy, exhausting evening in the Terroir kitchens. Bastian leaned back and stretched. "Hey to you too. How is LA?" he asked his fiancé, hoping to keep the news of their new caterer under wraps as long as possible.

"Lonely without you," Kian said, and it didn't matter how long they'd been dating; there was still a part—an embarrassingly large one that he would never, ever admit to owning—that still quivered and then collapsed into goo every time Kian said something sweet.

And since Kian was the sweetest man that Bastian had ever met, even though he still possessed a tough, exacting streak that could go toe-to-toe with Bastian's own, it happened a lot.

"Aren't Wyatt and Miles keeping you busy?" Bastian asked, clearing his throat. No matter how he tried, the bone-meltingly sweet things that Kian said so offhandedly didn't come quite so easily to him.

"Busy enough." Bastian could hear the slow, fond smile in Kian's voice—like he knew just how much Bastian wished he could vocalize better exactly how he felt. "Wyatt is thinking of getting another food truck."

"Ah," Bastian said noncommittally. Wyatt was an extraordinarily talented chef, and Bastian still wasn't sure how he felt about his ex-employee wasting his efforts by locking himself up in a tiny little kitchen on wheels. Still, food trucks were becoming more and more popular, and more accepted by the higher echelon of chefs as a legitimate business option.

"Bastian," Kian teased softly. "It's okay to be happy for him. I promise, no big bad Michelin inspector will come take your chef card away. Or your stars."

He didn't even bother trying to hide his bark of laughter. With Kian, he laughed more, and like the food trucks, he realized that more of that could only be a good thing.

"I'd like to see them try," Bastian retorted.

Kian laughed then, and it hit Bastian again, breaking over him like a never-ending wave of wonder: this man was going to stand up in front of every friend and family member they knew, nevermind every professional acquaintance that Bastian could think of, and promise to love and support him forever.

It was a heady, incredible feeling, tempered only by the slight concern he was still experiencing over the food. What if it was bad? He was Bastian Aquino;

he couldn't have terri*ble* food at his wedding. He couldn't even have mediocre food. That might even be more egregious.

"I miss you," Kian repeated, and his voice had gone soft and quiet, like he meant it even more this time than he had the last. "I shouldn't be here, hanging out with Miles and Wyatt, and trying to talk Wyatt out of letting Tony experiment on the innocent diners of Los Angeles. I should be up in Napa with you, getting ready for the wedding." He sounded almost *guilty*, which was not what Bastian wanted at all when he'd convinced him to go.

"Everything is fine," Bastian soothed. "I've got everything under control. You're clearly needed there, if Wyatt is letting Tony do *anything*." It wasn't *exactly* a lie. Bastian did mostly have everything under control. Xander had agreed to help cater the reception, with his staff and Bastian's own. It would be fine; it would be *better* than fine.

After all, it needed to be.

"If everything is fine, then why did Xander text me about menus?" Kian's voice, perplexed and a little hurt, said it all.

Merde. That little shit. Sometimes Bastian couldn't believe that Xander had worked for him for years, and he'd managed not to kill him during all that time. Now it seemed that every time he turned around, Xander was doing something annoying and/or frustrating that pushed every single one of Bastian's buttons. And there was no question of whether it was on purpose—Bastian knew the truth.

He also knew Xander had never wanted Kian to end up with him, but once it had actually happened, Xander seemed mostly okay with it. Still, that didn't apparently exempt Bastian from being continually hazed by him. Even three years into their relationship.

"Uh," Bastian hedged. "There may have been a *slight* problem with the caterer."

"Slight?"

"He came in to the restaurant today and quit. Quit *my* wedding!"

Kian laughed, which was a completely unfair reaction, because it wasn't funny. Not even a little.

"You mean *our* wedding?" Kian asked, not sounding annoyed or perturbed in the least. "I'm pretty sure we're getting married to each other, last time I checked anyway."

"I...yes. We are. We definitely are."

"So the caterer quit and you...hired Xander?"

"I know we agreed, none of your friends. But he shouldn't have to do much on the day. He can bring his entire staff and I'll lend him use anyone I can from Terroir. There should be plenty of help."

"I'm not." Kian chuckled. "I'm not mad. I'm just . . .shocked, honestly, that Xander would agree."

Something they had in common. "Maybe he wants to make up for all the headaches he's given me over the years," Bastian suggested.

"Maybe." Kian didn't sound convinced. Frankly, Bastian wasn't either. He still didn't know why Xander had agreed, but in the end, why did it matter? At least he could depend on Xander supplying food that was edible and would satisfy Bastian's requirement for excellence. As much of a pain in the ass as he was, Xander *was* a talented chef.

"What did he ask you about the menus?" Bastian asked. If Xander had questions, he should direct them to Bastian—not Kian.

"He mentioned something about turkey."

Bastian's eyebrows shot up to his hairline. He grabbed the glass of wine next to him and took a deep, bracing gulp. "*Turkey?*"

"You know," Bastian could picture Kian's breezy hand wave, which he almost always did when Bastian should be truly concerned, but Kian didn't want him to be, "Thanksgiving dinner. He had this idea to do a fall-themed dinner centered around turkey."

Bastian wasn't proud that Kian (though this could all be laid directly at Xander's door, like most things could), had shocked him into silence.

He should have settled the menu with Xander before he'd left Barrel House, but he'd stupidly assumed that Xander would be *reasonable* and would comprehend, at least a little bit, the kind of food that Bastian would expect to be served at his wedding.

Turkey was not on the list. And the list was extensive.

"I think it'll be great," Kian finished. And sounded like he actually, genuinely meant it.

They'd been dating for long enough by now that Bastian knew exactly what would happen if he expressed what he truly felt about the turkey idea. And how wretched he would feel later at Kian's disappointed moping.

That was the thing nobody ever told you about falling in love; suddenly your own very decisive wants and *not*-wants became entirely superseded by those of your lover. And you didn't even feel *bad* about it. You just wanted them to be happy.

"Turkey it is," Bastian said, though god knew, he couldn't fake enthusiasm about it.

Kian laughed. "Xander will do magnificent work, I promise."

"I know he will, it's the accompanying bad I always worry about," Bastian said, and he wouldn't realize until much, much later how portentous of a statement that truly was.

The day of the wedding dawned clear and perfect; the epitome of a slightly warm autumn day. The sky was an aching blue overhead, with not a single cloud to mar its perfection, and the leaves, turning their rich russet and rust and gold, complemented it flawlessly.

Bastian couldn't have asked for a more beautiful day for him to marry the love of his life.

And then Marcus, who was working—but not entirely succeeding—on replacing Kian as his intern, poked his head into Bastian's office, where he would get ready for the wedding. "You need to come see this," Marcus said, and the hysteria in his tone immediately set Bastian on edge.

"What's happened?" Bastian barked. The catering had seemed taken care of. Xander had come and grabbed about five cooks from the Terroir kitchen yesterday and claimed everything was under control with the turkey dinner.

Bastian had really, really wanted to believe that was true. When he'd suggested to Xander that he could check in with the food prep, Xander had firmly told him that his place was getting ready for the wedding, and working on his vows.

He'd considered telling Xander that his vows had been written for *months* already, that they'd been the easiest thing in the world to write because whenever he thought about committing his life to Kian for the entirety of it, his feelings about it were embarrassingly simple to verbalize. For maybe the first time ever. But he didn't tell Xander, because his reputation would likely never recover.

As he followed Marcus out of his office and deeper into the Terroir kitchens, Bastian realized he should have traded everything—including his stupid reputation—to see and possibly even taste the reception meal that Xander was so secretively preparing.

Bastian rounded a corner and, honest to god, actually *gasped*. Sitting on one of the long stainless steel prep counters was something unholy.

"I told you," Marcus said grimly, but Bastian was still speechless.

He took a step closer to the ugly aberration and confirmed that yes, *somehow* that was indeed a turkey, its normal gloriously burnished skin covered in . . .*red fur*?

"Oh my god." Bastian turned and saw Kian standing there, still dressed in jeans and a t-shirt.

"You're not supposed to be here," Marcus said at the exact same time that Bastian echoed, "What are you doing here?"

"I heard a rumor that Xander was doing something insane, and I had to check, because," Kian took a deep breath, "he's my friend, isn't he? If he fucks this up, it's on me."

"No." Bastian took an even deeper breath. He couldn't even look at the monstrosity sitting in front of them—it made his blood pressure raise in ways that couldn't be medically explained—but he *could* look at Kian. He took him aside and gazed at his fiancé and *only* at his fiancé. "If Xander has . . .gone insane . . .then that is one hundred percent on him. Not on you. Never on you."

"But . . ." Kian hesitated.

"No," Bastian repeated. "I hired him for this. I should have prevented this. I *will* prevent this."

"I'm not sure it's actually preventable at this point." Kian's voice was wry. "I mean that thing . . .that . . . whatever it is . . .it exists."

Bastian smiled grimly. "That doesn't mean he's going to get away with serving it. Not at our wedding."

"Oh, good, you're here." Bastian looked up then, if only because he had every intention of throttling Xander until he prepared something (*anything*) else.

"What the fuck were you thinking?" Except that Kian was already there, in his face, pointing to the offending poultry in front of them. "What *is* this?"

"Your turkey." Xander beamed. "It's a new recipe. I think you'll like it."

"This is our *wedding*. Do not test me," Bastian inserted, stalking over, glaring at the turkey. Except that from the very beginning of Xander's career at Terroir, he had been the very best at testing Bastian. Exactly why it had been a foolish idea to ever trust Xander with a job this monumentally important.

Marcus fled, probably because he sensed a record-setting confrontation.

But Xander continued like Bastian wasn't even there. He was giddy; a proposition more terrifying than the prospect of serving the cream of American culinary society that . . .that . . .*thing*.

"It's been dusted liberally with Flaming Hot Cheetos," Xander said. "And stuffed with two pounds of Velveeta."

Bastian's first instinct was to look over at Kian, who had bent over and was apparently choking on something? He rushed over and while patting his fiancé on the back, he wracked his brain, trying to figure out what Xander was even talking about. What were *Cheetos*? And *Velveeta?*

Finally, Kian lifted his head, and it appeared he'd been laughing so hard, there were tears in his eyes. "What the ever-living fuck, Xander," was all he could get out between bursts of unrestrained laughter.

"Get yourself together," Xander faux-ordered, amusement lighting his expression. "I'm going to carve it now, and you really don't want to miss this."

"Wait. First." Bastian wondered if he was taking his sanity into his own hands by asking, but he *had* to know. "What are . . .what are Cheetos? What is Velveeta?"

"Oh god," Kian got out between gasps of laughter. "Oh god, Xander, you are *so* dead."

"Cheetos are . . .well . . ." Xander rummaged around on the countertop behind him, and emerged with a metallic bag printed in eye-searing yellow and red, extending it towards Bastian. "Try one for yourself."

Bastian reached into the bag and dubiously eyed the bright red puff he pulled out. "I'm supposed to eat this?" he questioned.

Xander nodded vigorously, even as Kian continued to cackle behind him. Sometimes the man he loved was *not* helpful.

He cautiously popped it in his mouth. Artificial heat exploded on his tongue as he chewed, followed by hideously fake cheese taste, all wrapped up with a consistency resembling cardboard.

Leaning over, he spat into the nearby prep sink and took a quick drink of water from the faucet directly, swishing the liquid around in his mouth to try to eliminate the taste. "You put *that* on turkey? Are you insane?" Bastian cried.

Kian was still laughing. Bastian wouldn't be surprised if he was still hysterical by the time it came to walk down the aisle.

"As for the Velveeta, it's better to show you," Xander said slyly and beckoned them both closer. Bastian came only reluctantly.

Whipping out a pair of sharp kitchen shears, Xander started cutting down the spine of the turkey, instead of carving it in the traditional way.

"What is he doing?" Bastian asked Kian, not bothering to lower his voice.

But Kian just shrugged. "The ultimate Bastard practical joke?"

Bastian rolled his eyes. He understood all too well why he'd gotten that nickname. He was even proud of it, in a sort of fucked up way. To him, it meant that he pushed people to be the best they could be, and that he wouldn't ever accept anything less. Unfortunately, that wasn't always why ex-employees (and possibly current ones) liked to use it.

"I would hope that Xander had grown out of practical . . ." Bastian gave a shocked screech as the top of the bird finally cracked open, and inside was a massive lake of bright yellow melted cheese, dotted with nebulous reddish chunks that might have once been Flaming Hot Cheetos.

"That is . . ." Kian was staring open-mouthed at the abomination in front of them. "That's . . ."

"You are *not* serving this today," Bastian said as sternly as he ever had. He'd consider pulling his usual counter-clearing technique, but then that horrid-looking turkey *stuffing* might get everywhere, and his stomach rebelled at the thought of all that nastiness spreading all over his pristine kitchen.

"He's definitely not," Kian agreed. "But then, he already knew that, which is why I'm sure he has a handful of gorgeous roasted turkeys hiding somewhere. Don't you, Xander?"

Xander just chuckled. "Why would you think that?"

Bastian was inordinately proud; Kian's resulting glare even made the usually unflappable Xander flinch.

"Okay, you win. You two were never really fun, and you've unfortunately continued that streak today."

"Today, you mean . . ." Bastian glanced over at Kian, who was smiling again. "Are you really surprised we weren't interested in your little joke on our wedding day?"

"Shocking, I know," Xander said, and then broke into an even bigger smile. "Seriously you two, you shouldn't even be here. I said I'd take care of the food, and I will. I promise. It's going to be beautiful. Trust me."

"No turkeys with Cheetos, flaming or otherwise? Stuffed with something that isn't . . .viscous, fake cheese?" Kian inquired hopefully.

"I've got you," Xander said confidently. Bastian still nearly asked to see the preparations because after having his emotions played with on this level, he wasn't quite sure he trusted Xander the way Kian did.

Still, Kian trusted Xander—and Bastian trusted Kian completely, more than he'd ever trusted anyone else before. Maybe even more than he trusted his own *maman*. Or maybe he just trusted Kian differently. He'd trust Kian with Terroir, with everything he'd worked his entire life to build. When that had happened, all those years ago, he'd known that Kian was the only one for him. Because that trust didn't come easily, and it wouldn't fade or shift or ever break down.

"Come on, let's leave Xander to it," Kian said, reaching out for Bastian's hand. Holding hands in Terroir—that still wasn't something they did often, but once upon a time, it would have been unheard of. Bastian never would have allowed it—and god knew, he'd spent enough time denying both of them because he was so sure that becoming emotionally involved was a mistake.

"Marcus is right," Bastian said, "we're not supposed to be seeing each other today."

"It's a silly superstition, like pranking the culinary-obsessed groom with the threat of a catering disaster," Kian teased back lightly as they walked towards Bastian's office.

"Do you think . . ." Bastian hesitated. He'd learned a long time ago that if he didn't want to hear the truth from Kian, he didn't ask. Of course, he almost always ended up asking, because somehow hearing the truth from Kian was easier than hearing it from anybody else. "Do you think Xander got the caterer to quit?"

"So he could prank you? It's not impossible to imagine." The corner of Kian's mouth quirked up. "I'm sure we'll never know."

"No," Bastian said, pulling Kian closer to him despite that they were still technically in Terroir, and he tried very hard not to indulge in PDA. But it was their wedding day, and he was tired of resisting Kian's irresistible pull.

He leaned down and captured Kian's mouth with his own. He still felt that jolt of adrenaline and excitement every time it happened, just like that first time—when he'd been so desperate to convince Kian that he'd never felt this way about anybody before. It was just as true now as it had been then.

The kiss drew out, endlessly sweet with just an edge of spice, and then Kian drew away. "We're not supposed to do this here," he said, eyes sparkling.

"It's our wedding day," Bastian said. "I think we can do as we damn well please."

Kian reached and gave him one last peck. "Then, I guess I'll see you a little later," he teased.

"You'd better," Bastian faux-threatened as Kian sauntered off.

❧❧❧❧❧ ❦❦❦❦❦

It wasn't like Bastian genuinely expected anybody in the crowd of four hundred friends and family and professional acquaintances to object to him marrying the kindest, hardest-working guy that any of them knew.

They'd probably be smart to do it, but Bastian intended to fight anyone who made even the tiniest movement when the officiant asked, "Is there anybody here who objects to these two men being joined in committed matrimony?"

It was lucky, then, that nobody said a word. Like they all knew what would happen if they protested, nobody even moved. There wasn't a single flinch in the entire audience.

There'd been a time when Bastian might have counted himself on the side that didn't believe he and Kian could—or *should*—last. But the person in front of him, holding his hands as tightly as he held him every single night, had proven every single day that the place beside him was his and his alone.

It couldn't possibly belong to anyone else.

"Kian and Bastian have prepared their own vows," the officiant said, and then looked at Kian.

Everything inside Bastian trembled as Kian let go of one of his hands to pull a small folded square of paper from his pocket.

"Bastian Aquino, you changed my life," Kian said, and his voice was so clear, so confident, so *sure*, that Bastian wanted to cry right then. *Reputation*, he reminded himself. *If you cry now, you will never, ever live this down. Someone, somewhere is recording this, and they'll put it up on that video site and then nobody will ever take you seriously in a kitchen ever again.* "The first time I met you, I understood who you were, and what drove you to be the best version of yourself. And for the first time, who I was, and what I wanted, and everything I worked for finally made sense. All those hopes and ambitions I'd held inside for so long made sense because *you* made them make sense. You gave me a drive and a purpose, and somehow, impossibly, you wanted me to succeed even more than I wanted to succeed myself. You made me a better chef, but more importantly you made me a better man. I became who I was meant to be, only because you were next to me, supporting and loving me exactly the way I needed."

In the end, Bastian supposed it was inevitable that the world would see the complete and utter sap that Kian had made of him. And it felt particularly appropriate that they would see it on this day, the day Kian agreed to be his husband. A tear trickled down Bastian's cheek and he swallowed hard. He'd always tried so hard to be what Kian needed, even if it wasn't always what Kian thought he wanted, and most of all, what he always wanted most of all was to love Kian the way he deserved to be loved.

And if Kian felt that, felt that strongly enough to say so in their wedding vows, then he must be doing a pretty damn good job of it. That was the thought that pushed him over the edge and then caused the tears to fall. He'd done that, and he'd done it after nearly everyone believed that he couldn't. It was, Bastian knew, the crowning achievement of his life. Terroir had officially taken a backseat.

"Because you're always there for me, this is what I can promise you," Kian continued. "I will promise to love and cherish you through every good time and each bad one. I will be there for you, right next to you, for as long as you need me to be. I intend to love you and cook with you every single day for the rest of our lives."

Bastian squeezed Kian's hands hard, and wished, fervently, that this vow part was already done and they could be kissing already. Because the next time they kissed, they'd be married, and he'd be one of *those* guys, head over heels for his own husband and not caring who knew it.

"And now, Bastian," the officiant gently prodded, likely because Bastian was too busy gazing sappily into Kian's blue eyes to say his own vows.

He'd written these before he'd even proposed—properly, anyway—and then rewritten them so many times he didn't even need notes, because he knew exactly what he wanted to say to Kian.

The rest of the world? They just happened to be there, witnessing the greatest moment of his life.

"Before you came to work at Terroir, I thought I had the perfect life," Bastian said. "I had achieved everything I wanted for myself in my restaurant. I poured everything I had into it, and I thought there was nothing left—I didn't even want there to be anything left. But then you arrived, and you were so persistent, so stubborn, so determined to show me that there could be a different path for me. And it wasn't until we started down it that I realized that I had so much more I could give. So much hiding inside of me, that I had ignored for a very long time, but now I had someone to give it to. Love and companionship and friendship and *trust*. I know now that those things were waiting, laying dormant inside. They were waiting; they were waiting for *you*."

Kian brushed a tear off his own cheek, and laughed wetly, a little self-consciously.

"I vow to never forget that as much as I give to my work, and to Terroir, I will always have something left over, that is yours and yours alone."

"I pronounce you husband and husband," the officiant said, but already her words were fading away as he and Kian came together, and as amazing as all their other thousands of kisses had been—this one left them all in the dust.

"Always," Kian murmured under his breath, when the kiss finally ended.

"Always," Bastian agreed.

Everyone always told Bastian that weddings were a constant, frenetic experiment in chaos. There was never enough time to talk to everyone, to accept all the well-wishes, to even eat the food or sample the wine they'd selected. And even though Bastian had promised himself that they had plenty of time, he found himself wrapped up with Kian, lost in that feverish pace, bouncing from one table to the next.

At almost every single table, they complimented the food. Bastian grudgingly acknowledged more than once that Xander had been in charge of catering, and he rested easy that not only had the entire event been a complete success, Xander hadn't managed to fuck it up with his bizarre turkey after all.

Much, much later, after the guests had departed for the dance floor, thousands of lights twinkling above them in the darkened night sky, Bastian found Kian finally tucking into some of Xander's turkey dinner away from the crowd.

Except—it wasn't the beautiful sage and honey roasted turkey that everyone else had eaten.

"Is that?" Bastian asked with a shudder. "You *didn't*."

"I didn't want it to go to waste, and I wanted to try it, even if it was only supposed to give you a heart attack," Kian protested as his fork scooped up a whole puddle of congealed, Cheetos-dotted fake cheese.

"It was uncommonly successful at that," Bastian said, sitting down next to his husband and wrapping an arm around his shoulders.

"Besides, aren't you always the one telling me I can't judge something that I haven't tasted?"

Bastian flinched as Kian gamely stuck the forkful into his mouth. "I didn't mean that quite so literally."

Kian just shrugged. "It's not half-bad."

"You're lying," Bastian insisted.

Laughing, Kian shoved a forkful at Bastian's face. "Well, try it then, and see."

But even if Kian was willing to eat it, he had to know that Bastian, who would even be willing to bare his surprisingly tender heart for a crowd, wouldn't ever capitulate to eating Flaming Hot Cheetos Turkey. "Never change," Bastian said softly, pulling Kian in even closer. "Promise me."

Kian smiled back, his eyes luminous. "Only if you swear to me that you'll never change either. I love you exactly how you are. You might be a Bastard, but you're *my* Bastard."

INTERESTED IN READING MORE OF
BETH'S BOOKS?

CHECK OUT A FULL LIST OF TILES
BY SCANNING THE QR CODE
OR VISITING HER WEBSITE

WWW.BETHBOLDEN.COM/BOOKLIST

WANT TO FOLLOW BETH?

MAKE SURE YOU NEVER
MISS A RELEASE?

SCAN THE QR CODE BELOW
OR VISIT HER WEBSITE
FOR A SOCIAL MEDIA LIST,
NEWSLETTER SIGNUP,
AND SO MUCH MORE!

WWW.BETHBOLDEN.COM/ABOUT

www.ingramcontent.com/pod-product-compliance
Lightning Source LLC
Chambersburg PA
CBHW070358310726
48977CB00003B/483